[illegible] des Roys de Perse a Ispahan et du Meidan [illegible] la place la plus grande [illegible]
[illegible]

World Without End

ALSO BY KEN FOLLETT

The Modigliani Scandal

Paper Money

Eye of the Needle

Triple

The Key to Rebecca

The Man from St. Petersburg

On Wings of Eagles

Lie Down with Lions

The Pillars of the Earth

Night over Water

A Dangerous Fortune

A Place Called Freedom

The Third Twin

The Hammer of Eden

Code to Zero

Jackdaws

Hornet Flight

Whiteout

WORLD WITHOUT END

Dutton

DUTTON
Published by Penguin Group (USA) Inc.
375 Hudson Street, New York, New York 10014, U.S.A.
Penguin Group (Canada), 90 Eglinton Avenue East, Suite 700, Toronto, Ontario M4P 2Y3, Canada (a division of Pearson Penguin Canada Inc.); Penguin Books Ltd, 80 Strand, London WC2R 0RL, England; Penguin Ireland, 25 St Stephen's Green, Dublin 2, Ireland (a division of Penguin Books Ltd); Penguin Group (Australia), 250 Camberwell Road, Camberwell, Victoria 3124, Australia (a division of Pearson Australia Group Pty Ltd); Penguin Books India Pvt Ltd, 11 Community Centre, Panchsheel Park, New Delhi – 110 017, India; Penguin Group (NZ), 67 Apollo Drive, Rosedale, North Shore 0632, New Zealand (a division of Pearson New Zealand Ltd.); Penguin Books (South Africa) (Pty) Ltd, 24 Sturdee Avenue, Rosebank, Johannesburg 2196, South Africa

Penguin Books Ltd, Registered Offices: 80 Strand, London WC2R 0RL, England

Published by Dutton, a member of Penguin Group (USA) Inc.

First printing, October 2007

1 3 5 7 9 10 8 6 4 2

LIBRARY OF CONGRESS CATALOGING-IN-PUBLICATION DATA
Follett, Ken.
World without end / Ken Follett.
p. cm.
ISBN 978-0-525-95007-3
1. Black Death—England—Fiction. 2. Great Britain—History—14th century—Fiction. I. Title.
PR6056.O45W67 2007
823'.914—dc22 2007026639

Printed in the United States of America
Set in American Garamond
Designed by Amy Hill

PUBLISHER'S NOTE

This book is a work of fiction. Names, characters, places, and incidents either are the product of the author's imagination or are used fictitiously, and any resemblance to actual persons, living or dead, business establishments, events, or locales is entirely coincidental.

For Barbara

PART I
November 1,
1327

1

wenda was eight years old, but she was not afraid of the dark.

When she opened her eyes she could see nothing, but that was not what scared her. She knew where she was. She was at Kingsbridge Priory, in the long stone building they called the hospital, lying on the floor in a bed of straw. Her mother lay next to her, and Gwenda could tell, by the warm milky smell, that Ma was feeding the new baby, who did not yet have a name. Beside Ma was Pa, and next to him Gwenda's older brother, Philemon, who was twelve.

The hospital was crowded, and though she could not see the other families lying along the floor, squashed together like sheep in a pen, she could smell the rank odor of their warm bodies. When dawn broke it would be All Hallows, a Sunday this year and therefore an especially holy day. By the same token the night before was All Hallows Eve, a dangerous time when evil spirits roamed freely. Hundreds of people had come to Kingsbridge from the surrounding villages, as Gwenda's family had, to spend Halloween in the sanctified precincts of the priory, and to attend the All Hallows service at daybreak.

Gwenda was wary of evil spirits, like every sensible person; but she was more scared of what she had to do during the service.

She stared into the gloom, trying not to think about what frightened her. She knew that the wall opposite her had an arched window. There was no glass—only the most important buildings had glass windows—but a linen blind kept out the cold autumn air. However, she could not even see a faint patch of gray where the window should be. She was glad. She did not want the morning to come.

She could see nothing, but there was plenty to listen to. The straw that covered the floor whispered constantly as people stirred and shifted in their sleep. A child cried out, as if woken by a dream, and was quickly silenced by a murmured endearment. Now and again someone spoke, uttering the half-formed words of sleep talk. Somewhere there was the sound of two people doing the thing parents did but never spoke of, the thing Gwenda called grunting because she had no other word for it.

Too soon, there was a light. At the eastern end of the long room, behind the altar, a monk came through the door carrying a single candle. He put the candle down on the altar, lit a taper from it, and went around touching the flame to the wall lamps, his long shadow reaching up the wall each time like a reflection, his taper meeting the shadow taper at the wick of the lamp.

The strengthening light illuminated rows of humped figures on the floor, wrapped in their drab cloaks or huddled up to their neighbors for warmth. Sick people occupied the cots near the altar, where they could get the maximum benefit from the holiness of the place. At the opposite end, a staircase led to the upper floor, where there were rooms for aristocratic visitors: the earl of Shiring was there now with some of his family.

The monk leaned over Gwenda to light the lamp above her head. He caught her eye and smiled. She studied his face in the shifting light of the flame and recognized him as Brother Godwyn. He was young and handsome, and last night he had spoken kindly to Philemon.

Beside Gwenda was another family from her village: Samuel, a prosperous peasant with a large landholding, and his wife and two sons, the youngest of whom, Wulfric, was an annoying six-year-old who thought that throwing acorns at girls then running away was the funniest thing in the world.

Gwenda's family was not prosperous. Her father had no land at all, and hired himself out as a laborer to anyone who would pay him. There was always work in the summer, but after the harvest was gathered in and the weather began to turn cold, the family often went hungry.

That was why Gwenda had to steal.

She imagined being caught: a strong hand grabbing her arm, holding her in an unbreakable grip while she wriggled helplessly; a deep, cruel voice saying, "Well, well, a little thief"; the pain and humiliation of a whipping; and then, worst of all, the agony and loss as her hand was chopped off.

Her father had suffered this punishment. At the end of his left arm was a hideous wrinkled stump. He managed well with one hand—he could use a shovel, saddle a horse, and even make a net to catch birds—but all the same he was always the last laborer to be hired in the spring, and the first to be laid off in the autumn. He could never leave the village and seek work elsewhere, because the amputation marked him as a thief, so that people would refuse to hire him. When traveling, he tied a stuffed glove to the stump, to avoid being shunned by every stranger he met; but that did not fool people for long.

Gwenda had not witnessed Pa's punishment—it had happened before she was born—but she had often imagined it, and now she could not help thinking about the same thing happening to her. In her mind she saw the blade of the axe coming down on her wrist, slicing through her skin and her bones, and severing her hand from her arm, so that it could never be reattached; and she had to clamp her teeth together to keep from screaming out loud.

People were standing up, stretching and yawning and rubbing their faces. Gwenda got up and shook out her clothes. All her garments had previously belonged to her older brother. She wore a woolen shift that came down to her knees and a tunic over it, gathered at the waist with a belt made of hemp cord. Her shoes had once been laced, but the eyelets were torn and the laces gone, and she tied them to her feet with plaited straw. When she had tucked her hair into a cap made of squirrel tails, she had finished dressing.

She caught her father's eye, and he pointed surreptitiously to a family across the way, a couple in middle age with two sons a little older than Gwenda. The man was short and slight, with a curly red beard. He was buckling on a sword, which meant he was a man-at-arms or a knight: ordinary people were not allowed to wear swords. His wife was a thin woman with a brisk manner and a grumpy face. As Gwenda scrutinized them, Brother Godwyn nodded respectfully and said: "Good morning, Sir Gerald, Lady Maud."

Gwenda saw what had attracted her father's notice. Sir Gerald had a purse attached to his belt by a leather thong. The purse bulged. It looked as if it contained several hundred of the small, thin silver pennies, halfpennies, and farthings that were the English currency—as much money as Pa could earn in a year if he had been able to find employment. It would be more than enough to feed the family until the spring plowing. The purse might even contain a few foreign gold coins, florins from Florence or ducats from Venice.

Gwenda had a small knife in a wooden sheath hanging from a cord around her neck. The sharp blade would quickly cut the thong and cause the fat purse to fall into her small hand—unless Sir Gerald felt something strange and grabbed her before she could do the deed . . .

Godwyn raised his voice over the rumble of talk. "For the love of Christ, who teaches us charity, breakfast will be provided after the All Hallows service," he said. "Meanwhile, there is pure drinking water in the courtyard fountain. Please remember to use the latrines outside—no pissing indoors!"

The monks and nuns were strict about cleanliness. Last night, Godwyn had caught a six-year-old boy peeing in a corner, and had expelled the whole family. Unless they had a penny for a tavern, they would have had to spend the cold October night shivering on the stone floor of the cathedral's north porch. There was also a ban on animals. Gwenda's three-legged dog, Hop, had been banished. She wondered where he had spent the night.

When all the lamps were lit, Godwyn opened the big wooden door to the outside. The night air bit sharply at Gwenda's ears and the tip of her nose. The overnight guests pulled their coats around them and began to shuffle out. When Sir Gerald and his family moved off, Pa and Ma fell into line behind them, and Gwenda and Philemon followed suit.

Philemon had done the stealing until now, but yesterday he had almost been caught, at Kingsbridge Market. He had palmed a small jar of expensive oil from the booth of an Italian merchant, then he had dropped the jar, so that everyone saw it. Mercifully, it had not broken when it hit the ground. He had been forced to pretend that he had accidentally knocked it off the stall.

Until recently Philemon had been small and unobtrusive, like Gwenda, but in the last year he had grown several inches, developed a deep voice, and become awkward and clumsy, as if he could not get used to his new, larger body. Last night, after the incident with the jar of oil, Pa had announced that Philemon was now too big for serious thieving, and henceforth it was Gwenda's job.

That was why she had lain awake for so much of the night.

Philemon's name was really Holger. When he was ten years old, he had decided he was going to be a monk, so he told everyone he had changed his name to Philemon, which sounded more religious. Surprisingly, most people had gone along with his wish, though Ma and Pa still called him Holger.

They passed through the door and saw two lines of shivering nuns holding burning torches to light the pathway from the hospital to the great west door of Kingsbridge Cathedral. Shadows flickered at the edges of the torchlight, as if the imps and hobgoblins of the night were cavorting just out of sight, kept at a distance only by the sanctity of the nuns.

Gwenda half expected to see Hop waiting outside, but he was not there. Perhaps he had found somewhere warm to sleep. As they walked to the church, Pa made sure they stayed close to Sir Gerald. From behind, someone tugged painfully at Gwenda's hair. She squealed, thinking it was a goblin; but when she turned she saw Wulfric, her six-year-old neighbor. He darted out of her reach, laughing. Then his father growled: "Behave!" and smacked his head, and the little boy began to cry.

The vast church was a shapeless mass towering above the huddled crowd. Only the lowest parts were distinct, arches and mullions picked out in orange and red by the uncertain torchlight. The procession slowed as it approached the cathedral entrance, and Gwenda could see a group of townspeople coming from the opposite direction. There were hundreds of them, Gwenda thought, maybe thousands, although she was not sure how many people made a thousand, for she could not count that high.

The crowd inched through the vestibule. The restless light of the torches fell on the sculpted figures around the walls, making them dance madly. At the lowest level were demons and monsters. Gwenda stared uneasily at dragons and griffins, a bear with a man's head, a dog with two bodies and one muzzle. Some of the demons struggled with humans: a devil put a noose around a man's neck, a foxlike monster dragged a woman by her hair, an eagle with hands speared a naked man. Above these scenes the saints stood in a row under sheltering canopies; over them the apostles sat on thrones; then, in the arch over the main door, St. Peter with his key and St. Paul with a scroll looked adoringly upward at Jesus Christ.

Gwenda knew that Jesus was telling her not to sin, or she would be tortured by demons; but humans frightened her more than demons. If she failed to steal Sir Gerald's purse, she would be whipped by her father. Worse, there would be nothing for the family to eat but soup made with acorns. She and Philemon would be hungry for weeks on end. Ma's breasts would dry up, and the new baby would die, as the last two had. Pa would disappear for days, and come back with nothing for the pot but a scrawny heron or a couple of squirrels. Being hungry was worse than being whipped—it hurt longer.

She had been taught to pilfer at a young age: an apple from a stall, a new-laid egg from under a neighbor's hen, a knife dropped carelessly on a tavern table by a drunk. But stealing money was different. If she were caught robbing Sir Gerald, it would be no use bursting into tears and hoping to be treated as a naughty child, as she had once after thieving a pair of dainty leather shoes from a softhearted nun. Cutting the strings of a knight's purse was no childish peccadillo, it was a real grown-up crime, and she would be treated accordingly.

She tried not to think about it. She was small and nimble and quick, and she would take the purse stealthily, like a ghost—provided she could keep from trembling.

The wide church was already thronged with people. In the side aisles, hooded monks held torches that cast a restless red glow. The marching pillars of the nave reached up into darkness. Gwenda stayed close to Sir Gerald as the crowd pushed forward toward the altar. The red-bearded knight and his thin wife did not notice her. Their two boys paid no more attention to her than to the stone walls of the cathedral. Gwenda's family fell back and she lost sight of them.

The nave filled up quickly. Gwenda had never seen so many people in one place: it was busier than the cathedral green on market day. People greeted one another cheerfully, feeling safe from evil spirits in this holy place, and the sound of all their conversations mounted to a roar.

Then the bell tolled, and they fell silent.

Sir Gerald was standing by a family from the town. They all wore cloaks of fine cloth, so they were probably rich wool dealers. Next to the knight stood a girl about ten years old. Gwenda stood behind Sir Gerald and the girl. She tried to make herself inconspicuous but, to her dismay, the girl looked at her and smiled reassuringly, as if to tell her not to be frightened.

Around the edges of the crowd the monks extinguished their torches, one by one, until the great church was in utter darkness.

Gwenda wondered if the rich girl would remember her later. She had not merely glanced at Gwenda then ignored her, as most people did. She had noticed her, had thought about her, had anticipated that she might be scared, and had given her a friendly smile. But there were hundreds of children in the cathedral. She could not have got a very clear impression of Gwenda's features in the dim light . . . could she? Gwenda tried to put the worry out of her mind.

Invisible in the darkness, she stepped forward and slipped noiselessly between the two figures, feeling the soft wool of the girl's cloak on one side and the stiffer fabric of the knight's old surcoat on the other. Now she was in a position to get at the purse.

She reached into her neckline and took the little knife from its sheath.

The silence was broken by a terrible scream. Gwenda had been expecting it—Ma had explained what was going to happen during the service—but, all the same, she was shocked. It sounded like someone being tortured.

Then there was a harsh drumming sound, as of someone beating on a metal plate. More noises followed: wailing, mad laughter, a hunting horn, a rattle, animal noises, a cracked bell. In the congregation, a child started to cry, and others joined in. Some of the adults laughed nervously. They knew the noises were made by the monks, but all the same it was a hellish cacophony.

This was not the moment to take the purse, Gwenda thought fearfully. Everyone was tense, alert. The knight would be sensitive to any touch.

The devilish noise grew louder, then a new sound intervened: music. At first it was so soft that Gwenda was not sure she had really heard it, then gradually it grew louder. The nuns were singing. Gwenda felt her body flood with tension. The moment was approaching. Moving like a spirit, imperceptible as the air, she turned so that she was facing Sir Gerald.

She knew exactly what he was wearing. He had on a heavy wool robe gathered at the waist by a broad studded belt. His purse was tied to the belt with a leather thong. Over the robe he wore an embroidered surcoat, costly but worn, with yellowing bone buttons down the front. He had done up some of the buttons, but not all, probably out of sleepy laziness, or because the walk from the hospital to the church was so short.

With a touch as light as possible, Gwenda put one small hand on his coat. She imagined her hand was a spider, so weightless that he could not possibly feel it. She ran her spider hand across the front of his coat and found the opening. She slipped her hand under the edge of the coat and along his heavy belt until she came to the purse.

The pandemonium faded as the music grew louder. From the front of the congregation came a murmur of awe. Gwenda could see nothing, but she knew that a lamp had been lit on the altar, illuminating a reliquary, an elaborately carved ivory-and-gold box holding the bones of St. Adolphus, that had not been there when the lights went out. The crowd surged forward, everyone trying to get closer to the holy remains. As Gwenda felt herself squashed between Sir Gerald and the man in front of him, she brought up her right hand and put the edge of the knife to the thong of his purse.

The leather was tough, and her first stroke did not cut it. She sawed frantically with the knife, hoping desperately that Sir Gerald was too interested in the scene at the altar to notice what was happening under his nose. She glanced upward and realized she could just about see the outlines of people around her: the monks and nuns were lighting candles. The light would get brighter every moment. She had no time left.

She gave a fierce yank on the knife, and felt the thong give. Sir Gerald grunted quietly: had he felt something, or was he reacting to the spectacle at the altar? The purse dropped, and landed in her hand; but it was too big for her to grasp easily, and it slipped. For a terrifying moment she thought she was going to drop it and lose it on the floor among the heedless feet of the crowd; then she got a grip on it and held it.

She felt a moment of joyous relief: she had the purse.

But she was still in terrible danger. Her heart was beating so loudly she felt as if everyone must be able to hear it. She turned quickly so that her back was to the knight. In the same movement, she stuffed the heavy purse down the front of her tunic. She could feel that it made a bulge that would be conspicuous, hanging over her belt like an old man's belly. She shifted it around to her side, where it was partly covered by her arm. It would still be visible when the lights brightened, but she had nowhere else to put it.

She sheathed the knife. Now she had to get away quickly, before Sir Gerald noticed his loss—but the crush of worshippers, which had helped her take the purse unnoticed, now hindered her escape. She tried to step backward, hoping to force a gap in the bodies behind her, but everyone was still pressing forward to look at the bones of the saint. She was trapped, unable to move, right in front of the man she had robbed.

A voice in her ear said: "Are you all right?"

It was the rich girl. Gwenda fought down panic. She needed to be invisible. A helpful older child was the last thing she wanted. She said nothing.

"Be careful," the girl said to the people around. "You're squashing this little girl."

Gwenda could have screamed. The rich girl's thoughtfulness would get Gwenda's hand chopped off.

Desperate to get away, she put her hands on the man in front and shoved, pushing herself backward. She succeeded only in getting the attention of Sir Gerald. "You can't see anything down there, can you?" said her victim in a kindly voice; and, to her horror, he grasped her under the arms and lifted her up.

She was helpless. His big hand in her armpit was only an inch from the purse. She faced forward, so that he could see only the back of her head, and looked over the crowd to the altar, where the monks and nuns were lighting more candles and singing to the long-dead saint. Beyond them, a faint light showed through the big rose window at the east end of the building: dawn was breaking, chasing the evil spirits away. The clangor had stopped now, and the singing swelled. A tall, good-looking monk stepped up to the altar, and Gwenda recognized him as Anthony, the prior of Kingsbridge. Raising his hands in a blessing, he said loudly: "And so, once again, by the grace of Christ Jesus, the evil and darkness of this world are banished by the harmony and light of God's holy church."

The congregation gave a triumphant roar, then began to relax. The climax of the ceremony had passed. Gwenda wriggled, and Sir Gerald got the message and put her down. Keeping her face turned away from him, she pushed past him, heading toward the back of the crowd. People were no longer so eager to see the altar, and she was now able to force her way between the bodies. The farther back she went, the easier it became, until at last she found herself by the great west door, and saw her family.

Pa looked expectantly at her, ready to be angry if she had failed. She pulled the purse out of her shirt and thrust it at him, glad to get rid of it. He grabbed it, turned slightly, and furtively looked inside. She saw him grin with delight. Then he passed the purse to Ma, who quickly shoved it into the folds of the blanket that wrapped the baby.

The ordeal was over, but the risk had not yet passed. "A rich girl noticed me," Gwenda said, and she could hear the shrill fear in her own voice.

Pa's small, dark eyes flashed anger. "Did she see what you did?"

"No, but she told the others not to squash me, then the knight picked me up so I could see better."

Ma gave a low groan.

Pa said: "He saw your face, then."

"I tried to keep it turned away."

"Still, better if he doesn't come across you again," Pa said. "We won't return to the monks' hospital. We'll go to a tavern for our breakfast."

Ma said: "We can't hide away all day."

"No, but we can melt into the crowd."

Gwenda started to feel better. Pa seemed to think there was no real danger. Anyway, she was reassured just by his being in charge again, and taking the responsibility from her.

"Besides," he went on, "I fancy bread and meat, instead of the monks' watery porridge. I can afford it now!"

They went out of the church. The sky was pearly gray with dawn light. Gwenda wanted to hold Ma's hand, but the baby started to cry, and Ma was distracted. Then she saw a small three-legged dog, white with a black face, come running into the cathedral close with a familiar lopsided stride. "Hop!" she cried, and picked him up and hugged him.

2

Merthin was eleven, a year older than his brother Ralph; but, to his intense annoyance, Ralph was taller and stronger.

This caused trouble with their parents. Their father, Sir Gerald, was a soldier, and could not conceal his disappointment when Merthin proved unable to lift the heavy lance, or became exhausted before the tree was chopped down, or came home crying after losing a fight. Their mother, Lady Maud, made matters worse, embarrassing Merthin by being overprotective, when what he needed her to do was pretend not to notice. When Father showed his pride in Ralph's strength, Mother tried to compensate by criticizing Ralph's stupidity. Ralph was a bit slow on the uptake, but he could not help it, and being nagged about it only made him angry, so that he got into fights with other boys.

Both parents were tetchy on the morning of All Hallows Day. Father had not wanted to come to Kingsbridge at all. But he had been compelled. He owed money to the priory, and he could not pay. Mother said they would take away his lands: he was lord of three villages near Kingsbridge. Father reminded her that he was directly descended from the Thomas who became earl of Shiring in the year that Archbishop Becket was murdered by King Henry II. That Earl Thomas had been the son of Jack Builder, the architect of Kingsbridge Cathedral, and Lady Aliena of Shiring—a near-legendary couple whose story was told, on long winter evenings, along with the heroic tales of Charlemagne and Roland. With such ancestry, Sir Gerald could not have his land confiscated by any monk, he bellowed, least of all that old woman Prior Anthony. When he started shouting, a look of tired resignation came over Maud's face, and she turned away—though Merthin had heard her mutter: "The Lady Aliena had a brother, Richard, who was no good for anything but fighting."

Prior Anthony might be an old woman, but he had at least been man enough to complain about Sir Gerald's unpaid debts. He had gone to Gerald's overlord, the present earl of Shiring, who happened also to be Gerald's second cousin. Earl Roland had summoned Gerald to Kingsbridge today to meet with the prior and work out some resolution. Hence Father's bad temper.

Then Father was robbed.

He discovered the loss after the All Hallows service. Merthin had enjoyed the drama: the darkness, the weird noises, the music beginning so quietly and then swelling until it seemed to fill the huge church, and finally the slow illumination of candles. He had also noticed, as the lights began to come on, that some people had been taking advantage of the darkness to commit minor sins for which they could now be forgiven: he had seen two monks hastily stop kissing, and a sly merchant remove his hand from the plump breast of a smiling woman who appeared to be someone else's wife. Merthin was still in an excited mood when they returned to the hospital.

As they were waiting for the nuns to serve breakfast, a kitchen boy passed through the room and went up the stairs carrying a tray with a big jug of ale and a platter of hot salt beef. Mother said grumpily: "I would think your relative, the earl, might invite us to breakfast with him in his private room. After all, your grandmother was sister to his grandfather."

Father replied: "If you don't want porridge, we can go to the tavern."

Merthin's ears pricked up. He liked tavern breakfasts of new bread and salt butter. But Mother said: "We can't afford it."

"We can," Father said, feeling for his purse; and that was when he realized it was gone.

At first he looked around the floor, as if it might have fallen; then he noticed the cut ends of the leather thong, and he roared with indignation. Everyone looked at him except Mother, who turned away, and Merthin heard her mutter: "That was all the money we had."

Father glared accusingly at the other guests in the hospital. The long scar that ran from his right temple to his left eye seemed to darken with rage. The room went quiet with tension: an angry knight was dangerous, even one who was evidently down on his luck.

Then Mother said: "You were robbed in the church, no doubt."

Merthin guessed that must be right. In the darkness, people had been stealing more than kisses.

"Sacrilege, too!" said Father.

"I expect it happened when you picked up that little girl," Mother went on. Her face was twisted, as if she had swallowed something bitter. "The thief probably reached around your waist from behind."

"He must be found!" Father roared.

The young monk called Godwyn spoke up. "I'm very sorry this has happened, Sir Gerald," he said. "I will go and tell John Constable right away. He can look out for a poor townsman who has suddenly become rich."

That seemed to Merthin a very unpromising plan. There were thousands of townspeople and hundreds more visitors. The constable could not observe them all.

But Father was slightly mollified. "The rogue shall hang!" he said in a voice a little less loud.

"And, meanwhile, perhaps you and Lady Maud, and your sons, would do us the honor of sitting at the table that is being set up in front of the altar," Godwyn said smoothly.

Father grunted. He was pleased, Merthin knew, to be accorded higher status than the mass of guests, who would eat sitting on the floor where they had slept.

The moment of potential violence passed, and Merthin relaxed a little; but, as the four of them took their seats, he wondered anxiously what would happen to the family now. His father was a brave soldier—everyone said that. Sir Gerald had fought for the old king at Boroughbridge, where a Lancashire rebel's sword had given him the scar on his forehead. But he was unlucky. Some knights came home from battle with booty: plundered jewels, a cartload of costly Flemish cloth and Italian silk, or the beloved father of a noble family who could be ransomed for a thousand pounds. Sir Gerald never seemed to get much loot. But he still had to buy weapons, armor, and an expensive warhorse to enable him to do his duty and serve the king; and somehow the rents from his lands were never enough. So, against Mother's will, he had started to borrow.

The kitchen hands brought in a steaming cauldron. Sir Gerald's family was served first. The porridge was made with barley and flavored with rosemary and salt. Ralph, who did not understand the family crisis, started to talk excitedly about the All Hallows service, but the glum silence in which his comments were received shut him up.

When the porridge was eaten, Merthin went to the altar. Behind it he had stashed his bow and arrows. People would hesitate to steal something from an altar. They might overcome their fears, if the reward were tempting enough; but a homemade bow was not much of a prize; and, sure enough, it was still there.

He was proud of it. It was small, of course: to bend a full-size, six-foot bow took all the strength of a grown man. Merthin's was four feet long, and slender, but in other respects it was just like the standard English longbow that had killed so many Scots mountain men, Welsh rebels, and French knights in armor.

Father had not previously commented on the bow, and now he looked at it as if seeing it for the first time. "Where did you get the stave?" he said. "They're costly."

"Not this one—it's too short. A bowyer gave it me."

Father nodded. "Apart from that it's a perfect stave," he said. "It's taken from the inside of the yew, where the sapwood meets the heartwood." He pointed to the two different colors.

"I know," Merthin said eagerly. He did not often get the chance to impress his father. "The stretchy sapwood is best for the front of the bow, because it pulls back to its original shape; and the hard heartwood is best for the inside of the curve, because it pushes back when the bow is bent inwards."

"Exactly," Father said. He handed the bow back. "But remember, this is not a nobleman's weapon. Knights' sons do not become archers. Give it to some peasant boy."

Merthin was crestfallen. "I haven't even tried it yet!"

Mother intervened. "Let them play," she said. "They're only boys."

"True," Father said, losing interest. "I wonder if those monks would bring us a jug of ale?"

"Off you go," Mother said. "Merthin, take care of your brother."

Father grunted. "More likely to be the other way around."

Merthin was stung. Father had no idea what went on. Merthin could look after himself, but Ralph on his own would get into fights. However, Merthin knew better than to take issue with his father in this mood, and he left the hospital without saying anything. Ralph trailed behind him.

It was a clear, cold November day, and the sky was roofed with high pale-gray cloud. They left the cathedral close and walked down the main street, passing Fish Lane, Leather Yard, and Cookshop Street. At the bottom of the hill they crossed the wooden bridge over the river, leaving the old city for the suburb called Newtown. Here the streets of timber houses ran between pastures and gardens. Merthin led the way to a meadow called Lovers' Field. There, the town constable and his deputies had set up butts—targets for archery. Shooting practice after church was compulsory for all men, by order of the king.

Enforcement was not much needed: it was no hardship to loose off a few arrows on a Sunday morning, and a hundred or so of the young men of the town were lining up for their turn, watched by women, children, and men who considered themselves too old, or too dignified, to be archers. Some had their own weapons. For those too poor to afford a bow, John Constable had inexpensive practice bows made of ash or hazel.

It was like a feast day. Dick Brewer was selling tankards of ale from a barrel on a cart, and Betty Baxter's four adolescent daughters were walking around with trays of spiced buns for sale. The wealthier townspeople were done up in fur caps and new shoes, and even the poorer women had dressed their hair and trimmed their cloaks with new braid.

Merthin was the only child carrying a bow, and he immediately attracted the attention of other children. They crowded around him and Ralph, the boys asking envious questions, the girls looking admiring or disdainful according to temperament. One of the girls said: "How did you know how to make it?"

Merthin recognized her: she had stood near him in the cathedral. She was about a year younger than himself, he thought, and she wore a dress and cloak of expensive, close-woven wool. Merthin usually found girls of his own age tiresome: they giggled a lot and refused to take anything seriously. But this one looked at him and his bow with a frank curiosity that he liked. "I just guessed," he said.

"That's clever. Does it work?"

"I haven't tried it. What's your name?"

"Caris, from the Wooler family. Who are you?"

"Merthin. My father is Sir Gerald." Merthin pushed back the hood of his cape, reached inside it, and took out a coiled bowstring.

"Why do you keep the string in your hat?"

"So it won't get wet if there's rain. It's what the real archers do." He attached the twine to the notches at either end of the stave, bending the bow slightly so that the tension would hold the string in place.

"Are you going to shoot at the targets?"

"Yes."

Another boy said: "They won't let you."

Merthin looked at him. He was about twelve, tall and thin with big hands and feet. Merthin had seen him last night in the priory hospital with his family: his name was Philemon. He had been hanging around the monks, asking questions and helping to serve supper. "Of course they'll let me," Merthin told him. "Why shouldn't they?"

"Because you're too young."

"That's stupid." Even as he spoke, Merthin knew he should not be so sure: adults often were stupid. But Philemon's assumption of superior knowledge irritated him, especially after he had shown confidence in front of Caris.

He left the children and walked over to a group of men waiting to use a target. He recognized one of them: an exceptionally tall, broad-shouldered man called Mark Webber. Mark noticed the bow and spoke to Merthin in a slow, amiable voice. "Where did you get that?"

"I made it," Merthin said proudly.

"Look at this, Elfric," Mark said to his neighbor. "He's made a nice job of it."

Elfric was a brawny man with a sly look. He gave the bow a cursory glance. "It's too small," he said dismissively. "That'll never fire an arrow to penetrate a French knight's armor."

"Perhaps not," Mark said mildly. "But I expect the lad's got a year or two to go before he has to fight the French."

John Constable called out: "We're ready, let's get started. Mark Webber, you're first." The giant stepped up to the line. He picked up a stout bow and tested it, bending the thick wood effortlessly.

The constable noticed Merthin for the first time. "No boys," he said.

"Why not?" Merthin protested.

"Never mind why not, just get out of the way."

Merthin heard some of the other children snigger. "There's no reason for it!" he said indignantly.

"I don't have to give reasons to children," John said. "All right, Mark, take your shot."

Merthin was mortified. The oily Philemon had proved him wrong in front of everyone. He turned away from the targets.

"I told you so," said Philemon.

"Oh, shut up and go away."

"You can't make me go away," said Philemon, who was six inches taller than Merthin.

Ralph put in: "I could, though."

Merthin sighed. Ralph was unfailingly loyal, but he did not see that for him to fight Philemon would only make Merthin look like a weakling as well as a fool.

"I'm leaving anyway," said Philemon. "I'm going to help Brother Godwyn." He walked off.

The rest of the children began to drift away, seeking other curiosities. Caris said to Merthin: "You could go somewhere else to try the bow." She was obviously keen to see what would happen.

Merthin looked around. "But where?" If he was seen shooting unsupervised, the bow might be taken from him.

"We could go into the forest."

Merthin was surprised. Children were forbidden to go into the forest. Outlaws hid there, men and women who lived by stealing. Children might be stripped of their clothes, or made into slaves, and there were worse dangers that parents only hinted at. Even if they escaped such perils, the children were liable to be flogged by their fathers for breaking the rule.

But Caris did not seem to be afraid, and Merthin was reluctant to appear less bold than she. Besides, the constable's curt dismissal had made him feel defiant. "All right," he said. "But we'll have to make sure no one sees us."

She had the answer to that. "I know a way."

She walked toward the river. Merthin and Ralph followed. A small three-legged dog tagged along. "What's your dog's name?" Merthin asked Caris.

"He's not mine," she said. "But I gave him a piece of moldy bacon, and now I can't shake him off."

They walked along the muddy bank of the river, past warehouses and wharves and barges. Merthin covertly studied this girl who had so effortlessly become the leader. She had a square, determined face, neither pretty nor ugly, and there was mischief in her eyes, which were a greenish color with brown flecks. Her light brown hair was done in two plaits, as was the fashion among affluent women. Her clothes were costly, but she wore practical leather boots rather than the embroidered fabric shoes preferred by noble ladies.

She turned away from the river and led them through a timber yard, and suddenly they were in scrubby woodland. Merthin felt a pang of unease. Now that he was in the forest, where there might be an outlaw lurking behind any oak tree, he regretted his bravado; but he would be ashamed to back out.

They walked on, looking for a clearing big enough for archery. Suddenly Caris spoke in a conspiratorial voice. "You see that big holly bush?"

"Yes."

"As soon as we're past it, crouch down with me and keep silent."

"Why?"

"You'll see."

A moment later Merthin, Ralph, and Caris squatted behind the bush. The three-legged dog sat with them and looked hopefully at Caris. Ralph began to ask a question, but Caris hushed him.

A minute later a little girl came by. Caris jumped out and grabbed her. The girl screamed.

"Be quiet!" Caris said. "We're not far from the road, and we don't want to be heard. Why are you following us?"

"You've got my dog, and he won't come back!" the child sobbed.

"I know you, I met you in church this morning," Caris said to her in a softer voice. "All right, there's nothing to cry about, we aren't going to do you any harm. What's your name?"

"Gwenda."

"And the dog?"

"Hop." Gwenda picked up the dog, and he licked her tears.

"Well, you've got him now. You'd better come with us, in case he runs off again. Besides, you might not be able to find your way back to town on your own."

They went on. Merthin said: "What has eight arms and eleven legs?"

"I give up," Ralph said immediately. He always did.

"I know," said Caris with a grin. "It's us. Four children and the dog." She laughed. "That's good."

Merthin was pleased. People did not always get his jokes; girls almost never did. A moment later he heard Gwenda explaining it to Ralph: "Two arms, and two arms, and two arms, and two arms makes eight," she said. "Two legs . . ."

They saw no one, which was good. The small number of people who had legitimate business in the forest—woodcutters, charcoal burners, iron smelters—would not be working today, and it would be unusual to see an aristocratic hunting party on a Sunday. Anyone they met was likely to be an outlaw. But the chances were slim. It was a big forest, stretching for many miles. Merthin had never traveled far enough to see the end of it.

They came to a wide clearing and Merthin said: "This will do."

There was an oak tree with a broad trunk on the far edge, about fifty feet away. Merthin stood side-on to the target, as he had seen the men do. He took out one of his three arrows and fitted the notched end to the bowstring. The arrows had been as difficult to make as the bow. The wood was ash, and they had goose-feather flights. He had not been able to get iron for the points, so he had simply sharpened the ends then scorched the wood to harden it. He sighted on the tree, then pulled back on the bowstring. It took a great effort. He released the arrow.

It fell to the ground well short of the target. Hop the dog scampered across the clearing to fetch it.

Merthin was taken aback. He had expected the arrow to go winging through the air and embed its point in the tree. He realized that he had not bent the bow sufficiently.

He tried the bow in his right hand and the arrow in his left. He was unusual in this respect, that he was neither right-handed nor left-handed, but a mixture. With the second arrow, he pulled on the bowstring and pushed the bow with all his might, and succeeded in bending them farther than before. This time, the arrow almost reached the tree.

For his third shot he aimed the bow upward, hoping the arrow would fly through the air in an arc and come down into the trunk. But he overcompensated, and the arrow went into the branches, and fell to the ground amid a flurry of dry brown leaves.

Merthin was embarrassed. Archery was more difficult than he had imagined. The bow was probably all right, he guessed: the problem was his own proficiency, or lack of it.

Once again, Caris seemed not to notice his discomfiture. "Let me have a go," she said.

"Girls can't shoot," Ralph said, and he snatched the bow from Merthin. Standing sideways-on to the target, as Merthin had, he did not shoot straightaway, but flexed the bow several times, getting the feel of it. Like Merthin, he found it harder than he had at first expected, but after a few moments he seemed to get the hang of it.

Hop had dropped all three arrows at Gwenda's feet, and now the little girl picked them up and handed them to Ralph.

He took aim without drawing the bow, sighting the arrow at the tree trunk, while there was no pressure on his arms. Merthin realized he should have done the same. Why did these things come so naturally to Ralph, who could never answer a riddle? Ralph drew the bow, not effortlessly but with a fluid motion, seeming to take the strain with his thighs. He released the arrow and it hit the trunk of the oak tree, sinking an inch or more into the soft outer wood. Ralph laughed triumphantly.

Hop scampered after the arrow. When he reached the tree, he stopped, baffled.

Ralph was drawing the bow again. Merthin realized what he was intending to do. "Don't—" he said, but he was a moment too late. Ralph shot at the dog. The arrow hit the back of its neck and sunk in. Hop fell forward and lay twitching.

Gwenda screamed. Caris said: "Oh, no!" The two girls ran to the dog.

Ralph was grinning. "What about that?" he said proudly.

"You shot her dog!" Merthin said angrily.

"Doesn't matter—it only had three legs."

"The little girl was fond of it, you idiot. Look at her crying."

"You're just jealous because you can't shoot." Something caught Ralph's eye. With a smooth movement he notched another arrow, swept the bow around in an arc, and fired while it was still moving. Merthin did not see what he was shooting at until the arrow met its target, and a fat hare jumped into the air with the shaft sticking deep into its hindquarters.

Merthin could not hide his admiration. Even with practice, not everyone could hit a running hare. Ralph had a natural gift. Merthin *was* jealous, although he would never admit it. He longed to be a knight, bold and strong, and fight for the king as his father did; and it dismayed him when he turned out to be hopeless at things such as archery.

Ralph found a stone and crushed the hare's skull, putting it out of its misery.

Merthin knelt beside the two girls and Hop. The dog was not breathing. Caris gently drew the arrow out of its neck and handed it to Merthin. There was no gush of blood: Hop was dead.

For a moment no one spoke. In the silence, they heard a man shout.

Merthin sprang to his feet, heart thudding. He heard another shout, a different voice: there was more than one person. Both sounded aggressive and angry. Some kind of fight was going on. He was terrified, and so were the others. As they stood frozen, listening, they heard another sound, the noise made by a man running headlong through woodland, snapping fallen branches, flattening saplings, trampling dead leaves.

He was coming their way.

Caris spoke first. "The bush," she said, pointing to a big cluster of evergreen shrubs—probably the home of the hare Ralph had shot, Merthin thought. A moment later she was flat on her belly, crawling into the thicket. Gwenda followed, cradling the body of Hop. Ralph picked up the dead hare and joined them. Merthin was on his knees when he realized that they had left a telltale arrow sticking out of the tree trunk. He dashed across the clearing, pulled it out, ran back, and dived under the bush.

They heard the man breathing before they saw him. He was panting hard as he ran, drawing in ragged lungfuls of air in a way that suggested he was almost done in. The shouts were coming from his pursuers, calling to each other: "This way—over here!" Merthin recalled that Caris had said they were not far from the road. Was the fleeing man a traveler who had been set upon by thieves?

A moment later he burst into the clearing.

He was a knight in his early twenties, with both a sword and a long dagger attached to his belt. He was well dressed, in a leather traveling tunic and high boots with turned-over tops. He stumbled and fell, rolled over, got up, then stood with his back to the oak tree, gasping for breath, and drew his weapons.

Merthin glanced at his playmates. Caris was white with fear, biting her lip. Gwenda was hugging the corpse of her dog as if that made her feel safer. Ralph looked scared, too, but he was not too frightened to pull the arrow out of the hare's rump and stuff the dead animal down the front of his tunic.

For a moment the knight seemed to stare at the bush, and Merthin felt, with terror, that he must have seen the hiding children. Or perhaps he had noticed broken branches and crushed leaves where they had pushed through the foliage. Out of the corner of his eye, Merthin saw Ralph notch an arrow to the bow.

Then the pursuers arrived. They were two men-at-arms, strongly built and thuggish-looking, carrying drawn swords. They wore distinctive two-colored tunics, the left side yellow and the right green. One had a surcoat of cheap brown wool, the other a grubby black cloak. All three men paused, catching their breath. Merthin was sure he was about to see the knight hacked to death, and he suffered a shameful impulse to burst into tears. Then, suddenly, the knight reversed his sword and offered it, hilt first, in a gesture of surrender.

The older man-at-arms, in the black cloak, stepped forward and reached out with his left hand. Warily, he took the proffered sword, handed it to his partner, then accepted the knight's dagger. Then he said: "It's not your weapons I want, Thomas Langley."

"You know me, but I don't know you," said Thomas. If he was feeling any fear, he had it well under control. "By your coats, you must be the queen's men."

The older man put the point of his sword to Thomas's throat and pushed him up against the tree. "You've got a letter."

"Instructions from the earl to the sheriff on the subject of taxes. You're welcome to read it." This was a joke. The men-at-arms were almost certainly unable to read. Thomas had a cool nerve, Merthin thought, to mock men who seemed ready to kill him.

The second man-at-arms reached under the sword of the first and grasped the wallet attached to Thomas's belt. Impatiently, he cut the belt with his sword. He threw the belt aside and opened the wallet. He took out a smaller bag made of what appeared to be oiled wool, and drew from that a sheet of parchment, rolled into a scroll and sealed with wax.

Could this fight be about nothing more than a letter? Merthin wondered. If so, what was written on the scroll? It was not likely to be routine instructions about taxes. Some terrible secret must be inscribed there.

"If you kill me," the knight said, "the murder will be witnessed by whoever is hiding in that bush."

The tableau froze for a split second. The man in the black cloak kept his sword point pressed to Thomas's throat and resisted the temptation to look over his shoulder. The one in green hesitated, then looked at the bush.

At that point, Gwenda screamed.

The man in the green surcoat raised his sword and took two long strides across the clearing to the bush. Gwenda stood up and ran, bursting out of the foliage. The man-at-arms leaped after her, reaching out to grab her.

Ralph stood up suddenly, raised the bow and drew it in one fluid motion, and shot an arrow at the man. It went through his eye and sank several inches into his head. His left hand came up, as if to grasp the arrow and pull it out; then he went limp and fell like a dropped sack of grain, hitting the ground with a thump Merthin could feel.

Ralph ran out of the bush and followed Gwenda. At the edge of his vision Merthin perceived Caris going after them. Merthin wanted to flee too, but his feet seemed stuck to the ground.

There was a shout from the other side of the clearing, and Merthin saw that Thomas had knocked aside the sword that threatened him and had drawn, from somewhere about his person, a small knife with a blade as long as a man's hand. But the man-at-arms in the black cloak was alert, and jumped back out of reach. Then he raised his sword and swung at the knight's head.

Thomas dodged aside, but not fast enough. The edge of the blade came down on his left forearm, slicing through the leather jerkin and sinking into his flesh. He roared with pain, but did not fall. With a quick motion that seemed extraordinarily graceful, he swung his right hand up and thrust the knife into his opponent's throat; then, his hand continuing in an arc, he pulled the knife sideways, severing most of the neck.

Blood came like a fountain from the man's throat. Thomas staggered back, dodging the splash. The man in black fell to the ground, his head hanging from his body by a strip.

Thomas dropped the knife from his right hand and clutched his wounded left arm. He sat on the ground, suddenly looking weak.

Merthin was alone with the wounded knight, two dead men-at-arms, and the corpse of a three-legged dog. He knew he should run after the other children, but his curiosity kept him there. Thomas now seemed harmless, he told himself.

The knight had sharp eyes. "You can come out," he called. "I'm no danger to you in this state."

Hesitantly, Merthin got to his feet and pushed his way out of the bush. He crossed the clearing and stopped several feet away from the sitting knight.

Thomas said: "If they find out you've been playing in the forest, you'll be flogged."

Merthin nodded.

"I'll keep your secret, if you'll keep mine."

Merthin nodded again. In agreeing to the bargain, he was making no concessions. None of the children would tell what they had seen. There would be untold trouble if they did. What would happen to Ralph, who had killed one of the queen's men?

"Would you be kind enough to help me bind up this wound?" said Thomas. Despite all that had happened, he spoke courteously, Merthin observed. The knight's poise was remarkable. Merthin felt he wanted to be like that when he was grown up.

At last Merthin's constricted throat managed to produce a word. "Yes."

"Pick up that broken belt, then, and wrap it around my arm, if you would."

Merthin did as he was told. Thomas's undershirt was soaked with blood, and the flesh of his arm was sliced open like something on a butcher's slab. Merthin felt a little nauseated, but he forced himself to twist the belt around Thomas's arm so that it pulled the wound closed and slowed the bleeding. He made a knot, and Thomas used his right hand to pull it tight.

Then Thomas struggled to his feet.

He looked at the dead men. "We can't bury them," he said. "I'd bleed to death before the graves were dug." Glancing at Merthin, he added: "Even with you helping me." He thought for a moment. "On the other hand, I don't want them to be discovered by some courting couple looking for a place to . . . be alone. Let's lug the guts into that bush where you were hiding. Green coat first."

They approached the body.

"One leg each," said Thomas. With his right hand he grasped the dead man's left ankle. Merthin took the other limp foot in both hands and heaved. Together they hauled the corpse into the shrubbery, next to Hop.

"That will do," said Thomas. His face was white with pain. After a moment, he bent down and pulled the arrow out of the corpse's eye. "Yours?" he said with a raised eyebrow.

Merthin took the arrow and wiped it on the ground to get rid of some of the blood and brains adhering to the shaft.

In the same way they dragged the second body across the clearing, its loosely attached head trailing behind, and left it beside the first.

Thomas picked up the two men's dropped swords and threw them into the bush with the bodies. Then he found his own weapons.

"Now," said Thomas, "I have a great favor to ask." He proffered his dagger. "Would you dig me a small hole?"

"All right." Merthin took the dagger.

"Just here, right in front of the oak tree."

"How big?"

Thomas picked up the leather wallet that had been attached to his belt. "Big enough to hide this for fifty years."

Screwing up his courage, Merthin said: "Why?"

"Dig, and I'll tell you as much of it as I can."

Merthin scratched a square on the ground and began to loosen the cold earth with the dagger, then scoop it up with his hands.

Thomas picked up the scroll and put it into the wool bag, then fastened the bag inside the wallet. "I was given this letter to deliver to the earl of Shiring," he said. "But it contains a secret so dangerous that I realized the bearer was sure to be killed, to make certain he could never speak of it. So I needed to disappear. I decided I would take sanctuary in a monastery, become a monk. I've had enough of fighting, and I've a lot of sins to repent. As soon as I went missing, the people who gave me the letter started to search for me—and I was unlucky. I was spotted in a tavern in Bristol."

"Why did the queen's men come after you?"

"She, too, would like to prevent the spread of this secret."

When Merthin's hole was eighteen inches deep, Thomas said: "That will do." He dropped the wallet inside.

Merthin shoveled the earth back into the hole on top of the wallet, and Thomas covered the freshly turned earth with leaves and twigs until it was indistinguishable from the ground around it.

"If you hear that I've died," said Thomas, "I'd like you to dig up this letter and give it to a priest. Would you do that for me?"

"All right."

"Until that happens, you must tell no one. While they know I've got the letter, but they don't know where it is, they'll be afraid to do anything. But if you tell the secret, two things will happen. First, they will kill me. Then they will kill you."

Merthin was aghast. It seemed unfair that he should be in so much danger just because he helped a man by digging a hole.

"I'm sorry to scare you," said Thomas. "But, then, it's not entirely my fault. After all, I didn't ask you to come here."

"No." Merthin wished with all his heart that he had obeyed his mother's orders and stayed out of the forest.

"I'm going to return to the road. Why don't you go back the way you came? I bet you'll find your friends waiting somewhere not far from here."

Merthin turned to go.

"What's your name?" the knight called after him.

"Merthin, son of Sir Gerald."

"Really?" Thomas said, as if he knew Father. "Well, not a word, even to him."

Merthin nodded and left.

When he had gone fifty yards he vomited. After that he felt slightly better.

As Thomas had predicted, the others were waiting for him, right at the edge of the wood, near the timber yard. They crowded around him, touching him as if to make sure he was all right, looking relieved yet ashamed, as if they were guilty about having left him. They were all shaken, even Ralph. "That man," he said. "The one I shot. Was he badly hurt?"

"He's dead," Merthin said. He showed Ralph the arrow, still stained with blood.

"Did you pull it out of his eye?"

Merthin would have liked to say he had, but he decided to tell the truth. "The knight pulled it out."

"What happened to the other man-at-arms?"

"The knight cut his throat. Then we hid the bodies in the bush."

"And he just let you go?"

"Yes." Merthin said nothing about the buried letter.

"We have to keep this secret," Caris urged. "There will be terrible trouble if anyone finds out."

Ralph said: "I'll never tell."

"We should swear an oath," Caris said.

They stood in a little ring. Caris stuck out her arm so that her hand was in the center of the circle. Merthin placed his hand over hers. Her skin was soft and warm. Ralph added his hand, then Gwenda did the same, and they swore by the blood of Jesus.

Then they walked back into the town.

Archery practice was over, and it was time for the midday meal. As they crossed the bridge, Merthin said to Ralph: "When I grow up, I want to be like that knight—always courteous, never frightened, deadly in a fight."

"Me, too," said Ralph. "Deadly."

In the old city, Merthin felt an irrational sense of surprise that normal life was going on all around: the sound of babies crying, the smell of roasting meat, the sight of men drinking ale outside taverns.

Caris stopped outside a big house on the main street, just opposite the entrance to the priory precincts. She put an arm around Gwenda's shoulders and said: "My dog at home has had puppies. Do you want to see them?"

Gwenda still looked frightened and close to tears, but she nodded emphatically. "Yes, please."

That was clever as well as kind, Merthin thought. The puppies would be a comfort to the little girl—and a distraction, too. When she returned to her family, she would talk about the puppies and be less likely to speak of going into the forest.

They said good-bye, and the girls went into the house. Merthin found himself wondering when he would see Caris again.

Then his other troubles came back to him. What was his father going to do about his debts? Merthin and Ralph turned into the cathedral close, Ralph still carrying the bow and the dead hare. The place was quiet.

The guesthouse was empty but for a few sick people. A nun said to them: "Your father is in the church, with the earl of Shiring."

They went into the great cathedral. Their parents were in the vestibule. Mother was sitting at the foot of a pillar, on the outjutting corner where the round column met the square base. In the cold light that came through the tall windows, her face was still and serene, almost as if she were carved of the same gray stone as the pillar against which she leaned her head. Father stood beside her, his broad shoulders slumped in an attitude of resignation. Earl Roland faced them. He was older than Father, but with his black hair and vigorous manner he seemed more youthful. Prior Anthony stood beside the earl.

The two boys hung back at the door, but Mother beckoned them. "Come here," she said. "Earl Roland has helped us come to an arrangement with Prior Anthony that solves all our problems."

Father grunted, as if he was not as grateful as she for what the earl had done. "And the priory gets my lands," he said. "There'll be nothing for you two to inherit."

"We're going to live here, in Kingsbridge," Mother went on brightly. "We'll be corrodiaries of the priory."

Merthin said: "What's a corrodiary?"

"It means the monks will provide us with a house to live in and two meals a day, for the rest of our lives. Isn't that wonderful?"

Merthin could tell that she did not really think it was wonderful. She was pretending to be pleased. Father was clearly ashamed to have lost his lands. There was more than a hint of disgrace in this, Merthin realized.

Father addressed the earl. "What about my boys?"

Earl Roland turned and looked at them. "The big one looks promising," he said. "Did you kill that hare, lad?"

"Yes, Lord," Ralph said proudly. "Shot it with an arrow."

"He can come to me as a squire in a few years' time," the earl said briskly. "We'll teach him to be a knight."

Father looked pleased.

Merthin felt bewildered. Big decisions were being made too quickly. He was outraged that his younger brother should be so favored while no mention was made of himself. "That's not fair!" he burst out. "I want to be a knight, too!"

His mother said: "No!"

"But I made the bow!"

Father gave a sigh of exasperation and looked disgusted.

"You made the bow, did you, little one?" the earl said, and his face showed disdain. "In that case, you shall be apprenticed to a carpenter."

3

Caris's home was a luxurious wood-frame building with stone floors and a stone chimney. There were three separate rooms on the ground floor: the hall with the big dining table, the small parlor where Papa could discuss business privately, and the kitchen at the back. When Caris and Gwenda walked in, the house was full of the mouthwatering smell of a ham boiling.

Caris led Gwenda through the hall and up the internal staircase.

"Where are the puppies?" said Gwenda.

"I want to see my mother first," Caris replied. "She's ill."

They went into the front bedroom, where Mama lay on the carved wooden bedstead. She was small and frail: Caris was already the same height. Mama looked paler than usual, and her hair was not yet dressed, so it stuck to her damp cheeks. "How are you feeling?" Caris said.

"A little weak, today." The effort of speaking made Mama breathless.

Caris felt a familiar, painful jumble of anxiety and helplessness. Her mother had been ill for a year. It had started with pains in her joints. Soon she had ulcers inside her mouth and unaccountable bruises on her body. She had felt too weak to do anything. Last week she had caught a cold. Now she was running a fever and had trouble in catching her breath.

"Is there anything you need?" Caris asked.

"No, thank you."

It was the usual answer, but Caris felt maddened by powerlessness each time she heard it. "Should I fetch Mother Cecilia?" The prioress of Kingsbridge was the only person able to bring Mama some comfort. She had an extract of poppies that she mixed with honey and warm wine that eased the pain for a while. Caris regarded Cecilia as better than an angel.

"No need, dear," Mama said. "How was the All Hallows service?"

Caris noticed how pale her mother's lips were. "Scary," she said.

Mama paused, resting, then said: "What have you been doing this morning?"

"Watching the archery." Caris held her breath, frightened that Mama might guess her guilty secret, as she often did.

But Mama looked at Gwenda. "Who is your little friend?"

"Gwenda. I've brought her to see the puppies."

"That's lovely." Mama suddenly looked tired. She closed her eyes and turned her head aside.

The girls crept out quietly.

Gwenda was looking shocked. "What's wrong with her?"

"A wasting disease." Caris hated to talk about it. Her mother's illness gave her the unnerving feeling that nothing was certain, anything could happen, there was no safety in the world. It was even more frightening than the fight they had witnessed in the forest. If she thought about what might happen, and the possibility that her mother might die, she suffered a panicky fluttering sensation in her chest that made her want to scream.

The middle bedroom was used in summer by the Italians, wool buyers from Florence and Prato who came to do business with Papa. Now it was empty. The puppies were in the back bedroom, which belonged to Caris and her sister, Alice. They were seven weeks old, ready to leave their mother, who was growing impatient with them. Gwenda gave a sigh of joy and immediately got down on the floor with them.

Caris picked up the smallest of the litter, a lively female, always going off on her own to explore the world. "This is the one I'm going to keep," she said. "She's called Scrap." Holding the little dog soothed her, and helped her forget about the things that troubled her.

The other four clambered all over Gwenda, sniffing her and chewing her dress. She picked up an ugly brown dog with a long muzzle and eyes set too close together. "I like this one," she said. The puppy curled up in her lap.

Caris said: "Would you like to keep him?"

Tears came to Gwenda's eyes. "Could I?"

"We're allowed to give them away."

"Really?"

"Papa doesn't want any more dogs. If you like him, you can have him."

"Oh, yes," Gwenda said in a whisper. "Yes, please."

"What will you name him?"

"Something that reminds me of Hop. Perhaps I'll call him Skip."

"That's a good name." Skip had already gone to sleep in Gwenda's lap, Caris saw.

The two girls sat quietly with the dogs. Caris thought about the boys they had met, the little red-haired one with the golden brown eyes and his tall, handsome younger brother. What had made her take them into the forest? It was not the first time she had yielded to a stupid impulse. It tended to happen when someone in authority ordered her not to do something. Her aunt Petranilla was a great rule-maker. "Don't feed that cat, we'll never get rid of it. No ball games in the house. Stay away from that boy, his family are peasants." Rules that constrained her behavior seemed to drive Caris crazy.

But she had never done something this foolish. She felt shaky when she thought of it. Two men had died. But what might have happened was worse. The four children might have been killed, too.

She wondered what the fight had been about, and why the men-at-arms had been chasing the knight. Obviously it was not a simple robbery. They had spoken about a letter. But Merthin had said no more about that. Probably he had learned nothing further. It was just another of the mysteries of adult life.

Caris had liked Merthin. His boring brother, Ralph, was just like every other boy in Kingsbridge, boastful and aggressive and stupid, but Merthin seemed different. He had intrigued her right from the start.

Two new friends in one day, she thought, looking at Gwenda. The little girl was not pretty. She had dark brown eyes set close together above a beaky nose. She had picked a dog that looked a bit like her, Caris realized with amusement. Gwenda's clothes were old, and must have been worn by many children before her. Gwenda was calmer now. She no longer looked as if she might burst into tears at any moment. She, too, had been soothed by the puppies.

There was a familiar lopsided tread in the hall below, and a moment later a voice bellowed: "Bring me a flagon of ale, for the love of the saints, I've got a thirst like a cart horse."

"It's my father," Caris said. "Come and meet him." Seeing that Gwenda looked anxious, she added: "Don't worry, he always shouts like that, but he's really nice."

The girls went downstairs with their puppies. "What's happened to all my servants?" Papa roared. "Have they run away to join the fairy folk?" He came stomping out of the kitchen, trailing his twisted right leg as always, carrying a big wooden cup slopping over with ale. "Hello, my little buttercup," he said to Caris in a softer voice. He sat on the big chair at the head of the table and took a long draft from the cup. "That's better," he said, wiping his straggly beard with his sleeve. He noticed Gwenda. "A little daisy to go with my buttercup?" he said. "What's your name?"

"Gwenda, from Wigleigh, my lord," she said, awestruck.

"I gave her a puppy," Caris explained.

"That's a good idea!" Papa said. "Puppies need affection, and no one can love a puppy the way a little girl does."

On the stool beside the table Caris saw a cloak of scarlet cloth. It had to be imported, for English dyers did not know how to achieve such a bright red. Following her eye, Papa said: "It's for your mother. She's always wanted a coat of Italian red. I'm hoping it will encourage her to get well enough to wear it."

Caris touched it. The wool was soft and close-woven, as only the Italians could make it. "It's beautiful," she said.

Aunt Petranilla entered from the street. She bore some resemblance to Papa, but was purse-mouthed where he was hearty. She was more like her other brother, Anthony, the prior of Kingsbridge: they were both tall, imposing figures, whereas Papa was short, barrel-chested, and lame.

Caris disliked Petranilla. She was clever as well as mean, a deadly combination in an adult: Caris was never able to outwit her. Gwenda sensed Caris's dislike, and looked apprehensively at the newcomer. Only Papa was pleased to see her. "Come in, sister," he said. "Where are all my servants?"

"I can't think why you imagine I should know that, having just come from my own house at the other end of the street, but if I had to guess, Edmund, I should say that your cook is in the henhouse, hoping to find an egg to make you a pudding, and your maid is upstairs, helping your wife to a close stool, which she generally requires about midday. As for your apprentices, I hope they are both on guard duty at the warehouse by the riverside, making sure that no holiday revelers take it into their drunken heads to light a bonfire within a spark's fly of your wool store."

She often spoke like this, giving a little sermon in answer to a simple question. Her manner was supercilious, as always, but Papa did not mind, or pretended not to. "My remarkable sister," he said. "You're the one who inherited our father's wisdom."

Petranilla turned to the girls. "Our father was descended from Tom Builder, the stepfather and mentor of Jack Builder, architect of Kingsbridge Cathedral," she said. "Father vowed to give his firstborn to God but, unfortunately, his firstborn was a girl—me. He named me after Saint Petranilla—who was the daughter of Saint Peter, as I'm sure you know—and he prayed for a boy next time. But his first son was born deformed, and he did not want to give God a flawed gift, so he brought Edmund up to take over the wool business. Happily, his third child was our brother Anthony, a well behaved and God-fearing child, who entered the monastery as a boy and is now, we are all proud to say, the prior."

She would have become a priest, had she been a man, but as it was she had done the next best thing and brought up her son, Godwyn, to be a monk at the priory. Like Grandfather Wooler, she had given a child to God. Caris had always felt sorry for Godwyn, her older cousin, for having Petranilla as a mother.

Petranilla noticed the red coat. "Whose is this?" she said. "It's the most expensive Italian cloth!"

"I bought it for Rose," said Papa.

Petranilla stared at him for a moment. Caris could tell she thought he was a fool to buy such a coat for a woman who had not left the house for a year. But all she said was: "You're very good to her," which might have been a compliment or not.

Father did not care. "Go up and see her," he urged. "You'll cheer her up."

Caris doubted that, but Petranilla suffered no such misgivings, and she went up the stairs.

Caris's sister, Alice, came in from the street. She was eleven, a year older than Caris. She stared at Gwenda and said: "Who's she?"

"My new friend Gwenda," said Caris. "She's going to take a puppy."

"But she's got the one I wanted!" Alice protested.

She had not said that before. "Ooh—you never picked one!" Caris said, outraged. "You're just saying that to be mean."

"Why should she have one of our puppies?"

Papa intervened. "Now, now," he said. "We've got more puppies than we need."

"Caris should have asked me which one I wanted first!"

"Yes, she should," Papa said, even though he knew perfectly well that Alice was only making trouble. "Don't do it again, Caris."

"Yes, Papa."

The cook came in from the kitchen with jugs and cups. When Caris was learning to talk she had called the cook Tutty, no one knew why, but the name had stuck. Papa said: "Thank you, Tutty. Sit at the table, girls." Gwenda hesitated, not sure if she was invited, but Caris nodded at her, knowing that Papa intended her to be included—he generally asked everyone within his range of vision to come to dinner.

Tutty refilled Papa's cup with ale, then gave Alice, Caris, and Gwenda ale mixed with water. Gwenda drank all of hers immediately, with relish, and Caris guessed she did not often get ale: poor people drank cider made from crab apples.

Next, the cook put in front of each of them a thick slice of rye bread a foot square. Gwenda picked hers up to eat it, and Caris realized she had never dined at a table before. "Wait," she said quietly, and Gwenda put the bread down again. Tutty brought in the ham on a board and a dish of cabbage. Papa took a big knife and cut slices off the ham, piling it on their bread trenchers. Gwenda stared big-eyed at the quantity of meat she was given. Caris spooned cabbage leaves on top of the ham.

The chambermaid, Elaine, came hurrying down the stairs. "The mistress seems worse," she said. "Mistress Petranilla says we should send for Mother Cecilia."

"Then run to the priory and beg her to come," Papa said.

The maid hurried off.

"Eat up, children," said Papa, and he speared a slice of hot ham with his knife; but Caris could see that the dinner now had no relish for him, and he seemed to be looking at something far away.

Gwenda ate some cabbage and whispered: "This is food from Heaven." Caris tried it. The cabbage was cooked with ginger. Gwenda had probably never tasted ginger: only rich people could afford it.

Petranilla came down, put some ham on a wooden platter, and took it up for Mama; but she came back a few moments later with the food untouched. She sat at the table to eat it herself, and the cook brought her a bread trencher. "When I was a girl, we were the only family in Kingsbridge who had meat for dinner every day," she said. "Except on fast days—my father was very devout. He was the first wool merchant in town to deal directly with the Italians. Everyone does now—although my brother Edmund is still the most important."

Caris had lost her appetite, and she had to chew for a long time before she could swallow. At last Mother Cecilia arrived, a small, vital woman with a reassuringly bossy manner. With her was Sister Juliana, a simple person with a warm heart. Caris felt better as she watched them climb the stairs, a chirpy sparrow with a hen waddling behind. They would wash Mama in rose water to cool her fever, and the fragrance would lift her spirits.

Tutty brought in apples and cheese. Papa peeled an apple absentmindedly with his knife. Caris remembered how, when she was younger, he used to feed her peeled slices then eat the skin himself.

Sister Juliana came downstairs, a worried look on her pudgy face. "The prioress wants Brother Joseph to come and see Mistress Rose," she said. Joseph was the senior physician at the monastery: he had trained with the masters at Oxford. "I'll just go and fetch him," Juliana said, and she ran out through the door to the street.

Papa put his peeled apple down uneaten.

Caris said: "What is going to happen?"

"I don't know, buttercup. Will it rain? How many sacks of wool do the Florentines need? Will the sheep catch a murrain? Is the baby a girl, or a boy with a twisted leg? We never know, do we? That's . . ." He looked away. "That's what makes it so hard."

He gave her the apple. Caris gave it to Gwenda, who ate it entire, core and pips, too.

Brother Joseph arrived a few minutes later with a young assistant whom Caris recognized as Saul Whitehead, so called because his hair—what little he had left after his monkish haircut—was ash blond.

Cecilia and Juliana came downstairs, no doubt to make room for the two men in the small bedroom. Cecilia sat at the table, but did not eat. She had a small face with sharp features: a little pointed nose, bright eyes, a chin like the prow of a boat. She looked with curiosity at Gwenda. "Well, now," she said brightly, "who is this little girl, and does she love Jesus and His Holy Mother?"

Gwenda said: "I'm Gwenda, I'm Caris's friend." She looked anxiously at Caris, as if she feared it might have been presumptuous of her to claim friendship.

Caris said: "Will the Virgin Mary make my mama better?"

Cecilia raised her eyebrows. "Such a direct question. I could have guessed you're Edmund's daughter."

"Everyone prays to her, but not everyone gets well," Caris said.

"And do you know why that is?"

"Perhaps she never helps anyone, and it's just that the strong people get well and the weak don't."

"Now, now, don't be silly," said Papa. "Everyone knows the Holy Mother helps us."

"That's all right," Cecilia told him. "It's normal for children to ask questions—especially the bright ones. Caris, the saints are always powerful, but some prayers are more effective than others. Do you understand that?"

Caris nodded reluctantly, feeling not convinced so much as outwitted.

"She must come to our school," Cecilia said. The nuns had a school for the daughters of the nobility and of the more prosperous townspeople. The monks ran a separate school for boys.

Papa looked stubborn. "Rose has taught both girls their letters," he said. "And Caris knows her numbers as well as I do—she helps me in the business."

"She should learn more than that. Surely you don't want her to spend her life as your servant?"

Petranilla put in: "She has no need of book learning. She will marry extremely well. There will be crowds of suitors for both sisters. Sons of merchants, even sons of knights will be eager to marry into this family. But Caris is a willful child: we must take care she doesn't throw herself away on some penniless minstrel boy."

Caris noticed that Petranilla did not anticipate trouble with obedient Alice, who would probably marry whomever they picked for her.

Cecilia said: "God might call Caris to his service."

Papa said grumpily: "God has already called two from this family—my brother and my nephew. I'd have thought He would be satisfied by now."

Cecilia looked at Caris. "What do you think?" she said. "Will you be a wool merchant, a knight's wife, or a nun?"

The idea of being a nun horrified Caris. She would have to obey someone else's orders every hour of the day. It would be like remaining a child all your life, and having Petranilla for a mother. Being the wife of a knight, or of anyone else, seemed almost as bad, for women had to obey their husbands. Helping Papa, then perhaps taking over the business when he was too old, was the least unattractive option, but on the other hand it was not exactly her dream. "I don't want to be any of those," she said.

"Is there something you would like?" Cecilia asked.

There was, although Caris had not told anyone before, in fact had not fully realized it until now; but the ambition seemed fully formed, and suddenly she knew without doubt that it was her destiny. "I'm going to be a doctor," she said.

There was a moment of silence, then they all laughed.

Caris flushed, not knowing what was so funny.

Papa took pity and said: "Only men can be doctors. Didn't you know that, buttercup?"

Caris was bewildered. She turned to Cecilia. "But what about you?"

"I'm not a physician," Cecilia said. "We nuns care for the sick, of course, but we follow the instructions of trained men. The monks who have studied under the masters understand the humors of the body, the way they go out of balance in sickness, and how to bring them back to their correct proportions for good health. They know which vein to bleed for migraine, leprosy, or breathlessness; where to cup and cauterize; whether to poultice or bathe."

"Couldn't a woman learn those things?"

"Perhaps, but God has ordained it otherwise."

Caris felt frustrated with the way adults trotted out this truism every time they were stuck for an answer. Before she could say anything, Brother Saul came downstairs with a bowl of blood and went through the kitchen to the backyard to get rid of it. The sight made Caris feel weepy. All doctors used bloodletting as a cure, so it must be effective, she supposed; but all the same she hated to see her mother's life force in a bowl to be thrown away.

Saul returned to the sick room, and a few moments later he and Joseph came down. "I've done what I can for her," Joseph said solemnly to Papa. "And she has confessed her sins."

Confessed her sins! Caris knew what that meant. She began to cry.

Papa took six silver pennies from his purse and gave them to the monk. "Thank you, Brother," he said. His voice was hoarse.

As the monks left, the two nuns went back upstairs.

Alice sat on Papa's lap and buried her face in his neck. Caris cried and hugged Scrap. Petranilla ordered Tutty to clear the table. Gwenda watched everything with wide eyes. They sat around the table in silence, waiting.

4

Brother Godwyn was hungry. He had eaten his dinner, a stew of sliced turnips with salt fish, and it had not satisfied him. The monks nearly always had fish and weak ale for dinner, even when it was not a fast day.

Not all the monks, of course: Prior Anthony had a privileged diet. He would dine especially well today, for the prioress, Mother Cecilia, was to be his guest. She was accustomed to rich food. The nuns, who always seemed to have more money than the monks, killed a pig or a sheep every few days and washed it down with Gascony wine.

It was Godwyn's job to supervise the dinner, a hard task when his own stomach was rumbling. He spoke to the monastery cook, and checked on the fat goose in the oven and the pot of apple sauce bubbling on the fire. He asked the cellarer for a jug of cider from the barrel, and got a loaf of rye bread from the bakery—stale, for there was no baking on Sunday. He took the silver platters and goblets from the locked chest and set them on the table of the hall in the prior's house.

The prior and prioress dined together once a month. The monastery and the nunnery were separate institutions, with their own premises, and different sources of income. Prior and prioress were independently responsible to the bishop of Kingsbridge. Nevertheless they shared the great cathedral and several other buildings, including the hospital, where monks worked as doctors and nuns as nurses. So there were always details to discuss: cathedral services, hospital guests and patients, town politics. Anthony often tried to get Cecilia to pay costs that should, strictly speaking, have been divided equally—glass windows for the chapter house, bedsteads for the hospital, the repainting of the cathedral's interior—and she usually agreed.

Today, however, the talk was likely to center on politics. Anthony had returned yesterday from two weeks in Gloucester, where he had assisted at the interment of King Edward II, who had lost his throne in January and his life in September. Mother Cecilia would want to hear the gossip while pretending to be above it all.

Godwyn had something else on his mind. He wanted to talk to Anthony about his future. He had been anxiously awaiting the right moment ever since the prior returned home. He had rehearsed his speech, but had not yet found the opportunity to deliver it. He hoped to get a chance this afternoon.

Anthony entered the hall as Godwyn was putting a cheese and a bowl of pears on the sideboard. The prior looked like an older version of Godwyn. Both were tall, with regular features and light brown hair, and like all the family they had greenish eyes with flecks of gold. Anthony stood by the fire—the room was cold and the old building let in freezing drafts. Godwyn poured him a cup of cider. "Father Prior, today is my birthday," he said as Anthony drank. "I'm twenty-one."

"So it is," said Anthony. "I remember your birth very well. I was fourteen years old. My sister, Petranilla, screamed like a boar with an arrow in its guts as she brought you into the world." He raised his goblet in a toast, looking fondly at Godwyn. "And now you're a man."

Godwyn decided that this was his moment. "I've been at the priory ten years," he said.

"Is it that long?"

"Yes—as schoolboy, novice, and monk."

"My goodness."

"I hope I've been a credit to my mother and to you."

"We're both very proud of you."

"Thank you." Godwyn swallowed. "And now I want to go to Oxford."

The city of Oxford had long been a center for masters of theology, medicine, and law. Priests and monks went there to study and debate with teachers and other students. In the last century the masters had been incorporated into a company, or university, that had royal permission to set examinations and award degrees. Kingsbridge Priory maintained a branch or cell in the city, known as Kingsbridge College, where eight monks could carry on their lives of worship and self-denial while they studied.

"Oxford!" said Anthony, and an expression of anxiety and distaste came over his face. "Why?"

"To study. It's what monks are supposed to do."

"I never went to Oxford—and I'm prior."

It was true, but Anthony was sometimes at a disadvantage with his senior colleagues in consequence. The sacrist, the treasurer, and several other monastic officials, or obedientiaries, were graduates of the university, as were all the physicians. They were quick-thinking and skilled in argument, and Anthony sometimes appeared bumbling by comparison, especially in chapter, the daily meeting of all the monks. Godwyn longed to acquire the sharp logic and confident superiority he observed in the Oxford men. He did not want to be like his uncle.

But he could not say that. "I want to learn," he said.

"Why learn heresy?" Anthony said scornfully. "Oxford students question the teachings of the church!"

"In order to understand them better."

"Pointless and dangerous."

Godwyn asked himself why Anthony was making this fuss. The prior had never appeared concerned about heresy before, and Godwyn was not in the least interested in challenging accepted doctrines. He frowned. "I thought you and my mother had ambitions for me," he said. "Don't you want me to advance, and become an obedientiary, and perhaps one day prior?"

"Eventually, yes. But you don't have to leave Kingsbridge to achieve that."

You don't want me to advance too fast, in case I outstrip you; and you don't want me to leave town, in case you lose control of me, Godwyn thought in a flash of insight. He wished he had anticipated this resistance to his plans. "I don't want to study theology," he said.

"What, then?"

"Medicine. It's such an important part of our work here."

Anthony pursed his lips. Godwyn had seen the same disapproving expression on his mother's face. "The monastery can't afford to pay for you," Anthony said. "Do you realize that just one book costs at least fourteen shillings?"

Godwyn was taken by surprise. Students could hire books by the page, he knew; but that was not the main point. "What about the students already there?" he said. "Who pays for them?"

"Two are supported by their families, and one by the nuns. The priory pays for the other three, but we can't afford any more. In fact there are two places vacant in the college for lack of funds."

Godwyn knew the priory was in financial difficulties. On the other hand, it had vast resources: thousands of acres of land; mills and fishponds and woodland; and the enormous income from Kingsbridge market. He could not believe his uncle was refusing him the money to go to Oxford. He felt betrayed. Anthony was his mentor as well as a relative. He had always favored Godwyn over other young monks. But now he was trying to hold Godwyn back.

"Physicians bring money into the priory," he argued. "If you don't train young men, eventually the old ones will die and the priory will be poorer."

"God will provide."

This infuriating platitude was always Anthony's answer. For some years the priory's income from the annual Fleece Fair had been declining. The townspeople had urged Anthony to invest in better facilities for the wool traders—tents, booths, latrines, even a wool exchange building—but he always refused, pleading poverty. And when his brother, Edmund, told him the fair would eventually decline to nothing, he said: "God will provide."

Godwyn said: "Well, then, perhaps he will provide the money for me to go to Oxford."

"Perhaps he will."

Godwyn felt painfully disappointed. He had an urge to get away from his hometown and breathe a different air. At Kingsbridge College he would be subject to the same monastic discipline, of course—but nevertheless he would be far from his uncle and his mother, and that prospect was alluring.

He was not yet ready to give up the argument. "My mother will be very disappointed if I don't go."

Anthony looked uneasy. He did not want to incur the wrath of his formidable sister. "Then let her pray for the money to be found."

"I may be able to get it elsewhere," Godwyn said, extemporizing.

"How would you do that?"

He cast about for an answer, and found inspiration. "I could do what you do, and ask Mother Cecilia." It was possible. Cecilia made him nervous—she could be as intimidating as Petranilla—but she was more susceptible to his boyish charm. She might be persuaded to pay for a bright young monk's education.

The suggestion took Anthony by surprise. Godwyn could see him trying to think of an objection. But he had been arguing as if money were the main consideration, and it was difficult now for him to shift his ground.

While Anthony hesitated, Cecilia came in.

She wore a heavy cloak of fine wool, her only indulgence—she hated to be cold. After greeting the prior, she turned to Godwyn. "Your aunt Rose is gravely ill," she said. Her voice was musically precise. "She may not last the night."

"May God be with her." Godwyn felt a pang of pity. In a family where everyone was a leader, Rose was the only follower. Her petals seemed the more fragile for being surrounded by brambles. "It's not a shock," he added. "But my cousins, Alice and Caris, will be sad."

"Fortunately, they have your mother to console them."

"Yes." Consolation was not Petranilla's strong point, Godwyn thought—she was better at stiffening your spine and preventing you from backsliding—but he did not correct the prioress. Instead he poured her a goblet of cider. "Is it a little chilly in here, Reverend Mother?"

"Freezing," she said bluntly.

"I'll build up the fire."

Anthony said slyly: "My nephew Godwyn is being attentive because he wants you to pay for him to go to Oxford."

Godwyn glared furiously at him. Godwyn would have planned a careful speech and chosen the best time to deliver it. Now Anthony had blurted out the request in the most charmless fashion.

Cecilia said: "I don't think we can afford to finance *two* more."

It was Anthony's turn to be surprised. "Someone else has asked you for money to go to Oxford?"

"Perhaps I shouldn't say," Cecilia replied. "I don't want to get anyone into trouble."

"It's of no consequence," Anthony said huffily; then he recollected himself and added: "We are always grateful for your generosity."

Godwyn put more wood on the fire then went out. The prior's house was on the north side of the cathedral. The cloisters, and all the other priory buildings, were to the south of the church. Godwyn walked shivering across the cathedral green to the monastery kitchen.

He had thought Anthony might quibble about Oxford, saying he should wait until he was older, or until one of the existing students graduated—for Anthony was a quibbler by nature. But he was Anthony's protégé, and he had been confident that in the end his uncle would support him. Anthony's flat opposition had left him feeling shocked.

He asked himself who else had petitioned the prioress for support. Of the twenty-six monks, six were around Godwyn's age. It could be any one of them. In the kitchen the sub-cellarer, Theodoric, was helping the cook. Could he be the rival for Cecilia's money? Godwyn watched him put the goose on a platter with a bowl of apple sauce. Theodoric had brains enough to study. He could be a contender.

Godwyn carried the dinner back to the prior's house, feeling worried. If Cecilia decided to help Theodoric, he did not know what he would do. He had no fallback plan.

He wanted to be prior of Kingsbridge one day. He felt sure he could do the job better than Anthony. And if he was a successful prior, he might rise higher: bishop, archbishop, or perhaps a royal official or counselor. He had only a vague idea of what he would do with such power, but he felt strongly that he belonged in some elevated position in life. However, there were only two routes to such heights. One was aristocratic birth; the other, education. Godwyn came from a family of wool merchants: his only hope was the university. And for that, he was going to need Cecilia's money.

He put the dinner on the table. Cecilia was saying: "But how did the king die?"

"He suffered a fall," Anthony said.

Godwyn carved the goose. "May I give you some of the breast, Reverend Mother?"

"Yes, please. A fall?" she said skeptically. "You make the king sound like a doddering old man. He was forty-three!"

"It's what his jailers say." Having been deposed, the ex-king had been a prisoner at Berkeley Castle, a couple of days' ride from Kingsbridge.

"Ah, yes, his jailers," Cecilia said. "Mortimer's men." She disapproved of Roger Mortimer, the earl of March. Not only had he led the rebellion against Edward II, he had also seduced the king's wife, Queen Isabella.

They began to eat. Godwyn wondered whether there would be any left over.

Anthony said to Cecilia: "You sound as if you suspect something sinister."

"Of course not—but others do. There has been talk . . ."

"That he was murdered? I know. But I saw the corpse, naked. There were no marks of violence on the body."

Godwyn knew he should not interrupt, but he could not resist. "Rumor says that when the king died his screams of agony were heard by everyone in the village of Berkeley."

Anthony looked censorious. "When a king dies, there are always rumors."

"This king did not merely die," Cecilia said. "He was first deposed by Parliament—something that has never happened before."

Anthony lowered his voice. "The reasons were powerful. There were sins of impurity."

He was being enigmatic, but Godwyn knew what he meant. Edward had had "favorites"—young men he seemed unnaturally fond of. The first, Peter Gaveston, had been given so much power and privilege that he aroused jealousy and resentment among the barons, and in the end he had been executed for treason. But then there had been others. It was no wonder, people said, that the queen took a lover.

"I cannot believe such a thing," said Cecilia, who was a passionate royalist. "It may be true that outlaws in the forest give themselves up to such foul practices, but a man of royal blood could never sink so low. Is there any more of that goose?"

"Yes," Godwyn said, concealing his disappointment. He cut the last of the meat from the bird and gave it to the prioress.

Anthony said: "At least there is now no challenge to the new king." The son of Edward II and Queen Isabella had been crowned as King Edward III.

"He is fourteen years old, and he has been put on the throne by Mortimer," said Cecilia. "Who will be the real ruler?"

"The nobles are glad to have stability."

"Especially those of them who are Mortimer's cronies."

"Such as Earl Roland of Shiring, you mean?"

"He seemed ebullient today."

"You're not suggesting . . ."

"That he had something to do with the king's 'fall'? Certainly not." The prioress ate the last of the meat. "Such an idea would be dangerous to speak of, even among friends."

"Indeed."

There was a tap at the door, and Saul Whitehead came in. He was the same age as Godwyn. Could he be the rival? He was intelligent and capable, and he had the great advantage of being a distant relation of the earl of Shiring; but Godwyn doubted whether he had the ambition to go to Oxford. He was devout and shy, the kind of man for whom humility was no virtue because it came naturally. But anything was possible.

"A knight has come into the hospital with a sword wound," Saul said.

"Interesting," said Anthony, "but hardly shocking enough to justify interrupting the prior and the prioress at dinner."

Saul looked scared. "I beg your pardon, Father Prior," he stammered. "But there is a disagreement about the treatment."

Anthony sighed. "Well, the goose is all gone," he said, and he got to his feet.

Cecilia went with him, and Godwyn and Saul followed. They entered the cathedral by the north transept and walked through the crossing, out by the south transept, across the cloisters and into the hospital. The wounded knight lay on the bed nearest the altar, as befitted his rank.

Prior Anthony uttered an involuntary grunt of surprise. For a moment he showed shock and fear. But he recovered his composure quickly, and made his face expressionless.

However, Cecilia missed nothing. "Do you know this man?" she asked Anthony.

"I believe I do. He is Sir Thomas Langley, one of the earl of Monmouth's men."

He was a handsome man in his twenties, broad-shouldered and long-legged. He was naked to the waist, showing a muscular torso crisscrossed with the scars of earlier fights. He looked pale and exhausted.

"He was attacked on the road," Saul explained. "He managed to fight off his assailants, but then he had to drag himself a mile or more to the town. He's lost a lot of blood."

The knight's left forearm was split from elbow to wrist, a clean cut obviously made by a sharp sword.

The monastery's senior physician, Brother Joseph, stood beside the patient. Joseph was in his thirties, a small man with a big nose and bad teeth. He said: "The wound should be kept open and treated with an ointment to bring on a pus. That way, evil humors will be expelled and the wound will heal from the inside out."

Anthony nodded. "So where is the disagreement?"

"Matthew Barber has another idea."

Matthew was a barber-surgeon from the town. He had been standing back deferentially, but now he stepped forward, holding the leather case that contained his expensive, sharp knives. He was a small, thin man with bright blue eyes and a solemn expression.

Anthony did not acknowledge Matthew, but said to Joseph: "What's he doing here?"

"The knight knows him and sent for him."

Anthony spoke to Thomas. "If you want to be butchered, why did you come to the priory hospital?"

The ghost of a smile flickered across the knight's white face, but he seemed too tired to reply.

Matthew spoke up with surprising confidence, apparently undeterred by Anthony's scorn. "I've seen many wounds like this on the battlefield, Father Prior," he said. "The best treatment is the simplest: wash the wound with warm wine, then stitch it closed and bandage it." He was not as deferential as he looked.

Mother Cecilia interrupted. "I wonder if our two young monks have opinions on the question?" she asked.

Anthony looked impatient, but Godwyn realized what she was up to. This was a test. Perhaps Saul was the rival for her money.

The answer was easy, so Godwyn got in first. "Brother Joseph has studied the ancient masters," he said. "He must know best. I don't suppose Matthew can even read."

"I can, Brother Godwyn," Matthew protested. "And I have a book."

Anthony laughed. The idea of a barber with a book was silly, like a horse with a hat. "What book?"

"The *Canon* of Avicenna, the great Islamic physician. Translated from Arabic into Latin. I have read it all, slowly."

"And is your remedy proposed by Avicenna?"

"No, but—"

"Well, then."

Matthew persisted. "But I learned more about healing by traveling with armies and treating the wounded than I ever did from the book."

Mother Cecilia said: "Saul, what's your view?"

Godwyn expected Saul to give the same answer, so that the contest would be indecisive. But, although he looked nervous and shy, Saul contradicted Godwyn. "The barber may be right," he said. Godwyn was delighted. Saul went on arguing for the wrong side. "The treatment proposed by Brother Joseph might be more suitable for crushing or hammering injuries, such as we get on building sites, where the skin and flesh all around the cut is damaged, and to close the wound prematurely might seal evil humors inside the body. This is a clean cut, and the sooner it is closed the faster it will heal."

"Nonsense," said Prior Anthony. "How could a town barber be right and an educated monk be wrong?"

Godwyn smothered a triumphant grin.

The door flew open, and a young man in the robes of a priest strode in. Godwyn recognized Richard of Shiring, the younger of the two sons of Earl Roland. His nod to the prior and prioress was so perfunctory as to be impolite. He went straight to the bedside and spoke to the knight. "What the devil has happened?" he said.

Thomas lifted a weak hand and beckoned Richard closer. The young priest leaned over the patient. Thomas whispered in his ear.

Father Richard drew away as if shocked. "Absolutely not!" he said.

Thomas beckoned again, and the process was repeated: another whisper, another outraged reaction. This time, Richard said: "But why?"

Thomas did not reply.

Richard said: "You are asking for something that is not in our power to give."

Thomas nodded firmly, as if to say: *Yes, it is.*

"You're giving us no choice."

Thomas shook his head weakly from side to side.

Richard turned to Prior Anthony. "Sir Thomas wishes to become a monk here at the priory."

There was a moment of surprised silence. Cecilia was the first to react. "But he's a man of violence!"

"Come on, it's not unknown," Richard said impatiently. "A fighting man sometimes decides to abandon his life of warfare and seek forgiveness for his sins."

"In old age, perhaps," Cecilia said. "This man is not yet twenty-five. He's fleeing some danger." She looked hard at Richard. "Who threatens his life?"

"Curb your curiosity," Richard said rudely. "He wants to be a monk, not a nun, so you need not inquire further." It was a shocking way to talk to a prioress, but the sons of earls could get away with such rudeness. He turned to Anthony. "You must admit him."

Anthony said: "The priory is too poor to take on any more monks—unless there were to be a gift that would pay the costs . . ."

"It will be arranged."

"It would have to be adequate to the need—"

"It will be arranged!"

"Very well."

Cecilia was suspicious. She said to Anthony: "Do you know more about this man than you're telling me?"

"I see no reason to turn him away."

"What makes you think he's a genuine penitent?"

Everyone looked at Thomas. His eyes had closed.

Anthony said: "He will have to prove his sincerity during his novitiate, like anyone else."

She was clearly dissatisfied, but for once Anthony was not asking her for the money, so there was nothing she could do. "We'd better get on with treating this wound," she said.

Saul said: "He refused Brother Joseph's treatment. That's why we had to fetch the Father Prior."

Anthony leaned over the patient. In a loud voice, as if speaking to someone deaf, he said: "You must have the treatment prescribed by Brother Joseph. He knows best."

Thomas appeared unconscious.

Anthony turned to Joseph. "He is no longer objecting."

Matthew Barber said: "He could lose his arm!"

"You'd better leave," Anthony told him.

Looking angry, Matthew went out.

Anthony said to Richard: "Perhaps you would come to the prior's house for a cup of cider."

"Thank you."

As they left, Anthony said to Godwyn: "Stay here and help the Mother Prioress. Come to me before Vespers and tell me how the knight is recovering."

Prior Anthony did not normally worry about the progress of individual patients. Clearly he had a special interest in this one.

Godwyn watched as Brother Joseph applied ointment to the arm of the now-unconscious knight. He thought he had probably ensured Cecilia's financial support by giving the correct answer to the question, but he was keen to get her explicit agreement. When Brother Joseph had done, and Cecilia was bathing Thomas's forehead with rose water, he said: "I hope you will consider my request favorably."

She gave him a sharp look. "I might as well tell you now that I have decided to give the money to Saul."

Godwyn was shocked. "But I gave the right answer!"

"Did you?"

"Surely you didn't agree with the barber?"

She raised her eyebrows. "I won't be interrogated by you, Brother Godwyn."

"I'm sorry," he said immediately. "I just don't understand it."

"I know."

If she was going to be enigmatic, there was no point in talking to her. Godwyn turned away, shaking with frustration and disappointment. She was giving the money to Saul! Was it because he was related to the earl? Godwyn thought not: she was too independent-minded. It was Saul's showy piety that had tipped the balance, he decided. But Saul would never be leader of anything. What a waste. Godwyn wondered how he was going to break this news to his mother. She would be furious—but who would she blame? Anthony? Godwyn himself? A familiar feeling of dread came over him as he pictured his mother's wrath.

As he thought of her, he saw her enter the hospital by the door at the far end, a tall woman with a prominent bust. She caught his eye and stood by the door, waiting for him to come to her. He walked slowly, trying to figure out what to say.

"Your aunt Rose is dying," Petranilla said as soon as he was close.

"May God bless her soul. Mother Cecilia told me."

"You look shocked—but you know how ill she is."

"It's not Aunt Rose. I've had other bad news." He swallowed. "I can't go to Oxford. Uncle Anthony won't pay for it, and Mother Cecilia turned me down, too."

She did not explode immediately, to his great relief. However, her mouth tightened into a grim line. "But why?" she said.

"He hasn't got the money, and she is sending Saul."

"Saul Whitehead? He'll never amount to anything."

"Well, at least he's going to be a physician."

She looked him in the eye, and he shriveled. "I think you handled this badly," she said. "You should have discussed it with me beforehand."

He had feared she would take this line. "How can you say I mishandled it?" he protested.

"You should have let me speak to Anthony first. I would have softened him."

"He still might have said no."

"And before you approached Cecilia, you should have found out whether anyone else had asked her. Then you could have undermined Saul before speaking to her."

"How?"

"He must have a weakness. You could have found out what it is, and made sure it was brought to her attention. Then, when she was feeling disillusioned, you could have approached her yourself."

He saw the sense of what she was saying. "I never thought of that," he said. He bowed his head.

With controlled anger she said: "You have to plan these things, the way earls plan battles."

"I see that now," he said, not meeting her eye. "I'll never make the same mistake again."

"I hope not."

He looked at her again. "What am I going to do?"

"I'm not giving up." A familiar expression of determination came over her face. "I shall provide the money," she said.

Godwyn felt a surge of hope, but he could not imagine how his mother would fulfill such a promise. "Where will you get it?" he asked.

"I'll give up my house, and move in with my brother Edmund."

"Will he have you?" Edmund was a generous man, but he sometimes clashed with his sister.

"I think he will. He's going to be a widower soon, and he'll need a housekeeper. Not that Rose was ever very effective in that role."

Godwyn shook his head. "You'll still need money."

"For what? Edmund will give me bed and board, and pay for the few small necessities I may require. In return, I'll manage his servants and raise his daughters. And you shall have the money I inherited from your father."

She spoke firmly, but Godwyn could see the bitterness of regret expressed in the twist of her mouth. He knew what a sacrifice this would be for her. She was proud of her independence. She was one of the town's prominent women, the daughter of a wealthy man and the sister of the leading wool merchant, and she prized that status. She loved to invite the powerful men and women of Kingsbridge to dine with her and drink the best wine. Now she was proposing to move into her brother's house and live as a poor relation, working as a kind of servant and dependent on him for everything. It would be a terrible comedown. "It's too much to sacrifice," Godwyn said. "You can't do it."

Her face hardened, and she gave a little shake of the shoulders, as if preparing to take the weight of a heavy burden. "Oh, yes, I can," she said.

5

Gwenda told her father everything.

She had sworn on the blood of Jesus that she would keep the secret, so now she was going to Hell, but she was more frightened of her father than of Hell.

He began by asking her where she got Skip, the new puppy, and she was forced to explain how Hop had died; and in the end the whole story came out.

To her surprise, she was not whipped. In fact Pa seemed pleased. He made her take him to the clearing in the forest where the killings had happened. It was not easy to find the place again, but she got there, and they found the bodies of the two men-at-arms dressed in green-and-yellow livery.

First Pa opened their purses. Both contained twenty or thirty pennies. He was even more pleased with their swords, which were worth more than a few pennies. He began to strip the dead men, which was difficult for him with one hand, so he made Gwenda help him. The lifeless bodies were awkwardly heavy, so strange to touch. Pa made her take off everything they wore, even their muddy hose and their soiled underdrawers.

He wrapped their weapons in the clothing, making what looked like a bundle of rags. Then he and Gwenda dragged the naked corpses back into the evergreen bush.

He was in high spirits as they walked back into Kingsbridge. He took her to Slaughterhouse Ditch, a street near the river, and they went into a large but dirty tavern called the White Horse. He bought Gwenda a cup of ale to drink while he disappeared into the back of the house with the innkeeper, whom he addressed as "Davey boy." It was the second time Gwenda had drunk ale in one day. Pa reappeared a few minutes later without the bundle.

They returned to the main street and found Ma, Philemon, and the baby at the Bell Inn, next to the priory gates. Pa winked broadly at Ma and gave her a big handful of money to hide in the baby's blankets.

It was mid-afternoon, and most visitors had left to return to their villages; but it was too late to set out for Wigleigh, so the family would spend the night at the inn. As Pa kept saying, they could afford it now; although Ma said nervously: "Don't let people know you've got money!"

Gwenda felt weary. She had got up early and walked a long way. She lay down on a bench and quickly fell asleep.

She was awakened by the inn door banging open violently. She looked up, startled, to see two men-at-arms walk in. At first she thought they were the ghosts of the men who had been killed in the forest, and she suffered a moment of sheer terror. Then she realized they were different men wearing the same uniform, yellow on one side and green on the other. The younger of the two carried a familiar-looking bundle of rags.

The older spoke directly to Pa. "You're Joby from Wigleigh, aren't you?"

Gwenda instantly felt frightened again. There was a tone of serious menace in the man's voice. He was not posturing, just determined, but he gave her the impression he would do anything to get his way.

"No," Pa replied, lying automatically. "You've got the wrong man."

They ignored that. The second man put the bundle on the table and spread it out. It consisted of two yellow-and-green tunics wrapped around two swords and two daggers. He looked at Pa and said: "Where did these come from?"

"I've never seen them before, I swear by the Cross."

He was stupid to deny it, Gwenda thought fearfully: they would get the truth out of him, just as he had got the truth out of her.

The older man-at-arms said: "Davey, the landlord of the White Horse, says he bought these from Joby Wigleigh." His voice hardened with threat, and the handful of other customers in the room all got up from their seats and quickly slipped out of the inn, leaving only Gwenda's family.

"Joby left here a while ago," Pa said desperately.

The man nodded. "With his wife, two children, and a baby."

"Yes."

The man moved with sudden speed. He grabbed Pa's tunic in a strong hand and pushed him up against the wall. Ma screamed, and the baby began to cry. Gwenda saw that the man's right hand bore a padded glove covered with chain mail. He drew back his arm and punched Pa in the stomach.

Ma shouted: "Help! Murder!" Philemon began to cry.

Pa's face turned white with pain, and he went limp, but the man held him up against the wall, preventing him from falling, and punched him again, this time in the face. Blood spurted from Pa's nose and mouth.

Gwenda wanted to scream, and her mouth was open wide, but no noise would come from her throat. She thought her father was all-powerful—even though he often slyly pretended to be weak, or craven, in order to get sympathy, or turn aside anger—and it terrified her to see him so helpless.

The innkeeper appeared in the doorway that led to the back of the house. He was a big man in his thirties. A plump little girl peeped from behind him. "What's this?" he said in a voice of authority.

The man-at-arms did not look at him. "You keep out of it," he said, and he punched Pa in the stomach again.

Pa vomited blood.

"Stop that," said the innkeeper.

The man-at-arms said: "Who do you think you are?"

"I'm Paul Bell, and this is my house."

"Well, then, Paul Bell, you mind your own business, if you know what's good for you."

"I suppose you think you can do what you like, wearing that uniform." There was contempt in Paul's voice.

"That's about right."

"Whose livery is it, anyway?"

"The queen's."

Paul spoke over his shoulder. "Bessie, run and fetch John Constable. If a man is going to be murdered in my tavern, I want the constable to witness it." The little girl disappeared.

"There'll be no killing here," the man-at-arms said. "Joby has changed his mind. He's decided to lead me to the place where he robbed two dead men—haven't you, Joby?"

Pa could not speak, but he nodded. The man let him go, and he fell to his knees, coughing and retching.

The man looked at the rest of the family. "And the child that witnessed the fight . . . ?"

Gwenda screamed: "No!"

He nodded in satisfaction. "The rat-faced girl, obviously."

Gwenda ran to her mother. Ma said: "Mary, Mother of God, save my child."

The man grabbed Gwenda's arm and roughly pulled her away from her mother. She cried out. He said harshly: "Shut your noise, or you'll get the same as your miserable father."

Gwenda clamped her jaws together to stop herself screaming.

"Get up, Joby." The man dragged Pa to his feet. "Pull yourself together, you're going for a ride."

The second man picked up the clothes and the weapons.

As they left the inn, Ma called out frantically: "Just do everything they ask!"

The men had horses. Gwenda rode in front of the older man, and Pa was mounted in the same position on the other horse. Pa was helpless, groaning, so Gwenda directed them, remembering the way clearly now that she had followed it twice. They made rapid progress on horseback, but all the same the afternoon was darkening when they reached the clearing.

The younger man held on to Gwenda and Pa while the leader pulled the bodies of their comrades out from under the bush.

"That Thomas must be a rare fighter, to kill Harry and Alfred together," the older man mused, looking at the corpses. Gwenda realized that these men did not know about the other children. She would have confessed that she had not been alone, and that Ralph had killed one of the men; but she was too terrified to speak. "He's nearly cut Alfred's head off," the man went on. He turned and looked at Gwenda. "Was anything said about a letter?"

"I don't know!" she said, finding her voice. "I had my eyes shut because I was frightened, and I couldn't hear what they were saying! It's true, I'd tell you if I knew!"

"If they got the letter from him in the first place, he would have taken it back after he killed them anyway," the man said to his comrade. He looked at the trees around the clearing, as if the letter might have been hanging among the dying leaves. "He probably has it now, at the priory, where we can't get at him without violating the sanctity of the monastery."

The second man said: "At least we can report exactly what happened, and take the bodies home for a Christian burial."

There was a sudden commotion. Pa wrenched himself out of the grasp of the second man and dashed across the clearing. His captor moved to go after him, but was stopped by the older man-at-arms. "Let him go—what's the point in killing him now?"

Gwenda began to cry quietly.

"What about this child?" said the younger man.

They were going to murder her, Gwenda felt sure. She could see nothing through her tears, and she was sobbing too hard to plead for her life. She would die and go to Hell. She waited for the end.

"Let her go," said the older man. "I wasn't born to kill little girls."

The younger man released her and gave her a shove. She stumbled and fell to the ground. She got up, wiped her eyes so that she could see, and stumbled off.

"Go on, run away," the man called after her. "It's your lucky day!"

Caris could not sleep. She got up from her bed and went into Mama's room. Papa was sitting on a stool, staring at the still figure in the bed.

Mama's eyes were closed and her face glistened, in the candlelight, with a film of perspiration. She seemed to be hardly breathing. Caris took her pale hand: it was terribly cold. She held it between her own, trying to warm it.

She said: "Why did they take her blood?"

"They think illness sometimes comes from an excess of one of the humors. They hope to take it away with the blood."

"But it didn't make her better."

"No. In fact, she seems worse."

Tears came to Caris's eyes. "Why did you let them do it, then?"

"Priests and monks study the works of the ancient philosophers. They know more than we do."

"I don't believe that."

"It's hard to know what to believe, little buttercup."

"If I was a doctor, I'd only do things that made people better."

Papa was not listening. He was looking more intently at Mama. He leaned forward and slipped his hand under the blanket to touch her chest just below her left breast. Caris could see the shape of his big hand under the fine wool. He made a small choking sound in his throat, then moved his hand and pressed down more firmly. He held it there for a few moments.

He closed his eyes.

He seemed to fall slowly forward, until he was on his knees beside the bed, as if praying, with his big forehead resting on Mama's thigh, and his hand still on her chest.

She realized he was crying. It was the most frightening thing that had ever happened to her, much more frightening than seeing a man killed in the forest. Children cried, women cried, weak and helpless people cried, but Papa never cried. She felt as if the world was ending.

She had to get help. She let Mama's cold hand slip out of her own onto the blanket, where it lay motionless. She went back to her bedroom and shook the shoulder of the sleeping Alice. "You've got to wake up!" she said.

At first Alice would not open her eyes.

"Papa is crying!" Caris said.

Alice sat upright. "He can't be," she said.

"Get up!"

Alice got out of bed. Caris took her older sister's hand and they went together into Mama's room. Papa was standing up now, looking down at the still face on the pillow, his face wet with tears. Alice stared at him in shock. Caris whispered: "I told you so."

On the other side of the bed stood Aunt Petranilla.

Papa saw the girls standing in the doorway. He left his station by the bed and came to them. He put one arm around each of them, drew them both to him, and hugged them. "Your mama has gone to be with the angels," he said quietly. "Pray for her soul."

"Be brave, girls," said Petranilla. "From now on, I will be your mama."

Caris wiped the tears from her eyes and looked up at her aunt. "Oh, no, you won't," she said.

PART II

June 8 to 14,

1337

6

n Whitsunday in the year that Merthin was twenty-one, a river of rain fell on Kingsbridge Cathedral.

Great globules of water bounced off the slate roof; streams flooded the gutters; fountains gushed from the mouths of gargoyles; sheets of water unfolded down the buttresses; and torrents ran over the arches and down the columns, soaking the statues of the saints. The sky, the great church, and the town round about were all shades of wet gray paint.

Whitsunday commemorated the moment when the Holy Spirit descended on the disciples of Jesus. The seventh Sunday after Easter, it fell in May or June, soon after most of England's sheep had been sheared; and so it was always the first day of the Kingsbridge Fleece Fair.

As Merthin splashed through the downpour to the cathedral for the morning service, pulling his hood forward over his brow in a vain attempt to keep his face dry, he had to pass through the fair. On the broad green to the west of the church, hundreds of traders had set out their stalls—then hastily covered them with sheets of oiled sacking or felted cloth to keep the rain off. Wool traders were the key figures in the fair, from the small operators who collected the produce of a few scattered villagers, to the big dealers such as Edmund who had a warehouse full of woolsacks to sell. Around them clustered subsidiary stalls selling just about everything else money could buy: sweet wine from the Rhineland, silk brocade threaded with gold from Lucca, glass bowls from Venice, ginger and pepper from places in the East that few people could even name. And finally there were the workaday tradespeople who supplied visitors and stallholders with their commonplace needs: bakers, brewers, confectioners, fortune-tellers, and prostitutes.

The stallholders responded bravely to the rain, joking with one another, trying to create the carnival atmosphere; but the weather would be bad for their profits. Some people had to do business, rain or shine: Italian and Flemish buyers needed soft English wool for thousands of busy looms in Florence and Bruges. But more casual customers would stay at home: a knight's wife would decide she could manage without nutmeg and cinnamon; a prosperous peasant would make his old coat last another winter; a lawyer would judge that his mistress did not really need a gold bangle.

Merthin was not going to buy anything. He had no money. He was an unpaid apprentice, living with his master, Elfric Builder. He was fed at the family table, he slept on the kitchen floor, and he wore Elfric's cast-off clothes, but he got no wages. In the long winter evenings he carved ingenious toys that he sold for a few pennies—a jewel box with secret compartments, a cockerel whose tongue poked out when its tail was pressed—but in summer there was no spare time, for craftsmen worked until dark.

However, his apprenticeship was almost over. In less than six months, on the first day of December, he would become a full member of the carpenters' guild of Kingsbridge at the age of twenty-one. He could hardly wait.

The great west doors of the cathedral were open to admit the thousands of townspeople and visitors who would attend today's service. Merthin stepped inside, shaking the rain off his clothes. The stone floor was slippery with water and mud. On a fine day, the interior of the church would be bright with shafts of sunlight, but today it was murky, the stained-glass windows dim, the congregation shrouded in dark, wet clothes.

Where did all the rain go? There were no drainage ditches around the church. The water—thousands and thousands of gallons of it—just soaked into the ground. Did it go on down, farther and farther, until it fell as rain again in Hell? No. The cathedral was built on a slope. The water traveled underground, seeping down the hill from north to south. The foundations of large stone buildings were designed to let water flow through, for a buildup was dangerous. All this rain eventually passed into the river on the southern boundary of the priory grounds.

Merthin imagined he could feel the underground rush of the water, its drumming vibration transmitted through the foundations and the tiled floor and sensed by the soles of his feet.

A small black dog scampered up to him, wagging its tail, and greeted him joyfully. "Hello, Scrap," he said, and patted her. He looked up to see the dog's mistress, Caris; and his heart skipped a beat.

She wore a cloak of bright scarlet that she had inherited from her mother. It was the only splash of color in the gloom. Merthin smiled broadly, happy to see her. It was hard to say what made her so beautiful. She had a small, round face with neat, regular features; mid-brown hair; and green eyes flecked with gold. She was not so different from a hundred other Kingsbridge girls. But she wore her hat at a jaunty angle, there was a mocking intelligence in her eyes, and she looked at him with a mischievous grin that promised vague but tantalizing delights. He had known her for ten years, but it was only in the last few months that he had realized he loved her.

She drew him behind a pillar and kissed him on the mouth, the tip of her tongue running lightly across his lips.

They kissed every chance they got: in church, in the marketplace, when they met on the street, and—best of all—when he was at her house and they found themselves alone. He lived for those moments. He thought about kissing her before he went to sleep and again as soon as he woke up.

He visited her house two or three times a week. Her father, Edmund, liked him, though her aunt Petranilla did not. A convivial man, Edmund often invited Merthin to stay for supper, and Merthin accepted gratefully, knowing it would be a better meal than he would get at Elfric's house. He and Caris would play chess or checkers, or just sit talking. He liked to watch her while she told a story or explained something, her hands drawing pictures in the air, her face expressing amusement or astonishment, acting every part in a pageant. But, most of the time, he was waiting for those moments when he could steal a kiss.

He glanced around the church: no one was looking their way. He slipped his hand inside her coat and touched her through the soft linen of her dress. Her body was warm. He held her breast in his palm, small and round. He loved the way her flesh yielded to the press of his fingertips. He had never seen her naked, but he knew her breasts intimately.

In his dreams they went farther. Then, they were alone somewhere, a clearing in the woods or the big bedchamber of a castle; and they were both naked. But, strangely, his dreams always ended a moment too soon, just before he entered her; and he would wake up frustrated.

One day, he would think; one day.

They had not yet spoken about marriage. Apprentices could not marry, so he had to wait. Caris must, surely, have asked herself what they were going to do when he finished his term; but she had not voiced those thoughts. She seemed content to take life one day at a time. And he had a superstitious fear of talking about their future together. It was said that pilgrims should not spend too much time planning their journey, for they might learn of so many hazards that they would decide not to go.

A nun walked past, and Merthin withdrew his hand guiltily from Caris's bosom; but the nun did not notice them. People did all sorts of things in the vast space of the cathedral. Last year Merthin had seen a couple having sexual congress up against the wall of the south aisle, in the darkness of the Christmas Eve service—although they had been thrown out for it. He wondered if he and Caris could stay here throughout the service, dallying discreetly.

But she had other ideas. "Let's go to the front," she said. She took his hand and led him through the crowd. He knew many of the people there, though not all: Kingsbridge was one of the larger cities in England, with about seven thousand inhabitants, and no one knew everybody. He followed Caris to the crossing, where the nave met the transepts. There they came up against a wooden barrier blocking entrance to the eastern end, or chancel, which was reserved for clergy.

Merthin found himself standing next to Buonaventura Caroli, the most important of the Italian merchants, a heavyset man in a richly embroidered coat of thick wool cloth. He came originally from Florence—which he said was the greatest city in the Christian world, more than ten times the size of Kingsbridge—but he now lived in London, managing the large business his family had with English wool producers. The Carolis were so rich they loaned money to kings, but Buonaventura was amiable and unpretentious—though people said that in business he could be implacably hard.

Caris greeted the man in a casually familiar way: he was staying at her house. He gave Merthin a friendly nod, even though he must have guessed, from Merthin's age and hand-me-down clothing, that he was a mere apprentice.

Buonaventura was looking at the architecture. "I have been coming to Kingsbridge for five years," he said, making idle conversation, "but until today I have never noticed that the windows of the transepts are much bigger than those in the rest of the church." He spoke French with an admixture of words from the dialect of the Italian region of Tuscany.

Merthin had no trouble understanding. He had grown up, like most sons of English knights, speaking Norman French to his parents and English to his playmates; and he could guess the meanings of many Italian words because he had learned Latin in the monks' school. "I can tell you why the windows are like that," he said.

Buonaventura raised his eyebrows, surprised that an apprentice should claim such knowledge.

"The church was built two hundred years ago, when these narrow lancet windows in the nave and chancel were a revolutionary new design," Merthin went on. "Then, a hundred years later, the bishop wanted a taller tower, and he rebuilt the transepts at the same time, putting in the bigger windows that had by then come into fashion."

Buonaventura was impressed. "And how do you happen to know this?"

"In the monastery library there is a history of the priory, called *Timothy's Book*, that tells all about the building of the cathedral. Most of it was written in the time of the great Prior Philip, but later writers have added to it. I read it as a boy at the monks' school."

Buonaventura looked hard at Merthin for a moment, as if memorizing his face, then he said casually: "It's a fine building."

"Are the buildings very different in Italy?" Merthin was fascinated by talk of foreign countries, their life in general and their architecture in particular.

Buonaventura looked thoughtful. "I believe the principles of building are the same everywhere. But in England I have never seen domes."

"What's a dome?"

"A round roof, like half a ball."

Merthin was astonished. "I never heard of such a thing! How is it built?"

Buonaventura laughed. "Young man, I am a wool merchant. I can tell whether a fleece comes from a Cotswold sheep or a Lincoln sheep, just by rubbing the wool between my finger and thumb, but I don't know how a henhouse is built, let alone a dome."

Merthin's master, Elfric, arrived. He was a prosperous man, and he wore expensive clothes, but they always looked as if they belonged to someone else. A habitual sycophant, he ignored Caris and Merthin, but made a deep bow to Buonaventura and said: "Honored to have you in our city once again, sir."

Merthin turned away.

"How many languages do you think there are?" Caris said to him.

She was always saying crazy things. "Five," Merthin replied without thinking.

"No, be serious," she said. "There's English, and French, and Latin, that's three. Then the Florentines and the Venetians speak differently, though they have words in common."

"You're right," he said, entering into the game. "That's five already. Then there's Flemish." Few people could make out the tongue of the traders who came to Kingsbridge from the weaving towns of Flanders: Ypres, Bruges, Ghent.

"And Danish."

"The Arabs have their own language, and when they write, they don't even use the same letters as we do."

"And Mother Cecilia told me that all the barbarians have their own tongues that no one even knows how to write down—Scots, Welsh, Irish, and probably others. That makes eleven, and there might be people we haven't even heard of!"

Merthin grinned. Caris was the only person he could do this with. Among their friends of the same age, no one understood the thrill of imagining strange people and different ways of life. She would ask a random question: What is it like to live at the edge of the world? Are the priests wrong about God? How do you know you're not dreaming, right now? And they would be off on a speculative voyage, competing to come up with the most outlandish notions.

The roar of conversation in the church suddenly quieted, and Merthin saw that the monks and nuns were seating themselves. The choirmaster, Blind Carlus, came in last. Although he could not see, he walked without assistance in the church and the monastic buildings, moving slowly, but as confident as a sighted man, familiar with every pillar and flagstone. Now he sang a note in his rich baritone, and the choir began a hymn.

Merthin was quietly skeptical about the clergy. Priests had power that was not always matched by their knowledge—rather like his employer, Elfric. However, he liked going to church. The services induced a kind of trance in him. The music, the architecture, and the Latin incantations enchanted him, and he felt as if he were asleep with his eyes open. Once again he had the fanciful sensation that he could feel the rainwater flowing in torrents far beneath his feet.

His gaze roamed over the three levels of the nave—arcade, gallery, and clerestory. He knew that the columns were made by placing one stone on top of another, but they gave a different impression, at least at first glance.

The stone blocks were carved so that each column looked like a bundle of shafts. He traced the rise of one of the four giant piers of the crossing, from the huge square foot on which it stood, up to where one shaft branched north to form an arch across the side aisle, on up to the tribune level, where another shaft branched west to form the arcade of the gallery, on up to the westward springing of a clerestory arch, until the last remaining shafts separated, like a spray of flowers, and became the curving ribs of the ceiling vault far above. From the central boss at the highest point of the vault, he followed a rib all the way down again to the matching pier on the opposite corner of the crossing.

As he did so, something odd happened. His vision seemed momentarily to blur, and it looked as if the east side of the transept moved.

There was a low rumbling sound, so deep it was almost inaudible, and a tremor underfoot, as if a tree had fallen nearby.

The singing faltered.

In the chancel, a crack appeared in the south wall, right next to the pier Merthin had been looking at.

He found himself turning toward Caris. Out of the corner of his eye he saw masonry falling in the choir and the crossing. Then there was nothing but noise: women screaming, men shouting, and the deafening crash of huge stones hitting the floor. It lasted a long moment. When silence descended, Merthin found he was holding Caris, his left arm around her shoulders pressing her to him, his right arm protectively covering her head, his body interposed between her and the place where a part of the great church lay in ruins.

It was obviously a miracle that no one died.

The worst of the damage was in the south aisle of the chancel, which had been empty of people during the service. The congregation was not admitted to the chancel, and the clergy had all been in the central part, called the choir. Several monks had had narrow escapes, which only heightened the talk of miracles, and others had bad cuts and bruises from flying chips of stone. The congregation suffered no more than a few scratches. Evidently, they had all been supernaturally protected by St. Adolphus, whose bones were preserved under the high altar, and whose deeds included many instances of curing the sick and saving people from death. However, it was generally agreed that God had sent the people of Kingsbridge a warning. What he was warning them about was not yet clear.

An hour later, four men were inspecting the damage. Brother Godwyn, the cousin of Caris, was the sacrist, responsible for the church and all its treasures. Under him as matricularius, in charge of building operations and repairs, was Brother Thomas, who had been Sir Thomas Langley ten years ago. The contract for cathedral maintenance was held by Elfric, a carpenter by training and a general builder by trade. And Merthin tagged along as Elfric's apprentice.

The east end of the church was divided by pillars into four sections, called bays. The collapse had affected the two bays nearest the crossing. The stone vaulting over the south aisle was destroyed completely in the first bay and partially in the second. There were cracks in the tribune gallery, and stone mullions had fallen from the windows of the clerestory.

Elfric said: "Some weakness in the mortar allowed the vault to crumble, and that in turn caused the cracks at higher levels."

That did not sound right to Merthin, but he lacked an alternative explanation.

Merthin hated his master. He had first been apprenticed to Elfric's father, Joachim, a builder of wide experience who had worked on churches and bridges in London and Paris. The old man had delighted in explaining to Merthin the lore of the masons—what they called their "mysteries," which were mostly arithmetical formulas for building, such as the ratio between the height of a building and the depth of its foundations. Merthin liked numbers and lapped up everything Joachim could teach him.

Then Joachim died, and Elfric took over. Elfric believed the main thing an apprentice had to learn was obedience. Merthin found this difficult to accept, and Elfric punished him with short rations, thin clothing, and outdoor work in frosty weather. To make matters worse, Elfric's chubby daughter Griselda, the same age as Merthin, was always well fed and warmly dressed.

Three years ago Elfric's wife had died, and he had married Alice, the older sister of Caris. People thought Alice was the prettier sister, and it was true that she had more regular features, but she lacked Caris's captivating ways, and Merthin found her dull. Alice had always seemed to like Merthin almost as much as her sister did, and so he had hoped she would make Elfric treat him better. But the reverse happened. Alice seemed to think it was her wifely duty to join with Elfric in tormenting him.

Merthin knew that many other apprentices suffered in the same way, and they all put up with it because apprenticeship was the only way into a well-paid trade. The craft guilds efficiently kept out upstarts. No one could do business in a town without belonging to a guild. Even a priest, a monk, or a woman who wanted to deal in wool or brew ale for sale would have to get into a guild. And outside the towns there was little business to be done: peasants built their own houses and sewed their own shirts.

At the end of the apprenticeship, most boys would remain with the master, working as journeymen for a wage. A few would end up partners, taking over the enterprise when the old man died. That would not be Merthin's destiny. He hated Elfric too much. He would leave the moment he could.

"Let's look at it from above," said Godwyn.

They walked toward the east end. Elfric said: "It's good to see you back from Oxford, Brother Godwyn. But you must miss the company of all those learned people."

Godwyn nodded. "The masters are truly astonishing."

"And the other students—they must be remarkable young men, I imagine. Though we hear tales of bad behavior, too."

Godwyn looked rueful. "I'm afraid some of those stories are true. When a young priest or monk is away from home for the first time, he may suffer temptation."

"Still—we're fortunate to have the benefit of university-trained men here in Kingsbridge."

"Very kind of you to say so."

"Oh, but it's true."

Merthin wanted to say: Shut up, for pity's sake. But this was Elfric's way. He was a poor craftsman, his work inaccurate and his judgment shaky, but he knew how to ingratiate himself. Merthin had watched him do it, time and again—for Elfric could be as charming to people from whom he wanted something as he could be rude to those who had nothing he needed.

Merthin was more surprised at Godwyn. How could an intelligent and educated man fail to see through Elfric? Perhaps it was less obvious to the person who was the object of the compliments.

Godwyn opened a small door and led the way up a narrow spiral staircase concealed in the wall. Merthin felt excited. He loved to enter the hidden passageways of the cathedral. He was also curious about the dramatic collapse, and eager to figure out its cause.

The aisles were single-story structures that stuck out either side of the main body of the church. They had rib-vaulted stone ceilings. Above the vault, a lean-to roof rose from the outer edge of the aisle up to the base of the clerestory. Under that sloping roof was a triangular void, its floor the hidden side, or extrados, of the aisle's vaulted ceiling. The four men climbed into this void to look at the damage from above.

It was lit by window openings into the interior of the church, and Thomas had had the foresight to bring an oil lamp. The first thing Merthin noticed was that the vaults, viewed from above, were not exactly the same in each bay. The easternmost formed a slightly flatter curve than its neighbor, and the next one—partly destroyed—looked as though it was different again.

They walked along the extrados, staying close to the edge where the vault was strongest, until they were as near as they dared go to the collapsed portion. The vault was constructed in the same way as the rest of the church, of stones mortared together, except that ceiling stones were very thin and light. The vault was almost vertical at its springing, but as it rose it leaned inward, until it met the stonework coming up from the opposite edge.

Elfric said: "Well, the first thing to do is obviously to rebuild the vaulting over the first two bays of the aisle."

Thomas said: "It's a long time since anyone in Kingsbridge built rib-vaulting." He turned to Merthin. "Could you make the formwork?"

Merthin knew what he meant. At the edge of the vault, where the masonry was almost upright, the stones would stay in place by their own weight; but, higher up, as the curve turned toward the horizontal, some support was needed to keep everything in place while the mortar dried. The obvious method was to make a wooden frame, called formwork or centering, and lay the stones on top of that.

It was a challenging job for a carpenter, for the curves had to be just right. Thomas knew the quality of Merthin's craftsmanship, having closely supervised the work Merthin and Elfric carried out at the cathedral over several years. However, it was tactless of Thomas to address the apprentice rather than the boss, and Elfric reacted quickly. "Under my supervision he can do it, yes," he said.

"I can make the formwork," Merthin said, already thinking about how the frame would be supported by the scaffolding, and the platform on which the masons would have to stand. "But these vaults were not built with formwork."

"Don't talk nonsense, boy," Elfric said. "Of course they were. You know nothing about it."

Merthin knew it was unwise to argue with his employer. On the other hand, in six months he would be competing with Elfric for work, and he needed people such as Brother Godwyn to believe in his competence. Also, he was stung by the scorn in Elfric's voice, and he felt an irresistible desire to prove his master wrong. "Look at the extrados," he said indignantly. "Having finished one bay, surely the masons would have re-used the same formwork for the next. In which case, all the vaults would have the same curve. But, in fact, they're all different."

"Obviously they didn't re-use their formwork," Elfric said irritably.

"Why wouldn't they?" Merthin persisted. "They must have wanted to save on timber, not to mention the wages of skilled carpenters."

"Anyway, it's not possible to build vaulting without formwork."

"Yes, it is," Merthin said. "There's a method—"

"That's enough," Elfric said. "You're here to learn, not teach."

Godwyn put in: "Just a minute, Elfric. If the boy is right, it could save the priory a lot of money." He looked at Merthin. "What were you going to say?"

Merthin was half wishing he had not raised this subject. There would be hell to pay later. But he was committed now. If he backed off, they would think he did not know what he was talking about. "It's described in a book in the monastery library, and it's very simple," he said. "As each stone is laid, a rope is draped over it. One end of the rope is tied to the wall, the other weighted with a lump of wood. The rope forms a right angle over the edge of the stone, and keeps it from slipping off its bed of mortar and falling to the ground."

There was a moment of silence as they all concentrated, trying to visualize the arrangements. Then Thomas nodded. "It could work," he said.

Elfric looked furious.

Godwyn was intrigued. "What book is this?"

"It's called *Timothy's Book*," Merthin told him.

"I know of it, but I've never studied it. Obviously I should." Godwyn addressed the others. "Have we seen enough?"

Elfric and Thomas nodded. As the four men left the roof space, Elfric muttered to Merthin: "Do you realize you've just talked yourself out of several weeks' work? You won't do that when you're your own master, I'll bet."

Merthin had not thought of that. Elfric was right: by proving that formwork was unnecessary, he had also done himself out of a job. But there was something badly wrong with Elfric's way of thinking. It was unfair to allow someone to spend money unnecessarily, just to keep yourself in work. Merthin did not want to live by cheating people.

They went down the spiral staircase into the chancel. Elfric said to Godwyn: "I'll come to you tomorrow with a price for the work."

"Good."

Elfric turned to Merthin. "You stay here and count the stones in an aisle vault. Bring me the answer at home."

"Yes."

Elfric and Godwyn left, but Thomas lingered. "I got you into trouble," he said.

"You were trying to boost me."

The monk shrugged and made a what-can-you-do gesture with his right arm. His left arm had been amputated at the elbow ten years ago, after infection set in to the wound he received in the fight Merthin had witnessed.

Merthin hardly ever thought about that strange scene in the forest—he had become used to Thomas in a monk's robe—but he recalled it now: the men-at-arms, the children hiding in the bush, the bow and arrow, the buried letter. Thomas was always kind to him, and he guessed it was because of what happened that day. "I've never told anyone about that letter," he said quietly.

"I know," Thomas replied. "If you had, you'd be dead."

Most large towns were run by a guild merchant, an organization of the leading citizens. Under the guild merchant were numerous craft guilds, each dedicated to a particular trade: masons, carpenters, leather tanners, weavers, tailors. Then there were the parish guilds, small groups centered on local churches, formed to raise money for priestly robes and sacred ornaments, and for the support of widows and orphans.

Cathedral towns were different. Kingsbridge, like St. Albans and Bury St. Edmunds, was ruled by the monastery, which owned almost all the land in and around the town. The priors had always refused permission for a guild merchant. However, the most important craftsmen and traders belonged to the parish guild of St. Adolphus. No doubt this had started out, in the distant past, as a pious group that raised money for the cathedral, but it was now the most important organization in town. It made rules for the conduct of business, and elected an alderman and six wardens to enforce them. In the guildhall were kept the measures that standardized the weight of a woolsack, the width of a bolt of cloth, and the volume of a bushel for all Kingsbridge trade. Nevertheless, the merchants could not hold courts and dispense justice the way they did in borough towns—the Kingsbridge prior retained those powers for himself.

On the afternoon of Whitsunday, the parish guild gave a banquet at the guildhall for the most important visiting buyers. Edmund Wooler was the alderman, and Caris went with him to be hostess, so Merthin had to amuse himself without her.

Fortunately, Elfric and Alice were also at the banquet, so he could sit in the kitchen, listening to the rain and thinking. The weather was not cold, but there was a small fire for cooking, and its red glow was cheerful.

He could hear Elfric's daughter, Griselda, moving about upstairs. It was a fine house, although smaller than Edmund's. There was just a hall and a kitchen downstairs. The staircase led to an open landing, where Griselda slept, and a closed bedroom for the master and his wife. Merthin slept in the kitchen.

There had been a time, three or four years ago, when Merthin had been tormented at night by fantasies of climbing the stairs and slipping under the blankets next to Griselda's warm, plump body. But she considered herself superior to him, treating him like a servant, and she had never given him the least encouragement.

Sitting on a bench, Merthin looked into the fire and visualized the wooden scaffolding he would build for the masons who would reconstruct the collapsed vaulting in the cathedral. Wood was expensive, and long tree trunks were rare—the owners of woodland usually yielded to the temptation of selling the timber before it was fully mature. So builders tried to minimize the amount of scaffolding. Rather than build it up from floor level, they saved timber by suspending it from the existing walls.

While he was thinking, Griselda came into the kitchen and took a cup of ale from the barrel. "Would you like some?" she said. Merthin accepted, amazed by her courtesy. She surprised him again by sitting on a stool opposite him to drink.

Griselda's paramour, Thurstan, had disappeared three weeks ago. No doubt she now felt lonely, which would be why she wanted Merthin's company. The drink warmed his stomach and relaxed him. Searching for something to say, he asked: "What happened to Thurstan?"

She tossed her head like a frisky mare. "I told him I didn't want to marry him."

"Why not?"

"He's too young for me."

That did not sound right to Merthin. Thurstan was seventeen, Griselda twenty, but Griselda was not notably mature. More likely, he thought, Thurstan was too low-class. He had arrived in Kingsbridge from nowhere a couple of years ago and had worked as an unskilled laborer for several of the town's craftsmen. He had probably got bored, with Griselda or with Kingsbridge, and simply moved on.

"Where did he go?"

"I don't know, and I don't care. I should marry someone my own age, someone with a sense of responsibility—perhaps a man who could take over my father's enterprise one day."

It occurred to Merthin that she might mean him. Surely not, he thought; she's always looked down on me. Then she got up from her stool and came and sat on the bench beside him.

"My father is spiteful to you," she said. "I've always thought that."

Merthin was astonished. "Well, it's taken you long enough to say so—I've been living here six and a half years."

"It's hard for me to go against my family."

"Why is he so vile to me, anyway?"

"Because you think you know better than him, and you can't hide it."

"Maybe I do know better."

"See what I mean?"

He laughed. It was the first time she had ever made him laugh.

She shifted closer on the bench, so that her thigh in the woolen dress was pressed against his. He was in his worn linen shirt, which came to mid-thigh, with the undershorts that all men wore, but he could feel the warmth of her body through their clothes. What had brought this on? He looked incredulously at her. She had glossy dark hair and brown eyes. Her face was attractive in a fleshy way. She had a nice mouth for kissing.

She said: "I like being indoors in a rainstorm. It feels cozy."

He felt himself becoming aroused, and looked away from her. What would Caris think, he asked himself, if she walked in here now? He tried to quell his desire, but that only made it worse.

He looked back at Griselda. Her lips were moist and slightly parted. She leaned toward him. He kissed her. Immediately, she thrust her tongue into his mouth. It was a sudden, shocking intimacy that he found thrilling, and he responded in the same way. This was not like kissing Caris—

That thought arrested him. He tore himself away from Griselda and stood up.

She said: "What's the matter?"

He did not want to tell her the truth, so he said: "You never seemed to like me."

She looked annoyed. "I've told you, I had to side with my father."

"You've changed very suddenly."

She stood up and moved toward him. He stepped away until his back was to the wall. She took his hand and pressed it to her bosom. Her breasts were round and heavy, and he could not resist the temptation to feel them. She said: "Have you ever done it—the real thing—with a girl?"

He found he could not speak, but he nodded.

"Have you thought about doing it with me?"

"Yes," he managed.

"You can do it to me now, if you like, while they're out. We can go upstairs and lie on my bed."

"No."

She pressed her body to his. "Kissing you has made me go all hot and slippery inside."

He pushed her away. The shove was rougher than he intended, and she fell backward, landing on her well-cushioned bottom. "Leave me alone," he said.

He was not sure he meant it, but she took him at his word. "Go to hell, then," she swore. She got to her feet and stomped upstairs.

He stayed where he was, panting. Now that he had rejected her, he regretted it.

Apprentices were not very attractive to young women, who did not want to be forced to wait years before marrying. All the same, Merthin had courted several Kingsbridge girls. One, Kate Brown, had been sufficiently fond of him to let him go all the way, one warm summer afternoon a year ago, in her father's orchard. Then her father had died suddenly, and her mother had taken the family to live in Portsmouth. It was the only time Merthin had lain with a woman. Was he mad to turn down Griselda's offer?

He told himself he had had a lucky escape. Griselda was a mean-spirited girl who did not really like him. He should be proud of having resisted temptation. He had not followed his instinct like a dumb beast; he had made a decision, like a man.

Then Griselda started to cry.

Her weeping was not loud, but all the same he could hear everything. He went to the back door. Like every house in town, Elfric's had a long, narrow strip of land at the back with a privy and a rubbish dump. Most householders kept chickens and a pig, and grew vegetables and fruits, but Elfric's yard was used to store stacks of lumber and stones, coils of rope, buckets and barrows and ladders. Merthin stared at the rain falling on the yard, but Griselda's sobbing still reached his ears.

He decided to leave the house, and got as far as the front door, but then he could not think where to go. At Caris's house there was only Petranilla, who would not welcome him. He thought of going to his parents, but they were the last people he wanted to see when he was in this state. He could have talked to his brother, but Ralph was not due to arrive in Kingsbridge until later in the week. Besides, he realized, he could not leave the house without a coat—not because of the rain, he did not mind getting wet, but because of the bulge in front of his clothing that would not subside.

He tried to think of Caris. She would be sipping wine, he thought, and eating roast beef and wheat bread. He asked himself what she was wearing. Her best dress was a soft pinkish red with a square-cut neckline that showed off the pale skin of her slender neck. But Griselda's crying kept intruding on his thoughts. He wanted to comfort her, to tell her he was sorry to make her feel spurned, and explain to her that she was an attractive person but they were not right for one another.

He sat down, then stood up again. It was hard to listen to a woman in distress. He could not think about scaffolding while that sound filled the house. Can't stay, can't leave, can't sit still.

He went upstairs.

She was lying facedown on the straw-filled palliasse that was her bed. Her dress was rucked up around her chubby thighs. The skin on the back of her legs was very white and looked soft.

"I'm sorry," he said.

"Go away."

"Don't cry."

"I hate you."

He knelt down and patted her back. "I can't sit in the kitchen and listen to you crying."

She rolled over and looked at him, her face wet with tears. "I'm ugly and fat, and you hate me."

"I don't hate you." He wiped her wet cheeks with the back of his hand.

She took his wrist and drew him to her. "Don't you? Truly?"

"No. But . . ."

She put her hand behind his head, pulled him down, and kissed him. He groaned, more aroused than ever. He lay beside her on the mattress. I will leave her in a moment, he told himself. I'll just comfort her a little more, then I'll get up and go down the stairs.

She took his hand and pushed it up her skirt, placing it between her legs. He felt the wiry hair, the soft skin beneath, and the moist divide, and he knew he was lost. He stroked her roughly, his finger slipping inside. He felt as if he would burst. "I can't stop," he said.

"Quickly," she said, panting. She pulled up his shirt and pushed down his drawers, and he rolled onto her.

He felt himself losing control as she guided him inside her. The remorse hit him before it was over. "Oh, no," he said. The explosion began with his first thrust, and in an instant it was finished. He slumped on top of her, his eyes closed. "Oh, God," he said. "I wish I was dead."

7

Buonaventura Caroli made his shocking announcement at breakfast on Monday, the day after the big banquet at the guildhall.

Caris felt a little unwell as she took her seat at the oak table in the dining hall of her father's house. She had a headache and a touch of nausea. She ate a small dish of warm bread-and-milk to settle her stomach. Recalling that she had enjoyed the wine at the banquet, she wondered whether she had drunk too much of it. Was this the morning-after feeling that men and boys joked about when they boasted how much strong drink they could take?

Father and Buonaventura were eating cold mutton, and Aunt Petranilla was telling a story. "When I was fifteen, I was betrothed to a nephew of the earl of Shiring," she said. "It was considered a good match: his father was a knight of the middling sort, and mine a wealthy wool merchant. Then the earl and his only son both died in Scotland, at the battle of Loudon Hill. My fiancé, Roland, became the earl—and broke off the engagement. He is still the earl today. If I had married Roland before the battle, I would now be the countess of Shiring." She dipped toast in her ale.

"Perhaps it was not the will of God," said Buonaventura. He threw a bone to Scrap, who pounced on it as if she had not seen food for a week. Then he said to Papa: "My friend, there is something I should tell you before we begin the day's business."

Caris felt, from his tone of voice, that he had bad news; and her father must have had the same intuition, for he said: "This sounds ominous."

"Our trade has been shrinking for the last few years," Buonaventura went on. "Each year my family sells a little less cloth, each year we buy a little less wool from England."

"Business is always like that," said Edmund. "It goes up, it goes down, no one knows why."

"But now your king has interfered."

It was true. Edward III had seen the money being made in wool and had decided that more of it must go to the crown. He had introduced a new tax of one pound per woolsack. A sack was standardized at 364 pounds weight and sold for about four pounds in money; so the extra tax was a quarter of the value of the wool, a huge slice.

Buonaventura went on: "What is worse, he has made it difficult to export wool from England. I have had to pay large bribes."

"The ban on exports will be lifted shortly," Edmund said. "The merchants of the Wool Company in London are negotiating with royal officials—"

"I hope you are right," Buonaventura said. "But, with things as they are, my family feels I no longer need to visit two separate wool fairs in this part of the country."

"Quite right!" said Edmund. "Come here, and forget about the Shiring fair."

The town of Shiring was two days' travel from Kingsbridge. It was about the same size, and while it did not have a cathedral or a priory, it boasted the sheriff's castle and the county court. It held a rival wool fair once a year.

"I'm afraid I can't find the range of wool here. You see, the Kingsbridge Fleece Fair seems to be declining. More and more sellers go to Shiring. Their fair offers a greater variety of types and qualities."

Caris was dismayed. This could be disastrous for her father. She put in: "Why would sellers prefer Shiring?"

Buonaventura shrugged. "The guild merchant there has made the fair attractive. There's no long queue to enter the city gate; the dealers can hire tents and booths; there's a wool exchange building where everyone can do business when it rains like this . . ."

"We could do all that," she said.

Her father snorted. "If only."

"Why not, Papa?"

"Shiring is an independent borough, with a royal charter. The merchant guild there has the power to organize things for the benefit of the wool merchants. Kingsbridge belongs to the priory—"

Petranilla put in: "For the glory of God."

"No doubt," Edmund said. "But our parish guild can't do anything without the priory's approval—and priors are cautious and conservative people, my brother being no exception. The upshot is that most improvement plans get rejected."

Buonaventura went on: "Because of my family's long association with you, Edmund, and your father before you, we have continued to come to Kingsbridge; but in hard times we can't afford to be sentimental."

"Then let me ask you a small favor, for the sake of that long association," Edmund said. "Don't make a final decision yet. Keep an open mind."

That was clever, Caris thought. She was struck—as she often was—by how shrewd her father could be in a negotiation. He did not argue that Buonaventura should reverse his decision, for that would just make him dig his heels in. The Italian was much more likely to agree not to make the decision final. That committed him to nothing, but left the door open.

Buonaventura found it hard to refuse. "All right, but to what end?"

"I want the chance to improve the fair, and especially that bridge," Edmund replied. "If we could offer better facilities here at Kingsbridge than they have at Shiring, and attract more sellers, you would continue to visit us, wouldn't you?"

"Of course."

"Then that's what we'll have to do." He stood up. "I'll go and see my brother now. Caris, come with me. We'll show him the queue at the bridge. No, wait, Caris, go and fetch your clever young builder, Merthin. We might need his expertise."

"He'll be working."

Petranilla said: "Just tell his master that the alderman of the parish guild wants the boy." Petranilla was proud that her brother was alderman, and mentioned it at every opportunity.

But she was right. Elfric would have to release Merthin. "I'll go and find him," Caris said.

She put on a cape with a hood and went out. It was still raining, though not as heavily as yesterday. Elfric, like most of the leading citizens, lived on the main street that ran from the bridge up to the priory gates. The broad street was crowded with carts and people heading for the fair, splashing through puddles and streamlets of rain.

She was eager to see Merthin, as always. She had liked him ever since All Hallows Day ten years ago, when he had appeared at archery practice with his homemade bow. He was clever and funny. Like her, he knew that the world was a bigger and more fascinating place than most Kingsbridge citizens could conceive. But six months ago they had discovered something that was even more fun than being friends.

Caris had kissed boys before Merthin, though not often: she had never really seen the point. With him it was different, exciting and sexy. He had an impish streak that made everything he did seem mildly wicked.

She liked it when he touched her body, too. She wanted to do more—but she tried not to think about that. "More" meant marriage, and a wife had to be subordinate to her husband, who was her master—and Caris hated that idea. Fortunately she was not forced to think about it yet, for Merthin could not marry until his apprenticeship was over, and that was half a year away.

She reached Elfric's house and stepped inside. Her sister, Alice, was in the front room, at the table, with her stepdaughter, Griselda. They were eating bread with honey. Alice had changed in the three years since she had married Elfric. Her nature had always been harsh, like Petranilla's, and under the influence of her husband she had become more suspicious, resentful, and ungenerous.

But she was pleasant enough today. "Sit down, sister," she said. "The bread is fresh this morning."

"I can't, I'm looking for Merthin."

Alice looked disapproving. "So early?"

"Father wants him." Caris went through the kitchen to the back door and looked into the yard. Rain fell on a dismal landscape of builder's junk. One of Elfric's laborers was putting wet stones into a barrow. There was no sign of Merthin. She went back inside.

Alice said: "He's probably at the cathedral. He's been making a door."

Caris recalled that Merthin had mentioned this. The door in the north porch had rotted, and Merthin was working on a replacement.

Griselda added: "He's been carving virgins." She grinned, then put more bread-and-honey into her mouth.

Caris knew this, too. The old door was decorated with carvings illustrating the story Jesus told on the Mount of Olives, about the wise and foolish virgins, and Merthin had to copy it. But there was something unpleasant about Griselda's grin, Caris thought; almost as if she were laughing at Caris for being a virgin herself.

"I'll try the cathedral," Caris said, and with a perfunctory wave she left.

She climbed the main street and entered the cathedral close. As she threaded her way through the market stalls, it seemed to her that a dismal air hung over the fair. Was she imagining it, because of what Buonaventura had said? She thought not. When she recalled the fleece fairs of her childhood, it seemed to her that they had been busier and more crowded. In those days, the priory precincts had not been large enough to contain the fair, and the streets all around had been obstructed by unlicensed stalls—often just a small table covered with trinkets—plus hawkers with trays, jugglers, fortune-tellers, musicians, and itinerant friars calling sinners to redemption. Now it seemed to her there might have been room for a few more stalls within the precincts. "Buonaventura must be right," she said to herself. "The fair is shrinking." A trader gave her a strange look, and she realized she had spoken her thoughts out loud. It was a bad habit: people thought she was talking to spirits. She had taught herself not to do it, but she sometimes forgot, especially when she was anxious.

She walked around the great church to the north side.

Merthin was working in the porch, a roomy space where people often held meetings. He had the door standing upright in a stout wooden frame that held it still while he carved. Behind the new work, the old door was still in place in the archway, cracked and crumbling. Merthin stood with his back to her, so that the light fell over his shoulders onto the wood in front of him. He did not see her, and the sound of the rain drowned her footsteps, so she was able to study him for a few moments unnoticed.

He was a small man, not much taller than she. He had a large, intelligent head on a wiry body. His small hands moved deftly across the carving, shaving fine curls of wood with a sharp knife as he shaped the images. He had white skin and a lot of bushy red hair. "He's not very handsome," Alice had said, with a twist of her lip, when Caris admitted she had fallen in love with him. It was true that Merthin did not have the dashing good looks of his brother, Ralph, but Caris thought his face was quite marvelous: irregular and quirky and wise and full of laughter, just as he was.

"Hello," she said, and he jumped. She laughed. "It's not like you to be so easily spooked."

"You startled me." He hesitated, then kissed her. He seemed a little awkward, but that sometimes happened when he was concentrating on his work.

She looked at the carving. They were five virgins on each side of the door, the wise ones feasting at the wedding, and the foolish ones outside, holding their lamps upside down to show that they were empty of oil. Merthin had copied the design of the old door, but with subtle changes. The virgins stood in rows, five on one side and five on the other, like the arches in the cathedral; but, in the new door, they were not exactly alike. Merthin had given each girl a sign of individuality. One was pretty, another had curly hair, one wept, another closed one eye in a mischievous wink. He had made them real, and the scene on the old door now looked stiff and lifeless by comparison. "It's wonderful," Caris said. "But I wonder what the monks will think."

"Brother Thomas likes it," Merthin replied.

"What about Prior Anthony?"

"He hasn't seen it. But he'll accept it. He won't want to pay twice."

That was true, Caris thought. Her uncle Anthony was unadventurous, but parsimonious, too. The mention of the prior reminded her of her errand. "My father wants you to meet him and the prior at the bridge."

"Did he say why?"

"I think he's going to ask Anthony to build a new bridge."

Merthin put his tools into a leather satchel and quickly swept the floor, brushing sawdust and wood shavings out of the porch. Then he and Caris walked in the rain through the fair and down the main street to the wooden bridge. Caris told him what Buonaventura had said at the breakfast table. Merthin felt, as she did, that recent fairs had not been as bustling as those he remembered from childhood.

Despite that, there was a long queue of people and carts waiting to get into Kingsbridge. At the near end of the bridge was a small gatehouse where a monk sat taking a fee of one penny from every trader who entered the city with goods for sale. The bridge was narrow, so it was not possible for anyone to jump the queue, and in consequence people who did not need to pay—residents of the town, mainly—also had to stand in line. In addition, some of the boards that formed the surface were twisted and broken, so carts had to move slowly as they crossed. The result was that the queue stretched away along the road between the suburban hovels and disappeared into the rain.

The bridge was also too short. Once, no doubt, both its ends had given on to dry land. But either the river had widened or, more likely, the passage of carts and people over decades and centuries had flattened the banks, so that now people had to wade across muddy beaches on both sides.

Caris saw that Merthin was studying its structure. She knew that look in his eyes: he was thinking about how it stayed upright. She often caught him staring at something in that way, usually in the cathedral, but sometimes in front of a house or even something natural, a thorn tree in blossom or a sparrow hawk hovering. He became very still, his gaze bright and sharp, as if he were shining a light into a murky place, trying to make out what was there. If she asked him, he told her he was trying to see the insides of things.

She followed his gaze and strained to imagine what he perceived in the old bridge. It was sixty yards from end to end, the longest bridge she had ever seen. The roadbed was supported by massive oak piers in two rows, like the pillars that marched either side of the nave of the cathedral. There were five pairs of piers. The end ones, where the water was shallow, were quite short, but the three central pairs stood fifteen feet above the waterline.

Each pier consisted of four oak beams in a cluster, held together by plank braces. Legend said that the king had given Kingsbridge Priory the twenty-four best oak trees in England to build the three central pairs of piers. The tops were linked by beams in two parallel lines. Shorter beams crossed from one line to the other, forming the roadbed; and longitudinal planks had been laid on top to form the road surface. On each side was a wooden railing that served as a flimsy parapet. Every couple of years a drunk peasant would drive a cart through the rail and kill himself and his horse in the river.

"What are you looking at?" Caris asked Merthin.

"The cracks."

"I don't see any."

"The timbers on either side of the central pier are splitting. You can see where Elfric has reinforced them with iron braces."

Now that he pointed them out, Caris could see the flat metal strips nailed across the cracks. "You look worried," she said to him.

"I don't know why the timbers cracked in the first place."

"Does it matter?"

"Of course it does."

He was not very talkative this morning. She was about to ask him why, when he said: "Here comes your father."

She looked along the street. The two brothers made an odd pair. Tall Anthony fastidiously held up the skirts of his monkish robe and stepped gingerly around the puddles, wearing an expression of distaste on his pale indoor face. Edmund, more vigorous despite being the elder, had a red face and a long, untidy gray beard, and he walked carelessly, dragging his withered leg through the mud, speaking argumentatively and gesturing extravagantly with both arms. When Caris saw her father at a distance, the way a stranger might see him, she always felt a surge of love.

The dispute was in full swing when they got to the bridge, and they continued without pause. "Look at that queue!" Edmund shouted. "Hundreds of people *not* trading at the fair because they haven't got there yet! And you can be sure half of them will meet a buyer or seller while waiting, and conduct their business right then and there, then go home without even entering the city!"

"That's forestalling, and it's against the law," said Anthony.

"You could go and tell them that, if you could get across the bridge, but you can't, because it's too narrow! Listen, Anthony. If the Italians pull out, the Fleece Fair will never be the same again. Your prosperity and mine are based on the fair—we must not just let it go!"

"We can't force Buonaventura to do business here."

"But we can make our fair more attractive than Shiring's. We need to announce a big, symbolic project, right now, this week, something to convince them all that the Fleece Fair isn't finished. We have to tell them we're going to tear down this old bridge and build a new one, twice as wide." Without warning, he turned to Merthin. "How long would it take, young lad?"

Merthin looked startled, but he answered. "Finding the trees would be the hard part. You need very long timbers, well seasoned. Then the piers have to be driven into the river bed—that's tricky, because you're working in running water. After that it's just carpentry. You could finish it by Christmas."

Anthony said: "There's no certainty the Caroli family will change its plans if we build a new bridge."

"They will," Edmund said forcefully. "I guarantee it."

"Anyway, I can't afford to build a bridge. I don't have the money."

"You can't afford *not* to build a bridge," Edmund shouted. "You'll ruin yourself as well as the town."

"It's out of the question. I don't even know where I'm going to get the money for the repairs in the south aisle."

"So what will you do?"

"Trust in God."

"Those who trust in God and sow a seed may reap a harvest. But you're not sowing the seed."

Anthony got irritated. "I know this is difficult for you to understand, Edmund, but Kingsbridge Priory is not a commercial enterprise. We're here to worship God, not to make money."

"You won't worship God for long if you've nothing to eat."

"God will provide."

Edmund's red face flushed with anger, turning an purplish color. "When you were a boy, our father's business fed you and clothed you and paid for your education. Since you've been a monk, the citizens of this town and the peasants of the surrounding countryside have kept you alive by paying you rents, tithes, charges for market stalls, bridge tolls, and a dozen other different fees. All your life you've lived like a flea on the backs of hardworking people. And now you have the nerve to tell us that God provides."

"That's perilously close to blasphemy."

"Don't forget that I've known you since you were born, Anthony. You always had a talent for avoiding work." Edmund's voice, so often raised in a shout, now dropped—a sign, Caris knew, that he was really furious. "When it was time to empty out the privy, you went off to bed, so that you would be rested for school the next day. Father's gift to God, you always had the best of everything, and never lifted your hand to earn it. Strengthening food, the warmest bedroom, the best clothes—I was the only boy who wore his younger brother's cast-off outfits!"

"And you never let me forget it."

Caris had been waiting for the opportunity to halt the flow, and now she took it. "There ought to be a way around this."

They both looked at her, surprised to be interrupted.

She went on: "For example, couldn't the townspeople build a bridge?"

"Don't be ridiculous," said Anthony. "The town belongs to the priory. A servant doesn't furnish his master's house."

"But if your permission was sought, you would have no reason to refuse it."

Anthony did not immediately contradict that, which was encouraging; but Edmund was shaking his head. "I don't think I could persuade them to put up the money," he said. "It would be in their interests, long term, of course; but people are very reluctant to think in the long term when being asked to part with their money."

"Ha!" said Anthony. "Yet you expect me to think long term."

"You deal with eternal life, don't you?" Edmund shot back. "You of all people ought to be able to see beyond the end of next week. Besides, you get a penny toll from everyone who crosses the bridge. You'd get your money back *and* you'd benefit from the improvement in business."

Caris said: "But Uncle Anthony is a spiritual leader, and he feels it's not his role."

"But he owns the town!" Papa protested. "He's the only one who can do it!" Then he gave her an inquiring look, realizing that she would not have contradicted him without a reason. "What are you thinking?"

"Suppose the townspeople built a bridge, and were repaid out of the penny tolls?"

Edmund opened his mouth to express an objection, but could not think of one.

Caris looked at Anthony.

Anthony said: "When the priory was new, its only income came from that bridge. I can't give it away."

"But think what you would gain, if the Fleece Fair and the weekly market began to return to their former size: not just the bridge tolls, but stallholders' fees, the percentage you take of all transactions at the fair, and gifts to the cathedral, too!"

Edmund added: "And the profits on your own sales: wool, grain, hides, books, statues of the saints—"

Anthony said: "You planned this, didn't you?" He pointed an accusing finger at his older brother. "You told your daughter what to say, and the lad. He would never think up a scheme like this, and she's just a woman. It has your mark on it. This is all a plot to cheat me of my bridge tolls. Well, it's failed. Praise God, I'm not that stupid!" He turned away and splashed off through the mud.

Edmund said: "I don't know how my father ever sired someone with so little sense." And he, too, stomped off.

Caris turned to Merthin. "Well," she said, "what did you think of all that?"

"I don't know." He looked away, avoiding her eye. "I'd better get back to work." He went without kissing her.

"Well!" she said when he was out of earshot. "What on earth has got into him?"

8

The earl of Shiring came to Kingsbridge on the Tuesday of Fleece Fair week. He brought with him both his sons, various other family members, and an entourage of knights and squires. The bridge was cleared by his advance men, and no one was permitted to cross for an hour before his arrival, lest he should suffer the indignity of being made to wait alongside the common people. His followers wore his red-and-black livery, and they all splashed into town with banners flying, their horses' hooves spattering the citizens with rainwater and mud. Earl Roland had prospered in the last ten years—under Queen Isabella and, later, her son Edward III—and he wanted the world to know it, as rich and powerful men generally did.

In his company was Ralph, son of Sir Gerald and brother of Merthin. At the same time as Merthin had been apprenticed to Elfric's father, Ralph had become a squire in the household of Earl Roland, and he had been happy ever since. He had been well fed and clothed, he had learned to ride and fight, and he had spent most of his time hunting and playing sports and games. In six and a half years no one had asked him to read or write a word. As he rode behind the earl through the huddled stalls of the Fleece Fair, watched by faces both envious and fearful, he pitied the merchants and tradesmen grubbing for pennies in the mud.

The earl dismounted at the prior's house, on the north side of the cathedral. His younger son, Richard, did the same. Richard was bishop of Kingsbridge and the cathedral was, theoretically, his church. However, the bishop's palace was in the county town of Shiring, two days' journey away. This suited the bishop, whose duties were political as much as religious; and it suited the monks, who preferred not to be too closely supervised.

Richard was only twenty-eight, but his father was a close ally of the king, and that counted for more than seniority.

The rest of the entourage rode to the south end of the cathedral close. The earl's elder son, William, lord of Caster, told the squires to stable the horses while half a dozen knights settled in to the hospital. Ralph moved quickly to help William's wife, Lady Philippa, get down from her horse. She was a tall, attractive woman with long legs and deep breasts, and Ralph nurtured a hopeless love for her.

When the horses were settled, Ralph went to visit his mother and father. They lived rent-free in a small house in the southwest quarter of the town, by the river, in a neighborhood made malodorous by the work of leather tanners. As he approached the house, Ralph felt himself shriveling with shame inside his red-and-black uniform. He was grateful that Lady Philippa could not see the indignity of his parents' situation.

He had not seen them for a year, and they seemed older. There was a lot of gray in his mother's hair, and his father was losing his eyesight. They gave him cider made by the monks and wild strawberries Mother had gathered in the woods. Father admired his livery. "Has the earl made you a knight yet?" he asked eagerly.

It was the ambition of every squire to become a knight, but Ralph felt it more keenly than most. His father had never got over the humiliation, ten years ago, of being degraded to the position of pensioner of the priory. An arrow had pierced Ralph's heart that day. The pain would not be eased until he had restored the family honor. But not all squires became knights. Nevertheless, Father always talked as if it were only a matter of time for Ralph.

"Not yet," Ralph said. "But we're likely to go to war with France before long, and that will be my chance." He spoke lightly, not wishing to show how badly he yearned for the chance to distinguish himself in battle.

Mother was disgusted. "Why do kings always want war?"

Father laughed. "It's what men were made for."

"No, it's not," she said sharply. "When I gave birth to Ralph in pain and suffering, I didn't intend that he should live to have his head cut off by a Frenchman's sword or his heart pierced by a bolt from a crossbow."

Father flapped a hand at her in a dismissive gesture and said to Ralph: "What makes you say there will be war?"

"King Philip of France has confiscated Gascony."

"Ah. We can't have that."

English kings had ruled the western French province of Gascony for generations. They had given trade privileges to the merchants of Bordeaux and Bayonne, who did more business with London than with Paris. Still, there was always trouble.

Ralph said: "King Edward has sent ambassadors to Flanders to form alliances."

"Allies may want money."

"That's why Earl Roland has come to Kingsbridge. The king wants a loan from the wool merchants."

"How much?"

"The talk is of two hundred thousands pounds, nationwide, as an advance against the wool tax."

Mother said bleakly: "The king should take care not to tax the wool merchants to death."

Father said: "The merchants have plenty of money—just look at their fine clothes." There was bitterness in his tone, and Ralph observed that he had on a worn linen undershirt and old shoes. "Anyway, they want us to stop the French navy interfering with their trade." Over the last year, French ships had raided towns on the south coast of England, sacking the ports and setting fire to ships in the harbors.

"The French attack us, so we attack the French," said Mother. "What is the sense of it?"

"Women will never understand," Father replied.

"That's the truth," she said crisply.

Ralph changed the subject. "How is my brother?"

"He's a fine craftsman," said his father, and he sounded, Ralph thought, like a horse salesman saying that an undersize pony was a good mount for a woman.

Mother said: "He's smitten with Edmund Wooler's daughter."

"Caris?" Ralph smiled. "He always liked her. We played together as children. She was a bossy little minx, but Merthin never seemed to mind. Will he marry her?"

"I expect so," Mother said. "When he finishes his apprenticeship."

"He'll have his hands full." Ralph got up. "Where do you think he is now?"

"He's working in the north porch of the cathedral," Father said. "But he might be having his dinner."

"I'll find him." Ralph kissed them both and went out.

He returned to the priory and wandered through the fair. The rain had stopped and the sun was shining fitfully, glinting in the puddles and raising steam off the stallholders' wet covers. He saw a familiar profile, and the regular footsteps of his heart faltered. It was the straight nose and strong jaw of Lady Philippa. She was older than Ralph, about twenty-five, he guessed. She was standing at a stall, looking at bolts of silk from Italy, and he drank in the way her light summer dress draped itself lasciviously over the curves of her hips. He made her an unnecessarily elaborate bow.

She glanced up and gave a perfunctory nod.

"Beautiful materials," he said, trying to open a conversation.

"Yes."

At that moment, a diminutive figure with untidy carrot-colored hair approached: Merthin. Ralph was delighted to see him. "This is my clever older brother," he said to Philippa.

Merthin said to Philippa: "Buy the pale green—it matches your eyes."

Ralph winced. Merthin should not have addressed her in such a familiar way.

However, she did not seem to mind too much. She spoke in a tone of mild reproof, saying: "When I want a boy's opinion, I'll ask my son," but as she said it she gave him a smile that was almost flirtatious.

Ralph said: "This is the Lady Philippa, you fool! I apologize for my brother's cheek, my lady."

"What's his name, anyway?"

"I'm Merthin Fitzgerald, at your service anytime you find yourself hesitating over silks."

Ralph took his arm and led him away before he could say anything else indiscreet. "I don't know how you do it!" he said, with exasperation and admiration equally mixed. "It matches her eyes, does it? If I said something like that, she'd have me flogged." He was exaggerating, but it was true that Philippa usually responded sharply to insolence. He did not know whether to be amused or angry that she had been indulgent to Merthin.

"That's me," Merthin said. "Every woman's dream."

Ralph detected bitterness in his tone. "Is anything wrong?" he said. "How's Caris?"

"I've done something stupid," Merthin replied. "I'll tell you later. Let's look around while the sun's out."

Ralph noticed a stall where a monk with ash blond hair was selling cheese. "Watch this," he said to Merthin. He approached the stall and said: "This looks tasty, brother—where does it come from?"

"We make it at St.-John-in-the-Forest. It's a small cell, or branch, of Kingsbridge Priory. I'm the prior there—my name is Saul Whitehead."

"It makes me hungry to look at it. I wish I could buy some—but the earl keeps us squires penniless."

The monk cut a slice off the wheel of cheese and gave it to Ralph. "Then you shall have some for nothing, in the name of Jesus," he said.

"Thank you, Brother Saul."

As they walked away, Ralph grinned at Merthin and said: "See? As easy as taking an apple from a child."

"And about as admirable," Merthin said.

"But what a fool, to give his cheese away to anyone with a sob story!"

"He probably thinks it's better to risk being made a fool of than to deny food to a starving man."

"You're a bit sour today. How come you're allowed to cheek a noblewoman, but I can't talk a stupid monk into giving me free cheese?"

Merthin surprised him with a grin. "Just like when we were boys, eh?"

"Exactly!" Now Ralph did not know whether to be angry or amused. Before he could make up his mind, a pretty girl approached him with eggs on a tray. She was slim, with a small bust under a homespun dress, and he imagined her breasts to be pale and round like the eggs. He smiled at her: "How much?" he said, though he had no need of eggs.

"A penny for twelve."

"Are they good?"

She pointed at a nearby stall. "They're from these hens."

"And have the hens been well serviced by a healthy rooster?" Ralph saw Merthin roll up his eyes in mock despair at this sally.

However, the girl played along. "Yes, sir," she said with a smile.

"Lucky hens, eh?"

"I don't know."

"Of course not. A maid understands little of these things." Ralph scrutinized her. She had fair hair and a turned-up nose. She was about eighteen, he guessed.

She batted her eyelids and said: "Don't stare at me, please."

From behind the stall a peasant—no doubt the girl's father—called: "Annet! Come here."

"So your name is Annet," Ralph said.

She ignored the summons.

Ralph said: "Who is your father?"

"Perkin from Wigleigh."

"Really? My friend Stephen is lord of Wigleigh. Is Stephen good to you?"

"Lord Stephen is just and merciful," she said dutifully.

Her father called again. "Annet! You're wanted here."

Ralph knew why Perkin was trying to get her away. He would not mind if a squire wanted to marry his daughter: that would be a step up the social ladder for her. But he feared that Ralph wanted to dally with her then discard her. And he was right.

"Don't go, Annet Wigleigh," Ralph said.

"Not until you've bought what I'm offering."

Beside them, Merthin groaned: "One is as bad as the other."

Ralph said: "Why don't you put down the eggs and come with me. We could stroll along the riverbank." Between the river and the wall of the priory grounds there was a wide bank, covered at this time of year with wildflowers and bushes, where courting couples traditionally went.

But Annet was not that easy. "My father would be displeased," she said.

"Let's not worry about him." There was not much a peasant could do to oppose the will of a squire, especially when the squire was wearing the livery of a great earl. It was an insult to the earl to lay hands on one of his servants. The peasant might try to dissuade his daughter, but it would be risky for him to restrain her forcibly.

However, someone else came to Perkin's aid. A youthful voice said: "Hello, Annet, is all well?"

Ralph turned to the newcomer. He looked about sixteen, but he was almost as tall as Ralph, with broad shoulders and big hands. He was strikingly handsome, with regular features that might have been carved by a cathedral sculptor. He had thick, tawny hair and the beginnings of a beard the same color.

Ralph said: "Who the hell are you?"

"I'm Wulfric from Wigleigh, sir." Wulfric was deferential, but not afraid. He turned back to Annet and said: "I've come to help you sell some eggs."

The boy's muscular shoulder came between Ralph and Annet, his stance protecting the girl and at the same time excluding Ralph. It was mildly insolent, and Ralph felt a stirring of anger. "Get out of the way, Wulfric Wigleigh," he said. "You're not wanted here."

Wulfric turned again and gave him a level look. "I'm betrothed to this woman, sir," he said. Once again, the tone was respectful but the attitude fearless.

Perkin spoke up. "That's true, sir—they are to be married."

"Don't talk to me about your peasant customs," Ralph said contemptuously. "I don't care if she's married to the oaf." It angered him to be spoken to this way by his inferiors. It was not their place to tell him what to do.

Merthin butted in. "Let's go, Ralph," he said. "I'm hungry, and Betty Baxter is selling hot pies."

"Pies?" Ralph said. "I'm more interested in eggs." He picked up one of the eggs on her tray and fondled it suggestively, then he put it down and touched her left breast. It was firm to his fingertips, and egg-shaped.

"What do you think you're doing?" She sounded indignant, but she did not move away.

He squeezed gently, enjoying the sensation. "Examining the goods on offer."

"Take your hands off me."

"In a minute."

Then Wulfric shoved him violently.

Ralph was taken by surprise. He had not expected to be attacked by a peasant. He staggered back, stumbled, and fell to the ground with a thump. He heard someone laugh, and amazement gave way to humiliation. He sprang to his feet, enraged.

He was not wearing his sword, but he had a long dagger at his belt. However, it would be undignified to use weapons on an unarmed peasant: he could lose the respect of the earl's knights and the other squires. He would have to punish Wulfric with his fists.

Perkin stepped from behind his stall, speaking rapidly. "A clumsy mistake, sir, not intended, the lad is deeply sorry, I assure you—"

However, his daughter seemed unafraid. "Boys, boys!" she said in a tone of mock reprimand, but she seemed more pleased than anything else.

Ralph ignored them both. He took one step toward Wulfric and raised his right fist. Then, when Wulfric lifted both arms to defend his face from the blow, Ralph drove his left fist into the boy's belly.

It was not as soft as he had expected. All the same, Wulfric bent forward, his face twisted in agony, both hands going to his midriff; whereupon Ralph hit him full in the face with his right fist, catching him high on the cheekbone. The punch hurt his hand but brought joy to his soul.

To his astonishment, Wulfric hit him back.

Instead of crumpling to the floor and lying there waiting to be kicked, the peasant boy came back with a right-handed punch that had all the strength of his shoulders behind it. Ralph's nose seemed to explode in blood and pain. He roared with anger.

Wulfric stepped back, seeming to realize what a terrible thing he had done, and he dropped both arms, holding his palms upward.

But it was too late to be sorry. Ralph hit him with both fists on the face and body, a storm of blows that Wulfric feebly tried to ward off by holding up his arms and ducking his head. As he punched him, Ralph wondered vaguely why the boy did not run away, and guessed he was hoping to take his punishment now rather than face worse later. He had guts, Ralph realized; but that made him even angrier. He hit him harder, again and again, and he was filled with an emotion that was both rage and ecstasy. Merthin tried to intervene. "For the love of Christ, enough," he said, putting a hand on Ralph's shoulder; but Ralph shook him off.

At last Wulfric's hands fell to his sides and he staggered, dazed, his handsome face covered in blood, his eyes closing; then he fell down. Ralph started to kick him. Then a burly man in leather trousers appeared and spoke with a voice of authority: "Now, then, young Ralph, don't murder the boy."

Ralph recognized John, the town constable, and said indignantly: "He attacked me!"

"Well, he's not attacking you anymore, is he, sir? Lying on the ground like that with his eyes shut." John put himself in front of Ralph. "I'd rather do without the trouble of a coroner's inquiry."

People crowded around Wulfric: Perkin; Annet, who was flushed with excitement; the Lady Philippa; and several bystanders.

The ecstatic feeling left Ralph, and his nose hurt like hell. He could breathe only through his mouth. He tasted blood. "That animal punched my nose," he said, and he sounded like a man with a heavy cold.

"Then he shall be punished," said John.

Two men who looked like Wulfric appeared: his father and his elder brother, Ralph guessed. They helped Wulfric to his feet, shooting angry glances at Ralph.

Perkin spoke up. He was a fat man with a sly face. "The squire threw the first punch," he said.

Ralph said: "The peasant deliberately shoved me!"

"The squire insulted Wulfric's wife-to-be."

The constable said: "No matter what the squire may have said, Wulfric should know better than to lay hands on a servant of Earl Roland's. I should think the earl will expect him to be severely dealt with."

Wulfric's father spoke up. "Is there a new law, John Constable, that says a man in livery may do what he likes?"

There was a mutter of agreement from the small crowd now gathered. Young squires caused a lot of trouble, and often escaped punishment because they were wearing the colors of some baron; and this was deeply resented by law-abiding tradesmen and peasants.

Lady Philippa intervened. "I'm the earl's daughter-in-law, and I saw the whole thing," she said. Her voice was low and melodious, but she spoke with the authority of high rank. Ralph expected her to take his side, but to his dismay she went on: "I'm sorry to say that this was entirely Ralph's fault. He fondled the girl's body in a most outrageous way."

"Thank you, my lady," John Constable said deferentially. He lowered his voice to confer with her. "But I think the earl might not want the peasant lad to go unpunished."

She nodded thoughtfully. "We don't want this to be the start of a lengthy dispute. Put the boy in the stocks for twenty-four hours. It won't do him much harm, at his age, but everyone will know that justice has been done. That will satisfy the earl—I'll answer for him."

John hesitated. Ralph could see that the constable did not like taking orders from anyone but his master, the prior of Kingsbridge. However, Philippa's decision would surely satisfy all parties. Ralph himself would have liked to see Wulfric flogged, but he was beginning to suspect that he did not come out of this as a hero, and he would look worse if he demanded a harsh punishment. After a moment John said: "Very well, Lady Philippa, if you're willing to take responsibility."

"I am."

"Right." John took Wulfric by the arm and led him away. The lad had recovered fast, and was able to walk normally. His family followed. Perhaps they would bring him food and drink while he was in the stocks, and make sure he was not pelted.

Merthin said to Ralph: "How are you?"

Ralph felt as if the middle of his face were swelling like an inflated bladder. His vision was blurred, his speech was a nasal honk, and he was in pain. "I'm fine," he said. "Never better."

"Let's get a monk to look at your nose."

"No." Ralph was not afraid of fights, but he hated the things physicians did: bleeding and cupping and lancing boils. "All I need is a bottle of strong wine. Take me to the nearest tavern."

"All right," Merthin said, but he did not move. He was giving Ralph a queer look.

Ralph said: "What's the matter with you?"
"You don't change, do you?"
Ralph shrugged. "Does anyone?"

9

Godwyn was completely fascinated by *Timothy's Book*. It was a history of Kingsbridge Priory and, like most such histories, it began with the creation by God of Heaven and Earth. But mostly it recounted the era of Prior Philip, two centuries ago, when the cathedral was built—a time now regarded by the monks as a golden age. The author, Brother Timothy, claimed that the legendary Philip had been a stern disciplinarian as well as a man of compassion. Godwyn was not sure how you could be both.

On the Wednesday of Fleece Fair week, in the study hour before the service of Sext, Godwyn sat on a high stool in the monastery library, the book open on a lectern before him. This was his favorite place in the priory: a spacious room, well lit by high windows, with almost a hundred books in a locked cupboard. It was normally hushed, but today he could hear, from the far side of the cathedral, the muffled roar of the fair—a thousand people buying and selling, haggling and quarreling, calling their wares and shouting encouragement at cockfighting and bear-baiting.

At the back of the book, later authors had tracked the descendants of the cathedral builders down to the present day. Godwyn was pleased—and frankly surprised—to find confirmation of his mother's theory that she was descended from Tom Builder through Tom's daughter Martha. He wondered what family traits might have come down from Tom. A mason needed to be a shrewd businessman, he supposed, and Godwyn's grandfather and his uncle Edmund had that quality. His cousin Caris also showed signs of the same flair. Perhaps Tom had also had the green eyes flecked with yellow that they all shared.

Godwyn also read about Tom Builder's stepson, Jack, the architect of Kingsbridge Cathedral, who had married the Lady Aliena and fathered a dynasty of earls of Shiring. He was the ancestor of Caris's sweetheart, Merthin Fitzgerald. That made sense: young Merthin was already showing unparalleled ability as a carpenter. *Timothy's Book* even mentioned Jack's red hair, which had been inherited by Sir Gerald and Merthin, though not Ralph.

What interested him most was the book's chapter on women. It seemed there had been no nuns at Kingsbridge in Prior Philip's day. Women had been strictly forbidden to enter the monastery buildings. The author, quoting Philip, said that if possible a monk should never look at a female, for his own peace of mind. Philip disapproved of combined monastery-nunneries, saying the advantages of shared facilities were outweighed by the opportunities for the devil to introduce temptation. Where there was a double house, the separation of monks and nuns should be as rigid as possible, he added.

Godwyn felt the thrill of finding authoritative support for a preexisting conviction. At Oxford he had enjoyed the all-male environment of Kingsbridge College. The university teachers were men, as were the students, without exception. He had hardly spoken to a female for seven years and, if he kept his eyes on the ground as he walked through the city, he could even avoid looking at them. On his return to the priory, he had found it disturbing to see nuns so frequently. Although they had their own cloisters, refectory, kitchen, and other buildings, he met them constantly in the church, the hospital, and other communal areas. At this moment there was a pretty young nun called Mair just a few feet away, consulting an illustrated book on medicinal herbs. It was even worse to encounter girls from the town, with their close-fitting clothes and alluring hairstyles, casually walking through the priory grounds on everyday errands, bringing supplies to the kitchen or visiting the hospital.

Clearly, he thought, the priory had fallen from Philip's high standards—another example of the slackness that had crept in under the rule of Anthony, Godwyn's uncle. But perhaps there was something he could do about this.

The bell rang for Sext, and he closed the book. Sister Mair did the same, and smiled at him, her red lips forming a sweet curve as she did so. He looked away and hurried out of the room.

The weather was improving, the sun shining fitfully between showers of rain. In the church, the stained-glass windows brightened and faded as patchy clouds blew across the sky. Godwyn's mind was equally restless, distracted from his prayers by thoughts of how he could best use *Timothy's Book* to inspire a revival in the priory. He decided he would raise the subject at chapter, the daily meeting of all the monks.

The builders were getting on quickly with the repairs to the chancel after last Sunday's collapse, he noted. The rubble had been cleared away and the area had been roped off. There was a growing stack of thin, lightweight stones in the transept. The men did not stop work when the monks began to sing—there were so many services during the course of a normal day that the repairs would have been severely delayed. Merthin Fitzgerald, who had temporarily abandoned his work on the new door, was in the south aisle, constructing an elaborate spiderweb of ropes, branches, and hurdles on which the masons would stand as they rebuilt the vaulted ceiling. Thomas Langley, whose job it was to supervise the builders, was standing in the south transept with Elfric, pointing with his one arm at the collapsed vault, obviously discussing Merthin's work.

Thomas was effective as matricularius: he was decisive, and he never let things slip. Any morning the builders failed to show up—a frequent irritation—Thomas would go and find them and demand to know why. If he had a fault, it was that he was too independent: he rarely reported progress or asked Godwyn's opinion, but got on with the work as if he were his own master rather than Godwyn's subordinate. Godwyn had an annoying suspicion that Thomas doubted his ability. Godwyn was younger, but only slightly: he was thirty-one, Thomas thirty-four. Perhaps Thomas thought that Godwyn had been promoted by Anthony under pressure from Petranilla. However, he showed no other sign of resentment. He just did things his own way.

As Godwyn watched, murmuring the responses of the service automatically, Thomas's conversation with Elfric was interrupted. Lord William of Caster came striding into the church. He was a tall, black-bearded figure very like his father, and equally harsh, though people said he was sometimes softened by his wife, Philippa. He approached Thomas and waved Elfric away. Thomas turned to William, and something in his stance reminded Godwyn that Thomas had once been a knight, and had first arrived at the priory bleeding from the sword wound that had eventually necessitated the amputation of his left arm at the elbow.

Godwyn wished he could hear what Lord William was saying. William was leaning forward, speaking aggressively, pointing a finger. Thomas, unafraid, answered with equal vigor. Godwyn suddenly remembered Thomas having just such an intense, combative conversation ten years ago, on the day he arrived here. On that occasion, he had been arguing with William's younger brother, Richard—then a priest, now the bishop of Kingsbridge. Perhaps it was fanciful, but Godwyn imagined they were quarreling about the same thing today. What could it be? Could there really be an issue between a monk and a noble family that was still a cause of anger after ten years?

Lord William stamped off, evidently unsatisfied, and Thomas turned back to Elfric.

The argument ten years ago had resulted in Thomas's joining the priory.

Godwyn recalled that Richard had promised a donation to secure Thomas's admittance. Godwyn had never heard any more about that donation. He wondered if it had ever been paid.

In all that time, no one at the priory seemed to have learned much about Thomas's former life. That was curious: monks gossiped constantly. Living closely together in a small group—there were twenty-six at present—they tended to know almost everything about one another. What lord had Thomas served? Where had he lived? Most knights ruled over a few villages, receiving rents that enabled them to pay for horses, armor, and weapons. Had Thomas had a wife and children? If so, what had become of them? No one knew.

Apart from the mystery of his background, Thomas was a good monk, devout and hardworking. It seemed as if this existence suited him better than his life as a knight. Despite his former career of violence, there was something of the woman about him, as there was about many monks. He was very close to Brother Matthias, a sweet-natured man a few years younger than he. But, if they were committing sins of impurity, they were very discreet about it, for no accusation had ever been made.

Toward the end of the service Godwyn glanced into the deep gloom of the nave and saw his mother, Petranilla, standing as still as one of the pillars, a shaft of sunlight illuminating her proud gray head. She was alone. He wondered how long she had been there, watching. Laypeople were not encouraged to attend the weekday services, and Godwyn guessed she was here to see him. He felt the familiar mixture of pleasure and apprehension. She would do anything for him, he knew. She had sold her house and become her brother Edmund's housekeeper just so that he could study at Oxford; and when he thought of the sacrifice that entailed for his proud mother, he wanted to weep with gratitude. Yet her presence always made him anxious, as if he were going to be reprimanded for some transgression.

As the monks and nuns filed out, Godwyn peeled off from the procession and approached her. "Good morning, Mama."

She kissed his forehead. "You look thin," she said with maternal anxiety. "Aren't you getting enough to eat?"

"Salt fish and porridge, but there's plenty of it," he said.

"What are you so excited about?" She could always read his mood.

He told her about *Timothy's Book*. "I could read the passage during chapter," he said.

"Would others support you?"

"Theodoric and the younger monks would. A lot of them find it disturbing to see women all the time. After all, they have all chosen to live in an all-male community."

She nodded approvingly. "This casts you in the role of leader. Excellent."

"Besides, they like me because of the hot stones."

"Hot stones?"

"I introduced a new rule in the winter. On frosty nights, when we go into church for Matins, each monk is given a hot stone wrapped in a rag. It prevents them getting chilblains in their feet."

"Very clever. All the same, check your support before you make your move."

"Of course. But it fits in with what the masters teach at Oxford."

"Which is?"

"Mankind is fallible, so we should not rely on our own reasoning. We cannot hope to understand the world—all we can do is stand amazed at God's creation. True knowledge comes only from revelation. We should not question received wisdom."

Mother looked skeptical, as laypeople often did when educated men tried to explain high philosophy. "And this is what bishops and cardinals believe?"

"Yes. The University of Paris has actually banned the works of Aristotle and Aquinas because they are based on rationality rather than faith."

"Will this way of thinking help you find favor with your superiors?"

That was all she really cared about. She wanted her son to be prior, bishop, archbishop, even cardinal. He wanted the same, but he hoped he was not as cynical as she. "I'm sure of it," he replied.

"Good. But that's not why I came to see you. Your uncle Edmund has suffered a blow. The Italians are threatening to take their custom to Shiring."

Godwyn was shocked. "That will ruin his business." But he was not sure why she had made a special visit to tell him.

"Edmund thinks he can win them back if we improve the Fleece Fair, and in particular if we tear down the old bridge and build a new, wider one."

"Let me guess: Uncle Anthony refused."

"But Edmund has not given up."

"You want me to talk to Anthony?"

She shook her head. "You can't persuade him. But, if the subject comes up in chapter, you should support the proposal."

"And go against Uncle Anthony?"

"Whenever a sensible proposal is opposed by the old guard, you must be identified as leader of the reformers."

Godwyn smiled admiringly. "Mama, how do you know so much about politics?"

"I'll tell you." She looked away, her eyes focusing on the great rose window at the east end, her mind in the past. "When my father started to trade with the Italians, he was treated as an upstart by the leading citizens of Kingsbridge. They turned up their noses at him and his family, and did everything they could to prevent him implementing his new ideas. My mother was dead by then, and I was an adolescent, so I became his confidante, and he told me everything." Her face, normally fixed in an expression of frozen calm, twisted now into a mask of bitterness and resentment: her eyes narrowed, her lip curled, and her cheek flushed with remembered shame. "He decided he would never be free of them until he took control of the parish guild. So that's what he set out to do, and I helped him." She drew a deep breath, as if once again gathering her strength for a long war. "We divided the ruling group, set one faction against the other, made alliances then shifted them, ruthlessly undermined our opponents, and used our supporters until it suited us to discard them. It took us ten years, and at the end of it, he was alderman of the guild and the richest man in town."

She had told him the story of his grandfather before, but never in quite such bluntly honest terms. "So you were his aide, as Caris is to Edmund?"

She gave a short, harsh laugh. "Yes. Except that, by the time Edmund took over, we were the leading citizens. My father and I climbed the mountain, and Edmund just had to walk down the other side."

They were interrupted by Philemon. He came into the church from the cloisters, a tall, scrawny-necked man of twenty-two, walking like a bird, with short, pigeon-toed steps. He carried a broom: he was employed by the priory as a cleaner. He seemed excited. "I've been looking for you, Brother Godwyn."

Petranilla ignored his obvious hurry. "Hello, Philemon, haven't they made you a monk yet?"

"I can't raise the necessary donation, Mistress Petranilla. I come from a humble family."

"But it's not unknown for the priory to waive the donation in the case of an applicant who shows devotion. And you've been a servant of the priory, paid and unpaid, for years."

"Brother Godwyn has proposed me, but some of the older monks argued against me."

Godwyn put in: "Blind Carlus hates Philemon—I don't know why."

Petranilla said: "I'll speak to my brother Anthony. He should overrule Carlus. You're a good friend to my son—I'd like to see you get on."

"Thank you, Mistress."

"Well, you're obviously bursting to tell Godwyn something that can't be said in front of me, so I'll take my leave." She kissed Godwyn. "Remember what I said."

"I will, Mama."

Godwyn felt relieved, as if a storm cloud had passed overhead and gone on to drench some other town.

As soon as Petranilla was out of earshot, Philemon said: "It's Bishop Richard!"

Godwyn raised his eyebrows. Philemon had a way of learning people's secrets. "What have you found out?"

"He's in the hospital, right now, in one of the private rooms upstairs—with his cousin Margery!"

Margery was a pretty girl of sixteen. Her parents—a younger brother of Earl Roland and a sister of the countess of Marr—were both dead, and she was Roland's ward. He had arranged for her to marry a son of the earl of Monmouth, in a political alliance that would greatly strengthen Roland's position as the leading nobleman of southwest England. "What are they doing?" Godwyn said, though he could guess.

Philemon lowered his voice. "Kissing!"

"How do you know?"

"I'll show you."

Philemon led the way out of the church via the south transept, through the monks' cloisters, and up a flight of steps to the dormitory. It was a plain room with two rows of simple wooden bedsteads, each having a straw mattress. It shared a party wall with the hospital. Philemon went to a large cupboard that contained blankets. With an effort, he pulled it forward. In the wall behind it there was a loose stone. Momentarily Godwyn wondered how Philemon had come across this peephole, and guessed he might have hidden something in the gap. Philemon lifted the stone out, careful to make no noise, and whispered: "Look, quick!"

Godwyn hesitated. In a low voice he said: "How many other guests have you observed from here?"

"All of them," Philemon replied, as if that should have been obvious.

Godwyn thought he knew what he was going to see, and he did not relish it. Peeping at a misbehaving bishop might be all right for Philemon, but it seemed shamefully underhand. However, his curiosity urged him on. In the end he asked himself what his mother would advise, and knew immediately that she would tell him to look.

The hole in the wall was a little below eye level. He stooped and peeked through.

He was looking into one of the two private guest rooms upstairs at the hospital. In one corner stood a prie-dieu facing a wall painting of the crucifixion. There were two comfortable chairs and a couple of stools. When there was a crowd of important guests, the men took one room and the women the other; and this was clearly the women's room, for on a small table were several distinctly feminine articles: combs, ribbons, and mysterious small jars and vials.

On the floor were two straw mattresses. Richard and Margery lay on one of them. They were doing more than kissing.

Bishop Richard was an attractive man with wavy mid-brown hair and regular features. Margery was not much more than half his age, a slender girl with white skin and dark eyebrows. They lay side by side. Richard was kissing her face and speaking into her ear. A smile of pleasure played upon his fleshy lips. Margery's dress was pushed up around her waist. She had beautiful long white legs. His hand was between her thighs, moving with a practised, regular motion: although Godwyn had no experience of women, somehow he knew what Richard was doing. Margery looked at Richard adoringly, her mouth half-open, panting with excitement, her face flushed with passion. Perhaps it was mere prejudice, but Godwyn sensed intuitively that Richard saw Margery as a plaything of the moment, whereas Margery believed Richard was the love of her life.

Godwyn stared at them for a horrified moment. Richard moved his hand, and suddenly Godwyn was looking at the triangle of coarse hair between Margery's thighs, dark against her white skin, like her eyebrows. Quickly, he looked away.

"Let me see," said Philemon.

Godwyn moved away from the wall. This was shocking, but what should he do about it—if anything?

Philemon looked through the hole and gave a gasp of excitement. "I can see her cunt!" he whispered. "He's rubbing it!"

"Come away from there," Godwyn said. "We've seen enough—too much."

Philemon hesitated, fascinated; then, reluctantly, he moved away and replaced the loose stone. "We must expose the bishop's fornication at once!" he said.

"Shut your mouth and let me think," Godwyn said. If he did as Philemon suggested, he would make enemies of Richard and his powerful family—and to no purpose. But surely there was a way something like this could be turned to advantage? Godwyn tried to think about it as his mother would. If there was nothing to be gained by revealing Richard's sin, was it possible to make a virtue of concealing it? Perhaps Richard would be grateful to Godwyn for keeping it secret.

That was more promising. But for it to work, Richard had to know that Godwyn was protecting him.

"Come with me," Godwyn said to Philemon.

Philemon moved the cupboard back into place. Godwyn wondered whether the sound of the wood scraping on the floor was audible in the next room. He doubted it—and, anyway, Richard and Margery were surely too absorbed in what they were doing to notice noises from beyond the wall.

Godwyn led the way down the stairs and through the cloisters. There were two staircases to the private rooms: one led up from the hospital's ground floor, and the other was outside the building, permitting important guests to come and go without passing through the common people's quarters. Godwyn hurried up the outside stairs.

He paused outside the room where Richard and Margery were and spoke to Philemon quietly. "Follow me in," he said. "Do nothing. Say nothing. Leave when I leave."

Philemon put down his broom.

"No," Godwyn said. "Carry it."

"All right."

Godwyn threw open the door and strode in. "I want this chamber immaculately clean," he said loudly. "Sweep every corner—oh! I beg your pardon! I thought the room was empty!"

In the time it had taken Godwyn and Philemon to rush from the dormitory to the hospital, the lovers had progressed. Richard now lay on top of Margery, his long clerical robe lifted in front. Her shapely white legs stuck straight up in the air either side of the bishop's hips. There was no mistaking what they were doing.

Richard ceased his thrusting motion and looked at Godwyn, his expression a mixture of angry frustration and frightened guilt. Margery gave a cry of shock and she, too, stared at Godwyn with fear in her eyes.

Godwyn drew the moment out. "Bishop Richard!" he said, feigning bewilderment. He wanted Richard to be in no doubt that he had been recognized. "But how . . . and Margery?" He pretended to understand suddenly. "Forgive me!" He spun on his heel. He shouted at Philemon: "Get out! Now!" Philemon scuttled back through the door, still clutching his broom.

Godwyn followed, but he turned at the door, to make sure Richard got a good look at him. The two lovers remained frozen in position, locked in sexual congress, but their faces had changed. Margery's hand had flown to her mouth in the eternal gesture of surprised guilt. Richard's expression had become frantically calculating. He wanted to speak but he could not think what to say. Godwyn decided to put them out of their misery. He had done everything he needed to do.

He stepped out—then, before he could close the door, a shock made him stop. A woman was coming up the stairs. He suffered a moment of panic. It was Philippa, the wife of the earl's other son.

He realized instantly that Richard's guilty secret would lose its value if someone else knew it. He had to warn Richard. "Lady Philippa!" he said in a loud voice. "Welcome to Kingsbridge Priory!"

Urgent scuffling noises came from behind him. Out of the corner of his eye, he saw Richard leap to his feet.

Luckily, Philippa did not march straight past, but stopped and spoke to Godwyn. "Perhaps you can help me." From where she stood, she could not quite see into the room, he thought. "I've lost a bracelet. It's not precious, just carved wood, but I'm fond of it."

"What a shame," Godwyn said sympathetically. "I'll ask all the monks and nuns to look out for it."

Philemon said: "I haven't seen it."

Godwyn said to Philippa: "Perhaps it slipped from your wrist."

She frowned. "The odd thing is, I haven't actually worn it since I got here. I took it off when I arrived, and put it on the table, and now I can't find it."

"Perhaps it rolled into a dark corner. Philemon here will look for it. He cleans the guest rooms."

Philippa looked at Philemon. "Yes, I saw you as I was leaving, an hour or so ago. You didn't spot it when you swept the room?"

"I didn't sweep. Miss Margery came in just as I was getting started."

Godwyn said: "Philemon has just come back to clean your room, but Miss Margery is . . . ," he looked into the room, ". . . at prayer," he finished. Margery was kneeling on the prie-dieu, eyes closed—begging forgiveness for her sin, Godwyn hoped. Richard stood behind her, head bowed, hands clasped, lips moving in a murmur.

Godwyn stepped aside to let Philippa enter the room. She gave her brother-in-law a suspicious look. "Hello, Richard," she said. "It's not like you to pray on a weekday."

He put his finger to his lips in a shushing gesture, and pointed to Margery on the prayer stool.

Philippa said briskly: "Margery can pray as much as she likes, but this is the women's room, and I want you out."

Richard concealed his relief and left, closing the door on the two women.

He and Godwyn stood face to face in the hallway. Godwyn could tell that Richard did not know what line to take. He might be inclined to say *How dare you burst into a room without knocking?* However, he was so badly in the wrong that he probably could not summon up the nerve to bluster. On the other hand, he could hardly beg Godwyn to keep quiet about what he had seen, for that would be to acknowledge himself in Godwyn's power. It was a moment of painful awkwardness.

While Richard hesitated, Godwyn spoke. "No one shall hear of this from me."

Richard looked relieved, then glanced at Philemon. "What about him?"

"Philemon wants to be a monk. He is learning the virtue of obedience."

"I'm in your debt."

"A man should confess his own sins, not those of others."

"All the same, I'm grateful, Brother . . ."

"Godwyn, the sacrist. I'm the nephew of Prior Anthony." He wanted Richard to know that he was sufficiently well connected to make serious trouble. But, to take the edge off the threat, he added: "My mother was betrothed to your father, many years ago, before your father became the earl."

"I've heard that story."

Godwyn wanted to add: And your father spurned my mother, just as you're planning to spurn the wretched Margery. But instead he said pleasantly: "We might have been brothers."

"Yes."

The bell rang for dinner. Relieved of their embarrassment, the three men parted company: Richard to Prior Anthony's house, Godwyn to the monks' refectory, and Philemon to the kitchen to help serve.

Godwyn was thoughtful as he walked through the cloisters. He was upset by the animal scene he had witnessed, but he felt he had handled it well. At the end, Richard had seemed to trust him.

In the refectory Godwyn sat next to Theodoric, a bright monk a couple of years younger than he. Theodoric had not studied at Oxford, and in consequence he looked up to Godwyn. Godwyn treated him as an equal, which flattered Theodoric. "I've just read something that will interest you," Godwyn said. He summarized what he had read about the revered Prior Philip's attitude to women in general and nuns in particular. "It's what you've always said," he finished. In fact, Theodoric had never expressed an opinion on the subject, but he always agreed when Godwyn complained about Prior Anthony's slackness.

"Of course," Theodoric said. He had blue eyes and fair skin, and now he flushed with excitement. "How can we have pure thoughts when we are constantly distracted by females?"

"But what can we do about it?"

"We must confront the prior."

"In chapter, you mean," Godwyn said, as if it were Theodoric's idea rather than his own. "Yes, excellent plan. But would others support us?"

"The younger monks would."

Young men probably agreed with more or less any criticism of their elders, Godwyn thought. But he also knew that many monks shared his own preference for a life in which women were absent or, at least, invisible. "If you talk to anyone between now and chapter, let me know what they say," he said. That would encourage Theodoric to go around whipping up support.

The dinner arrived, a stew of salt fish and beans. Before Godwyn could begin to eat, he was prevented by Friar Murdo.

Friars were monks who lived among the people instead of secluding themselves in monasteries. They felt that their self-denial was more rigorous than that of institutional monks, whose vow of poverty was compromised by their splendid buildings and extensive landholdings. Traditionally friars had no property, not even churches—although many had slipped from this ideal after pious admirers gave them land and money. Those who still lived by the original principles scrounged their food and slept on kitchen floors. They preached in marketplaces and outside taverns, and were rewarded with pennies. They did not hesitate to sponge off ordinary monks for food and lodging anytime it suited their convenience. Not surprisingly, their assumption of superiority was resented.

Friar Murdo was a particularly unpleasant example: fat, dirty, greedy, often drunk, and sometimes seen in the company of prostitutes. But he was also a charismatic preacher who could hold a crowd of hundreds with his colorful, theologically dubious sermons.

Now he stood up, uninvited, and began to pray in a loud voice. "Our Father, bless this food to our foul, corrupt bodies, as full of sin as a dead dog is full of maggots . . ."

Murdo's prayers were never short. Godwyn put down his spoon with a sigh.

There was always a reading in chapter—usually from the Rule of St. Benedict, but often from the Bible, and occasionally other religious books. As the monks were taking their places on the raked stone benches around the octagonal chapter house, Godwyn sought out the young monk who was due to read today and told him, quietly but firmly, that he, Godwyn, would be reading instead. Then, when the moment came, he read the crucial page from *Timothy's Book*.

He felt nervous. He had returned from Oxford a year ago, and he had been quietly talking to people about reforming the priory ever since; but, until this moment, he had not openly confronted Anthony. The prior was weak and lazy, and needed to be shocked out of his lethargy. Furthermore, St. Benedict had written: "All must be called to chapter, for the Lord often reveals to a younger member what is best." Godwyn was perfectly entitled to speak out in chapter and call for stricter compliance with monastic rules. All the same, he suddenly felt he was running a risk, and wished he had taken longer to think about his tactics in using *Timothy's Book*.

But it was too late for regrets. He closed the book and said: "My question, to myself and my brethren, is this: Have we slipped below the standards of Prior Philip in the matter of separation between monks and females?" He had learned, in student debates, to put his argument in the form of a question whenever he could, giving his opponent as little as possible to argue against.

The first to reply was Blind Carlus, the subprior, Anthony's deputy. "Some monasteries are located far from any center of population, on an uninhabited island, or deep in the forest, or perched on a lonely mountaintop," he said. His slow, deliberate speech made Godwyn fidget with impatience. "In such houses, the brothers seclude themselves from all contact with the secular world," he went on unhurriedly. "Kingsbridge has never been like that. We're in the heart of a great city, the home of seven thousand souls. We care for one of the most magnificent cathedrals in Christendom. Many of us are physicians, because St. Benedict said: 'Special care must be taken of the sick, so that in very deed they be looked after as if it were Christ himself.' The luxury of total isolation has not been granted to us. God has given us a different mission."

Godwyn had expected something like this. Carlus hated furniture to be moved, for then he would stumble over it; and he opposed any other kind of change, out of a parallel anxiety about coping with the unfamiliar.

Theodoric had a quick answer to Carlus. "All the more reason for us to be strict about the rules," he said. "A man who lives next door to a tavern must be extra careful to avoid drunkenness."

There was a murmur of pleased agreement: the monks enjoyed a smart riposte. Godwyn gave a nod of approval. The fair-skinned Theodoric blushed with gratification.

Emboldened, a novice called Juley said in a loud whisper: "Women don't bother Carlus, he can't see them." Several monks laughed, though others shook their heads in disapproval.

Godwyn felt it was going well. He seemed to be winning the argument, so far. Then Prior Anthony said: "Exactly what are you proposing, Brother Godwyn?" He had not been to Oxford, but he knew enough to press for his opponent's real agenda.

Reluctantly, Godwyn put his cards on the table. "We might consider reverting to the position as it was in the time of Prior Philip."

Anthony persisted: "What do you mean by that, exactly? No nuns?"

"Yes."

"But where would they go?"

"The nunnery could be removed to another location, and become a remote cell of the priory, like Kingsbridge College, or St.-John-in-the-Forest."

That shocked them. There was a clamor of comment, which the prior suppressed with difficulty. The voice that emerged from the hubbub was that of Joseph, the senior physician. He was a clever man, but proud, and Godwyn was wary of him. "How would we run a hospital without nuns?" he said. His bad teeth caused him to slur his sibilants, making him sound drunk, but he spoke with no less authority. "They administer medicines, change dressings, feed the incapable, comb the hair of senile old men—"

Theodoric said: "Monks could do all that."

"Then what about childbirth?" Joseph said. "We often deal with women who are having difficulty bringing a baby into the world. How could monks help them without nuns to do the actual . . . handling?"

Several men voiced their agreement, but Godwyn had anticipated this question, and now he said: "Suppose the nuns removed to the old lazar house?" The leper colony—or lazar house—was on a small island in the river on the south side of the town. In the old days it had been full of sufferers, but leprosy seemed to be dying out, and now there were only two occupants, both elderly.

Brother Cuthbert, who was a wit, muttered: "I wouldn't want to be the one to tell Mother Cecilia she's being moved to a leper colony." There was a ripple of laughter.

"Women should be ruled by men," said Theodoric.

Prior Anthony said: "And Mother Cecilia is ruled by Bishop Richard. He would have to make a decision such as this."

"Heaven forbid that he should," said a new voice. It was Simeon, the treasurer. A thin man with a long face, he spoke against every proposal that involved spending money. "We could not survive without the nuns," he said.

Godwyn was taken by surprise. "Why not?" he said.

"We don't have enough money," Simeon said promptly. "When the cathedral needs repair, who do you think pays the builders? Not us—we can't afford it. Mother Cecilia pays. She buys supplies for the hospital, parchment for the scriptorium, and fodder for the stables. Anything used communally by both monks and nuns is paid for by her."

Godwyn was dismayed. "How can this be? Why are we dependent on them?"

Simeon shrugged. "Over the years, many devout women have given the nunnery land and other assets."

That was not the whole story, Godwyn felt sure. The monks also had extensive resources. They collected rent and other charges from just about every citizen of Kingsbridge, and they held thousands of acres of farmland, too. The way the wealth was husbanded must be a factor. But there was no point going into that now. He had lost the argument. Even Theodoric was silent.

Anthony said complacently: "Well, that was a most interesting discussion. Thank you, Godwyn, for asking the question. And now let us pray."

Godwyn was too angry for prayer. He had gained nothing of what he wanted, and he was unsure where he had gone wrong.

As the monks filed out, Theodoric gave him a frightened look and said: "I didn't know the nuns paid for so much."

"None of us knew," Godwyn said. He realized he was glaring at Theodoric, and made amends hastily, adding: "But you were splendid—you debated better than many an Oxford man."

It was just the right thing to say, and Theodoric looked happy.

This was the hour for monks to read in the library or walk in the cloisters, meditating, but Godwyn had other plans. Something had been nagging him all through dinner and chapter. He had thrust it to the back of his mind, because more important things had intervened, but now it came back. He thought he knew where Lady Philippa's bracelet might be.

There were few hiding places in a monastery. The monks lived communally: no one but the prior had a room to himself. Even in the latrine they sat side by side over a trough that was continuously flushed by a stream of piped water. They were not permitted to have personal possessions, so no one had his own cupboard or even box.

But today Godwyn had seen a hiding place.

He went upstairs to the dormitory. It was empty. He pulled the blanket cupboard away from the wall and removed the loose stone, but he did not look through the hole. Instead, he put his hand into the gap, exploring. He felt the top, bottom, and sides of the hole. To the right there was a small fissure. Godwyn eased his fingers inside and touched something that was neither stone nor mortar. Scrabbling with his fingertips, he drew the object out.

It was a carved wooden bracelet.

Godwyn held it to the light. It was made of some hard wood, probably oak. The inner surface was smoothly polished, but the outside was carved with an interlocking design of bold squares and diagonals, executed with pleasing precision: Godwyn could see why Lady Philippa was fond of it.

He put it back, restored the loose stone, and returned the cupboard to its usual position.

What did Philemon want with such a thing? He might be able to sell it for a penny or two, though that would be dangerous because it was so recognizable. But he certainly could not wear it.

Godwyn left the dormitory and went down the stairs to the cloisters. He was in no mood for study or meditation. He needed to talk over the day's events. He felt the need to see his mother.

The thought made him apprehensive. She might berate him for his failure in chapter. But she would praise him for his handling of Bishop Richard, he felt sure, and he was eager to tell her the story. He decided to go in search of her.

Strictly speaking, this was not allowed. Monks were not supposed to roam about the streets of the town at will. They needed a reason, and in theory they were supposed to ask the prior's permission before leaving the precincts. But in practice, the obedientiaries—monastic officials—had dozens of excuses. The priory did business constantly with merchants, buying food, cloth, shoes, parchment, candles, garden tools, tack for horses—all the necessities of everyday life. The monks were landlords, owning almost the entire city. And any one of the physicians might be called to see a patient who was unable to walk to the hospital. So it was common to see monks in the streets, and Godwyn, the sacrist, was not likely to be asked to explain what he was doing out of the monastery.

Nevertheless it was wise to be discreet, and he made sure he was not observed as he left the priory. He passed through the busy fair and went quickly along the main street to his uncle Edmund's house.

As he hoped, Edmund and Caris were out doing business, and he found his mother alone but for the servants. "This is a treat for a mother," she said. "To see you twice in one day! And it gives me a chance to feed you up." She poured him a big tankard of strong ale and told the cook to bring a plate of cold beef. "What happened in chapter?" she said.

He told her the story. "I was in too much of a hurry," he said at the end.

She nodded. "My father used to say: never call a meeting until the outcome is a foregone conclusion."

Godwyn smiled. "I must remember that."

"All the same, I don't think you've done any harm."

That was a relief. She was not going to be angry. "But I lost the argument," he said.

"You also established your position as leader of the reformist younger group."

"Even though I made a fool of myself?"

"Better than being a nonentity."

He was not sure she was right about that but, as usual when he doubted the wisdom of his mother's advice, he did not challenge her, but resolved to think about it later. "Something very odd happened," he said, and he told her about Richard and Margery, leaving out the gross physical details.

She was surprised. "Richard must be mad!" she said. "The wedding will be called off if the earl of Monmouth finds out that Margery isn't a virgin. Earl Roland will be furious. Richard could be unfrocked."

"But a lot of bishops have mistresses, don't they?"

"That's different. A priest may have a 'housekeeper' who is his wife in all but name. A bishop may have several. But to take the virginity of a noblewoman shortly before her wedding—even the son of an earl might find it difficult to survive as a clergyman after that."

"What do you think I should do?"

"Nothing. You've handled it perfectly so far." He glowed with pride.

She added: "One day this information will be a powerful weapon. Just remember it."

"There's one more thing. I wondered how Philemon had come across the loose stone, and it occurred to me that he might have used it initially as a hiding place. I was right—and I found a bracelet that Lady Philippa had lost."

"Interesting," she said. "I have a strong feeling that Philemon will be useful to you. He'll do anything, you see. He has no scruples, no morals. My father had an associate who was always willing to do his dirty work—start rumors, spread poisonous gossip, foment strife. Such men can be invaluable."

"So you don't think I should report the theft."

"Certainly not. Make him give the bracelet back, if you think it's important—he can just say he found it while sweeping. But don't expose him. You'll reap the benefit, I guarantee."

"So I should protect him?"

"As you would a mad dog that mauls intruders. He's dangerous, but he's worth it."

10

On Thursday, Merthin completed the door he was carving.

He had finished work in the south aisle, for the present. The scaffolding was in place. There was no need for him to make formwork for the masons, as Godwyn and Thomas were determined to save money by trying Merthin's method of building without it. So he returned to his carving and realized there was little left to do. He spent an hour improving a wise virgin's hair, and another on a foolish virgin's silly smile, but he was not sure he was making them any better. He found it difficult to make decisions, because his mind kept wandering to Caris and Griselda.

He had hardly been able to bring himself to speak to Caris all week. He felt so ashamed of himself. Every time he saw Caris, he thought of how he had embraced Griselda, and kissed her, and done with her the most loving act of human life—a girl he did not like, let alone love. Although he had formerly spent many happy hours imagining the moment when he would do that with Caris, now the prospect was filled with dread. There was nothing wrong with Griselda—well, there was, but that was not what disturbed him. He would have felt the same if it had been any woman other than Caris. He had taken away the meaning of the act by doing it with Griselda. And now he could not face the woman he loved.

While he was staring at his work, trying to stop thinking about Caris and decide whether the door was finished or not, Elizabeth Clerk walked into the north porch. She was a pale, thin beauty of twenty-five with a cloud of fair curls. Her father had been the bishop of Kingsbridge before Richard. He had lived, like Richard, in the bishop's palace at Shiring, but on his frequent visits to Kingsbridge he had fallen for a serving wench at the Bell—Elizabeth's mother. Because of her illegitimacy, Elizabeth was sensitive about her social position, alert to the least slight and quick to take offense. But Merthin liked her because she was clever, and because when he was eighteen she had kissed him and let him feel her breasts, which were high on her chest and flat, as if molded from shallow cups, with nipples that hardened at the gentlest touch. Their romance had ended over something that seemed trivial to him and unforgivable to her—a joke he had made about randy priests—but he still liked her.

She touched his shoulder and looked at the door. Her hand went to her mouth, and she drew in her breath. "They seem alive!" she said.

He was thrilled. Her praise was not lightly given. All the same, he felt an impulse to be modest. "It's only that I've made each one individual. On the old door, the virgins were identical."

"It's more than that. They look as if they might step forward and talk to us."

"Thank you."

"But it's so different from everything else in the cathedral. What will the monks say?"

"Brother Thomas likes it."

"What about the sacrist?"

"Godwyn? I don't know what he'll think. But if there's a fuss I'll appeal to Prior Anthony—who won't want to commission another door and pay twice."

"Well," she said thoughtfully, "the Bible doesn't say that they were all alike, of course—just that five had the sense to get ready well in advance, and the other five left arrangements until the last minute and ended up missing the party. But what about Elfric?"

"It's not for him."

"He's your master."

"He only cares about getting the money."

She was not convinced. "The problem is that you're a better craftsman than he. That's been obvious for a couple of years, and everyone knows it.

Elfric would never admit it, but that's why he hates you. He may make you regret this."

"You always see the black side."

"Do I?" She was offended. "Well, we'll see if I'm right. I hope I'm wrong." She turned to go.

"Elizabeth?"

"Yes."

"I'm really pleased you think it's good."

She did not reply, but she seemed a bit mollified. She waved good-bye and left.

Merthin decided the door was finished. He wrapped it in coarse sacking. He would have to show it to Elfric, and now was as good a time as any: the rain had stopped, for a while at least.

He got one of the laborers to help him carry the door. The builders had a technique for carrying heavy, awkward objects. They laid two stout poles on the ground, parallel, then placed boards crosswise on the poles in the center to provide a firm base. They manhandled the object onto the boards. Then they stood between the poles, one man at each end, and lifted. The arrangement was called a stretcher, and it was also used for carrying sick people to the hospital.

Even so, the door was very heavy. However, Merthin was used to difficult lifting. Elfric had never allowed him to make an excuse of his slight stature, and the result was that he had become surprisingly strong.

The two men reached Elfric's house and carried the door inside. Griselda was sitting in the kitchen. She seemed to be getting more voluptuous by the day—her large breasts appeared to be growing even bigger. Merthin hated to be at odds with people, so he tried to be friendly. "Do you want to see my door?" he said as they passed her.

"Why would I want to look at a door?"

"It's carved. The story of the wise and foolish virgins."

She gave a humorless laugh. "Don't tell me about virgins."

They carried it through to the yard. Merthin did not understand women. Griselda had been cold to him ever since they had made love. If that was how she felt, why had she done it? She was making it clear she did not want to do it again. He could have reassured her that he felt the same way—in fact he loathed the prospect—but that would be insulting, so he said nothing.

They put down the stretcher and Merthin's helper left. Elfric was in the yard, his brawny body bent over a stack of timber, counting planks, tapping each beam with a piece of square-cut wood a couple of feet long, sticking his tongue into his cheek as he did whenever he faced a mental challenge. He glared at Merthin and carried on, so Merthin said nothing, but unwrapped the door and stood it up against a pile of stone blocks. He was extraordinarily proud of what he had done. He had followed the traditional pattern, but at the same time he had done something original that made people gasp. He could hardly wait to see the door installed in the church.

"Forty-seven," Elfric said, then he turned to Merthin.

"I finished the door," Merthin said proudly. "What do you think?"

Elfric looked at the door for a moment. He had a big nose, and his nostrils twitched in surprise. Then, without warning, he hit Merthin across the face with the stick he had been using to count. It was a solid piece of wood and the blow was hard. Merthin cried out in sudden agony, staggered back, and fell to the ground.

"You piece of filth!" Elfric yelled. "You defiled my daughter!"

Merthin tried to sputter a protest, but his mouth was full of blood.

"How dare you!" Elfric bellowed.

As if at a signal, Alice appeared from inside the house. "Snake!" she screamed. "You slithered into our home and deflowered our little girl!"

They were pretending to be spontaneous, but they must have planned this, Merthin thought. He spat blood and said: "Deflowered? She was no virgin!"

Elfric lashed out again with his improvised club. Merthin rolled out of the way, but the blow landed painfully on his shoulder.

Alice said: "How could you do this to Caris? My poor sister—when she finds out, it will break her heart."

Merthin was stung into a response. "And you'll be sure to tell her, won't you, you bitch."

"Well, you're not going to marry Griselda in secret," Alice said.

Merthin was astonished. "Marry? I'm not marrying her. She hates me!"

With that, Griselda appeared. "I certainly don't want to marry you," she said. "But I'll have to. I'm pregnant."

Merthin stared at her. "That's not possible—we only did it once."

Elfric laughed harshly. "It only takes once, you young fool."

"I'm still not marrying her."

"If you don't, you'll be sacked," Elfric said.

"You can't do that."

"Why not?"

"I don't care, I'm not going to marry her."

Elfric dropped the club and picked up an axe.

Merthin said: "Jesus Christ!"

Alice took a step forward. "Elfric, don't commit murder."

"Get out of the way, woman." Elfric lifted the axe.

Merthin, still on the ground, scooted away, in fear of his life.

Elfric brought the axe down, not on Merthin, but on his door.

Merthin shouted: "No!"

The sharp blade sank into the face of the long-haired virgin and split the wood along the grain.

Merthin yelled: "Stop it!"

Elfric lifted the axe again and brought it down even harder. It split the door in two.

Merthin got to his feet. To his horror, he felt his eyes fill with tears. "You have no right!" He was trying to shout, but his voice came out in a whisper.

Elfric lifted the axe and turned toward him. "Stay back, boy—don't tempt me."

Merthin saw a mad light in Elfric's eye, and backed away.

Elfric brought the axe down on the door again.

Merthin stood and watched with tears pouring down his face.

11

The two dogs, Skip and Scrap, greeted one another with joyful enthusiasm. They were from the same litter, though they did not look similar: Skip was a brown boy dog and Scrap a small black female. Skip was a typical village dog, lean and suspicious, whereas the city-dwelling Scrap was plump and contented.

It was ten years since Gwenda had picked Skip out of a litter of mongrel puppies, on the floor of Caris's bedroom in the wool merchant's big house, the day Caris's mother died. Since then, Gwenda and Caris had become close friends. They met only two or three times a year, but they shared their secrets. Gwenda felt she could tell Caris everything, and the information would never get back to her parents or anyone else in Wigleigh. She assumed Caris felt the same: because Gwenda did not talk to any other Kingsbridge girls, there could be no risk of her letting something slip in a careless moment.

Gwenda arrived in Kingsbridge on the Friday of Fleece Fair week. Her father, Joby, went to the fairground in front of the cathedral to sell the furs of squirrels he had trapped in the forest near Wigleigh. Gwenda went straight to Caris's house, and the two dogs were reunited.

As always, Gwenda and Caris talked about boys. "Merthin is in a strange mood," Caris said. "On Sunday he was his normal self, kissing me in church—then, on Monday, he could hardly look me in the eye."

"He's feeling guilty about something," Gwenda said immediately.

"It's probably connected with Elizabeth Clerk. She's always had her eye on him, though she's a cold bitch and much too old for him."

"Have you and Merthin done it yet?"

"Done what?"

"You know . . . When I was little, I used to call it grunting, because that was the noise grown-ups made while they were doing it."

"Oh, that? No, not yet."

"Why not?"

"I don't know . . ."

"Don't you want to?"

"Yes, but . . . don't you worry about spending your life doing some man's bidding?"

Gwenda shrugged. "I don't like the idea but, on the other hand, I don't worry about it."

"What about you? Have you done it yet?"

"Not properly. I said yes to a boy from the next village, years ago, just to see what it was like. It's a nice warm glow, like drinking wine. That was the only time. But I'd let Wulfric do it any time he liked."

"Wulfric? This is new!"

"I know. I mean, I've known him since we were small, when he used to pull my hair and run away. Then one day, soon after Christmas, I looked at him as he came into church, and I realized he'd become a man. Well, not just a man, but a really gorgeous man. He had snow in his hair and a sort of mustard-colored scarf around his neck, and he just looked glowing."

"Do you love him?"

Gwenda sighed. She did not know how to say what she felt. It was not just love. She thought about him all the time, and she did not know how she could live without him. She daydreamed about kidnapping him and locking him up in a hut deep in the forest so that he could never escape from her.

"Well, the look on your face answers my question," Caris said. "Does he love you?"

Gwenda shook her head. "He never even speaks to me. I wish he'd do something to show that he knows who I am, even if it was only pulling my hair. But he's in love with Annet, the daughter of Perkin. She's a selfish cow, but he adores her. Her father and his are the two wealthiest men in the village. Her father raises laying hens and sells them, and his father has fifty acres."

"You make it sound hopeless."

"I don't know. What's hopeless? Annet might die. Wulfric might suddenly realize he's always loved me. My father might be made earl and order him to marry me."

Caris smiled. "You're right. Love is never hopeless. I'd like to see this boy."

Gwenda stood up. "I was hoping you'd say that. Let's go and find him."

They left the house, the dogs following at their heels. The rainstorms that had lashed the town earlier in the week had given way to occasional showers, but the main street was still a stream of mud. Because of the fair, the mud was mixed with animal droppings, rotten vegetables, and all the litter and filth of a thousand visitors.

As they splashed through the disgusting puddles, Caris asked about Gwenda's family.

"The cow died," Gwenda said. "Pa needs to buy another, but I don't know how he's going to do it. He only has a few squirrel furs to sell."

"A cow costs twelve shillings this year," Caris said with concern. "That's a hundred and forty-four silver pennies." Caris always did arithmetic in her head: she had learned Arabic numbers from Buonaventura Caroli, and she said that made it easy.

"For the last few winters that cow has kept us alive—especially the little ones." The pain of extreme hunger was familiar to Gwenda. Even with the cow to give milk, four of Ma's babies had died. No wonder Philemon had longed to be a monk, she thought: it was worth almost any sacrifice to have hearty meals provided every day without fail.

Caris said: "What will your father do?"

"Something underhand. It's difficult to steal a cow—you can't slip it into your satchel—but he'll have a crafty scheme." Gwenda was sounding more confident than she felt. Pa was dishonest, but not clever. He would do anything he could, legal or not, to get another cow, but he might just fail.

They passed through the priory gates into the wide fairground. The traders were wet and miserable on the sixth day of bad weather. They had exposed their stock to the rain and got little in return.

Gwenda felt awkward. She and Caris almost never talked about the disparity in wealth between the two families. Every time Gwenda visited, Caris would quietly give her a present to take home: a cheese, a smoked fish, a bolt of cloth, a jar of honey. Gwenda would thank her—and she was always profoundly grateful—but no more would be said. When Pa tried to make her take advantage of Caris's trust by stealing from the house, Gwenda would argue that she would then be unable to visit again, whereas this way she came home with something two or three times a year. Even Pa could see the sense of that.

Gwenda looked for the stall where Perkin would be selling his hens. Annet would probably be there and, wherever Annet was, Wulfric would not be far away. Gwenda was right. There was Perkin, fat and sly, greasily polite to his customers, curt to everyone else. Annet was carrying a tray of eggs, smiling coquettishly, the tray pulling her dress tight against her breasts, her fair hair straying from her hat in wisps that played around her pink cheeks and her long neck. And there was Wulfric, looking like an archangel who had lost his way and wandered among humankind by mistake.

"There he is," Gwenda murmured. "The tall one with—"

"I can tell which one he is," Caris said. "He looks good enough to eat."

"You see what I mean."

"He's a bit young, isn't he?"

"Sixteen. I'm eighteen. Annet is eighteen too."

"All right."

"I know what you're thinking," Gwenda said. "He's too handsome for me."

"No—"

"Handsome men never fall for ugly women, do they?"

"You're not ugly—"

"I've seen myself in a glass." The memory was painful, and Gwenda grimaced. "I cried when I realized what I looked like. I have a big nose and my eyes are too close together. I resemble my father."

Caris protested: "You have beautiful soft brown eyes, and wonderful thick hair."

"But I'm not in Wulfric's class."

Wulfric was standing side-on to Gwenda and Caris, giving them a good view of his carved profile. They both admired him for a moment—then he turned, and Gwenda gasped. The other side of his face was completely different: bruised and swollen, with one eye closed.

She ran up to him. "What happened to you?" she cried.

He was startled. "Oh, hello, Gwenda. I had a fight." He half-turned away, obviously embarrassed.

"Who with?"

"Some squire of the earl's."

"You're hurt!"

He looked impatient. "Don't worry, I'm fine."

He did not understand why she was concerned, of course. Perhaps he even thought she was reveling in his misfortune. Then Caris spoke. "Which squire?" she said.

Wulfric looked at her with interest, realizing from her dress that she was a wealthy woman. "His name is Ralph Fitzgerald."

"Oh—Merthin's brother!" Caris said. "Was he hurt?"

"I broke his nose." Wulfric looked proud.

"Weren't you punished?"

"A night in the stocks."

Gwenda gave a little cry of anguish. "Poor you!"

"It wasn't so bad. My brother made sure no one pelted me."

"Even so . . ." Gwenda was horrified. The idea of being imprisoned in any way seemed to her the worst kind of torture.

Annet finished with a customer and joined in the conversation. "Oh, it's you, Gwenda," she said coldly. Wulfric might be oblivious to Gwenda's feelings, but Annet was not, and she treated Gwenda with a mixture of hostility and scorn. "Wulfric fought a squire who insulted me," she said, unable to conceal her satisfaction. "He was just like a knight in a ballad."

Gwenda said sharply: "I wouldn't want him to get his face hurt for my sake."

"Fortunately, that's not very likely, is it?" Annet smiled triumphantly.

Caris said: "One never knows what the future may hold."

Annet looked at her, startled by the interruption, and showed surprise that Gwenda's companion was so expensively dressed.

Caris took Gwenda's arm. "Such a pleasure to meet you Wigleigh folk," she said graciously. "Good-bye."

They walked on. Gwenda giggled. "You were terribly condescending to Annet."

"She annoyed me. Her kind give women a bad name."

"She was so pleased that Wulfric got beaten up for her sake! I'd like to poke out her eyes."

Caris said thoughtfully: "Apart from his good looks, what is he actually like?"

"Strong, proud, loyal—just the type to get into a fight on someone else's behalf. But he's the kind of man who will provide tirelessly for his family, year in and year out, until the day he drops dead."

Caris said nothing.

Gwenda said: "He doesn't appeal to you, does he?"

"You make him sound a bit dull."

"If you'd grown up with my father, you wouldn't think a good provider was dull."

"I know." Caris squeezed Gwenda's arm. "I think he's wonderful for you—and, to prove it, I'm going to help you get him."

Gwenda was not expecting that. "How?"

"Come with me."

They left the fairground and walked to the north end of the town. Caris led Gwenda to a small house in a side street near St. Mark's parish church. "A wise woman lives here," she said. Leaving the dogs outside, they ducked through a low doorway.

The single, narrow downstairs room was divided by a curtain. In the front half were a chair and a bench. The fireplace had to be at the back, Gwenda thought, and she wondered why someone would want to hide whatever went on in the kitchen. The room was clean, and there was a strong smell, herby and slightly acid, hardly a perfume but not unpleasant. Caris called out: "Mattie, it's me."

After a moment, a woman of about forty pulled aside the curtain and came through. She had gray hair and pale indoor skin. She smiled when she saw Caris. Then she gave Gwenda a hard look and said: "I see your friend is in love—but the boy hardly speaks to her."

Gwenda gasped: "How did you know?"

Mattie sat on the chair heavily: she was stout, and short of breath. "People come here for three reasons: sickness, revenge, and love. You look healthy, and you're too young for revenge, so you must be in love. And the boy must be indifferent to you, otherwise you wouldn't need my help."

Gwenda glanced at Caris, who looked pleased and said: "I told you she was wise." The two girls sat on the bench and looked expectantly at the woman.

Mattie went on: "He lives close to you, probably in the same village; but his family are wealthier than yours."

"All true." Gwenda was amazed. No doubt Mattie was guessing, but she was so accurate it seemed as if she must have second sight.

"Is he handsome?"

"Very."

"But he's in love with the prettiest girl in the village."

"If you like that type."

"And her family, too, is wealthier than yours."

"Yes."

Mattie nodded. "A familiar story. I can help you. But you must understand something. I have nothing to do with the spirit world. Only God can work miracles."

Gwenda was puzzled. Everyone knew that the spirits of the dead controlled all of life's hazards. If they were pleased with you, they would guide rabbits to your traps, give you healthy babies, and make the sun shine on your ripening corn. But if you did something to anger them, they could put worms in your apples, cause your cow to give birth to a deformed calf, and make your husband impotent. Even the physicians at the priory admitted that prayers to the saints were more efficacious than their medicines.

Mattie went on: "Don't despair. I can sell you a love potion."

"I'm sorry, I have no money."

"I know. But your friend Caris is extraordinarily fond of you, and she wants you to be happy. She came here prepared to pay for the potion. However, you must administer it correctly. Can you get the boy alone for an hour?"

"I'll find a way."

"Put the potion in his drink. Within a short time he will become amorous. That's when you must be alone with him—if there is another girl in sight he may fall for her instead. So keep him away from other women, and be very sweet to him. He will think you the most desirable woman in the world. Kiss him, tell him he's wonderful, and—if you want—make love to him. After a while, he will sleep. When he wakes up, he will remember that he spent the happiest hour of his life in your arms, and he'll want to do it again as soon as he can."

"But won't I need another dose?"

"No. The second time, your love and desire and femininity will be enough. A woman can make any man blissfully happy if he gives her the chance."

The very thought made Gwenda feel lustful. "I can't wait."

"Then let's make up the mixture." Mattie heaved herself out of the chair. "You can come behind the curtain," she said. Gwenda and Caris followed her. "It's only there for the ignorant."

The kitchen had a clean stone floor and a big fireplace equipped with stands and hooks for cooking and boiling, far more than one woman would need for her own food. There was a heavy old table, stained and scorched but scrubbed clean; a shelf with a row of pottery jars; and a locked cupboard, presumably containing the more precious ingredients used in Mattie's potions. Hanging on the wall was a large slate with numbers and letters scratched on it, presumably recipes. "Why do you need to hide all this behind a curtain?" Gwenda said.

"A man who makes ointments and medicines is called an apothecary, but a woman who does the same runs the risk of being called a witch. There's a woman in town called Crazy Nell who goes around shouting about the devil. Friar Murdo has accused her of heresy. Nell is mad, it's true, but there's no harm in her. All the same, Murdo is insisting on a trial. Men like to kill a woman, every now and again, and Murdo will give them an excuse, and collect their pennies afterwards as alms. That's why I always tell people that only God works miracles. I don't conjure spirits. I just use the herbs of the forest and my powers of observation."

While Mattie talked, Caris was moving about the kitchen as freely as if she were at home. She put a mixing bowl and a vial on the table. Mattie handed her a key, and she opened the cupboard. "Put three drops of essence of poppies into a spoonful of distilled wine," Mattie said. "We must be careful not to make the mixture over-strong, or he will go to sleep too soon."

Gwenda was astonished. "Are *you* going to make the potion, Caris?"

"I sometimes help Mattie. Don't say anything to Petranilla; she would disapprove."

"I wouldn't tell her if her hair was on fire." Caris's aunt disliked Gwenda, probably for the same reason she would disapprove of Mattie: they were both low-class, and such things mattered to Petranilla.

But why was Caris, the daughter of a wealthy man, working like an apprentice in the kitchen of a side-street medicine woman? While Caris made up the mixture, Gwenda recalled that her friend had always been intrigued by illness and cures. As a little girl, Caris had wanted to be a physician, not understanding that only priests were allowed to study medicine. Gwenda remembered her saying, after her mother had died: "But *why* do people have to fall sick?" Mother Cecilia had told her it was because of sin; Edmund had said that no one really knew. Neither response had satisfied Caris. Perhaps she was still seeking the answer here in Mattie's kitchen.

Caris poured the liquid into a tiny jar, stoppered it, and bound the stopper tightly with cord, tying the ends in a knot. Then she handed the jar to Gwenda.

Gwenda tucked it into the leather purse attached to her belt. She wondered how on earth she was going to get Wulfric on his own for an hour. She had glibly said that she would find a way but, now that she had the love potion in her possession, the task seemed nearly impossible. He showed signs of restlessness if she merely spoke to him. He wanted to be with Annet any free time he had. What reason would Gwenda give for needing to be alone with him? *I want to show you a place where we can get wild duck eggs.* But why would she show him and not her father? Wulfric was a little naïve, but not stupid: he would know she was up to something.

Caris gave Mattie twelve silver pennies—two weeks' wages for Pa. Gwenda said: "Thank you, Caris. I hope you'll come to my wedding."

Caris laughed. "That's what I like to see—confidence!"

They left Mattie and headed back to the fair. Gwenda decided to begin by finding out where Wulfric was staying. His family was too well off to claim poverty, so they could not stay free at the priory. They would probably be lodging in a tavern. She could just casually ask him, or his brother, and follow up with a question about the standard of accommodation, as if she were interested to know which of the town's many inns was the best.

A monk passed by, and Gwenda realized with a guilty start that she had not even thought about trying to see her brother, Philemon. Pa would not visit him, for they had hated one another for years; but Gwenda was fond of him. She knew that he was sly, untruthful, and malicious, but all the same he loved her. They had been through many hungry winters together. She would seek him out later, she resolved, after she had seen Wulfric again.

But before she and Caris reached the fairground, they met Gwenda's father.

Joby was near the priory gates, outside the Bell. With him was a rough-looking man in a yellow tunic, with a pack on his back—and a brown cow.

He waved Gwenda over. "I've found a cow," he said.

Gwenda looked more closely. It was two years old, and thin, with a bad-tempered look, but it appeared healthy. "It seems fine," she said.

"This is Sim Chapman," he said, jerking a thumb at the yellow tunic. A chapman traveled from village to village selling small necessities—needles, buckles, hand mirrors, combs. He might have stolen the cow, but that would not bother Pa, if the price was right.

Gwenda said to her father: "Where did you get the money?"

"I'm not paying, exactly," he replied, looking shifty.

Gwenda had expected him to have some scheme. "What, then?"

"It's more of a swap."

"What are you giving him in exchange for the cow?"

"You," said Pa.

"Don't be silly," she said, and then she felt a loop of rope dropped over her head and tightened around her body, pinning her arms to her sides.

She felt bewildered. This could not be happening. She struggled to free herself, but Sim just pulled the rope tighter.

"Now, don't make a fuss," Pa said.

She could not believe they were serious. "What do you think you're doing?" she said incredulously. "You can't sell me, you fool!"

"Sim needs a woman, and I need a cow," Pa said. "It's very simple."

Sim spoke for the first time. "She's ugly enough, your daughter."

"This is ridiculous!" Gwenda said.

Sim smiled at her. "Don't worry, Gwenda," he said. "I'll be good to you, as long as you behave yourself, and do as you're told."

They meant it, Gwenda saw. They actually thought they could make this exchange. A cold needle of fear entered her heart as she realized it might even happen.

Caris spoke up. "This joke has gone on long enough," she said in a loud, clear voice. "Release Gwenda immediately."

Sim was not intimidated by her air of command. "And who are you, to give orders?"

"My father is alderman of the parish guild."

"But you're not," Sim said. "And even if you were, you'd have no authority over me or my friend Joby."

"You can't trade a girl for a cow!"

"Why not?" said Sim. "It's my cow, and the girl is his daughter."

Their raised voices attracted the attention of passers-by, who stopped to stare at the girl tied up with a rope. Someone said: "What's happening?" Another replied: "He's sold his daughter for a cow." Gwenda saw a look of panic cross her father's face. He was wishing he had done this up a quiet alley—but he was not smart enough to have foreseen the public reaction. Gwenda realized the bystanders might be her only hope.

Caris waved to a monk who came out of the priory gates. "Brother Godwyn!" she called. "Come and settle an argument, please." She looked triumphantly at Sim. "The priory has jurisdiction over all bargains agreed at the Fleece Fair," she said. "Brother Godwyn is the sacrist. I think you'll have to accept his authority."

Godwyn said: "Hello, cousin Caris. What's the matter?"

Sim grunted with disgust. "Your cousin, is he?"

Godwyn gave him a frosty look. "Whatever the dispute is here, I shall try to give a fair judgment, as a man of God—you can depend on me for that, I hope."

"And very glad to hear it, sir," Sim said, becoming obsequious.

Joby was equally oily. "I know you, Brother—my son Philemon is devoted to you. You've been the soul of kindness to him."

"All right, enough of that," Godwyn said. "What's going on?"

Caris said: "Joby here wants to sell Gwenda for a cow. Tell him he can't."

Joby said: "She's my daughter, sir, and she's eighteen years old and a maid, so she's mine to do with what I will."

Godwyn said: "All the same, it seems a shameful business, selling your children."

Joby became pathetic. "I wouldn't do it, sir, only I've three more at home, and I'm a landless laborer, with no means to feed the children through the winter, unless I have a cow, and our old one has died."

There was a sympathetic murmur from the growing crowd. They knew about winter hardship, and the extremes to which a man might have to go to feed his family. Gwenda began to despair.

Sim said: "Shameful you may think it, Brother Godwyn, but is it a sin?" He spoke as if he already knew the answer, and Gwenda guessed he might have had this argument before, in a different place.

With obvious reluctance, Godwyn said: "The Bible does appear to sanction selling your daughter into slavery. The book of Exodus, chapter twenty-one."

"Well, there you are, then!" said Joby. "It's a Christian act!"

Caris was outraged. "The book of Exodus!" she said scornfully.

One of the bystanders joined in. "We are not the children of Israel," she said. She was a small, chunky woman with an underbite that gave her jaw a determined look. Although dressed poorly, she was assertive. Gwenda recognized her as Madge, the wife of Mark Webber. "There is no slavery today," Madge said.

Sim said: "Then what of apprentices, who get no pay, and may be beaten by their master? Or novice monks and nuns? Or those who skivvy for bed and board in the palaces of the nobility?"

Madge said: "Their life may be hard, but they can't be bought and sold—can they, Brother Godwyn?"

"I don't say that the trade is lawful," Godwyn responded. "I studied medicine at Oxford, not law. But I can find no reason, in Holy Scripture or the teachings of the Church, to say that what these men are doing is a sin." He looked at Caris and shrugged. "I'm sorry, cousin."

Madge Webber folded her arms across her chest. "Well, chapman, how are you going to take the girl out of town?"

"At the end of a rope," he said. "Same way I brought the cow in."

"Ah, but you didn't have to get the cow past me and these people."

Gwenda's heart leaped with hope. She was not sure how many of the bystanders supported her, but if it came to a fight they were more likely to side with Madge, who was a townswoman, than with Sim, an outsider.

"I've dealt with obstinate women before," Sim said, and his mouth twisted as he spoke. "They've never given me much trouble."

Madge put her hand on the rope. "Perhaps you've been lucky."

He snatched the rope away. "Keep your hands off my property and you won't get hurt."

Deliberately, Madge put a hand on Gwenda's shoulder.

Sim shoved Madge roughly, and she staggered back; but there was a murmur of protest from the crowd.

A bystander said: "You wouldn't do that if you'd seen her husband."

There was a ripple of laughter. Gwenda recalled Madge's husband Mark, a gentle giant. If only he would show up!

But it was John Constable who arrived, his well-developed nose for trouble bringing him to any crowd almost as soon as it gathered. "We'll have no shoving," he said. "Are you causing trouble, chapman?"

Gwenda became hopeful again. Chapmen had a bad reputation, and the constable was assuming Sim was the cause of the trouble.

Sim turned obsequious, something he could obviously do quicker than changing his hat. "Beg pardon, Master Constable," he said. "But when a man has paid an agreed price for his purchase, he must be allowed to leave Kingsbridge with his goods intact."

"Of course." John had to agree. A market town depended on its reputation for fair dealing. "But what have you bought?"

"This girl."

"Oh." John looked thoughtful. "Who sold her?"

"I did," said Joby. "I'm her father."

Sim went on: "And this woman with the big chin threatened to stop me taking the girl away."

"So I did," said Madge. "For I've never heard of a woman being bought and sold in Kingsbridge Market, and nor has anyone else around here."

Joby said: "A man may do as he will with a child of his own." He looked around the crowd appealingly. "Is there anyone here who will disagree with that?"

Gwenda knew that no one would. Some people treated their children kindly, and some harshly, but all were agreed that the father must have absolute power over the child. She burst out angrily: "You wouldn't stand there, deaf and dumb, if you had a father like him. How many of you were sold by your parents? How many of you were made to steal, when you were children and had hands small enough to slide into folks' wallets?"

Joby started to look worried. "She's raving, now, Master Constable," he said. "No child of mine ever stole."

"Never mind that," said John. "Everyone listen to me. I shall make a ruling on this. Those who disagree with my decision can complain to the prior. If there's any shoving, by anyone, or any other kind of rough stuff, I shall arrest everyone involved in it. I hope that's clear." He looked around belligerently. No one spoke: they were eager to hear his decision. He went on: "I know of no reason why this trade is unlawful, therefore Sim Chapman is allowed to go his way, with the girl."

Joby said: "I told you so, didn't—"

"Shut your damn mouth, Joby, you fool," said the constable. "Sim, get going, and make it quick. Madge Webber, if you raise a hand I'll put you in the stocks, and your husband won't stop me either. And not a word from you, Caris Wooler, please—you may complain to your father about me if you wish."

Before John had finished speaking, Sim jerked hard on the rope. Gwenda was tipped forward, and stuck a foot out in front of her to keep from falling to the ground; then, somehow, she was moving along, stumbling and half-running down the street. Out of the corner of her eye, she saw Caris alongside her. Then John Constable seized Caris by the arm, she turned to protest to him, and a moment later she disappeared from Gwenda's sight.

Sim walked quickly down the muddy main street, hauling on the rope, keeping Gwenda just off balance. As they approached the bridge, she began to feel desperate. She tried jerking back on the rope, but he responded with an extra strong heave that threw her down in the mud. Her arms were still pinioned, so she could not use her hands to protect herself, and she fell flat, bruising her chest, her face squelching into the ooze. She struggled to her feet, giving up all resistance. Roped like an animal, hurt, frightened, and covered in filthy mud, she staggered after her new owner, across the bridge and along the road that led into the forest.

ஃ

Sim Chapman led Gwenda through the suburb of Newtown to the crossroads known as Gallows Cross, where criminals were hanged. There he took the road south, toward Wigleigh. He tied her rope to his wrist so that she could not break away, even when his attention wandered. Her dog, Skip, followed them, but Sim threw stones at him and, after one hit him full on the nose, he retreated with his tail between his legs.

After several miles, as the sun began to set, Sim turned into the forest. Gwenda had seen no feature beside the road to mark the spot, but Sim seemed to have chosen carefully for, a few hundred paces into the trees, they came upon a pathway. Looking down, Gwenda could see the neat impressions of dozens of small hooves in the earth, and she realized it was a deer path. It would lead to water, she guessed. Sure enough, they came to a little brook, the vegetation on either side trodden into mud.

Sim knelt beside the stream, filled his cupped hands with clear water, and drank. Then he moved the rope so that it was around her neck, freeing her hands, and motioned her to the water.

She washed her hands in the stream then drank thirstily.

"Wash your face," he ordered. "You're ugly enough by nature."

She did as she was told, wondering wearily why he cared how she looked.

The path continued on the farther side of the drinking hole. They walked on. Gwenda was a strong girl, capable of walking all day, but she was defeated and miserable and scared, and that made her feel exhausted. Whatever fate awaited her at their destination, it was probably worse than this, but all the same she yearned to get there so that she could sit down.

Darkness was falling. The deer path wound through trees for a mile then petered out at the foot of a hill. Sim stopped beside a particularly massive oak tree and gave a low whistle.

A few moments later, a figure materialized out of the half-lit woodland and said: "All right, Sim."

"All right, Jed."

"What you got there, a fruit tart?"

"You shall have a slice, Jed, same as the others, so long as you've got sixpence."

Gwenda realized what Sim had planned. He was going to prostitute her. The realization hit her like a blow, and she staggered and fell to her knees.

"Sixpence, eh?" Jed's voice seemed to come from far away, but all the same she could hear the excitement in his voice. "How old is she?"

"Her father claimed she was eighteen." Sim jerked on the rope. "Stand up, you lazy cow, we're not there yet."

Gwenda got to her feet. That's why he wanted me to wash my face, she thought, and for some reason the realization made her cry.

She wept hopelessly as she stumbled along in Sim's footsteps until they came to a clearing with a fire in the middle. Through her tears, she perceived fifteen or twenty people lying around the edge of the clearing, most of them wrapped in blankets or cloaks. Almost all those watching her in the firelight were male, but she caught sight of a white female face, hard in expression but smooth-chinned, that stared at her briefly then disappeared back into a bundle of ragged bedding. An upturned wine barrel and a scattering of wooden cups testified to a drunken party.

Gwenda realized that Sim had brought her to a den of outlaws.

She groaned. How many of them would she be forced to submit to?

As soon as she asked herself the question, she knew the answer: all of them.

Sim dragged her across the clearing to a man who was sitting upright, his back against a tree. "All right, Tam," said Sim.

Gwenda knew instantly who the man must be: the most famous outlaw in the county, he was called Tam Hiding. He had a handsome face, though it was reddened by drink. People said he was noble-born, but they always said that about famous outlaws. Looking at him, Gwenda was surprised by his youth: he was in his mid-twenties. But then, to kill an outlaw was no crime so, in all probability, few lived to be old.

Tam said: "All right, Sim."

"I traded Alwyn's cow for a girl."

"Well done." Tam's speech was only slightly slurred.

"We're going to charge the boys sixpence, but of course you can have a free go. I expect you'd like to be first."

Tam peered at her with bloodshot eyes. Perhaps it was wishful thinking, but she imagined she saw a hint of pity in his look. He said: "No, thanks, Sim. You go ahead and let the boys have a good time. Though you might want to leave it until tomorrow. We got a barrel of good wine from a pair of monks who were taking it to Kingsbridge, and most of the lads are dead drunk now."

Gwenda's heart leaped with hope. Perhaps her torture would be postponed.

"I'll have to consult Alwyn," Sim said doubtfully. "Thanks, Tam." He turned away, pulling Gwenda behind him.

A few yards away, a broad-shouldered man was struggling to his feet.

Sim said: "All right, Alwyn." The phrase seemed to serve the outlaws as a greeting and a recognition code.

Alwyn was at the bad-tempered phase of drunkenness. "What have you got?"

"A fresh young girl."

Alwyn took Gwenda's chin in his hand, gripping unnecessarily hard, and turned her face to the firelight. She was forced to look into his eyes. He was young, like Tam Hiding, but with the same unhealthy air of dissipation. His breath smelled of drink. "By Christ, you picked an ugly one," he said.

For once Gwenda was happy to be thought ugly: perhaps Alwyn would not want to do anything to her.

"I took what I could get," Sim said testily. "If the man had a beautiful daughter he wouldn't sell her for a cow, would he? He'd marry her to the son of a rich wool merchant instead."

The thought of her father made Gwenda angry. He must have known, or suspected, that this would happen. How could he do it to her?

"All right, all right, it doesn't matter," Alwyn said to Sim. "With only two women in the group, most of the lads are desperate."

"Tam said we should wait until tomorrow, because they're all too drunk tonight—but it's up to you."

"Tam's right. Half of them are asleep already."

Gwenda's fear retreated a little. Anything could happen overnight.

"Good," Sim said. "I'm dog tired anyway." He looked at Gwenda. "Lie down, you." He never called her by her name.

She lay down, and he used the rope to tie her feet together and her hands behind her back. Then he and Alwyn lay down either side of her. In a few moments, both men were asleep.

Gwenda was exhausted, but she had no thought of sleep. With her arms behind her back, every position was painful. She tried to move her wrists within the rope, but Sim had pulled it tight and knotted it well. All she achieved was broken skin, so that the rope burned her flesh.

Despair turned to helpless rage, and she pictured herself taking revenge on her captors, lashing them all with a whip as they cowered in front of her. It was a pointless fantasy. She turned her mind to practical means of escape.

First she would have to make them untie her. That done, she would have to get away. Ideally, she would somehow ensure they could not follow her and recapture her.

It seemed impossible.

12

Gwenda was cold when she woke up. It was midsummer, but the weather was cool, and she had no covering but her light dress. The sky was turning from black to gray. She looked around the clearing in the faint light: no one was moving.

She needed to pee. She thought of doing it there, and soaking her dress. If she made herself disgusting, so much the better. Almost as soon as the thought occurred to her she dismissed it. That would be giving up. She was not giving up.

But what was she going to do?

Alwyn was sleeping beside her, with his long dagger in its sheath still attached to his belt, and that gave her the glimmer of an idea. She was not sure she had the nerve to carry out the plan that was forming in her mind. But she refused to think about how scared she was. She just had to do it.

Although her ankles were tied together, she could move her legs. She kicked Alwyn. At first he did not seem to feel it. She kicked him again, and he moved. The third time, he sat upright. "Was that you?" he said blearily.

"I have to pee," she said.

"Not in the clearing. It's one of Tam's rules. Go twenty paces for a piss, fifty for a shit."

"So, even outlaws live by rules."

He stared uncomprehendingly at her. The irony escaped him. He was not a clever man, she realized. That was helpful. But he was strong, and mean. She would have to be very cautious.

She said: "I can't go anywhere tied up."

Grumbling, he undid the rope around her ankles.

The first part of her plan had worked. Now she was even more frightened.

She struggled to her feet. All the muscles of her legs ached from a night of constriction. She took a step, stumbled, and fell down again. "It's so hard with my hands tied," she said.

He ignored that.

The second part of her plan had not worked.

She would have to keep trying.

She got up again and walked into the trees, with Alwyn following her. He was counting paces on his fingers. The first time he got to ten, he started again. The second time, he said: "Far enough."

She looked at him helplessly. "I can't lift my dress," she said.

Would he fall for this?

He stared dumbly at her. She could almost hear his brain working, rumbling like the gears of a water mill. He could lift her dress while she peed, but that was the kind of thing a mother did for a toddler, and he would find it humiliating. Alternatively, he could untie her hands. With hands and feet free, she might make a run for it. But she was small, weary and cramped: there was no way she could outrun a man with long, muscular legs. He must be thinking that the risk was not serious.

He untied the rope around her wrists.

She looked away from him, so that he would not see her look of triumph.

She rubbed her forearms to restore the circulation. She wanted to poke his eyeballs out with her thumbs, but instead she smiled as sweetly as she could and said: "Thank you," as if he had performed an act of kindness.

He said nothing, but stood watching her, waiting.

She expected him to look away when she hitched up the skirt of her dress and squatted, but he only stared more intensely. She held his gaze, unwilling to act ashamed while she did what was natural. His mouth opened slightly and she could tell he was breathing harder.

Now came the hardest part.

She stood up slowly, letting him get a good look before she dropped her dress. He licked his lips, and she knew she had him.

She went closer and stood in front of him. "Will you be my protector?" she said, using a little-girl voice that did not come naturally to her.

He showed no sign of suspicion. He did not speak, but grasped her breast in his rough hand and squeezed.

She gasped with pain. "Not so hard!" She took his hand in hers. "Be more gentle." She moved his hand against her breast, rubbing the nipple so that it stood up. "It's nicer if you're gentle."

He grunted, but continued to rub softly. Then he took the neckline of her dress in his left hand and drew his dagger. The knife was a foot long, with a point, and the blade gleamed with recent sharpening. He obviously intended to cut her dress off. That would not do—it would leave her naked.

She took his wrist in a light grip, restraining him momentarily. "You don't need the knife," she said. "Look." She stepped back, undid her belt and, with a quick movement, pulled the dress off over her head. It was her only garment.

She stretched it out on the ground then lay on it. She tried to smile at him. She felt sure the result was a horrible grimace. Then she parted her legs.

He hesitated only for a moment.

Keeping the knife in his right hand, he pushed down his underdrawers and knelt between her thighs. He pointed the dagger at her face and said: "Any trouble, and I'll slice your cheek open."

"You won't need to do that," she said. She was trying desperately to think what words such a man would like to hear from a woman. "My big, strong protector," she said.

He showed no reaction to that.

He lay over her, thrusting blindly. "Not so fast," she said, gritting her teeth against the pain of his clumsy stabs. She reached between her legs and guided him inside, throwing her legs up to make the entrance easier.

He reared over her, taking his weight on his arms. He put the dagger on the grass beside her head, covering the hilt with his right hand. He groaned as he moved inside her. She moved with him, keeping up the pretense of willingness, watching his face, forcing herself not to glance sideways at the dagger, waiting for her moment. She was both scared and disgusted, but a small part of her mind remained calm and calculating.

He closed his eyes and lifted his head like an animal scenting the breeze. His arms were straight, holding him up. She risked a look at the knife. He had moved his hand slightly, so that it only partly covered the hilt. She could grab it now, but how fast would he react?

She looked at his face again. His mouth was twisted in a rictus of concentration. He thrust faster, and she matched his motion.

To her dismay, she felt a glow spread through her loins. She was appalled at herself. The man was a murdering outlaw, little better than a beast, and he was planning to prostitute her for sixpence a time. She was doing this to save her life, not for enjoyment! Yet there was a gush of moisture inside her, and he thrust faster.

She sensed that his moment of climax was near. It was now or never. He gave a groan that sounded like surrender, and she moved.

She snatched the knife from under his hand. There was no change in the expression of ecstasy on his face: he had not noticed her movement. Terrified that he would see what she was doing and stop her at the last moment, she did not hesitate but jabbed upward, jerking her shoulders up from the lying position as she did so. He sensed her movement and opened his eyes. Shock and fear showed on his face. Stabbing wildly, she stuck the knife into his throat just below the jaw. She cursed, knowing she had missed the most vulnerable parts of the neck—the breathing pipe and the jugular vein. He roared with pain and rage, but he was not incapacitated, and she knew she was as close to death as she had ever been.

She moved instinctively, without forethought. Using her left arm, she struck at the inside of his elbow. He could not prevent the bending of his arm, and involuntarily he slumped. She pushed harder at the foot-long dagger, and his weight dragged him down on to the blade. As the knife entered his head from below, blood gushed from his open mouth, falling on her face, and she jerked her head aside reflexively; but she kept pushing on the knife. The blade met resistance for a moment, then slipped through, until his eyeball seemed to explode, and she saw the point emerge from the eye socket in a spray of blood and brains. He slumped on top of her, dead or nearly so. His weight knocked the breath out of her. It was like being stuck under a fallen tree. For a moment she was helpless to move.

To her horror, she felt him ejaculate inside her.

She was filled with superstitious terror. He was more frightening like this than when he had threatened her with a knife. Panicking, she wriggled out from under him.

She scrambled to her feet shakily, breathing hard. She had his blood on her breasts and his seed on her thighs. She glanced fearfully toward the outlaws' camp. Had anyone been awake to hear Alwyn's shout? If they had all been asleep, had the sound wakened any of them?

Trembling, she pulled her dress over her head and buckled her belt. She had her wallet and her own small knife, mainly used for eating. She hardly dared take her eyes off Alwyn: she had a dreadful feeling he might still be alive. She knew she should finish him off, but she could not bring herself to do it. A sound from the direction of the clearing startled her. She needed to get away fast. She looked around, getting her bearings, then headed in the direction of the road.

There was a sentry near the big oak tree, she recalled with a sudden start of fear. She walked softly through the woods, careful to make no sound, as she approached the tree. Then she saw the sentry—Jed, his name was—fast asleep on the ground. She tiptoed past him. It took all her willpower not to break into a mad run. But he did not stir.

She found the deer path and followed it to the brook. It seemed there was no one on her tail. She washed the blood off her face and chest, then splashed cold water on her private parts. She drank deeply, knowing she had a long walk ahead.

Feeling slightly less frantic, she continued along the deer path. As she walked, she listened. How soon would the outlaws find Alwyn? She had not even tried to conceal the body. When they figured out what had happened they would surely come after her, for they had given a cow for her, and that was worth twelve shillings, half a year's pay for a laborer such as her father.

She reached the road. For a woman traveling alone, the open road was almost as hazardous as a forest track. Tam Hiding's group were not the only outlaws, and there were plenty of other men—squires, peasant boys, bands of men-at-arms—who might take advantage of a defenseless woman. But her first priority was to get away from Sim Chapman and his cronies, so speed was paramount.

Which direction should she take? If she went home to Wigleigh, Sim might follow her there and claim her back—and there was no telling how her father would deal with that. She needed friends she could trust. Caris would help her.

She set off for Kingsbridge.

It was a clear day, but the road was muddy from many days of rain, and walking was that much more difficult. After a while she reached the top of a hill. Looking back, she could see along the road for about a mile. At the far limit of her vision, she saw a lone figure striding along. He wore a yellow tunic.

Sim Chapman.

She broke into a run.

The case against Crazy Nell was heard in the north transept of the cathedral on Saturday at noon. Bishop Richard presided over the ecclesiastical court, with Prior Anthony on his right, and on his left his personal assistant, Archdeacon Lloyd, a dour black-haired priest who was said to do all the actual work of the bishopric.

There was a big crowd of townspeople. A heresy trial was good entertainment, and Kingsbridge had not seen one for years. Many craftsmen and laborers finished work at midday on Saturdays. Outside, the Fleece Fair was coming to an end, tradespeople dismantling their stalls and packing up their unsold goods, buyers preparing for the journey home or arranging to consign their purchases by raft downriver to the seaport of Melcombe.

Waiting for the trial to begin, Caris thought gloomily of Gwenda. What was she doing now? Sim Chapman would force her to have sex with him, for sure—but that might not be the worst thing to happen to her. What else would she have to do as his slave? Caris had no doubt Gwenda would try to escape—but would she succeed? And, if she failed, how would Sim punish her? Caris realized she might never find out.

It had been a strange week. Buonaventura Caroli had not changed his mind: the Florentine buyers would not return to Kingsbridge, at least until the priory improved facilities for the Fleece Fair. Caris's father and the other leading wool merchants had spent half the week shut up with Earl Roland. Merthin continued in a strange mood, withdrawn and gloomy. And it was raining again.

Nell was dragged into church by John Constable and Friar Murdo. Her only garment was a sleeveless surcoat, fastened at the front but revealing her bony shoulders. She had no hat or shoes. She struggled feebly in the men's grasp, shouting imprecations.

When they got her quieted down, a series of townspeople came forward to attest that they had heard her call upon the devil. They were telling the truth. Nell threatened people with the devil all the time—for refusing to give her a handout, for standing in her way on the street, for wearing a good coat, or for no reason at all.

Each witness related some misfortune that had followed the curse. A goldsmith's wife had lost a valuable brooch; an innkeeper's chickens had all died; a widow developed a painful boil on her bottom—a complaint that caused laughter, but also carried conviction, for witches were known to have a malicious sense of humor.

While this was going on, Merthin appeared beside Caris. "This is so stupid," Caris said to him indignantly. "Ten times the number of witnesses could come forward to say that Nell cursed them and nothing bad ensued."

Merthin shrugged. "People just believe what they want to believe."

"Ordinary people, perhaps. But the bishop and the prior should know better—they are educated."

"I've got something to tell you," Merthin said.

Caris perked up. Perhaps she was about to learn the reason for his bad mood. She had been looking at him sidelong, but now she turned and saw that he had a huge bruise on the left side of his face. "What happened to you?"

The crowd roared with laughter at some interjection of Nell's, and Archdeacon Lloyd had to call repeatedly for quiet. When Merthin could be heard again he said: "Not here. Can we go somewhere quiet?"

She almost turned to leave with him, but something stopped her. All week long he had bewildered and wounded her by his coldness. Now, at last, he had decided he was ready to say what was on his mind—and she was expected to jump at his command. Why should he set the timetable? He had made her wait five days—why should she not make him wait an hour or so? "No," she said. "Not now."

He looked surprised. "Why not?"

"Because it doesn't suit my convenience," she said. "Now let me listen." As she turned from him, she saw a hurt look cross his face, and straightaway she wished she had not been so cold; but it was too late, and she was not going to apologize.

The witnesses had finished. Bishop Richard said: "Woman, do you say that the devil rules the earth?"

Caris was outraged. Heretics worshipped Satan because they believed he had jurisdiction over the earth, and God only ruled Heaven. Crazy Nell could not even understand such a sophisticated credo. It was disgraceful that Richard was going along with Friar Murdo's ridiculous accusation.

Nell shouted back: "You can shove your prick up your arse."

The crowd laughed, delighted by this coarse insult to the bishop.

Richard said: "If that's her defense . . ."

Archdeacon Lloyd intervened. "Someone should speak on her behalf," he said. He spoke respectfully, but he seemed comfortable correcting his superior. No doubt the lazy Richard relied on Lloyd to remind him of the rules.

Richard looked around the transept. "Who will speak for Nell?" he called out.

Caris waited, but no one volunteered. She could not allow this to happen. Someone must point out how irrational this whole procedure was. When no one else spoke, Caris stood up. "Nell is mad," she said.

Everyone looked around, wondering who was foolish enough to side with Nell. There was a murmur of recognition—most people knew Caris—but no great sense of surprise, for she had a reputation for doing the unexpected.

Prior Anthony leaned over and said something in the bishop's ear. Richard said: "Caris, the daughter of Edmund Wooler, tells us that the accused woman is mad. We had reached that conclusion without her assistance."

Caris was goaded by his cool sarcasm. "Nell has no idea what she is saying! She calls upon the devil, the saints, the moon and the stars. It has no more meaning than the barking of a dog. You might as well hang a horse for neighing at the king." She could not keep the note of scorn from her voice, though she knew it was unwise to let your contempt show when addressing the nobility.

Some of the crowd murmured agreement. They liked a spirited argument.

Richard said: "But you have heard people testify to the damage done by her curses."

"I lost a penny yesterday," Caris rejoined. "I boiled an egg, and it was bad. My father lay awake all night coughing. But no one cursed us. Bad things just happen."

There was much head-shaking at this. Most people believed there was some malign influence behind every misfortune, great or small. Caris had lost the support of the crowd.

Prior Anthony, her uncle, knew her views, and had argued with her before. Now he leaned forward and said: "Surely you don't believe that *God* is responsible for illness and misfortune and loss?"

"No—"

"Who, then?"

Caris imitated Anthony's prissy tone. "Surely you don't believe that every misfortune in life is the responsibility of either God or Crazy Nell?"

Archdeacon Lloyd said sharply: "Speak respectfully to the prior." He did not realize Anthony was Caris's uncle. The townspeople laughed: they knew the prim prior and his independent-minded niece.

Caris finished: "I believe Nell is harmless. Mad, yes, but harmless."

Suddenly Friar Murdo was on his feet. "My lord bishop, men of Kingsbridge, friends," he said in his sonorous voice. "The evil one is everywhere among us, tempting us to sin—to lying, greed of food, drunkenness with wine, puffed-up pride, and fleshly lust." The crowd liked this: Murdo's descriptions of sin called to the imagination delightful scenes of indulgence that were sanctified by his brimstone disapproval. "But he cannot go unobserved," Murdo went on, his voice rising with excitement. "As the horse presses his hoofprints into the mud, as the kitchen mouse makes dainty tracks across the butter, as the lecher deposits his vile seed to grow in the womb of the deceived maid, so the devil must leave—his mark!"

They shouted their approval. They knew what he meant, and so did Caris.

"The servants of the evil one may be known by the mark he leaves upon them. For he sucks their hot blood as a child sucks the sweet milk from its mother's swollen breasts. And, like the child, he needs a teat from which to suck—a third nipple!"

He had the audience rapt, Caris observed. He began each sentence in a low, quiet voice, then built it up, piling one emotive phrase on another to his climax; and the crowd responded eagerly, listening in silence while he spoke, then shouting their approval at the end.

"This mark is dark in color, ridged like a nipple, and rises from the clear skin around it. It may be on any part of the body. Sometimes it lies in the soft valley between a woman's breasts, the unnatural manifestation cruelly mimicking the natural. But the devil best likes it to be in the secret places of the body: in the groin, on the private parts, especially—"

Bishop Richard said loudly: "Thank you, Friar Murdo, you need go no further. You are demanding that the woman's body be examined for the devil's mark."

"Yes, my lord bishop, for—"

"All right, no need for further argument, your point is well made." He looked around. "Is Mother Cecilia close by?"

The prioress was sitting on a bench on one side of the court, with Sister Juliana and some of the senior nuns. Crazy Nell's naked body could not be examined by men, so women would have to do it in private and report back. The nuns were the obvious choice.

Caris did not envy them their task. Most townspeople washed their hands and faces every day, and the smellier parts of their bodies once a week. All-over bathing was at best a twice-a-year ritual, necessary though dangerous to the health. However, Crazy Nell never seemed to wash at all. Her face was grimy, her hands were filthy, and she smelled like a dunghill.

Cecilia stood up. Richard said: "Please take this woman to a private room, remove her clothing, examine her body carefully, and come back to report faithfully what you find."

The nuns got up immediately and approached Nell. Cecilia spoke soothingly to the madwoman and took her gently by the arm. But Nell was not fooled. She twisted away, throwing her arms into the air.

At that point, Friar Murdo shouted: "I see it! I see it!"

Four of the nuns managed to hold Nell still.

The friar said: "No need to take off her clothes. Just look under her right arm." As Nell started to wriggle again, he strode over to her and lifted her arm himself, holding it high above her head. "There!" he said, pointing into her armpit.

The crowd surged forward. "I see it!" someone shouted, and others repeated the cry. Caris could see nothing other than normal armpit hair, and she was unwilling to commit the indignity of peering. She had no doubt that Nell had some kind of blemish or growth there. Lots of people had marks on their skin, especially the elderly.

Archdeacon Lloyd called for order, and John Constable beat the crowd back with a stick. When at last the church was quiet, Richard stood up. "Crazy Nell of Kingsbridge, I find you guilty of heresy," he said. "You shall now be tied to the back of a cart and whipped through the town, then taken to the place known as Gallows Cross, where you shall be hanged by the neck until you die."

The crowd cheered. Caris turned away in disgust. With justice like this, no woman was safe. Her eye lit on Merthin, waiting patiently for her. "All right," she said bad-temperedly. "What is it?"

"It's stopped raining," he said. "Come down to the river."

The priory had a string of ponies for the senior monks and nuns to use when traveling, plus some carthorses for transporting goods. These were kept, along with the mounts of prosperous visitors, in a run of stone stables at the south end of the cathedral close. The nearby kitchen garden was manured with the straw from the stalls.

Ralph was in the stable yard, with the rest of Earl Roland's entourage. Their horses were saddled, ready to begin the two-day journey back to Roland's residence at Earlscastle, near Shiring. They were waiting only for the earl.

Ralph was holding his horse, a bay called Griff, and talking to his parents. "I don't know why Stephen was made lord of Wigleigh while I got nothing," he said. "We're the same age, and he's no better than I am at riding or jousting or fencing."

Every time they met, Sir Gerald asked the same hopeful questions, and Ralph had to give him the same inadequate answers. Ralph could have borne his disappointment more easily had it not been for his father's pathetic eagerness to see him elevated.

Griff was a young horse. He was a hunter: a mere squire did not merit a costly warhorse. But Ralph liked him. He responded gratifyingly well when Ralph urged him on in the hunt. Griff was excited by all the activity in the yard, and impatient to get going. Ralph murmured in his ear: "Quiet, my lovely lad, you shall stretch your legs later." The horse calmed down at the sound of his voice.

"Be constantly on the alert for ways to please the earl," Sir Gerald said. "Then he will remember you when there is a post to be filled."

That was all very well, Ralph thought, but the real opportunities came only in battle. However, war might be a little nearer today than it had been a week ago. Ralph had not been in on the meetings between the earl and the wool merchants, but he gathered that the merchants were willing to lend money to King Edward. They wanted the king to take some decisive action against France, in retaliation for French attacks on the south coast ports.

Meanwhile, Ralph longed for some way to distinguish himself and begin to win back the honor the family had lost ten years ago—not just for his father, but for his own pride.

Griff stamped and tossed his head. To calm him, Ralph began to walk him up and down, and his father walked with him. His mother stood apart. She was upset about his broken nose.

With Father he walked past Lady Philippa, who was holding the bridle of a spirited courser with a firm hand while she talked to her husband, Lord William. She wore close-fitting clothes, which were suitable for a long ride but also emphasized her full bosom and long legs. Ralph was always on the lookout for excuses to talk to her, but it did him no good: he was just one of her father-in-law's followers, and she never spoke to him unless she had to.

As Ralph watched, she smiled at her husband and tapped him on the chest with the back of her hand in a gesture of mock reprimand. Ralph was filled with resentment. Why should it not be him with whom she was sharing such a moment of private amusement? No doubt she would if he were lord of forty villages, as William was.

Ralph felt that his life was all aspiration. When would he actually achieve something? He and his father walked the length of the yard then turned and came back.

He saw a one-armed monk come out of the kitchen and cross the yard, and was struck by how familiar the man looked. A moment later, he remembered how he knew the face. This was Thomas Langley, the knight who had killed two men-at-arms in the forest ten years ago. Ralph had not seen the man since that day, but his brother Merthin had, for the knight-become-monk was now responsible for supervising repairs to the priory buildings. Thomas wore a drab robe instead of the fine clothes of a knight, and had his head shaved in the monkish tonsure. He was heavier around the waist, but still carried himself like a fighting man.

As Thomas walked past, Ralph said casually to Lord William: "There he goes—the mystery monk."

William said sharply: "What do you mean?"

"Brother Thomas. He used to be a knight, and no one knows why he joined the monastery."

"What the devil do you know of him?" William's tone showed anger, although Ralph had said nothing offensive. Perhaps he was in a bad mood, despite the affectionate smiles of his beautiful wife.

Ralph wished he had not begun the conversation. "I was here the day he came to Kingsbridge," he said. He hesitated, recalling the oath the children had sworn that afternoon. Because of that, and because of William's inexplicable annoyance, Ralph did not tell the whole story. "He staggered into town bleeding from a sword wound," he went on. "A boy remembers such things."

Philippa said: "How curious." She looked at her husband. "Do you know what Brother Thomas's story is?"

"Certainly not," William snapped. "How would I know a thing like that?"

She shrugged and turned away.

Ralph walked on, glad to get away. "Lord William was lying," he said to his father in a low voice. "I wonder why."

"Don't ask any more questions about that monk," Father said anxiously. "It's obviously a touchy subject."

At last Earl Roland appeared. Prior Anthony was with him. The knights and squires mounted up. Ralph kissed his parents and swung himself into the saddle. Griff danced sideways, eager to be off. The motion made Ralph's broken nose hurt like fire. He gritted his teeth: there was nothing he could do but endure it.

Roland went up to his horse, Victory, a black stallion with a white patch over one eye. He did not mount, but took the bridle and began to walk, still in conversation with the prior. William called out: "Sir Stephen Wigleigh and Ralph Fitzgerald, ride ahead and clear the bridge."

Ralph and Stephen rode across the cathedral green. The grass was trampled and the ground muddy from the Fleece Fair. A few stalls were still doing business, but most were closing, and many had already gone. They passed out through the priory gates.

On the main street, Ralph saw the boy who had given him a broken nose. Wulfric, his name was, and he came from Stephen's village of Wigleigh. The left side of his face was bruised and swollen where Ralph had repeatedly punched him. Wulfric was outside the Bell Inn with his father, mother, and brother. They appeared to be about to leave.

You'd better hope you never meet me again, Ralph thought.

He tried to think of some insult to shout, but he was distracted by the sound of a crowd.

As he and Stephen rode down the main street, their horses stepping adroitly through the mud, they saw ahead of them a mob of people. Halfway down the hill, they were forced to stop.

The street was jammed by hundreds of men, women, and children shouting, laughing, and jostling for space. They all had their backs to Ralph. He looked over their heads.

At the front of this unruly procession was a cart drawn by an ox. Tied to the back of the cart was a half-naked woman. Ralph had seen this kind of thing before: to be whipped through the town was a common punishment. The woman wore only a skirt of rough wool secured at the waist by a cord. Her face, when he could see it, was begrimed, and her hair was filthy, so that at first he thought she was old. Then he saw her breasts and realized she was only in her twenties.

Her hands were bound together and attached by the same rope to the back end of the cart. She stumbled along behind it, sometimes falling and being dragged writhing through the mud until she managed to get back on her feet. The town constable followed, vigorously lashing her bare back with a bullwhip, a strip of leather at the end of a stick.

The crowd, led by a knot of young men, were taunting the woman, shouting insults, laughing, and throwing mud and rubbish. She delighted them by responding, screaming imprecations and spitting at anyone who got near her.

Ralph and Stephen urged their horses into the crowd. Ralph raised his voice. "Clear the way!" he shouted at the top of his voice. "Make way for the earl!"

Stephen did the same.

No one took any notice.

∽

To the south of the priory, the ground sloped steeply down to the river. The bank on that side was rocky, unsuitable for loading barges and rafts, so all the wharves were on the more accessible south side, in the suburb of Newtown. The quiet north side bloomed at this time of year with shrubbery and wildflowers. Merthin and Caris sat on a low bluff overlooking the water.

The river was swollen with rain. It moved faster than it used to, Merthin noticed, and he could see why: the channel was narrower than formerly. That was because of the development of the riverside. When he was a child, most of the south bank had been a wide, muddy beach with a swampy field beyond. The river then had flowed at a stately pace, and as a boy he had floated on his back from one side to the other. But the new wharves, protected from flooding by stone walls, squeezed the same quantity of water into a smaller funnel, through which it hurried as if eager to get past the bridge. Beyond the bridge, the river widened and slowed around Leper Island.

"I've done something terrible," Merthin said to Caris.

Unfortunately, she looked particularly lovely today. She wore a dark red linen dress, and her skin seemed to glow with vitality. She had been angry at the trial of Crazy Nell, but now she just seemed worried, and that gave her a vulnerable look that tugged at Merthin's heart. She must have noticed how he had been unable to meet her eye all week. But what he had to tell her was probably worse than anything she had imagined.

He had spoken to no one about this since the row with Griselda, Elfric, and Alice. No one even knew that his door had been destroyed. He was longing to unburden himself, but he had held back. He did not want to talk to his parents: his mother would be judgmental and his father would just tell him to be a man. He might have talked to Ralph, but there had been a coolness between them since the fight with Wulfric: Merthin thought Ralph had behaved like a bully, and Ralph knew it.

He dreaded telling Caris the truth. For a moment he asked himself why. It was not that he was afraid of what she would do. She might be scornful—she was good at that—but she could not say anything worse than the things he said to himself constantly.

What he truly feared, he realized, was hurting her. He could bear her anger: it was her pain he could not face.

She said: "Do you still love me?"

He was not expecting the question, but he answered without hesitation. "Yes."

"And I love you. Anything else is just a problem we can solve together."

He wished she were right. He wished it so badly that tears came to his eyes. He looked away so that she would not see. A mob of people was moving onto the bridge, following a slow-moving cart, and he realized this must be Crazy Nell being whipped through the town on her way to Gallows Cross in Newtown. The bridge was already crowded with departing stallholders and their carts, and the traffic was almost at a standstill.

"What's the matter?" Caris said. "Are you crying?"

"I lay with Griselda," Merthin said abruptly.

Caris's mouth dropped open. *"Griselda?"* she said unbelievingly.

"I'm so ashamed."

"I thought it must be Elizabeth Clerk."

"She's too proud to offer herself."

Caris's reaction to that surprised him. "Oh, so you would have done it with her, too, if she'd suggested it?"

"That's not what I meant!"

"Griselda! Dear Saint Mary, I thought I was worth more than that."

"You are."

"Lupa," she said, using the Latin word for a whore.

"I don't even like her. I hated it."

"Is that supposed to make me feel better? Are you saying you wouldn't be so sorry if you'd enjoyed it?"

"No!" Merthin was dismayed. Caris seemed determined to misinterpret everything he said.

"Whatever got into you?"

"She was crying."

"Oh, for God's sake! Do you do that to every girl you see crying?"

"Of course not! I was just trying to explain to you how it happened even though I really didn't want it to."

Her scorn got worse with everything he said. "Don't talk rubbish," she said. "If you hadn't wanted it to happen, it wouldn't have."

"Listen to me, please," he said frustratedly. "She asked me, and I said no. Then she cried, and I put my arm around her to comfort her, then—"

"Oh, spare me the sickening details—I don't want to know."

He began to feel resentful. He knew he had done wrong, and he expected her to be angry, but her contempt stung. "All right," he said, and he shut up.

But silence was not what she wanted. She stared at him in dissatisfaction, then said: "What else?"

He shrugged. "What's the point in my speaking? You just pour scorn on everything I say."

"I don't want to listen to pathetic excuses. But there's something you haven't told me—I can feel it."

He sighed. "She's pregnant."

Caris's reaction surprised him again. All the anger left her. Her face, until now taut with indignation, seemed to collapse. Only sadness remained. "A baby," she said. "Griselda is going to have your baby."

"It may not happen," he said. "Sometimes . . ."

Caris shook her head. "Griselda is a healthy girl, well fed. There's no reason she should miscarry."

"Not that I'd wish it," he said, though he was not quite sure that was true.

"But what will you do?" she said. "It will be your child. You will love it, even if you hate its mother."

"I've got to marry her."

Caris gasped. "Marry! But that would be forever."

"I've fathered a child, so I should take care of it."

"But to spend your whole life with Griselda!"

"I know."

"You don't have to," she said decisively. "Think. Elizabeth Clerk's father didn't marry her mother."

"He was a bishop."

"There's Maud Roberts, in Slaughterhouse Ditch—she has three children, and everyone knows the father is Edward Butcher."

"He's already married, and has four other children with his wife."

"I'm saying they don't always force people to marry. You could just carry on as you are."

"No, I couldn't. Elfric would throw me out."

She looked thoughtful. "So, you've already talked to Elfric?"

"Talked?" Merthin touched his bruised cheek. "I thought he was going to kill me."

"And his wife—my sister?"

"She screamed at me."

"So she knows."

"Yes. She said I have to marry Griselda. She never wanted me to be with you, anyway. I don't know why."

Caris muttered: "She wanted you for herself."

That was news to Merthin. It seemed unlikely that the haughty Alice would be attracted to a lowly apprentice. "I never saw any sign of that."

"Only because you never looked at her. That's what made her so cross. She married Elfric in frustration. You broke my sister's heart—and now you're breaking mine."

Merthin looked away. He barely recognized this picture of himself as a heartbreaker. How had things gone so wrong? Caris went quiet. Merthin stared moodily along the river to the bridge.

The crowd had come to a standstill, he saw. A heavy cart loaded with woolsacks was stuck at the southern end, probably with a broken wheel. The cart pulling Nell had stopped, unable to pass. The crowd was swarming around both carts, and some people had climbed onto the woolsacks for a better view. Earl Roland was also trying to leave. He was at the town end of the bridge, on horseback, with his entourage; but even they were having trouble getting the citizens to give way. Merthin spotted his brother, Ralph, on his horse, chestnut colored with a black mane and tail. Prior Anthony, who had evidently come to see the earl off, stood wringing his hands with anxiety while Roland's men forced their horses into the mob, trying in vain to clear a passage.

Merthin's intuition rang an alarm. Something was badly wrong, he felt sure, though at first he did not know what. He looked more closely at the bridge. He had noticed, on Monday, that the massive oak beams stretching from one piling to another across the length of the bridge were showing cracks on the upstream side; and that the beams had been strengthened with iron braces nailed across the cracks. Merthin had not been involved in this job, which was why he had not previously looked hard at the work. On Monday he had wondered why the beams were cracking. The weakness was not halfway between the uprights, as he would have expected if the timbers had simply deteriorated over time. Rather, the cracks were near the central pier, where the strain should have been less.

He had not thought about it since Monday—there was too much else on his mind—but now an explanation occurred to him. It was almost as if that central pier was not supporting the beams, but dragging them down. That would mean that something had undermined the foundation beneath the pier—and, as soon as that thought occurred to him, he realized how it could have happened. It must be the faster flow of the river, scouring the river bed from under the pier.

He remembered walking barefoot on a sandy beach, as a child, and noticing that when he stood at the sea's edge, letting the water wash over his feet, the outgoing waves would suck the sand from under his toes. That kind of phenomenon had always fascinated him.

If he was right, the central pier, with nothing underneath to support it, was now hanging from the bridge—hence the cracks. Elfric's iron braces had not helped; in fact, they might have worsened the problem, by making it impossible for the bridge to settle slowly into a new, stable position.

Merthin guessed that the other pier of the pair—on the farther, downstream side of the bridge—was still grounded. The current surely spent most of its force on the upstream pier, and attacked the second of the pair with reduced violence. Only one pier was affected; and it seemed that the rest of the structure was knitted together strongly enough for the entire bridge to stay upright—as long as it was not subjected to extraordinary strain.

But the cracks seemed wider today than on Monday. And it was not difficult to guess why. Hundreds of people were on the bridge, a much greater load than it normally took; and there was a heavily laden wool cart, with twenty or thirty people sitting on the sacks of wool to add to the burden.

Fear gripped Merthin's heart. He did not think the bridge could withstand that level of strain for long.

He was vaguely aware that Caris was speaking, but her meaning did not penetrate his thoughts until she raised her voice and said: "You're not even listening!"

"There's going to be a terrible accident," he said.

"What do you mean?"

"We have to get everyone off the bridge."

"Are you mad? They're all tormenting Crazy Nell. Even Earl Roland can't get them to move. They're not going to listen to you."

"I think it could collapse."

"Oh, look!" said Caris, pointing. "Can you see someone running along the road from the forest, approaching the south end of the bridge?"

Merthin wondered what that had to do with anything, but he followed her pointing finger. Sure enough, he saw the figure of a young woman running, her hair flying.

Caris said: "It looks like Gwenda."

Behind her, in hot pursuit, was a man in a yellow tunic.

Gwenda was more tired than she had ever been in her life.

She knew that the fastest way to cover a long distance was to run twenty paces then walk twenty paces. She had started to do that half a day ago, when she spotted Sim Chapman a mile behind her. For a while she lost sight of him but, when once again the road provided her with a long rearward view, she saw that he, too, was walking and running alternately. As mile succeeded mile and hour followed hour he gained on her. By midmorning she had known that at this rate he would catch her before she reached Kingsbridge.

In desperation, she had taken to the forest. But she could not stray far from the road for fear of losing her way. Eventually she heard running steps and heavy breathing, and peered through the undergrowth to see Sim go by on the road. She realized that as soon as he came to a long clear stretch he would guess what she had done. Sure enough, some time later she saw him come back.

She had pressed on through the forest, stopping every few minutes to stand in silence and listen. For a long time she had evaded him, and she knew he would have to search the woods on both sides of the road to make sure she was not in hiding. But her progress was also slow, for she had to fight her way through the summer undergrowth, and keep checking that she had not strayed too far from the road.

When she heard the sound of a distant crowd, she knew she could not be far from the city, and she thought she was going to escape after all. She made her way to the road and cautiously looked out from a bush. The way was clear in both directions—and, a quarter of a mile to the north, she could see the tower of the cathedral.

She was almost there.

She heard a familiar bark, and her dog, Skip, emerged from the bushes at the side of the road. She bent to pat him, and he wagged joyfully, licking her hands. Tears came to her eyes.

Sim was not in sight, so she risked the open road. She wearily resumed her twenty paces of running and twenty of walking, now with Skip trotting happily beside her, thinking this was a new game. Each time she switched, she looked back over her shoulder. The third time she did so, she saw Sim.

He was only a couple of hundred yards behind.

Despair washed over her like a tidal wave. She wanted to lie down and die. But she was in the suburbs now, and the bridge was only a quarter of a mile away. She forced herself to keep going.

She tried to sprint, but her legs refused to obey orders. A staggering jog was the best she could manage. Her feet hurt. Looking down, she saw blood seeping through the holes in her tattered shoes. As she turned the corner at Gallows Cross, she saw a huge crowd on the bridge ahead of her. They were all looking at something, and no one noticed her running for her life, with Sim Chapman close behind.

She had no weapons other than her eating knife, which would just about cut through a baked hare, but would hardly disable a man. She wished with all her heart that she had had the nerve to pull Alwyn's long dagger out of his head and bring it away with her. Now she was virtually defenseless.

She had a row of small houses on one side of her—the suburban homes of people too poor to live in the city—and, on the other side, the pasture called Lovers' Field, owned by the priory. Sim was so close behind her that she could hear his breathing, harsh and ragged like her own. Terror gave her a last burst of energy. Skip barked, but there was more fear than defiance in his note—he had not forgotten the stone that hit him on the nose.

The approach to the bridge was a swamp of sticky mud, churned up by boots, hooves, and cartwheels. Gwenda waded through it, desperately hoping that the heavier Sim would be hampered even more than she.

At last she reached the bridge. She pushed into the crowd, which was less dense at this end. They were all looking the other way, where a heavy cart loaded with wool was blocking the passage of an ox cart. She had to get to Caris's house, almost in sight now on the main street. "Let me through!" she screamed, fighting her way forward. Only one person seemed to hear her. A head turned to look, and she saw the face of her brother Philemon. His mouth dropped open in alarm, and he tried to move toward her, but the crowd resisted him as it resisted her.

Gwenda tried to push past the team of oxen drawing the wool cart, but an ox tossed its massive head and knocked her sideways. She lost her footing—and, at that moment, a big hand grasped her arm in a powerful grip, and she knew she was recaptured.

"I've got you, you bitch," Sim gasped. He pulled her to him and slapped her across the face as hard as he could. She had no strength left to resist him. Skip snapped ineffectually at his heels. "You won't get away from me again," he said.

Despair engulfed her. It had all been for nothing: seducing Alwyn, murdering him, running for miles. She was back where she had started, the captive of Sim.

Then the bridge seemed to move.

13

Merthin saw the bridge bend.

Over the central pier on the near side, the entire roadbed sagged like a horse with a broken back. The people tormenting Nell suddenly found the surface beneath their feet unsteady. They staggered, grabbing their neighbors for support. One fell backward over the parapet into the river; then another, then another. The shouts and catcalls directed at Nell were quickly drowned out by yells of warning and screams of fright.

Merthin said: "Oh, no!"

Caris screamed: "What's happening?"

All those people, he wanted to say—*people we grew up with, women who have been kind to us, men we hate, children who admire us; mothers and sons, uncles and nieces; cruel masters and sworn enemies and panting lovers—they're going to die.* But he could not get any words out.

For a moment—less than a breath—Merthin hoped the structure might stabilize in the new position; but he was disappointed. The bridge sagged again. This time, the interlocked timbers began to tear free of their joints. The longitudinal planks on which the people were standing sprang from their wooden pegs; the transverse joints that supported the roadbed twisted out of their sockets; and the iron braces that Elfric had hammered across the cracks were ripped out of the wood.

The central part of the bridge seemed to lurch downward on the side nearest Merthin, the upstream side. The wool cart tilted, and the spectators standing and sitting on the piled woolsacks were hurled into the river. Great timbers snapped and flew through the air, killing everyone they struck. The insubstantial parapet gave way, and the cart slid slowly off the edge, its helpless oxen lowing in terror. It fell with nightmare slowness through the air and hit the water with a thunderclap. Suddenly there were dozens of people jumping or falling into the river, then scores of them. Those already in the water were struck by the falling bodies of those who came after, and by the disintegrating timbers, some small, some huge. Horses fell, with and without riders, and carts fell on top of them.

Merthin's first thought was of his parents. Neither of them had gone to the trial of Crazy Nell, and they would not have wanted to watch her punishment: his mother thought such public spectacles beneath her dignity, and his father was not interested when there was no more at stake than the life of a madwoman. Instead, they had gone to the priory to say good-bye to Ralph.

But Ralph was now on the bridge.

Merthin could see his brother fighting to control his horse, Griff, which was rearing and kicking out with its front hooves. "Ralph!" he yelled uselessly. Then the timbers under Griff fell into the water. "No!" Merthin shouted as horse and rider disappeared from view.

Merthin's gaze flashed to the other end, where Caris had spotted Gwenda, and he saw her struggling with a man in a yellow tunic. Then that part gave way, and both ends of the bridge were dragged into the water by the collapsing middle.

The river was now a mass of writhing people, panicking horses, splintered timbers, smashed carts, and bleeding bodies. Merthin realized that Caris was no longer by his side when he saw her hurrying along the bank toward the bridge, clambering over rocks and running along the muddy strand. She looked back at him and yelled: "Hurry up! What are you waiting for? Come and help!"

This must be what a battlefield is like, Ralph thought: the screaming, the random violence, the people falling, the horses mad with fear. It was the last thought he had before the ground dropped away beneath him.

He suffered a moment of sheer terror. He did not understand what had happened. The bridge had been there, under his horse's hooves, but now it was not, and he and his mount were tumbling through the air. Then he could no longer feel the familiar bulk of Griff between his thighs, and he realized they had separated. An instant later he hit the cold water.

He went under and held his breath. The panic left him. Now he felt scared, but calm. He had played in the sea as a child—a seaside village had been among his father's domains—and he knew he would rise to the surface, though it might seem to take a long time. He was weighed down by his thick traveling clothes, now saturated, and by his sword. If he had been wearing armor, he would have sunk to the bottom and stayed there forever. But at last his head broke the surface and he gasped for breath.

He had swum a good deal as a boy, but that was many years ago. All the same, the technique came back to him, more or less, and he was able to keep his head above water. He began to thrash his way toward the north bank. Beside him, he recognized the chestnut coat and black mane of Griff, doing the same as he was, swimming for the nearest shore.

The horse's gait changed, and he realized it had found its footing. Ralph let his feet drift down to the riverbed and found that he, too, could stand. He waded through the shallows. The sticky mud of the bottom seemed to be trying to suck him back into midstream. Griff hauled himself onto a narrow strip of beach below the priory wall. Ralph did the same.

He turned and looked back. There were several hundred people in the water, many bleeding, many screaming, many dead. Near the edge he saw a figure wearing the red-and-black livery of the earl of Shiring, floating facedown. He stepped back into the water, grabbed the man by the belt, and hauled him ashore.

He turned the heavy body over, and his heart lurched with recognition. It was his friend Stephen. The face was unmarked, but Stephen's chest appeared to have caved in. His eyes were wide open, showing no sign of life. There was no breath. The body was too damaged even for Ralph to feel for a heartbeat. A few minutes ago I was envying him, Ralph thought. Now I'm the lucky one.

Feeling irrationally guilty, he closed Stephen's eyes.

He thought of his parents. Only a few minutes ago he had left them in the stable yard. Even if they had followed him, they could not have reached the bridge yet. They must be safe.

Where was Lady Philippa? Ralph cast his mind back to the scene on the bridge just before the collapse. Lord William and Philippa had been at the rear of the earl's procession and had not yet ridden onto the bridge.

But the earl had.

Ralph could picture the scene quite clearly. Earl Roland had been close behind him, impatiently urging his horse, Victory, forward through the gap in the crowd made by Ralph on Griff. Roland must have fallen close to Ralph.

Ralph heard again his father's words: *Be constantly on the alert for ways to please the earl.* Perhaps this was the big chance he had been looking for, he thought excitedly. He might not have to wait for a war. He could distinguish himself today. He would save Earl Roland—or even just Victory.

The thought energized him. He scanned the river. The earl had been wearing a distinctive purple robe and a black velvet surcoat. It was hard to pick out an individual in the seething mass of bodies, alive and dead. Then he saw a black stallion with a distinctive white patch over one eye, and his heart leaped: it was Roland's mount. Victory was thrashing around in the water, apparently unable to swim in a straight line, probably having broken one or more legs.

Floating next to the horse was a tall figure in a purple robe.

This was Ralph's moment.

He threw off his outer clothing: it would hamper his swimming. Wearing only his underdrawers, he plunged back into the river and swam toward the earl. He had to force his way through a mass of men, women, and children. Many of the living grabbed desperately at him, delaying his progress. He fought them off ruthlessly with merciless blows of his fists.

At last he reached Victory. The beast's struggles were weakening. It was still for a moment and started to sink; then, when its head dipped into the water, it began to struggle again. "Easy, boy, easy," Ralph said into its ear; but he felt sure it was going to drown.

Roland was floating on his back, eyes closed, unconscious or dead. One foot was caught in a stirrup, and that seemed to be what was keeping his body from going down. He had lost his hat, and the top of his head was a bloody mess. Ralph could not see how a man could live after such an injury. All the same, he would rescue him. There would surely be some reward just for the corpse, when it was that of an earl.

He tried to pull Roland's foot from the stirrup, but he found the strap was twisted tight around the ankle. He felt for his knife and realized it was attached to his belt, which he had left on the shore with the rest of his outer clothing. But the earl had weapons. Ralph fumbled Roland's dagger from its sheath.

Victory's convulsions made it difficult for Ralph to cut the strap. Each time he caught hold of the stirrup, the dying horse jerked it from his grasp before he could bring the knife to bear on the leather. He cut the back of his own hand in the struggle. Finally he braced himself against the horse's side with both feet, for stability, and in that position he was able to slice through the stirrup strap.

Now he had to drag the unconscious earl to the bank. Ralph was not a strong swimmer, and he was already panting with exhaustion. To make matters worse, he could not breathe through his broken nose, so his mouth kept filling with river water. He paused for a moment, leaning his weight on the doomed Victory, trying to catch his breath; but the earl's body, now unsupported, began to sink, and Ralph realized he could not rest.

He grabbed Roland's ankle in his right hand and started to swim for the shore. He found it harder to keep his head above the surface when he had only one hand free for swimming. He did not look back at Roland: if the earl's head went under water there was nothing Ralph could do about it. After a few seconds he was gasping for air and his limbs were aching.

He was not used to this. He was young and strong, and his whole life was spent hunting, jousting, and fencing. He could ride all day then win a wrestling match the same evening. But now he seemed to be relying on disused muscles. His neck hurt from the effort of keeping his head up. He could not help breathing water in, and that made him cough and choke. He flapped his left arm madly and just managed to keep himself afloat. He heaved at the bulky body of the earl, made heavier by its water-soaked clothing. He approached the shore with agonizing slowness.

At last he was close enough to put his feet on the riverbed. Gulping air, he began to wade, still dragging Roland. When the water was thigh-high he turned, picked up the earl in his arms, and carried him the last few steps to the shore.

He put the body on the ground and collapsed beside it, exhausted. With the last of his energy, he felt the chest. There was a strong heartbeat.

Earl Roland was alive.

The collapse of the bridge paralyzed Gwenda with fear. Then, an instant later, the sudden immersion in cold water shocked her back to normal.

When her head came above the surface, she found herself surrounded by brawling, yelling people. Some had found a piece of wood to keep them afloat, but every other man tried to keep himself above water by leaning on someone else. Those leaned upon felt themselves being pushed under, and lashed out with their fists to get free. Many of the blows missed. Those that connected were returned. It was like being outside a Kingsbridge tavern at midnight. It would have been comical, except that people were dying.

Gwenda gasped air and went under. She could not swim.

She came up again. To her horror, Sim Chapman was immediately in front of her, blowing water out of his mouth like a fountain. He began to go under, obviously as unable to swim as she was. In desperation, he grabbed her shoulder and tried to use her for support. She immediately sank. Finding her inadequate to keep him on the surface, he let her go.

Under the water, holding her breath, fighting off panic, she thought: I can't drown now, after all I've been through.

Next time she surfaced, she felt herself shoved aside by a heavy body, and she saw, out of the corner of her eye, the ox that had knocked her over a moment before the bridge fell apart. It was apparently unharmed and swimming strongly. She reached out, kicking her feet, and managed to get hold of one of its horns. She pulled its head sideways for a moment, then the powerful neck pulled back and its head came upright again.

Gwenda managed to hang on.

Her dog, Skip, appeared beside her, swimming effortlessly, and yelped for joy to see her face.

The ox was heading for the suburban shore. Gwenda clung to its horn, even though her arm felt as if it was about to drop off.

Someone grabbed her, and she looked over her shoulder to see Sim again. Trying to use her to keep himself afloat, he pulled her under. Without letting go of the ox, she pushed Sim off with her free hand. He dropped back, his head close to her feet. Taking careful aim, she kicked him as hard as she could in the face. He gave a cry of pain that was quickly silenced as his head went under.

The ox found its footing and lumbered out of the water, splashing and snorting. Gwenda let go as soon as she could stand on the bottom.

Skip gave a frightened bark, and Gwenda looked around warily. Sim was not on the bank. She scanned the river, looking for the flash of a yellow tunic among the bodies and the floating timbers.

She saw him, keeping himself afloat by holding on to a plank, kicking with his legs and coming straight toward her.

She could not run. She had no strength left, and her dress was waterlogged. On this side of the river, there was no place to hide. And, now that the bridge was down, there was no way to cross to the Kingsbridge side.

But she was not going to let him take her.

She saw that he was struggling, and that gave her hope. The plank would have kept him afloat if he had remained still, but he was kicking for the shore, and his thrashing destabilized him. He would push down on the plank to lift himself up, then kick to swim for shore, and his head would go under again. He might not make it to the bank.

She realized she could make certain of that.

She looked around quickly. The water was full of bits of wood, from huge load-bearing timbers to splinters. Her eye lit on a stout timber about a yard long. She stepped into the water and grabbed it. Then she waded out into the river to meet her owner.

She had the satisfaction of seeing the light of fear in his eyes.

He paused in his paddling. Ahead of him was the woman he had tried to enslave—angry, determined, and wielding a formidable club. Behind him, death by drowning.

He came forward.

Gwenda stood up to her waist in water and waited for her moment.

She saw Sim pause again, and guessed from his movements that he was trying to find the bottom with his feet.

Now or never.

Gwenda raised the wood over her head and stepped forward. Sim saw what she was about to do, and scrabbled desperately to get out of the way; but he was off balance, neither swimming nor wading, and he could not dodge. Gwenda brought the timber down on top of his head with all her might.

Sim's eyes rolled up and he slumped unconscious.

She reached forward and grabbed him by the yellow tunic. She was not going to let him float away he might survive. She pulled him to her, then took his head in both hands and pushed it under the water.

It was more difficult than she had imagined to keep a body under, even though he was out cold. His greasy hair was slippery. She had to grasp his head under her arm then lift her feet off the bottom, so that her weight carried them both down.

She began to feel she might have overcome him. How long did it take to drown a man? She had no idea. Sim's lungs must be filling with water already. How would she know when she could let go?

Suddenly he twisted. She tightened her grip on his head. For a moment she struggled to hold him. She was not sure whether he had come round, or was undergoing an unconscious convulsion. His spasms were strong, but seemed random. Her feet found the bottom again and she braced herself and held on.

She looked around. No one was watching: they were all too busy saving themselves.

After a few moments, Sim's movements became weaker. Soon he was still. Gradually she relaxed her grip. Sim sank slowly to the bottom.

He did not come up again.

Panting for breath, Gwenda waded to the shore. She sat down heavily on the muddy ground. She felt for the leather purse on her belt: it was still there. The outlaws had not got around to stealing it from her, and she had kept it through all her trials. It contained the precious love potion made by Mattie Wise. She opened the purse to check—and found nothing but shards of pottery. The little vial had been smashed.

She started to cry.

ഗ

The first person Caris saw doing anything sensible was Merthin's brother, Ralph. He was wearing nothing but a soaking wet pair of underdrawers. He was uninjured, apart from his red and swollen nose, which he had had before. Ralph pulled the earl of Shiring out of the water and laid him on the shore next to a body in the earl's livery. The earl had a grisly head injury that might be fatal. Ralph appeared exhausted by his efforts and unsure what to do next. Caris considered what she should tell him.

She looked around. On this side, the riverbank consisted of small, muddy beaches separated by rocky outcrops. There was not much room to lay out the dead and injured here: they would have to be taken elsewhere.

A few yards away, a flight of stone steps led up from the river to a gate in the priory wall. Caris made a decision. Pointing, she said to Ralph: "Take the earl that way into the priory. Lay him down carefully in the cathedral, then run to the hospital. Tell the first nun you see to fetch Mother Cecilia immediately."

Ralph seemed glad to have someone decisive to obey, and did as he was told right away.

Merthin started to wade into the water, but Caris stopped him. "Look at that crowd of idiots," she said, pointing to the city end of the ruined bridge. Dozens of people were standing gawping at the scene of carnage in front of them. "Get all the strong men down here," she went on. "They can start pulling people out of the water and carrying them to the cathedral."

He hesitated. "They can't get down here from there."

Caris saw his point. They would have to clamber over the wreckage, and that would probably lead to more injuries. But the houses on this side of the main street had gardens that backed up against the priory walls; and the house on the corner, belonging to Ben Wheeler, had a small door in the wall so that he could come to the river directly from his garden.

Merthin was thinking the same. He said: "I'll bring them through Ben's house and across his yard."

"Good."

He clambered over the rocks, pushed open the door, and disappeared.

Caris looked across the water. A tall figure was wading onto the bank nearby, and she recognized Philemon. Gasping, he said: "Have you seen Gwenda?"

"Yes—just before the bridge collapsed," Caris replied. "She was running from Sim Chapman."

"I know—but where is she now?"

"I don't see her. The best thing you can do is start pulling people out of the water."

"I want to find my sister."

"If she's alive, she'll be among those who need to get out of the river."

"All right." Philemon splashed back into the water.

Caris was desperate to find out where her own family was—but there was too much to do here. She promised herself she would look for her father as soon as possible.

Ben Wheeler emerged from his gate. A squat man with big shoulders and a thick neck, he was a carter, and got through life more by the use of his muscles than his brain. He scrambled down to the beach, then looked around, not knowing what to do.

On the ground at Caris's feet was one of Earl Roland's men, wearing the red-and-black livery, apparently dead. She said: "Ben, carry this man into the cathedral."

Ben's wife, Lib, appeared, carrying a toddler. She was a little brighter than her husband, and she asked: "Shouldn't we deal with the living first?"

"We have to get them out of the water before we can tell whether they're dead or alive—and we can't leave bodies here on the bank because they will get in the way of rescuers. Take him to the church."

Lib saw the sense of that. "You'd better do as Caris says, Ben," she said.

Ben picked up the body effortlessly and moved off.

Caris realized they could move the bodies more quickly if they carried them on the kind of stretchers the builders used. The monks could organize those. Where were the monks? She had told Ralph to alert Mother Cecilia, but so far no one had appeared. The injured would need wound dressings, ointments, and cleansing fluids: every nun and monk would be needed. Matthew Barber must be summoned: there would be many broken bones to set. And Mattie Wise, to give potions to the injured to ease their pain. Caris needed to raise the alarm, but she was reluctant to leave the riverside before the rescue operation was properly organized. Where was Merthin?

A woman was crawling to the shore. Caris stepped into the water and pulled her to her feet. It was Griselda. Her wet dress clung to her, and Caris could see her full breasts and the swell of her thighs. Knowing that she was pregnant, Caris said anxiously: "Are you all right?"

"I think so."

"You're not bleeding?"

"No."

"Thank God." Caris looked around and was grateful to see Merthin coming from Ben Wheeler's garden at the head of a line of men, some of them wearing the earl's livery. She called to him: "Take Griselda's arm. Help her up the steps to the priory. She should sit down and rest for a while." She added reassuringly: "She's all right, though."

Both Merthin and Griselda looked at her strangely, and she realized in a flash how peculiar this situation was. The three of them stood for a moment in a frozen triangle: the mother-to-be, the father of her child, and the woman who loved him.

Then Caris turned away, breaking the spell, and began to give orders to the men.

Gwenda cried for a few moments, then stopped. It was not really the broken vial that made her so sad: Mattie could make up another love potion, and Caris would pay for it, if either of them was still alive. Her tears were for everything she had been through in the last twenty-four hours, from her father's treachery to her bleeding feet.

She had no regrets about the two men she had killed. Sim and Alwyn had tried to enslave her then prostitute her. They deserved to die. Killing them was not even murder, for it was no crime to do away with an outlaw. All the same, she could not stop her hands shaking. She was exultant that she had beaten her enemies and won her freedom, and at the same time she felt sickened by what she had done. She would never forget the way the dying body of Sim had twitched at the end. And she feared that the vision of Alwyn with the point of his own knife sticking out of his eye socket might appear in her dreams. She could not help trembling in the grip of such strong contradictory feelings.

She tried to put the killings out of her mind. Who else was dead? Her parents had been planning to leave Kingsbridge yesterday. But what about her brother, Philemon? Caris, her greatest friend? Wulfric, the man she loved?

She looked across the river and was immediately reassured about Caris. She was on the far side with Merthin, and they appeared to be organizing a gang of men to pull people out of the water. Gwenda felt a surge of gratitude: at least she had not been left completely alone in the world.

But what about Philemon? He was the last person she had seen before the collapse. He should have fallen near her, all other things being equal; but she could not see him now.

And where was Wulfric? She doubted whether he would have cared to watch the spectacle of a witch being flogged through the town. However, he had been planning to return home to Wigleigh with his family today, and it was possible—God forbid, she thought—that they had been crossing the bridge on their way home when the collapse happened. She scanned the surface frantically, looking for his distinctive tawny hair, praying that she would see him swimming vigorously for the shore, rather than floating facedown. But she could not see him at all.

She decided to cross over. She could not swim, but she thought that if she had a sizeable piece of wood to keep her afloat she might be able to kick herself across. She found a plank, pulled it from the water, and walked fifty yards upstream, to get well clear of the mass of bodies. Then she reentered the water. Skip followed fearlessly. It was more taxing than she had expected, and her wet dress was a drag on progress, but she reached the far shore.

She ran to Caris, and they embraced. Caris said: "What happened?"

"I escaped."

"And Sim?"

"He was an outlaw."

"Was?"

"He's dead."

Caris looked startled.

Gwenda added hastily: "Killed when the bridge collapsed." She did not want even her best friend to know the exact circumstances. She went on: "Have you seen any of my family?"

"Your parents left town yesterday. I saw Philemon a few moments ago—he's looking for you."

"Thank God! What about Wulfric?"

"I don't know. He hasn't been brought out of the river. His fiancée left yesterday, but his parents and his brother were in the cathedral this morning, at the trial of Crazy Nell."

"I have to look for him."

"Good luck."

Gwenda ran up the steps to the priory and across the green. A few of the stallholders were still packing up their effects, and it seemed incredible to her that they could go about their normal business when hundreds of people had just been killed in an accident—until she realized that they probably did not yet know: it had happened only minutes ago, though it felt like hours.

She passed through the priory gates into the main street. Wulfric and his family had been staying at the Bell. She ran inside.

An adolescent boy stood beside the ale barrel, looking frightened.

Gwenda said: "I'm looking for Wulfric Wigleigh."

"There's no one here," the boy said. "I'm the apprentice, they left me to guard the beer."

Someone had summoned everyone to the riverside, Gwenda guessed.

She ran out again. As she passed through the doorway, Wulfric appeared.

She was so relieved that she threw her arms around him. "You're alive—thank God!" she cried.

"Someone said the bridge collapsed," he said. "Is it true, then?"

"Yes—it's dreadful. Where are the rest of your family?"

"They left a while ago. I stayed behind to collect a debt." He held up a small leather money bag. "I hope they weren't on the bridge when it fell."

"I know how we can find out," Gwenda said. "Come with me."

She took his hand. He let her lead him into the priory precincts without withdrawing his hand. She had never touched him for so long. His hand was large, the fingers rough with work, the palm soft. It sent thrills through her, despite all that had happened.

She took him across the green and inside the cathedral. "They're pulling people out of the river and bringing them here," she explained.

There were already twenty or thirty bodies on the stone floor of the nave, with more arriving continually. A handful of nuns attended to the injured, dwarfed by the mighty pillars around them. The blind monk who normally led the choir seemed to be in charge. "Put the dead on the north side," he called out as Gwenda and Wulfric entered the nave. "Wounded to the south."

Suddenly Wulfric let out a cry of shock and dismay. Gwenda followed his gaze, and saw David, his brother, lying among the wounded. They both knelt beside him on the floor. David was a couple of years older than Wulfric, and the same large build. He was breathing, and his eyes were open, but he seemed not to see them. Wulfric spoke to him. "Dave!" he said in a low, urgent voice. "Dave, it's me, Wulfric."

Gwenda felt something sticky, and realized David was lying in a pool of blood.

Wulfric said: "Dave—where are Ma and Pa?"

There was no response.

Gwenda looked around and saw Wulfric's mother. She was on the far side of the nave, in the north aisle, where Blind Carlus was telling people to put the dead. "Wulfric," Gwenda said quietly.

"What?"

"Your ma."

He stood up and looked. "Oh, no," he said.

They crossed the wide church. Wulfric's mother was lying next to Sir Stephen, the lord of Wigleigh—his equal now. She was a petite woman—it was amazing that she had given birth to two such big sons. In life she had been wiry and full of energy, but now she looked like a fragile doll, white and thin. Wulfric put his hand on her chest, feeling for a heartbeat. When he pressed down, a trickle of water came from her mouth.

"She drowned," he whispered.

Gwenda put her arm around his wide shoulders, trying to console him with her touch. She could not tell whether he noticed.

A man-at-arms wearing Earl Roland's red-and-black livery came up carrying the lifeless body of a big man. Wulfric gasped again: it was his father.

Gwenda said: "Lay him here, next to his wife."

Wulfric was stunned. He said nothing, seeming unable to take it in. Gwenda herself was bewildered. What could she say to the man she loved in these circumstances? Every phrase that came to mind seemed stupid. She was desperate to give him some kind of comfort, but she did not know how.

As Wulfric stared at the bodies of his mother and father, Gwenda looked across the church at his brother. David seemed very still. She walked quickly to his side. His eyes were staring up blindly, and he was no longer breathing. She felt his chest: no heartbeat.

How could Wulfric bear it?

She wiped tears from her own eyes and returned to him. There was no point in hiding the truth. "David is dead, too," she said.

Wulfric looked blank, as if he did not understand. The dreadful thought occurred to Gwenda that the shock might have caused him to lose his mind.

But he spoke at last. "All of them," he said in a whisper. "All three. All dead." He looked at Gwenda, and she saw tears come to his eyes.

She put her arms around him, and felt his big body shake with helpless sobs. She squeezed him tightly. "Poor Wulfric," she said. "Poor, beloved Wulfric."

"Thank God I've still got Annet," he said.

An hour later, the bodies of the dead and wounded covered most of the floor of the nave. Blind Carlus, the subprior, stood in the middle of it all, with thin-faced Simeon, the treasurer, beside him to be his eyes. Carlus was in charge because Prior Anthony was missing. "Brother Theodoric, is that you?" he said, apparently recognizing the tread of the fair-skinned, blue-eyed monk who had just walked in. "Find the gravedigger. Tell him to get six strong men to help him. We're going to need at least a hundred new graves, and in this season we don't want to delay burial."

"Right away, Brother," said Theodoric.

Caris was impressed by how effectively Carlus could organize things despite his blindness.

Caris had left Merthin efficiently managing the rescue of bodies from the water. She had made sure the nuns and monks were alerted to the disaster, then she had found Matthew Barber and Mattie Wise. Finally she had checked on her own family.

Only Uncle Anthony and Griselda had been on the bridge at the time of the collapse. She had found her father at the guildhall with Buonaventura Caroli. Edmund had said: "They'll have to build a new bridge now!" Then he had gone limping down to the riverbank to help pull people out of the water. The others were safe: Aunt Petranilla had been at home, cooking; Caris's sister, Alice, had been with Elfric at the Bell Inn; her cousin Godwyn had been in the cathedral, checking on the repairs to the south side of the chancel.

Griselda had now gone home to rest. Anthony was still unaccounted for. Caris was not fond of her uncle, but she would not wish him dead, and she looked anxiously for him every time a new body was brought into the nave from the river.

Mother Cecilia and the nuns were washing wounds, applying honey as an antiseptic, affixing bandages, and giving out restorative cups of hot spiced ale. Matthew Barber, the briskly efficient battlefield surgeon, was working with a panting, overweight Mattie Wise, Mattie administering a calming medicine a few minutes before Matthew set the broken arms and legs.

Caris walked to the south transept. There, away from the noise, the bustle, and the blood in the nave, the senior physician-monks were clustered around the still-unconscious figure of the earl of Shiring. His wet clothes had been removed, and he had been covered with a heavy blanket. "He's alive," said Brother Godwyn. "But his injury is very serious." He pointed to the back of the head. "Part of his skull has shattered."

Caris peered over Godwyn's shoulder. She could see the skull, like a broken pie crust, stained with blood. Through the gaps she could see gray matter underneath. Surely nothing could be done for such a dreadful injury?

Brother Joseph, the oldest of the physicians, felt the same. He rubbed his large nose and spoke through a mouth full of bad teeth. "We must bring the relics of the saint," he said, slurring his sibilants like a drunk, as always. "They are his best hope for recovery."

Caris had little faith in the power of the bones of a long-dead saint to heal a living man's broken head. She said nothing, of course: she knew she was peculiar in this respect, and she kept her views to herself most of the time.

The earl's sons, Lord William and Bishop Richard, stood looking on. William, with his tall, soldierly figure and black hair, was a younger version of the unconscious man on the table. Richard was fairer and rounder. Merthin's brother, Ralph, was with them. "I pulled the earl out of the water," he said. It was the second time Caris had heard him say it.

"Yes, well done," said William.

William's wife, Philippa, was as dissatisfied as Caris with Brother Joseph's pronouncement. "Isn't there something *you* can do to help the earl?" she said.

Godwyn replied: "Prayer is the most effective cure."

The relics were kept in a locked compartment under the high altar. As soon as Godwyn and Joseph left to fetch them, Matthew Barber bent over the earl, peering at the head wound. "It will never heal like that," he said. "Not even with the help of the saint."

William said sharply: "What do you mean?" Caris thought he sounded just like his father.

"The skull is a bone like any other," Matthew answered. "It can mend itself, but the pieces need to be in the right place. Otherwise it will grow back crooked."

"Do you think you know better than the monks?"

"My lord, the monks know how to call upon the help of the spirit world. I only set broken bones."

"And where did you get this knowledge?"

"I was surgeon with the king's armies for many years. I marched alongside your father, the earl, in the Scottish wars. I have seen broken heads before."

"What would you do for my father now?"

Matthew was nervous under William's aggressive questioning, Caris felt; but he seemed sure of what he was saying. "I would take the pieces of broken bone out of the brain, clean them, and try to fit them together again."

Caris gasped. She could hardly imagine such a bold operation. How did Matthew have the nerve to propose it? And what if it went wrong?

William said: "And he would recover?"

"I don't know," Matthew replied. "Sometimes a head wound has strange effects, impairing a man's ability to walk, or speak. All I can do is mend his skull. If you want miracles, ask the saint."

"So you can't promise success."

"Only God is all-powerful. Men must do what they can and hope for the best. But I believe your father will die of this injury if it remains untreated."

"But Joseph and Godwyn have read the books written by the ancient medical philosophers."

"And I have seen wounded men die or recover on the battlefield. It's for you to decide whom to trust."

William looked at his wife. Philippa said: "Let the barber do what he can, and ask Saint Adolphus to help him."

William nodded. "All right," he said to Matthew. "Go ahead."

"I want the earl lying on a table," Matthew said decisively. "Near the window, where a strong light will fall on his injury."

William snapped his fingers at two novice monks. "Do whatever this man asks," he ordered.

Matthew said: "All I need is a bowl of warm wine."

The monks brought a trestle table from the hospital and set it up below the big window in the south transept. Two squires lifted Earl Roland on to the table.

"Facedown, please," said Matthew.

They turned him over.

Matthew had a leather satchel containing the sharp tools from which barbers got their name. He first took out a small pair of scissors. He bent over the earl's head and began to cut away the hair around the wound. The earl had thick black hair that was naturally oily. Matthew snipped the locks and tossed them aside so that they landed on the floor. When he had clipped a circle around the wound, the damage was more clearly visible.

Brother Godwyn reappeared, carrying the reliquary, the carved ivory-and-gold box containing the skull of St. Adolphus and the bones of one arm and a hand. When he saw Matthew operating on Earl Roland, he said indignantly: "What is going on here?"

Matthew looked up. "If you would place the holy relics on the earl's back, as close as possible to his head, I believe the saint will steady my hands."

Godwyn hesitated, clearly angry that a mere barber had taken charge.

Lord William said: "Do as he says, Brother, or the death of my father may be laid at your door."

Still Godwyn did not obey. Instead he spoke to Blind Carlus, standing a few yards away. "Brother Carlus, I am ordered by Lord William to—"

"I heard what Lord William said," Carlus interrupted. "You'd better do as he wishes."

It was not the answer Godwyn had been hoping for. His face showed angry frustration. With evident distaste, he placed the sacred container on Earl Roland's broad back.

Matthew picked up a fine pair of forceps. With a delicate touch, he grasped the visible edge of a piece of bone and lifted it, without touching the gray matter beneath. Caris watched, entranced. The bone came right away from the head, with skin and hair attached. Matthew put it gently into the bowl of warm wine.

He did the same with two more small pieces of bone. The noise from the nave—the groans of the wounded and the sobs of the bereaved—seemed to recede into the background. The people watching Matthew stood silent and still in a circle around him and the unconscious earl.

Next, he worked on the shards that remained attached to the rest of the skull. In each case he snipped away the hair, washed the area carefully with a piece of linen dipped in wine, then used the forceps to press the bone gently into what he thought was its original position.

Caris could hardly breathe, the tension was so great. She had never admired anyone as much as she admired Matthew Barber at this moment. He had such courage, such skill, such confidence. And he was performing this inconceivably delicate operation on an earl! If it went wrong, they would probably hang him. Yet his hands were as steady as the hands of the angels carved in stone over the cathedral doorway.

Finally he replaced the three detached shards that he had put in the bowl of wine, fitting them together as if he were mending a broken jar.

He pulled the skin of the scalp across the wound and sewed it together with swift, precise stitches.

Now Roland's skull was complete.

"The earl must sleep for a day and a night," he said. "If he wakes, give him a strong dose of Mattie Wise's sleeping draft. Then he must lie still for forty days and forty nights. If necessary, strap him down."

Then he asked Mother Cecilia to bandage the head.

Godwyn left the cathedral and ran down to the riverbank, feeling frustrated and annoyed. There was no firm authority: Carlus was letting everyone do as they wished. Prior Anthony was weak, but he was better than Carlus. He had to be found.

Most of the bodies were out of the water now. Those who were merely bruised and shocked had walked away. Most of the dead and wounded had been carried to the cathedral. Those left were somehow entangled with the wreckage.

Godwyn was both excited and frightened by the thought that Anthony might be dead. He longed for a new regime at the priory: a stricter interpretation of Benedict's rule, along with meticulous management of the finances. But, at the same time, he knew that Anthony was his patron, and that under another prior he might not continue to be promoted.

Merthin had commandeered a boat. He and two other young men were out in midstream, where most of what had been the bridge was now floating in the water. Wearing only their underdrawers, the three were trying to lift a heavy beam in order to free someone. Merthin was small in stature, but the other two looked strong and well fed, and Godwyn guessed they were squires from the earl's entourage. Despite their evident fitness, they were finding it difficult to get leverage on the heavy timbers, standing as they were in the well of a small rowing boat.

Godwyn stood with a crowd of townspeople, watching, torn by fear and hope, as the two squires raised a heavy beam and Merthin pulled a body from beneath it. After a short examination, he called out: "Marguerite Jones—dead."

Marguerite was an elderly woman of no account. Impatiently, Godwyn shouted out: "Can't you see Prior Anthony?"

A look passed between the men on the boat, and Godwyn realized he had been too peremptory. But Merthin called back: "I can see a monk's robe."

"Then it's the prior!" Godwyn shouted. Anthony was the only monk still unaccounted for. "Can you tell how he is?"

Merthin leaned over the side of the boat. Apparently unable to get close enough from there, he eased himself into the water. Eventually he called out: "Still breathing."

Godwyn felt both elated and disappointed. "Then get him out, quickly!" he shouted. "Please," he added.

There was no acknowledgment of what he said, but he saw Merthin duck under a partly submerged plank, then relay instructions to the other two. They eased the beam they were holding to one side, letting it slip gently into the water, then they leaned over the prow of the little boat to get hold of the plank Merthin was under. Merthin seemed to be struggling to detach Anthony's clothing from a tangle of boards and splinters.

Godwyn watched, frustrated that he could do nothing to speed the process. He spoke to two of the bystanders. "Go to the priory and get two monks to bring a stretcher. Tell them Godwyn sent you." The two men went up the steps and into the priory grounds.

At last Merthin managed to pull the unconscious figure from the wreckage. He drew him close, then the other two heaved the prior into the boat. Merthin scrambled in after, and they poled to the bank.

Eager volunteers took Anthony from the boat and put him on the stretcher brought by the monks. Godwyn examined the prior quickly. He was breathing, but his pulse was weak. His eyes were closed and his face was ominously white. His head and chest were only bruised, but his pelvis seemed smashed, and he was bleeding.

The monks picked him up. Godwyn led the way across the priory grounds into the cathedral. "Make way!" he shouted. He took the prior along the nave and into the chancel, the holiest part of the church. He told the monks to lay the body in front of the high altar. The sodden robe clearly outlined Anthony's hips and legs, which were twisted so far out of shape that only his top half looked human.

Within a few moments, all the monks had gathered around the

unconscious body of their prior. Godwyn retrieved the reliquary from Earl Roland and placed it at Anthony's feet. Joseph placed a jeweled crucifix on his chest and wrapped Anthony's hands around it.

Mother Cecilia knelt beside Anthony. She wiped his face with a cloth soaked in some soothing liquid. She said to Joseph: "He seems to have broken many bones. Do you want Matthew Barber to look at him?"

Joseph shook his head silently.

Godwyn was glad. The barber would have defiled the holy sanctuary. Better to leave the outcome to God.

Brother Carlus performed the last rites, then led the monks in a hymn.

Godwyn did not know what to hope for. For some years he had been looking forward to the end of Prior Anthony's rule. But in the last hour he had got a glimpse of what might replace Anthony: joint rule by Carlus and Simeon. They were Anthony's cronies, and would be no better.

Suddenly he saw Matthew Barber at the edge of the crowd, looking over the monks' shoulders, studying Anthony's lower half. Godwyn was about to order him indignantly to leave the chancel, when he gave an almost imperceptible shake of the head and walked away.

Anthony opened his eyes.

Brother Joseph cried: "Praise God!"

The prior seemed to want to speak. Mother Cecilia, who was still kneeling beside him, leaned over his face to catch his words. Godwyn saw Anthony's mouth move, and wished he could hear. After a moment, the prior fell silent.

Cecilia looked shocked. "Is that true?" she said.

They all stared. Godwyn said: "What did he say, Mother Cecilia?"

She did not answer.

Anthony's eyes closed. A subtle change came over him. He went very still.

Godwyn bent over his body. There was no breath. He placed a hand over Anthony's heart, and felt no beat. He grasped the wrist, feeling for a pulse: nothing.

He stood up. "Prior Anthony has left this world," he said. "May God bless his soul and welcome him into His holy presence."

All the monks said: "Amen."

Godwyn thought: Now there will have to be an election.

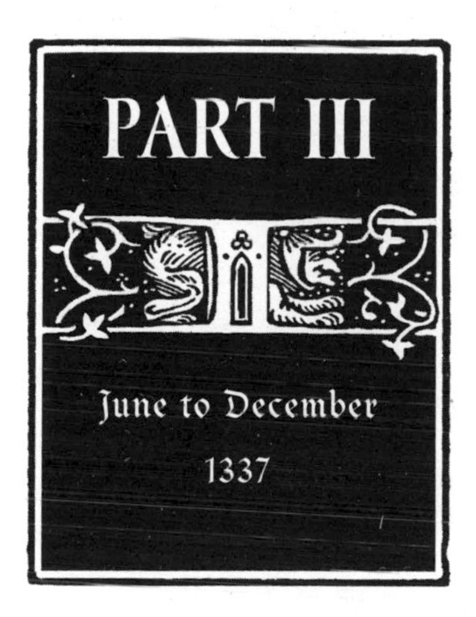

PART III

June to December

1337

14

ingsbridge Cathedral was a place of horror. Wounded people groaned in pain and cried out for help to God, or the saints, or their mothers. Every few minutes, someone searching for a loved one would find him or her dead and would scream with the shock of sudden grief. The living and the dead were grotesquely twisted with broken bones, covered in blood, their clothing ripped and sodden. The stone floor of the church was slippery with water, blood, and riverside mud.

In the middle of the horror, a small zone of calm and efficiency was centered on the figure of Mother Cecilia. Like a small, quick bird, she went from one horizontal figure to the next. She was followed by a little flock of hooded nuns, among them her long-time assistant, Sister Juliana, now respectfully known as Old Julie. As she examined each patient, she gave orders: for washing, for ointments, for bandages, for herbal medicines. In the more serious cases she would summon Mattie Wise, Matthew Barber, or Brother Joseph. She always spoke quietly but clearly, her instructions simple and decisive. She left most patients soothed, and their relatives reassured and hopeful.

It reminded Caris, with dreadful vividness, of the day her mother died. There had been terror and confusion then, though only in her heart. In the same way, Mother Cecilia had seemed to know what to do. Mama had died despite Cecilia's help, just as many of today's wounded would die; but there had been an orderliness about the death, a sense that everything possible had been done.

Some people appealed to the Virgin and the saints when someone was sick, but that only made Caris more uncertain and frightened, for there was no way to know if the spirits would help, or even whether they had heard. Mother Cecilia was not as powerful as the saints, the ten-year-old Caris had known; but all the same her assured, practical presence had given Caris both hope and resignation in a combination that brought peace to her soul.

Now Caris became part of Cecilia's entourage, without really making a decision or even thinking about it. She followed the commands of the most assertive person in the vicinity, just as people had obeyed her directions at the riverside immediately after the collapse, when no one else seemed to know what to do. Cecilia's brisk practicality was infectious, and those around her acquired some of the same cool competence. Caris found herself holding a small bowl of vinegar, while a beautiful novice nun called Mair dipped a rag in it and washed the blood from the face of Susanna Chepstow, the timber merchant's wife.

After that it was nonstop until well after dark. Thanks to the long summer evening, all the floating bodies were retrieved from the river before nightfall—though perhaps no one would ever know how many drowned people had sunk to the bottom or drifted downstream. There was no trace of Crazy Nell, who must have been pulled under by the cart to which she was tied. Unjustly, Friar Murdo had survived, having suffered nothing worse than a twisted ankle, and had limped off to the Bell to recuperate with hot ham and strong ale.

However, the treatment of the injured continued, after nightfall, by candlelight. Some of the nuns became exhausted and had to stop; others were overwhelmed by the scale of the tragedy and fell apart, misunderstanding what they were told and becoming clumsy, so that they had to be dismissed; but Caris and a small core group carried on until there was no more to do. It must have been midnight when the last knot was tied in the last bandage, and Caris staggered across the green to her father's house.

Papa and Petranilla sat together in the dining hall, holding hands, grieving for the death of their brother, Anthony. Edmund's eyes were wet with tears, and Petranilla was crying inconsolably. Caris kissed them both, but she could think of nothing to say. If she had sat down, she would have gone to sleep in the chair; so she climbed the stairs. She got into bed next to Gwenda, who was staying with her, as always. Gwenda was deep in an exhausted sleep, and did not stir.

Caris closed her eyes, her body weary and her heart aching with sorrow. Her father was mourning one person among the many, but she felt the weight of them all. She thought of her friends, neighbors, and acquaintances lying dead on the cold stone floor of the cathedral; and she imagined the sadness of their parents, their children, their brothers and sisters; and the sheer volume of grief overwhelmed her. She sobbed into her pillow. Without speaking, Gwenda put an arm around her and hugged her. After a few moments exhaustion overtook her, and she fell asleep.

She got up again at dawn. Leaving Gwenda still fast asleep, she returned to the cathedral and continued the work. Most of the injured were sent home. Those who still needed to be watched over—such as the still-unconscious Earl Roland—were moved into the hospital. The dead bodies were laid out in neat rows in the chancel, the eastern end of the church, to await burial.

The time flew by, with hardly a moment to rest. Then, late on Sunday afternoon, Mother Cecilia told Caris to take a break. She looked around and realized that most of the work was done. That was when she started to think of the future.

Until that moment she had felt, unconsciously, that ordinary life was over, and she was living in a new world of horror and tragedy. Now she realized that this, like everything else, would pass. The dead would be buried, the injured would heal, and somehow the town would struggle back to normal. And she remembered that, just before the bridge collapsed, there had been another tragedy, violent and devastating in its own way.

She found Merthin down by the river, with Elfric and Thomas Langley, organizing the cleanup with the help of fifty or more volunteers. Merthin's quarrel with Elfric had clearly been set aside in the emergency. Most of the loose timber had been retrieved from the water and stacked on the bank. But much of the woodwork was still joined together, and a mass of interlocked timber floated on the surface, moving slightly on the rise and fall of the water, with the innocent tranquillity of a great beast after it has killed and eaten.

The men were trying to break up the wreckage into manageable proportions. It was a dangerous job, with a constant risk that the bridge would collapse further and injure the volunteers. They had tied a rope around the central part of the bridge, now partly submerged, and a team of men stood on the bank hauling on the rope. In a boat in midstream were Merthin and giant Mark Webber with an oarsman. When the men on the bank rested, the boat was rowed in close to the wreckage, and Mark, directed by Merthin, attacked the beams with a huge forester's axe. Then the boat moved to a safe distance, Elfric gave a command, and the rope team pulled again.

As Caris watched, a big section of the bridge came free. Everyone cheered, and the men dragged the tangled woodwork to the shore.

The wives of some of the volunteers arrived with loaves of bread and jugs of ale. Thomas Langley ordered a break. While the men were resting, Caris got Merthin on his own. "You can't marry Griselda," she said without preamble.

The sudden assertion did not surprise him. "I don't know what to do," he said. "I keep thinking about it."

"Will you walk with me?"

"All right."

They left the crowd at the riverside and went up the main street. After the bustle of the Fleece Fair, the town was graveyard quiet. Everyone was staying indoors, tending the sick or mourning the dead. "There can't be many families in town that don't have someone dead or injured," she said. "There must have been a thousand people on the bridge, either trying to leave town or tormenting Crazy Nell. There are more than a hundred bodies in the church, and we've treated about four hundred wounded."

"And five hundred lucky ones," Merthin said.

"We could have been on the bridge, or near it. You and I might be lying on the floor of the chancel, now, cold and still. But we've been given a gift—the rest of our lives. And we mustn't waste that gift because of one mistake."

"It's not a mistake," he said sharply. "It's a baby—a person, with a soul."

"You're a person with a soul, too—an exceptional one. Look at what you've been doing just now. Three people are in charge down there at the river. One is the town's most prosperous builder. Another is the matricularius at the priory. And the third is . . . a mere apprentice, not yet twenty-one. Yet the townsmen obey you as readily as they obey Elfric and Thomas."

"That doesn't mean I can shirk my responsibilities."

They turned into the priory close. The green in front of the cathedral was rutted and trampled from the fair, and there were boggy patches and wide puddles. In the three great west windows of the church Caris could see the reflection of a watery sun and ripped clouds, a picture divided, like a three-sided altarpiece. A bell began to ring for Evensong.

Caris said: "Think how often you've talked of going to see the buildings of Paris and Florence. Will you give all that up?"

"I suppose so. A man can't abandon his wife and child."

"So you're already thinking of her as your wife."

He rounded on her. "I'll never think of her as my wife," he said bitterly. "You know who I love."

For once she could not think of a clever answer. She opened her mouth to speak, but no words came to her. Instead, she felt a constriction in her throat. She blinked away tears, and looked down to hide her emotions.

He grasped her arms and pulled her close to him. "You know, don't you?"

She forced herself to meet his eye. "Do I?" Her vision blurred.

He kissed her mouth. It was a new kind of kiss, different from anything she had experienced before. His lips moved gently but insistently against hers, as if he was determined to remember the moment; and she realized, with dread, that he was thinking this would be their last kiss.

She clung to him, wanting it to go on forever, but all too soon he drew away.

"I love you," he said. "But I'm going to marry Griselda."

Life and death went on. Children were born and old people died. On Sunday Emma Butchers attacked her adulterous husband, Edward, with his largest cleaver in a fit of jealous rage. On Monday one of Bess Hampton's chickens went missing, and was found boiling in a pot over Glynnie Thompson's kitchen fire, whereupon Glynnie was stripped and flogged by John Constable. On Tuesday Howell Tyler was working on the roof of St. Mark's church when a rotten beam gave way beneath him and he fell, crashing through the ceiling, to the floor below, and died immediately.

By Wednesday the wreckage of the bridge had been cleared, all but the stumps of two of the main piers, and the timber was stacked on the bank. The waterway was open, and barges and rafts were able to leave Kingsbridge for Melcombe with wool and other goods from the Fleece Fair consigned to Flanders and Italy.

When Caris and Edmund went to the riverside to check on progress, Merthin was using the salvaged timbers to build a raft to ferry people across the river. "It's better than a boat," he explained. "Livestock can walk on and off, and carts can be driven on, too."

Edmund nodded gloomily. "It will have to do, for the weekly market. Fortunately, we should have a new bridge by the time of the next Fleece Fair."

"I don't think so," Merthin said.

"But you told me it would take a year to build a new bridge!"

"A wooden bridge, yes. But if we build another wooden one it, too, will fall down."

"Why?"

"Let me show you." Merthin took them to a pile of timber. He pointed to a group of mighty posts. "These formed the piers—they're probably the famous twenty-four best oak trees in the land, given to the priory by the king. Notice the ends."

Caris could see that the huge posts had originally been sharpened into points, though their outlines had been softened by years under water.

Merthin said: "A timber bridge has no foundations. The posts are simply driven into the riverbed. That's not good enough."

"But this bridge has stood for hundreds of years!" Edmund said indignantly. He always sounded quarrelsome when he argued.

Merthin was used to him, and paid no attention to his tone of voice. "And now it has fallen down," he said patiently. "Something has changed. Wooden piers were once firm enough, but no longer."

"What can have changed? The river is the river."

"Well, for one thing you built a barn and a jetty on the bank, and protected the property with a wall. Several other merchants did the same. The old mud beach where I used to play on the south shore has mostly gone. So the river can no longer spread itself into the fields. As a result, the water flows faster than it used to—especially after the kind of heavy rain we've had this year."

"So it will have to be a stone bridge?"

"Yes."

Edmund looked up and saw Elfric standing by, listening. "Merthin says a stone bridge will take three years."

Elfric nodded. "Three building seasons."

Most building was done in the warmer months, Caris knew. Merthin had explained to her that stone walls could not be constructed when there was a risk that the mortar might freeze before it had begun to set.

Elfric went on: "One season for the foundations, one for the arches, and one for the roadbed. After each stage, the mortar must be left for three or four months to set hard before the next stage can be laid on top of it."

"Three years with no bridge," Edmund said gloomily.

"Four years, unless you get started right away."

"You'd better prepare an estimate of the cost for the priory."

"I've already started, but it's a long job. It will take me another two or three days."

"Quick as you can."

Edmund and Caris left the riverside and walked up the main street,

Edmund with his energetically lopsided stride. He would never lean on anyone's arm, despite his withered leg. To keep his balance, he swung his arms as if he were sprinting. The townspeople knew to give him plenty of room, especially when he was in a hurry. "Three years!" he said as they walked. "It will do terrible damage to the Fleece Fair. I don't know how long it will take us to get back to normal. Three years!"

When they got home, they found Caris's sister, Alice, there. Her hair was tied up in her hat in an elaborate new style copied from Lady Philippa. She was sitting at the table with Aunt Petranilla. Caris knew immediately, from the looks on their faces, that they had been talking about her.

Petranilla went to the kitchen and came back with ale, bread, and fresh butter. She filled a cup for Edmund.

Petranilla had cried on Sunday, but since then she had shown little sign of bereavement for her dead brother, Anthony. Surprisingly Edmund, who had never liked Anthony, seemed to grieve more: tears would come to his eyes at unexpected moments during the day, though they would disappear just as quickly.

Now he was full of news of the bridge. Alice was inclined to question Merthin's judgment, but Edmund dismissed that notion impatiently. "The boy's a genius," he said. "He knows more than many master builders, yet he isn't out of his apprenticeship."

Caris said bitterly: "All the more shame that he's going to spend his life with Griselda."

Alice leaped to the defense of her stepdaughter. "There's nothing wrong with Griselda."

"Yes, there is," Caris said. "She doesn't love him. She seduced him because her boyfriend left town, that's all."

"Is that the story Merthin's telling you?" Alice laughed sarcastically. "If a man doesn't want to do it, he doesn't do it—take my word."

Edmund grunted. "Men can be tempted," he said.

"Oh, so you're siding with Caris, are you, Papa?" Alice said. "I shouldn't be surprised, you usually do."

"It's not a question of taking sides," Edmund replied. "A man may not want to do a thing beforehand, and he may regret it afterward, yet for a brief moment his wishes may change—especially when a woman uses her wiles."

"Wiles? Why do you assume that she threw herself at him?"

"I didn't say that. But I understand it began when she cried, and he comforted her."

Caris herself had told him this.

Alice made a disgusted sound. "You've always had a soft spot for that insubordinate apprentice."

Caris ate some bread with butter, but she had no appetite. She said: "I suppose they'll have half a dozen fat children, and Merthin will inherit Elfric's business, and become just another town tradesman, building houses for merchants and fawning on clergymen for contracts, just like his father-in-law."

Petranilla said: "And very lucky so to do! He'll be one of the leading men of the town."

"He's worthy of a better destiny."

"Is he, really?" Petranilla said in mock amazement. "And him the son of a knight who fell from grace and hasn't a shilling to buy shoes for his wife! What exactly do you believe him to be destined for?"

Caris was stung by this mockery. It was true that Merthin's parents were poor corrodiaries, dependent on the priory for their food and drink. For him to inherit a successful building business would indeed mean a jump up the social ladder. Yet she still felt he deserved better. She could not say exactly what future she had in mind for him. She just knew that he was different from everyone else in town, and she could not bear the thought of his becoming like the rest.

On Friday, Caris took Gwenda to see Mattie Wise.

Gwenda was still in town because Wulfric was there, attending to the burial of his family. Elaine, Edmund's housemaid, had dried Gwenda's dress in front of the fire, and Caris had bandaged her feet and given her an old pair of shoes.

Caris felt that Gwenda was not telling the full truth about her adventure in the forest. She said that Sim had taken her to the outlaws, and she had escaped; he had chased after her, and he had died in the bridge collapse. John Constable was satisfied with that story: outlaws were outside the law, as their name indicated, so there was no question of Sim bequeathing his property. Gwenda was free. But something else had happened in the forest, Caris felt sure; something Gwenda did not want to talk about. Caris did not press her friend. Some things were best buried.

Funerals were the business of the town this week. The extraordinary manner of the deaths made little difference to the rituals of interment. The bodies had to be washed, the shrouds sewn for the poor, the coffins nailed for the rich, the graves dug, and the priests paid. Not all the monks were qualified as priests, but several were, and they worked in shifts, all day, every day, conducting obsequies in the cemetery on the north side of the cathedral. There were half a dozen small parish churches in Kingsbridge, and their priests were also busy.

Gwenda was helping Wulfric with the arrangements, performing the traditional woman's tasks, washing the bodies and making the shrouds, doing what she could to comfort him. He was in a kind of daze. He managed the details of the burial well enough, but spent hours gazing into space, with a slightly puzzled frown, as if trying to make sense of a massive conundrum.

By Friday the funerals were over, but the acting prior, Carlus, had announced a special service on Sunday for the souls of all those killed, so Wulfric was staying until Monday. Gwenda reported to Caris that he seemed grateful for the company of someone from his own village, but showed animation only when talking about Annet. Caris offered to buy her another love potion.

They found Mattie Wise in her kitchen, brewing medicines. The little house smelled of herbs, oil, and wine. "I used just about everything I had on Saturday and Sunday," she said. "I need to restock."

"You must have made some money, anyway," Gwenda said.

"Yes—if I can collect it."

Caris was shocked. "Do people welsh on you?"

"Some do. I always try to collect the fee in advance, while they're still in pain. But if they haven't got the money there and then, it's hard to refuse them treatment. Most pay up afterwards, but not all."

Caris felt indignant on behalf of her friend. "What do they say?"

"All sorts of things. They can't afford it, the potion did them no good, they were given it against their will, anything. But don't worry. There are enough honest people for me to continue. What's on your mind?"

"Gwenda lost her love potion in the accident."

"That's easily remedied. Why don't you prepare it for her?"

While Caris was making up the mixture, she asked Mattie: "How many pregnancies end in a miscarriage?"

Gwenda knew why she was asking. Caris had told her all about Merthin's dilemma. The two girls had spent most of their time together discussing either Wulfric's indifference or Merthin's high principles. Caris had even been tempted to buy a love potion herself, and use it on Merthin; though something held her back.

Mattie gave her a sharp look, but answered noncommittally. "No one knows. Many times, a woman misses one month but comes on again the next. Did she get pregnant and lose the baby, or was there some other reason? It's impossible to tell."

"Oh."

"Neither of you is pregnant, though, if that's what you're worried about."

Gwenda said quickly: "How do you know?"

"By looking at you. A woman changes almost immediately. Not just her belly and her breasts, but her complexion, her way of moving, her mood. I see these things better than most people—that's why they call me wise. So who is pregnant?"

"Griselda, Elfric's daughter."

"Oh, yes, I've seen her. She's three months gone."

Caris was astonished. "How long?"

"Three months, or very nearly. Take a look at her. She was never a thin girl, but she's even more voluptuous now. So why are you so shocked? I suppose it's Merthin's baby, is it?"

Mattie always guessed these things.

Gwenda said to Caris: "I thought you told me it happened recently."

"Merthin didn't say exactly when, but he gave me the impression it was not long ago, and it only happened once. Now it seems he's been doing it to her for months!"

Mattie frowned. "Why would he lie?"

"To make himself look not so bad?" Gwenda suggested.

"How could it be worse?"

"Men are peculiar, the way they think."

"I'm going to ask him," Caris said. "Right now." She put down the jar and the measuring spoon.

Gwenda said: "What about my love potion?"

"I'll finish making it," Mattie said. "Caris is in too much of a hurry."

"Thank you," Caris said, and she went out.

She marched down to the riverside, but for once Merthin was not there. She failed to find him at Elfric's house either. She decided he must be in the mason's loft.

In the west front of the cathedral, neatly fitted into one of the towers, was a workroom for the master mason. Caris reached it by climbing a narrow spiral staircase in a buttress of the tower. It was a wide room, well lit by tall lancet windows. All along one wall were stacked the beautifully shaped wooden templates used by the original cathedral stone carvers, carefully preserved and used now for repairs.

Underfoot was the tracing floor. The floorboards were covered with a layer of plaster, and the original master mason, Jack Builder, had scratched his plans in the mortar with iron drawing instruments. The marks thus made were white at first, but they faded over time, and new drawings could be scratched on top of the old. When there were so many designs that it became hard to tell the new from the old, a fresh layer of plaster was laid on top, and the process began again.

Parchment, the thin leather on which monks copied out the books of the Bible, was much too expensive to be used for drawings. In Caris's lifetime a new writing material had appeared, paper, but it came from the Arabs, so monks rejected it as a heathen Muslim invention. Anyway, it had to be imported from Italy and was no cheaper than parchment. And the tracing floor had another advantage: a carpenter could lay a piece of wood on the floor, on top of the drawing, and carve his template exactly to the lines drawn by the master mason.

Merthin was kneeling on the floor, carving a piece of oak in accordance with a drawing, but he was not making a template. He was carving a cogwheel with sixteen teeth. On the floor close by was another, smaller wheel, and Merthin stopped carving for a moment to put the two together and see how well they fitted. Caris had seen such cogs, or gears, in water mills, connecting the mill paddle to the grindstone.

He must have heard her footsteps on the stone staircase, but he was too absorbed in his work to glance up. She regarded him for a second, anger competing with love in her heart. He had the look of total concentration that she knew so well: his slight body bent over his work, his strong hands and dextrous fingers making fine adjustments, his face immobile, his gaze unwavering. He had the perfect grace of a young deer bending its head to drink from a stream. This was what a man looked like, she thought, when he was doing what he was born to do. He was in a state like happiness, but more profound. He was fulfilling his destiny.

She burst out: "Why did you lie to me?"

His chisel slipped. He cried out in pain and looked at his finger. "Christ," he said, and put his finger in his mouth.

"I'm sorry," Caris said. "Are you hurt?"

"Nothing much. When did I lie to you?"

"You gave me the impression that Griselda seduced you one time. The truth is that the two of you have been at it for months."

"No, we haven't." He sucked his bleeding finger.

"She's three months pregnant."

"She can't be, it happened two weeks ago."

"She is, you can tell by her figure."

"Can you?"

"Mattie Wise told me. Why did you lie?"

He looked her in the eye. "But I didn't lie," he said. "It happened on the Sunday of Fleece Fair week. That was the first and only time."

"Then how could she be sure she's pregnant, after only two weeks?"

"I don't know. How soon can women tell, anyway?"

"Don't you know?"

"I've never asked. Anyway, three months ago Griselda was still with . . ."

"Oh, God!" Caris said. A spark of hope flared in her breast. "She was still with her old boyfriend—Thurstan." The spark blazed into a flame. "It must be his baby, Thurstan's—not yours. You're not the father!"

"Is it possible?" Merthin seemed hardly to dare to hope.

"Of course—it explains everything. If she had suddenly fallen in love with you, she'd be after you every chance she gets. But you said she hardly speaks to you."

"I thought that was because I was reluctant to marry her."

"She's never liked you. She just needed a father for her baby. Thurstan ran away—probably when she told him she was pregnant—and you were right there in the house, and stupid enough to fall for her trick. Oh, thank God!"

"Thank Mattie Wise," said Merthin.

She caught sight of his left hand. Blood was welling from a finger. "Oh, I made you hurt yourself!" she cried. She took his hand and examined the cut. It was small, but deep. "I'm so sorry."

"It's not that bad."

"But it is," she said, not knowing whether she was talking about the cut or something else. She kissed his hand, feeling his hot blood on her lips. She put his finger in her mouth, sucking the wound clean. It was so intimate that it felt like a sexual act, and she closed her eyes, feeling ecstatic. She swallowed, tasting his blood, and shuddered with pleasure.

A week after the bridge collapsed, Merthin had built a ferry.

It was ready at dawn on Saturday morning, in time for the weekly Kingsbridge market. He had worked on it by lamplight all Friday night, and Caris guessed he had not had time to speak to Griselda and tell her he knew the baby was Thurstan's. Caris and her father came down to the riverside to see the new sensation as the first traders arrived—women from the surrounding villages with baskets of eggs, peasants with cartloads of butter and cheese, and shepherds with flocks of lambs.

Caris admired Merthin's work. The raft was large enough to carry a horse and cart without taking the beast out of the shafts, and it had a firm wooden railing to keep sheep from falling overboard. New wooden platforms at water level on both banks made it easy for carts to roll on and off. Passengers paid a penny, collected by a monk—the ferry, like the bridge, belonged to the priory.

Most ingenious was the system Merthin had devised for moving the raft from one bank to the other. A long rope ran from the south end of the raft across the river, around a post, back across the river, around a drum, and back to the raft, where it was attached again at the north end. The drum was connected by wooden gears to a wheel turned by a pacing ox: Caris had seen Merthin carving the gears yesterday. A lever altered the gears so that the drum turned in either direction, depending on whether the raft was going or coming back—and there was no need to take the ox out of its traces and turn it around.

"It's quite simple," Merthin said when she marveled at it—and it was, when she looked closely. The lever simply lifted one large cogwheel up out of the chain and moved into its place two smaller wheels, the effect being to reverse the direction in which the drum turned. All the same, no one in Kingsbridge had seen anything like it.

During the course of the morning, half the town came to look at Merthin's amazing new machine. Caris was bursting with pride in him. Elfric stood by, explaining the mechanism to anyone who asked, taking the credit for Merthin's work.

Caris wondered where Elfric got the nerve. He had destroyed Merthin's door—an act of violence that would have scandalized the town, had it not been overtaken by the greater tragedy of the bridge collapse. He had beaten Merthin with a stick, and Merthin still had the bruise on his face. And he had colluded in a deception intended to make Merthin marry Griselda and raise another man's child. Merthin had continued to work with him, feeling that the emergency outweighed their quarrel. But Caris did not know how Elfric could continue to hold his head up.

The ferry was brilliant—but inadequate.

Edmund pointed this out. On the far side of the river, carts and traders were queuing all along the road through the suburbs as far as the eye could see.

"It would go faster with two oxen," Merthin said.

"Twice as fast?"

"Not quite, no. I could build another ferry."

"There's already a second one," Edmund said, pointing. He was right: Ian Boatman was rowing foot passengers across. Ian could not take carts, he refused livestock, and he charged twopence. Normally he had trouble scraping a living: he took a monk across to Leper Island twice a day and found little other business. But today he, too, had a queue.

Merthin said: "Well, you're right. In the end, a ferry is not a bridge."

"This is a catastrophe," Edmund said. "Buonaventura's news was bad enough. But this—this could kill the town."

"Then you must have a new bridge."

"It's not me, it's the priory. The prior is dead, and there's no telling how long they will take to elect a new one. We'll just have to pressure the acting prior to make a decision. I'll go and see Carlus now. Come with me, Caris."

They walked up the street and entered the priory. Most visitors had to go to the hospital, and tell one of the servants that they wanted to speak to a monk; but Edmund was too important a personage, and too proud, to beg the favor of an audience in that way. The prior was lord of Kingsbridge, but Edmund was alderman of the guild, leader of the merchants who made the town what it was, and he treated the prior as a partner in the governance of the town. Besides, for the last thirteen years the prior had been his younger brother. So he went straight to the prior's house on the north side of the cathedral.

It was a timber-framed house like Edmund's, with a hall and a parlor on the ground floor and two bedrooms upstairs. There was no kitchen, for the prior's meals were prepared in the monastery kitchen. Many bishops and priors lived in palaces—and the bishop of Kingsbridge had a fine place in Shiring—but the prior of Kingsbridge lived modestly. However, the chairs were comfortable, the wall was hung with tapestries of Bible scenes, and there was a big fireplace to keep the house cozy in winter.

Caris and Edmund arrived mid-morning, the time when younger monks were supposed to labor, and their elders to read. Edmund and Caris found Blind Carlus in the hall of the prior's house, deep in conversation with Simeon, the treasurer. "We must talk about the new bridge," Edmund said immediately.

"Very well, Edmund," Carlus said, recognizing him by his voice. The welcome was not warm, Caris noted, and she wondered if they had come at a bad time.

Edmund was just as sensitive as she to atmosphere, but he always blustered through. Now he took a chair and said: "When do you think you'll hold the election for the new prior?"

"You can sit down, too, Caris," said Carlus. She had no idea how he knew she was there. "No date has been set for the election," he went on. "Earl Roland has the right to nominate a candidate, but he has not yet recovered consciousness."

"We can't wait," Edmund said. Caris thought he was being too abrupt, but this was his way, so she said nothing. "We have to start work on the new bridge right away," her father continued. "Timber's no good, we have to build in stone. It's going to take three years—four, if we delay."

"A stone bridge?"

"It's essential. I've been talking to Elfric and Merthin. Another wooden bridge would fall down like the old."

"But the cost!"

"About two hundred and fifty pounds, depending on the design. That's Elfric's calculation."

Brother Simeon said: "A new wooden bridge would cost fifty pounds, and Prior Anthony rejected that last week because of the price."

"And look at the result! A hundred people dead, many more injured, livestock and carts lost, the prior dead, and the earl at death's door."

Carlus said stiffly: "I hope you don't mean to blame all that on the late Prior Anthony."

"We can't pretend his decision worked out well."

"God has punished us for sin."

Edmund sighed. Caris felt frustrated. Whenever they were in the wrong, monks would bring God into the argument. Edmund said: "It is hard for us mere men to know God's intentions. But one thing we do know is that, without a bridge, this town will die. We're already losing out to Shiring. Unless we build a new stone bridge as fast as we possibly can, Kingsbridge will soon become a small village."

"That may be God's plan for us."

Edmund began to show his exasperation. "Is it possible that God is so displeased with you monks? For, believe me, if the Fleece Fair and the Kingsbridge market die, there will not be a priory here with twenty-five monks and forty nuns and fifty employees, and a hospital and a choir and a school. There may not be a cathedral, either. The bishop of Kingsbridge has always lived in Shiring—what if the prosperous merchants there offer to build him a splendid new cathedral in their own town, out of the profits from their ever-growing market? No Kingsbridge market, no town, no cathedral, no priory—is that what you want?"

Carlus looked dismayed. Clearly it had not occurred to him that the long-term consequences of the bridge collapse could actually affect the status of the priory.

But Simeon said: "If the priory can't afford to build a wooden bridge, there's certainly no prospect of a stone one."

"But you must!"

"Will the masons work free?"

"Certainly not. They have to feed their families. But we've already explained how the townspeople could raise the money and lend it to the priory against the security of the bridge tolls."

"And take away our income from the bridge!" Simeon said indignantly. "You're back to that swindle, are you?"

Caris put in: "You've got no bridge tolls at all now."

"On the contrary, we're collecting fares on the ferry."

"You found the money to pay Elfric for that."

"A lot less than a bridge—and even so it emptied our coffers."

"The fares will never amount to much—the ferry is too slow."

"The time may come, in the future, when the priory is able to build a new bridge. God will send the means, if he wishes it. And then we will still have the tolls."

Edmund said: "God has already sent the means. He inspired my daughter to dream up a way of raising the money that has never been thought of before."

Carlus said primly: "Please leave it to us to decide what God has done."

"Very well." Edmund stood up, and Caris did the same. "I'm very sorry you're taking this attitude. It's a catastrophe for Kingsbridge and everyone who lives here, including the monks."

"I must be guided by God, not you."

Edmund and Caris turned to leave.

"One more thing, if I may," said Carlus.

Edmund turned at the door. "Of course."

"It's not acceptable for laypeople to enter priory buildings at will. Next time you wish to see me, please come to the hospital, and send a novice or a priory servant to seek me out, in the usual way."

"I'm alderman of the parish guild!" Edmund protested. "I've always had direct access to the prior."

"No doubt the fact that Prior Anthony was your brother made him reluctant to impose the usual rules. But those days are over."

Caris looked at her father's face. He was repressing fury. "Very well," he said tightly.

"God bless you."

Edmund went out, and Caris followed.

They walked across the muddy green together, passing a pitifully small cluster of market stalls. Caris felt the weight of her father's obligations. Most people just worried about feeding their families. Edmund worried about the entire town. She glanced at him and saw that his expression was twisted into an anxious frown. Unlike Carlus, Edmund would not throw his hands in the air and say that God's will would be done. He was racking his brains for a solution to the problem. She felt a surge of compassion for him, straining to do the right thing with no help from the powerful priory. He never complained of the responsibility, he just took it on. It made her want to weep.

They left the precincts and crossed the main street. As they came to their front door, Caris said: "What are we going to do?"

"It's obvious, isn't it?" said her father. "We've got to make sure Carlus doesn't get elected prior."

15

Godwyn wanted to be prior of Kingsbridge. He longed for it with all his heart. He itched to reform the priory's finances, tightening up the management of its lands and other assets, so that the monks no longer had to go to Mother Cecilia for money. He yearned for the stricter separation of monks from nuns, and both from townspeople, so that they might all breathe the pure air of sanctity. But as well as these irreproachable motives, there was something else. He lusted for the authority and distinction of the title. At night, in his imagination, he was already prior.

"Clean up that mess in the cloister!" he would say to a monk.

"Yes, Father Prior, right away."

Godwyn loved the sound of *Father Prior.*

"Good day, Bishop Richard," he would say, not obsequiously, but with friendly courtesy.

And Bishop Richard would reply, as one distinguished clergyman to another: "And a good day to you, too, Prior Godwyn."

"I trust everything is to your satisfaction, Archbishop?" he might say, more deferentially this time, but still as a junior colleague of the great man, rather than as an underling.

"Oh, yes, Godwyn, you've done extraordinarily well here."

"Your Reverence is very kind."

And perhaps, one day, strolling in the cloister side by side with a richly dressed potentate: "Your Majesty does us great honor to visit our humble priory."

"Thank you, Father Godwyn, but I come to ask your advice."

He wanted this position—but he was not sure how to get it. He pondered the question all week, as he supervised a hundred burials and planned the big Sunday service that would be both Anthony's funeral and a remembrance for the souls of all the Kingsbridge dead.

Meanwhile, he spoke to no one of his hopes. It was only ten days ago that he had learned the price of being guileless. He had gone to the chapter with *Timothy's Book* and a strong argument for reform—and the old guard had turned on him with perfect coordination, as if they had rehearsed it, and squashed him like a frog under a cartwheel.

He would not let that happen again.

On Sunday morning, as the monks were filing into the refectory for breakfast, a novice whispered to Godwyn that his mother would like to see him in the north porch of the cathedral. He slipped away discreetly.

He felt apprehensive as he passed quietly through the cloisters and the church. He could guess what had happened. Something had occurred yesterday to trouble Petranilla. She had lain awake half the night worrying about it. This morning she had woken up at dawn with a plan of action—and he was part of it. She would be at her most impatient and domineering. Her plan would probably be good—but even if it was not, she would insist he carry it out.

She stood in the gloom of the porch in a wet cloak—it was raining again. "My brother Edmund came to see Blind Carlus yesterday," she said. "He tells me Carlus is acting as if he is already prior, and the election is a mere formality."

There was an accusing note in her voice, as if this was Godwyn's fault, and he answered defensively. "The old guard swung behind Carlus before Uncle Anthony's body was cold. They won't hear talk of rival candidates."

"Hm. And the youngsters?"

"They want me to run, of course. They liked the way I stood up to Prior Anthony over *Timothy's Book*—even though I was overruled. But I've said nothing."

"Any other candidates?"

"Thomas Langley is the outsider. Some disapprove of him because he used to be a knight, and has killed people, by his own admission. But he's capable, does his job with quiet efficiency, never bullies the novices . . ."

His mother looked thoughtful. "What's his story? Why did he become a monk?"

Godwyn's apprehension began to ease. It seemed she was not going to berate him for inaction. "Thomas just says he always hankered for the sanctified life and, when he came here to get a sword wound attended to, he resolved never to leave."

"I remember that. It was ten years ago. But I never did hear how he got the wound."

"Nor I. He doesn't like to talk about his violent past."

"Who paid for his admission to the priory?"

"Oddly enough, I don't know." Godwyn often marveled at his mother's ability to ask the revealing question. She might be tyrannical, but he had to admire her. "It might have been Bishop Richard—I recall him promising the usual gift. But he wouldn't have had the resources personally—he wasn't a bishop, then, just a priest. Perhaps he was speaking for Earl Roland."

"Find out."

Godwyn hesitated. He would have to look through all the charters in the priory's library. The librarian, Brother Augustine, would not presume to question the sacrist, but someone else might. Then Godwyn would have the awkwardness of inventing a plausible story to explain what he was doing. If the gift had been cash, rather than land or other property—unusual, but possible—he would have to go through the account rolls . . .

"What's the matter?" his mother said sharply.

"Nothing. You're right." He reminded himself that her domineering attitude was a sign of her love for him, perhaps the only way she knew how to express it. "There must be a record. Come to think of it . . ."

"What?"

"A gift like that is usually trumpeted. The prior announces it in church, and calls down blessings on the head of the donor, then preaches a sermon on how people who give lands to the priory are rewarded in Heaven. But I don't remember anything like that happening at the time Thomas came to us."

"All the more reason to seek out the charter. I think Thomas is a man with a secret. And a secret is always a weakness."

"I'll look into it. What do you think I should say to people who want me to stand for election?"

Petranilla smiled slyly. "I think you should tell them you're not going to be a candidate."

Breakfast was over by the time Godwyn left his mother. Latecomers were not allowed to eat, by a longstanding rule. But the kitchener, Brother Reynard, could always find a morsel for someone he liked. Godwyn went to the kitchen and got a slice of cheese and a heel of bread. He ate it standing up, while around him the priory servants brought the breakfast bowls back from the refectory and scrubbed out the iron pot in which the porridge had been cooked.

As he ate, he mulled over his mother's advice. The more he thought about it, the cleverer it seemed. Once he had announced he would not stand for election, everything else he said would carry the authority of a disinterested commentator. He could manipulate the election without being suspected of selfish motives. Then he could make his move at the last moment. He felt a warm glow of loving gratitude for the shrewdness of his mother's restless brain, and the loyalty of her indomitable heart.

Brother Theodoric found him there. Theodoric's fair complexion was flushed with indignation. "Brother Simeon spoke to us at breakfast about Carlus becoming prior," he said. "It was all about continuing the wise traditions of Anthony. He's not going to change anything!"

That was sly, Godwyn thought. Simeon had taken advantage of Godwyn's absence to say, with authority, things that Godwyn would have challenged if he had been present. He said sympathetically: "That's disgraceful."

"I asked whether the other candidates would be permitted to address the monks at breakfast in the same way."

Godwyn grinned. "Good for you!"

"Simeon said there was no need for other candidates. 'We're not holding an archery contest,' he said. In his view, the decision has already been made: Prior Anthony chose Carlus as his successor by making him subprior."

"That's complete rubbish."

"Exactly. The monks are furious."

This was very good, Godwyn thought. Carlus had offended even his supporters by trying to take away their right to vote. He was undermining his own candidacy.

Theodoric went on: "I think we should press Carlus to withdraw himself from the contest."

Godwyn wanted to say: *Are you mad?* He bit his tongue and tried to look as if he were mulling over what Theodoric had said. "Is that the best way to deal with it?" he asked, as if genuinely unsure.

Theodoric was surprised by the question. "What do you mean?"

"You say the brothers are all furious with Carlus and Simeon. If this goes on, they won't vote for Carlus. But if Carlus withdraws, the old guard will come up with another candidate. They could make a better choice the second time. It might be someone popular—Brother Joseph, for example."

Theodoric was thunderstruck. "I never thought of it that way."

"Perhaps we should hope that Carlus remains the choice of the old guard. Everyone knows he's against any kind of change. The reason he's a monk is that he likes to know that every day will be the same: he'll walk the same paths, sit in the same seats, eat and pray and sleep in the same places. Perhaps it's because of his blindness, though I suspect he might have been like that anyway. The cause doesn't matter. He believes that nothing here needs changing. Now, there aren't many monks who are *that* contented—which makes Carlus relatively easy to beat. A candidate who represented the old guard but advocated a few minor reforms would be much more likely to win." Godwyn realized he had forgotten to seem tentative and had started laying down the law. Backtracking quickly, he added: "I don't know—what do you think?"

"I think you're a genius," said Theodoric.

I'm not a genius, Godwyn thought, but I learn fast.

He went to the hospital, where he found Philemon sweeping out the private guest rooms upstairs. Lord William was still here, watching over his father, waiting for him to wake up or die. Lady Philippa was with him. Bishop Richard had returned to his palace in Shiring, but was expected back today for the big funeral service.

Godwyn took Philemon to the library. Philemon could barely read, but he would be useful for getting out the charters.

The priory had more than a hundred charters. Most were deeds to landholdings, the majority near Kingsbridge, some scattered around far parts of England and Wales. Other charters entitled the monks to establish their priory, to build a church, to take stone from a quarry on the earl of Shiring's land without payment, to parcel the land around the priory into house plots and rent them out, to hold courts, to have a weekly market, to charge a toll for crossing the bridge, to have an annual Fleece Fair, and to ship goods by river to Melcombe without paying taxes to the lords of any of the lands through which the river passed.

The documents were written with pen and ink on parchment, thin leather painstakingly cleaned and scraped and bleached and stretched to form a writing surface. Longer ones were rolled up and tied with a fine leather thong. They were kept in an ironbound chest. The chest was locked, but the key was in the library, in a small carved box.

Godwyn frowned with disapproval when he opened the chest. The charters were not lined up in neat stacks, but tumbled in the box in no apparent order. Some had small rips and frayed edges, and all were covered with dust. They should be kept in date sequence, he thought, each one numbered, and the numbered list fixed to the inside of the lid, so that any particular charter could be quickly located. If I become prior . . .

Philemon took the charters out one by one, blew off the dust, and laid them on a table for Godwyn. Most people disliked Philemon. One or two of the older monks mistrusted him, but Godwyn did not: it was hard to mistrust someone who treated you like a god. Most of the monks were just used to him—he had been around for so long. Godwyn remembered him as a boy, tall and awkward, always hanging around the priory, asking the monks which saint was best to pray to, and had they ever witnessed a miracle.

Most of the charters had originally been written out twice on a single sheet. The word "chirograph" had been written in large letters between the two copies, then the sheet had been cut in half with a zigzag line through the word. Each of the parties kept half the sheet, and the match between the zigzags was taken as proof that both documents were genuine.

Some of the sheets had holes, probably where the living sheep had been bitten by an insect. Others appeared to have been nibbled, at some point in their history, presumably by mice.

They were written in Latin, of course. The more recent ones were easier to read, but the older style of handwriting was sometimes hard for Godwyn to decipher. He scanned each until he came to a date. He was looking for something written soon after All Hallows Day ten years ago.

He examined every sheet and found nothing.

The nearest was a deed dated some weeks later in which Earl Roland gave permission to Sir Gerald to transfer his lands to the ownership of the priory, in exchange for which the priory would forgive Gerald's debts and support him and his wife for the rest of their lives.

Godwyn was not really disappointed. Rather the contrary. Either Thomas had been admitted without the usual gift—which would in itself be curious—or the charter was kept somewhere else, away from prying eyes. Either way, it seemed increasingly likely that Petranilla's instinct was right, and Thomas had a secret.

There were not many private places in a monastery. Monks were supposed to have no personal property and no secrets. Although some wealthy monasteries had built private cells for the senior monks, at Kingsbridge they slept in one big room—all except the prior himself. Almost certainly, the charter that had secured Thomas's admission was in the prior's house.

Which was now occupied by Carlus.

That made things difficult. Carlus would not let Godwyn search the place. Searching might hardly be necessary; there was probably a box or satchel somewhere in plain sight containing the late Prior Anthony's personal documents: a notebook from his novice days, a friendly letter from the archbishop, some sermons. Carlus had probably examined the contents after Anthony died. But he had no reason to permit Godwyn to do the same.

Godwyn frowned, thinking. Could someone else search? Edmund or Petranilla might ask to see their late brother's possessions, and it would be hard for Carlus to deny such a request. But he might remove any priory documents beforehand. No, the search had to be clandestine.

The bell rang for Terce, the morning office. Godwyn realized that the only time he could be certain Carlus would not be in the prior's house was during a service in the cathedral.

He would have to skip Terce. He could think up a plausible excuse. It would not be easy—he was the sacrist, the one person who should never skip services. But there was no alternative.

"I want you to come to me in the church," he said to Philemon.

"All right," said Philemon, though he looked worried: priory employees were not supposed to enter the chancel during worship.

"Come right after the verse. Whisper in my ear. It doesn't matter what you say. Take no notice of my reaction, just continue."

Philemon frowned anxiously, but he nodded assent. He would do anything for Godwyn.

Godwyn left the library and joined the procession into the church. There was only a handful of people standing in the nave: most of the town would come later in the day to attend the mass for the victims of the bridge collapse. The monks took their places in the chancel, and the ritual began. "Oh, God, incline unto mine aid," Godwyn said along with the rest.

They finished the verse and began the first hymn, and Philemon appeared. All the monks stared at him, as people always did stare at anything out of the ordinary that occurred during a familiar rite. Brother Simeon frowned disapprovingly. Carlus, conducting the singing, sensed a disturbance and looked puzzled. Philemon came to Godwyn's seat and bent over. "Blessed is the man that walketh not in the counsel of the ungodly," he whispered.

Godwyn pretended to be surprised, and continued to listen while Philemon recited Psalm number one. After a few moments he shook his head vigorously, as if denying a request. Then he listened some more. He was going to have to think up an elaborate story to account for this pantomime. Perhaps he would say that his mother had insisted on speaking to him immediately about the funeral of her brother, Prior Anthony, and that she was threatening to come into the chancel herself unless Philemon took a message to Godwyn. Petranilla's overbearing personality, combined with family grief, made the story just about credible. As Philemon finished the psalm, Godwyn made a resigned face and got up and followed Philemon out of the chancel.

They hurried around the cathedral to the prior's house. A young employee was sweeping the floor. He would not dare to question a monk. He might tell Carlus that Godwyn and Philemon had been here—but it would be too late then.

Godwyn thought the prior's house was a disgrace. It was smaller than Uncle Edmund's home in the main street. A prior should have a palace befitting his station, as the bishop did. There was nothing glorious about this building. A few tapestries covered the walls, depicting biblical scenes and keeping out the drafts, but overall the decor was dull and unimaginative—rather like the late Anthony.

They searched the place quickly and soon found what they were looking for. Upstairs in the bedroom, in a chest beside the prie-dieu, was a large wallet. It was made of soft ginger-brown goatskin and beautifully sewn with scarlet thread: Godwyn felt sure it had been a pious gift from one of the town's leatherworkers.

Watched intently by Philemon, he opened it.

Inside were about thirty sheets of parchment, laid flat and interleaved with protective linen cloths. Godwyn examined them quickly.

Several bore study notes on the Psalms: Anthony must at some time have contemplated writing a book of commentaries, but the work appeared to have been abandoned. The most surprising was a love poem, in Latin. Headed *Virent Oculi*, it was addressed to a man with green eyes. Uncle Anthony had green eyes flecked with gold, like all his family.

Godwyn wondered who had written it. Not many women could write Latin well enough to compose a poem. Had a nun loved Anthony? Or was the poem from a man? The parchment was old and yellowing: the love affair, if such it was, had happened in Anthony's youth. But he had kept the poem. Perhaps he had not been quite as dull as Godwyn had imagined.

Philemon said: "What is it?"

Godwyn felt guilty. He had peeped into a deeply private corner of his uncle's life, and he wished he had not. "Nothing," he said. "Just a poem." He picked up the next sheet—and struck gold.

It was a charter dated Christmas ten years ago. It concerned a landholding of five hundred acres near Lynn, in Norfolk. The lord had recently died. The deed assigned the vacant lordship to Kingsbridge Priory, and specified the annual dues—grain, fleeces, calves, and chickens—payable to the priory by the serfs and tenants who farmed the land. It nominated one of the peasants to be a bailiff with the responsibility of delivering the produce to the priory annually. It also assigned money payments that could be offered instead of the actual produce—a practice that was now predominant, especially where the land was many miles from the residence of the lord.

It was a typical charter. Every year, after the harvest, representatives of dozens of similar communities made the pilgrimage to the priory to deliver what they owed. Those from nearby showed up early in the autumn; others came at intervals through the winter, with a few from long distances not arriving until after Christmas.

The deed also specified that the gift was given in consideration of the priory's accepting Sir Thomas Langley as a monk. That, too, was routine.

But one feature of this document was not commonplace. It was signed by Queen Isabella.

That was interesting. Isabella was the unfaithful wife of King Edward II. She had rebelled against her royal husband and installed, in his place, their fourteen-year-old son. Shortly afterward the deposed king had died, and Prior Anthony had been present at his burial in Gloucester. Thomas had come to Kingsbridge at around the same time.

For a few years the queen and her lover, Roger Mortimer, had ruled England; but, before long, Edward III had asserted his authority, despite his youth. The new king was now twenty-four and firmly in control. Mortimer was dead, and Isabella, now forty-two, lived in opulent retirement at Castle Rising in Norfolk, not far from Lynn.

"This is it!" Godwyn said to Philemon. "It was Queen Isabella who arranged for Thomas to become a monk."

Philemon frowned. "But why?"

Though uneducated, Philemon was shrewd. "Why indeed?" Godwyn answered. "Presumably she wanted to reward him, or silence him, or perhaps both. And this happened in the year of her coup."

"He must have performed some service for her."

Godwyn nodded. "He carried a message, or opened the gates of a castle, or betrayed the king's plans to her, or secured for her the support of some important baron. But why is it a secret?"

"It's not," said Philemon. "The treasurer must know about it. And everyone in Lynn. The bailiff must talk to a few people when he comes here."

"But no one knows that the whole arrangement was made for the benefit of Thomas—unless they have seen this charter."

"So that's the secret—that Queen Isabella made this gift for Thomas's sake."

"Exactly." Godwyn packed up the documents, carefully interleaving the sheets of parchment with linen cloths, and replaced the wallet in the chest.

Philemon asked: "But why is it a secret? There's nothing dishonest or shameful about such an arrangement—it happens all the time."

"I don't know why it's a secret, and perhaps we don't need to know. The fact that people want to keep it hidden may be sufficient for our purpose. Let's get out of this house."

Godwyn felt satisfied. Thomas had a secret and Godwyn knew about it. That gave Godwyn power. Now he felt confident enough to risk putting Thomas forward as a candidate for prior. He also felt apprehensive: Thomas was no fool.

They returned to the cathedral. The office of Terce ended a few moments later, and Godwyn began to prepare the church for the big funeral service. On his instructions, six monks lifted Anthony's coffin and placed it on a stand in front of the altar, then surrounded it with candles. Townspeople began to gather in the nave. Godwyn nodded to his cousin Caris, who had covered her everyday headgear in black silk. Then he spotted Thomas, carrying in a large, ornate chair, with the help of a novice. This was the bishop's throne, or cathedra, that gave the church its special cathedral status.

Godwyn touched Thomas's arm. "Let Philemon do that."

Thomas bristled, thinking that Godwyn was offering help because of his missing arm. "I can manage."

"I know you can. I want a word."

Thomas was older—he was thirty-four, Godwyn thirty-one—but Godwyn was his superior in the monastic hierarchy. All the same, Godwyn was always a little afraid of Thomas. The matricularius usually showed the appropriate deference to the sacrist, but all the same Godwyn felt he was getting just as much respect as Thomas thought he merited, and no more. Though Thomas conformed in every way to the discipline of St. Benedict's

Rule, nevertheless he seemed to have brought into the priory with him a quality of independence and self-sufficiency that he never lost.

It would not be easy to deceive Thomas—but that was exactly what Godwyn planned to do.

Thomas allowed Philemon to take his side of the throne, and Godwyn drew him into the aisle. "They're talking about you as possibly the next prior," Godwyn said.

"They're saying the same about you," Thomas rejoined.

"I shall refuse to stand."

Thomas raised his eyebrows. "You surprise me, Brother."

"Two reasons," Godwyn said. "One, I think you would do a better job."

Thomas looked more surprised. He probably had not suspected Godwyn of such modesty. He was right: Godwyn was lying.

"Two," Godwyn continued, "you're more likely to win." Now Godwyn was telling the truth. "The youngsters like me, but you're popular across the range of all ages."

Thomas's handsome face looked quizzical. He was waiting for the catch.

"I want to help you," Godwyn said. "I believe the only important thing is to have a prior who will reform the monastery and improve its finances."

"I think I could do that. But what do you want in return for your support?"

Godwyn knew better than to ask for nothing. Thomas would not believe that. He invented a plausible lie. "I'd like to be your subprior."

Thomas nodded, but did not immediately consent. "How would you help me?"

"First, by gaining you the support of the townspeople."

"Just because Edmund Wooler is your uncle?"

"It's not that simple. The townspeople are worried about the bridge. Carlus won't say when he'll begin building, if ever. They're desperate to stop him becoming prior. If I tell Edmund that you'll start work on the bridge as soon as you're elected, you'll have the whole town behind you."

"That won't win me the votes of many monks."

"Don't be so sure. Remember, the monks' choice has to be ratified by the bishop. Most bishops are prudent enough to consult local opinion—and Richard is as keen as anyone to avoid trouble. If the townspeople come out for you, it will make a difference."

Godwyn could see that Thomas did not trust him. The matricularius studied him, and Godwyn felt a bead of sweat trickle down his spine as he fought to remain expressionless under that keen gaze. But Thomas was listening to his arguments. "There's no doubt we need a new bridge," he said. "Carlus is foolish to prevaricate."

"So you would be promising something you intend to do anyway."

"You're very persuasive."

Godwyn held up his hands in a defensive gesture. "I don't mean to be. You must do what you feel is God's will."

Thomas looked skeptical. He did not believe that Godwyn was so dispassionate. But he said: "All right." Then he added: "I'll pray about it."

Godwyn sensed he would get no stronger commitment out of Thomas today, and it might be counterproductive to push any harder. "So will I," he said, and he turned away.

Thomas would do exactly what he had promised, and pray about it. He had little in the way of personal desires. If he thought it was God's will he would stand as prior, and if not, not. Godwyn could do no more with him, for the moment.

There was now a blaze of candles around Anthony's coffin. The nave was filling with townspeople and peasants from the surrounding villages. Godwyn raked the crowd for the face of Caris, which he had spotted a few minutes earlier. He located her in the south transept, looking at Merthin's scaffolding in the aisle. He had affectionate memories of Caris as a child, when he had been her all-knowing grown-up cousin.

She had been looking glum since the bridge collapse, he had noticed, but today she seemed cheerful. He was glad: he had a soft spot for her. He touched her elbow. "You look happy."

"I am." She smiled. "A romantic knot just came untangled. But you wouldn't understand."

"Of course not." You have no idea, he thought, how many romantic tangles there are among monks. But he said nothing: laypeople were best left in ignorance of sins that took place in the priory. He said: "Your father should speak to Bishop Richard about rebuilding the bridge."

"Really?" she said skeptically. As a child she had hero-worshipped him, but nowadays she was less in awe. "What's the point? It's not his bridge."

"The monks' choice for prior has to be approved by the bishop. Richard could let it be known that he won't approve anyone who refuses to rebuild the bridge. Some monks might be defiant, but others will say there's no point in voting for someone who isn't going to be ratified."

"I see. You really think my father could help?"

"Absolutely."

"Then I'll suggest it."

"Thank you."

The bell rang. Godwyn slipped out of the church and again joined the procession forming up in the cloisters. It was midday.

He had done a good morning's work.

16

Wulfric and Gwenda left Kingsbridge early on Monday morning to walk the long road back to their village of Wigleigh.

Caris and Merthin watched them cross the river on Merthin's new ferry. Merthin was pleased by how well it was working. The wooden gears would wear out quite quickly, he knew. Iron gears would be better, but . . .

Caris had other thoughts. "Gwenda is so much in love," she sighed.

"She has no chance with Wulfric," Merthin said.

"You never know. She's a determined girl. Look how she escaped from Sim Chapman."

"But Wulfric's engaged to that Annet—who is much prettier."

"Good looks aren't everything in a romance."

"For which I thank God every day."

She laughed. "I love your funny face."

"But Wulfric fought my brother over Annet. He must love her."

"Gwenda's got a love potion."

Merthin gave her a disapproving look. "So you think it's all right for a girl to maneuver a man into marrying her when he loves someone else?"

She was struck silent for a moment. The soft skin of her throat turned pink. "I never thought of it that way," she said. "Is it really the same thing?"

"It's similar."

"But she's not coercing him—she just wants to make him love her."

"She should try to do that without a potion."

"Now I feel ashamed of helping her."

"Too late." Wulfric and Gwenda were getting off the ferry on the far side. They turned to wave, then headed along the road through the suburbs with Skip, the dog, at their heels.

Merthin and Caris walked back up the main street. Caris said: "You haven't spoken to Griselda yet."

"I'm going to do it now. I don't know whether I'm looking forward to it or dreading it."

"You've got nothing to fear. She's the one who lied."

"That's true." He touched his face. The bruise had almost healed. "I just hope her father doesn't get violent again."

"Do you want me to come with you?"

He would have been glad of her support, but he shook his head. "I made this mess, and I have to straighten it out."

They stopped outside Elfric's house. Caris said: "Good luck."

"Thanks." Merthin kissed her lips briefly, resisted the temptation to kiss her again, and walked in.

Elfric was sitting at the table eating bread and cheese. A cup of ale stood in front of him. Beyond him, Merthin could see Alice and the maid in the kitchen. There was no sign of Griselda.

Elfric said: "Where have you been?"

Merthin decided that if he had nothing to fear he had better act fearlessly. He ignored Elfric's question. "Where's Griselda?"

"Still in bed."

Merthin shouted up the stairs: "Griselda! I want to talk to you."

Elfric said: "No time for that. We've got work to do."

Again Merthin ignored him. "Griselda! You'd better get up now."

"Hey!" Elfric said. "Who do you think you are, to give orders?"

"You want me to marry her, don't you?"

"So what?"

"So she'd better get used to doing what her husband tells her." He raised his voice again. "Get down here now, or you'll just have to hear what I've got to say from someone else."

She appeared at the top of the stairs. "I'm coming!" she said irritably. "What's all the fuss about?"

Merthin waited for her to come down, then said: "I've found out who the father of the baby is."

Fear flashed in her eyes. "Don't be stupid, it's you."

"No, it's Thurstan."

"I never lay with Thurstan!" She looked at her father. "Honestly I didn't."

Elfric said: "She doesn't lie."

Alice came out of the kitchen. "That's right," she said.

Merthin said: "I lay with Griselda on the Sunday of Fleece Fair week—fifteen days ago. Griselda is three months pregnant."

"I'm not!"

Merthin looked hard at Alice. "You knew, didn't you?" Alice looked away. Merthin went on: "And yet you lied—even to Caris, your own sister."

Elfric said: "You don't know how long pregnant she is."

"Look at her," Merthin replied. "You can see the bulge in her belly. Not much, but it's there."

"What do you know of such things? You're just a boy."

"Yes—you were all relying on my ignorance, weren't you? And it almost worked."

Elfric wagged his finger. "You lay with Griselda, and now you'll marry Griselda."

"Oh, no I won't. She doesn't love me. She lay with me to get a father for her baby, after Thurstan ran away. I know I did wrong, but I'm not going to punish myself for the rest of my life by marrying her."

Elfric stood up. "You are, you know."

"No."

"You've got to."

"No."

Elfric's face turned red, and he shouted: "You will marry her!"

Merthin said: "How long do you want me to keep on saying no?"

Elfric realized he was serious. "In that case, you're dismissed," he said. "Get out of my house and never come back."

Merthin had been expecting this, and it came as a relief. It meant the argument was over. "All right." He tried to step past Elfric.

Elfric blocked his way. "Where do you think you're going?"

"To the kitchen, to get my things."

"Your tools, you mean."

"Yes."

"They're not yours. I paid for them."

"An apprentice is always given his tools at the end of his . . ." Merthin tailed off.

"You haven't finished your apprenticeship, so you don't get your tools."

Merthin had not expected this. "I've done six and a half years!"

"You're supposed to do seven."

Without tools Merthin could not earn his living. "That's unfair. I'll appeal to the carpenters' guild."

"I look forward to it," Elfric said smugly. "It will be interesting to hear you argue that an apprentice who is sacked for lying with his master's daughter should be rewarded with a free set of tools. The carpenters in the guild have all got apprentices, and most of them have daughters. They'll throw you out on your arse."

Merthin realized he was right.

Alice said: "There you are, you're in real trouble now, aren't you?"

"Yes," Merthin said. "But whatever happens, it won't be as bad as life with Griselda and her family."

Later that morning, Merthin went to St. Mark's Church for the funeral of Howell Tyler. He attended because he hoped someone there would give him a job.

Looking up at the timber ceiling—the church did not have a stone vault—Merthin could see a man-shaped hole in the painted wood, grim testament to the manner of Howell's death. Everything up there was rotten, the builders at the funeral said knowingly; but they said it after the accident, their sagacity coming too late to save Howell. It was now clear that the roof was too weak to be repaired, but must be demolished completely and rebuilt from scratch. That meant closing the church.

St. Mark's was a poor church. It had a pitiful endowment, a single farm ten miles away that was kept by the priest's brother and just about managed to feed the family. The priest, Father Joffroi, had to get his income from the eight or nine hundred citizens of his parish in the poorer north end of town. Those who were not actually destitute generally pretended to be, so their tithes brought in only a modest sum. He made his living by christening, marrying, and burying them, charging a lot less than the monks at the cathedral. His parishioners married early, had many children, and died young, so there was plenty of work for him, and in the end he did well enough. But if he closed the church, his income would dry up—and he would not be able to pay the builders.

Consequently the work on the roof had stopped.

All the town's builders came to the funeral, including Elfric. Merthin tried to look unashamed as he stood in the church, but it was difficult: most of them knew he had been dismissed. He had been unjustly treated but, unfortunately, he was not completely innocent.

Howell had had a young wife who was friendly with Caris, and now Caris walked in with the widow and the bereaved family. Merthin moved next to Caris and told her what had happened with Elfric.

Father Joffroi conducted the service dressed in an old robe. Merthin thought about the roof. It seemed to him there must be a way to dismantle it without closing the church. The standard approach, when repairs had been postponed too long and the timbers were too badly rotted to bear the weight of workmen, was to build scaffolding around the church and knock the timbers down into the nave. The building was then open to the elements until the new roof was finished and tiled. But it should be possible to build a swiveling hoist, supported by the thick side wall of the church, which would lift the roof timbers up one by one, instead of pushing them down, and swing them across the wall and down into the graveyard. That way, the wooden ceiling could be left intact, and replaced only after the roof had been rebuilt.

At the graveside, he looked at the men one by one, wondering which of them was most likely to employ him. He decided to approach Bill Watkin, the town's second largest builder and no admirer of Elfric's. Bill had a bald dome with a fringe of black hair, a natural version of the monkish tonsure. He did most of the house building in Kingsbridge. Like Elfric, he employed a stonemason and a carpenter, a handful of laborers and one or two apprentices.

Howell had not been prosperous, and his body was lowered into the grave in a shroud, without a coffin.

When Father Joffroi had departed, Merthin approached Bill Watkin. "Good day, Master Watkin," he said formally.

Bill's response was not warm. "Well, young Merthin?"

"I've parted company with Elfric."

"I know that," said Bill. "And I know why."

"You've heard Elfric's side of the story."

"I've heard all I need to hear."

Elfric had been talking to people before and during the service, Merthin realized. He was sure Elfric had left out of his account the fact that Griselda had tried to make Merthin the substitute father for Thurstan's baby. But he felt he would do himself no good by making excuses. Better to admit his fault. "I realize I did wrong, and I'm sorry, but I'm still a good carpenter."

Bill nodded agreement. "The new ferry testifies to that."

Merthin was encouraged. "Will you hire me?"

"As what?"

"As a carpenter. You said I was a good one."

"But where are your tools?"

"Elfric wouldn't give them to me."

"And he was right—because you haven't finished your apprenticeship."

"Then take me on as an apprentice for six months."

"And give you a new set of tools for nothing at the end of it? I can't afford that kind of generosity." Tools were expensive because iron and steel were costly.

"I'll work as a laborer, and save up to buy my own tools." It would take a long time, but he was desperate.

"No."

"Why not?"

"Because I've got a daughter, too."

This was outrageous. "I'm not a menace to maidens, you know."

"You're an example to apprentices. If you get away with this, what's to stop the others trying their luck?"

"That is so unjust!"

Bill shrugged. "You might think so. But ask any other master carpenter in town. I think you'll find they feel as I do."

"But what am I to do?"

"I don't know. You should have thought of that before you shagged her."

"You don't care about losing a good carpenter?"

Bill shrugged again. "All the more work for the rest of us."

Merthin turned away. That was the trouble with guilds, he thought bitterly: it was in their interest to exclude people, for good or bad reasons. A shortage of carpenters would just drive up their wages. They had no incentive to be fair.

Howell's widow left, accompanied by her mother. Caris, liberated from her duty of commiseration, came over to Merthin. "Why do you look unhappy?" she said. "You hardly knew Howell."

"I may have to leave Kingsbridge," he said.

She went pale. "Why on earth would you do that?"

He told her what Bill Watkin had said. "So, you see, no one in Kingsbridge will hire me, and I can't work on my own account for I've no tools. I could live with my parents, but I can't take the food from their mouths. So I'll have to seek work someplace where no one knows about Griselda. In time, perhaps I can save up enough money to buy a hammer and chisel and then move to another town and try to gain admittance to the carpenters' guild."

As he explained this to Caris, he began to appreciate the full misery of the situation. He saw her familiar features as if for the first time, and he was enchanted again by her sparkling green eyes, her small, neat nose, and the determined set of her jaw. Her mouth, he realized, did not quite fit the rest of her face: it was too wide, and the lips were too full. It unbalanced the regularity of her physiognomy the way her sensual nature subverted her tidy mind. It was a mouth made for sex, and the thought that he might have to go away and never kiss it again filled him with despair.

Caris was furious. "This is iniquitous! They have no right."

"That's what I think. But there seems to be nothing I can do about it. I just have to accept it."

"Wait a minute. Let's think about this. You can live with your parents, and have your dinner at my house."

"I don't want to become a dependent, like my father."

"Nor should you. You can buy Howell Tyler's tools—his widow was just telling me she's asking a pound for them."

"I haven't any money."

"Ask my father for a loan. He's always liked you, I'm sure he'll do it."

"But it's against the rules for anyone to employ a carpenter who isn't in the guild."

"Rules can be broken. There must be someone in town desperate enough to defy the guild."

Merthin realized he had allowed the old men to quench his spirit, and he was grateful to Caris for refusing to accept defeat. She was right, of course: he should stay in Kingsbridge and fight this unjust ruling. And he knew someone who was in desperate need of his talents. "Father Joffroi," he said.

"Is he desperate? Why?"

Merthin explained about the roof.

"Let's go and see him," Caris said.

The priest lived in a small house next to the church. They found him preparing a dinner of salt fish in a stew with spring greens. Joffroi was in his thirties, built like a soldier, tall with broad shoulders. His manner was brusque, but he had a reputation for sticking up for the poor.

Merthin said: "I can repair your roof without closing your church."

Joffroi looked wary. "You're an answer to prayer if you can."

"I'll build a hoist that will lift the roof timbers and deposit them in the graveyard."

"Elfric sacked you." The priest shot an embarrassed look in Caris's direction.

She said: "I know what happened, Father."

Merthin said: "He dismissed me because I would not marry his daughter. But the child she is bearing is not mine."

Joffroi nodded. "Some say you were treated unjustly. I can believe it. I have no great love for the guilds—their decisions are rarely unselfish. All the same, you haven't completed your apprenticeship."

"Can any member of the carpenters' guild repair your roof without closing your church?"

"I heard you haven't even got any tools."

"Leave that problem to me to solve."

Joffroi looked thoughtful. "How much do you want to be paid?"

Merthin stuck his neck out. "Four pence a day, plus the cost of materials."

"That's a journeyman carpenter's wage."

"If I don't have the skill of a qualified carpenter, you shouldn't hire me."

"You're cocky."

"I'm just saying what I can do."

"Arrogance is not the worst sin in the world. And I can afford four pence a day if I can keep my church open. How long will it take you to build your hoist?"

"Two weeks at the most."

"I'm not going to pay you until I can be sure it will work."

Merthin breathed in. He would be penniless, but he could cope with that. He could live with his parents and eat at Edmund Wooler's table. He would get by. "Pay for the materials, and save my wages up until the first roof timber is removed and safely brought to ground."

Joffroi hesitated. "I'll be unpopular . . . but I have no choice." He held out his hand.

Merthin shook it.

17

All the way from Kingsbridge to Wigleigh—a distance of twenty miles, a full day's walk—Gwenda was hoping for a chance to use the love potion; but she was disappointed.

It was not that Wulfric was wary. On the contrary, he was open and friendly. He talked about his family, and told her how he wept every morning when he woke up and realized their deaths were not a dream. He was considerate, asking whether she was tired and needed to rest. He told her that he felt land was a trust, something a man held for a lifetime then passed to his heirs, and that when he improved his land—by weeding fields, fencing sheepfolds, or clearing stones from pasture—he was fulfilling his destiny.

He even patted Skip.

By the end of the day she was more in love with him than ever. Unfortunately, he showed no sign of feeling anything for her more than a kind of camaraderie, caring but not passionate. In the forest with Sim Chapman, she had wished with all her heart that men were not so much like wild beasts; but now she wanted Wulfric to have a bit more of the beast in him. All day she did little things to arouse his interest. As if by accident, she let him see her legs, which were firm and shapely. When the terrain was hilly, she made it an excuse to take deep breaths and stick out her chest. At every opportunity she brushed against him, touched his arm, or put a hand on his shoulder. None of it had the least effect. She was not pretty, she knew, but there was something about her that often made men look hard at her and breathe through their mouths—but it was not working on Wulfric.

They stopped for a rest at noon, and ate the bread and cheese they carried with them; but they drank water from a clear stream, using their hands as cups, and she had no opportunity to give him the potion.

All the same, she was happy. She had him all to herself for a whole day. She could look at him, talk to him, make him laugh, sympathize with him, and occasionally touch him. She pretended to herself that she could kiss him anytime she liked, but that at the moment she was not so disposed. It was almost like being married. And it was over too soon.

They arrived in Wigleigh early in the evening. The village stood on a rise, its fields sloping away to all sides, and it was always windy. After two weeks in the bustle of Kingsbridge, the familiar place seemed small and quiet, just a scatter of rough dwellings along the road that led to the manor house and the church. The manor was as large as a Kingsbridge merchant's home, with bedrooms on an upper floor. The priest's house was also a fine dwelling, and a few of the peasant houses were substantial. But most of the homes were two-room hovels, one room normally being occupied by livestock and the other serving as kitchen and bedroom for all the family. Only the church was built of stone.

The first of the more substantial houses belonged to Wulfric's family. Its doors and shutters were closed, giving it a desolate look. He walked past it to the second big house, which was where Annet lived with her parents. He gave Gwenda a casual wave of farewell and went inside, smiling in anticipation.

She felt the sharp tug of loss, as if she had just woken out of a delightful dream. She swallowed her discontent and set out across the fields. The early June rain had been good for the crops, and the wheat and barley were green, but now they needed sunshine to ripen them. Village women were moving along the rows of grain, bent double, pulling up weeds. Some waved to her.

As she approached her home, Gwenda felt a mixture of apprehension and anger. She had not seen her parents since the day her father had sold her to Sim Chapman for a cow. Almost certainly, Pa thought she was still with Sim. Her appearance would come as a shock. What would he say when he saw her? And what was she going to say to the father who had betrayed her trust?

She felt sure her mother knew nothing of the sale. Pa had probably told Ma some story about Gwenda running off with a boy. Ma was going to fly into a fearsome rage.

She felt happy at the prospect of seeing the little ones—Cath, Joanie, and Eric. She realized now how much she had missed them.

On the far side of the hundred-acre field, half-hidden in the trees at the edge of the forest, was her home. It was even smaller than the peasants' hovels, having only one room, which was shared with the cow at night. It was made of wattle and daub: tree branches stuck upright in the ground, with twigs interwoven basket-fashion, the gaps plugged with a sticky mixture of mud, straw, and cow dung. There was a hole in the thatched roof to let out the smoke of the fire in the middle of the earth floor. Such houses lasted only a few years then had to be rebuilt. It now seemed meaner than ever to Gwenda. She was determined not to spend her life in such a place, having babies every year or two, most of whom died for lack of food. She would not live like her mother. She would rather die.

When she was still a hundred yards from the house, she saw her father coming toward her. He was carrying a jug, probably going to buy ale from Peggy Perkins, Annet's mother, who was the village brewster. Pa always had money at this time of year, for there was plenty of work to be had in the fields.

At first he did not see her.

She studied his thin figure as he walked along the narrow gap between two field strips. He wore a long smock that came to his knees, a battered cap, and homemade sandals tied to his feet with straw. His gait managed to be both furtive and jaunty: he always looked like a nervous foreigner defiantly pretending to be at home. His eyes were set closely either side of a big nose, and he had a wide jaw with a knob of a chin, so that his face looked like a lumpy triangle: Gwenda knew that she resembled him in that. He glanced sidelong at the women he passed in the field, as if he did not want them to know he was observing them.

As he came close, he threw her one of his sneaky looks, up from under his lowered eyelids. He looked down instantly, then looked up again. She lifted her chin and stared back at him haughtily.

Astonishment spread across his face. "You!" he said. "What happened?"

"Sim Chapman wasn't a tinker, he was an outlaw."

"And where is he now?"

"He's in hell, Pa. You'll meet him there."

"Did you kill him?"

"No." She had long ago decided to lie about this. "God killed him. The bridge at Kingsbridge collapsed while Sim was crossing it. God punished him for his sin. Has he punished you yet?"

"God forgives good Christians."

"Is that all you have to say to me? That God forgives good Christians?"

"How did you escape?"

"I used my wits."

A crafty look came over his face. "You're a good girl," he said.

She stared at him suspiciously. "What mischief are you planning now?"

"You're a good girl," he repeated. "Go in to your mother now. You shall have a cup of ale with your supper." He walked on.

Gwenda frowned. Pa did not seem afraid of what Ma would say when she learned the truth. Perhaps he thought Gwenda would not tell her, out of shame. Well, he was wrong.

Cath and Joanie were outside the house, playing in the dirt. When they saw Gwenda, they jumped up and ran to her. Skip barked hysterically. Gwenda hugged her sisters, remembering how she had thought she would never see them again; and at that moment she was fiercely glad she had stuck a long knife into Alwyn's head.

She went inside. Ma was sitting on a stool, giving little Eric some milk, helping him hold the cup steady so that he did not spill any. She gave a cry of joy when she saw Gwenda. She put down the cup, stood up, and embraced her. Gwenda began to weep.

Once she had started crying, it was hard to stop. She cried because Sim had led her out of town on a rope, and because she had let Alwyn fuck her, and for all the people who had died when the bridge collapsed, and because Wulfric loved Annet.

When her sobs subsided enough for her to speak again, she said: "Pa sold me, Ma. He sold me for a cow, and I had to go with outlaws."

"That was wrong," her mother said.

"It was worse than wrong! He's wicked, evil—he's a devil."

Ma withdrew from the embrace. "Don't say such things."

"They're true!"

"He's your father."

"A father doesn't sell his children like livestock. I have no father."

"He's fed you for eighteen years."

Gwenda stared uncomprehendingly. "How can you be so hard? He sold me to outlaws!"

"And he got us a cow. So there's milk for Eric, even though my breasts have dried up. And you're here, aren't you?"

Gwenda was shocked. "You're defending him!"

"He's all I've got, Gwenda. He's not a prince. He's not even a peasant. He's a landless laborer. But he's done everything he can for this family for almost twenty-five years. He worked when he could and thieved when he had to. He kept you alive, and your brother, and with a fair wind he'll do the same for Cath and Joanie and Eric. Whatever his faults, we'd be worse off without him. So don't you call him a devil."

Gwenda was struck dumb. She had hardly got used to the idea that her father had betrayed her. Now she had to face the fact that her mother was as bad. She felt disoriented. It was like when the bridge had moved under her feet: she could hardly understand what was happening to her.

Her father came into the house carrying the jug of ale. He seemed not to notice the atmosphere. He took three wooden cups from the shelf over the fireplace. "Now, then," he said cheerfully. "Let's drink to the return of our big girl."

Gwenda was hungry and thirsty after walking all day. She took the cup and drank deeply. But she knew her father in this mood. "What are you planning?" she said.

"Well, now," he said. "It's the Shiring Fair next week, isn't it?"

"So what?"

"Well . . . we could do it again."

She could hardly believe what she was hearing. "Do what again?"

"I sell you, you go with the buyer, then you escape and come home. You're none the worse."

"None the worse?"

"And we've got a cow worth twelve shillings! Why, it takes me near half a year of laboring to earn twelve shillings."

"And after that? What then?"

"Well, there's other fairs—Winchester, Gloucester, I don't know how many." He refilled her cup from the ale jug. "Why—this could be better than the year you stole Sir Gerald's purse!"

She did not drink. There was a bitter taste in her mouth, as if she had eaten something corrupt. She thought of arguing with him. Harsh words came to her lips, angry accusations, curses—but she did not speak them. The way she felt was beyond rage. What was the point of having a row? She could never trust her father again. And because Ma refused to be disloyal to him, Gwenda could not trust her either.

"What am I to do?" she said aloud, but she did not want an answer from anyone in the room: the question was to herself. In this family she had become a commodity, to be sold at city fairs. If she was not prepared to accept that, what could she do?

She could leave.

She realized with a shock that this house was no longer a home to her. The blow shook the foundations of her existence. She had lived here since before she could remember. Now she did not feel safe here. She had to get out.

Not next week, she realized; not even tomorrow morning—she had to go now.

She had nowhere to go, but that made no difference. To stay here, and eat the bread her father put on the table, would be to yield to his authority. She would be accepting his evaluation of her, as a commodity to be sold. She was sorry she had drunk the first cup of ale. Her only chance was to reject him immediately and get out from under his roof.

Gwenda looked at her mother. "You're wrong," she said. "He is a devil. And the old stories are right: when you make a bargain with the devil, you end up paying more than you thought."

Ma looked away.

Gwenda stood up. The refilled cup was still in her hand. She tipped it, pouring the ale on the floor. Skip immediately started to lick it up.

Her father said angrily: "I paid a farthing for this jug of ale!"

"Good-bye," said Gwenda, and she walked out.

18

On the following Sunday, Gwenda attended the court hearing that would decide the fate of the man she loved.

The manorial court was held in the church after the service. It was the forum in which the village took collective action. Some of the questions it addressed were disputes—arguments over field boundaries, accusations of theft or rape, quarrels about debts—but more often it made pragmatic decisions, such as when to begin plowing with the communal eight-ox team.

In theory, the lord of the manor sat in judgment over his serfs. But Norman law—brought to England by invaders from France almost three centuries earlier—compelled lords to follow the customs of their predecessors; and in order to find out what those customs were, they had to formally consult twelve men of good standing in the village—a jury. So, in practice, the proceedings often became a negotiation between lord and villagers.

On this particular Sunday, Wigleigh had no lord. Sir Stephen had been killed in the collapse of the bridge. Gwenda had brought this news to the village. She also reported that Earl Roland, who had the task of appointing Stephen's replacement, had been gravely injured. On the day before she left Kingsbridge, the earl had recovered consciousness for the first time—but he had woken into a fever so violent that he was unable to speak a coherent sentence. So there was no prospect of a new lord of Wigleigh yet.

This was not an unusual circumstance. Lords were frequently away: at war, in Parliament, fighting lawsuits, or just attending on their earl or the king. Earl Roland always appointed a deputy, usually one of his sons—but, in this case, he had not been able to do so. In the absence of an overlord, the bailiff had to manage the landholding as best he could.

The job of a bailiff or reeve was, in theory, to carry out the lord's decisions, but this inevitably gave him a degree of power over his fellows. Exactly how much power depended on the lord's personal preference: some held tight control, others were lax. Sir Stephen had kept a loose rein, but Earl Roland was notoriously strict.

Nate Reeve had been bailiff to Sir Stephen and to Sir Henry before him, and would presumably be bailiff to whoever came next. He was a hunchback, a small, bent figure, thin and energetic. He was shrewd and greedy, careful to make the most of his limited power by demanding bribes from the villagers at every opportunity.

Gwenda disliked Nate. It was not his greed she objected to: all bailiffs had that vice. But Nate was a man twisted by resentment as much as by his physical defect. His father had been bailiff to the earl of Shiring, but Nate had not inherited that grand position, and he blamed his hump for the fact that he had ended up in the small village of Wigleigh. He seemed to hate all young, strong, handsome people. In his leisure hours he liked to drink wine with Perkin, Annet's father—who always paid for the liquor.

The question before the court today was what to do about Wulfric's family's land.

It was a large holding. Peasants were not all equal, and they did not have equal lands. The standard was a virgate, which was thirty acres in this part of England. In theory a virgate was the area of land one man could farm, and normally yielded enough to feed one family. However, most Wigleigh peasants had a half virgate, fifteen acres, or thereabouts. They were obliged to find additional means of support for their families: netting birds in the woods, trapping fish in the stream that ran through Brookfield, making belts or sandals from cheap leather offcuts, weaving cloth from yarn for Kingsbridge merchants, or poaching the king's deer in the forest. A few had more than a virgate. Perkin had a hundred acres, and Wulfric's father, Samuel, had had ninety. Such wealthy peasants needed help to farm their land, either from their sons and other relatives, or from hired laborers such as Gwenda's father.

When a serf died, his land might be inherited by his widow, his sons, or a married daughter. In any event, the handover had to be licensed by the lord, and a stiff tax, called a heriot, was due. In normal circumstances Samuel's land would automatically have been inherited by his two sons, and there would have been no need for a court hearing. They would have clubbed together to pay the heriot, then either divided up the land or farmed it together, and made some arrangement for their mother. But one of Samuel's sons had died with him, which complicated matters.

Every adult in the village attended the court, in general. Gwenda had a particular interest today. Wulfric's future would be decided, and the fact that he planned to spend that future with another woman did not dampen Gwenda's concern. Perhaps she should have wished him a miserable life with Annet, she sometimes thought; but she could not. She wanted him to be happy.

When the service was over, a large wooden chair and two benches were brought in from the manor house. Nate took the chair and the jurymen sat on the benches. Everyone else stood.

Wulfric spoke simply. "My father held ninety acres of the lord of

Wigleigh," he said. "Fifty acres were held by his father before him, and forty by his uncle who died ten years ago. As my mother is dead, and so is my brother, and I have no sisters, I am the sole heir."

"How old are you?" said Nate.

"Sixteen years."

"You can't even call yourself a man yet."

It seemed Nate was going to make things difficult. Gwenda knew why. He wanted a bribe. But Wulfric had no money.

"Years aren't everything," Wulfric said. "I'm taller and stronger than most grown men."

Aaron Appletree, one of the jurors, said: "David Johns inherited from his father when he was eighteen."

Nate said: "Eighteen isn't sixteen. I don't recall an instance where a sixteen-year-old was allowed to inherit."

David Johns was not a juror, and he was standing next to Gwenda. "I didn't have no ninety acres, neither," he said, and there was a ripple of laughter. David had a half virgate, like most of them.

Another juror spoke. "Ninety acres is too much for one man, let alone a boy. Why, it was farmed by three until now." The speaker was Billy Howard, a man in his middle twenties who had wooed Annet unsuccessfully—which might be why he wanted to side with Nate in putting obstacles in Wulfric's way. "I've got forty acres, and I have to hire laborers at harvest time."

Several of the men nodded agreement. Gwenda began to feel pessimistic. It was not going Wulfric's way.

"I can get help," Wulfric said.

Nate said: "Have you got money to pay laborers?"

Wulfric looked a bit desperate, and Gwenda's heart went out to him. "My father's purse was lost when the bridge collapsed, and I spent what money I had on the funeral," he said. "But I can offer my laborers a share of the harvest."

Nate shook his head. "Everyone in the village is already working full-time on their own lands, and those who have no land are already employed. And no one is likely to give up a job that pays cash for one that offers a share of an uncertain crop."

"I will get the harvest in," Wulfric said with passionate determination. "I can work day and night, if I have to. I'll prove to you all that I can handle it."

There was so much yearning on his handsome face that Gwenda wanted to jump up and shout her support for him. But the men were shaking their heads. Everyone knew that one man could not harvest ninety acres on his own.

Nate turned to Perkin. "He's engaged to your daughter. Can't you do something for him?"

Perkin looked thoughtful. "Perhaps you should transfer the land to me, for the time being. I could pay the heriot. Then, when he marries Annet, he could take over his land."

"No!" Wulfric said immediately.

Gwenda knew why he was so against the idea. Perkin was nothing if not sly. He would spend every waking minute between now and the wedding trying to figure out a way of keeping Wulfric's land for himself.

Nate said to Wulfric: "If you have no money, how will you pay the heriot?"

"I'll have money when I get the harvest in."

"If you get the harvest in. And then it may not be enough. Your father paid three pounds for his father's lands and two pounds for his uncle's."

Gwenda gasped. Five pounds was a fortune. It seemed impossible that Wulfric could raise so much money. It would probably have taken all his family's savings.

Nate went on: "Besides, the heriot is normally paid before the inheritor takes possession—not after the harvest."

Aaron Appletree said: "In the circumstances, Nate, you might show leniency on that point."

"Might I? A lord may show leniency, for he holds sway over his own possessions. But if a bailiff shows leniency, he's giving away someone else's gold."

"But we will only be making a recommendation, in any case. Nothing will be final until approved by the new lord of Wigleigh, whoever he may be."

That was true, strictly speaking, Gwenda thought; but in practice it was unlikely a new lord would overturn an inheritance from father to son.

Wulfric said: "Sir, my father's heriot was not so much as five pounds."

"We must check the rolls." Nate's response was so quick that Gwenda guessed he had been waiting for Wulfric to challenge the amount. Nate often engineered a pause of some kind in the middle of a hearing, she reflected. She presumed it was to give the parties an opportunity to offer him a bribe. Perhaps he thought Wulfric was concealing some money.

Two jurors brought from the vestry the chest containing the manorial rolls, the record of the manor court's decisions, written on long strips of parchment rolled into cylinders. Nate could read and write—a bailiff had to be literate, in order to compile accounts for the lord. He searched through the box for the right one.

Gwenda felt that Wulfric was doing badly. His plain speaking and evident honesty were not enough. Nate wanted above all else to make sure he collected the lord's heriot. Perkin was maneuvering to get the land for himself. Billy Howard wanted to do Wulfric down out of sheer malice. And Wulfric had no money for a bribe.

He was also guileless. He believed that if he stated his case he would get justice. He had no sense of managing the situation.

Perhaps she could help him. A child of Joby's could not grow up without learning something about guile.

Wulfric had not appealed to the villagers' self-interest in his arguments. She would do so for him. She turned to David Johns, standing beside her. "I'm surprised you men aren't more worried about this," she said.

He gave her a shrewd look. "What are you getting at, lass?"

"Despite the sudden deaths, this is an inheritance from father to son. If you let Nate quibble about this one, he'll question them all. He can always dream up some reason for arguing about a legacy. Aren't you afraid he'll interfere with your own sons' rights?"

David looked worried. "You might have a point, there, girl," he said, and he turned to talk to his neighbor on the other side.

Gwenda also felt it was a mistake for Wulfric to demand a final ruling today. Better to ask for a temporary judgment, which the jurymen would grant more readily. She went to speak to Wulfric. He was arguing with Perkin and Annet. When Gwenda appeared, Perkin looked suspicious, and Annet put her nose in the air, but Wulfric was as courteous as ever. "Hello, my traveling companion," he said. "I heard you left your father's house."

"He threatened to sell me."

"A second time?"

"As many times as I could escape. He thinks he's found a bottomless purse."

"Where are you living?"

"Widow Huberts took me in. And I've been working for the bailiff, on the lord's lands. A penny a day, sunrise to sunset—Nate likes his laborers to go home tired. Do you think he'll give you what you want?"

Wulfric made a face. "He seems reluctant."

"A woman would handle it so differently."

He looked surprised. "How so?"

Annet glared at her, but Gwenda ignored the look. "A woman would not demand a ruling, especially when everyone knows that today's decision isn't final. She would not risk a no for the chance of a maybe."

Wulfric looked thoughtful. "What would she do?"

"She would just ask to be allowed to continue working the land, for now. She would let the binding decision wait until the new lord is appointed. She would know that in the interim everyone would get used to her being in possession, so that when the new lord showed up his approval would seem like a formality. She would gain her objective without giving people much chance to argue about it."

Wulfric was not sure. "Well . . ."

"It's not what you want, but it's the most you can get today. And how can Nate refuse you, when he has no one else to bring in the harvest?"

Wulfric nodded. He was working out the possibilities. "People would see me reaping the crop, and become accustomed to the idea. After that, it would seem unjust to deny me the inheritance. And I'd be able to pay the heriot, or some of it."

"You'd be a lot closer to your goal than you are now."

"Thank you. You're very wise." He touched her arm, then turned back to Annet. She said something sharp to him in an undertone. Her father looked annoyed.

Gwenda turned away. Don't tell me I'm wise, she thought. Tell me I'm . . . what? Beautiful? Never. The love of your life? That's Annet. A true friend? To hell with that. So what do I want? Why am I desperate to help you?

She had no answer.

She noticed David Johns speaking emphatically to one of the jurors, Aaron Appletree.

Nate flourished the manor roll. "Wulfric's father, Samuel, paid thirty shillings to inherit from his father, and a pound to inherit from his uncle." A shilling was twelve pennies. There was no shilling coin, but everyone talked about shillings just the same. Twenty shillings made a pound. The sum Nate had announced was exactly half what he had originally said.

David Johns spoke up. "A man's lands should go to his son," he said. "We don't want to give our new lord, whoever he may be, the impression that he can pick and choose who shall inherit."

There was a murmur of agreement.

Wulfric stepped forward. "Bailiff, I know you can't make a final decision today, and I'm content to wait until the new lord is appointed. All I ask is that I should be allowed to continue to work the land. I will bring in the harvest, I swear it. But nothing is lost to you if I fail. And nothing is promised to me if I succeed. When the new lord comes, I will throw myself on his mercy."

Nate looked cornered. Gwenda felt sure he had been hoping for some way of making money out of this. Perhaps he had expected a bribe from Perkin, Wulfric's prospective father-in-law. She watched Nate's face as he tried to think of a way to refuse Wulfric's more modest request. As he hesitated, one or two villagers began to mutter, and he realized he was doing himself no good by revealing his reluctance. "Very well," he said with a show of grace that was not very convincing. "What does the jury say?"

Aaron Appletree conferred briefly with his fellow jurors, then said: "Wulfric's request is modest and reasonable. He should occupy the lands of his father until the new lord of Wigleigh is appointed."

Gwenda sighed with relief.

Nate said: "Thank you, jurymen."

The court broke up and people began to head home for dinner. Most of the villagers could afford to eat meat once a week, and Sunday was the usual day they chose. Even Joby and Ethna could generally manage a stew of squirrel or hedgehog, and at this time of year there were plenty of young rabbits to be caught. Widow Huberts had a neck of mutton in a pot on the fire.

Gwenda caught Wulfric's eye as they were leaving the church. "Well done," she said as they strolled out together. "He couldn't refuse you, though he seemed to want to."

"It was your idea," he said admiringly. "You knew exactly what I needed to say. I don't know how to thank you."

She resisted the temptation to tell him. They walked through the graveyard. She said: "How will you manage the harvest?"

"I don't know."

"Why don't you let me come and labor for you?"

"I've no money."

"I don't care, I'll work for food."

He stopped at the gate, turned, and gave her a candid look. "No, Gwenda. I don't think that would be a good plan. Annet wouldn't like it and, to be frank, she'd be right."

Gwenda found herself blushing. There was no doubt what he meant. If he had wanted to reject her because she might be too weak, or something, there would have been no need for the direct look, or for the mention of his fiancée's name. He knew, she realized with mortification, that she was in love with him, and he was refusing her offer of help because he did not want to encourage her hopeless passion. "All right," she whispered, looking down. "Whatever you say."

He smiled warmly. "But thank you for the offer."

She made no reply and, after a moment, he turned and walked away.

19

Gwenda got up while it was still dark.

She slept in the straw on the floor of Widow Huberts's house. Somehow her sleeping mind knew the time, and woke her just before dawn. The widow, lying next to her, did not stir when Gwenda unwrapped her blanket and stood up. Finding her way by touch, she opened the back door and stepped into the yard. Skip followed her, shaking himself.

She stood still for a moment. There was a fresh breeze, as always in Wigleigh. The night was not totally black, and she could make out vague shapes: the duck house, the privy, the pear tree. She could not see the neighboring house, which was Wulfric's; but she heard a low growl from his dog, tethered outside the small sheepfold, and she murmured a quiet phrase so that it would recognize her voice and be reassured.

It was a peaceful time—but nowadays there were too many such moments in her day. All her life she had lived in a tiny house full of babies and children, and at any instant at least one of them was clamoring for food, crying because of a minor hurt, shouting a protest, or screaming with helpless infantile rage. She would never have guessed she might miss that. But she did, living with the quiet widow, who chatted amiably enough but was equally comfortable with silence. Sometimes Gwenda longed to hear a child cry, just so that she could pick it up and comfort it.

She found the old wooden bucket and washed her hands and face, then went back inside. She located the table in the dark, opened the bread box, and cut a thick slice from the week-old loaf. Then she set out, eating the bread as she walked.

The village was silent: she was the first up. Peasants worked from sunup to sundown, and at this time of year it was a long, weary day. They treasured every moment of rest. Only Gwenda also used the hour between dawn and sunrise, and the hour of twilight at the end of the day.

Dawn broke as she left the houses behind and set out across the fields. Wigleigh had three great fields: Hundredacre, Brookfield, and Longfield. Different crops were grown on each in a three-year cycle. Wheat and rye, the most valuable grains, were sown in the first year; then lesser crops such as oats, barley, peas, and beans in the second year; and in the third year the field was left fallow. This year, Hundredacre was in wheat and rye, Brookfield in various secondary crops, and Longfield was fallow. Each field was divided into strips of about one acre; and each serf's land consisted of a number of strips scattered across all three fields.

Gwenda went to Hundredacre and began weeding one of Wulfric's strips, pulling up the persistent new growth of dockweed, marigolds, and dog fennel from between his stalks of wheat. She was happy working on his land, helping him, whether he knew about it or not. Every time she bent down, she was saving his back the same effort; every time she pulled a weed, she made his crop greater. It was like giving him presents. As she worked she thought of him, picturing his face when he laughed, hearing his voice, the deep voice of a man yet with the eagerness of a boy. She touched the green shoots of his wheat and imagined she was stroking his hair.

She weeded until sunrise then moved to the demesne lands—those strips farmed by the lord, or his laborers—and worked for pay. Although Sir Stephen was dead, his crops still had to be reaped, and his successor would demand a strict account of what had been done with the proceeds. At sundown, having earned her daily bread, Gwenda would move to another part of Wulfric's holding and work there until dark—longer, if there was a moon.

She had said nothing to Wulfric. But, in a village of only two hundred people, few things remained secret for long. Widow Huberts had asked her, with gentle curiosity, what she hoped to achieve. "He's going to marry Perkin's girl, you know—you can't prevent that."

"I just want him to succeed," Gwenda had replied. "He deserves it. He's an honest man with a good heart, and he's willing to work until he drops. I want him to be happy, even if he does marry that bitch."

Today the demesne workers were in Brookfield, harvesting the lord's early peas and beans, and Wulfric was nearby, digging a drainage ditch: the land was swampy after the heavy rain of early June. Gwenda watched him working, wearing only his drawers and boots, his broad back bending over the spade. He moved as tirelessly as a millwheel. Only the sweat glistening on his skin betrayed the effort he was making. At midday Annet came to him, looking pretty with a green ribbon in her hair, carrying a jug of ale and some bread and cheese wrapped in a piece of sacking.

Nate Reeve rang a bell, and everyone stopped work and retreated to the fringe of trees at the north end of the field. Nate gave out cider, bread, and onions to the demesne workers: dinner was included in their remuneration. Gwenda sat with her back against a hornbeam tree and studied Wulfric and Annet with the fascination of a condemned man watching the carpenter build the gallows.

At first, Annet was her usual flirtatious self, tilting her head, batting her eyelids, playfully striking Wulfric in mock punishment for something he said. Then she became serious, speaking to him insistently while he seemed to protest innocence. They both looked at Gwenda, and she guessed they were talking about her. She presumed Annet had found out about her working on Wulfric's strips in the mornings and evenings. Eventually Annet left, looking petulant, and Wulfric finished his dinner in thoughtful solitude.

After eating, everyone rested for the remainder of the dinner hour. The older people lay full length on the ground and dozed while the youngsters chatted. Wulfric came to where Gwenda sat and crouched beside her. "You've been weeding my strips," he said.

Gwenda was not going to apologize. "I suppose Annet scolded you."

"She doesn't want you working for me."

"What would she like me to do, put the weeds back in the earth?"

He glanced around and lowered his voice, not wanting others to hear—although everyone could surely guess what he and Gwenda were saying to one another. "I know you mean well, and I'm grateful, but it's causing trouble."

She enjoyed being this close to him. He smelled of earth and sweat. "You need help," she said. "And Annet isn't much use."

"Please don't criticize her. In fact, don't speak of her at all."

"All right, but you can't get the harvest in alone."

He sighed. "If only the sun would shine." Automatically, he looked up at the sky, a peasant reflex. There was thick cloud from horizon to horizon. All the grain crops were struggling in the cool, damp weather.

"Let me work for you," Gwenda begged. "Tell Annet you need me. A man is supposed to be master of his wife, not the other way around."

"I'll think about it," he said.

But the next day he hired a laborer.

He was a traveling man who showed up at the end of the afternoon. The villagers gathered around him in the twilight to hear his story. His name was Gram and he came from Salisbury. He said his wife and children had been killed when his house burned down. He was on his way to

Kingsbridge, where he hoped to get employment, perhaps at the priory. His brother was a monk there.

Gwenda said: "I probably know him. My brother, Philemon, has worked at the priory for years. What's your brother's name?"

"John." There were two monks called John but, before Gwenda could ask which was Gram's brother, he went on: "When I started out, I had a little money to buy food along the way. Then I was robbed by outlaws, and now I'm penniless."

There was a lot of sympathy for the man. Wulfric invited him to sleep at his house. The next day, Saturday, he started to work for Wulfric, accepting board and lodging and a share of the harvest as his remuneration.

Gram worked hard all day Saturday. Wulfric was shallow-plowing his fallow land in Longfield to destroy thistles. It was a two-man job: Gram led the horse, whipping it on when it flagged, while Wulfric guided the plow. On Sunday they rested.

In church on Sunday, Gwenda burst into tears when she saw Cath, Joanie, and Eric. She had not realized how badly she missed them. She held Eric through the service. Afterward, her mother spoke harshly to her. "You're breaking your heart for that Wulfric. Weeding his strips won't make him love you. He's cross-eyed for that worthless Annet."

"I know," Gwenda said. "But I want to help him anyway."

"You should leave the village. There's nothing for you here."

She knew her mother was right. "I will," she said. "I'll leave the day after their wedding."

Ma lowered her voice. "If you must stay, watch out for your father. He hasn't given up hope of another twelve shillings."

"What do you mean?" Gwenda asked.

Ma just shook her head.

"He can't sell me now," Gwenda said. "I've left his house. He doesn't feed or shelter me. I work for the lord of Wigleigh. I'm not Pa's to dispose of any longer."

"Just watch out," said Ma, and she would say no more.

Outside the church the traveling man, Gram, talked to Gwenda, asking her questions about herself, and suggested they take a stroll together after dinner. She guessed what he meant by a "stroll" and turned him down flat, but later she saw him with yellow-haired Joanna, the daughter of David Johns, who was only fifteen and stupid enough to fall for the blandishments of a traveling man.

On Monday, Gwenda was weeding Wulfric's wheat on Hundredacre in the half light before sunrise when Wulfric came across the field toward her at a run. His face was grim with fury.

She had continued to defy his wishes, working on his lands every morning and evening, and it looked as if she had driven him too far. What would he do—beat her up? After the way she had provoked him, he could probably do violence to her with impunity—people would say she had asked for it, and she had no one to stick up for her now that she had left her parents' home. She felt scared. She had seen Wulfric break Ralph Fitzgerald's nose.

Then she told herself not to be foolish. Although he had been in many fights, she had never known him to strike a woman or a child. All the same, his anger made her tremble.

But it was nothing like that. As soon as he got within hailing distance, he shouted: "Have you seen Gram?"

"No, why?"

He came closer and stopped, breathing hard. "How long have you been here?"

"I got up before dawn."

Wulfric's shoulders slumped. "Then, if he came this way, he's out of reach by now."

"What's happened?"

"He's disappeared—and so has my horse."

That explained Wulfric's rage. A horse was a valuable asset—only wealthy peasants such as his father could afford one. Gwenda recalled how quickly Gram had changed the subject when she said she might know his brother. He did not have a brother at the priory, of course, nor had he lost his wife and child in a fire. He was a liar who had wormed his way into the confidence of the villagers with the intention of stealing. "What fools we were to listen to his story," she said.

"And I the biggest fool of all, to take him into my house," Wulfric said bitterly. "He stayed just long enough for the animals to get to know him, so that the horse was willing to go with him, and the dog didn't bark when he left."

Gwenda's heart ached for Wulfric, losing the horse at a time when he needed it most. "I don't think he came this way," she said thoughtfully. "He can't have left before me—the night was too dark. And if he had followed me, I would have seen him." There was only one road into and out of the village, and it dead-ended at the manor house. But there were numerous pathways across the fields. "He probably took the lane between Brookfield and Longfield—it's the quickest way into the forest."

"The horse can't move very fast in the woods. I might catch him yet." Wulfric turned and ran back the way he had come.

"Good luck," Gwenda called after him, and he waved acknowledgment without turning his head.

However, he did not have good luck.

Late that afternoon, as Gwenda was carrying a sack of peas from Brookfield to the lord's barn, she walked past Longfield and saw Wulfric again. He was digging over his fallow land with a spade. Obviously he had not caught up with Gram, or retrieved his horse.

She put down the sack and crossed the field to speak to him. "You can't do this," she said. "You've got thirty acres here, and you've plowed, what, ten? No man can dig over twenty acres."

He did not meet her eye. He carried on digging, his face set. "I can't plow," he said. "I've no horse."

"Put yourself in harness," she said. "You're strong, and it's a light plow—you're only killing thistles."

"I've no one to guide the plow."

"Yes, you have."

He stared at her.

"I'll do it," she said.

He shook his head.

She said: "You've lost your family, and now you've lost your horse. You can't manage on your own. You have no choice. You have to let me help you."

He looked away, across the fields, toward the village, and she knew he was thinking about Annet.

"I'll be ready first thing tomorrow morning," Gwenda said.

His gaze returned to her. His face worked with emotion. He was torn between love of the land and a desire to please Annet.

"I'll knock on your door," Gwenda said. "We'll plow the rest together." She turned and walked away, then stopped and looked back.

He did not say yes.

But he did not say no.

⁂

They plowed for two days, then made hay, then picked spring vegetables.

Now that Gwenda was no longer earning money to pay Widow Huberts for bed and board, she needed somewhere else to sleep, so she moved into Wulfric's cowshed. She explained the reason, and he made no objection.

After the first day, Annet ceased to bring Wulfric's dinner at midday, so Gwenda would prepare food for them both from his cupboard: bread, ale in a jug, boiled eggs or cold bacon, and spring onions or beets. Once again, Wulfric accepted the change without comment.

She still had the love potion. The little pottery vial was in a tiny leather bag attached to a thong around her neck. It hung between her breasts, hidden from view. She could have dosed his ale at any dinnertime, but she would not be able to take advantage of its effects out in the fields in the middle of the day.

Every evening he went to Perkin's house and had supper with Annet and her family, so Gwenda sat alone in his kitchen. When he returned he often looked grim, but he said nothing to Gwenda, so she assumed he must have overruled Annet's objections. He went to bed without taking anything more to eat or drink, so she was not able to use the potion.

On the Saturday after Gram ran off, Gwenda made herself a supper of greens boiled with salt pork. Wulfric's house was stocked with food for four adults, so there was plenty to eat. The evenings were cool, even though it was now July, and after she had eaten she put another log on the kitchen fire and sat watching it catch alight, thinking of the simple, predictable life she had led until a few short weeks ago, marveling at how that life had collapsed as completely as the bridge at Kingsbridge.

When the door opened, she thought it was Wulfric coming home. She always retired to the cowshed when he came back, but she enjoyed the few friendly words they exchanged before going to bed. She looked up eagerly, expecting to see his handsome face; but she suffered an unpleasant shock.

It was not Wulfric, but her father.

With him was a rough looking stranger.

She leaped to her feet, full of fear. "What do you want?"

Skip gave a hostile bark, but retreated from Joby in fear.

Joby said: "Now, then, my little girl, no need to be afraid, I'm your pa."

She recalled, with dismay, her mother's vague warning in church. "Who is he?" she said, pointing at the stranger.

"This here is Jonah from Abingdon, a dealer in hides."

Jonah might once have been a merchant, Gwenda thought grimly, and he might even come from Abingdon, but his boots were worn, his clothes were filthy, and his matted hair and straggly beard showed that he had not visited a city barber for some years.

Showing more courage than she felt, Gwenda said: "Get away from me."

"I told you she was feisty," Joby said to Jonah. "But she's a good girl, and strong."

Jonah spoke for the first time. "Not to worry," he said. He licked his lips as he studied Gwenda, and she wished she were wearing more than her light wool dress. "I've broken in a few fillies in my time," he added.

Gwenda had no doubt that her father had carried out his threat and sold her again. She had thought that leaving his house would make her safe. Surely the villagers would not permit the abduction of a laborer employed by one of their number? But it was dark now, and she might be far away before anyone realized what had happened.

There was no one to help her.

All the same, she was not going without a fight.

She looked around desperately, searching for a weapon. The log she had put on a few minutes ago was blazing at one end, but it was about eighteen inches long, and the other end stuck out invitingly. She bent quickly and snatched it up.

"Now, then, no need for that sort of thing," said Joby. "You don't want to hurt your old pa, do you?" He stepped closer.

A rush of rage overwhelmed her. How dare he speak of himself as her old pa when he was trying to sell her? Suddenly she did want to hurt him. She leaped at him, screaming with rage, thrusting the burning log at his face.

He jumped back, but she kept coming, mad with fury. Skip yapped frantically. Joby lifted his arms to protect himself, trying to knock the brand away, but she was strong, too. His flailing arms failed to stop her rush, and she pushed the red-hot end of the log into his face. He screamed in pain as it scorched his cheek. His dirty beard caught fire, and there was a sickening smell of roasting flesh.

Then Gwenda was grabbed from behind. Jonah's arms encircled her, pinning her own arms to her side. She dropped the burning log. Flames leaped up immediately from the straw on the floor. Skip, terrified of fire, ran out of the house. Gwenda struggled, wriggling in Jonah's grasp, throwing herself from side to side, but he was surprisingly strong. He lifted her off her feet.

A tall figure appeared in the doorway. Gwenda saw only the shape, then it disappeared again. Gwenda felt herself thrown to the ground. For a moment she was stunned. When she came to her senses, Jonah was kneeling on her, tying her hands with a rope.

The tall figure reappeared, and Gwenda recognized Wulfric. This time he was carrying a big oak bucket. Swiftly, he emptied the bucket onto the burning straw, putting out the flames. Then he changed his grip, swung the bucket, and hit the kneeling Jonah a mighty blow on top of the head.

Jonah's grip on Gwenda relaxed. She pulled her wrists apart and felt the rope loosen. Wulfric swung the bucket and hit Jonah a second time, even harder. Jonah's eyes closed and he slumped to the floor.

Joby put out the flames of his burning beard by pressing his sleeve against it, then sank to his knees, moaning in agony.

Wulfric picked up the unconscious Jonah by his tunic front. "Who on earth is this?"

"His name is Jonah. My father wanted to sell me to him."

Wulfric lifted the man by the belt, carried him to the front door, and threw him out into the road.

Joby groaned. "Help me, my face is burned."

"Help you?" said Wulfric. "You've set fire to my house and attacked my laborer, and you want me to help you? Get out!"

Joby got to his feet, moaning piteously, and staggered to the front door. Gwenda searched her heart and found no compassion. What little love she might have had left for him had been destroyed tonight. As he went out through the door, she hoped he would never speak to her again.

Perkin came to the back door, carrying a rush light. "What happened?" he said. "I thought I heard a scream." Gwenda saw Annet hovering behind him.

Wulfric answered the question. "Joby came here with another ruffian. They tried to take Gwenda away."

Perkin grunted. "You seem to have dealt with the problem."

"Without difficulty." Wulfric realized he still had the bucket in his hand, and he put it down.

Annet said: "Are you hurt?"

"Not in the least."

"Do you need anything?"

"I just want to go to sleep."

Perkin and Annet took the hint and went away. No one else seemed to have heard the commotion. Wulfric closed the doors.

He looked at Gwenda in the firelight. "How do you feel?"

"Shaky." She sat on the bench and leaned her elbows on the kitchen table.

He went to the cupboard. "Drink a little wine to steady yourself." He took out a small barrel, put it on the table, and got two cups off the shelf.

Gwenda was suddenly alert. Could this be her chance? She tried to pull herself together. She would have to act quickly.

Wulfric poured wine into the cups, then returned the barrel to the cupboard.

Gwenda had only a second or two. While his back was turned, she reached into her bosom and pulled out the bag that hung around her neck on its leather thong. She fumbled the vial from the bag. With a trembling hand she unstoppered it and emptied it into his cup.

He turned around as she was pushing the bag back into her neckline. She patted herself as if she had merely been straightening her clothing. Typical man, he noticed nothing amiss, and sat opposite her at the table.

She picked up her cup and raised it in a toast. "You saved me," she said. "Thank you."

"Your hand is shaking," he said. "You've had a nasty shock."

They both drank.

Gwenda wondered how long the potion would take to have its effect.

Wulfric said: "You saved me, by helping me in the fields. Thank you."

They drank again.

"I don't know what's worse," Gwenda said. "To have a father like mine, or to be like you and have no father at all."

"I feel sorry for you," Wulfric said thoughtfully. "At least I have good memories of my parents." He emptied his cup. "I don't usually drink wine—I don't like that woozy feeling—but this is great."

She watched him carefully. Mattie Wise had said that he would become amorous. Gwenda looked for the signs. Sure enough, he soon began to stare as if seeing her for the first time. After a while he said: "You know, you've got such a nice face. There's a lot of kindness in it."

Now she was supposed to use her feminine wiles to seduce him. But, she realized with a panicky feeling, she had had no practice at this. Women such as Annet did it all the time. However, when she thought of the things Annet did—smilingly coyly, touching her hair, fluttering her eyelashes—she could not bring herself even to try. She would just feel stupid.

"You're kind," she said, talking to gain time. "But your face shows something else."

"What?"

"Strength. The kind that comes, not from big muscles, but from determination."

"I feel strong tonight." He grinned. "You said no man could dig over twenty acres—but I feel as if I could, right now."

She put her hand over his on the table. "Enjoy your rest," she said. "There's plenty of time for digging."

He looked at her small hand on his large one. "We've got different color skin," he said, as if discovering an amazing fact. "Look: yours is brown, mine's pink."

"Different skin, different hair, different eyes. I wonder what our babies would be like?"

He smiled at the thought. Then his expression changed as he realized something was wrong with what she had said. Abruptly, his face became grave. The change might have been comical if she had not cared so much about his feelings for her. He said solemnly: "We're not going to have babies." He took his hand away.

"Let's not think about that," she said desperately.

"Don't you sometimes wish . . ." He tailed off.

"What?"

"Don't you sometimes wish the world could be different from the way it is?"

She got up, walked around the table, and sat close to him. "Don't wish," she said. "We're alone, and it's night. You can do anything you want." She looked directly into his eyes. "Anything."

He stared back at her. She saw the yearning in his face, and realized with a thrill of triumph that he desired her. It had required a potion to bring it out, but it was unmistakably genuine. Right now he wanted nothing in the world other than to make love to her.

Still he made no move.

She took his hand. He did not resist as she drew it to her lips. She held the big, rough fingers, then pressed the palm to her mouth. She kissed it, then licked it with the tip of her tongue. Then she pressed his hand to one breast.

His hand closed over it, making it seem very small. His mouth opened a fraction, and she could see that he was breathing hard. She tilted her head back, ready to be kissed, but he did nothing.

She stood up and quickly pulled her dress up over her head and threw it to the floor. She stood naked in front of him in the firelight. He gazed at her, eyes wide, mouth open, as if he were witnessing a miracle.

She took his hand again. This time, she touched it to the soft place between her thighs. It covered the triangle of hair there. She was so wet that his finger slipped inside her, and she gave an involuntary groan of pleasure.

But he did nothing of his own volition, and she understood that he was paralyzed by indecision. He wanted her, but he had not forgotten Annet. Gwenda could move him like a puppet all night, perhaps even have sex with his inert body, but that would change nothing. She needed him to take the initiative.

She leaned forward, still holding his hand against her groin. "Kiss me," she said. She moved her face closer to his. "Please," she said. She was an inch away from his mouth. She would not get nearer: he had to close the gap.

Suddenly, he moved.

He withdrew his hand, turned away from her, and stood up. "This is wrong," he said.

And she knew that she had lost.

Tears came to her eyes. She picked up her dress from the floor and held it in front of her, covering her nakedness.

"I'm sorry," he said. "I shouldn't have done any of those things. I misled you. I've been cruel."

No, you haven't, she thought. I've been cruel. I've misled you. But you were too strong. You're too loyal, too faithful. You're too good for me.

But she said nothing.

He kept his gaze steadfastly away from her. "You must go to the cowshed," he said. "Go to sleep. We'll feel differently in the morning. It might be all right then."

She ran out through the back door, not bothering to get dressed. It was moonlight, but there was no one to see her, and she would not have cared anyway. She was inside the cowshed in seconds.

At one end of the wooden building was a raised loft where clean straw was kept. That was where she made her bed each night. She climbed the ladder and threw herself down, too miserable to care about the sharp prickle of straw on her bare skin. She wept with disappointment and shame.

When eventually she calmed down, she stood up and put her dress on, then wrapped a blanket around her. As she did so, she thought she heard a step outside. She looked through a gap in the rough wattle-and-daub of the wall.

The moon was almost full, and she could see clearly. Wulfric was outside. He walked toward the door of the cowshed. Gwenda's heart leaped. Perhaps it was not all over yet. But he hesitated at the door, then walked away. He returned to the house, turned at the kitchen door, came back to the cowshed, and turned again.

She watched him pace up and down, her heart thudding, but she did not move. She had done all she could to encourage him. He had to take the last step himself.

He stopped at the kitchen door. His body was profiled by the moonlight, a silver line running from his forelock to his boots. She saw clearly as he reached into his drawers. She knew what he was going to do: she had seen her older brother do the same thing. She heard Wulfric groan as he began to rub himself with the motion that caricatured lovemaking. She stared at him, beautiful in the moonlight, wasting his desire, and she felt as if her heart would break.

20

Godwyn moved against Blind Carlus on the Sunday before the birthday of St. Adolphus.

On that Sunday every year, a special service was held in Kingsbridge Cathedral. The bones of the saint were carried around the church by the prior, followed by the monks in procession; and they prayed for good harvest weather.

As always, it was Godwyn's job to prepare the church for the service—placing candles, getting incense ready, and moving furniture—helped by novices and employees such as Philemon. The Feast of St. Adolphus required a secondary altar, an elaborately carved wooden table set on a platform that could be moved about the church as required. Godwyn placed this altar on the eastern edge of the crossing and put on it a pair of silver-gilt candlesticks. As he did so, he anxiously mulled over his position.

Now that he had persuaded Thomas to stand for election as prior, his next step was to eliminate the opposition. Carlus ought to be an easy target—but in a way, that was a disadvantage, for Godwyn did not want to appear callous.

He placed in the center of the altar a reliquary cross, a bejeweled gold crucifix with a core of wood from the True Cross. This, the actual timber upon which Christ was killed, had been miraculously found a thousand years ago by Helena, the mother of Constantine the Great, and pieces of it had found their way to churches all over Europe.

As Godwyn was arranging the ornaments on the altar, he saw Mother Cecilia nearby and broke off from his work to speak to her. "I understand that Earl Roland has recovered his mind," he said. "Praise God."

"Amen," she said. "The fever was on him so long that we feared for his life. Some evil humor must have entered his brain after his skull was fractured. Nothing he said made sense. Then, this morning, he woke up and spoke normally."

"You cured him."

"God cured him."

"Still, he should be grateful to you."

She smiled. "You're young, Brother Godwyn. You'll learn that men of power never show gratitude. Whatever we give them, they accept as their right."

Her condescension annoyed Godwyn, but he concealed his irritation. "At any rate, we can now hold the election for prior, at last."

"Who will win?"

"Ten monks have promised firmly to vote for Carlus, and only seven for Thomas. With the candidates' own votes, that makes the score eleven to eight, with six uncommitted."

"So it could go either way."

"But Carlus is in the lead. Thomas could do with your support, Mother Cecilia."

"I don't have a vote."

"But you have influence. If you were to say that the monastery needs stricter control and a measure of reform, and you felt Thomas was more likely to deliver such a program, it would sway some of the waverers."

"I ought not to take sides."

"Perhaps not, but you could say that you will not continue to subsidize the monks unless they manage their money better. What could be wrong with that?"

Her bright eyes glittered with amusement: she was not so easily persuaded. "That would be a coded message of support for Thomas."

"Yes."

"I am strictly neutral. I will happily work with whomever the monks choose. And that's my last word, Brother."

He bowed his head deferentially. "I respect your decision, of course."

She nodded and moved away.

Godwyn was pleased. He had never expected her to endorse Thomas. She was conservative. Everyone assumed she favored Carlus. But Godwyn could now spread the word that she would be content with either candidate. In effect, he had undermined her implicit support for Carlus. She might even be cross when she heard what use he was making of her words, but she would not withdraw her statement of neutrality.

I am so clever, he thought; I really deserve to be prior.

Neutralizing Cecilia was helpful, but it would not be enough to crush Carlus. Godwyn needed to give the monks a vivid demonstration of how incompetent Carlus was to lead them. He was hoping anxiously for such an opportunity today.

Carlus and Simeon were in the church now, rehearsing the service. Carlus was the acting prior, so he had to lead the procession, carrying the ivory-and-gold reliquary that contained the bones of the saint. Simeon, the treasurer and Carlus's crony, was walking him through it, and Godwyn could see Carlus counting his paces, so that he would be able to do it on his own. The congregation was impressed when Carlus moved around confidently despite his blindness: it seemed like a minor miracle.

The procession always began at the east end of the church, where the relics were stored under the high altar. The prior would unlock the cupboard and remove the reliquary. He would carry it along the north aisle of the chancel, around the north transept, down the north aisle of the nave, across the west end, and back up the center of the nave and into the crossing. There he would climb two steps to place it on the second altar that Godwyn had put in position ready. The holy relics would remain there, for the congregation to stare at, throughout the service.

Looking around the church, Godwyn's eye fell on the repairs in the south aisle of the chancel, and he stepped closer to see how they were coming along. Merthin was no longer involved, having been sacked by Elfric, but his startlingly simple method was still being operated. Instead of expensive wooden formwork supporting the new masonry while the mortar set, each stone was held in place by a simple rope, draped over the long edge of the stone and weighted with a rock. The system could not be used to build the ribs of the vault, which were composed of long, slender stones laid end to end, so formwork had to be made for those elements; but, all the same, Merthin had saved the priory a small fortune in carpentry.

Godwyn recognized Merthin's genius, but still felt uneasy with him, and preferred to work with Elfric. Elfric could be trusted always to be a willing tool, never to make trouble; whereas Merthin was all too likely to walk his own road.

Carlus and Simeon left. The church was ready for the service. Godwyn sent away the men who had been helping him, all but Philemon, who was sweeping the floor of the crossing.

For a moment, the great cathedral was empty but for the two of them.

This was Godwyn's chance. The plan he had half-formulated now appeared complete in his mind. He hesitated, for it was dreadfully risky. But he decided to gamble.

He beckoned to Philemon. "Now," he said. "Quickly—move the platform forward a yard."

Much of the time, the cathedral was no more than a place of work to Godwyn. It was a space to be used, a building to be repaired, a source of income and at the same time a financial burden. But, on an occasion such as this, its majesty was renewed. The candle flames flickered, their reflections glinting on the gold of the candlesticks; the robed monks and nuns glided between the ancient stone pillars; and the voices of the choir soared to the high vault. No wonder the crowd of hundreds of townspeople was hushed as they stood watching.

Carlus led the procession. As the monks and nuns sang, he opened the compartment under the high altar—working by touch—and took out the ivory-and-gold reliquary. Holding it high, he began to process around the church. He was the picture of a holy innocent, with his white beard and unseeing eyes.

Would he fall into Godwyn's trap? It was so simple—it seemed too easy. Godwyn, following a few paces behind Carlus, bit his lip and tried to remain calm.

The congregation was awestruck. Godwyn never failed to marvel at how willing they were to be manipulated. They could not see the bones and, if they had, they could not have distinguished them from any other human remains. But, because of the costly extravagance of the box, the eerie beauty of the singing, the uniform robes of the monks and nuns, and the towering architecture that dwarfed them all, they felt the presence of something holy.

Godwyn watched Carlus carefully. As he reached the precise midpoint of the westernmost bay of the north aisle, he turned sharply left. Simeon stood ready to correct him if he misjudged, but it was not necessary. Good: the more confident Carlus was, the more likely he was to stumble at the crucial moment.

Counting his paces, Carlus marched to the exact center of the nave then turned again, heading straight for the altar. On cue, the singing stopped, and the procession carried on in a reverent hush.

It must be a bit like finding your way to the latrine in the middle of the night, Godwyn thought. Carlus had followed this route several times a year for most of his life. He was now doing it as leader of the procession, which must make him tense; but he appeared calm, only the slight movement of his lips betraying the fact that he was counting. But Godwyn had ensured that his count would be wrong. Would he make a fool of himself? Or would he somehow recover?

The congregation fell back fearfully as the sacred bones went by. Touching the casket could work miracles, they knew, but they also believed that any disrespect shown to the relics would have disastrous consequences. The spirits of the dead were ever present, watching over their remains while they waited for the day of judgment; and those who had led holy lives enjoyed almost unlimited powers to reward or punish the living.

The thought crossed Godwyn's mind that St. Adolphus might be displeased with him for what was about to happen in Kingsbridge Cathedral. He shivered with momentary terror. Then he reassured himself that he was acting for the good of the priory that housed the sacred bones, and that the all-wise saint, who could see into men's hearts, would understand that this was for the best.

Carlus slowed as he approached the altar, but his paces were the same measured length. Godwyn stopped breathing. Carlus seemed to hesitate as he took the step that should, by his own calculations, bring him just short of the platform on which the altar stood. Godwyn watched helplessly, dreading some last-moment change of routine.

Then, confidently, Carlus walked on.

His foot struck the edge of the platform a yard sooner than expected. In the silence, the sound of his sandal on the hollow wood resounded loudly. He let out a cry of shock and fear. His momentum carried him forward.

Godwyn's heart was lifted by a surge of triumph—but it lasted only an instant, then disaster struck.

Simeon reached out to grab Carlus's arm, but he was too late. The casket flew from Carlus's hands. The congregation gave a collective gasp of horror. The precious box hit the stone floor and burst open, scattering the bones of the saint. Carlus crashed into the heavy carved-wood altar, pushing it back off the platform, sending its ornaments and candles tumbling to the floor.

Godwyn was horrified. This was much worse than he had intended.

The skull of the saint rolled across the floor and came to rest at Godwyn's feet.

His plan had worked—but too well. He had wanted Carlus to fall, and appear helpless, but he had not intended the holy remains to be desecrated. He stared, horrified, at the skull on the ground, and its empty eyes seemed to look back at him accusingly. What dreadful punishment would befall him?

Could he ever make restitution for such a crime?

Because he had been expecting an incident, he was slightly less shocked than everyone else, and he regained his composure first. Standing over the bones, he raised both arms in the air and shouted over the hubbub: "Everyone—on your knees! We must pray!"

Those at the front knelt down, and the rest quickly followed suit.

Godwyn began a familiar prayer, and the monks and nuns joined in. As the chanting filled the church, he righted the reliquary, which seemed undamaged. Then, moving with theatrical slowness, he picked up the skull in both hands. He was shaking with superstitious dread, but he managed to hold it. Speaking the Latin words of the prayer, he carried the skull to the casket and placed it inside.

He saw that Carlus was struggling to his feet. He pointed at two nuns. "Help the subprior to the hospital," he said. "Brother Simeon, Mother Cecilia, will you go with him?"

He picked up another bone. He was frightened, knowing that he more than Carlus was to blame for what had happened; but his intentions had been pure, and he still hoped to mollify the saint. At the same time, he was aware that his actions must look good in the eyes of everyone present: he was taking charge in a crisis, like a true leader.

However, this moment of awe and horror could not be allowed to last too long. He needed to gather up the bones more quickly. "Brother Thomas," he said. "Brother Theodoric. Come and help me." Philemon stepped forward, but Godwyn waved him back: he was not a monk, and only men of God should touch the bones.

Carlus limped out of the church, helped by Simeon and Cecilia, leaving Godwyn the undisputed master of the occasion.

Godwyn beckoned Philemon and another employee, Otho, and told them to right the altar. They set it straight on the platform. Otho picked up the candlesticks and Philemon the jeweled crucifix. They placed them reverently on the altar then retrieved the scattered candles.

All the bones were picked up. Godwyn tried to close the lid of the reliquary, but it had buckled and did not quite fit. Making the best of it, he ceremoniously placed the casket on the altar.

Godwyn remembered, just in time, that he was seeking to show Thomas, not himself, in the light of leader of the priory—for the present. He picked up the book Simeon had been carrying and handed it to Thomas. Thomas did not need to be told what to do. He opened the book, found the correct page, and read the verse. The monks and nuns formed lines either side of the altar, then Thomas led them in singing the psalm.

Somehow, they got through the service.

ᔕ

Godwyn began to tremble again as soon as he got out of the church. It had been a near-disaster, but he seemed to have got away with it.

The monks burst into excited chatter as the procession reached the cloisters and broke up. Godwyn leaned against a pillar, struggling to regain his composure. He listened to the comments of the monks. Some felt the desecration of the relics was a sign that God did not want Carlus to be prior—the reaction Godwyn had intended. But, to his dismay, most expressed compassion for Carlus. That was not what Godwyn wanted. He realized he might have given Carlus the benefit of a sympathetic backlash.

He pulled himself together and hurried to the hospital. He needed to get to Carlus while the man was still demoralized, and before he got wind of the monks' understanding.

The subprior was sitting up in bed with one arm in a sling and a bandage around his head. He was pale and looked shaken, and every few moments his face would twitch nervously. Simeon was sitting beside him.

Simeon gave Godwyn a filthy look. "I suppose you're pleased," he said.

Godwyn ignored him. "Brother Carlus, you'll be glad to know that the relics of the saint have been restored to their usual place with hymns and prayers. The saint will surely forgive us all for this tragic accident."

Carlus shook his head. "There are no accidents," he said. "Everything is ordained by God."

Godwyn's hopes lifted. This was promising.

Simeon's thoughts followed the same lines, and he tried to restrain Carlus. "Don't say anything hasty, Brother."

"It's a sign," Carlus said. "God is telling us he does not want me to be prior."

This was what Godwyn had been hoping for.

Simeon said: "Nonsense." He picked up a cup from a table beside the bed. Godwyn guessed it contained warm wine and honey, Mother Cecilia's prescription for most ills. Simeon put the cup into Carlus's hand. "Drink."

Carlus drank, but he was not to be diverted from his theme. "It would be a sin to ignore such a portent."

"Portents are not so easily interpreted," Simeon protested.

"Perhaps not. But even if you're right, will the brothers vote for a prior who can't carry the relics of the saint without falling over?"

Godwyn said: "Some of them might, in fact, be drawn to you in commiseration, rather than repelled."

Simeon shot him a puzzled look, wondering what he was up to.

Simeon was right to be suspicious. Godwyn was playing devil's advocate because he wanted more than vague expressions of doubt from Carlus. Could he possibly extract a definitive withdrawal?

As he hoped, Carlus argued with him. "A man should be made prior because the brothers respect him and believe he can lead them wisely—not out of pity." He spoke with the bitter conviction of a lifetime of disability.

"I suppose that's true," Godwyn said with feigned reluctance, as if the admission had been wrung from him against his will. Taking a risk, he added: "But perhaps Simeon is right, and you should postpone any final decision until you feel more yourself."

"I'm as well as I'm ever going to be," Carlus retorted, refusing to admit to weakness in front of young Godwyn. "Nothing is going to change. I'll feel tomorrow the way I feel today. I will not stand for election as prior."

Those were the words Godwyn had been waiting for. He stood up abruptly and bowed his head as if in acknowledgment, hiding his face for fear he might reveal his sense of triumph. "You are as clear as always, Brother Carlus," he said. "I will convey your wishes to the rest of the monks."

Simeon opened his mouth to protest, but he was forestalled by Mother Cecilia, coming into the room from the stairwell. She looked flustered. "Earl Roland is demanding to see the subprior," she said. "He's threatening to get out of bed, but he must not move, for his skull may not yet be fully healed. But Brother Carlus should not move either."

Godwyn looked at Simeon. "We'll go," he said.

They went together up the stairs.

Godwyn was feeling good. Carlus did not even know that he had been routed. Of his own accord, he had withdrawn himself from the contest, leaving only Thomas. And Godwyn could eliminate Thomas anytime he liked.

The plan had been astonishingly successful—so far.

Earl Roland was lying on his back, and his head was thickly bandaged, but all the same he managed to look like a man in power. The barber must have visited him, for his face was shaved and his black hair—as much of it as was not covered by the bandage—had been neatly trimmed. He wore a short purple tunic and new hose, the two legs fashionably dyed different colors, one red and one yellow. Despite lying in bed, he wore a belt with a dagger and short leather boots. His elder son, William, and William's wife, Philippa, stood by the bed. His young secretary, Father Jerome, in priestly robes, sat at a nearby writing desk with pens and sealing wax ready.

The message was clear: the earl was back in charge.

"Is the subprior there?" he said in a clear, strong voice.

Godwyn was quicker-thinking than Simeon, and he replied first. "Subprior Carlus has suffered a fall and is himself lying here in this hospital,

Lord," he said. "I am the sacrist, Godwyn, and with me is the treasurer, Simeon. We thank God for your miraculous recovery, for He guided the hands of the physician-monks who have been attending you."

"It was the barber who mended my broken head," said Roland. "Thank him."

Because the earl was lying on his back, looking up at the ceiling, Godwyn could not see his face well; but he had the impression that the earl's expression was curiously blank, and he wondered whether the injury had done some permanent damage. He said: "Do you have everything you need to make you comfortable?"

"If I don't, you'll soon know. Now, listen. My niece, Margery, is to marry Monmouth's younger son, Roger. I presume you know this."

"Yes." Godwyn had a sudden flash of memory: Margery lying on her back in this very room, her white legs in the air, fornicating with her cousin Richard, the bishop of Kingsbridge.

"The wedding has been unduly delayed by my injuries."

That was not true, Godwyn reflected. The collapse of the bridge had taken place only a month ago. The truth was probably that the earl needed to prove that the injury had not diminished him, and he was still a power worthy of an alliance with the earl of Monmouth.

Roland went on: "The wedding will take place in Kingsbridge Cathedral three weeks from today."

Strictly speaking the earl should have made a request, not issued a command, and an elected prior might have bristled at his high-handedness; but, of course, there was no prior. Anyway, Godwyn could think of no reason why Roland should not have his wish. "Very well, my lord," he said. "I will make the necessary preparations."

"I want the new prior installed in time for the service," Roland went on.

Simeon grunted in surprise.

Godwyn quickly calculated that haste would suit his plans remarkably well. "Very good," he replied. "There were two candidates, but today Subprior Carlus withdrew his name, leaving only Brother Thomas, the matricularius. We can hold the election as soon as you like." He could hardly believe his luck.

Simeon knew he was looking defeat in the face. "Wait a minute," he said.

But Roland was not listening. "I don't want Thomas," he said.

Godwyn had not been expecting that.

Simeon grinned, pleased at this last-minute reprieve.

Shocked, Godwyn said: "But, my lord—"

Roland did not permit him to interrupt. "Summon my nephew, Saul Whitehead, from St.-John-in-the-Forest," he said.

Godwyn's heart filled with foreboding. Saul was his contemporary. As novices, they had been friends. They had gone to Oxford together—but there they had grown apart, Saul becoming more devout and Godwyn more worldly. Saul was now the competent prior of the remote cell of St. John. He took very seriously the monastic virtue of humility, and he would never have put forward his own name. But he was bright, devout, and liked by everyone.

"Get him here as soon as possible," said Roland. "I shall nominate him as the next prior of Kingsbridge."

21

Merthin sat on the roof of St. Mark's Church, at the north end of Kingsbridge. From here he could see the whole town. To the southeast, a bend in the river cradled the priory in the crook of its elbow. A quarter of the town was taken up by the priory buildings and the grounds around them—cemetery, marketplace, orchard, and vegetable garden—with the cathedral rising from its surroundings like an oak in a field of nettles. He could see priory employees picking vegetables in the garden, mucking out a stable, and unloading barrels from a cart.

The center of town was the wealthy neighborhood, especially the main street, climbing the slope from the river as the first monks must have climbed it hundreds of years ago. Several wealthy merchants, identifiable by the glowing colors of their fine wool coats, walked purposefully along the street: merchants were always busy. Another wide thoroughfare, the high street, ran west to east through the middle of the town, bisecting the main street at right angles near the northwest corner of the priory. On the same corner he could see the broad roof of the guildhall, the largest building in town outside the priory.

On the main street next to the Bell were the priory gates, with Caris's house opposite, taller than most of the other buildings. Outside the Bell, Merthin could see a crowd gathered around Friar Murdo. The friar, who did not seem to be attached to any particular fraternal order, had stayed in Kingsbridge after the bridge collapse. Shocked and bereaved people were particularly susceptible to his emotional roadside sermons, and he was raking in the silver halfpennies and farthings. Merthin thought he was a fraud, his holy anger faked and his tears a cover for cynicism and greed—but Merthin was in a minority.

At the bottom of the main street, the stumps of the bridge still stuck up out of the water, and next to them Merthin's ferry was crossing the water bearing a cart loaded with tree trunks. To the southwest was the industrial sector, where large houses on broad plots encompassed abattoirs, tanneries, breweries, bakeries, and workshops of all kinds—too smelly and dirty for the town's leading citizens, but nevertheless a district where plenty of money was made. The river widened there, dividing into two channels either side of Leper Island. Merthin could see Ian Boatman rowing his small craft to the island, his passenger a monk, probably carrying food to the one remaining leper. The south bank of the river was lined with wharves and warehouses, and rafts and barges were being unloaded at several of them. Beyond was the suburb of Newtown, where rows of poor houses ran between orchards, pastures, and gardens in which priory employees produced food for the monks and nuns.

The north end of town, where St. Mark's stood, was the poor quarter, and the church was surrounded by the huddled homes of laborers, widows, the unsuccessful, and the old. It was a poor church—luckily for Merthin.

Four weeks ago, a desperate Father Joffroi had hired Merthin to build a hoist and repair his roof. Caris had persuaded Edmund to lend Merthin the money to buy tools. Merthin had hired a fourteen-year-old boy, Jimmie, to labor for a halfpenny a day. And today the hoist was finished.

Somehow, word had got around that Merthin was about to try out a new machine. Everyone had been impressed by his ferry, and people were fascinated to see what he had come up with now. Down in the graveyard a small crowd had gathered, mostly idlers but including Father Joffroi, Edmund and Caris, and some of the town's builders, notably Elfric. If Merthin failed today, he would fail in front of his friends and enemies.

That was not the worst of it. This job had saved him from the need to leave town in search of work. But such a fate still hung over him. If the hoist went wrong, people would conclude that hiring Merthin brought bad luck. They would say that the spirits did not want him in town. He would be under greater pressure to leave. He would have to say good-bye to Kingsbridge—and to Caris.

Over the last four weeks, as he had shaped the wood and joined the pieces of his hoist, he had for the first time seriously thought about losing her; and it dismayed him. He had realized that she was all the joy in his world. If the weather was fine, he wanted to walk in the sunshine with her; if he saw something beautiful, he wanted to show it to her; if he heard something funny, his first thought was to tell her, and see her smile. His work gave him pleasure, especially when he came up with clever solutions to intractable problems; but it was a cold, cerebral satisfaction, and he knew that his life would be a long winter without Caris.

He stood up. It was time to put his skill to the test.

He had built a normal hoist with one innovative feature. Like all hoists, it had a rope that ran through a series of pulleys. On top of the church wall, at the edge of the roof, Merthin had built a timber structure like a gallows, with an arm that reached across the roof. The rope ran out to the end of the arm. At the other end of the rope, on the ground in the graveyard, was a treadwheel, which wound up the rope when operated by the boy Jimmie. All this was standard. The innovation was that the gallows incorporated a swivel, so that the arm could swing.

To save himself from the fate of Howell Tyler, Merthin had a belt under his arms that was tied to a sturdy stone pinnacle: if he fell, he would not fall far. So protected, he had removed the slates from a section of the roof then tied the rope of the hoist to a timber. Now he called down to Jimmie: "Turn the wheel!"

Then he held his breath. He was sure it would work—it had to—but, all the same, this was a moment of high anxiety.

Jimmie, inside the great treadmill on the ground, began to walk. The wheel could move only one way. It had a brake pressing on its asymmetric teeth: one side of each tooth was gently angled, so that the brake moved gradually along the slope; but the other side was vertical, so that any reverse movement was immediately arrested.

As the wheel turned, the roof timber rose.

When the timber was clear of the roof structure, Merthin shouted: "Whoa!"

Jimmie stopped, the brake engaged, and the timber hung in the air, swinging gently. So far, so good. The next part was where things might go wrong.

Merthin turned the hoist, so that its arm began to swing. He watched it, holding his breath. New strains were brought to bear on the structure as the weight of the load moved its position. The wood of the hoist creaked. The arm swung through half a circle, bringing the timber from its original location over the roof to a new point over the graveyard. There was a collective murmur of wonder from the crowd: they had never seen a hoist that could swivel.

"Let it down!" Merthin called.

Jimmie operated the brake, allowing the load to fall jerkily, a foot at a time, as the wheel turned and the rope unwound.

Everyone watched in silence. When the timber touched the ground there was a round of applause.

Jimmie detached the timber from the rope.

Merthin permitted himself a moment of triumph. It had worked.

He climbed down the ladder. The crowd cheered. Caris kissed him. Father Joffroi shook his hand. "It's a marvel," the priest said. "I've never seen anything like it."

"No one has," Merthin said proudly. "I invented it."

Several more men congratulated him. Everyone was pleased to have been among the first to witness the phenomenon—all but Elfric, looking cross at the back of the crowd.

Merthin ignored him. He said to Father Joffroi: "Our agreement was that you would pay me if it worked."

"Gladly," said Joffroi. "I owe you eight shillings so far, and the sooner I have to pay you for removing the rest of the timbers and rebuilding the roof, the happier I'll be." He opened the wallet at his waist and took out some coins tied up in a rag.

Elfric said loudly: "Wait a moment!"

Everyone looked at him.

"You can't pay this boy, Father Joffroi," he said. "He's not a qualified carpenter."

Surely this could not happen, Merthin thought. He had done the work—it was too late now to deny him the wages. But Elfric cared nothing for fairness.

"Nonsense!" said Joffroi. "He's done what no other carpenter in town could do."

"All the same, he's not in the guild."

"I wanted to join," Merthin put in. "You would not admit me."

"That's the prerogative of the guild."

Joffroi said: "I say that's unjust—and many people in town would agree. He's done six and a half years of his apprenticeship, with no wages but his food and a bed on the kitchen floor, and everyone knows he's been doing the work of a qualified carpenter for years. You should not have turned him out without his tools."

There was a murmur of assent from the men gathered around. Elfric was generally thought to have gone a bit too far.

Elfric said: "With due respect to your reverence, that is for the guild to decide, not you."

"All right." Joffroi folded his arms. "You tell me not to pay Merthin—even though he is the only man in town who can repair my church without closing it. I defy you." He handed the coins to Merthin. "Now you can take the case to court."

"The prior's court." Elfric's face twisted in spite. "When a man has a grievance against a priest, is he likely to get a fair hearing in a court run by monks?"

There was some sympathy in the crowd for this. They knew of too many instances where the prior's court had unjustly favored the clergy.

But Joffroi shot back: "Can an apprentice get a fair hearing in a guild run by masters?"

The crowd laughed at that: they appreciated clever arguments.

Elfric looked crushed. Whatever the court, he could win a dispute between himself and Merthin, but he could not so easily prevail against a priest. Resentfully, he said: "It's a bad day for the town when apprentices defy their masters and priests support the boys." But he sensed he had lost, and he turned away.

Merthin felt the weight of the coins in his hand: eight shillings, ninety-six silver pennies, two-fifths of a pound. He knew he should count them, but he was too happy to bother. He had earned his first wages.

He turned to Edmund. "This is your money," he said.

"Pay me five shillings now, the rest later," Edmund said generously. "Keep some money for yourself—you deserve it."

Merthin smiled. That would leave him three shillings to spend—more money than he had ever had in his life. He did not know what to do with it. Perhaps he would buy his mother a chicken.

It was midday, and the crowd began to disperse, heading home for dinner. Merthin went with Caris and Edmund. He felt his future was secure. He had proved himself as a carpenter, and few people would hesitate to employ him now that Father Joffroi had set the precedent. He could earn a living. He could have a house of his own.

He could get married.

Petranilla was waiting for them. As Merthin counted out five shillings for Edmund, she put on the table a fragrant dish of fish baked with herbs. In celebration of Merthin's triumph, Edmund poured sweet Rhenish wine into cups for all of them.

But Edmund was not a man to linger over the past. "We must get on with the new bridge," he said impatiently. "Five weeks have gone by and nothing has been done!"

Petranilla said: "I hear the earl's health is rapidly returning to normal, so perhaps the monks will hold the election soon. I must ask Godwyn—but I haven't seen him since yesterday, when Blind Carlus fell over during the service."

"I'd like to have a bridge design ready," Edmund said. "Then work could begin as soon as the new prior is elected."

Merthin's ears pricked up. "What have you got in mind?"

"We know it has to be a stone bridge. I want it wide enough for two carts to pass."

Merthin nodded. "And it should be ramped at both ends, so that people will step off the bridge onto dry ground, not a muddy beach."

"Yes—excellent."

Caris said: "But how do you build stone walls in the middle of a river?"

Edmund said: "I've no idea, but it must be possible. There are lots of stone bridges."

Merthin said: "I've heard men talk about this. You have to build a special structure called a cofferdam to keep the water out of the area where you're building. It's quite simple, but they say you have to be very careful to make sure it's watertight."

Godwyn came in, looking anxious. He was not supposed to make social calls in the town—in theory, he could leave the priory only on a specific errand. Merthin wondered what had happened.

"Carlus withdrew his name from the election," he said.

"Good news!" Edmund said. "Have a cup of this wine."

"Don't celebrate yet," Godwyn said.

"Why not? That leaves Thomas as the only candidate—and Thomas wants to build the new bridge. Our problem is solved."

"Thomas is no longer the only candidate. The earl is nominating Saul Whitehead."

"Oh." Edmund was thoughtful. "Is that necessarily bad?"

"Yes. Saul is well liked and has shown himself a competent prior of St.-John-in-the-Forest. If he accepts the nomination, he's likely to get the votes of former supporters of Carlus—which means he could win. Then, as the earl's nominee, and his cousin, too, Saul is likely to do his sponsor's bidding—and the earl may oppose the building of the new bridge, on the grounds that it might take business away from Shiring market."

Edmund looked worried. "Is there anything we can do?"

"I hope so. Someone has to go to St. John to tell Saul the news and bring him to Kingsbridge. I've volunteered for that job, and I'm hoping there's some way I can persuade him to refuse."

Petranilla spoke. "That may not solve the problem," she said. Merthin listened carefully to her: he did not like her, but she was clever. She went on: "The earl might nominate another candidate. Any nominee of his could oppose the bridge."

Godwyn nodded agreement. "So, assuming I can keep Saul out of the contest, we must make sure the earl's second choice is someone who can't possibly get elected."

"Who do you have in mind?" his mother asked.

"Friar Murdo."

"Excellent."

Caris said: "But he's awful!"

"Exactly," Godwyn said. "Greedy, drunken, a sponger, a self-righteous rabble-rouser. The monks will never vote for him. That's why we want him to be the earl's candidate."

Godwyn was like his mother, Merthin realized, in having a talent for this kind of plotting.

Petranilla said: "How shall we proceed?"

"First, we need to persuade Murdo to put his name forward."

"That won't be hard. Just tell him he's in with a chance. He'd love to be prior."

"Agreed. But I can't do it. Murdo would immediately suspect my motives. Everyone knows I'm backing Thomas."

"I'll speak to him," said Petranilla. "I'll tell him you and I are at odds, and I don't want Thomas. I'll say the earl is looking for someone to nominate, and Murdo could be the right man. He's popular in the town, especially among the poor and ignorant, who labor under the delusion that he's one of them. All he needs to do, to get the nomination, is make it clear that he's willing to be the earl's pawn."

"Good." Godwyn stood up. "I'll try to be present when Murdo speaks to Earl Roland." He kissed his mother's cheek and went out.

The fish was all gone. Merthin ate his bread trencher, rich with juices. Edmund offered him more wine, but he declined: he was afraid he might fall off the roof of St. Mark's this afternoon if he drank too much. Petranilla went into the kitchen and Edmund retired to the parlor to sleep. Merthin and Caris were left alone.

He moved to sit on the bench next to her, and kissed her.

She said: "I'm so proud of you."

He glowed. He was proud of himself. He kissed her again, this time with a long, moist kiss that gave him an erection. He touched her breast through the linen of her robe, squeezing her nipple gently with his fingertips.

She touched his erection and giggled. "Do you want me to bring you off?" she whispered.

She did that sometimes late in the evening, when her father and Petranilla were asleep, and Merthin and she were alone on the ground floor of the house. But this was broad daylight, and someone could walk in at any moment. "No!" he said.

"I could do it quickly." She tightened her grasp.

"I'm too embarrassed." He stood up and moved to the other side of the table.

"I'm sorry."

"Well, maybe we won't have to do this much longer."

"Do what?"

"Hide, and worry about people walking in."

She looked hurt. "Don't you like it?"

"Of course I do! But it would be nicer for us to be alone. I could take a house, now that I'm getting paid."

"You've only been paid once."

"That's true . . . but you seem very pessimistic all of a sudden. Have I said something wrong?"

"No, but . . . why do you want to change the way things are?"

He was baffled by this question. "I just want more of the same, in private."

She looked defiant. "I'm happy now."

"Well, so am I . . . but nothing goes on forever."

"Why not?"

He felt as if he were explaining something to a child. "Because we can't spend the rest of our lives living with our parents and stealing kisses when no one's looking. We have to get a home of our own, and live as man and wife, and sleep together every night, and have real sex instead of bringing each other off, and raise a family."

"Why?" she said.

"I don't know why," he said in exasperation. "That's the way it is, and I'm not going to try to explain anymore, because I think you're determined not to understand; or, at least, to pretend you don't understand."

"All right."

"And besides, I have to go back to work."

"Go on, then."

This was incomprehensible. He had been frustrated, during the last half year, by not being able to marry Caris, and he had assumed she felt the same. Now it seemed she did not. Indeed, she resented his assumption. But did she really believe that they could continue this adolescent relationship indefinitely?

He looked at her, trying to read her face, and saw only a sulky obstinacy there. He turned away and went out through the door.

He hesitated on the street outside. Perhaps he should go back in and make her say what was on her mind. But, remembering the look on her face, he knew this was not the moment to try to make her do anything. So he walked on, heading for St. Mark's, thinking: How did such a wonderful day turn so bad?

22

Godwyn was preparing Kingsbridge Cathedral for the big wedding. The church had to look its best. In addition to the earl of Monmouth and the earl of Shiring, there would be several barons and hundreds of knights in attendance. Broken flagstones had to be replaced, chipped masonry repaired, crumbling moldings carved anew, walls whitewashed, pillars painted, and everything scrubbed clean.

"And I want the repairs to the south aisle of the chancel finished," Godwyn said to Elfric as they walked through the church.

"I'm not sure that's possible—"

"It must be done. We can't have scaffolding in the chancel during a wedding of this importance." He saw Philemon waving urgently at him from the south transept door. "Excuse me."

"I haven't got the men!" Elfric called after him.

"You shouldn't be so quick to sack them," Godwyn said over his shoulder.

Philemon was looking excited. "Friar Murdo is asking to see the earl," he said.

"Good!" Petranilla had spoken to the friar last night, and this morning Godwyn had instructed Philemon to lurk near the hospital and watch out for Murdo. He had been expecting an early visit.

He hurried to the hospital, with Philemon in tow. He was relieved to see that Murdo was still waiting in the big room on the ground floor. The fat friar had smartened up his appearance: his face and hands were clean, the fringe of hair around his tonsure was combed, and he had sponged the worst of the stains off his robe. He did not look like a prior, but he almost looked like a monk.

Godwyn ignored him and went up the stairs. Standing guard outside the earl's room he saw Merthin's brother, Ralph, who was one of the earl's squires. Ralph was handsome, except for a broken nose, a recent injury. Squires were always breaking bones. "Hello, Ralph," Godwyn said amiably. "What happened to your nose?"

"I had a fight with a peasant bastard."

"You should have got it set properly. Did that friar come up here?"

"Yes. They asked him to wait."

"Who's with the earl?"

"Lady Philippa and the clerk, Father Jerome."

"Ask if they'll see me."

"Lady Philippa says the earl must not see anyone."

Godwyn gave Ralph a man-to-man grin. "But she's only a woman."

Ralph grinned back, then opened the door and put his head inside. "Brother Godwyn, the sacrist?" he said.

There was a pause, and then Lady Philippa stepped out and closed the door behind her. "I told you no visitors," she said angrily. "Earl Roland is not getting the rest he needs."

Ralph said: "I know, my lady, but Brother Godwyn wouldn't bother the earl unnecessarily."

Something in Ralph's tone made Godwyn look at him. Although Ralph's words were mundane, the expression on his face was adoring. Godwyn noticed, then, how voluptuous Philippa was. She wore a dark red dress belted at the waist, and the fine wool clung to her breasts and hips. She looked like a statue representing Temptation, Godwyn thought, and he wished, yet again, that he could find a way to ban women from the priory. It was bad enough if a squire fell in love with a married woman, but for a monk to do the same would be a catastrophe.

"I regret the need to trouble the earl," Godwyn said. "But there's a friar waiting downstairs to see him."

"I know—Murdo. Is his business so urgent?"

"On the contrary. But I need to forewarn the earl what to expect."

"So you know what the friar is going to say?"

"I believe I do."

"Well, I think it's best if the two of you see the earl together."

Godwyn said: "But—" then pretended to stifle a protest.

Philippa looked at Ralph. "Get the friar up here, please."

Ralph summoned Murdo, and Philippa ushered him and Godwyn into the room. Earl Roland was on the bed, fully dressed as before, but this time he was sitting up, his bandaged head cushioned with feather pillows. "What's this?" he said with his usual bad temper. "A meeting of the chapter? What do you monks want?"

Looking at his visage directly for the first time since the bridge collapse, Godwyn was shocked to see that the entire right side of his face was paralyzed: the eyelid drooped, the cheek hardly moved, and the mouth was slack. What made it so startling was that the left side was animated. When Roland spoke, the left side of his forehead frowned, his left eye opened wide and seemed to blaze with authority, and he spoke vehemently out of the left side of his mouth. The doctor in Godwyn was fascinated. He knew that head injuries could have unpredictable effects, but he had never heard of this particular manifestation.

"Don't gawk at me," the earl said impatiently. "You look like a pair of cows staring over a hedge. State your business."

Godwyn pulled himself together. He had to tread carefully over the next few minutes. He knew that Roland would reject Murdo's application to be nominated as prior. All the same, he wanted to plant in Roland's mind the idea of Murdo as a possible alternative to Saul Whitehead. Therefore Godwyn's job was to strengthen Murdo's application. He would do this, paradoxically, by objecting to Murdo, thereby showing Roland that Murdo would owe no allegiance to the monks—for Roland wanted a prior who served him alone. But, on the other hand, Godwyn must not protest too strongly, for he did not want the earl to realize what a truly hopeless candidate Murdo actually was. It was a tortuous path to walk.

Murdo spoke first, in his sonorous pulpit voice. "My lord, I come to ask you to consider me for the position of prior of Kingsbridge. I believe—"

"Not so loud, for the love of the saints," Roland protested.

Murdo lowered his voice. "My lord, I believe that I—"

"Why do you want to be prior?" Roland said, interrupting him again. "I thought a friar was a monk without a church—by definition." This point of view was old-fashioned. Friars originally were travelers who held no property, but nowadays some of the fraternal orders were as wealthy as traditional monks. Roland knew this, and was just being provocative.

Murdo gave the standard answer. "I believe that God accepts both forms of sacrifice."

"So you're willing to turn your coat."

"I have come to think that the talents he gave me could be put to better use in a priory, so yes, I would be happy to embrace the rule of St. Benedict."

"But why should I consider you?"

"I am also an ordained priest."

"No shortage of those."

"And I have a following in Kingsbridge and the surrounding countryside such that, if I may be allowed to boast, I must be the most influential man of God in the area."

Father Jerome spoke for the first time. He was a confident young man with an intelligent face, and Godwyn sensed that he was ambitious. "It's true," he said. "The friar is extraordinarily popular."

He was not popular with the monks, of course—but neither Roland nor Jerome knew that, and Godwyn was not about to enlighten them.

Nor was Murdo. He bowed his head and said unctuously: "I thank you from my heart, Father Jerome."

Godwyn said: "He is popular with the ignorant multitude."

"As was our Savior," Murdo shot back.

"Monks should lead lives of poverty and self-denial," Godwyn said.

Roland put in: "The friar's clothes look poor enough. And as for self-denial, it seems to me that Kingsbridge monks eat better than many peasants."

"Friar Murdo has been seen drunk in taverns!" Godwyn protested.

Murdo said: "St. Benedict's Rule permits monks to drink wine."

"Only if they are sick, or laboring in the fields."

"I preach in the fields."

Murdo was a formidable opponent in an argument, Godwyn noted. He was glad that he did not actually want to win this one. He turned to Roland. "All I can say is that as the sacrist here I strongly counsel your lordship against nominating Murdo as prior of Kingsbridge."

"Noted," Roland said coldly.

Philippa gave Godwyn a look of mild surprise, and he realized he had yielded a little too easily. But Roland had not noticed: he did not deal in nuances.

Murdo had not finished. "The prior of Kingsbridge must serve God, of course; but, in all things temporal, he should be guided by the king, and the king's earls and barons."

That was about as plain as could be, Godwyn thought. Murdo might as well have said: "I will be your man." It was an outrageous declaration. The monks would be horrified. It would wipe out any support there might have been among them for Murdo's candidacy.

Godwyn made no comment, but Roland looked inquiringly at him. "Anything to say to that, sacrist?"

"I'm sure the friar did not mean to say that the priory of Kingsbridge should be in subjection to the earl of Shiring in any matter, temporal or otherwise—did you, Murdo?"

"I have said what I have said," Murdo replied in his pulpit voice.

"Enough," said Roland, bored now with the game. "You're wasting your time, both of you. I shall nominate Saul Whitehead. Off you go."

St.-John-in-the-Forest was a miniature version of Kingsbridge Priory. The church was small, as were the stone-built cloisters and dormitory; and the rest of the buildings were simple wood-frame structures. There were eight monks and no nuns. In addition to their lives of prayer and meditation, they grew most of their own food and made a goats' cheese that was famous throughout southwest England.

Godwyn and Philemon had been riding for two days, and it was early evening when the road emerged from the forest and they saw a wide acreage of cleared land with the church in the middle. Godwyn knew at once that his fears were true, and reports that Saul Whitehead was doing a good job as prior of this cell were, if anything, understated. There was a look of order and neatness about everything: the hedges trimmed, the ditches straight, the trees planted at measured intervals in the orchard, the fields of ripening grain free of weeds. He felt sure he would find that the services were held at the correct times and conducted reverently. He had to hope that Saul's evident fitness for leadership had not made him ambitious.

As they rode along the path through the fields, Philemon said: "Why is the earl so keen to make his cousin prior of Kingsbridge?"

"For the same reason that he had his younger son made bishop of Kingsbridge," Godwyn replied. "Bishops and priors are powerful. The earl wants to make sure that any influential man in his neighborhood is an ally, not an enemy."

"What might they quarrel about?"

Godwyn was interested to see that young Philemon was beginning to be intrigued by the chess game of power politics. "Land, taxes, rights, privileges . . . for example, the prior might want to build a new bridge at Kingsbridge, to bring more business to the Fleece Fair; and the earl might oppose such a scheme, on the grounds that it would take business away from his own fair at Shiring."

"But I don't really see how the prior could fight against the earl. A prior has no soldiers . . ."

"A clergyman can influence the mass of the people. If he preaches a sermon against the earl, or calls upon the saints to bring misfortune to the earl, people will begin to believe that the earl is cursed. Then they will discount his power, mistrust him, and expect all his projects to be doomed. It can be very hard for a nobleman to oppose a truly determined cleric. Look what happened to King Henry II after the murder of Thomas Becket."

They rode into the farmyard and dismounted. The horses immediately drank from the trough. There was no one about but a monk with his robe hitched up, mucking out a pigsty behind the stables. He was sure to be a youngster, doing a job like that. Godwyn called to him. "Hey, you, lad! Come and help us with our horses."

"Righto!" the monk called back. He finished cleaning out the sty with a few more passes of his rake, then leaned the tool up against the stable wall and walked toward the newcomers. Godwyn was about to tell him to get a move on when he recognized the blond fringe of Saul.

Godwyn disapproved. A prior should not muck out a pigsty. Ostentatious humility was, after all, ostentation. However, in this case Saul's meekness might suit Godwyn's purpose.

He gave Saul a friendly smile. "Hello, Brother. I didn't mean to order the prior to unsaddle my horse."

"Why not?" said Saul. "Someone must do it, and you've been traveling all day." Saul led the horses into the stable. "The brothers are in the fields," he called out. "But they'll be back soon for Evensong." He reemerged. "Come into the kitchen."

They had never been close. Godwyn could not helping feeling criticized by Saul's piety. Saul was never unfriendly, but with quiet determination he simply did things differently. Godwyn had to take care not to become irritated. He felt stressed enough already.

Godwyn and Philemon followed Saul across the farmyard and into a one-story building with a high roof. Although made of wood, it had a stone fireplace and chimney. They sat gratefully on a rough bench at a scrubbed table. Saul drew two generous cups of ale from a large barrel.

He sat opposite them. Philemon drank thirstily, but Godwyn just sipped. Saul offered no food, and Godwyn guessed they would get nothing more until after Evensong. He felt too tense to eat, anyway.

This was another delicate moment, he reflected anxiously. He had had to protest against Murdo's nomination in such a way as not to dissuade Roland. Now he had to invite Saul to stand in a way that he could not possibly accept. He knew what he was going to say, but he had to say it right. If he made a false step, Saul would become suspicious, and then anything could happen.

Saul gave him no time for further worry. "What brings you here, Brother?" he said.

"Earl Roland has recovered his wits."

"I thank God."

"This means we can hold the election for prior."

"Good. We should not go too long without one."

"But who should it be?"

Saul sidestepped the question. "Have any names been put forward?"

"Brother Thomas, the matricularius."

"He'd be a good manager. No one else?"

Godwyn told a half truth. "Not formally."

"What about Carlus? When I came to Kingsbridge for Prior Anthony's funeral, the subprior was the leading candidate."

"He feels he is not capable of the job."

"Because of his blindness?"

"Perhaps." Saul did not know about Carlus falling over during the service for St. Adolphus's birthday. Godwyn decided not to tell him. "At any rate, he has thought and prayed about it, and made his decision."

"Has the earl not made a nomination?"

"He's thinking about it." Godwyn hesitated. "That's why we're here. The earl is . . . considering nominating you." This was not really a lie, Godwyn told himself; just a misleading emphasis.

"I'm honored."

Godwyn studied him. "But not completely surprised, perhaps?"

Saul flushed. "Forgive me. The great Philip was in charge here at St. John and then became prior of Kingsbridge, and others have followed the same route. That is not to say that I'm worthy as they were, of course. But the thought had crossed my mind, I confess."

"Nothing to be ashamed of. How would you feel about being nominated?"

"How would I feel?" Saul seemed mystified. "Why ask that? If the earl wishes, he will nominate me; and if my brethren want me, they'll vote for me; and I will consider myself called by God. It makes no difference how I feel about it."

This was not the answer Godwyn wanted. He needed Saul to make up his own mind. Talk of God's will was counterproductive. "It's not quite so simple," he said. "You don't have to accept the nomination. That's why the earl sent me here."

"It's not like Roland to ask where he might command."

Godwyn almost winced. Never forget how shrewd Saul is, he told himself. He backpedaled hastily. "No, indeed. However, if you think you might refuse, he needs to know as soon as possible, so that he can nominate someone else." That was probably true, though Roland had not said it.

"I didn't realize it was done this way."

It is not done this way, Godwyn thought. But he said: "Last time it happened, when Prior Anthony was elected, you and I were both novices, so we didn't know what went on."

"True."

"Do you feel you have the ability to fill the role of prior of Kingsbridge?"

"Certainly not."

"Ah." Godwyn pretended disappointment, though he had been relying on Saul's humility to produce that answer.

"However . . ."

"What?"

"With God's help, who knows what might be accomplished?"

"How true." Godwyn concealed his annoyance. The humble answer had just been a formality. The truth was that Saul thought he could do the job. "Of course, you should reflect and pray about it tonight."

"I'm sure I'll think of little else." They heard distant voices. "The brothers are returning from their work."

"We can talk again in the morning," Godwyn said. "If you decide to be a candidate, you must come back to Kingsbridge with us."

"Very well."

There was a serious danger of Saul's accepting, Godwyn feared. But he had one more arrow to shoot. "Something else you might bear in mind in your prayers," he said. "A nobleman never offers a free gift."

Saul looked worried. "What do you mean?"

"Earls and barons dispense titles, land, positions, monopolies—but these things always have a price."

"And in this case?"

"If you are elected, Roland will expect you to make recompense. You are his cousin, anyway; and you'll owe your position to him. You will be his voice in chapter, making sure the priory's actions don't interfere with his interests."

"Will he make that an explicit condition of the nomination?"

"Explicit? No. But, when you return with me to Kingsbridge, he will question you, and the questions will be designed to reveal your intentions. If you insist that you will be an independent prior, showing no special favor to your cousin and sponsor, he will nominate someone else."

"I had not thought of that."

"Of course, you may simply give him the answers he wants to hear and then change your mind after the election."

"But that would be dishonest."

"Some would think so."

"God would think so."

"That's something for you to pray about tonight."

A group of young monks came into the kitchen, muddy from the fields, talking loudly; and Saul got up to serve them ale, but the worried look remained on his face. It stayed there when they went into the little church, with its wall painting of the Day of Judgment over the altar, for Evensong. It was still there when at last the evening meal was served and Godwyn's hunger was assuaged by the delicious cheese the monks made.

Godwyn lay awake that night, although he ached from two days on horseback. He had confronted Saul with an ethical dilemma. Most monks would have been willing to shade their position while talking to Roland, and speak words which promised a degree of subservience to the earl much greater than they really intended. But not Saul. He was driven by moral imperatives. Would he find a way through the dilemma, and accept the nomination? Godwyn did not see how he could.

Saul still wore the worried look when the monks got up, at first light, for the service of Lauds.

After breakfast, he told Godwyn he could not accept the nomination.

Godwyn could not get used to Earl Roland's face. It was the strangest thing to look at. The earl was now wearing a hat to cover the bandages on his head; but, by making his appearance more normal, the hat emphasized the paralysis of the right side of his face. Roland also seemed even more bad-tempered than usual, and Godwyn guessed he was still suffering severe headaches.

"Where is my cousin Saul?" he said as soon as Godwyn walked into the room.

"Still at St. John, my lord. I gave him your message—"

"Message? It was a command!"

Lady Philippa, standing beside the bed, said softly: "Don't excite yourself, lord—you know it makes you feel ill."

Godwyn said: "Brother Saul simply said that he cannot accept the nomination."

"Why the devil not?"

"He thought and prayed—"

"Of course he prayed, that's what monks do. What reason did he give for defying me?"

"He does not feel himself capable of such a challenging role."

"Nonsense. What challenge? He's not being asked to lead a thousand knights into battle—just make sure a handful of monks sing their hymns at the right times of day."

That was rubbish, so Godwyn bowed his head and said nothing.

The earl's tone changed suddenly. "I've just realized who you are. You're the son of Petranilla, aren't you?"

"Yes, Lord." That Petranilla whom you jilted, Godwyn thought.

"She was sly, and I'll bet you are too. How do I know you didn't talk Saul out of accepting? You want Thomas Langley to be prior, don't you?"

My plan is a lot more devious than that, you fool, Godwyn thought. He said: "Saul did ask me what you might want in return for nominating him."

"Ah, now we come to it. What did you tell him?"

"That you would expect him to listen to one who was his cousin, his sponsor, and his earl."

"And he was too pigheaded to accept that, I suppose. Right. That settles it. I shall nominate that fat friar. Now, get out of my sight."

Godwyn had to hide his elation as he bowed out of the room. The penultimate stage of his plan had worked perfectly. Earl Roland had not the least suspicion of how he had been nudged into nominating the most hopeless candidate Godwyn could think of.

Now for the final step.

He left the hospital and entered the cloisters. It was the hour of study before the midday service of Sext, and most of the monks were standing or sitting around reading, being read to, or meditating. Godwyn spotted Theodoric, his young ally, and summoned him with a jerk of the head.

In a low voice, he said: "Earl Roland has nominated Friar Murdo as prior."

Theodoric said loudly: "What?"

"Hush."

"It's impossible!"

"Of course it is."

"No one will vote for him."

"That's why I'm pleased."

Understanding dawned on Theodoric's face. "Oh . . . I see. So it's good for us, really."

Godwyn wondered why he always had to explain these things, even to intelligent men. No one saw below the surface, except him and his mother. "Go around telling everyone—quietly. No need to show your outrage. They'll get angry enough without encouragement."

"Should I say that this is good for Thomas?"

"Absolutely not."

"Right," said Theodoric. "I understand."

He evidently did not, but Godwyn felt he could be trusted to follow instructions.

Godwyn left him and went in search of Philemon. He found him sweeping out the refectory. "Do you know where Murdo is?" he asked.

"Probably in the kitchen."

"Find him and ask him to meet you in the prior's house when all the monks are in church for Sext. I don't want anyone to see you there with him."

"All right. What do I tell him?"

"First of all, you say: 'Brother Murdo, no one must ever know that I told you this.' Is that clear?"

"No one must ever know that I told you this. All right."

"Then show him the charter we found. You remember where it is—in the bedroom beside the prie-dieu, there's a chest with a ginger-colored leather wallet inside."

"Is that all?"

"Point out that the land Thomas brought to the priory belonged originally to Queen Isabella, and that this fact has been kept secret for ten years."

Philemon looked puzzled. "But we don't know what Thomas is trying to hide."

"No. But there's always a reason for a secret."

"Don't you think Murdo will try to use this information against Thomas?"

"Of course."

"What will Murdo do?"

"I don't know but, whatever it is, it's sure to be bad for Thomas."

Philemon frowned. "I thought we were supposed to be helping Thomas."

Godwyn smiled. "That's what everyone thinks."

The bell rang for Sext.

Philemon went off in search of Murdo, and Godwyn joined the rest of the monks in church. In unison with the others he said: "Oh, God, incline unto mine aid." On this occasion he prayed with unusual earnestness. Despite the confidence he had shown Philemon, he knew he was gambling. He had staked everything on Thomas's secret, but he did not know what the face of the card would show when he turned it up.

However, it was clear he had succeeded in stirring up the monks. They were restless and talkative, and Carlus had to call for quiet twice during the psalms. They disliked friars in general, for taking an attitude of moral superiority on the question of earthly possessions while, at the same time, sponging off those they condemned. And they disliked Murdo in particular for being pompous, greedy, and drunk. They would have anyone rather than him.

As they left the church after the service, Simeon spoke to Godwyn. "We cannot have the friar," he said.

"I agree."

"Carlus and I will not be putting forward another name. If the monks appear divided, the earl will be able to present his candidate as a necessary compromise. We must sink our differences and rally round Thomas. If we show the world a united front, it will be difficult for the earl to oppose us."

Godwyn stopped and faced Simeon. "Thank you, Brother," he said, forcing himself to look humble and hide the exultation he felt.

"We're doing it for the good of the priory."

"I know. But I appreciate your generosity of spirit."

Simeon nodded and walked away.

Godwyn smelled victory.

The monks went into the refectory for dinner. Murdo joined them. He missed services, but not meals. All monasteries had a general rule that any monk or friar was welcomed at the table—though few people exploited the practice as thoroughly as Murdo. Godwyn studied his face. The friar looked excited, as if he had news he was bursting to share. However, he contained himself while dinner was served, and remained silent throughout the meal, listening to a novice read.

The passage chosen was the story of Susanna and the Elders. Godwyn disapproved: the story was too sexy to be read aloud in a celibate community.

But today even the attempts of two lascivious old men to blackmail a woman into having sex with them failed to capture the monks' attention. They kept whispering among themselves, looking sidelong at Murdo.

When the food was finished, and the prophet Daniel had saved Susanna from execution by interrogating the elders separately and showing that they told inconsistent stories, the monks got ready to leave. At that moment, Murdo spoke to Thomas.

"When you came here, Brother Thomas, you had a sword wound, I believe."

He spoke loudly enough for everyone to hear, and the other monks stopped to listen.

Thomas looked at him stonily. "Yes."

"The wound that eventually caused you to lose your left arm. I wonder, did you receive that wound in the service of Queen Isabella?"

Thomas turned pale. "I've been a monk of Kingsbridge for ten years. My previous life is forgotten."

Murdo carried on unperturbed. "I ask because of the parcel of land that you brought with you when you joined the priory. A very productive little village in Norfolk. Five hundred acres. Near Lynn—where the queen lives."

Godwyn interrupted, pretending to be indignant. "What does an outsider know of our property?"

"Oh, I've read the charter," Murdo said. "These things aren't secret."

Godwyn looked at Carlus and Simeon, sitting side by side. Both men looked startled. As subprior and treasurer, they knew already. They must be wondering how Murdo had got sight of the deed. Simeon opened his mouth to speak.

Murdo said: "Or, at least, they're not supposed to be secret."

Simeon closed his mouth again. If he demanded to know how Murdo had found out, he would himself face questions about why he had kept the secret.

Murdo went on: "And the farm at Lynn was donated to the priory by . . ." He paused for dramatic effect. "Queen Isabella," he finished.

Godwyn looked around. There was consternation among the monks, all but Carlus and Simeon, who both looked stone-faced.

Friar Murdo leaned across the table. Green herbs from the dinnertime stew adhered to his teeth. "I ask you again," he said aggressively. "Did you receive your wound in the service of Queen Isabella?"

Thomas said: "Everyone knows what I did before I was a monk. I was a knight, I fought battles, I killed men. I have confessed and received absolution."

"A monk may put his past behind him—but the prior of Kingsbridge carries a heavier burden. He may be asked whom he killed, and why, and—most importantly—what reward he received."

Thomas stared back at Murdo without speaking. Godwyn tried to read Thomas's face. It was rigidly set in an expression of some strong emotion—but what? There was no sign of guilt, or even embarrassment: whatever the secret was, Thomas did not feel he had done something shameful. The look was not rage, either. Murdo's sneering tone might have provoked many men to violence, but Thomas did not look as if he were about to lash out. No, what Thomas seemed to be feeling was something different, colder than embarrassment, quieter than rage. It was, Godwyn realized at last, fear. Thomas was afraid. Of Murdo? Hardly. No, he feared something that might happen because of Murdo, some consequence of Murdo's having discovered the secret.

Murdo continued like a dog with a bone. "If you don't answer the question here in this room, it will be asked elsewhere."

Godwyn's calculations called for Thomas to give up at this point. But it was not a certainty. Thomas was tough. For ten years he had shown himself to be quiet, patient, and resilient. When approached by Godwyn to stand as prior, he must have decided that the past could be buried. He must now realize he had been wrong. But how would he react to that realization? Would he see his mistake and back away? Or would he grit his teeth and see it through? Godwyn bit his lip and waited.

Thomas spoke at last. "I think you may be right about the question being asked elsewhere," he said. "Or, at least, I think you will do everything in your power, no matter how unbrotherly or dangerous, to make your forecast come true."

"I don't know if you're implying—"

"You need say no more!" Thomas said, rising abruptly to his feet. Murdo recoiled. Thomas's height and soldierly physique, combined with a sharp rise in his voice, achieved the rare result of silencing the friar.

"I have never answered questions about my past," Thomas said. His voice was quiet again, and every monk in the room was still and silent, straining to hear. "I never will." He pointed at Murdo. "But this . . . slug . . . makes me realize that if I became your prior, such questions would never cease. A monk may keep his past to himself, but a prior is different, I now see. A prior may have enemies, and any mystery is a weakness. And then, of course, by the leader's vulnerability the institution itself is threatened. My brain should have led me where Friar Murdo's malice led him—to the conclusion that a man who does not want to answer questions about his past cannot be a prior. Therefore—"

Young Theodoric said: "No!"

"Therefore I now withdraw my candidacy in the coming election."

Godwyn breathed a long sigh of satisfaction. He had achieved his object.

Thomas sat down; Murdo looked smug; and everyone else tried to speak at the same time.

Carlus banged the table, and slowly they quieted down. He said: "Friar Murdo, as you don't have a vote in this election, I must ask you to leave us now."

Murdo slowly walked out, looking triumphant.

When he had gone, Carlus said: "This is a catastrophe—Murdo the only candidate!"

Theodoric said: "Thomas cannot be allowed to withdraw."

"But he has!"

Simeon said: "There must be another candidate."

"Yes," said Carlus. "And I propose Simeon."

"No!" said Theodoric.

"Let me speak," said Simeon. "We must choose the one among us who is most certain to unite the brethren against Murdo. That is not myself. I know I don't have enough backing among the youngsters. I think we all know who would gather most support from all sections."

He turned and looked at Godwyn.

"Yes!" Theodoric said. "Godwyn!"

The younger monks cheered, and the older ones looked resigned. Godwyn shook his head, as if reluctant even to respond to them. They began to bang the tables and chant his name: "God-wyn! God-wyn!"

At last he stood up. His heart was full of elation, but he kept his face straight. He held up his hands for quiet. Then, when the room was silent, he said in a low, modest voice: "I shall obey the will of my brethren."

The room erupted in cheering.

23

Godwyn delayed the election. Earl Roland was going to be angry at the result, and Godwyn wanted to give him as little time as possible to fight the decision before the wedding.

The truth was that Godwyn was frightened. He was going up against one of the most powerful men in the kingdom. There were only thirteen earls. Together with about forty lesser barons, twenty-one bishops, and a handful of others, they governed England. When the king summoned Parliament, they were the Lords, the aristocratic group, by contrast with the Commons, who were knights, gentry, and merchants. The earl of Shiring was one of the more powerful and prominent men of his class. And yet Brother Godwyn, age thirty-one, son of the widow Petranilla, who had risen no higher than sacrist of Kingsbridge Priory, was in conflict with the earl—and, what was even more dangerous, he was winning.

So he dithered—but, six days before the wedding, Roland put his foot down and said: "Tomorrow!"

Guests were already arriving for the nuptials. The earl of Monmouth had moved into the hospital, using the private room next to Roland's. Lord William and Lady Philippa had had to remove to the Bell Inn. Bishop Richard was sharing the prior's house with Carlus. Lesser barons and knights filled the taverns, along with their wives and children, squires and servants and horses. The town enjoyed a surge of spending, much needed after the disappointing profits from the rain-drenched Fleece Fair.

On the morning of the election Godwyn and Simeon went to the treasury, a small windowless room behind a heavy oak door off the library. The precious ornaments used for special services were there, locked in an ironbound chest. Simeon as treasurer held the keys.

The election was a foregone conclusion, or so thought everyone except Earl Roland. No one suspected Godwyn's hidden hand. He had suffered one tense moment, when Thomas had wondered aloud how Friar Murdo got to know about the Isabella charter. "He can't have discovered it accidentally—he's never been seen reading in the library, and anyway that deed isn't kept with the others," Thomas had said to Godwyn. "Someone must have told him about it. But who? Only Carlus and Simeon knew of it. Why would they have let the secret out? They didn't want to help Murdo." Godwyn had said nothing, and Thomas had remained baffled.

Godwyn and Simeon dragged the treasure chest into the light of the library. The cathedral jewels were wrapped in blue cloth and cushioned in protective sheets of leather. As they sorted through the box, Simeon unwrapped some of the items, admiring them and checking that they were undamaged. There was a plaque a few inches wide made of ivory, delicately carved, showing the crucifixion of St. Adolphus, at which the saint had asked God to grant good health and long life to all those who venerated his memory. There were numerous candlesticks and crucifixes, all of gold or silver, most decorated with precious stones. In the strong light from the tall library windows the gems glittered and the gold glowed. These things had been given to the priory, over the centuries, by devout worshippers. Their combined value was awesome: there was more wealth here than most people ever saw in one place.

Godwyn had come for a ceremonial crosier, or shepherd's crook, made of wood encased in gold, with an elaborately jeweled handle. This was ritually handed to the new prior at the end of the election process. The crook was at the bottom of the chest, not having been used for thirteen years. As Godwyn drew it out, Simeon let out an exclamation.

Godwyn looked up sharply. Simeon was holding a large crucifix on a stand, intended to be placed on an altar. "What's the matter?" Godwyn said.

Simeon showed him the back of the cross and pointed to a shallow cup-shaped indentation just below the crosspiece. Godwyn immediately saw that a ruby was missing. "It must have fallen out," he said. He glanced around the library: they were alone.

They were both worried. As treasurer and sacrist they shared responsibility. They would be blamed for any loss.

Together they examined every item in the chest. They unwrapped each one and shook out every blue cloth. They looked at all the leather sheets. Frantically, they scrutinized the empty box and the floor all around. The ruby was nowhere to be seen.

Simeon said: "When was the crucifix last used?"

"At the feast of St. Adolphus, when Carlus fell. He knocked it off the table."

"Perhaps the ruby fell out then. But how is it possible that no one noticed?"

"The stone was on the back of the cross. But surely someone would have seen it on the floor?"

"Who picked up the crucifix?"

"I don't remember," Godwyn said quickly. "The situation was confused." In fact he remembered perfectly well.

It was Philemon.

Godwyn could picture the scene. Philemon and Otho together had righted the altar, setting it squarely on its platform. Then Otho had picked up the candlesticks and Philemon the cross.

With a growing feeling of dismay, Godwyn recalled the disappearance of Lady Philippa's bracelet. Had Philemon stolen again? He trembled to think how it might affect him. Everyone knew that Philemon was Godwyn's unofficial acolyte. Such a dreadful sin—stealing a jewel from a sacred ornament—would bring shame on everyone associated with the perpetrator. It could easily upset the election.

Simeon obviously did not recollect the scene exactly, and he accepted without question Godwyn's feigned inability to remember who had picked up the cross. But others among the monks would surely recall seeing it in Philemon's hands. Godwyn had to put this right quickly, before suspicion could fall on Philemon. But first he had to get Simeon out of the way.

"We must search for the ruby in the church," Simeon said.

"But the service was two weeks ago," Godwyn protested. "A ruby can't have lain on the floor unnoticed for that length of time."

"It's unlikely, but we must check."

Godwyn saw that he had to go with Simeon, and wait for an opportunity to get away from him and seek out Philemon. "Of course," he said.

They put the ornaments away and locked the treasury door. As they left the library, Godwyn said: "I suggest we say nothing about this until we're sure the jewel has been lost. No point in bringing blame on our heads prematurely."

"Agreed."

They hurried around the cloisters and entered the church. They stood in the center of the crossing and scanned the ground all around them. A month ago, the idea that a ruby could lie hidden somewhere on the church floor would have been more plausible; but recently the flagstones had been repaired, and the cracks and chips had disappeared. A ruby would have stood out.

Simeon said: "Now that I come to think of it, wasn't it Philemon who picked up the crucifix?"

Godwyn looked at Simeon's face. Was there accusation in the expression? He could not tell. "It may have been Philemon," Godwyn said. Then he saw a chance to get away. "I'll go and fetch him," he suggested. "Perhaps he will be able to recall exactly where he was standing at the time."

"Good idea. I'll wait here." Simeon got down on his knees and began to pat the floor with his hands, as if the ruby might be found by touch more easily than by sight.

Godwyn hurried out. He went first to the dormitory. The blanket cupboard was in the same place. He pulled it away from the wall, found the loose stone, and removed it. He put his hand into the hidey-hole where Philemon had stashed Lady Philippa's bracelet.

He found nothing there.

He cursed. It was not going to be that easy.

I'll have to dismiss Philemon from the monastery, he thought as he strode through the priory buildings looking for him. If he has stolen this ruby, I can't cover up for him again. He's out.

Then he realized, with a shock of dismay, that he could not dismiss Philemon—not now, perhaps not ever. It was Philemon who had told Friar Murdo about the Isabella charter. If dismissed, Philemon could confess what he had done, and reveal that he had done it at Godwyn's instigation. And he would be believed. Godwyn recalled Thomas's puzzling over who had told Murdo the secret, and why. Philemon's revelation would gain conviction by answering that question.

There would be an outcry at such underhand work. Even if the disclosure were made after the election, it would undermine Godwyn's authority and cripple his ability to lead the monks. The ominous truth dawned on him that he now had to protect Philemon in order to protect himself.

He found Philemon sweeping the hospital floor. He beckoned him outside and led him around to the back of the kitchen, where it was unlikely that anyone would see them.

He looked Philemon in the eye and said: "There's a ruby missing."

Philemon looked away. "How terrible."

"It's from the altar crucifix that was knocked to the floor when Carlus fell over."

Philemon pretended innocence. "How could it have gone missing?"

"The ruby may have become dislodged when the crucifix hit the floor. But it's not on the floor now—I've just looked. Someone found it—and kept it."

"Surely not."

Godwyn felt angered by Philemon's false air of innocence. "You fool, everyone saw you pick up that crucifix!"

Philemon's voice rose to a higher pitch. "I know nothing about it!"

"Don't waste time lying to me! We have to put this right. I could lose the election on your account." Godwyn pushed Philemon up against the wall of the bakehouse. "Where is it?"

To his astonishment, Philemon began to cry.

"For the love of the saints," Godwyn said disgustedly. "Stop this nonsense—you're a grown man!"

Philemon continued to sob. "I'm sorry," he said. "I'm sorry."

"If you don't stop that—" Godwyn checked himself. Nothing was to be gained by berating Philemon. The man was truly pathetic. Speaking more gently, he said: "Try to pull yourself together. Where is the ruby?"

"I hid it."

"Yes . . ."

"In the refectory chimney."

Godwyn immediately turned away, heading for the refectory. "Mary save us, it could fall into the fire!"

Philemon followed, his tears drying. "There's no fire in August. I would have moved it before the cold weather."

They entered the refectory. At one end of the long room was a wide fireplace. Philemon put his arm up the chimney and fumbled for a moment. Then he produced a ruby the size of a sparrow's egg, covered with soot. He wiped it clean on his sleeve.

Godwyn took it. "Now come with me," he said.

"What are we going to do?"

"Simeon is going to find this."

They went to the church. Simeon was still searching on hands and knees. "Now," Godwyn said to Philemon. "Try to remember exactly where you were when you picked up the crucifix."

Simeon looked at Philemon and, seeing signs of emotion on his face, spoke kindly to him. "Don't be afraid, lad, you've done nothing wrong."

Philemon positioned himself on the east side of the crossing, close to the steps leading up to the chancel. "I think it was here," he said.

Godwyn climbed the two steps and looked under the choir stalls, pretending to search. Surreptitiously, he placed the ruby under one of the rows of seats, close to the near end, where it was not visible to a casual glance. Then, as if changing his mind about the likeliest place to look, he moved to the south side of the chancel. "Come and search under here, Philemon," he said.

As he had hoped, Simeon then moved to the north side and got down on his knees to look under the stalls, murmuring a prayer as he did so.

Godwyn expected Simeon to see the ruby immediately. He pretended to search the south aisle, waiting for Simeon to find it. He began to think there must be something wrong with Simeon's eyesight. He might have to go over there and "find" it himself. Then at last Simeon called out: "Oh! Here!"

Godwyn pretended to be excited. "Have you found it?"

"Yes! Hallelujah!"

"Where was it?"

"Here—under the choir stalls!"

"Praise be to God," said Godwyn.

Godwyn told himself not to be frightened of Earl Roland. As he climbed the stone stairs of the hospital to the guest rooms, he asked himself what the earl could do to him. Even if Roland had been capable of getting out of his bed and drawing a sword, he would not be foolish enough to attack a monk within the precincts of a monastery—even a king would hardly get away with that.

Ralph Fitzgerald announced him, and he went into the room.

The earl's sons stood either side of the bed: tall William, in soldierly brown hose and muddy boots, his hair already receding from his forehead; and Richard, in bishop's purple, his growing roundness of figure evidence of a sybaritic nature and the means to indulge it. William was thirty, a year younger than Godwyn; he had his father's strength of will, but it was sometimes softened by the influence of his wife, Philippa. Richard was twenty-eight, and presumably took after his late mother, for he had little of the earl's imposing bearing and forcefulness.

"Well, monk?" said the earl, speaking out of the left side of his mouth. "Have you held your little election?"

Godwyn suffered a moment of resentment for this discourteous form of address. One day, he vowed silently, Roland would call him Father Prior. Indignation gave him the courage he needed to tell the earl the news. "We have, Lord," he said. "I have the honor to tell you that the monks of Kingsbridge have chosen me as their prior."

"What?" the earl bellowed. "You?"

Godwyn bowed his head in an affectation of humility. "No one could be more surprised than I."

"You're nothing but a boy!"

The insult stung Godwyn into a rejoinder. "I'm older than your son, the bishop of Kingsbridge."

"How many votes did you get?"

"Twenty-five."

"And how many for Friar Murdo?"

"None. The monks were unanimous—"

"None?" Roland roared. "There must have been a conspiracy—this is treason!"

"The election was held in strict accordance with the rules."

"I don't care a pig's prick for your rules. I won't be ignored by a bunch of effeminate monks."

"I am the choice of my brothers, my lord. The inauguration ceremony will be held this coming Sunday, before the wedding."

"The monks' choice must be ratified by the bishop of Kingsbridge. And I can tell you he will not ratify you. Rerun the election, and this time bring me the result I want."

"Very good, Earl Roland." Godwyn went to the door. He had several more cards in his hand, but he was not going to lay them on the table all at once. He turned and addressed Richard. "My lord bishop, when you wish to speak to me about this, you will find me in the prior's house."

He stepped outside. "You're not the prior!" Roland shouted as he shut the door.

Godwyn was trembling. Roland was formidable, especially when angry, and he was often angry. But Godwyn had stood his ground. Petranilla would be proud of him.

He went down the stairs on shaky legs and made his way to the prior's house. Carlus had already moved out. For the first time in fifteen years, Godwyn would have a bedroom to himself. His pleasure was only slightly damped by having to share the place with the bishop, who traditionally stayed there while visiting. The bishop was, technically, the abbot of Kingsbridge ex officio and, though his power was limited, his status was above that of the prior. Richard was rarely in the house during the day, but returned every night to sleep in the best bedroom.

Godwyn entered the ground-floor hall and sat in the big chair, waiting. It would not be long before Bishop Richard appeared, his ears burning with his father's scorching instructions. Richard was a rich and powerful man, but not frightening in the way the earl was. All the same, it was a bold monk who defied his bishop. However, Godwyn had an advantage in this confrontation, for he knew something shameful about Richard, and that was as good as a knife up his sleeve.

Richard bustled in a few minutes later, showing a confidence that Godwyn knew to be faked. "I've struck a bargain for you," he said without preamble. "You can be subprior under Murdo. You'll be in charge of day-today management of the priory. Murdo doesn't want to be an administrator, anyway—he just wants the prestige. You'll have all the power, but my father will be satisfied."

"Let me get this straight," said Godwyn. "Murdo agrees to make me his subprior. Then we tell the rest of the monks that he is the only one you'll ratify. And you think they will accept that."

"They have no choice!"

"I have an alternative suggestion. Tell the earl that the monks will not have anyone but me—and that I must be ratified before the wedding, otherwise the monks will not take part in the nuptials. The nuns, too, will refuse." Godwyn did not know whether the monks would go along with this—let alone Mother Cecilia and the nuns—but he was too far gone for caution.

"They wouldn't dare!"

"I'm afraid they would."

Richard looked panicky. "My father won't be bullied!"

Godwyn laughed. "Small chance of that. But I hope he may be made to see reason."

"He'll say the wedding must go ahead anyway. I'm the bishop, I can marry the couple, I don't need monks to help me."

"Of course. But there will be no singing, no candles, no psalms, no incense—just you and Archdeacon Lloyd."

"They will still be married."

"How will the earl of Monmouth feel about such a mean wedding for his son?"

"He'll be furious, but he'll accept it. The alliance is the important thing."

That was probably right, Godwyn thought, and he felt the cold draft of imminent failure.

It was time to draw his concealed knife.

"You owe me a kindness," he said.

At first, Richard pretended not to know what he was talking about. "Do I?"

"I concealed a sin you committed. Don't pretend to have forgotten, it was only a couple of months ago."

"Ah, yes, that was generous of you."

"I saw, with my own eyes, you and Margery on the bed in the guest room."

"Hush, for pity's sake!"

"Now is your chance to repay me that kindness. Intercede with your father. Tell him to give in. Argue that the wedding is more important. Insist on ratifying me."

Richard's face showed desperation. He looked crushed by opposing forces. "I can't!" he said, and there was panic in his voice. "My father won't be defied. You know what he's like."

"Try."

"I've already tried! I forced him to concede that you could be subprior."

Godwyn doubted that Roland had conceded any such thing. Richard had almost certainly made it up, knowing that such a promise could easily be broken. All the same, Godwyn said: "I thank you for that." Then he added: "But it's not enough."

"Just think about it," Richard pleaded. "That's all I ask."

"I will. And I suggest you ask your father to do the same."

"Oh, God," Richard groaned. "This is going to be a catastrophe."

The wedding was scheduled for Sunday. On the Saturday, in place of the service of Sext, Godwyn ordered a rehearsal, beginning with the ceremony of inauguration of the new prior and continuing with the marriage service. Outside it was another sunless day, the sky full of low, gray cloud heavy with rain, and the inside of the cathedral was gloomy. After the rehearsal, as the monks and nuns headed off for dinner and the novices began to tidy up the church, Godwyn was approached by Carlus and Simeon, both looking solemn.

"I think that went very smoothly, don't you?" Godwyn said brightly.

Simeon said: "Is there actually going to be an inauguration for you?"

"Absolutely."

"We hear the earl has ordered the election to be rerun."

"Do you think he has the right to do that?"

"Indeed not," said Simeon. "He has the power of nomination, that's all. But he says Bishop Richard will not ratify you as prior."

"Has Richard told you that?"

"Not himself, no."

"I thought not. Trust me, the bishop will ratify me." Godwyn heard his own voice sounding sincere and confident, and wished his feelings matched it.

Carlus said anxiously. "Did you tell Richard the monks would refuse to take part in the wedding?"

"I did."

"That's very hazardous. We're not here to oppose the will of noblemen."

Godwyn could have predicted that Carlus would weaken at the first sign of serious opposition. Fortunately, he was not planning to test the monks' resolve. "We won't have to do it, don't worry. It's just an empty threat. But don't tell the bishop I said so."

"So you're not planning to ask the monks to boycott the wedding?"

"No."

Simeon said: "You're playing a dangerous game."

"Perhaps—but I trust no one is in danger except me."

"You did not even want to be prior. You would not allow your name to be put forward. You only accepted when all else failed."

"I don't want to be prior," Godwyn lied. "But the earl of Shiring must not be allowed to choose for us, and that's more important than my personal feelings."

Simeon looked at him with respect. "You're being very honorable."

"Like you, Brother, I'm just trying to do the will of God."

"May He bless your efforts."

The two old monks left him. He felt a twinge of conscience for allowing them to believe that he was acting unselfishly. They saw him as some kind of martyr. But it was true, he told himself, that he was only trying to do the will of God.

He looked around: the church was back to normal. He was about to go to the prior's house for dinner when his cousin Caris appeared, her blue dress a startling splash of color in the dim, gray church. "Are you going to be inaugurated tomorrow?" she said.

He smiled. "Everyone's asking the same question. The answer is yes."

"We hear the earl is putting up a fight."

"He's going to lose it."

Her shrewd green eyes gave him a penetrating stare. "I've known you since you were a child, and I can tell when you're lying."

"I'm not lying."

"You're pretending to be more certain than you actually feel."

"That's not a sin."

"My father is worried about the bridge. Friar Murdo is even more likely to obey the earl's will than Saul Whitehead was."

"Murdo is not going to be prior of Kingsbridge."

"There you go again."

Godwyn was annoyed by her perspicacity. "I don't know what to say to you," he snapped. "I've been elected, and I mean to take the post. Earl

Roland would like to stop me, but he doesn't have the right, and I'm fighting him with all the means at my disposal. Am I scared? Yes. But I still intend to beat him."

She grinned. "That's what I wanted to hear." She punched his shoulder. "Go and see your mother. She's in your house, waiting for you. That's what I came to tell you." With that she turned and left.

Godwyn went out through the north transept. Caris was clever, he thought with a mixture of admiration and irritation. She had cajoled him into giving her an assessment of the situation more candid than anything he had said to anyone else.

But he was glad of the chance to talk to his mother. Everyone else doubted his power to win this fight. She would have confidence—and perhaps some strategic ideas.

He found Petranilla in the hall, sitting at the table, which was laid for two with bread, ale, and a platter of salted fish. He kissed her forehead, said grace, and sat down to eat. He allowed himself a moment of triumphant pleasure. "Well," he said. "I'm the prior-elect, at least, and here we are having dinner in the prior's house."

"But Roland is still fighting you," she said.

"Harder than I expected. After all, he has the right of nomination, not selection. It's inherent in his position that his choice will not always be elected."

"Most earls would accept that, but not him," Petranilla said. "He's felt superior to everyone he's ever met." There was a bitterness in her tone which, Godwyn guessed, sprang from memories of their aborted engagement more than thirty years ago. She smiled vengefully. "Soon he will realize how badly he's underestimated us."

"He knows I'm your son."

"Then that will be a factor. You probably remind him of the dishonorable way he behaved to me. That's enough to make him hate you."

"It's a shame." Godwyn lowered his voice in case a servant might be listening outside the door. "Until this point, your plan has worked perfectly. Withdrawing myself from the contest, then discrediting everyone else, was brilliant."

"Perhaps. But we may be about to lose everything. Have you said any more to the bishop?"

"No. I've reminded him that we know about Margery. He was scared, but not scared enough to defy his father, it seems."

"He should be. If this comes out, he won't be forgiven. He could end up a lowly knight on the level of Sir Gerald, wasting his days as a pensioner. Doesn't he realize that?"

"Perhaps he thinks I don't have the courage to reveal what I know."

"Then you'll have to go to the earl with the information."

"Heavens! He'll explode!"

"Steel your nerve."

She always said this kind of thing. It was why he looked forward with such apprehension to meetings with her. She always wanted him to be a little more daring, and take greater risks, than was his inclination. But he could never refuse her.

She went on: "If it came out that Margery's not a virgin, the marriage would be called off. Roland doesn't want that. He'll accept the lesser evil of you as prior."

"But he'll be my enemy for the rest of his life."

"He'll be that whatever happens."

Small consolation, Godwyn thought; but he did not argue, for he could see that his mother was right.

There was a tap at the door, and Lady Philippa walked in.

Godwyn and Petranilla stood up.

"I need to talk to you," Philippa said to Godwyn.

He said: "May I present my mother, Petranilla?"

Petranilla curtsied, then said: "I'd better leave. You're obviously here to broker a deal, my lady."

Philippa gave her an amused look. "If you know that much, you know everything of importance. Perhaps you should stay."

As the two women stood facing one another, Godwyn noticed that they were similar: same height, same statuesque build, and the same imperious air. Philippa was younger, of course, by something like twenty years; and she had a relaxed authority, and a touch of humor, that contrasted with Petranilla's tight-wound determination—perhaps because Philippa had a husband and Petranilla had lost hers. But Philippa was a strong-willed woman who exercised power through a man—Lord William—and, Godwyn now realized, Petranilla also wielded influence through a man—himself.

"Let's sit down," Philippa said.

Petranilla said: "Has the earl approved whatever you're about to propose?"

"No." Philippa made a helpless gesture with her hands. "Roland is too proud to agree in advance to something that might then be rejected by the other side. If I can get Godwyn's agreement to what I'm about to suggest, then I've got a chance of persuading Roland to compromise."

"I thought as much."

Godwyn said: "Would you like something to eat, my lady?"

Philippa dismissed the offer with an impatient wave. "As things stand, everyone is going to lose," she began. "The wedding will take place, but without the proper pomp and ceremony; so that Roland's alliance with the earl of Monmouth will be blighted from the start. The bishop will refuse to ratify you as prior, Godwyn, so the archbishop will be called in to resolve the dispute; and he will dismiss both you and Murdo, and nominate someone new, probably a member of his staff whom he wants to be rid of. No one will get what they want. Am I right?"

She directed the question at Petranilla, who made a noncommittal sound.

"So why not anticipate the archbishop's compromise?" Philippa went on. "Bring forward the third candidate now. Only"—she pointed a finger at Godwyn—"the candidate is chosen by you—and he promises to make you subprior."

Godwyn considered. This would relieve him of the need to confront the earl eyeball-to-eyeball and threaten him with the revelation of his son's behavior. But the compromise would doom him to be subprior for an indefinite period—and then, when the new prior died, he would have to fight the battle all over again. He was inclined to refuse, despite his apprehension.

He glanced at his mother. She gave an almost imperceptible shake of the head. She did not like it either.

"I'm sorry," Godwyn said to Philippa. "The monks have held an election, and the result must stand."

Philippa stood up. "In that case, I must give you the message that is my official reason for coming here. Tomorrow morning the earl will rise from his sickbed. He wishes to inspect the cathedral and make sure all is ready in plenty of time for the wedding. You are to meet him in the church at eight o'clock. All the monks and nuns must be robed and ready, and the church dressed with the usual ornaments."

Godwyn bowed his head in acknowledgment, and she went out.

~

At the appointed hour Godwyn stood in a bare, silent church.

He was alone: there were no monks or nuns with him. No furniture was to be seen, except for the fixed choir stalls. There were no candles, no crucifixes, no chalices, no flowers. The watery sun that had shone fitfully through rain clouds much of this summer now cast a weak, cold light into the nave. Godwyn held his hands tightly together behind his back to keep them from shaking.

On time, the earl walked in.

With him were Lord William, Lady Philippa, Bishop Richard, Richard's assistant Archdeacon Lloyd, and the earl's clerk Father Jerome. Godwyn would have liked to surround himself with an entourage, but none of the monks knew quite how risky his scheme was, and if they had known, they might not have had the nerve to back him up; so he had decided to face the earl alone.

The bandages had been removed from Roland's head. He walked slowly but steadily. He must surely feel shaky after so many weeks in bed, Godwyn thought, but he seemed determined not to show it. He looked normal apart from the paralysis of half his face. His message to the world today would be that he was fully recovered and back in charge. And Godwyn was threatening to spoil that design.

The others looked with incredulity at the empty church, but the earl showed no surprise. "You're an arrogant monk," he said to Godwyn, speaking as always out of the left side of his mouth.

Godwyn was risking everything, and had nothing further to lose by being defiant, so he said: "You're an obstinate earl."

Roland put his hand on the hilt of his sword. "I ought to run you through for that."

"Go ahead." Godwyn held his arms out sideways, ready to be crucified. "Murder the prior of Kingsbridge, here in the cathedral, just as King Henry's knights murdered Archbishop Thomas Becket in Canterbury. Send me to Heaven and yourself to eternal damnation."

Philippa gasped with shock at Godwyn's disrespect. William moved as if to silence Godwyn. Roland restrained him with a gesture, and said to Godwyn: "Your bishop orders you to ready the church for the wedding. Don't monks take a vow of obedience?"

"The lady Margery cannot be married here."

"Why not—because you want to be prior?"

"Because she is not a virgin."

Philippa's hand flew to her mouth. Richard groaned. William drew his sword. Roland said: "This is treason!"

Godwyn said: "Put away your sword, Lord William—you can't restore her maidenhead with that."

Roland said: "What do you know of such things, monk?"

"Two men of this priory witnessed the act, which took place in a private room of the hospital, the very room where you, my lord, are staying."

"I don't believe you."

"The earl of Monmouth will."

"You would not dare to tell him."

"I must explain to him why his son cannot marry Margery in Kingsbridge Cathedral—at least until she has confessed her sin and received absolution."

"You have no proof of this slander."

"I have two witnesses. But ask the girl. I believe she will confess. I imagine she favors the lover who took her virginity over the political match chosen by her uncle." Once again Godwyn was going out on a limb. But he had seen Margery's face when Richard was kissing her, and at that moment he had felt sure she was in love. Having to marry the earl's son must be breaking her heart. It would be very difficult for such a young woman to lie convincingly if her emotions were as turbulent as Godwyn guessed.

The animated half of Roland's face was working with fury. "And who is this man who you claim committed this crime? For, if you can prove what you allege, the villain will hang, I swear. And, if not, you will. So let him be sent for, and we'll see what he has to say."

"He's already here."

Roland looked with incredulity at the four men with him—his two sons, William and Richard, plus two priests, Lloyd and Jerome.

Godwyn stared at Richard.

Roland followed the direction of Godwyn's stare. In a moment, they were all looking at Richard.

Godwyn held his breath. What would Richard say? Would he bluster? Would he accuse Godwyn of lying? Would he fly into a rage and attack his accuser?

But his face showed defeat, not anger, and after a moment he bowed his head and said: "It's no good. The damned monk is right—she will not withstand interrogation."

Earl Roland went white. "You did this?" he said. For once he was not shouting, but that seemed to make him more terrifying. "The girl I betrothed to an earl's son—you fucked her?"

Richard made no reply, but looked down at the ground.

"You fool," the earl said. "You traitor. You—"

Philippa interrupted him. "Who else knows?"

That stopped the tirade. They all looked at her.

"Perhaps the wedding may still take place," she said. "Thank God, the earl of Monmouth isn't here." She looked at Godwyn. "Who knows about this, other than the people here now, and the two men of the priory who witnessed the act?"

Godwyn tried to calm his thudding heart. He was so close to success that he seemed to taste it. "No one else knows, my lady," he said.

"All of us on the earl's side can keep the secret," she said. "What about your men?"

"They will obey their elected prior," he said, with the slightest emphasis on the word "elected."

Philippa turned to Roland. "Then the wedding can take place."

Godwyn added: "Provided the inauguration ceremony is held first."

Everyone looked at the earl.

He took a step forward and suddenly hit Richard in the face. It was a powerful blow struck by a soldier who knew how to put all his weight into it. Although he used his open hand, Richard was knocked to the ground.

Richard lay still, looking terrified, blood trickling from his mouth.

Earl Roland's face was white and sweating: the blow had used up all his reserves, and he now looked shaky. Several silent seconds passed. At last he seemed to recover his strength. With a contemptuous glance at the purple-robed figure cowering on the floor, he turned on his heel and walked, slowly but steadily, out of the church.

24

Caris stood on the green in front of Kingsbridge Cathedral, along with at least half the population of the town, waiting for the bride and groom to emerge from the great west door of the church.

Caris was not sure why she was here. She had been feeling negative about marriage ever since the day Merthin had finished his hoist, and they had had an abrasive conversation about their future. She felt angry with him, even though everything he had said made perfect sense. Of course he wanted to have his own house and live with her in it; of course he wanted to sleep with her every night and have children. That was what everyone wanted—everyone, it seemed, except Caris.

And in fact she wanted all those things, too, in a way. She would have liked to lie down beside him every evening, and put her arms around his slim body anytime she wanted, and feel his clever hands on her skin when she woke up in the morning, and give birth to a miniature version of him that they could both love and care for. But she did not want the things that went with marriage. She wanted a lover, not a master; she wanted to live with him, not dedicate her life to him. And she was angry with Merthin for forcing her to face up to the dilemma. Why could they not go on just as they were?

For three weeks she had hardly spoken to him. She pretended to have a summer cold, and in fact she developed a painful sore on her lip that gave her an excuse not to kiss him. He still took his meals at her house, and talked amiably with her father; but he did not linger after Edmund and Petranilla went to bed.

Now Caris's sore had healed and her anger had cooled. She still did not want to become Merthin's property, but she wished he would start kissing her again. However, he was not with her now. He was in the crowd, some distance away, talking to Bessie Bell, daughter of the landlord of the Bell Inn. She was a small girl with a curvy body and the kind of grin that men called saucy and women called tarty. Merthin was making her laugh. Caris looked away.

The big wooden church door opened. A cheer went up from the crowd, and the bride emerged. Margery was a pretty girl of sixteen, dressed in white, with flowers in her hair. The groom followed her out, a tall, serious-looking man about ten years older than she.

They both looked completely miserable.

They hardly knew each other. Until this week, they had met only once, six months ago, when the two earls had arranged the marriage. There was a rumor that Margery loved someone else, but of course there was no question of her disobeying Earl Roland. And her new husband had a studious air, as if he would prefer to be in a library somewhere, reading a book about geometry. What would their life together be like? It was hard to imagine their developing the kind of passion for one another that Caris and Merthin enjoyed.

She saw Merthin coming toward her through the crowd, and suddenly she was struck by the thought that she was ungrateful. How lucky she was not to be the niece of an earl! No one was going to force her into an arranged marriage. She was free to marry the man she loved—and all she could do was find reasons not to.

She greeted him with a hug and a kiss on the lips. He looked surprised, but made no comment. Some men would have been unnerved by her change of mood, but Merthin had a bedrock equanimity that was hard to shake.

They stood together and watched as Earl Roland came out of the church, followed by the earl and countess of Monmouth, then Bishop Richard and Prior Godwyn. Caris noticed that her cousin Godwyn looked both pleased and apprehensive—almost as if he were the groom. The reason, no doubt, was that he had just been inaugurated as prior.

An escort of knights formed up, the Shiring men in Roland's red-and-black livery, the Monmouth men in yellow and green. The procession moved off, heading for the guildhall. There Earl Roland was giving a banquet for the wedding guests. Edmund was going, but Caris had managed to get out of it, and Petranilla was to accompany him.

As the bridal party left the precincts, a light shower of rain began to fall. Caris and Merthin took shelter in the cathedral porch. "Come with me to the chancel," Merthin said. "I want to look at Elfric's repairs."

The wedding guests were still leaving the church. Moving against the flow, Merthin and Caris pushed through the crowd in the nave and went to the south aisle of the chancel. This part of the church was reserved for the clergy, and they would have disapproved of Caris's being there, but the monks and nuns had already left. Caris glanced around, but there was no one to see her except one unfamiliar woman, a well-dressed redhead of about thirty, presumably a wedding guest, apparently waiting for someone.

Merthin craned his neck to look up at the vaulted ceiling over the aisle. The repairs were not quite finished: a small section of the vault was still open, and a sheet of canvas, painted white, was stretched across the gap, so that the ceiling looked complete to a casual glance.

"He's doing a decent job," Merthin said. "I wonder how long it will last."

"Why wouldn't it last indefinitely?" Caris asked.

"Because we don't know why the vault crumbled. These things don't happen for no reason—they're not acts of God, regardless of what the priests may say. Whatever caused the stonework to collapse once will, presumably, do so again."

"Is it possible to discover the cause?"

"It's not easy. Elfric certainly can't do it. I might."

"But you've been sacked."

"Exactly." He stood there for a few moments, head tilted back, then said: "I want to see this from above. I'm going into the loft."

"I'll come with you."

They both looked around, but there was no one nearby except for the red-haired wedding guest, who was still loitering in the south transept. Merthin led Caris to a small door that opened on a narrow spiral staircase. She followed him up, wondering what the monks would think if they knew a woman was exploring their secret passageways. The staircase emerged into an attic over the south aisle.

Caris was intrigued to see the vault from the other side. "What you're looking at is called the extrados," Merthin said. She liked the casual way he gave her architectural information, assuming she would be interested and knowing she would understand. He never made stupid jokes about women not grasping technicalities.

He moved along the narrow walkway then lay down to examine the new stonework closely. Mischievously, she lay beside him and put her arm around him, as if they were in bed. Merthin touched the mortar between the new stones then put his finger on his tongue. "It's drying out quite quickly," he said.

"I'm sure it's very dangerous if there's moisture in the cleft."

He looked at her. "I'll give you moisture in the cleft."

"You already have."

He kissed her. She closed her eyes to enjoy it more.

After a minute she said: "Let's go to my house. We'll have it to ourselves—my father and my aunt are both at the wedding banquet."

They were about to get up when they heard voices. A man and a woman had come into the south aisle, immediately below the repair work. What they said was only a little muffled by the canvas sheet covering the hole in the ceiling. "Your son is thirteen now," the woman said. "He wants to be a knight."

"All boys do," came the reply.

Merthin whispered: "Don't move—they'll hear us."

Caris presumed the female voice to be that of the wedding guest. The male voice was familiar, and she had the feeling the speaker was a monk—but a monk could not have a son.

"And your daughter is twelve. She's going to be beautiful."

"Like her mother."

"A little." There was a pause, then the woman went on: "I can't stay long—the countess may look for me."

So she was in the entourage of the countess of Monmouth. She might be a lady-in-waiting, Caris guessed. She seemed to be giving news of children to a father who had not seen them for years. Who could it be?

He said: "Why did you want to meet me, Loreen?"

"Just to look at you. I'm sorry you lost your arm."

Caris gasped, then covered her mouth, hoping she had not been heard. There was only one monk who had lost an arm: Thomas. Now that the name had come into her mind, she knew that the voice was his. Could it be that he had a wife? And two children? Caris looked at Merthin and saw that his face was a mask of incredulity.

"What do you tell the children of me?" Thomas asked.

"That their father is dead," Loreen replied harshly. Then she began to cry. "Why did you do it?"

"I had no choice. If I had not come here, I would have been killed. Even now, I almost never leave the precincts."

"Why would anyone want to kill you?"

"To protect a secret."

"I'd be better off if you'd died. As a widow, I could find a husband, someone to be a father to my children. But this way I have all the burdens of a wife and mother but no one to help me . . . no one to put his arms around me in the night."

"I'm sorry I'm still alive."

"Oh, I didn't mean that. I don't wish you dead. I loved you once."

"And I loved you as much as a man of my kind can love a woman."

Caris frowned. What did he mean by "a man of my kind"? Was he one of those men who loved other men? Monks often were.

Whatever he meant, Loreen seemed to understand, for she said gently: "I know you did."

There was a long silence. Caris knew she and Merthin should not be eavesdropping on such an intimate conversation—but it was now too late to reveal themselves.

Loreen said: "Are you happy?"

"Yes. I was not made to be a husband, or a knight. I pray for my children every day—and for you. I ask God to wash from my hands the blood of all the men I killed. This is the life I always wanted."

"In that case, I wish you well."

"You're very generous."

"You'll probably never see me again."

"I know."

"Kiss me, and say good-bye."

There was a long silence, then light footsteps receded. Caris lay still, hardly daring to breathe. After another pause, she heard Thomas crying. His sobs were muffled, but seemed to come from deep inside. Tears came to her own eyes as she listened.

Eventually Thomas got himself under control. He sniffed, coughed, and muttered something that might have been a prayer; then she heard his steps as he walked away.

At last she and Merthin could move. They stood up and walked back along the loft and down the spiral stairs. Neither spoke as they went down the nave of the great church. Caris felt as if she had been staring at a painting of high tragedy, the figures frozen in their dramatic attitudes of the moment, their past and future only to be guessed at.

Like a painting, the scene aroused different emotions in different people, and Merthin's reaction was not the same as hers. As they emerged into a damp summer afternoon, he said: "What a sad story."

"It makes me angry," Caris said. "That woman has been ruined by Thomas."

"You can hardly blame him. He had to save his life."

"And now her life is over. She has no husband, but she can't marry again. She's forced to raise two children alone. At least Thomas has the monastery."

"She has the court of the countess."

"How can you compare the two?" Caris said irritably. "She's probably a distant relation, kept on as an act of charity, asked to perform menial tasks, helping the countess dress her hair and choose her clothes. She's got no choice—she's trapped."

"So is he. You heard him say he can't leave the precincts."

"But Thomas has a role, he's the matricularius, he makes decisions, he does something."

"Loreen has her children."

"Exactly! The man takes care of the most important building for miles around, and the woman is stuck with her children."

"Queen Isabella had four children, and for a while she was one of the most powerful people in Europe."

"But she had to get rid of her husband first."

They went on in silence, walking out of the priory grounds into the main street, and stopped in front of Caris's house. She realized that this was another quarrel, and it was on the same subject as last time: marriage.

Merthin said: "I'm going to the Bell for dinner."

That was Bessie's father's inn. "All right," Caris said despondently.

As Merthin walked away, she called after him: "Loreen would be better off if she'd never married."

He spoke over his shoulder. "What else would she do?"

That was the problem, Caris thought resentfully as she entered her house. What else was a woman to do?

The place was empty. Edmund and Petranilla were at the banquet, and the servants had the afternoon off. Only Scrap the dog was there to welcome Caris with a lazy wag of her tail. Caris patted her black head absentmindedly, then sat at the table in the hall, brooding.

Every other young woman in Christendom wanted nothing more than to marry the man she loved—why was Caris so horrified by the prospect? From where had she got such unconventional feelings? Certainly not from her own mother. Rose had wanted only to be a good wife to Edmund. She had believed what men said about the inferiority of women. Her subordination had embarrassed Caris and, though Edmund never complained, Caris suspected that he had been bored by it. Caris had more respect for her forceful, unlovable aunt Petranilla than for her compliant mother.

Even Petranilla had allowed her life to be shaped by men. For years she had worked to maneuver her father up the social ladder until he became alderman of Kingsbridge. Her strongest emotion was resentment: toward Earl Roland because he had jilted her, and toward her husband because he had died. As a widow she had dedicated herself to Godwyn's career.

Queen Isabella had been similar. She had deposed her husband, King Edward II; but the result had been that her lover, Roger Mortimer, had effectively ruled England until her son grew old enough and confident enough to oust him.

Was that what Caris should do—live her life through men? Her father wanted her to work with him in the wool business. Or she could manage Merthin's career, helping him secure contracts to construct churches and bridges, expanding his business until he was the richest and most important builder in England.

She was roused from her thoughts by a tap at the door, and the birdlike figure of Mother Cecilia walked briskly in.

"Good afternoon!" Caris said in surprise. "I was just asking myself whether all women are doomed to live their lives through men—and here you are, an obvious counterexample."

"You're not quite right," Cecilia said with a friendly smile. "I live through Jesus Christ, who was a man, though he is God, too."

Caris was not sure whether that counted. She opened the cupboard and took out a small barrel of the best wine. "Would you like a cup of my father's Rhenish?"

"Just a little, mixed with water."

Caris half-filled two cups with wine then topped up the drinks with water from a jug. "You know that my father and aunt are at the banquet."

"Yes. I came to see you."

Caris had guessed as much. The prioress did not wander around the town making social calls without a purpose.

Cecilia sipped, then went on: "I've been thinking about you, and the way you acted on the day the bridge collapsed."

"Did I do something wrong?"

"On the contrary. You did everything perfectly. You were gentle but firm with the injured, and you obeyed my orders but at the same time used your initiative. I was impressed."

"Thank you."

"And you seemed . . . not to enjoy it, exactly, but at least to find satisfaction in the work."

"People were in distress, and we brought them relief—what could be more satisfying?"

"That's how I feel, and it's why I'm a nun."

Caris saw where this was going. "I couldn't spend my life in the priory."

"The natural aptitude you showed for looking after the sick is only part of what I noticed. When people first started to walk into the cathedral carrying the injured and dead, I asked who had told them what to do. The answer was Caris Wooler."

"It was obvious what should be done."

"Yes—to you." Cecilia leaned forward earnestly. "The talent for organization is given to few people. I know—I have it, and I recognize it in others. When everyone around us is baffled, or panicked, or terrified, you and I take charge."

Caris felt this was true. "I suppose so," she said reluctantly.

"I've watched you for ten years—since the day your mother died."

"You brought her relief in her distress."

"I knew then, just by talking to you, that you were going to grow up into an exceptional woman. My feeling was confirmed when you attended the nuns' school. You're twenty now. You must be thinking about what to do with your life. I believe that God has work for you."

"How do you know what God thinks?"

Cecilia bristled. "If anyone else in town asked me that question, I'd order them down on their knees to pray for forgiveness. But you're sincere, so I'll answer. I know what God thinks because I accept the teachings of His church. And I'm convinced he wants you to be a nun."

"I like men too much."

"Always a problem for me, as a youngster—but, I can assure you, a problem that diminishes with every passing year."

"I can't be told how to live."

"Don't be a Beguine."

"What's that?"

"Beguines are nuns who accept no rules and consider their vows to be temporary. They live together, cultivate their lands and graze their cattle, and refuse to be governed by men."

Caris was always intrigued to hear of women who defied the rules. "Where are they to be found?"

"Mostly in the Netherlands. They had a leader, Marguerite Porete, who wrote a book called *The Mirror of Simple Souls*."

"I'd like to read it."

"Out of the question. The Beguines have been condemned by the church for the heresy of the Free Spirit—the belief that we can attain spiritual perfection here on earth."

"Spiritual perfection? What does that mean? It's just a phrase."

"If you're determined to close your mind to God, you'll never understand it."

"I'm sorry, Mother Cecilia, but every time I'm told something about God by a mere human, I think: But humans are fallible, so the truth might be different."

"How could the church be wrong?"

"Well, the Muslims have different beliefs."

"They're heathens!"

"They call us infidels—it's the same thing. And Buonaventura Caroli says there are more Muslims than Christians in the world. So somebody's church is wrong."

"Be careful," Cecilia said severely. "Don't allow your passion for argument to lead you into blasphemy."

"Sorry, Mother." Caris knew that Cecilia enjoyed sparring with her, but there always came a moment when the prioress stopped arguing and started preaching, and Caris had to back down. It left her feeling slightly cheated.

Cecilia stood up. "I know I can't persuade you against your will, but I wanted you to know the tendency of my thoughts. You could do nothing better than to join our nunnery, and dedicate your life to the sacrament of healing. Thank you for the wine."

As Cecilia was leaving, Caris said: "What happened to Marguerite Porete? Is she still alive?"

"No," said the prioress. "She was burned at the stake." She went out into the street, shutting the door behind her.

Caris stared at the closed door. A woman's life was a house of closed doors: she could not be an apprentice, she could not study at the university, she could not be a priest or a physician, or shoot a bow or fight with a sword, and she could not marry without submitting herself to the tyranny of her husband.

She wondered what Merthin was doing now. Was Bessie sitting at his table at the Bell Inn, watching him drink her father's best ale, giving him that inviting smile, pulling the front of her dress tight to make sure he could see what nice breasts she had? Was he being charming and amusing to her, making her laugh? Was she parting her lips to show him her even teeth, and throwing back her head so that he could appreciate the soft skin of her white throat? Was he talking to her father, Paul Bell, asking respectful and interested questions about his business, so that later Paul would tell his daughter that Merthin was a good sort, a fine young man? Would Merthin get drunk and put his arm around Bessie's waist, resting his hand on her hip then slyly inching his fingertips toward that sensitive place between her thighs that was already itching for his touch—just as he once had with Caris?

Tears came to her eyes. She felt she was a fool. She had the best man in town and here she was handing him over to a barmaid. Why did she do these things to herself?

At that moment he walked in.

She looked at him through a mist of tears. Her vision was so blurred that she could not read his expression. Had he come to make friends again—or to berate her, venting his anger with the courage of several tankards of ale?

She stood up. For a moment she was held in suspense, as he closed the door behind him and came slowly to stand in front of her. Then he said: "No matter what you do or say, I still love you."

She threw her arms around him and burst out crying.

He stroked her hair and said nothing, which was just right.

After a while they started to kiss. She felt the familiar hunger, but stronger than ever: she wanted his hands all over her, his tongue in her mouth, his fingers inside her. She felt differently and she wanted their love to find a new expression. "Let's take off all our clothes," she said. They had never done that before.

He smiled with pleasure. "All right, but what if someone comes in?"

"They'll be at the banquet for hours. And anyway we can go upstairs."

They went to her bedroom. She kicked off her shoes. Suddenly she felt shy. What would he think when he saw her naked? She knew he loved her body bit by bit: her breasts, her legs, her throat, her cunt—he always told her how beautiful they were as he kissed and caressed them. But would he now notice that her hips were too wide, her legs a little short, her breasts quite small?

He seemed to have no such inhibitions. He threw off his shirt, pulled down his underdrawers, and stood unself-consciously before her. His body was slight but strong, and he seemed full of pent-up energy, like a young deer. She noticed for the first time that the hair at his groin was the color of autumn leaves. His cock stood up eagerly. Desire overcame her shyness, and she pulled her dress quickly over her head.

He stared at her bare body, but she no longer felt embarrassed—his look inflamed her like an intimate caress. "You're beautiful," he said.

"So are you."

They lay side by side on the straw-filled palliasse that was her bed. As they kissed and touched one another, she realized that today she was not going to be satisfied with the games they usually played. "I want to do it properly," she said.

"You mean go the whole way?"

The thought of pregnancy surfaced in her mind, but she pushed it back down. She was too heated to think of consequences. "Yes," she whispered.

"So do I."

He lay on top of her. Half her life she had wondered what this moment would be like. She looked up at his face. It wore the concentrated expression that she loved so much, the look he had when he was working, his small hands shaping wood with tenderness and skill. His fingertips softly spread the petals of her sex. She was slippery and yearning for him.

He said: "Are you sure?"

Once again she suppressed the thought of pregnancy. "I'm sure."

She felt a moment of fear when he entered her. She tightened involuntarily, and he hesitated, feeling her body resisting him. "It's all right," she said. "You can push harder. You won't hurt me." She was wrong about that, and there was a sudden sharp pain as he thrust. She could not help crying out.

"I'm sorry," he whispered.

"Just wait a minute," she said.

They lay still. He kissed her eyelids and her forehead and the tip of her nose. She stroked his face and looked into his golden brown eyes. Then the pain was gone and the desire came back, and she began to move, rejoicing in the feeling of having the man she loved deep inside her body for the first time. She thrilled to see the intensity of his pleasure. He stared at her, a faint smile on his lips, a deep hunger in his eyes, as they moved faster.

"I can't stop," he said breathlessly.

"Don't stop, don't stop."

She watched him intently. In a few moments he was overwhelmed by pleasure, his eyes shut tight and his mouth open and his whole body as taut as a bowstring. She felt his spasms inside her, and the jet of his ejaculation, and she thought that nothing in life had prepared her for such happiness. A moment later she herself was convulsed with ecstasy. She had had this sensation before, but not so powerfully, and she closed her eyes and gave herself up to it, pulling his body hard against her own as she shook like a tree in the wind.

When it was over, they lay still for a long while. He buried his face in her neck, and she felt his panting breath on her skin. She stroked his back. His skin was damp with perspiration. Gradually her heartbeat slowed, and a deep contentment stole over her like twilight on a summer evening.

"So," she said after a while, "that's what all the fuss is about."

25

The day after Godwyn was confirmed as prior of Kingsbridge, Edmund Wooler came to Merthin's parents' house early in the morning.

Merthin tended to forget what an important personage Edmund was, for Edmund treated him as a member of the family; but Gerald and Maud acted as if receiving an unexpected royal visitation. They were embarrassed that Edmund should see how poor their house was. There was only one room. Merthin and his parents slept on straw mattresses on the floor. There was a fireplace and a table and a small yard at the back.

Fortunately, the family had been up since sunrise, and had washed and dressed and tidied the place. All the same, when Edmund came stomping into the house with his uneven gait, Merthin's mother dusted a stool, patted her hair, closed the back door then opened it again, and put a log on the fire. His father bowed several times, put on a surcoat, and offered Edmund a cup of ale.

"No, thank you, Sir Gerald," said Edmund, no doubt knowing that the family had none to spare. "However, I'll take a small bowl of your pottage, Lady Maud, if I may." Every family kept a pot of oats on the fire to which they added bones, apple cores, pea pods, and other scraps, to be slow-cooked for days. Flavored with salt and herbs, the result was a soup that never tasted the same twice. It was the cheapest food.

Pleased, Maud ladled some pottage into a bowl and put it on the table with a spoon and a plate of bread.

Merthin was still feeling the euphoria of the previous afternoon. It was like being slightly drunk. He had gone to sleep thinking of Caris's naked body and woken up smiling. But he was suddenly reminded of his confrontation with Elfric over Griselda. A false instinct told him that Edmund was going to scream, "You defiled my daughter!" and hit him across the face with a length of timber.

It was only a momentary vision, and it vanished as Edmund sat at the table. He picked up the spoon but, before he began to eat, he said to Merthin: "Now that we've got a prior, I want to start work on the new bridge as soon as possible."

"Good," said Merthin.

Edmund swallowed a spoonful and smacked his lips. "This is the best pottage I've ever tasted, Lady Maud." Merthin's mother looked pleased.

Merthin was grateful to Edmund for being charming to his parents. They felt the humiliation of their reduced status, and it was balm to the wound to have the town's alderman eating at their table and calling them Sir Gerald and Lady Maud.

Now his father said: "I almost didn't marry her, Edmund—did you know that?"

Merthin was sure Edmund had heard the story before, but he replied: "Good lord, no—how did that happen?"

"I saw her in church on Easter Sunday, and fell in love with her instantly. There must have been a thousand people in Kingsbridge Cathedral, and she was the most beautiful woman there."

"Now, Gerald, no need to exaggerate," Maud said crisply.

"Then she disappeared into the crowd, and I couldn't find her! I didn't know her name. I asked people who was the pretty girl with the fair hair, and they said all the girls were pretty and fair."

Maud said: "I hurried away after the service. We were staying at the

Holly Bush Inn, and my mother was unwell, so I went back to take care of her."

Gerald said: "I looked all over town, but I couldn't find her. After Easter, everyone went home. I was living in Shiring, and she in Casterham, though I didn't know that. I thought I'd never see her again. I imagined she might have been an angel, come to earth to make sure everyone was attending the service."

She said: "Gerald, please."

"But my heart was lost. I took no interest in other women. I expected to spend my life longing for the Angel of Kingsbridge. This went on for two years. Then I saw her at a tournament in Winchester."

She said: "This complete stranger came up to me and said: 'It's you—after all this time! You must marry me before you disappear again.' I thought he was mad."

"Amazing," said Edmund.

Merthin thought Edmund's goodwill had been stretched far enough. "Anyway," he said, "I've drawn some designs on the tracing floor in the mason's loft at the cathedral."

Edmund nodded. "A stone bridge wide enough for two carts?"

"As you specified—and ramped at both ends. And I've found a way to reduce the price by about a third."

"That's astonishing! How?"

"I'll show you, as soon as you've finished eating."

Edmund spooned up the last of the pottage and stood. "I'm done. Let's go." He turned to Gerald and inclined his head in a slight bow. "Thank you for your hospitality."

"It's a pleasure to have you here, alderman."

Merthin and Edmund stepped out into a light drizzle. Instead of heading for the cathedral, Merthin led Edmund toward the river. Edmund's lopsided stride was instantly recognizable, and every second person on the street greeted him with a friendly word or a respectful bow.

Merthin suddenly felt nervous. He had been thinking about the bridge design for months. While he worked at St Mark's, supervising the carpenters who were constructing the new roof as the old was demolished, he mulled over the greater challenge of the bridge. Now for the first time his ideas would come under scrutiny by someone else.

As yet, Edmund had no idea how radical Merthin's plan was.

The muddy street wound downhill through houses and workshops. The city ramparts had fallen into disrepair during two centuries of civil peace, and in some places all that remained were humps of earth that now formed parts of garden walls. At the river's edge were industries that used large quantities of water, especially wool dyers and leather tanners.

Merthin and Edmund emerged onto the muddy foreshore between a slaughterhouse that gave off a strong smell of blood and a smithy where hammers clanged on iron. Directly in front of them, across a narrow stretch of water, was Leper Island. Edmund said: "Why are we here? The bridge is a quarter of a mile upstream."

"It was," said Merthin. He took a breath and said: "I think we should build the new one here."

"A bridge to the island?"

"And another from the island to the far shore. Two small bridges instead of one big one. Much cheaper."

"But people will have to walk across the island from one bridge to the other."

"Why not?"

"Because it's a leper colony!"

"There's only one leper left. He can be moved elsewhere. The disease seems to be dying out."

Edmund looked thoughtful. "So everyone who comes to Kingsbridge will arrive at this spot, where we're standing."

"We'll have to build a new street, and knock down some of these buildings—but the cost will be small by comparison with the money saved on the bridge."

"And on the other side . . ."

"A pasture that belongs to the priory. I can see the whole layout when I'm on the roof of St. Mark's. That's how come I thought of it."

Edmund was impressed. "That's very clever. I wonder why the bridge wasn't put here originally."

"The first bridge was erected hundreds of years ago. The river probably had a different shape then. Riverbanks must move their position as the centuries go by. The channel between the island and the pasture could have been wider at one time. Then there would have been no advantage in building here."

Edmund peered across the water, and Merthin followed his gaze. The leper colony was a scatter of tumbledown wooden buildings spread over three or four acres. The island was too rocky for cultivation, but there were some trees and scrubby grass. The place was infested with rabbits, which the townspeople would not eat because of a superstition that they were the souls of dead lepers. At one time the ostracized inhabitants had kept their own chickens and pigs. Now, however, it was simpler for the priory to supply food to the last remaining inhabitant. "You're right," Edmund said. "There hasn't been a new case of leprosy in the town for at least ten years."

"I've never seen a leper," Merthin said. "As a child, I thought people were saying 'leopard.' I imagined that island to be occupied by spotted lions."

Edmund laughed. Turning his back on the river, he looked at the buildings around. "There will be some political work to do," he mused. "The people whose homes must be demolished will have to be convinced that they're the lucky ones, being moved to new and better houses while their neighbors missed out. And the island may have to be cleansed with holy water to convince people that it's safe. But we can handle all that."

"I've drawn both bridges with pointed arches, like the cathedral," Merthin said. "They will be beautiful."

"Show me."

They left the riverside and walked uphill through the town to the priory. The cathedral dripped with rain under a layer of low cloud like smoke from a damp fire. Merthin was looking forward to seeing his drawings again—he had not been to the loft for a week or so—and to explaining them to Edmund. He had thought a great deal about the way the current had undermined the old bridge, and how he could protect the new one from the same fate.

He led Edmund through the north porch and up the spiral staircase. His wet shoes slipped on the worn stone steps. Edmund energetically hauled his withered leg up behind him.

Several lamps were burning in the mason's loft. At first Merthin was pleased, for that meant they would be able to see his drawings more clearly. Then he saw Elfric working on the tracing floor.

He felt momentarily frustrated. The enmity between himself and his former master was as great as ever. Elfric had failed to prevent townspeople from employing Merthin, but he continued to block Merthin's application to join the carpenters' guild—leaving Merthin in an anomalous position, illegitimate but accepted. Elfric's attitude was pointless, but spiteful.

Elfric's presence here would put a damper on Merthin's conversation with Edmund. He told himself not to be so sensitive. Why should it not be Elfric who was made uncomfortable?

He held the door for Edmund, and together they crossed the room to the tracing floor. Then he suffered a shock.

Elfric was bent over the tracing floor, drawing with a pair of compasses—on a fresh layer of plaster. He had re-covered the floor, totally obliterating Merthin's drawings.

Merthin said incredulously: "What have you done?"

Elfric looked contemptuously at him and went on with his drawing, saying nothing.

"He's wiped out my work," Merthin said to Edmund.

"What's your explanation, man?" Edmund demanded.

Elfric could not ignore his father-in-law. "There's nothing to explain," he said. "A tracing floor has to be renewed at intervals."

"But you've covered over important designs!"

"Have I? The prior has not commissioned this boy to make any drawings, and the boy has not asked permission to use the tracing floor."

Edmund was never slow to anger, and Elfric's cool insolence was getting under his skin. "Don't act stupid," he said. "I asked Merthin to prepare drawings for the new bridge."

"I'm sorry, but only the prior has authority to do that."

"Damn it, the guild is providing the money."

"A loan, to be repaid."

"It still gives us the right to a say on the design."

"Does it? You'll have to speak to the prior about that. I don't think he'll be impressed by your choice of an inexperienced apprentice as your designer, though."

Merthin was looking at the drawings Elfric had scratched in the new plaster. "I suppose this is your bridge design," he said.

"Prior Godwyn has commissioned me to build it," Elfric said.

Edmund was shocked. "Without asking us?"

Elfric said resentfully: "What's the matter—don't you want the work to go to your own daughter's husband?"

"Round arches," Merthin said, still studying Elfric's drawing. "And narrow openings. How many piers will you have?"

Elfric was reluctant to answer, but Edmund was staring expectantly at him. "Seven," he said.

"The wooden bridge only had five!" Merthin said. "Why are they so thick, and the openings so narrow?"

"To bear the weight of a stone-paved roadway."

"You don't need thick piers for that. Look at this cathedral—its columns bear the entire weight of the roof, but they're slim and widely spaced."

Elfric sneered. "No one's going to drive a cart across the roof of a church."

"That's true, but—" Merthin stopped. The rain on the cathedral's vast expanse of roof probably weighed more than an oxcart loaded with stone, but why should he explain this to Elfric? It was not his role to educate an incompetent builder. Elfric's design was poor, but Merthin did not want to improve it, he wanted to replace it with his own, so he shut up.

Edmund also realized he was wasting his breath. "This decision is not going to be made by you two," he said, and he stomped off.

John Constable's baby daughter was christened in the cathedral by Prior Godwyn. This honor was granted because he was an important employee of the priory. All the leading townspeople attended. Although John was neither wealthy nor well connected—his father had worked in the priory stables—Petranilla said that respectable people should take care to show friendship toward him and support for him. Caris thought they condescended to John because they needed him to protect their property.

It was raining again, and the people grouped around the font were wetter than the infant who was sprinkled with holy water. Strange feelings stirred in Caris as she looked at the tiny, helpless child. Since lying with Merthin she had simply refused to let herself think about pregnancy but, all the same, she felt a warm surge of protective emotion when she saw the baby.

She was named Jesca, after Abraham's niece.

Caris's cousin Godwyn had never been comfortable with babies and, as soon as the brief rite was over, he turned to leave. But Petranilla grabbed the sleeve of his Benedictine robe. "What about this bridge?" she said.

She spoke in a low voice, but Caris heard, and made up her mind to listen to the rest.

Godwyn said: "I've asked Elfric to prepare drawings and estimates."

"Good. We should keep it in the family."

"Elfric is the priory's builder."

"Other people may want to horn in."

"I shall decide who builds the bridge."

Caris was annoyed enough to intervene. "How dare you," she said to Petranilla.

"I was not speaking to you," her aunt said.

Caris ignored that. "Why should Merthin's design not be considered?"

"Because he isn't family."

"He practically lives with us!"

"But you're not married to him. If you were, it might be different."

Caris knew she was at a disadvantage there, so she shifted her ground.

"You've always been prejudiced against Merthin," she said. "But everyone knows he's a better builder than Elfric."

Her sister, Alice, heard that and joined in the argument. "Elfric taught Merthin everything, and now Merthin pretends he knows better!"

That was dishonest, Caris knew, and she felt angry. "Who built the ferry?" she said, raising her voice. "Who repaired the roof of St. Mark's?"

"Merthin was working with Elfric when he built the ferry. And no one asked Elfric about St. Mark's."

"Because they knew he wouldn't be able to solve the problem!"

Godwyn interrupted. "Please!" he said, with his hands raised in front of himself protectively. "I know you're my family, but I'm the prior and this is the cathedral. I can't be harangued by womenfolk in public."

Edmund joined the circle. "Just what I was going to say. Keep your voices down."

Alice said accusingly: "You should be supporting your son-in-law."

It occurred to Caris that Alice was getting more like Petranilla. Although she was only twenty-one, and Petranilla was more than twice that age, Alice had the same purse-mouthed look of disapproval. She was also becoming more stout, her bosom filling out the front of her dress like wind in a sail.

Edmund looked sternly at Alice. "This decision will not be made on the basis of family relationships," he said. "The fact that Elfric is married to my daughter won't help his bridge stay upright."

He had strong views on this subject, Caris knew. He believed you should always do business with the most reliable supplier, always hire the best man for the job, regardless of friendship or family ties. "Any man who needs to surround himself with loyal acolytes doesn't really believe in himself," he would say. "And if he doesn't believe in himself, why should I?"

Petranilla said: "So how will the choice be made?" She gave him a shrewd look. "You've obviously got a plan."

"The priory and the guild will consider Elfric's design and Merthin's—and any others that may be put forward," Edmund said decisively. "All designs must be drawn and costed. The costing must be independently checked by other builders."

Alice muttered: "I've never heard of such goings-on. It's like an archery contest. Elfric is the priory's builder; he should do the job."

Her father ignored her. "Finally, the designers will be questioned by the leading citizens of the town at a meeting of the parish guild. And then"—he looked at Godwyn, who was pretending not to be bewildered by the way the decision process had been taken out of his hands—"and then Prior Godwyn will make his choice."

The meeting took place in the guildhall on the main street. It had a stone undercroft below and a timber superstructure, topped by a tiled roof and two stone chimneys. In the basement were the large kitchen that prepared food for the banquets, a jail, and an office for the constable. The main floor was as spacious as a church, a hundred feet long and thirty feet wide. At one end was a chapel. Because it was so wide, and because timbers long enough to span a thirty-foot roof were rare and expensive, the main room was divided by a row of wooden pillars supporting the joists.

It appeared an unpretentious building, made of the materials used in the humblest dwellings, glorifying nobody. But, as Edmund often said, the money made by the people here paid for the limestone-and-stained-glass majesty of the cathedral. And the guildhall was comfortable in its unostentatious way. There were tapestries on the walls and glass in the windows, and two huge fireplaces kept it warm in winter. When business was booming, the food served here was fit for royalty.

The parish guild had been formed hundreds of years ago, when Kingsbridge was a small town. A few merchants had got together to raise money to buy ornaments for the cathedral. But when wealthy men eat and drink in a group they inevitably discuss their common concerns, and fund-raising soon became secondary to politics. From the start the guild was dominated by wool merchants, which was why a huge pair of scales and a standard weight for a woolsack—364 pounds—stood at one end of the hall. As Kingsbridge grew, other guilds had been formed, representing crafts—carpenters, masons, brewers, goldsmiths—but their leading members also belonged to the parish guild, which retained its primacy. It was a less powerful version of the guild merchant that ruled most English towns, but was prohibited here by the town's landlord, Kingsbridge Priory.

Merthin had never attended a meeting or banquet here, but he had been inside several times on more mundane business. He liked to crane back his neck and study the complex geometry of the roof timbers, a lesson in how the weight of a broad expanse of roof could be funneled down to a few slender wooden pillars. Most of the elements made sense, but one or two pieces of wood seemed to him to be superfluous, or even detrimental, transferring weight to weaker zones. That was because no one really knew what made buildings stand up. Builders went by instinct and experience, and sometimes got it wrong.

This evening Merthin was in a state of high anxiety, too nervous to really appreciate the woodwork. The guild was about to pass judgment on his bridge design. It was far superior to Elfric's—but would they see that?

Elfric had had the benefit of the tracing floor. Merthin might have asked Godwyn for permission to use it, but he had been afraid of further sabotage by Elfric, so he had devised an alternative. He had stretched a large piece of parchment across a wooden frame, and had drawn his design on the skin with a pen and ink. Tonight this might work to his advantage, for he had brought his design with him to the guildhall, so that members would have it in front of them, whereas Elfric's would only be in their memories.

He placed his framed drawing at the front of the hall, on a three-legged stand he had devised for the purpose. Everyone came and looked at it as they arrived, although they had all seen it at least once over the last few days. They had also climbed the spiral staircase to the loft and looked at Elfric's drawings. Merthin thought most people preferred his design, but some were wary of backing a youngster against an experienced man. Many had kept their opinions to themselves.

The noise level rose as the hall filled up with men and a few women. They dressed up for the guild, as they did for church, the men in expensive wool coats despite the mild summer weather, the women in elaborate headdresses. Although everyone paid lip service to the untrustworthiness and general inferiority of women, in practice several of the town's wealthiest and most important citizens were female. There was Mother Cecilia, sitting now at the front with her personal assistant, a nun known as Old Julie. Caris was here—everyone acknowledged that she was Edmund's right hand. Merthin experienced a jolt of desire as she sat on the bench next to him, her thigh warm against his own. Anyone carrying on a trade in the town had to belong to a guild—outsiders could do business only on market days. Even monks and priests were compelled to join if they wanted to trade, which they often did. When a man died, it was common for his widow to continue his enterprise. Betty Baxter was the town's most prosperous baker; Sarah Taverner kept the Holly Bush Inn. It would have been difficult and cruel to prevent such women earning a living. Much easier to include them in the guild.

Edmund normally chaired these meetings, sitting on a big wooden throne on a raised platform at the front. Today, however, there were two chairs on the platform. Edmund sat in one and, when Prior Godwyn arrived, Edmund invited him to take the other. Godwyn was accompanied by all the senior monks, and Merthin was pleased to see Thomas among them.

Philemon was also in the entourage, lanky and awkward, and Merthin wondered briefly what on earth Godwyn had brought him for.

Godwyn was looking pained. Opening the proceedings, Edmund was careful to acknowledge that the prior was in charge of the bridge, and the choice of design was ultimately his. But everyone knew that, in fact, Edmund had taken the decision out of Godwyn's hands by calling this meeting. Provided there was a clear consensus tonight, Godwyn would have great difficulty in going against the expressed will of the merchants in a matter of commerce rather than religion. Edmund asked Godwyn to begin with a prayer, and Godwyn obliged, but he knew he had been outmaneuvered, and that was why he looked as if there was a bad smell.

Edmund stood up and said: "These two designs have been costed by Elfric and Merthin, who have used the same methods of calculation."

Elfric interjected: "Of course we have—he learned them from me." There was a ripple of laughter from the older men.

It was true. There were formulae for calculating costs per square foot of wall, per cubic yard of infill, per foot of a roof span, and for more intricate work such as arches and vaulting. All builders used the same methods, though with their individual variations. The bridge calculations had been complex, but easier than for a building such as a church.

Edmund went on: "Each man has checked the other's calculations, so there is no room for dispute."

Edward Butcher called out: "Yes—all builders overcharge by the same amount!" That got a big laugh. Edward was popular with the men for his quick wit, and with the women for his good looks and brown bedroom eyes. He was not so popular with his wife, who knew about his infidelities and had recently attacked him with one of his own heavy knives; he still had a bandage on his left arm.

"Elfric's bridge will cost two hundred and eighty-five pounds," Edmund said as the laughter died away. "Merthin's comes out at three hundred and seven. The difference is twenty-two pounds, as most of you will have worked out faster than me." There was a quiet chuckle at that: Edmund was often teased for having his daughter do his arithmetic for him. He still used the old Latin numerals, because he could not get used to the new Arabic digits that made calculation so much easier.

A new voice said: "Twenty-two pounds is a lot of money." It was Bill Watkin, the builder who had refused to hire Merthin, looking like one of the monks with his bald dome.

Dick Brewer said: "Yes, but Merthin's bridge is twice as wide. It ought to cost twice as much—but it doesn't, because it's a cleverer design." Dick was fond of his own product, ale, and in consequence had a protruding round belly like a pregnant woman.

Bill rejoined: "How many days a year do we need a bridge wide enough for two carts?"

"Every market day and all of Fleece Fair week."

"Not so," said Bill. "It's only for an hour in the morning and another in the afternoon."

"I've waited two hours with a cartload of barley before now."

"You should have the sense to bring your barley in on quiet days."

"I bring barley in every day." Dick was the largest brewer in the county. He owned a huge copper kettle that held five hundred gallons, in consequence of which his tavern was called the Copper.

Edmund interrupted this spat. "There are other problems caused by delays on the bridge," he said. "Some traders go to Shiring, where there's no bridge and no queue. Others do their business while waiting in line, then go home without ever entering the town, and save themselves the bridge toll and the market taxes. It's forestalling, and it's illegal, but we've never succeeded in stopping it. And then there's the question of how people think of Kingsbridge. Right now we're the town whose bridge collapsed. If we're going to attract back all the business we're losing, we need to change that. I'd like us to become known as the town with the best bridge in England."

Edmund was hugely influential, and Merthin began to scent victory.

Betty Baxter, an enormously fat woman in her forties, stood up and pointed to something on Merthin's drawing. "What's this, here in the middle of the bridge parapet, over the pier?" she said. "There's a little pointed bit that sticks out over the water, like a viewing platform. What is it for, fishing?" The others laughed.

"It's a pedestrian refuge," Merthin answered. "If you're walking over the bridge, and suddenly the earl of Shiring rides across with twenty mounted knights, you can step out of their way."

Edward Butcher said: "I hope it's big enough to fit Betty in."

Everyone laughed, but Betty persisted with her questioning. "Why is the pier underneath it pointed like that all the way down to the water? Elfric's piers aren't pointed."

"To deflect debris. Look at any river bridge—you'll see the piers are chipped and cracked. What do you think causes that damage? It must be the large pieces of wood—tree trunks, or timbers from demolished buildings—that you see floating downstream and crashing into piers."

"Or Ian Boatman when he's drunk," said Edward.

"Boats or debris, they will cause less damage to my pointed piers. Elfric's will suffer the full impact."

Elfric said: "My walls are too strong to be knocked down by bits of wood."

"On the contrary," said Merthin. "Your arches are narrower than mine, therefore the water will be drawn through them faster, and the debris will strike the piers with greater force, causing more damage."

He could see from Elfric's face that the older man had not even thought of that. But the audience were not builders—how could they judge what was right?

Around the base of each pier, Merthin had drawn a pile of rough stones, known to builders as riprap. This would prevent the current undermining his piers the way it had those of the old wooden bridge. But no one asked him about the riprap, so he did not explain it.

Betty had more questions. "Why is your bridge so long? Elfric's begins at the water's edge. Yours starts several yards inland. Isn't that unnecessary expense?"

"My bridge is ramped at both ends," Merthin explained. "That's so that you step off the bridge onto dry land, instead of a swamp. No more oxcarts getting bogged down on the beach and blocking the bridge for an hour."

"Cheaper to put down a paved road," said Elfric.

Elfric was beginning to sound desperate. Then Bill Watkin stood up. "I'm having trouble deciding who's right and who's wrong," he said. "When these two argue, it's difficult to make up your mind. And I'm a builder—it must be worse for those who aren't." There was a murmur of agreement. Bill went on: "So I think we should look at the men, not the designs."

Merthin had been afraid of this. He listened with increasing despair.

"Which of the two do you know best?" said Bill. "Which can you rely on? Elfric has been a builder in this town, man and boy, for twenty years. We can look at houses he's put up and see they're still standing. We can see the repairs he's done on the cathedral. On the other hand, here's Merthin—a clever lad, we know, but a bit of a tearaway, and never finished his apprenticeship. There's not a lot to indicate that he's capable of taking charge of the largest building project Kingsbridge has seen since the construction of the cathedral. I know which one I trust." He sat down.

Several men voiced their approval. They would not judge the designs—they would decide on personalities. It was maddeningly unfair.

Then Brother Thomas spoke up. "Has anyone in Kingsbridge ever been involved in a project that involved building below water level?"

Merthin knew the answer was no. He felt a surge of hope. This could rescue it for him.

Thomas went on: "I would like to know how both men would handle that problem."

Merthin was ready with his solution—but he was afraid that if he spoke first Elfric would simply echo him. He compressed his lips, hoping that Thomas—who usually helped him—would get the message.

Thomas caught Merthin's eye, and said: "Elfric, what would you do?"

"The answer is simpler than you think," Elfric said. "You just have to drop loose rubble into the river at the point where your pier will stand. The rubble rests on the river bottom. You put more and more in until the pile is visible above water level. Then you build your pier on that foundation."

As Merthin had expected, Elfric had come up with the crudest solution to the problem. Now Merthin said: "There are two snags with Elfric's method. One is that a pile of rubble is no more stable under water than on land. Over time, it will shift and drop, and when that happens the bridge will subside. If you want a bridge to last only a few years, fine. But I think we should build for the long term."

He heard a quiet rumble of concurrence.

"The second problem is the shape of the pile. It will naturally slope outwards below the waterline, restricting the passage of boats, especially when the river is low. And Elfric's arches are already narrow."

Elfric said irritably: "What would you do instead?"

Merthin suppressed a smile. That was what he had wanted to hear—Elfric admitting that he did not know a better answer. "I'll tell you," he said. And I'll show everyone that I know better than the idiot who chopped my door to pieces, he thought. He looked around. They were all listening. Their decision hung on what he would say next.

He took a deep breath. "First, I would take a pointed wooden stake and pile-drive it into the riverbed. Then I would bang in another next to it, touching; then another. In that way I would build a ring of stakes around the place in the river where I want to put my pier."

"A ring of stakes?" Elfric jeered. "That will never keep the water out."

Brother Thomas, who had asked the question, said: "Listen to him, please. He listened to you."

Merthin said: "Next, I would build a second ring inside the first, with a gap between them of half a foot." He sensed that he had his audience's attention now.

"It still won't be waterproof," said Elfric.

Edmund said: "Shut up, Elfric, this is interesting."

Merthin went on: "Then I would pour a clay mortar into the gap between the two rings. The mixture would displace the water, being heavier. And it would plug any chinks between the wood stakes, making the ring watertight. This is called a cofferdam."

The room was quiet.

"Finally, I would remove the water from inside by bucket, exposing the riverbed, and build a mortared stone foundation."

Elfric was dumbstruck. Both Edmund and Godwyn were staring at Merthin.

Thomas said: "Thank you both. Speaking for myself, that makes the decision an easy one."

"Yes, said Edmund. "I rather think it does."

Caris was surprised that Godwyn had wanted Elfric to design the bridge. She understood that Elfric would seem a safer choice—but Godwyn was a reformer, not a conservative, and she had expected him to be enthusiastic about Merthin's clever, radical design. Instead he had timidly favored the cautious option.

Fortunately, Edmund had been able to outmaneuver Godwyn, and now Kingsbridge would have a well-built, beautiful bridge that would allow two carts to cross at the same time. But Godwyn's eagerness to appoint the unimaginative sycophant rather than the bold man of talent was an ominous sign for the future.

And Godwyn had never been a good loser. When he was a boy Petranilla had taught him to play chess, letting him win to encourage him, and he had challenged his uncle Edmund; but after being beaten twice he had sulked and refused to play again. He was in the same mood after the meeting in the guildhall, she could tell. It was probably not that he was particularly attracted to Elfric's design. But he undoubtedly resented having the decision taken out of his hands. Next day, when she and her father went to the prior's house, she anticipated trouble.

Godwyn greeted them coolly and did not offer any refreshment. As always, Edmund pretended not to notice slights. "I want Merthin to start work on the bridge immediately," he said as he sat down at the table in the hall. "I have pledges of money for the full amount of Merthin's budget—"

"From whom?" Godwyn interrupted.

"The town's wealthiest traders."

Godwyn continued to look inquiringly at Edmund.

Edmund shrugged and said: "Fifty pounds from Betty Baxter, eighty from Dick Brewer, seventy from myself, and ten pounds each from eleven others."

"I didn't know our citizens possessed such riches," Godwyn said. He seemed both awestruck and envious. "God has been kind."

Edmund added: "Kind enough to reward people for a lifetime's hard work and worry."

"No doubt."

"Which is why I need to give them reassurances about the return of their money. When the bridge is built, the tolls will come to the parish guild, which will use them to repay loans—but who will collect the pennies as the passengers cross the bridge? I think it has to be a servant of the guild."

"I never agreed to this," Godwyn said.

"I know, that's why I'm raising it now."

"I mean, I never agreed to pay the tolls to the parish guild."

"What?"

Caris stared at Godwyn, flabbergasted. Of course he had agreed to it—what was he talking about? He had spoken to her as well as to Edmund and assured them that Brother Thomas—

"Oh," she said. "You promised that Thomas would build the bridge, if he was elected prior. Then, when Thomas withdrew and you became the candidate, we assumed . . ."

"You assumed," Godwyn said. A smirk of triumph played about his lips.

Edmund could barely contain himself. "This is not square dealing, Godwyn!" he said in a choked voice. "You knew what the understanding was!"

"I knew no such thing, and you should call me Father Prior."

Edmund's voice got louder. "Then we're back where we were with Prior Anthony three months ago! Except that now, instead of an inadequate bridge, we have no bridge at all. Don't imagine it will be built at no cost to you. Citizens may lend their life savings to the priory, on the security of income from the bridge tolls, but they will not give their money away . . . Father Prior."

"Then they must manage without a bridge. I have only just become prior—how can I start by alienating a right that has belonged to my priory for hundreds of years?"

"But it's only temporary!" Edmund exploded. "And if you don't do this no one will gain any money from bridge tolls because there will be no cursed bridge!"

Caris was furious, but she bit her tongue and tried to figure out what Godwyn was up to. He was getting his revenge for last night, but did he really mean it? "What do you want?" she said to him.

Edmund looked surprised by the question, but he said nothing: the reason he brought Caris with him to meetings was that she often saw things he missed, and asked questions he had not thought of.

"I don't know what you mean," Godwyn replied.

"You've pulled a surprise," she said. "You've caught us wrong-footed. Very well. We admit we made an assumption that may have been unwarranted. But what's your purpose? Just to make us feel stupid?"

"You asked for this meeting, not I."

Edmund burst out: "What kind of way is that to talk to your uncle and your cousin?"

"Just a minute, Papa," Caris said. Godwyn did have a secret agenda, she felt sure, but he did not want to admit it. All right, she thought, I'll have to guess it. "Give me a minute to think," she said. Godwyn still wanted the bridge—he had to, nothing else made sense. The business about alienating the priory's ancient rights was rhetoric, the kind of pompous prating that all students were taught at Oxford. Did he want Edmund to break down and agree to Elfric's design? She did not think so. Godwyn clearly resented the way Edmund had appealed over his head to the citizenry, but he must see that Merthin was offering twice as much bridge for almost the same money. So what else could it be?

Perhaps he just wanted a better deal.

He had looked hard at the priory's finances, she guessed. Having railed comfortably against Anthony's inefficiency for many years, he was now confronted with the reality of having to do the job better himself. Perhaps it was not going to be as easy as he had imagined. Perhaps he was not as clever about money and management as he had thought. In desperation, he wanted the bridge *and* the money from tolls. But how did he think that could happen?

She said: "What could we offer you that would make you change your mind?"

"Build the bridge without taking the tolls," he said instantly.

So that was his agenda. You always were a bit sneaky, Godwyn, she thought.

A flash of inspiration struck her, and she said: "How much money are we talking about?"

Godwyn looked suspicious. "Why do you want to know that?"

Edmund said: "We can work it out. Not counting citizens, who don't pay the toll, about a hundred people cross the bridge every market day, and carts pay twopence. It's much less now, with the ferry, of course."

Caris said: "Say a hundred and twenty pennies a week, or ten shillings, which comes to twenty-six pounds a year."

Edmund said: "Then, during Fleece Fair week, about a thousand on the first day, and another two hundred each subsequent day."

"That's two thousand two hundred, plus carts, call it two thousand four hundred pennies, which is ten pounds. Total, thirty-six pounds a year." Caris looked at Godwyn. "Is that about right?"

"Yes," he acknowledged grudgingly.

"So, what you want from us is thirty-six pounds a year."

"Yes."

"Impossible!" said Edmund.

"Not necessarily," Caris said. "Suppose the priory were to grant the parish guild a lease on the bridge—" Thinking on her feet, she added: "Plus an acre of ground at either end, and the island in the middle—for thirty-six pounds a year, in perpetuity." Once the bridge was built, that land would be priceless, she knew. "Would that give you what you want, Father Prior?"

"Yes."

Godwyn clearly thought he was getting thirty-six pounds a year for something worthless. He had no idea how much rent could be charged for a plot of land at the end of a bridge. The worst negotiator in the world is a man who believes he's clever, Caris thought.

Edmund said: "But how would the guild recoup the cost of construction?"

"With Merthin's design, the number of people and carts crossing should rise. Theoretically it could double. Everything over thirty-six pounds is the guild's. Then we could put up buildings either side to service travelers—taverns, stables, cook shops. They should be profitable—we could charge a good rent."

"I don't know," said Edmund. "It seems very risky to me."

For a moment, Caris felt furious with her father. She had come up with a brilliant solution, and he seemed to be finding unnecessary fault with it. Then she realized he was faking. She could see the light of enthusiasm in his eyes, not quite concealed. He loved the idea, but he did not want Godwyn to know how keen he was. He was hiding his feelings, for fear the prior would try to negotiate a better bargain. It was a ploy father and daughter had used before, when bargaining over wool.

Having figured out what he was up to, Caris played along, pretending to share his misgivings. "I know it's hazardous," she said gloomily. "We could lose everything. But what alternative do we have? We've got our backs to the wall. If we don't build the bridge, we'll go out of business."

Edmund shook his head dubiously. "All the same, I can't agree to this on behalf of the guild. I'll have to talk to the people who are putting up the money. I can't say what their reply will be." He looked Godwyn in the eye. "But I'll do my best to persuade them, if this is your best offer."

Godwyn had not actually made an offer, Caris reflected; but he had forgotten that. "It is," he said firmly.

Got you, Caris thought triumphantly.

"You're really very shrewd," Merthin said.

He was lying between Caris's legs, his head on her thigh, toying with her pubic hair. They had just made love for the second time ever, and he had found it even more joyous than the first. As they dozed in the pleasant daydream of satisfied lovers, she had told him about her negotiation with Godwyn. He was impressed.

Caris said: "The best of it is, he thinks he's driven a hard bargain. In fact, a perpetual lease on the bridge and the land around it is priceless."

"All the same, it's a bit dismaying if he's going to be no better at managing the priory's money than your uncle Anthony was."

They were in the forest, in a clearing hidden by brambles and shaded by a stand of tall beech trees, where a stream ran over rocks to form a pool. It had probably been used by lovers for hundreds of years. They had stripped naked and bathed in the pool before making love on the grassy bank. Anyone traveling clandestinely through the woods would skirt the thicket, so they were not likely to be discovered, unless by children picking blackberries—which was how Caris had originally discovered the glade, she told Merthin.

Now he said idly: "Why did you ask for that island?"

"I'm not sure. It's obviously not as valuable as the land at either end of the bridge, and it's no good for cultivation, but it could still be developed. The truth is, I guessed he wouldn't object, so I just threw it in."

"Will you take over your father's wool business one day?"

"No."

"So definite? Why?"

"It's too easy for the king to tax the wool trade. He has just imposed an extra duty of a pound per sack of wool—that's on top of the existing tax of two-thirds of a pound. The price of wool is now so high that the Italians are looking for wool from other countries, such as Spain. The business is too much at the mercy of the monarch."

"Still, it's a living. What else would you do?" Merthin was edging the conversation toward marriage, a subject she never raised.

"I don't know." She smiled. "When I was ten, I wanted to be a doctor. I thought that if I had known about medicine I could have saved my mother's life. They all laughed at me. I didn't realize only men could be physicians."

"You could be a wise woman, like Mattie."

"That would shock the family. Imagine what Petranilla would say! Mother Cecilia thinks it's my destiny to be a nun."

He laughed. "If she could see you now!" He kissed the soft inside of her thigh.

"She'd probably want to do what you're doing," Caris said. "You know what people say about nuns."

"Why would she think you wanted to join the convent?"

"It's because of what we did after the bridge collapsed. I helped her take care of the injured. She said I had a natural gift for it."

"You have. Even I could see it."

"I just did what Cecilia said."

"But people seemed to feel better as soon as you spoke to them. And then you always listened to what they had to say before telling them what they should do."

She stroked his cheek. "I couldn't be a nun. I'm too fond of you."

Her triangle of hair was reddish-brown with golden lights. "You've got a little mole," he said. "Right here, on the left, beside the cleft."

"I know. It's been there since I was a little girl. I used to think it was ugly. I was so pleased when my hair grew, because I thought that meant my husband wouldn't see it. I never imagined anyone would look as closely as you."

"Friar Murdo would call you a witch—you'd better not let him see it."

"Not if he were the last man on earth."

"This is the blemish that saves you from blasphemy."

"What are you talking about?"

"In the Arab world, every work of art has a tiny flaw, so that it doesn't sacrilegiously compete with the perfection of God."

"How do you know that?"

"One of the Florentines told me. Listen, do you think the parish guild will want the island?"

"Why do you ask?"

"Because I'd like to own it."

"Four acres of rock and rabbits. Why?"

"I'd build a dock and a builder's yard. Stone and timber coming by river could be delivered directly to my dock. When the bridge is finished, I'd build a house on the island."

"Nice idea. But they wouldn't give it to you free."

"How about as part payment for building the bridge? I could take, say, half wages for two years."

"You charge four pence a day . . . so the price of the island would be just over five pounds. I should think the guild would be pleased to get that much for barren land."

"Do you think it's a good idea?"

"I think you could build houses there and rent them, as soon as the bridge is finished and people can travel to and from the island easily."

"Yes," said Merthin thoughtfully. "I'd better talk to your father about it."

26

Returning to Earlscastle at the end of a day's hunting, when all the men in Earl Roland's entourage were in a good mood, Ralph Fitzgerald was happy.

They crossed the drawbridge like an invading army, knights and squires and dogs. Rain was falling in a light drizzle, coolly welcome to the men and animals, who were hot and tired and content. They had taken several summer-fat hinds that would make good eating, plus a big old stag, too tough for anything but dog meat, killed for its magnificent antlers.

They dismounted in the outer compound, within the lower circle of the figure-eight moat. Ralph unsaddled Griff, murmured a few words of thanks in his ear, fed him a carrot, and handed him to a groom to be rubbed down. Kitchen boys dragged away the bloody carcasses of the deer. The men were noisily recalling the day's incidents, boasting and jeering and laughing, remembering remarkable jumps and dangerous falls and hairsbreadth escapes. Ralph's nostrils filled with a smell he loved, a mixture of sweating horses, wet dogs, leather, and blood.

Ralph found himself next to Lord William of Caster, the earl's elder son. "A great day's sport," he said.

"Tremendous," William agreed. He pulled off his cap and scratched his balding head. "I'm sorry to lose old Bruno, though."

Bruno, the leader of the dog pack, had gone in for the kill a few moments too early. When the stag was too exhausted to run any farther, and turned to face the hounds, its heaving shoulders covered with blood, Bruno had leaped for its throat—but, with a last burst of defiance, the deer had dipped its head and swung its muscular neck and impaled the soft belly of the dog on the points of its antlers. The effort finished the beast off, and a moment later the other dogs were tearing it apart; but, as it thrashed its life away, Bruno's guts unraveled across the antlers like a tangled rope, and William had had to put him out of his misery, slashing his throat with a long dagger. "He was a brave dog," Ralph said, and put a hand on William's shoulder in commiseration.

"Like a lion," William agreed.

On the spur of the moment, Ralph decided to speak about his prospects. There would never be a better moment. He had been Roland's man for seven years; he was brave and strong; and he had saved his lord's life after the bridge collapsed—yet he had been given no promotion, and was still a squire. What more could be asked of him?

Yesterday he had met his brother, by chance, at a tavern on the road from Kingsbridge to Shiring. Merthin, on his way to the priory's quarry, had been full of news. He was going to build the most beautiful bridge in England. He would be rich and famous. Their parents were thrilled. It had made Ralph feel even more frustrated.

Now, speaking to Lord William, he could not think of a neat way to introduce the subject that was on his mind, so he just plunged in. "It's three months since I saved your father's life at Kingsbridge."

"Several people claim that honor," William said. The harsh look that came over his face reminded Ralph strongly of Roland.

"I pulled him out of the water."

"And Matthew Barber mended his head, and the nuns changed his bandages, and the monks prayed for him. God saved his life, though."

"Amen," Ralph said. "All the same, I was hoping for some sign of favor."

"My father's a hard man to please."

William's brother, Richard, was standing nearby, red-faced and sweating, and he overheard the remark. "That's as true as the Bible," he said.

"Don't complain," William said. "Our father's hardness made us strong."

"As I recall, it made us miserable."

William turned away, probably not wanting to argue the point in front of an underling.

When the horses were stabled, the men drifted across the compound, past the kitchens and barracks and chapel, to a second drawbridge that led to a small inner compound, the top loop of the figure eight. Here the earl lived in a traditional keep, with ground-floor storerooms, a great hall above, and a small upper story for the earl's private bedchamber. A colony of rooks inhabited the high trees around the keep, and strutted on the battlements like sergeants, cawing their dissatisfaction. Roland was in the great hall, having changed out of his dirty hunting clothes into a purple robe. Ralph stood near the earl, determined to raise the question of his promotion at the first opportunity.

Roland was arguing good-naturedly with William's wife, Lady Philippa—one of the few people who could contradict him and get away with it. They were talking about the castle. "I don't think it's changed for a hundred years," Philippa said.

"That's because it's such a good design," Roland said, speaking out of the left side of his mouth. "The enemy expends most of his strength getting into the lower compound, then he faces a whole new battle to reach the keep."

"Exactly!" said Philippa. "It was built for defense, not comfort. But when was the last time a castle in this part of England came under attack? Not in my lifetime."

"Nor in mine." He grinned with the mobile half of his face. "Probably because our defenses are so strong."

"There was a bishop who scattered acorns on the road wherever he traveled, to protect him from lions," Philippa said. "When they told him there were no lions in all England, he said: 'It's more effective than I thought.'"

Roland laughed.

Philippa added: "Most noble families nowadays live in more comfortable homes."

Ralph did not care for luxury, but he cared for Philippa. He gazed at her voluptuous figure as she talked, unaware of him. He imagined her lying beneath him, twisting her naked body, crying out in pleasure, or pain, or both. If he were a knight, he could have a woman like that.

"You should knock down this old keep and build a modern house," she was saying to her father-in-law. "One with big windows and lots of fireplaces. You could have the hall at ground level, with the family apartments at one end, so that we could all have somewhere private to sleep when we come to visit you; and the kitchens at the other end, so that the food is still hot when it reaches the table."

Suddenly Ralph realized he could make a contribution to this conversation. "I know who could design such a house for you," he said.

They turned to him in surprise. What would a squire know of house design? "Who?" said Philippa.

"My brother, Merthin."

She looked thoughtful. "The funny-faced boy who tells me to buy green silk to match my eyes?"

"He meant no disrespect."

"I'm not sure what he meant. Is he a builder?"

"He's the best," Ralph said proudly. "He devised the new ferry at Kingsbridge, then he figured out how to repair the roof of St. Mark's when no one else could, and now he's been commissioned to build the most beautiful bridge in England."

"Somehow I'm not surprised," she said.

"What bridge?" said Roland.

"The new one at Kingsbridge. It will have pointed arches, like a church, and be wide enough for two carts!"

"I've heard nothing of this," Roland said.

Ralph realized the earl was displeased. What had annoyed him? "The bridge must be rebuilt, mustn't it?" Ralph said.

"I'm not so sure," Roland replied. "Nowadays there's hardly enough business for two markets as close together as Kingsbridge and Shiring. But, if we must accept the Kingsbridge market, that doesn't mean we have to countenance a blatant attempt by the priory to steal customers from Shiring." Bishop Richard had come in, and now Roland rounded on him. "You didn't tell me about the new bridge at Kingsbridge."

"Because I don't know about it," Richard answered.

"You ought to, you're the bishop."

Richard flushed at the reproof. "The bishop of Kingsbridge has lived in or near Shiring ever since the civil war between King Stephen and the Empress Maud, two centuries ago. The monks prefer it that way, and so do most bishops."

"That doesn't prevent you keeping your ear to the ground. You should have some idea of what's happening there."

"Since I don't, perhaps you'd be kind enough to tell me what you've learned."

That kind of cool insolence passed over Roland's head. "It's going to be wide enough for two carts. It will take business away from my market at Shiring."

"There's nothing I can do about it."

"Why not? You're the abbot, ex officio. The monks are supposed to do what you say."

"They don't, though."

"Perhaps they will if we take away their builder. Ralph, can you persuade your brother to give up the project?"

"I can try."

"Offer him a better prospect. Tell him I want him to build a new palace for me here at Earlscastle."

Ralph was excited to get a special commission from the earl, but he was daunted, too. He had never been able to talk Merthin into anything—it was always the other way around. "All right," he said.

"Will they be able to go ahead without him?"

"He got the job because no one else in Kingsbridge knew how to build under water."

Richard said: "He's not the only man in England who can design a bridge, obviously."

William said: "Still, taking away their builder would surely delay them. They probably couldn't start for another year."

"Then it's worth doing," Roland said decisively. A look of hatred came over the animated half of his face, and he added: "That arrogant prior has to be put in his place."

Things had changed in the life of Gerald and Maud, Ralph discovered. His mother wore a new green dress to church, and his father had leather shoes. Back at home there was a goose stuffed with apples roasting over the fire, filling the little house with a mouthwatering smell, and a loaf of wheat bread, the most expensive kind, standing on the table.

The money came from Merthin, Ralph soon learned. "He gets paid four pence a day every day he works on St. Mark's," Maud said proudly. "And he's building a new house for Dick Brewer. That's as well as getting ready to build the new bridge."

Merthin received a lower wage for working on the bridge, he explained while his father carved the goose, because he had been given Leper Island in part payment. The last remaining leper, old and bedridden, had been moved to a small house in the monks' orchard on the far side of the river.

Ralph found that his mother's evident happiness left a sour taste in his mouth. He had believed, since he was a boy, that the destiny of the family lay in his hands. He had been sent away, at the age of fourteen, to join the household of the earl of Shiring, and he had known even then that it was up to him to wipe out his father's humiliation by becoming a knight, perhaps a baron, even an earl. Merthin, by contrast, had been apprenticed to a carpenter, and set on a road that could only lead farther down the social hill. Builders were never made knights.

It was some consolation that their father was unimpressed by Merthin's success. He showed signs of impatience when Maud talked about building projects. "My elder son seems to have inherited the blood of Jack Builder, my only low-born ancestor," he said, and his tone was amazed rather than proud. "But, Ralph, tell us how you're getting on at the court of Earl Roland."

Unfortunately, Ralph had so far mysteriously failed to rise in the nobility, whereas Merthin was buying his parents new clothes and expensive dinners. Ralph knew he should just be grateful that one of them had won success, and that even if his parents remained humble they could at least be comfortable. But, though his mind told him to rejoice, his heart seethed with resentment.

And now he had to persuade his brother to give up the bridge. The trouble with Merthin was that he would never see anything simply. He was not like the knights and squires with whom Ralph had spent the last seven years. They were fighting men. In their world loyalties were clear, bravery was the virtue, and the issue was life or death. There was never much need for deep thought. But Merthin thought about everything. He could not play a game of checkers without suggesting a change in the rules.

He was explaining to their parents why he had accepted four acres of barren rock in part payment for his work on the bridge. "Everyone thinks the land is worthless because it's an island," he said. "What they don't realize is that when the bridge is built the island will become part of the city. Townspeople will walk across the bridge just as they walk along the main street. And four acres of city land is very valuable. If I build houses on it, the rents will be worth a fortune."

Gerald said: "You've a few years to wait before then."

"I'm getting some income from it already. Jake Chepstow is renting half an acre to use as a timber yard. He's bringing logs from Wales."

"Why from Wales?" Gerald asked. "The New Forest is nearer—their wood should be cheaper."

"It should be, but the earl of Shaftesbury charges a toll or a tax at every river ford and bridge in his territory."

It was a familiar gripe. Many lords found ways to tax goods that passed through their territories.

As they started to eat, Ralph said to Merthin: "I bring you news of another opportunity. The earl wants to build a new palace at Earlscastle."

Merthin looked suspicious. "He sent you to ask me to design it?"

"I suggested you. Lady Philippa was berating him about how old-fashioned the keep is, and I said I knew the right person to talk to."

Maud was thrilled. "Isn't that wonderful?"

Merthin remained skeptical. "And the earl said he wanted me?"

"Yes."

"Amazing. A few months ago I couldn't get a job. Now I've got too much to do. And Earlscastle is two days away. I don't see how I could build a palace there and a bridge here at the same time."

"Oh, you'll have to give up the bridge," Ralph said.

"What?"

"Work for the earl has to take precedence over everything else, naturally."

"I'm not sure that's right."

"Take it from me."

"Did he say that?"

"Yes, as a matter of fact, he did."

Their father joined in. "This is a marvelous opportunity, Merthin," he said. "To build a palace for an earl!"

"Of course it is," Merthin replied. "But a bridge for this town is at least as important."

"Don't be stupid," his father said.

"I do my best not to be," Merthin said sarcastically.

"The earl of Shiring is one of the great men of the land. The prior of Kingsbridge is a nobody, by comparison."

Ralph cut a slice of goose thigh and put it in his mouth, but he could hardly swallow. He had been afraid of this. Merthin was going to be difficult. He would not take orders from their father, either. He had never been obedient, even as a child.

Ralph felt desperate. "Listen," he said. "The earl doesn't want the new bridge to be built. He thinks it will take business away from Shiring."

"Aha," said Gerald. "You don't want to go up against the earl, Merthin."

"Is that what's behind this, Ralph?" Merthin asked. "Is Roland offering me this job just to prevent the building of the bridge?"

"Not just for that reason."

"But it's a condition. If I want to build his palace, I must abandon the bridge."

Gerald said with exasperation: "You don't have a choice, Merthin! The earl doesn't request, he commands."

Ralph could have told him that an argument based on authority was not the way to persuade Merthin.

Merthin said: "I don't think he can command the prior of Kingsbridge, who has commissioned me to build this bridge."

"But he can command you."

"Can he? He's not my lord."

"Don't be foolish, son. You can't win a fight with an earl."

"I don't think Roland's quarrel is with me, Father. This is between the earl and the prior. Roland wants to use me, as a hunter uses a dog, but I think I'd do better to stay out of the fight."

"I think you should do what the earl says. Don't forget, he's your kinsman, too."

Merthin tried a different argument. "Has it occurred to you what a betrayal this would be of Prior Godwyn?"

Gerald made a disgusted noise. "What loyalty do we owe the priory? It was the monks who forced us into penury."

"And your neighbors? The people of Kingsbridge, among whom you've lived for ten years? They need the bridge—it's their lifeline."

"We are of the nobility," his father said. "We're not required to take into account the needs of mere merchants."

Merthin nodded. "You may feel that way, but as a mere carpenter I can't share your view."

"This isn't just about you!" Ralph burst out. He had to come clean, he realized. "The earl has given me a mission. If I succeed, he may make me a knight, or at least a minor lord. If I fail, I could remain a squire."

Maud said: "It's very important that we all try to please the earl."

Merthin looked troubled. He was always willing to go head-to-head with their father, but he did not like to argue with Mother. "I've agreed to build the bridge," he said. "The town is counting on me. I can't give it up."

"Of course you can," Maud said.

"I don't want to get a reputation for unreliability."

"Everyone would understand if you gave the earl precedence."

"They might understand, but they wouldn't respect me for it."

"You should put your family first."

"I fought for this bridge, Mother," Merthin said stubbornly. "I made a beautiful design, and I persuaded the whole town to have faith in me. No one else can build it—not the way it should be done."

"If you defy the earl, it will affect Ralph's whole life!" she said. "Don't you see that?"

"His whole life shouldn't depend on something like this."

"But it does. Are you willing to sacrifice your brother, just for the sake of a bridge?"

Merthin said: "I suppose it's a bit like my asking him to save men's lives by not going to war."

Gerald said: "Come, now, you can't compare a carpenter to a soldier."

That was tactless, Ralph thought. It showed Gerald's preference for the younger son. Merthin felt the sting, Ralph could tell. His brother's face reddened and he bit his lip as if to restrain himself from a combative reply.

After a pause, Merthin spoke in a quiet voice that Ralph knew to be a sign that he had made up his mind irrevocably. "I didn't ask to be a carpenter," he said. "Like Ralph, I wanted to be a knight. A foolish aspiration for me, I know that now. All the same, it was your decision that I should be what I am. As things have turned out, I'm good at it. I'm going to make a success of what you forced me into. One day I'd like to build the tallest building in England. This is what you made me—so you'd better learn to live with it."

Before Ralph went back to Earlscastle with the bad news, he racked his brains for a way to turn defeat into victory. If he could not talk his brother into abandoning the bridge, was there some other way he could get the project canceled or delayed?

There was no point talking to Prior Godwyn or Edmund Wooler, he was sure. They would be more committed to the bridge even than Merthin, and anyway they would not be persuaded by a mere squire. What could the earl do? He might send a troop of knights to kill the construction workers, but that could cause more problems than it solved.

It was Merthin who gave him the idea. He had said that Jake Chepstow, the timber merchant who was using Leper Island as a store yard, was buying trees from Wales to avoid the taxes charged by the earl of Shaftesbury.

"My brother feels he must accept the authority of the prior of Kingsbridge," Ralph said to Earl Roland on his return. Before the earl had time to get angry, he added: "But there may be a better way to delay the building of the bridge. The priory's quarry is in the heart of your earldom, between Shiring and Earlscastle."

"But it belongs to the monks," Roland growled. "The king gave it to them centuries ago. We can't stop them taking stone."

"You could tax them, though," Ralph said. He felt guilty: he was sabotaging a project dear to his brother's heart. But it had to be done, and he quelled his conscience. "They will be transporting their stone through your earldom. Their heavy carts will wear away your roads and churn up your river fords. They ought to pay."

"They'll squeal like pigs. They'll go to the king."

"Let them," Ralph said, sounding more confident than he felt. "It will take time. There are only two months left of this year's building season—they have to stop work before the first frost. With luck, you could delay the start of the bridge until next year."

Roland gave Ralph a hard look. "I may have underestimated you," he said. "Perhaps you're good for more than pulling drowning earls out of rivers."

Ralph concealed a triumphant smile. "Thank you, my lord."

"But how shall we enforce this tax? Usually there's a crossroads, a ford in a river, some place every cart has to pass through."

"Since we're only interested in blocks of stone, we could simply camp a troop of men outside the quarry."

"Excellent," said the earl. "And you can lead them."

Two days later Ralph was approaching the quarry with four men-at-arms on horseback and two boys leading a string of packhorses carrying tents and food for a week. He was pleased with himself, so far. He had been given an impossible task and turned it around. The earl thought he was good for more than river rescue work. Things were looking up.

He was deeply uncomfortable about what he was doing to Merthin. He had lain awake much of the night recalling their childhood together. He had always revered his clever older brother. They had often fought, and Ralph had felt worse when he won than when he lost. They had always made friends afterward, in those days. But grown-up fights were harder to forget.

He was not very anxious about the coming confrontation with the monks' quarrymen. It should not prove too challenging for a group of military men. He had no knights with him—such work was beneath their dignity—but he had Joseph Woodstock, whom he knew to be a hard man, and three others. All the same, he would be glad when it was over and he had achieved his aim.

It was just after dawn. They had camped the night before in the forest a few miles from the quarry. Ralph planned to get there in time to challenge the first cart that attempted to leave this morning.

The horses stepped daintily along a road muddied by the hooves of oxen and deeply rutted by the wheels of heavy carts. The sun rose into a sky of rain clouds broken by scraps of blue. Ralph's group were in a good mood, looking forward to exercising their power over unarmed men, with no serious risk to themselves.

Ralph smelled wood burning, then saw the smoke of several fires rising over the trees. A few moments later, the road widened into a muddy clearing in front of the largest hole in the ground he had ever seen. It was a hundred yards wide and stretched for at least a quarter of a mile. A mud ramp led down to the tents and wooden huts of the quarrymen, who were clustered around their fires cooking breakfast. A few were already at work, farther along the site, and Ralph could hear the dull thud of hammers driving wedges into cracks in the rock, splitting great slabs from the mass of stone.

The quarry was a day's journey from Kingsbridge, so most carters arrived in the evening and left the following morning. Ralph could see several carts dotted about the quarry, some being loaded with stone, and one already making its slow way along the track through the diggings toward the exit ramp.

The men in the quarry looked up, alerted by the sound of horses, but no one approached. Workers were never in a hurry to converse with men-at-arms. Ralph waited patiently. There appeared to be only one way out of the quarry, the long slope of mud that led to where he was.

The first cart lumbered slowly up the ramp, the carter urging the ox on with a long-tailed whip, the ox putting one foot in front of the other with mute resentment. Four huge stones were piled on its flatbed, rough-hewn and incised with the mark of the man who had quarried them. Each man's output was counted once at the quarry and again at the building site, and he was paid per stone.

As the cart came closer, Ralph saw that the carter was a Kingsbridge man, Ben Wheeler. He looked a bit like his ox, with a thick neck and massive shoulders. His face wore a similar expression of dull hostility. He might try to make trouble, Ralph guessed. However, he could be subdued.

Ben drove his ox toward the line of horses blocking the road. Instead of halting at a distance, he let the beast come closer and closer. The horses were not combat-trained destriers but everyday hacks, and they snorted nervously and backed. The ox stopped of its own accord.

Ben's attitude angered Ralph, who called out: "You're a cocksure oaf."

Ben said: "Why do you stand in my way?"

"To collect the tax."

"There's no tax."

"To carry stone across the territory of the earl of Shiring, you must pay a penny per cartload."

"I have no money."

"Then you must get some."

"Do you bar my passage?"

The fool was not as scared as he should have been, which infuriated Ralph. "Don't presume to question me," Ralph said. "The stone stays here until someone has paid tax for it."

Ben glared back at him for a long moment, and Ralph had the strongest feeling that the man was wondering whether to knock him off his horse. "But I have no money," he said eventually.

Ralph wanted to run him through with his sword, but he reined in his temper. "Don't pretend to be even more stupid than you are," he said contemptuously. "Just go to the master quarryman and tell him the earl's men will not let you leave."

Ben stared at him a little longer, mulling this over; then, without speaking, he turned and walked back down the ramp, leaving his cart.

Ralph waited, fuming, staring at the ox.

Ben entered a wooden hut halfway along the quarry. He emerged a few minutes later accompanied by a slight man in a brown tunic. At first, Ralph presumed the second man was the quarrymaster. However, the figure looked familiar and, as the two came closer, Ralph recognized his brother, Merthin.

"Oh, no," he said aloud.

He was not prepared for this. He felt tortured by shame as he watched Merthin walk up the long ramp. He knew he was here to betray his brother, but he had not expected Merthin to be here to see it.

"Hello, Ralph," said Merthin as he came closer. "Ben says you won't let him pass."

Merthin had always been able to overcome him in an argument, Ralph recalled dismally. He decided to be formal. It would hide his emotions, and he could hardly get into trouble if he simply repeated his instructions. He said stiffly: "The earl has decided to exercise his right to collect taxes from consignments of stone using his roads."

Merthin ignored that. "Aren't you going to get down off your horse to talk to your brother?"

Ralph would have preferred to stay mounted, but he did not want to refuse what seemed like some kind of challenge, so he got down. Then he felt as if he had already been bested.

"There's no tax on stone from here," Merthin said.

"There is now."

"The monks have been working this quarry for hundreds of years. Kingsbridge Cathedral is built of this stone. It has never been taxed."

"Perhaps the earl forgave the tax for the sake of the church," Ralph said, improvising. "But he won't do it for a bridge."

"He just doesn't want the town to have a new bridge. That's the reason for this. First he sends you to bribe me, then when that fails he invents a new tax." Merthin looked thoughtfully at Ralph. "This was your idea, wasn't it?"

Ralph was mortified. How had he guessed? "No!" he said, but he felt himself redden.

"I can see from your face that it was. I gave you the notion, I'm sure, when I spoke of Jake Chepstow importing logs from Wales to avoid the earl of Shaftesbury's tax."

Ralph was feeling more foolish and angry with every moment. "There's no connection," he said stubbornly.

"You berated me for putting my bridge before my brother, but you're happy to wreck my hopes for the sake of your earl."

"It doesn't matter whose idea it was, the earl has decided to tax the stone."

"But he doesn't have the right."

Ben Wheeler was following the conversation intently, standing beside Merthin with his legs apart and his hands on his hips. Now he said to Merthin: "Are you saying these men don't have the right to stop me?"

"That's exactly what I'm saying," said Merthin.

Ralph could have told Merthin it was a mistake to treat such a man as if he was intelligent. Ben now took Merthin's words for permission to leave. He flicked his whip over his ox's shoulders. The beast leaned into its wooden collar and took the strain.

Ralph shouted angrily: "Halt!"

Ben whipped the ox again and called: "Hup!"

The ox pulled harder and the cart started forward with a jerk that startled the horses. Joseph Woodstock's mount whinnied and reared up, eyes rolling.

Joseph sawed at the reins and got the horse under control. Then he pulled from his saddlebag a long wooden club. "You keep still when you're told," he said to Ben. He urged his horse forward and lashed out with the club.

Ben dodged the blow, grabbed the club, and pulled.

Joseph was already leaning out from his saddle. The sudden jerk unbalanced him, and he fell off his horse.

Merthin cried: "Oh, no!"

Ralph knew why Merthin was dismayed. A man-at-arms could not overlook such humiliation. There was no avoiding violence now. But Ralph himself was not sorry. His brother had failed to treat the earl's men with the deference they merited, and now he would see the consequences.

Ben was holding Joseph's club in a two-handed grip. Joseph leaped to his feet. Seeing Ben brandishing the club, he reached for his dagger. But Ben was quicker—the carter must have fought in battle at some time, Ralph realized. Ben swung the club and landed a mighty blow on the top of Joseph's head. Joseph fell to the ground and lay motionless.

Ralph roared with rage. He drew his sword and ran at the carter.

Merthin shouted: "No!"

Ralph stabbed Ben in the chest, thrusting the sword between his ribs as forcefully as he could. It passed through Ben's thick body and came out the other side. Ben fell back and Ralph pulled the sword out. Blood spurted from the carter in a fountain. Ralph felt a jolt of triumphant satisfaction. There would be no more insolence from Ben Wheeler.

He knelt beside Joseph. The man's eyes stared sightlessly. There was no heartbeat. He was dead.

In a way that was good. It simplified the explanations. Ben Wheeler had murdered one of the earl's men, and had died for it. No one would see any injustice in that—least of all Earl Roland, who had no mercy for those who defied his authority.

Merthin did not see it the same way. His face was twisted as if in pain. "What have you done?" he said incredulously. "Ben Wheeler has a two-year-old son! They call him Bennie!"

"The widow had better look for another husband, then," said Ralph. "This time, she should choose a man who knows his place."

27

It was a poor harvest. There was so little sunshine in August that the grain had barely ripened by September. In the village of Wigleigh, spirits were low. There was none of the usual euphoria of harvest time: the dances, the drinking, the sudden romances. Wet crops were liable to rot. Many villagers would go hungry before spring.

Wulfric reaped his barley in the driving rain, scything the wet stalks while Gwenda followed behind binding the sheaves. On the first sunny day of September they started to harvest the wheat, the most valuable crop, in the hope that the fine weather would last long enough to dry it.

At some point Gwenda realized that Wulfric was powered by fury. The sudden loss of his entire family had enraged him. He would have blamed someone for his bereavement, if he could; but the collapse of the bridge seemed a random event, an act of evil spirits, or a punishment by God; so he had no outlet for his passion except work. She herself was driven by love, which was just as potent.

They were in the fields before the crack of dawn, and they did not stop until it was too dark to see. Gwenda went to sleep with an aching back every night and woke when she heard Wulfric bang the kitchen door before dawn. Still they lagged behind everyone else.

Gradually, she sensed a change in the attitude of the village toward her and Wulfric. All her life, she had been looked down upon as the daughter of the disreputable Joby; and the women had disapproved of her even more when they realized she wanted to snatch Wulfric away from Annet. Wulfric was hard to dislike, but some felt that his desire to inherit such a big landholding was greedy and impractical. However, people could hardly fail to be impressed by their efforts to get the harvest in. A boy and a girl were trying to do the work of three men, and they were getting on better than anyone had expected. Men began to look at Wulfric with admiration, and women at Gwenda with sympathy.

In the end the villagers rallied around to help them. The priest, Father Gaspard, turned a blind eye to their working on Sundays. When Annet's family had got their harvest in, her father, Perkin, and her brother, Rob, joined Gwenda on Wulfric's land. Even Gwenda's mother, Ethna, showed up. As they carted the last of the sheaves to Wulfric's barn, there was a hint of the traditional harvest spirit, with everyone singing the old songs as they walked home behind the cart.

Annet was there, in violation of the saying that you should first follow the plow if you want to dance the harvest jig. She walked by Wulfric's side, as was her right, being his acknowledged fiancée. Gwenda watched her from behind, noting sourly how she swayed her hips, tossed her head, and laughed prettily at everything he said. How could he be so stupid as to fall for that? Had he not noticed that Annet had done no work on his land?

No day had yet been fixed for the wedding. Perkin was nothing if not shrewd, and he would not let his daughter commit herself until the question of the inheritance was settled.

Wulfric had proved his ability to farm the land. No one would question that now. His age had come to seem irrelevant. The only remaining obstacle was the heriot. Would he be able to raise the money to pay the inheritance tax? It would depend how much he got for his cash crops. The harvest was poor but, if the bad weather had been widespread, the price of wheat would probably be high. In normal circumstances, a prosperous peasant family would have money saved up for the heriot; but Wulfric's family's savings were at the bottom of the river in Kingsbridge. So nothing was settled. And Gwenda could continue to dream that Wulfric would inherit the land and, somehow, transfer his affections to her. Anything was possible.

As they were unloading the cart into the barn, Nathan Reeve arrived. The hunchbacked bailiff was in a state of high excitement. "Come to the church, quickly," he said. "Everybody! Stop what you're doing."

Wulfric said: "I'm not leaving my crops out in the open—it might rain."

Gwenda said: "We'll just drag the cart inside. What's the emergency, Nate?"

The bailiff was already hurrying to the next house. "The new lord is arriving!" he said.

"Wait!" Wulfric ran after him. "Will you recommend that I inherit?"

Everyone stood still, watching, waiting for the answer.

Nathan turned reluctantly and faced Wulfric. He had to look up, for Wulfric was taller by a foot. "I don't know," he said slowly.

"I've proved I can farm the land—you can see that. Just look in the barn!"

"You've done well, no question. But can you pay the heriot?"

"It depends on the price of wheat."

Annet spoke. "Father?" she said.

Gwenda wondered what was coming.

Perkin looked hesitant.

Annet prompted him again. "You remember what you promised me."

"Yes, I remember," Perkin said at last.

"Tell Nate, then."

Perkin turned to the bailiff. "I'll guarantee the heriot, if the lord will let Wulfric inherit."

Gwenda's hand flew to her mouth.

Nathan said: "You'll pay it for him? It's two pounds and ten shillings."

"If he's short, I'll lend him what he needs. Of course, they'll have to be married first."

Nathan lowered his voice. "And, in addition . . . ?"

Perkin said something so quietly that Gwenda could not hear it, but she could guess what it was. Perkin was offering Nathan a bribe, probably a tenth of the tax, which would be five shillings.

"Very well," Nathan said. "I'll make the recommendation. Now get yourselves to the church, quickly!" He ran off.

Wulfric smiled broadly and kissed Annet. Everyone shook his hand.

Gwenda was heartsick. Her hopes were dashed. Annet had been too clever. She had persuaded her father to lend Wulfric the money he needed. He would inherit his land—and he would marry Annet.

Gwenda forced herself to help push the cart into the barn. Then she followed the happy couple as they walked through the village to the church. It was all over. A new lord, not knowing the village or the people, was unlikely to go against his bailiff's advice on a question such as this. The fact that Nathan had gone to the trouble of negotiating a bribe indicated his confidence.

It was partly her fault, of course. She had broken her back to make sure Wulfric got his harvest in, in the vain hope that somehow he would realize how much better a wife she would make than Annet. All summer long she had been digging her own grave, she thought as she walked through the cemetery to the church door. But she would do the same again. She could not have borne to see him struggle alone. Whatever happens, she thought, he'll always know I was the one who stuck it out with him. It was small consolation.

Most of the villagers were already in the church. They had not needed much urging from Nathan. They were eager to be among the first to pay their respects to their new lord, and curious to see what he was like: young or old, ugly or handsome, cheerful or dyspeptic, clever or stupid, and—most important of all—cruel or kind. Everything about him would affect their lives for as long as he remained lord, which might be years or decades. If he were reasonable, he could do a lot to make Wigleigh a happy and prosperous village. If he were a fool, they would have unwise decisions and unjust rulings, oppressive taxes and harsh punishments. And one of his first decisions would be whether to let Wulfric inherit.

The rumble of conversation died away, and a jingle of harness was heard. Gwenda heard Nathan's voice, low and obsequious, then the authoritative tone of a lord—a big man, she thought, confident, but young. Everyone looked at the church door. It flew open.

Gwenda gasped with shock.

The man who strode in was no more than twenty. He was well dressed in an expensive wool surcoat, and armed with sword and dagger. He was tall, and his expression was proud. He seemed pleased to be lord of Wigleigh, though there was a hint of insecurity in the haughty look. He had wavy dark hair and a handsome face disfigured by a broken nose.

He was Ralph Fitzgerald.

ꟃ

Ralph's first manorial court was held the following Sunday.

In the interim, Wulfric was depressed. Gwenda wanted to weep every time she looked at him. He walked around with his eyes cast down, his broad shoulders slumped. All summer he had seemed tireless, working in the fields with the uncomplaining dependability of a plowhorse; but now he looked weary. He had done all a man could do, but his fate had been given into the hands of one who hated him.

She would have liked to say something hopeful, in an attempt to cheer him up, but the truth was that she shared his pessimism. Lords were often petty and vindictive, and nothing about Ralph encouraged her to believe that he would be magnanimous. As a child, he had been stupid and brutal. She would never forget the day he had killed her dog with Merthin's bow and arrow.

There was no sign that he had improved since then. He had moved into the manor house with his sidekick, a beefy young squire called Alan Fernhill, and the two of them were drinking the best wine, eating the chickens, and squeezing the breasts of the female servants with the carelessness typical of their class.

Nathan Reeve's attitude confirmed her fears. The bailiff was not bothering to negotiate an increased bribe—a sure sign that he expected failure.

Annet, too, seemed to have a poor view of Wulfric's prospects. Gwenda saw an unmistakable change in her. She did not toss her hair so gaily, or walk with that swish of her hips, and the waterfall tinkle of her laughter was not heard so often. Gwenda hoped Wulfric would not see the difference in Annet: he had enough to be gloomy about. But it seemed to her that he did not stay so late at Perkin's house in the evenings, and when he returned home he was taciturn.

She was surprised to learn, on Sunday morning, that Wulfric still harbored the ghost of a hope. When the service ended, and Father Gaspard gave place to Lord Ralph, she saw that Wulfric's eyes were closed and his lips were moving, presumably in a prayer to his favorite saint, the Virgin Mary.

All the villagers were in church, of course, including Joby and Ethna. Gwenda did not stand with her parents. She talked to her mother sometimes, but only when her father was not around. Joby had an angry red patch on his cheek where she had burned him with the blazing log. He never met her eye. She was still afraid of him, but she sensed that he was now also afraid of her.

Ralph sat on the big wooden chair, staring at his serfs with the appraising look of a buyer at a cattle market. The court proceedings on this day consisted of a series of announcements. Nathan proclaimed the arrangements for getting the harvest in from the lord's fields, stating on which days of the coming week different villagers would be required to perform their customary duty on the lord's lands. No discussion was invited. Clearly Ralph did not intend to govern by consensus.

There were other details of the kind Nathan dealt with every week: gleaning should be completed in Hundredacre by Monday night so that livestock could graze the stubble from Tuesday morning, and autumn plowing of Longfield would begin on Wednesday. Normally there would have been minor disputes about these plans, with the more argumentative villagers finding reasons to propose different arrangements, but today they were all quiet, waiting to get the measure of the new lord.

When the decision came, it seemed curiously low-key. As if he were simply stating another schedule of work, Nathan said: "Wulfric will not be permitted to inherit his father's landholding, because he is only sixteen."

Gwenda looked at Ralph. He was trying to smother a triumphant grin. His hand went to his face—unconsciously, she thought—and he touched his broken nose.

Nathan went on: "Lord Ralph will consider what to do with the lands and give his judgment later."

Wulfric groaned loud enough for everyone to hear. It was the decision he had been expecting, but its confirmation was bitter. She watched as he turned his back on the crowd in the church, hiding his face, and leaned against the wall as if to stop himself falling.

"That's all for today," said Nathan.

Ralph stood up. He walked down the aisle slowly, his eyes continually turning to the distraught Wulfric. What kind of lord would he be, Gwenda thought, if his first instinct was to use his power for revenge? Nathan followed Ralph, looking at the floor: he knew that an injustice had been done. As they left the church, a buzz of comment arose. Gwenda spoke to no one, but watched Wulfric.

He turned from the wall, his face a picture of misery. His eyes raked the crowd and found Annet. She looked furious. Gwenda waited for her to meet Wulfric's eye, but she seemed determined not to look at him. Gwenda wondered what was going through her mind.

Annet walked toward the door, head held high. Her father, Perkin, and the family followed. Would she not even speak to Wulfric?

The same thought must have occurred to him, for he went after her. "Annet!" he said. "Wait."

The place went quiet.

Annet turned. Wulfric stood before her. "We'll still get married, won't we?" he said. Gwenda winced to hear the undignified note of pleading in his voice. Annet stared at him, apparently about to speak, but she said nothing for a long moment, and Wulfric spoke again. "Lords need good serfs to farm the land. Perhaps Ralph will give me a smaller holding—"

"You broke his nose," she said harshly. "He will never give you anything."

Gwenda recalled how pleased Annet had been, at the time, to have two men fighting over her.

Wulfric said: "Then I'll be a laborer. I'm strong, I'll never lack for work."

"But you'll be poor all your life. Is that what you're offering me?"

"We'll be together—just as we dreamed, that day in the forest, when you told me you loved me, don't you remember?"

"And what would life be like for me, married to a landless laborer?" Annet demanded angrily. "I'll tell you." She lifted her arm and pointed at Gwenda's mother, Ethna, standing with Joby and the three little ones. "I would be like her—grim-faced with worry and as thin as a broom handle."

Joby was stung by this. He waved the stump of his severed arm at Annet. "You watch your mouth, you haughty minx."

Perkin stepped in front of his daughter and made a patting gesture with both hands. "Forgive her, Joby, she's overwrought, she means no harm."

Wulfric said: "No disrespect to Joby, but I'm not like him, Annet."

"But you are!" she said. "You've got no land. It's why he's poor, and it's why you'll be poor, and your children will be hungry and your wife will be drab."

It was true. In hard times the landless were the first to suffer. Dismissing your employees was the quickest way to save money. All the same, Gwenda found it hard to believe that a woman would turn down the chance of spending her life with Wulfric.

Yet that seemed to be what Annet was doing.

Wulfric thought so, too. Plaintively, he said: "Don't you love me anymore?"

He had lost all his dignity and he looked pathetic; yet, at that moment, Gwenda felt more passion for him than ever before.

"I can't eat love," Annet said, and she walked out of the church.

Two weeks later, she married Billy Howard.

Gwenda went to the wedding, as did everyone in the village except Wulfric. Despite the poor harvest, there was a good feast. By this marriage two large landholdings were united: Perkin's hundred acres with Billy's forty. Furthermore, Perkin had asked Ralph to give him Wulfric's family's lands. If Ralph agreed, Annet's children could be heirs to almost half the village. But Ralph had gone to Kingsbridge, promising a decision as soon as he returned.

Perkin broached a barrel of his wife's strongest ale and slaughtered a cow. Gwenda ate and drank heartily. Her future was too uncertain for her to turn down good food.

She played with her little sisters, Cathie and Joanie, throwing and catching a wooden ball; then she took baby Eric on her knee and sang to him. After a while her mother sat beside her and said: "What will you do now?"

In her heart Gwenda was not completely reconciled with Ethna. They talked, and Ma asked concerned questions. Gwenda still resented her mother for forgiving Joby, but she answered the questions. "I'll live in Wulfric's barn as long as I can," she said. "Perhaps I can stay there indefinitely."

"And if Wulfric moves out—leaves the village, say?"

"I don't know."

For now, Wulfric was still working in the fields, plowing-in the stubble and harrowing the fallow on the land that had been his family's, and Gwenda was helping him. They were paid the daily laborer's rate by Nathan, as they would have no part of the next harvest. Nathan was keen for them to stay, otherwise the land would deteriorate rapidly. They would continue until Ralph announced who the new tenant would be. At that point, they would have to offer themselves for hire.

"Where is Wulfric now?" Ethna asked.

"I assume he's not disposed to celebrate this wedding."

"How does he feel about you?"

Gwenda gave her mother a candid look. "He tells me I'm the best friend he's ever had."

"What does that mean?"

"I don't know. But it doesn't mean 'I love you,' does it?"

"No," said her mother. "No, it doesn't mean that."

Gwenda heard music. Aaron Appletree was playing a bagpipe, running up and down the scale in preparation for a tune. She saw Perkin coming out of his house with a pair of small drums attached to his belt. The dancing was about to begin.

She was in no mood to dance. She could have talked to the old women, but they would only ask the same questions as her mother, and she did not want to spend the rest of the day explaining her predicament. She recalled the last village wedding, and Wulfric slightly drunk, dancing around with great leaps, embracing all the women, though still favoring Annet. Without him there was no festival for Gwenda. She gave Eric back to her mother and drifted away. Her dog, Skip, stayed behind, knowing that such parties provided a banquet of dropped food and discarded scraps.

She went into Wulfric's house, half-hoping he might be there, but the place was empty. It was a sturdy timber house, of post-and-beam construction, but with no chimney—such luxuries were for the rich. She looked in both ground-floor rooms and the upstairs bedroom. The place was as tidy and clean as it had been when his mother was alive, but that was because he used only one room. He ate and slept in the kitchen. The place was cold and unhomely. It was a family house with no family.

She went to the barn. It was full of bundled hay, for winter fodder, and sheaves of barley and wheat waiting to be threshed. She climbed the ladder to the loft and lay down in the hay. After a while she fell asleep.

When she woke up, it was dark. She had no idea what time it was. She stepped outside to look at the sky. There was a low moon behind streaks of cloud, and she calculated that it was only an hour or two after nightfall. As she stood by the barn door, still half-asleep, she heard weeping.

She knew instantly that it was Wulfric. She had heard him cry once before, when he saw the bodies of his parents and his brother lying on the floor of Kingsbridge Cathedral. He cried with great sobs that seemed torn from the depths of his chest. Tears came to her own eyes as she listened to his grief.

After a while, she went into the house.

She could see him by the light of the moon. He lay facedown in the straw, his back heaving as he sobbed. He must have heard her lift the latch, but he was too distraught to care, and he did not look up.

Gwenda knelt beside him and tentatively touched his mane of hair. He made no response. She rarely touched him, and to stroke his hair was an unknown delight. Her caress seemed to soothe him, for his weeping subsided.

After a while, she dared to lie down beside him. She expected him to push her away, but he did not. He turned his face to her, eyes closed. She dabbed at his cheeks with her sleeve, wiping away the tears. She was thrilled to be this close to him, and to be permitted these small intimacies. She longed to kiss his closed eyelids, but she was afraid that would be a step too far, and she restrained herself.

A few moments later, she realized he was asleep.

She was pleased. It was a sign of how comfortable he felt with her, and it meant she could stay with him, at least until he woke up.

It was autumn, and the night was cold. As Wulfric's breathing became slower and steadier, she got up stealthily and took his blanket from its hook on the wall. She draped it over him. He slept on undisturbed.

Despite the chill in the air, she slipped her dress over her head and lay beside him naked, arranging the blanket so that it covered them both.

She moved close to him and laid her cheek against his chest. She could hear his heartbeat and feel the breeze of his breath on the top of her head. The heat of his big body warmed her. In time, the moon went down, and the room became pitch dark. She felt she could have stayed like this forever.

She did not sleep. She had no intention of wasting any of this precious time. She savored every moment, knowing it might never happen again. She touched him cautiously, careful not to wake him. Through his light wool shift, her fingertips explored the muscles of his chest and back, the bones of his ribs and hips, the turn of his shoulder and the knob of his elbow.

He moved in his sleep several times. He turned and lay flat on his back, whereupon she put her head on his shoulder and her arm across his flat belly. Later he turned away, and then she moved really close, fitting herself into the S-shape of his body, pressing her breasts against his broad back, her hips into his, her knees into the backs of his knees. Then he turned back to her, flinging one arm across her shoulders and one leg over her thighs. His leg was painfully heavy, but she relished the ache as proof that she was not dreaming.

He dreamed, though. In the middle of the night he suddenly kissed her, thrusting his tongue roughly into her mouth, grasping her breast with one big hand. She felt his erection as he rubbed up against her clumsily. For a moment she was bewildered. He could have her whatever way he wanted, but it was unlike him to be anything but gentle. She put her hand to his groin and grasped his penis, which was sticking out through the slit in his underdrawers. Then, just as suddenly, he turned away and lay on his back, breathing rhythmically, and she realized that he had never woken up, but had touched her in a dream. He was undoubtedly dreaming of Annet, she realized ruefully.

She did not sleep, but she daydreamed. She imagined him introducing her to a stranger, saying: "This is my wife, Gwenda." She saw herself pregnant, but still working in the fields, and fainting in the middle of the day; and in her fantasy he picked her up and carried her home, and bathed her face with cold water. She saw him as an old man, playing with their grandchildren, indulging them, giving them apples and honeycombs.

Grandchildren? she thought wryly. It was a big edifice to build on the strength of his allowing her to put her arm around him while he cried himself to sleep.

When she was thinking that it must be almost dawn, and her stay in paradise might soon be over, he begin to stir. His breathing changed. He rolled onto his back. Her arm fell across his chest and she left it there, tucking her hand under his arm. After a few moments she sensed that he was awake, thinking. She lay still, afraid that if she spoke or moved she would break the spell.

Eventually he rolled back toward her. He put his arm around her, and she felt his hand on the bare skin of her back. He stroked her there, but she did not know what the caress meant: he seemed to be exploring, surprised to find that she was naked. His hand went up to her neck and all the way down to the curve of her hip.

At last he spoke. As if afraid of being overheard, he whispered: "She married him."

Gwenda whispered back: "Yes."

"Her love is weak."

"True love is never weak."

His hand remained on her hip, maddeningly close to the places where she wanted him to touch her.

He said: "Will I ever stop loving her?"

Gwenda took his hand and moved it. "She has two breasts, like these," she said, still whispering. She did not know why she did it: intuition was guiding her, and she followed it for good or ill.

He groaned, and she felt his hand close gently over one, then the other.

"And she has hair down here, like this," she said, moving his hand again. His breathing became faster. Leaving his hand there, she explored his body beneath his wool shift, and found that he had an erection. She grasped it and said: "Her hand feels just like this." He began to move his hips rhythmically.

She suddenly felt afraid that the act would be over before it was fully consummated. She did not want that. It was all or nothing now. She pushed him gently on to his back, then quickly raised herself and straddled him. "Inside, she's hot and wet," she said, and she lowered herself onto him. Although she had done it before, it had not been anything like this; she felt filled up and yet she wanted more. She moved down against the thrust of his hips, then up as he withdrew. She lowered her face to his and kissed his bearded mouth.

He held her head in his hands and kissed her back.

"She loves you," Gwenda whispered to him. "She loves you so much."

He cried out with passion, and she was rocked up and down, riding his hips like a wild pony, until at last she felt him come inside her, and he gave one last cry, then said: "Oh, I love you too! I love you, Annet!"

28

Wulfric went back to sleep, but Gwenda lay awake. She was too excited to sleep. She had won his love—she knew it. It hardly mattered that she had had to half-pretend to be Annet. He had made love to her with such hunger, and had kissed her afterward with such tenderness and gratitude, that she felt he was hers forever.

When her heart stopped racing and her mind calmed down, she thought about his inheritance. She was not willing to give up on it, especially now. As dawn broke outside, she racked her brains for some way to save it. When Wulfric woke up, she said: "I'm going to Kingsbridge."

He was startled. "Why?"

"To find out whether there's some way you can still inherit."

"How?"

"I don't know. But Ralph hasn't given the land to anyone else yet, so there's still a chance. And you deserve it—you've worked so hard and suffered so much."

"What will you do?"

"I'll see my brother Philemon. He understands these things better than we do. He'll know what we need to do."

Wulfric looked at her strangely.

She said: "What is it?"

He said: "You really love me, don't you?"

She smiled, full of happiness, and said: "Let's do it again, shall we?"

On the following morning she was at Kingsbridge Priory, sitting on the stone bench by the vegetable garden, waiting for Philemon. During the long walk from Wigleigh she had gone over every second of Sunday night in her mind, relishing the physical pleasures, puzzling over the words spoken. Wulfric still had not said that he loved her, but he had said: "You really love me." And he had seemed pleased that she loved him, albeit a bit bewildered by the strength of her passion.

She longed to win back his birthright. She yearned for it almost as much as she had yearned for him. She wanted it for both of them. Even if he were a landless laborer like her father, she would marry him, given the chance; but she wanted better for them both, and she was determined to get it.

When Philemon came out of the priory into the garden to greet her, she saw immediately that he was wearing the robes of a novice monk. "Holger!" she said, using his real name in her shock. "You're a novice—what you've always wanted!"

He smiled proudly, and benignly overlooked the use of his old name. "It was one of Godwyn's first acts as prior," he said. "He is a wonderful man. It's such an honor to serve him." He sat beside her on the bench. It was a mild autumn day, cloudy but dry.

"And how are you getting on with your lessons?"

"Slowly. It's hard to learn to read and write when you're grown-up." He grimaced. "The small boys progress faster than I do. But I can copy out the Lord's Prayer in Latin."

She envied him. She could not even write her name. "That's wonderful!" she said. Her brother was on his way to achieving his life's dream, and becoming a monk. Perhaps the status of novice might ameliorate the feelings of worthlessness that, she felt sure, accounted for his sometimes being sly and deceitful.

"But what about you?" he said. "Why have you come to Kingsbridge?"

"Did you know that Ralph Fitzgerald has become lord of Wigleigh?"

"Yes. He's here in town, staying at the Bell, living it up."

"He has refused to let Wulfric inherit his father's land." She told Philemon the story. "I want to know whether the decision can be contested."

Philemon shook his head. "The short answer is no. Wulfric could appeal to the earl of Shiring, of course, asking him to overturn Ralph's decision, but the earl won't intervene unless he has a personal stake. Even if he thinks the decision unjust—which it obviously is—he won't undermine the authority of a new appointee. But what's your interest? I thought Wulfric was going to marry Annet."

"When Ralph announced his decision, Annet jilted Wulfric and married Billy Howard."

"And now you have a chance with Wulfric."

"I think so." She felt herself blush.

"How do you know?" he asked shrewdly.

"I took advantage of him," she confessed. "When he was distraught over the wedding, I went to his bed."

"Don't worry. We who are born poor have to use cunning to get what we want. Scruples are for the privileged."

She did not really like to hear him talk that way. Sometimes he seemed to think that any behavior could be excused by their difficult childhood. But she was too disappointed to worry about that. "Is there really nothing I can do?"

"Oh, I didn't say that. It can't be contested, I said. But Ralph might be talked around."

"Not by me, I'm sure."

"I don't know. Why don't you go and see Godwyn's cousin Caris? You've been friends with her since you were girls. She'll help you if she can. And she's close to Ralph's brother, Merthin. Perhaps he can think of something."

Any hope was better than none. Gwenda stood up to go. "I'll see her right away." She leaned forward to kiss her brother good-bye, then realized that he was forbidden such contact now. Instead, she clasped his hand, which seemed peculiar.

"I'll pray for you," he said.

Caris's house was opposite the priory gates. When Gwenda went in, there was no one in the dining hall, but she heard voices in the parlor, where Edmund usually did business. The cook, Tutty, told her Caris was with her father. Gwenda sat down to wait, tapping her foot impatiently, but after a few minutes the door opened.

Edmund came out accompanied by a man she did not recognize. He was tall, and had flared nostrils that gave his face a supercilious look. He wore the black robe of a priest, but no cross or other sacred symbol. Edmund nodded amiably to Gwenda and said to the stranger: "I'll walk you back to the priory."

Caris followed the two men out of the parlor and embraced Gwenda. "Who was that man?" Gwenda asked as soon as he had left.

"His name is Gregory Longfellow. He's the lawyer hired by Prior Godwyn."

"Hired for what?"

"Earl Roland has stopped the priory taking stone from its quarry. He's trying to charge a penny a cartload. Godwyn is going to appeal to the king."

"Are you involved?"

"Gregory thinks we must argue that the town will be unable to pay its taxes without a bridge. That's the best way to persuade the king, he says. So my father will go with Godwyn to testify at the royal court."

"Will you go, too?"

"Yes. But tell me why you're here?"

"I lay with Wulfric."

Caris smiled. "Really? At last! How was it?"

"It was wonderful. I lay beside him all night while he slept, then when he woke up I . . . persuaded him."

"Tell me more, I want all the details."

Gwenda told Caris the story. At the end, even though she was impatient to get on to the real purpose of her visit, she said: "But something tells me you have news of the same kind."

Caris nodded. "I lay with Merthin. I told him I didn't want to get married, and he went off to see that fat sow Bessie Bell, and I got upset at the thought of her sticking out her big tits at him—then he came back, and I was so pleased I just had to do it with him."

"Did you like it?"

"I loved it. It's the best thing ever. And it gets better. We do it whenever we get the chance."

"What if you get pregnant?"

"I'm not even thinking about that. I don't care if I die. One time—" She lowered her voice. "One time, we bathed in a pool in the forest, and afterwards he licked me . . . down there."

"Oh, disgusting! What was it like?"

"Nice. He liked it, too."

"You didn't do the same to him."

"Yes."

"But did he . . . ?"

Caris nodded. "In my mouth."

"Wasn't it foul?"

Caris shrugged. "It tastes funny . . . but it's so exciting to feel that happen. And he enjoyed it so much."

Gwenda was shocked but intrigued. Perhaps she should do that to Wulfric. She knew a place where they could bathe, a stream in the forest far from any roads . . .

Caris said: "But you didn't come all this way just to tell me about Wulfric."

"No. It's about his inheritance." Gwenda explained Ralph's decision. "Philemon thought perhaps Merthin could persuade Ralph to change his mind."

Caris shook her head pessimistically. "I doubt it. They've quarreled."

"Oh, no!"

"It was Ralph who stopped the carts leaving the quarry. Unfortunately, Merthin was there at the time. There was a fight. Ben Wheeler killed one of the earl's ruffians, and Ralph killed Ben."

Gwenda gasped. "But Lib Wheeler has a two-year-old!"

"And now little Bennie has no father."

Gwenda was dismayed for herself as well as for Lib. "So a brother's influence won't help."

"Let's go and see Merthin anyway. He's working on Leper Island today."

They left the house and walked down the main street to the riverside. Gwenda was discouraged. Everyone believed her chances were slender. It was so unfair.

They got Ian Boatman to row them across to the island. Caris explained that the old bridge was to be replaced by two new ones which would use the island as a stepping stone.

They found Merthin with his boy assistant, fourteen-year-old Jimmie, laying out the abutments of the new bridge. His measuring stick was an iron pole more than twice the height of a man, and he was hammering pointed stakes into the rocky ground to mark where the foundations must be dug.

Gwenda watched the way Caris and Merthin kissed. It was different.

There was a cozy relish in one another's bodies that seemed new. It matched how Gwenda herself felt about Wulfric. His body was not just desirable, it was hers to enjoy. It seemed to belong to her the way her own body did.

She and Caris watched while Merthin finished what he was doing, tying a length of twine between two stakes. Then he told Jimmie to pack up the tools.

Gwenda said: "I suppose there's not much you can do without stone."

"There are some preparations we can make. But I've sent all the masons to the quarry. They're dressing the stones there, instead of here on-site. We're building a stockpile."

"So, if you win your case in the royal court, you can start building right away."

"I hope so. It depends on how long the case takes—and the weather. We can't build in deepest winter, in case the frost freezes the mortar. It's October already. We normally stop around the middle of November." He looked up at the sky. "We might have a bit longer this year—rain clouds keep the earth warm."

Gwenda told him what she wanted.

"I wish I could help you," Merthin said. "Wulfric is a decent man, and that fight was entirely Ralph's fault. But I've quarreled with my brother. Before asking him a favor, I'd have to make friends. And I can't forgive him for killing Ben Wheeler."

It was the third negative response in a row, Gwenda thought glumly. Perhaps this was a foolish errand.

Caris said: "You may have to do this on your own."

"Yes, I will," Gwenda said decisively. It was time to stop asking for other people's help and start relying on herself—the way she had all her life. "Ralph is here in town, isn't he?"

"Yes," Merthin said. "He came to tell our parents the good news about his promotion. They're the only people in the county who are celebrating."

"But he's not staying with them."

"He's too grand for that now. He's at the Bell."

"What would be the best way to persuade him?"

Merthin thought for a few moments. "Ralph feels our father's humiliation—a knight reduced to the status of a pensioner of the priory. He'll do anything that seems to enhance his social position."

Gwenda thought about that as Ian Boatman rowed them all back to the city. How could she present her request as a way for Ralph to raise his standing? It was midday as she walked up the main street with the others.

Merthin was going to Caris's house for dinner, and Caris invited Gwenda to join them, but she was impatient to see Ralph, and she went on to the Bell.

A potboy told her Ralph was upstairs in the best room. Most lodgers slept in a communal dormitory: Ralph was emphasizing his new position by taking an entire room—paid for, Gwenda thought sourly, out of the meager harvests of Wigleigh peasants.

She knocked at the door and went in.

Ralph was there with his squire, Alan Fernhill, a boy of about eighteen with big shoulders and a small head. On the table between them stood a jug of ale, a loaf, and a joint of hot beef with a wisp of steam coming from it. They were finishing their dinner and looked thoroughly contented with their lot in life, Gwenda thought. She hoped they were not too drunk: men in that state could not talk to women; all they could do was make ribald remarks and laugh helplessly at each other's wit.

Ralph peered at her: the room was not well lit. "You're one of my serfs, aren't you?"

"No, my lord, but I'd like to be. I'm Gwenda, and my father is Joby, a landless laborer."

"And what are you doing so far from the village? It's not market day."

She moved a step farther into the room so that she could see his face more clearly. "Sir, I come to plead for Wulfric, son of the late Samuel. I know that he behaved disrespectfully to you once but, since then, he has suffered the torments of Job. His parents and brother were killed when the bridge collapsed, all the family's money was lost, and now his fiancée has married someone else. I hope you might feel that God has punished him harshly for the wrong he did you, and it is time for you to show mercy." Remembering what Merthin had advised, she added: "The mercy characteristic of the true nobleman."

He belched fruitily and sighed. "What do you care whether Wulfric inherits?"

"I love him, my lord. Now that he has been rejected by Annet, I hope he may marry me—with your gracious permission, of course."

"Come closer," he said.

She moved into the center of the room and stood in front of him.

His eyes roamed all over her body. "You're not a pretty girl," he said. "But there's something about you. Are you a virgin?"

"Lord—I . . . I . . ."

"Obviously not," he laughed. "Have you lain with Wulfric yet?"

"No!"

"Liar." He grinned, enjoying himself. "Well, now, what if I let Wulfric have his father's lands after all? Perhaps I should. What then?"

"You would be called a true nobleman by Wigleigh and all the world."

"The world won't care. But will you be grateful to me?"

Gwenda had a horrible feeling that she knew where this was leading. "Of course, deeply grateful."

"And how would you show it?"

She backed toward the door. "Any way I could without shame."

"Would you take off your dress?"

Her heart sank. "No, lord."

"Ah. Not so grateful, then."

She reached the door and touched the handle, but she did not go out. "What . . . what are you asking me, lord?"

"I want to see you naked. Then I'll decide."

"Here?"

"Yes."

She looked at Alan. "In front of him?"

"Yes."

It did not seem much, to show herself to these two men—not by comparison with the prize, winning Wulfric's inheritance back.

Swiftly, she undid her belt and pulled her dress over her head. She held the dress in her hand, keeping the other hand on the doorknob, and stared defiantly at Ralph. He looked greedily at her body, then glanced over at his companion with a grin of triumph; and Gwenda saw that this was about showing his power as much as anything else.

Ralph said: "An ugly cow, but nice udders—eh, Alan?"

Alan replied: "I wouldn't climb over her to get at you."

Ralph laughed.

Gwenda said: "Now will you grant my petition?"

Ralph put his hand to his crotch and began to stroke himself. "Lie with me," he said. "On that bed."

"No."

"Come on—you've already done it with Wulfric, you're no virgin."

"No."

"Think of the lands—ninety acres, all that his father had."

She thought. If she agreed, Wulfric would have his heart's desire—and the two of them could look forward to a life of plenty. If she continued to refuse, Wulfric would be a landless laborer, like Joby, struggling all his life to make enough to feed his children, and often failing.

Still the thought revolted her. Ralph was an unpleasant man, petty and vengeful, a bully—so different from his brother. His being tall and handsome made little difference. It would be disgusting to lie with someone she disliked so much.

The fact that she had done it with Wulfric only yesterday made the prospect of sex with Ralph even more repellent. After her night of happy intimacy with Wulfric, it would be a terrible betrayal to do the same with another man.

Don't be a fool, she told herself. For the sake of five minutes of unpleasantness, will you condemn yourself to a life of hardship? She thought of her mother, and the babies that had died. She remembered the stealing she and Philemon had been forced to do. Was it not better to prostitute herself to Ralph one time, for just a few moments, than to condemn her unborn children to a life of poverty?

Ralph remained quiet while she vacillated. He was wise: any words from him would only have strengthened her revulsion. Silence served him better.

"Please," Gwenda said at last. "Don't make me do this."

"Ah," he said. "That tells me you're willing."

"It's a sin," she said desperately. She did not often talk about sin, but she thought there was a chance it might move him. "A sin for you to ask, and a sin for me to agree."

"Sins can be forgiven."

"What would your brother think of you?"

That gave him pause. For a moment he seemed to hesitate.

"Please," she said. "Just let Wulfric inherit."

His face hardened again. "I've made my decision. I'm not going to reverse it—unless you can persuade me. And just saying please won't work." His eyes glistened with desire, and he was breathing a little faster, his mouth open, his lips moist behind his beard.

She dropped her dress to the floor and walked to the bed.

"Kneel on the mattress," Ralph said. "No, facing away from me."

She did as he said.

"Better view from this side," he said, and Alan laughed loudly. Gwenda wondered if Alan was going to stay to watch, but then Ralph said: "Leave us alone." A moment later the door slammed.

Ralph knelt on the bed behind Gwenda. She closed her eyes and prayed for forgiveness. She felt his thick fingers exploring her. She heard him spit, then he rubbed a wet hand on her. A moment later he entered her. She groaned with shame.

Ralph misinterpreted the sound and said: "You like that, eh?"

She wondered how long this would take. He began to move rhythmically. To ease the discomfort she moved with him, and he laughed triumphantly, thinking he had excited her lust. Her greatest fear was that this would sour her entire experience of lovemaking. In future, when she lay with Wulfric, would she think of this moment?

And then, to her horror, a warm flush of pleasure began to spread through her loins. She felt her face redden in shame. Despite her profound repugnance, her body betrayed her, and moisture flooded inside her, easing the friction of his thrusts. He sensed the change and moved faster. Disgusted with herself, she ceased to match his rhythm; but he grabbed her hips, pushing and pulling alternately, and she was helpless to resist. She remembered with dismay that her body had undermined her in the same way with Alwyn in the forest. Then as now, she had wanted her body to be a wooden statue, numb and impassive; both times, it had responded against her will.

She had killed Alwyn with his own knife.

She could not do the same to Ralph, even if she had wanted to, because he was behind her. She could not see him, and she had little control over her body. She was in his hands. She was glad when she sensed that he was approaching the climax. Soon it would be over. She felt an answering pressure in her own loins. She tried to make her body limp and her mind blank: it would be too humiliating if she, too, reached a climax. She felt Ralph ejaculate inside her, and she shuddered, not with pleasure but with loathing.

He sighed with satisfaction, withdrew from her, and lay flat on the bed.

She got up and quickly pulled on her dress.

"That was better than I expected," Ralph said, as if he were paying her some kind of polite compliment.

She went out and slammed the door behind her.

On the following Sunday, before church, Nathan Reeve came to Wulfric's house.

Gwenda and Wulfric were sitting in the kitchen. They had had breakfast and swept the room, and now Wulfric was sewing a pair of leather trousers while Gwenda wove a belt from cords. They sat close to the window, for better light—it was raining again.

Gwenda was pretending to live in the barn, so that Father Gaspard would not be offended, but she spent every night with Wulfric. He had not mentioned marriage, which disappointed her. However, they were living more or less as man and wife, in the way that people often did when they intended to marry as soon as they got around to the formalities. The nobility and the gentry were permitted no such laxity, but it was routinely overlooked among the peasantry.

As she had feared, she felt strange making love to him. The more she tried to put Ralph out of her mind, the more he intruded. Fortunately, Wulfric never noticed her mood. He made love to her with such enthusiasm and joy that it almost swamped her guilty conscience—but not quite.

And she had the consolation of knowing that he would inherit his family's lands after all. That made up for everything. She could not tell him this, of course, for then she would have needed to explain what had changed Ralph's mind. She had told him about her conversations with Philemon, Caris, and Merthin, and had given him a partial version of her encounter with Ralph, saying only that he had promised to reconsider. So Wulfric was hopeful, rather than triumphant.

"Come to the manor house, right away, both of you," Nathan said, putting his wet head around the door.

Gwenda said: "What does the Lord Ralph want?"

"Will you refuse to go if the proposed topic of discussion fails to interest you?" Nathan said sarcastically. "Don't ask stupid questions, just come."

She put a blanket over her head to walk to the big house. She still did not have a cloak. Wulfric had money, from the sale of his crops, and could have bought her a cloak, but he was saving for the heriot.

They hurried through the rain to the manor house. It was a small version of a nobleman's castle, having a great hall with a long dining table, plus a small upper story, called the solar, for the lord's private chamber. Now it bore the signs of a house occupied by men without wives: the walls were bare of tapestries, the straw on the floor gave up a pungent smell, the dogs snarled at the newcomers, and a mouse nibbled a crust on the sideboard.

Ralph sat at the head of the table. On his right was Alan, who gave Gwenda a smirk she did her best to ignore. A minute later, Nathan came in. Behind him followed fat, sly Perkin, rubbing his hands and bowing obsequiously, his hair so oily it looked like a leather skullcap. With Perkin was his new son-in-law, Billy Howard. Billy shot a triumphant glance at Wulfric: I've got your girl, he was thinking, and now I'm going to get your land. He had a shock coming.

Nathan sat on Ralph's left. The rest of them remained standing.

Gwenda had been looking forward to this moment. It was the reward for her sacrifice. She eagerly anticipated the expression on Wulfric's face when he learned that he had inherited after all. He would be overjoyed—

and she would, too. Their future would be secure, or at least as secure as was possible in a world of unpredictable weather and oscillating grain prices.

Ralph said: "Three weeks ago, I said that Wulfric, son of Samuel, could not inherit his father's land because he's too young." He spoke slowly and ponderously. He loves this, Gwenda thought: sitting at the head of the table, pronouncing judgment, everyone hanging on his words. "Wulfric has been working the land since then, while I have considered who should succeed old Samuel." He paused, then said: "But I've come to doubt my rejection of Wulfric."

Perkin started. He had been confident of success, and this shocked him.

Billy Howard said: "What's this? I thought Nate—" Then Perkin nudged him, and he shut up.

Gwenda could not restrain a smile of triumph.

Ralph said: "Despite his youth, Wulfric has shown himself capable."

Perkin glared at Nathan. Gwenda guessed that Nathan had promised the land to Perkin. Perhaps the bribe had already been paid.

Nathan was just as shocked as Perkin. He stared openmouthed at Ralph for a moment, turned to Perkin with a baffled expression, then looked suspiciously at Gwenda.

Ralph added: "In this he has been well supported by Gwenda, whose strength and loyalty have impressed me."

Nathan stared at her speculatively. She could tell what he was thinking. He realized she had intervened, and he was wondering how she had managed to change Ralph's mind. He might even be guessing the truth. She did not care if he did, so long as Wulfric remained ignorant.

Suddenly Nathan seemed to make a decision. He stood up and leaned his twisted torso across the table. He spoke to Ralph quietly. Gwenda could not hear what he said.

"Really?" Ralph said in a normal voice. "How much?"

Nathan turned to Perkin and murmured something to him.

Gwenda said: "Wait a minute! What's all this whispering?"

Perkin looked angry, but said reluctantly: "Yes, all right."

"All right to what?" Gwenda said fearfully.

"Double?" said Nathan.

Perkin nodded.

Gwenda had a feeling of dread.

Nathan said aloud: "Perkin offers to pay double the normal heriot, which would be five pounds."

Ralph said: "That makes a difference."

Gwenda cried: "No!"

Wulfric spoke for the first time. "The heriot is laid down by custom, recorded in the manor rolls," he said in his slow, boy-man voice. "It's not for negotiation."

Nathan said quickly: "Heriots can change, though. They're not in the Domesday Book."

Ralph said: "Are you two lawyers? If not, shut up. The heriot is two pounds and ten shillings. Any other money that changes hands is none of your business."

Gwenda realized with horror that Ralph was on the point of reneging on their deal. She spoke in a low, accusing voice, slow but clear. "You made me a promise."

"Why would I do something like that?" Ralph said.

It was the one question she could not answer. "Because I pleaded with you," she replied feebly.

"And I said I would think again. But I made no promise."

She was powerless to make him keep his word. She wanted to kill him. "Yes, you did!" she said.

"Lords don't bargain with peasants."

She stared at him, lost for words. It had all been for nothing: the long walk to Kingsbridge, the humiliation of appearing naked in front of him and Alan, the shameful act she had performed on Ralph's bed. She had betrayed Wulfric, and he still would not inherit. She pointed a finger at Ralph and said bitterly: "God damn you to hell, Ralph Fitzgerald."

He went pale. The curse of a genuinely wronged woman was known to be powerful. "Watch what you say," he replied. "We have a punishment for a witch who casts spells."

Gwenda drew back. No woman could take such a threat lightly. The accusation of witchcraft was easy to make and hard to refute. Still she could not resist saying: "Those who escape justice in this life will find it in the next."

Ralph ignored that and turned to Perkin. "Where is the money?"

Perkin had not got rich by telling people where he kept his cash. "I'll fetch it right away, lord," he said.

Wulfric said: "Come on, Gwenda. There's no mercy for us here."

Gwenda fought back tears. Anger had been replaced by grief. They had lost the battle, after all they had done. She turned away, head lowered to hide her emotions.

Perkin said: "Wait, Wulfric. You need employment—and I need help. Work for me. I'll pay you a penny a day."

Wulfric flushed with the shame of being offered a job as a laborer on lands his family had owned.

Perkin added: "Gwenda, too. You're both young and willing."

He did not intend to be malicious, Gwenda saw. He was single-minded in the pursuit of his own interests, and he was eager to hire two strong young laborers to help him farm his amalgamated holding. He did not care, or perhaps did not even know, that for Wulfric this was the final humiliation.

Perkin said: "That's a shilling a week between you. You'll have plenty."

Wulfric looked bitter. "Work for a wage, on lands that my family has owned for decades?" he said. "Never." He turned away and left the house.

Gwenda followed, thinking: What are we going to do now?

29

Westminster Hall was huge, bigger than the inside of some cathedrals. It was dauntingly long and wide, and its distant ceiling was supported by a double row of tall pillars. It was the most important room in the Palace of Westminster.

Earl Roland was perfectly at home here, Godwyn thought resentfully. The earl and his son William swaggered about in their fashionable clothes, with one leg of their hose red and the other black. Every earl knew all the others, and most of the barons too, and they clapped their friends on the shoulders, mocked each other facetiously, and hooted with laughter at their own humor. Godwyn wanted to remind them that the courts held in this room had the power to sentence any one of them to death, even if they were the nobility.

He and his entourage were quiet, speaking only to one another, and then in hushed tones. This was not out of reverence, he had to admit, but nervousness. Godwyn, Edmund, and Caris were ill at ease here. None of them had been to London before. The only person they knew was Buonaventura Caroli, and he was out of town. They did not know their way around, their clothes looked old-fashioned, and the money they had brought—which they had thought would be plenty—was running out.

Edmund was not cowed by anything, and Caris seemed distracted—as if she had something more important on her mind, though it hardly seemed possible—but Godwyn was tormented by anxiety. He was a newly elected prior, challenging one of the greatest noblemen in the land. The issue was the future of the town. Without the bridge, Kingsbridge would die. The priory, currently the beating heart of one of England's great cities, would dwindle to a lonely outpost in a small village, where a few monks did their devotions in the echoing emptiness of a crumbling cathedral. Godwyn had not fought to be prior only to see his prize turn to dust.

With so much at stake, he wanted to be in control of events, confident that he was cleverer than almost everyone else, as he was in Kingsbridge. But here he felt the opposite, and the insecurity drove him to distraction.

His consolation was Gregory Longfellow. A friend of Godwyn's from university days, Gregory had a devious mind well suited to the law. The royal court was familiar to him. Aggressive and cocksure, he had guided Godwyn through the legal maze. He had presented the priory's petition to Parliament, as he had presented many petitions before. It was not debated by Parliament, of course, but passed to the king's council, which was overseen by the chancellor. The chancellor's team of lawyers—all of them friends or acquaintances of Gregory's—might have referred the matter to the king's bench, the court that dealt with disputes in which the king had an interest, but, again as Gregory had foreseen, they had decided this was too petty to bother the king with, and had instead sent the case to the common bench, or court of common pleas.

All this had taken a full six weeks. It was late November, and the weather was getting colder. The building season was nearly over.

Today at last they stood before Sir Wilbert Wheatfield, an experienced judge who was said to be liked by the king. Sir Wilbert was the younger son of a northern baron. His elder brother had inherited the title and the estate, and Wilbert had trained as a priest, studied law, come to London, and found favor at the royal court. His inclination would be to side with an earl against a monk, Gregory warned; but he would put the king's interests ahead of all else.

The judge sat on a raised bench against the east wall of the palace, between windows that looked out onto the Green Yard and the River Thames. In front of him were two clerks at a long table. There were no seats for the litigants.

"Sir, the earl of Shiring has sent armed men to blockade the quarry owned by Kingsbridge Priory," Gregory said as soon as Sir Wilbert looked at him. His voice quivered with simulated indignation. "The quarry, which is within the earldom, was granted to the priory by King Henry I some two hundred years ago. A copy of the charter has been lodged with the court."

Sir Wilbert had a pink face and white hair, and looked handsome until he spoke, when he showed rotten teeth. "I have the charter before me," he said.

Earl Roland spoke without waiting to be invited. "The monks were given the quarry so that they could build their cathedral," he said, speaking in a bored-sounding drawl.

Gregory said quickly: "But the charter does not restrict their use of it to any one purpose."

"Now they want to build a bridge," Roland said.

"To replace the bridge that collapsed at Whitsun—a bridge that itself was built, many hundreds of years ago, with timber that was a gift of the king!" Gregory spoke as if he was outraged by the earl's every word.

"They don't need permission to rebuild a preexisting bridge," Sir Wilbert said briskly. "And the charter does say that the king wishes to encourage the building of the cathedral, but it does not say they have to relinquish their rights when the church is finished, nor that they are forbidden to use the stone for any other purpose."

Godwyn was heartened. The judge seemed to have seen the priory's side of the argument immediately.

Gregory made a spreading gesture with his hands, palms up, as if the judge had said something blindingly obvious. "And, indeed, sir, that has been the understanding of priors of Kingsbridge and earls of Shiring for three centuries."

That was not quite right, Godwyn knew. There had been disputes about the charter in the time of Prior Philip. But Sir Wilbert did not know that, nor did Earl Roland.

Roland's attitude was haughty, as if it was beneath his dignity to squabble with lawyers, but this was deceptive: he had a firm grip on the argument. "The charter does not say the priory may escape tax."

Gregory said: "Why, then, has the earl never imposed such a tax until now?"

Roland had his answer ready. "Former earls forgave the tax, as their contribution to the cathedral. It was a pious act. But no piety compels me to subsidize a bridge. Yet the monks refuse to pay."

Suddenly the argument had swung the other way. How fast it moved,

Godwyn thought; not like arguments in the monks' chapter house, which could go on for hours.

Gregory said: "And the earl's men prevent movement of stones from the quarry, and have killed a poor carter."

Sir Wilbert said: "Then the dispute had better be resolved as soon as possible. What does the priory say to the argument that the earl has the right to tax consignments passing through his earldom, using roads and bridges and fords that belong to him, regardless of whether he has actually enforced this right in the past or not?"

"That since the stones are not passing through his lands, but originate there, the tax is tantamount to charging the monks for the stones, contrary to the charter of Henry I."

Godwyn saw with dismay that the judge seemed unimpressed by this.

However, Gregory had not finished. "And that the kings who gave Kingsbridge a bridge and a quarry did so for a good reason: they wanted the priory and the town to prosper. And the town's alderman is here to testify that Kingsbridge cannot prosper without a bridge."

Edmund stepped forward. With his unkempt hair and provincial clothes he looked like a country bumpkin, by contrast with the gorgeously robed noblemen around; but, unlike Godwyn, he did not appear intimidated. "I'm a wool merchant, sir," he said. "Without the bridge, there's no trade. And without trade, Kingsbridge will pay no taxes to the king."

Sir Wilbert leaned forward. "How much did the town yield in the last tenth?"

He was speaking of the tax, imposed by Parliament from time to time, of one-tenth or one-fifteenth of each individual's movable property. No one ever paid a tenth, of course—everyone understated their wealth—so the amount payable by each town or county had become fixed, and the burden was shared out more or less fairly, with poor men and lowly peasants paying nothing at all.

Edmund had been expecting this question, and he replied promptly: "One thousand and eleven pounds, sir."

"And the effect of the loss of the bridge?"

"Today, I estimate that a tenth would raise less than three hundred pounds. But our citizens are continuing to trade in the hope that the bridge will be rebuilt. If that hope were to be dashed in this court today, the annual Fleece Fair and the weekly market would almost disappear, and the yield from a tenth would fall below fifty pounds."

"Next to nothing, in the scale of the king's needs," the judge said. He did not say what they all knew: that the king was in dire need of money because in the last few weeks he had declared war on France.

Roland was needled. "Is this hearing about the king's finances?" he said scornfully.

Sir Wilbert was not to be browbeaten, even by an earl. "This is the king's court," he said mildly. "What would you expect?"

"Justice," Roland replied.

"And you shall have it." The judge implied, but did not say, *Whether you like it or not.* "Edmund Wooler, where is the nearest alternative market?"

"Shiring."

"Ah. So the business you lose will move to the earl's town."

"No, sir. Some will move, but much will vanish. Many Kingsbridge traders will be unable to get to Shiring."

The judge turned to Roland. "How much does a tenth yield from Shiring?"

Roland conferred briefly with his secretary, Father Jerome, then said: "Six hundred and twenty pounds."

"And with the increased trade at Shiring market, could you pay one thousand six hundred and twenty pounds?"

"Of course not," the earl said angrily.

The judge continued in his mild tone. "Then your opposition to this bridge would cost the king dear."

"I have my rights," Roland said sulkily.

"And the king has his. Is there any way you could compensate the royal treasury for the loss of a thousand pounds every year or so?"

"By fighting alongside him in France—which wool merchants and monks will never do!"

"Indeed," said Sir Wilbert. "But your knights will require payment."

"This is outrageous," said Roland. He knew he was losing the argument. Godwyn tried not to look triumphant.

The judge did not like his proceedings being called outrageous. He fixed Roland with a look. "When you sent your men-at-arms to blockade the priory's quarry, I feel sure you did not intend to damage the king's interests." He paused expectantly.

Roland sensed a trap, but there was only one answer he could give. "Certainly not."

"Now that it has been made clear to the court, and to you, how the building of the new bridge serves the king's purposes, as well as those of Kingsbridge Priory and the town, I imagine you will agree to the reopening of the quarry."

Godwyn realized Sir Wilbert was being clever. He was forcing Roland to consent to his ruling, making it difficult for him to appeal personally to the king later.

After a long pause, Roland said: "Yes."

"And to the transport of stones through your territory without tax."

Roland knew he had lost. There was fury in his voice as he said again: "Yes."

"So ordered," the judge said. "Next case."

∽

It was a great victory, but it had probably come too late.

November had turned into December. Building normally stopped about now. Because of the rainy weather, the frosts would come late this year but, even so, there were at most a couple of weeks left. Merthin had hundreds of stones stockpiled at the quarry, cut and shaped and ready to be laid. However, it would take months to cart them all to Kingsbridge. Although Earl Roland had lost the court case, he had almost certainly succeeded in delaying the building of the bridge by a year.

Caris returned to Kingsbridge, with Edmund and Godwyn, in a somber mood. Reining in on the suburban side of the river, she saw that Merthin had already constructed his cofferdams. In each of the channels that ran either side of Leper Island, the ends of wooden boards stuck a couple of feet above the surface in a big circle. She recalled Merthin explaining, in the guildhall, how he planned to drive stakes into the riverbed in a double ring then fill the gap between the rings with clay mortar to make a watertight seal. The water inside the coffer could then be taken out so that the builders could lay a foundation on the riverbed.

One of Merthin's workmen, Harold Mason, was on the ferry as they crossed the river, and Caris asked him if the cofferdams had been drained. "Not yet," he said. "The master wants to leave it until we're ready to start building."

Caris noticed with pleasure that Merthin was now called the master, despite his youth. "But why?" she said. "I thought we wanted everything ready for a quick start."

"He says the force of the river puts more strain on the dam when there's no water inside."

Caris wondered how Merthin knew such things. He had learned the basics from his first master, Joachim, Elfric's father. He always talked a lot to strangers who came to town, especially men who had seen tall buildings in Florence and Rome. And he had read all about the construction of the cathedral in *Timothy's Book*. But he seemed also to have remarkable intuition about these matters. She would never have guessed that an empty dam would be weaker than a full one.

Although they were subdued as they entered the town, they wanted to tell Merthin the good news right away and find out what, if anything, he could get done before the end of the season. Pausing only to entrust their horses to stableboys, they went in search of him. They found him in the mason's loft, high in the northwest tower of the cathedral, working by the light of several oil lamps, scratching a design for a parapet on the tracing floor.

He looked up from his drawing, saw their faces, and grinned widely. "We won?" he said.

"We won," said Edmund.

"Thanks to Gregory Longfellow," Godwyn added. "He cost a lot of money, but he was worth it."

Merthin embraced both men—his quarrel with Godwyn forgotten, at least for now. He kissed Caris tenderly. "I missed you," he murmured. "It's been eight weeks! I felt as if you were never coming back."

She made no reply. She had something momentous to say to him, but she wanted privacy.

Her father did not notice her reticence. "Well, Merthin, you can start building right away."

"Good."

Godwyn said: "You can begin carting stones from the quarry tomorrow—but I suppose it's too late to get much building done before the winter frosts."

"I've been thinking about that," Merthin said. He glanced at the windows. It was mid-afternoon, the December day already darkening to evening. "There might be a way to do it."

Edmund was immediately enthusiastic. "Well, out with it, lad! What's your idea?"

Merthin turned to the prior. "Would you grant an indulgence to volunteers who bring stones from the quarry?" An indulgence was a special act of forgiveness of sins. Like a gift of money, it could either pay for past debts or stand in credit for future liabilities.

"I could," Godwyn said. "What have you got in mind?"

Merthin turned to Edmund. "How many people in Kingsbridge own a cart?"

"Let me think," Edmund said, frowning. "Every substantial trader has one . . . so it must come to a couple of hundred, at least."

"Suppose we were to go around the town tonight and ask every one of them to drive to the quarry tomorrow and pick up stones."

Edmund stared at Merthin, and a grin slowly spread across his face. "Now," he said delightedly, "that's an idea!"

"We'll tell each one that everybody else is going," Merthin went on. "It will be like a holiday. Their families can go along, and they can take food and beer. If each one brings back a cartload of stone or rubble, in two days' time we'll have enough to build the piers of the bridge."

That was brilliant, Caris thought wonderingly. It was typical of him, to think of something no one else could have imagined. But would it work?

"What about the weather?" said Godwyn.

"The rain has been a curse for the peasants, but it's held off the deep cold. We've a week or two yet, I think."

Edmund was excited, stomping up and down the loft with his lopsided gait. "But if you can build the piers in the next few days . . ."

"By the end of next year we can finish the bulk of the work."

"Could we use the bridge the following year?"

"No . . . but wait. We could put a temporary wooden roadbed on top in time for the Fleece Fair."

"So we would have a usable bridge by the year after next—and miss only one Fleece Fair!"

"We'd have to finish the stone roadbed after the Fleece Fair, then it would harden in time to be used normally in the third year."

"Damn it, we've got to do it!" Edmund said excitedly.

Godwyn said cautiously: "You have yet to empty the water out of the cofferdams."

Merthin nodded. "That's hard work. In my original plan I allowed two weeks for it. But I've got an idea about that, too. However, let's get the carts organized first."

They all moved to the door, animated with enthusiasm. As Godwyn and Edmund started down the narrow spiral staircase, Caris caught Merthin by the sleeve and held him back. He thought she wanted to kiss, and he put his arms around her, but she pushed him away. "I've got some news," she said.

"More?"

"I'm pregnant."

She watched his face. He was startled at first, and his red brown eyebrows rose. Then he blinked, tilted his head to one side, and shrugged, as if to say: *Nothing surprising about that.* He grinned, at first ruefully, then with unmixed happiness. At the end he was beaming. "That's wonderful!" he said.

She hated him momentarily for his stupidity. "No, it's not!"

"Why not?"

"Because I don't want to spend my life as a slave to anyone, even if it is my own child."

"A slave? Is every mother a slave?"

"Yes! How could you possibly not know that I feel that way?"

He looked baffled and hurt, and a part of her wanted to back off, but she had been nursing her anger too long. "I did know, I suppose," he said. "But then you lay with me, so I thought . . ." He hesitated. "You must have known it might happen—*would* happen, sooner or later."

"Of course I knew, but I acted as if I didn't."

"Yes, I can understand that."

"Oh, stop being so understanding. You're such a weakling."

His face froze. After a long pause he said: "All right, then, I'll stop being so understanding. Just give me the information. What's your plan?"

"I don't have a plan, you fool. I just know I don't want to have a baby."

"So you don't have a plan, and I'm a fool and a weakling. Do you want anything from me?"

"No!"

"Then what are you doing here?"

"Don't be so logical!"

He sighed. "I'm going to stop trying to be what you tell me to be, because you make no sense." He went around the room putting out the lamps. "I'm glad we're having a baby, and I'd like us to be married and look after the child together—assuming this mood you're in is only temporary." He put his drawing implements in a leather bag and slung it over his shoulder. "But for now, you're so cantankerous that I'd rather not speak to you at all. And besides, I have work to do." He went to the door, then paused. "On the other hand, we could kiss and make up."

"Go away!" she yelled.

He ducked through the low door and disappeared into the stairwell.

Caris began to cry.

Merthin had no idea whether the people of Kingsbridge would rally to the cause. They all had work and worries of their own: would they see the communal effort to build the bridge as being more important? He was not sure. He knew, from his reading of *Timothy's Book*, that at moments of crisis

Prior Philip had often prevailed by calling on the ordinary people to make a massive effort. But Merthin was not Philip. He had no right to lead people. He was just a carpenter.

They made a list of cart owners and divided it up by streets. Edmund rounded up ten leading citizens, and Godwyn picked ten senior monks, and they went around in pairs. Merthin was teamed with Brother Thomas.

The first door they knocked on was Lib Wheeler's. She was continuing Ben's business with hired labor. "You can have both my carts," she said. "And the men to drive them. Anything to give that damned earl a poke in the eye."

But their second call brought a refusal. "I'm not well," said Peter Dyer, who had a cart for delivering the bales of woolen cloth he dyed yellow and green and pink. "I can't travel."

He looked perfectly all right, Merthin thought; he was probably scared of a confrontation with the earl's men. There would be no fight, Merthin felt sure; but he could understand the fear. What if all the citizens felt that way?

Their third call was on Harold Mason, a young builder who was hoping for several years of work building the bridge. He agreed immediately. "Jake Chepstow will come, too," he said. "I'll make sure of that." Harold and Jake were pals.

After that, almost everybody said yes.

They did not need to be told how important the bridge was—everyone who had a cart was a trader, obviously—and they had the additional incentive of a pardon for their sins. But the most important factor seemed to be the promise of an unexpected holiday. Most people said: "Is so-and-so going?" When they heard that their friends and neighbors had volunteered, they did not want to be left out.

When they had made all their calls, Merthin left Thomas and went down to the ferry. They had to take the carts across overnight, to be ready to leave at sunrise. The ferry carried only one cart at a time—two hundred carts would take several hours. That was why they needed a bridge, of course.

An ox was revolving the great wheel, and carts were already crossing the river. On the other side, the owners turned their beasts out to graze in the pasture, then came back on the ferry and went to bed. Edmund had got John Constable and half a dozen of his deputies to spend the night in Newtown, guarding carts and beasts.

The ferry was still working when Merthin went to bed an hour or so after midnight. He lay thinking about Caris for a while. Her quirkiness and unpredictability were part of what he loved, but sometimes she was impossible. She was the cleverest individual in Kingsbridge, but also hopelessly irrational at times.

Most of all, though, he hated to be called weak. He was not sure he would ever forgive Caris for that jibe. Earl Roland had humiliated him, ten years ago, by saying he could not be a squire, and was fit only to be apprenticed to a carpenter. But he was not weak. He had defied Elfric's tyranny, he had routed Prior Godwyn over the bridge design, and he was about to save the entire town. I might be small, he thought, but by God I'm strong.

Still he did not know what to do about Caris, and he fell asleep worrying.

Edmund woke him at first light. By then almost every cart in Kingsbridge was on the far side of the river, in a straggly line that led through the suburb of Newtown and half a mile into the forest. It took a couple more hours to ferry the people over. The excitement of organizing what was effectively a pilgrimage diverted Merthin's mind from the problem of Caris and her pregnancy. Soon the pasture on the far side was a scene of good-natured chaos, as dozens of people caught their horses and oxen, led them to their carts, and backed them into the traces. Dick Brewer brought over a huge barrel of ale and gave it away—"to encourage the expedition," he said—with mixed results: some people were so encouraged they had to lie down.

A crowd of spectators gathered on the city side of the river, watching. As the line of carts at last began to move off, a great cheer went up.

But stones were only half the problem.

Merthin turned his attention to the next challenge. If he were to begin laying stones as soon as they arrived from the quarry, he had to empty the cofferdams in two days instead of two weeks. As the cheering died down, he raised his voice and addressed the crowd. This was the moment to catch their interest, when the excitement was fading and they were beginning to wonder what to do next.

"I need the strongest men left in town!" he shouted. They went quiet, intrigued. "Are there any strong men in Kingsbridge?" This was partly a come-on: the work would be heavy, but asking only for strong people also threw down a challenge that the young men would find hard to resist. "Before the carts get back from the quarry tomorrow night, we have to empty the water out of the cofferdams. It will be the hardest work you've ever done—so no weaklings, please." As he said this, he looked at Caris in the crowd and caught her eye, and he saw her flinch: she remembered using that word, and she knew she had insulted him. "Any woman who thinks she is the equal of the men can join in," he went on. "I need you to find a bucket and meet me on the shore opposite Leper Island as soon as possible. Remember—only the strongest!"

He was not sure whether he had won them over. As he finished, he spotted the tall figure of Mark Webber, and pushed through the throng to him. "Mark, will you encourage them?" he said anxiously.

Mark was a gentle giant, much liked in the town. Even though he was poor, he had influence, especially among adolescents. "I'll make sure the lads join in," he said.

"Thank you."

Next, Merthin found Ian Boatman. "I'm going to need you all day, I hope," he said. "Ferrying people out to the cofferdams and back. You can work for pay or an indulgence—your choice." Ian was excessively fond of his wife's younger sister, and would probably prefer the indulgence, either for a past sin or for one he was hoping to commit soon.

Merthin made his way through the streets to the shore where he was preparing to build the bridge. Could the cofferdams be emptied in two days? He really had no idea. He wondered how many gallons of water were in each. Thousands? Hundreds of thousands? There must be a way of calculating. The Greek philosophers had probably worked out a method but, if they had, it had not been taught at the priory school. To find out, he would probably have to go to Oxford, where there were mathematicians famous all over the world, according to Godwyn.

He waited at the river's edge, wondering if anyone would come.

The first to arrive was Megg Robbins, the strapping daughter of a corn dealer, with muscles enlarged by years of lifting sacks of grain. "I can outdo most of the men in this town," she said, and Merthin did not doubt it.

A group of young men came next, then three novice monks.

As soon as Merthin had ten people with buckets, he got Ian to row them and him to the nearer of the two dams.

Inside the rim of the dam, he had built a ledge just above water level, strong enough for men to stand on. From the ledge four ladders reached all the way down to the riverbed. In the center of the dam, floating on the surface, was a large raft. Between the raft and the ledge there was a gap of about two feet, and the raft was held in a central position by protruding wooden spokes that reached almost to the wall and prevented movement of more than a few inches in any direction.

"You work in pairs," he told them. "One on the raft, one on the ledge. The one on the raft fills his bucket and passes it to the one on the ledge, who tosses the water over the edge into the river. As the empty bucket is passed back, another full one is passed forward."

Megg Robbins said: "What happens when the water level inside falls, and we can't reach one another?"

"Good thinking, Megg. You'd better be my forewoman in charge here. When you can no longer reach, you work in threes, with one on a ladder."

She caught on fast. "And then fours, with two on a ladder . . ."

"Yes. Though by then we'll need to rest the men and bring in fresh ones."

"Right."

"Get started. I'll bring over another ten—you've got plenty of room still."

Megg turned away. "Pick your partners, everyone!" she called.

The volunteers started to dip their buckets. He heard Megg say: "Let's keep a rhythm going. Dip, lift, pass, chuck! One, two, three, four. How about a song to give us the swing of it?" She raised her voice in a lusty contralto. "Oh, *there* was *once* a *come*ly *knight* . . ."

They knew the song, and all joined in the next line: "His *blade* was *straight* and *true, oh!*"

Merthin watched. Everyone was soaking wet in a few minutes. He could see no apparent fall in the level of the water. It was going to be a long job.

He climbed over the side and into Ian's boat.

By the time he reached the bank there were thirty more volunteers with buckets.

He got the second cofferdam started, with Mark Webber as foreman, then doubled the numbers in both locations, then started replacing tired workers with fresh ones. Ian Boatman became exhausted and handed the oars over to his son. The water inside the dams fell inch by wearisome inch. As the level fell, the work went ever more slowly, for the buckets had to be lifted greater and greater distances to the rim.

Megg was the first to discover that a person could not hold a full bucket in one hand and an empty one in the other and still keep balance on a ladder. She devised a one-way bucket chain, with full buckets going up one ladder and empty ones down another. Mark instituted the same system in his dam.

The volunteers worked an hour and rested an hour, but Merthin did not stop. He was organizing the teams, supervising the transport of volunteers to and from the dams, replacing buckets that broke. Most of the men drank ale during their rest periods, and in consequence there were several accidents during the afternoon, with people dropping buckets and falling off ladders. Mother Cecilia came to take care of the injured, with the help of Mattie Wise and Caris.

Too soon, the light began to fail, and they had to stop. But both coffers were more than half-empty. Merthin asked everyone to come back in the morning, then went home. After a few spoonfuls of his mother's soup he fell asleep at the table, waking only long enough to wrap a blanket around himself and lie down in the straw. When he woke the next morning, his first thought was to wonder whether any of the volunteers would show up for the second day.

He hurried down to the river at first light with an anxious heart. Both Mark Webber and Megg Robbins were there already, Mark eating his way through a doorstep of bread and Megg lacing a pair of high boots in the hope of keeping her feet dry. No one else showed up for the next half hour, and Merthin began to wonder what he would do with no volunteers. Then some of the young men arrived, carrying their breakfast with them, followed by the novice monks, then a whole crowd.

Ian Boatman turned up, and Merthin got him to row Megg out with some volunteers, and they began again.

The work was harder today. Everyone was aching from yesterday's efforts. Every bucket had to be lifted ten feet or more. But the end was in sight. The levels continued to drop, and the volunteers began to glimpse the riverbed.

In the middle of the afternoon, the first of the carts arrived back from the quarry. Merthin directed the owner to unload his stone in the pasture and ferry his cart back across the river to the town. A short while later, in Megg's coffer, the raft bumped the riverbed.

There was more to be done. When the last of the water was lifted out, the raft itself had to be dismantled and raised, plank by plank, up the ladders and out. Then dozens of fish were revealed, flapping in muddy pools on the bottom, and they had to be netted and shared out among the volunteers. But, when that was finished, Merthin stood on the ledge, weary but jubilant, and looked down a twenty-foot hole at the flat mud of the riverbed.

Tomorrow he would drop several tons of rubble into each hole, and drench the rubble with mortar, forming a massive, immovable foundation.

Then he would start building the bridge.

Wulfric was in a depression.

He ate almost nothing and forgot to wash himself. He got up automatically at daybreak and lay down again when it got dark, but he did not work, and he did not make love to Gwenda in the night. When she asked him what was the matter, he would say: "I don't know, really." He answered all questions with such uninformative replies, or just with grunts.

There was little to do in the fields anyway. This was the season when villagers sat by their fires, sewing leather shoes and carving oak shovels, eating salt pork and soft apples and cabbage preserved in vinegar. Gwenda was not worried about how they were going to feed themselves: Wulfric still had money from the sale of his crops. But she was desperately anxious about him.

Wulfric had always lived for his work. Some villagers grumbled constantly and were happy only on rest days, but he was not like that. The fields, the crops, the beasts, and the weather were what he cared about. On Sundays he had always been restless until he found some occupation that was not forbidden, and on holidays he had done all he could to circumvent the rules.

She knew she had to get him to return to his normal state of mind. Otherwise he might fall sick with some physical illness. And his money would not last forever. Sooner or later they must both work.

However, she did not give him her news until two full moons had passed, and she was sure.

Then, one morning in December, she said: "I have something to tell you."

He grunted. He was sitting at the kitchen table, whittling a stick, and he did not look up from this idle occupation.

She reached across the table and held his wrists, stopping the whittling. "Wulfric, would you please look at me?"

He did so with a surly expression on his face, resentful at being ordered but too lethargic to defy her.

"It's important," she said.

He looked at her in silence.

"I'm going to have a baby," she said.

His expression did not change, but he dropped the knife and stick.

She looked back at him for a long moment. "Do you understand me?" she said.

He nodded. "A baby," he said.

"Yes. We will have a child."

"When?"

She smiled. It was the first question he had asked for two months. "Next summer, before the harvest."

"The child must be cared for," he said. "You, too."

"Yes."

"I must work." He looked depressed again.

She held her breath. What was coming?

He sighed, then set his jaw. "I'll go and see Perkin," he said. "He'll need help with his winter plowing."

"And manuring," she said happily. "I'll come with you. He offered to hire us both."

"All right." He was still staring at her. "A child," he said, as if it were a marvel. "Boy or girl, I wonder."

She got up and walked around the table to sit on the bench next to him. "Which would you prefer?"

"A little girl. It was all boys in my family."

"I want a boy, a miniature version of you."

"We might have twins."

"One of each."

He put his arm around her. "We should get Father Gaspard to marry us properly."

Gwenda sighed contentedly and leaned her head on his shoulder. "Yes," she said. "Perhaps we should."

Merthin moved out of his parents' house just before Christmas. He had built a one-room house for himself on Leper Island, which was now his land. He said he needed to guard the growing stockpile of valuable building materials he was keeping on the island—timber, stones, lime, ropes, and iron tools.

At the same time, he stopped coming to Caris's house for meals.

On the last but one day of December, she went to see Mattie Wise.

"No need to tell me why you're here," said Mattie. "Three months gone?"

Caris nodded and avoided her eye. She looked around the little kitchen, with its bottles and jars. Mattie was heating something in a small iron pot, and it gave off an acrid smell that made Caris want to sneeze.

"I don't want to have a baby," Caris said.

"I wish I had a chicken for every time I've heard that said."

"Am I wicked?"

Mattie shrugged. "I make potions, not judgments. People know the difference between right and wrong—and if they don't, that's what priests are for."

Caris was disappointed. She had been hoping for sympathy. More coolly, she said: "Do you have a potion to get rid of this pregnancy?"

"I do . . ." Mattie looked uneasy.

"Is there a snag?"

"The way to get rid of a pregnancy is to poison yourself. Some girls drink a gallon of strong wine. I make up a dose with several toxic herbs. Sometimes it works, sometimes it doesn't. But it always makes you feel dreadful."

"Is it dangerous? Could I die?"

"Yes, though it's not as risky as childbirth."

"I'll take it."

Mattie took her pot off the fire and put it on a stone slab to cool. Turning to her scarred old workbench, she took a small pottery bowl from a cupboard and poured into it small quantities of different powders.

Caris said: "What's the matter? You say you don't make judgments, but you look disapproving."

Mattie nodded. "You're right. I do make judgments, of course; everyone does."

"And you're judging me."

"I'm thinking that Merthin is a good man and you love him, but you don't seem able to find happiness with him. That makes me sad."

"You think I should be like other women, and throw myself at the feet of some man."

"It seems to make them happy. But I chose a different way of life. And so will you, I suppose."

"Are you happy?"

"I wasn't born to be happy. But I help people, I make a living, and I'm free." She poured her mixture into a cup, added some wine, and stirred, dissolving the powders. "Have you had breakfast?"

"Just some milk."

She dripped a little honey into the cup. "Drink this, and don't bother to eat dinner—you'll only throw it up."

Caris took the cup, hesitated, then swallowed the draft. "Thank you." It had a vilely bitter taste that was only partly masked by the sweetness of the honey.

"It should be all over by tomorrow morning—one way or the other."

Caris paid her and left. Walking home, she felt an odd mixture of elation and sadness. Her spirits were lifted by having made a decision, after all the weeks of worry; but she also felt a tug of loss, as if she were saying good-bye to someone—Merthin, perhaps. She wondered if their separation would be permanent. She could contemplate the prospect calmly, because she still felt angry with him, but she knew she would miss him terribly. He would find another lover eventually—Bessie Bell, perhaps—but Caris felt sure she would not do the same. She would never love anyone as she had loved Merthin.

When she got home, the smell of roasting pork in the house nauseated her, and she went out again. She did not want to gossip with other women in the main street or talk business with the men at the guildhall, so she drifted into the priory grounds, her heavy wool cloak wrapped around her for warmth, and sat on a tombstone in the graveyard, looking at the north wall of the cathedral, marveling at the perfection of its carved moldings and the grace of its flying buttresses.

It was not long before she felt ill.

She puked on a grave, but her stomach was empty, and nothing came up except a sour fluid. Her head began to ache. She wanted to lie down, but she was reluctant to go home because of the kitchen smell. She decided to go to the priory hospital. The nuns would let her lie down for a minute. She left the graveyard, crossed the green in front of the cathedral, and entered the hospital. Suddenly she was terribly thirsty.

She was greeted by the kindly, podgy face of Old Julie. "Oh, Sister Juliana," Caris said gratefully. "Would you bring me a cup of water?" The priory had water piped from upstream, cool and clear and safe to drink.

"Are you ill, child?" said Old Julie anxiously.

"A little nauseated. If I may, I'll just lie down for a moment."

"Of course. I'll fetch Mother Cecilia."

Caris lay down on one of the straw mattresses lined up neatly on the floor. For a few moments she felt better, then the headache became worse. Julie returned with a jug and a cup, and Mother Cecilia. Caris drank some water, threw up, and drank some more.

Cecilia asked her some questions then said: "You've eaten something corrupt. You need to be purged."

Caris hurt so much she could make no response. Cecilia left and returned moments later with a bottle and a spoon. She gave Caris a spoonful of treacly medicine that tasted of cloves.

Caris lay back with her eyes closed and longed for the pain to go away. After a while, she was afflicted with stomach cramps, followed by uncontrollable diarrhea. She assumed vaguely that it had been brought on by the treacle. After an hour it went away. Julie undressed her, washed her, gave her a nun's robe instead of her own soiled dress, and put her on a clean mattress. She lay down and closed her eyes, exhausted.

Prior Godwyn came to see her and said she must be bled. Another monk came to do the job. He made her sit up and stretch out her arm with her elbow over a large bowl. Then he took a sharp knife and opened the vein in the crook of her arm. She hardly noticed the pain of the cut or the slow throb of the bleeding. After a while the monk put a dressing on the cut and told her to hold it there firmly. He took away the bowl of blood.

She was vaguely conscious of people coming to see her: her father, Petranilla, Merthin. Old Julie put a cup to her lips from time to time, and she always drank, for she was insatiably thirsty. At some point she noticed candles, and realized it must be night. Eventually she fell into a troubled sleep, and had terrifying dreams about blood. Every time she woke, Julie gave her water.

At last she woke to daylight. The pain had receded, leaving only a dull headache. The next thing she realized was that someone was washing her thighs. She raised herself on her elbow.

A novice nun with the face of an angel crouched beside the mattress. Caris's dress was up around her waist, and the nun was bathing her with a cloth dipped in warm water. After a moment, she remembered the girl's name. "Mair," she said.

"Yes," the novice answered with a smile.

As she squeezed out the cloth into a bowl, Caris was frightened to see that it was red. "Blood!" she said fearfully.

"Don't worry," said Mair. "It's just your monthly cycle. Heavy, but normal."

Caris saw that her dress and the mattress were soaked with blood.

She lay back, looking up at the ceiling. Tears came to her eyes, but she did not know whether she was crying out of relief or sadness.

She was no longer pregnant.

PART IV
June 1338 to
May 1339

30

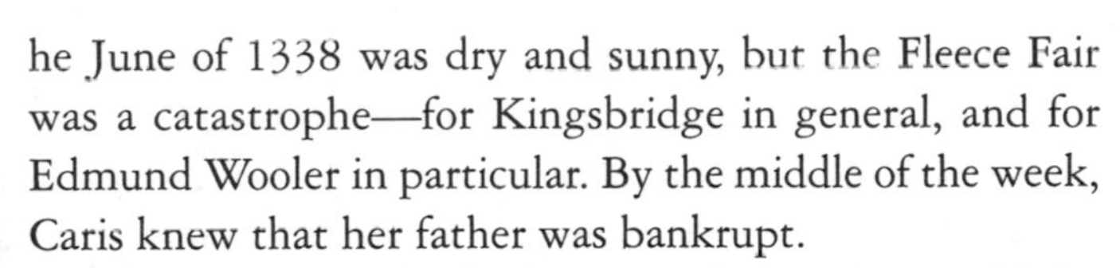

he June of 1338 was dry and sunny, but the Fleece Fair was a catastrophe—for Kingsbridge in general, and for Edmund Wooler in particular. By the middle of the week, Caris knew that her father was bankrupt.

The townspeople had expected that it would be difficult, and had done all they could to prepare. They commissioned Merthin to build three large rafts that could be poled across the river, to supplement the ferry and Ian's boat. He could have built more, but there was no room to land them on the banks. The priory's grounds were opened a day early, and the ferry operated all night, by torchlight. They persuaded Godwyn to give permission for Kingsbridge shopkeepers to cross to the suburban side and sell to the queue, in the hope that Dick Brewer's ale and Betty Baxter's buns would mollify the people waiting.

It was not enough.

Fewer people than usual came to the fair, but the queues were worse than ever. The extra rafts were insufficient but, even so, the shore on both sides became so swampy that carts were constantly getting stuck in the mud and having to be towed out by teams of oxen. Worse, the rafts were difficult to steer, and on two occasions there were collisions that threw passengers into the water, though fortunately no one drowned.

Some traders anticipated these problems and stayed away. Others turned back when they saw the length of the queue. Of those willing to wait half a day to get into the city, some then did such paltry business that they left after a day or two. By Wednesday the ferry was taking more people away than it was bringing in.

That morning, Caris and Edmund made a tour of the bridge works with Guillaume of London. Guillaume was not as big a customer as Buonaventura Caroli, but he was the best they had this year, and they were making a fuss over him. He was a tall, beefy man in a cloak of expensive Italian cloth, bright red.

They borrowed Merthin's raft, which had a raised deck and a built-in hoist for transporting building materials. His young assistant, Jimmie, poled them out into the river.

The midstream piers that Merthin had constructed in such a rush last December were still surrounded by their cofferdams. He had explained to Edmund and Caris that he would leave the dams in place until the bridge was almost finished, to protect the stonework from accidental damage by his own workmen. When he demolished them, he would put in their place a pile of loose large stones, called riprap, which he said would prevent the current undermining the piers.

The massive stone columns had now grown, like trees, spreading their arches sideways toward smaller piers built in the shallower water near the banks. These in turn were growing arches, on one side toward the central piers and on the other toward abutments on the bank. A dozen or more masons were busy on the elaborate scaffolding that clung to the stonework like gulls' nests on a cliff.

They landed on Leper Island and found Merthin with Brother Thomas, supervising the masons building the abutment from which the bridge would spring across the northern branch of the river. The priory still owned and controlled the bridge, even though the land was leased to the parish guild and the construction was financed by loans from individual townspeople. Thomas was often on-site. Prior Godwyn took a proprietorial interest in the work, and especially in how the bridge would look, evidently feeling it was going to be some kind of monument to him.

Merthin looked up at the visitors with his golden brown eyes, and Caris's heart seemed to beat faster. She hardly saw him, these days, and when they spoke it was always about business; but she still felt strange in his presence. She had to make an effort to breathe normally, to meet his eye with feigned indifference, and to slow her speech to a moderate speed.

They had never patched up their quarrel. She had not told him about her abortion, so he did not know whether her pregnancy had terminated spontaneously or otherwise. Neither of them had ever referred to it. On two occasions since then he had come to talk to her, solemnly, and had begged her to make a fresh start with him. Both times, she had told him that she would never love another man, but she was not going to spend her life as someone's wife and someone else's mother. "How *will* you spend your life, then?" he had asked, and she had replied simply that she did not know.

Merthin was not as impish as he used to be. His hair and beard were neatly trimmed—he was now a regular customer of Matthew Barber. He was dressed in a russet tunic, like the masons, but he wore a yellow cape trimmed with fur, a sign of his status as a master, and a cap with a feather in it, which made him look a bit taller.

Elfric, whose enmity continued, had objected to Merthin dressing like a master, on the grounds that he was not a member of any guild. Merthin's reply was that he was a master, and the solution to the problem was for him to be admitted to a guild. And there the matter remained, unresolved.

Merthin was still only twenty-one, and Guillaume looked at him and said: "He's young!"

Caris said defensively: "He's been the best builder in town since he was about seventeen."

Merthin said a few more words to Thomas then came over. "The abutments of a bridge need to be heavy, with deep foundations," he said, explaining the massive bulwark of stone he was constructing.

Guillaume said: "Why is that, young man?"

Merthin was used to being condescended to, and he took it lightly. With a small smile, he said: "Let me show you. Stand with your feet as far apart as you can, like this." Merthin demonstrated, and Guillaume—after a moment's hesitation—imitated him. "Your feet feel as if they might slide farther apart, don't they?"

"Yes."

"And the ends of a bridge tend to spread, like your feet. This puts a strain on the bridge, just as you're now feeling the tension in your groin." Merthin stood upright and placed his own booted foot firmly up against Guillaume's soft leather shoe. "Now your foot can't move, and the strain on your groin has eased, hasn't it?"

"Yes."

"The abutment has the same effect as my foot, in bracing your foot and relieving the strain."

"Very interesting," Guillaume said thoughtfully as he straightened up, and Caris knew he was telling himself not to underestimate Merthin.

"Let me show you around," Merthin said.

The island had changed completely in the last six months. All signs of the old leper colony had gone. Much of the rocky land was now taken up with stores: neat piles of stone, barrels of lime, stacks of timber, and coils of rope. The place was still infested with rabbits—but they were now competing for space with the builders. There was a smithy, where a blacksmith was repairing old tools and forging new ones; several masons' lodges; and Merthin's new house, small but carefully built and beautifully proportioned. Carpenters, stone carvers, and mortar makers were laboring to keep the men on the scaffolding supplied with materials.

"There seem to be more people at work than usual," Caris murmured in Merthin's ear.

He grinned. "I've put as many as possible in highly visible positions," he replied quietly. "I want every visitor to notice how fast we're working to build the new bridge. I want them to believe the fair will be back to normal next year."

At the west end of the island, away from the twin bridges, were storage yards and warehouses on plots of land Merthin had rented to Kingsbridge merchants. Although his rents were lower than what tenants would have to pay within the city walls, Merthin was already earning a good deal more than the token sum he paid every year for the lease.

He was also seeing a lot of Elizabeth Clerk. Caris thought she was a cold bitch, but she was the only other woman in town with the brains to challenge Merthin. She had a small box of books she had inherited from her father, the bishop, and Merthin spent evenings at her house, reading. Whether anything else went on, Caris did not know.

When the tour was over, Edmund took Guillaume back across the water, but Caris stayed behind to talk to Merthin. "Good customer?" he asked as they watched the raft being poled away.

"We've just sold him two sacks of cheap wool for less than we paid." A sack was 364 pounds weight of wool, washed clean and dried. This year, the cheap wool was selling for thirty-six shillings a sack, the good quality for about double that.

"Why?"

"When prices are falling, it's better to have cash than wool."

"But surely you anticipated a poor fair."

"We didn't expect it to be this bad."

"I'm surprised. In the past, your father has always had a supernatural ability to foresee trends."

Caris hesitated. "It's the combination of slack demand and the lack of a bridge." In truth, she was surprised, too. She had watched her father buy fleeces in the same quantity as usual, despite the poor prospects, and had wondered why he did not play safe by reducing his purchases.

"I suppose you'll try to sell your surplus at the Shiring Fair," Merthin said.

"It's what Earl Roland wants everyone to do. The trouble is, we're not regulars there. The locals will cream off the best of the business. It's what happens in Kingsbridge: my father and two or three others strike large deals with the biggest buyers, leaving smaller operators and outsiders to scrabble for the leftovers. I'm sure the Shiring merchants do the same. We might sell a few sacks there, but there's no real chance we can get rid of it all."

"What will you do?"

"That's why I've come to talk to you. We may have to stop work on the bridge."

He stared at her. "No," he said quietly.

"I'm very sorry, but my father doesn't have the money. He's put it all into fleeces that he can't sell."

Merthin looked as if he had been slapped. After a moment he said: "We have to find another way!"

Her heart went out to him, but she could think of nothing hopeful to say. "My father pledged seventy pounds to the bridge. He's paid out half already. The rest, I'm afraid, is in woolsacks at his warehouse."

"He can't be completely penniless."

"Very nearly. And the same applies to several other citizens who promised money for the bridge."

"I could slow down," Merthin said desperately. "Lay off some craftsmen, and run down the stocks of materials."

"Then you wouldn't have a bridge ready by next year's fair, and we'd be in worse trouble."

"Better than giving up altogether."

"Yes, it would be," she said. "But don't do anything yet. When the Fleece Fair is over, we'll think again. I just wanted you to know the situation."

Merthin still looked pale. "I appreciate it."

The raft came back, and Jimmie waited to take her to the shore. As she walked on board, Caris said casually: "And how is Elizabeth Clerk?"

Merthin pretended to be a little surprised by the question. "She's fine, I think," he said.

"You seem to be seeing a lot of her."

"Not especially. We've always been friends."

"Yes, of course," Caris said, though it was not really true. Merthin had completely ignored Elizabeth for most of last year, when he and Caris were spending so much time together. But it would have been undignified to contradict him, so she said no more.

She waved good-bye and Jimmie pushed the raft off. Merthin was trying to give the impression that his relationship with Elizabeth was not a romance. Perhaps that was true. Or perhaps he was embarrassed to admit to Caris that he was in love with someone else. She could not tell. One thing she felt sure of: it was a romance on Elizabeth's side. Caris could tell, just by the way Elizabeth looked at him. Elizabeth might be an ice maiden, but she was hot for Merthin.

The raft bumped against the opposite bank. Caris stepped off and walked up the hill into the center of the city.

Merthin had been deeply shaken by her news. Caris felt like crying when she recalled the shock and dismay on his face. That was how he had looked when she had refused to rekindle their love affair.

She still did not know how she was going to spend her life. She had always assumed that, whatever she did, she would live in a comfortable house paid for by a profitable business. Now even that ground was moving under her feet. She racked her brains for some way out of the mess. Her father was oddly serene, as if he had not yet grasped the scale of his losses; but she knew that something had to be done.

Walking up the main street, she passed Elfric's daughter, Griselda, carrying her six-month-old baby. It was a boy, and she had named him Merthin, a permanent reproach to the original Merthin for not marrying her. Griselda was still maintaining a pretense of injured innocence. Everyone else now accepted that Merthin was not the father, though some townspeople still thought he should have married her anyway, as he had lain with her.

As Caris came to her own house, her father came out. She stared at him in astonishment. He was dressed only in his underwear: a long undershirt, drawers, and hose. "Where are your clothes?" she said.

He looked down at himself and made a disgusted sound. "I'm getting absentminded," he said, and he went back indoors.

He must have taken his coat off to go to the privy, she thought, then forgotten to put it on again. Was that just his age? He was only forty-eight, and besides, it seemed worse than mere forgetfulness. She felt unnerved.

He returned normally dressed, and they crossed the main street together and entered the priory grounds. Edmund said: "Did you tell Merthin about the money?"

"Yes. He was terribly shocked."

"What did he say?"

"That he could spend less by slowing the pace."

"But then we wouldn't have a bridge in time for next year."

"But, as he said, that would be better than abandoning the bridge half-built."

They came to the stall of Perkin Wigleigh, selling laying hens. His flirtatious daughter, Annet, had a tray of eggs held up by a strap around her neck. Behind the counter Caris saw her friend Gwenda, who was now working for Perkin. Eight months pregnant, with heavy breasts and a swollen belly, Gwenda stood with one hand on her hip, stretching in the classic pose of the expectant mother with an aching back.

Caris calculated that she would now be eight months pregnant, if she had not taken Mattie's potion. After the abortion her breasts had leaked milk, and she could not help feeling that this was her body's reproach for what she had done. She suffered pangs of regret but, whenever she thought about it logically, she knew that if she had her time over again she would do the same.

Gwenda caught Caris's eye and smiled. Against all the odds, Gwenda had got what she wanted: Wulfric for her husband. He was there now, strong as a horse and twice as handsome, lifting a stack of wooden crates onto the flatbed of a cart. Caris was thrilled for Gwenda. "How do you feel today?" she said.

"My back's been hurting all morning."

"Not long, now."

"A couple of weeks, I think."

Edmund said: "Who's this, my dear?"

"Don't you remember Gwenda?" said Caris. "She's been a guest at your house at least once a year for the past ten years!"

Edmund smiled. "I didn't recognize you, Gwenda—it must be the pregnancy. You look well, though."

They moved on. Wulfric had not been given his inheritance, Caris knew: Gwenda had failed in that task. Caris was not sure exactly what had gone on last September, when Gwenda had gone to plead with Ralph, but it seemed Ralph had made some kind of promise then reneged. Anyway, Gwenda now hated Ralph with a passion that was almost frightening.

Nearby was a line of stalls at which local cloth merchants were selling brown burel, the loosely woven fabric that was bought by all but the rich for their homemade clothing. They seemed to be doing good business, unlike the wool merchants. Raw wool was a wholesale business—the absence of a few big buyers could ruin the market. But cloth was retail. Everyone needed it, everyone bought it. A bit less, perhaps, when times were hard, but they still needed clothes.

A vague thought formed in the back of Caris's mind. When merchants could not sell their wool, they sometimes had it woven and tried to sell it as cloth. But it was a lot of work, and there was not much profit in brown burel. Everyone bought the cheapest, and sellers had to keep the price down.

She looked at the cloth stalls with new eyes. "I wonder what fetches the most money," she said. The burel was twelve pence per yard. You had to pay half as much again for cloth that had been fulled—thickened by pounding in water—and still more for colors other than the natural dull brown. Peter Dyer's stall featured green, yellow, and pink cloth at two shillings—twenty-four pence—per yard, even though the colors were not very bright.

She turned to her father, to tell him the notion that was forming in her mind; but, before she could speak, something happened to distract her.

Being at the Fleece Fair reminded Ralph unpleasantly of the same event a year ago, and he touched his misshapen nose. How had that occurred? It had started with him harmlessly teasing the peasant girl, Annet, then teaching her oafish paramour a lesson in respect; but somehow it had ended up in humiliation for Ralph.

As he approached Perkin's stall, he consoled himself by reflecting on what had happened since. He had saved Earl Roland's life after the collapse of the bridge; he had pleased the earl by his decisive behavior at the quarry; and he had at last been made a lord, albeit over nothing more than the little village of Wigleigh. He had killed a man, Ben Wheeler—a carter, so there was no honor in it, but all the same he had proved to himself that he could do it.

He had even made up his quarrel with his brother. Their mother had forced the issue, inviting them both to dinner on Christmas day, insisting that they shake hands. It was a misfortune, their father had said, that they served masters who were rivals, but each had a duty to do his best, like soldiers who found themselves on opposing sides in a civil war. Ralph was pleased, and he thought Merthin felt the same.

He had been able to take a satisfying revenge on Wulfric, by denying him his inheritance and, at the same time, his girl. The eye-catching Annet was now married to Billy Howard, and Wulfric had to content himself with the ugly, though passionate, Gwenda.

It was a pity Wulfric did not look more crushed. He seemed to walk tall and proud around the village, as if he, not Ralph, owned the place. All his neighbors liked him, and his pregnant wife worshipped him. Despite the defeats Ralph had inflicted, Wulfric somehow emerged as the hero. Perhaps it was because his wife was so lusty.

Ralph would have liked to tell Wulfric about Gwenda's visit to him at the Bell. "I lay with your wife," he wanted to say. "And she liked it." That would wipe the proud look off Wulfric's face. But then Wulfric would also know that Ralph had made a promise and, shamefully, broken it—which would just make Wulfric feel superior all over again. Ralph shuddered when he thought of the contempt Wulfric and others would feel for him if they ever found out about that betrayal. His brother, Merthin, in particular, would despise him for it. No, his tumble with Gwenda would have to remain a secret.

They were all at the stall. Perkin was the first to see Ralph approaching, and greeted his lord as obsequiously as ever. "Good day, Lord Ralph," he said, bowing; and his wife, Peggy, curtseyed behind him. Gwenda was there, rubbing her back as if it hurt. Then Ralph saw Annet with her tray of eggs, and he remembered touching her small breast, round and firm like the eggs on the tray. She saw him looking, and dropped her eyes demurely. He wanted to touch her breast again. Why not? he thought—I'm her lord. Then he saw Wulfric, at the back of the stall. The boy had been loading crates onto a cart, but now he stood still, looking at Ralph. His face was carefully expressionless, but his gaze was level and steady. His look could not be called insolent, but for Ralph there was no mistaking the threat. It could not have been clearer if Ralph had said, *Touch her and I'll kill you.*

Perhaps I should do it, Ralph thought. Let him attack me. I'll run him through with my sword. I will be completely in the right, a lord defending himself against a peasant maddened with hatred. Holding Wulfric's gaze, he lifted his hand to fondle Annet's breast—and then Gwenda let out a sharp cry of pain and distress, and all eyes turned to her.

31

Caris heard a cry of pain, and recognized the voice of Gwenda. She felt a throb of fear. Something was wrong. In a few hurried steps she was at Perkin's stall.

Gwenda was sitting on a stool, looking pale, her face twisted in a grimace of pain, her hand on her hip again. Her dress was wet.

Perkin's wife, Peg, said briskly: "Her waters have broken. Her labor is beginning."

"It's early," Caris said anxiously.

"The baby is coming anyway."

"This is dangerous." Caris made a decision. "Let's take her to the hospital." Women did not normally go to the hospital to give birth, but they would admit Gwenda if Caris insisted. An early baby could be vulnerable; everyone knew that.

Wulfric appeared. Caris was struck by how young he looked. He was seventeen and about to become a father.

Gwenda said: "I feel a bit wobbly. I'll be all right in a minute."

"I'll carry you," Wulfric said, and he picked her up effortlessly.

"Follow me," said Caris. She walked ahead of him through the stalls, calling: "Stand aside, please—stand aside!" In a minute they were at the hospital.

The door was wide open. Overnight visitors had been tipped out hours ago, and their straw mattresses were now piled high against one wall. Several employees and novices were energetically washing the floor with mops and buckets. Caris addressed the nearest cleaner, a middle-aged woman with bare feet. "Fetch Old Julie, quickly—tell her Caris sent you."

Caris found a reasonably clean mattress and spread it on the floor near the altar. She was not sure how effective altars were at helping sick people, but she followed the convention. Wulfric put Gwenda down on the bed as carefully as if she had been made of glass. She lay with her knees up and her legs parted.

A few moments later Old Julie arrived, and Caris thought how often in her life she had been comforted by this nun, who was probably not much past forty but seemed ancient. "This is Gwenda Wigleigh," said Caris. "She may be fine, but the baby is coming several weeks early, and I thought it a sensible precaution to bring her here. We were just outside, anyway."

"Very wise," said Julie, gently pushing Caris aside to kneel by the bed. "How do you feel, my dear?" she said to Gwenda.

While Julie talked to Gwenda in a low voice, Caris looked at Wulfric. His handsome young face was contorted with anxiety. Caris knew that he had never intended to marry Gwenda—he had always wanted Annet. However, he now seemed as concerned for her as if he had loved her for years.

Gwenda cried out in pain. "There, there," said Julie. She knelt between

Gwenda's feet and looked up her dress. "Baby's coming quite soon," she said.

Another nun appeared, and Caris recognized Mair, the novice with the angel face. She said: "Shall I get Mother Cecilia?"

"No need to bother her," said Julie. "Just go to the storeroom and fetch me the wooden box with 'Birth' written on the top."

Mair hurried away.

Gwenda said: "Oh, God, it hurts."

"Keep pushing," said Julie.

Wulfric said: "What's wrong, for God's sake?"

"Nothing's wrong," said Julie. "This is normal. This is how women give birth. You must be the youngest of your family, otherwise you would have seen your mother like this."

Caris, too, was the young sibling in her family. She knew that childbirth was painful, but she had never actually watched it, and she was shocked by how bad it was.

Mair returned and placed a wooden box on the floor next to Julie.

Gwenda stopped groaning. Her eyes closed, and she looked almost as if she might have been asleep. Then, a few minutes later, she cried out again.

Julie said to Wulfric: "Sit beside her and hold her hand." He obeyed immediately.

Julie was still looking up Gwenda's dress. "Stop pushing now," she said after a while. "Take lots of short breaths." She panted to show Gwenda what she meant. Gwenda complied, and it seemed to ease her distress for a few minutes. Then she cried out again.

Caris could hardly stand it. If this was normal, what was childbirth like when there were difficulties? She lost her sense of time: everything was happening very quickly, but Gwenda's torment seemed endless. Caris had the powerless feeling that she hated so much, the feeling that had overwhelmed her when her mother died. She wanted to help, but she did not know what to do, and it made her so anxious that she bit her lip until she tasted blood.

Julie said: "Here comes baby." She reached between Gwenda's legs. The dress fell away, and suddenly Caris could clearly see the baby's head, facedown, covered in wet hair, emerging from an opening that seemed impossibly stretched. "God help us, no wonder it hurts!" she said in horror.

Julie supported the head with her left hand. The baby slowly turned sideways, then its tiny shoulders came out. Its skin was slippery with blood and some other fluid. "Just relax now," Julie said. "It's nearly over. Baby looks beautiful."

Beautiful? Caris thought. To her it looked horrible.

The baby's torso came out with a fat, pulsing blue cord attached to its navel. Then its legs and feet came all in a rush. Julie picked up the baby in both hands. It was tiny, its head not much bigger than the palm of Julie's hand.

Something seemed wrong. Caris realized the baby was not breathing.

Julie brought the baby's face close to her own and blew into its miniature nostrils.

The baby suddenly opened its mouth, gasped air, and cried.

"Praise God," said Julie.

She wiped the baby's face with the sleeve of her robe, tenderly cleaning around the ears, eyes, nose, and mouth. Then she pressed the newborn to her bosom, closing her eyes; and in that instant Caris saw a lifetime of self-denial. The moment passed, and Julie laid the baby on Gwenda's chest.

Gwenda looked down. "Is it a boy or a girl?"

Caris realized that none of them had looked. Julie leaned over and parted the baby's knees. "A boy," she said.

The blue cord stopped pulsing and shriveled, turning white. Julie took from the box two short lengths of string and tied off the umbilical cord. Then she took out a small, sharp knife and cut the cord between the two knots.

Mair took the knife from her and handed her a tiny blanket from the box. Julie took the baby from Gwenda, wrapped him in the blanket, and gave him back. Mair found some pillows and propped Gwenda up. Gwenda pushed down the neck of her shift and took out a swollen breast. She gave the baby the nipple, and he began to suck. After a minute, he seemed to sleep.

The other end of the cord was still hanging out of Gwenda. A few minutes later it moved, and a shapeless red mass slipped out: the afterbirth. Blood soaked the mattress. Julie lifted the mass, handed it to Mair and said: "Burn this."

Julie scrutinized Gwenda's pelvic area and frowned. Caris followed her gaze, and saw that the blood was still flowing. Julie wiped the stains away from Gwenda's body, but the red streaks reappeared immediately.

When Mair came back, Julie said: "Fetch Mother Cecilia, please, right away."

Wulfric said: "Is something wrong?"

"The bleeding should have stopped by now," Julie answered.

Suddenly there was tension in the air. Wulfric looked frightened. The baby cried, and Gwenda gave him the nipple again. He suckled briefly and slept again. Julie kept looking at the doorway.

At last Cecilia appeared. She looked at Gwenda and said: "Has the afterbirth come out?"

"A few minutes ago."

"Did you put the baby to the breast?"

"As soon as we had cut the cord."

"I'll get a physician." Cecilia walked quickly away.

She was gone some minutes. When she returned, she was carrying a small glass vessel containing a yellowish fluid. "Prior Godwyn has prescribed this," she said.

Caris was indignant. "Doesn't he want to examine Gwenda?"

"Certainly not," Cecilia said crisply. "He's a priest as well as a monk. Such men don't look upon women's private parts."

"Podex," Caris said contemptuously. It was the Latin for asshole.

Cecilia pretended not to hear. She knelt beside Gwenda. "Drink this, my dear."

Gwenda drank the potion, but she continued to bleed. She was pale, and looked weaker than she had immediately after the birth. The baby slept contentedly on her breast, but everyone else was scared. Wulfric kept standing up and sitting down again. Julie wiped the blood off Gwenda's thighs and looked as if she might cry. Gwenda asked for something to drink, and Mair brought a cup of ale.

Caris took Julie aside and said in a whisper: "She's bleeding to death!"

"We've done what we can," Julie said.

"Have you seen cases like this before?"

"Yes, three."

"How did they end?"

"The women died."

Caris gave a low groan of despair. "There must be something we can do!"

"She's in God's hands now. You could pray."

"That's not what I meant by doing something."

"You be careful what you say."

Caris immediately felt guilty. She did not want to quarrel with someone as kindly as Julie. "I'm sorry, sister. I didn't mean to deny the power of prayer."

"I should hope not."

"But I'm not yet ready to leave Gwenda in the hands of God."

"What else is there to do?"

"You'll see." Caris hurried out of the hospital.

She pushed impatiently through the customers strolling around the fair. It seemed amazing to her that people could still be buying and selling when a drama of life and death was going on a few yards away. But there had been many occasions when she had heard that a mother-to-be had gone into labor, and she had never stopped what she was doing, just wished the woman well and carried on.

She emerged from the priory grounds and ran through the streets of the town to Mattie Wise's house. She knocked on the door and opened it. To her relief, Mattie was at home.

"Gwenda's just had her baby," she said.

"What's gone wrong?" Mattie said immediately.

"The baby's all right, but Gwenda's still bleeding."

"Has the afterbirth come out?"

"Yes."

"The bleeding should have stopped."

"Can you help her?"

"Perhaps. I'll try."

"Hurry, please!"

Mattie took a pot off the fire and put on her shoes, then the two of them left, Mattie locking her door behind her.

Caris said vehemently: "I'm never going to have a baby, I swear."

They rushed to the priory and went into the hospital. Caris noticed the strong smell of blood.

Mattie was careful to acknowledge Old Julie. "Good afternoon, Sister Juliana."

"Hello, Mattie." Julie looked disapproving. "Do you believe you can help this woman, when the holy prior's remedies have not been blessed with success?"

"If you pray for me and for the patient, Sister, who knows what may happen?"

It was a diplomatic answer, and Julie was mollified.

Mattie knelt beside mother and child. Gwenda was becoming paler. Her eyes were closed. The baby sought blindly for the nipple, but Gwenda seemed too tired to help him.

Mattie said: "She must keep drinking—but not strong liquor. Please bring her a jug of warm water with a small glass of wine mixed into it. Then ask the kitchener if he has a clear soup, warm but not hot."

Mair looked questioningly at Julie, who hesitated, then said: "Go—but don't tell anyone that you're doing Mattie's bidding." The novice hurried off.

Mattie pushed Gwenda's dress up as high as it would go, exposing all of her abdomen. The skin that had been stretched so taut a few hours ago was now flabby and folded. Mattie grasped the loose flesh, digging her fingers gently but firmly into Gwenda's belly. Gwenda grunted, but it was a sound of discomfort rather than pain.

Mattie said: "The womb is soft. It has failed to contract. That's why she's bleeding."

Wulfric, who seemed close to tears, said: "Can you do anything for her?"

"I don't know." Mattie began to massage, her fingers apparently pressing Gwenda's womb through the skin and flesh of her belly. "Sometimes this provokes the womb to shrink," she said.

Everyone watched in silence. Caris was almost afraid to breathe.

Mair came back with the water-and-wine mixture. "Give her some, please," Mattie said without pausing in her massage. Mair held a cup to Gwenda's lips and she drank thirstily. "Not too much," Mattie warned. Mair took the cup away.

Mattie continued to massage, glancing from time to time at Gwenda's pelvis. Julie's lips moved in silent prayer. The blood flowed without letup.

Looking worried, Mattie changed her position. She put her left hand on Gwenda's belly just below the navel, then her right hand over the left. She pressed down, slowly putting on more pressure. Caris was afraid it must hurt the patient, but Gwenda seemed only half-conscious. Mattie leaned farther over Gwenda until she seemed to be putting all her weight onto her hands.

Julie said: "She's stopped bleeding!"

Mattie did not change her position. "Can anyone here count to five hundred?"

"Yes," Caris said.

"Slowly, please."

Caris began to count aloud. Julie wiped the blood off Gwenda again, and this time the streaks did not reappear. She began to pray aloud. "Holy Mary, Mother of the Lord Jesus Christ . . ."

Everyone was still, like a group of statuary: the mother and baby on the bed, the wise woman pressing down on the mother's belly; the husband, the praying nun, and Caris counting: "A hundred and eleven, a hundred and twelve . . ."

As well as her own voice and Julie's, Caris could hear the sound of the fair outside, the roar of hundreds of people all speaking at once. The strain of pressing down began to show on Mattie's face, but she did not move. Wulfric was crying silently, tears streaming down his sunburned cheeks.

When Caris reached five hundred, Mattie slowly eased her weight off Gwenda's abdomen. Everyone looked at her vagina, dreading the gush of blood.

It did not come.

Mattie breathed a long sigh of relief. Wulfric smiled. Julie said: "Praise God!"

Mattie said: "Give her another drink, please."

Once again, Mair put a full cup to Gwenda's lips. Gwenda opened her eyes and drank it all.

"You're going to be all right now," Mattie said.

Gwenda whispered: "Thank you." Then she closed her eyes.

Mattie looked at Mair. "Perhaps you should go and see about that soup," she said. "The woman must rebuild her strength, otherwise her milk will dry up."

Mair nodded and left.

The baby cried. Gwenda seemed to revive. She moved the baby to her other breast and helped him find the nipple. Then she looked up at Wulfric and smiled.

Julie said: "What a beautiful little boy."

Caris looked at the baby again. For the first time, she saw him as an individual. What would he be like—strong and true like Wulfric, or weak and dishonest like his grandfather Joby? He did not resemble either, she thought. "Who does he look like?" she said.

Julie said: "He has his mother's coloring."

That was right, Caris thought. The baby had dark hair and beige skin, where Wulfric had fair skin and a mane of dark blond hair. The baby's face reminded her of someone, and after a moment she realized it was Merthin. A foolish thought crossed her mind, and she dismissed it immediately. All the same, the resemblance was there. "You know who he reminds me of?" she said.

Suddenly she caught a look from Gwenda. Her eyes widened, an expression of panic crossed her face, and she gave a barely perceptible shake of her head. It was gone in an instant, but the message was unmistakable: *Shut up!* Caris clamped her teeth together.

"Who?" said Julie innocently.

Caris hesitated, desperately thinking of something to say. At last she was inspired. "Philemon, Gwenda's brother," she said.

"Of course," said Julie. "Someone should tell him to come and see his new nephew."

Caris was bewildered. So the baby was not Wulfric's? Then whose? It could not be Merthin's. He might have lain with Gwenda—he was certainly vulnerable to temptation—but he could never have kept it secret from Caris afterward. If not Merthin . . .

Caris was struck by a dreadful thought. What *had* gone on that day when Gwenda went to plead with Ralph for Wulfric's inheritance? Could the baby be *Ralph*'s? It was too grim to contemplate.

She looked at Gwenda, then at the baby, then at Wulfric. Wulfric was smiling with joy, though his face was still wet with tears. He had no suspicions.

Julie said: "Have you thought about the baby's name?"

"Oh, yes," said Wulfric. "I want to name him Samuel."

Gwenda nodded, looking down at the baby's face. "Samuel," she said. "Sammy. Sam."

"After my father," Wulfric said happily.

32

One year after the death of Anthony, Kingsbridge Priory was a different place, Godwyn thought, with satisfaction, as he stood in the cathedral on the Sunday after the Fleece Fair.

The main difference was the separation of monks and nuns. They no longer mingled in the cloisters, the library, or the scriptorium. Even here in the church, a new carved oak screen running down the center of the choir prevented them from looking at one another during the services. Only in the hospital were they sometimes forced to mix.

In his sermon, Prior Godwyn said the collapse of the bridge a year ago had been God's punishment for laxity in the monks and nuns, and for sin among the townspeople. The new spirit of rigor and purity at the priory, and piety and submission in the town, would lead to a better life for all, in this world and the hereafter. He felt it went down quite well.

Afterward he had dinner with Brother Simeon, the treasurer, in the prior's house. Philemon served them stewed eel and cider. "I want to build a new prior's house," Godwyn said.

Simeon's long, thin face seemed to get longer. "Any particular reason?"

"I'm sure I am the only prior in Christendom who lives in a house like a leather tanner's. Think of the people who have been guests here in the last twelve months—the earl of Shiring, the bishop of Kingsbridge, the earl of Monmouth—this building isn't appropriate for such folk. It gives a poor impression of us and of our order. We need a magnificent building to reflect the prestige of Kingsbridge Priory."

"You want a palace," said Simeon.

Godwyn detected a disapproving note in Simeon's tone of voice, as if Godwyn's aim were to glorify himself rather than the priory. "Call it a palace, if you wish," he said stiffly. "Why not? Bishops and priors live in palaces. It's not for their own comfort, but for that of their guests, and for the reputation of the institution they represent."

"Of course," said Simeon, giving up that line of argument. "But you can't afford it."

Godwyn frowned. In theory, his senior monks were encouraged to debate with him, but the truth was that he hated to be opposed. "That's ridiculous," he said. "Kingsbridge is one of the richest monasteries in the land."

"So it is always said. And we do own vast resources. But the price of wool has fallen this year, for the fifth year in succession. Our income is shrinking."

Philemon suddenly interjected: "They say the Italian merchants are buying fleeces in Spain."

Philemon was changing. Since achieving his ambition and becoming a novice monk, he had lost the awkward-boy look and had grown in confidence to the point where he could join in a conversation between prior and treasurer—and make an interesting contribution.

"Could be," said Simeon. "Also, the Fleece Fair was smaller, because there's no bridge, so we earned a lot less in duty and tolls than we usually do."

Godwyn said: "But we hold thousands of acres of farmland."

"In this part of the country, where most of our lands are, there was a poor harvest last year, after all that rain. Many of our serfs struggled to stay alive. It's hard to force them to pay their rents when they're hungry—"

"They must pay, all the same," Godwyn said. "Monks get hungry, too."

Philemon spoke again. "If the bailiff of a village says that a serf has defaulted on his rent, or that part of the land is untenanted therefore no rent is due, you haven't really got any way of checking that he's telling the truth. Bailiffs can be bribed by serfs."

Godwyn felt frustrated. He had had numerous conversations like this in the past year. He had been determined to tighten up control of the priory's finances, but every time he tried to change things he ran into barriers. "Have you got a suggestion?" he said irritably to Philemon.

"Send an inspector on a tour of the villages. Let him speak to bailiffs, look at the land, go into the cottages of serfs who are said to be starving."

"If the bailiff can be bribed, so can the inspector."

"Not if he's a monk. What use have we for money?"

Godwyn recalled Philemon's old inclination to stealing. It was true that monks had no use for personal money, at least in theory, but that did not mean they were incorruptible. However, a visit from the prior's inspector would certainly put bailiffs on their toes. "It's a good idea," Godwyn said. "Would you like to be the inspector?"

"I'd be honored."

"Then it's settled." Godwyn turned back to Simeon. "All the same, we still have a huge income."

"And huge costs," Simeon replied. "We pay a subvention to our bishop. We feed, clothe, and house twenty-five monks, seven novices, and nineteen pensioners of the priory. We employ thirty people as cleaners, cooks, stable boys, and so on. We spend a *fortune* on candles. Monks' robes—"

"All right, I've grasped your point," Godwyn said impatiently. "But I still want to build a palace."

"Where will you go for the money, then?"

Godwyn sighed. "Where we always go, in the end. I'll ask Mother Cecilia."

He saw her a few minutes later. Normally he would have asked her to come to him, as a sign of the superiority of the male within the church; but on this occasion he thought it best to flatter her.

The prioress's house was an exact copy of the prior's, but it had a different feel. There were cushions and rugs, flowers in a bowl on the table, embroidered samplers on the wall illustrating Bible stories and texts, and a cat asleep in front of the fireplace. Cecilia was finishing a dinner of roast lamb and dark red wine. She put on a veil when Godwyn arrived, in accordance with a rule Godwyn had introduced, for occasions when monks had to talk to nuns.

He found Cecilia difficult to read, veiled or not. She had formally welcomed his election as prior, and had gone along unprotestingly with his stricter rules about separation of monks and nuns, making only the occasional practical point about the efficient running of the hospital. She had never opposed him, and yet he felt she was not really on his side. It seemed he was no longer able to charm her. When he was younger, he had been able to make her laugh like a girl. Now she was no longer susceptible—or perhaps he had lost the knack.

Small talk was difficult with a woman in a veil, so he plunged straight into his topic. "I think we should build two new houses for entertaining noble and high-ranking guests," he said. "One for men, one for women. They would be called the prior's house and the prioress's house, but their main purpose would be to accommodate visitors in the style to which they're accustomed."

"That's an interesting idea," Cecilia said. As ever, she was compliant without being enthusiastic.

"We should have impressive stone buildings," Godwyn went on. "After all, you have been prioress here for more than a decade—you are one of the most senior nuns in the kingdom."

"We want the guests to be impressed, not by our wealth, but by the holiness of the priory and the piety of the monks and nuns, of course," she said.

"Indeed—but the buildings should symbolize that, as the cathedral symbolizes the majesty of God."

"Where do you think the new buildings should be sited?"

This was good, Godwyn thought—she was already getting down to details. "Close to where the old houses are now."

"So, yours near the east end of the church, next to the chapter house, and mine down here by the fishpond."

It crossed Godwyn's mind that she might be mocking him. He could not see her expression. Imposing a veil on women had its disadvantages, he reflected. "You might prefer a new location," he said.

"Yes, I might."

There was a short silence. Godwyn was finding it hard to broach the subject of money. He was going to have to change the rule about veils—make an exception for the prioress, perhaps. It was just too difficult to negotiate like this.

He was forced to plunge again. "Unfortunately, I would not be able to make any contribution to the building costs. The monastery is very poor."

"To the cost of the prioress's house, you mean?" she said. "I wouldn't expect it."

"No, actually, I meant the cost of the prior's house."

"Oh. So you want the nunnery to pay for your new house as well as mine."

"I'm afraid I would have to ask you that, yes. I hope you don't mind."

"Well, if it's for the prestige of Kingsbridge Priory . . ."

"I knew you would see it that way."

"Let me see . . . Right now I'm building new cloisters for the nuns, as we no longer share with the monks."

Godwyn made no comment. He was irritated that Cecilia had employed Merthin to design the cloisters, rather than the cheaper Elfric, which was a wasteful extravagance; but this was not the moment to say so.

Cecilia went on: "And when that's done, I need to build a nuns' library and buy some books for it, as we can't use your library anymore."

Godwyn tapped his foot impatiently. This seemed irrelevant.

"And then we need a covered walkway to the church, as we now take a different route to that used by the monks, and we have no protection in bad weather."

"Very reasonable," Godwyn commented, though he wanted to say: *Stop dithering!*

"So," she said with an air of finality, "I think we could consider this proposal in three years' time."

"Three years? I want to start now!"

"Oh, I don't think we can contemplate that."

"Why not?"

"We have a budget for building, you see."

"But isn't this more important?"

"We must stick to our budget."

"Why?"

"So that we remain financially strong and independent," she said, then she added pointedly: "I wouldn't like to go begging."

Godwyn did not know what to say. Worse, he had a ghastly feeling that she was laughing at him behind the veil. He could not stand to be laughed at. He stood up abruptly. "Thank you, Mother Cecilia," he said coldly. "We'll talk about this again."

"Yes," she said, "in three years' time. I look forward to it."

Now he was sure she was laughing. He turned away and left as quickly as he could.

Back in his own house, he threw himself in a chair, fuming. "I hate that woman," he said to Philemon, who was still there.

"She said no?"

"She said she would consider it in three years' time."

"That's worse than a no," said Philemon. "It's a three-year no."

"We're always in her power, because she has money."

"I listen to the talk of the older men," Philemon said, apparently irrelevantly. "It's surprising how much you learn."

"What are you getting at?"

"When the priory first built mills, and dug fishponds, and fenced off rabbit warrens, the priors made a law that townspeople had to use the monks' facilities, and pay for them. They weren't allowed to grind their corn at home, or full cloth by treading it, nor could they have their own ponds and warrens—they had to buy from us. The law ensured that the priory got back its costs."

"But the law fell out of use?"

"It changed. Instead of a prohibition, people were allowed their own facilities if they paid a fine. Then *that* fell out of use, in Prior Anthony's time."

"And now there's a hand mill in every house."

"And all the fishmongers have ponds, there are half a dozen warrens, and dyers full their own cloth by making their wives and children tread it, instead of bringing it to the priory's fulling mill."

Godwyn was excited. "If all those people paid a fine for the privilege of having their own facilities . . ."

"It could be quite a lot of money."

"They would squeal like pigs." Godwyn frowned. "Can we prove what we say?"

"There are plenty of people who remember the fines. But it's bound to be written in the priory records somewhere—probably in *Timothy's Book*."

"You'd better find out exactly how much the fines were. If we're resting on the ground of precedent, we'd better get it right."

"If I may make a suggestion . . ."

"Of course."

"You could announce the new regime from the pulpit of the cathedral on Sunday morning. That would serve to emphasize that it's the will of God."

"Good idea," said Godwyn. "That's exactly what I'll do."

33

"I've got the solution," Caris said to her father.

He sat back in the big wooden seat at the head of the table, a slight smile on his face. She knew that look. It was skeptical, but willing to listen. "Go on," he said.

She was a little nervous. She felt sure her idea would work—saving her father's fortune and Merthin's bridge—but could she convince Edmund? "We take our surplus wool and have it woven into cloth and dyed," she said simply. She held her breath, waiting for his reaction.

"Wool merchants often try that in hard times," he said. "But tell me why you think it would work. What would it cost?"

"For cleaning, spinning, and weaving, four shillings per sack."

"And how much cloth would that make?"

"A sack of poor-quality wool, that you bought for thirty-six shillings, and wove for four more shillings, would make forty-eight yards of cloth."

"Which you would sell for . . . ?"

"Undyed, brown burel sells for a shilling a yard, so forty-eight shillings—eight more than we would have paid out."

"It's not much, considering the work we would have put in."

"But that's not the best of it."

"Keep going."

"Weavers sell their brown burel because they're in a hurry to get the money. But if you spend another twenty shillings fulling the cloth, to thicken it, then dyeing and finishing it, you can get double the price—two shillings a yard, ninety-six shillings for the whole lot—thirty-six shillings more than you paid!"

Edmund looked dubious. "If it's so easy, why don't more people do it?"

"Because they don't have the money to lay out."

"Nor do I!"

"You've got three pounds from Guillaume of London."

"Am I to have nothing with which to buy wool next year?"

"At these prices, you're better off out of the business."

He laughed. "By the saints, you're right. Very well, try it out with some cheap stuff. I've got five sacks of coarse Devon wool that the Italians never want. I'll give you a sack of that, and see if you can do what you say."

Two weeks later, Caris found Mark Webber smashing up his hand mill.

She was shocked to see a poor man destroying a valuable piece of equipment—so much so that, for a moment, she forgot her own troubles.

The hand mill consisted of two stone disks, each slightly roughened on one face. The smaller sat on the larger, fitting perfectly into a shallow indentation, rough side to rough. A protruding wooden handle enabled the upper stone to be turned while the lower remained still. Ears of grain placed between the two stones would be rapidly ground to flour.

Most Kingsbridge people of the lower class had a hand mill. The very poor could not afford one, and the affluent did not need one—they could buy flour already ground by a miller. But for families such as the Webbers, who needed every penny they earned to feed their children, a hand mill was a money-saving godsend.

Mark had laid his on the ground in front of his small house. He had borrowed from somewhere a long-handled sledgehammer with an iron head. Two of his children were watching, a thin girl in a ragged dress and a naked toddler. He lifted the hammer over his head and swung it in a long arc. It was a sight to see: he was the biggest man in Kingsbridge, with shoulders like a carthorse. The stone crazed like an eggshell and fell into pieces.

Caris said: "What on earth are you doing?"

"We must grind corn at the prior's watermills, and forfeit one sack in twenty-four as a fee," Mark replied.

He seemed phlegmatic about it, but she was horrified. "I thought the new rules applied only to unlicensed windmills and watermills."

"Tomorrow I have to go around with John Constable, searching people's homes, breaking up illicit hand mills. I can't have them saying I've got one of my own. That's why I'm doing this in the street, where everyone can see."

"I didn't realize Godwyn intended to take the bread out of the mouths of the poor," Caris said grimly.

"Luckily for us, we've got some weaving to do—thanks to you."

Caris turned her mind to her own business. "How are you getting on?"

"Finished."

"That was quick!"

"It takes longer in winter. But in summer, with sixteen hours of daylight, I can weave six yards in a day, with Madge helping."

"Wonderful!"

"Come inside and I'll show you."

His wife, Madge, was standing over the cooking fire at the back of the one-room house, with a baby on one arm and a shy boy at her side. Madge was shorter than her husband by more than a foot, but her build was chunky. She had a large bust and a jutting behind, and she made Caris think of a plump pigeon. Her protruding jaw gave her an aggressive air that was not entirely misleading. Although combative, she was good-hearted, and Caris liked her. She offered her visitor a cup of cider, which Caris refused, knowing the family could not afford it.

Mark's loom was a wooden frame, more than a yard square, on a stand. It took up most of the living space. Behind it, close to the back door, was a table with two benches. Obviously they all slept on the floor around the loom.

"I make narrow dozens," Mark explained. "A narrow dozen is a cloth a yard wide and twelve yards long. I can't make broadcloth, because I haven't room for such a wide loom." Four rolls of brown burel were stacked against the wall. "One sack of wool makes four narrow dozens," he said.

Caris had brought him the raw fleeces in a standard woolsack. Madge had arranged for the wool to be cleaned, sorted, and spun into yarn. The spinning was done by the poor women of the town, and the cleaning and sorting by their children.

Caris felt the cloth. She was excited: she had completed the first stage of her plan. "Why is it so loosely woven?" she asked.

Mark bristled. "Loose? My burel is the tightest weave in Kingsbridge!"

"I know—I didn't mean to sound critical. But Italian cloth feels so different—yet they make it from our wool."

"Partly it depends on the weaver's strength, and how hard he can press down the batten to pack the wool."

"I don't think the Italian weavers are all stronger than you."

"Then it's their machines. The better the loom, the closer the weave."

"I was afraid of that." The implication was that Caris could not compete with high-quality Italian wool unless she bought Italian looms, which seemed impossible.

One problem at a time, she told herself. She paid Mark, counting out four shillings, of which he would have to give about half to the women who had done the spinning. Caris had made eight shillings profit, theoretically. Eight shillings would not pay for much work on the bridge. And at this rate it would take years to weave all her father's surplus wool. "Is there any way we can produce cloth faster?" she said to Mark.

Madge answered. "There are other weavers in Kingsbridge, but most of them are committed to work for existing cloth merchants. I can find you more outside the town, though. The larger villages often have a weaver with a loom. He usually makes cloth for the villagers from their own yarn. Such men can easily switch to another job, if the money's good."

Caris concealed her anxiety. "All right," she said. "I'll let you know. Meanwhile, will you deliver these cloths to Peter Dyer for me?"

"Of course. I'll take them now."

Caris went home for dinner, deep in thought. To make any real difference, she would have to spend most of what money her father had left. If things went wrong, they would be even worse off. But what was the alternative? Her plan was risky, but no one else had any kind of plan at all.

When she arrived home, Petranilla was serving a mutton stew. Edmund sat at the head of the table. The financial setback of the Fleece Fair seemed to have affected him more severely than Caris would have expected. His normal exuberance was subdued, and he often appeared thoughtful, not to say distracted. Caris was worried about him.

"I saw Mark Webber smashing up his hand mill," she said as she sat down. "Where's the sense in that?"

Petranilla put her nose in the air. "Godwyn is entirely within his rights," she said.

"Those rights are out of date—they haven't been enforced for years. Where else does a priory do such things?"

"In St. Albans," Petranilla said triumphantly.

Edmund said: "I've heard of St. Albans. The townspeople periodically riot against the monastery."

"Kingsbridge Priory is entitled to recoup the money it spent building mills," Petranilla argued. "Just as you, Edmund, want to get back the money you're putting into the bridge. How would you feel if someone built a second bridge?"

Edmund did not answer her, so Caris did. "It would depend entirely on how soon it happened," she said. "The priory's mills were built hundreds of years ago, as were the warrens and fishponds. No one has the right to hold back the development of the town forever."

"The prior has a right to collect his dues," she said stubbornly.

"Well, if he carries on like this, there will be no one to collect dues from. People will go and live in Shiring. They're allowed hand mills there."

"Don't you understand that the needs of the priory are sacred?" Petranilla said angrily. "The monks serve God! By comparison with that, the lives of the townspeople are insignificant."

"Is that what your son Godwyn believes?"

"Of course."

"I was afraid of that."

"Don't you believe the prior's work is sacred?"

Caris had no answer to that, so she just shrugged, and Petranilla looked triumphant.

The dinner was good, but Caris was too tense to eat much. As soon as the others had finished, she said: "I have to go and see Peter Dyer."

Petranilla protested: "Are you going to spend more? You've already given Mark Webber four shillings of your father's money."

"Yes—and the cloth is worth twelve shillings more than the wool was, so I've made eight shillings."

"No, you haven't," Petranilla said. "You haven't sold the cloth yet."

Petranilla was expressing doubts that Caris shared, in her more pessimistic moments, but she was stung into denial. "I will sell it, though—especially if it's dyed red."

"And what will Peter charge for dyeing and fulling four narrow dozens?"

"Twenty shillings—but the red cloth will be worth double the brown burel, so we'll make another twenty-eight shillings."

"If you sell it. And if you don't?"

"I'll sell it."

Her father intervened. "Let her be," he said to Petranilla. "I've told her she can give this a try."

Shiring Castle stood on top of a hill. It was the home of the county sheriff. At the foot of the hill stood the gallows. Whenever there was a hanging, the prisoner was brought down from the castle on a cart, to be hanged in front of the church.

The square in which the gallows stood was also the marketplace. The Shiring Fair was held here, between the guildhall and a large timber building called the Wool Exchange. The bishop's palace and numerous taverns also stood around the square.

This year, because of the troubles at Kingsbridge, there were more stalls than ever, and the fair spilled into the streets off the marketplace. Edmund had brought forty sacks of wool on ten carts, and could get more brought from Kingsbridge before the end of the week, if necessary.

To Caris's dismay, it was not necessary. He sold ten sacks on the first day, then nothing until the end of the fair, when he sold another ten by reducing the price below what he had paid. She could not remember seeing him so down.

She put her four lengths of dull brownish red cloth on his stall, and over the week, yard by yard, she sold three of the four. "Look at it this way," she said to her father on the last day of the fair. "Before, you had a sack of unsaleable wool and four shillings. Now you've got thirty-six shillings and a length of cloth."

But her cheerfulness was only for his benefit. She was deeply depressed. She had boasted bravely that she could sell cloth. The result was not a complete failure, but it was no triumph. If she could not sell the cloth for more than it cost, then she did not have the solution to the problem. What was she going to do? She left the stall and went to survey other cloth sellers.

The best cloth came from Italy, as always. Caris stopped at the stall of Loro Fiorentino. Cloth merchants such as Loro were not wool buyers, though they often worked closely with buyers. Caris knew that Loro gave his English takings to Buonaventura, who used it to pay English merchants for their raw wool. Then, when the wool reached Florence, Buonaventura's family would sell it, and with the proceeds pay back Loro's family. That way, they all avoided the hazards of transporting barrels of gold and silver coins across Europe.

Loro had on his stall only two rolls of cloth, but the colors were much brighter than anything the local people could produce. "Is this all you brought?" Caris asked him.

"Of course not. I've sold the rest."

She was surprised. "Everyone else is having a bad fair."

He shrugged. "The finest cloth always sells."

An idea was taking shape in Caris's head. "How much is the scarlet?"

"Only seven shillings per yard, mistress."

That was seven times the price of burel. "But who can afford it?"

"The bishop took a lot of my red, Lady Philippa some blue and green, a few daughters of the brewers and bakers in town, some lords and ladies from the villages round about . . . Even when times are hard, someone is prospering. This vermilion will be so beautiful on you." With a swift motion, he unrolled the bale and draped a length over Caris's shoulder. "Marvelous. See how everyone is looking at you already."

She smiled. "I can see why you sell so much." She handled the cloth. It was closely woven. She already had a cloak of Italian scarlet that she had inherited from her mother. It was her favorite garment. "What dye do they use to get this red?"

"Madder, the same as everyone."

"But how do they make it so bright?"

"It's no secret. They use alum. It brightens the color and also fixes it, so it won't fade. A cloak in this color, for you, would be wonderful, a joy forever."

"Alum," she repeated. "Why don't English dyers use it?"

"It's very expensive. It comes from Turkey. Such luxury is only for special women."

"And the blue?"

"Like your eyes."

Her eyes were green, but she did not correct him. "It's such a deep color."

"English dyers use woad, but we get indigo from Bengal. Moorish traders bring it from India to Egypt, and then our Italian merchants buy it in Alexandria." He smiled. "Think how far it has traveled—to complement your outstanding beauty."

"Yes," said Caris. "Just think of that."

The riverside workshop of Peter Dyer was a house as big as Edmund's, but built of stone, and with no interior walls or floors—just a shell. Two iron cauldrons stood over great fires. Beside each was a hoist, like the ones Merthin made for building work. These were used to lift huge sacks of wool or cloth and lower them into the vats. The floors were permanently wet and the air was thick with steam. The apprentices worked barefoot, in their underdrawers because of the heat, their faces running with sweat, their hair gleaming with damp. There was an acrid smell that bit at the back of Caris's throat.

She showed Peter her unsold length of cloth. "I want the bright scarlet that the Italian cloths have," she said. "That's what sells best."

Peter was a lugubrious man who always looked injured, no matter what you said to him. Now he nodded glumly, as if acknowledging a justified criticism. "We'll dye it again with madder."

"And with alum, to fix the color and make it brighter."

"We don't use alum. Never have. I don't know anyone who does."

Caris cursed inwardly. She had not thought to check this. She had assumed a dyer would know everything about dyes. "Can't you try it?"

"I haven't got any."

Caris sighed. Peter seemed to be one of those craftsmen for whom everything is impossible unless they have done it before. "Suppose I could get you some?"

"Where from?"

"Winchester, I suppose, or London. Or perhaps from Melcombe." That was the nearest big port. Ships came from all over Europe to Melcombe.

"If I had some, I wouldn't know how to use it."

"Can't you find out?"

"Who from?"

"I'll try to find out, then."

He shook his head pessimistically. "I don't know . . ."

She did not want to quarrel with him: he was the only large-scale dyer in town. "We'll cross that bridge when we come to it," she said in a conciliatory tone. "I won't take up any more of your time discussing it now. First I'll see if I can get some alum."

She left him. Who in town might know about alum? She wished now that she had asked Loro Fiorentino more questions. The monks ought to know about things like this, but they were no longer allowed to talk to women. She decided to see Mattie Wise. Mattie was forever mixing strange ingredients—maybe alum was one of them. More importantly, if she did not know she would admit her ignorance, unlike a monk or an apothecary who might make something up for fear of being thought foolish.

Mattie's first words were: "How is your father?"

"He seems a bit shaken by the failure of the Fleece Fair," Caris said. It was typical of Mattie to know what she was worried about. "He's becoming forgetful. He seems older."

"Take care of him," said Mattie. "He's a good man."

"I know." Caris was not sure what Mattie was getting at.

"Petranilla is a self-centered cow."

"I know that, too."

Mattie was grinding something with a mortar and pestle. She pushed the bowl toward Caris. "If you do this for me, I'll pour you a cup of wine."

"Thank you." Caris began to grind.

Mattie poured yellow wine from a stone jug into two wooden cups. "Why are you here? You're not ill."

"Do you know what alum is?"

"Yes. In small quantities, we use it as an astringent, to close wounds. It can also stop diarrhea. But in large quantities it's poisonous. Like most poisons, it makes you vomit. There was alum in the potion I gave you last year."

"What is it, a herb?"

"No, it's an earth. The Moors mine it in Turkey and Africa. Tanners employ it in the preparation of leather, sometimes. I suppose you want to use it to dye cloth."

"Yes." As always, Mattie's guesswork seemed supernaturally accurate.

"It acts as a mordant—it helps the dye to bite the wool."

"And where do you get it?"

"I buy it in Melcombe," said Mattie.

Caris made the two-day journey to Melcombe, where she had been several times before, accompanied by one of her father's employees as a bodyguard. At the quayside she found a merchant who dealt in spices, cage birds, musical instruments, and all kinds of curiosities from remote parts of the world. He sold her both the red dye made from the root of the madder plant, cultivated in France, and a type of alum known as Spiralum that he said came from Ethiopia. He charged her seven shillings for a small barrel of madder and a pound for a sack of alum, and she had no idea whether she was paying fair prices or not. He sold her his entire stock, and promised to get more from the next Italian ship to come into port. She asked him what quantities of dye and alum she should use, but he did not know.

When she got home, she began to dye pieces of her unsold cloth in a cooking pot. Petranilla objected to the smell, so Caris built a fire in the backyard. She knew that she had to put the cloth in a solution of dye and boil it, and Peter Dyer told her the correct strength of the dye solution. However, no one knew how much alum she needed or how she should use it.

She began a frustrating process of trial and error. She tried soaking the cloth in alum before dyeing it; putting the alum in at the same time as the dye; and boiling the dyed cloth in a solution of alum afterward. She tried using the same quantity of alum as dye, then more, then less. At Mattie's suggestion she experimented with other ingredients: oak galls, chalk, lime water, vinegar, urine.

She was short of time. In all towns, no one could sell cloth but members of the guild—except during a fair, when the normal rules were relaxed. And all fairs were held in summer. The last was St. Giles's Fair, which took place on the downs to the east of Winchester on St. Giles's Day, September 12. It was now mid-July, so she had eight weeks.

She started early in the morning and worked until long after dark. Agitating the cloth continuously and lifting it in and out of the pot made her back ache. Her hands became red and sore from constant dipping in the harsh chemicals, and her hair began to smell. But, despite the frustration, she occasionally felt happy, and sometimes she hummed or even sang as she worked, old tunes whose words she could barely remember from childhood. Neighbors in their own backyards watched her curiously across the fences.

Now and again there came into her mind the thought: Is this my fate?

More than once she had said that she did not know what to do with her life. But she might not have a free choice. She was not to be allowed to be a physician; becoming a wool merchant looked like a bad idea; she did not want to enslave herself to a husband and children—but she had never dreamed that she might end up as a dyer. When she thought about it, she knew that this was not what she wanted to do. Having started it, she was determined to succeed—but it was not going to be her destiny.

At first she could only get the cloth to turn brownish red or pale pink. When she began to approach the right shade of scarlet she found, maddeningly, that it faded when she dried it in the sun, or it came out when washed. She tried double-dyeing, but the effect proved temporary. Peter told her, rather late, that the material would soak up dye more completely if she worked with the yarn before it was woven, or even with raw fleeces; and that improved the shade, but not the fastness.

"There's only one way to learn dyeing, and that's from a master," Peter said several times. They all thought that way, Caris realized. Prior Godwyn learned medicine by reading books that were hundreds of years old, and prescribed medicines without even looking at his patient. Elfric had punished Merthin for carving the parable of the virgins in a new way. Peter had never even tried to dye cloth scarlet. Only Mattie based her decisions on what she could see for herself, rather than on some venerated authority.

Caris's sister Alice stood watching her late one evening, with folded arms and pursed lips. As darkness gathered in the corners of the yard, the light of Caris's fire reddened Alice's disapproving face. "How much of our father's money have you spent on this foolishness?" she said.

Caris added it up. "Seven shillings for the madder, a pound for the alum, twelve shillings for the cloth—thirty-nine shillings."

"God save us!" Alice was horrified.

Caris herself was daunted. It was more than a year's wages for most people in Kingsbridge. "It is a lot, but I'll make more," she said.

Alice was angry. "You have no right to spend his money like this."

"No right?" Caris said. "I have his permission—what more do I need?"

"He's showing signs of age. His judgment is not what it was."

Caris pretended not to know this. "His judgment is fine, and a lot better than yours."

"You're spending our inheritance!"

"Is *that* what's bothering you? Don't worry, I'm making you money."

"I don't want to take the risk."

"You're not taking the risk, he is."

"He shouldn't throw away money that should come to us!"

"Tell him that."

Alice went away defeated, but Caris was not as confident as she pretended. She might never get it just right. And then what would she and her father do?

When finally she found the right formula, it was remarkably simple: an ounce of madder and two ounces of alum for every three ounces of wool. She boiled the wool in the alum first, then added the madder to the pot without reboiling the liquid. The extra ingredient was lime water. She could hardly believe the result. It was more successful than she could have hoped. The red was bright, almost like the Italian red. She felt sure it would fade, and give her another disappointment; but the color remained the same through drying, rewashing, and fulling.

She gave Peter the formula, and under her close supervision, he used all her remaining alum to dye twelve yards of best-quality wool cloth in one of his giant vats. When it had been fulled, Caris paid a finisher to draw off the loose threads with a teazle, the prickly head of a wildflower, and to repair small blemishes.

She went to St Giles's Fair with a bale of perfect bright red cloth.

As she was unrolling it, she was addressed by a man with a London accent. "How much is that?" he said.

She looked at him. His clothes were expensive without being ostentatious, and she guessed he was wealthy but not noble. Trying to mask the trembling in her voice, she said: "Seven shillings a yard. It's the best—"

"No, I meant how much for the whole cloth."

"It's twelve yards, so that would be eighty-four shillings."

He rubbed the cloth between finger and thumb. "It's not as close-woven as Italian cloth, but it's not bad. I'll give you twenty-seven gold florins."

The gold coin of Florence was in common use, because England had no gold currency of its own. It was worth about three shillings, thirty-six English silver pennies. The Londoner was offering to buy her entire cloth for only three shillings less than she would get selling it yard by yard. But she sensed that he was not very serious about haggling—otherwise he would have started lower. "No," she said, marveling at her own temerity. "I want the full price."

"All right," he said immediately, confirming her instinct. She watched, thrilled, as he took out his purse. A moment later she held in her hand twenty-eight gold florins.

She examined one carefully. It was a bit larger than a silver penny. On one side was St. John the Baptist, the patron saint of Florence, and on the other the flower of Florence. She placed it on a balance to compare its weight with that of a new-minted florin her father kept for the purpose. The coin was good.

"Thank you," she said, hardly believing her success.

"I'm Harry Mercer of Cheapside, London," he said. "My father is the largest cloth merchant in England. When you've got more of this scarlet, come to London. We'll buy as much as you can bring us."

"Let's weave it all!" she said to her father when she returned home. "You've got forty sacks of wool left. We'll turn it all into red cloth."

"It's a big enterprise," he said thoughtfully.

Caris was sure her scheme would work. "There are plenty of weavers, and they're all poor. Peter isn't the only dyer in Kingsbridge, we can teach the others to use the alum."

"Others will copy you, once the secret gets out."

She knew he was right to think of snags, but all the same she felt impatient. "Let them copy," she said. "They can make money, too."

He was not going to be pushed into anything. "The price will come down if there's a lot of cloth for sale."

"It will have to fall a long way before the business becomes unprofitable."

He nodded. "That's true. But can you sell that much in Kingsbridge and Shiring? There aren't that many rich people."

"Then I'll take it to London."

"All right." He smiled. "You're so determined. It's a good plan—but even if it were a bad one, you'd probably make it work."

She went immediately to Mark Webber's house and arranged for him to begin work on another sack of wool. She also arranged for Madge to take one of Edmund's oxcarts and four sacks of wool, and go around neighboring villages looking for weavers.

But the rest of Caris's family were not happy. Next day, Alice came to dinner. As they sat down, Petranilla said to Edmund: "Alice and I think you should reconsider your cloth-making project."

Caris wanted him to tell her that the decision was made and it was too late to go back. But instead he said mildly: "Really? Tell me why."

"You'll be risking just about every penny you've got, that's why!"

"Most of it's at risk now," he said. "I've got a warehouse full of wool that I can't sell."

"But you could make a bad situation worse."

"I've decided to take that chance."

Alice broke in: "It's not fair on me!"

"Why not?"

"Caris is spending my inheritance!"

His face darkened. "I'm not dead yet," he said.

Petranilla clamped her mouth shut, recognizing the undertone in his low voice; but Alice did not notice how angry he was, and plowed on. "We have to think about the future," she said. "Why should Caris be allowed to spend my birthright?"

"Because it's not yours yet, and perhaps it never will be."

"You can't just throw away money that should come to me."

"I won't be told what to do with my money—especially by my children," he said, and his voice was so taut with anger that even Alice noticed.

More quietly, she said: "I didn't intend to annoy you."

He grunted. It was not much of an apology, but he could never remain grumpy for long. "Let's have dinner and say no more about it," he said; and Caris knew that her project had survived another day.

After dinner she went to see Peter Dyer, to warn him of the large quantity of work coming his way. "It can't be done," he said.

That took her by surprise. He always looked gloomy, but he normally did what she wanted. "Don't worry, you won't have to dye it all," she said. "I'll give some of the work to others."

"It's not the dyeing," he said. "It's the fulling."

"Why?"

"We're not allowed to full the cloth ourselves. Prior Godwyn has issued a new edict. We have to use the priory's fulling mill."

"Well, then, we'll use it."

"It's too slow. The machinery is old, and keeps breaking down. It's been repaired again and again, so the wood is a mixture of new and old, which never sorts well. It's no faster than a man treading in a bath of water. And there's only one mill. It will barely cope with the normal work of Kingsbridge weavers and dyers."

This was maddening. Surely her whole scheme could not fail because of a stupid ruling by her cousin Godwyn? She said indignantly: "But if the mill can't do the work, the prior must permit us to tread the cloth by foot!"

Peter shrugged. "Tell him that."

"I will!"

She marched off toward the priory, but before she got there, she thought again. The hall of the prior's house was used for his meetings with townspeople, but all the same it would be unusual for a woman to go in alone without an appointment, and Godwyn was increasingly touchy about such things. Moreover, a straight confrontation might not be the best way to change his mind. She realized she would do better to think this through. She returned to her house and sat down with her father in the parlor.

"Young Godwyn is on weak ground here," Edmund said immediately. "There never was a charge for using the fulling mill. According to legend, it was built by a townsman, Jack Builder, for the great Prior Philip; and, when Jack died, Philip gave the town the right to use the mill in perpetuity."

"Why did people stop using it?"

"It fell into disrepair, and I think there was an argument about who should pay for its upkeep. The argument was never resolved, and people went back to treading cloth themselves."

"Why, then, he has no right to charge a fee, nor to force people to use it!"

"No, indeed."

Edmund sent a message to the priory asking when it might be convenient for Godwyn to see him, and the reply came back saying he was free right away, so Edmund and Caris crossed the street and went to the prior's house.

Godwyn had changed a lot in a year, Caris thought. There was no boyish eagerness left. He seemed wary, as if he expected them to be aggressive. She was beginning to wonder whether he had the strength of character to be prior.

Philemon was with him, pathetically eager as ever to fetch chairs and pour drinks, but with a new touch of assurance in his manner, the look of someone who knew he belonged here.

"So, Philemon, you're an uncle now," Caris said. "What do you think of your new nephew, Sam?"

"I'm a novice monk," he said prissily. "We give up all worldly relations."

Caris shrugged. She knew he was fond of his sister Gwenda, but if he wanted to pretend otherwise, she was not going to argue.

Edmund laid out the problem starkly for Godwyn. "Work on the bridge will have to stop if the wool merchants of Kingsbridge can't improve their fortunes. Happily, we have come up with a new source of income. Caris has discovered how to produce high-quality scarlet cloth. Only one thing stands in the way of the success of this new enterprise: the fulling mill."

"Why?" said Godwyn. "The scarlet cloth can be fulled at the mill."

"Apparently not. It's old and inefficient. It can barely handle the existing production of cloth. It has no capacity for extra. Either you build a new fulling mill—"

"Out of the question," Godwyn interrupted. "I have no spare cash for that sort of thing."

"Very well, then," said Edmund. "You'll have to permit people to full cloth in the old way, by putting it in a bath of water and stamping on it with their bare feet."

The look that came over Godwyn's face was familiar to Caris. It was compounded of resentment, injured pride, and mulish obstinacy. In childhood he had looked like that whenever he was opposed. It meant he would try to bully the other children into submission or, failing that, stamp his foot and go home. Wanting his own way was only part of it. He seemed, Caris thought, to feel humiliated by disagreement, as if the idea that someone might think him wrong was too wounding to be borne. Whatever the explanation, she knew as soon as she saw the look that he was not going to be reasonable.

"I knew you would oppose me," he said petulantly to Edmund. "You seem to think the priory exists for the benefit of Kingsbridge. You'll just have to realize that it's the other way around."

Edmund rapidly became exasperated. "Don't you see that we depend on one another? We thought you understood that interrelationship—that's why we helped you get elected."

"I was elected by the monks, not the merchants. The town may depend on the priory, but there was a priory here before there was a town, and we can exist without you."

"You can exist, perhaps, but as an isolated outpost, rather than as the throbbing heart of a bustling city."

Caris put in: "You must want Kingsbridge to prosper, Godwyn—why else would you have gone to London to oppose Earl Roland?"

"I went to the royal court to defend the ancient rights of the priory—as I am trying to do here and now."

Edmund said indignantly: "This is treachery! We supported you as prior because you led us to believe you would build a bridge!"

"I owe you nothing," Godwyn replied. "My mother sold her house to send me to the university—where was my rich uncle then?"

Caris was amazed that Godwyn was still resentful over what had happened ten years ago.

Edmund's expression became coldly hostile. "I don't think you have the right to force people to use the fulling mill," he said.

A glance passed between Godwyn and Philemon, and Caris realized they knew this. Godwyn said: "There may have been times when the prior generously allowed the townspeople to use the mill without charge."

"It was the gift of Prior Philip to the town."

"I know nothing of that."

"There must be a document in your records."

Godwyn became angry. "The townspeople have allowed the mill to fall into disrepair, so that the priory has to pay to put it right. That is enough to annul any gift."

Edmund was right, Caris realized: Godwyn was on weak ground. He knew about Prior Philip's gift, but he intended to ignore it.

Edmund tried again. "Surely we can settle this between us?"

"I will not back down from my edict," Godwyn said. "It would make me appear weak."

That was what really bothered him, Caris realized. He was frightened that the townspeople would disrespect him if he changed his mind. His obstinacy came, paradoxically, from a kind of timidity.

Edmund said: "Neither of us wants the trouble and expense of another visit to the royal court."

Godwyn bristled. "Are you threatening me with the royal court?"

"I'm trying to avoid it. But . . ."

Caris closed her eyes, praying that the two men would not push their argument to the brink. Her prayer was not answered.

"But what?" said Godwyn challengingly.

Edmund sighed. "But yes, if you force the townspeople to use the fulling mill, and prohibit home fulling, I will appeal to the king."

"So be it," said Godwyn.

34

The deer was a young female, a year or two old, sleek across the haunches, well muscled under a soft leather skin. She was on the far side of a clearing, pushing her long neck through the branches of a bush to reach a patch of scrubby grass. Ralph Fitzgerald and Alan Fernhill were on horseback, the hooves of their mounts muffled by the carpet of wet autumn leaves, and their dogs were trained to silence. Because of this, and perhaps because she was concentrating on straining to reach her fodder, the deer did not hear their approach until it was too late.

Ralph saw her first, and pointed across the clearing. Alan was carrying his longbow, grasping it and the reins in his left hand. With the speed of long practice, he fitted an arrow to the string in a heartbeat, and shot.

The dogs were slower. Only when they heard the thrum of the bowstring and the whistle of the arrow as it flew through the air did they react. Barley, the bitch, froze in place, head up, ears erect; and Blade, her puppy, now grown larger than his mother, uttered a low, startled woof.

The arrow was a yard long, flighted with swan feathers. Its tip was two inches of solid iron with a socket into which the shaft fitted tightly. It was a hunting arrow, with a sharp point: a battle arrow would have had a square head, so that it would punch through armor without being deflected.

Alan's shot was good, but not perfect. It struck the deer low in the neck. She jumped with all four feet—shocked, presumably, by the sudden, agonizing stab. Her head came up out of the bush. For an instant, Ralph thought she was going to fall down dead, but a moment later she bounded away. The arrow was still buried in her neck, but the blood was oozing rather than spurting from the wound, so it must have lodged in her muscles, missing the major blood vessels.

The dogs leaped forward as if they, too, had been shot from bows; and the two horses followed without urging. Ralph was on Griff, his favorite hunter. He felt the rush of excitement that was what he mainly lived for. It was a tingling in the nerves, a constriction in the neck, an irresistible impulse to yell at the top of his voice; a thrill so like sexual excitement that he could hardly have said what the difference was.

Men such as Ralph existed to fight. The king and his barons made them lords and knights, and gave them villages and lands to rule over, for a reason: so that they would be able to provide themselves with horses, squires, weapons, and armor whenever the king needed an army. But there was not a war every year. Sometimes two or three years would go by without so much as a minor police action on the borders of rebellious Wales or barbarian Scotland. Knights needed something to do in the interim. They had to keep fit and maintain their horsemanship and—perhaps most important of all—their bloodlust. Soldiers had to kill, and they did it better when they longed for it.

Hunting was the answer. All noblemen, from the king down to minor lords such as Ralph, hunted whenever they got the chance, often several times a week. They enjoyed it, and it ensured they were fit for battle whenever called upon. Ralph hunted with Earl Roland on his frequent visits to Earlscastle, and often joined Lord William's hunt at Casterham. When he was at his own village of Wigleigh, he went out with his squire, Alan, in the forests round about. They usually killed boar—there was not much meat on the wild pigs, but they were exciting to hunt because they put up a good fight. Ralph also went after foxes and the occasional, rare, wolf. But a deer was best: agile, fast, and a hundred pounds of good meat to take home.

Now Ralph thrilled to the feel of Griff beneath him, the horse's weight and strength, the powerful action of its muscles and the drumbeat of its tread. The deer disappeared into the vegetation, but Barley knew where it had gone, and the horses followed the dogs. Ralph carried a spear ready in his right hand, a long shaft of ash with a fire-hardened point. As Griff swerved and jumped, Ralph ducked under overhanging branches and swayed with the horse, his boots firmly in the stirrups, keeping his seat effortlessly by the pressure of his knees.

In the undergrowth the horses were not as nimble as the deer, and they fell behind; but the dogs had the advantage, and Ralph heard frantic barking as they closed in. Then there was a lull, and in a few moments Ralph found out why: the deer had broken out of the vegetation onto a pathway and was leaving the dogs behind. Here, however, the horses had the advantage, and they quickly passed the dogs and began to gain on the deer.

Ralph could see that the beast was weakening. He saw blood on its rump, and deduced that one of the dogs had got a bite. Its gait became irregular as it struggled to get away. It was a sprinter, made for the sudden quick dash, and it could not keep up its initial pace for long.

His blood raced as he closed on his prey. He tightened his grip on the lance. It took a great deal of strength to force a wooden point into the tough body of a big animal: the skin was leathery, the muscles dense, the bones hard. The neck was the softest target, if you could contrive to miss the vertebrae and hit the jugular vein. You had to choose the exact moment, then thrust quickly with all your might.

Seeing the horses almost upon it, the deer made a desperate turn into the bushes. This gave it a few seconds' respite. The horses slowed as they crashed through undergrowth over which the deer had bounded without pause. But the dogs caught up again, and Ralph saw that the deer could not go much farther.

The usual pattern was that the dogs would inflict more and more wounds, slowing the deer until the horses could catch it and the hunter could deliver the death blow. But, on this occasion, there was an accident.

When the dogs and the horses were almost upon the deer, she dodged sideways. Blade, the younger dog, went after her with more enthusiasm than sense, and swerved in front of Griff. The horse was going too fast to stop or even avoid the dog, and kicked him with a mighty foreleg. The dog was a mastiff, weighing seventy or eighty pounds, and the impact caused the horse to stumble.

Ralph was thrown. He let go of his spear as he flew through the air. His greatest fear, in that instant, was that his horse would fall on him. But he saw, in the moment before he landed, that Griff had somehow regained his balance.

Ralph fell into a thorn bush. His hands and face were scratched painfully, but the branches broke his fall. All the same, he was enraged.

Alan reined in. Barley went after the deer but returned in a few moments: the beast had obviously got away. Ralph struggled to his feet, cursing. Alan caught Griff then dismounted, holding both horses.

Blade lay motionless on the dead leaves, blood dripping from his mouth. He had been struck on the head by Griff's iron horseshoe. Barley went up to him, sniffed, nudged him with her nose, and licked the blood on his face, then turned away, looking bewildered. Alan prodded the dog with the toe of his boot. There was no response. Blade was not breathing. "Dead," Alan said.

"Damn fool dog deserved to die," Ralph said.

They walked the horses through the woods, looking for a place to rest. After a while Ralph heard running water. Following the sound, he came to a fast-flowing stream. He recognized the stretch of water: they were only a little way beyond the fields of Wigleigh. "Let's have some refreshment," he said. Alan tied up the horses then took from his saddlebag a stoppered jug, two wooden cups, and a canvas sack of food.

Barley went to the stream and lapped the cold water thirstily. Ralph sat on the bank, resting his back against a tree. Alan sat beside him and handed him a cup of ale and a wedge of cheese. Ralph took the drink and refused the food.

Alan knew his boss in a bad mood, and said nothing while Ralph drank, wordlessly refilling Ralph's cup from the jug. In the silence they both heard female voices. Alan looked at Ralph with a raised eyebrow. Barley growled. Ralph stood up, shushing the dog, and walked softly in the direction of the sound. Alan followed.

A few yards downstream Ralph stopped, looking through the vegetation. A small group of village women were doing laundry on the near bank of the stream, where the water flowed fast over an outcrop of rocks. It was a damp October day, cool but not cold, and they wore their sleeves rolled up and the skirts of their shifts raised to thigh level to keep them dry.

Ralph studied them one by one. There was Gwenda, all muscular forearms and calves, with her baby—now four months old—strapped to her back. He identified Peg, the wife of Perkin, scrubbing her husband's underdrawers with a stone. His own housemaid, Vira, was there, a hard-faced woman of about thirty who had looked so stonily at him when he patted her arse that he never touched her again. The voice that he had heard belonged to the Widow Huberts, a great talker, no doubt because she lived alone. The widow was standing in midstream, calling out to the others, carrying on a gossipy conversation at a distance.

And there was Annet.

She stood on a rock, washing some small garment, bending to dip it in the stream then standing upright to scrub it. She had long, white legs that disappeared enchantingly into her rucked-up dress. Every time she bent over, her neckline fell open to reveal the pale fruit of her small breasts hanging like temptation on a tree. Her fair hair was wet at the ends, and there was a petulant look on her pretty face, as if she felt she had not been born for this kind of work.

They had been there for some time, Ralph guessed, and their presence might have remained unknown to him, had not Widow Huberts raised her voice to call out. He lowered himself to the ground and knelt behind a bush, peering through the leafless twigs. Alan squatted beside him.

Ralph liked spying on women. He had often done it as an adolescent. They scratched themselves, sprawled on the ground with their legs apart, and talked about things they would never speak of if they knew a man was listening. In fact they acted like men.

He feasted his eyes on the unsuspecting women of his village, and strained to hear what they were saying. He watched Gwenda, looking at her small, strong body, remembering her naked, kneeling on the bed, and reliving how it had felt to hold her hips and pull her to him. He recalled how her attitude had changed. At first she had been coldly passive, struggling to conceal her resentment and distaste for the act she was performing; then he had seen a slow alteration. The skin on her neck had flushed, her chest had betrayed her excited breathing, and she had bent her head and closed her eyes in what seemed to him to be a mixture of shame and pleasure. The memory made him breathe faster and brought out a film of perspiration on his brow, despite the chill October air. He wondered if he would get another chance to lie with Gwenda.

Too soon, the women prepared to depart. They folded the damp washing and packed it into baskets, or wrapped it in bundles to be balanced on their heads, and then began to move away along the pathway beside the stream. Then an argument began between Annet and her mother. Annet had done only half the laundry she had brought. She was proposing to take the dirty half home, and it seemed Peg thought she should stay and finish it. In the end Peg stomped off and Annet stayed, looking sulky.

Ralph could hardly believe his luck.

In a low voice he said to Alan: "We'll have some fun with her. Sneak around and cut off her retreat."

Alan disappeared.

Ralph watched as Annet dipped the remaining laundry perfunctorily in the stream, then sat on the bank staring at the water grumpily. When he judged that the other women were out of earshot and Alan must be in place, he stood up and walked forward.

She heard him pushing through the undergrowth and looked up, startled. He enjoyed seeing the expression on her face change from surprise and curiosity to fear as she realized she was alone with him in the forest. She leaped to her feet, but by that time he was next to her, holding her arm in a light but firm grip. "Hello, Annet," he said. "What are you doing here . . . all alone?"

She looked over his shoulder—hoping, he guessed, that he might be accompanied by others who would restrain him, and her face registered dismay when she saw only Barley. "I'm going home," she said. "My mother's just left."

"Don't rush," he said. "You look so attractive like this, with your hair damp and your knees bare."

She tried hastily to push the skirt of her dress down. With his free hand, he held the point of her chin and made her look at him. "How about a smile?" he said. "Don't look so worried. I wouldn't harm you—I'm your lord."

She attempted a smile. "I'm just a bit flustered," she said. "You startled me." She mustered a trace of her habitual coquetry. "Perhaps you would escort me home," she said with a simper. "A girl needs protection in the forest."

"Oh, I'll protect you. I'll look after you much better than that fool Wulfric, or your husband." He took his hand from her chin and grasped her breast. It was as he remembered, small and firm. He released her arm so that he could use both hands, one on each breast.

But as soon as he let go of her, she fled. He laughed as she ran along the path and into the trees. A moment later he heard her give a cry of shock. He stayed where he was, and Alan brought her to him, her arm twisted behind her back so that her chest stuck out invitingly.

Ralph drew his knife, a sharp dagger with a blade a foot long. "Take off your dress," he said.

Alan let her go, but she did not immediately comply. "Please, lord," she said. "I've always shown you respect—"

"Take off your dress, or I'll cut your cheeks and scar you for ever."

It was a well-chosen threat for a vain woman, and she gave in immediately. She began to cry as she lifted the plain brown wool shift over her head. At first she held the crumpled garment in front of her, covering her nakedness, but Alan snatched it from her and threw it aside.

Ralph stared at her naked body. She stood with her eyes down, tears on her face. She had slim hips with a prominent bush of dark blond hair. "Wulfric never saw you like this, did he?" Ralph said.

She shook her head in negation without raising her eyes.

He thrust his hand between her legs. "Did he ever touch you here?"

She said: "Please, lord, I'm a married woman—"

"All the better—you've no virginity to lose, nothing to worry about. Lie down."

She tried to back away from him, and bumped into Alan, who expertly tripped her, so that she fell on her back. Ralph grabbed her ankles, so that she could not get up, but she wriggled desperately. "Hold her down," Ralph said to Alan.

Alan forced her head down then put his knees on her upper arms and his hands on her shoulders.

Ralph got his cock out and rubbed it to make it harder. Then he knelt between Annet's thighs.

She began to scream, but no one heard her.

35

Fortunately, Gwenda was one of the first people to see Annet after the incident.

Gwenda and Peg brought home the laundry and hung it to dry around the fire in the kitchen of Perkin's house. Gwenda was still working as a laborer for Perkin but now, in autumn, when there was less to do in the fields, she helped Peg with her domestic chores. When they had dealt with the laundry they began to prepare the midday meal for Perkin, Rob, Billy Howard, and Wulfric. After an hour Peg said: "What can have happened to Annet?"

"I'll go and see." Gwenda first checked on her baby. Sammy was lying in a basketwork crib, wrapped in an old bit of brown blanket, his alert dark eyes watching the smoke from the fire gathering in curls under the ceiling. Gwenda kissed his forehead then went to look for Annet.

She retraced her steps across the windy fields. Lord Ralph and Alan Fernhill galloped past her, heading up to the village, their day's hunting apparently cut short. Gwenda entered the forest and followed the short path that led to the spot where the women did laundry. Before she got there she met Annet coming the other way.

"Are you all right?" Gwenda said. "Your mother is worried."

"I'm fine," Annet replied.

Gwenda could tell something was wrong. "What has happened?"

"Nothing." Annet would not meet her eye. "Nothing happened, leave me alone."

Gwenda stood squarely in front of Annet and looked her up and down. Her face told Gwenda unmistakably that there had been some calamity. At first glance she did not appear to be physically hurt—though most of her body was covered by the long wool shift—but then Gwenda saw dark smears on her dress that looked like bloodstains.

Gwenda recalled Ralph and Alan galloping past. "Did Lord Ralph do something to you?"

"I'm going home." Annet tried to push past Gwenda. Gwenda grabbed her arm to stop her. She did not squeeze hard, but nevertheless Annet cried out in pain, her hand flying to her upper arm.

"You're hurt!" Gwenda exclaimed.

Annet burst into tears.

Gwenda put her arm around Annet's shoulders. "Come home," she said. "Tell your mother about it."

Annet shook her head. "I'm not telling anyone," she said.

Too late for that, Gwenda thought.

Walking Annet back to Perkin's house, Gwenda ran over the possibilities in her mind. Clearly Annet had suffered some kind of assault. She might have been attacked by one or more travelers, though there was no road nearby. Outlaws were always a possibility, but it was a long time since any had been seen near Wigleigh. No, the likeliest suspects were Ralph and Alan.

Peg was brisk. She sat Annet down on a stool and pulled her dress down over her shoulders. Both upper arms showed swollen red bruises. "Someone held you down," Peg said angrily.

Annet made no reply.

Peg persisted. "Am I right? Answer me, child, or you'll be in worse trouble. Did someone hold you down?"

Annet nodded.

"How many men? Come on, out with it."

Annet did not speak, but held up two fingers.

Peg reddened with fury. "Did they fuck you?"

Annet nodded.

"Who were they?"

Annet shook her head.

Gwenda knew why she did not want to say. It was dangerous for a serf to accuse a lord of a crime. She said to Peg: "I saw Ralph and Alan riding away."

Peg said to Annet: "Was it them—Ralph and Alan?"

Annet nodded.

Peg's voice fell almost to a whisper. "I suppose Alan held you down while Ralph did it."

Annet nodded again.

Peg softened, now that she had got the truth. She put her arms around her daughter and hugged her. "You poor child," she said. "My poor baby."

Annet began to sob.

Gwenda left the house.

The men would be home soon for their midday dinner, and they would quickly find out that Ralph had raped Annet. Annet's father, her brother, her husband, and her former lover would be mad with rage. Perkin was too old to do anything foolish, Rob would do what Perkin told him, and Billy Howard probably was not brave enough to make trouble— but Wulfric would be incandescent. He would kill Ralph.

And then he would be hanged.

Gwenda had to turn the course of events; otherwise she would lose her husband. She hurried through the village, speaking to no one, and went to the manor house. There, she hoped to be told that Ralph and Alan had finished their dinner and gone out again; but it was a little too early and, to her dismay, they were still at home.

She found them in the stable behind the house, looking at a horse with an infected hoof. Normally she was uncomfortable in the presence of Ralph or Alan, for she felt sure that whenever they looked at her they remembered the sight of her kneeling naked on the bed at the Bell in Kingsbridge. But today the thought hardly entered her head. Somehow she had to make them leave the village—now, before Wulfric found out what they had done. What was she going to say?

For a moment she was struck dumb. Then in desperation she said: "Lord, there was a messenger here from Earl Roland."

Ralph was surprised. "When was this?"

"An hour ago."

Ralph looked at the groom who was holding the horse's foot up for inspection. The man said: "No one came here."

Naturally, a messenger would have come to the manor house and spoken to the lord's servants. Ralph said to Gwenda: "Why did he give this message to *you*?"

She improvised desperately. "I met him on the road just outside the village. He asked for Lord Ralph, and I told him you were out hunting and you would be back for dinner—but he wouldn't stay."

This was unusual behavior for a messenger, who would normally stop to eat and drink and rest his horse. Ralph said: "Why was he in such a hurry?"

Inventing excuses extempore, Gwenda said: "He had to get to Cowford by sundown . . . I didn't make so bold as to question him."

Ralph grunted. The last part was plausible: a messenger from Earl Roland was not likely to subject himself to cross-examination by a peasant woman. "Why didn't you tell me this earlier?"

"I came across the fields to meet you, but you didn't see me and galloped past."

"Oh. I think I did see you. No matter—what's the message?"

"Earl Roland summons you to Earlscastle as soon as possible." She took a breath and added another layer of implausibility. "The messenger said to tell you not to wait to eat your dinner, but take fresh horses and leave at once." It was barely credible, but she had to get Ralph away before Wulfric showed up.

"Really? Did he say why he needs me in such a terrible hurry?"

"No."

"Hm." Ralph looked thoughtful and said nothing for a few moments.

Gwenda said anxiously: "So, will you go now?"

He glared at her. "That's no concern of yours."

"It's just that I wouldn't want it to be said that I hadn't made the urgency clear enough."

"Oh, wouldn't you? Well, I don't care what you would or wouldn't want. Be off."

Gwenda had to go.

She returned to Perkin's house. She arrived just as the men were coming in from the fields. Sam was quiet and happy in his crib. Annet was sitting in the same place, with her dress pulled down to show the bruises on her arms. Peg said accusingly: "Where have you been?"

Gwenda did not answer, and Peg was distracted by Perkin coming in and saying: "What's this? What's the matter with Annet?"

Peg said: "She had the misfortune to meet Ralph and Alan when she was alone in the forest."

Perkin's face darkened with anger. "Why was she alone?"

"It's my fault," Peg said, and she began to cry. "Only she was so lazy about the laundry, as she always is, and I made her stay back and finish it, after the other women went home, and that's when those two animals must have come along."

"We saw them a while ago, riding across Brookfield," Perkin said. "They must have just come from the place." He looked frightened. "This is very dangerous," he said. "It's the kind of thing that can ruin a family."

"But *we've* done nothing wrong!" Peg protested.

"Ralph's guilt will make him hate us for our innocence."

That was probably true, Gwenda realized. Perkin was shrewd, beneath his obsequious manner.

Annet's husband, Billy Howard, came in, wiping his muddy hands on his shirt. Her brother, Rob, was close behind. Billy looked at his wife's bruises and said: "What happened to you?"

Peg answered for her. "It was Ralph and Alan."

Billy stared at his wife. "What did they do to you?"

Annet lowered her eyes and said nothing.

"I'll kill them both," Billy said furiously, but it was obviously an idle threat: Billy was a mild-mannered man, slim built, and had never been known to fight, even when drunk.

Wulfric was the last to come through the door. Too late, Gwenda realized how attractive Annet was looking. She had a long neck and pretty shoulders, and the tops of her breasts were showing. The ugly bruises only emphasized her other charms. Wulfric stared at her with undisguised admiration—he never could hide his feelings. Then, after a moment, he registered the angry bruises, and he frowned.

Billy said: "Did they rape you?"

Gwenda was watching Wulfric. As he grasped the significance of the scene, his expression registered shock and dismay, and his fair skin flushed with emotion.

Billy said: "Did they, woman?"

Gwenda felt a surge of compassion for the unlovable Annet. Why did everyone feel they had the right to ask her bullying questions?

At last, Annet answered Billy's question with a silent nod.

Wulfric's face was suffused with black rage. "Who?" he growled.

Billy said: "This is none of your business, Wulfric. Go home."

Perkin said tremulously: "I don't want trouble. We mustn't let this destroy us."

Billy looked angrily at his father-in-law. "What are you saying? That we should do nothing?"

"If we make an enemy of Lord Ralph, we could suffer for the rest of our lives."

"But he's raped Annet!"

Wulfric said incredulously: "Ralph did this?"

Perkin said: "God will punish him."

"So will I, by Christ," said Wulfric.

Gwenda said: "Please, Wulfric, no!"

Wulfric made for the door.

Gwenda went to him, frantic with fright, and grabbed his arm. Only a few minutes had gone by since she had given Ralph the fake message. Even if he believed it, she did not know how seriously he would take the urgency. There was a good chance he had not left the village yet. "Don't go to the manor house," she pleaded with Wulfric. "Please."

He shook her off roughly. "Get away from me," he said.

"Look at your baby!" she cried, pointing at Sammy in the crib. "Are you going to leave him without a father?"

Wulfric went out.

Gwenda followed, and the other men came after. Wulfric marched through the village like the angel of death, fists clenched at his sides, staring straight ahead, his face twisted into a rictus of fury. Other villagers, on their way home for the midday meal, spoke to him but got no reply.

Some followed him. In the few minutes it took to walk to the manor house he gathered a small crowd. Nathan Reeve came out of his house and asked Gwenda what was happening, but all she could say was: "Stop him, someone, please!" It was useless: none of them could have restrained Wulfric even if they had dared to try.

He threw open the front door of the manor house and marched in. Gwenda was right behind him, and the crowd pushed through after them. The housekeeper, Vira, said indignantly: "You're supposed to knock!"

"Where is your master?" said Wulfric.

Vira saw the expression on Wulfric's face and looked scared. "He went to the stable," she said. "He's about to leave for Earlscastle."

Wulfric pushed past her and went through the kitchen. As he and Gwenda stepped out of the back door, they saw Ralph and Alan mounting up. Gwenda could have screamed—they were just seconds too early!

Wulfric jumped forward. With desperate inspiration, Gwenda stuck out her foot and hooked it around Wulfric's ankle.

Wulfric fell flat on his face in the mud.

Ralph did not see either of them. He kicked his horse and it trotted out of the yard. Alan saw them, read the situation, decided to avoid trouble, and followed Ralph. As they left the yard Alan urged his horse into a canter, passing Ralph, whereupon Ralph's horse eagerly increased its pace.

Wulfric leaped to his feet, cursing, and chased them. Gwenda ran after him. Wulfric could not catch the horses, but Gwenda was terrified that Ralph would look behind, and rein in to see what the fuss was about.

But the two men were enjoying the lively energy of fresh horses, and without a backward glance they raced away along the track that led out of the village. In seconds they disappeared.

Wulfric slumped on his knees in the mud.

Gwenda caught up with him and took his arm to help him to his feet. He pushed her aside so forcefully that she staggered and almost fell. She was shocked: it was completely out of character for him to be rough with her.

"You tripped me up," he said as he got to his feet unaided.

"I saved your life," she said.

He stared at her with hatred in his eyes and said: "I will never forgive you."

When Ralph reached Earlscastle he was told that Roland had not sent for him at all, never mind urgently. The rooks on the battlements laughed mockingly at him.

Alan conjectured an explanation. "It's to do with Annet," he said. "Just as we left, I saw Wulfric coming out of the back door of the manor house. I thought nothing of it at the time, but maybe he was intending to confront you."

"I'll bet he was," Ralph said. He touched the long dagger at his belt. "You should have told me—I'd welcome an excuse to stick my knife in his belly."

"And no doubt Gwenda knows that, so perhaps she invented the message to get you away from her murderous husband."

"Of course," said Ralph. "That would explain why no one else saw this messenger—he never existed. Crafty bitch."

She should be punished, but it might be difficult. She would probably say she did it for the best, and Ralph could hardly argue that she had been wrong to prevent her husband attacking the lord of the manor. Worse, if he made a fuss about her deception he would call attention to the fact that she had outwitted him. No, there would be no formal penalty—though he might find unofficial ways to chastise her.

As he was at Earlscastle, he took the opportunity to go hunting with the earl and his entourage, and he forgot about Annet—until the end of the second day, when Roland called him into his private chamber. Only the earl's clerk, Father Jerome, was with him. Roland did not ask Ralph to sit down. "The priest of Wigleigh is here," he said.

Ralph was surprised. "Father Gaspard? At Earlscastle?"

Roland did not bother to answer these rhetorical questions. "He complains that you raped a woman called Annet, the wife of Billy Howard, one of your serfs."

Ralph's heart missed a beat. He had not imagined the peasants would have the nerve to complain to the earl. It was very difficult for a serf to accuse a lord in a court of law. But they could be sly, and someone in Wigleigh had cleverly persuaded the priest to make the complaint.

Ralph put on an expression of carelessness. "Rubbish," he said. "All right, I lay with her, but she was willing." He gave Roland a man-to-man grin. "More than willing."

An expression of distaste came over Roland's face, and he turned to Father Jerome with an inquiring look.

Jerome was an educated, ambitious young man, a type Ralph particularly disliked. He had a snooty look as he said: "The girl is here. Woman, I should say, though she is only nineteen. She has massive bruises on her arms and a bloodstained dress. She says you encountered her in the forest, and your squire knelt on her to hold her down. And a man called Wulfric is here to say that you were seen riding away from the scene."

Ralph guessed it was Wulfric who had persuaded Father Gaspard to come here to Earlscastle. "It's not true," he said, trying to put a note of indignation into his voice.

Jerome looked skeptical. "Why would she lie?"

"Maybe someone saw us and told her husband. He gave her the bruises, I expect. She cried rape to stop him beating her. Then she stained her dress with chicken blood."

Roland sighed. "It's a bit oafish, isn't it, Ralph?"

Ralph was not sure what he meant. Did he expect his men to behave like damned monks?

Roland went on: "I was warned you'd be like this. My daughter-in-law always said you'd give me problems."

"Philippa?"

"Lady Philippa, to you."

Enlightenment dawned on Ralph, and he said incredulously: "Is that why you didn't promote me after I saved your life—because a *woman* was against me? What sort of an army will you have if you let girls pick your men?"

"You're right, of course, and that's why I went against her judgment in the end. What women never realize is that a man without some bile in him is good for nothing but tilling the land. We can't take milksops into battle. But she was right when she warned me that you would cause trouble. I don't want to be bothered, in peacetime, with damned priests whining about serfs' wives being raped. Don't do it again. I don't care if you lie with the peasant women. If it comes to that, I don't care if you lie with the men. But if you take a man's wife, willing or otherwise, be prepared to compensate the husband in some way. Most peasants can be bought. Just don't let it become my problem."

"Yes, lord."

Jerome said: "What am I to do with this Gaspard?"

"Let me see," Roland said thoughtfully. "Wigleigh is on the edge of my territory, not far from my son William's landholding, is it not?"

"Yes," Ralph said.

"How far were you from the border when you met this girl?"

"A mile. We were only just outside Wigleigh."

"No matter." He turned to Jerome. "Everyone will know this is just an excuse, but tell Father Gaspard that the incident took place in Lord William's territory, so I can't adjudicate."

"Very good, my lord."

Ralph said: "What if they go to William?"

"I doubt that they will. But if they persist, you'll have to come to some arrangement with William. The peasants will tire of complaining eventually."

Ralph nodded, relieved. For a moment, he had suffered the dread thought that he had made a terrible error of judgment, and that after all he might be made to pay the price for raping Annet. But, in the end, he had got away with it, as he had expected to.

"Thank you, my lord," he said.

He wondered what his brother would say about this. The thought filled him with shame. But perhaps Merthin would never find out.

"We must complain to Lord William," said Wulfric when they got back to Wigleigh.

The entire village gathered in the church to discuss the matter. Father Gaspard and Nathan Reeve were there, but somehow Wulfric seemed to be the leader, despite his youth. He had gone to the front, leaving Gwenda and baby Sammy in the crowd.

Gwenda was praying that they would decide to drop the matter. It was not that she wanted Ralph to go unpunished—on the contrary, she would have liked to see him boiled alive. She herself had killed two men for merely threatening her with rape, something she remembered, every now and again during the discussion, with a shudder. But she did not like Wulfric taking the leading role. It was partly because he was driven by the unquenched flame of his feeling for Annet, which hurt and saddened Gwenda. But, more importantly, she feared for him. The enmity between him and Ralph had already cost Wulfric his inheritance. What other vengeance would Ralph take?

Perkin said: "I'm the father of the victim, and I don't want any more trouble over this. It's very dangerous to complain of the actions of a lord. He always finds a way to punish the complainers, right or wrong. Let's drop it."

"Too late for that," said Wulfric. "We've already complained, or at least our priest has. There's nothing to be gained by backing down now."

"We've gone far enough," Perkin argued. "Ralph has been embarrassed in front of his earl. He knows now that he can't do just whatever he pleases."

"On the contrary," said Wulfric. "He thinks he's got away with it. I'm afraid he'll do it again. No woman in the village will be safe."

Gwenda herself had said to Wulfric all the things Perkin was saying. Wulfric had not answered her. He had hardly spoken to her since she tripped him up at the back door of the manor house. At first, she had told herself that he was merely sulking because he had felt foolish. She had expected him to have forgotten about it by the time he returned from Earlscastle. But she had been wrong. He had not touched her, in bed or out of it, for a week; he rarely met her eye; and he talked to her in monosyllables and grunts. It was beginning to depress her.

Nathan Reeve said: "You'll never win against Ralph. Serfs never overcome lords."

"I'm not so sure," Wulfric said. "Everyone has enemies. We might not be the only people who would like to see Ralph reined in. Perhaps we will never see him convicted in court—but we must inflict the maximum of trouble and embarrassment on him if we want him to hesitate before doing this sort of thing again."

Several villagers nodded agreement, but no one spoke in support of Wulfric, and Gwenda began to hope that he would lose the argument. However, her husband was nothing if not determined, and he now turned to the priest. "What do you think, Father Gaspard?"

Gaspard was young, poor, and earnest. He had no fear of the nobility. He was not ambitious—he did not want to become a bishop and join the ruling class—so he felt no need to please aristocrats. He said: "Annet has been cruelly violated, the peace of our village has been criminally broken, and Lord Ralph has committed a wicked, vile sin which he must confess and repent. For the sake of the victim, for our own self-respect, and to save Lord Ralph from the flames of Hell, we must go to Lord William."

There was a rumble of assent.

Wulfric looked at Billy Howard and Annet, sitting side by side. In the end, Gwenda thought, people would probably do what Annet and Billy wanted. "I don't want trouble," Billy said. "But we should finish what we've started, for the sake of all the women in the village."

Annet did not raise her eyes from the floor, but she nodded assent, and Gwenda realized with dismay that Wulfric had won.

"Well, you got what you wanted," she said to him as they left the church.

He grunted.

She persisted: "So, I suppose you will continue to risk your life for the honor of Billy Howard's wife, while refusing to speak to your own wife."

He said nothing. Sammy sensed the hostility and began to cry.

Gwenda felt desperate. She had moved heaven and earth to get the man she loved, she had married him and had his baby, and now he was treating her like an enemy. Her father had never behaved this way to her mother—not that Joby's behavior was a model for anyone. But she had no idea how to deal with him. She had tried using Sammy, holding him in one arm while touching Wulfric with the other hand, in an attempt to win back his affection by associating herself with the baby boy he loved; but he just moved away, rejecting them both. She had even tried sex, pressing her breasts against his back at night, brushing her hand across his belly, touching his penis, but it did not work—as she might have known, remembering how resistant he had been last summer, before Annet married Billy.

Now, in frustration, she cried out: "What is wrong with you? I only tried to save your life!"

"You should not have done it," he said.

"If I'd let you kill Ralph, you'd have been hanged!"

"You had no right."

"What does it matter if I had the right or not?"

"That's your father's philosophy, isn't it?"

She was startled. "What do you mean?"

"Your father believes it doesn't matter whether or not he has the right to do something. If it's for the best, he does it. Like selling you to feed his family."

"They sold me to be raped! I tripped you up to save you from the gallows. That's completely different."

"As long as you go on telling yourself that, you'll never understand him or me."

She realized she was not going to win back his affection by trying to prove him wrong. "Well . . . I don't understand, then."

"You took away my power to make my own decisions. You treated me the way your father treated you, as a thing to be controlled, not as a person. It doesn't matter whether I was right or wrong. What matters is that it was up to me to decide, not you. But you can't see that, just as your father can't see what he took away from you when he sold you."

She still thought the two things were completely different, but she did not argue the point, because she was beginning to see what had made him angry. He was passionate about his independence—something she could empathize with, for she felt the same way. And she had robbed him of that. She said falteringly: "I . . . I think I understand."

"Do you?"

"At any rate, I'll try not to do anything of that kind again."

"Good."

She only half believed she had been wrong, but she was desperate to end the war between them, so she said: "I'm very sorry."

"All right."

He wasn't saying much, but she sensed he might be softening. "You know that I don't want you to complain to Lord William about Ralph—but, if you're determined to, I won't try to stop you."

"I'm glad."

"In fact," she said, "I might be able to help you."

"Oh?" he said. "How?"

36

The home of Lord William and Lady Philippa, at Casterham, had once been a castle. There was still a round stone keep with battlements, though it was in ruins and used as a cowshed. The wall around the courtyard was intact, but the moat had dried up, and the ground in the slight remaining dip was used to grow vegetables and fruit trees. Where once there had been a drawbridge, a simple ramp now led up to the gatehouse.

Gwenda, carrying Sammy, passed under the arch of the gatehouse with Father Gaspard, Billy Howard, Annet, and Wulfric. A young man-at-arms was lolling on a bench, presumably on guard, but he saw the priest's robe and did not challenge them. The relaxed atmosphere encouraged Gwenda. She was hoping to get a private audience with Lady Philippa.

They entered the house by the main door and found themselves in a traditional great hall, with high windows like those of a church. It seemed to take up about half the total space of the house. The rest, presumably, would be personal chambers, in the modern fashion, which emphasized the privacy of the noble family and played down military defenses.

A middle-aged man in a leather tunic was sitting at a table counting notches on a tally stick. He glanced up at them, finished his count, made a note on a slate, then said: "Good day to you, strangers."

"Good day, Master Bailiff," said Gaspard, deducing the man's occupation. "We've come to see Lord William."

"He's expected back by suppertime, Father," the bailiff said politely. "What's your business with him, may I ask?"

Gaspard began to explain, and Gwenda slipped back outside.

She went around the house to the domestic end. There was a wooden extension that she guessed was the kitchen. A maid sat on a stool by the kitchen door with a sack of cabbages, washing the mud off in a big bowl of water. The maid was young, and looked fondly at the baby. "How old is he?" she said.

"Four months, nearly five. His name is Samuel. We call him Sammy, or Sam."

The baby smiled at the girl, and she said: "Ah."

Gwenda said: "I'm just an ordinary woman, like you, but I need to speak to the Lady Philippa."

The girl frowned and looked troubled. "I'm only the kitchen maid," she said.

"But you must see her sometimes. You could speak to her for me."

She glanced behind her, as if worried about being overheard. "I don't like to."

Gwenda realized this might be more difficult than she had anticipated. "Couldn't you just give her a message for me?" she said.

The maid shook her head.

Then a voice came from inside: "Who wants to send me a message?"

Gwenda tensed, wondering if she was in trouble. She looked toward the kitchen door.

A moment later, Lady Philippa stepped out.

She was not quite beautiful, and certainly not pretty, but she was good-looking. She had a straight nose and a strong jaw, and her green eyes were large and clear. She was not smiling, in fact she wore a slight frown, but nevertheless there was something friendly and understanding about her face.

Gwenda answered her question. "I'm Gwenda from Wigleigh, my lady."

"Wigleigh." Philippa's frown deepened. "And what do you have to say to me?"

"It's about Lord Ralph."

"I was afraid it might be. Well, come inside and let's warm that baby by the kitchen fire."

Many noble ladies would have refused to speak to someone as lowly as Gwenda, but she had guessed that Philippa had a big heart underneath that rather formidable exterior. She followed Philippa inside. Sammy began to grizzle, and Gwenda gave him the breast.

"You can sit down," Philippa said.

That was even more unusual. A serf would normally remain standing when talking to a lady. Philippa was being kind because of the baby, Gwenda guessed.

"All right, out with it," Philippa said. "What has Ralph done?"

"You may remember, lady, a fight at the Fleece Fair in Kingsbridge last year."

"I certainly do. Ralph groped a peasant girl, and her handsome young fiancé broke his nose. The boy shouldn't have done it, of course, but Ralph is a brute."

"Indeed he is. Last week he came across the same girl, Annet, in the woods. His squire held her down while Ralph raped her."

"Oh, God save us." Philippa looked distressed. "Ralph is an animal, a pig, a wild boar. I knew he should never have been made a lord. I told my father-in-law not to promote him."

"A pity the earl didn't follow your advice."

"And I suppose the fiancé wants justice."

Gwenda hesitated. She was not sure how much of the complicated story to tell. But she sensed it would be a mistake to hold anything back. "Annet is married, lady, but to a different man."

"So what lucky girl got Mr. Handsome?"

"As it happens, Wulfric married me."

"Congratulations."

"Though Wulfric is here, with Annet's husband, to bear witness."

Philippa gave Gwenda a sharp look, and seemed about to comment, then changed her mind. "So why have you come here? Wigleigh is not in my husband's territory."

"The incident happened in the forest, and the earl says it was on Lord William's land, so he can't adjudicate."

"That's an excuse. Roland adjudicates anything he likes. He just doesn't want to punish a man he's recently elevated."

"Anyway, our village priest is here to tell Lord William what happened."

"And what do you want me to do?"

"You're a woman, you understand. You know how men make excuses for rape. They say the girl must have been flirting, or doing something provocative."

"Yes."

"If Ralph gets away with this, he might do it again—perhaps to me."

"Or me," said Philippa. "You should see the way he stares at me—like a dog looking at a goose on the pond."

That was encouraging. "Perhaps you can make Lord William understand how important it is that Ralph should not get away with this."

Philippa nodded. "I think I can."

Sammy had stopped sucking and gone to sleep. Gwenda stood up. "Thank you, lady."

"I'm glad you came to me," said Philippa.

Lord William summoned them the next morning. They met with him in the great hall. Gwenda was glad to see Lady Philippa sitting beside him. She gave Gwenda a friendly look, and Gwenda hoped that meant she had spoken to her husband.

William was tall and black-haired, like his father the earl, but he was going bald, and the dome above the dark beard and eyebrows suggested a more thoughtful kind of authority, matching his reputation. He examined the bloodstained dress and looked at Annet's bruises, which were blue now, rather than the original angry red. All the same, they brought a look of fury to Lady Philippa's face. Gwenda guessed it was not so much the severity of the injuries as the grim picture they conjured up of a brawny squire kneeling on a girl's arms to hold her down while another man raped her.

"Well, you've done everything correctly so far," William said to Annet. "You went immediately to the nearest village, you showed your injuries to men of good reputation there, and you named your attacker. Now you have to offer a bill to a justice of the peace in the Shiring County Court."

She looked anxious. "What does that mean?"

"A bill is an accusation, written in Latin."

"I can't write English, lord, let alone Latin."

"Father Gaspard can do it for you. The justice will put the bill before an indicting jury, and you will tell them what happened. Can you do that? They may ask for embarrassing details."

Annet nodded determinedly.

"If they believe you, they will order the sheriff to summon Lord Ralph to the court a month later to be tried. Then you will need two sureties, people who will pledge a sum of money to guarantee that you will appear at the trial."

"But who will be my sureties?"

"Father Gaspard can be one, and I will be the other. I'll put up the money."

"Thank you, lord!"

"Thank my wife, who has persuaded me that I can't allow the king's peace to be breached on my territory by an act of rape."

Annet shot a grateful look at Philippa.

Gwenda looked at Wulfric. She had told her husband about her conversation with the lord's wife. Now he met her eye and gave an almost imperceptible nod of acknowledgment. He knew she had made this happen.

William went on: "At the trial, you will tell your story again. Your friends will all have to be witnesses: Gwenda will say she saw you coming from the forest in your bloodstained dress, Father Gaspard will say you told him what happened, Wulfric will say he saw Ralph and Alan riding away from the scene."

They all nodded solemnly.

"One more thing. Having started something like this, you can't stop it. Withdrawing an appeal is an offense, and you would be severely punished—to say nothing of what revenge Ralph might take on you."

Annet said: "I won't change my mind. But what will happen to Ralph? How will he be punished?"

"Oh, there's only one penalty for rape," said Lord William. "He'll be hanged."

They all slept in the great hall of the castle, with William's servants and squires and dogs, wrapping their cloaks around them and nestling into the carpet of rushes on the floor. As the light from the embers in the huge fireplace dimmed to a glow, Gwenda hesitantly reached for her husband, putting a tentative hand on his arm, stroking the wool of his cloak. They had not made love since the rape, and she was unsure whether he wanted her or not. She had angered him grievously by tripping him up: would he feel that her intervention with Lady Philippa made up for that?

He responded immediately, drawing her to him and kissing her lips. She relaxed gratefully into his arms. They toyed with each other for a while. Gwenda was so happy she wanted to weep.

She waited for him to roll on top of her, but he did not do so. She could tell he wanted to, for he was being very affectionate, and his penis was hard in her hand; but perhaps he hesitated to do it in the company of so many others. People did have sex in halls like this, of course; it was normal, and no one took any notice. But perhaps Wulfric felt shy.

However, Gwenda was determined to seal the repair of their love, and after a while she climbed onto him, drawing her cloak over them both. As they began to move together, she saw an adolescent boy watching them, wide-eyed, a few yards away. Adults would politely look the other way, of course, but he was at the age where sex was a captivating mystery, and he obviously could not tear his gaze away. Gwenda was feeling so happy that she hardly cared. She met his eye, then smiled at him, without ceasing to move. His mouth fell open in shock, and he was struck by agonizing embarrassment. Looking mortified, he rolled over and covered his eyes with his arm.

Gwenda pulled her cloak up over her head and Wulfric's, buried her face in his neck, and gave herself up to pleasure.

37

Caris felt confident the second time she went to the royal court. The vast interior of Westminster Hall no longer intimidated her, nor did the mass of wealthy and powerful people crowding around the judges' benches. She had been here before, she knew the ropes, everything that had seemed so strange a year ago was now familiar. She even wore a dress in the London fashion, green on the right side and blue on the left. She enjoyed studying those around her, and reading their lives in their faces: cocksure or desperate, bewildered or sly. She could spot people who were new to the capital by their wide-eyed gaze and their air of uncertainty, and she felt pleasantly knowledgeable and superior.

If she had any misgivings, they centred on her lawyer, Francis Bookman. He was young and well informed, and—like most lawyers, she thought—he seemed very sure of himself. A small man with sandy hair, quick in his movements and always ready for an argument, he made her think of a cheeky bird on a window ledge, pecking crumbs and aggressively chasing away rivals. He had told them that their case was incontrovertible.

Godwyn had Gregory Longfellow, of course. Gregory had won the case against Earl Roland, and Godwyn had naturally asked him to represent the priory again. He had proved his ability, whereas Bookman was an unknown. However, Caris had a weapon up her sleeve, something that would come as a shock to Godwyn.

Godwyn showed no awareness that he had betrayed Caris, her father, and the entire city of Kingsbridge. He had always presented himself as a reformer, impatient of stick-in-the-mud Prior Anthony, sympathetic with the needs of the town, eager for the prosperity of monks and merchants alike. Then, within a year of becoming prior, he had turned to face the opposite way and become even more of a traditionalist than Anthony. Yet he appeared to feel no shame. Caris flushed with anger every time she thought of it.

He had no right to force the townspeople to use the fulling mill. His other impositions—the ban on hand mills, the fines for private fishponds and warrens—were technically correct, albeit outrageously harsh. But the fulling mill should be free, and Godwyn knew it. Caris wondered whether he believed that any deceit was pardonable provided it was done for the sake of God's work. Surely men of God should be *more* scrupulous about honesty than laymen, not less?

She put the point to her father, as they hung around the court, waiting for their case to come up. He said: "I never trust anyone who proclaims his morality from the pulpit. That high-minded type can always find an excuse for breaking his own rules. I'd rather do business with an everyday sinner who thinks it's probably to his advantage, in the long run, to tell the truth and keep his promises. He's not likely to change his mind about that."

In moments such as that, when Papa was his old self, Caris realized how much he had changed. Nowadays he was not often shrewd and quick-witted. More usually, he was forgetful and distracted. Caris suspected the decline had begun some months before she had noticed, and it probably accounted for his disastrous failure to anticipate the collapse of the wool market.

After several days' wait, they were called before Sir Wilbert Wheatfield, the pink-faced judge with rotten teeth who had ruled for the priory against Earl Roland a year ago. Caris's confidence began to ebb away as the judge took his seat on the bench against the east wall. It was frightening that a mere mortal should have such power. If he made the wrong decision, Caris's new cloth manufacturing enterprise would be blighted, her father would be ruined, and no one would be able to pay for the new bridge.

Then, as her lawyer began to speak, she started to feel better. Francis commenced with the history of the fulling mill, saying how it had been invented by the legendary Jack Builder, who built the first one, and how Prior Philip had given the townspeople the right to use it free.

He then dealt with Godwyn's counterarguments, disarming the prior in advance. "It is true that the mill is in bad repair, slow, and prone to frequent breakdowns," he said. "But how can the prior argue that the people have lost the right to it? The mill is the priory's property, and it is for the priory to keep it in good repair. The fact that he has failed in this duty makes no difference. The people have no right to repair the mill, and they certainly have no obligation so to do. Prior Philip's grant was not conditional."

At this point, Francis produced his secret weapon. "In case the prior should attempt to claim that the grant *was* conditional, I invite the court to read this copy of Prior Philip's will."

Godwyn was astonished. He had tried to pretend that the will had been lost. But Thomas Langley had agreed to look for it, as a favor to Merthin; and he had sneaked it out of the library, for a day, time enough for Edmund to have it copied.

Caris could not help enjoying the look of shock and outrage on Godwyn's face when he found that his deception had been foiled. He stepped forward and said indignantly: "How was this obtained?"

The question was revealing. He did not ask: "Where was it found?"—which would have been the logical inquiry if it had really been lost.

Gregory Longfellow looked annoyed, and waved at him with a hushing gesture; and Godwyn closed his mouth and stepped back, realizing he had given himself away—but it was surely too late, Caris thought. The judge must see that the only reason for Godwyn to be angry was that he knew the document favored the townspeople, and had attempted to suppress it.

Francis wound up quickly after that—a good decision, Caris thought, for Godwyn's duplicity would be fresh in the judge's mind while Gregory made the case for the defense.

But Gregory's approach took them all completely by surprise.

He stepped forward and said to the judge: "Sir, Kingsbridge is not a chartered borough." He stopped there, as if that was all he had to say.

It was true, technically. Most towns had a royal charter giving them the freedom to trade and hold markets without obligations to the local earl or baron. Their citizens were free men, owing allegiance to no one but the king. However, a few towns such as Kingsbridge remained the property of an overlord, usually a bishop or a prior: St. Albans and Bury St. Edmunds were examples. Their status was less clear.

The judge said: "That makes a difference. Only free men can appeal to the royal court. What do you have to say to that, Francis Bookman? Are your clients serfs?"

Francis turned to Edmund. In a low, urgent voice he said: "Have the townspeople appealed to the royal court before?"

"No. The prior has—"

"But not the parish guild? Even before your time?"

"There's no record of it—"

"So we can't argue from precedent. Damn." Francis turned back to the judge. His face changed from worried to confident in a flash, and he spoke as if condescending to deal with something trivial. "Sir, the townspeople are free. They enjoy burgess tenure."

Gregory said quickly: "There is no universal pattern of burgess tenure. It means different things in different places."

The judge said. "Is there a written statement of customs?"

Francis looked at Edmund, who shook his head. "No prior would ever agree to such things being written down," he muttered.

Francis turned back to the judge. "There is no written statement, sir, but clearly—"

"Then this court must decide whether or not you are free men," the judge said.

Edmund spoke directly to the judge. "Sir, the citizens have the freedom to buy and sell their homes." This was an important right not granted to serfs, who needed their lord's permission.

Gregory said: "But you have feudal obligations. You must use the prior's mills and fishponds."

Sir Wilbert said: "Forget fishponds. The key factor is the citizens' relationship to the system of royal justice. Does the town freely admit the king's sheriff?"

Gregory answered that. "No, he must ask permission to enter the town."

Edmund said indignantly: "That is the prior's decision, not ours!"

Sir Wilbert said: "Very well. Do the citizens serve on royal juries, or claim exemption?"

Edmund hesitated. Godwyn looked exultant. Serving on juries was a time-consuming chore that everyone avoided if they could. After a pause, Edmund said: "We claim exemption."

"Then that settles the matter," the judge said. "If you refuse that duty on the grounds that you are serfs, you cannot appeal over the head of your landlord to the king's justice."

Gregory said triumphantly: "In the light of that, I beg you to dismiss the townspeople's application."

"So ruled," said the judge.

Francis appeared outraged. "Sir, may I speak?"

"Certainly not," said the judge.

"But, sir—"

"Another word and I'll hold you in contempt."

Francis closed his mouth and bowed his head.

Sir Wilbert said: "Next case."

Another lawyer began to speak.

Caris was dazed.

Francis addressed her and her father in tones of protest. "You should have told me you were serfs!"

"We're not."

"The judge has just ruled that you are. I can't win cases on partial information."

She decided not to squabble with him. He was the type of young man who could not admit a mistake.

Godwyn was so pleased with himself that he looked as if he might burst. As he left, he could not resist a parting shot. He wagged a finger at Edmund and Caris. "I hope that, in future, you'll see the wisdom of submitting to the will of God," he said solemnly.

Caris said: "Oh, piss off," and turned her back.

She spoke to her father. "This makes us completely powerless! We proved we had the right to use the fulling mill free, but Godwyn can still withhold that right!"

"So it seems," he said.

She turned to Francis. "There must be *something* we can do," she said angrily.

"Well," he said, "you could get Kingsbridge made into a proper borough, with a royal charter setting out your rights and freedoms. Then you would have access to the royal court."

Caris saw a glimmer of hope. "How do we go about that?"

"You apply to the king."

"Would he grant it?"

"If you argued that you need this to be able to pay your taxes, he would certainly listen."

"Then we must try."

Edmund warned: "Godwyn will be furious."

"Let him," Caris said grimly.

"Don't underestimate the challenge," her father persisted. "You know how ruthless he is, even over small disputes. Something like this will lead to total war."

"So be it," said Caris bleakly. "Total war."

"Oh, Ralph, how could you do it?" said his mother.

Merthin studied his brother's face in the dim light of their parents' home. Ralph appeared torn between outright denial and self-justification.

In the end, Ralph said: "She led me on."

Maud was distressed more than angry. "But, Ralph, she is another man's wife!"

"A peasant's wife."

"Even so."

"Don't worry, Mother, they'll never convict a lord on the word of a serf."

Merthin was not so sure. Ralph was a minor lord, and it seemed he had incurred the enmity of William of Caster. There was no telling how the trial would come out.

Their father said sternly: "Even if they don't convict you—which I pray for—just think of the shame of it! You're the son of a knight—how could you forget that?"

Merthin was horrified and upset, but not surprised. That streak of violence had always been in Ralph's nature. In their boyhood he had ever been ready for a fight, and Merthin had often steered him away from fisticuffs, deflating a confrontation with a conciliatory word or a joke. Had anyone other than his brother committed this horrible rape, Merthin would have been hoping to see the man hang.

Ralph kept glancing at Merthin. He was worried about Merthin's disapproval—perhaps more so than his mother's. He had always looked up to his older brother. Merthin just wished there was some way Ralph could be shackled to prevent his attacking people, now that he no longer had Merthin nearby to keep him out of trouble.

The discussion with their distraught parents was set to go on for some time, but there was a knock at the door of the modest house, and Caris came in. She smiled at Gerald and Maud, though her face changed when she saw Ralph.

Merthin guessed she wanted him. He stood up. "I didn't know you were back from London," he said.

"Just arrived," she replied. "Can we have a few words?"

He pulled a cloak around his shoulders and stepped outside with her into the dim gray light of a cold December day. It was a year since she had terminated their love affair. He knew that her pregnancy had ended in the hospital, and he guessed she had somehow brought on the abortion deliberately. Twice in the following few weeks he had asked her to come back to him, but she had refused. It was bewildering: he sensed that she still loved him, but she was adamant. He had given up hope, and assumed that in time he would cease to grieve. So far, that had not happened. His heart still beat faster when he saw her, and he was happier talking to her than doing anything else in the world.

They walked to the main street and turned into the Bell. In the late afternoon the tavern was quiet. They ordered hot spiced wine.

"We lost the case," Caris said.

Merthin was shocked. "How is that possible? You had Prior Philip's will—"

"It made no difference." She was bitterly disappointed, Merthin could see. She explained: "Godwyn's smart lawyer argued that Kingsbridge people are serfs of the prior, and serfs have no right to appeal to the royal court. The judge dismissed the case."

Merthin felt angry. "But that's stupid. It means the prior can do anything he likes, regardless of laws and charters—"

"I know."

Merthin realized she was impatient because he was saying things she had said to herself many times. He suppressed his indignation and tried to be practical. "What are you going to do?"

"Apply for a borough charter. That would free the town from the control of the prior. Our lawyer thinks we have a strong case. Mind you, he thought we would win against the fulling mill. However, the king is desperate for money for this war against France. He needs prosperous towns to pay his taxes."

"How long would it take to get a charter?"

"That's the bad news—at least a year, perhaps more."

"And in that time, you can't manufacture scarlet cloth."

"Not with the old fulling mill."

"So we'll have to stop work on the bridge."

"I can't see any way out of it."

"Damn." It seemed so unreasonable. Here they had at their fingertips the means to restore the town's prosperity, and one man's stubbornness was preventing them. "How we all misjudged Godwyn," Merthin said.

"Don't remind me."

"We've got to escape from his control."

"I know."

"But sooner than a year from now."

"I wish there was a way."

Merthin racked his brains. At the same time, he was studying Caris. She was a wearing a new dress from London, particolored in the current fashion, which gave her a playful look, even though she was solemn and anxious. The colors, deep green and mid-blue, seemed to make her eyes sparkle and her skin glow. This happened every so often. He would be deep in conversation with her over some problem to do with the bridge—they rarely talked of anything else—then suddenly he would realize how lovely she was.

Even while he was thinking about that, the problem-solving part of his mind came up with a proposal. "We should build our own fulling mill."

Caris shook her head. "It would be illegal. Godwyn would order John Constable to pull it down."

"What if it were outside the town?"

"In the forest, you mean? That's illegal, too. You'd have the king's verderers on your back." Verderers enforced the laws of the forest.

"Not in the forest, then. Somewhere else."

"Wherever you went, you'd need the permission of some lord."

"My brother's a lord."

A look of distaste crossed Caris's face at the mention of Ralph, then her expression changed as she thought through what Merthin was saying. "Build a fulling mill at Wigleigh?"

"Why not?"

"Is there a fast-flowing stream to turn the mill wheel?"

"I believe so—but if not, it can be driven by an ox like the ferry."

"Would Ralph let you?"

"Of course. He's my brother. If I ask him, he'll say yes."

"Godwyn will go mad with rage."

"Ralph doesn't care about Godwyn."

Caris was pleased and excited, Merthin could see; but what were her feelings toward him? She was glad they had a solution to their problem, and eager to outwit Godwyn, but beyond that he could not read her mind.

"Let's think this through before we rejoice," she said. "Godwyn will make a rule saying cloth can't be taken out of Kingsbridge to be fulled. Lots of towns have laws like that."

"Very hard for him to enforce such a rule without the cooperation of a guild. And, if he does, you can get around it. Most of the cloth is being woven in the villages anyway, isn't it?"

"Yes."

"Then don't bring it into the city. Send it from the weavers to Wigleigh. Dye it there, full it in the new mill, then take it to London. Godwyn will have no jurisdiction."

"How long would it take to build a mill?"

Merthin considered. "The timber building can be put up in a couple of days. The machinery will be wooden, too, but it will take longer, as it has to be precisely measured. Getting the men and materials there will take the most time. I could have it finished a week after Christmas."

"That's wonderful," she said. "We'll do it."

Elizabeth rolled the dice and moved her last counter into the home position on the board. "I win!" she said. "That's three out of three. Pay up."

Merthin handed her a silver penny. Only two people ever beat him at tabula: Elizabeth and Caris. He did not mind losing. He was grateful for a worthy opponent.

He sat back and sipped his pear wine. It was a cold Saturday afternoon in January, and already dark. Elizabeth's mother was asleep in a chair near the fire, snoring gently with her mouth open. She worked at the Bell, but she was always at home when Merthin visited her daughter. He preferred it that way. It meant he never had to decide whether to kiss Elizabeth or not. It was a question he did not want to confront. He would have liked to kiss her, of course. He remembered the touch of her cool lips and the firmness of her flat breasts. But it would mean admitting that his love affair with Caris was over forever, and he was not yet ready for that.

"How is the new mill at Wigleigh?" Elizabeth asked.

"Finished, and rolling," Merthin said proudly. "Caris has been fulling cloth there for a week."

Elizabeth raised her eyebrows. "Herself?"

"No, that was a figure of speech. As a matter of fact, Mark Webber is running the mill, though he is training some of the village men to take over."

"It will be good for Mark if he becomes Caris's second-in-command. He's been poor all his life—this is a big opportunity."

"Caris's new enterprise will be good for us all. It will mean I can finish the bridge."

"She's a clever girl," Elizabeth said in a level voice. "But what does Godwyn have to say?"

"Nothing. I'm not sure he knows about it yet."

"He will, though."

"I don't believe there's anything he can do."

"He's a prideful man. If you've outwitted him, he'll never forgive you."

"I can live with that."

"And what about the bridge?"

"Despite all the problems, the work is only a couple of weeks behind schedule. I've had to spend money to catch up, but we will be able to use the bridge—with a temporary wooden roadbed—for the next Fleece Fair."

"You and Caris between you have saved the town."

"Not yet—but we will."

There was a knock at the door, and Elizabeth's mother woke up with a start. "Now who could that be?" she said. "It's dark out."

It was one of Edmund's apprentice boys. "Master Merthin is wanted at the parish guild meeting," he said.

"What for?" Merthin asked him.

"Master Edmund said to tell you, you're wanted at the parish guild meeting," the boy said. He had obviously learned the message off by heart and knew nothing more.

"Something about the bridge, I expect," Merthin said to Elizabeth. "They're worried about the cost." He picked up his cloak. "Thank you for the wine—and the game."

"I'll play you anytime you like," she said.

He walked beside the apprentice to the guildhall on the main street. The guild was holding a business meeting, not a banquet. The twenty or so most important people in Kingsbridge were sitting at a long trestle table, some drinking ale or wine, talking in low voices. Merthin sensed tension and anger, and he became apprehensive.

Edmund was at the head of the table. Prior Godwyn sat next to him. The prior was not a member of the guild: his presence suggested that Merthin's surmise had been right, and the meeting was about the bridge. However, Thomas the matricularius was not present, although Philemon was. That was odd.

Merthin had recently had a small dispute with Godwyn. His contract had been for a year at two pence a day plus the lease on Leper Island. It was due for renewal, and Godwyn had proposed to continue paying him two pence a day. Merthin had insisted on four pence, and in the end Godwyn had conceded the point. Had he complained about this to the guild?

Edmund spoke with characteristic abruptness. "We've called you here because Prior Godwyn wishes to dismiss you as master builder in charge of the bridge."

Merthin felt as if he had been punched in the face. He was not expecting anything like this. "What?" he said. "But Godwyn appointed me!"

Godwyn said: "And therefore I have the right to dismiss you."

"But why?

"The work is behind schedule and over budget."

"It's behind schedule because the earl closed the quarry—and it's over budget because I had to spend money to catch up."

"Excuses."

"Am I inventing the death of a carter?"

Godwyn shot back: "Killed by your own brother!"

"What has that to do with anything?"

Godwyn ignored the question. "A man who is accused of rape!" he added.

"You can't dismiss a master builder because of his brother's behavior."

"Who are you to say what I can do?"

"I'm the builder of your bridge!" Then it occurred to Merthin that much of his work as master builder was complete. He had designed all the most complicated parts and made wooden templates to guide the stonemasons. He had built the cofferdams, which no one else knew how to do. And he had constructed the floating cranes and hoists needed to move the heavy stones into position in midstream. Any builder could now finish the job, he realized with dismay.

"There is no guarantee of renewal of your contract," Godwyn said.

It was true. Merthin looked around the room for support. No one would meet his eye. They had already argued this out with Godwyn, he deduced. Despair overwhelmed him. Why had this happened? It was not because the bridge was behind schedule and over budget—the delay was not Merthin's fault, and anyway he was catching up. What was the real reason? As soon as he had asked the question, the answer came into his mind. "This is because of the fulling mill at Wigleigh!" he said.

Godwyn said primly: "The two things are not necessarily connected."

Edmund said quietly but distinctly: "Lying monk."

Philemon spoke for the first time. "Take care, Alderman!" he said.

Edmund was undeterred. "Merthin and Caris outwitted you, didn't they, Godwyn? Their mill at Wigleigh is entirely legitimate. You brought defeat on yourself by your greed and obstinacy. And this is your revenge."

Edmund was right. No one was as capable a builder as Merthin. Godwyn must know that, but clearly he did not care. "Who will you hire instead of me?" Merthin asked. Then he answered the question himself. "Elfric, I suppose."

"That has to be decided."

Edmund said: "Another lie."

Philemon spoke again, his voice more shrill. "You can be brought before the ecclesiastical court for talk like that!"

Merthin wondered if this might be no more than a move in the game, a way for Godwyn to renegotiate his contract. He said to Edmund: "Is the parish guild in agreement with the prior on this?"

Godwyn said: "It is not for them to agree or disagree!"

Merthin ignored him and looked expectantly at Edmund.

Edmund was shamefaced. "It cannot be denied that the prior has the right. The guildsmen are financing the bridge by loans, but the prior is overlord of the town. This was agreed from the start."

Merthin turned to Godwyn. "Do you have anything else to say to me, Lord Prior?" He waited, hoping in his heart that Godwyn would come out with his real demands.

But Godwyn said stonily: "No."

"Good night, then."

He waited a second longer. No one spoke. The silence told him it was all over.

He left the room.

Outside the building, he took a deep breath of the cold night air. He could hardly believe what had happened. He was no longer master of the bridge.

He walked through the dark streets. It was a clear night, and he could find his way by starlight. He walked past Elizabeth's house: he did not want to talk to her. He hesitated outside Caris's, but passed that, too, and went down to the waterside. His small rowboat was tied up opposite Leper Island. He got in and rowed himself across.

When he reached his house, he paused outside and looked up at the stars, fighting back tears. The truth was that in the end he had *not* outwitted Godwyn—rather the reverse. He had underestimated the lengths to which the prior would go to punish those who opposed him. Merthin had thought himself clever, but Godwyn had been cleverer, or at least more ruthless. He was prepared to damage the town and the priory, if necessary, to avenge a wound to his pride. And that had given him victory.

Merthin went inside and lay down, alone and beaten.

38

Ralph lay awake all through the night before his trial.

He had seen many people die by hanging. Every year, twenty or thirty men and a few women rode the sheriff's cart from the prison in

Shiring Castle down the hill to the market square where the gallows stood waiting. It was a common occurrence, but those men had remained in Ralph's memory, and on this night they returned to torment him.

Some died fast, their necks snapped by the drop; but not many. Most strangled slowly. They kicked and struggled and opened their mouths wide in silent, breathless screaming. They pissed and shat themselves. He recalled an old woman convicted of witchcraft: when she dropped, she bit right through her tongue and spat it out, and the crowd around the gallows had backed away in fright from the bloody lump of flesh as it flew through the air and fell on the dusty ground.

Everyone told Ralph he was not going to be hanged, but he could not get the thought out of his mind. People said that Earl Roland could not allow one of his lords to be executed on the word of a serf. However, so far the earl had done nothing to intervene.

The preliminary jury had returned an indictment against Ralph to the justice of the peace in Shiring. Like all such juries, it had consisted mainly of knights of the county owing allegiance to Earl Roland—but, despite this, they had acted on the evidence of the Wigleigh peasants. The men—jurors were never women, of course—had not flinched from indicting one of their own. In fact the jurors had shown, by their questions, some distaste for what Ralph had done, and several had refused to shake his hand afterward.

Ralph had planned to prevent Annet testifying again, at the trial proper, by imprisoning her in Wigleigh before she could leave for Shiring. However, when he went to her house to seize her, he found she had already departed. She must have anticipated his move and left earlier to foil him.

Today another jury would hear the case but, to Ralph's dismay, at least four of the men had been on the preliminary jury, too. Since the evidence on both sides was likely to be exactly the same, he could not see how this group could return a different verdict, unless some kind of pressure was put on the jurors—and it was getting very late for that.

He got up at first light and went downstairs to the ground floor of the Courthouse Inn on the market square of Shiring. He found a shivering boy breaking the ice on the well in the backyard and told him to fetch bread and ale. Then he went to the communal dormitory and woke his brother, Merthin.

They sat together in the cold parlor, with the stale smell of last night's ale and wine, and Ralph said: "I'm afraid they'll hang me."

"So am I," said Merthin.

"I don't know what to do." The boy brought two tankards and half a loaf. Ralph picked up his ale in a shaking hand and took a long draft.

Merthin ate some bread automatically, frowning and looking upward out of the corners of his eyes in the way he always did when he was racking his brains. "The only thing I can think of is to try to persuade Annet to drop the charge and come to a settlement. You'll have to offer her compensation."

Ralph shook his head. "She can't back out—it's not allowed. They'll punish her if she does."

"I know. But she could deliberately give weak evidence, making room for doubt. That's how it's usually done, I believe."

Hope sparked in Ralph's heart. "I wonder if she would consent."

The potboy brought in an armful of logs and knelt before the fireplace to start a fire.

Merthin said thoughtfully: "How much money could you offer Annet?"

"I've got twenty florins." That was worth three pounds of English silver pennies.

Merthin ran a hand through his untidy red hair. "It's not much."

"It's a lot to a peasant girl. On the other hand, her family is rich, for peasants."

"Doesn't Wigleigh yield you much money?"

"I've had to buy armor. When you're a lord you need to be ready to go to war."

"I could lend you money."

"How much have you got?"

"Thirteen pounds."

Ralph was so astonished that for a moment he forgot his troubles. "Where did you get all that?"

Merthin looked faintly resentful. "I work hard and I'm paid well."

"But you were sacked as master builder of the bridge."

"There's plenty more work. And I rent out land on Leper Island."

Ralph was indignant. "So a carpenter is richer than a lord!"

"Luckily for you, as it happens. How much do you think Annet will want?"

Ralph thought of a snag, and his spirits fell again. "It's not her, it's Wulfric. He's the ringleader in this."

"Of course." Merthin had spent a lot of time in Wigleigh while building the fulling mill, and he knew that Wulfric had married Gwenda only after being jilted by Annet. "Then let's talk to him."

Ralph did not think it would do any good, but he had nothing to lose.

They went out into the bleak gray daylight, pulling their cloaks around their shoulders against a cold February wind. They crossed the marketplace and entered the Bell, where the Wigleigh folk were staying—paid for, Ralph presumed, by Lord William, without whose help they would not have begun this process. But Ralph had no doubt that his real enemy was William's voluptuous, malevolent wife, Philippa, who seemed to hate Ralph, even though—or perhaps because—he found her fascinating and alluring.

Wulfric was up, and they found him eating porridge with bacon. When he saw Ralph, his face turned thunderous and he rose from his seat.

Ralph put his hand on his sword, ready to fight there and then, but Merthin hastily stepped forward, holding his hands open in front of him in a conciliatory gesture. "I come as a friend, Wulfric," he said. "Don't get angry, or you'll end up on trial instead of my brother."

Wulfric remained standing with his hands at his sides. Ralph was disappointed: the agony of his suspense would have been eased by a fight.

Wulfric spat a piece of bacon rind on the floor and swallowed, then said: "What do you want, if not trouble?"

"To make a settlement. Ralph is willing to pay Annet ten pounds by way of recompense for what he did."

Ralph was startled by the amount. Merthin would have to pay most of it—but he showed no hesitation.

Wulfric said: "Annet can't withdraw the charge—it's not allowed."

"But she can alter her evidence. If she says that at first she consented, then changed her mind when it was too late, the jury wouldn't convict Ralph."

Ralph watched Wulfric's face eagerly for a sign of willingness, but his expression remained stony, and he said: "So you're offering her a bribe to commit perjury?"

Ralph began to despair. He could see that Wulfric did not want Annet to be paid money. Revenge was his aim, not compensation. He wanted a hanging.

Merthin said reasonably: "I'm offering her a different kind of justice."

"You're trying to get your brother off the hook."

"Wouldn't you do the same? You had a brother once." Ralph recalled that Wulfric's brother had been killed, along with his parents, when the bridge collapsed. Merthin went on: "Wouldn't you try to save his life—even if he had done wrong?"

Wulfric appeared startled by this appeal to family feeling. Clearly it had never occurred to him to think of Ralph as someone with kinfolk who loved him. But he recovered after a moment and said: "My brother David would never have done what Ralph did."

"Of course," Merthin said soothingly. "All the same, you can't blame me for wanting to find a way to save Ralph, especially if it can be managed without doing an injustice to Annet."

Ralph admired his brother's smooth way of talking. He could charm a bird out of a tree, he thought.

But Wulfric was not easily persuaded. "The villagers want to see the back of Ralph. They're afraid he might do the same thing again."

Merthin sidestepped that. "Perhaps you should put our offer to Annet. It should be her decision, surely."

Wulfric looked thoughtful. "How could we be certain you would pay the money?"

Ralph's heart leaped. Wulfric was softening.

Merthin replied: "We'll give the cash to Caris Wooler before the trial. She will pay Annet after Ralph is declared innocent. You trust Caris, and we do, too."

Wulfric nodded. "As you say, it's not my decision. I'll put it to her." He went upstairs.

Merthin let out his breath in a long sigh. "By heaven, there's an angry man."

"You talked him round, though," Ralph said admiringly.

"He's only agreed to pass on a message."

They sat at the table Wulfric had vacated. A potboy asked them if they wanted breakfast, but they both refused. The parlor was full of guests calling for ham and cheese and ale. The inns were crowded with people attending the court. Unless they had a good excuse, all the knights of the shire were obliged to come, as were most other prominent men of the county: senior clergymen, wealthy merchants, and anyone with an income over forty pounds a year. Lord William, Prior Godwyn, and Edmund Wooler were all included. Ralph and Merthin's father, Sir Gerald, had been a regular attender before his fall from grace. They had to offer themselves as jurors and transact other business, such as paying their taxes or electing their Members of Parliament. In addition there was a host of accused men, victims, witnesses, and sureties. A court brought a lot of business to the inns of a town.

Wulfric kept them waiting. Ralph said: "What do you think they're talking about, up there?"

Merthin said: "Annet may be inclined to take the money. Her father would support her in that, and perhaps her husband, Billy Howard, too. But Wulfric is the type who thinks telling the truth is more important than money. His wife, Gwenda, will support him out of loyalty, and Father Gaspard will do the same on principle. Most importantly, they'll have to consult Lord William; and he'll do what Lady Philippa wants. She hates you, for some reason. On the other hand, a woman is more likely to choose reconciliation over confrontation."

"So it could go either way."

"Exactly."

The patrons of the inn finished their breakfasts and began to drift out, heading across the square to the Courthouse Inn, where the session would be held. Soon it would be too late.

At last Wulfric reappeared. "She says no," he said abruptly, and he turned away.

"Just a minute!" Merthin said.

Wulfric took no notice, and disappeared again up the stairs.

Ralph cursed. For a while he had hoped for a reprieve. Now he was in the hands of the jury.

He heard the sound of a handbell being rung vigorously outside. A sheriff's deputy was summoning all concerned to the court. Merthin stood up. Reluctantly, Ralph followed suit.

They walked back to the courthouse and went into the large back room. At the far end, the justice's "bench" stood on a raised dais. Although always called a bench, it was in fact a carved wooden chair like a throne. The justice was not seated, but his clerk was at a table in front of the dais, reading a scroll. Two long benches for the jurymen stood to one side. There were no other seats in the room: everyone else would stand wherever he wished. Order was maintained by the power of the justice to sentence instantly anyone who misbehaved: no trial was necessary for a crime that the judge had himself witnessed. Ralph spotted Alan Fernhill, looking terrified, and stood beside him without speaking.

Ralph began to think he should never have come here. He could have made an excuse: sickness, a misunderstanding about dates, a horse lamed on the road. But that would only have brought him a postponement. Eventually the sheriff would have come, with armed deputies, to arrest him; and if he evaded them, he would have been declared an outlaw.

However, that was better than hanging. He wondered if he should flee now. He could probably fight his way out of the tavern. But he would not get far on foot. He would be chased by half the town, and if they did not catch him, the sheriff's deputies would follow on horseback. And his flight would be seen as an admission of guilt. As things stood, he still had a chance of acquittal. Annet might be too intimidated to give her evidence clearly. Perhaps key witnesses would fail to show up. There could be some last-minute intervention by Earl Roland.

The courtroom filled up: Annet, the villagers, Lord William and Lady Philippa, Edmund Wooler and Caris, Prior Godwyn and his slimy assistant Philemon. The clerk banged on his table for quiet, and the justice came through a side door. It was Sir Guy de Bois, a large landholder. He had a bald head and a fat belly. He was an old comrade-in-arms of the earl's, which might stand in Ralph's favor; but, on the other side of the balance, he was Lady Philippa's uncle, and she might have whispered malice in his ear. He had the flushed look of a man who has breakfasted on salt beef and strong ale. He sat down, farted loudly, sighed with satisfaction, and said: "All right, let's get on with it."

Earl Roland was not present.

Ralph's case came first: it was the one that most interested everybody, including the justice. The indictment was read, and Annet was called to give her evidence.

Ralph found it strangely difficult to concentrate. He had heard it all before, of course, but he should have been listening hard for any discrepancy in the story Annet told today, any sign of uncertainty, any hesitation or faltering. But he felt fatalistic. His enemies were out in full force. His one powerful friend, Earl Roland, was absent. Only his brother stood beside him, and Merthin had already tried his best to help, and failed. Ralph was doomed.

The witnesses followed: Gwenda, Wulfric, Peg, Gaspard. Ralph had thought he had absolute power over these people, but somehow they had conquered him. The foreman of the jury, Sir Herbert Montain, was one of those who had refused to shake Ralph's hand, and he asked questions that seemed designed to emphasize the horror of the crime: How bad was the pain? How much blood? Was she weeping?

When it was Ralph's turn to speak, he told the story that had been disbelieved by the jury of indictment, and he told it in a low voice, stumbling over his words. Alan Fernhill did better, saying firmly that Annet had been eager to lie with Ralph, and that the two lovers had asked him to make himself scarce while they enjoyed one another's favors beside the stream. But the jury did not believe him: Ralph could tell by their faces. He began to feel almost bored by the proceedings, wishing they would be over, and his fate sealed.

As Alan stepped back, Ralph was conscious of a new figure at his shoulder, and a low voice said: "Listen to me."

Ralph glanced behind and saw Father Jerome, the earl's clerk, and the thought crossed his mind that a court such as this had no power over priests, even if they committed crimes.

The justice turned to the jury and asked for their verdict.

Father Jerome murmured: "Your horses stand outside, saddled and ready to go."

Ralph froze. Was he hearing correctly? He turned and said: "What?"

"Run for it."

Ralph looked behind him. A hundred men barred his way to the door, many of them armed. "It's not possible."

"Use the side door," Jerome said, indicating with a slight inclination of his head the entrance through which the justice had come. Ralph saw immediately that only the Wigleigh people stood between him and the side door.

The foreman of the jury, Sir Herbert, stood up, looking self-important.

Ralph caught the eye of Alan Fernhill, standing beside him. Alan had heard everything and looked expectant.

"Go now!" whispered Jerome.

Ralph put his hand on his sword.

"We find Lord Ralph of Wigleigh guilty of rape," said the foreman.

Ralph drew his sword. Waving it in the air, he dashed for the door.

There was a second of stunned silence, then everyone shouted at once. But Ralph was the one man in the room with a weapon in his hand, and he knew it would take the others a moment to draw.

Only Wulfric tried to stop him, stepping into his path heedlessly, not even looking scared, just determined. Ralph raised his sword and brought it down, as hard as he could, aiming at the middle of Wulfric's skull, intending to cleave it in two. But Wulfric stepped nimbly back and to the side. Nevertheless, the point of the sword sliced through the left side of his face, cutting it open from the temple to the jaw. Wulfric cried out in sudden agony, and his hands flew to his cheek; and then Ralph was past him.

He flung open the door, stepped through, and turned. Alan Fernhill dashed past him. The foreman of the jury was close behind Alan, sword drawn and raised. Ralph experienced a moment of pure elation. This was how things should be settled—by a fight, not a discussion. Win or lose, he preferred it this way.

With a yell of exhilaration he thrust at Sir Herbert. The point of his sword touched the foreman's chest, ripping through his leather tunic; but the man was too distant for the blow to penetrate the ribs, and it merely cut his skin then glanced off the bones. All the same, Herbert cried out—more in fear than pain—and stumbled back, colliding with those behind him. Ralph slammed the door on them.

He found himself in a passage that ran the length of the house, with a door to the market square at one end and another to the stable yard at the other. Where were the horses? Jerome had said only that they were outside. Alan was already running for the back door, so Ralph followed. As they burst into the yard, a hubbub behind them told him that the courtroom door had been opened and the crowd was after him.

There was no sign of their horses in the yard.

Ralph ran under the arch that led to the front.

There stood the most welcome sight in the world: his hunter, Griff, saddled and pawing the ground, with Alan's two-year-old Fletch beside him, both held by a barefoot stable boy with his mouth full of bread.

Ralph seized the reins and jumped on his horse. Alan did the same. They kicked their beasts just as the mob from the courtroom came through the arch. The stable boy threw himself out of the way, terrified. The horses surged forward and away.

Someone in the crowd threw a knife. It stuck a quarter of an inch into Griff's flank, then fell away, serving only to spur the horse on.

They galloped flat out through the streets, scattering townspeople before them, careless of men, women, children, and livestock. They charged through a gate in the old wall and passed into a suburb of houses interspersed with gardens and orchards. Ralph looked behind. No pursuers were in sight.

The sheriff's men would come after them, of course, but they had first to fetch horses and saddle them. Ralph and Alan were already a mile from the market square, and their mounts showed no signs of tiring. Ralph was filled with glee. Five minutes ago he had reconciled himself to being hanged. Now he was free!

The road forked. Choosing at random, Ralph turned left. A mile away across the fields he could see woodland. Once there, he would turn off the track, and disappear.

But what would he do then?

39

"Earl Roland was clever," Merthin said to Elizabeth Clerk. "He allowed justice to take its course almost to the end. He didn't bribe the judge or influence the jury or intimidate the witnesses, and he avoided a quarrel with his son, Lord William. But he escaped the humiliation of seeing one of his men hanged."

"Where is your brother now?" she said.

"No idea. I haven't spoken to him or even seen him since that day."

They were sitting in Elizabeth's kitchen on Sunday afternoon. She had made dinner for him: boiled ham with stewed apples and winter greens, and a small jug of wine that her mother had bought, or perhaps stolen, from the inn where she worked.

Elizabeth said: "What will happen now?"

"The sentence of death still hangs over him. He can't return to Wigleigh, or come here to Kingsbridge, without getting arrested. In effect, he's declared himself an outlaw."

"Is there nothing he can do?"

"He could get a pardon from the king—but that costs a fortune, far more money than he or I could raise."

"And how do you feel about him?"

Merthin winced. "Well, he deserves punishment for what he did, of course. All the same, I can't wish it on him. I just hope he's all right, wherever he is."

He had told the story of Ralph's trial many times in the last few days, but Elizabeth had asked the most astute questions. She was intelligent and sympathetic. The thought crossed his mind that it would be no hardship to spend every Sunday afternoon this way.

Her mother, Sairy, was dozing by the fire, as usual, but now she opened her eyes and said: "My soul! I've forgotten the pie." She stood up, patting her mussed gray hair. "I promised to ask Betty Baxter to make a pie with ham and eggs for the leather-tanners guild. They're holding their last-before-Lent dinner at the Bell tomorrow." She draped a blanket around her shoulders and went out.

It was unusual for them to be left alone together, and Merthin felt slightly awkward, but Elizabeth seemed relaxed enough. She said: "What are you doing with yourself, now that you no longer work on the bridge?"

"I'm building a house for Dick Brewer, among other things. Dick's ready to retire and hand over to his son, but he says he'll never stop work while he's living at the Copper, so he wants a house with a garden outside the old city walls."

"Oh—is that the building site beyond Lovers' Field?"

"Yes. It will be the biggest house in Kingsbridge."

"A brewer is never short of money."

"Would you like to see it?"

"The site?"

"The house. It's not finished, but it's got four walls and a roof."

"Now?"

"There's still an hour of daylight."

She hesitated, as if she might have had another plan; but then she said: "I'd love to."

They put on heavy cloaks with hoods and went out. It was the first day of March. Flurries of snow chased them down the main street. They took the ferry to the suburban side.

Despite the ups and downs of the wool trade, the town seemed to grow a little every year, and the priory turned more and more of its pasture and orchards into house plots for rent. Merthin guessed there must be fifty dwellings that had not been here when he first came to Kingsbridge, as a boy, twelve years ago.

Dick Brewer's new home was a two-story structure set back from the road. As yet it had no window shutters or doors, so the gaps in the walls had been temporarily covered with hurdles, wood frames filled in with woven reeds. The front entrance was thus blocked, but Merthin took Elizabeth to the back, where there was a temporary wooden door with a lock.

Merthin's sixteen-year-old assistant, Jimmie, was in the kitchen, guarding the place from thieves. He was a superstitious boy, always crossing himself and throwing salt over his shoulder. He was sitting on a bench in front of a big fire, but he looked anxious. "Hello, master," he said. "Now that you're here, may I go and get my dinner? Lol Turner was supposed to bring it, but he hasn't come."

"Make sure you're back before it gets dark."

"Thank you." He hurried off.

Merthin stepped through the doorway to the interior of the house. "Four rooms downstairs," he said, showing her.

She was incredulous. "What will they use them all for?"

"Kitchen, parlor, dining room, and hall." There was no staircase yet, but Merthin climbed a ladder to the upper floor, and Elizabeth followed. "Four bedrooms," he said as she reached the top.

"Who will live here?"

"Dick and his wife, his son Danny and *his* wife, and his daughter, who probably won't remain single for ever."

Most Kingsbridge families lived in one room, and all slept side by side on the floor: parents, children, grandparents, and in-laws. Elizabeth said: "This place has more rooms than a palace!"

It was true. A nobleman with a big entourage might still live in two rooms: a bedchamber for himself and his wife, and a great hall for everyone else. But Merthin had now designed several houses for wealthy Kingsbridge merchants, and the luxury they all craved was privacy. It was a new trend, he thought.

"I suppose there will be glass in the windows," Elizabeth said.

"Yes." That was another trend. Merthin could remember the time when there was no glazier in Kingsbridge, just an itinerant who called every year or two. Now the city had a resident glazier.

They returned to the ground floor. Elizabeth sat on Jimmie's bench in front of the fire and warmed her hands. Merthin sat beside her. "I'll build a house like this for myself, one day," he said. "In a big garden with fruit trees."

To his surprise, she leaned her head on his shoulder. "What a nice dream," she said.

They both stared into the fire. Her hair tickled Merthin's cheek. After a moment, she laid a hand on his knee. In the silence, he could hear her breathing, and his own, and the crackle of burning logs.

"In your dream, who's in the house?" she said.

"I don't know."

"Just like a man. I can't see my house, but I know who's in it: a husband, some babies, my mother, an elderly parent-in-law, and three servants."

"Men and women have different dreams."

She lifted her head, looked at him, and touched his face. "And when you put them together, you have a life." She kissed his mouth.

He closed his eyes. He remembered the soft touch of her lips from years ago. Her mouth lingered on his for just a moment, then she drew back.

He felt oddly detached, as if he were watching himself from a corner of the room. He did not know how he felt. He looked at her and saw again how lovely she was. He asked himself what was so striking about her, and realized immediately that everything was in harmony, like the parts of a beautiful church. Her mouth, her chin, her cheekbones, and her forehead were just as he would have drawn them if he had been God creating a woman.

She looked back at him with calm blue eyes. "Touch me," she said. She opened her cloak.

He took her breast gently in his hand. He remembered doing this, too. Her breasts were firm and flat against her chest. Her nipple hardened immediately to his touch, betraying her calm demeanor.

"I want to be in your dream house," she said, and she kissed him again.

She was not acting on the spur of the moment; Elizabeth never did. She had been thinking about this. While he had been casually visiting her, enjoying her company without thinking any farther, she had been imagining their life together. Perhaps she had even planned this scene. That would explain why her mother had left them with an excuse about a pie. He had almost spoiled her plan by proposing to show her Dick Brewer's house, but she had improvised.

There was nothing wrong with such an unemotional approach. She was a reasoning person. It was one of the things he liked about her. He knew that passions burned nonetheless beneath the surface.

What seemed wrong was his own lack of feeling. It was not his way to be coolly rational about women—quite the reverse. When he had felt love, it had taken him over, making him feel rage and resentment as well as lust and tenderness. Now he felt interested, flattered, and titillated, but he was not out of control.

She sensed that his kiss was lukewarm, and drew back. He saw the ghost of an emotion on her face, fiercely suppressed, but he knew there was fear behind the mask. She was so poised, by nature, that it must have cost her a lot to be so forward, and she dreaded rejection.

She drew away from him, stood up, and lifted the skirt of her dress. She had long, shapely legs covered with nearly invisible fine blond hair. Although she was tall and slim, her body widened just below the hips in a delightfully womanly way. His gaze homed in helplessly on the delta of her sex. Her hair was so fair that he could see through it, to the pale swelling of the lips and the delicate line between them.

He looked up to her face and read desperation there. She had tried everything, and she saw that it had not worked.

Merthin said: "I'm sorry."

She dropped her skirts.

"Listen," he said. "I think—"

She interrupted him. "Don't speak." Her desire was turning to anger. "Whatever you say now will be a lie."

She was right. He had been trying to formulate some soothing half-truth: he was not feeling well, or Jimmie might be back at any moment.

But she did not want to be mollified. She had been rebuffed, and feeble excuses would only make her feel patronized as well.

She stared at him, grief struggling with rage on the battleground of her beautiful face. Tears of frustration came to her eyes. "Why not?" she cried; but when he opened his mouth to reply she said: "Don't answer! It won't be the truth"; and again she was right.

She turned to go, then came back. "It's Caris," she said, her face working with emotion. "That witch has cast a spell on you. She won't marry you, but no one else can have you. She's evil!"

At last she walked away. She flung open the door and stepped out. He heard her sob once, then she was gone.

Merthin stared into the fire. "Oh, hell," he said.

"There's something I need to explain to you," Merthin said to Edmund a week later, as they were leaving the cathedral.

Edmund's face took on a look of mild amusement that was familiar to Merthin. *I'm thirty years older than you,* the look said, *and you should be listening to me, not giving me lessons; but I enjoy youthful enthusiasm. Besides, I'm not yet too old to learn something.* "All right," he said. "But explain it in the Bell. I want a cup of wine."

They went into the tavern and sat close to the fire. Elizabeth's mother brought their wine, but she stuck her nose in the air and did not talk to them. Edmund said: "Is Sairy angry with you or me?"

"Never mind that," said Merthin. "Have you ever stood at the edge of the ocean, with your bare feet on the sand, and felt the sea wash over your toes?"

"Of course. All children play in water. Even I was a boy once."

"Do you remember how the action of the waves, flowing in and out, seems to scour the sand from under the edges of your feet, making a little channel?"

"Yes. It's a long time ago, but I think I know what you mean."

"That's what happened to the old wooden bridge. The flowing river scoured the earth from under the central pier."

"How do you know?"

"By the pattern of cracks in the woodwork just before the collapse."

"What's your point?"

"The river hasn't changed. It will undermine the new bridge just as surely as it did the old—unless we prevent it."

"How?"

"In my drawing, I showed a pile of large, loose stones surrounding each of the piers of the new bridge. They will break up the current and enfeeble its effect. It's the difference between being tickled by loose thread and being flogged with a tightly woven rope."

"How do you know?"

"I asked Buonaventura about it, immediately after the bridge collapsed, before he went back to London. He said he had seen such piles of stones around the piers of bridges in Italy, and he had often wondered what they were for."

"Fascinating. Are you telling me this for general enlightenment, or is there some more specific purpose?"

"People like Godwyn and Elfric don't understand this, and wouldn't listen if I told them. Just in case Elfric takes it into his fool head not to follow my design exactly, I want to be sure that at least one person in town knows the reason for the pile of stones."

"But one person does—you."

"I'm leaving Kingsbridge."

That shocked him. "Leaving?" he said. "You?"

At that moment, Caris appeared. "Don't stay here too long," she said to her father. "Aunt Petranilla is preparing dinner. Do you want to join us, Merthin?"

Edmund said: "Merthin's leaving Kingsbridge."

Caris paled.

Seeing her reaction, Merthin felt a jolt of satisfaction. She had rejected him, but she was dismayed to hear that he was leaving town. He immediately felt ashamed of such an unworthy emotion. He was too fond of her to want her to suffer. All the same, he would have felt worse if she had received the news with equanimity.

"Why?" she said.

"There's nothing for me here. What am I going to build? I can't work on the bridge. The town already has a cathedral. I don't want to do nothing but merchants' houses for the rest of my life."

In a quiet voice, she said: "Where will you go?"

"Florence. I've always wanted to see the buildings of Italy. I'll ask Buonaventura Caroli for letters of introduction. I might even be able to travel with one of his consignments."

"But you own property here in Kingsbridge."

"I wanted to speak to you about that. Would you manage it for me? You could collect my rents, take a commission, and give the balance to Buonaventura. He can transfer money to Florence by letter."

"I don't want a damn commission," she said huffily.

Merthin shrugged. "It's work, you should be paid."

"How can you be so cold about it?" she said. Her voice was shrill, and around the parlor of the Bell several people looked up. She took no notice. "You'll be leaving all your friends!"

"I'm not cold about it. Friends are great. But I'd like to get married."

Edmund put in: "Plenty of girls in Kingsbridge would marry you. You're not handsome, but you're prosperous, and that's worth more than good looks."

Merthin smiled wryly. Edmund could be disarmingly blunt. Caris had inherited the trait. "For a while I thought I might marry Elizabeth Clerk," he said.

Edmund said: "So did I."

Caris said: "She's a cold fish."

"No, she's not. But when she asked me, I backed off."

Caris said: "Oh—so that's why she's so bad-tempered lately."

Edmund said: "And why her mother won't look at Merthin."

"Why did you refuse her?" Caris asked.

"There's only one woman in Kingsbridge I could marry—and she doesn't want to be anyone's wife."

"But she doesn't want to lose you."

Merthin became angry. "What should I do?" he said. His voice was loud, and people around them stopped their conversations to listen. "Godwyn has fired me, you've rejected me, and my brother is an outlaw. In God's name, why should I stay here?"

"I don't want you to go," she said.

"That's not enough!" he shouted.

The room was silent now. Everyone there knew them: the landlord, Paul Bell, and his curvy daughter Bessie; the gray-haired barmaid Sairy, Elizabeth's mother; Bill Watkin, who had refused to employ Merthin; Edward Butcher, the notorious adulterer; Jake Chepstow, Merthin's tenant; Friar Murdo, Matthew Barber, and Mark Webber. They all knew the history of Merthin and Caris, and they were fascinated by the quarrel.

Merthin did not care. Let them listen. He said furiously: "I'm not going to spend my life hanging around you, like your dog Scrap, waiting for your attention. I'll be your husband, but I won't be your pet."

"All right, then," she said in a small voice.

Her sudden change of tone surprised him, and he was not sure what she meant. "All right, what?"

"All right, I'll marry you."

For a moment, he was too shocked to speak. Then he said suspiciously: "Do you mean it?"

She looked up at him at last and smiled shyly. "Yes, I mean it," she said. "Just ask me."

"All right." He took a deep breath. "Will you marry me?"

"Yes, I will," she said.

Edmund shouted: "Hoorah!"

Everyone in the tavern cheered and clapped.

Merthin and Caris started laughing. "Will you, really?" he said.

"Yes."

They kissed, then he put his arms around her and squeezed as hard as he could. When he let her go, he saw that she was crying.

"Some wine for my betrothed," he called out. "A barrel, in fact—give everyone a cup, so they can all drink our health!"

"Coming right up," said the landlord, and they all cheered again.

A week later, Elizabeth Clerk became a novice nun.

40

Ralph and Alan were miserable. They were living on venison and cold water, and Ralph found himself dreaming about food he would normally scorn: onions, apples, eggs, milk. They slept in a different place every night, always lighting a fire. They each had a good cloak, but it was not enough out in the open, and they woke shivering every dawn. They robbed any vulnerable people they met on the road, but most of the loot was either paltry or useless: ragged clothes, animal fodder, and money, which would buy nothing in the forest.

Once they stole a big barrel of wine. They rolled it a hundred yards into the woods, drank as much as they could, and fell asleep. When they woke up, hungover and ill-tempered, they realized they could not take the three-quarters-full barrel with them, so they just left it there.

Ralph thought nostalgically of his former life: the manor house, the roaring fires, the servants, the dinners. But, in his realistic moments, he knew he did not want that life either. It was too dull. That was probably why he had raped the girl. He needed excitement.

After a month in the forest, Ralph decided they had to get organized. They needed a base where they could build some kind of shelter and store food. And they had to plan their robberies so that they stole items that would be really valuable to them, such as warm clothing and fresh food.

Around the time he was coming to this realization, their wanderings brought them to a range of hills a few miles from Kingsbridge. Ralph recalled that the hillsides, bleak and bare in winter, were used for summer grazing by shepherds, who had built rough stone shelters in the folds of the landscape. As adolescents he and Merthin had discovered these crude buildings while out hunting, and had lit fires and cooked the rabbits and partridges they shot with their bows. Even in those days, he recalled, he had craved the thrill of the hunt: chasing and shooting a terrified creature, finishing it off with a knife or club—the ecstatic sense of power that came from taking a life.

No one would come here until the new season's grass was thick. The traditional day was Whitsunday, also the opening day of the Fleece Fair, still two months away. Ralph selected a hut that looked sturdy, and they made it their home. There were no doors or windows, just a low entrance, but there was a hole in the roof to let smoke out, and they lit a fire and slept warm for the first time in a month.

Proximity to Kingsbridge gave Ralph another bright idea. The time to rob people, he realized, was when they were on their way to market. They were carrying cheeses, flagons of cider, honey, oatcakes: all the things that were produced by villagers and needed by townspeople—and by outlaws.

Kingsbridge market was on a Sunday. Ralph had lost track of the days of the week, but he found out by asking a traveling friar, before robbing him of three shillings and a goose. On the following Saturday, he and Alan made camp not far from the road to Kingsbridge, and stayed awake all night by their fire. At dawn they made their way to the road and lay in wait.

The first group to come along were carting fodder. Kingsbridge had hundreds of horses and very little grass, so the town constantly needed supplies of hay. However, it was no use to Ralph: Griff and Fletch had no end of grazing in the forest.

Ralph was not bored waiting. Preparing an ambush was like watching a woman get undressed. The longer the anticipation, the more intense the thrill.

Soon afterward they heard singing. The hairs on the back of Ralph's neck stood up: it sounded like angels. The morning was hazy, and when he first saw the singers, they seemed to have halos. Alan, obviously thinking the same as Ralph, even gave a sob of fear. But it was only the weak winter sun lighting the mist behind the travelers. They were peasant women, each carrying a basket of eggs—hardly worth robbing. Ralph let them go by without revealing himself.

The sun rose a little higher. Ralph began to worry that soon the road would become sufficiently crowded with marketgoers to make robbery difficult. Then along came a family: a man and woman in their thirties with two adolescent children, a boy and a girl. They were vaguely familiar: no doubt he had seen them at Kingsbridge market during the years he lived there. They carried an assortment of goods. The husband had a heavy basket of vegetables on his back; the wife balanced on her shoulder a long pole bearing several live chickens, trussed; the boy had a heavy ham on his shoulder and the girl a crock that probably contained salted butter. Ralph's mouth watered at the thought of ham.

The excitement rose in his guts, and he gave Alan a nod.

As the family drew level, Ralph and Alan came out of the bushes at a run.

The woman screamed and the boy gave a shout of fear.

The man tried to shrug off his basket but, before it fell from his shoulders, Ralph ran him through, his sword piercing the man's abdomen under the ribs and then rising up. The man's scream of agony was cut off abruptly as the point of the sword penetrated his heart.

Alan swung at the woman and cut through most of her neck, so that blood spurted from her severed throat in a sudden red jet.

Exhilarated, Ralph turned to the son. The lad was quick to react: he had already dropped his ham and drawn a knife. While Ralph's weapon was still on the upswing, the boy darted close and stabbed him. It was an unprofessional blow, too wild to do much damage. The knife completely missed Ralph's chest, but the point caught in the flesh of his upper right arm, and the sudden agonizing pain made him drop his sword. The boy turned and ran away, going in the direction of Kingsbridge.

Ralph looked at Alan. Before turning to the girl, Alan finished off the mother, and the delay almost cost him his life. Ralph saw the girl throw her crock of butter at Alan. Either accurate or lucky, she hit him square on the back of the head, and Alan fell to the ground as if poleaxed.

Then she ran after her brother.

Ralph stooped, picked up his sword in his left hand, and gave chase.

They were young and fleet, but he had long legs, and he soon gained on them. The boy looked over his shoulder and saw Ralph coming close. To Ralph's astonishment the lad stopped, turned, and came running back at him, screaming, knife raised in his fist.

Ralph stopped running and lifted his sword. The boy ran at him—then stopped outside his reach. Ralph stepped forward and lunged, but it was a feint. The boy dodged the blow; then, thinking to catch Ralph off balance, tried to step inside his guard and stab him at close quarters. But that was exactly what Ralph was expecting. He stepped nimbly back, stood on the balls of his feet, and thrust his sword precisely into the boy's throat, pushing it through until the point came out of the back of his neck.

The boy fell dead, and Ralph withdrew his sword, pleased with the accuracy and efficiency of the death blow.

He looked up to see the girl disappearing into the distance. He saw immediately that he could not catch her on foot; and by the time he fetched his horse, she would be in Kingsbridge.

He turned and looked back. To his surprise, Alan was struggling to his feet. "I thought she'd killed you," Ralph said. He wiped his sword on the dead boy's tunic, sheathed his blade, and clamped his left hand over the wound in his right arm, trying to stop the bleeding.

"My head hurts like Satan," Alan replied. "Did you kill them all?"

"The girl got away."

"Do you think she knew us?"

"She might know me. I've seen this family before."

"In that case, we're now branded as murderers."

Ralph shrugged. "Better to hang than starve." He looked at the three bodies. "All the same, let's get these peasants off the road before someone comes along."

With his left hand he dragged the man to the edge of the road. Alan picked up the body and threw it into the bushes. They did the same with the woman and the boy. Ralph made sure the corpses were not visible to passersby. The blood on the road was already darkening to the color of the mud into which it was soaking.

Ralph cut a strip off the woman's dress and tied it around the cut in his arm. It still hurt, but the flow of blood was less. He felt the slight depression that always followed a fight, like the sadness after sex.

Alan began to collect up the loot. "A nice haul," he said. "Ham, chickens, butter . . . ," he looked into the basket the man had been carrying, ". . . and onions! Last year's, of course, but still good."

"Old onions taste better than no onions. My mother says that."

As Ralph bent to pick up the butter crock that had felled Alan, he felt a sharp iron point stick into his ass. Alan was in front of him, dealing with the trussed chickens. Ralph said: "Who . . . ?"

A harsh voice said: "Don't move."

Ralph never obeyed such instructions. He sprang forward, away from the voice, and spun around. Six or seven men had materialized from nowhere. He was bewildered, but he managed, left-handed, to draw his sword. The man nearest him—who presumably had prodded him—raised his sword to fight, but the others were grabbing the loot, snatching chickens and fighting over the ham. Alan's sword flashed in defense of his chickens as Ralph engaged with his antagonist. He realized that another group of outlaws was trying to rob him. He was filled with indignation: he had killed people for this stuff, and now they wanted to take it from him! He felt no fear, only anger. He attacked his opponent with the energy of outrage, despite being forced to fight left-handed. Then an authoritative voice said loudly: "Put away your blades, you fools."

All the newcomers stood still. Ralph held his sword at the ready, suspicious of a trick, and looked toward the voice. He saw a handsome man in his twenties with something of the nobility about him. He wore clothes that looked expensive but were filthy dirty: a cloak of Italian scarlet covered with leaves and twigs, a rich brocade coat marked with what appeared to be food stains, and hose of a rich chestnut leather, scratched and muddy.

"It amuses me to steal from thieves," the newcomer said. "It's not a crime, you see."

Ralph knew he was in a tight spot but, all the same, he was intrigued. "Are you the one they call Tam Hiding?" he said.

"There were stories of Tam Hiding when I was a child," the man replied. "But every now and again someone comes along to act the part, like a monk impersonating Lucifer in a mystery play."

"You're not a common type of outlaw."

"Nor are you. I'm guessing that you're Ralph Fitzgerald."

Ralph nodded.

"I heard about your escape, and I've been wondering when I'd run into you." Tam looked up and down the road. "We happened upon you by accident. What made you choose this spot?"

"I picked the day and time, first. It's Sunday, and at this hour the peasants are taking their produce to market in Kingsbridge, which is on this road."

"Well, well. Ten years I've been living outside the law, and I never thought of doing that. Perhaps we should team up. Are you going to put your weapon away?"

Ralph hesitated, but Tam was unarmed, so he could not see the disadvantage. Anyway, he and Alan were so heavily outnumbered that it would be best to avoid a fight. Slowly, he sheathed his sword.

"That's better." Tam put an arm around Ralph's shoulders, and Ralph realized they were the same height. Not many people were as tall as Ralph. Tam walked him into the woods, saying: "The others will bring the loot. Come this way. We've got a lot to talk about, you and I."

Edmund rapped on the table. "I've called this emergency meeting of the parish guild to discuss the outlaw problem," he said. "But, as I'm getting old and lazy, I've asked my daughter to summarize the situation."

Caris was a member of the parish guild now, by virtue of her success as a manufacturer of scarlet cloth. The new business had rescued her father's fortunes. Numerous other Kingsbridge people were prospering because of it, notably the Webber family. Her father had been able to fulfill his pledge to lend money for the building of the bridge, and in the general upturn several other merchants had done the same. Bridge building continued apace—supervised now by Elfric, not Merthin, unfortunately.

Her father took little initiative these days. The moments when he was his sharp-witted former self were becoming rarer. She was worried about him, but there was nothing she could do. She felt the rage that had possessed her during her mother's illness. Why was there no help for him? Nobody understood what was wrong; no one could even put a name to his malady. They said it was old age, but he was not yet fifty!

She prayed he would live to see her wedding. She was going to marry Merthin in Kingsbridge Cathedral on the Sunday after the Fleece Fair, now just a month away. The wedding of the daughter of the town's alderman would be a big event. There would be a banquet in the guildhall for the leading citizens, and a picnic in Lovers' Field for several hundred more guests. Some days her father would spend hours planning the menus and the entertainment, only to forget everything he had said and start again from scratch the next day.

She put that out of her mind, and turned her attention to a problem she hoped would be more tractable. "In the last month there has been a big increase in attacks by outlaws," she said. "They take place mainly on Sundays, and the victims are invariably people bringing produce to Kingsbridge."

She was interrupted by Elfric. "It's your fiancé's brother that's doing it!" he said. "Talk to Merthin, not us."

Caris suppressed a flash of exasperation. Her sister's husband never missed a chance to snipe at her. She was painfully aware of Ralph's likely involvement. It was a cause of agony to Merthin. Elfric relished that.

Dick Brewer said: "I think it's Tam Hiding."

"Perhaps it's both," Caris said. "I believe that Ralph Fitzgerald, who has some military training, may have joined forces with an existing band of outlaws and simply made them more organized and effective."

Fat Betty Baxter, the town's most successful baker, said: "Whoever it is, they'll be the ruination of this town. No one comes to market anymore!"

That was an exaggeration, but attendance at the weekly market was down drastically, and the effects were felt by just about every enterprise in town, from bakeries to brothels. "That's not the worst of it, though," Caris said. "In four weeks' time we've got the Fleece Fair. Several people here have invested enormous sums of money in the new bridge, which should be ready for use, with a temporary timber roadbed, in time for the opening. Most of us depend on the annual fair for our prosperity. I personally have a warehouse full of costly scarlet cloth to sell. If it gets around that people coming to Kingsbridge are likely to be robbed by outlaws, we may have no customers."

She was even more worried than she let herself appear. Neither she nor her father had any cash left. Everything they had was either invested in the bridge or tied up in raw wool and scarlet cloth. The Fleece Fair was their chance to get their money back. If attendance was poor, they would be in deep trouble. Among other things, who would pay for the wedding?

She was not the only worried citizen. Rick Silvers, the head of the jewelers' guild, said: "That would be the third bad year in succession." He was a prim, fussy man, always immaculately dressed. "It would finish some of my people," he went on. "We do half our year's business at the Fleece Fair."

Edmund said: "It would finish this town. We can't let it happen."

Several others joined in. Caris, who was unofficially presiding, let them grumble. A heightened sense of urgency would predispose them to accept the radical solution she was going to propose.

Elfric said: "The sheriff of Shiring ought to do something about it. What's he paid for, if not to keep the peace?"

Caris said: "He can't search the entire forest. He doesn't have enough men."

"Earl Roland has."

This was wishful thinking, but again Caris let the discussion run, so that when she proposed her solution they would be aware that there were no real alternatives.

Edmund said to Elfric: "The earl won't help us—I've already asked him."

Caris, who had in fact written Edmund's letter to Roland, said: "Ralph was the earl's man, and still is. You notice the outlaws don't attack people going to Shiring market."

Elfric said indignantly: "Those Wigleigh peasants should never have made a complaint against a squire of the earl's—who do they think they are?"

Caris was about to respond indignantly, but Betty Baxter beat her to it. "Oh, so you think lords should be allowed to rape anyone they like?"

Edmund intervened. "That's a different question," he said briskly, showing some of his old authority. "It's happened, and Ralph is preying on us, so what are we going to do? The sheriff can't help us and the earl won't."

Rick Silvers said: "What about Lord William? He took the side of the Wigleigh people—it's his fault that Ralph's an outlaw."

"I asked him, too," Edmund said. "He said we're not in his territory."

Rick said: "That's the trouble with having the priory as your landlord—what use is a prior when you need protection?"

Caris said: "Another reason why we are applying to the king for a borough charter. We'd be under royal protection then."

Elfric said: "We've got our own constable, what's he doing?"

Mark Webber spoke. He was one of the constable's deputies. "We're ready to do whatever's necessary," he said. "Just give us the word."

Caris said: "No one doubts your bravery. But your role is to deal with troublemakers within the town. John Constable doesn't have the expertise to hunt down outlaws."

Mark, who was close to Caris because he ran her fulling mill at Wigleigh, was mildly indignant. "Well, who does, then?"

Caris had been leading the discussion toward this question. "As a matter of fact, there is an experienced soldier who is willing to help us," she said. "I took the liberty of asking him to come here tonight, and he's waiting in the chapel." She raised her voice. "Thomas, will you join us?"

Thomas Langley came out of the little chapel at the end of the hall.

Rick Silvers said skeptically: "A monk?"

"Before he was a monk, he was a soldier," Caris explained. "That's how he lost his arm."

Elfric said grumpily: "Guild members' permission should have been sought before he was invited." No one took any notice, Caris was pleased to see: they were too interested to hear what Thomas would have to say.

"You need to form a militia," Thomas began. "By all accounts there are twenty or thirty outlaws in the troop. That's not many. Most townsmen can use a longbow effectively, thanks to the Sunday morning practice sessions. A hundred of you, well prepared and intelligently led, could overcome the outlaws easily."

"That's all very well," said Rick Silvers. "But we have to find them."

"Of course," said Thomas. "But I feel sure there is someone in Kingsbridge who knows where they are."

Merthin had asked the timber merchant, Jake Chepstow, to bring him a piece of slate from Wales—the largest piece he could find. Jake had come back from his next logging expedition with a thin sheet of gray Welsh slate about four feet square. Merthin had encased it in a wooden frame, and he used it for sketching plans.

This evening, while Caris was at the parish guild, Merthin was at his own house on Leper Island, working on a map of the island. Renting parts of it for wharves and warehouses was the least of his ambitions. He foresaw an entire street of inns and shops crossing the island from one bridge to the other. He would construct the buildings himself and rent them to enterprising Kingsbridge traders. It excited him to look into the future of the town and imagine the buildings and streets it was going to need. This was the kind of thing the priory would have done, if it had had better leadership.

Included in the plan was a new house for him and Caris. This little place would be cozy when they were first married, but they would need more room eventually, especially if they had children. He had marked out a site on the southern shore, where they would get fresh air off the river. Most of the island was rocky, but the patch he had in mind featured a small area of cultivable soil where he might be able to grow some fruit trees. As he planned the house, he relished the vision of the two of them living side by side, day by day, always.

His dream was interrupted by a knock at the door. He was startled. Normally no one came to the island at night—except Caris, and she would not knock. "Who is it?" he called nervously.

Thomas Langley came in.

"Monks are supposed to be asleep at this time," Merthin said.

"Godwyn doesn't know I'm here." Thomas looked at the slate. "You draw left-handed?"

"Left or right, it makes no difference. Would you like a cup of wine?"

"No, thanks. I'll have to be up for Matins in a few hours, so I don't want to get sleepy."

Merthin liked Thomas. There had been a bond between them ever since that day, twelve years ago, when he had promised that if Thomas should die he would take a priest to the place where the letter was buried. Later, when they had worked together on cathedral repairs, Thomas had always been clear in his instructions and gracious to apprentices. He managed to be sincere about his religious calling without becoming prideful: all men of God should be like that, Merthin thought.

He waved Thomas to a chair by the fire. "What can I do for you?"

"It's about your brother. He has to be stopped."

Merthin winced, as if at a sudden stab of pain. "If I could do anything, I would. But I haven't seen him, and when I do, I'm not sure he will listen to me. There was a time when he looked to me for guidance, but I think those days are over."

"I've just come from a meeting of the parish guild. They asked me to organize a militia."

"Don't expect me to be part of it."

"No, I didn't come for that purpose." Thomas gave a wry smile. "Your many amazing talents don't actually include military skills."

Merthin nodded ruefully. "Thanks."

"But there is something you could do to help me, if you would."

Merthin felt uneasy. "Well, ask me."

"The outlaws must have a hideout somewhere not far from Kingsbridge. I want you to think about where your brother might be. It's probably a place you both know—a cave, perhaps, or an abandoned verderer's hut in the forest."

Merthin hesitated.

Thomas said: "I know you'd hate to betray him. But think of that first family he attacked: a decent, hardworking peasant, his pretty wife, a lad of fourteen, and a little girl. Now three of them are dead and the little girl has no parents. Even though you love your brother, you have to help us catch him."

"I know."

"Can you think where he might be?"

Merthin was not yet ready to answer the question. "Will you take him alive?"

"If I can."

Merthin shook his head. "Not good enough. I need a guarantee."

Thomas was silent for a few moments. At last he said: "All right. I'll take him alive. I don't know how, but I'll find a way. I promise."

"Thank you." Merthin paused. He knew he had to do this, but his heart rebelled. After a moment, he forced himself to speak. "When I was about thirteen we used to go hunting, often with older boys. We would stay out all day and cook whatever we shot. Sometimes we used to go as far as the Chalk Hills and meet the families who spend the summer up there grazing sheep. Shepherdesses tend to be quite free and easy—some would let you kiss them." He smiled briefly. "In winter, when they weren't there, we used their huts for shelter. That might be where Ralph is hiding out."

"Thank you," said Thomas. He stood up.

"Remember your promise."

"I will."

"You trusted me with a secret twelve years ago."

"I know."

"I never betrayed you."

"I realize that."

"Now I'm trusting you." Merthin knew that his words could be interpreted two ways: either as a plea for reciprocity, or as a veiled threat. That was all right. Let Thomas take it how he wished.

Thomas put out his one hand, and Merthin clasped it. "I'll keep my word," Thomas said. Then he went out.

Ralph and Tam rode side by side up the hill, followed by Alan Fernhill on his horse and the rest of the outlaws on foot. Ralph was feeling good: it had been another successful Sunday morning's work. Spring had arrived, and the peasants were beginning to bring the new season's produce to market. The members of the gang were carrying half a dozen lambs, a jar of honey, a stoppered jug of cream, and several leather bottles of wine. As usual, the outlaws had suffered only minor injuries, a few cuts and bruises inflicted by the more foolhardy of their victims.

Ralph's partnership with Tam had been extraordinarily successful. A couple of hours' easy fighting brought them all they needed for a week of living in luxury. They spent the rest of their time hunting in the day and drinking in the evenings. There were no clodhopping serfs to badger them about boundary disputes or cheat them of rent. All they lacked were women, and today they had remedied that, by kidnapping two plump girls, sisters of about thirteen and fourteen years.

His only regret was that he had never fought for the king. It had been his ambition since boyhood, and he still felt the tug. Being an outlaw was too easy. He could not feel very proud of killing unarmed serfs. The boy in him longed yet for glory. He had never proved, to himself and others, that he had in him the soul of a true knight.

However, he would not allow that thought to lower his spirits. As he breasted the rise that hid the upland pasture where their hideout was, he looked forward to a feast tonight. They would roast a lamb on a spit and drink cream with honey. And the girls . . . Ralph decided he would make them lie side by side, so that each would see her sister being violated by one man after another. The thought made his heart beat faster.

They came within sight of the stone shelters. They would not be able to use these much longer, Ralph reflected. The grass was growing and the shepherds would be here soon. Easter had been early this year, so Whitsun would come soon after May Day. The outlaws would have to find another base.

When he was fifty yards from the nearest hut, he was shocked to see someone walk out of it.

He and Tam both reined in, and the outlaws gathered around them, hands on their weapons.

The man approached them, and Ralph saw that it was a monk. Tam, beside Ralph, said: "What in the name of heaven . . . ?"

One sleeve of the monk's robe flapped empty, and Ralph recognized him as Brother Thomas from Kingsbridge. Thomas walked up to them as if meeting them by chance on the main street. "Hello, Ralph," he said. "Remember me?"

Tam said to Ralph: "Do you know this man?"

Thomas came up on the right side of Ralph's horse and extended his good right arm to shake hands. What the hell was he doing here? On the other hand, what harm could there be in a one-armed monk? Baffled, Ralph reached down and took the proffered hand. Thomas slipped his hand up Ralph's arm and grasped his elbow.

Out of the corner of his eye, Ralph saw movement near the stone huts. Glancing up, he saw a man step out through the doorway of the nearest building, closely followed by a second man, then three more; then he saw that they were pouring out of all the huts—and fitting arrows to the tall longbows they carried. He realized that he and his band had been ambushed—but, in that moment, the grip on his elbow tightened and, with a sudden strong heave, he was pulled off his horse.

A shout went up from the outlaws. Ralph crashed to the ground, landing on his back. His horse, Griff, skittered sideways, frightened. As Ralph tried to get up, Thomas fell on him like a tree, flattening him to the ground, and lay on top of him like a lover. "Lie still and you won't get killed," he said in Ralph's ear.

Then Ralph heard the sound of dozens of arrows being shot simultaneously from longbows, a deadly swish that was unmistakable, like the sudden wind of a flash thunderstorm. The noise was tremendous—there must have been a hundred archers, he thought. They had obviously crammed themselves into the shelters. Thomas's grasping Ralph's arm must have been the signal for them to come out and shoot.

He considered fighting Thomas off, and thought better of it. He could hear the cries of the outlaws as the arrows struck home. From ground level he could not see much, but some of his men were drawing their swords. However, they were too far from the archers: if they ran at their enemy, they would be shot down before they could engage. It was a massacre, not a battle. Hooves drummed the earth, and Ralph wondered whether Tam was charging the archers or riding away.

Confusion reigned, but not for long. Within moments he could tell that the outlaws were in full retreat.

Thomas got off him, pulled a long dagger from under his Benedictine robe, and said: "Don't even think about drawing your sword."

Ralph stood up. He looked at the archers, and recognized many of them: fat Dick Brewer, randy Edward Butcher, convivial Paul Bell, grumpy Bill Watkin—timid, law-abiding citizens of Kingsbridge, every one. He had been captured by tradesmen. But that was not the most surprising thing.

He looked curiously at Thomas. "You saved my life, monk," he said.

"Only because your brother asked me to," Thomas replied crisply. "If it had been up to me, you would have been dead before you hit the ground."

The Kingsbridge jail was in the basement of the guildhall. The pen had stone walls, a dirt floor, and no windows. There was no fire either, and prisoners occasionally died of cold in the winter; but this was May, and Ralph had a wool cloak to keep him warm at night. He also had a few items of furniture—a chair, a bench, and a small table—rented from John Constable and paid for by Merthin. On the other side of the barred oak door was John Constable's office. On market days and during the fair he and his deputies sat there waiting to be summoned to deal with trouble.

Alan Fernhill was in the cell with Ralph. A Kingsbridge archer had brought him down with an arrow in the thigh, and although the wound was not serious he had been unable to run. However, Tam Hiding had got away.

Today was their last here. The sheriff was due at midday to take them to Shiring. They had already been sentenced to death, in their absence, for the rape of Annet, and for the crimes they had committed in that court under the judge's eye: wounding the foreman of the jury, wounding Wulfric, and escaping. When they got to Shiring they would be hanged.

An hour before noon, Ralph's parents brought them dinner: hot ham, new bread, and a jug of strong ale. Merthin came with them, and Ralph surmised that this was good-bye.

His father confirmed it. "We'll not follow you to Shiring," he said.

His mother added: "We don't want to see you—" She broke down, but he knew what she was going to say. They would not journey to Shiring to see him hang.

Ralph drank the ale but found it difficult to eat. He was going to the gallows, and food seemed pointless. Anyway, he had no appetite. Alan tucked in: he seemed to have no sense of the doom that awaited him.

The family sat in an awkward silence. Although these were their last minutes together, no one knew what to say. Maud wept quietly, Gerald looked thunderous, and Merthin sat with his head in his hands. Alan Fernhill just looked bored.

Ralph had a question for his brother. Part of him did not want to ask it, but now he realized that this was his last chance. "When Brother Thomas pulled me off my horse, protecting me from the arrows, I thanked him for saving my life," he said. Looking at his brother, he went on: "Thomas said he did it for you, Merthin."

Merthin just nodded.

"Did you ask him to?"

"Yes."

"So you knew what was going to happen."

"Yes."

"So . . . how did Thomas know where to find me?"

Merthin did not answer.

Ralph said: "You told him, didn't you?"

Their father was shocked. "Merthin!" he said. "How could you?"

Alan Fernhill said: "You treacherous swine."

Merthin said to Ralph: "You were murdering people! Innocent peasants and their wives and children! You had to be stopped!"

Ralph did not feel angry, somewhat to his surprise. He felt a choking sensation. He swallowed, then said: "But why did you ask Thomas to spare my life? Was it because you preferred that I should hang?"

Maud said: "Ralph, don't," and sobbed.

"I don't know," Merthin said. "Perhaps I just wanted you to live a little longer."

"But you did betray me." Ralph found that he was on the verge of breaking down. Tears seemed to gather behind his eyes, and he felt the pressure in his head. "You betrayed me," he repeated.

Merthin stood up and said angrily: "By God, you deserved it!"

Maud said: "Don't fight."

Ralph shook his head sadly. "We're not going to fight," he said. "Those days are over."

The door opened and John Constable stepped in. "The sheriff is outside," he announced.

Maud put her arms around Ralph and clung to him, weeping. After a few moments, Gerald gently pulled her away.

John walked out and Ralph followed him. He was surprised not to be tied up or chained. He had escaped once before—were they not afraid he would do the same again? He walked through the constable's office and out into the open air. His family came behind.

It must have been raining earlier, for now bright sunshine reflected off the wet street, and Ralph had to screw up his eyes against the glare. As he adjusted to the light, he recognized his own horse, Griff, saddled ready. The sight gladdened his heart. He took the reins and spoke into the horse's ear. "You never betrayed me, boy, did you, eh?" The horse blew through its nostrils and stamped, pleased to have its master back.

The sheriff and several deputies were waiting, mounted and armed to the teeth: they were going to let Ralph ride to Shiring, but they were not taking any risks with him. There would be no escape this time, he realized.

Then he looked again. The sheriff was here, but the other armed riders were not his deputies. They were Earl Roland's men. And there was the earl himself, black-haired and black-bearded, mounted on a gray charger. What was he doing here?

Without dismounting, the earl leaned down and handed a rolled sheet of parchment to John Constable. "Read that, if you can," Roland said, speaking as always out of one side of his mouth. "It is a writ from the king. All the prisoners in the county are pardoned and freed—on condition they come with me to join the king's army."

Gerald shouted: "Hoorah!!" Maud burst into tears. Merthin looked over the constable's shoulder and read the writ.

Ralph looked at Alan, who said: "What does it mean?"

"It means we're free!" Ralph said.

John Constable said: "It does, if I read it aright." He looked at the sheriff. "Do you confirm this?"

"I do," said the sheriff.

"Then there is no more to be said. These men are free to go with the earl." The constable rolled up the parchment.

Ralph looked at his brother. Merthin was weeping. Were they tears of joy, or frustration?

He was given no more time to wonder. "Come on," said Roland impatiently. "We've completed the formalities, let's get on the road. The king is in France—we've a long way to go!" He wheeled his horse and rode down the main street.

Ralph kicked Griff's sides, and the horse eagerly broke into a trot and followed the earl.

41

"You can't win," Gregory Longfellow said to Prior Godwyn, sitting in the large chair in the hall of the prior's house. "The king is going to grant a borough charter to Kingsbridge."

Godwyn stared at him. This was the lawyer who had won two cases for him at the royal court, one against the earl and the other against the alderman. If such a champion declared himself beaten then, surely, defeat must be inevitable.

It was not to be borne. If Kingsbridge became a royal borough, the priory would be sidelined. For hundreds of years, the prior had ruled the town. In Godwyn's eyes, the town existed only to serve the priory, which served God. Now the priory would become just part of a town ruled by merchants, serving the god of Money. And the Book of Life would show that the prior who let this happen was Godwyn.

Dismayed, he said: "Are you quite certain?"

"I'm always quite certain," said Gregory.

Godwyn was aggravated. Gregory's cocksure attitude was all very well when he was sneering at your opponents, but when he turned it on you it became infuriating. Angrily, Godwyn said: "You came all the way to Kingsbridge to tell me you can't do what I asked for?"

"And to collect my fee," Gregory said blithely.

Godwyn wished he could have him thrown into the fishpond in his London clothes.

It was the Saturday of Whitsun weekend, the day before the opening of the Fleece Fair. Outside, on the green to the west of the cathedral, hundreds of traders were setting up their stalls, and their conversations and cries to one another combined to make a roar that could be heard here in the hall of the prior's house, where Godwyn and Gregory sat at either end of the dining table.

Philemon, sitting on the bench at the side, said to Gregory: "Perhaps you could explain to the lord prior how you have reached this pessimistic conclusion?" He was developing a tone of voice that sounded half obsequious and half contemptuous. Godwyn was not sure he liked it.

Gregory did not react to the tone. "Of course," he said. "The king is in France."

Godwyn said: "He has been there for almost a year, but nothing much has happened."

"You will hear of action this winter."

"Why?"

"You must have heard of the French raids on our southern ports."

"I have," Philemon said. "They say the French sailors raped nuns at Canterbury."

"We always claim the enemy has raped nuns," Gregory said with condescension. "It encourages the common people to support the war. But they did burn Portsmouth. And there has been serious disruption to shipping. You may have noticed a fall in the price you get for your wool."

"We certainly have."

"That's partly due to the difficulty of shipping it to Flanders. And the price you're paying for wine from Bordeaux is up for the same reason."

We couldn't afford wine at the old prices, Godwyn thought; but he did not say so.

Gregory went on: "These raids appear to be no more than preliminaries. The French are assembling an invasion fleet. Our spies say they already have more than two hundred vessels anchored in the mouth of the Zwyn River."

Godwyn noted that Gregory talked of "our spies" as if he were part of the government. In reality he was only retailing gossip. All the same, it sounded convincing. "But what does the French war have to do with whether or not Kingsbridge becomes a borough?"

"Taxes. The king needs money. The parish guild has argued that the town will be more prosperous, and therefore will pay more tax, if the merchants are freed from the control of the priory."

"And the king believes this?"

"It has proved true before. That's why kings create boroughs. Boroughs generate trade, and trade produces tax revenue."

Money again, Godwyn thought with disgust. "Is there nothing we can do?"

"Not in London. I advise you to concentrate on the Kingsbridge end. Can you persuade the parish guild to withdraw the application? What's the old alderman like? Can he be bribed?"

"My uncle Edmund? He's in poor health, and fading fast. But his daughter, my cousin Caris, is the real driving force behind this."

"Ah, yes, I remember her at the trial. Rather arrogant, I felt."

There was a case of the pot calling the kettle black, Godwyn thought sourly. "She's a witch," he said.

"Is she, now? That might help."

"I didn't mean literally."

Philemon said: "As a matter of fact, Lord Prior, there have been rumors."

Gregory raised his eyebrows. "Interesting!"

Philemon went on: "She is a great friend of a wise woman called Mattie, who mixes potions for gullible townspeople."

Godwyn was about to pour scorn on the witchcraft idea, then he decided to shut up. Any weapon that might shoot down the notion of a borough charter must surely have been sent by God. Perhaps Caris does use witchcraft, he thought; who knows?

Gregory said: "I see you hesitate. Of course, if you are fond of your cousin . . ."

"I was when we were younger," Godwyn said, and he felt a pang of regret for the old simplicities. "But I regret to say she has not grown into a God-fearing woman."

"In that case . . ."

"I must investigate this," Godwyn said.

Gregory said: "If I might make a suggestion?"

Godwyn had had enough of Gregory's suggestions, but he did not quite have the nerve to say so. "Of course," he said with slightly exaggerated politeness.

"Heresy investigations can be . . . mucky. You shouldn't get your own hands soiled. And people may be nervous about talking to a prior. Delegate the task to someone less intimidating. This young novice, for example." He indicated Philemon, who glowed with pleasure. "His attitude strikes me as . . . sensible."

Godwyn recalled that it was Philemon who had discovered Bishop Richard's weakness—his affair with Margery. He was certainly the man for any dirty work. "All right," he said. "See what you can find out, Philemon."

"Thank you, Lord Prior," said Philemon. "Nothing would give me more pleasure."

On Sunday morning, people were still pouring into Kingsbridge. Caris stood and watched them streaming over Merthin's two wide bridges on foot, on horseback, or driving two-wheeled and four-wheeled horse carts and oxcarts laden with goods for the fair. The sight gladdened her heart. There had been no grand opening ceremony—the bridge was not really finished, but was usable thanks to a temporary timber roadbed—but, all the same, word had got around that it was open, and that the roads were safe from outlaws. Even Buonaventura Caroli was here.

Merthin had suggested a different way of collecting the tolls, which the parish guild had adopted eagerly. Instead of a single booth at the end of the bridge, creating a bottleneck, they had stationed ten men on Leper Island in temporary booths spread across the road between the two bridges. Most people handed over their penny without breaking stride. "There isn't even a queue," Caris said aloud, talking to herself.

And the weather was sunny and mild with no sign of rain. The fair was going to be a triumph.

Then, a week from today, she would marry Merthin.

She still had misgivings. The idea of losing her independence, and becoming someone's property, had not ceased to terrify her, even though she knew Merthin was not the kind of man to take advantage by bullying his wife. On the rare occasions when she had confessed this feeling—to Gwenda, for example, or to Mattie Wise—she had been told that she thought like a man. Well, so be it, that was how she felt.

But the prospect of losing him had seemed even more bleak. What would she have left, except for a cloth manufacturing business that did not inspire her? When he finally announced his intention of leaving town, the future had suddenly seemed empty. And she had realized that the only thing worse than being married to him might be not being married to him.

At least, that was what she told herself in her more positive moments. Then, sometimes, when she lay awake in the middle of the night, she saw herself backing out at the last minute, often in the middle of the wedding, refusing to take the vows and rushing out of the church, to the consternation of the entire congregation.

That was nonsense, she felt now in the light of day, with everything going so well. She would marry Merthin and be happy.

She left the riverbank and walked through the town to the cathedral, already crowded with worshippers waiting for the morning service. She remembered Merthin feeling her up behind a pillar. She felt nostalgic for the thoughtless passion of their early relationship; the long, intense conversations and the stolen kisses.

She found him near the front of the congregation, studying the south aisle of the choir, the part of the church that had collapsed in front of their eyes two years ago. She recalled going up into the space over the vaulting with Merthin, and overhearing that dreadful interaction between Brother Thomas and his estranged wife, the conversation that had crystallized all her fears and made her turn Merthin down. She put the thought out of her mind. "The repairs seem to be holding," she said, guessing what he was thinking about.

He looked dubious. "Two years is a short time in the life of a cathedral."

"There's no sign of deterioration."

"That's what makes it difficult. An invisible weakness can work away for years, unsuspected, until something comes tumbling down."

"Perhaps there is no weakness."

"There must be," he said with a touch of impatience. "There was a reason why that collapse took place two years ago. We never found out what it was, so we haven't put it right. If it hasn't been put right, it's still a weakness."

"It might have corrected itself spontaneously."

She was just being argumentative, but he took her seriously. "Buildings don't usually repair themselves—but you're right, it's possible. There might have been some seepage of water, for example from a blocked gargoyle, which somehow became diverted to a less harmful route."

The monks began to enter in procession, singing, and the congregation went quiet. The nuns appeared from their separate entrance. One of the novice nuns looked up, a beautiful pale face in the line of hooded heads. It was Elizabeth Clerk. She saw Merthin and Caris together, and the sudden malice in her eyes made Caris shudder. Then Elizabeth bowed her head and disappeared back into her anonymous uniform.

"She hates you," Merthin said.

"She thinks I stopped you marrying her."

"She's right."

"No, she's not—you could have married anyone you wanted!"

"But I only wanted you."

"You toyed with Elizabeth."

"It must have seemed that way to her," Merthin said regretfully. "But I just liked talking to her. Especially after you turned to ice."

She felt uncomfortable. "I know. But Elizabeth feels cheated. The way she looks at me makes me nervous."

"Don't be afraid. She's a nun, now. She can't do you any harm."

They were quiet for a while, standing side by side, their shoulders touching intimately, watching the ritual. Bishop Richard sat on the throne at the east end, presiding over the service. Merthin liked this sort of thing, Caris knew. He always felt better afterward, and he said that was what going to church was supposed to do for you. Caris went because people noticed if she stayed away, but she had doubts about the whole business. She believed in God, but she was not sure He revealed His wishes exclusively to men such as her cousin Godwyn. Why would a god want praise, for example? Kings and earls required worship, and the more petty their rank the more deference they demanded. It seemed to her that an almighty God would not care one way or another whether the people of Kingsbridge sang His praises, any more than she cared whether the deer in the forest feared her. She occasionally gave voice to these ideas, but no one took her seriously.

Her thoughts drifted to the future. The signs were good that the king would grant Kingsbridge a borough charter. Her father would probably be the first mayor, if his health recovered. Her cloth business would continue to grow. Mark Webber would be rich. With increased prosperity, the parish guild could build a Wool Exchange, so that everyone could do business comfortably even in bad weather. Merthin could design the building. Even the priory was going to be better off, though Godwyn would not thank her.

The service came to an end, and the monks and nuns began to process out. A novice monk broke out of line and entered the congregation. It was Philemon. To Caris's surprise, he approached her. "May I have a word?" he said.

She repressed a shudder. There was something loathsome about Gwenda's brother. "What about?" she replied, barely politely.

"I want to ask your advice, really," he said, with an attempt at a charming smile. "You know Mattie Wise."

"Yes."

"What do you think of her methods?"

She gave him a hard look. Where was this going? She decided she had better defend Mattie anyway. "She has never studied the texts of the ancients, of course. Despite that, her remedies work—sometimes better than those of the monks. I think it's because she bases her treatments on what has worked previously, rather than on a theory about the humors."

People standing nearby were listening with curiosity, and some of them now joined in uninvited.

"She gave our Nora a potion that brought her fever down," said Madge Webber.

John Constable said: "When I broke my arm, her medicine took the pain away while Matthew Barber set the bone."

Philemon said: "And what kind of spells does she pronounce when she's making her mixtures?"

"No spells!" Caris said indignantly. "She tells people to pray when they take their medicines, because only God can heal—she says."

"Could she be a witch?"

"No! It's a ridiculous idea."

"Only there has been a complaint to the ecclesiastical court."

A chill gripped Caris. "From whom?"

"I can't say. But I've been asked to investigate."

Caris was mystified. Who could Mattie's enemy be? She said to Philemon: "Well, you of all people know Mattie's worth—she saved the life of your sister when she gave birth to Sam. Gwenda would have bled to death if not for Mattie."

"So it seems."

"Seems? Gwenda's alive, isn't she?"

"Yes, of course. So you feel sure Mattie does not call on the devil?"

Caris noticed that he asked the question in a slightly raised voice, as if he wanted to make sure the listeners around heard it. She was puzzled, but she had no doubt of her answer. "Of course I'm sure! I'll swear an oath if you want."

"Not necessary," Philemon said smoothly. "Thank you for your advice." He inclined his head in a sort of bow and slithered away.

Caris and Merthin walked toward the exit. "What rubbish!" Caris said. "Mattie a witch!"

Merthin looked troubled. "You would expect Philemon to want evidence against her, wouldn't you?"

"Yes."

"So why did he come to you? He could have guessed that you, of all people, would deny the charge. Why would he be keen to clear her name?"

"I don't know."

They passed through the great west doorway and out on to the green. The sun was shining on hundreds of stalls loaded with colorful goods. "It doesn't make sense," Merthin said. "And that troubles me."

"Why?"

"It's like the cause of weakness in the south aisle. If you can't see it, it may be working away invisibly to undermine you—and you won't know it until everything comes crashing down all around."

The scarlet cloth on Caris's market stall was not as good as that sold by Loro Fiorentino, although you had to have a sharp eye for wool to see the difference. The weave was not so close, because the Italian looms were somehow superior. The color was just as bright, but it was not perfectly even over the length of the bale, no doubt because Italian dyers were more skilled. In consequence, she charged one-tenth less than Loro.

All the same, it was easily the best English scarlet that had ever been seen at Kingsbridge, and business was brisk. Mark and Madge sold it retail by the yard, measuring and cutting for individual customers, and Caris dealt with wholesale buyers, negotiating reductions for one bale or six with drapers from Winchester, Gloucester, and even London. By midday on Monday she knew she would sell out before the end of the week.

When business slowed down for the dinner break, she strolled around the fair. She felt a profound sense of satisfaction. She had triumphed over adversity, and so had Merthin. She stopped at Perkin's stall to talk to the Wigleigh folk. Even Gwenda had triumphed. Here she was, married to Wulfric—something that had seemed impossible—and there was her baby, Sammy, a year old, sitting on the ground, fat and happy. Annet was selling eggs from a tray, as always. And Ralph had gone to France to fight for the king, and might never come back.

Farther on she saw Joby, Gwenda's father, selling his squirrel furs. There was a wicked man. But he seemed to have lost his power to hurt Gwenda.

Caris stopped at her own father's stall. She had persuaded him to buy fleece in smaller quantities this year. The international wool market could not possibly thrive when the French and English were raiding one another's ports and burning ships. "How is business?" she asked him.

"Steady," he said. "I think I've judged it about right." He forgot that it had been her judgment, not his, that had counseled caution. But that was all right.

Their cook, Tutty, appeared with Edmund's dinner: mutton stew in a pot, a loaf of bread, and a jug of ale. It was important to look prosperous but not overly so. Edmund had explained to Caris, many years ago, that although customers needed to believe they were buying from a successful business, they would resent contributing to the wealth of someone who appeared to be rolling in money.

"Are you hungry?" he asked her.

"Starving."

He stood up to reach for the stew pot. Then he staggered, made an odd sound halfway between a grunt and a cry, and fell to the ground.

The cook screamed.

Caris cried: "Father!" But she knew he would not respond. She could tell he was unconscious by the way he hit had the earth, inertly heavy, like a sack of onions. She fought down the urge to scream. She knelt beside him. He was alive, and breathing hoarsely. She grasped his wrist and felt his pulse: it was strong, but slow. His face seemed flushed. It was always reddish, but now it seemed more so than usual.

Tutty said: "What is it? What is it?"

Caris forced herself to speak calmly. "He's had a fit," she said. "Fetch Mark Webber. He can carry Father into the hospital."

The cook ran off. People from the neighboring stalls gathered around. Dick Brewer appeared and said: "Poor Edmund—what can I do?"

Dick was too old and fat to lift Edmund. Caris said: "Mark's coming to take him to the hospital." She began to cry. "I hope he'll be all right," she said.

Mark appeared. He lifted Edmund easily, cradling him gently in his strong arms, and walked toward the hospital, negotiating his way through the crowds, calling: "Mind out, there! Out of the way, please! Injured man, injured man."

Caris followed, distraught. She could hardly see through her tears, so she stayed close to Mark's broad back. They reached the hospital building and went inside. Caris was grateful to see the familiar knobbly face of Old Julie. "Fetch Mother Cecilia, as quick as you can!" Caris said to her. The old nun hurried away, and Mark laid Edmund on a pallet near the altar.

Edmund was still unconscious, eyes closed, breathing hoarsely. Caris felt his forehead: he was neither hot nor cold. What had caused this? It had been so sudden. One moment he had been talking normally, the next he fell down unconscious. How could such a thing happen?

Mother Cecilia came. Her bustling efficiency was reassuring. She knelt beside the pallet and felt Edmund's heart, then his pulse. She listened to his breathing and touched his face. "Get him a pillow and a blanket," she said to Julie. "Then fetch one of the monk physicians."

She stood up and looked at Caris. "He's had a fit," she said. "He may recover. All we can do is make him comfortable. The physician may recommend bleeding, but apart from that the only treatment is prayer."

That was not good enough for Caris. "I'm going for Mattie," she said.

She ran out of the building and dodged through the fair, remembering that she had done exactly the same thing a year ago, rushing to fetch Mattie when Gwenda was bleeding to death. This time it was her father, and she felt a different kind of panic. She had been desperately worried about Gwenda, but now it was as if the world was falling apart. The fear that her father might die gave her the dreadful feeling she sometimes got in dreams, when she found herself on the roof of Kingsbridge Cathedral with no way down but to jump.

The physical effort of running through the streets calmed her a little, and she was in control of her emotions by the time she came to Mattie's house. Mattie would know what to do. She would say: "I've seen this before, I know what will happen next, here's the treatment that helps."

Caris banged on the door. Hearing no immediate answer, she impatiently tried the latch and found it open. She dashed inside, saying: "Mattie, you have to come to the hospital right away, it's my father!"

The front room was empty. Caris pulled aside the curtain that screened off the kitchen. Mattie was not there, either. Caris said aloud: "Oh, why would you be out of the house at this very moment?" She looked around for some clue as to where Mattie might have gone. Then she noticed how stripped the room appeared. All the little jars and bottles had gone, leaving the shelves bare. There were none of the mortars and pestles Mattie used for grinding ingredients, none of her small pots for melting and boiling, no knives for chopping herbs. Caris returned to the front half of the house and saw that Mattie's personal possessions had also disappeared: her sewing box, her polished wood cups for wine, the embroidered shawl she had hung on the wall for decoration, the carved bone comb she treasured.

Mattie had packed up and gone.

And Caris could guess why. Mattie must have heard about Philemon's questions in church yesterday. Traditionally, the ecclesiastical court held a session on the Saturday of Fleece Fair week. Only two years ago the monks had used the occasion for the trial of Crazy Nell on the absurd charge of heresy.

Mattie was no heretic, of course, but it was difficult to prove that, as many old women had learned. She had calculated her chances of surviving a trial and found the answer frightening. Without telling anyone, she had packed up her possessions and left town. Probably she had found a peasant returning home after selling his produce and persuaded him to take her on his oxcart. Caris imagined her leaving at first light, her box beside her on the cart, the hood of her cloak pulled forward to hide her face. No one could even guess where she had gone.

"What am I going to do?" Caris said to the empty room. Mattie knew better than anyone else in Kingsbridge how to help sick people. This was the worst possible moment for her to disappear, just when Edmund lay unconscious in the hospital. Caris felt despair.

She sat down on Mattie's chair, still panting from the effort of running. She wanted to run back to the hospital, but there was no point. She would not be able to help her father. Nobody could.

The town must have a healer, she thought; one who does not rely on prayers and holy water, or bleeding, but uses simple treatments that have been shown to work. And, as she sat in Mattie's empty house, she realized that there was one person who could fill the role, someone who knew Mattie's methods and believed in her practical philosophy. That person was Caris herself.

The thought burst on her with the blinding light of a revelation, and she sat dead still, bewildered by the implications. She knew the recipes for Mattie's main potions: one for easing pain, one to cause vomiting, one for washing wounds, one to bring down a fever. She knew the uses of all the common herbs: dill for indigestion, fennel for fever, rue for flatulence, watercress for infertility. She knew the treatments Mattie *never* prescribed: poultices made with dung, medicines containing gold and silver, verses written on vellum and bound to the ailing part of the body.

And she had an instinct for it. Mother Cecilia had said so, had practically pleaded with Caris to become a nun. Well, she was not going to enter the priory, but she might perhaps take Mattie's place. Why not? The cloth business could be run by Mark Webber—he was doing most of the work anyway.

She would seek out other wise women—in Shiring, in Winchester, perhaps in London—and question them about their methods, what succeeded and what failed. Men were secretive about their craft skills—their "mysteries" as they called them, as if there were something supernatural about tanning leather or making horseshoes—but women were usually willing to share knowledge with other women.

She would even read some of the monks' ancient texts. There might be some truth in them. Perhaps the instinct that Cecilia attributed to her would help her winnow the seeds of practical treatment from the chaff of priestly mumbo-jumbo.

She stood up and left the house. She walked slowly back, dreading what she would find at the hospital. She felt fatalistic now. Her father would either be all right, or he would not. All she could do was carry out her resolution so that in future, when the people she loved were sick, she would know she was doing everything possible to help them.

She fought back tears as she made her way through the fair to the priory buildings. When she entered the hospital, she hardly dared look at her father. She approached the bed, which was surrounded by people: Mother Cecilia, Old Julie, Brother Joseph, Mark Webber, Petranilla, Alice, Elfric.

What must be, must be, she thought. She touched the shoulder of her sister, Alice, who moved aside, making room. At last Caris looked at her father.

He was alive and conscious, though he looked pale and tired. His eyes were open, and he looked straight at her and tried a weak smile. "I'm afraid I gave you a scare," he said. "I'm sorry, my dear."

"Oh, thank God," said Caris, and she began to cry.

*

On Wednesday morning Merthin came to Caris's stall in consternation. "Betty Baxter just asked me a strange question," he said. "She wanted to know who was going to stand against Elfric in the election for alderman."

"What election?" Caris said. "My father is alderman . . . oh." She realized what must be going on. Elfric was telling people that Edmund was too old and sick to fulfill the role, and the town needed someone new. And he was presenting himself as a candidate. "We must tell my father right away."

Caris and Merthin left the fairground and crossed the main street to the house. Edmund had left the priory hospital yesterday, saying—correctly—that there was nothing the monks could do for him but bleed him, which made him feel worse. He had been carried home, and a bed had been made up for him in the parlor on the ground floor.

This morning he was reclining on a stack of pillows in his improvised bed. He looked so weak that Caris hesitated to bother him with the news, but Merthin sat down beside him and laid out the facts starkly.

"Elfric is right," Edmund said when Merthin had finished. "Look at me. I can hardly sit upright. The parish guild needs strong leadership. It's no job for a sick man."

"But you'll be better soon!" Caris exclaimed.

"Perhaps. But I'm getting old. You must have noticed how absentminded I've become. I forget things. And I was fatally slow to react to the downturn in the market for raw wool—I lost a lot of money last year. Thank God, we've rebuilt our fortune with the scarlet cloth—but you did that, Caris, not me."

She knew all that, of course, but still she felt indignant. "Are you just going to let Elfric take over?"

"Certainly not. He would be a disaster. He's too much in thrall to Godwyn. Even after we become a borough, we'll need an alderman who can stand up to the priory."

"Who else could do the job?"

"Talk to Dick Brewer. He's one of the richest men in town, and the alderman must be rich, to have the respect of the other merchants. Dick's not afraid of Godwyn or any of the monks. He'd be a good leader."

Caris found herself reluctant to do as he said. It seemed like accepting that he was going to die. She could not remember a time when her father had not been alderman. She did not want her world to change.

Merthin understood her reluctance, but urged her on. "We have to accept this," he said. "If we ignore what's happening, we could end up with Elfric in charge. He would be a disaster—he might even withdraw the application for the borough charter."

That decided her. "You're right," she said. "Let's find Dick."

Dick Brewer had several carts in different locations in the fairground. Each bore a huge barrel. His children, grandchildren, and in-laws were selling ale from the barrels as fast as they could pour it. Caris and Merthin found him setting an example by drinking a large pot of his own brew while he watched his family making money for him. They took him aside and explained what was going on.

Dick said to Caris: "When your father dies, I suppose his fortune will be divided equally between you and your sister?"

"Yes." Edmund had already told Caris that this was in his will.

"When Alice's inheritance is added to Elfric's existing wealth, he will be very rich."

Caris realized that half the money she was making from her scarlet cloth might go to her sister. She had not thought of this before, because she had not thought about her father dying. It came as a shock. Money itself was not important to her, but she did not want to help Elfric become alderman. "It's not just a question of who is the richest man," she said. "We need someone who will stand up for the merchants."

"Then you must put up a rival candidate," Dick said.

"Will you stand?" she asked him directly.

He shook his head. "Don't bother trying to persuade me. At the end of this week I'm handing over to my eldest son. I'm planning to spend the rest of my days drinking beer instead of brewing it." He took a long draft from his tankard and belched contentedly.

Caris felt she had to accept that: he seemed quite sure. She said: "Who do you think we might approach?"

"There's only one real possibility," he said. "You."

Caris was astonished. "Me! Why?"

"You're the driving force behind the campaign for a borough charter. Your fiancé's bridge has saved the Fleece Fair, and your cloth business has pretty much rescued the town's prosperity after the wool slump. You're the child of the existing alderman and, although it's not an inherited office, people think leaders breed leaders. And they're right. You've actually been acting as alderman for almost a year, ever since your father's powers started to fail."

"Has the town ever had a woman alderman?"

"Not as far as I know. Nor one as young as you. Both these things will count heavily against you. I'm not saying you're going to win. I'm telling you no one else has a better chance of beating Elfric."

Caris had a faintly dizzy feeling. Was it possible? Could she do the job? What about her vow to become a healer? Were there not many other people in town who would be better than she as alderman? "What about Mark Webber?" she said.

"He'd be good, especially with that shrewd wife of his at his side. But people in this town still think of Mark as a poor weaver."

"He's prosperous now."

"Thanks to your scarlet cloth. But people are suspicious of new money. They would just say Mark is a jumped-up weaver. They want an alderman from a well-established family—someone whose father was rich, and preferably grandfather too."

Caris wanted to beat Elfric, but she did not feel sure of her ability. She thought of her father's patience and shrewdness, his hearty conviviality, his inexhaustible energy. Did she have any such qualities? She looked at Merthin.

He said: "You would be the best alderman the town has ever had."

His unhesitating confidence decided her. "All right," she said. "I'll do it."

Godwyn invited Elfric to dine with him on the Friday of the fair. He ordered an expensive dinner: swan cooked with ginger and honey. Philemon served them, and sat down to eat with them.

The citizens had decided to elect a new alderman and, in a remarkably short time, two candidates had emerged as the principal contestants: Elfric and Caris.

Godwyn did not like Elfric, but he was useful. He was not a particularly good builder, but he had successfully ingratiated himself with Prior Anthony, and thereby gained the contract for cathedral repairs. When Godwyn took office, he had seen in Elfric a servile toady and had kept him on. Elfric was not well liked, but he either employed or subcontracted most of the building craftsmen and suppliers in town, and they in their turn courted him in the hope of work. Having won his confidence, they all wanted him to continue in a position where he could grant them favors. And that gave him a power base.

"I don't like uncertainty," Godwyn said.

Elfric tasted the swan and grunted appreciatively. "In what context?"

"The election of a new alderman."

"By its nature, an election is uncertain—unless there is only one candidate."

"Which would be my preference."

"Mine, too, provided that candidate was me."

"That's what I'm suggesting."

Elfric looked up from his dinner. "Really?"

"Tell me, Elfric—how badly do you want to be alderman?"

Elfric swallowed his mouthful. "I want it," he said. His voice sounded a little hoarse, and he slurped some wine. "I deserve it," he went on, a note of indignation creeping into his tone. "I'm as good as any of them, am I not? Why should I not be alderman?"

"Would you proceed with the application for a borough charter?"

Elfric stared at him. Thoughtfully, he said: "Are you asking me to withdraw it?"

"If you're elected alderman, yes."

"Are you offering to help me get elected?"

"Yes."

"But how?"

"By eliminating the rival candidate."

Elfric looked skeptical. "I don't see how you could achieve that."

Godwyn nodded to Philemon, who said: "I believe Caris is a heretic."

Elfric dropped his knife. "You're going to try Caris as a witch?"

"You must not tell anyone about this," Philemon said. "If she hears about it beforehand, she may flee."

"As Mattie Wise did."

"I have let some townspeople believe that Mattie has been captured, and it is she who will be tried on Saturday at the ecclesiastical court. But, at the last minute, a different person will be accused."

Elfric nodded. "And, as it's an ecclesiastical court, there is conveniently no need for indictments or juries." He turned to Godwyn. "And you will be judge."

"Unfortunately, no," Godwyn said. "Bishop Richard will preside. So we must prove our point."

"Have you any evidence?" Elfric said skeptically.

Godwyn replied: "Some, but we'd like more. What we already have would be plenty if the accused were some old woman with no family or friends, like Crazy Nell. But Caris is well known and comes from a wealthy and influential family, as I need hardly tell you."

Philemon put in: "It's extremely fortunate for us that her father is too ill to leave his bed—God has ordained it so that he will not be able to defend her."

Godwyn nodded. "Nevertheless, she has many friends. So our evidence must be strong."

"What have you got in mind?" said Elfric.

Philemon answered. "It would be helpful if a member of her family were to come forward and say that she had called upon the devil, or turned a crucifix upside down, or spoken to some presence in an empty room."

For a moment, Elfric looked as if he did not understand; then enlightenment dawned. "Oh!" he said. "You mean me?"

"Think very carefully before you answer."

"You're asking me to help send my sister-in-law to Gallows Cross."

Godwyn said: "Your sister-in-law; my cousin. Yes."

"All right, I'm thinking."

Godwyn saw on Elfric's face ambition, greed, and vainglory, and he marveled at the way God used even men's weaknesses to His holy purpose. He could guess what Elfric was thinking. The position of alderman was a burdensome task for an unselfish man such as Edmund, who exercised his power for the benefit of the town's merchants; but for someone with his eye on the main chance it offered endless opportunities for profit and self-aggrandizement.

Philemon continued in a smooth, assured voice. "If you have never witnessed anything suspicious, then of course that is the end of the matter. But I beg you to search your memory carefully."

Godwyn noticed again how much Philemon had learned in the last two years. The awkward priory servant had vanished. He talked like an archdeacon.

"There may have been incidents that seemed at the time perfectly harmless, but which take on a sinister cast in the light of what you have been told today. On mature reflection, you may feel that these events were not as innocent as they at first appeared."

"I get your meaning, Brother," Elfric said.

There was a long silence. None of them ate. Godwyn waited patiently for Elfric's decision.

Philemon said: "And, of course, if Caris were dead, then Edmund's entire fortune would come to the other sister, Alice . . . your wife."

"Yes," Elfric said. "I'd thought of that."

"Well?" said Philemon. "Is there anything you can think of that might help us?"

"Oh, yes," Elfric said at last. "I can think of quite a lot."

42

Caris was unable to find out the truth about Mattie Wise. Some people said she had been captured and was locked in a cell in the priory. Others thought she would be tried in her absence. A third strand of opinion claimed that someone else entirely would stand trial for heresy. Godwyn refused to answer Caris's questions, and the rest of the monks said they knew nothing.

Caris went to the cathedral on Saturday morning determined to defend Mattie whether she was present or not, and to stand up for any other poor old woman who suffered this absurd accusation. Why did monks and priests hate women so? They worshipped their Blessed Virgin, but treated every other female as an incarnation of the devil. What was the matter with them?

In a secular court there would have been a jury of indictment and a preliminary hearing, and Caris would have been able to find out in advance what the evidence against Mattie might be. But the church made its own rules.

Whatever they alleged, Caris would say loud and clear that Mattie was a genuine healer who used herbs and drugs and told people to pray to God to make them well. Some of the many townspeople who had been helped by Mattie would surely speak up for her.

Caris stood with Merthin in the north transept and remembered the Saturday two years ago when Crazy Nell had been tried. Caris had told the court Nell was mad but harmless. It had done no good.

Today, as then, there was a big crowd of townspeople and visitors in the cathedral, hoping for drama: accusations, counteraccusations, quarrels, hysterics, curses, and the spectacle of a woman being flogged through the streets and then hanged at Gallows Cross. Friar Murdo was present. He always showed up for sensational trials. They provided an opportunity for him to do what he did best: whip up hysteria in a congregation.

While they were waiting for the clergy, Caris's mind wandered. Tomorrow, in this church, she would marry Merthin. Betty Baxter and her four daughters were already busy making the bread and pastry for the feast. Tomorrow night, Caris and Merthin would sleep together in his house on Leper Island.

She had stopped worrying about the marriage. She had made her decision and she would take the consequences. In truth she felt very happy. Sometimes she wondered how she could have been so scared. Merthin could not make anyone his slave—it was not in his nature. He was even kind to his boy laborer Jimmie.

Most of all she loved their sexual intimacy. It was the best thing that had ever happened to her. What she looked forward to most was having a home and a bed of their own, and being able to make love whenever they wanted to, on going to bed or on waking up, in the middle of the night or even the middle of the day.

At last the monks and nuns came in, led by Bishop Richard with his assistant, Archdeacon Lloyd. When they had taken their seats, Prior Godwyn stood up and said: "We are here today to try the charge of heresy against Caris, daughter of Edmund Wooler."

The crowd gasped.

Merthin shouted: "No!"

Everyone turned to look at Caris. She felt sick with fear. She had had no suspicion of this. It hit her like a punch in the dark. Bewildered, she said: "Why?" No one answered her.

She remembered her father warning her that Godwyn would have an extreme reaction to the threat of a borough charter. "You know how ruthless he is, even over small disputes," Edmund had said. "Something like this will lead to total war." Caris shuddered now to remember her reply: "So be it—total war."

Even so, Godwyn's chance of success would have been slender indeed if her father had been in good health. Edmund would have fought Godwyn to a standstill, and probably destroyed him. But Caris alone was a different matter. She did not have her father's power, authority, or popular support—not yet. Without him, she had become vulnerable.

She noticed her aunt Petranilla in the crowd. She was one of the few people *not* looking at Caris. How could she stand there in silence? Of course she supported her son, Godwyn, in general—but surely she would try to stop him condemning Caris to death? She had once said she wanted to be like a mother to Caris. Would she remember that? Somehow, Caris felt she would not. Her devotion to her son was too great. That was why she could not meet Caris's eye. She had already made up her mind not to stand in Godwyn's way.

Philemon stood up. "My lord bishop," he said, formally addressing the judge. But he immediately turned to the crowd. "As everyone knows, the woman Mattie Wise has fled, too frightened and guilty to be tried. Caris has been a regular visitor to Mattie's house for some years. Only days ago she defended the woman, in front of witnesses, here in the cathedral."

So that was why Philemon had questioned her about Mattie, Caris realized. She caught Merthin's eye. He had been worried because he could not figure out what Philemon was up to. He had been right to worry. Now they knew.

At the same time, part of her mind marveled at the transformation of Philemon. That awkward, unhappy boy was now a confident, arrogant man, standing in front of the bishop, the prior, and the townspeople, as full of spite as a snake about to strike.

Philemon said: "She offered to swear on oath that Mattie is no witch. Why would she do that—unless to cover her own guilt?"

Merthin shouted out: "Because she's innocent, and so is Mattie, you mendacious hypocrite!"

He might have been put in the stocks for that, but others were shouting at the same time, and his insult passed without comment.

Philemon went on: "Recently, Caris has miraculously dyed wool the exact shade of Italian scarlet, something Kingsbridge dyers have never been able to do. How has this been achieved? By a magic spell!"

Caris heard the rumble of Mark Webber's bass voice: "This is a lie!"

"She could not do this by daylight, of course. She lit a fire in her backyard at night, as was seen by people living nearby."

Philemon had been assiduous, Caris noted with foreboding. He had interviewed her neighbors.

"And she chanted strange rhymes. Why?" Caris had sung to herself out of boredom, as she boiled up dyes and dipped the cloth, but Philemon had the ability to turn innocent trivia into evidence of evil. He dropped his voice to a thrilling stage whisper and said: "Because she was calling for the secret aid of the Prince of Darkness . . . ," he raised his voice to a shout, ". . . Lucifer!"

The crowd groaned with dread.

"That cloth is Satan's scarlet!"

Caris looked at Merthin. He was aghast. "The fools are starting to believe him!" he said.

Caris's courage began to return. "Don't despair," she said. "I haven't had my say yet."

He took her hand.

"This is not the only spell she has used," Philemon continued in a more normal voice. "Mattie Wise also made love potions." He looked accusingly around the crowd. "There may even be wicked girls in this church now who have made use of Mattie's powers to bewitch a man."

Including your own sister, Caris thought. Did Philemon know about that?

He said: "This novice nun will testify."

Elizabeth Clerk stood up. She spoke in a quiet voice, eyes lowered, the picture of nunlike modesty. "I say this on my oath as I hope to be saved," she began. "I was betrothed to Merthin Builder."

Merthin called out: "Liar!"

"We were in love and very happy," Elizabeth went on. "Suddenly he changed. He seemed like a stranger to me. He became cold."

Philemon asked her: "Did you notice anything else unusual, Sister?"

"Yes, Brother. I saw him hold his knife in his left hand."

The crowd gasped. This was an acknowledged sign of bewitchment—although, as Caris knew, Merthin was ambidextrous.

Elizabeth said: "Then he announced he was going to marry Caris."

It was amazing, Caris thought, how the truth could be just a little skewed so that it sounded sinister. She knew what had really happened. Merthin and Elizabeth had been friends until Elizabeth made it clear she wanted to be more than a friend, at which point he had told her that he did not share her feelings, and they had parted. But a satanic spell made a much better story.

Elizabeth might have convinced herself that she was telling the truth. But Philemon knew this was a lie. And Philemon was Godwyn's tool. How could Godwyn reconcile his conscience with this level of wickedness? Was he telling himself that anything was justified in the service of the priory?

Elizabeth finished: "I can never love another man. That is why I have decided to give my life to God." She sat down.

It was powerful evidence, Caris realized, and her dismay darkened like a winter sky. The fact that Elizabeth had become a nun lent conviction to her testimony. She was operating a kind of sentimental blackmail: How can you disbelieve me when I have made such a sacrifice?

The townspeople were quieter now. This was not the hilarious spectacle of a mad old woman being condemned. They were watching a battle for the life of a fellow citizen.

Philemon said: "Most damning of all, my lord bishop, is the final witness, a close member of the accused woman's own family: her brother-in-law, Elfric Builder."

Caris gasped. She had been accused by her cousin, Godwyn; by her best friend's brother, Philemon; and by Elizabeth—but this was worse. For her sister's husband to speak against her was astonishing treachery. Surely no one would ever respect Elfric again.

Elfric stood up. The expression of defiance on his face told Caris he was ashamed of himself. "I say this on my oath as I hope to be saved," he began.

Caris looked around for her sister, Alice, but did not see her. If she had been here, she would surely have stopped Elfric. No doubt Elfric had ordered her to stay at home on some pretext. She probably knew nothing of this.

Elfric said: "Caris speaks to unseen presences in empty rooms."

"Spirits?" Philemon prompted.

"I fear so."

A murmur of horror came from the crowd.

Caris was aware that she often talked aloud to herself. She had always thought of it as a harmless, if mildly embarrassing, habit. Her father said all imaginative people did it. Now it was being used to condemn her. She bit back a protest. It was better to let the prosecution run its course, then refute the accusations one by one.

"When does she do this?" Philemon asked Elfric.

"When she thinks she is alone."

"And what does she say?"

"The words are difficult to make out. She might be speaking a foreign tongue."

The crowded reacted to that, too: witches and their familiars were said to have their own language that no one else could understand.

"What does she seem to be saying?"

"To judge by her tone of voice, she is asking for help, pleading for good luck, cursing those who cause her misfortune, that sort of thing."

Merthin shouted: "This is not evidence!" Everyone looked at him, and he added: "He has admitted he did not understand the words—he's just making this up!"

There was a rumble of support from the more levelheaded citizens, but it was not as loud or as indignant as Caris would have liked.

Bishop Richard spoke for the first time. "Be quiet," he said. "Men who disrupt the proceedings will be put outside by the constable. Carry on, please, Brother Philemon, but do not invite witnesses to fabricate evidence when they have admitted they do not know the truth."

That was at least evenhanded, Caris thought. Richard and his family had no love for Godwyn after the quarrel over Margery's wedding. On the other hand, as a cleric Richard might not want the town to pass out of the priory's control. Perhaps he would at least be neutral in this. Her hopes rose a little.

Philemon said to Elfric: "Do you think the familiars she speaks to help her in any way?"

"Most certainly," Elfric replied. "Caris's friends, those she favors, are lucky. Merthin has become a successful builder although he never even completed his apprenticeship as a carpenter. Mark Webber was a poor man, but now he is rich. Caris's friend Gwenda is married to Wulfric, even though Wulfric was betrothed to someone else. How are these things achieved, if not with unnatural help?"

"Thank you."

Elfric sat down.

As Philemon summarized his evidence, Caris fought down a rising feeling of terror. She tried to put out of her mind the vision of Crazy Nell being flogged behind a cart. She struggled to concentrate on what she should say to defend herself. She could ridicule every statement made about her, but that might not be enough. She needed to explain why people had lied about her, and show what their motives were.

When Philemon was finished, Godwyn asked her if she had anything to say. In a loud voice that sounded more confident than she felt, she replied: "Of course I do." She made her way to the front of the crowd: she would not let her accusers monopolize the position of authority. She took her time, making them all wait for her. She walked up to the throne and looked Richard in the eye. "My lord bishop, I say this on my oath as I hope to be saved . . . ," she turned to the crowd and added, ". . . which I notice Philemon did not say."

Godwyn interrupted: "As a monk, he does not need to swear."

Caris raised her voice. "And a good thing for him, otherwise he would burn in Hell for the lies he has told today!"

Score a point to me, she thought, and her hopes rose another notch.

She spoke to the crowd. Although the decision would be made by the bishop, he would be heavily influenced by the reaction of the townspeople. He was not a man of high principle.

"Mattie Wise healed many people in this town," she began. "On this day two years ago, when the old bridge collapsed, she was one of the foremost in tending to the injured, working alongside Mother Cecilia and the nuns. Looking around the church today I see many people who benefited from her care at that terrible time. Did anyone hear her invoke the devil on that day? If so, let him speak now."

She paused to let the silence impress itself on her audience.

She pointed at Madge Webber. "Mattie gave you a potion that brought down your child's fever. What did she say to you?"

Madge looked scared. No one was comfortable being called as a witness in the defense of a witch. But Madge owed a lot to Caris. She straightened her shoulders, looked defiant, and said: "Mattie said to me: 'Pray to God, for only He can heal.'"

Caris pointed at the constable. "John, she eased your pain while Mathew Barber set your broken bones. What did she say to you?"

John was used to being on the prosecuting side, and he, too, looked uneasy, but he told the truth in a strong voice. "She said: 'Pray to God, for only He can heal.'"

Caris turned to the crowd. "Everyone knows that Mattie was no witch. In that case, says Brother Philemon, why did she flee? Easy question. She was afraid that lies would be told about her—as they have been told about me. Which of you women, if falsely accused of heresy, would feel confident about proving your innocence to a court of priests and monks?" She looked around, letting her eyes rest on the prominent women of the town: Lib Wheeler, Sarah Taverner, Susanna Chepstow.

"Why did I mix dyes at night?" she resumed. "Because the days were short! Like many of you, my father failed to sell all his fleeces last year, and I wanted to turn the raw wool into something I could market. It was very difficult to discover the formula, but I did it, by hard work, over many hours, day and night—but without the help of Satan." She paused for breath.

When she began again, she used a different tone of voice, more playful. "I am accused of bewitching Merthin. I have to admit that the case against me is strong. Look at Sister Elizabeth. Stand up, please, Sister."

Reluctantly, Elizabeth stood.

"She is beautiful, isn't she?" Caris said. "She is also clever. And she is the daughter of a bishop. Oh, forgive me, my lord bishop, I meant no disrespect."

The crowd chuckled at that cheeky stab. Godwyn looked outraged, but Bishop Richard smothered a smile.

"Sister Elizabeth cannot see why any man would prefer me to her. Nor can I. Unaccountably, Merthin loves me, plain as I am. I cannot explain it." There was more giggling. "I'm sorry Elizabeth is so angry. If we lived in Old Testament times, Merthin could have two wives and everyone would be happy." They laughed loudly at that. She waited for the sound to subside, then said gravely: "What I am most sorry about is that the commonplace jealousy of a disappointed woman should become the pretext, in the untrustworthy mouth of a novice monk, for a charge as serious as that of heresy."

Philemon stood up to protest the charge of untrustworthiness, but Bishop Richard flapped a hand at him, saying: "Let her speak, let her speak."

Caris decided she had made her point about Elizabeth, and moved on. "I confess that I sometimes use vulgar words when I am alone—especially if I stub my toe. But you may ask why my own brother-in-law would testify against me, and tell you that my mutterings were invocations to evil spirits. I'm afraid I can answer that." She paused, then spoke solemnly. "My father is ill. If he dies, his fortune will be divided between me and my sister. But, if I die first, my sister will get it all. And my sister is Elfric's wife."

She paused, looking quizzically at the crowd. "Are you shocked?" she said. "So am I. But men kill for less money than that."

She moved away, as if she had finished, and Philemon got up from his bench. Caris turned around and addressed him in Latin. *"Caput tuum in ano est."*

The monks laughed loudly, and Philemon flushed.

Caris turned to Elfric. "You didn't understand that, did you, Elfric?"

"No," he said sulkily.

"Which is why you might have thought I was using some sinister witchcraft tongue." She turned back to Philemon. "Brother, you know what language I was using, don't you?"

"Latin," Philemon replied.

"Perhaps you would tell us what I just said to you."

Philemon looked an appeal at the bishop. But Richard was amused, and just said: "Answer the question."

Looking furious, Philemon obeyed. "She said: 'You've got your head up your ass.'"

The townspeople roared with laughter, and Caris walked back to her place.

When the noise died down, Philemon began to speak, but Richard interrupted him. "I don't need to hear any further from you," he said. "You've made a strong case against her, and she has mounted a vigorous defense. Does anyone else have anything to say about this accusation?"

"I do, my lord bishop." Friar Murdo came forward. Some of the townspeople cheered, others groaned: Murdo aroused contrary reactions. "Heresy is an evil," he began, his voice modulating into fruity preaching mode. "It corrupts the souls of women and men—"

"Thank you, Brother, but I know what heresy does," said Richard. "Do you have anything else to say? If not—"

"Just this," Murdo replied. "I agree with, and reiterate—"

"If it has been said before—"

"—your own comment that the case is strong, and the defense similar."

"In which case—"

"I have a solution to propose."

"All right, Brother Murdo, what is it? In the minimum number of words."

"She must be examined for the Devil's Mark."

Caris's heart seemed to stop.

"Of course," said the bishop. "I seem to remember you making the same suggestion at an earlier trial."

"Indeed, lord, for the devil greedily sucks the hot blood of his acolytes through his own special nipple, as the newborn babe sucks the swollen breasts—"

"Yes, thank you, friar, no need for further details. Mother Cecilia, will you and two other nuns please take the accused woman to a place of examination?"

Caris looked at Merthin. He was pale with horror. They were both thinking the same.

Caris had a mole.

It was tiny, but the nuns would find it—in just the kind of place they thought the devil was most interested in: on the left side of her vulva, just beside the cleft. It was dark brown, and the red gold hair around did not hide it. The first time Merthin had noticed it, he had joked: "Friar Murdo would call you a witch—you'd better not let him see it." And Caris had laughed and said: "Not if he were the last man on earth."

How could they have spoken of it in such a carefree way? Now she would be condemned to death for it.

She looked around desperately. She would have run, but she was surrounded by hundreds of people, some of whom would stop her. She saw Merthin's hand on the knife at his belt; but even if the knife had been a sword and he had been a great fighter—which he was not—he could not have cut his way through such a crowd.

Mother Cecilia came to her and took her hand.

Caris decided she would escape as soon as she got outside the church. Crossing the cloisters she could easily break free.

Then Godwyn said: "Constable, take one of your deputies and escort the woman to the place of examination, and stand outside the door until it is done."

Cecilia could not have held Caris, but two men could.

John looked at Mark Webber, normally his first choice among the deputies. Caris felt a faint hope: Mark was a loyal friend to her. But the constable apparently had the same thought, for he turned from Mark and pointed to Christopher Blacksmith.

Cecilia tugged gently on Caris's hand.

As if sleepwalking, Caris allowed herself to be led out of the church. They left by the north door, Cecilia and Caris followed by Sister Mair and Old Julie, with John Constable and Christopher Blacksmith close behind. They crossed the cloisters, entered the nuns' quarters, and made their way to the dormitory. The two men stayed outside.

Cecilia closed the door.

"No need to examine me," Caris said dully. "I've got a mark."

"We know," said Cecilia.

Caris frowned. "How?"

"We have washed you." She indicated Mair and Julie. "All three of us. When you were in the hospital, two Christmases ago. You had eaten something that poisoned you."

Cecilia did not know, or was pretending not to have guessed, that Caris had taken a potion to end her pregnancy.

She went on: "You were puking and shitting all over the place, and bleeding down there. You had to be washed several times. We all saw the mole."

Hopeless despair washed over Caris in an irresistible tide. She closed her eyes. "So now you will condemn me to death," she said in a voice so low it was almost a whisper.

"Not necessarily," said Cecilia. "There could be another way."

Merthin was distraught. Caris was trapped. She would be condemned to death, and there was nothing he could do. He could not have rescued her even if he had been Ralph, with big shoulders and a sword and a relish for violence. He stared, horrified, at the door through which she had disappeared. He knew where Caris's mole was, and he felt sure the nuns would find it—that was just the kind of place where they would look most carefully.

All around him the noise of excited chatter rose from the crowd. People were arguing for or against Caris, rerunning the trial, but he seemed to be inside a bubble, and he could hardly follow what anyone said. In his ears, their talk sounded like the random beating of a hundred drums.

He found himself staring at Godwyn, wondering what he was thinking. Merthin could understand the others—Elizabeth was eaten up with jealousy, Elfric was possessed by greed, and Philemon was pure malevolence—but the prior mystified him. Godwyn had grown up with his cousin Caris, and he knew she was not a witch. Yet he was prepared to see her die. How could he do something so wicked? What excuse did he make to himself? Did he tell himself that this was all for the glory of God? Godwyn had once seemed to be a man of enlightenment and decency, the antidote to Prior Anthony's narrow conservatism. But he had turned out to be worse than Anthony: more ruthless in the pursuit of the same obsolete aims.

If Caris dies, Merthin thought, I'm going to kill Godwyn.

His parents came up to him. They had been in the cathedral throughout the trial. His father said something, but Merthin could not understand him. "What?" he said.

Then the north door opened, and the crowd became silent. Mother Cecilia walked in alone and closed the door behind her. There was a murmur of curiosity. What now?

Cecilia walked up to the bishop's throne.

Richard said: "Well, Mother Prioress? What do you have to report to the court?"

Cecilia said slowly: "Caris has confessed—"

There was a roar of shock from the crowd.

Cecilia raised her voice. ". . . confessed her sins."

They went quiet again. What did this mean?

"She has received absolution—"

"From whom?" Godwyn interrupted. "A nun cannot give absolution!"

"From Father Joffroi."

Merthin knew Joffroi. He was the priest at St. Mark's, the church where Merthin had repaired the roof. Joffroi had no love for Godwyn.

But what was going on? Everyone waited for Cecilia to explain.

She said: "Caris has applied to become a novice nun here at the priory—"

Once again she was interrupted by a shout of shock from the assembled townspeople.

She yelled over their voices: "—and I have accepted her!"

There was uproar. Merthin could see Godwyn yelling at the top of his voice, but his words were lost. Elizabeth was enraged; Philemon stared at Cecilia with poisonous hatred; Elfric looked bewildered; Richard was amused. Merthin's own mind reeled with the implications. Would the bishop accept this? Did it mean the trial was over? Had Caris been saved from execution?

Eventually the tumult died down. As soon as he could be heard, Godwyn spoke, his face white with fury. "Did she, or did she not, confess to heresy?"

"The confessional is a sacred trust," Cecilia replied imperturbably. "I don't know what she said to the priest, and if I did I could not tell you or anyone else."

"Does she bear the mark of Satan?"

"We did not examine her." This answer was evasive, Merthin realized, but Cecilia quickly added: "It was not necessary once she had received absolution."

"This is unacceptable!" Godwyn bellowed. He had dropped the pretense that Philemon was the prosecutor. "The prioress cannot frustrate the proceedings of the court in this way!"

Bishop Richard said: "Thank you, Father Prior—"

"The order of the court must be carried out!"

Richard raised his voice. "That will do!"

Godwyn opened his mouth to protest further, then thought better of it.

Richard said: "I don't need to hear any more argument. I have made my decision, and I will now announce my judgment."

Silence fell.

"The proposal that Caris be permitted to enter the nunnery is an interesting one. If she is a witch, she will be unable to do any harm in the holiness of her surroundings. The devil cannot enter here. On the other hand, if she is not a witch, we will have been saved from the error of condemning an innocent woman. Perhaps the nunnery would not have been Caris's choice as a way of life, but her consolation will be an existence dedicated to serving God. On balance, then, I find this a satisfactory solution."

Godwyn said: "What if she should leave the nunnery?"

"Good point," said the bishop. "That is why I am formally sentencing her to death, but suspending the sentence for as long as she remains a nun. If she should renounce her vows, the sentence would be carried out."

That's it, thought Merthin in despair; a life sentence; and he felt tears of rage and grief come to his eyes.

Richard stood up. Godwyn said: "The court is adjourned!" The bishop left, followed by the monks and nuns in procession.

Merthin moved in a daze. His mother spoke to him in a consoling voice, but he ignored her. He let the crowd carry him to the great west door of the cathedral and out on to the green. The traders were packing up their leftover goods and dismantling their stalls: the Fleece Fair was over for another year. Godwyn had got what he wanted, he realized. With Edmund dying and Caris out of the way, Elfric would become alderman and the application for a borough charter would be withdrawn.

He looked at the gray stone walls of the priory buildings: Caris was in there somewhere. He turned that way, moving across the tide of the crowd, and headed for the hospital.

The place was empty. It had been swept clean, and the straw-filled palliasses used by the overnight visitors were stacked neatly against the walls. A candle burned on the altar at the eastern end. Merthin walked slowly the length of the room, not sure what to do next.

He recalled, from *Timothy's Book,* that his ancestor Jack Builder had briefly become a novice monk. The author had hinted that Jack had been a reluctant recruit, and had not taken easily to monastic discipline; at any rate, his novitiate had ended abruptly in circumstances over which Timothy drew a tactful veil.

But Bishop Richard had stated that if Caris ever left the nunnery she would be under sentence of death.

A young nun came in. When she recognized Merthin she looked scared. "What do you want?" she said.

"I must speak to Caris."

"I'll go and ask," she said, and hurried out.

Merthin looked at the altar, and the crucifix, and the triptych on the wall showing Elizabeth of Hungary, the patron saint of hospitals. One panel showed the saint, who had been a princess, wearing a crown and feeding the poor; the second showed her building her hospital; and the third illustrated the miracle in which the food she carried beneath her cloak was turned into roses. What would Caris do in this place? She was a skeptic, doubtful of just about everything the church taught. She did not believe that a princess could turn bread into roses. "How do they know that?" she would say to stories that everyone else accepted without question—Adam and Eve, Noah's ark, David and Goliath, even the Nativity. She would be a caged wildcat in here.

He had to talk to her, to find out what was in her mind. She must have some plan that he was not able to guess at. He waited impatiently for the nun to return. She did not come back, but Old Julie appeared. "Thank heaven!" he said. "Julie, I have to see Caris, quickly!"

"I'm sorry, young Merthin," she said. "Caris doesn't want to see you."

"Don't be ridiculous," he said. "We're betrothed—we're supposed to get married tomorrow. She has to see me!"

"She's a novice nun now. She won't be getting married."

Merthin raised his voice. "If that's true, don't you think she should tell me herself?"

"It's not for me to say. She knows you're here, and she won't see you."

"I don't believe you." Merthin pushed past the old nun and went through the door by which she had entered. He found himself in a small lobby. He had never been here before: few men had ever entered the nuns' area of the priory. He passed through another door and found himself in the nuns' cloisters. Several of them stood there, some reading, some walking around the square meditatively, some talking in quiet voices.

He ran along the arcade. A nun caught sight of him and screamed. He ignored her. Seeing a staircase, he ran up it and entered the first room. He found himself in a dormitory. There were two lines of mattresses, with neatly folded blankets on top. No one was there. He went a few steps along the corridor and tried another door. It was locked. "Caris!" he shouted. "Are you in there? Speak to me!" He banged on the door with his fist. He scraped the skin of his knuckles, which started to bleed, but he hardly felt the pain. "Let me in!" he yelled. "Let me in!"

A voice behind him said: "I'll let you in."

He spun around to see Mother Cecilia.

She took a key from her belt and calmly unlocked the door. Merthin threw it open. Beyond it was a small room with a single window. All around the walls were shelves packed with folded clothes.

"This is where we keep our winter robes," Cecilia said. "It's a storeroom."

"Where is she?" Merthin shouted.

"She's in a room that is locked by her own request. You won't find the room and, if you did, you couldn't get in. She will not see you."

"How do I know she's not dead?" Merthin heard his voice crack with emotion, but he did not care.

"You know me," Cecilia said. "She's not dead." She looked at his hand. "You've hurt yourself," she said sympathetically. "Come with me and let me put some ointment on your cuts."

He looked at his hand, and then at her. "You're a devil," he said.

He ran from her, back the way he had come, into the hospital, past a scared-looking Julie, out into the open. He made his way through the end-of-fair chaos in front of the cathedral and emerged onto the main street. He thought of speaking to Edmund, but decided against it: someone else could tell Caris's ailing father the terrible truth. Whom could he trust? He thought of Mark Webber.

Mark and his family had moved to a big house on the main street, with a large stone-built ground-floor storeroom for bales of cloth. There was no loom in their kitchen now: all the weaving was done by others whom they organized. Mark and Madge were sitting on a bench, looking solemn. When Merthin walked in, Mark jumped up. "Have you seen her?" he cried.

"They won't let me."

"That's outrageous!" Mark said. "They don't have the right to stop her seeing the man she's supposed to marry!"

"The nuns say she doesn't want to see me."

"I don't believe them."

"Nor do I. I went in and looked for her, but I couldn't find her. There are a lot of locked doors."

"She must be there somewhere."

"I know. Will you come back with me, and bring a hammer, and help me break down every door until we find her?"

Mark looked uncomfortable. Strong as he was, he hated violence.

Merthin said: "I have to find her—she might be dead!"

Before he could reply, Madge said: "I've got a better idea."

The two men looked at her.

"I'll go to the nunnery," Madge said. "The nuns won't be so nervous of a woman. Perhaps they will persuade Caris to see me."

Mark nodded. "At least then we'll know that she's alive."

Merthin said: "But . . . I need more than that. What is she thinking? Is she going to wait until the fuss dies down, then escape? Should I try to break her out of there? Or should I just wait—and, if so, how long? A month? A year? Seven years?"

"I'll ask her, if they'll let me in." Madge stood up. "You wait here."

"No, I'm coming with you," Merthin said. "I'll wait outside."

"In that case, Mark, why don't you come, too, to keep Merthin company?"

To keep Merthin out of trouble, she meant, but he made no objection. He had asked for their help. And he was grateful to have two people he trusted on his side.

They hurried back to the priory close. Mark and Merthin waited outside the hospital while Madge went in. Merthin saw that Caris's old dog, Scrap, was sitting at the door, waiting for her to reappear.

After Madge had been gone for half an hour, Merthin said: "I think they must have let her in, otherwise she'd be back by now."

"We'll see," said Mark.

They watched the last of the traders pack up and depart, leaving the cathedral green a sea of churned mud. Merthin paced up and down while Mark sat like a statue of Samson. One hour followed another. Despite his impatience, Merthin was glad of the delay, for almost certainly Madge was talking to Caris.

The sun was sinking over the west side of town when at last Madge emerged. Her expression was solemn and her face was wet with tears. "Caris is alive," she said. "And there's nothing wrong with her, physically or mentally. She's in her right mind."

"What did she say?" Merthin asked urgently.

"I'll tell you every word. Come, let's sit in the garden."

They went to the vegetable patch and sat on the stone bench, looking at the sunset. Madge's equanimity gave Merthin a bad feeling. He would have preferred her to be spitting with rage. Her manner told him the news was bad. He felt hopeless. He said: "Is it true that she doesn't want to see me?"

Madge sighed. "Yes."

"But why?"

"I asked her that. She said it would break her heart."

Merthin began to cry.

Madge went on in a low, clear voice. "Mother Cecilia left us alone, so that we could speak frankly, without being overheard. Caris believes that Godwyn and Philemon are determined to get rid of her, because of the application for a borough charter. She's safe in the nunnery, but if she ever leaves they will find her and kill her."

"She could escape and I could take her to London!" Merthin said. "Godwyn would never find us there!"

Madge nodded. "I said that to her. We discussed it for a long time. She feels the two of you would be fugitives for the rest of your lives. She's not willing to condemn you to that. It's your destiny to be the greatest builder of your generation. You will be famous. But, if she is with you, you will always have to lie about your identity and hide from the light of day."

"I don't care about that!"

"She told me you would say that. But she believes you do care about it, and what is more she thinks you should. Anyway, she cares about it. She will not take away your destiny, even if you ask her to."

"She could say this to me herself!"

"She's afraid you would talk her around."

Merthin knew Madge was telling the truth. Cecilia had been telling the truth, too. Caris did not want to see him. He felt choked with grief. He swallowed, wiped the tears from his face with his sleeve, and struggled to speak. "But what will she do?" he said.

"Make the best of it. Try to be a good nun."

"She hates the church!"

"I know she has never been very respectful of the clergy. In this town, it's not surprising. But she believes she can find some kind of consolation in a life dedicated to healing her fellow women and men."

Merthin thought about that. Mark and Madge watched him in silence. He could imagine Caris working in the hospital, taking care of sick people. But how would she feel about spending half the night singing and praying? "She might kill herself," he said after a long pause.

"I don't think so," Madge said with conviction. "She's terribly sad, but I don't see her taking that way out."

"She might kill someone else."

"That's more likely."

"Then again," Merthin said slowly and reluctantly, "she might find a kind of happiness."

Madge said nothing. Merthin looked hard at her. She nodded.

That was the terrible truth, he realized. Caris might be happy. She was losing her home, her freedom, and her husband-to-be; but she might still be happy, in the end.

There was nothing more to say.

Merthin stood up. "Thank you for being my friends," he said. He began to walk away.

Mark said: "Where are you going?"

Merthin stopped and turned back. There was a thought spinning in his head, and he waited for it to become clear. When it did, he was astonished. But he saw immediately that the idea was right. It was not merely right, it was perfect.

He wiped the tears from his face and looked at Mark and Madge in the red light of the dying sun.

"I'm going to Florence," he said. "Good-bye."

PART V

March 1346 to
December 1348

43

ister Caris left the nuns' cloisters and walked briskly into the hospital. There were three patients lying in beds. Old Julie was now too infirm to attend services or climb the stairs to the nuns' dormitory. Bella Brewer, the wife of Dick Brewer's son Danny, was recovering from a complicated birth. And Rickie Silvers, aged thirteen, had a broken arm which Matthew Barber had set. Two other people sat on a bench to one side, talking: a novice nun called Nellie, and a priory servant, Bob.

Caris's experienced gaze swept the room. Beside each bed was a dirty dinner plate. The dinner hour was long over. "Bob!" she said. He leaped to his feet. "Take away these plates. This is a monastery, and cleanliness is a virtue. Jump to it!"

"Sorry, Sister," he said.

"Nellie, have you taken Old Julie to the latrine?"

"Not yet, Sister."

"She always needs to go after dinner. My mother was the same. Take her quick, before she has an accident."

Nellie began to get the old nun up.

Caris was trying to develop the quality of patience, but after seven years as a nun she still had not succeeded, and she became frustrated by having to repeat instructions again and again. Bob knew he should clear away as soon as dinner was over—Caris had told him often. Nellie knew Julie's needs. Yet they sat on a bench gossiping until Caris surprised them with a lightning inspection.

She picked up the bowl of water that had been used for hand washing and walked the length of the room to throw it outside. A man she did not know was relieving himself against the outside wall. She guessed he was a traveler hoping for a bed. "Next time, use the latrine behind the stable," she snapped.

He leered at her, holding his penis in his hand. "And who are you?" he said insolently.

"I'm in charge of this hospital, and if you want to stay here tonight you'll have to improve your manners."

"Oh!" he said. "The bossy type, eh?" He took his time shaking the drops off.

"Put away your pathetic prick, or you won't be allowed to spend a night in this town, let alone at the priory." Caris threw the bowl of water at his middle. He jumped back, shocked, his hose soaked.

She went back inside and refilled the bowl at the fountain. There was an underground pipe running through the priory that brought clean water from upstream of the town and fed fountains in the cloisters, the kitchens, and the hospital. A separate branch of the subterranean stream flushed the latrines. One day, Caris wanted to build a new latrine adjacent to the hospital, so that senile patients such as Julie would not have to go so far.

The stranger followed her in. "Wash your hands," she said, handing him the bowl.

He hesitated, then took the bowl from her.

She looked at him. He was about her own age, twenty-nine. "Who are you?" she said.

"Gilbert of Hereford, a pilgrim," he said. "I've come to reverence the relics of St. Adolphus."

"In that case, you'll be welcome to stay a night here at the hospital, provided you speak respectfully to me—and to anyone else here, for that matter."

"Yes, Sister."

Caris returned to the cloisters. It was a mild spring day, and the sun shone on the smooth old stones of the courtyard. Along the west walk, Sister Mair was teaching the girls' school a new hymn, and Caris paused to observe. People said that Mair looked like an angel: she had clear skin, bright eyes, and a mouth shaped like a bow. The school was technically one of Caris's responsibilities—she was guest master, in charge of everyone who came into the nunnery from the outside world. She had attended this school herself, almost twenty years ago.

There were ten pupils, aged from nine to fifteen. Some were the daughters of Kingsbridge merchants; others were noblemen's children. The hymn, on the theme that God is good, came to an end, and one of the girls asked: "Sister Mair, if God is good, why did he let my parents die?"

It was the child's personal version of a classic question, one asked by all intelligent youngsters sooner or later: How can bad things happen? Caris had asked it herself. She looked with interest at the questioner. She was Tilly Shiring, twelve-year-old niece of Earl Roland, a girl with an impish look that Caris liked. Tilly's mother had bled to death after giving birth to her, and her father had broken his neck in a hunting accident not long afterward, so she had been brought up in the earl's household.

Mair gave a bland answer about God's mysterious ways. Tilly clearly was not satisfied, but was unable to articulate her misgivings, and fell silent. The question would come up again, Caris felt sure.

Mair started them singing the hymn again, then stepped over to speak to Caris.

"A bright girl," Caris said.

"The best in the class. In a year or two she'll be arguing with me fiercely."

"She reminds me of someone," Caris said, frowning. "I'm trying to remember her mother . . ."

Mair touched Caris's arm lightly. Gestures of affection were prohibited between nuns, but Caris was not strict about such things. "She reminds you of yourself," Mair said.

Caris laughed. "I was never that pretty."

But Mair was right: even as a child, Caris had asked skeptical questions. Later, when she became a novice nun, she had started an argument at every theology class. Within a week, Mother Cecilia had been obliged to order her to be silent during lessons. Then Caris had begun breaking the nunnery rules, and responding to correction by questioning the rationale behind convent discipline. Once again she had been enjoined to silence.

Before long, Mother Cecilia had offered her a deal. Caris could spend most of her time in the hospital—a part of the nuns' work she did believe in—and skip services whenever necessary. In exchange, Caris had to stop flouting discipline and keep her theological ideas to herself. Caris had agreed, reluctantly and sulkily, but Cecilia was wise, and the arrangement had worked. It was still working, for Caris now spent most of her time supervising the hospital. She missed more than half the services, and rarely said or did anything openly subversive.

Mair smiled. "You're pretty now," she said. "Especially when you laugh."

Caris found herself momentarily spellbound by Mair's blue eyes. Then she heard a child scream.

She turned away. The scream had come not from the group in the cloisters, but from the hospital. She hurried through the little lobby. Christopher Blacksmith was carrying a girl of about eight into the hospital. The child, whom Caris recognized as his daughter Minnie, was screaming in pain.

"Lay her on a mattress," Caris said.

Christopher put the child down.

"What happened?"

Christopher was a strong man in a panic, and he spoke in a strangely high-pitched voice. "She stumbled in my workshop and fell with her arm against a bar of red-hot iron. Do something for her, quickly, Sister, she's in such agony!"

Caris touched the child's cheek. "There, there, Minnie, we'll ease the pain very soon." Poppy-seed extract was too strong, she thought: it might kill such a small child. She needed a milder potion. "Nellie, go to my pharmacy and fetch the jar marked 'Hemp essence.' Walk quickly, but don't run—if you should stumble and break the vial, it will take hours to make up a new batch." Nellie hurried away.

Caris studied Minnie's arm. She had a nasty burn but, fortunately, it was restricted to the arm, nothing like as dangerous as the all-over burns people got in house fires. There were large angry blisters over most of the girl's forearm, and in the middle the skin was burned away to reveal charred flesh underneath.

Caris looked up for help and saw Mair. "Go to the kitchen and get me half a pint of wine and the same quantity of olive oil, in two separate jugs, please. Both need to be warm but not hot." Mair left.

Caris spoke to the child. "Minnie, you must try to stop screaming. I know it hurts, but you need to listen to me. I'm getting you some medicine. It will ease the pain." The screaming abated somewhat, and began to turn into sobbing.

Nellie arrived with the hemp essence. Caris poured some onto a spoon, then thrust the spoon into Minnie's open mouth and held her nose. The child swallowed. She screamed again, but after a minute she began to calm down.

"Give me a clean towel," Caris said to Nellie. They used a lot of towels in the hospital, and the cupboard behind the altar was always full of clean ones, by Caris's edict.

Mair came back from the kitchen with the oil and wine. Caris put a towel on the floor beside Minnie's mattress and moved the burned arm over the towel. "How do you feel?" she asked.

"It hurts," Minnie wailed.

Caris nodded in satisfaction. Those were the first coherent words the patient had uttered. The worst was over.

Minnie began to look sleepy as the hemp took effect. Caris said: "I'm going to put something on your arm to make it better. Try to keep still, will you?"

Minnie nodded.

Caris poured a little of the warm wine onto Minnie's wrist, where the burn was least bad. The child flinched, but did not try to snatch her arm away. Encouraged, Caris slowly moved the jug up the arm, pouring the wine over the worst of the burn to cleanse it. Then she did the same with the olive oil, which would soothe the place and protect the flesh from bad influences in the air. Finally she took a fresh towel and wrapped it lightly around the arm to keep the flies off.

Minnie was moaning, but half-asleep. Caris looked anxiously at her complexion. Her face was flushed pink with strain. That was good—if she had been turning pale, it would have been a sign that the dose had been too strong.

Caris was always nervous about drugs. The strength varied from batch to batch, and she had no precise way of measuring it. When weak, the medicine was ineffectual; when strong, dangerous. She was especially frightened of overdosing children, though the parents always pressured her for powerful medicine because they were so distressed by their children's pain.

At that point Brother Joseph came in. He was old now—somewhere in his late fifties—and all his teeth had fallen out, but he was still the priory's best monk-physician. Christopher Blacksmith immediately leaped to his feet. "Oh, Brother Joseph, thank God you're here," he said. "My little girl has a terrible burn."

"Let's have a look," said Joseph.

Caris stood back, hiding her irritation. Everyone believed the monks were powerful doctors, able to work near-miracles, whereas the nuns just fed the patients and cleared up. Caris had long ago stopped fighting that attitude, but it still annoyed her.

Joseph took off the towel and looked at the patient's arm. He prodded the burned flesh with his fingers. Minnie whimpered in her drugged sleep. "A bad burn, but not fatal," he said. He turned to Caris. "Make up a poultice of three parts chicken fat, three parts goat's dung, and one part white lead, and cover the burn with it. That will bring forth the pus."

"Yes, Brother." Caris was doubtful of the value of poultices. She had noticed that many injuries healed well without bringing forth the pus that monks thought such a healthy sign. In her experience, wounds sometimes became corrupt beneath such ointments. But the monks disagreed—except for Brother Thomas, who was convinced he had lost his arm because of the poultice prescribed by Prior Anthony almost twenty years ago. However, this was another battle Caris had given up. The monks' techniques had the authority of Hippocrates and Galen, the ancient writers on medicine, and everyone agreed they must be right.

Joseph left. Caris made sure that Minnie was comfortable and her father was reassured. "When she wakes up, she will be thirsty. Make sure she gets plenty to drink—weak ale or watered wine."

She was in no hurry to make the poultice. She would give God a few hours to work unaided before she began Joseph's treatment. The likelihood that the monk-physician would come back later to check on his patient was small. She sent Nellie out to collect goat dung from the green to the west of the cathedral; then she went to her pharmacy.

It was next to the monks' library. Unfortunately, she did not have large windows matching those in the library. The room was small and dark. However, it had a workbench, some shelves for her jars and vials, and a small fireplace for heating ingredients.

In a cupboard she kept a small notebook. Parchment was expensive, and a text block of identical sheets would be used only for holy scriptures. However, she had gathered a stack of odd-shaped offcuts and sewn them together. She kept a record of every patient with a serious complaint. She wrote down the date, the patient's name, the symptoms, and the treatment given; then later she added the results, always noting exactly how many hours or days had passed before the patient got better or worse. She often looked back over past cases to refresh her memory on how effective different treatments had been.

When she wrote down Minnie's age, it occurred to her that her own child would have been eight this year, if she had not taken Mattie Wise's potion. For no good reason, she thought her baby would have been a girl. She wondered how she would have reacted if her own daughter had suffered an accident. Would she have been able to deal so coolly with the emergency? Or would she have been almost hysterical with fear, like Christopher Blacksmith?

She had just finished logging the case when the bell rang for Evensong, and she went to the service. Afterward it was time for the nuns' supper. Then they went to bed, to get some sleep before they had to rise for Matins at three o'clock in the morning.

Instead of going to bed, Caris went back to her pharmacy to make the poultice. She did not mind the goat's dung—anyone who worked in a hospital saw worse things. But she wondered how Joseph could imagine it was a good thing to put on burned flesh.

She would not be able to apply it until morning, now. Minnie was a healthy child: her recovery would be well advanced by then.

While she was working, Mair came in.

Caris looked at her curiously. "What are you doing out of bed?"

Mair stood beside her at the workbench. "I came to help you."

"It doesn't take two people to make a poultice. What did Sister Natalie say?" Natalie was the subprioress, in charge of discipline, and no one could leave the dormitory at night without her permission.

"She's fast asleep. Do you really think you're not pretty?"

"Did you get out of bed to ask me that?"

"Merthin must have thought you were."

Caris smiled. "Yes, he did."

"Do you miss him?"

Caris finished mixing the poultice and turned away to wash her hands in a bowl. "I think about him every day," she said. "He is now the richest architect in Florence."

"How do you know?"

"I get news of him every Fleece Fair from Buonaventura Caroli."

"Does Merthin get news of you?"

"What news? There's nothing to tell. I'm a nun."

"Do you long for him?"

Caris turned back and gave Mair a direct look. "Nuns are forbidden to long for men."

"But not for women," Mair said, and she leaned forward and kissed Caris on the mouth.

Caris was so surprised that for a second she froze. Mair held the kiss. The touch of a woman's lips was soft, not like Merthin's. Caris was shocked, though not horrified. It was seven years since anyone had kissed her, and she realized suddenly how much she missed it.

In the silence, there was a loud noise from the library next door.

Mair jerked away guiltily. "What was that?"

"It sounded like a box being dropped on the floor."

"Who could it be?"

Caris frowned. "There shouldn't be anyone in the library at this time of night. Monks and nuns are in bed."

Mair looked scared. "What should we do?"

"We'd better go and look."

They left the pharmacy. Although the library was adjacent, they had to walk through the nuns' cloisters and into the monks' cloisters to reach the library door. It was a dark night, but they had both lived here for years, and they could find their way blindfolded. When they reached their destination, they saw a flickering light in the high windows. The door, normally locked at night, was ajar.

Caris pushed it open.

For a moment, she could not make out what she was looking at. She saw a closet door standing open, a box on a table, a candle next to it, and a shadowy figure. After a moment, she realized that the closet was the treasury, where charters and other valuables were kept, and the box was the chest containing the jeweled gold and silver ornaments used in the cathedral for special services. The shadowy man was taking objects out of the box and putting them in some kind of bag.

The figure looked up, and Caris recognized the face. It was Gilbert of Hereford, the pilgrim who had arrived earlier today. Except that he was no pilgrim, and he probably was not even from Hereford. He was a thief.

They stared at each other for a moment, no one moving.

Then Mair screamed.

Gilbert put out the candle.

Caris pulled the door shut, to delay him a second longer. Then she dashed along the cloisters and darted into a recess, pulling Mair with her.

They were at the foot of the stairs that led to the monks' dorm. Mair's scream would have awakened the men, but they might be slow to react. "Tell the monks what's happening!" Caris yelled at Mair. "Go on, run!" Mair dashed up the stairs.

Caris heard a creak, and guessed that the library door was opening. She listened for the sound of footsteps on the flagstones of the cloisters, but Gilbert must have been a practised burglar, for he walked silently. She held her breath and listened for his. Then a commotion broke out upstairs.

The thief must have realized then that he had only a few seconds to escape, for he broke into a run, and Caris heard his tread.

She did not care greatly for the precious cathedral ornaments, believing that gold and jewels probably pleased the bishop and the prior more than they pleased God; but she had taken a dislike to Gilbert, and she hated the idea that he might get rich by robbing the priory. So she stepped out of her recess.

She could hardly see, but there was no mistaking the running steps hurtling toward her. She held her arms out to protect herself, and he cannoned into her. She was knocked off balance, but grasped his clothing, and they both fell to the ground. There was a clatter as his sack of crucifixes and chalices hit the paving stones.

The pain of the fall enraged Caris, and she let go of his clothes and reached for where she thought his face might be. She encountered skin and dragged her fingernails across it, digging deep. He roared with pain and she felt blood flow under her fingertips.

But he was stronger. He grappled with her and swung himself on top. A light appeared from the head of the monks' stairs, and suddenly she could see Gilbert—and he could see her. Kneeling astride her, he punched her face, first with his right fist, then with his left, then with the right again. She cried out in agony.

There was more light. The monks were stumbling down the stairs. Caris heard Mair scream: "Leave her alone, you devil!" Gilbert leaped to his feet and scrabbled for his sack, but he was too late: suddenly Mair was flying at him with some kind of blunt instrument. He took a blow to the head, turned to retaliate, and fell beneath a tidal wave of monks.

Caris got to her feet. Mair came to her and they hugged.

Mair said: "What did you do?"

"Tripped him up then scratched his face. What did you hit him with?"

"The wooden cross off the dormitory wall."

"Well," said Caris, "so much for turning the other cheek."

44

Gilbert Hereford was tried before the ecclesiastical court, found guilty, and sentenced, by Prior Godwyn, to an appropriate punishment for those who robbed churches: he would be flayed alive. His skin would be cut off him, while he was fully conscious, and he would bleed to death.

On the day of the flaying, Godwyn had his weekly meeting with Mother Cecilia. Their deputies would also attend: Subprior Philemon and Subprioress Natalie. Waiting in the hall of the prior's house for the nuns to arrive, Godwyn said to Philemon: "We must try to persuade them to build a new treasury. We can no longer keep our valuables in a box in the library."

Philemon said thoughtfully: "Would it be a shared building?"

"It would have to be. We can't afford to pay for it."

Godwyn thought regretfully of the ambitions he had once had, as a young man, to reform the monastery's finances and make it rich again. This had not happened, and he still did not understand why. He had been tough, forcing the townspeople to use and pay for the priory's mills, fishponds, and warrens, but they seemed to find ways around his rules—like building mills in neighboring villages. He had imposed harsh sentences on men and women caught poaching or illegally cutting down trees in the priory's forests. And he had resisted the blandishments of those who would tempt him to spend the priory's money by building mills, or waste the priory's timber by licensing charcoal burners and iron smelters. He felt sure his approach was right, but it had not yet yielded the increased income he felt he deserved.

"So you will ask Cecilia for the money," Philemon said thoughtfully. "There might be advantages in keeping our wealth in the same place as the nuns'."

Godwyn saw which way Philemon's devious mind was leading him. "But we wouldn't say that to Cecilia."

"Of course not."

"All right, I'll propose it."

"While we're waiting . . ."

"Yes?"

"There's a problem you need to know about in the village of Long Ham."

Godwyn nodded. Long Ham was one of dozens of villages that paid homage—and feudal dues—to the priory.

Philemon explained: "It has to do with the landholding of a widow, Mary-Lynn. When her husband died, she agreed to let a neighbor farm her land, a man called John Nott. Now the widow has remarried, and she wants the land back so that her new husband can farm it."

Godwyn was puzzled. This was a typical peasant squabble, too trivial to require his intervention. "What does the bailiff say?"

"That the land should revert to the widow, since the arrangement was always intended to be temporary."

"Then that is what must happen."

"There is a complication. Sister Elizabeth has a half brother and two half sisters in Long Ham."

"Ah." Godwyn might have guessed there would be a reason for Philemon's interest. Sister Elizabeth, formerly Elizabeth Clerk, was the nuns' matricularius, in charge of their buildings. She was young and bright, and would rise farther up the hierarchy. She could be a valuable ally.

"They are the only family she's got, apart from her mother, who works at the Bell," Philemon went on. "Elizabeth is fond of her peasant relatives, and they in turn revere her as the holy one of the family. When they come to Kingsbridge they bring gifts to the nunnery—fruit, honey, eggs, that sort of thing."

"And . . . ?"

"John Nott is the half brother of Sister Elizabeth."

"Has Elizabeth asked you to intervene?"

"Yes. And she also asked that I should not tell Mother Cecilia of the request."

Godwyn knew that this was just the kind of thing Philemon liked. He loved to be regarded as a powerful person who could use his influence to favor one side or the other in a dispute. Such things fed his ego, which was never satisfied. And he was drawn to anything clandestine. The fact that Elizabeth did not want her superior to know about this request delighted Philemon. It meant he knew her shameful secret. He would store the information away like miser's gold.

"What do you want to do?" Godwyn asked.

"It's for you to say, of course, but I suggest we let John Nott keep the land. Elizabeth would be in our debt, and that cannot fail to be useful at some point in the future."

"That's hard on the widow," Godwyn said uneasily.

"I agree. But that must be balanced against the interests of the priory."

"And God's work is more important. Very well. Tell the bailiff."

"The widow will receive her reward in the hereafter."

"Indeed." There had been a time when Godwyn had hesitated to authorize Philemon's underhand schemes, but that was long ago. Philemon had proved too useful—as Godwyn's mother, Petranilla, had forecast all those years ago.

There was a tap at the door, and Petranilla herself came in.

She now lived in a comfortable small house in Candle Court, just off the main street. Her brother Edmund had left her a generous bequest, enough to last her the rest of her life. She was fifty-eight years old, her tall figure was now stooped and frail, and she walked with a stick, but she still had a mind like a bear trap. As always, Godwyn was glad to see her but also apprehensive that he might have done something to displease her.

Petranilla was the head of the family now. Anthony had been killed in the bridge collapse and Edmund had died seven years ago, so she was the last survivor of her generation. She never hesitated to tell Godwyn what to do. She was the same with her niece Alice. Alice's husband, Elfric, was the alderman, but she gave him orders, too. Her authority even extended to her stepgranddaughter Griselda, and she terrorized Griselda's eight-year-old son, Little Merthin. Her judgment was as sound as ever, so they all obeyed her most of the time. If for some reason she did not take command, they would usually ask her opinion anyway. Godwyn was not sure how they would manage without her. And on the rare occasions when they did not do her bidding, they worked very hard to hide the fact. Only Caris stood up to her. "Don't you dare tell me what to do," she had said to Petranilla more than once. "You would have let them kill me."

Petranilla sat down and looked around the room. "This is not good enough," she said.

She was often abrupt, but all the same Godwyn became edgy when she spoke like this. "What do you mean?"

"You should have a better house."

"I know." Eight years ago, Godwyn had tried to persuade Mother Cecilia to pay for a new palace. She had promised to give him the money three years later but, when the time came, she said she had changed her mind. He felt sure it was because of what he had done to Caris. After that heresy trial, his charm had ceased to work on Cecilia, and it had become difficult to get money out of her.

Petranilla said: "You need a palace for entertaining bishops and archbishops, barons and earls."

"We don't get many of those, nowadays. Earl Roland and Bishop Richard have been in France for much of the last few years." King Edward had invaded northeast France in 1339 and spent all of 1340 there; then in 1342 he had taken his army to northwest France and fought in Brittany. In 1345 English troops had done battle in the southwestern wine district of Gascony. Now Edward was back in England, but assembling another army of invasion.

"Roland and Richard aren't the only noblemen," Petranilla said testily.

"The others never come here."

Her voice hardened. "Perhaps that's because you can't accommodate them in the style they expect. You need a banqueting hall, and a private chapel, and spacious bedchambers."

She had been awake all night thinking about this, he guessed. That was her way: she brooded over things then shot off her ideas like arrows. He wondered what had brought on this particular complaint. "It sounds very extravagant," he said, playing for time.

"Don't you understand?" she snapped. "The priory is not as influential as it might be, simply because you don't ever see the powerful men of the land. When you've got a palace with beautiful rooms for them, they will come."

She was probably right. Wealthy monasteries such as Durham and St. Albans even complained about the number of noble and royal visitors they were obliged to entertain.

She went on: "Yesterday was the anniversary of my father's death." So that's what brought this on, Godwyn thought: she's been remembering Grandfather's glorious career. "You've been prior here for almost nine years," she said. "I don't want you to get stuck. The archbishops and the king should be considering you for a bishopric, a major abbey such as Durham, or a mission to the pope."

Godwyn had always assumed that Kingsbridge would be his springboard to higher things but, he realized now, he had let his ambition wane. It seemed only a little while ago that he had won the election for prior. He felt he had only just got on top of the job. But she was right, it was more than eight years.

"Why aren't they thinking of you for more important posts?" she asked rhetorically. "Because they don't know you exist! You are prior of a great monastery, but you haven't told anyone about it. Display your magnificence! Build a palace. Invite the archbishop of Canterbury to be your first guest. Dedicate the chapel to his favorite saint. Tell the king you have built a royal bedchamber in the hope that he will visit."

"Wait a moment, one thing at a time," Godwyn protested. "I'd love to build a palace, but I haven't got the money."

"Then get it," she said.

He wanted to ask her how, but at that moment the two leaders of the nunnery came into the room. Petranilla and Cecilia greeted one another with wary courtesy, then Petranilla took her leave.

Mother Cecilia and Sister Natalie sat down. Cecilia was fifty-one now, with gray in her hair and poor eyesight. She still darted about the place like a busy bird, poking her beak into every room, chirping her instructions to nuns, novices, and servants; but she had mellowed with the years, and would go a long way to avoid a conflict.

Cecilia was carrying a scroll. "The nunnery has received a legacy," she said as she made herself comfortable. "From a pious woman of Thornbury."

Godwyn said: "How much?"

"One hundred and fifty pounds in gold coins."

Godwyn was startled. It was a huge sum. It was enough to build a modest palace. "The nunnery has received it—or the priory?"

"The nunnery," she said firmly. "This scroll is our copy of her will."

"Why did she leave you so much money?"

"Apparently we nursed her when she fell ill on her way home from London."

Natalie spoke. She was a few years older than Cecilia, a round-faced woman with a mild disposition. "Our problem is, where are we going to keep the money?"

Godwyn looked at Philemon. Natalie had given them an opening for the topic they had planned to raise. "What do you do with your money at present?" he asked her.

"It's in the prioress's bedroom, which can be reached only by going through the dormitory."

As though thinking of it for the first time, Godwyn said: "Perhaps we should spend a little of the bequest on a new treasury."

"I think that's necessary," said Cecilia. "A simple stone building with no windows and a stout oak door."

"It won't take long to construct," Godwyn said. "And shouldn't cost more than five or ten pounds."

"For safety, we think it should be part of the cathedral."

"Ah." That was why the nuns had to discuss the plan with Godwyn. They would not have needed to consult him about building within their own area of the priory, but the church was common to monks and nuns. He said: "It could go up against the cathedral wall, in the corner formed by the north transept and the choir, but be entered from inside the church."

"Yes—that's just the kind of thing I had in mind."

"I'll speak to Elfric today, if you like, and ask him to give us an estimate."

"Please do."

Godwyn was happy to have extracted from Cecilia a fraction of her windfall, but he was not satisfied. After the conversation with his mother, he yearned to get his hands on more of it. He would have liked to grab it all. But how?

The cathedral bell tolled, and the four of them stood up and went out.

The condemned man was outside the west end of the church. He was naked, and tied tightly by his hands and feet to an upright wooden rectangle like a door frame. A hundred or so townspeople stood waiting to watch the execution. The ordinary monks and nuns had not been invited: it was considered improper for them to see bloodshed.

The executioner was Will Tanner, a man of about fifty whose skin was brown from his trade. He wore a clean canvas apron. He stood by a small table on which he had laid out his knives. He was sharpening one of them on a stone, and the scrape of steel on granite made Godwyn shudder.

Godwyn said several prayers, ending with an extempore plea in English that the death of the thief would serve God by deterring others from the same sin. Then he nodded to Will Tanner.

Will stood behind the tethered thief. He took a small knife with a sharp point and inserted it into the middle of Gilbert's neck, then drew it downward in a long straight line to the base of the spine. Gilbert roared with pain, and blood welled out of the cut. Will made another slash across the man's shoulders, forming the shape of the letter T.

Will then changed his knife, selecting one with a long, thin blade. He inserted it carefully at the point where the two cuts met, and pulled away a corner of skin. Gilbert cried out again. Then, holding the corner in the fingers of his left hand, Will began carefully to cut the skin of Gilbert's back away from his body.

Gilbert began to scream.

Sister Natalie made a noise in her throat, turned away, and ran back into the priory. Cecilia closed her eyes and began to pray. Godwyn felt nauseated. Someone in the crowd fell to the ground in a dead faint. Only Philemon seemed unmoved.

Will worked quickly, his sharp knife slicing through the subcutaneous fat to reveal the woven muscles below. Blood flowed copiously, and he stopped every few seconds to wipe his hands on his apron. Gilbert screamed in undiminished agony at every cut. Soon the skin of his back hung in two broad flaps.

Will knelt on the ground, his knees an inch deep in blood, and began to work on the legs.

The screaming stopped suddenly: Gilbert appeared to have passed out. Godwyn was relieved. He had intended the man to suffer agony for trying to rob a church—and he had wanted others to witness the thief's torment—but, all the same, he had found it hard to listen to that screaming.

Will continued his work phlegmatically, apparently unconcerned whether his victim was conscious or not, until all the back skin—body, arms, and legs—was detached. Then he went around to the front. He cut around the ankles and wrists, then detached the skin so that it hung from the victim's shoulders and hips. He worked upward from the pelvis, and Godwyn realized he was going to try to take the entire skin off in one piece. Soon there was no skin left attached except for the head.

Gilbert was still breathing.

Will made a careful series of cuts around the skull. Then he put down his knives and wiped his hands one more time. Finally he grasped Gilbert's skin at the shoulders and gave a sudden jerk upward. The face and scalp were ripped off the head, yet remained attached to the rest of the skin.

Will held Gilbert's bloody hide up in the air like a hunting trophy, and the crowd cheered.

Caris was uneasy about sharing the new treasury with the monks. She pestered Beth with so many questions about the safety of their money that in the end Beth took her to inspect the place.

Godwyn and Philemon were in the cathedral at the time, as if by chance, and they saw the nuns and followed them.

They passed through a new arch in the south wall of the choir into a little lobby and halted in front of a formidable studded door. Sister Beth took out a big iron key. She was a humble, unassuming woman, like most nuns. "This is ours," she said to Caris. "We can enter the treasury anytime we like."

"I should think so, since we paid for it," said Caris crisply.

They entered a small, square room. It contained a counting table with a stack of parchment rolls, a couple of stools, and a big ironbound chest.

"The chest is too big to be taken out through the door," Beth pointed out.

Caris said: "So how did you it get in here?"

Godwyn answered: "In pieces. It was put together by the carpenter here in the room."

Caris gave Godwyn a cold look. This man had tried to kill her. Ever since the witchcraft trial she had looked at him with loathing and avoided speaking to him if at all possible. Now she said flatly: "The nuns will need a key to the chest."

"Not necessary," Godwyn said quickly. "It contains the jeweled cathedral ornaments, which are in the care of the sacrist, who is always a monk."

Caris said: "Show me."

She could see that he was offended by her tone, and had half a mind to refuse her, but he wanted to appear open and guileless, so he conceded. He took a key from the wallet at his belt and opened the chest. As well as the cathedral ornaments, it contained dozens of scrolls, the priory's charters.

"Not just the ornaments, then," Caris said, her suspicions vindicated.

"The records, too."

"Including the nuns' charters," she persisted

"Yes."

"In which case we will have a key."

"My idea is that we copy all our charters, and keep the copies in the library. Whenever we need to read a charter, we consult the library copy, so that the precious originals can remain under lock and key."

Beth hated conflict, and intervened nervously. "That sounds like quite a sensible idea, Sister Caris."

Caris said grudgingly: "So long as the nuns always have access to their documents in some form." The charters were a secondary issue. Addressing Beth, rather than Godwyn, she said: "More importantly, where do we keep the money?"

Beth said: "In hidden vaults in the floor. There are four of them—two for the monks and two for the nuns. If you look carefully you can see the loose stones."

Caris studied the floor, and after a moment said: "I wouldn't have noticed if you hadn't told me, but I can see them now. Can they be locked?"

"I suppose they could," said Godwyn. "But then it would be obvious where they were, which would defeat the purpose of hiding them under flagstones."

"But this way the monks and nuns have access to one another's money."

Philemon spoke up. He looked accusingly at Caris and said: "Why are you here? You're the guest master—nothing to do with the treasury."

Caris's attitude to Philemon was simple loathing. She felt he was not fully human. He seemed to have no sense of right and wrong, no principles or scruples. Whereas she despised Godwyn as a wicked man who knew when he was doing evil, she felt that Philemon was more like a vicious animal, a mad dog or a wild boar. "I have an eye for detail," she told him.

"You're very mistrustful," he said resentfully.

Caris gave a humorless laugh. "Coming from you, Philemon, that's ironic."

He pretended to be hurt. "I don't know what you can mean."

Beth spoke again, trying to keep the peace. "I just wanted Caris to come and look because she asks questions I don't think of."

Caris said: "For example, how can we be sure that the monks don't take the nuns' money?"

"I'll show you," said Beth. Hanging on a hook on the wall was a stout length of oak. Using it as a lever, she prized up a flagstone. Underneath was a hollow space containing an ironbound chest. "We've had a locked casket made to fit each of these vaults," she said. She reached inside and lifted out the chest.

Caris examined it. It seemed strongly made. The lid was hinged, and the clasp was secured by a barrel padlock made of iron. "Where did we get the lock?" she asked.

"Christopher Blacksmith made it."

That was good. Christopher was a well-establish Kingsbridge citizen who would not risk his reputation by selling duplicate keys to thieves.

Caris was not able to fault the arrangements. Perhaps she had worried unnecessarily. She turned to go.

Elfric appeared, accompanied by an apprentice with a sack. "Is it all right to put up the warning?" Elfric said.

Philemon replied: "Yes, please, go ahead."

Elfric's assistant took from his sack something that looked like a big piece of leather.

Beth said: "What's that?"

"Wait," said Philemon. "You'll see."

The apprentice held the object up against the door.

"I've been waiting for it to dry out," Philemon said. "It's Gilbert Hereford's skin."

Beth gave a cry of horror.

Caris said: "That's disgusting."

The skin was turning yellow, and the hair was falling out of the scalp, but you could still make out the face: the ears, two holes for the eyes, and a gash of a mouth that seemed to grin.

"That should scare thieves away," Philemon said with satisfaction.

Elfric took out a hammer and began to nail the hide to the treasury door.

The two nuns left. Godwyn and Philemon waited for Elfric to finish his gruesome task, then they went back inside the treasury.

Godwyn said: "I think we're safe."

Philemon nodded: "Caris is a suspicious woman, but all her questions were answered satisfactorily."

"In which case . . ."

Philemon closed the door and locked it. Then he lifted the stone slab over one of the nuns' two vaults and took out the chest.

"Sister Beth keeps a small amount of cash for everyday needs somewhere in the nuns' quarters," he explained to Godwyn. "She comes in here only to deposit or withdraw larger sums. She always goes to the other vault, which contains mostly silver pennies. She almost never opens this chest, which contains the bequest."

He turned the box around and looked at the hinge at the back. It was fixed to the wood by four nails. He took from his pocket a thin steel chisel and a pair of pliers for gripping. Godwyn wondered where he had got the tools, but did not ask. Sometimes it was best not to know too many details.

Philemon slipped the sharp blade of the chisel under the edge of the iron hinge and pushed. The hinge came away from the wood slightly, and he pushed the blade in a little farther. He worked delicately and patiently, careful to make sure that the damage would not be visible to a casual glance. Gradually the flat plate of the hinge became detached, the nails coming out with it. When he had made enough room for the pliers to grip the nailheads, he pulled them out. Then he was able to detach the hinge and lift the lid.

"Here's the money from the pious woman of Thornbury," he said.

Godwyn looked into the chest. The money was in Venetian ducats. These gold coins showed the doge of Venice kneeling before St. Mark on one side and, on the other, the Virgin Mary, surrounded by stars to indicate that she was in Heaven. Ducats were intended to be interchangeable with florins from Florence, and were the same size, weight, and purity of metal. They were worth three shillings, or thirty-six English silver pennies. England had its own gold coins now, an innovation of King Edward's—nobles, half nobles, and quarter nobles—but these had been in circulation less than two years and had not yet displaced foreign gold coins.

Godwyn took fifty ducats, worth seven pounds and ten shillings. Philemon closed the lid of the chest. He wrapped each of the nails in a thin strip of leather, to make them a tight fit, and reattached the hinge. He put the chest back in the vault and lowered the slab over the hole.

"Of course they will notice the loss, sooner or later," he said.

"It may not be for years," Godwyn said. "We'll cross that bridge when we come to it."

They went out, and Godwyn locked the door.

Godwyn said: "Find Elfric, and meet me in the cemetery."

Philemon left. Godwyn went to the eastern end of the graveyard, just beyond the existing prior's house. It was a blowy May day, and the fresh wind made his robe flap around his legs. A loose goat was grazing among the tombstones. Godwyn watched it meditatively.

He was risking a terrible row with the nuns, he knew. He did not think they would discover their loss for a year or more, but he could not be sure. When they did find out, there would be hell to pay. But what, exactly, could they do? He was not like Gilbert Hereford, stealing money for himself. He had taken the bequest of a pious woman to use for holy purposes.

He thrust his worries aside. His mother was right: he needed to glorify his role as prior of Kingsbridge if he was going to make further progress.

When Philemon returned with Elfric, Godwyn said: "I want to build the prior's palace here, well to the east of the present building."

Elfric nodded. "A very good location, if I may say so, Lord Prior—close to the chapter house and the east end of the cathedral, but separated from the marketplace by the graveyard, so you'll have privacy and quiet."

"I want a big dining hall downstairs for banquets," Godwyn went on. "About a hundred feet long. It must be a really prestigious, impressive room, for entertaining the nobility, perhaps even royalty."

"Very good."

"And a chapel at the east end of the ground floor."

"But you'll be just a few steps from the cathedral."

"Noble guests don't always want to expose themselves to the people. They must be able to worship in private if they wish."

"And upstairs?"

"The prior's own chamber, of course, with room for an altar and a writing desk. And three large chambers for guests."

"Splendid."

"How much will it cost?"

"More than a hundred pounds—perhaps two hundred. I'll make a drawing then give you a more accurate estimate."

"Don't let it go above a hundred and fifty pounds. That's all I can afford."

If Elfric wondered where Godwyn had suddenly acquired a hundred and fifty pounds, he did not ask. "I'd better start stockpiling the stone as soon as possible," he said. "Can you give me some money to begin with?"

"How much would you like—five pounds?"

"Ten would be better."

"I'll give you seven pounds ten shillings, in ducats," Godwyn said, and handed over the fifty gold coins he had taken from the nuns' reserves.

Three days later, as the monks and nuns were filing out of the cathedral after the dinnertime service of Nones, Sister Elizabeth spoke to Godwyn.

Nuns and monks were not supposed to talk to one another casually, so she had to contrive a pretext. As it happened, there was a dog in the nave, and it had barked during the service. Dogs were always getting into the church and making a minor nuisance of themselves, but they were generally ignored. However, on this occasion Elizabeth left the procession to shoo the dog out. She was obliged to cross the line of monks, and timed her move so that she walked in front of Godwyn. She smiled apologetically at him and said: "I beg your pardon, Father Prior." Then she lowered her voice and said: "Meet me in the library, as if by accident." She chased the dog out of the west door.

Intrigued, Godwyn made his way to the library and sat down to read the Rule of St. Benedict. Shortly afterward, Elizabeth appeared and took out the Gospel of St. Matthew. The nuns had built their own library, after Godwyn took over as prior, in order to improve the separation between males and females; but when they removed all their books from the monks' library, the place had been denuded, and Godwyn had reversed his decision. The nuns' library building was now used as a schoolroom in cold weather.

Elizabeth sat with her back to Godwyn, so that anyone coming in would not get the impression that they were conspiring, but she was close enough for him to hear her clearly. "Something I felt I should tell you," she said. "Sister Caris doesn't like the nuns' money being kept in the new treasury."

"I knew that already," Godwyn said.

"She has persuaded Sister Beth to count the money, to make sure it's all still there. I thought you might like to know that, just in case you have . . . borrowed from them."

Godwyn's heart missed a beat. An audit would find the reserves short by fifty ducats. And he was going to need the rest to build his palace. He had not been expecting this so soon. He cursed Caris. How had she guessed what he had done so secretly?

"When?" he said, and there was a catch in his voice.

"Today. I don't know at what hour—it could be anytime. But Caris was most emphatic that you should have no advance warning."

He was going to have to put the ducats back, and fast. "Thank you very much," he said. "I appreciate your telling me this."

"It's because you showed favor to my family in Long Ham," she said; and she got up and went out.

Godwyn hurried after her. What luck that Elizabeth felt indebted to him! Philemon's instinct for intrigue was invaluable. As that thought crossed his mind, he saw Philemon in the cloisters. "Get those tools and meet me in the treasury!" he whispered. Then he left the priory.

He hurried across the green and into the main street. Elfric's wife, Alice, had inherited the house of Edmund Wooler, one of the largest homes in town, along with all the money Caris had made dyeing cloth. Elfric now lived in great luxury.

Godwyn knocked on the door and entered the hall. Alice was sitting at the table amid the remains of dinner. With her was her stepdaughter Griselda, and Griselda's son, Little Merthin. No one now believed that Merthin Fitzgerald was the little boy's father—he looked just like Griselda's runaway boyfriend Thurstan. Griselda had married one of her father's employees, Harold Mason. Polite people called the eight-year-old Merthin Haroldson, and the others called him Merthin Bastard.

Alice leaped up from her seat when she saw Godwyn. "Well, Cousin Prior, what a pleasure to have you in our house! Will you take a little wine?"

Godwyn ignored her polite hospitality. "Where's Elfric?"

"He's upstairs, taking a short nap before he goes back to work. Sit in the parlor, and I'll fetch him."

"Right away, if you please." Godwyn stepped into the next room. There were two comfortable-looking chairs, but he paced up and down.

Elfric came in rubbing his eyes. "Sorry about this," he said. "I was just—"

"Those fifty ducats I gave you three days ago," Godwyn said. "I need them back."

Elfric was startled. "But the money was for stone."

"I know what it was for! I have to have it right now."

"I've spent some of it, paying carters to bring the stones from the quarry."

"How much?"

"About half."

"Well, you can make that up out of your own funds, can't you?"

"Don't you want a palace anymore?"

"Of course I do, but I must have that money. Don't ask why, just give it to me."

"What am I to do with the stones I've bought?"

"Just keep them. You'll get the money again, I just need it for a few days. Hurry!"

"All right. Wait here. If you will."

"I'm not going anywhere."

Elfric went out. Godwyn wondered where he kept his money. In the hearth, under the firestone was the usual place. Being a builder, Elfric might have a more cunning hidey-hole. Wherever it was, he was back in a few moments.

He counted fifty gold coins into Godwyn's hand.

Godwyn said: "I gave you ducats—some of these are florins." The florin was the same size, but stamped with different images: John the Baptist on one side and a flower on the other.

"I don't have the same coins! I told you I've spent some of them. They're all worth the same, aren't they?"

They were. Would the nuns notice the difference?

Godwyn thrust the money into the wallet at his belt and left without another word.

He hurried back to the cathedral and found Philemon in the treasury. "The nuns are going to carry out an audit," he explained breathlessly. "I've got the money back from Elfric. Open that chest, quickly."

Philemon opened the vault in the floor, took out the chest, and removed the nails. He lifted the lid.

Godwyn sifted through the coins. They were all ducats.

It could not be helped. He dug down into the money and pushed his florins to the bottom. "Close it up and put it back," he said.

Philemon did so.

Godwyn felt a moment of relief. His crime was partly concealed. At least now it would not be glaringly obvious.

"I want to be here when she counts it," he said to Philemon. "I'm worried about whether she'll notice that she's now got some florins mixed in with her ducats."

"Do you know when they intend to come?"

"No."

"I'll put a novice to sweeping the choir. When Beth shows up, he can come and fetch us." Philemon had a little coterie of admiring novice monks eager to do his bidding.

However, the novice was not needed. As they were about to leave the treasury, Sister Beth and Sister Caris arrived.

Godwyn pretended to be in the middle of a conversation about accounts. "We'll have to look in an earlier account roll, Brother," he said to Philemon. "Oh, good day, sisters."

Caris opened both nuns' vaults and took out the two chests.

"Something I can help you with?" Godwyn said.

Caris ignored him.

Beth said: "We're just checking something, thank you, Father Prior. We won't be long."

"Go ahead, go ahead," he said benevolently, though his heart was hammering in his chest.

Caris said irritably: "There's no need to apologize for our being here, Sister Beth. It's our treasury and our money."

Godwyn opened an account roll at random, and he and Philemon pretended to study it. Beth and Caris counted the silver in the first chest: farthings, halfpennies, pennies, and a few Luxembourgs, forged pennies crudely made of adulterated silver and used as small change. There were a few assorted gold coins, too: florins, ducats, and similar coins—the genovino from Genoa and the reale from Naples—plus some larger French moutons and new English nobles. Beth checked the totals against a small notebook. When they had finished she said: "Exactly right."

They replaced all the coins in the chest, locked it, and put it back in its underfloor vault.

They began counting the gold coins in the other chest, putting them in piles of ten. When they got toward the bottom of the chest, Beth frowned and made a puzzled sound.

"What is it?" Caris said.

Godwyn felt a guilty dread.

Beth said: "This chest contains only the bequest from the pious woman of Thornbury. I kept it separate."

"And . . . ?"

"Her husband traded with Venice. I was sure the entire amount was in ducats. But there are some florins here, too."

Godwyn and Philemon froze, listening.

"That's odd," Caris said.

"Perhaps I made a mistake."

"It's a bit suspicious."

"Not really," Beth said. "Thieves don't put money into your treasury, do they?"

"You're right, they don't," Caris said reluctantly.

They finished counting. They had one hundred stacks of ten coins, worth a hundred and fifty pounds. "That's the exact figure in my book," Beth said.

"So every pound and penny is correct," Caris said.

Beth said: "I told you so."

45

Caris spent many hours thinking about Sister Mair.

She had been startled by the kiss, but more surprised at her own reaction to it. She had found it exciting. Until now, she had not felt attracted to Mair or any other woman. In fact there was only one person who had ever made her yearn to be touched and kissed and penetrated, and that was Merthin. In the nunnery she had learned to live without physical contact. The only hand that touched her sexually was her own, in the darkness of the dormitory, when she remembered the days of her courtship, and buried her face in the pillow so that the other nuns would not hear her panting.

She did not feel for Mair the same happy lust that Merthin inspired in her. But Merthin was a thousand miles away and seven years in the past. And she was fond of Mair. It was something to do with her angelic face, something about her blue eyes, some response to her gentleness in the hospital and the school.

Mair always spoke sweetly to Caris and, when no one was looking, touched her arm, or her shoulder, and once her cheek. Caris did not rebuff her, but she held back from responding. It was not that she thought it would be a sin. She felt sure God was much too wise to make a rule against women harmlessly pleasuring themselves or each other. But she was afraid of disappointing Mair. Instinct told her that Mair's feelings were strong and definite, whereas her own were uncertain. She's in love with me, Caris thought, but I'm not in love with her. If I kiss her again, she may hope that the two of us will be soul mates for life, and I can't promise her that.

So she did nothing, until Fleece Fair week.

The Kingsbridge fair had recovered from the slump of 1338. The trade in raw wool was still suffering from interference by the king, and the Italians came only every second year, but the new business of weaving and dyeing compensated. The town was still not as prosperous as it might have been, for Prior Godwyn's prohibition of private mills had driven the industry out of the city and into the surrounding villages; but most of the cloth was sold in the market, indeed it had become known as Kingsbridge Scarlet. Merthin's bridge had been finished by Elfric, and people poured across the wide double span with their packhorses and wagons.

So, on the Saturday night before the official opening of the fair, the hospital was full to bursting with visitors.

And one of them was ill.

His name was Maldwyn Cook, and his trade was to make salty little savories with flour and scraps of meat or fish, cook them quickly in butter over a fire, and sell them six for a farthing. Soon after he arrived, he was afflicted with a sudden, savage bellyache, followed by vomiting and diarrhea. There was nothing Caris could do for him other than give him a bed near the door.

She had long wanted to give the hospital its own latrine, so that she could supervise its cleanliness. But that was only one of the improvements she hoped for. She needed a new pharmacy, adjacent to the hospital, a spacious, well-lit room where she could prepare medicines and make her notes. And she was trying to figure out a way to give patients more privacy. At present everyone in the room could see a woman giving birth, a man having a fit, a child vomiting. People in distress should have small rooms of their own, she felt, like the side chapels in a large church. But she was not sure how to achieve this: the hospital was not big enough. She had had several discussions with Jeremiah Builder—who had been Merthin's apprentice Jimmie, many years ago—but he had not come up with a satisfactory solution.

Next morning, three more people had the same symptoms as Maldwyn Cook.

Caris fed the visitors breakfast and tipped them out into the market. Only the sick were allowed to stay behind. The floor of the hospital was filthier than usual, and she had it swept and swabbed. Then she went to the service in the cathedral.

Bishop Richard was not present. He was with the king, preparing to invade France again—he had always regarded his bishopric mainly as a means of supporting his aristocratic lifestyle. In his absence the diocese was run by Archdeacon Lloyd, who collected the bishop's tithes and rents, baptized children, and conducted services with dogged but unimaginative efficiency—a trait he illustrated by giving a tedious sermon on why God was more important than money, an odd note on which to open one of England's great commercial fairs.

Nevertheless, everyone was in high spirits, as was usual on the first day. The Fleece Fair was the high point of the year for the townspeople and the peasants of the surrounding villages. People made money at the fair and lost it gambling in the inns. Strapping village girls allowed themselves to be seduced by slick city boys. Prosperous peasants paid the town's prostitutes for services they dared not ask their wives to perform. There was usually a murder, often several.

Caris spotted the heavyset, richly dressed figure of Buonaventura Caroli in the congregation, and her heart faltered. He might have news of Merthin. She went through the service distractedly, mumbling the psalms. On the way out she managed to catch Buonaventura's eye. He smiled at her. She tried to indicate, with an inclination of her head, that she wanted him to meet her afterward. She was not sure whether he got the message.

However, she went to the hospital—the only place in the priory where a nun could meet a man from outside—and Buonaventura came in not long afterward. He wore a costly blue coat and pointed shoes. He said: "Last time I saw you, you had just been consecrated a nun by Bishop Richard."

"I'm guest master now," she said.

"Congratulations! I never expected you to take so well to convent life." Buonaventura had known her since she was a little girl.

"Nor did I," she laughed.

"The priory seems to be doing well."

"What makes you say that?"

"I see that Godwyn is building a new palace."

"Yes."

"He must be prospering."

"I suppose he is. How about you? Is trade good?"

"We have some problems. The war between England and France has disrupted transport, and your King Edward's taxes make English wool more expensive than the Spanish. But it's also better quality."

They always complained about taxes. Caris came to the subject that really interested her. "Any news of Merthin?"

"As a matter of fact, there is," Buonaventura said; and although his manner was as urbane as ever, she detected a hesitation. "Merthin is married."

Caris felt as if she had been punched. She had never expected this, never even thought of it. How could Merthin do this? He was . . . They were . . .

There was no reason at all why he should not get married, of course. She had rejected him more than once, and on the last occasion she had made her rejection final by entering the nunnery. It was only remarkable that he had waited so long. She had no right to feel hurt.

She forced a smile. "How splendid!" she said. "Please send him my congratulations. Who is the girl?"

Buonaventura pretended not to notice her distress. "Her name is Silvia," he said, as casually as if he were passing on harmless gossip. "She's the younger daughter of one of the city's most prominent citizens, Alessandro Christi, a trader in oriental spices who owns several ships."

"How old?"

He grinned. "Alessandro? He must be about my age . . ."

"Don't tease me!" She was grateful to Buonaventura for lightening the tone. "How old is Silvia?"

"Twenty-three."

"Six years younger than me."

"A beautiful girl . . ."

She sensed the unspoken qualification. "But . . . ?"

He tilted his head to one side apologetically. "She has the reputation of being sharp-tongued. Of course, people say all sorts of things . . . but perhaps that is why she remained single so long—girls in Florence generally marry before the age of eighteen."

"I'm sure it's true," Caris said. "The only girls Merthin liked in Kingsbridge were me and Elizabeth Clerk, and we're both shrews."

Buonaventura laughed. "Not so, not so."

"When was the wedding?"

"Two years ago. Not long after I last saw you."

Caris realized that Merthin had remained single until she had been consecrated as a nun. He would have heard, via Buonaventura, that she had taken the final step. She thought of him waiting and hoping, for more than four years, in a foreign country; and her brittle facade of good cheer began to crack.

Buonaventura said: "And they have a child, a little baby girl called Lolla."

That was too much. All the grief Caris had felt seven years ago—the pain she thought had gone forever—came back in a rush. She had not truly lost him back then in 1339, she realized. He had remained loyal to her memory for years. But she had lost him now, finally, eternally.

She was shaken as if by a fit, and she knew she could not hold out much longer. Trembling, she said: "It's such a pleasure to see you, and catch up with the news, but I must get back to my work."

His face showed concern. "I hope I haven't upset you too much. I thought you would prefer to know."

"Don't be kind to me—I can't stand it." She turned from him and hurried away.

She bent her head to hide her face as she walked from the hospital into the cloisters. Searching for somewhere to be alone, she ran up the stairs to the dormitory. There was no one there in the daytime. She began to sob as she walked the length of the bare room. At the far end was Mother Cecilia's bedroom. No one was allowed in there without an invitation, but Caris went in anyway, slamming the door behind her. She fell on Cecilia's bed, not caring that her nun's cap had fallen off. She buried her face in the straw mattress and wept.

After a while she felt a hand on her head, stroking her short-cropped hair. She had not heard the person enter the room. She did not care who it was. All the same she was slowly, gradually soothed. Her sobs became less wrenching, her tears dried, and the storm of her emotions began to die down. She rolled over and looked up at her comforter. It was Mair.

Caris said: "Merthin is married—he has a baby girl." She began to cry again.

Mair lay down on the bed and cradled Caris's head in her arms. Caris pressed her face into Mair's soft breasts, letting the woolen robe soak up the tears. "There, there," said Mair.

After a while, Caris calmed down. She was too drained to feel any more sorrow. She thought of Merthin holding a dark-haired little Italian baby, and saw how happy he would be. She was glad that he was happy, and she drifted into an exhausted sleep.

The illness that had started with Maldwyn Cook spread like a summer fire through the crowds at the Fleece Fair. On Monday it leaped from the hospital to the taverns, then on Tuesday from the visitors to the townspeople. Caris noted its characteristics in her book: it began with stomach pains, led quickly to vomiting and diarrhea, and lasted between twenty-four and forty-eight hours. It left adults not much the worse, but killed old people and small babies.

On Wednesday, it struck the nuns and the children in the girls' school. Both Mair and Tilly were affected. Caris sought out Buonaventura, at the Bell, and worriedly asked him whether Italian doctors had any treatment for such diseases. "There's no cure," he said. "None that works, anyway, though doctors nearly always prescribe something just to get more money out of people. But some Arab physicians believe you can retard the spread of such illnesses."

"Oh, really?" Caris was interested. Traders said that Muslim doctors were superior to their Christian counterparts, although the priest-physicians denied this hotly. "How?"

"They believe the disease is acquired when a sick person looks at you. Sight functions by beams that issue from the eyes and touch the things we see—rather like extending a finger to feel whether something is warm, or dry, or hard. But the beams may also project sickness. Therefore you can avoid the disease by never being in the same room as a sufferer."

Caris did not think illness could be transmitted by looks. If that were true then, after an important service in the cathedral, everyone in the congregation would acquire any illness the bishop had. Whenever the king was ill, he would infect all the hundreds of people who saw him. And surely someone would have noticed that.

However, the notion that you should not share a room with someone who was ill did seem convincing. Here in the hospital, Maldwyn's illness seemed to spread from a sufferer to those nearby: the sick man's wife and family were the first to catch it, followed by people in neighboring beds.

She had also observed that certain kinds of illness—stomach upsets, coughs and colds, and poxes of all sorts—seemed to flare up during fairs and markets; so it seemed obvious that they were passed from one person to another by some means.

On Wednesday night at supper, half the guests in the hospital were suffering from the illness; then by Thursday morning every one of them had it. Several priory servants also succumbed, so Caris was short of people to clean up.

Surveying the chaos at breakfasttime, Mother Cecilia suggested closing the hospital.

Caris was ready to consider anything. She felt dismayed at her own powerlessness to combat the disease, and devastated by the filth of her hospital. "But where would the people sleep?" she said.

"Send them to the taverns."

"The taverns have the same problem. We could put them in the cathedral."

Cecilia shook her head. "Godwyn won't have peasants puking in the nave while services go on in the choir."

"Wherever they sleep, we ought to separate the sick from the well. That's the way to retard the spread of the illness, according to Buonaventura."

"It makes sense."

Caris was struck by a new idea, something that suddenly seemed very obvious, though she had not thought of it before. "Perhaps we shouldn't just improve the hospital," she said. "Maybe we should build a new one, just for sick people, and keep the old one for pilgrims and other healthy visitors."

Cecilia looked thoughtful. "It would be costly."

"We've got a hundred and fifty pounds." Caris's imagination began to work. "It could incorporate a new pharmacy. We could have private rooms for people who are chronically ill."

"Find out what it would cost. You could ask Elfric."

Caris hated Elfric. She had disliked him even before he had given evidence against her. She did not want him to build her new hospital. "Elfric is busy building Godwyn's new palace," she said. "I'd rather consult Jeremiah."

"By all means."

Caris felt a rush of affection for Cecilia. Although she was a martinet, tough on discipline, she gave her deputies room to make their own decisions. She had always understood the conflicting passions that drove Caris. Instead of trying to suppress those passions, Cecilia had found ways to make use of them. She had given Caris work that engaged her and provided outlets for her rebellious energy. Here I am, Caris thought, plainly incapable of dealing with the crisis in front of me, and my superior is calmly telling me to forge ahead with a new long-term project. "Thank you, Mother Cecilia," she said.

Later that day she walked around the priory grounds with Jeremiah and explained her aspirations. He was as superstitious as ever, seeing the work of saints and devils in the most trivial of everyday incidents. Nevertheless, he was an imaginative builder, open to new ideas: he had learned from Merthin. They quickly settled on the best location for the new hospital, immediately to the south of the existing kitchen block. It would be apart from the rest of the buildings, so that sick people would have less contact with the healthy, but food would not have to be carried far, and the new building could still be accessed conveniently from the nuns' cloisters. With the pharmacy, the new latrines, and an upper floor with private rooms, Jeremiah thought it would cost about a hundred pounds—most of the legacy.

Caris discussed the site with Mother Cecilia. It was land that belonged neither to the monks nor the nuns, so they went to see Godwyn about it.

They found him on the site of his own building project, the new palace. The shell was up and the roof was on. Caris had not visited the site for some weeks, and she was surprised at its size—it was going to be as big as her new hospital. She saw why Buonaventura had called it impressive: the dining hall was larger than the nuns' refectory. The site was swarming with workmen, as if Godwyn was in a hurry to get it finished. Masons were laying a floor of colored tiles in a geometric pattern, several carpenters were making doors, and a master glazier had set up a furnace to make the windows. Godwyn was spending a lot of money.

He and Philemon were showing the new building to Archdeacon Lloyd, the bishop's deputy. Godwyn broke off as the nuns approached. Cecilia said: "Don't let us interrupt you—but, when you're finished, will you meet me outside the hospital? There's something I need to show you."

"By all means," said Godwyn.

Caris and Cecilia walked back through the marketplace in front of the cathedral. Friday was bargain day at the Fleece Fair, when traders sold their remaining stocks at reduced prices so that they would not have to carry the goods home. Caris saw Mark Webber, round-faced and round-bellied now, wearing a coat of his own bright scarlet. His four children were helping at his stall. Caris was especially fond of Dora, now fifteen, who had her mother's bustling confidence in a slimmer body.

"You're looking prosperous," Caris said to Mark with a smile.

"The wealth should have come to you," he replied. "You invented the dye. I just did what you said. I almost feel as if I cheated you."

"You've been rewarded for hard work," she said. She did not mind that Mark and Madge had done so well out of her invention. Although she had always enjoyed the challenge of doing business, she had never lusted for money—perhaps because she had always taken it for granted, growing up in her father's wealthy household. Whatever the reason, she felt no pang of regret that the Webbers were making a fortune that might have been hers. The cashless life of the priory seemed to suit her well. And she was thrilled to see the Webber children healthy and well dressed. She remembered when all six of them had to find sleeping space on the floor of a single room, most of which was taken up by a loom.

She and Cecilia went to the south end of the priory grounds. The land around the stables looked like a farmyard. There were a few small buildings: a dovecote, a henhouse, and a tool shed. Chickens scratched in the dirt, and pigs rooted in the kitchen garbage. Caris itched to tidy it up.

Godwyn and Philemon joined them soon, with Lloyd tagging along. Cecilia indicated the patch of land next to the kitchens, and said: "I'm going to build a new hospital, and I want to put it there. What do you think?"

"A new hospital?" Godwyn said. "Why?"

Caris thought he looked anxious, which puzzled her.

Cecilia said: "We want a hospital for the sick and a separate guest house for healthy visitors."

"What an extraordinary idea."

"It's because of the stomach illness that started with Maldwyn Cook. This is a particularly virulent example, but diseases often flare up at markets, and part of the reason they spread so fast may be that we have the sick and the well eating and sleeping and going to the latrine together."

Godwyn took umbrage. "Oho!" he said. "So the nuns are the physicians now, are they?"

Caris frowned. This kind of sneering was not Godwyn's style. He used charm to get his way, especially with powerful people such as Cecilia. This fit of pique was covering something else.

"Of course not," Cecilia said. "But we all know that some illnesses spread from one sufferer to the next—that's obvious."

Caris put in: "The Muslim physicians believe illness is transmitted by looking at the sick person."

"Oh, do they? How interesting!" Godwyn spoke with ponderous sarcasm. "Those of us who have spent seven years studying medicine at the university are always glad to be lectured on illness by young nuns barely out of their novitiate."

Caris was not intimidated. She felt no inclination to show respect to a lying hypocrite who had tried to murder her. She said: "If you don't believe in the transmission of illness, why don't you prove your sincerity by coming to the hospital tonight and sleeping alongside a hundred people suffering from nausea and diarrhea?"

Cecilia said: "Sister Caris! That will be enough." She turned to Godwyn. "Forgive her, Father Prior. It wasn't my intention to engage you in a discussion about disease with a mere nun. I just want to make sure you don't object to my choice of site."

"You can't build it now, anyway," Godwyn said. "Elfric is too busy with the palace."

Caris said: "We don't want Elfric—we're using Jeremiah."

Cecilia turned on her. "Caris, be quiet! Remember your place. Don't interrupt my conversation with the lord prior again."

Caris realized she was not helping Cecilia, and—against her inclination—she lowered her head and said: "I'm sorry, Mother Prioress."

Cecilia said to Godwyn: "The question is not *when* we build, it's *where*."

"I'm afraid I don't approve of this," he said stiffly.

"Where would you prefer the new building to be sited?"

"I don't think you need a new hospital at all."

"Forgive me, but I am in charge of the nunnery," Cecilia said with asperity. "You can't tell me how I should spend our money. However, we normally consult one another before putting up new buildings—although it has to be said that you forgot this little courtesy when planning your palace. Nevertheless, I am consulting you—merely on the question of the location of the building." She looked at Lloyd. "I'm sure the archdeacon will agree with me on this."

"There must be agreement," Lloyd said noncommittally.

Caris frowned, baffled. Why did Godwyn care? He was building his palace on the north side of the cathedral. It made no difference to him if the nuns put up a new building down here in the south, where most monks hardly ever came. What was he worried about?

Godwyn said: "I'm telling you that I do not approve of the location nor of the building, so that is the end of the matter!"

Caris suddenly saw, in a flash of inspiration, the reason for Godwyn's behavior. She was so shocked that she blurted it out. "You stole our money!"

Cecilia said: "Caris! I told you—"

"He's stolen the legacy of the woman of Thornbury!" Caris said, overriding Cecilia in her outrage. "That's where he got the money for his palace, of course. And now he's trying to stop us building because he knows we'll go to the treasury and find that our money has vanished!" She felt so indignant she might burst.

Godwyn said: "Don't be preposterous."

As a response, it was so muted that Caris knew she must have touched a nerve. Confirmation made her even angrier. "Prove it!" she yelled. She forced herself to speak more calmly. "We'll go to the treasury now and check the vaults. You wouldn't object to that, would you, Father Prior?"

Philemon chipped in: "It would be a completely undignified proceeding, and there is no question of the prior submitting himself to it."

Caris ignored him. "There should be one hundred and fifty pounds in gold in the nuns' reserves."

"Out of the question," said Godwyn.

Caris said: "Well, clearly the nuns will have to check the vaults anyway, now that the accusation has been made." She looked at Cecilia, who nodded in agreement. "So, if the prior prefers not to be present, no doubt the archdeacon will be happy to attend as a witness."

Lloyd looked as if he would have preferred not to get involved in this dispute, but it was hard for him to refuse to play the role of umpire, so he muttered: "If I can help both sides, of course . . ."

Caris's mind was racing on. "How did you open the chest?" she said. "Christopher Blacksmith made the lock, and he's too honest to give you a duplicate key and help you steal from us. You must have broken the box open, then repaired it somehow. What did you do, take off the hinge?" She saw Godwyn glance involuntarily at his subprior. "Ah," Caris said triumphantly, "so *Philemon* took the hinge off. But the prior took the money, and gave it to Elfric."

Cecilia said: "Enough speculation. Let's settle the matter. We'll all go to the treasury and open the box, and that will be an end to it."

Godwyn said: "It wasn't stealing."

Everyone stared at him. There was a shocked silence.

Cecilia said: "You're admitting it!"

"It wasn't stealing," Godwyn repeated. "The money is being used for the benefit of the priory and the glory of God."

Caris said: "It makes no difference. It wasn't your money!"

"It's God's money," Godwyn said stubbornly.

Cecilia said: "It was left to the nunnery. You know that. You saw the will."

"I know nothing of any will."

"Of course you do. I gave it to you, to make a copy . . ." Cecilia tailed off.

Godwyn said again: "I know nothing of any will."

Caris said: "He's destroyed it. He said he would make a copy, and put the original in the chest, in the treasury . . . but he destroyed it."

Cecilia was staring openmouthed at Godwyn. "I should have known," she said. "After what you tried to do to Caris—I should never have trusted you again. But I thought your soul might yet have been saved. I was so wrong."

Caris said: "It's a good thing we made our own copy of the will, before handing it over." She was inventing this in desperation.

Godwyn said: "A forgery, obviously."

Caris said: "If the money was yours in the first place, you will have had no need to break open the casket to get it. So let's go and look. That will settle it one way or another."

Philemon said: "The fact that the hinge has been tampered with proves nothing."

"So I was right!" said Caris. "But how do you know about the hinge?

Sister Beth has not opened the vault since the audit, and the box was fine then. You must have removed it from the vault yourself, if you know that it has been interfered with."

Philemon looked bewildered, and had no answer.

Cecilia turned to Lloyd. "Archdeacon, you are the bishop's representative. I think it's your duty to order the prior to return this money to the nuns."

Lloyd looked worried. He said to Godwyn: "Have you got any of the money left?"

Caris said furiously: "When you've caught a thief, you don't ask him whether he can afford to relinquish his ill-gotten gains!"

Godwyn said: "More than half has already been spent on the palace."

"Building must stop immediately," Caris said. "The men must be dismissed today, the building torn down and the materials sold. You have to return every penny. What you can't pay in cash, after the palace has been demolished, you must make up in land or other assets."

"I refuse," Godwyn said.

Cecilia addressed Lloyd again. "Archdeacon, please do your duty. You cannot allow one of the bishop's subordinates to steal from another, no matter that they both do God's work."

Lloyd said: "I can't adjudicate a dispute such as this myself. It's too serious."

Caris was speechless with fury and dismay at Lloyd's weakness.

Cecilia protested: "But you must!"

He looked trapped, but he shook his head stubbornly. "Accusations of theft, destruction of a will, a charge of forgery . . . This must go to the bishop himself!"

Cecilia said: "But Bishop Richard is on his way to France—and no one knows when he will be back. Meanwhile, Godwyn is spending the stolen money!"

"I can't help that, I'm afraid," Lloyd said. "You must appeal to Richard."

"Very well, then," said Caris. Something in her tone made them all look at her. "In that case there's only one thing to do. We'll go and find our bishop."

46

In July of 1346, King Edward III assembled the largest invasion fleet England had ever seen, almost a thousand ships, at Portsmouth. Contrary winds delayed the armada, but they finally set sail on July 11, their destination a secret.

Caris and Mair arrived in Portsmouth two days later, just missing Bishop Richard, who had sailed with the king.

They decided to follow the army to France.

It had not been easy to get approval even for the trip to Portsmouth. Mother Cecilia had invited the nuns in chapter to discuss the proposal, and some had felt that Caris would be in moral and physical danger. But nuns did leave their convents, not just on pilgrimages, but on business errands to London, Canterbury, and Rome. And the Kingsbridge sisters wanted their stolen money back.

However, Caris was not sure that she would have got permission to cross the Channel. Fortunately she was not able to ask.

She and Mair could not have followed the army immediately, even if they had known the king's destination, because every seaworthy vessel on the south coast of England had been commandeered for the invasion. So they fretted with impatience at a nunnery just outside Portsmouth and waited for news.

Caris learned later that King Edward and his army disembarked on a broad beach at St.-Vaast-la-Hogue, on the north coast of France near Barfleur. However, the fleet did not return immediately. Instead, the ships followed the coast eastward for two weeks, tracking the invading army as far as Caen. There they loaded their holds with booty: jewelry, expensive cloth, and gold and silver plate looted by Edward's army from the prosperous burgesses of Normandy. Then they returned.

One of the first back was the *Grace,* which was a cog—a broad-built cargo ship with rounded prow and stern. Her captain, a leather-faced salt called Rollo, was full of praise for the king. He had been paid at scarcity rates for his ship and his men, and he had gained a good share of the plunder himself. "Biggest army I've ever seen," Rollo said with relish. He thought there were at least fifteen thousand men, about half of them archers, and probably five thousand horses. "You'll have your work cut out to catch up with them," he said. "I'll take you to Caen, the last place I know them to have been, and you can pick up their trail there. Whatever direction they've taken, they'll be about a week ahead of you."

Caris and Mair negotiated a price with Rollo then went aboard the *Grace* with two sturdy ponies, Blackie and Stamp. They could not travel any faster than the army's horses, but the army had to stop and fight every so often, Caris reasoned, and that should enable her to catch up.

When they reached the French side and sailed into the estuary of the Orne, early on a sunny August morning, Caris sniffed the breeze and noticed the unpleasant smell of old ashes. Studying the landscape on either side of the river, she saw that the farmland was black. It looked as if the crops had been burned in the fields. "Standard practice," Rollo said. "What the army can't take must be destroyed, otherwise it could benefit the enemy." As they neared the port of Caen, they passed the hulks of several burned-out ships, presumably fired for the same reason.

"No one knows the king's plan," Rollo told them. "He may go south and advance on Paris, or swing northeast to Calais and hope to meet up there with his Flemish allies. But you'll be able to follow his trail. Just keep the blackened fields on either side of you."

Before they disembarked, Rollo gave them a ham. "Thank you, but we've got some smoked fish and hard cheese in our saddlebags," Caris said to him. "And we have money—we can buy anything else we need."

"Money may not be much use to you," the captain replied. "There may be nothing to buy. An army is like a plague of locusts, it strips the country bare. Take the ham."

"You're very kind. Good-bye."

"Pray for me, if you would, Sister. I've committed some heavy sins in my time."

Caen was a city of several thousand houses. Like Kingsbridge, its two halves, Old Town and New Town, were divided by a river, the Odon, which was spanned by St. Peter's Bridge. On the riverbank near the bridge, a few fishermen were selling their catch. Caris asked the price of an eel. She found the answer difficult to understand: the fisherman spoke a dialect of French she had never heard. When at last she was able to make out what he was saying, the price took her breath away. Food was so scarce, she realized, that it was more precious than jewels. She was grateful for Rollo's generosity.

They had decided that if they were questioned they would say they were Irish nuns traveling to Rome. Now, however, as she and Mair rode away from the river, Caris wondered nervously whether local people would know from her accent that she was English.

There were not many local people to be seen. Broken-down doors and smashed shutters revealed empty houses. There was a ghostly hush—no vendors crying their wares, no children quarreling, no church bells. The only work being done was burial. The battle had taken place more than a week ago, but small groups of grim-faced men were still bringing corpses out of buildings and loading them onto carts. It looked as if the English army had simply massacred men, women and children. They passed a church where a huge pit had been dug in the churchyard, and saw the bodies being tipped into a mass grave, without coffins or even shrouds, while a priest intoned a continuous burial service. The stench was unspeakable.

A well-dressed man bowed to them and asked if they needed assistance. His proprietorial manner suggested that he was a leading citizen concerned to make sure no harm came to religious visitors. Caris declined his offer of help, noting that his Norman French was no different from that of a nobleman in England. Perhaps, she thought, the lower orders all had their different local dialects, while the ruling class spoke with an international accent.

The two nuns took the road east out of town, glad to leave the haunted streets behind. The countryside was deserted, too. The bitter taste of ash was always on Caris's tongue. Many of the fields and orchards on either side of the road had been fired. Every few miles they rode through a heap of charred ruins that had been a village. The peasants had either fled before the army or died in the conflagration, for there was little life: just the birds, the occasional pig or chicken overlooked by the army's foragers, and sometimes a dog, nosing through the debris in a bewildered way, trying to pick up the scent of its master in a pile of cold embers.

Their immediate destination was a nunnery half a day's ride from Caen. Whenever possible, they would spend the night at a religious house—nunnery, monastery, or hospital—as they had on the way from Kingsbridge to Portsmouth. They knew the names and locations of fifty-one such institutions between Caen and Paris. If they could find them, as they hurried in the scorched footprints of King Edward, their accommodation and food would be free and they would be safe from thieves—and, Mother Cecilia would add, from fleshly temptations such as strong drink and male company.

Cecilia's instincts were sharp, but she had not sensed that a different kind of temptation was in the air between Caris and Mair. Because of that, Caris had at first refused Mair's request to come with her. She was focused on moving fast, and she did not want to complicate her mission by entering into a passionate entanglement—or by refusing so to do. On the other hand, she needed someone courageous and resourceful as her companion. Now she was glad of her choice: of all the nuns, Mair was the only one with the guts to go chasing the English army through France.

She had planned to have a frank talk before they left, saying that there should be no physical affection between them while they were away. Apart from anything else, they could get into terrible trouble if they were seen. But somehow she had never got around to the frank talk. So here they were in France with the issue still hanging unmentioned, like an invisible third traveler riding between them on a silent horse.

They stopped at midday by a stream on the edge of a wood, where there was an unburned meadow for the ponies to graze. Caris cut slices from Rollo's ham, and Mair took from their baggage a loaf of stale bread from Portsmouth. They drank the water from the stream, though it had the taste of cinders.

Caris suppressed her eagerness to get going, and forced herself to let the horses rest for the hottest hour of the day. Then, as they were getting ready to leave, she was startled to see someone watching her. She froze, with the ham in one hand and her knife in the other.

Mair said: "What is it?" Then she followed Caris's gaze, and understood.

Two men stood a few yards away, in the shade of the trees, staring at them. They looked quite young, but it was hard to be sure, for their faces were sooty and their clothing was filthy.

After a moment, Caris spoke to them in Norman French. "God bless you, my children."

They made no reply. Caris guessed they were unsure what to do. But what possibilities were they considering? Robbery? Rape? They had a predatory look.

She was scared, but she made herself think calmly. Whatever else they might want, they must be starving, she calculated. She said to Mair: "Quickly, give me two trenchers of that bread."

Mair cut two thick slices off the big loaf. Caris cut corresponding slabs from the ham. She put the ham on the bread, then said to Mair: "Give them one each."

Mair looked terrified, but she walked across the grass with an unhesitating step and offered the food to the men.

They both snatched it and began to wolf it down. Caris thanked her stars that she had guessed right.

She quickly put the ham in her saddlebag and the knife in her belt, then climbed onto Blackie. Mair followed suit, stowing the bread and mounting Stamp. Caris felt safer on horseback.

The taller of the two men came toward them, moving quickly. Caris was tempted to kick her pony and take off, but she did not quite have time; and then the man's hand was holding her bridle. He spoke through a mouthful of food. "Thank you," he said with the heavy local accent.

Caris said: "Thank God, not me. He sent me to help you. He is watching over you. He sees everything."

"You have more meat in your bag."

"God will tell me who to give it to."

There was a pause, while the man thought that over, then he said: "Give me your blessing."

Caris was reluctant to extend her right arm in the traditional gesture of blessing—it would take her hand too far away from the knife at her belt. It was only a short-bladed food knife of the kind carried by every man and woman, but it was enough to slash the back of the hand that held her bridle and cause the man to let go.

Then she was inspired. "Very well," she said. "Kneel down."

The man hesitated.

"You must kneel to receive my blessing," she said in a slightly raised voice.

Slowly, the man knelt, still holding his food in his hand.

Caris turned her gaze on his companion. After a moment, the second man did the same.

Caris blessed them both, then kicked Blackie and quickly trotted away. After a moment she looked back. Mair was close behind her. The two starving men stood staring at them.

Caris mulled over the incident anxiously as they rode through the afternoon. The sun shone cheerfully, as on a fine day in Hell. In some places, smoke was rising fitfully from a patch of woodland or a smoldering barn. But the countryside was not totally deserted, she realized gradually. She saw a pregnant woman harvesting beans in a field that had escaped the English torches; the scared faces of two children looking out from the blackened stones of a manor house; and several small groups of men, usually flitting through the fringes of woodland, moving with the alert purposefulness of scavengers. The men worried her. They looked hungry, and hungry men were dangerous. She wondered whether she should stop fretting about speed and worry instead about safety.

Finding their way to the religious houses where they planned to stop was also going to be more difficult than Caris had thought. She had not anticipated that the English army would leave such devastation in its wake. She had assumed there would be peasants around to direct her. It could be hard enough in normal times to get such information from people who had never traveled farther than the nearest market town. Now her interlocutors would also be elusive, terrified, or predatory.

She knew by the sun that she was heading east, and she thought, judging by the deep cartwheel ruts in the baked mud, that she was on the main road. Tonight's destination was a village named, after the nunnery at its center, Hôpital-des-Soeurs. As the shadow in front of her grew longer, she looked about with increasing urgency for someone whom she could ask for directions.

Children fled from their approach in fear. Caris was not yet desperate enough to risk getting close to the hungry-looking men. She hoped to come across a woman. There were no young women anywhere, and Caris had a bleak suspicion about the fate they might have met at the hands of the marauding English. Occasionally she saw, in the far distance, a few lonely figures harvesting a field that had escaped burning; but she was reluctant to go too far from the road.

At last they found a wrinkled old woman sitting under an apple tree next to a substantial stone house. She was eating small apples wrenched from the tree long before they were ripe. She looked terrified. Caris dismounted, to seem less intimidating. The old woman tried to hide her poor meal in the folds of her dress, but she seemed not to have the strength to run away.

Caris addressed her politely. "Good evening, mother. Will this road take us to Hôpital-des-Soeurs, may I ask?"

The woman seemed to pull herself together, and answered intelligently. Pointing in the direction in which they were heading, she said: "Through the woods and over the hill."

Caris saw that she had no teeth. It must have been almost impossible to eat unripe apples with your gums, she thought with pity. "How far?" she asked.

"A long way."

All distances were long at her age. "Can we get there by nightfall?"

"On a horse, yes."

"Thank you, mother."

"I had a daughter," said the old woman. "And two grandsons. Fourteen years and sixteen. Fine boys."

"I'm very sorry to hear that."

"The English," said the old woman. "May they all burn in Hell."

Evidently it did not occur to her that Caris and Mair might be English. That answered Caris's question: local people could not tell the nationality of strangers. "What were the boys' names, mother?"

"Giles and Jean."

"I will pray for the souls of Giles and Jean."

"Have you any bread?"

Caris looked around, to make sure there was no one else lurking nearby, ready to pounce, but they were alone. She nodded to Mair, who took from her saddlebag the remains of the loaf and offered it to the old woman.

The woman snatched it from her and began to gnaw it with her gums.

Caris and Mair rode away.

Mair said: "If we keep giving our food away, we're going to starve."

"I know," said Caris. "But how can you refuse?"

"We can't fulfill our mission if we're dead."

"But we are nuns, after all," Caris said with asperity. "We must help the needy, and leave it to God to decide when it's time for us to die."

Mair was startled. "I've never heard you talk like that before."

"My father hated people who preached about morality. We're all good when it suits us, he used to say: that doesn't count. It's when you want so badly to do something wrong—when you're about to make a fortune from a dishonest deal, or kiss the lovely lips of your neighbor's wife, or tell a lie to get yourself out of terrible trouble—that's when you need the rules. Your integrity is like a sword, he would say: you shouldn't wave it until you're about to put it to the test. Not that he knew anything about swords."

Mair was silent for a while. She might have been mulling over what Caris had said, or she might simply have given up the argument: Caris was not sure.

Talk of Edmund always made Caris realize how much she missed him. After her mother died he had become the cornerstone of her life. He had always been there, standing at her shoulder, as it were, ready when she needed sympathy and understanding, or shrewd advice, or just information: he had known so much about the world. Now, when she turned in that direction, there was just an empty space.

They passed through a patch of woodland then breasted a rise, as the old woman had forecast. Looking down on a shallow valley, they saw another burned village, the same as all the rest but for a cluster of stone buildings that looked like a small convent. "This must be Hôpital-des-Soeurs," said Caris. "Thank God."

She realized, as she approached, how used to nunnery life she had become. As they rode down the hill, she found herself looking forward to the ritual washing of hands, a meal taken in silence, bedtime at nightfall, even the sleepy peacefulness of Matins at three o'clock in the morning. After what she had seen today, the security of those gray stone walls was alluring, and she kicked the tired Blackie into a trot.

There was no one moving about the place, but that was not really surprising: it was a small house in a village, and you would not expect the kind of hustle and bustle seen at a major priory such as Kingsbridge. Still, at this time of day there should have been a column of smoke from a kitchen fire as the evening meal was prepared. However, as she came closer she saw further ominous signs, and a sense of dismay slowly engulfed her. The nearest building, which looked like a church, appeared to have no roof. The windows were empty sockets, lacking shutters or glass. Some of the stone walls were blackened, as if by smoke.

The place was silent: no bells, no cries of hostlers or kitchen hands. It was deserted, Caris realized despondently as she reined in. And it had been fired, like every other building in the village. Most of the stone walls were still standing, but the timber roofs had fallen in, doors and other woodwork had burned, and glass windows had shattered in the heat.

Mair said unbelievingly: "They set fire to a nunnery?"

Caris was equally shocked. She had believed that invading armies invariably left ecclesiastical buildings intact. It was an iron rule, people said. A commander would not hesitate to put to death a soldier who violated a holy place. She had accepted that without question. "So much for chivalry," she said.

They dismounted and walked, stepping cautiously around charred beams and scorched rubble, to the domestic quarters. As they approached the kitchen door, Mair gave a shriek and said: "Oh, God, what's that?"

Caris knew the answer. "It's a dead nun." The corpse on the ground was naked, but had the cropped hair of a nun. The body had somehow survived the fire. The woman was about a week dead. The birds had already eaten her eyes, and parts of her face had been nibbled by some scavenging animal.

Also, her breasts had been cut off with a knife.

Mair said in amazement: "Did the *English* do this?"

"Well, it wasn't the French."

"Our soldiers have foreigners fighting alongside them, don't they? Welshmen and Germans and so on. Perhaps it was them."

"They're all under the orders of our king," Caris said with grim disapprobation. "He brought them here. What they do is his responsibility."

They stared at the hideous sight. As they looked, a mouse came out of the corpse's mouth. Mair screamed and turned away.

Caris hugged her. "Calm down," she said firmly, but she stroked Mair's back to comfort her. "Come on," she said after a moment. "Let's get away from here."

They returned to their horses. Caris resisted an impulse to bury the dead nun: if they delayed, they would still be here at nightfall. But where were they to go? They had planned to spend the night here. "We'll go back to the old woman with the apple tree," she said. "Her house is the only intact building we've seen since we left Caen." She glanced anxiously at the setting sun. "If we push the horses, we can be there before it's full dark."

They urged their tired ponies forward, and headed back along the road. Directly ahead of them the sun sank all too quickly below the horizon. The last of the light was fading when they arrived back at the house by the apple tree.

The old woman was happy to see them, expecting them to share their food, which they did, eating in the dark. Her name was Jeanne. There was no fire, but the weather was mild, and the three women rolled up side by side in their blankets. Not fully trusting their hostess, Caris and Mair lay down clutching the saddlebags that contained their food.

Caris lay awake for a while. She was pleased to be on the move after such a long delay in Portsmouth, and they had made good progress in the last two days. If she could find Bishop Richard, she felt sure he would force Godwyn to repay the nuns' money. He was no paragon of integrity, but he was open-minded, and in his lackadaisical way he dispensed justice evenhandedly. Godwyn had not had things all his own way even in the witchcraft trial. She felt sure she could persuade Richard to give her a letter ordering Godwyn to sell priory assets in order to give back the stolen cash.

But she was worried about her safety and Mair's. Her assumption that soldiers would leave nuns alone had been quite wrong: what they had seen at Hôpital-des-Soeurs had made that clear. She and Mair needed a disguise.

When she woke up at first light, she said to Jeanne: "Your grandsons—do you still have their clothes?"

The old woman opened a wooden chest. "Take what you want," she said. "I have no one to give them to." She picked up a bucket and went off to fetch water.

Caris began to sort through the garments in the chest. Jeanne had not asked for payment. Clothes had little monetary value after so many people had died, she guessed.

Mair said: "What are you up to?"

"Nuns aren't safe," Caris said. "We're going to become pages in the service of a minor lord—Pierre, *sieur* of Longchamp in Brittany. Pierre is a common name and there must be lots of places called Longchamp. Our master has been captured by the English, and our mistress has sent us to find him and negotiate his ransom."

"All right," Mair said eagerly.

"Giles and Jean were fourteen and sixteen, so with luck their clothes will fit us."

Caris picked out a tunic, leggings, and a cape with a hood, all in the dull brown of undyed wool. Mair found a similar outfit in green, with short sleeves and an undershirt. Women did not usually wear underdrawers, but men did, and fortunately Jeanne had lovingly washed the linen garments of her dead family. Caris and Mair could keep their own shoes: the practical footwear of nuns was no different from what men wore.

"Shall we put them on?" said Mair.

They pulled off their nuns' robes. Caris had never seen Mair undressed, and she could not resist a peek. Her companion's naked body took her breath away. Mair's skin seemed to glow like a pink pearl. Her breasts were generous, with pale girlish nipples, and she had a luxuriant bush of fair pubic hair. Caris was suddenly conscious that her own body was not as beautiful. She looked away, and quickly began to put on the clothes she had chosen.

She pulled the tunic over her head. It was just like a woman's dress except that it stopped at the knee instead of the ankles. She pulled up the linen underdrawers and the leggings, then put her shoes and belt back on.

Mair said: "How do I look?"

Caris studied her. Mair had put a boy's cap over her short blond hair, and tilted it at an angle. She was grinning. "You look so happy!" Caris said in surprise.

"I've always liked boys' clothes." Mair swaggered up and down the small room. "This is how they walk," she said. "Always taking more space than they need." It was such an accurate imitation that Caris burst out laughing.

Caris was struck by a thought. "Are we going to have to pee standing up?"

"I can do it, but not in undershorts—too inaccurate."

Caris giggled. "We can't leave off the drawers—a sudden flurry of wind could expose our . . . pretenses."

Mair laughed. Then she began to stare at Caris in a way that was strange but not entirely unfamiliar, looking her up and down, meeting her eyes and holding her gaze.

"What are you doing?" said Caris.

"This is how men look at women, as if they own us. But be careful—if you do it to a man, he becomes aggressive."

"This could be more difficult than I thought."

"You're too beautiful," Mair said. "You need a dirty face." She went to the fireplace and blackened her hand with soot. Then she smeared it on Caris's face. Her touch was like a caress. My face isn't beautiful, Caris thought; no one ever judged it so—except Merthin, of course . . .

"Too much," Mair said after a minute, and wiped some off with her other hand. "That's better." She smeared Caris's hand and said: "Now do me."

Caris spread a faint smudge on Mair's jawline and throat, making it look as if she might have a light beard. It felt very intimate, to be looking so hard at her face, and touching her skin so softly. She dirtied Mair's forehead and cheeks. Mair looked like a pretty boy—but she did not look like a woman.

They studied one another. A smile played on the red bow of Mair's lips. Caris felt a sense of anticipation, as if something momentous was about to happen. Then a voice said: "Where are the nuns?"

They both turned around guiltily. Jeanne stood in the doorway, holding a heavy bucket of fresh water, looking frightened. "What have you done to the nuns?" she said.

Caris and Mair burst out laughing, and then Jeanne recognized them. "How you have changed yourselves!" she exclaimed.

They drank some of the water, and Caris shared out the rest of the smoked fish for breakfast. It was a good sign, she thought as they ate, that Jeanne had not recognized them. If they were careful, perhaps they could get away with this.

They took their leave of Jeanne and rode off. As they breasted the rise before Hôpital-des-Soeurs, the sun came up directly ahead of them, casting a red light on the nunnery, making the ruins look as if they were still burning. Caris and Mair trotted quickly through the village, trying not to think about the mutilated corpse of the nun lying there in the debris, and rode on into the sunrise.

47

By Tuesday, August 22, the English army was on the run.

Ralph Fitzgerald was not sure how it had happened. They had stormed across Normandy from west to east, looting and burning, and no one had been able to withstand them. Ralph had been in his element. On the march, a soldier could take anything he saw—food, jewelry, women—and kill any man who stood in his way. It was how life ought to be lived.

The king was a man after Ralph's own heart. Edward III loved to fight. When he was not at war he spent most of his time organizing elaborate tournaments, costly mock battles with armies of knights in specially designed uniforms. On the campaign, he was always ready to lead a sortie or raiding party, hazarding his life, never pausing to balance risks against benefits like a Kingsbridge merchant. The older knights and earls commented on his brutality, and had protested about incidents such as the systematic rape of the women of Caen, but Edward did not care. When he had heard that some of the Caen citizens had thrown stones at soldiers who were ransacking their homes, he had ordered that everyone in the town should be killed, and only relented after vigorous protests by Sir Godfrey de Harcourt and others.

Things had started to go wrong when they came to the River Seine. At Rouen they had found the bridge destroyed, and the town—on the far side of the water—heavily fortified. King Philippe VI of France was there in person, with a mighty army.

The English marched upstream, looking for a place to cross, but they found that Philippe had been there before them, and one bridge after another was either strongly defended or in ruins. They went as far as Poissy, only twenty miles from Paris, and Ralph thought they would surely attack the capital—but older men shook their heads sagely and said it was impossible. Paris was a city of fifty thousand men, and they must by now have heard the news from Caen, so they would be prepared to fight to the death, knowing they could expect no mercy.

If the king did not intend to attack Paris, Ralph asked, what was his plan? No one knew, and Ralph suspected that Edward had no plan other than to wreak havoc.

The town of Poissy had been evacuated, and the English engineers were able to rebuild its bridge—fighting off a French attack at the same time—so at last the army crossed the river.

By then it was clear that Philippe had assembled an army larger by far than the English, and Edward decided on a dash to the north, with the aim of joining up with an Anglo-Flemish force invading from the northeast.

Philippe gave chase.

Today the English were encamped south of another great river, the Somme, and the French were playing the same trick as they had at the Seine. Sorties and reconnaissance parties reported that every bridge had been destroyed, every riverside town heavily fortified. Even more ominously, an English detachment had seen, on the far bank, the flag of Philippe's most famous and frightening ally, John, the blind king of Bohemia.

Edward had started out with fifteen thousand men in total. In six weeks of campaigning many of those had fallen, and others had deserted, to find their way home with their saddlebags full of gold. He had about ten thousand left, Ralph calculated. Reports of spies suggested that in Amiens, a few miles upstream, Philippe now had sixty thousand foot soldiers and twelve thousand mounted knights, an overwhelming advantage in numbers. Ralph was more worried than he had been since he first set foot in Normandy. The English were in trouble.

Next day they marched downstream to Abbeville, location of the last bridge before the Somme widened into an estuary; but the burgesses of the town had spent money, over the years, strengthening the walls, and the English could see it was impregnable. So cocksure were the citizens that they sent out a large force of knights to attack the vanguard of the English army, and there was a fierce skirmish before the locals withdrew back inside their walled town.

When Philippe's army left Amiens, and started advancing from the south, Edward found himself trapped in the point of a triangle: on his right the estuary, on his left the sea, and behind him the French army, baying for the blood of the barbaric invaders.

That afternoon, Earl Roland came to see Ralph.

Ralph had been fighting in Roland's retinue for seven years. The earl no longer regarded him as an untried boy. Roland still gave the impression that he did not much like Ralph, but he certainly respected him, and would always use him to shore up a weak point in the line, lead a sally, or organize a raid. Ralph had lost three fingers from his left hand, and had walked with a limp when tired ever since a Frenchman's pikestaff had cracked his shinbone outside Nantes in 1342. Nevertheless, the king had not yet knighted Ralph, an omission which caused Ralph bitter resentment. For all the loot he had garnered—most of it held for safekeeping by a London goldsmith—Ralph was unfulfilled. He knew that his father would be equally dissatisfied. Like Gerald, Ralph fought for honor, not money;

but in all this time he had not climbed a single step up the staircase of nobility.

When Roland appeared, Ralph was sitting in a field of ripening wheat that had been trampled to shreds by the army. He was with Alan Fernhill and half a dozen comrades, eating a gloomy dinner, pea soup with onions: food was running out, and there was no meat left. Ralph felt as they did, tired from constant marching, dispirited by repeated encounters with broken bridges and well-defended towns, and scared of what would happen when the French army caught up with them.

Roland was now an old man, his hair and beard gray, but he still walked erect and spoke with authority. He had learned to keep his expression stonily impassive, so that people hardly noticed that the right side of his face was paralyzed. He said: "The estuary of the Somme is tidal. At low tide, the water may be shallow in places. But the bottom is thick mud, making it impassable."

"So we can't cross," said Ralph. But he knew Roland had not come just to give him bad news, and his spirits lifted optimistically.

"There may be a ford—a point where the bottom is firmer," Roland went on. "If there is, the French will know."

"You want me to find out."

"As quick as you like. There are some prisoners in the next field."

Ralph shook his head. "Soldiers might have come from anywhere in France, or even other countries. It's the local people who will have the information."

"I don't care who you interrogate. Just come to the king's tent with the answer by nightfall." Roland walked away.

Ralph drained his bowl and leaped to his feet, glad to have something aggressive to do. "Saddle up, lads," he said.

He still had Griff. Miraculously, his favorite horse had survived seven years of war. Griff was somewhat smaller than a warhorse, but had more spirit than the oversize destriers most knights preferred. He was now experienced in battle, and his iron-shod hooves gave Ralph an extra weapon in the melee. Ralph was more fond of him than of most of his human comrades. In fact the only living creature to whom he felt closer was his brother, Merthin, whom he had not seen for seven years—and might never see again, for Merthin had gone to Florence.

They headed northeast, toward the estuary. Every peasant living within half a day's walk would know of the ford if there was one, Ralph calculated. They would use it constantly, crossing the river to buy and sell livestock, to attend the weddings and funerals of relatives, to go to markets and fairs and religious festivals. They would be reluctant to give information to the invading English, of course—but he knew how to solve that problem.

They rode away from the army, into territory that had not yet suffered from the arrival of thousands of men, where there were sheep in the pastures and crops ripening in the fields. They came to a village from which the estuary could be seen in the far distance. They kicked their horses into a canter along the grassy track that led into the village. The one-room and two-room hovels of the serfs reminded Ralph of Wigleigh. As he expected, the peasants fled in all directions, the women carrying babies and children, most of the men holding an axe or a sickle.

Ralph and his companions had played out this drama twenty or thirty times in the past few weeks. They were specialists in gathering intelligence. Usually, the army's leaders wanted to know where local people had hidden their stocks. When they heard the English were coming, the sly peasants drove their cattle and sheep into woods, stashed sacks of flour in holes in the ground, and hid bales of hay in the bell tower of the church. They knew they would probably starve to death if they revealed where their food was, but they always told sooner or later. On other occasions the army needed directions, perhaps to an important town, a strategic bridge, a fortified abbey. The peasants would usually answer such inquiries unhesitatingly, but it was necessary to make sure they were not lying, for the shrewder among them might try to deceive the invading army, knowing the soldiers were not able to return to punish them.

As Ralph and his men chased the fleeing peasants across gardens and fields, they ignored the men and concentrated on the women and children. Ralph knew that if he captured them, their husbands and fathers would come back.

He caught up with a girl of about thirteen. He rode alongside her for a few seconds, watching her terrified expression. She was dark-haired and dark-skinned, with plain, homely features, young but with a rounded woman's body—the type he liked. She reminded him of Gwenda. In slightly different circumstances he would have enjoyed her sexually, as he had several similar girls in the last few weeks.

But today he had other priorities. He turned Griff to cut her off. She tried to dodge him, tripped over her own feet, and fell flat in a vegetable patch. Ralph leaped off his horse and grabbed her as she got up. She screamed and scratched his face, so he punched her in the stomach to quiet her. Then he grabbed her long hair. Walking his horse, he began to drag her back to the village. She stumbled and fell, but he just kept going, dragging her along by the hair; and she struggled to her feet, crying in pain. After that, she did not fall again.

They gathered in the little wooden church. The eight English soldiers had captured four women, four children, and two babies in arms. They made them sit on the floor in front of the altar. A few moments later a man ran in, babbling in the local French, begging and pleading. Four others followed.

Ralph was pleased.

He stood at the altar, which was only a wooden table painted white. "Quiet!" he shouted. He waved his sword. They fell silent. He pointed at a young man. "You," he said. "What are you?"

"A leather worker, lord. Please don't harm my wife and child, they've done you no wrong."

He pointed to another man. "You?"

The girl he had captured gasped, and Ralph concluded that they were related; father and daughter, he guessed.

"Just a poor cowherd, lord."

"A cowherd?" That was good. "And how often do you take cattle across the river?"

"Once or twice a year, lord, when I go to market."

"And where is the ford?"

He hesitated. "Ford? There is no ford. We have to cross the bridge at Abbeville."

"Are you sure?"

"Yes, lord."

He looked around. "All of you—is this the truth?"

They nodded.

Ralph considered. They were scared—terrified—but they could still be lying. "If I fetch the priest, and he brings a Bible, will you all swear on your immortal souls that there is no ford across the estuary?"

"Yes, lord."

But that would take too long. Ralph looked at the girl he had captured. "Come here."

She took a step back.

The cowherd fell to his knees. "Please, lord, don't harm an innocent child, she is only thirteen—"

Alan Fernhill picked up the girl as if she were a sack of onions and threw her to Ralph, who caught her and held her. "You're lying to me, all of you. There is a ford, I'm sure there is. I just need to know exactly where it is."

"All right," said the cowherd. "I'll tell you, but leave the child alone."

"Where is the ford?"

"It's a mile downstream from Abbeville."

"What's the name of the village?"

The cowherd was thrown by the question for a moment, then he said: "There is no village, but you can see an inn on the far side."

He was lying. He had never traveled, so he did not realize that there was always a village by a ford.

Ralph took the girl's hand and placed it on the altar. He drew his knife. With a swift movement, he cut off one of her fingers. His heavy blade easily split her small bones. The girl screamed in agony, and her blood spurted red over the white paint of the altar. All the peasants cried out with horror. The cowherd took an angry step forward, but was stopped by the point of Alan Fernhill's sword.

Ralph kept hold of the girl with one hand, and held up the severed finger on the point of his knife.

"You are the devil himself," the cowherd said, shaking with shock.

"No, I'm not." Ralph had heard that accusation before, but it still stung him. "I'm saving the lives of thousands of men," he said. "And if I have to, I'll cut off the rest of her fingers, one by one."

"No, no!"

"Then tell me where the ford really is." He brandished the knife.

The cowherd shouted: "The Blanchetaque, it's called the Blanchetaque, please leave her alone!"

"The Blanchetaque?" said Ralph. He was pretending skepticism, but in fact this was promising. It was an unfamiliar word, but it sounded as if it might mean a white platform, and it was not the kind of thing that a terrified man would invent on the spur of the moment.

"Yes, lord, they call it that because of the white stones on the river bottom that enable you to cross the mud." He was panic-stricken, tears streaming down his face, so he was almost certainly telling the truth, Ralph thought with satisfaction. The cowherd babbled on: "People say the stones were put there in olden times, by the Romans, please leave my little girl alone."

"Where is it?"

"Ten miles downstream from Abbeville."

"Not a mile?"

"I'm telling the truth this time, lord, as I hope to be saved!"

"And the name of the village?"

"Saigneville."

"Is the ford always passable, or only at low tide?"

"Only at low tide, lord, especially with livestock or a cart."

"But you know the tides."

"Yes."

"Now, I have only one more question for you, but it is a very important one. If I even suspect you may be lying to me, I will cut off her whole hand." The girl screamed. Ralph said: "You know I mean it, don't you?"

"Yes, lord, I'll tell you anything!"

"When is low tide tomorrow?"

A look of panic came over the cowherd. "Ah—ah—let me work it out!" The man was so wrought up he could barely think.

The leather worker said: "I'll tell you. My brother crossed yesterday, so I know. Low tide tomorrow will be in the middle of the morning, two hours before noon."

"Yes!" said the cowherd. "That's right! I was just trying to calculate. Mid-morning, or a little after. Then again in the evening."

Ralph kept hold of the girl's bleeding hand. "How sure are you?"

"Oh, lord, as sure as I am of my own name, I swear!"

The man probably did not know his own name right now, he was so distracted with terror. Ralph looked at the leather worker. There was no sign of deceit on his face, no defiance or eagerness to please in his expression: he just looked a bit ashamed of himself, as if he had been forced, against his will, to do something wrong. This is the truth, Ralph thought exultantly; I've done it.

He said: "The Blanchetaque. Ten miles downstream from Abbeville, at the village of Saigneville. White stones on the river bottom. Low tide at mid-morning tomorrow."

"Yes, lord."

Ralph let go of the girl's wrist, and she ran sobbing to her father, who put his arms around her. Ralph looked down at the pool of blood on the white altar table. There was a lot of it, for a slip of a girl. "All right, men," he said. "We're finished here."

The trumpets woke Ralph at first light. There was no time to light a fire or eat breakfast: the army struck camp immediately. Ten thousand men had to travel six miles by mid-morning, most of them on foot.

The prince of Wales's division led the march off, followed by the king's division, then the baggage train, then the rear guard. Scouts were sent out to check how far away the French army was. Ralph was in the vanguard, with the sixteen-year-old prince, who had the same name as his father, Edward.

They hoped to surprise the French by crossing the Somme at the ford. Last night the king had said: "Well done, Ralph Fitzgerald." Ralph had long ago learned that such words meant nothing. He had performed numerous useful or brave tasks for King Edward, Earl Roland, and other nobles, but he still had not been knighted. On this occasion he felt little resentment. His life was in as much danger today as it had ever been, and he was so glad to have found an escape route for himself that he hardly cared whether anyone gave him credit for saving the entire army.

As they marched, dozens of marshals and undermarshals patrolled constantly, heading the army in the right direction, keeping the formation together, maintaining the separation of divisions, and rounding up stragglers. The marshals were all noblemen, for they had to have the authority to give orders. King Edward was fanatical about orderly marching.

They headed north. The land rose in a gentle slope to a ridge from which they could see the distant glint of the estuary. From there they descended through cornfields. As they passed through villages the marshals ensured there was no looting, because they did not want to carry extra baggage across the river. They also refrained from setting fire to the crops, for fear the smoke might betray their exact position to the enemy.

The sun was about to rise when the leaders reached Saigneville. The village stood on a bluff thirty feet above the river. From the lip of the bank, Ralph looked over a formidable obstacle: a mile and a half of water and marshland. He could see the whitish stones on the bottom marking the ford. On the other side of the estuary was a green hill. As the sun appeared on his right, he saw on the far slope a glint of metal and a flash of color, and his heart filled with dismay.

The strengthening light confirmed his suspicion: the enemy was waiting for them. The French knew where the ford was, of course, and a wise commander had provided for the possibility that the English might discover its location. So much for surprise.

Ralph looked at the water. It was flowing west, showing that the tide was going out; but it was still too deep for a man to wade. They would have to wait.

The English army continued to build up at the shore, hundreds more men arriving every minute. If the king had tried now to turn the army around and go back, the confusion would have been nightmarish.

A scout returned, and Ralph listened as the news was related to the prince of Wales. King Philippe's army had left Abbeville and was approaching on this bank of the river.

The scout was sent to determine how fast the French army was moving.

There was no turning back, Ralph realized with fear in his heart; the English had to cross the water.

He studied the far side, trying to figure out how many French were on the north bank. More than a thousand, he thought. But the greater danger was the army of tens of thousands coming up from Abbeville. Ralph had learned, in many encounters with the French, that they were extraordinarily brave—foolhardy, sometimes—but they were also undisciplined. They marched in disarray, they disobeyed orders, and they sometimes attacked, to prove their valor, when they would have been wiser to wait. But if they could overcome their disorderly habits, and get here in the next few hours, they would catch King Edward's army in midstream. With the enemy on both banks, the English could be wiped out.

After the devastation they had wrought in the last six weeks, they could expect no mercy.

Ralph thought about armor. He had a fine suit of plate armor that he had taken from a French corpse at Cambrai seven years ago, but it was on a wagon in the baggage train. Furthermore, he was not sure he could wade through a mile and a half of water and mud so encumbered. He was wearing a steel cap and a short cape of chain mail, which was all he could manage on the march. It would have to do. The others had similar light protection. Most of the infantry carried their helmets hanging from their belts, and they would put them on before coming within range of the enemy; but no one marched in full armor.

The sun rose high in the east. The water level fell until it was just knee-deep. The noblemen came from the king's entourage with orders to begin the crossing. Earl Roland's son, William of Caster, brought the instructions to Ralph's group. "The archers go first, and begin firing as soon as they are near enough to the other side," William told them. Ralph looked at him stonily. He had not forgotten that William had tried to have him hanged for doing what half the English army had done in the last six weeks. "Then, when you get to the beach, the archers scatter left and right to let the knights and men-at-arms through." It sounded simple, Ralph thought; orders always did. But it was going to be bloody. The enemy would be perfectly positioned, on the slope above the river, to pick off the English soldiers struggling unprotected through the water.

The men of Hugh Despenser led the advance, carrying his distinctive black-on-white banner. His archers waded in, holding their bows above the water line, and the knights and men-at-arms splashed along behind. Roland's men followed, and soon Ralph and Alan were riding through the water.

A mile and a half was not far to walk but, Ralph now realized, it was a long way to wade, even for a horse. The depth varied: in some places they walked on swampy ground above the surface, in others the water came up to the waists of the infantry. Men and animals tired quickly. The August sun beat down on their heads while their wet feet grew numb with cold. And all the time, as they looked ahead, they could see, more and more clearly, the enemy waiting for them on the north bank.

Ralph studied the opposing force with growing trepidation. The front line, along the shore, consisted of crossbowmen. He knew that these were not Frenchmen but Italian mercenaries, always called Genoese but in fact coming from various parts of Italy. The crossbow had a slower rate of fire than the longbow, but the Genoese were going to have plenty of time to reload while their targets lumbered through the shallows. Behind the archers, on the green rise, stood foot soldiers and mounted knights ready to charge.

Looking back, Ralph saw thousands of English crossing the river behind him. Once again, turning back was not an option; in fact, those behind were pressing forward, crowding the leaders.

Now he could see the enemy ranks clearly. Ranged along the shore were the heavy wooden shields, called pavises, used by the crossbowmen. As soon as the English came within range, the Genoese began to shoot.

At a distance of three hundred yards, their aim was inaccurate, and the bolts fell with diminished force. All the same, a handful of horses and men were hit. The injured fell and drifted downstream to drown. Wounded horses thrashed in the water, turning it bloody. Ralph's heart beat faster.

As the English came closer to the shore, the accuracy of the Genoese improved, and the bolts landed with greater power. The crossbow was slow, but it fired a steel-tipped iron bolt with terrible force. All around Ralph, men and horses fell. Some of those hit died instantly. There was nothing he could do to protect himself, he realized with an apprehension of doom: either he would be lucky, or he would die. The air filled with the awful noise of battle: the swish of deadly arrows, the curses of wounded men, the screams of horses in agony.

The archers at the front of the English column shot back. Their six-foot longbows dragged their ends in the water, so they had to hold them at an unfamiliar angle, and the river bottom beneath their feet was slippery, but they did their best.

Crossbow bolts could penetrate armor plate at close range, but none of the English were wearing any serious armor anyway. Apart from their helmets, they had little protection from the deadly hail.

Ralph would have turned and run if he could. However, behind him ten thousand men and half as many horses were pressing forward, and would have trampled him and drowned him if he had tried to go back. He had no alternative but to lower his head to Griff's neck and urge him on.

The survivors among the leading English archers at last reached shallow water and began to deploy their longbows more effectively. They shot in a trajectory, over the top of the pavises. Once they got started, English bowmen could shoot twelve arrows a minute. The shafts were made of wood—usually ash—but they had steel tips, and when they fell like rain they were terrifying. Suddenly the shooting from the enemy side lessened. Some of the shields fell. The Genoese were driven back, and the English began to reach the foreshore.

As soon as the archers got their feet on solid ground they dispersed left and right, leaving the shore clear for the knights, who charged out of the shallows at the enemy lines. Ralph, still wading across the river, had seen enough battles to know what the French tactics should be at this point: they needed to hold their line and let the crossbowmen continue to slaughter the English on the beach and in the water. But the chivalric code would not permit the French nobility to hide behind low-born archers, and they broke the line to ride forth and engage with the English knights—thereby throwing away much of the benefit of their position. Ralph felt a glimmer of hope.

The Genoese fell back, and the beach was a melee. Ralph's heart pounded with fear and excitement. The French still had the advantage of charging downhill, and they were fully armored: they slaughtered Hugh Despenser's men wholesale. The vanguard of the charge splashed into the shallows, cutting down the men still in the water.

Earl Roland's archers reached the edge just ahead of Ralph and Alan. Those who survived gained the shore and divided. Ralph felt that the English were doomed, and he was sure to die, but there was nowhere to go except forward, and suddenly he was charging, head down by Griff's neck, sword in the air, straight at the French line. He ducked a scything sword and reached dry ground. He struck uselessly at a steel helmet, then Griff cannoned into another horse. The French horse was larger but younger, and it stumbled, throwing its rider to the mud. Ralph whirled Griff around, went back, and prepared to charge again.

His sword was of limited use against plate armor, but he was a big man on a spirited horse, and his best hope was to knock enemy soldiers off their mounts. He charged again. At this point in a battle he felt no fear. Instead, he was possessed by an exhilarating rage that drove him to kill as many of the enemy as he could. When battle was joined, time stood still, and he fought from moment to moment. Later, when the action came to an end, if he was still alive, he would be astonished to see that the sun was setting and a whole day had gone by. Now he rode at the enemy again and again, dodging their swords, thrusting where he saw an opportunity; never slowing his pace, for that was fatal.

At some point—it might have been after a few minutes or a few hours—he realized, with incredulity, that the English were no longer being slaughtered. In fact, they seemed to be winning ground and gaining hope. He detached himself from the melee and paused, panting, to take stock.

The beach was carpeted with corpses, but there were as many French as English, and Ralph realized the folly of the French charge. As soon as the knights on both sides engaged, the Genoese crossbowmen had stopped firing, for fear of hitting their own side, so the enemy had no longer been able to pick off the English in the water like ducks on a pond. Ever since then the English had streamed out of the estuary in their hordes, all following the same orders, archers spreading left and right, knights and infantrymen pushing relentlessly forward, so that the French were inundated by sheer weight of numbers. Glancing back at the water, Ralph saw that the tide was now rising again, so those English still in the river were desperate to get out, regardless of the fate that might await them on the beach.

As he was catching his breath, the French lost their nerve. Forced off the beach, chased up the hill, overwhelmed by the army stampeding out of the rising water, they began to retreat. The English pressed forward, hardly able to believe their luck; and, as so often happened, it took remarkably little time for retreat to turn into flight, with every man for himself.

Ralph looked back over the estuary. The baggage train was in midstream, horses and oxen pulling the heavy carts across the ford, lashed by drivers frantic to beat the tide. There was scrappy fighting on the far bank now. The vanguard of King Philippe's army must have arrived and engaged a few stragglers, and Ralph thought he recognized, in the sunlight, the colors of the Bohemian light cavalry. But they were too late.

He slumped in his saddle, suddenly weak with relief. The battle was over. Incredibly, against all expectations, the English had slipped out of the French trap.

For today, they were safe.

48

Caris and Mair arrived in the vicinity of Abbeville on August 25, and were dismayed to find the French army already there. Tens of thousands of foot soldiers and archers were camped in the fields around the town. On the road they heard, not just regional French accents, but the tongues of places farther afield: Flanders, Bohemia, Italy, Savoy, Majorca.

The French and their allies were chasing King Edward of England and his army—as were Caris and Mair. Caris wondered how she and Mair could ever get ahead in the race.

When they passed through the gates and entered the town, late in the afternoon, the streets were crowded with French noblemen. Caris had never seen such a display of costly clothing, fine weapons, magnificent horses, and new shoes, not even in London. It seemed as if the entire aristocracy of France was here. The innkeepers, bakers, street entertainers, and prostitutes of the town were working nonstop to fulfill the needs of their guests. Every tavern was full of counts and every house had knights sleeping on the floor.

The abbey of St. Peter was on the list of religious houses where Caris and Mair had planned to take shelter. But even if they had still been dressed as nuns they would have had trouble getting into the guest quarters: the king of France was staying there, and his entourage took up all the available space. The two Kingsbridge nuns, disguised now as Christophe de Longchamp and Michel de Longchamp, were directed to the grand abbey church, where several hundred of the king's squires, grooms, and other attendants were bedding down at night on the cold stone floor of the nave. However, the marshal in charge told them there was no room, and they would have to sleep in the fields like everyone else of low station.

The north transept was a hospital for the wounded. On the way out, Caris paused to watch a surgeon sewing up a deep cut on the cheek of a groaning man-at-arms. The surgeon was quick and skillful, and when he had finished Caris said admiringly: "You did that very well."

"Thank you," he said. Glancing at her he added: "But how would you know, laddie?"

She knew because she had watched Matthew Barber at work many times, but she had to make up a story quickly, so she said: "Back in Longchamp, my father is surgeon to the *sieur*."

"And are you with your *sieur* now?"

"He has been captured by the English, and my lady has sent me and my brother to negotiate his ransom."

"Hmm. You might have done better to go straight to London. If he isn't there now, he soon will be. However, now that you're here, you can earn a bed for the night by helping me."

"Gladly."

"Have you seen your father wash wounds with warm wine?"

Caris could wash wounds in her sleep. In a few moments she and Mair were doing what they knew best, taking care of sick people. Most of the men had been hurt the previous day, in a battle at a ford over the River Somme. Injured noblemen had been attended to first, and now the surgeon was getting around to the common soldiers. They worked nonstop for several hours. The long summer evening turned to twilight, and candles were brought. At last all the bones had been set, the crushed extremities amputated, and the wounds sewn up; and the surgeon, Martin Chirurgien, took them to the refectory for supper.

They were treated as part of the king's entourage and fed stewed mutton with onions. They had not tasted meat for a week. They even had good red wine. Mair drank with relish. Caris was glad they had the opportunity to build up their strength, but she was still anxious about catching up with the English.

A knight at their table said. "Do you realize that in the abbot's dining room, next door, four kings and two archbishops are eating supper?" He counted on his fingers as he named them: "The kings of France, Bohemia, Rome, and Majorca, and the archbishops of Rouen and Sens."

Caris decided she had to see. She went out of the room by the door that seemed to lead to the kitchen. She saw servants carrying laden platters into another room, and peeped through the door.

The men around the table were undoubtedly high-ranking—the board was loaded with roasted fowls, huge joints of beef and mutton, rich puddings, and pyramids of sugared fruits. The man at the head was presumably King Philippe, fifty-three years old, with a scatter of gray hairs in his blond beard. Beside him, a younger man who resembled him was holding forth. "The English are not noblemen," he said, red-faced with fury. "They are like thieves, who steal in the night and then run away."

Martin appeared at Caris's shoulder and murmured in her ear: "That's my master—Charles, count of Alençon, the king's brother."

A new voice said: "I disagree." Caris saw immediately that the speaker was blind, and concluded that he must be King Jean of Bohemia. "The English cannot run much longer. They are low on food, and they're tired."

Charles said: "Edward wants to join forces with the Anglo-Flemish army that has invaded northeast France from Flanders."

Jean shook his head. "We learned today that that army has gone into retreat. I think Edward has to stand and fight. And, from his point of view, the sooner the better, for his men are only going to become more dispirited as the days go by."

Charles said excitedly: "Then we may catch them tomorrow. After what they have done to Normandy, every one of them should die—knights, noblemen, even Edward himself!"

King Philippe put a hand on Charles's arm, silencing him. "Our brother's anger is understandable," he said. "The crimes of the English are disgusting. But remember: when we encounter the enemy, the most important thing is to put aside any differences there may be between us—forget our quarrels and grudges—and trust one another, at least for the course of the battle. We outnumber the English, and we should vanquish them easily—but we must fight together, as one army. Let us drink to unity."

That was an interesting toast, Caris decided as she discreetly withdrew. Clearly the king could not take it for granted that his allies would act as a team. But what worried her about the conversation was the likelihood that there would be a battle soon, perhaps tomorrow. She and Mair would have to take care not to get mixed up in it.

As they returned to the refectory, Martin said quietly: "Like the king, you have an unruly brother."

Caris saw that Mair was getting drunk. She was overplaying her boyish role, sitting with her legs splayed and her elbows on the table. "By the saints, that was a good stew, but it's making me fart like the devil," said the sweet-faced nun in men's clothing. "Sorry about the stink, lads." She refilled her wine cup and drank deeply.

The men laughed at her indulgently, amused by the sight of a boy getting drunk for the first time, doubtless remembering embarrassing incidents in their own pasts.

Caris took her arm. "Time you were in bed, baby brother," she said. "Off we go."

Mair went willingly enough. "My big brother acts like an old woman," she said to the company. "But he loves me—don't you, Christophe?"

"Yes, Michel, I love you," Caris said, and the men laughed again.

Mair held on tightly to her. Caris walked her back to the church and found the spot in the nave where they had left their blankets. She made Mair lie down, and covered her with her blanket.

"Kiss me good night, Christophe," said Mair.

Caris kissed her lips, then said: "You're drunk. Go to sleep. We have to start early in the morning."

Caris lay awake for some time, worrying. She felt she had had terribly bad luck. She and Mair had almost caught up with the English army and Bishop Richard—but at exactly the same moment the French had also caught up with them. She should keep well away from the battlefield. On the other hand, if she and Mair got stuck in the rear of the French army they might never catch the English.

On balance she thought she had better set off first thing in the morning, and try to get ahead of the French. An army this big could not move fast—it would take hours just to form up into marching order. If she and Mair were nimble, they should be able to stay ahead. It was risky—but they had done nothing but take risks since leaving Portsmouth.

She drifted off to sleep, and woke when the bell rang for Matins soon after three o'clock in the morning. She roused Mair, and was unsympathetic when she complained of a headache. While the monks sang psalms in the church, Caris and Mair went to the stables and found their horses. The sky was clear, and they could see by starlight.

The town's bakers had been working all night, so they were able to buy loaves for their journey. But the city gates were still closed: they had to wait impatiently until dawn, shivering in the cool air, eating the new bread.

At about half past four they at last left Abbeville and headed northwest along the right bank of the Somme, the direction the English army was said to be taking.

They were only a quarter of a mile away when the trumpets sounded a reveille on the walls of the town. Like Caris, King Philippe had decided on an early start. In the fields, the soldiers and men-at-arms began to stir. The marshals must have got their orders last night, for they seemed to know what to do, and before long some of the army joined Caris and Mair on the road.

Caris still hoped to reach the English ahead of these troops. The French would obviously have to stop and regroup before joining battle. That ought to give Caris and Mair time to reach their countrymen and find some safe place beyond the battlefield. She did not want to get caught between the two sides. She was beginning to think she had been foolhardy to set out on this mission. Knowing nothing of war, she had not been able to imagine the difficulties and dangers. But it was too late now for regrets. And they had got this far without coming to harm.

The soldiers on the road were not French but Italian. They carried steel crossbows and sheaves of iron arrows. They were friendly, and Caris chatted to them in a mixture of Norman French, Latin, and the Italian she had picked up from Buonaventura Caroli. They told her that in battle they always formed the front line, and fired from behind their heavy wooden pavises, which at the moment were in wagons somewhere behind them. They grumbled about their hasty breakfast, disparaged French knights as impulsive and quarrelsome, and spoke with admiration of their leader, Ottone Doria, who could be seen a few yards ahead.

The sun climbed in the sky and everyone got hot. Because the crossbowmen knew they might do battle today, they were wearing heavy quilted coats and carrying iron helmets and knee guards as well as their bows and arrows. Toward noon, Mair declared that she would faint unless they stopped for a break. Caris, too, felt exhausted—they had been riding since dawn—and she knew their horses also needed rest. So, against her inclination, she was forced to stop while thousands of crossbowmen overtook them.

Caris and Mair watered their ponies in the Somme and ate some more bread. When they set off again, they found themselves marching with French knights and men-at-arms. Caris recognized Philippe's choleric brother Charles at the head of the group. She was in the thick of the French army, but there was nothing to do but keep moving and hope for a chance to get ahead.

Soon after midday an order came down the line. The English were not west of here, as previously believed, but north; and the French king had ordered that his army should swing in that direction—not in a column, but all at the same time. The men around Caris and Mair, led by Count Charles, turned off the riverside road down a narrow path through the fields. Caris followed with a sinking heart.

A familiar voice hailed her, and Martin Chirurgien came alongside. "This is chaos," he said grimly. "The marching order has completely broken down."

A small group of men on fast horses appeared across the fields and hailed Count Charles. "Scouts," said Martin, and he went forward to hear what they had to say. Caris and Mair's ponies went too, with the natural instinct of horses to stick together.

"The English have halted," they heard. "They've taken up a defensive position on a ridge near the town of Crécy."

Martin said: "That's Henri le Moine, an old comrade of the king of Bohemia."

Charles was pleased by the news. "Then we shall have battle today!" he said, and the knights around him gave a ragged cheer.

Henri raised a hand in caution. "We're suggesting that all units stop and regroup," he said.

"Stop now?" Charles roared. "When the English are at last willing to stand and fight? Let's get at them!"

"Our men and horses need rest," Henri said quietly. "The king is far in the rear. Give him a chance to catch up and look at the battlefield. He can make his dispositions today for an attack tomorrow, when the men will be fresh."

"To hell with dispositions. There are only a few thousand English. We'll just overrun them."

Henri made a helpless gesture. "It is not for me to command you, my lord. But I will ask your brother the king for his orders."

"Ask him! Ask him!" said Charles, and he rode on.

Martin said to Caris: "I don't know why my master is so intemperate."

Caris said thoughtfully: "I suppose he has to prove that he's brave enough to rule, even though by an accident of birth he's not the king."

Martin shot her a sharp look. "You're very wise, for a mere boy."

Caris avoided his eye, and vowed to remember her false identity. There was no hostility in Martin's voice, but he was suspicious. As a surgeon, he would be familiar with the subtle differences in bone structure between men and women, and he might have noticed that Christophe and Michel de Longchamp were abnormal. Fortunately, he did not press the matter.

The sky began to cloud over, but the air was still warm and humid. Woodland appeared on the left, and Martin told Caris this was the Forest of Crécy. They could not be far from the English—but now Caris wondered how she was going to detach herself from the French and join the English without being killed by one side or the other.

The effect of the forest was to crowd the left flank of the marching army, so that the road on which Caris was riding became jam-packed with troops, the different divisions getting hopelessly mixed up.

Couriers came down the line with new orders from the king: the army was instructed to halt and make camp. Caris's hopes rose: now she would have a chance to get ahead of the French army. There was an altercation between Charles and a courier, and Martin went to Charles's side to listen. He came back looking incredulous. "Count Charles is refusing to obey the orders!" he said.

"Why?" Caris asked in dismay.

"He thinks his brother is overcautious. He, Charles, will not be so lily-livered as to halt before such a weak enemy."

"I thought everyone had to obey the king in battle."

"They should. But nothing is more important to French noblemen than their code of chivalry. They would die rather than do something cowardly."

The army marched on in defiance of its orders. "I'm glad you two are here," Martin said. "I'm going to need your help again. Win or lose, there will be a lot of wounded men by sundown."

Caris realized she could not escape. But somehow she no longer wanted to get away. In fact she felt a strange eagerness. If these men were mad enough to maim one another with swords and arrows, she could at least come to the aid of the wounded.

Soon the crossbowmen's leader, Ottone Doria, came riding back through the crowd—not without difficulty, given the crush—to speak to Charles of Alençon. "Halt your men!" he shouted at the count.

Charles took offense. "How dare you give orders to me!"

"The orders come from the king! We are to halt—but my men can't stop, because of yours pushing from behind!"

"Then let them march on."

"We are within sight of the enemy. If we go any farther we'll have to do battle."

"So be it."

"But the men have been marching all day. They're hungry and thirsty and tired. And my crossbowmen don't have their pavises."

"Are they too cowardly to fight without shields?"

"Are you calling my men cowards?"

"If they won't fight, yes."

Ottone was quiet for a moment. Then he spoke in a low voice, and Caris could only just hear his words. "You're a fool, Alençon. And you'll be in Hell by nightfall." Then he turned his horse and rode away.

Caris felt water on her face, and looked up at the sky. It was beginning to rain.

49

The shower was heavy but brief and, when it cleared, Ralph looked down over the valley and saw, with a thrill of fear, that the enemy had arrived.

The English occupied a ridge that ran from southwest to northeast. At their backs, to the northwest, was a wood. In front and on both sides the hill sloped down. Their right flank looked over the town of Crécy-en-Ponthieu, which nestled in the valley of the River Maye.

The French were approaching from the south.

Ralph was on the right flank, with Earl Roland's men, commanded by the young prince of Wales. They were drawn up in the harrow formation that had proved so effective against the Scots. To the left and right, triangular formations of archers stood, like the two teeth of a harrow. Between the teeth, set well back, were dismounted knights and men-at-arms. This was a radical innovation, and one which many knights still resisted: they liked their horses and felt vulnerable on foot. But the king was implacable: everyone on foot. In the ground in front of the knights, the men had dug pitfalls—holes in the ground a foot deep and a foot square—to trip the French horses.

On Ralph's right, at the end of the ridge, was a novelty: three new machines called bombards, or cannons, that used explosive powder to shoot round stones. They had been dragged all the way across Normandy but so far had never been fired, and no one was sure whether they would work. Today King Edward needed to use every means at his disposal, for the enemy's superiority was somewhere between four-to-one and seven-to-one.

On the English left flank, the earl of Northampton's men were drawn up in the same harrow formation. Behind the front lines, a third battalion led by the king stood in reserve. Behind the king were two fallback positions. The baggage wagons formed the first, drawn up in a circle, with noncombatants—cooks, engineers, and hostlers—inside the circle with the horses. The second was the wood itself where, in the event of a rout, the remnants of the English army could flee, and the mounted French knights would find it difficult to follow.

They had been here since early morning, with nothing to eat but pea soup with onions. Ralph was wearing his armor, and had been sweltering in the heat, so the rainstorm had been welcome. It had also muddied the slope up which the French would have to charge, making their approach treacherously slippery.

Ralph could guess what the French tactics would be. The Genoese crossbowmen would shoot from behind their shields, to soften up the English line. Then, when they had done enough damage, they would step aside, and the French knights would charge on their warhorses.

There was nothing so terrifying as that charge. Called the *furor fransiscus,* it was the ultimate weapon of the French nobility. Their code made them disregard their own safety. Those huge horses, with riders so completely armored that they looked like iron men, simply rolled over archers, shields, swords, and men-at-arms.

Of course, it did not always work. The charge could be repulsed, especially where the terrain favored the defenders, as it did here. However, the French were not easily discouraged: they would charge again. And they had such enormous superiority in numbers that Ralph could not see how the English could hold them off indefinitely.

He was scared, but all the same he did not regret being with the army. For seven years he had lived the life of action he had always wanted, in which strong men were kings and the weak counted for nothing. He was twenty-nine, and men of action rarely lived to be old. He had committed foul sins, but had been absolved of them all, most recently this morning, by the bishop of Shiring, who was now standing next to his father, the earl, armed with a vicious-looking mace—priests were not supposed to shed blood, a rule they acknowledged cursorily by using blunt weapons on the battlefield.

The crossbowmen in their white coats reached the foot of the slope. The English archers, who had been sitting down, their arrows stuck point-first into the ground in front of them, now began to stand up and string their bows. Ralph guessed that most of them felt what he did, a mixture of relief that the long wait was over and fear at the thought of the odds against them.

Ralph thought there was plenty of time. He could see that the Genoese did not have the heavy wooden pavises that were an essential element of their tactics. The battle would not start until the shields were brought, he felt sure.

Behind the crossbowmen, thousands of knights were pouring into the valley from the south, spreading left and right behind the crossbowmen. The sun came out again, lighting up the bright colors of their banners and the horses' coats. Ralph recognized the coat of arms of Charles, count of Alençon, King Philippe's brother.

The crossbowmen stopped at the foot of the slope. There were thousands of them. As if at a signal, they all gave a terrific shout. Some jumped up in the air. Trumpets sounded.

It was their war cry, meant to terrify the enemy, and it might have worked on some foes, but the English army consisted of experienced fighting men who were at the end of a six-week campaign, and it took more than shouting to scare them. They looked on impassively.

Then, to Ralph's utter astonishment, the Genoese lifted their crossbows and shot.

What were they doing? They had no shields!

The sound was sudden and terrifying, five thousand iron bolts flying through the air. But the crossbowmen were out of range. Perhaps they had failed to take account of the fact that they were shooting uphill; and the afternoon sun behind the English lines must have been shining in their eyes. Whatever the reason, their bolts fell uselessly short.

There was a flash of flame and a crash like thunder from the middle of the English front line. Amazed, Ralph saw smoke rising from where the new bombards were. Their sound was impressive, but when he returned his gaze to the enemy ranks he saw little actual damage. However, many of the crossbowmen were shocked enough to pause in their reloading.

At that moment, the prince of Wales shouted the order for his archers to shoot.

Two thousand longbows were raised. Knowing they were too distant to shoot in a straight line parallel with the ground, the archers aimed into the sky, intuitively plotting a shallow trajectory for their arrows. All the bows bent simultaneously, like blades of wheat in a field blown by a sudden summer breeze; then the arrows were released with a collective sound like a church bell tolling. The shafts, flying faster than the swiftest bird, rose into the air then turned downward and fell on the crossbowmen like a hailstorm

The enemy ranks were densely packed, and the padded Genoese coats gave little protection. Without their shields, the crossbowmen were horribly vulnerable. Hundreds of them fell dead or wounded.

But that was only the beginning.

While the surviving crossbowmen were rewinding their weapons, the English fired again and again. It took an archer only four or five seconds to pull an arrow from the ground, nock it, draw the bow, take aim, shoot, and reach for another. Experienced, practised men could do it faster. In the space of a minute, twenty thousand arrows fell on the unprotected crossbowmen.

It was a massacre, and the consequence was inevitable: they turned and ran.

In moments the Genoese were out of range, and the English held their fire, laughing at their unexpected triumph and jeering at the enemy. But then the crossbowmen encountered another hazard. The French knights were moving forward. A dense herd of fleeing crossbowmen came head to head with massed horsemen itching to charge. For a moment there was chaos.

Ralph was amazed to see the enemy begin to fight among themselves. The knights drew their swords and started to hack the bowmen, who discharged their bolts at the knights, then fought on with knives. The French noblemen should have been trying to stop the carnage but, as far as Ralph could see, those in the most expensive armor and riding the largest horses were at the forefront of the fight, attacking their own side with ever-greater fury.

The knights drove the crossbowmen back up the slope until they were again within longbow range. Once again the prince of Wales gave the order for the English archers to shoot. Now the hail of arrows fell among knights as well as bowmen. In seven years of warfare Ralph had seen nothing like this. Hundreds of the enemy lay dead and wounded, and not a single English soldier had been so much as scratched.

At last the French knights retreated, and the remaining crossbowmen scattered. They left the slope below the English position littered with bodies. Welsh and Cornish knifemen ran forward from the English ranks onto the battlefield and began finishing off the French wounded, retrieving undamaged arrows for the longbowmen to reuse, and no doubt robbing the corpses while they were at it. At the same time, boy runners got fresh stocks of arrows from the supply train and brought them to the English front line.

There was a pause, but it did not last long.

The French knights regrouped, reinforced by new arrivals who were appearing in their hundreds and thousands. Peering into their ranks, Ralph could see that the colors of Alençon had been joined by those of Flanders and Normandy. The standard of the count of Alençon moved to the front, then the trumpets sounded, and the horsemen began to move.

Ralph put his faceplate down and drew his sword. He thought of his mother. He knew she prayed for him every time she went to church, and he felt a moment of warm gratitude to her. Then he watched the enemy.

The huge horses were slow to start, encumbered as they were by riders in full plate armor. The setting sun glinted off the French visors, and the flags snapped in the evening breeze. Gradually the pounding of the hooves grew louder and the pace of the charge picked up. The knights yelled encouragement to their mounts and to one another, waving their swords and spears. They came like a wave onto a beach, seeming to get bigger and faster as they got nearer. Ralph's mouth was dry and his heart beat like a big drum.

They came within bowshot, and again the prince gave the order to shoot. Once more, the arrows rose into the air and fell like deadly rain.

The charging knights were fully armored, and it was a lucky shot indeed that found the weak spot in the joints between plates. But their mounts had only faceplates and chain-mail neck cowls. So it was the horses that were vulnerable. When the arrows pierced their shoulders and their haunches, some stopped dead, some fell, and some turned and tried to flee. The screams of beasts in pain filled the air. Collisions between horses caused more knights to fall to the ground, joining the bodies of Genoese crossbowmen. Those behind were going too fast to take evasive action, so they just rode over the fallen.

But there were thousands of knights, and they kept coming.

The range shortened for the archers, and their trajectory flattened. When the charge was a hundred yards away, they switched to a different type of arrow, with a flattened steel tip for punching through armor, instead of a point. Now they could kill the riders, although a shot that hit a horse was almost as good.

The ground was already wet with rain, and now the charge encountered the pitfalls dug earlier by the English. The horses' momentum was such that few of them could step into a hole a foot deep without stumbling, and many fell, pitching their riders onto the ground in the path of other horses.

The oncoming knights shied away from the archers so, as the English had planned, the charge was funneled into a narrow killing field, fired upon from left and right.

This was the key to the English tactics. At this point, the wisdom of forcing the English knights to dismount became clear. If they had been on horseback, they could not have resisted the urge to charge—and then the archers would have had to cease shooting, for fear of killing their own side. But, because the knights and men-at-arms remained in their lines, the enemy could be slaughtered wholesale, with no casualties on the English side.

But it was not enough. The French were too numerous and too brave. Still they came on, and at last they reached the line of dismounted knights and men-at-arms in the fork between the two masses of archers, and the real fighting began.

The horses trampled over the front ranks of English, but their charge had been slowed by the muddy uphill slope, and they were brought up short by the densely packed English line. Ralph was suddenly in the thick of it, avoiding deadly downward blows from mounted knights, swinging his sword at the legs of their horses, aiming to cripple the beasts by the easiest and most reliable method, cutting their hamstrings. The fighting was fierce: the English had nowhere to go, and the French knew that if they retreated they would have to ride back through the same lethal hail of arrows.

Men fell all around Ralph, hacked down by swords and battleaxes, then tramped by the mighty iron-shod hooves of the warhorses. He saw Earl Roland go down to a French sword. Roland's son, Bishop Richard, swung his mace to protect his fallen father, but a warhorse shouldered Richard aside, and the earl was trampled.

The English were forced back, and Ralph realized that the French had a target: the prince of Wales.

Ralph had no affection for the privileged sixteen-year-old heir to the throne, but he knew it would be a crushing blow to English morale if the prince were captured or killed. Ralph moved back and to his left, joining several others who thickened the shield of fighting men around the prince. But the French intensified their efforts, and they were on horseback.

Then Ralph found himself fighting shoulder-to-shoulder with the prince, recognizing him by his quartered surcoat, with fleurs-de-lis on a blue background and heraldic lions on red. A moment later, a French horseman swung at the prince with an axe, and the prince fell to the ground.

It was a bad moment.

Ralph sprang forward and lunged at the attacker, sliding his long sword into the man's armpit, where the armor was jointed. He had the satisfaction of feeling the point penetrate flesh, and saw blood spurt from the wound.

Someone else straddled the fallen prince and swung a big sword two-handed at men and horses alike. Ralph saw that it was the prince's standard-bearer, Richard FitzSimon, who had dropped the flag over his supine master. For a few moments Richard and Ralph fought savagely to defend the king's son, not knowing if he was alive or dead.

Then reinforcements arrived. The earl of Arundel appeared with a large force of men-at-arms, all fresh to the fight. The newcomers joined the battle with vigor, and they turned the tables. The French began to fall back.

The prince of Wales got to his knees. Ralph put up his visor and helped the prince to his feet. The boy seemed to be hurt, but not seriously, and Ralph turned away and fought on.

A moment later the French broke. Despite the lunacy of their tactics, their courage had almost enabled them to sever the English line—but not quite. Now they fled, many more falling as they ran the gauntlet of archers, stumbling down the bloody slope back to their own lines; and a cheer went up from the English, weary but jubilant.

Once again the Welsh invaded the battlefield, cutting the throats of the wounded and collecting thousands of arrows. The archers, too, picked up spent shafts to replenish their stocks. From the rear, cooks appeared with jugs of beer and wine, and surgeons rushed to attend injured noblemen.

Ralph saw William of Caster bend over Earl Roland. Roland was breathing, but his eyes were closed and he looked near to death.

Ralph wiped his bloody sword on the ground and put his visor up to drink a tankard of ale. The prince of Wales approached him and said: "What's your name?"

"Ralph Fitzgerald of Wigleigh, my lord."

"You fought bravely. You shall be Sir Ralph tomorrow, if the king listens to me."

Ralph glowed with pleasure. "Thank you, lord."

The prince nodded graciously and moved away.

50

Caris watched the early stages of the battle from the far side of the valley. She saw the Genoese crossbowmen try to flee, only to be cut down by knights of their own side. Then she saw the first great charge, with the colors of Charles of Alençon leading thousands of knights and men-at-arms.

She had never seen battle, and she was utterly sickened. Hundreds of knights fell to the English arrows, to be trampled by the hooves of the great warhorses. She was too far away to be able to follow the hand-to-hand fighting, but she saw the swords flash and the men fall, and she wanted to weep. As a nun, she had seen severe injuries—men who had fallen from high scaffolding, hurt themselves with sharp tools, suffered hunting accidents—and she always felt the pain and the waste of a lost hand, a crushed leg, a damaged brain. To see men inflicting such wounds on one another intentionally revolted her.

For a long time it seemed the fight could go either way. If she had been at home, hearing news of the war from afar, she might have hoped for an English victory; but after what she had seen in the last two weeks she felt a sort of disgusted neutrality. She could not identify with the English who had murdered peasants and burned their crops, and it made no difference to her that they had committed these atrocities in Normandy. Of course, they would say the French deserved what they got because they had burned Portsmouth, but that was a stupid way to think—so stupid that it led to scenes of horror such as this.

The French retreated, and she assumed they would regroup and reorganize, and wait for the king to arrive to develop a new battle plan. They still had overwhelming superiority in numbers, she could see: there were tens of thousands of troops in the valley, with more still arriving.

But the French did not regroup. Instead, every new battalion that arrived went straight into the attack, throwing themselves suicidally up the hill at the English position. The second and subsequent charges fared worse than the first. Some were cut down by archers even before they reached the English lines; the rest were beaten off by foot soldiers. The slope below the ridge became shiny with the gushing blood of hundreds of men and horses.

After the first charge, Caris looked only occasionally at the battle. She was too busy tending those French wounded who were lucky enough to be able to leave the field. Martin Chirurgien had realized that she was as good a surgeon as he. Giving her free access to his instruments, he left her and Mair to work independently. They washed, sewed, and bandaged hour after hour.

News of prominent casualties came back to them from the front line. Charles of Alençon was the first high-ranking fatality. Caris could not help feeling that he deserved his fate. She had witnessed his foolish enthusiasm and careless indiscipline. Hours later, King Jean of Bohemia was reported dead, and she wondered what madness drove a blind man to battle.

"In God's name, why don't they stop?" she said to Martin when he brought her a cup of ale to refresh her.

"Fear," he replied. "They're scared of disgrace. To leave the field without striking a blow would be shameful. They would prefer to die."

"A lot of them have had that wish granted," said Caris grimly, and she emptied her tankard and went back to work. Her knowledge and understanding of the human body was growing by leaps and bounds, she reflected. She saw inside every part of a living man: the brains beneath shattered skulls, the pipework of the throat, the muscles of the arms sliced open, the heart and lungs within smashed rib cages, the slimy tangle of the intestines, the articulation of the bones at hip and knee and ankle. She discovered more in an hour on the battlefield than in a year at the priory hospital. This was how Matthew Barber had learned so much, she realized. No wonder he was confident.

The carnage continued until night fell. The English lit torches, afraid of a sneak attack under cover of darkness. But Caris could have told them they were safe. The French were routed. She could hear the calls of French soldiers searching the battlefield for fallen kinsmen and comrades. The king, who had arrived in time to join one of the last hopeless charges, left the field. After that the exit became general.

A fog came up from the river, filling the valley and obscuring the distant flares. Once again, Caris and Mair worked by firelight long into the night, patching up the wounded. All those who could walk or hobble left as soon as they could, putting as much distance as possible between themselves and the English, hoping to avoid tomorrow's inevitable bloodthirsty mopping-up operation. When Caris and Mair had done all they could for the victims, they slipped away.

This was their chance.

They located their ponies and led them forward by the light of a burning torch. They reached the bottom of the valley and found themselves in no-man's-land. Hidden by fog and darkness, they slipped out of their boys' clothing. For a moment they were terribly vulnerable, two naked women in the middle of a battlefield. But no one could see them, and a second later they were pulling their nuns' robes over their heads. They packed up their male garments in case they should need them again: it was a long way home.

Caris decided to abandon the torch, in case an English archer should take it into his head to shoot at the light and ask questions afterward. Holding hands so that they would not get separated they went forward, still leading the horses. They could see nothing: the fog obscured whatever light might have come from moon or stars. They headed uphill toward the English lines. There was a smell like a butcher's shop. So many bodies of horses and men covered the ground that they could not walk around them. They had to grit their teeth and step on the corpses. Soon their shoes were covered with a mixture of mud and blood.

The bodies on the ground thinned out, and soon there were none. Caris began to feel a deep sense of relief as she approached the English army. She and Mair had traveled hundreds of miles, lived rough for two weeks, and risked their lives, for this moment. She had almost forgotten the outrageous theft by Prior Godwyn of one hundred and fifty pounds from the nuns' treasury—the reason for her journey. Somehow it seemed less important after all this bloodshed. Still, she would appeal to Bishop Richard and win justice for the nunnery.

The walk seemed farther than Caris had imagined when she looked across the valley in daylight. She wondered nervously if she had become disoriented. She might have turned in the wrong direction and just walked straight past the English. Perhaps the army was now behind her. She strained to hear some noise—ten thousand men could not be silent, even if most of them had fallen into exhausted sleep—but the fog muffled sound.

She clung to the conviction that, as King Edward had positioned his forces on the highest land, she must be approaching him as long as she was walking uphill. But the blindness was unnerving. If there had been a precipice, she would have stepped right over it.

The light of dawn was turning the fog to the color of pearl when at last she heard a voice. She stopped. It was a man speaking in a low murmur. Mair squeezed her hand nervously. Another man spoke. She could not make out the language. She feared that she might have walked in a full circle and arrived back on the French side.

She turned toward the voice, still holding Mair's hand. The red glow of flames became visible through the gray mist, and she headed for it gratefully. As she came nearer, she heard the talk more clearly, and realized with immense relief that the men were speaking English. A moment later she made out a group of men around a fire. Several lay asleep, rolled in blankets, but three sat upright, legs crossed, looking into the flames, talking. A moment later Caris saw a man standing, peering into the fog, presumably on sentry duty, though the fact that he had not noticed her approach proved his job was impossible.

To get their attention, Caris said in a low voice: "God bless you, men of England."

She startled them. One gave a shout of fear. The sentry said belatedly: "Who goes there?"

"Two nuns from Kingsbridge Priory," Caris said. The men stared at her in superstitious dread, and she realized they thought she might be an apparition. "Don't worry, we're flesh and blood, and so are these ponies."

"Did you say Kingsbridge?" said one of them in surprise. "I know you," he said, standing up. "I've seen you before."

Caris recognized him. "Lord William of Caster," she said.

"I am the earl of Shiring, now," he said. "My father died of his wounds an hour ago."

"May his soul rest in peace. We have come here to see your brother, Bishop Richard, who is our abbot."

"You're too late," William said. "My brother, too, is dead."

Later in the morning, when the fog had lifted and the battlefield looked like a sunlit slaughterhouse, Earl William took Caris and Mair to see King Edward.

Everyone was astonished at the tale of the two nuns who had followed the English army all through Normandy, and soldiers who had faced death only yesterday were fascinated by their adventures. William told Caris that the king would want to hear the story from her own lips.

Edward III had been king for nineteen years, but he was still only thirty-three years old. Tall and broad-shouldered, he was imposing rather than handsome, with a face that might have been molded for power: a big nose, high cheekbones, and luxuriant long hair just beginning to recede from his high forehead. Caris saw why people called him a lion.

He sat on a stool in front of his tent, fashionably dressed in two-colored hose and a cape with a scalloped border. He wore no armor or weapons: the French had vanished, and in fact a force of vengeful troops had been sent out to hunt down and kill any stragglers. A handful of barons stood around.

As Caris told how she and Mair had sought food and shelter in the devastated landscape of Normandy, she wondered if the king felt criticized by her tale of hardship. However, he seemed not to think the sufferings of the people reflected on him. He was as delighted with her exploits as if he were hearing of someone who had been brave during a shipwreck.

She ended by telling him of her disappointment on finding, after all her travails, that Bishop Richard, from whom she had hoped for justice, was dead. "I beg Your Majesty to order the prior of Kingsbridge to restore to the nuns the money he stole."

Edward smiled ruefully. "You're a brave woman, but you know nothing of politics," he said with condescension. "The king can't get involved in an ecclesiastical quarrel such as this. We would have all our bishops banging on our door in protest."

That might be so, Caris reflected, but it did not prevent the king interfering with the church when it suited his own purposes. However, she said nothing.

Edward went on: "And it would do your cause harm. The church would be so outraged that every cleric in the land would oppose our ruling, regardless of its merits."

There might be something in that, she judged. But he was not as powerless as he pretended. "I know you will remember the wronged nuns of Kingsbridge," she said. "When you appoint the new bishop of Kingsbridge, please tell him our story."

"Of course," said the king, but Caris had the feeling he would forget.

The interview seemed to be over, but then William said: "Your Majesty, now that you have graciously confirmed my elevation to my father's earldom, there is the question of who is to be lord of Caster."

"Ah, yes. Our son the prince of Wales suggests Sir Ralph Fitzgerald, who was knighted yesterday for saving his life."

Caris murmured: "Oh, no!"

The king did not hear her, but William did, and he obviously felt the same way. He was not quite able to hide his indignation as he said: "Ralph was an outlaw, guilty of numerous thefts, murders, and rapes, until he obtained a royal pardon by joining your majesty's army."

The king was not as moved by this as Caris expected. He said: "All the same, Ralph has fought with us for seven years now. He has earned a second chance."

"Indeed he has," William said diplomatically. "But, given the trouble we've had with him in the past, I'd like to see him settle down peacefully for a year of two before he's ennobled."

"Well, you will be his overlord, so you'll have to deal with him," Edward granted. "We won't impose him on you against your will. However, the prince is keen that he should have some further reward." The king thought for a few moments, then said: "Don't you have a cousin who is eligible for marriage?"

"Yes, Matilda," said William. "We call her Tilly."

Caris knew Tilly. She was at the nunnery school.

"That's right," said Edward. "She was your father Roland's ward. Her father had three villages near Shiring."

"Your Majesty has a good memory for detail."

"Marry Lady Matilda to Ralph and give him her father's villages," said the king.

Caris was appalled. "But she's only twelve!" she burst out.

William said to her: "Hush!"

King Edward turned a cold gaze on her. "The children of the nobility must grow up fast, Sister. Queen Philippa was fourteen when I married her."

Caris knew she should shut up, but she could not. Tilly was only four years older than the daughter she might have had, if she had given birth to Merthin's baby. "There's a big difference between twelve and fourteen," she said desperately.

The young king became even more frosty. "In the royal presence, people give their opinions only when asked. And the king almost never asks for the opinions of women."

Caris realized she had taken the wrong tack. Her objection to the marriage was not based on Tilly's age so much as Ralph's character. "I know Tilly," she said. "You can't marry her to that brute Ralph."

Mair said in a scared whisper: "Caris! Remember who you're speaking to!"

Edward looked at William. "Take her away, Shiring, before she says something that cannot be overlooked."

William took Caris's arm and firmly marched her out of the royal presence. Mair followed. Behind them, Caris heard the king say: "I can see how she survived in Normandy—the locals must have been terrified of her." The noblemen around him laughed.

"You must be mad!" William hissed.

"Must I?" Caris said. They were out of earshot of the king now, and she raised her voice. "In the last six weeks the king has caused the deaths of thousands of men, women, and children, and burned their crops and their homes. And I have tried to save a twelve-year-old girl from being married to a murderer. Tell me again, Lord William, which of us is mad?"

51

In the year 1347 the peasants of Wigleigh suffered a poor harvest. The villagers did what they always did in such times: they ate less food, postponed the purchase of hats and belts, and slept closer together for warmth. Old Widow Huberts died earlier than expected; Janey Jones succumbed to a cough that she might have survived in a good year; and Joanna David's new baby, who might otherwise have had a chance, failed to make it to his first birthday.

Gwenda kept an anxious eye on her two little boys. Sam, the eight-year-old, was big for his age, and strong: he had Wulfric's physique, people said, though Gwenda knew that in truth he was like his real father, Ralph Fitzgerald. Even so, Sam was visibly thinner by December. David, named after Wulfric's brother who had died when the bridge collapsed, was six. He resembled Gwenda, being small and dark. The poor diet had weakened him, and all through the autumn he suffered minor ailments: a cold, then a skin rash, then a cough.

All the same, she took the boys with her when she went with Wulfric to finish sowing the winter wheat on Perkin's land. A bitterly cold wind swept across the open fields. She dropped seeds into the furrows, and Sam and David chased off the daring birds who tried to snatch the corn before Wulfric turned the earth over. As they ran, and jumped, and shouted, Gwenda marveled that these two fully functioning miniature human beings had come from inside her body. They turned the chasing of the birds into some kind of competitive game, and she delighted in the miracle of their imagination. Once part of her, they were now able to have thoughts she did not know about.

Mud clung to their feet as they tramped up and down. A fast-running stream bordered the big field, and on the far bank stood the fulling mill Merthin had built nine years ago. The distant rumble of its pounding wooden hammers accompanied their work. The mill was run by two eccentric brothers, Jack and Eli—both unmarried men with no land—and an apprentice boy who was their nephew. They were the only villagers who had not suffered on account of the bad harvest: Mark Webber paid them the same wages all winter long.

It was a short midwinter day. Gwenda and her family finished sowing just as the gray sky began to darken, and the twilight gathered mistily in the distant woods. They were all tired.

There was half a sack of seed leftover, so they took it to Perkin's house. As they approached the place, they saw Perkin himself coming from the opposite direction. He was walking beside a cart on which his daughter, Annet, was riding. They had been to Kingsbridge to sell the last of the year's apples and pears from Perkin's trees.

Annet still retained her girlish figure, although she was now twenty-eight, and had had a child. She called attention to her youthfulness with a dress that was a little too short and a hairstyle that was charmingly disarrayed. She looked silly, Gwenda thought. Her opinion was shared by every woman in the village and none of the men.

Gwenda was shocked to see that Perkin's cart was full of fruit. "What happened?" she said.

Perkin's face was grim. "Kingsbridge folk are having a hard winter just like us," he said. "They've no money to buy apples. We shall have to make cider with this lot."

That was bad news. Gwenda had never known Perkin to come home from the market with so much unsold produce.

Annet seemed unworried. She held out a hand to Wulfric, who helped her down from the cart. As she stepped to the ground, she stumbled, and fell against him with her hand on his chest. "Oops!" she said, and smiled at him as she recovered her balance. Wulfric flushed with pleasure.

You blind idiot, Gwenda thought.

They went inside. Perkin sat at the table, and his wife, Peggy, brought him a bowl of pottage. He cut a thick slice from the loaf on the board. Peggy served her own family next. Annet, her husband Billy Howard, Annet's brother Rob, and Rob's wife. She gave a little to Annet's four-year-old daughter, Amabel, and to Rob's two small boys. Then she invited Wulfric and his family to sit down.

Gwenda spooned up the broth hungrily. It was thicker than the pottage she made: Peggy was putting stale bread in, whereas in Gwenda's house the bread never lasted long enough to go stale. Perkin's family got cups of ale, but Gwenda and Wulfric were not offered any: hospitality went only so far in hard times.

Perkin was jocular with his customers, but otherwise a sourpuss, and the atmosphere in his house was always more or less dismal. He talked in a disheartened way about the Kingsbridge market. Most of the traders had had a bad day. The only ones doing any business were those who sold essentials such as corn, meat, and salt. No one was buying the now-famous Kingsbridge Scarlet cloth.

Peggy lit a lamp. Gwenda wanted to go home, but she and Wulfric were waiting for their wages. The boys began to misbehave, running around the room and bumping into adults. "It's getting near their bedtime," said Gwenda, though it was not really.

At last Wulfric said: "If you'll give us our wages, Perkin, we'll leave."

"I haven't got any money," Perkin said.

Gwenda stared at him. He had never said anything like this in the nine years she and Wulfric had been working for him.

Wulfric said: "We must have our wages. We've got to eat."

"You've had some pottage, haven't you?" Perkin said.

Gwenda was outraged. "We work for money, not pottage!"

"Well, I haven't got any money," Perkin repeated. "I went to market to sell my apples, but no one bought them, so I've got more apples than we can eat, and no money."

Gwenda was so shocked that she did not know what to say. It had never occurred to her that Perkin might not pay them. She felt a stab of fear as she realized there was nothing she could do about it.

Wulfric said slowly: "Well, what's to be done about it? Shall we go to the Long Field and take the seeds back out of the ground?"

"I'll have to owe you this week's wages," Perkin said. "I'll pay you when things get better."

"And next week?"

"I won't have any money next week, either—where do you think it's to come from?"

Gwenda said: "We'll go to Mark Webber. Perhaps he can employ us at the fulling mill."

Perkin shook his head. "I spoke to him yesterday, in Kingsbridge, and asked if he could hire you. He said no. He's not selling enough cloth. He'll continue to employ Jack and Eli and the boy, and stockpile the cloth until trade picks up, but he can't take on any extra hands."

Wulfric was bewildered. "How are we to live? How will you get your spring plowing done?"

"You can work for food," Perkin offered.

Wulfric looked at Gwenda. She choked back a scornful retort. She and her family were in deep trouble, and this was not the moment to antagonize anyone. She thought fast. They did not have much choice: eat or starve. "We'll work for food, and you'll owe us the money," she said.

Perkin shook his head. "What you're suggesting may be fair—"

"It is fair!"

"All right, it is fair, but just the same I can't do it. I don't know when I'll have the money. Why, I could owe you a pound come Whitsun! You can work for food, or not at all."

"You'll have to feed all four of us."

"Yes."

"But only Wulfric will work."

"I don't know—"

"A family wants more than food. Children need clothes. A man must have boots. If you can't pay me, I will have to find some other way of providing such things."

"How?"

"I don't know." She paused. The truth was, she had no idea. She fought down panic. "I may have to ask my father how he manages."

Peggy put in: "I wouldn't do that, if I were you—Joby will tell you to steal."

Gwenda was stung. What right did Peggy have to take a supercilious attitude? Joby had never employed people then told them at the end of the week that he could not pay them. But she bit her tongue and said mildly: "He fed me through eighteen winters, even if he did sell me to outlaws at the end."

Peggy tossed her head and abruptly began to pick up the bowls from the table.

Wulfric said: "We should go."

Gwenda did not move. Whatever advantages she could gain had to be won now. When she left this house, Perkin would consider that a bargain had been struck, and could not be renegotiated. She thought hard. Remembering how Peggy had given ale only to her own family, she said: "You won't fob us off with stale fish and watery beer. You'll feed us exactly the same as yourself and your family—meat, bread, ale, whatever it may be."

Peggy made a deprecating noise. She had been planning to do just what Gwenda feared, it seemed.

Gwenda added: "That is, if you want Wulfric to do the same work as you and Rob." They all knew perfectly well that Wulfric did more work than Rob and twice as much as Perkin.

"All right," Perkin said.

"And this is strictly an emergency arrangement. As soon as you get money, you have to start paying us again at the old rate—a penny a day each."

"Yes."

There was a short silence. Wulfric said: "Is that it?"

"I think so," Gwenda said. "You and Perkin should shake hands on the bargain."

They shook hands.

Taking their children, Gwenda and Wulfric left. It was now full dark. Clouds hid the stars, and they had to make their way by the glimmer of light shining through cracks in shutters and around doors. Fortunately they had walked from Perkin's house to their own a thousand times before.

Wulfric lit a lamp and built up the fire while Gwenda put the boys to bed. Although there were bedrooms upstairs—they were still living in the large house that had been occupied by Wulfric's parents—nevertheless they all slept in the kitchen, for warmth.

Gwenda felt depressed as she wrapped the boys in blankets and settled them near the fire. She had grown up determined not to live the way her mother did, in constant worry and want. She had aspired to independence:

a patch of land, a hardworking husband, a reasonable lord. Wulfric yearned to get back the land his father had farmed. In all those aspirations they had failed. She was a pauper, and her husband a landless laborer whose employer could not even pay him a penny a day. She had ended up exactly like her mother, she thought; and she felt too bitter for tears.

Wulfric took a pottery bottle from a shelf and poured ale into a wooden cup. "Enjoy it," Gwenda said sourly. "You won't be able to buy your own ale for a while."

Wulfric said conversationally: "It's amazing that Perkin has no money. He's the richest man in the village, apart from Nathan Reeve."

"Perkin has money," Gwenda said. "There's a jar of silver pennies under his fireplace. I've seen it."

"Then why won't he pay us?"

"He doesn't want to dip into his savings."

Wulfric was taken aback. "But he could pay us, if he wanted to?"

"Of course."

"Then why am I going to work for food?"

Gwenda let out an impatient grunt. Wulfric was so slow on the uptake. "Because the alternative was no work at all."

Wulfric was feeling that they had been hoodwinked. "We should have insisted on payment."

"Then why didn't you?"

"I didn't know about the jar of pennies under the fireplace."

"For God's sake, do you think a man as rich as Perkin can be impoverished by failing to sell one cartload of apples? He's been the largest landholder in Wigleigh ever since he got hold of your father's acres ten years ago. Of course he has savings!"

"Yes, I see that."

She stared into the fire while he finished the ale, then they went to bed. He put his arms around her, and she rested her head on his chest, but she did not want to make love. She was too angry. She told herself she should not take it out on her husband: Perkin had let them down, not Wulfric. But she *was* angry with Wulfric—furious. As she sensed him drifting off to sleep, she realized that her anger was not about their wages. That was the kind of misfortune that afflicted everyone from time to time, like bad weather and barley mold.

What, then?

She recalled the way Annet had fallen against Wulfric as she stepped down from the cart. When she remembered Annet's coquettish smile, and

Wulfric's flush of pleasure, she wanted to slap his face. I'm angry with you, she thought, because that worthless, empty-headed flirt can still make you look such a damn fool.

On the Sunday before Christmas, a manor court was held in the church after the service. It was cold, and the villagers huddled together, wrapped in cloaks and blankets. Nathan Reeve was in charge. The lord of the manor, Ralph Fitzgerald, had not been seen in Wigleigh for years. So much the better, Gwenda thought. Besides, he was Sir Ralph now, with three other villages in his fiefdom, so he would not take much interest in ox teams and cow pasture.

Alfred Shorthouse had died during the week. He was a childless widower with ten acres. "He has no natural heirs," said Nate Reeve. "Perkin is willing to take over his land."

Gwenda was surprised. How could Perkin think of taking on more land? She was too startled to respond immediately, and Aaron Appletree, the bagpipe player, spoke first. "Alfred has been in poor health since the summer," he said. "He's done no autumn plowing and sown no winter wheat. All the work is to be done. Perkin will have his hands full."

Nate said aggressively: "Are you asking for the land yourself?"

Aaron shook his head. "In a few more years, when my boys are big enough to help, I'll jump at such a chance," he said. "I couldn't handle it now."

"I can manage it," Perkin said.

Gwenda frowned. Nate obviously wanted Perkin to have the land. No doubt a bribe had been promised. She had known all along that Perkin had money. But she had little interest in exposing Perkin's duplicity. She was thinking of how she could exploit this situation to her advantage, and get her family out of poverty.

Nate said: "You could take on another laborer, Perkin."

"Wait a minute," Gwenda said. "Perkin can't pay the laborers he's got now. How can he take on more land?"

Perkin was taken aback, but he could hardly deny what Gwenda was saying, so he remained silent.

Nate said: "Well, who else can cope with it?"

Gwenda said quickly: "We'll take it."

Nate looked surprised.

She added quickly: "Wulfric is working for food. I have no work. We need land."

She noticed several nodding heads. No one in the village liked what Perkin had done. They all feared that one day they might end up in the same situation.

Nate saw the danger of his plan going awry. "You can't afford the entry fee," he said.

"We'll pay it a little at a time."

Nate shook his head. "I want a tenant who can pay right away." He looked around the assembled villagers. However, no one volunteered. "David Johns?"

David was a middle-aged man whose sons had land of their own. "I would have said yes a year ago," he said. "But the rain at harvest time knocked me back."

The offer of an extra ten acres would normally have had the more ambitious villagers fighting among themselves, but it was a bad year. Gwenda and Wulfric were different. For one thing, Wulfric had never ceased to long for land of his own. Alfred's acres were not Wulfric's birthright, but they were better than nothing. Anyway, Gwenda and Wulfric were desperate.

Aaron Appletree said: "Give it to Wulfric, Nate. He's a hard worker, he'll get the plowing done in time. And he and his wife deserve some good luck—they've had more than their fair share of bad."

Nate looked bad-tempered, but there was a loud rumble of assent from the peasants. Wulfric and Gwenda were well respected despite their poverty.

This was a rare combination of circumstances that could get Gwenda and her family started on the road to a better life, and she felt growing excitement as it began to seem possible.

But Nate was still looking dubious. "Sir Ralph hates Wulfric," he said.

Wulfric's hand went to his cheek, and he touched the scar made by Ralph's sword.

"I know," said Gwenda. "But Ralph's not here."

52

When Earl Roland died the day after the battle of Crécy, several people moved a step up the ladder. His elder son, William, became the earl, overlord of the county of Shiring, answerable to the king. A cousin of William's, Sir Edward Courthose, became lord of Caster, took over the rule of the forty villages of that fiefdom as a subtenant of the earl, and moved into William and Philippa's old house in Casterham. And Sir Ralph Fitzgerald became lord of Tench.

For the next eighteen months, none of them went home. They were all too busy traveling with the king and killing French people. Then, in 1347, the war reached a stalemate. The English captured and held the valuable port city of Calais, but otherwise there was little to show for a decade of war—except, of course, a great deal of booty.

In January 1348 Ralph took possession of his new property. Tench was a large village with a hundred peasant families, and the manor included two smaller villages nearby. He also retained Wigleigh, which was half a day's ride away.

Ralph felt a thrill of pride as he rode through Tench. He had looked forward to this moment. The serfs bowed and their children stared. He was lord of every person and owner of every object in the place.

The house was set in a compound. Riding in, followed by a cart loaded with French loot, Ralph saw immediately that the defensive walls had long ago fallen into disrepair. He wondered whether he should restore them. The burghers of Normandy had neglected their defenses, by and large, and that had made it relatively easy for Edward III to overrun them. On the other hand, the likelihood of an invasion of southern England was now very small. Early in the war, most of the French fleet had been wiped out at the port of Sluys, and thereafter the English had controlled the sea channel that separated the two countries. Apart from minor raids by freelance pirates, every battle since Sluys had been fought on French soil. On balance it hardly seemed worthwhile to rebuild the compound walls.

Several grooms appeared and took the horses. Ralph left Alan Fernhill to supervise the unloading, and walked toward his new house. He was limping: his injured leg always hurt after a long ride. Tench Hall was a stone-built manor house. It was impressive, he noted with satisfaction, though it needed repairs—not surprisingly, for it had remained unoccupied since Lady Matilda's father died. However, it was modern in design. In old-fashioned houses, the lord's private chamber was an afterthought stuck on to the end of the all-important great hall, but Ralph could see, from the outside, that here the domestic apartments took up half the building.

He entered the hall, and was annoyed to find Earl William there.

At the far end of the room was a large chair made of dark wood, elaborately carved with powerful symbols: angels and lions on the back and arms, snakes and monsters on the legs. It was obviously the chair of the lord of the manor. But William was sitting in it.

Much of Ralph's pleasure evaporated. He could not enjoy his mastery of the new manor under the scrutiny of his own overlord. It would be like going to bed with a woman while her husband listened outside the door.

He masked his displeasure and formally greeted Earl William. The earl introduced the man standing next to him. "This is Daniel, who has been bailiff here for twenty years, and has taken good care of the place, on my father's behalf, during Tilly's minority."

Ralph acknowledged the bailiff stiffly. William's message was clear: he wanted Ralph to let Daniel continue in the job. But Daniel had been Earl Roland's man and now he would be Earl William's. Ralph had no intention of letting his domain be managed by the earl's man. His bailiff would be loyal to him alone.

William waited expectantly for Ralph to say something about Daniel. However, Ralph was not going to have that discussion. Ten years ago he would have jumped feet first into an argument, but he had learned a lot in the time he had spent with the king. He was not obliged to get his earl's approval for his choice of bailiff, so he would not seek it. He would say nothing until William had gone, then he would tell Daniel he was being assigned to other duties.

Both William and Ralph remained stubbornly silent for a few moments, then the deadlock was broken. A large door opened at the domestic end of the hall and the tall, elegant figure of Lady Philippa came in. It was many years since Ralph had seen her, but his youthful passion returned with a shock that felt like a punch, leaving him breathless. She was older—she had to be forty, he guessed—but she was in her prime. Perhaps she was a little heavier than he remembered, her hips more rounded, her breasts fuller, but that only added to her allure. She still walked like a queen. As always, the sight of her made him ask resentfully why he could not have a wife like that.

In the past she had barely deigned to notice his presence, but today she smiled and shook his hand and said: "Are you getting to know Daniel?"

She, too, wanted him to continue to employ the earl's retainer—that was why she was being courteous. All the more reason to get rid of the man, he thought with secret relish. "I've just arrived," he said noncommittally.

Philippa explained their presence. "We wanted to be here when you met young Tilly—she's part of our family."

Ralph had commanded the nuns of Kingsbridge Priory to bring his fiancée here to meet him today. Interfering busybodies, the nuns had obviously told Earl William what was happening. "Lady Matilda was the ward of Earl Roland, rest his soul," Ralph said, emphasizing that the wardship had ended with Roland's death.

"Yes—and I would have expected the king to transfer her wardship to my husband, as Roland's heir." Clearly Philippa would have preferred that.

"But he did not," Ralph said. "He gave her to me to wed." Although no ceremony had yet taken place, the girl had immediately become Ralph's responsibility. Strictly speaking, William and Philippa had no business to invite themselves here today, as if playing the role of Tilly's parents. But William was Ralph's overlord, so he could visit whenever he pleased.

Ralph did not want to quarrel with William. It was too easy for William to make Ralph's life difficult. On the other hand, the new earl was overreaching his authority here—probably under pressure from his wife. But Ralph was not going to be bullied. The last seven years had given him the confidence to defend such independence as he was entitled to.

Anyway, he was enjoying crossing swords with Philippa. It gave him an excuse to stare at her. He rested his gaze on the assertive line of her jaw and the fullness of her lips. Despite her hauteur, she was forced to engage with him. This was the longest conversation he had ever had with her.

"Tilly is very young," said Philippa.

"She will be fourteen this year," Ralph said. "That's the age our queen was when she married our king—as the king himself pointed out, to me and to Earl William, after the battle of Crécy."

"The aftermath of a battle is not necessarily the best moment to decide the fate of a young girl," Philippa said in a lowered voice.

Ralph was not going to let that pass. "Speaking for myself, I feel obliged to comply with the decisions of His Majesty."

"As do we all," she muttered.

Ralph felt he had vanquished her. It was a sexual feeling, almost as if he had lain with her. Satisfied, he turned to Daniel. "My wife-to-be should arrive in time for dinner," he said. "Make sure we have a feast."

Philippa said: "I have already seen to that."

Ralph slowly turned his head until his eyes were on her again. She had overstepped the bounds of courtesy by going into his kitchen and giving orders.

She knew it, and reddened. "I didn't know what time you would get here," she said.

Ralph said nothing. She would not apologize, but he was content in having forced her to explain herself—a climb-down for a woman as proud as she.

For a short while there had been the noise of horses outside, and now Ralph's parents came in. He had not seen them for some years, and he hurried to embrace them.

They were both in their fifties, but his mother had aged faster, it seemed to him. Her hair was white and her face was lined. She had the slight stoop of elderly women. His father seemed more vigorous. It was partly the excitement of the moment: he was flushed with pride, and shook Ralph's hand as if pumping water from a well. But there was no gray in his red beard, and his slim figure still appeared spry. They were both wearing new clothes—Ralph had sent the money. Sir Gerald had a heavy wool surcoat and Lady Maud a fur cloak.

Ralph snapped his fingers at Daniel. "Bring wine," he said. For an instant, the bailiff looked as though he might protest at being treated like a maidservant; then he swallowed his pride and hurried off to the kitchen.

Ralph said: "Earl William, Lady Philippa, may I present my father, Sir Gerald, and my mother, Lady Maud."

He was afraid that William and Philippa would look down their noses at his parents, but they acknowledged them courteously enough.

Gerald said to William: "I was a comrade-in-arms of your father, may he rest in peace. In fact, Earl William, I knew you as a boy, though you won't remember me."

Ralph wished his father would not call attention to his glorious past. It only emphasized how far he had fallen.

But William seemed not to notice. "Well, d'you know, I think I do remember," he said. He was probably just being kind, but Gerald was pleased. "Of course," William added, "I recall you as a giant at least seven feet tall."

Gerald, who was short in stature, laughed delightedly.

Maud looked around and said: "My, this is a fine house, Ralph."

"I wanted to decorate it with all the treasures I've brought back from France," he said. "But I've only just got here."

A kitchen girl brought a jug of wine and goblets on a tray, and they all took some refreshment. The wine was good Bordeaux, Ralph noticed, clear and sweet. Due credit to Daniel for keeping the house well supplied, he thought at first; then he reflected that for many years no one had been here to drink it—except, of course, Daniel.

He said to his mother: "Any news of my brother, Merthin?"

"He's doing very well," she said proudly. "Married with a daughter, and rich. He's building a palace for the family of Buonaventura Caroli."

"But they haven't made him a *conte* yet, I suppose?" Ralph pretended to be joking, but he was pointing out that Merthin, for all his success, had not gained a noble title; and that it was he, Ralph, who had fulfilled their father's hopes by taking the family back into the nobility.

"Not yet," said his father gaily, as if it were a real possibility that Merthin might become an Italian count; which annoyed Ralph, but only momentarily.

His mother said: "Could we see our rooms?"

Ralph hesitated. What did she mean by "our rooms"? The dreadful thought crossed his mind that his parents might think they were going to live here. He could not have that: they would be a constant reminder of the family's years of shame. Besides, they would cramp his style. On the other hand, he now realized, it was also shameful for a nobleman to let his parents live in a one-room house as pensioners of a priory.

He would have to think more about that. For now he said: "I haven't had a chance to look at the private quarters myself yet. I hope I can make you comfortable for a few nights."

"A few nights?" his mother said quickly. "Are you going to send us back to our hovel in Kingsbridge?"

Ralph was mortified that she should mention that in front of William and Philippa. "I don't think there's room for you to live here."

"How do you know, if you haven't yet looked at the chambers?"

Daniel interrupted. "There's a villager here from Wigleigh, Sir Ralph—name of Perkin. Wants to pay his respects and discuss an urgent matter."

Ralph would normally have told the man off for butting into a conversation, but on this occasion he was grateful for the diversion. "Have a look at the rooms, Mother," he said. "I'll deal with this peasant."

William and Philippa went off with his parents to inspect the domestic quarters, and Daniel brought Perkin to the table. Perkin was as obsequious as ever. "So happy to see your lordship safe and whole after the French wars," he said.

Ralph looked at his left hand, with three fingers missing. "Well, almost whole," he said.

"All the people of Wigleigh are sorry for your wounds, lord, but the rewards! A knighthood, and three more villages, and Lady Matilda to wed!"

"Thank you for your felicitations, but what was the urgent matter you needed to discuss?"

"Lord, it doesn't take long to tell. Alfred Shorthouse died without a natural heir to his ten acres, and I offered to take on the land, even though times have been very hard, after this year's thunderstorms in August—"

"Never mind the weather."

"Of course. In brief, Nathan Reeve made a decision that I feel you would not approve."

Ralph felt impatient. He really did not care which peasant farmed Alfred's ten acres. "Whatever Nathan decided—"

"He gave the land to Wulfric."

"Ah."

"Some of the villagers said Wulfric deserved it, as he had no land; but he can't pay the entry fee, and anyway—"

"You don't need to convince me," Ralph said. "I will not allow that troublemaker to hold land in my territory."

"Thank you, lord. Shall I tell Nathan Reeve that you wish me to have the ten acres?"

"Yes," Ralph said. He saw the earl and countess emerge from the private quarters, with his parents in tow. "I'll be there to confirm it in person within the next two weeks." He dismissed Perkin with a wave.

At that moment, Lady Matilda arrived.

She entered the hall with a nun on either side of her. One was Merthin's old girlfriend, Caris, who had tried to tell the king that Tilly was too young to marry. On the other side was the nun who had traveled to Crécy with Caris, an angel-faced woman whose name Ralph did not know. Behind them, presumably acting as their bodyguard, was the one-armed monk who had captured Ralph so cleverly nine years ago, Brother Thomas.

And in the center was Tilly. Ralph saw immediately why the nuns wanted to protect her from marriage. Her face had a look of childish innocence. She had freckles on her nose and a gap between her two front teeth. She stared about her with frightened eyes. Caris had heightened the childish look by dressing her in a plain white nun's robe and a simple cap, but the clothing failed to hide the womanly curves of the body underneath. Caris had obviously wanted to make Tilly seem too young for wedlock. The effect on Ralph was the opposite of what was intended.

One of the things Ralph had learned in the king's service was that, in many situations, a man could take charge simply by speaking first. He said loudly: "Come here, Tilly."

The girl stepped forward and came to him. Her escort hesitated, then stayed where they were.

"I am your husband," Ralph said to her. "My name is Sir Ralph Fitzgerald, Lord of Tench."

She looked terrified. "I'm happy to meet you, sir."

"This is your home now, as it was when you were a child and your father was lord here. You are now the Lady of Tench, as your mother once was. Are you happy to be back in your family home?"

"Yes, lord." She looked anything but happy.

"I'm sure the nuns have told you that you must be an obedient wife, and do all you can to please your husband, who is your lord and master."

"Yes, lord."

"And here are my mother and father, who are your parents, too, now."

She made a little curtsey to Gerald and Maud.

Ralph said: "Come here." He held out his hands.

Automatically, Tilly reached out, then she saw his maimed left hand. She made a disgusted sound and flinched back.

An angry curse came to Ralph's lips, but he suppressed it. With some difficulty he forced himself to speak in a light tone of voice. "Don't be afraid of my wounded hand," he said. "You should be proud of it. I lost those fingers in the service of the king." He kept both arms stretched out expectantly.

With an effort, she took his hands.

"Now you can kiss me, Tilly."

He was seated, and she was standing in front of him. She leaned forward and offered her cheek. He put his wounded hand at the back of her head and turned her face, then he kissed her lips. He sensed her uncertainty and guessed that she had not been kissed by a man before. He let his mouth linger on hers, partly because it was so sweet, and partly to enrage those watching. Then, with slow deliberation, he pressed his good hand against her chest, and felt her breasts. They were full and round. She was no child.

He released her and sighed with satisfaction. "We must get married soon," he said. He turned to Caris, who was visibly suppressing anger. "In Kingsbridge Cathedral, four weeks from Sunday," he said. He looked at Philippa but addressed William. "As we're getting married by the express wish of His Majesty King Edward, I would be honored if you would attend, Earl William."

William nodded curtly.

Caris spoke for the first time. "Sir Ralph, the prior of Kingsbridge sends you greetings, and says he will be honored to perform the ceremony, unless of course the new bishop wishes to do so."

Ralph nodded graciously.

She then added: "But those of us who have had charge of this child believe she is still too young to live with her husband conjugally."

Philippa said: "I concur."

Ralph's father spoke. "You know, son, I waited years to marry your mother."

Ralph did not want to hear that story all over again. "Unlike you, Father, I have been ordered by the king to marry Lady Matilda."

His mother said: "Perhaps you should wait, son."

"I have waited more than a year! She was twelve when the king gave her to me."

Caris said: "Marry the child, yes, with all due ceremony—but then let her return to the nunnery for a year. Let her grow fully into her womanhood. Then bring her to your home."

Ralph snorted scornfully. "I could be dead in a year, especially if the king decides to go back to France. Meanwhile, the Fitzgeralds need an heir."

"She is a child—"

Ralph interrupted, raising his voice. "She is no child—look at her! That stupid nun's habit can't disguise her breasts."

"Puppy fat—"

"Does she have a woman's hair?" Ralph demanded.

Tilly gasped at his crude frankness, and her cheeks reddened with shame.

Caris hesitated.

Ralph said: "Perhaps my mother should examine her on my behalf and tell me."

Caris shook her head. "That won't be necessary. Tilly has hair where a woman has it and a child does not."

"I knew as much. I have seen—" Ralph stopped, realizing that he did not want everyone here to know in what circumstances he had seen the naked bodies of girls of Tilly's age. "I guessed, from her figure," he amended, avoiding his mother's eye.

A rarely heard pleading tone entered Caris's voice. "But, Ralph, in her mind she is still a child."

I don't care about her mind, Ralph thought, but he did not say so. "She has four weeks to learn what she does not know," he said. He gave Caris a knowing look. "I'm sure you can teach her everything."

Caris flushed. Nuns were not supposed to know about marital intimacy, of course, but she had been his brother's girlfriend.

His mother said: "Perhaps a compromise—"

"You just don't understand, Mother, do you?" he said, rudely interrupting her. "No one is really concerned about her age. If I were going to marry the daughter of a Kingsbridge butcher, they wouldn't care if she was nine. It's because Tilly is noble-born, don't you see that? They think they're superior to us!" He knew he was shouting, and he could see the amazed expressions of everyone around him, but he did not care. "They don't want a cousin of the earl of Shiring to marry the son of an impoverished knight. They want to put off the marriage in the hope that I'll be killed in battle before it's consummated." He wiped his mouth. "But this son of an impoverished knight fought at the battle of Crécy, and saved the life of the prince of Wales. That's what matters to the king." He looked at each of them in turn: haughty William, scornful Philippa, furious Caris, and his astonished parents. "So you might as well accept the facts. Ralph Fitzgerald is a knight and a lord, and a comrade-in-arms of the king. And he's going to marry Lady Matilda, the cousin of the earl—whether you like it or not!"

There was a shocked silence for several moments.

At last Ralph turned to Daniel. "You can serve dinner now," he said.

53

In the spring of 1348, Merthin woke up as if from a nightmare he could not quite remember. He felt frightened and weak. He opened his eyes to a room lit by bars of bright sunshine coming through half-open shutters. He saw a high ceiling, white walls, red tiles. The air was mild. Reality returned slowly. He was in his bedroom, in his house, in Florence. He had been ill.

The illness came back to him first. It had begun with a skin rash, purplish-black blotches on his chest, then his arms, then everywhere. Soon afterward he developed a painful lump or bubo in his armpit. He had a fever, sweating in his bed, tangling the sheets as he writhed. He had vomited and coughed blood. He had thought he would die. Worst of all was a terrible, unquenchable thirst that had made him want to throw himself into the River Arno with his mouth open.

He was not the only sufferer. Thousands of Italians had fallen ill with this plague, tens of thousands. Half the workmen on his building sites had disappeared, as had most of his household servants. Almost everyone who caught it died within five days. They called it *la moria grande,* the big death.

But he was alive.

He had a nagging feeling that while ill he had reached a momentous decision, but he could not remember it. He concentrated for a moment. The harder he thought, the more elusive the memory became, until it vanished.

He sat up in bed. His limbs felt feeble and his head spun for a moment. He was wearing a clean linen nightshirt, and he wondered who had put it on him. After a pause, he stood.

He had a four-story house with a courtyard. He had designed and built it himself, with a flat facade instead of the traditional overhanging floors, and architectural features such as round window arches and classical columns. The neighbors had called it a *palagetto,* a mini-palace. That was seven years ago. Several prosperous Florentine merchants had asked him to build *palagetti* for them, and that had got his career here started.

Florence was a republic, with no ruling prince or duke, dominated by an elite of squabbling merchant families. The city was populated by thousands of weavers, but it was the merchants who made fortunes. They spent their money building grand houses, which made the city a perfect place for a talented young architect to prosper.

He went to the bedroom door and called his wife. "Silvia! Where are you?" It came naturally to him to speak the Tuscan dialect now, after nine years.

Then he remembered. Silvia had been ill, too. So had their daughter, who was three years old. Her name was Laura, but they had adopted her childish pronunciation, Lolla. His heart was gripped by a terrible fear. Was Silvia alive? Was Lolla?

The house was quiet. So was the city, he realized suddenly. The angle of the sunlight slanting into the rooms told him it was mid-morning. He should have been hearing the cries of street hawkers, the clop of horses and the rumble of wooden cartwheels, the background murmur of a thousand conversations—but there was nothing.

He went up the stairs. In his weakness, the effort made him breathless. He pushed open the door to the nursery. The room looked empty. He broke out in a sweat of fear. There was Lolla's cot, a small chest for her clothes, a box of toys, a miniature table with two tiny chairs. Then he heard a noise. There in the corner was Lolla, sitting on the floor in a clean dress, playing with a small wooden horse with articulated legs. Merthin gave a strangled cry of relief. She heard him and looked up. "Papa," she observed in a matter-of-fact tone.

Merthin picked her up and hugged her. "You're alive," he said in English.

There was a sound from the next room, and Maria walked in. A gray-haired woman in her fifties, she was Lolla's nurse. "Master!" she said. "You got up—are you better?"

"Where is your mistress?" he said.

Maria's face fell. "I'm so sorry, master," she said. "The mistress died."

Lolla said: "Mama's gone."

Merthin felt the shock like a blow. Stunned, he handed Lolla to Maria. Moving slowly and carefully, he turned away and walked out of the room, then down the stairs to the *piano nobile,* the principal floor. He stared at the long table, the empty chairs, the rugs on the floor, and the pictures on the walls. It looked like someone else's home.

He stood in front of a painting of the Virgin Mary with her mother. Italian painters were superior to the English or any others, and this artist had given Saint Anne the face of Silvia. She was a proud beauty, with flawless olive skin and noble features, but the painter had seen the sexual passion smoldering in those aloof brown eyes.

It was hard to comprehend that Silvia no longer existed. He thought of her slim body, and remembered how he had marveled, again and again, at her perfect breasts. That body, with which he had been so completely intimate, now lay in the ground somewhere. When he imagined that, tears came to his eyes at last, and he sobbed with grief.

Where was her grave? he wondered in his misery. He remembered that funerals had ceased in Florence: people were terrified to leave their houses. They simply dragged the bodies outside and laid them on the street. The city's thieves, beggars, and drunks had acquired a new profession: they were called corpse carriers or *becchini,* and they charged exorbitant fees to take the bodies away and put them in mass graves. Merthin might never know where Silvia lay.

They had been married four years. Looking at her picture, garbed in St. Anne's conventional red dress, Merthin suffered an access of painful honesty, and asked himself whether he had really loved her. He was very fond of her, but it was not an all-consuming passion. She had an independent spirit and a sharp tongue, and he was the only man in Florence with the nerve to woo her, despite her father's wealth. In return, she had given him complete devotion. But she had accurately gauged the quality of his love. "What are you thinking about?" she used to say sometimes, and he would give a guilty start, because he had been remembering Kingsbridge. Soon she changed it to: "Who are you thinking about?" He never spoke Caris's name, but Silvia said: "It must be a woman, I can tell by the look on your face." Eventually she began to talk about "your English girl." She would say: "You're remembering your English girl," and she was always right. But she seemed to accept it. Merthin was faithful to her. And he adored Lolla.

After a while, Maria brought him soup and bread. "What day is it?" he asked her.

"Tuesday."

"How long was I in bed?"

"Two weeks. You were so ill."

He wondered why he had survived. Some people never succumbed to the disease, as if they had natural protection; but those who caught it nearly always died. However, the tiny minority who recovered were doubly fortunate, for no one had ever caught the illness a second time.

When he had eaten, he felt stronger. He had to rebuild his life, he realized. He suspected that he had already made this decision once, when he was ill, but again he was tantalized by the thread of a memory slipping from his grasp.

His first task was to find out how much of his family was left.

He took his dishes to the kitchen, where Maria was feeding Lolla bread dipped in goat's milk. He asked her: "What about Silvia's parents? Are they alive?"

"I don't know," she said. "I haven't heard. I go out only to buy food."

"I'd better find out."

He got dressed and went downstairs. The ground floor of the house was a workshop, with the yard at the rear used for storing wood and stone. No one was at work, either inside or out.

He left the house. The buildings around him were mostly stone-built, some of them very grand: Kingsbridge had no houses to compare with these. The richest man in Kingsbridge, Edmund Wooler, had lived in a timber house. Here in Florence, only the poor lived in such places.

The street was deserted. He had never seen it this way, not even in the middle of the night. The effect was eerie. He wondered how many people had died: a third of the population? Half? Were their ghosts still lingering in alleyways and shadowed corners, enviously watching the lucky survivors?

The Christi house was on the next street. Merthin's father-in-law, Alessandro Christi, had been his first and best friend in Florence. A schoolmate of Buonaventura Caroli, Alessandro had given Merthin his first commission, a simple warehouse building. He was, of course, Lolla's grandpa.

The door of Alessandro's *palagetto* was locked. That was unusual in itself. Merthin banged on the woodwork and waited. Eventually it was opened by Elizabetta, a small, plump woman who was Alessandro's laundress. She stared at him in shock. "You're alive!" she said.

"Hello, Betta," he said. "I'm glad to see that you're alive, too."

She turned and called back into the house: "It's the English lord!"

He had told them he was not a lord, but the servants did not believe him. He stepped inside. "Alessandro?" he said.

She shook her head and began to cry.

"And your mistress?"

"Both dead."

The stairs led from the entrance hall to the main floor. Merthin walked up slowly, surprised by how weak he still felt. In the main room he sat down to catch his breath. Alessandro had been wealthy, and the room was a showplace of rugs and hangings, paintings and jeweled ornaments and books.

"Who else is here?" he asked Elizabetta.

"Just Lena and her children." Lena was an Asiatic slave, unusual but by no means unique in prosperous Florentine households. She had two small children by Alessandro, a boy and a girl, and he had treated them just like his legitimate offspring; in fact Silvia had said acidly that he doted on them more than he ever had on her and her brother. The arrangement was considered eccentric rather than scandalous by the sophisticated Florentines.

Merthin said: "What about Signor Gianni?" Gianni was Silvia's brother.

"Dead. And his wife. The baby is here with me."

"Dear God."

Betta said tentatively: "And your family, lord?"

"My wife is dead."

"I am so sorry."

"But Lolla is alive."

"Thank God!"

"Maria is taking care of her."

"Maria is a good woman. Would you like some refreshment?"

Merthin nodded, and she went away.

Lena's children came to stare at him: a dark-eyed boy of seven who looked like Alessandro, and a pretty four-year-old with her mother's Asiatic eyes. Then Lena herself came in, a beautiful woman in her twenties with golden skin and high cheekbones. She brought him a silver goblet of dark red Tuscan wine and a tray of almonds and olives.

She said: "Will you come to live here, lord?"

Merthin was surprised. "I don't think so—why?"

"The house is yours now." She waved a hand to indicate the Christi family's wealth. "Everything is yours."

Merthin realized she was right. He was Alessandro Christi's only surviving adult relative. That made him the heir—and the guardian of three children in addition to Lolla.

"Everything," Lena repeated, giving him a direct look.

Merthin met her candid gaze, and realized that she was offering herself.

He considered the prospect. The house was beautiful. It was home to Lena's children, and a familiar place to Lolla, and even to Gianni's baby: all the children would be happy here. He had inherited enough money to live on for the rest of his life. Lena was a woman of intelligence and experience, and he could readily imagine the pleasures of becoming intimate with her.

She read his mind. She took his hand and pressed it to her bosom. Her breasts felt soft and warm through the light wool dress.

But this was not what he wanted. He drew Lena's hand to him and kissed it. "I will provide for you and your children," he said. "Don't worry."

"Thank you, lord," she said, but she looked disappointed, and something in her eyes told Merthin that her offer had not been merely practical. She had genuinely hoped he might be more to her than just her new owner. But that was part of the problem. He could not imagine sex with someone he owned. The idea was distasteful to the point of revulsion.

He sipped his wine and felt stronger. If he was not drawn to an easy life of luxury and sensual gratification, what *did* he want? His family was almost gone: only Lolla was left. But he still had his work. Around the city were three sites where designs of his were under construction. He was not going to give up the job he loved. He had not survived the great death to become an idler. He recalled his youthful ambition to build the tallest building in England. He would pick up where he had left off. He would recover from the loss of Silvia by throwing himself into his building projects.

He got up to leave. Lena flung her arms around him. "Thank you," she said. "Thank you for saying you will take care of my children."

He patted her back. "They are Alessandro's grandchildren," he said. In

Florence, the children of slaves were not themselves enslaved. "When they grow up they will be rich." He detached her arms gently and went down the stairs.

All the houses were locked and shuttered. On some doorsteps he saw a shrouded form that he presumed was a dead body. There were a few people on the streets, but mostly the poorer sort. The desolation was unnerving. Florence was the greatest city in the Christian world, a noisy commercial metropolis producing thousands of yards of fine woolen cloth every day, a market where vast sums of money were paid over on no more security than a letter from Antwerp or the verbal promise of a prince. Walking through these silent, empty streets was like seeing an injured horse that has fallen and cannot get up: immense strength was suddenly brought to nothing. He saw no one from his circle of acquaintance. His friends were keeping indoors, he presumed—those that were still alive.

He went first to a square nearby, in the old Roman city, where he was building a fountain for the municipality. He had devised an elaborate system to recycle almost all the water during Florence's long, dry summers.

But, when he reached the square, he could see immediately that no one was working on the site. The underground pipes had been put in and covered over before he fell ill, and the first course of masonry for the stepped plinth around the pool had been laid. However, the dusty, neglected look of the stones told him that no work had been done for days. Worse, a small pyramid of mortar on a wooden board had hardened into a solid mass that gave off a puff of dust when he kicked it. There were even some tools lying on the ground. It was a miracle they had not been stolen.

The fountain was going to be stunning. In Merthin's workshop, the best stone carver in the city was sculpting the centerpiece—or had been. Merthin was disappointed that work had stopped. Surely not all the builders had died? Perhaps they were waiting to see whether Merthin would recover.

This was the smallest of his three projects, albeit a prestigious one. He left the square and headed north to inspect another one. But as he walked he worried. He had not yet met anyone knowledgeable enough to give him a wider perspective. What was left of the city government? Was the plague easing off or getting worse? What about the rest of Italy?

One thing at a time, he told himself.

He was building a home for Giulielmo Caroli, the older brother of Buonaventura. It was to be a real palazzo, a high double-fronted house designed around a grand staircase wider than some of the city's streets. The ground-floor wall was already up. The facade was battered, or inclined, at ground level, the slight protrusion giving an impression of fortification; but above were elegant pointed-arch two-light windows with a trefoil. The design said that the people inside were both powerful and refined, which was what the Caroli family wanted.

The scaffolding had been erected for the second floor, but no one was working. There should have been five masons laying stones. The only person on-site was a elderly man who acted as caretaker and lived in a wooden hut at the back. Merthin found him cooking a chicken over a fire. The fool had used costly marble slabs for his hearth. "Where is everyone?" Merthin said abruptly.

The caretaker leaped to his feet. "Signor Caroli died, and his son Agostino wouldn't pay the men, so they left, those that weren't already dead themselves."

That was a blow. The Caroli family was one of the richest in Florence. If they felt they could no longer afford to build, the crisis was severe indeed.

"So Agostino is alive?"

"Yes, master, I saw him this morning."

Merthin knew young Agostino. He was not as clever as his father or his uncle Buonaventura, so he compensated by being extremely cautious and conservative. He would not recommence building until he was sure the family finances had recovered from the effects of the plague.

However, Merthin felt confident his third and largest project would continue. He was building a church for an order of friars much favored by the city's merchants. The site was south of the river, so he crossed the new bridge.

This bridge had been finished only two years ago. In fact Merthin had done some work on it, under the leading designer, the painter Taddeo Gaddi. The bridge had to withstand fast-flowing water when the winter snows melted, and Merthin had helped with the design of the piers. Now, as he crossed, he was dismayed to see that all the little goldsmiths' shops on the bridge were closed—another bad sign.

The Church of Sant' Anna dei Frari was his most ambitious project to date. It was a big church, more like a cathedral—the friars were rich—though nothing like the cathedral at Kingsbridge. Italy had Gothic cathedrals, Milan being one of the greatest, but modern-minded Italians did not like the architecture of France and England: they regarded huge windows and flying buttresses as a foreign fetish. The obsession with light, which made sense in the gloomy northwest of Europe, seemed perverse in sunny Italy, where people sought shade and coolness. Italians identified with the classical architecture of ancient Rome, the ruins of which were all around them. They liked gable ends and round arches, and they rejected ornate exterior sculpture in favor of decorative patterns of different-colored stone and marble.

But Merthin was going to surprise even the Florentines with this church. The plan was a series of squares, each topped by a dome—five in a row, and two either side of the crossing. He had heard about domes back in England, but had never seen one until he visited Siena Cathedral. There were none in Florence. The clerestory would be a row of round windows, or oculi. Instead of narrow pillars that reached yearningly for Heaven, this church would have circles, complete in themselves, with the air of earthbound self-sufficiency that characterized the commercial people of Florence.

He was disappointed, but not surprised, to see that there were no masons on the scaffolding, no laborers moving the great stones, no mortar-making women stirring with their giant paddles. This site was as quiet as the other two. However, in this case he felt confident he could get the project restarted. A religious order had a life of its own, independent of individuals. He walked around the site and entered the friary.

The place was silent. Monasteries were supposed to be so, of course, but there was a quality to this silence that unnerved him. He passed from the vestibule into the waiting room. There was usually a brother on duty here, studying the scriptures in between attending to visitors, but today the room was empty. With grim apprehension, Merthin went through another door and found himself in the cloisters. The quadrangle was deserted. "Hello!" he called out. "Is anyone there?" His voice echoed around the stone arcades.

He searched the place. All the friars were gone. In the kitchen he found three men sitting at the table, eating ham and drinking wine. They wore the costly clothes of merchants, but they had matted hair, untrimmed beards, and dirty hands: they were paupers wearing dead men's garments. When he walked in, they looked guilty but defiant. He said: "Where are the holy brothers?"

"All dead," said one of the men.

"All?"

"Every one. They took care of the sick, you see, and so they caught the disease."

The man was drunk, Merthin could see. However, he seemed to be telling the truth. These three were too comfortable, sitting in the monastery, eating the friars' food and drinking their wine. They clearly knew there was no one left to object.

Merthin returned to the site of the new church. The walls of the choir and transepts were up, and the oculi in the clerestory were visible. He sat in the middle of the crossing, amid stacks of stones, looking at his work. For how long would the project be stalled? If all the friars were dead, who would get their money? As far as he knew, they were not part of a larger order. The bishop might claim the inheritance, and so might the pope. There was a legal tangle here that could take years to resolve.

This morning he had resolved to throw himself into his work as a way of healing the wound of Silvia's death. Now it was clear that, at least for the present, he had no work. Ever since he began to repair the roof of St. Mark's church in Kingsbridge, ten years ago, he had had at least one building project on the go. Without one, he was lost. It made him feel panicky.

He had woken up to find his whole life in ruins. The fact that he was suddenly very rich only heightened the sense of nightmare. Lolla was the only part of his life he had left.

He did not even know where to go next. He would go home, eventually, but he could not spend all day playing with his three-year-old and talking to Maria. So he stayed where he was, sitting on a carved stone disc intended for a column, looking along what would be the nave.

As the sun rolled down the curve of the afternoon, he began to remember his illness. He had felt sure he would die. So few survived that he did not expect to be among the lucky ones. In his more lucid moments, he had reviewed his life as if it were over. He had come to some grand realization, he knew, but since recovering he had been unable to recall what it was. Now, in the tranquility of the unfinished church, he recalled concluding that he had made one huge mistake in his life. What was it? He had quarreled with Elfric, he had had sex with Griselda, he had rejected Elizabeth Clerk . . . All these decisions had caused trouble, but none counted as the mistake of a lifetime.

Lying on the bed, sweating, coughing, tormented by thirst, he had almost wanted to die; but not quite. Something had kept him alive—and now it came back to him.

He had wanted to see Caris again.

That was his reason for living. In his delirium he had seen her face, and had wept with grief that he might die here, thousands of miles away from her. The mistake of his life had been to leave her.

As he at last retrieved that elusive memory, and realized the blinding truth of the revelation, he was filled with an odd kind of happiness.

It did not make sense, he reflected. She had joined the nunnery. She had refused to see him and explain herself. But his soul was not rational, and it was telling him that he should be where she was.

He wondered what she was doing now, while he sat in a half-built church in a city nearly destroyed by a plague. The last he had heard was that she had been consecrated by the bishop. That decision was irrevocable—or so they said: Caris had never accepted what other people told her were the rules. On the other hand, once she had made her own decision, it was generally impossible to change her mind. There was no doubt she was strongly committed to her new life.

It made no difference. He wanted to see her again. Not to do so would be the second biggest mistake of his life.

And now he was free. His ties with Florence were all broken. His wife was dead, and so were all his relations by marriage except for three children. The only family he had here was his daughter, Lolla, and he would take her with him. She was so young he felt she would hardly notice that they had left.

It was a momentous move, he told himself. He would first have to prove Alessandro's will, and make arrangements for the children—Agostino Caroli would help him with that. Then he would have to turn his wealth into gold and arrange for it to be transferred to England. The Caroli family could do that, too, if their international network was still intact. Most daunting, he would have to undertake the thousand-mile journey from Florence across Europe to Kingsbridge. And all that without having any idea how Caris would receive him when at last he arrived.

It was a decision that required long and careful thought, obviously.

He made up his mind in a few moments.

He was going home.

54

Merthin left Italy in company with a dozen merchants from Florence and Lucca. They took a ship from Genoa to the ancient French port of Marseilles. From there they traveled overland to Avignon, home of the pope for the last forty years or more, and the most lavish court in Europe—as well as the smelliest city Merthin had ever known. There they joined a large group of clergymen and returning pilgrims heading north.

Everyone traveled in groups, the larger the better. The merchants were carrying money and expensive trading goods, and they had men-at-arms to protect them from outlaws. They were happy to have company: priestly robes and pilgrim badges might deter robbers, and even ordinary travelers such as Merthin helped just by swelling the numbers.

Merthin had entrusted most of his fortune to the Caroli family in Florence. Their relatives in England would give him cash. The Carolis carried on this kind of international transaction all the time, and indeed Merthin had used their services nine years ago to transfer a smaller fortune from Kingsbridge to Florence. All the same, he knew that the system was not completely infallible—such families sometimes went bankrupt, especially if they got involved in lending money to untrustworthy types such as kings and princes. That was why he had a large sum in gold florins sewn into his undershirt.

Lolla enjoyed the journey. As the only child in the caravan, she was much fussed over. During the long days on horseback, she sat on the saddle in front of Merthin, his arms holding her safe while his hands held the reins. He sang songs, repeated rhymes, told stories, and talked to her about the things they saw—trees, mills, bridges, churches. She probably did not understand half of what he said, but the sound of his voice kept her happy.

He had never before spent this much time with his daughter. They were together all day, every day, week after week. He hoped the intimacy would make up, in part, for the loss of her mother. It certainly worked the other way around: he would have been terribly lonely without her. She no longer spoke about Mama, but every now and then she would put her arms around his neck and cling to him with desperation, as if frightened to let him go.

He felt regret only when he stood in front of the great cathedral at Chartres, sixty miles outside Paris. There were two towers at its west end. The north tower was unfinished, but the south tower was three hundred and fifty feet high. It reminded him that he had once yearned to design such buildings. He was unlikely to achieve that ambition in Kingsbridge.

He lingered in Paris for two weeks. The plague had not reached here, and it was an immense relief to see the normal life of a great city, with people buying and selling and walking around, instead of empty streets with corpses on the doorsteps. His spirits lifted, and it was only then that he realized how stricken he had been by the horror he had left behind in Florence. He looked at Paris's cathedrals and palaces, making sketches of details that interested him. He had a small notebook made of paper, a new writing material popular in Italy.

Leaving Paris, he teamed up with a noble family returning to Cherbourg.

Hearing Lolla talk, the people assumed Merthin was Italian, and he did not disabuse them, for the English were hated passionately in northern France. With the family and their entourage, Merthin crossed Normandy at a leisurely pace, with Lolla on the saddle in front of him and their packhorse following on a leading rein, looking at those churches and abbeys that had survived the devastation of King Edward's invasion almost two years ago.

He could have moved faster, but he told himself he was making the most of an opportunity that might not come again, the chance to see a rich variety of architecture. However, when he was honest with himself he had to admit that he was afraid of what he might find when he reached Kingsbridge.

He was going home to Caris, but she would not be the same Caris he had left behind nine years ago. She might have changed, physically and mentally. Some nuns became grossly fat, their only pleasure in life being food. More likely, Caris might have become ethereally thin, starving herself in an ecstasy of self-denial. By now she could be obsessed with religion, praying all day and flagellating herself for imaginary sins. Or she might be dead.

Those were his wildest nightmares. In his heart he knew she would not be enormously fat or a religious fanatic. And if she were dead he would have heard, as he had heard of the death of her father, Edmund. She was going to be the same Caris, small and neat, quick-witted, organized, and determined. But he was seriously concerned about how she would receive him. How did she feel about him after nine years? Did she think of him with indifference, as a part of her past too remote to care about, the way he thought of, say, Griselda? Or did she still long for him, somewhere deep in her soul? He had no idea, and that was the true cause of his anxiety.

They sailed to Portsmouth and traveled with a party of traders. They left the group at Mudeford Crossing, the traders going on to Shiring while Merthin and Lolla forded the shallow river on horseback and took the Kingsbridge road. It was a pity, Merthin thought, that there was no visible sign of the way to Kingsbridge. He wondered how many traders continued on to Shiring simply because they did not realize that Kingsbridge was nearer.

It was a warm summer day, and the sun was shining when they came within sight of their destination. The first thing he saw was the top of the cathedral tower, visible over the trees. At least it had not fallen down, Merthin thought: Elfric's repairs had held for eleven years. It was a pity the tower could not be seen from Mudeford Crossing—what a difference that would make to the numbers visiting the town.

As they came closer, he began to suffer a strange mixture of excitement and fear that made him feel nauseous. For a few moments he was afraid he would have to dismount and throw up. He tried to make himself calm. What could happen? Even if Caris proved to have become indifferent to him, he would not die.

He saw several new buildings on the outskirts of the suburb of Newtown. The splendid new home he had built for Dick Brewer was no longer on the edge of Kingsbridge, for the town had grown past it.

He momentarily forgot his apprehension when he saw his bridge. It rose in an elegant curve from the riverbank and landed gracefully on the midstream island. On the far side of the island, the bridge sprang again to span the second channel. Its white stone gleamed in the sun. People and carts were crossing in both directions. The sight made his heart swell with pride. It was everything he had hoped it would be: beautiful, useful, and strong. I did that, he thought, and it's good.

But he suffered a shock when he got closer. The masonry of the nearer span was damaged around the central pier. He could see cracks in the stonework, repaired with iron braces in a clumsy fashion that bore the hallmark of Elfric. He was appalled. Brown dribbles of rust dripped from the nails that fixed the ugly braces in the stonework. The sight took him back eleven years, to Elfric's repairs to the old wooden bridge. Everyone can make mistakes, he thought, but people who don't learn from their mistakes just make the same ones again. "Bloody fools," he said aloud.

"Bloody fools," Lolla repeated. She was learning English.

He rode on to the bridge. The roadbed had been finished properly, he was happy to see, and he was pleased with the design of the parapet, a sturdy barrier with a carved capstone that recalled the moldings in the cathedral.

Leper Island was still overrun with rabbits. Merthin continued to hold a lease on the island. In his absence, Mark Webber had been collecting rents from tenants, paying the nominal rent due to the priory every year, subtracting an agreed collection fee, and sending the balance annually to Merthin in Florence via the Caroli family. After all the deductions it was a small sum, but it grew a little every year.

Merthin's house on the island had an occupied look, the shutters open, the doorstep swept. He had arranged for Jimmie to live there. The boy must now be a man, he thought.

At the near end of the second span, an old man Merthin did not recognize sat in the sun collecting the tolls. Merthin paid him a penny.

The man gave him a hard stare, as if trying to recall where he had seen him before, but he said nothing.

The town was both familiar and strange. Because it was almost the same, the changes struck Merthin as miraculous, as if they had happened overnight: a row of hovels knocked down and replaced by fine houses; a busy inn where once there had been a big gloomy house occupied by a wealthy widow; a well dried up and paved over; a gray house painted white.

He went to the Bell Inn on the main street, next to the priory gates. It was unchanged: a tavern in such a good location would probably last hundreds of years. He left his horses and baggage with a hostler and went inside, holding hands with Lolla.

The Bell was like taverns everywhere: a big front room furnished with rough tables and benches, and a back area where the barrels of beer and wine were racked and food was cooked. Because it was popular and profitable, the straw on the floor was changed frequently and the walls were freshly whitewashed, and in winter a huge fire blazed. Now, in the heat of summer, all the windows were open, and a mild breeze blew through the front room.

After a moment, Bessie Bell came out from the back. Nine years ago she had been a curvy girl; now she was a voluptuous woman. She looked at him without recognition, but he saw her appraise his clothes and judge him an affluent customer. "Good day to you, traveler," she said. "What can we do to make you and your child comfortable?"

Merthin grinned. "I'd like to take your private room, please, Bessie."

She knew him as soon as he spoke. "My soul!" she cried. "It's Merthin Bridger!" He put out his hand to shake, but she threw her arms around him and hugged him. She had always had a soft spot for him. She released him and studied his face. "Such a beard you've grown! I would have recognized you sooner otherwise. Is this your little girl?"

"Her name is Lolla."

"Well, aren't you a pretty thing! Your mother must be beautiful."

Merthin said: "My wife died."

"How sad. But Lolla is young enough to forget. My husband died, too."

"I didn't know you were married."

"I met him after you left. Richard Brown, from Gloucester. I lost him a year ago."

"I'm sorry to hear that."

"My father's gone to Canterbury, on a pilgrimage, so I'm running this tavern all on my own at the moment."

"I always liked your father."

"He was fond of you, too. He always takes to men with a bit of spirit. He was never very keen on my Richard."

"Ah." Merthin felt the conversation had become too intimate, too fast. "What news of my parents?"

"They're not here in Kingsbridge. They're staying at your brother's new home in Tench."

Merthin had heard, through Buonaventura, that Ralph had become lord of Tench. "My father must be very pleased."

"Proud as a peacock." She smiled, then looked concerned. "You must be hungry and tired. I'll tell the boys to take your bags upstairs, then I'll bring you a tankard of ale and some pottage." She turned to go into the back room.

"That's kind, but . . ."

Bessie paused at the door.

"If you would give Lolla some soup, I'd be grateful. There's something I have to do."

Bessie nodded. "Of course." She bent down to Lolla. "Do you want to come with Auntie Bessie? I expect you could eat a piece of bread. Do you like new bread?"

Merthin translated the question into Italian, and Lolla nodded happily.

Bessie looked at Merthin. "Going to see Sister Caris, are you?"

Absurdly, he felt guilty. "Yes," he said. "She's still here, then?"

"Oh, yes. She's guest master at the nunnery now. I'll be surprised if she isn't prioress one day." She took Lolla's hand and led her into the back room. "Good luck," she called over her shoulder.

Merthin went out. Bessie could be a little suffocating, but her affection was sincere, and it warmed his heart to be welcomed back with such enthusiasm. He entered the priory grounds. He paused to look at the soaring west front of the cathedral, almost two hundred years old now and as awe-inspiring as ever.

He noticed a new stone building to the north of the church, beyond the graveyard. It was a medium-size palace, with an imposing entrance and an upper story. It had been built close to where the old timber prior's house used to be, so presumably it had replaced that modest building as the residence of Godwyn. He wondered where Godwyn had found the money.

He went closer. The palace was very grand, but Merthin did not like the design. None of the levels related in any way to the cathedral that loomed over it. The details were careless. The top of the ostentatious doorcase blocked part of an upper-story window. Worst of all, the palace was built on a different axis from that of the church, so that it stood at an awkward angle.

It was Elfric's work, no doubt of that.

A plump cat sat on the doorstep in the sun. It was black with a white tip to its tail. It glared malevolently at Merthin.

He turned away and walked slowly to the hospital. The cathedral green was quiet and deserted: there was no market today. The excitement and apprehension rose again in his stomach. He might see Caris at any moment. He reached the entrance and went in. The long room looked brighter and smelled fresher than he remembered: everything had a scrubbed look. There were a few people lying on mattresses on the floor, most of them elderly. At the altar a young novice was saying prayers aloud. He waited for her to finish. He was so anxious that he was sure he felt more ill than the patients on the beds. He had come a thousand miles for this moment. Was it a wasted journey?

At last the nun said "Amen" for the last time and turned around. He did not know her. She approached him and said politely: "May God bless you, stranger."

Merthin took a deep breath. "I've come to see Sister Caris," he said.

*

The nuns' chapter meetings now took place in the refectory. In the past they had shared with the monks the elegant octagonal chapter house at the northeast corner of the cathedral. Sadly, mistrust between monks and nuns was now so great that the nuns did not want to risk the monks' eavesdropping on their deliberations. So they met in the long bare room where they took their meals.

The nunnery officials sat behind a table, Mother Cecilia in the middle. There was no subprioress: Natalie had died a few weeks ago, at the age of fifty-seven, and Cecilia had not yet replaced her. On Cecilia's right was the treasurer, Beth, and her matricularius, Elizabeth, formerly Elizabeth Clerk. On Cecilia's left were the cellarer, Margaret, in charge of all supplies, and her subordinate Caris, the guest master. Thirty nuns sat on rows of benches facing the senior officials.

After the prayer and the reading, Mother Cecilia made her announcements. "We have received a letter from our lord bishop in response to our complaint about Prior Godwyn stealing our money," she said. There was a murmur of anticipation from the nuns.

The reply had been a long time coming. King Edward had taken almost a year to replace Bishop Richard. Earl William had lobbied hard for Jerome, his father's able administrator, but in the end Edward had chosen Henri of Mons, a relative of his wife's from Hainault in northern France. Bishop Henri had come to England for the ceremony, then traveled to Rome to be confirmed by the pope, then returned and settled into his palace at Shiring, before replying to Cecilia's formal letter of complaint.

Cecilia went on: "The bishop declines to take any action over the theft, saying that the events took place during the time of Bishop Richard, and the past is past."

The nuns gasped. They had accepted the delay patiently, feeling confident they would get justice in the end. This was a shocking rejection.

Caris had seen the letter earlier. She was not as astonished as the rest of the nuns. It was not so remarkable that the new bishop did not wish to begin his period of office by quarreling with the prior of Kingsbridge. The letter told her that Henri would be a pragmatic ruler, not a man of principle. He was no different, in that respect, from the majority of men who were successful in church politics.

However, she was no less disappointed for being unsurprised. The decision meant that she had to abandon, for the foreseeable future, her dream of building a new hospital where sick people could be isolated from healthy guests. She told herself she should not grieve: the priory had existed for hundreds of years without such a luxury, so it could wait another decade or more. On the other hand, it angered her to see the rapid spread of diseases like the vomiting sickness that Maldwyn Cook had brought to the Fleece Fair the year before last. No one understood exactly how these things were transmitted—by looking at a sick person, by touching him, or just by being in the same room—but there could be no doubt that many illnesses did hop from one victim to the next, and proximity was a factor. However, she had to forget all that for now.

A rumble of resentful muttering came from the nuns on the benches. Mair's voice rose above the others, saying: "The monks will be cock-a-hoop."

She was right, Caris thought. Godwyn and Philemon had got away with daylight robbery. They had always argued that it was not theft for the monks to use the nuns' money, since it was all for the glory of God in the end; and they would now consider that the bishop had vindicated them. It was a bitter defeat, especially for Caris and Mair.

But Mother Cecilia was not going to waste time on regrets. "This is not the fault of any of us, except perhaps me," she said. "We have simply been too trusting."

You trusted Godwyn, but I did not, Caris thought, but she kept her mouth clamped shut. She waited to hear what Cecilia would say next. She knew that the prioress was going to make changes among the nunnery officials, but no one knew what had been decided.

"However, we must be more careful in the future. We will build a treasury of our own, to which the monks will not have access; indeed, I hope they will not even know where it is. Sister Beth will retire as treasurer, with our thanks for long and faithful service, and Sister Elizabeth will take her place. I have complete faith in Elizabeth."

Caris tried to control her face so that her disgust would not be seen. Elizabeth had testified that Caris was a witch. It was nine years ago, and Cecilia had forgiven Elizabeth, but Caris never would. However, that was not the only reason for Caris's antipathy. Elizabeth was sour and twisted, and her resentments interfered with her judgment. Such people could never be trusted, in Caris's opinion: they were always liable to make decisions based on their prejudices.

Cecilia went on: "Sister Margaret has asked permission to step down from her duties, and Sister Caris will take her place as cellarer."

Caris was disappointed. She had hoped to be made subprioress, Cecilia's deputy. She tried to smile as if pleased, but she found it difficult. Cecilia was obviously not going to appoint a subprioress. She would have two rival subordinates, Caris and Elizabeth, and let them fight it out. Caris caught Elizabeth's eye, and saw barely suppressed hatred in her look.

Cecilia went on: "Under Caris's supervision, Sister Mair will become guest master."

Mair beamed with pleasure. She was glad to be promoted and even happier that she would be working under Caris. Caris, too, liked the decision. Mair shared her obsession with cleanliness and her mistrust of priests' remedies such as bleeding.

Caris had not got what she wanted, but she tried to look happy as Cecilia announced a handful of lesser appointments. When the meeting closed, she went to Cecilia and thanked her.

"Don't imagine it was an easy decision," the prioress said. "Elizabeth has brains and determination, and she's steady where you're volatile. But you're imaginative, and you get the best out of people. I need you both."

Caris could not argue with Cecilia's analysis of her. She really knows me, Caris thought ruefully; better than anyone else in the world, now that my father is dead and Merthin has gone. She felt a surge of affection. Cecilia was like a mother bird, always moving, always busy, taking care of her fledglings. "I'll do everything I can to live up to your expectations," Caris vowed.

She left the room. She needed to check on Old Julie. No matter what she said to the younger nuns, no one looked after Julie the way she did. It was as if they believed that a helpless old person did not need to be kept comfortable. Only Caris made sure Julie was given a blanket in cool weather, and got something to drink when she was thirsty, and was helped to the latrine at those times of day when habitually she needed to go. Caris decided to take her a hot drink, an infusion of herbs that seemed to cheer the old nun up. She went to her pharmacy and put a small pan of water on the fire to boil.

Mair came in and closed the door. "Isn't this wonderful?" she said. "We'll still be working together!" She threw her arms around Caris and kissed her lips.

Caris hugged her, then detached herself from the embrace. "Don't kiss me like that," she said.

"It's because I love you."

"And I love you, too, but not in the same way."

It was true. Caris was very fond of Mair. They had become highly intimate in France, when they had risked their lives together. Caris had even found herself attracted by Mair's beauty. One night in a tavern in Calais, when the two of them had had a room with a door that could be locked, Caris had at last succumbed to Mair's advances. Mair had fondled and kissed Caris in all her most private places, and Caris had done the same to Mair. Mair had said it was the happiest day of her life. Unfortunately, Caris had not felt the same. For her the experience was pleasant but not thrilling, and she had not wanted to repeat it.

"That's all right," Mair said. "As long as you love me, even just a little bit, I'm happy. You won't ever stop, will you?"

Caris poured boiling water on the herbs. "When you're as old as Julie, I promise I'll bring you an infusion to keep you healthy."

Tears came to Mair's eyes. "That's the nicest thing anyone has ever said to me."

Caris had not meant it to be a vow of eternal love. "Don't be sentimental," she said gently. She strained the infusion into a wooden cup. "Let's go and check on Julie."

They crossed the cloisters and entered the hospital. A man with a bushy red beard was standing near the altar. "God bless you, stranger," Caris said. The man seemed familiar. He did not reply to her greeting, but looked hard at her with intense golden brown eyes. Then she recognized him. She dropped the cup. "Oh, God!" she said. "You!"

The few moments before she saw him were exquisite, and Merthin knew he would treasure them all his life, whatever else happened. He stared hungrily at the face he had not seen for nine years, and remembered, with a shock that was like plunging into a cold river on a hot day, how dear that face had been to him. She had hardly changed at all: his fears had been groundless. She did not even look older. She would be thirty now, he calculated, but she was as slim and perky as she had been at twenty. She walked quickly into the hospital with an air of brisk authority, carrying a wooden cup full of some medicine; then she looked at him, paused, and dropped the cup.

He grinned at her, feeling happy.

"You're here!" she said. "I thought you were in Florence!"

"I'm very pleased to be back," he replied.

She looked at the liquid on the floor. The nun with her said: "Don't worry about this, I'll clear up. Go and talk to him." The second nun was pretty, and had tears in her eyes, Merthin noticed, but he was too excited to pay much attention.

Caris said: "When did you come back?"

"I arrived an hour ago. You look well."

"And you look . . . such a man."

Merthin laughed.

She said: "What made you decide to return?"

"It's a long story," he replied. "But I'd love to tell it to you."

"We'll step outside." She touched his arm lightly and led him out of the building. Nuns were not supposed to touch people, or to have private conversations with men, but for her such rules had always been optional. He was glad she had not acquired a respect for authority in the last nine years.

Merthin pointed to the bench by the vegetable garden. "I sat on that seat with Mark and Madge Webber, the day you entered the convent, nine years ago. Madge told me you had refused to see me."

She nodded. "It was the most unhappy day of my life—but I knew that seeing you would make it even worse."

"I felt the same way, except that I wanted to see you, no matter how miserable it made me."

She gave him a direct look, her gold-flecked green eyes as candid as ever. "That sounds a bit like a reproach."

"Perhaps it is. I was very angry with you. Whatever you decided to do, I felt you owed me an explanation." He had not intended the conversation to go this way, but he found he could not help himself.

She was unapologetic. "It's really quite simple. I could hardly bear to leave you. If I had been forced to speak to you, I think I would have killed myself."

He was taken aback. For nine years he had thought she had been selfish on that day of parting. Now it looked as if he had been the selfish one, in making such demands on her. She had always had this ability to make him revise his attitudes, he recalled. It was an uncomfortable process, but she was often right.

They did not sit on the bench, but turned away and walked across the cathedral green. The sky had clouded over, and the sun had gone. "There is a terrible plague in Italy," he said. "They call it *la moria grande.*"

"I've heard about it," she said. "Isn't it in southern France, too? It sounds dreadful."

"I caught the disease. I recovered, which is unusual. My wife, Silvia, died."

She looked shocked. "I'm so sorry," she said. "You must feel terribly sad."

"All her family died, and so did all my clients. It seemed like a good moment to come home. And you?"

"I've just been made cellarer," she said with evident pride.

To Merthin that seemed somewhat trivial, especially after the slaughter he had seen. However, such things were important in the life of the nunnery. He looked up at the great church. "Florence has a magnificent cathedral," he said. "Lots of patterns in colored stone. But I prefer this: carved shapes, all the same shade." As he studied the tower, gray stone against gray sky, it started to rain.

They went inside the church for shelter. A dozen or so people were scattered around the nave: visitors to the town looking at the architecture, devout locals praying, a couple of novice monks sweeping. "I remember feeling you up behind that pillar," Merthin said with a grin.

"I remember it, too," she said, but she did not meet his eye.

"I still feel the same about you as I did on that day. That's the real reason I came home."

She turned and looked at him with anger in her eyes. "But you got married."

"And you became a nun."

"But how could you marry her—Silvia—if you loved me?"

"I thought I could forget you. But I never did. Then, when I thought I was dying, I realized I would never get over you."

Her anger vanished as quickly as it had appeared, and tears came to her eyes. "I know," she said, looking away.

"You feel the same."

"I never changed."

"Did you try?"

She met his eye. "There's a nun . . ."

"The pretty one who was with you in the hospital?"

"How did you guess?"

"She cried when she saw me. I wondered why."

Caris looked guilty, and Merthin guessed she was feeling the way he had felt when Silvia used to say: "You're thinking about your English girl."

"Mair is dear to me," Caris said. "And she loves me. But . . ."

"But you didn't forget me."

"No."

Merthin felt triumphant, but he tried not to let it show. "In that case," he said, "you should renounce your vows, leave the nunnery, and marry me."

"Leave the nunnery?"

"You'll need first to get a pardon for the witchcraft conviction, I realize that, but I'm sure it can be done—we'll bribe the bishop and the archbishop and even the pope if necessary. I can afford it—"

She was not sure it would be as easy as he thought. But that was not her main problem. "It's not that I'm not tempted," she said. "But I promised Cecilia I would vindicate her faith in me . . . I have to help Mair take over as guest master . . . we need to build a new treasury . . . and I'm the only one who takes care of Old Julie properly . . ."

He was bewildered. "Is all that so important?"

"Of course it is!" she said angrily.

"I thought the nunnery was just old women saying prayers."

"And healing the sick, and feeding the poor, and managing thousands of acres of land. It's at least as important as building bridges and churches."

He had not anticipated this. She had always been skeptical of religious observance. She had gone into the nunnery under duress, when it was the only way to save her own life. But now she seemed to have grown to love her punishment. "You're like a prisoner who is reluctant to leave the dungeon, even when the door is opened wide," he said.

"The door isn't open wide. I would have to renounce my vows. Mother Cecilia—"

"We'll have to work on all these problems. Let's begin right away."

She looked miserable. "I'm not sure."

She was torn, he could see. It amazed him. "Is this you?" he said incredulously. "You used to hate the hypocrisy and falsehood that you saw in the priory. Lazy, greedy, dishonest, tyrannical—"

"That's still true of Godwyn and Philemon."

"Then leave."

"And do what?"

"Marry me, of course."

"Is that all?"

Once again he was bewildered. "It's all I want."

"No, it's not. You want to design palaces and castles. You want to build the tallest building in England."

"If you need someone to take care of . . ."

"What?"

"I've got a little girl. Her name is Lolla. She's three."

That seemed to settle Caris's mind. She sighed. "I'm a senior official in a convent of thirty-five nuns, ten novices, and twenty-five employees, with a school and a hospital and a pharmacy—and you're asking me to throw all that up to nursemaid one little girl I've never met."

He gave up arguing. "All I know is that I love you and I want to be with you."

She laughed humorlessly. "If you had said that and nothing else, you might have talked me into it."

"I'm confused," he said. "Are you refusing me, or not?"

"I don't know," she said.

55

Merthin lay awake much of the night. He was accustomed to bedding down in taverns, and the sounds Lolla made in her sleep only soothed him; but tonight he could not stop thinking about Caris. He was shocked by her reaction to his return. He realized, now, that he had never thought logically about how she would feel when he reappeared. He had indulged in unrealistic nightmares about how she might have changed, and in his heart he had hoped for a joyous reconciliation. Of course she had not forgotten him; but he could have figured out that she would not have spent nine years moping for him: she was not the type.

All the same, he would never have guessed that she would be so committed to her work as a nun. She had always been more or less hostile to the church. Given how dangerous it was to criticize religion in any way, she might well have concealed the true depth of her skepticism even from him. So it was a terrible shock to find her reluctant to leave the nunnery. He had anticipated fear of Bishop Richard's death sentence, or anxiety about being permitted to renounce her vows, but he had not suspected she might have found life in the priory so fulfilling that she hesitated to leave it to become his wife.

He felt angry with her. He wished he had said: "I've traveled a thousand miles to ask you to marry me—how can you say you're not sure?" He thought of a lot of biting remarks he might have made. Perhaps it was a good thing they had not occurred to him then. Their conversation had ended with her asking him to give her time to get over the shock of his sudden return and think about what she wanted to do. He had consented—he had no alternative—but it had left him hanging in agony like a man crucified.

Eventually he drifted into a troubled sleep.

Lolla woke him early, as usual, and they went down to the parlor for porridge. He repressed the impulse to go straight to the hospital and speak to Caris again. She had asked for time, and it would do his cause no good to pester her. It occurred to him that there might be more shocks in store for him, and that he had better try to catch up with what had been happening in Kingsbridge. So after breakfast he went to see Mark Webber.

The Webber family lived on the main street in a large house they had bought soon after Caris got them started in the cloth business. Merthin remembered the days when they and their four children had lived in one room that was not much bigger than the loom on which Mark worked. Their new house had a large stone-built ground floor used as a storeroom and shop. The living quarters were in the timber-built upper story. Merthin found Madge in the shop, checking a cartload of scarlet cloth that had just arrived from one of their out-of-town mills. She was almost forty now, with strands of gray in her dark hair. A short woman, she had become quite plump, with a prominent bosom and a vast behind. She made Merthin think of a pigeon, but an aggressive one, because of her jutting chin and assertive manner.

With her were two youngsters, a beautiful girl of about seventeen and a strapping boy a couple of years older. Merthin recalled her two older children—Dora, a thin girl in a ragged dress, and John, a shy boy—and realized that these were the same, grown up. Now John was effortlessly lifting the heavy bales of cloth while Dora counted them by notching a stick. It made Merthin feel old. I'm only thirty-two, he thought; but that seemed old when he looked at John.

Madge gave a cry of surprise and pleasure when she saw him. She hugged him and kissed his bearded cheeks, then made a fuss over Lolla. "I thought she could come and play with your children," Merthin said ruefully. "Of course they're much too old."

"Dennis and Noah are at the priory school," she said. "They're thirteen and eleven. But Dora will entertain Lolla—she loves children."

The young woman picked Lolla up. "The cat next door has kittens," she said. "Do you want to see them?"

Lolla replied with a stream of Italian, which Dora took for assent, and they went off.

Madge left John to finish unloading the cart and took Merthin upstairs. "Mark has gone to Melcombe," she said. "We export some of our cloth to Brittany and Gascony. He should be back today or tomorrow."

Merthin sat in her parlor and accepted a cup of ale. "Kingsbridge seems to be prospering," he said.

"The trade in fleeces has declined," she said. "It's because of war taxes. Everything has to be sold through a handful of large traders so that the king can collect his share. There are still a few dealers here in Kingsbridge—Petranilla carries on the business Edmund left—but it's nothing like it used to be. Luckily, the trade in finished cloth has grown to replace it, in this town at least."

"Is Godwyn still prior?"

"Unfortunately, yes."

"Is he still making difficulties?"

"He's so conservative. He objects to any change and vetoes all progress. For example, Mark proposed opening the market on Saturday as well as Sunday, as an experiment."

"What possible objection could Godwyn have to that?"

"He said it would enable people to come to market without going to church, which would be a bad thing."

"Some of them might have gone to church on Saturday, too."

"Godwyn's cup is always half-empty, never half-full."

"Surely the parish guild opposes him?"

"Not very often. Elfric is alderman now. He and Alice got almost everything Edmund left."

"The alderman doesn't have to be the richest man in town."

"But he usually is. Remember, Elfric employs lots of craftsmen—carpenters, stonemasons, mortar makers, scaffolders—and buys from everyone who trades in building materials. The town is full of people who are more or less bound to support him."

"And Elfric has always been close to Godwyn."

"Exactly. He gets all the priory's building work—which means every public project."

"And he's such a shoddy builder!"

"Strange, isn't it?" Madge said in a musing tone. "You'd think Godwyn would want the best man for the job. But he doesn't. For him, it's all about who will be compliant, who will obey his wishes unquestioningly."

Merthin felt a bit depressed. Nothing had changed: his enemies were still in power. It might prove difficult for him to resume his old life. "No good news for me there, then." He stood up. "I'd better take a look at my island."

"I'm sure Mark will seek you out as soon as he returns from Melcombe."

Merthin went next door for Lolla, but she was having such a good time that he left her with Dora, and strolled through the town to the riverside. He took another look at the cracks in his bridge, but he did not need to study them long: the cause was obvious. He made a tour of Leper Island. Little had changed: there were a few wharves and storehouses at the west end and just one house, the one he had lent to Jimmie, at the east end, beside the road that led from one span of the bridge to the other.

When he first took possession of the island, he had had ambitious plans for developing it. Nothing had happened, of course, during his exile. Now he thought he could do something. He paced the ground, making rough measurements and visualizing buildings and even streets, until it was time for the midday meal.

He picked Lolla up and returned to the Bell. Bessie served a tasty pork stew thickened with barley. The tavern was quiet, and Bessie joined them for dinner, bringing a jug of her best red wine. When they had eaten, she poured him another cup, and he told her about his ideas. "The road across the island, from one bridge to the other, is an ideal place to put shops," he said.

"And taverns," she pointed out. "This place and the Holly Bush are the busiest inns in town simply because they are close to the cathedral.

Any place where people are continually passing by is a good location for a tavern."

"If I built a tavern on Leper Island, you could run it."

She gave him a direct look. "We could run it together."

He smiled at her. He was full of her good food and wine, and any man would have loved to tumble into bed with her and enjoy her soft, round body; but it was not to be. "I was very fond of my wife, Silvia," he said. "But, all the time we were married, I kept thinking about Caris. And Silvia knew it."

Betty looked away. "That's sad."

"I know. And I'll never do it to another woman. I won't get married again, unless it's to Caris. I'm not a good man, but I'm not that bad."

"Caris may never marry you."

"I know."

She stood up, picking up their bowls. "You are a good man," she said. "Too good." She returned to the kitchen.

Merthin put Lolla to bed for a nap, then sat on a bench in front of the tavern, looking down the hillside at Leper Island, sketching on a big slate, enjoying the September sunshine. He did not get much work done because every other person who walked past wanted to welcome him home and ask what he had been doing for the last nine years.

Late in the afternoon he saw the massive figure of Mark Webber coming up the hill driving a cart bearing a barrel. Mark had always been a giant but now, Merthin observed, he was a plump giant.

Merthin shook his enormous hand. "I've been to Melcombe," Mark said. "I go every few weeks."

"What's in the barrel?"

"Wine from Bordeaux, straight off the ship—which also brought news. You know that Princess Joan was on her way to Spain?"

"Yes." Every well-informed person in Europe knew that the fifteen-year-old daughter of King Edward was to marry Prince Pedro, heir to the throne of Castile. The marriage would forge an alliance between England and the largest of the Iberian kingdoms, ensuring that Edward could concentrate on his interminable war against France without worrying about interference from the south.

"Well," said Mark, "Joan died of the plague in Bordeaux."

Merthin was doubly shocked: partly because Edward's position in France had suddenly become shaky, but mainly because the plague had spread so far. "They have the plague in Bordeaux?"

"Bodies piled in the streets, the French sailors told me."

Merthin was unnerved. He had thought he had left *la moria grande* behind him. Surely it would not come as far as England? He did not fear it personally: no one had ever caught it twice, so he was safe, and Lolla was among those who for some reason did not succumb to it. But he was afraid for everyone else—especially Caris.

Mark had other things on his mind. "You've returned at just the right time. Some of the younger merchants are getting fed up with Elfric as alderman. A lot of the time he's just a dogsbody for Godwyn. I'm planning to challenge him. You could be influential. There's a meeting of the parish guild tonight—come along and we'll get you admitted right away."

"Won't it matter that I never finished my apprenticeship?"

"After what you've built, here and abroad? Hardly."

"All right." Merthin needed to be a guild member if he was going to develop the island. People always found reasons to object to new buildings, and he might need support himself. But he was not as confident of his acceptance as Mark.

Mark took his barrel home and Merthin went inside to give Lolla her supper. At sundown Mark returned to the Bell, and Merthin walked with him up the main street as the warm afternoon turned into a chilly evening.

The guildhall had seemed like a fine building to Merthin years ago, when he had stood here and presented his bridge design to the parish guild. But it appeared awkward and shabby now that he had seen the grand public buildings of Italy. He wondered what men such as Buonaventura Caroli and Loro Fiorentino must think of its rough stone undercroft, with the prison and the kitchen, and its main hall with a row of pillars running awkwardly down the middle to support the roof.

Mark introduced him to a handful of men who had arrived in Kingsbridge, or had come to prominence, in Merthin's absence. However, most of the faces were familiar, albeit a little older. Merthin greeted those few he had not already encountered in the last two days. Among these was Elfric, ostentatiously dressed in a brocade surcoat made with silver thread. He showed no surprise—someone had obviously told him Merthin was back—but glared with undisguised hostility.

Also present were Prior Godwyn and his subprior, Brother Philemon. Godwyn at forty-two was looking more like his uncle Anthony, Merthin observed, with downsloping lines of querulous discontent around his mouth. He put on a pretense of affability that might have fooled someone who did not know him. Philemon, too, had changed. He was no longer lean and awkward. He had filled out like a prosperous merchant, and carried himself with an air of arrogant self-assurance—although Merthin fancied he could still see, underneath the facade, the anxiety and self-hatred of the fawning toady. Philemon shook his hand as if touching a snake. It was depressing to realize that old hatreds were so long-lived.

A handsome, dark-haired young man crossed himself when he saw Merthin, then revealed that he was Merthin's former protégé, Jimmie, now known as Jeremiah Builder. Merthin was delighted to find that he was doing well enough to belong to the parish guild. However, it seemed he was still as superstitious as ever.

Mark mentioned the news about Princess Joan to everyone he spoke to. Merthin answered one or two anxious questions about the plague, but the Kingsbridge merchants were more concerned that the collapse of the alliance with Castile would prolong the French war, which was bad for business.

Elfric sat on the big chair in front of the giant woolsack scales and opened the meeting. Mark immediately proposed that Merthin should be admitted as a member.

Not surprisingly, Elfric objected. "He was never a member of the guild because he did not finish his apprenticeship."

"Because he wouldn't marry your daughter, you mean," said one of the men, and they all laughed. Merthin took a few moments to identify the speaker: it was Bill Watkin, the house builder, the black hair around his bald dome now turning gray.

"Because he is not a craftsman of the required standard," Elfric persisted stubbornly.

"How can you say that?" Mark protested. "He has built houses, churches, palaces—"

"And our bridge, which is cracking after only eight years."

"You built that, Elfric."

"I followed Merthin's design exactly. Clearly the arches are not strong enough to bear the weight of the roadbed and the traffic upon it. The iron braces I have installed have not been sufficient to prevent the cracks widening. Therefore I propose to reinforce the arches either side of the central pier, on both bridges, with a second course of masonry, doubling their thickness. I thought this subject might come up tonight, so I have prepared estimates of the cost."

Elfric must have started to plan this attack the moment he heard that Merthin was back in town. He had always seen Merthin as an enemy: nothing had changed. However, he had failed to understand the problem with the bridge, and that gave Merthin his chance.

He spoke to Jeremiah in a low voice. "Would you do something for me?"

"After all you did for me? Anything!"

"Run to the priory now and ask to speak to Sister Caris urgently. Tell her to find the original drawing I made for the bridge. It should be in the priory library. Bring it here right away."

Jeremiah slipped out of the room.

Elfric went on: "I must tell guildsmen that I have already spoken to Prior Godwyn, who says the priory cannot afford to pay for this repair. We will have to finance it, as we financed the original cost of building the bridge, and be repaid out of penny tolls."

They all groaned. There followed a long and bad-tempered discussion about how much money each member of the guild should put up. Merthin felt animosity building up toward him in the room. This was undoubtedly what Elfric had intended. Merthin kept looking at the door, willing Jeremiah to reappear.

Bill Watkin said: "Maybe Merthin should pay for the repairs, if it's his design that's at fault."

Merthin could not stay out of the discussion any longer. He threw caution to the winds. "I agree," he said.

There was a startled silence.

"If my design has caused the cracks, I'll repair the bridge at my own expense," he went on recklessly. Bridges were costly: if he was wrong about the problem, it could cost half his fortune.

Bill said: "Handsomely said, I'm sure."

Merthin said: "But I have something to say, first, if guildsmen will permit." He looked at Elfric.

Elfric hesitated, obviously trying to think of a reason for refusing; but Bill said: "Let him speak," and there was a chorus of assent.

Elfric nodded reluctantly.

"Thank you," said Merthin. "When an arch is weak, it cracks in a characteristic pattern. The stones at the top of the arch are pressed downwards, so that their lower edges splay apart, and a crack appears at the crown of the arch on the intrados—the underside."

"That's true," said Bill Watkin. "I've seen that sort of crack many a time. It's not usually fatal."

Merthin went on: "This is *not* the type of cracking you're seeing on the bridge. Contrary to what Elfric said, those arches *are* strong enough: the thickness of the arch is one-twentieth of its diameter at the base, which is the standard proportion, in every country."

The builders in the room nodded. They all knew that ratio.

"The crown is intact. However, there are horizontal cracks at the springing of the arch either side of the central pier."

Bill spoke again. "You sometimes see that in a quadripartite vault."

"Which this bridge is *not,*" Merthin pointed out. "The vaults are simple."

"What's causing it, then?"

"Elfric did not follow my original design."

Elfric said: "I did!"

"I specified a pile of large, loose stones at both ends of the piers."

"A pile of stones?" Elfric said mockingly. "And you say that's what was going to keep your bridge upright?"

"Yes, I do," Merthin said. He could tell that even the builders in the room agreed with Elfric's skepticism. But they did not know about bridges, which were different from any other kind of building because they stood in water. "The piles of stones were an essential part of the design."

"They were never in the drawings."

"Would you like to show us my drawings, Elfric, to prove your point?"

"The tracing floor is long gone."

"I did a drawing on parchment. It should be in the priory library."

Elfric looked at Godwyn. At that moment the complicity between the two men was blatant, and Merthin hoped the rest of the guild could see it. Godwyn said: "Parchment is costly. That drawing was scraped and reused long ago."

Merthin nodded as if he believed Godwyn. There was still no sign of Jeremiah. Merthin might have to win the argument without the help of the original plans. "The stones *would* have prevented the problem that is now causing the cracks," he said.

Philemon put in: "You would say that, wouldn't you? But why should we believe you? It's just your word against Elfric's."

Merthin realized he would have to stick his neck out. All or nothing, he thought. "I will tell you what the problem is, and prove it to you, in daylight, if you will meet me at the riverside tomorrow at dawn."

Elfric's face showed that he wanted to refuse this challenge, but Bill Watkin said: "Fair enough! We'll be there."

"Bill, can you bring two sensible boys who are good swimmers and divers?"

"Easy."

Elfric had lost control of the meeting, and Godwyn intervened, revealing himself as the puppet master. "What kind of a mockery are you planning?" he said angrily.

But it was too late. The others were curious now. "Let him make his point," said Bill. "If it's a mockery, we'll all know soon enough."

Just then, Jeremiah came in. Merthin was pleased to see that he was carrying a wooden frame with a large sheet of parchment stretched across it. Elfric stared at Jeremiah, shocked.

Godwyn looked pale and said: "Who gave you that?"

"A revealing question," Merthin commented. "The lord prior doesn't ask what the drawing shows, nor where it came from—he seems to know all that already. He just wonders who handed it over."

Bill said: "Never mind all that. Show us the drawing, Jeremiah."

Jeremiah stood in front of the scales and turned the frame around so that everyone could see the drawing. There at the ends of the piers were the piles of stones Merthin had spoken of.

Merthin stood up. "In the morning, I'll explain how they work."

Summer was turning into autumn, and it was chilly on the riverbank at dawn. News had somehow got around that a drama would take place and, as well as the members of the parish guild, there were two or three hundred people waiting to see the clash between Merthin and Elfric. Even Caris was there. This was no longer merely an argument about an engineering problem, Merthin realized. He was the youngster challenging the authority of the old bull, and the herd understood that.

Bill Watkin produced two lads of twelve or thirteen, stripped to their undershorts and shivering. It turned out they were Mark Webber's younger sons, Dennis and Noah. Dennis, the thirteen-year-old, was short and chunky, like his mother. He had red-brown hair the color of leaves in autumn. Noah, the younger by two years, was taller, and would probably grow up to be as big as Mark. Merthin identified with the short redhead. He wondered whether Dennis was embarrassed, as Merthin himself had been at that age, to have a younger brother who was bigger and stronger.

Merthin thought Elfric might object to Mark's sons being the divers, on the grounds that they might have been briefed in advance by their father and told what to say. However, Elfric said nothing. Mark was too transparently honest for anyone to suspect him of such duplicity, and perhaps Elfric realized that—or, more likely, Godwyn realized it.

Merthin told the boys what to do. "Swim out to the central pier, then dive. You'll find the pier is smooth for a long way down. Then there's the foundation, a great lump of stones held together with mortar. When you reach the riverbed, feel underneath the foundation. You probably won't be able to see anything—the water will be too muddy. But hold your breath for as long as you can and investigate thoroughly all around the base. Then come up to the surface and tell us exactly what you find."

They both jumped into the water and swam out. Merthin spoke to the assembled townspeople. "The bed of this river is not rock but mud. The current swirls around the piers of a bridge and scours the mud out from underneath the pillars, leaving a depression filled only with water. This happened to the old wooden bridge. The oak piers were not resting on the riverbed at all, but hanging from the superstructure. That's why the bridge collapsed. To prevent the same thing happening to the new bridge, I specified piles of large rough stones around the feet of the piers. Such piles break up the current so that its action is haphazard and weak. However, the piles were not installed and so the piers have been undermined. They are no longer supporting the bridge, but hanging from it—and that's why there are cracks where the pier joins the arch."

Elfric snorted skeptically, but the other builders looked intrigued. The two boys reached midstream, touched the central pier, took deep breaths, and disappeared.

Merthin said: "When they come back, they will tell us that the pier is not resting on the riverbed, but hanging over a depression, filled with water, large enough for a man to climb into."

He hoped he was right.

Both boys stayed under water for a surprisingly long time. Merthin found himself feeling breathless, as it were, in sympathy with them. At last a wet head of red hair broke the surface, then a brown one. The two boys conversed briefly, nodding, as if establishing that they had both observed the same thing. Then they struck out for the shore.

Merthin was not completely sure of his diagnosis, but he could think of no other explanation for the cracks. And he had felt the need to appear supremely confident. If he now turned out to be wrong, he would look all the more foolish.

The boys reached the bank and waded out of the water, panting. Madge gave them blankets which they pulled around their shaking shoulders. Merthin allowed them a few moments to catch their breath, then said: "Well? What did you find?"

"Nothing," said Dennis, the elder.

"What do you mean, nothing?"

"There's nothing there, at the bottom of the pillar."

Elfric looked triumphant. "Just the mud of the riverbed, you mean."

"No!" said Dennis. "No mud—just water."

Noah put in: "There's a hole you could climb into—easily! That big pillar is just hanging in the water, with nothing under it."

Merthin tried not to look relieved.

Elfric blustered: "There's still no authority for saying a pile of loose stones would have solved the problem." But no one was listening to him. In the eyes of the crowd, Merthin had proved his point. They gathered around him, commenting and questioning. After a few moments, Elfric walked away alone.

Merthin felt a momentary pang of compassion. Then he recalled how, when he was an apprentice, Elfric had hit him across the face with a length of timber; and his pity evaporated into the cold morning air.

56

The following morning, a monk came to see Merthin at the Bell. When he pulled back his hood, Merthin did not at first recognize him. Then he saw that the monk's left arm was cut off at the elbow, and he realized it was Brother Thomas, now in his forties, with a gray beard and deep-set lines around his eyes and mouth. Was his secret still dangerous after all these years? Merthin wondered. Would Thomas's life be in danger, even now, if the truth came out?

But Thomas had not come to talk about that. "You were right about the bridge," he said.

Merthin nodded. There was a sour satisfaction in it. He had been right, but Prior Godwyn had fired him, and in consequence his bridge would never be perfect. "I wanted to explain the importance of the rough stones, back then," he said. "But I knew Elfric and Godwyn would never listen to me. So I told Edmund Wooler, then he died."

"You should have told me."

"I wish I had."

"Come with me to the church," Thomas said. "Since you can read so much from a few cracks, I'd like to show you something, if I may."

He led Merthin to the south transept. Here and in the south aisle of the choir Elfric had rebuilt the arches, following the partial collapse eleven years ago. Merthin saw immediately what Thomas was worrying about: the cracks had reappeared.

"You said they would come back," Thomas said.

"Unless you discovered the root cause of the problem, yes."

"You were right. Elfric was wrong twice."

Merthin felt a spark of excitement. If the tower needed to be rebuilt . . . "You understand that, but does Godwyn?"

Thomas did not answer the question. "What do you think the root cause might be?"

Merthin concentrated on the immediate problem. He had thought about this, on and off, for years. "This is not the original tower, is it?" he said. "According to *Timothy's Book,* it has been rebuilt, and made higher."

"About a hundred years ago, yes—when the raw wool business was booming. Do you think they made it too high?"

"It depends on the foundations." The site of the cathedral sloped gently to the south, toward the river, and that might be a factor. He walked through the crossing, under the tower, to the north transept. He stood at the foot of the massive pillar at the northeast corner of the crossing and looked up at the arch that stretched over his head, across the north aisle of the choir, to the wall.

"It's the south aisle I'm worried about," Thomas said, slightly peevishly. "There are no problems here."

Merthin pointed up. "There's a crack on the underside of the arch—the intrados—at the crown," he said. "You get that in a bridge, when the piers are inadequately grounded, and start to splay apart."

"What are you saying—that the tower is moving away from the north transept?"

Merthin went back through the crossing and looked at the matching arch on the south side. "This one is cracked, too, but on the upper side, the extrados, do you see? The wall above it is cracked, too."

"They aren't very big cracks."

"But they tell us what is happening. On the north side, the arch is being stretched; on the south side, it's being pinched. That means the tower is moving south."

Thomas looked up warily. "It seems straight."

"You can't see it with the eye. But if you climb up into the tower, and drop a plumb line from the top of one of the columns of the crossing, just below the springing of the arch, you will see that by the time the line touches the floor it will be adrift of the column to the south by several inches. And, as the tower leans, it's separating from the wall of the choir, which is where the damage shows worst."

"What can be done?"

Merthin wanted to say: *You have to commission me to build a new tower.* But that would have been premature. "A lot more investigation, before any building," he said, suppressing his excitement. "We have established that the cracks have appeared because the tower is moving—but *why* is it moving?"

"And how will we learn that?"

"Dig a hole," Merthin said.

In the end Jeremiah dug the hole. Thomas did not want to employ Merthin directly. It was difficult enough as it was, he said, to get the money for the investigation out of Godwyn, who seemed never to have any money to spare. But he could not give the job to Elfric, who would have said there was nothing to investigate. So the compromise was Merthin's old apprentice.

Jeremiah had learned from his master and liked to work fast. On the first day, he lifted the paving stones in the south transept. Next day, his men started excavating the earth around the huge southeast pier of the crossing.

As the hole got deeper, Jeremiah built a timber hoist for lifting out loads of earth. By the second week he had to build wooden ladders down the sides of the hole so that the laborers could get to the bottom.

Meanwhile, the parish guild gave Merthin the contract for the repair of the bridge. Elfric was against the decision, of course, but he was in no position to claim that he was the best man for the job, and he hardly bothered to argue.

Merthin went to work with speed and energy. He built cofferdams around the two problem piers, drained the dams, and began to fill the holes under the piers with rubble and mortar. Next he would surround the piers with the piles of large rough stones he had envisaged from the start. Finally, he would remove Elfric's ugly iron braces and fill the cracks with mortar. Provided the repaired foundations were sound, the cracks would not reopen.

But the job he really wanted was the rebuilding of the tower.

It would not be easy. He would have to get his design accepted by the priory and the parish guild, currently run by his two worst enemies, Godwyn and Elfric. And Godwyn would have to find the money.

As a first step, Merthin encouraged Mark to put himself forward for election as alderman, to replace Elfric. The alderman was elected once a year, on All Hallows Day, the first of November. In practice, most aldermen were reelected unopposed until they retired or died. However, there was no doubt that a contest was permitted. Indeed, Elfric himself had put his name forward while Edmund Wooler was still in office.

Mark required little prompting. He was itching to put an end to Elfric's rule. Elfric was so close to Godwyn that there was not much point in having a parish guild at all. The town was in effect run by the priory—narrow, conservative, mistrustful of new ideas, careless of the interests of the townspeople.

So the two candidates began drumming up support. Elfric had his followers, mainly people he either employed or bought materials from. However, he had lost face badly in the argument over the bridge, and those who took his side were downcast. Mark's supporters, by contrast, were ebullient.

Merthin visited the cathedral every day and examined the foundations of the mighty column as they were exposed by Jeremiah's digging. The foundations were made of the same stone as the rest of the church, laid in mortared courses, but less carefully trimmed, as they would not be visible. Each course was a little wider than the one above, in a pyramid shape. As the excavation went deeper, he examined every layer for weakness, and found none. But he felt confident that eventually he would.

Merthin told no one what was in his mind. If his suspicions were correct, and the thirteenth-century tower was simply too heavy for the twelfth-century foundations, the solution would be drastic: the tower would have to be demolished—and a new one built. And the new tower could be the tallest in England . . .

One day in the middle of October, Caris appeared at the digging. It was early in the morning, and a winter sun was shining through the great east window. She stood on the edge of the hole with her hood around her head like a halo. Merthin's heart beat faster. Perhaps she had an answer for him. He climbed up the ladder eagerly.

She was as beautiful as ever, though in the strong sunlight he could see the little differences that nine years had made to her face. Her skin was not quite as smooth, and there were now the tiniest of creases at the corners of her lips. But her green eyes still shone with that alert intelligence that he loved so much.

They walked together down the south aisle of the nave and stopped near the pillar that always reminded him of how he had once felt her up here. "I'm happy to see you," he said. "You've been hiding away."

"I'm a nun, I'm supposed to hide away."

"But you're thinking about renouncing your vows."

"I haven't made a decision."

He was crestfallen. "How much time do you need?"

"I don't know."

He looked away. He did not want to show her how badly he was hurt by her hesitation. He said nothing. He could have told her she was being unreasonable, but what was the point?

"You'll be going to visit your parents in Tench at some point, I suppose," she said.

He nodded. "Quite soon—they will want to see Lolla." He was eager to see them, too, and had delayed only because he had become so deeply involved in his work on the bridge and the tower.

"In that case, I wish you would talk to your brother about Wulfric in Wigleigh."

Merthin wanted to talk about himself and Caris, not Wulfric and Gwenda. His response was cool. "What do you want me to say to Ralph?"

"Wulfric is laboring for no money—just food—because Ralph won't give him even a small acreage to farm."

Merthin shrugged. "Wulfric broke Ralph's nose." He felt the conversation begin to descend into a quarrel, and he asked himself why he was angry. Caris had not spoken to him for weeks, but she had broken her silence for the sake of Gwenda. He resented Gwenda's place in her heart, he realized. That was an unworthy emotion, he told himself; but he could not shake it.

Caris flushed with annoyance. "That was twelve years ago! Isn't it time Ralph stopped punishing him?"

Merthin had forgotten the abrasive disagreements he and Caris used to have, but now he recognized this friction as familiar. He spoke dismissively. "Of course he should stop—in my opinion. But Ralph's opinion is the one that counts."

"Then see if you can change his mind," she said.

He resented her imperious attitude. "I'm yours to command," he said facetiously.

"Why the irony?"

"Because I'm *not* yours to command, of course, but you seem to think I am. And I feel a bit foolish for going along with you."

"Oh, for heaven's sake," she said. "You're offended that I've asked you?"

For some reason, he felt sure she had made up her mind to reject him, and stay in the nunnery. He tried to control his emotions. "If we were a couple, you could ask me anything. But while you're keeping open the option of rejecting me, it seems a bit presumptuous of you." He knew he was sounding pompous, but he could not stop. If he revealed his true feelings he would burst into tears.

She was too wrapped up in her indignation to notice his distress. "But it's not even for myself!" she protested.

"I realize it's your generosity of spirit that makes you do it, but I still feel you're using me."

"All right, then, don't do it."

"Of course I'll *do* it." Suddenly he could no longer contain himself. He turned and walked away from her. He was shaking with some passion he could not identify. As he strode up the aisle of the great church, he struggled to get himself under control. He reached the excavation. This was stupid, he thought. He turned and looked back, but Caris had vanished.

He stood at the lip of the hole, looking down, waiting for the storm inside him to subside.

After a while he realized that the excavation had reached a crucial stage. Thirty feet below him, the men had dug down past the masonry foundations and were beginning to reveal what was beneath. There was nothing more he could do about Caris right now. It would be best to concentrate on his work. He took a deep breath, swallowed, and went down the ladder.

This was the moment of truth. His distress over Caris began to ease as he watched the men dig farther down. Shovelful after shovelful of heavy mud was dug up and taken away. Merthin studied the stratum of earth that was revealed below the foundations. It looked like a mixture of sand and small stones. As the men removed the mud, the sandy stuff dribbled into the hole they were making.

Merthin ordered them to stop.

He knelt down and picked up a handful of the sandy material. It was nothing like the soil all around. It was not natural to the site, therefore it must be something that had been put there by builders. The excitement of discovery rose inside him, overmastering his grief about Caris. "Jeremiah!" he called. "See if you can find Brother Thomas—quick as you like."

He told the men to carry on digging, but to make a narrower hole: at this point the excavation itself could be dangerous to the structure. After a while Jeremiah returned with Thomas, and the three of them watched as the men took the hole farther down. Eventually the sandy layer came to an end, and the next stratum was revealed to be the natural muddy earth.

"I wonder what that sandy stuff is," Thomas said.

"I think I know," Merthin said. He tried not to look triumphant. He had predicted, years ago, that Elfric's repairs would not work unless the root of the problem was discovered, and he had been right—but it was never wise to say "I told you so."

Thomas and Jeremiah looked at him in anticipation.

He explained. "When you've dug a foundation hole, you cover the bottom with a mixture of rubble and mortar. Then you lay the masonry on top of that. It's a perfectly good system, as long as the foundations are proportional to the building above."

Thomas said impatiently: "We both know this."

"What happened here was that a much higher tower was erected on foundations that were not designed for it. The extra weight, acting over a hundred years, has crushed that layer of rubble-and-mortar to sand. The sand has no cohesion, and under pressure it has spread outward into the surrounding soil, allowing the masonry above it to sink down. The effect is worse on the south side simply because the site naturally slopes that way." He felt a profound satisfaction at having figured this out.

The other two looked thoughtful. Thomas said: "I suppose we will have to reinforce the foundations."

Jeremiah shook his head. "Before we can put any reinforcement under the stonework, we'd have to remove the sandy stuff, and that would leave the foundations unsupported. The tower would fall down."

Thomas was perplexed. "So what *can* we do?"

They both looked at Merthin. He said: "Build a temporary roof over the crossing, erect scaffolding, and take down the tower, stone by stone. Then reinforce the foundations."

"Then we'd have to build a new tower."

That was what Merthin wanted, but he did not say so. Thomas might suspect that his judgment had been colored by his aspiration. "I'm afraid so," he said with feigned regret.

"Prior Godwyn won't like that."

"I know," Merthin said. "But I don't think he's got any choice."

Next day Merthin rode out of Kingsbridge with Lolla on the saddle in front of him. As they traveled through the forest, he obsessively ran over his fraught exchange with Caris. He knew he had been ungenerous. How foolish that was, when he was trying to win back her love. What had got into him? Caris's request was perfectly reasonable. Why would he not wish to perform a small service for the woman he wanted to marry?

But she had not agreed to marry him. She was still reserving the right to reject him. That was the source of his anger. She was exercising the privileges of a fiancée without making the commitment.

He could see now that it was petty of him to object on these grounds. He had been stupid, and turned what could have been a delightful moment of intimacy into a squabble.

On the other hand, the underlying cause of his distress was all too real. How long did Caris expect him to wait for an answer? How long was he prepared to wait? He did not like to think about that.

Anyway, it would do him nothing but good if he could persuade Ralph to stop persecuting poor Wulfric.

Tench was on the far side of the county, and on the way Merthin spent a night at windy Wigleigh. He found Gwenda and Wulfric thin after a rainy summer and the second poor harvest in a row. Wulfric's scar seemed to stand out more on a hollowed cheek. Their two small sons looked pale, and had runny noses and sores on their lips.

Merthin gave them a leg of mutton, a small barrel of wine, and a gold florin that he pretended were gifts from Caris. Gwenda cooked the mutton over the fire. She was possessed by rage, and she hissed and spat like the turning meat as she talked of the injustice that had been done to them. "Perkin has almost half the land in the village!" she said. "The only reason he can manage it all is that he's got Wulfric, who does the work of three men. Yet he must demand more, and keep us in poverty."

"I'm sorry that Ralph still bears a grudge," Merthin said.

"Ralph himself provoked that fight!" Gwenda said. "Even Lady Philippa said so."

"Old quarrels," Wulfric said philosophically.

"I'll try to get him to see reason," Merthin said. "In the unlikely event that he listens to me, what do you really want from him?"

"Ah," said Wulfric, and he got a faraway look in his eyes, which was unusual for him. "What I pray for every Sunday is to get back the lands that my father farmed."

"That will never happen," Gwenda said quickly. "Perkin is too well entrenched. And, if he should die, he has a son and a married daughter waiting to inherit, and a couple of grandsons growing taller every day. But we'd like a piece of land of our own. For the last eleven years Wulfric has been working hard to feed other men's children. It's time he got some of the benefit of his strength."

"I'll tell my brother he has punished you long enough," Merthin said.

Next day he and Lolla rode from Wigleigh to Tench. Merthin was even more resolved to do something for Wulfric. It was not just that he wanted to please Caris, and atone for his curmudgeonly attitude. He also felt sad and indignant that two such honest and hardworking people as Wulfric and Gwenda should be poor and thin, and their children sickly, just because of Ralph's vindictiveness.

His parents were living in a house in the village, not in Tench Hall itself. Merthin was shocked by how much his mother had aged, though she perked up when she saw Lolla. His father looked better. "Ralph is very good to us," Gerald said in a defensive way that made Merthin think the opposite. The house was pleasant enough, but they would have preferred to live at the hall with Ralph. Merthin guessed that Ralph did not want his mother watching everything he did.

They showed him around their home, and Gerald asked Merthin how things were in Kingsbridge. "The town is still prospering, despite the effects of the king's French war," Merthin replied.

"Ah—but Edward must fight for his birthright," his father said. "He is the legitimate heir to the throne of France, after all."

"I think that's a dream, Father," said Merthin. "No matter how many times the king invades, the French nobility will not accept an Englishman as their king. And a king can't rule without the support of his earls."

"But we had to stop the French raids on our south coast ports."

"That hasn't been a major problem since the battle of Sluys, when we destroyed the French fleet—which was eight years ago. Anyway, burning the crops of the peasants won't stop pirates—it might even add to their numbers."

"The French support the Scots, who keep invading our northern counties."

"Don't you think the king would be better able to deal with Scottish incursions if he were in the north of England rather than the north of France?"

Gerald looked baffled. It had probably never occurred to him to question the wisdom of the war. "Well, Ralph has been knighted," he said. "And he brought your mother a silver candlestick from Calais."

That was about the size of it, Merthin thought. The real reason for the war was booty and glory.

They all walked to the manor house. Ralph was out hunting with Alan Fernhill. In the great hall was a huge carved wooden chair, obviously the lord's. Merthin saw what he thought was a young servant girl, heavily pregnant, and was dismayed to be introduced to her as Ralph's wife, Tilly. She went to the kitchen to fetch wine.

"How old is she?" Merthin said to his mother while she was gone.

"Fourteen."

It was not unknown for girls to become pregnant at fourteen, but all the same Merthin felt that decent people behaved otherwise. Such early pregnancies usually happened in royal families, for whom there was intense political pressure to produce heirs, and among the lowest and most ignorant of peasants, who knew no better. The middle classes maintained higher standards. "She's a bit young, isn't she?" he said quietly.

Maud replied: "We all asked Ralph to wait, but he would not." Clearly she, too, disapproved.

Tilly returned with a servant carrying a jug of wine and a bowl of apples. She might have been pretty, Merthin thought, but she looked worn out. His father addressed her with forced jollity. "Cheer up, Tilly! Your husband will be home soon—you don't want to greet him with a long face."

"I'm fed up with being pregnant," she said. "I just wish the baby would come as soon as possible."

"It won't be long now," Maud said. "Three or four weeks, I'd say."

"It seems like forever."

They heard horses outside. Maud said: "That sounds like Ralph."

Waiting for the brother he had not seen for nine years, Merthin had mixed feelings, as ever. His affection for Ralph was always contaminated by his knowledge of the evil Ralph had done. The rape of Annet had been only the beginning. During his days as an outlaw Ralph had murdered innocent men, women, and children. Merthin had heard, traveling through Normandy, of the atrocities perpetrated by King Edward's army and, while he did not know specifically what Ralph had done, it would have been foolish to hope that Ralph had held himself aloof from that orgy of rape, burning, looting, and slaughter. But Ralph was his brother.

Ralph, too, would have mixed feelings, Merthin was sure. He might not have forgiven Merthin for giving away the location of his outlaw hideout. And, although Merthin had made Brother Thomas promise not to kill Ralph, he had known that Ralph, once captured, was likely to be hanged. The last words Ralph had spoken to Merthin, in the jail in the basement of the guildhall at Kingsbridge, were: "You betrayed me."

Ralph came in with Alan, both muddy from the hunt. Merthin was shocked to see that he walked with a limp. Ralph took a moment to recognize Merthin. Then he smiled broadly. "My big brother!" he said heartily. It was an old joke: Merthin was the elder, but had long been smaller.

They embraced. Merthin felt a surge of warmth, despite everything. At least we're both alive, he thought, despite war and plague. When they had parted, he had wondered whether they would ever meet again.

Ralph threw himself into the big chair. "Bring some beer, we're thirsty!" he said to Tilly.

There were to be no recriminations, Merthin gathered.

He studied his brother. Ralph had changed since that day in 1339 when he had ridden off to war. He had lost some of the fingers of his left hand, presumably in battle. He had a dissipated look: his face was veined from drink and his skin seemed dry and flaky. "Did you have good hunting?" Merthin asked.

"We brought home a roe deer as fat as a cow," he replied with satisfaction. "You shall have her liver for supper."

Merthin asked him about fighting in the army of the king, and Ralph related some of the highlights of the war. Their father was enthusiastic. "An English knight is worth ten of the French!" he said. "The battle of Crécy proved that."

Ralph's response was surprisingly measured. "An English knight is not much different from a French knight, in my opinion," he said. "But the French haven't yet understood the harrow formation in which we line up, with archers either side of dismounted knights and men-at-arms. They are still charging us suicidally, and long may they continue. But they will figure it out one day, and then they will change their tactics. Meanwhile, we are almost unbeatable in defense. Unfortunately, the harrow formation is irrelevant to attack, so we have ended up winning very little."

Merthin was struck by how his brother had grown up. Warfare had given him a depth and subtlety he had never previously possessed.

In turn, Merthin talked about Florence: the incredible size of the city, the wealth of the merchants, the churches and palaces. Ralph was particularly fascinated by the notion of slave girls.

Darkness fell and the servants brought lamps and candles, then supper. Ralph drank a lot of wine. Merthin noticed that he hardly spoke to Tilly. Perhaps it was not surprising. Ralph was a thirty one year-old soldier who had spent half his adult life in an army, and Tilly was a girl of fourteen who had been educated in a nunnery. What would they have to talk about?

Late in the evening, when Gerald and Maud had returned to their own house and Tilly had gone to bed, Merthin broached the subject Caris had asked him to raise. He felt more optimistic than previously. Ralph was showing signs of maturity. He had forgiven Merthin for what had happened in 1339, and his cool analysis of English and French tactics had been impressively free from tribal chauvinism.

Merthin said: "On my way here, I spent a night in Wigleigh."

"I see that fulling mill stays busy."

"The scarlet cloth has become a good business for Kingsbridge."

Ralph shrugged. "Mark Webber pays the rent on time." It was beneath the dignity of noblemen to discuss business.

"I stayed with Gwenda and Wulfric," Merthin went on. "You know that Gwenda has been Caris's friend since childhood."

"I remember the day we all met Sir Thomas Langley in the forest."

Merthin shot a quick glance at Alan Fernhill. They had all kept their childish vows and had not told anyone about that incident. Merthin wanted the secrecy to continue, for he sensed it was still important to Thomas, though he had no idea why. But Alan showed no reaction: he had drunk a lot of wine, and had no ear for hints.

Merthin moved on quickly. "Caris asked me to speak to you about Wulfric. She thinks you've punished him enough for that fight. And I agree."

"He broke my nose!"

"I was there, remember? You weren't an innocent party." Merthin tried to make light of it. "You did feel up his fiancée. What was her name?"

"Annet."

"If her tits weren't worth a broken nose, you've only got yourself to blame."

Alan laughed, but Ralph was not amused. "Wulfric almost got me hanged, by stirring Lord William up after Annet pretended I'd raped her."

"But you weren't hanged. And you cut Wulfric's cheek open with your sword when you escaped from the courthouse. It was a terrible wound—you could see his back teeth through it. He'll never lose the scar."

"Good."

"You've punished Wulfric for eleven years. His wife is thin and his children are ill. Haven't you done enough, Ralph?"

"No."

"What do you mean?"

"It's not enough."

"Why?" Merthin cried in frustration. "I don't understand you."

"I will continue to punish Wulfric and hold him back, and humiliate him and his women."

Merthin was startled by Ralph's frankness. "For heaven's sake, to what end?"

"I wouldn't normally answer that question. I've learned that it rarely does you any good to explain yourself. But you're my big brother, and from childhood I've always needed your approval."

Ralph had not really changed, Merthin realized, except insofar as he seemed to know and understand himself in a way he never had when younger.

"The reason is simple," Ralph went on. "Wulfric is not afraid of me. He wasn't scared that day at the Fleece Fair, and he's still not scared of me, even after all I've done to him. That's why he must continue to suffer."

Merthin was horrified. "That's a life sentence."

"The day I see fear in his eyes when he looks at me, he shall have anything he likes."

"Is that so important to you?" Merthin said incredulously. "That people fear you?"

"It's the most important thing in the world," said Ralph.

57

Merthin's return affected the whole town. Caris observed the changes with amazement and admiration. It started with his victory over Elfric in the parish guild. People realized the town could have lost its bridge because of Elfric's incompetence, and that jolted them out of their apathy. But everyone knew that Elfric was a tool of Godwyn, so the priory was the ultimate focus of their resentment.

And people's attitude to the priory was changing. There was a mood of defiance. Caris felt optimistic. Mark Webber had a good chance of winning the election on the first day of November and becoming alderman. If that happened, Prior Godwyn would no longer have things all his own way, and perhaps the town could begin to grow: markets on Saturdays, new mills, independent courts that traders could have faith in.

But she spent most of her time thinking about her own position. Merthin's return was an earthquake that shook the foundations of her life. Her first reaction had been horror at the prospect of abandoning all that she had worked for over the last nine years; her position in the convent hierarchy; maternal Cecilia and affectionate Mair and ailing Old Julie; and most of all her hospital, so much more clean and efficient and welcoming than it had been before.

But as the days became shorter and colder, and Merthin repaired his bridge and began laying out the foundations of the street of new buildings he wanted to create on Leper Island, Caris's resolve to remain a nun weakened. Monastic restrictions that she had stopped noticing began to chafe again. The devotion of Mair, which had been a pleasant romantic diversion, now became irritating. She started to think about what kind of life she might lead as Merthin's wife.

She thought a lot about Lolla, and about the child she might have had with Merthin. Lolla was dark-eyed and black-haired, presumably like her Italian mother. Caris's daughter might have had the green eyes of the Wooler family. The idea of giving up everything to take care of another woman's daughter had appalled Caris in theory, but as soon as she met the little girl she softened.

She could not talk to anyone in the priory about this, of course. Mother Cecilia would tell her she must keep her vows; Mair would beg her to stay. So she agonized alone at night.

Her quarrel with Merthin over Wulfric made her despair. After he walked away from her, she had gone back to her pharmacy and cried. Why were things so difficult? All she wanted was to do the right thing.

While Merthin was at Tench, she confided in Madge Webber.

Two days after Merthin left, Madge came into the hospital soon after dawn, when Caris and Mair were doing their rounds. "I'm worried about my Mark," she said.

Mair said to Caris: "I went to see him yesterday. He had been to Melcombe and come back with a fever and an upset stomach. I didn't tell you because it didn't seem serious."

"Now he's coughing blood," Madge said.

"I'll go," Caris said. The Webbers were old friends: she preferred to attend Mark herself. She picked up a bag containing some basic medicines and went with Madge to her house in the main street.

The living area was upstairs, over the shop. Mark's three sons loitered anxiously in the dining hall. Madge took Caris into a bedroom that smelled bad. Caris was used to the odor of a sick room, a mixture of sweat, vomit, and human waste. Mark lay on a straw mattress, perspiring. His huge belly stuck up in the air as if he were pregnant. The daughter, Dora, stood by the bed.

Caris knelt beside Mark and said: "How do you feel?"

"Rough," Mark said in a croaky voice. "Can I have something to drink?"

Dora handed Caris a cup of wine, and Caris held it to Mark's lips. She found it strange to see a big man helpless. Mark had always seemed invulnerable. It was unnerving, like finding an oak tree that has been there all your life suddenly felled by lightning.

She touched his forehead. He was burning up: no wonder he was thirsty.

"Let him have as much to drink as he wants," she said. "Weak beer is better than wine."

She did not tell Madge that she was puzzled and worried by Mark's illness. The fever and the stomach upset were routine, but his coughing blood was a dangerous sign.

She took a vial of rose water from her bag, soaked a small piece of woolen cloth, and bathed his face and neck. The action soothed him immediately. The water would cool him a little, and the perfume masked the bad smells in the room. "I'll give you some of this from my pharmacy," she said to Madge. "The physicians prescribe it for an inflamed brain. A fever is hot and humid, and roses are cool and dry, so the monks say. Whatever the reason, it will give him some ease."

"Thank you."

But Caris knew of no effective treatment for bloody sputum. The monk-physicians would diagnose an excess of blood, and recommend bleeding, but they prescribed that for almost everything, and Caris did not believe in it.

As she bathed Mark's throat, she noticed a symptom Madge had not mentioned. There was a rash of purple black spots on Mark's neck and chest.

This was an illness she had not come across before, and she was mystified, but she did not let Madge know that. "Come back with me, and I'll give you the rose water."

The sun was rising as they walked from the house to the hospital. "You've been very good to my family," Madge said. "We were the poorest people in town, until you started the scarlet business."

"It was your energy and industry that made it work."

Madge nodded. She knew what she had done. "All the same, it wouldn't have happened without you."

On impulse, Caris decided to take Madge through the nuns' cloisters to her pharmacy so that they could talk privately. Laypeople were not normally allowed inside, but there were exceptions, and Caris was now senior enough to decide when the rules could be broken.

They were alone in the cramped little room. Caris filled a pottery bottle with rose water and asked Madge for sixpence. Then she said: "I'm thinking of renouncing my vows."

Madge nodded, unsurprised. "Everybody's wondering what you're going to do."

Caris was shocked that the townspeople had guessed her thoughts. "How do they know?"

"It doesn't take a clairvoyant. You entered the nunnery only to escape a death sentence for witchcraft. After the work you've done here, you should be able to get a pardon. You and Merthin were in love, and always seemed so right for one another. Now he's come back. You must at least be thinking about marrying him."

"I just don't know what my life would be like as someone's wife."

Madge shrugged. "A bit like mine, perhaps. Mark and I run the cloth business together. I have to organize the household as well—all husbands expect that—but it's not so difficult, especially if you have the money for servants. And the children will always be your responsibility rather than his. But I manage, and so would you."

"You don't make it sound very exciting."

She smiled. "I assume you already know about the good parts: feeling loved and adored; knowing there's one person in the world who will always be on your side; getting into bed every night with someone strong and tender who wants to fuck you . . . that's happiness, for me."

Madge's simple words painted a vivid picture, and Caris was suddenly filled with a longing that was almost unbearable. She felt she could hardly wait to quit the cold, hard, loveless life of the priory, in which the greatest sin was to touch another human being. If Merthin had walked into the room at that moment she would have torn off his clothes and taken him there on the floor.

She saw that Madge was watching her with a little smile, reading her thoughts, and she blushed.

"It's all right," Madge said. "I understand." She put six silver pennies down on the bench and picked up the bottle. "I'd better go home and look after my man."

Caris recovered her composure. "Try to keep him comfortable, and come and fetch me immediately there's any change."

"Thank you, Sister," said Madge. "I don't know what we'll do without you."

Merthin was thoughtful on the journey back to Kingsbridge. Even Lolla's bright, meaningless chatter did not bring him out of his mood. Ralph had learned a lot, but he had not changed deep down. He was still a cruel man. He neglected his child-wife, barely tolerated his parents, and was vengeful to the point of mania. He enjoyed being a lord, but felt little obligation to care for the peasants in his power. He saw everything around him, people included, as being there for his gratification.

However, Merthin felt optimistic about Kingsbridge. All the signs were that Mark would become alderman on All Hallows Day, and that could be the start of a boom.

Merthin got back on the last day of October, All Hallows Eve. It was a Friday this year, so there was not the influx of crowds that came when the night of evil spirits fell on a Saturday, as it had in the year that Merthin was eleven, and he met the ten-year-old Caris. All the same the people were nervous, and everyone planned to be in bed by nightfall.

On the main street he saw Mark Webber's eldest son, John. "My father is in the hospital," the boy said. "He has a fever."

"This is a bad time for him to fall sick," Merthin said.

"It's an ill-starred day."

"I didn't mean because of the date. He has to be present at the parish guild meeting tomorrow. An alderman can't be elected in his absence."

"I don't think he'll be going to any meetings tomorrow."

That was worrying. Merthin took his horses to the Bell and left Lolla in the care of Betty.

Entering the priory grounds, he ran into Godwyn with his mother. He guessed they had dined together and now Godwyn was walking her to the gate. They were deep in an anxious conversation, and Merthin guessed they were worried about the prospect of their placeman Elfric losing the post of alderman. They stopped abruptly when they saw him. Petranilla said unctuously: "I'm sorry to hear that Mark is unwell."

Forcing himself to be civil, Merthin replied: "It's just a fever."

"We will pray that he gets well quickly."

"Thank you."

Merthin entered the hospital. He found Madge distraught. "He's been coughing blood," she said. "And I can't quench his thirst." She held a cup of ale to Mark's lips.

Mark had a rash of purple blotches on his face and arms. He was perspiring, and his nose was bleeding.

Merthin said: "Not so good today, Mark?"

Mark did not seem to see him, but he croaked: "I'm very thirsty." Madge gave him the cup again. She said: "No matter how much he drinks, he's always thirsty." She spoke with a note of panic that Merthin had never heard in her voice before.

Merthin was filled with dread. Mark made frequent trips to Melcombe, where he talked to sailors from plague-ridden Bordeaux.

Tomorrow's meeting of the parish guild was the least of Mark's worries now. And the least of Merthin's, too.

Merthin's first impulse was to cry out to everyone the news that they were in mortal danger. But he clamped his mouth shut. No one listened to a man in a panic, and besides he was not yet sure. There was a small chance Mark's illness was not what he feared. When he was certain, he would get Caris alone and speak to her calmly and logically. But it would have to be soon.

Caris was bathing Mark's face with a sweet-smelling fluid. She wore a stony expression that Merthin recognized: she was hiding her feelings. She obviously had some idea of how serious Mark's illness was.

Mark was clutching something that looked like a scrap of parchment. Merthin guessed it would have a prayer written on it, or a verse of the Bible, or perhaps a magic spell. That would be Madge's idea—Caris had no faith in writing as a remedy.

Prior Godwyn came into the hospital, trailed as usual by Philemon. "Stand away from the bed!" Philemon said immediately. "How will the man get well if he cannot see the altar?"

Merthin and the two women stood back, and Godwyn bent over the patient. He touched Mark's forehead and neck, then felt his pulse. "Show me the urine," he said.

The monk-physicians set great store by examination of the patient's urine. The hospital had special glass bottles, called urinals, for the purpose. Caris handed one to Godwyn. It did not take an expert to see that there was blood in Mark's urine.

Godwyn handed it back. "This man is suffering from overheated blood," he said. "He must be bled, then fed sour apples and tripes."

Merthin knew, from his experience of the plague in Florence, that Godwyn was talking rubbish, but he made no comment. In his mind there was no longer much room for doubt about what was wrong with Mark. The skin rash, the bleeding, the thirst: this was the illness he himself had suffered in Florence, the one that had killed Silvia and all her family. This was *la moria grande.*

The plague had come to Kingsbridge.

❧

As darkness fell on All Hallows Eve, Mark Webber's breathing became more difficult. Caris watched him weaken. She felt the angry impotence that possessed her when she was unable to help a patient. Mark passed into a state of troubled unconsciousness, sweating and gasping although his eyes were closed and he showed no awareness. At Merthin's quiet suggestion, Caris felt in Mark's armpits, and found large boil-like swellings there. She did not ask Merthin the significance of this: she would question him later. The nuns prayed and sang hymns while Madge and her four children stood around, helplessly distraught.

At the end Mark convulsed, and blood jetted from his mouth in a sudden flood. Then he fell back, lay still, and stopped breathing.

Dora wailed loudly. The three sons looked bewildered, and struggled to hold back unmanly tears. Madge wept bitterly. "He was the best man in the world," she said to Caris. "Why did God have to take him?"

Caris had to fight back her own grief. Her loss was nothing compared with theirs. She did not know why God so often took the best people and left the wicked alive to do more wrong. The whole idea of a benevolent deity watching over everyone seemed unbelievable at moments such as this. The priests said sickness was a punishment for sin. Mark and Madge loved one another, cared for their children, and worked hard: why should they be punished?

There were no answers to religious questions, but Caris had some urgent practical inquiries to make. She was deeply worried by Mark's illness, and she could guess that Merthin knew something about it. She swallowed her tears.

First she sent Madge and her children home to rest, and told the nuns to prepare the body for burial. Then she said to Merthin: "I want to talk to you."

"And I to you," he said.

She noticed that he looked frightened. That was rare. Her fear deepened. "Come to the church," she said. "We can talk privately there."

A wintry wind swept across the cathedral green. It was a clear night, and they could see by starlight. In the chancel, monks were preparing for the All Hallows dawn service. Caris and Merthin stood in the northwest corner of the nave, away from the monks, so that they could not be overheard. Caris shivered and pulled her robe closer around her. She said: "Do you know what killed Mark?"

Merthin took a shaky breath. "It's the plague," he said. *"La moria grande."*

She nodded. This was what she had feared. But all the same she challenged him. "How do you know?"

"Mark goes to Melcombe and talks to sailors from Bordeaux, where the bodies are piled in the streets."

She nodded. "He's just back." But she did not want to believe Merthin. "All the same, can you be sure it's the plague?"

"The symptoms are the same: fever, purple-black spots, bleeding, buboes in the armpits, and most of all the thirst. I remember it, by Christ. I was one of the few to recover. Almost everyone dies within five days, often less."

She felt as if doomsday had come. She had heard the terrible stories from Italy and southern France: entire families wiped out, unburied bodies rotting in empty palaces, orphaned toddlers wandering the streets crying, livestock dying untended in ghost villages. Was this to happen to Kingsbridge? "What did the Italian doctors do?"

"Prayed, sang hymns, took blood, prescribed their favorite nostrums, and charged a fortune. Everything they tried was useless."

They were standing close together and speaking in low tones. She could see his face by the faint light of the monks' distant candles. He was staring at her with a strange intensity. He was deeply moved, she could tell, but it did not seem to be grief for Mark that possessed him. He was focused on her.

She asked: "What are the Italian doctors like, compared with our English physicians?"

"After the Muslims, the Italian doctors are supposed to be the most knowledgeable in the world. They even cut up dead bodies to learn more about sickness. But they never cured a single sufferer from this plague."

Caris refused to accept such complete hopelessness. "We can't be utterly helpless."

"No. We can't cure it, but some people think you can escape it."

Caris said eagerly: "How?"

"It seems to spread from one person to another."

She nodded. "Lots of diseases do that."

"Usually, when one in a family gets it, they all do. Proximity is the key factor."

"That makes sense. Some say you fall ill from looking at sick people."

"In Florence, the nuns counseled us to stay at home as much as possible, and avoid social gatherings, markets, and meetings of guilds and councils."

"And church services?"

"No, they didn't say that, though lots of people stayed home from church too."

This chimed with what Caris had been thinking for years. She felt renewed hope: perhaps her methods could stave off the plague. "What about the nuns themselves, and the physicians, people who have to meet the sick and touch them?"

"Priests refused to hear confessions in whispers, so that they did not have to get too near. Nuns wore linen masks over their mouths and noses so that they would not breathe the same air. Some washed their hands in vinegar every time they touched a patient. The priest-physicians said none of this would do any good, but most of them left the city anyway."

"And did these precautions help?"

"It's hard to say. None of this was done until the plague was rampant. And it wasn't systematic—just everyone trying different things."

"All the same, we must make the effort."

He nodded. After a pause he said: "However, there is one precaution that is sure."

"What's that?"

"Run away."

This was what he had been waiting to say, she realized.

He went on: "The saying goes: 'Leave early, go far, and stay long.' People who did that escaped the sickness."

"We can't go away."

"Why not?"

"Don't be silly. There are six or seven thousand people in Kingsbridge—they can't all leave town. Where would they go?"

"I'm not talking about them—just you. Listen, you may not have caught the plague from Mark. Madge and the children almost certainly have, but you spent less time close to him. If you're still all right, we could escape. We could leave today, you and me and Lolla."

Caris was appalled by the way he assumed it had spread by now. Was she doomed already? "And . . . and go where?"

"To Wales, or Ireland. We need to find a remote village where they don't see a stranger from one year to the next."

"You've had the sickness. You told me people don't get it twice."

"Never. And some people don't catch it at all. Lolla must be like that. If she didn't pick it up from her mother, she's not likely to get it from anyone else."

"So why do you want to go to Wales?"

He just stared at her with that intense look, and she realized that the fear she had detected in him was for her. He was terrified that she would die. Tears came to her eyes. She remembered what Madge had said: "Knowing there's one person in the world who will always be on your side." Merthin tried to look after her, no matter what she did. She thought of poor Madge, blasted by grief at the loss of the one who was always on her side. How could she, Caris, even think of rejecting Merthin?

But she did. "I can't leave Kingsbridge," she said. "Of all times, not now. They rely on me if someone is sick. When the plague strikes, I'm the one they will turn to for help. If I were to flee . . . well, I don't know how to explain this."

"I think I understand," Merthin said. "You'd be like a soldier who runs away as soon as the first arrow is shot. You'd feel a coward."

"Yes—and a cheat, after all these years of being a nun, and saying that I live to serve others."

"I knew you would feel this way," Merthin said. "But I had to try." The sadness in his voice nearly broke her heart as he added: "And I suppose this means you won't be renouncing your vows in the foreseeable future."

"No. The hospital is where they come for help. I have to be here at the priory, to play my role. I have to be a nun."

"All right, then."

"Don't be too downhearted."

With wry sorrow he said: "And why should I not be downhearted?"

"You said that it killed half the population of Florence?"

"Something like that."

"So at least half the people just didn't catch it."

"Like Lolla. No one knows why. Perhaps they have some special strength. Or maybe the disease strikes at random, like arrows fired into the enemy ranks, killing some and missing others."

"Either way, there's a good chance I'll escape the illness."

"One chance in two."

"Like the toss of a coin."

"Heads or tails," he said. "Life or death."

58

Hundreds of people came to Mark Webber's funeral. He had been one of the town's leading citizens, but it was more than that. Poor weavers arrived from the surrounding villages, some of them having walked for hours. He had been unusually well loved, Merthin reflected. The combination of his giant's body and his gentle temperament cast a spell.

It was a wet day, and the bared heads of rich and poor men were soaked as they stood around the grave. Cold rain mingled with hot tears on the faces of the mourners. Madge stood with her arms around the shoulders of her two younger sons, Dennis and Noah. They were flanked by the eldest son, John, and the daughter, Dora, who were both much taller than their mother, and looked as if they might be the parents of the three short people in the middle.

Merthin wondered grimly whether Madge or one of her children would be the next to die.

Six strong men grunted with the effort of lowering the extra-large coffin into the grave. Madge sobbed helplessly as the monks sang the last hymn. Then the gravediggers started to shovel the sodden earth back into the hole, and the crowd began to disperse.

Brother Thomas approached Merthin, pulling up his hood to keep the rain off. "The priory has no money to rebuild the tower," he said. "Godwyn has commissioned Elfric to demolish the old tower and just roof the crossing."

Merthin tore his mind away from apocalyptic thoughts of the plague. "How will Godwyn pay Elfric for that?"

"The nuns are putting up the money."

"I thought they hated Godwyn."

"Sister Elizabeth is the treasurer. Godwyn is careful to be kind to her family, who are tenants of the priory. Most of the other nuns do hate him, it's true—but they need a church."

Merthin had not given up his hope of rebuilding the tower higher than before. "If I could find the money, would the priory build a new tower?"

Thomas shrugged. "Hard to say."

That afternoon, Elfric was reelected alderman of the parish guild. After the meeting Merthin sought out Bill Watkin, the largest builder in town after Elfric. "Once the foundations of the tower are repaired, it could be built even higher," he said.

"No reason why not," Bill agreed. "But what would be the point?"

"So that it could be seen from Mudeford Crossing. Many travelers—pilgrims, merchants, and so on—miss the road for Kingsbridge and go on to Shiring. The town loses a lot of custom that way."

"Godwyn will say he can't afford it."

"Consider this," Merthin said. "Suppose the new tower could be financed the same way as the bridge? The town merchants could lend the money and be repaid out of bridge tolls."

Bill scratched his monklike fringe of gray hair. This was an unfamiliar concept. "But the tower is nothing to do with the bridge."

"Does that matter?"

"I suppose not."

"The bridge tolls are just a way of guaranteeing that the loan is repaid."

Bill considered his self-interest. "Would I be commissioned to do any of the work?"

"It would be a big project—every builder in town would get a piece of it."

"That would be useful."

"All right. Listen, if I design a large tower, will you back me, here at the parish guild, at the next meeting?"

Bill looked dubious. "The guild members aren't likely to approve of extravagance."

"I don't think it needs to be extravagant, just high. If we put a domed ceiling over the crossing, I can build that with no centering."

"A dome? That's a new idea."

"I saw domes in Italy."

"I can see how it would save money."

"And the tower can be topped by a slender wooden spire, which will save money and look wonderful."

"You've got this all worked out, haven't you?"

"Not really. But it's been at the back of my mind ever since I returned from Florence."

"Well, it sounds good to me—good for business, good for the town."

"And good for our eternal souls."

"I'll do my best to help you push it through."

"Thank you."

Merthin mulled over the design of the tower as he went about his more mundane work, repairing the bridge and building new houses on Leper Island. It helped turn his mind away from dreadful, obsessive visions of Caris ill with the plague. He thought a lot about the south tower at Chartres. It was a masterpiece, albeit a little old-fashioned, having been built about two hundred years ago.

What Merthin had liked about it, he recalled very clearly, was the transition from the square tower to the octagonal spire above. At the top of the tower, perched on each of the four corners, were pinnacles facing diagonally outward. On the same level, at the midpoint of each side of the square, were dormer windows similar in shape to the pinnacles. These eight structures matched the eight sloping sides of the tower rising behind them, so that the eye hardly noticed the change of shape from square to octagon.

However, Chartres was unnecessarily chunky by the standards of the fourteenth century. Merthin's tower would have slender columns and large window openings, to lighten the weight on the pillars below, and to reduce stress by allowing the wind to blow through.

He made his own tracing floor at his workshop on the island. He enjoyed himself planning the details, doubling and quadrupling the narrow lancets of the old cathedral to make the large windows of the new tower, updating the clusters of columns and the capitals.

He hesitated over the height. He had no way to calculate how high it had to be in order to be visible from Mudeford Crossing. That could be done only by trial and error. When he had finished the stone tower he would have to erect a temporary spire, then go to Mudeford on a clear day and determine whether it could be seen. The cathedral was built on elevated ground, and at Mudeford the road breasted a rise just before descending to the river crossing. His instinct told him that if he went a little higher than Chartres—say about four hundred feet—that would be sufficient.

The tower at Salisbury Cathedral was four hundred and four feet high.

Merthin planned his to be four hundred and five.

While he was bent over the tracing floor, drawing the roof pinnacles, Bill Watkin appeared. "What do you think of this?" Merthin said to him. "Does it need a cross on top, to point to heaven? Or an angel, to watch over us?"

"Neither," said Bill. "It's not going to get built."

Merthin stood up, holding a straightedge in his left hand and a sharpened iron drawing needle in his right. "What makes you say that?"

"I've had a visit from Brother Philemon. I thought I might as well let you know as soon as possible."

"What did that snake have to say?"

"He pretended to be friendly. He wanted to give me a piece of advice for my own good. He said it wouldn't be wise of me to support any plan for a tower designed by you."

"Why not?"

"Because it would annoy Prior Godwyn, who was not going to approve your plans, regardless."

Merthin could hardly be surprised. If Mark Webber had become alderman, the balance of power in the town would have changed, and Merthin might have won the commission to build the new tower. But Mark's death meant the odds were against him. He had clung to hope, however, and now he felt the deep ache of heavy disappointment. "I suppose he'll commission Elfric?"

"That was the implication."

"Will he never learn?"

"When a man is proud, that counts for more than common sense."

"Will the parish guild pay for a stumpy little tower designed by Elfric?"

"Probably. They may not get excited about it, but they'll find the money. They are proud of their cathedral, despite everything."

"Elfric's incompetence almost cost them the bridge!" Merthin said indignantly.

"They know that."

He allowed his wounded feelings to show. "If I hadn't diagnosed the problem with the tower, it would have collapsed—and it might have brought down the entire cathedral."

"They know that, too. But they're not going to fight with the prior just because he's treated you badly."

"Of course not," said Merthin, as if he thought that was perfectly reasonable; but he was hiding his bitterness. He had done more for Kingsbridge than Godwyn, and he was hurt that the townspeople had not put up more of a fight for him. But he also knew that most people most of the time acted in their own immediate self-interest.

"People are ungrateful," Bill said. "I'm sorry."

"Yes," Merthin said. "That's all right." He looked at Bill, then looked away; and then he threw down his drawing implements and walked off.

~

During the predawn service of Lauds, Caris was surprised to look down the nave and see a woman in the north aisle, on her knees, in front of a wall painting of Christ Risen. She had a candle by her side and, in its unsteady light, Caris made out the chunky body and jutting chin of Madge Webber.

Madge stayed there throughout the service, not paying any attention to the psalms, apparently deep in prayer. Perhaps she was asking God to forgive Mark's sins and let him rest in peace—not that Mark had committed many sins, as far as Caris knew. More likely, Madge was asking Mark to send her good fortune from the spirit world. Madge was going to carry on the cloth business with the help of her two older children. It was the usual thing, when a trader died leaving a widow and a thriving enterprise. Still, no doubt she felt the need of her dead husband's blessing on her efforts.

But this explanation did not quite satisfy Caris. There was something intense in Madge's posture, something about her stillness that suggested great passion, as if she were begging Heaven to grant her some terribly important boon.

When the service ended, and the monks and nuns began to file out, Caris broke away from the procession and walked through the vast gloom of the nave toward the candle's glow.

Madge stood up at the sound of her footsteps. When she recognized Caris's face, she spoke with a note of accusation. "Mark died of the plague, didn't he?"

So that was it. "I think so," said Caris.

"You didn't tell me."

"I'm not sure, and I didn't want to frighten you—not to mention the whole town—on the basis of a guess."

"I've heard it's come to Bristol."

So the townspeople had been talking about it. "And London," Caris said. She had heard this from a pilgrim.

"What will happen to us all?"

Sorrow stabbed Caris like a pain in the heart. "I don't know," she lied.

"It spreads from one to another, I hear."

"Many illnesses do."

The aggression went out of Madge, and her face took on a pleading look that broke Caris's heart. In a near-whisper she asked: "Will my children die?"

"Merthin's wife got it," Caris said. "She died, and so did all her family, but Merthin recovered, and Lolla didn't catch it at all."

"So my children will be all right?"

That was not what Caris had said. "They may be. Or some may catch it and others escape."

That did not satisfy Madge. Like most patients, she wanted certainties, not possibilities. "What can I do to protect them?"

Caris looked at the painting of Christ. "You're doing all you can," she said. She began to lose control. As a sob rose in her throat, she turned away to hide her feelings, and walked quickly out of the cathedral.

She sat in the nuns' cloisters for a few minutes, pulling herself together, then went to the hospital, as usual at this hour.

Mair was not there. She had probably been called to attend a sick person in the town. Caris took charge, overseeing the serving of breakfast to guests and patients, making sure the place was cleaned thoroughly, checking on those who were sick. The work eased her distress about Madge. She read a psalm to Old Julie. When all the chores were done, Mair still had not appeared, so Caris went in search of her.

She found her in the dormitory, lying facedown on her bed. Caris's heart quickened. "Mair! Are you all right?" she said.

Mair rolled over. She was pale and sweating. She coughed, but did not speak.

Caris knelt beside her and placed a hand on her forehead. "You've got a fever," she said, suppressing the dread that rose in her belly like nausea. "When did it begin?"

"I was coughing yesterday," Mair said. "But I slept all right, and got up this morning. Then, when I went in to breakfast, I suddenly felt I was going to throw up. I went to the latrine, then came here and lay down. I think I might have been sleeping . . . What time is it?"

"The bell is about to ring for Terce. But you're excused." It could just be an ordinary illness, Caris told herself. She touched Mair's neck, then pulled the cowl of her robe down.

Mair smiled weakly. "Are you trying to look at my chest?"

"Yes."

"You nuns are all the same."

There was no rash, as far as Caris could see. Perhaps it was just a cold. "Any pains?"

"There's a dreadfully tender place in my armpit."

That did not tell Caris much. Painful swellings in the armpits or groin were a feature of other illnesses as well as the plague. "Let's get you down to the hospital," she said.

As Mair lifted her head, Caris saw bloodstains on the pillow.

She felt the shock like a blow. Mark Webber had coughed blood. And Mair had been the first person to attend Mark at the start of his illness—she had gone to the house the day before Caris did.

Caris hid her fear and helped Mair up. Tears came to her eyes, but she controlled herself. Mair put her arm around Caris's waist and her head on her shoulder, as if she needed support walking. Caris put her arm around Mair's shoulder. Together they walked down the stairs and through the nuns' cloisters to the hospital.

Caris took Mair to a mattress near the altar. She fetched a cup of cold water from the fountain in the cloisters. Mair drank thirstily. Caris bathed her face and neck with rose water. After a while, Mair seemed to sleep.

The bell rang for Terce. Caris was normally excused this service, but today she felt the need for a few moments of quiet. She joined the file of nuns walking into the church. The old gray stones seemed cold and hard today. She chanted automatically, while in her heart a storm raged.

Mair had the plague. There was no rash, but she had the fever, she was thirsty, and she had coughed blood. She would probably die.

Caris felt a terrible guilt. Mair loved her devotedly. Caris had never been able to return Mair's love, not in the way Mair longed for. Now Mair was dying. Caris wished she could have been different. She ought to have been able to make Mair happy. She should be able to save her life. She cried as she sang the psalm, hoping that anyone who noticed her tears would assume she was moved by religious ecstasy.

At the end of the service, a novice nun was waiting anxiously for her outside the south transept door. "There's someone asking for you urgently in the hospital," the girl said.

Caris found Madge Webber there, her face white with fear.

Caris did not need to ask what Madge wanted. She picked up her medical bag and the two of them rushed out. They crossed the cathedral green in a biting November wind and went to the Webber house in the main street. Upstairs, Madge's children were waiting in the living room. The two older children were sitting at the table, looking frightened; the young boys were both lying on the floor.

Caris examined them quickly. All four were feverish. The girl had a nosebleed. The three boys were coughing.

They all had a rash of purplish black spots on their shoulders and necks.

Madge said: "It's the same, isn't it? This is what Mark died of. They've got the plague."

Caris nodded. "I'm sorry."

"I hope I die, too," Madge said. "Then we can all be together in Heaven."

59

In the hospital, Caris instituted the precautions Merthin had told her about. She cut up strips of linen for the nuns to tie over their mouths and noses while they were dealing with people who had the plague. And she compelled everyone to wash their hands in vinegar and water every time they touched a patient. The nuns all got chapped hands.

Madge brought her four children in, then fell ill herself. Old Julie, whose bed had been next to Mark Webber's while he was dying, also succumbed. There was little Caris could do for any of them. She bathed their faces to cool them, gave them cold clear water to drink from the fountain in the cloisters, cleaned up their bloody vomit, and waited for them to die.

She was too busy to think about her own death. She observed a kind of fearful admiration in the townspeople's eyes when they saw her soothing the brows of infectious plague victims, but she did not feel like a selfless martyr. She saw herself as the kind of person who disliked brooding and preferred to act. Like everyone else, she was haunted by the question: Who's next? But she firmly put it out of her mind.

Prior Godwyn came in to see the patients. He refused to wear the face mask, saying it was women's nonsense. He made the same diagnosis as before, overheated blood, and prescribed bleeding and a diet of sour apples and ram's tripe.

It did not matter much what the patients ate, as they threw everything up toward the end; but Caris felt sure that taking blood from them made the illness worse. They were already bleeding too much: they coughed blood, vomited blood, and pissed blood. But the monks were the trained physicians, so she had to follow their instructions. She did not have time to be angry whenever she saw a monk or nun kneeling at the bedside of a patient, holding an arm out straight, cutting into a vein with a small sharp knife, and supporting the arm while a pint or more of precious blood dripped into a bowl on the floor.

Caris sat with Mair at the end, holding her hand, not caring if anyone disapproved. To ease her torment, she gave her a tiny amount of the euphoric drug Mattie had taught her to make from poppies. Mair still coughed, but it did not hurt her so much. After a coughing fit, her breathing would be easier for a short while, and she could talk. "Thank you for that night in Calais," she whispered. "I know you didn't really enjoy it, but I was in heaven."

Caris tried not to cry. "I'm sorry I couldn't be what you wanted."

"You loved me, though, in your own way. I know that."

She coughed again. When the fit ended, Caris wiped the blood from her lips.

"I love you," Mair said, and closed her eyes.

Caris let the tears come, then, not caring who saw or what they thought. She watched Mair, through a watery film, as she grew paler and breathed more shallowly, until at last her breathing stopped.

Caris remained where she was, on the floor beside the mattress, holding the hand of the corpse. Mair was still beautiful, even like this, white and forever still. It occurred to Caris that one other person loved her as Mair had, and that was Merthin. How strange that she had rejected his love, too. There was something wrong with her, she thought; some malformation of the soul that prevented her from being like other women and embracing love gladly.

Later that night, the four children of Mark Webber died; and so did Old Julie.

Caris was distraught. Was there nothing she could do? The plague was spreading fast and killing everyone. It was like living in a prison and wondering which of the inmates would be next to go to the gallows. Was Kingsbridge to be like Florence and Bordeaux, with bodies in the streets? Next Sunday there would be a market on the green outside the cathedral. Hundreds of people from every village within walking distance would come to buy and sell and mingle with the townspeople in churches and taverns. How many would go home fatally ill? When she felt like this, excruciatingly helpless up against terrible forces, she understood why people threw up their hands and said everything was controlled by the spirit world. But that had never been her way.

Whenever a member of the priory died there was always a special burial service, involving all the monks and nuns, with extra prayers for the departed soul. Both Mair and Old Julie had been well loved, Julie for her kind heart and Mair for her beauty, and many of the nuns wept. Madge's children were included in the funeral, with the result that several hundred townspeople came. Madge herself was too ill to leave the hospital.

They all gathered in the graveyard under a slate-gray sky. Caris thought she could smell snow in the cold north wind. Brother Joseph said the graveside prayers, and six coffins were lowered into the ground.

A voice in the crowd asked the question that was on everyone's mind. "Are we all going to die, Brother Joseph?"

Joseph was the most popular of the monk-physicians. Now close to sixty years old and with no teeth, he was intellectual but had a warm bedside manner. Now he said: "We're all going to die, friend, but none of us knows when. That's why we must always be prepared to meet God."

Betty Baxter spoke up, ever the probing questioner. "What can we do about the plague?" she said. "It is the plague, isn't it?"

"The best protection is prayer," Joseph said. "And, in case God has decided to take you regardless, come to church and confess your sins."

Betty was not so easily fobbed off. "Merthin says that in Florence people stayed in their homes to avoid contact with the sick. Is that a good idea?"

"I don't think so. Did the Florentines escape the plague?"

Everyone looked at Merthin, standing with Lolla in his arms. "No, they didn't escape," he said. "But perhaps even more would have died if they had done otherwise."

Joseph shook his head. "If you stay at home, you can't go to church. Holiness is the best medicine."

Caris could not remain silent. "The plague spreads from one person to another," she said angrily. "If you stay away from other people, you've got a better chance of escaping infection."

Prior Godwyn spoke up. "So the women are the physicians now, are they?"

Caris ignored him. "We should cancel the market," she said. "It would save lives."

"Cancel the market!" he said scornfully. "And how would we do that? Send messengers to every village?"

"Shut the city gates," she replied. "Block the bridge. Keep all strangers out of the town."

"But there are already sick people in town."

"Close all taverns. Cancel meetings of all guilds. Prohibit guests at weddings."

Merthin said: "In Florence they even abandoned meetings of the city council."

Elfric spoke up. "Then how are people to do business?"

"If you do business, you'll die," Caris said. "And you'll kill your wife and children, too. So choose."

Betty Baxter said: "I don't want to close my shop—I'd lose a lot of money. But I'll do it to save my life." Caris's hopes lifted at this, but then Betty dashed them again. "What do the doctors say? They know best." Caris groaned aloud.

Prior Godwyn said: "The plague has been sent by God to punish us for our sins. The world has become wicked. Heresy, lasciviousness, and disrespect are rife. Men question authority, women flaunt their bodies, children disobey their parents. God is angry, and His rage is fearsome. Don't try to run from His justice! It will find you, no matter where you hide."

"What should we do?"

"If you want to live, you should go to church, confess your sins, pray, and lead a better life."

Caris knew it was useless to argue, but all the same she said: "A starving man should go to church, but he should also eat."

Mother Cecilia said: "Sister Caris, you need say no more."

"But we could save so many—"

"That will do."

"This is life and death!"

Cecilia lowered her voice. "But no one is listening to you. Drop it."

Caris knew Cecilia was right. No matter how long she argued, people would believe the priests, not her. She bit her lip and said no more.

Blind Carlus started a hymn, and the monks began to process back into the church. The nuns followed, and the crowd dispersed.

As they passed from the church into the cloisters, Mother Cecilia sneezed.

ᔕ

Every evening Merthin put Lolla to bed in the room at the Bell. He would sing to her, or recite poems, or tell her stories. This was the time when she talked to him, asking him the strangely unexpected questions of a three-year-old, some childish, some profound, some hilarious.

Tonight, while he was singing a lullaby, she burst into tears.

He asked her what the trouble was.

"Why did Dora die?" she wailed.

So that was it. Madge's daughter, Dora, had taken to Lolla. They had spent time together, playing counting games and plaiting one another's hair. "She had the plague," Merthin said.

"My mama had the plague," Lolla said. She switched to the Italian she had not quite forgotten. *"La moria grande."*

"I had it, too, but I got better."

"So did Libia." Libia was the wooden doll she had carried all the way from Florence.

"Did Libia have the plague?"

"Yes. She sneezed, felt hot, and had spots, but a nun made her better."

"I'm very pleased. That means she's safe. Nobody gets it twice."

"You're safe, aren't you?"

"Yes." That seemed like a good note on which to end. "Go to sleep now."

"Good night," she said.

He went to the door.

"Is Bessie safe?" she said.

"Go to sleep."

"I love Bessie."

"That's nice. Good night." He closed the door.

Downstairs, the parlor was empty. People were nervous about going to crowded places. Despite what Godwyn said, Caris's message had gone home.

He could smell a savory soup. Following his nose, he went into the kitchen. Bessie was stirring a pot on the fire. "Bean soup with ham," she said.

Merthin sat at the table with her father, Paul, a big man in his fifties. He helped himself to bread while Paul poured him a tankard of ale. Bessie served the soup.

Bessie and Lolla were becoming fond of one another, he realized. He had employed a nanny to take care of Lolla during the day, but Bessie often watched Lolla in the evening, and Lolla preferred her.

Merthin owned a house on Leper Island, but it was a small place, especially by comparison with the *palagetto* he had become used to in Florence. He was happy to let Jimmie go on living there. Merthin was comfortable here at the Bell. The place was warm and clean, and there was plenty of hearty food and good drink. He paid his bill every Saturday, but in other respects he was treated like a member of the family. He was in no hurry to move into a place of his own.

On the other hand, he could not live here forever. And when he did move out, Lolla might be upset to leave Bessie behind. Too many of the people in her life had left it. She needed stability. Perhaps he should move out now, before she became too attached to Bessie.

When they had eaten, Paul retired to bed. Bessie gave Merthin another cup of ale, and they sat by the fire. "How many people died in Florence?" she said.

"Thousands. Tens of thousands, probably. No one could keep count."

"I wonder who's next in Kingsbridge."

"I think about it all the time."

"It might be me."

"I'm afraid so."

"I'd like to lie with a man one more time, before I die."

Merthin smiled, but said nothing.

"I haven't been with a man since my Richard passed away, and that's more than a year."

"You miss him."

"How about you? How long is it since you had a woman?"

Merthin had not had sex since Silvia fell ill. Remembering her, he felt a stab of grief. He had been insufficiently grateful for her love. "About the same," he said.

"Your wife?"

"Yes, rest her soul."

"It's a long time to go without loving."

"Yes."

"But you're not the type to go with just anybody. You want someone to love."

"I suppose you're right."

"I'm the same. It's wonderful to lie with a man, the best thing in the world, but only if you love one another truly. I've only ever had one man, my husband. I never went with anyone else."

Merthin wondered if that was true. He could not be sure. Bessie seemed sincere. But it was the kind of thing a woman would say anyway.

"What about you?" she said. "How many women?"

"Three."

"Your wife, and before that Caris, and . . . who else? Oh, I remember—Griselda."

"I'm not saying who they were."

"Don't worry, everyone knows."

Merthin smiled ruefully. Of course, everyone did know. Perhaps they could not be sure, but they guessed, and they usually guessed right.

"How old is Griselda's little Merthin now—seven? Eight?"

"Ten."

"I've got fat knees," Bessie said. She pulled up the skirt of her dress to show him. "I've always hated my knees, but Richard used to like them."

Merthin looked. Her knees were plump and dimpled. He could see her white thighs.

"He would kiss my knees," she said. "He was a sweet man." She adjusted her dress, as if straightening it, but she lifted it, and for a moment he glimpsed the dark inviting patch of hair at her groin. "He would kiss me all over, sometimes, especially after bathing. I used to like that. I liked everything. A man can do what he likes to a woman who loves him. Don't you agree?"

This had gone far enough. Merthin stood up. "I think you're probably right, but this kind of talk leads only one way, so I'm going to bed before I commit a sin."

She gave him a sad smile. "Sleep well," she said. "If you get lonely, I'll be here by the fire."

"I'll remember that."

They put Mother Cecilia on a bedstead, not a mattress, and placed it immediately in front of the altar, the holiest place in the hospital. Nuns sang and prayed around her bed all day and all night, in shifts. There was always someone to bathe her face with cool rose water, always a cup of clear fountain water at her side. None of it made any difference. She declined as fast as the others, bleeding from her nose and her vagina, her breathing becoming more and more labored, her thirst unquenchable.

On the fourth night after she sneezed, she sent for Caris.

Caris was heavily asleep. Her days were exhausting: the hospital was overflowing. She was deep in a dream in which all the children in Kingsbridge had the plague, and as she rushed around the hospital trying to care for them all she suddenly realized that she, too, had caught it. One of the children was tugging at her sleeve, but she was ignoring it and desperately trying to figure out how she would cope with all these patients while she was so ill—and then she realized someone was shaking her shoulder with increasing urgency, saying: "Wake up, Sister, please, the mother prioress needs you!"

She came awake. A novice knelt by her bed with a candle. "How is she?" Caris asked.

"She's sinking, but she can still speak, and she wants you."

Caris got out of bed and put on her sandals. It was a bitterly cold night. She was wearing her nun's robe, and she took the blanket from her bed and pulled it around her shoulders. Then she ran down the stone stairs.

The hospital was full of dying people. The mattresses on the floor were lined up like fish bones, so that those patients who were able to sit upright could see the altar. Families clustered around the beds. There was a smell of blood. Caris took a clean length of linen from a basket by the door and tied it over her mouth and nose.

Four nuns knelt beside Cecilia's bed, singing. Cecilia lay back with her eyes closed, and at first Caris was afraid she had arrived too late. Then the old prioress seemed to sense her presence. She turned her head and opened her eyes.

Caris sat on the edge of the bed. She dipped a rag in a bowl of rose water and wiped a smear of blood from Cecilia's upper lip.

Cecilia's breathing was tortured. In between gasps, she said: "Has anyone survived this terrible illness?"

"Only Madge Webber."

"The one who didn't want to live."

"All her children died."

"I'm going to die soon."

"Don't say that."

"You forget yourself. We nuns have no fear of death. All our lives we long to be united with Jesus in Heaven. When death comes, we welcome it." The long speech exhausted her. She coughed convulsively.

Caris wiped blood from her chin. "Yes, Mother Prioress. But those who are left behind may weep." Tears came to her eyes. She had lost Mair and Old Julie, and now she was about to lose Cecilia.

"Don't cry. That's for the others. You have to be strong."

"I don't see why."

"I think God has you in mind to take my place, and become prioress."

In that case he has made a very odd choice, Caris thought. He usually picks people whose view of Him is more orthodox. But she had long ago learned that there was no point in saying these things. "If the sisters choose me, I'll do my best."

"I think they'll choose you."

"I'm sure Sister Elizabeth will want to be considered."

"Elizabeth is clever, but you're loving."

Caris bowed her head. Cecilia was probably right. Elizabeth would be too harsh. Caris was the best person to run the nunnery, even though she was skeptical of lives spent in prayer and hymn singing. She did believe in the school and the hospital. Heaven forbid that Elizabeth should end up running the hospital.

"There's something else." Cecilia lowered her voice, and Caris had to lean closer. "Something Prior Anthony told me when he was dying. He had kept it secret until the last, and now I've done the same."

Caris was not sure she wanted to be burdened with such a secret. However, the deathbed seemed to overrule such scruples.

Cecilia said: "The old king did not die of a fall."

Caris was shocked. It had happened more than twenty years ago, but she remembered the rumors. The killing of a king was the worst offense imaginable, a double outrage, combining murder with treason, both of them capital crimes. Even knowing about such a thing was dangerous. No wonder Anthony had kept it a secret.

Cecilia went on: "The queen and her lover, Mortimer, wanted Edward II out of the way. The heir to the throne was a little boy. Mortimer became king in all but name. In the upshot, it didn't last as long as he might have hoped, of course—young Edward III grew up too fast." She coughed again, more weakly.

"Mortimer was executed while I was an adolescent."

"But even Edward didn't want anyone to know what had really happened to his father. So the secret was kept."

Caris was awestruck. Queen Isabella was still alive, living in lavish circumstances in Norfolk, the revered mother of the king. If people found out that she had her husband's blood on her hands, there would be a political earthquake. Caris felt guilt just knowing about it.

"So he was murdered?" she asked.

Cecilia made no reply. Caris looked harder. The prioress was still, her face immobile, her eyes staring upward. She was dead.

60

The day after Cecilia died, Godwyn asked Sister Elizabeth to have dinner with him.

This was a dangerous moment. Cecilia's death unbalanced the power structure. Godwyn needed the nunnery, because the monastery on its own was not viable: he had never succeeded in improving its finances. Yet most of the nuns were now angry about the money he had taken from them, and bitterly hostile to him. If they fell under the control of a prioress bent on revenge—Caris, perhaps—it could mean the end of the monastery.

He was frightened of the plague, too. What if he caught it? What if Philemon died? Such flashes of nightmare unnerved him, but he succeeded in pushing them to the back of his mind. He was determined not to be distracted from his long-term purpose by the plague.

The election of the prioress was an immediate danger. He had visions of the monastery closing down, and himself leaving Kingsbridge in disgrace, being forced to become an ordinary monk in some other place, subordinate to a prior who would discipline and humiliate him. If that happened he thought he might kill himself.

On the other hand, this was an opportunity as well as a threat. If he handled things cleverly he might get a prioress sympathetic to him who would be content to let him take the lead. And Elizabeth was his best bet.

She would make an imperious leader, one who would stand on her dignity. But he could work with her. She was pragmatic: she had proved that, the time she had warned him that Caris was planning to audit the treasury. She would be his ally.

She walked in with her head held high. She knew she had suddenly become important, and she was enjoying it, Godwyn realized. He wondered anxiously if she would go along with the plan he was about to propose. She might need careful handling.

She looked around the grand dining hall. "You built a splendid palace," she said, reminding him that she had helped him get the money for it.

She had never been inside the place, he realized, although it had been finished a year ago. He preferred not to have females in the monks' part of the priory. Only Petranilla and Cecilia had been admitted here, until today. He said: "Thank you. I believe it wins us respect from the noble and powerful. Already we have entertained the archbishop of Monmouth here."

He had used the last of the nuns' florins to buy tapestries showing scenes from the lives of the prophets. She studied a picture of Daniel in the lions' den. "This is very good," she said.

"From Arras."

She raised an eyebrow. "Is that your cat under the sideboard?"

Godwyn tutted. "I can't get rid of it," he lied. He shooed it out of the room. Monks were not supposed to have pets, but he found the cat a soothing presence.

They sat at one end of the long banqueting table. He hated having a woman here, sitting down to dinner as if she were just as good as a man; but he hid his discomfort.

He had ordered an expensive dish, pork cooked with ginger and apples. Philemon poured wine from Gascony. Elizabeth tasted the pork and said: "Delicious."

Godwyn was not very interested in food, except as a means of impressing people, but Philemon tucked in greedily.

Godwyn got down to business. "How do you plan to win this election?"

"I believe I'm a better candidate than Sister Caris," she said.

Godwyn sensed the suppressed emotion with which she uttered the name. Clearly she was still angry that Merthin had rejected her in favor of Caris. Now she was about to enter another contest with her old rival. She would kill to win this time, he thought.

That was good.

Philemon said to her: "Why do you think you're better?"

"I'm older than Caris," Elizabeth said. "I've been a nun longer, and a priory officer longer. And I was born and brought up in a deeply religious household."

Philemon shook his head dismissively. "None of that will make any difference."

She raised her eyebrows, startled by his bluntness, and Godwyn hoped

Philemon would not be too brutal. *We need her compliant,* he wanted to whisper. *Don't get her back up.*

Philemon went on remorselessly. "You've only got one year of experience more than Caris has. And your father, the bishop—rest his soul—will count against you. After all, bishops aren't supposed to have children."

She flushed. "Priors aren't supposed to have cats."

"We're not discussing the prior," he said impatiently. His manner was insolent, and Godwyn winced. Godwyn was good at masking his hostility, and putting on a facade of friendly charm, but Philemon had never learned that art.

However, Elizabeth took it coolly. "So, did you ask me here to tell me I can't win?" She turned to Godwyn. "It's not like you to cook with costly ginger just for the pleasure of it."

"You're quite right," said Godwyn. "We want you to become prioress, and we're going to do everything we can to help you."

Philemon said: "And we're going to start by taking a realistic look at your prospects. Caris is liked by everyone—nuns, monks, merchants, and nobility. The job she does is a great advantage to her. Most of the monks and nuns, and hundreds of townspeople, have come to the hospital with ailments and been helped by her. By contrast, they rarely see you. You're the treasurer, thought of as cold and calculating."

"I appreciate your frankness," Elizabeth said. "Perhaps I should give up now."

Godwyn could not tell whether she was being ironic.

"You can't win," Philemon said. "But she can lose."

"Don't be enigmatic, it's tiresome," Elizabeth snapped. "Just tell me in plain words what you're getting at."

I can see why she's not popular, Godwyn thought.

Philemon pretended not to notice her tone. "Your task in the next few weeks is to destroy Caris," he said. "You have to transform her, in the nuns' minds, from a likeable, hardworking, compassionate sister into a monster."

A glint of eagerness came into Elizabeth's eye. "Is that possible?"

"With our help, yes."

"Go on."

"Is she still ordering nuns to wear linen masks in the hospital?"

"Yes."

"And wash their hands?"

"Yes."

"There is no basis for these practices in Galen or any other medical authority, and certainly none in the Bible. It seems a mere superstition."

Elizabeth shrugged. "Apparently the Italian doctors believe the plague spreads through the air. You catch it by looking at sick people, or touching them, or breathing their breath. I don't see how—"

"And where did the Italians get this idea?"

"Perhaps just by observing patients."

"I have heard Merthin say that the Italian doctors are the best—except for the Arabs."

Elizabeth nodded. "I've heard that."

"So this whole business of wearing masks probably comes from the Muslims."

"Possibly."

"In other words, it is a heathen practice."

"I suppose so."

Philemon sat back, as if he had proved a point.

Elizabeth did not yet get it. "So we outmaneuver Caris by saying she has introduced a heathen superstition into the nunnery?"

"Not exactly," said Philemon with a crafty smile. "We say she is practising witchcraft."

She saw it then. "Of course! I had almost forgotten about that."

"You testified against her at the trial!"

"It was a long time ago."

"I would think you'd never forget that your enemy was once accused of such a crime," Philemon said.

Philemon himself certainly never forgot such things, Godwyn reflected. Knowing people's weaknesses, and exploiting them shamelessly, was his specialty. Godwyn sometimes felt guilty about the sheer depth of Philemon's malice. But that malice was so useful to Godwyn that he always suppressed his misgivings. Who else could have dreamed up this way of poisoning the nuns' minds against the beloved Caris?

A novice brought apples and cheese, and Philemon poured more wine. Elizabeth said: "All right, this makes sense. Have you thought about how, in detail, we should bring this up?"

"It's important to prepare the ground," Philemon said. "You should never make an accusation such as this formally until it's already believed by large numbers of people."

Philemon was very good at this, Godwyn thought admiringly.

Elizabeth said: "And how do you suggest we achieve that?"

"Actions are better than words. Refuse to wear the mask yourself. When asked, shrug and say quietly that you have heard it is a Muslim practice, and you prefer Christian means of protection. Encourage your friends to refuse the mask, as a sign of support for you. Don't wash your hands too often, either. When you notice people following Caris's precepts, frown disapprovingly—but say nothing."

Godwyn nodded agreement. Philemon's slyness sometimes approached the level of genius.

"Should we not even mention heresy?"

"Talk about it as much as you like, without connecting it directly to Caris. Say that you've heard of a heretic being executed in another city, or a devil-worshipper who succeeded in depraving an entire nunnery, perhaps in France."

"I wouldn't wish to say anything that was not true," Elizabeth said stiffly.

Philemon sometimes forgot that not everyone was as unscrupulous as he. Godwyn said hastily: "Of course not—Philemon just means that you should repeat such stories if and when you hear them, to remind the nuns of the ever-present danger."

"Very good." The bell rang for Nones, and Elizabeth stood up. "I mustn't miss the service. I don't want someone to notice my absence and guess that I've been here."

"Quite right," said Godwyn. "Anyway, we've agreed our plan."

She nodded. "No masks."

Godwyn could see that she was nursing a doubt. He said: "You don't imagine they're effective, do you?"

"No," she replied. "No, of course not. How could they be?"

"Exactly."

"Thank you for dinner." She went out.

That had gone well, Godwyn reflected, but he was still worried. He said anxiously to Philemon: "Elizabeth on her own might not be able to convince people that Caris is still a witch."

"I agree. We may need to help with the process."

"Perhaps with a sermon?"

"Exactly."

"I'll speak about the plague from the cathedral pulpit."

Philemon looked thoughtful. "It might be dangerous to attack Caris directly. That could backfire."

Godwyn agreed. If there were open strife between himself and Caris, the townspeople would probably support her. "I won't mention her name."

"Just sow the seeds of doubt, and let people come to their own conclusions."

"I'll blame heresy, devil worship, and heathenish practices."

Godwyn's mother, Petranilla, came in. She was very stooped, and walked with two canes, but her large head still jutted forward assertively on her bony shoulders. "How did that go?" she said. She had urged Godwyn to attack Caris, and had approved Philemon's plan.

"Elizabeth will do exactly as we wish," Godwyn said, feeling pleased. He enjoyed giving her good news.

"Good. Now I want to talk to you about something else." She turned to Philemon. "We won't need you."

For a moment, Philemon looked hurt, like a child unexpectedly smacked. Brutally abrasive himself, he was easily wounded. However, he recovered quickly, and pretended to be untroubled and even a bit amused by her high-handedness. "Of course, madam," he said with exaggerated deference.

Godwyn said to him: "Take charge of Nones for me, will you?"

"Very good."

When he had gone, Petranilla sat at the big table and said: "I know it was me who urged you to foster that young man's talents, but I have to admit that nowadays he makes my flesh crawl."

"He's more useful than ever."

"You can never really trust a ruthless man. If he will betray others, why should he not betray you?"

"I'll remember that," Godwyn said, though he felt he was now so bound up with Philemon that it was hard to imagine operating without him. However, he did not want to tell his mother that. Changing the subject, he said: "Would you like a cup of wine?"

She shook her head. "I'm already too liable to fall over. Sit down and listen to me."

"Very well, Mother." He sat beside her at the table.

"I want you to leave Kingsbridge before this plague gets much worse."

"I can't do that. But you could go—"

"I don't matter! I'm going to die soon anyway."

The thought filled Godwyn with panic. "Don't say that!"

"Don't be stupid. I'm sixty years old. Look at me—I can't even stand upright. It's time for me to go. But you're only forty-two—and you've got so much ahead! You could be bishop, archbishop, even cardinal."

As always, her limitless ambition for him made Godwyn feel dizzy.

Was he really capable of becoming a cardinal? Or was it just a mother's blindness? He did not really know.

"I don't want you to die of the plague before you've achieved your destiny," she finished.

"Mother, you're not going to die."

"Forget about me!" she said angrily.

"I can't leave town. I have to make sure the nuns don't make Caris prioress."

"Get them to hold the election quickly. Failing that, get out anyway and leave the election in God's hands."

He was terrified of the plague, but he feared failure, too. "I could lose everything if they elect Caris!"

Her voice softened. "Godwyn, listen to me. I have only one child, and that's you. I can't bear to lose you."

Her sudden change of tone shocked him into silence.

She went on: "Please, I beg you, get out of this city and go to some place where the plague can't reach you."

He had never known her to plead. It was unnerving. He felt scared. Just to stop her, he said: "Let me think about it."

"This plague," she said. "It's like a wolf in the forest. When you see it, you don't think—you run."

Godwyn gave the sermon on the Sunday before Christmas.

It was a dry day with high, pale cloud roofing the cold vault of heaven. The central tower of the cathedral was covered by a bird's nest of rope-and-branch scaffolding where Elfric was demolishing it from the top down. At the market on the green, shivering traders did desultory business with a few preoccupied customers. Beyond the market, the frozen grass of the cemetery was quilted with the brown rectangles of more than a hundred fresh graves.

But the church was full. The frost that Godwyn had noticed on the inside walls during Prime had been dispersed by the warmth of thousands of bodies by the time he entered the church to perform the Christmas service. They huddled in their heavy earth-colored coats and cloaks, looking like cattle in a pen. They had come because of the plague, he knew. The congregation of thousands of townspeople had been augmented by hundreds more from the surrounding countryside, all in search of God's protection against an illness that had already struck at least one family in every city street and rural village. Godwyn sympathized. Even he had been praying more fervently lately.

Normally only the people at the front solemnly followed the service. Those behind chatted to their friends and neighbors, and the youngsters amused themselves at the back. But today there was little noise from the nave. All heads were turned to the monks and nuns, watching with unusual attention as they performed the rituals. The crowd murmured the responses scrupulously, desperate to acquire what defensive holiness they could. Godwyn studied their faces, reading their expressions. What he saw there was dread. Like him, they were wondering fearfully who would be the next to sneeze, or suffer a nosebleed, or come out in a rash of purple-black spots.

Right at the front he could see Earl William with his wife, Philippa, their two grown sons, Roland and Richard, and their much younger daughter, Odila, who was fourteen. William ruled the county in the same style as his father, Roland, with order and justice and a firm hand that was occasionally cruel. He looked worried: an outbreak of plague in his earldom was something he could not control, no matter how harsh he was. Philippa had her arm around the young girl, as if to protect her.

Next to them was Sir Ralph, lord of Tench. Ralph had never been any good at hiding his feelings, and now he looked terrified. His child-wife was carrying a tiny baby boy. Godwyn had recently christened the child Gerald, after its grandfather, who stood nearby with the grandmother, Maud.

Godwyn's eye moved along the line to Ralph's brother, Merthin. When Merthin had returned from Florence, Godwyn had hoped that Caris would renounce her vows and leave the nunnery. He thought she might be less of a nuisance as the mere wife of a citizen. But it had not happened. Merthin was holding the hand of his little Italian daughter. Next to them was Bessie from the Bell Inn. Bessie's father, Paul Bell, had succumbed to the plague already.

Not far away was the family Merthin had spurned: Elfric, with his daughter, Griselda, the little boy they had named Merthin—now ten—and Harry Mason, the husband Griselda had wed after she gave up hope of the original Merthin. Next to Elfric was his second wife, Godwyn's cousin Alice. Elfric kept looking up. He had built a temporary ceiling over the crossing while he tore down the tower, and he was either admiring his work or worrying about it.

Conspicuously absent was the bishop of Shiring, Henri of Mons. The bishop normally gave the sermon on Christmas Day. However, he had not come. So many clergy had died of the plague that the bishop was frantically busy visiting parishes and searching for replacements. There was already talk of easing the requirements for priests, and ordaining under-twenty-fives and even illegitimate men.

Godwyn stepped forward to speak. He had a delicate task. He needed to whip up fear and hatred of the most popular person in Kingsbridge. And he had to do it without mentioning her name, indeed without even letting people think he was hostile to her. They must turn on her with fury but, when they did, they had to believe it was their own idea, not his.

Not every service featured a sermon. Only at major solemnities, attended by large crowds, did he address the congregation, and then he did not always preach. Often there were announcements, messages from the archbishop or the king about national events—military victories, taxes, royal births and deaths. But today was special.

"What is sickness?" he said. The church was already quiet, but the congregation became very still. He has asked the question that was on everybody's mind.

"Why does God send illnesses and plagues to torment and kill us?" He caught the eye of his mother, standing behind Elfric and Alice, and he was suddenly reminded of her forecast that she would die soon. For a moment he froze, paralyzed with fear, unable to speak. The congregation shifted restlessly, waiting. Knowing he was losing their attention, he felt panicky, and that made his paralysis worse. Then the moment passed.

"Sickness is a punishment for sin," he resumed. Over the years he had developed a preaching style. He was not a ranter, like Friar Murdo. He spoke in a more conversational manner, sounding like a reasonable man rather than a demagogue. He wondered how suitable that was for whipping up the kind of hatred he wanted them to feel. But Philemon said it made him sound more convincing.

"The plague is a special sickness, so we know God is inflicting a special punishment on us." There was a low collective sound, between a murmur and a moan, from the crowd. This was what they wanted to hear. He was encouraged.

"We must ask ourselves what sins we have committed, to merit such punishment." As he said this, he noticed Madge Webber, standing alone. Last time she came to church she had had a husband and four children. He thought of making the point that she had enriched herself using dyes concocted by witchcraft, but he decided against that tactic. Madge was too well liked and respected.

"I say to you that God is punishing us for heresy. There are people in the world—in this town—even in this great cathedral today—who question the authority of God's holy church and its ministers. They doubt that the sacrament turns bread into the true body of Christ; they deny the efficacy of masses for the dead; they claim that it is idolatry to pray before statues of the saints." These were the usual heresies debated among student priests at Oxford. Few people in Kingsbridge cared about such arguments, and Godwyn saw disappointment and boredom on the faces in the crowd. He sensed he was losing them again, and he felt the panic rise. Desperately, he added: "There are people in this city who practise witchcraft."

That got their attention. There was a collective gasp.

"We must be vigilant against false religion," he said. "Remember that only God can cure sickness. Prayer, confession, communion, penance—these are the remedies sanctioned by Christianity." He raised his voice a little. "All else is blasphemy!"

This was not clear enough, he decided. He needed to be more specific.

"For if God sends us a punishment, and we try to escape it, are we not defying His will? We may pray to Him to forgive us, and perhaps in his wisdom he will heal our sickness. But heretical cures will only make matters worse." The audience was rapt, and he warmed up. "I warn you! Magic spells, appeals to the fairy folk, unchristian incantations, and especially heathen practices—all are witchcraft, all are forbidden by God's holy church."

His real audience today was the thirty-two nuns standing behind him in the choir of the church. So far only a few had registered their opposition to Caris, and their support for Elizabeth, by refusing to wear the mask against the plague. As things stood, Caris would easily win next week's election. He needed to give the nuns the clear message that Caris's medical ideas were heretical.

"Anyone who is guilty of such practices . . . ," he paused for effect, leaning forward and staring at the congregation, ". . . anyone in town . . . ," he turned and looked behind him, at the monks and nuns in the choir, ". . . or even in the priory . . ." He turned back. "I say, anyone guilty of such practices should be shunned."

He paused for effect.

"And may God have mercy on their souls."

61

Paul Bell was buried three days before Christmas. All those who stood at his frosty graveside in the December cold were invited to the Bell to drink to his memory. His daughter, Bessie, now owned the place. She did not want to grieve alone, so she poured the tavern's best ale generously. Lennie Fiddler played sad tunes on his five-stringed instrument, and the mourners became tearful and maudlin as they got drunker.

Merthin sat in the corner with Lolla. At yesterday's market he had bought some sweet raisins from Corinth—an expensive luxury. He was sharing them with Lolla, teaching her numbers at the same time. He counted nine raisins for himself, but when he was counting out hers he missed every other number, saying: "One, three, five, seven, nine."

"No!" she said. "That's not right!" She was laughing, knowing that he was only teasing.

"But I counted nine each," he protested.

"But you've got more!"

"Well, how did that happen?"

"You didn't count them right, silly."

"You'd better count them, then, and see if you can do better."

Bessie sat with them. She was wearing her best dress, which was a bit tight. "Can I have some raisins?" she said.

Lolla said: "Yes, but don't let Daddy count them."

"Don't worry," Bessie said. "I know his tricks."

"Here you are," Merthin said to Bessie. "One, three, nine, thirteen—oh, thirteen is too many. I'd better take some away." He took back three raisins. "Twelve, eleven, ten. There, now you've got ten raisins."

Lolla thought this was hysterically funny. "But she's only got one!" she said.

"Did I count them wrong again?"

"Yes!" She looked at Bessie. "We know his tricks."

"You count them, then."

The door opened, letting in a blast of icy air. Caris came in, wrapped in a heavy cloak. Merthin smiled: every time he saw her, he felt glad she was still alive.

Bessie looked at her warily, but spoke a welcome. "Hello, Sister," she said. "It's kind of you to remember my father."

Caris said: "I'm very sorry you have lost him. He was a good man." She, too, was being formally polite. Merthin realized that these two women saw themselves as rivals for his affections. He did not know what he had done to deserve such devotion.

"Thank you," Bessie said to Caris. "Will you have a cup of ale?"

"That's very kind, but no. I need to speak to Merthin."

Bessie looked at Lolla. "Shall we roast some nuts on the fire?"

"Yes, please!"

Bessie took Lolla away.

"They get on well together," Caris said.

Merthin nodded. "Bessie has a warm heart, and no children of her own."

Caris looked sad. "I have no children . . . but perhaps I haven't got the warm heart."

Merthin touched her hand. "I know better," he said. "You have such a warm heart you have to take care of not just one or two children but dozens of people."

"It's kind of you to see it that way."

"It's true, that's all. How are things at the hospital?"

"Unbearable. The place is full of people dying, and I can't do anything for them except bury them."

Merthin felt a surge of compassion. She was always so competent, so reliable, but the strain told on her, and she was willing to show it to him, if to no one else. "You look tired," he said.

"I am, God knows."

"I suppose you're worrying about the election, too."

"I came to ask for your help with that."

Merthin hesitated. He was torn by contradictory feelings. Part of him wanted her to achieve her ambition and become prioress. But then would she ever be his wife? He had a shamefully selfish hope that she would lose the election and renounce her vows. All the same, he wanted to give her whatever help she asked for, just because he loved her. "All right," he said.

"Godwyn's sermon yesterday hurt me."

"Will you never be rid of that old accusation of witchcraft? It's so absurd!"

"People are stupid. The sermon had a big impact on the nuns."

"As was intended, of course."

"No doubt of it. Few of them believed Elizabeth when she said that my linen masks were heathenish. Only her close friends discarded the mask: Cressie, Elaine, Jeannie, Rosie, and Simone. But when the others heard the message from the pulpit of the cathedral, it was different. The more impressionable sisters have all now discarded the mask. A few avoid making an obvious choice by never coming into the hospital. Only a handful still wear it: me and four nuns I'm close to."

"I was afraid of this."

"Now that Mother Cecilia, Mair, and Old Julie are dead, there are only thirty-two nuns eligible to vote. Seventeen votes are all you need to win. Elizabeth originally had five sworn supporters. The sermon has given her eleven more. With her own vote, that makes seventeen. I have only five, and even if all the waverers came over to me, I would lose."

Merthin felt angry on her behalf. It must be hurtful to be rejected like this after all she had done for the nunnery. "What can you do?"

"The bishop is my last hope. If he sets his face against Elizabeth, and announces that he will not ratify her election, some of her support may fall away, and I could have a chance."

"How can you influence him?"

"I can't, but you could—or, at least, the parish guild could."

"I suppose so . . ."

"They have a meeting this evening. You'll be there, I imagine."

"Yes."

"Think about it. Godwyn already has the town in a stranglehold. He's close to Elizabeth—her family are tenants of the priory, and Godwyn has always been careful to favor them. If she becomes prioress, she will be as compliant as Elfric. Godwyn will have no opposition in or out of the priory. It will be the death of Kingsbridge."

"That's true, but whether the guildsmen will agree to intercede with the bishop . . ."

Suddenly she looked terribly disheartened. "Just try. If they turn you down, so be it."

Her desperation touched him, and he wished he could be more optimistic. "I will, of course."

"Thank you." She stood up. "You must have conflicting feelings about this. Thank you for being a true friend."

He smiled wryly. He wanted to be her husband, not her friend. But he would take what he could get.

She went out into the cold.

Merthin joined Bessie and Lolla at the fireside, and sampled their roasted nuts, but he was preoccupied. Godwyn's influence was malign, but all the same his power never ceased to grow. Why was that? Perhaps because he was an ambitious man with no conscience—a potent combination.

As darkness fell, he put Lolla to bed and paid a neighbor's daughter to watch her. Bessie left the barmaid, Sairy, in charge of the tavern. Wearing heavy cloaks, they walked up the main street to the guildhall for the midwinter meeting of the parish guild.

At the back of the long room there was a seasonal barrel of ale for the members. The merrymaking seemed to have a driven quality this Christmas, Merthin thought. They had been drinking hard at Paul Bell's wake, and some of those people now followed Merthin in and filled their tankards again as eagerly as if they had not tasted ale for a week. Perhaps it took their minds off the plague.

Bessie was one of four people introduced as new members. The other three were eldest sons of leading merchants who had died. Godwyn, as overlord of the townspeople, must be enjoying a rise in his income from inheritance tax, Merthin realized.

When the routine business had been dealt with, Merthin raised the subject of the election of the new prioress.

"That's none of our business," Elfric said immediately.

"On the contrary, the result will affect commerce in this town for years to come, perhaps decades," Merthin argued. "The prioress is one of the richest and most powerful people in Kingsbridge, and we ought to do what we can to get one who will do nothing to fetter trade."

"But there's nothing we can do—we have no vote."

"We have influence. We could petition the bishop."

"It's never been done before."

"That's not much of an argument."

Bill Watkin interrupted. "Who are the candidates?"

Merthin replied: "Sorry, I thought you'd know. Sister Caris and Sister Elizabeth. I think we should support Caris."

"Of course you do," said Elfric. "And we all know why!"

There was a ripple of laughter. Everyone knew about the longstanding on-off love affair between Merthin and Caris.

Merthin smiled. "Go on, laugh—I don't mind. Just remember that Caris grew up in the wool business and helped her father, so she understands the problems and challenges that merchants face—whereas her rival is the daughter of a bishop, and more likely to sympathize with the prior."

Elfric was looking red in the face—partly because of the ale he had drunk, Merthin thought, but mainly through anger. "Why do you hate me, Merthin?" he said.

Merthin was surprised. "I thought it was the other way around."

"You seduced my daughter, then refused to marry her. You tried to prevent my building the bridge. I thought we'd got rid of you, then you came back and humiliated me over the cracks in the bridge. You hadn't been back more than a few days before you tried to get me ousted as alderman and replaced by your friend Mark. You even hinted that the cracks in the cathedral were my fault, although it was built before I was born. I repeat, why do you hate me?"

Merthin did not know what to say. How could Elfric not know what he had done to Merthin? But Merthin did not want to have this argument in front of the parish guild—it seemed childish. "I don't hate you, Elfric. You were a cruel master when I was an apprentice, and you're a slipshod builder, and you toady to Godwyn, but all the same I don't hate you."

One of the new members, Joseph Blacksmith, said: "Is this what you do at the parish guild—have stupid arguments?"

Merthin felt hard done by. It was not he who had introduced the personal note. But for him to say that would be seen as continuing a stupid argument. So he said nothing, and reflected that Elfric was ever sly.

"Joe's right," said Bill Watkin. "We didn't come here to listen to Elfric and Merthin squabbling."

Merthin was troubled by Bill's willingness to put him and Elfric on the same level. Generally, the guildsmen liked him and felt mildly hostile to Elfric, since the dispute over the bridge cracks. Indeed, they would have ousted Elfric if Mark had not died. But something had changed.

Merthin said: "Can we return to the matter in hand, which is petitioning the bishop to favor Caris as prioress?"

"I'm against it," Elfric said. "Prior Godwyn wants Elizabeth."

A new voice spoke up. "I'm with Elfric. We don't want to quarrel with the father prior." It was Marcel Chandler, who had the contract to supply wax candles to the priory. Godwyn was his biggest customer. Merthin was not surprised.

However, the next speaker shocked him. It was Jeremiah Builder, who said: "I don't think we should favor someone who has been accused of heresy." He spat on the floor twice, left and right, and crossed himself.

Merthin was too surprised to reply. Jeremiah had always been fearfully superstitious, but Merthin would never have imagined it would lead him to betray his mentor.

It was left to Bessie to defend Caris. "That charge was always ludicrous," she said.

"It was never disproved, though," said Jeremiah.

Merthin stared at him, but Jeremiah would not meet his eye. "What's got into you, Jimmie?" Merthin said.

"I don't want to die of the plague," Jeremiah said. "You heard the sermon.

Anyone practising heathen remedies should be shunned. We're talking about asking the bishop to make her prioress—that's not shunning her!"

There was a murmur of assent, and Merthin realized that the tide of opinion had turned. The others were not as credulous as Jeremiah, but they shared his fear. The plague had spooked them all, undermining their rationality. Godwyn's sermon had been more effective than Merthin had imagined.

He was ready to give up—then he thought of Caris, and how weary and demoralized she had looked, and he gave it one more try. "I've lived through this once, in Florence," he said. "I warn you now, priests and monks won't save anyone from the plague. You'll have handed the town to Godwyn on a plate, and all for nothing."

Jeremiah said: "That sounds awfully close to blasphemy."

Merthin looked around. The others agreed with Jeremiah. They were too scared to think straight. There was nothing more he could do.

They decided to take no action on the election for prioress, and soon afterward the meeting broke up in somewhat bad humor, the members taking burning sticks from the fire to light their way home.

Merthin decided it was too late to report to Caris—the nuns, like the monks, went to bed at nightfall and got up in the early hours of the morning. However, there was a figure wrapped in a big wool cloak waiting outside the guildhall, and to his surprise his torch revealed the troubled face of Caris. "What happened?" she said anxiously.

"I failed," he said. "I'm sorry."

In the torchlight she looked wounded. "What did they say?"

"They won't intervene. They believed the sermon."

"Fools."

Together they walked down the main street. At the priory gates, Merthin said: "Leave the nunnery, Caris. Not for my sake, but for your own. You can't work under Elizabeth. She hates you, and she'll block everything you want to do."

"She hasn't won yet."

"She will, though—you said so yourself. Renounce your vows, and marry me."

"Marriage is a vow. If I break my vow to God, why would you trust me to keep my promise to you?"

He smiled. "I'll risk it."

"Let me think about it."

"You've been thinking about it for months," Merthin said with resentment. "If you don't leave now, you never will."

"I can't leave now. People need me more than ever."

He began to feel angry. "I won't keep asking forever."

"I know."

"In fact, I won't ask you again, after tonight."

She began to cry. "I'm sorry, but I can't abandon the hospital in the midst of a plague."

"The hospital."

"And the people of the town."

"But what about yourself?"

The flame of his torch made her tears glisten. "They need me so badly."

"They're ungrateful, all of them—nuns, monks, townspeople. I should know, by God."

"It makes no difference."

He nodded, accepting her decision, suppressing his selfish anger. "If that's how you feel, you must do your duty."

"Thank you for understanding."

"I wish this had turned out differently."

"So do I."

"You'd better take this torch."

"Thank you."

She took the burning branch from his hand and turned away. He watched her, thinking: Is this how it ends? Is this all? She walked away with her characteristic stride, determined and confident, but her head was bowed. She passed through the gateway and disappeared.

The lights of the Bell shone cheerfully through the gaps around the shutters and the door. He went inside.

The last few customers were saying drunken farewells, and Sairy was collecting tankards and wiping tables. Merthin checked on Lolla, who was fast asleep, and paid the girl who had been watching her. He thought of going to bed, but he knew he would not sleep. He was too upset. Why had he run out of patience tonight, as opposed to any other time? He had got angry. But his anger came from fear, he realized as he calmed down. Underneath it all, he was terrified that Caris would catch the plague and die.

He sat on a bench in the parlor of the inn and took off his boots. He stayed there, staring into the fire, wondering why he could not have the one thing in life that he wanted most.

Bessie came in and hung up her cloak. Sairy left, and Bessie locked up. She sat opposite Merthin, taking the big chair that her father had always used. "I'm sorry about what happened at the guild," she said. "I'm not sure who's right, but I know you're disappointed."

"Thank you for supporting me, anyway."

"I'll always support you."

"Perhaps it's time for me to stop fighting Caris's battles."

"I agree with that. But I can see that it makes you sad."

"Sad and angry. I seem to have wasted half my life waiting for Caris."

"Love is never wasted."

He looked up at her, surprised. After a pause, he said: "You're a wise person."

"There's no one else in the house, except for Lolla," she said. "All the Christmas guests have left." She got up from her chair and knelt in front of him. "I'd like to comfort you," she said. "Any way I can."

He looked at her round, friendly face and felt his body stir in response. It was such a long time since he had held the soft body of a woman in his arms. But he shook his head. "I don't want to use you."

She smiled. "I'm not asking you to marry me. I'm not even asking you to love me. I've just buried my father, and you've been disappointed by Caris, and we're both in need of someone warm to hold on to."

"To dull the pain, like a jug of wine."

She took his hand and kissed the palm. "Better than wine," she said. She pressed his hand to her breast. It was big and soft, and he sighed as he caressed it. She turned her face up, and he leaned down and kissed her lips. She gave a little moan of pleasure. The kiss was delicious, like a cold drink on a hot day, and he did not want to stop.

Eventually she broke away from him, panting. She stood upright and pulled her woolen dress over her head. Her naked body looked rosy in the firelight. She was all curves: round hips, round belly, round breasts. Still seated, he put his hands on her waist and drew her to him. He kissed the warm skin of her belly, then the pink tips of her breasts. He looked up at her flushed face. "Do you want to go upstairs?" he murmured.

"No," she said breathlessly. "I can't wait that long."

62

The election for prioress was held on the day after Christmas. That morning, Caris felt so depressed she could hardly get out of bed. When the bell rang for Matins in the early hours, she was strongly tempted to put her head under the blankets and say that she did not feel well. But she could not pretend when so many were dying, so in the end she forced herself.

She shuffled around the ice-cold flagstones of the cloisters side by side with Elizabeth, the two of them at the head of the procession to the church. This protocol had been agreed because neither would yield precedence to the other while they were competing in the election. But Caris no longer cared. The result was a foregone conclusion. She stood yawning and shivering in the choir through the psalms and readings. She was angry. Later today, Elizabeth would be elected prioress. Caris resented the nuns for rejecting her, she hated Godwyn for his enmity, and she despised the town's merchants for refusing to intervene.

She felt as if her life had been a failure. She had not built the new hospital she had dreamed of, and now she never would.

She also resented Merthin, for making her an offer she could not accept. He did not understand. For him, their marriage would be an adjunct to his life as an architect. For her, marriage would have to *replace* the work to which she had dedicated herself. That was why she had vacillated for so many years. It was not that she did not want him. She longed for him with a hunger that she could hardly bear.

She mumbled the last of the responses and then, mechanically, walked out of the church at the front of the line. As they walked around the cloisters again, someone behind her sneezed. She was too dispirited even to look and see who it was.

The nuns climbed the stairs to their dormitory. When Caris entered the room she heard heavy breathing, and realized that someone had stayed behind. Her candle revealed the novice mistress, Sister Simone—a dour middle-aged woman, normally a conscientious nun, not one to malinger. Caris bound a strip of linen around her own face then knelt by Simone's mattress. Simone was perspiring and looking scared.

Caris said: "How do you feel?"

"Awful," Simone said. "I've had strange dreams."

Caris touched her forehead. She was burning hot.

Simone said: "Can I have something to drink?"

"In a moment."

"It's just a cold, I expect."

"You're certainly running a fever."

"I haven't got the plague, though, have I? It's not that bad."

"We'll take you to the hospital anyway," Caris said evasively. "Can you walk?"

Simone struggled to her feet. Caris took a blanket off the bed and wrapped it around Simone's shoulders.

As they were heading for the door, Caris heard a sneeze. This time she could see that it came from Sister Rosie, the plump matricularius. Caris looked hard at Rosie, who appeared scared.

Caris picked another nun at random. "Sister Cressie, take Simone to the hospital while I look at Rosie."

Cressie took Simone's arm and led her down the stairs.

Caris held her candle up to Rosie's face. She, too, was perspiring. Caris pulled down the neck of her robe. There was a rash of small purple spots over her shoulders and breasts.

"No," Rosie said. "No, please."

"It may be nothing at all," Caris lied.

"I don't want to die of the plague!" Rosie said, her voice cracking.

Caris said quietly: "Just keep calm and come with me." She took Rosie's arm firmly.

Rosie resisted. "No, I'll be all right!"

"Try saying a prayer," Caris said. "Ave Maria, come on."

Rosie began to pray, and a moment later Caris was able to lead her away.

The hospital was crammed with dying people and their families, most of them awake despite the hour. There was a strong odor of sweaty bodies, vomit, and blood. The place was dimly lit by tallow lamps and the candles on the altar. A handful of nuns attended to the patients, bringing water and cleaning up. Some wore the mask, others did not.

Brother Joseph was there, the oldest of the monk-physicians and the most well liked. He was giving the last rites to Rick Silvers, the head of the jewelers' guild, bending to hear the man's whispered confession, surrounded by the children and grandchildren.

Caris made a space for Rosie and persuaded her to lie down. One of the nuns brought her a cup of clear fountain water. Rosie lay still, but her eyes shifted restlessly this way and that. She knew her fate, and she was frightened. "Brother Joseph will come and see you shortly," Caris told her.

"You were right, Sister Caris," said Rosie.

"What do you mean?"

"Simone and I were among the original friends of Sister Elizabeth who refused to wear the mask—and look what has happened to us."

Caris had not thought of this. Would she be proved horribly right by the deaths of those who disagreed with her? She would rather be wrong.

She went to look at Simone. She was lying down and holding the hand of Cressie. Simone was older and calmer than Rosie, but there was fear in her eyes, and she was gripping Cressie's hand hard.

Caris glanced at Cressie. There was a dark stain above her lip. Caris reached out and wiped it with her sleeve.

Cressie, too, was among the original group who had abandoned the mask.

She looked at the mark on Caris's sleeve. "What is it?" she said.

"Blood," said Caris.

⁂

The election took place in the refectory an hour before dinnertime. Caris and Elizabeth were side by side behind a table at one end of the room, and the nuns sat on benches in rows.

Everything had changed. Simone, Rosie, and Cressie lay in the hospital, stricken by the plague. Here in the refectory the other two who had originally refused the mask, Elaine and Jeannie, were both showing early symptoms, Elaine sneezing and Jeannie sweating. Brother Joseph, who had been treating plague victims without a mask since the beginning, had at last succumbed. All the remaining nuns had resumed wearing the masks in the hospital. If the mask was still a sign of support for Caris, she had won.

They were tense and restless. Sister Beth, the former treasurer and now the oldest nun, read a prayer to open the meeting. Almost before she had finished, several nuns spoke at once. The voice that prevailed was that of Sister Margaret, the former cellarer. "Caris was right, and Elizabeth was wrong!" she cried. "Those who refused the mask are now dying."

There was a collective rumble of agreement.

Caris said: "I wish it were otherwise. I'd rather have Rosie and Simone and Cressie sitting here voting against me." She meant it. She was sick of seeing people die. It made her think how trivial everything else was.

Elizabeth stood up. "I propose we postpone the election," she said. "Three nuns are dead and three more are in the hospital. We should wait until the plague is over."

That took Caris by surprise. She had thought there was nothing Elizabeth could do to avoid defeat—but she had been wrong. No one would now vote for Elizabeth, but her supporters might prefer to avoid making any choice at all.

Caris's apathy vanished. Suddenly she remembered all the reasons why she wanted to be prioress: to improve the hospital, to teach more girls to read and write, to help the town prosper. It would be a catastrophe if Elizabeth were elected instead.

Elizabeth was immediately supported by old Sister Beth. "We shouldn't hold the election in a panic, and make a choice we might regret later when things have calmed down." Her statement sounded rehearsed: Elizabeth had obviously planned this. But the argument was not unreasonable, Caris thought with some trepidation.

Margaret said indignantly: "Beth, you only say that because you know Elizabeth is going to lose."

Caris held back from speaking, for fear of prompting the same argument against herself.

Sister Naomi, who was not committed to either side, said: "The trouble is, we have no leader. Mother Cecilia, rest her soul, never appointed a subprioress after Natalie died."

"Is that so bad?" Elizabeth said.

"Yes!" Margaret said. "We can't even make up our minds who is to go first in the procession!"

Caris decided to risk making a practical point. "There is a long list of decisions that need to be made, especially about inheritance of nunnery properties whose tenants have died of the plague. It would be difficult to go much longer with no prioress."

Sister Elaine, one of the original five friends of Elizabeth, now argued against postponement. "I hate elections," she said. She sneezed, then went on: "They set sister against sister and cause acrimony. I want to get this over with so that we can be united in the face of this dreadful plague."

That raised a cheer of support.

Elizabeth glared angrily at Elaine. Elaine caught her eye and said: "You see, I can't even make a pacific remark like that without Elizabeth looking at me as if I've betrayed her!"

Elizabeth dropped her gaze.

Margaret said: "Come on, let's vote. Whoever is for Elizabeth, say: 'Aye.'"

For a moment, no one spoke. Then Beth said quietly: "Aye."

Caris waited for someone else to speak, but Beth was the only one.

Caris's heart beat faster. Was she about to achieve her ambition?

Margaret said: "Who is for Caris?"

The response was instant. There was a shout of "Aye!" It seemed to Caris that almost all the nuns voted for her.

I've done it, she thought. I'm prioress. Now we can really begin.

Margaret said: "In that case—"

A male voice suddenly said: "Wait!"

Several nuns gasped, and one screamed. They all looked at the door. Philemon stood there. He must have been listening outside, Caris thought.

He said: "Before you go any farther—"

Caris was not having this. She stood up and interrupted him. "How dare you enter the nunnery!" she said. "You do not have permission and you are not welcome. Leave now!"

"I'm sent by the lord prior—"

"He has no right—"

"He is the senior religious in Kingsbridge, and in the absence of a prioress or a subprioress he has authority over the nuns."

"We are no longer without a prioress, Brother Philemon." Caris advanced toward him. "I have just been elected."

The nuns hated Philemon, and they all cheered.

He said: "Father Godwyn refuses to permit this election."

"Too late. Tell him *Mother* Caris is now in charge of the nunnery—and she threw you out."

Philemon backed away. "You are not prioress until your election has been ratified by the bishop!"

"Out!" said Caris.

The nuns took up the chant. "Out! Out! Out!"

Philemon was intimidated. He was not used to being defied. Caris took another step toward him, and he took another back. He looked amazed by what was happening, but also scared. The chanting got louder. Suddenly he turned around and scurried out.

The nuns laughed and cheered.

But Caris realized that his parting remark had been true. Her election would have to be ratified by Bishop Henri.

And Godwyn would do everything in his power to prevent that.

❧

A team of volunteers from the town had cleared an acre of rough woodland on the far side of the river, and Godwyn was in the process of consecrating the new land as a cemetery. Every churchyard within the town walls was full, and the available space in the cathedral graveyard was shrinking fast.

Godwyn paced the borders of the plot in a biting cold wind, sprinkling holy water that froze when it hit the ground, while monks and nuns marched behind him, singing a psalm. Although the service was not yet over, the gravediggers were already at work. Humps of raw earth stood in neat lines beside straight-sided pits, placed as close together as possible to save space. But an acre would not last long, and men were already at work clearing the next patch of woodland.

At moments such as this, Godwyn had to struggle to keep his composure. The plague was like an incoming tide, submerging everyone in its path, unstoppable. The monks had buried a hundred people during the week before Christmas and the numbers were still rising. Brother Joseph had died yesterday, and two more monks were now ill. Where would it end? Would everyone in the world die? Would Godwyn himself die?

He was so scared that he stopped, staring at the gold aspergillum with which he was sprinkling the holy water as if he had no idea how it had got into his hand. For a moment he was so panicked that he could not move. Then Philemon, at the head of the procession, pushed him gently from behind. Godwyn stumbled forward and resumed his march. He had to thrust these frightening thoughts from his mind.

He turned his brain to the problem of the nuns' election. Reaction to his sermon had been so favorable that he had thought Elizabeth's victory secure. The tide had turned with shocking rapidity, and the infuriating revival in Caris's popularity had taken him by surprise. Philemon's last-ditch intervention had been a desperate measure taken just too late. When he thought of it, Godwyn wanted to scream.

But it was not yet over. Caris had mocked Philemon, but the truth was that she could not consider her position safe until she had Bishop Henri's approval.

Unfortunately, Godwyn had not yet had a chance to ingratiate himself with Henri. The new bishop, who spoke no English, had visited Kingsbridge only once. Because he was so new, Philemon had not yet learned whether he had any fatal weaknesses. But he was a man, and a priest, so he ought to side with Godwyn against Caris.

Godwyn had written to Henri saying that Caris had bewitched the nuns into thinking she could save them from the plague. He had detailed Caris's history: the accusation of heresy, the trial and sentence eight years ago, the rescue by Cecilia. He hoped Henri would arrive in Kingsbridge with his mind firmly prejudiced against Caris.

But when would Henri come? It was extraordinary for the bishop to miss the Christmas service in the cathedral. A letter from the efficient, unimaginative Archdeacon Lloyd had explained that Henri was busy appointing clergy to replace those who had died of the plague. Lloyd might be against Godwyn: he was Earl William's man, owing his position to William's late brother Richard; and the father of William and Richard, Earl Roland, had hated Godwyn. But Lloyd would not make the decision,

Henri would. It was hard to know what might happen. Godwyn felt he had lost control. His career was threatened by Caris and his life was threatened by a remorseless plague.

A light snowfall began as the ceremony of consecration came to an end. Just beyond the cleared plot, seven funeral processions were at a standstill, waiting for the cemetery to be ready. At Godwyn's signal, they moved forward. The first body was in a coffin, but the rest were in shrouds on biers. In the best of times coffins were a luxury for the prosperous, but now that timber had become expensive and coffin-makers were overworked it was only the very rich that could afford to be buried in a wooden casket.

At the head of the first procession was Merthin, with snowflakes caught in his copper-red hair and beard. He was carrying his little girl. The wealthy deceased in the coffin must be Bessie Bell, Godwyn deduced. Bessie had died without relatives and left the tavern to Merthin. Money sticks to that man like wet leaves, Godwyn thought sourly. Merthin already had Leper Island and the fortune he had made in Florence. Now he owned the busiest tavern in Kingsbridge.

Godwyn knew about Bessie's will because the priory was entitled to an inheritance tax and had taken a fat percentage of the value of the place. Merthin had paid the money in gold florins without hesitation.

The one good consequence of the plague was that the priory suddenly had plenty of cash.

Godwyn conducted one burial service for all seven bodies. This was now the norm: one funeral in the morning and one in the afternoon, regardless of the number of dead. There were not enough priests in Kingsbridge to bury each person individually.

That thought renewed Godwyn's feeling of dread. He stumbled over the words of the service, seeing himself in one of the graves; then he managed to take hold of himself and continue.

At last the service was over, and he led the procession of monks and nuns back to the cathedral. They entered the church and fell out of formation in the nave. The monks returned to their normal duties. A novice nun approached Godwyn nervously and said: "Father Prior, would you kindly come to the hospital?"

Godwyn did not like to receive bossy messages via novices. "What for?" he snapped.

"I'm sorry, Father, I don't know—I was just told to ask you."

"I'll come as soon as I can," he said irritably. He did not have anything urgent to do, but just to make the point he delayed in the cathedral, speaking to Brother Eli about the monks' robes.

A few minutes later he crossed the cloisters and entered the hospital.

Nuns were crowded around a bedstead that had been set up in front of the altar. They must have an important patient, he thought. He wondered who it was. One of the attendant nuns turned to him. She wore a linen mask over her nose and mouth, but he recognized the gold-flecked green eyes that he and all his family shared: it was Caris. Although he could see so little of her face, he read an odd expression in her look. He expected dislike and contempt, but instead he saw compassion.

He moved closer to the bed with a feeling of trepidation. When the other nuns saw him they moved aside deferentially. A moment later, he saw the patient.

It was his mother.

Petranilla's large head lay on a white pillow. She was sweating, and there was a steady trickle of blood from her nose. A nun was in the act of wiping it away, but it reappeared. Another nun offered the patient a cup of water. There was a rash of purple spots on the wrinkled skin of Petranilla's throat.

Godwyn cried out as if he had been struck. He stared in horror. His mother gazed at him with suffering eyes. There was no room for doubt: she had fallen victim to the plague. "No!" he shouted. "No! No!" He felt an unbearable pain in his chest, as if he had been stabbed.

He heard Philemon, beside him, say in a frightened voice: "Try to stay calm, Father Prior," but he could not. He opened his mouth to scream, but no sound came. He suddenly felt detached from his body, with no control over his movements. Then a black mist arose from the floor and engulfed him, gradually rising up his body until it covered his nose and mouth, so that he could not breathe, and then his eyes, so that he was blind; and at last he lost consciousness.

~

Godwyn was in bed for five days. He ate nothing and drank only when Philemon put a cup to his lips. He could not think straight. He could not move, for it seemed he had no way of deciding what to do. He sobbed, and slept, then woke up and sobbed again. He was vaguely aware of a monk feeling his forehead, taking a urine sample, diagnosing brain fever, and bleeding him.

Then, on the last day of December, a scared-looking Philemon brought him the news that his mother was dead.

Godwyn got up. He had himself shaved, put on a new robe, and went to the hospital.

The nuns had washed and dressed the body. Petranilla's hair was brushed and she wore a dress of costly Italian wool. Seeing her like that, with the pallor of death on her face and her eyes forever closed, Godwyn felt a resurgence of the panic that had overwhelmed him; but this time he was able to fight it down. "Take her body to the cathedral," he ordered. Normally the honor of lying in state in the cathedral was reserved for monks, nuns, senior clergymen, and the aristocracy; but Godwyn knew that no one would dare to contradict him.

When she had been moved into the church, and placed in front of the altar, he knelt beside her and prayed. Prayer helped him calm his terror, and gradually he figured out what to do. When at last he stood up, he ordered Philemon to call a meeting in the chapter house immediately.

He felt shaky, but he knew he had to pull himself together. He had always been blessed with the power of persuasion. Now he had to use it to the utmost.

When the monks had gathered, he read to them from the Book of Genesis. "And it came to pass after these things, that God did tempt Abraham, and said unto him, Abraham: and he said, Behold, here I am. And he said, Take now thy son, thine only son Isaac, whom thou lovest, and get thee into the land of Moriah; and offer him there for a burnt offering upon one of the mountains which I will tell thee of. And Abraham rose up early in the morning, and saddled his ass, and took two of his young men with him, and Isaac his son, and clave the wood for the burnt offering, and rose up, and went unto the place of which God had told him."

Godwyn looked up from the book. The monks were watching him intently. They all knew the story of Abraham and Isaac. They were more interested in him, Godwyn. They were alert, wary, wondering what would come next.

"What does the story of Abraham and Isaac teach us?" he asked rhetorically. "God tells Abraham to kill his son—not just his eldest son, but his only son, born when he was a hundred years old. Did Abraham protest? Did he plead for mercy? Did he argue with God? Did he point out that to kill Isaac would be murder, infanticide, a terrible sin?" Godwyn let the question hang for a moment, then looked down at the book and read: "And Abraham rose up early in the morning, and saddled his ass . . ."

He looked up again. "God may tempt us, too. He may order us to perform acts which seem wrong. Perhaps he will tell us to do something that appears to be a sin. When that happens, we must remember Abraham."

Godwyn was speaking in what he knew was his most persuasive preaching style, rhythmic yet conversational. He could tell that he had their rapt attention by the quiet in the octagonal chapter house: no one fidgeted, whispered, or shuffled.

"We must not question," he said. "We must not argue. When God leads us, we must follow—no matter how foolish, sinful, or cruel his wishes may seem to our feeble human minds. We are weak and humble. Our understanding is fallible. It is not given to us to make decisions or choices. Our duty is simple. It is to obey."

Then he told them what they had to do.

∽

The bishop arrived after dark. It was almost midnight when the entourage entered the precinct: they had ridden by torchlight. Most of the priory had been in bed for hours, but there was a group of nuns at work in the hospital, and one of them came to wake Caris. "The bishop is here," she said.

"Why does he want me?" Caris asked sleepily.

"I don't know, Mother Prior."

Of course she didn't. Caris pulled herself out of bed and put on a cloak.

She paused in the cloisters. She took a long drink of water, and for a few moments she breathed deeply of the cold night air, clearing her head of sleep. She wanted to make a good impression on the bishop, so that there would be no trouble about his ratifying her election as prioress.

Archdeacon Lloyd was in the hospital, looking tired, the pointed tip of his long nose red with cold. "Come and greet your bishop," he said crossly, as if she ought to have been up and waiting.

She followed him out. A servant stood outside the door with a burning torch. They walked across the green to where the bishop sat on his horse.

He was a small man in a big hat, and he looked thoroughly fed up.

Caris said in Norman French: "Welcome to Kingsbridge Priory, my lord bishop."

Henri said peevishly: "Who are you?"

Caris had seen him before but had never spoken to him. "I am Sister Caris, prioress-elect."

"The witch."

Her heart sank. Godwyn must have already tried to poison Henri's mind against her. She felt indignant. "No, my lord bishop, there are no witches here," she said with more acerbity than was prudent. "Just a group of ordinary nuns doing their best for a town that has been stricken by the plague."

He ignored that. "Where is Prior Godwyn?"

"In his palace."

"No, he's not!"

Archdeacon Lloyd explained: "We've been there. The building is empty."

"Really?"

"Yes," the archdeacon said irritably. "Really."

At that moment, Caris spotted Godwyn's cat, with the distinctive white tip to its tail. The novices called it Archbishop. It walked across the west front of the cathedral and looked into the spaces between the pillars, as if searching for its master.

Caris was taken aback. "How strange . . . Perhaps Godwyn decided to sleep in the dormitory with the other monks."

"And why would he do that? I hope there's no impropriety going on."

Caris shook her head dismissively. The bishop suspected unchastity, but Godwyn was not prone to that particular sin. "He reacted badly when his mother caught the plague. He had some kind of fit and collapsed. She died today."

"If he's been unwell I should have thought he was all the more likely to sleep in his own bed."

Anything might have happened. Godwyn was slightly unhinged by Petranilla's illness. Caris said: "Would the lord bishop like to speak to one of his deputies?"

Henri answered crossly: "If I could find one, yes!"

"Perhaps if I take Archdeacon Lloyd to the dormitory . . ."

"As soon as you like!"

Lloyd got a torch from a servant, and Caris led him quickly through the cathedral into the cloisters. The place was silent, as monasteries generally were at this time of night. They reached the foot of the staircase that led up to the dormitory, and Caris stopped. "You'd better go up alone," she said. "A nun should not see monks in bed."

"Of course." Lloyd went up the stairs with his torch, leaving her in darkness. She waited, curious. She heard him shout: "Hello?" There was a strange silence. Then, after a few moments, he called down to her in an odd voice: "Sister?"

"Yes?"

"You can come up."

Mystified, she climbed the stairs and entered the dormitory. She stood beside Lloyd and peered into the room by the unsteady light of the burning torch. The monks' straw mattresses lay neatly in their places along either side of the room—but not one of them was occupied. "There's no one here," Caris said.

"Not a soul," Lloyd agreed. "What on earth has happened?"

"I don't know, but I can guess," said Caris.

"Then enlighten me, please."

"Isn't it obvious?" she said. "They've run away."

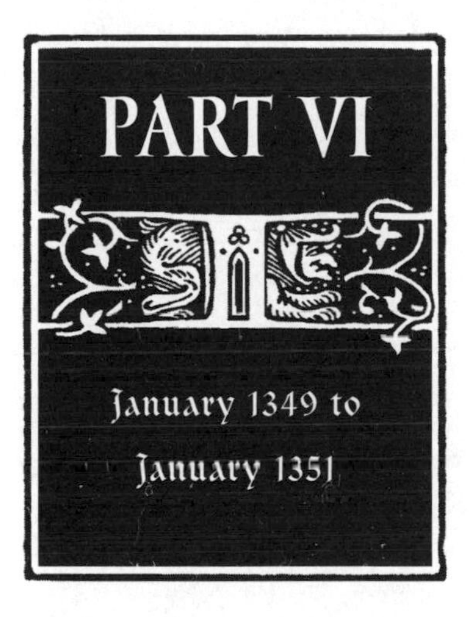
PART VI
January 1349 to
January 1351

63

hen Godwyn left, he took with him all the valuables from the monks' treasury and all the charters. This included the nuns' charters, which they had never succeeded in retrieving from his locked chest. He also took the sacred relics, including the bones of St. Adolphus in their priceless reliquary.

Caris discovered this on the morning afterward, the first day of January, the Feast of the Circumcision of Christ. She went with Bishop Henri and Sister Elizabeth to the treasury off the south transept. Henri's attitude to her was stiffly formal, which was worrying; but he was a peevish character, so perhaps he was like that with everyone.

The flayed skin of Gilbert Hereford was still nailed to the door, slowly turning hard and yellow, and giving off a faint but distinct whiff of rottenness.

But the door was not locked.

They went in. Caris had not been inside this room since Prior Godwyn stole the nuns' one hundred and fifty pounds to build his palace. After that they had built their own treasury.

It was immediately obvious what had happened. The flagstones that disguised the vaults in the floor had been lifted and not put back, and the lid of the ironbound chest stood open. Vaults and chest were empty.

Caris felt that her contempt for Godwyn was vindicated. A trained physician, a priest and the leader of the monks, he had fled just at the moment when the people needed him most. Now, surely, everyone would realize his true nature.

Archdeacon Lloyd was outraged. "He took everything!"

Caris said to Henri: "And this is the man who wanted you to annul my election."

Bishop Henri grunted noncommittally.

Elizabeth was desperate to find an excuse for Godwyn's behavior. "I'm sure the lord prior took the valuables with him for safekeeping."

That stung the bishop into a response. "Rubbish," he said crisply. "If your servant empties your purse and disappears without warning, he's not keeping your money safe, he's stealing it."

Elizabeth tried a different tack. "I believe this was Philemon's idea."

"The subprior?" Henri looked scornful. "Godwyn is in charge, not Philemon. Godwyn is responsible."

Elizabeth shut up.

Godwyn must have recovered from the death of his mother, Caris thought, at least temporarily. It was quite an achievement to persuade every single one of the monks to follow him. She wondered where they had gone.

Bishop Henri was thinking the same thing. "Where did the wretched cowards go?"

Caris remembered Merthin trying to persuade her to leave. *To Wales, or Ireland,* he had said. *A remote village where they don't see a stranger from one year to the next.* She said to the bishop: "They will be hiding out in some isolated place where no one ever goes."

"Find out exactly where," he said.

Caris realized that all opposition to her election had vanished with Godwyn. She felt triumphant, and made an effort not to look too pleased. "I'll make some inquiries in the town," she said. "Somebody must have seen them leave."

"Good," said the bishop. "However, I don't think they're coming back soon, so in the meantime you're going to have to manage as best you can with no men. Continue the services as normally as possible with the nuns. Get a parish priest to come into the cathedral for mass, if you can find one still alive. You cannot perform the mass, but you can hear confessions—there has been a special dispensation from the archbishop, because so many clergymen have died."

Caris was not going to let him slide past the question of her election. "Are you confirming me as prioress?" she said.

"Of course," he said irritably.

"In that case, before I accept the honor—"

"You have no decision to make, Mother Prioress," he said indignantly. "It is your duty to obey me."

She wanted the post desperately, but she resolved to pretend otherwise. She was going to drive a hard bargain. "We live in strange times, don't we?" she said. "You've given nuns authority to hear confessions. You've shortened the training for priests, but you still can't ordain them fast enough to keep up with deaths from the plague, I hear."

"Is it your intention to exploit the difficulties the church is facing for some purpose of your own?"

"No, but there is something you need to do to make it possible for me to carry out your instructions."

Henri sighed. Clearly he did not like being spoken to in this way. But, as Caris had suspected, he needed her more than she needed him. "Very well, what is it?"

"I want you to convene an ecclesiastical court and reopen my trial for witchcraft."

"For heaven's sake, why?"

"To declare me innocent, of course. Until that happens, it could be difficult for me to exercise authority. Anyone who disagrees with my decisions can all too easily undermine me by pointing out that I stand condemned."

The tidy secretarial mind of Archdeacon Lloyd liked that idea. "It would be good to have the issue disposed of once and for all, my lord bishop."

"Very well, then," said Henri.

"Thank you." She felt a surge of delight and relief, and bowed her head for fear that her triumph would show in her face. "I will do my best to bring honor to the position of prioress of Kingsbridge."

"Lose no time in inquiring after Godwyn. I'd like some kind of answer before I leave town."

"The alderman of the parish guild is a crony of Godwyn's. He'll know where they've gone if anyone does. I'll go and see him."

"Right away, please."

Caris left. Bishop Henri was charmless, but he seemed competent, and she thought she could work with him. Perhaps he would be the kind of leader who made decisions based on the merits of the case, instead of siding with whomever he perceived as an ally. That would be a pleasant change.

Passing the Bell, she was tempted to go in and tell Merthin her good news. However, she thought she had better find Elfric first.

In the street in front of the Holly Bush she saw Duncan Dyer lying on the ground. His wife, Winnie, was sitting on the bench outside the tavern, crying. Caris thought the man must have been hurt, but Winnie said: "He's drunk."

Caris was shocked. "It isn't even dinnertime yet!"

"His uncle, Peter Dyer, caught the plague and passed away. His wife and children died, too, so Duncan inherited all his money, and he just spends it on wine. I don't know what to do."

"Let's get him home," Caris said. "I'll help you lift him." They each took an arm and got Duncan to his feet. Holding him upright, they half-dragged him down the street to his house. They put him on the floor and covered him with a blanket. Winnie said: "He's like this every day. He's says it's not worth working, because we're all going to die of the plague. What shall I do?"

Caris thought for a moment. "Bury the money in the garden, now, while he's sleeping. When he wakes up, tell him he lost it all gambling with a chapman who left town."

"I might do that," Winnie said.

Caris crossed the street to Elfric's house and went inside. Her sister, Alice, was sitting in the kitchen sewing stockings. They had not been close since Alice married Elfric, and what little was left of their relationship had been destroyed by Elfric's testifying against Caris in the heresy trial. Forced to choose between sister and husband, Alice had been loyal to Elfric. Caris understood that, but it meant her sister had become like a stranger to her.

When Alice saw her, she stood up and dropped her sewing. "What are you doing here?" she said.

"The monks have all disappeared," Caris told her. "They must have left in the night."

"So that was what it was!" Alice said.

"Did you see them?"

"No, but I heard a whole crowd of men and horses. They weren't loud—in fact, now that I think of it, they must have been making an effort to be quiet—but you can't keep horses silent, and men make a noise just walking along the street. They woke me, but I didn't get up to see—it was too cold. Is that why you've entered my house for the first time in ten years?"

"You didn't know they were going to run off?"

"Is that what they've done, run off? Because of the plague?"

"I assume so."

"Surely not. What's the use of physicians who flee from sickness?" Alice was troubled by this behavior on the part of her husband's patron. "I can't understand it."

"I was wondering if Elfric knew anything about it."

"If he does, he hasn't told me."

"Where will I find him?"

"St. Peter's. Rick Silvers left some money to the church, and the priest decided to pave the floor of the nave."

"I'll go and ask him." Caris wondered if she should make an attempt to be courteous. Alice had no children of her own, but she had a stepdaughter. "How is Griselda?" Caris said.

"Very well and happy," Alice said with a touch of defiance, as if she thought Caris might prefer to hear otherwise.

"And your grandson?" Caris could not bring herself to use the child's name, which was Merthin.

"Lovely. And another grandchild on the way."

"I'm pleased for her."

"Yes. It's just as well she didn't marry your Merthin, the way things have turned out."

Caris refused to be drawn. "I'll go and find Elfric."

St. Peter's Church was at the western end of the town. As Caris was threading her way through the winding streets, she came upon two men fighting. They were shouting curses at one another and punching wildly. Two women, presumably their wives, were screeching abuse, while a small crowd of neighbors looked on. The door of the nearest house had been broken down. On the ground nearby was a cage made of twigs and rushes containing three live chickens.

Caris went up to the men and stepped between them. "Stop it this instant," she said. "I command you in the name of God."

They did not take much persuading. They had probably expended their wrath with the first few blows, and might even be grateful for an excuse to stop. They stepped back and dropped their arms.

"What's this about?" Caris demanded.

They both started speaking at once, and so did their wives.

"One at a time!" Caris said. She pointed at the larger of the two men, a dark-haired fellow whose good looks were spoiled by a swelling around his eye. "You're Joe Blacksmith, aren't you? Explain."

"I caught Toby Peterson stealing Jack Marrow's chickens. He broke down the door."

Toby was a smaller man with a gamecock bravado. He spoke through bleeding lips. "Jack Marrow owed me five shillings—I'm entitled to those chickens!"

Joe said: "Jack and all his family died of the plague two weeks ago. I've been feeding his chickens ever since. They'd be dead but for me. If anyone should take them, it ought to be me."

Caris said: "Well, you're both entitled to them, aren't you? Toby because of the debt, and Joe because he kept them alive at his own expense."

They looked taken aback at the thought that they might both be right.

Caris said: "Joseph, take one of the chickens out of the cage."

Toby said: "Wait a moment—"

"Trust me, Toby," Caris said. "You know I wouldn't treat you unjustly, don't you?"

"Well, I can't deny that . . ."

Joe opened the cage and picked up a scrawny brown-feathered chicken by its feet. The bird's head turned jerkily from side to side, as if it was bewildered to see the world upside-down.

Caris said: "Now give it to Toby's wife."

"What?"

"Would I cheat you, Joseph?"

Joe reluctantly handed the chicken to Toby's wife, a pretty, sulky type. "There you are, then, Jane."

Jane took it with alacrity.

Caris said to her: "Now thank Joe."

Jane looked petulant, but she said: "I thank you, Joseph Blacksmith."

Caris said: "Now, Toby, give a chicken to Ellie Blacksmith."

Toby obeyed, with a sheepish grin. Joe's wife, Ellie, who was heavily pregnant, smiled and said: "Thank you, Toby Peterson."

They were returning to normal, and beginning to realize the foolishness of what they had been doing.

Jane said: "What about the third chicken?"

"I'm coming to that," Caris said. She looked at the watching crowd and pointed at a sensible-looking girl of eleven or twelve. "What's your name?"

"I'm Jesca, Mother Prior—the daughter of John Constable."

"Take the other chicken to St. Peter's Church and give it to Father Michael. Say that Toby and Joe will be coming to ask forgiveness for the sin of covetousness."

"Yes, Sister." Jesca picked up the third chicken and went off.

Joe's wife, Ellie, said: "You may remember, Mother Caris, that you helped my husband's baby sister, Minnie, when she burned her arm in the forge."

"Oh, yes, of course," Caris said. It had been a nasty burn, she remembered. "She must be ten now."

"That's right."

"Is she well?"

"Right as rain, thanks to you, and God's grace."

"I'm glad to hear it."

"Would you care to step into my house for a cup of ale, Mother Prioress?"

"I'd love to, but I'm in a hurry." She turned to the men. "God bless you, and no more fighting."

Joe said: "Thank you."

Caris walked away.

Toby called after her: "Thank you, Mother."

She waved without looking back.

She noticed several more houses that appeared to have been broken into, presumably to be looted after the occupants died. Someone ought to do something about it, she thought. But with Elfric as alderman, and a disappearing prior, there was no one to take the initiative.

She reached St. Peter's and found Elfric with a team of paviors and their apprentices in the nave. Stone slabs were stacked all around, and the men were preparing the ground, pouring sand and smoothing it with sticks. Elfric was checking that the surface was level, using a complicated piece of apparatus with a wooden frame and a dangling cord with a lead point at its end. The apparatus looked like a miniature gallows, and it reminded Caris that Elfric had tried to get her hanged for witchcraft ten years ago. She was surprised to find that she felt no hatred for him. He was too mean-spirited and small-minded for that. When she looked at him, she felt nothing but contempt.

She waited for him to finish, then said abruptly: "Did you know that Godwyn and all the monks have run away?"

She intended to surprise him, and she knew by his look of astonishment that he had no foreknowledge. "Why would they . . . ? When . . . ? Oh, last night?"

"You didn't see them."

"I heard something."

"I saw them," said a pavior. He leaned on his spade to talk. "I was coming out of the Holly Bush. It was dark, but they had torches. The prior was riding, and the rest walking, but they had a sight of baggage: wine casks and wheels of cheese and I don't know what."

Caris already knew that Godwyn had emptied the monks' food stores. He had not tried to take any of the nuns' supplies, which were kept separately. "What time was that?"

"Not late—nine or ten o'clock."

"Did you speak to them?"

"Just to say good night."

"Any clue as to where they might have been headed?"

The pavior shook his head. "They went over the bridge, but I didn't see which road they took at Gallows Cross."

Caris turned to Elfric. "Think back over the past few days. Did Godwyn say anything to you that, with hindsight, might relate to this? Mention any place names—Monmouth, York, Antwerp, Bremen?"

"No. I had no clue." Elfric looked grumpy about not having been forewarned, which made Caris think he was telling the truth.

If Elfric was surprised, it was unlikely that anyone else had known what Godwyn planned. Godwyn was fleeing from the plague, and clearly he did not want anyone to follow him, bringing the disease with them. *Leave early, go far, and stay long,* Merthin had said. Godwyn could be anywhere.

"If you hear from him, or any of the monks, please tell me," Caris said.

Elfric said nothing.

Caris raised her voice to make sure the workmen heard. "Godwyn has stolen all the precious ornaments," she said. There was a rumble of indignation. The men felt proprietorial about the cathedral ornaments—indeed, the wealthier craftsmen had probably helped pay for some of them. "The bishop wants them back. Anyone who helps Godwyn, even just by concealing his whereabouts, is guilty of sacrilege."

Elfric looked bewildered. He had based his life on ingratiating himself with Godwyn. Now his patron had gone. He said: "There may be some perfectly innocent explanation . . ."

"If there is, why did Godwyn tell no one? Or even leave behind a letter?"

Elfric could not think of anything to say.

Caris realized she was going to have to speak to all the leading merchants, and the sooner the better. "I'd like you to call a meeting," she said to Elfric. Then she thought of a more persuasive way of putting it. "The bishop wants the parish guild to meet today, after dinner. Please inform the members."

"Very well," said Elfric.

They would all be there, Caris knew, agog with curiosity.

She left St. Peter's and headed back toward the priory. As she passed the White Horse Tavern, she saw something that made her pause. A young girl was talking to an older man, and there was something about the interaction that raised Caris's hackles. She always felt the vulnerability of girls very sharply—perhaps because she remembered herself as an adolescent, perhaps because of the daughter she had never had. She drew back into a doorway and studied them.

The man was poorly dressed except for a costly fur hat. Caris did not know him, but she guessed he was a laborer and had inherited the hat. So many people had died that there was a glut of finery, and you saw odd sights like this all the time. The girl was about fourteen years old, and pretty, with an adolescent figure. She was trying to be coquettish, Caris saw with disapproval; though she was not very convincing. The man took money from his purse, and they seemed to be arguing. Then the man fondled the girl's small breast.

Caris had seen enough. She marched up to the pair. The man took one look at her nun's habit and walked quickly away. The girl looked both guilty and resentful. Caris said: "What are you doing—trying to sell your body?"

"No, Mother."

"Tell the truth! Why did you let him feel your breast?"

"I don't know what to do! I haven't got anything to eat, and now you've chased him away." She burst into tears.

Caris could believe the girl was hungry. She looked thin and pale. "Come with me," Caris said. "I'll give you something to eat."

She took the girl's arm and steered her toward the priory. "What's your name?" she asked.

"Ismay."

"How old are you?"

"Thirteen."

They reached the priory and Caris took Ismay to the kitchen, where the nuns' dinner was being prepared under the supervision of a novice called Oonagh. The kitchener, Josephine, had fallen to the plague. "Give this child some bread and butter," Caris said to Oonagh.

She sat and watched the girl eat. Ismay obviously had not had food for days. She ate half of a four-pound loaf before slowing down.

Caris poured her a cup of cider. "Why were you starving?" she asked.

"All my family died of the plague."

"What was your father?"

"A tailor, and I can sew very neatly, but no one is buying clothes—they can get anything they want from the homes of dead people."

"So that's why you were trying to prostitute yourself."

She looked down. "I'm sorry, Mother Prioress. I was so hungry."

"Was that the first time that you tried?"

She shook her head and would not look at Caris.

Tears of rage welled up in Caris's eyes. What kind of man would have sexual congress with a starving thirteen-year-old? What kind of God would drive a girl to such desperation? "Would you like to live here, with the nuns, and work in the kitchen?" she said. "You would have plenty to eat."

Ismay looked up with eagerness. "Oh, yes, Mother, I'd like that."

"Then you shall. You can begin by helping to prepare the nuns' dinner. Oonagh, here's a new kitchen hand."

"Thank you, Mother Caris, I need all the help I can get."

Caris left the kitchen and went thoughtfully into the cathedral for the service of Sext. The plague was not just a physical sickness, she was beginning to realize. Ismay had escaped the disease, but her soul had been in peril.

Bishop Henri took the service, leaving Caris free to think. At the parish guild meeting she needed to talk about more than just the flight of the monks, she decided. It was time to get the town organized to deal with the effects of the plague. But how?

She mulled over the problems through dinner. For all sorts of reasons, this was a good time to make big decisions. With the bishop here to back up her authority, she might be able to push through measures that could otherwise meet with opposition.

This was also a good moment to get what she wanted from the bishop. That was a fertile thought . . .

After dinner she went to see the bishop in the prior's house, where he was staying. He was at table with Archdeacon Lloyd. They had been fed by the nuns' kitchen and were drinking wine while a priory servant cleared the table. "I hope you enjoyed your dinner, my lord bishop," she said formally.

He was a little less peevish than usual. "It was fine, thank you, Mother Caris—a very tasty pike. Any news of the runaway prior?"

"He seems to have been careful to leave no clue as to his destination."

"Disappointing."

"As I walked through the town, making inquiries, I saw several incidents that disturbed me: a thirteen-year-old girl prostituting herself; two normally law-abiding citizens fighting over a dead man's property; a man dead drunk at midday."

"These are the effects of the plague. It's the same everywhere."

"I believe we must act to counter those effects."

He raised his eyebrows. It seemed he had not thought of taking such action. "How?"

"The prior is overlord of Kingsbridge. He is the one to take the initiative."

"But he has vanished."

"As bishop, you are technically our abbot. I believe you must stay here in Kingsbridge permanently, and take charge of the town."

This was in fact the last thing she wanted. Fortunately, there was little chance of the bishop agreeing: he had far too much to do elsewhere. She was just trying to back him into a corner.

He hesitated, and for a moment she worried that she might have misjudged him, and he might accept her suggestion. Then he said: "Out of the question. Every town in the diocese has the same problems. Shiring is worse. I have to try to hold together the fabric of Christianity here while my priests are dying. I have no time to worry about drunks and prostitutes."

"Well, somebody must act as prior of Kingsbridge. The town needs a moral leader."

Archdeacon Lloyd put in: "My lord bishop, there is also the question of who is to receive monies owed to the priory, maintain the cathedral and other buildings, manage the lands and the serfs . . ."

Henri said: "Well, you will have to do all that, Mother Caris."

She pretended to consider the suggestion as if she had not already thought of it. "I could handle all the less important tasks—managing the monks' money and their lands—but I could not do what you can do, my lord bishop. I could not perform the holy sacraments."

"We've already discussed that," he said impatiently. "I'm creating new priests as fast as I can. But you can do everything else."

"It almost seems as if you're asking me to be acting prior of Kingsbridge."

"That's exactly what I want."

Caris was careful not to show her elation. It seemed too good to be true. She was prior for all purposes except those she did not care about. Were there any hidden snags she had not thought of?

Archdeacon Lloyd said: "You'd better let me write her a letter to that effect, in case she needs to enforce her authority."

Caris said: "If you want the town to abide by your wishes, you may need to impress upon them that this is your personal decision. A meeting of the parish guild is about to begin. If you're willing, Bishop, I'd like you to attend it and make an announcement."

"All right, let us go."

They left Godwyn's palace and walked up the main street to the guildhall. The members were all waiting to hear what had happened to the monks. Caris began by telling them what she knew. Several people had seen or heard the exodus yesterday after dark, although no one had realized or even suspected that every single one of the monks was leaving.

She asked them to be alert for talk among travelers about a large group of monks on the road with a lot of baggage.

"But we have to accept the likelihood that the monks will not return soon. And in connection with that, the lord bishop has an announcement." She wanted the words to come from him, not her.

Henri cleared his throat and said: "I have confirmed the election of Caris as prioress, and I have appointed her acting prior. You will all please treat her as my representative and your overlord in all matters, excepting only those reserved to ordained priests."

Caris watched the faces. Elfric was furious. Merthin smiled faintly, guessing that she had maneuvered herself into this position, pleased for her and for the town, the rueful twist to his mouth showing that he knew this would keep her out of his arms. Everyone else seemed glad. They knew and trusted her, and she had won even more loyalty by staying while Godwyn fled.

She would make the most of it. "Three matters I want to take care of urgently on my first day as acting prior," she said. "First, drunkenness. Today I saw Duncan Dyer unconscious in the street before dinnertime. I believe this contributes to an atmosphere of debauchery in the town, which is the last thing we need during this dreadful crisis."

There were loud sounds of approval. The parish guild was dominated by the older and more conservative of the town merchants. If they ever got drunk in the morning, they did it at home where no one could see.

Caris went on: "I want to give John Constable an extra deputy and instruct him to arrest anyone found drunk in daylight. He can put them in the jail until they sober up."

Even Elfric was nodding.

"Second is the question of what happens to the property of people who die without heirs. This morning I found Joseph Blacksmith and

Toby Peterson fighting in the street over three chickens belonging to Jack Marrow."

There was laughter at the idea of grown men fighting over such trifles.

Caris had thought out her solution to that problem. "In principle, such property reverts to the lord of the manor, which for Kingsbridge residents means the priory. However, I don't want the monastery buildings filled up with old clothes, so I propose to waive the rule for anyone whose possessions are worth less than two pounds. Instead, the two nearest neighbors should lock up the house, to make sure nothing is taken; then the property should be inventoried by the parish priest, who will also hear the claims of any creditors. Where there is no priest, they can come to me. When any debts have been paid, the deceased's personal possessions—clothing, furniture, food and drink—will be divided up among the neighbors, and any cash given to the parish church."

There was widespread approval for this, too, most people nodding and murmuring agreement.

"Finally, I found a thirteen-year-old orphan girl trying to sell her body outside the White Horse. Her name is Ismay, and she did it because she had nothing to eat." Caris looked around the room with a challenging stare. "Can anyone tell me how such a thing could possibly happen in a Christian town? All her family are dead—but did they have no friends or neighbors? Who allows a child to starve?"

Edward Butcher said in a low voice: "Ismay Taylor is a rather badly behaved child."

Caris was not accepting excuses. "She's thirteen!"

"I'm just saying that she might have been offered help and spurned it."

"Since when did we allow children to make such decisions for themselves? If a child is orphaned, it is the duty of every one of us to take care of her. What does your religion mean, if not that?"

They all looked shamefaced.

"In future, whenever a child is orphaned, I want the two nearest neighbors to bring the child to me. Those who cannot be placed with a friendly family will move into the priory. The girls can live with the nuns, and we will turn the monks' dormitory into a bedroom for boys. They can all have lessons in the morning and do suitable work in the afternoon."

There was general approval for that, too.

Elfric spoke up. "Have you finished, Mother Caris?"

"I think so, unless anyone wants to discuss the details of what I have suggested."

No one spoke up, and the members began to move in their seats as if the meeting was over.

Then Elfric said: "Some of the men here may remember that they elected *me* as alderman of the guild."

His voice was full of resentment. Everyone fidgeted impatiently.

"We have now seen the prior of Kingsbridge accused of theft and condemned without trial," he went on.

That went down badly. There was a rumble of dissent. No one thought Godwyn innocent.

Elfric ignored the mood of the room. "And we have sat here like slaves and let a woman dictate the laws of the city to us. By whose authority are drunks to be imprisoned? Hers. Who is the ultimate judge of inheritance? She is. Who will dispose of the city's orphans? She will. What have you come to? Are you not men?"

Betty Baxter said: "No."

The men laughed.

Caris decided not to intervene. It was unnecessary. She glanced at the bishop, wondering if he would assert himself against Elfric, and saw that he was sitting back, mouth clamped shut: plainly he, too, had realized that Elfric was fighting a losing battle.

Elfric raised his voice. "I say we reject a female prior, even acting prior, and we deny the right of the prioress to come to the parish guild and issue commandments!"

Several muttered mutinously. Two or three stood up, as if about to walk out in disgust. Someone called out: "Forget it, Elfric."

He persisted. "And this is a woman who was convicted of witchcraft and sentenced to death!"

All the men were standing, now. One walked out of the door.

"Come back!" Elfric shouted. "I haven't closed the meeting!"

No one took any notice.

Caris joined the group at the door. She made way for the bishop and the archdeacon. She was the last to leave. She turned back at the exit and looked at Elfric. He sat alone at the head of the room.

She went out.

64

It was twelve years since Godwyn and Philemon had visited the cell of St.-John-in-the-Forest. Godwyn remembered being impressed by the neatness of the fields, the trimmed hedges, the cleared ditches, and the apple trees in straight lines in the orchard. It was the same today. Evidently Saul Whitehead had not changed, either.

Godwyn and his caravan crossed a checkerboard of frozen fields toward the clustered buildings of the monastery. As they came closer, Godwyn saw that there had been some developments. Twelve years ago the little stone church with its cloister and dormitory had been surrounded by a scatter of small wooden structures: kitchen, stables, dairy, bakery. Now the flimsy timber outbuildings had gone, and the stone-built complex attached to the church had grown correspondingly. "The compound is more secure than it used to be," Godwyn remarked.

"Because of the increase in outlawry by soldiers coming home from the French wars, I'd guess," Philemon said.

Godwyn frowned. "I don't recall being asked for my permission for the building program."

"You were not."

"Hmm." Unfortunately, he could hardly complain. Someone might ask how it was possible for Saul to have carried out such a program without Godwyn's knowledge, unless Godwyn had neglected his duty of supervision.

Besides, it suited his purpose now for the place to be easily closed to intruders.

The two day journey had somewhat calmed him. The death of his mother had thrown him into a frenzy of fear. Every hour he remained in Kingsbridge, he had felt he was sure to die. He had got just enough grip on his emotions to address the meeting in the chapter house and organize the exodus. Despite his eloquence, a few of the monks had had misgivings about fleeing. Fortunately, they were all sworn to obedience, and the habit of doing as they were told had prevailed. Nevertheless, he had not begun to feel safe until his group had crossed the double bridge, torches blazing, and headed off into the night.

He still felt close to the edge. Every now and again he would be mulling something over and would decide to ask Petranilla what she thought, then he would realize he could not ask her advice ever again, and panic would rise like bile in his throat.

He was fleeing from the plague—but he should have done it three months ago, when Mark Webber died. Was he too late? He fought down terror. He would not feel safe until he was locked away from the world.

He wrenched his thoughts back to the present. There was no one in the fields at this time of year, but in a yard of beaten earth in front of the monastery he saw a handful of monks working: one shoeing a horse, another mending a plow, and a small group turning the lever of a cider press.

They all stopped what they were doing and stared, astonished, at the crowd of visitors approaching them: twenty monks, half a dozen novices, four carts, and ten packhorses. Godwyn had left nobody behind but the priory servants.

One of those at the cider press detached himself from the group and came forward. Godwyn recognized him as Saul Whitehead. They had met on Saul's annual visits to Kingsbridge, but now for the first time Godwyn noticed touches of gray in Saul's distinctive ash blond hair.

Twenty years ago they had been students together at Oxford. Saul had been the star pupil, quick to learn and agile in argument. He had also been the most devoutly religious of them all. He might have become prior of Kingsbridge if he had been less spiritual, and had thought strategically about his career instead of leaving such matters to God. As it was, when Prior Anthony had died and the election was held, Godwyn had easily outmaneuvered Saul.

All the same, Saul was not weak. He had a streak of stubborn righteousness that Godwyn feared. Would he go along obediently with Godwyn's plan today, or would he make trouble? Once again Godwyn fought down panic and struggled to remain cool.

He studied Saul's face carefully. The prior of St. John was surprised to see him, and clearly displeased. His expression was carefully composed into a look of polite welcome, but he was not smiling.

During the election campaign, Godwyn had made everyone believe that he himself did not want the job, but he had eliminated every other reasonable candidate, including Saul. Did Saul suspect how he had been hoodwinked?

"Good day to you, Father Prior," Saul said as he approached. "This is an unexpected blessing."

So he was not going to be openly hostile. No doubt he would think that such behavior conflicted with his vow of obedience. Godwyn was relieved. He said: "God bless you, my son. It is too long since I have visited my children at St. John."

Saul looked at the monks, the horses, and the carts loaded with supplies. "This appears to be more than a simple visit." He did not offer to help Godwyn down from his horse. It was as if he wanted an explanation before he would invite them in—which was ridiculous: he had no right to turn away his superior.

All the same, Godwyn found himself explaining. "Have you heard about the plague?"

"Rumors," Saul said. "There are few visitors to bring us news."

That was good. The lack of visitors was what drew Godwyn here. "The disease has killed hundreds in Kingsbridge. I feared it might wipe out the priory. That's why I've brought the monks here. It may be the only way to ensure our survival."

"You are welcome here, of course, whatever the reason for your visit."

"It goes without saying," Godwyn said stiffly. He felt angry that he had been nudged into justifying himself.

Saul looked thoughtful. "I'm not sure where everyone's going to sleep . . ."

"I shall decide that," Godwyn said, reasserting his authority. "You can show me around while your kitchen is preparing our supper." He got down from his horse unaided and walked into the monastery.

Saul was obliged to follow.

The whole place had a bare, scrubbed look that expressed how serious Saul was about the monkish vow of poverty. But today Godwyn was more interested in how readily the place could be closed to outsiders. Fortunately, Saul's belief in order and control had led him to design buildings with few entrances. There were only three ways into the priory: through the kitchen, the stable, or the church. Each entrance had a stout door that could be firmly barred.

The dormitory was small, normally accommodating nine or ten monks, and there was no separate bedroom for the prior. The only way to fit twenty extra monks in was the let them sleep in the church.

Godwyn thought of taking over the dormitory for himself, but there was nowhere in the room to hide the cathedral treasures, and he wanted to keep them close. Fortunately, the little church had a small side chapel that could be closed off, and Godwyn took that for his own room. The rest of the Kingsbridge monks spread straw on the stamped earth floor of the nave and made the best of it.

The food and wine went to the kitchen and the cellar, but Philemon brought the ornaments into Godwyn's chapel-bedroom. Philemon had been chatting to the St. John monks. "Saul has his own way of running things," he reported. "He demands rigid obedience to God and the Rule of St. Benedict, but they say he doesn't set himself up on a pedestal. He sleeps in the dorm, eats the same food as the others, and in general takes no privileges. Needless to say, they like him for that. But there's one monk who is constantly being punished—Brother Jonquil."

"I remember him." Jonquil had always been in trouble while a novice at Kingsbridge—for lateness, slovenliness, laziness, and greed. He was without self-control, and had probably been drawn to the monastic life as a way of getting someone else to enforce the restraint he could not impose on himself. "I doubt that he will be much help to us."

"He will break ranks, given half a chance," Philemon said. "But he doesn't carry any authority. No one will follow him."

"And they have no complaints about Saul? Doesn't he sleep late, or dodge unpleasant chores, or take the best wine for himself?"

"Apparently not."

"Hmm." Saul was as upright as ever. Godwyn was disappointed, but not very surprised.

During Evensong, Godwyn noted how solemn and disciplined the St. John men were. Over the years, he had always sent problem monks here: the mutinous, the mentally ill, those inclined to question the church's teachings and take an interest in heretical ideas. Saul had never complained, never sent anyone back. It seemed he was able to turn such people into model monks.

After the service, Godwyn sent most of the Kingsbridge men to the refectory for supper, keeping only Philemon and two strong young monks behind. When they had the church to themselves, he told Philemon to guard the door that gave entrance from the cloisters, then ordered the youngsters to move the carved wooden altar and dig a hole beneath where it normally stood.

When the hole was deep enough, Godwyn brought the cathedral ornaments from his chapel, ready to be buried beneath the altar. But before he could complete the job Saul came to the door.

Godwyn heard Philemon say: "The lord prior wishes to be alone."

Next came Saul's voice. "Then he may tell me so himself."

"He has asked me to say so."

Saul's voice rose. "I will not be shut out of my own church—least of all by you!"

"Will you offer violence to me, the subprior of Kingsbridge?"

"I will pick you up and throw you in the fountain, if you continue to stand in my way."

Godwyn intervened. He would have preferred to keep Saul in ignorance, but it was not to be. "Let him in, Philemon," he called.

Philemon stepped aside and Saul marched in. He saw the baggage and, without asking permission, opened the neck of a sack and looked inside. "My soul!" he exclaimed, drawing out a silver-gilt altar cruet. "What's all this?"

Godwyn was tempted to tell him not to interrogate his superiors. Saul might have accepted such a reproof: he believed in humility, at least in principle. But Godwyn did not want to let suspicion ferment in Saul's mind, so he said: "I've brought the cathedral treasures with me."

Saul made a face of distaste. "I realize that such gewgaws are thought appropriate in a great cathedral, but they will seem out of place at a humble cell in the forest."

"You won't have to look at them. I'm going to hide them. There's no harm in your knowing where, though I intended to spare you the burden of that knowledge."

Saul looked suspicious. "Why bring them at all?"

"For safekeeping."

Saul was not so easily reassured. "I'm surprised the bishop was willing to let them be taken away."

The bishop had not been asked, of course, but Godwyn did not say that. "At the moment, things are so bad in Kingsbridge that we're not sure the ornaments are safe even at the priory."

"Safer than here, though, surely? We are surrounded by outlaws, you know. Thank God you didn't meet them on the road."

"God is watching over us."

"And over his jewelry, I hope."

Saul's attitude amounted almost to insubordination, but Godwyn did not reprimand him, fearing that an overreaction would suggest guilt. However, he noted that Saul's humility had its limits. Perhaps after all Saul did know that he had been hoodwinked twelve years ago.

Now Godwyn said: "Please ask all the monks to stay in the refectory after supper. I will address them as soon as I have finished here."

Saul accepted this dismissal and went out. Godwyn buried the ornaments, the priory charters, the relics of the saint, and almost all the money. The monks replaced the soil in the hole, tamped it down, and put the altar back in its place. There was some loose earth left over, which they took outside and scattered.

Then they went to the refectory. The little room was crowded now, with the addition of the Kingsbridge men. A monk stood at the lectern, reading a passage from Mark's gospel, but he fell silent when Godwyn walked in.

Godwyn motioned the reader to a seat and took his place. "This is a holy retreat," he began. "God has sent this terrible plague to punish us for our sins. We have come here to purge those sins far away from the corrupting influence of the city."

Godwyn had not intended to open a discussion, but Saul sang out: "What sins in particular, Father Godwyn?"

Godwyn improvised. "Men have challenged the authority of God's holy church; women have become lascivious; monks have failed to separate themselves completely from female society; nuns have turned to heresy and witchcraft."

"And how long will it take to purge these sins?"

"We will know we have triumphed when the plague dies away."

Another St. John monk spoke up, and Godwyn recognized Jonquil, a large, uncoordinated man with a wild look in his eyes. "How will you purge yourself?"

Godwyn was surprised that the monks here felt so free to question their superiors. "By prayer, meditation, and fasting."

"The fasting is a good idea," said Jonquil. "We haven't got much food to spare."

There was a little laughter at that.

Godwyn was worried that he might lose control of his audience. He banged the lectern for quiet. "From now on, anyone who comes here from the outside world is a danger to us," he said. "I want all doors to the precinct barred from the inside day and night. No monk is to go outside without my personal permission, which will be granted only in emergency. All callers are to be turned away. We are going to lock ourselves in until this terrible plague is over."

Jonquil said: "But what if—"

Godwyn interrupted him. "I haven't asked for comments, Brother." He glared around the room, staring them all into silence. "You are monks, and it is your duty to obey," he said. "And now, let us pray."

⁂

The crisis came the very next day.

Godwyn sensed that his orders had been accepted by Saul and the other monks in a provisional way. Everyone was taken by surprise, and on the spur of the moment they could think of no great objections; and so, in default of a strong reason for rebellion, they instinctively obeyed their superior. But he knew the time would come when they would have to make a real decision. However, he did not expect it so soon.

They were singing the office of Prime. It was freezing cold in the little church. Godwyn was stiff and aching after an uncomfortable night. He missed his palace with its fireplaces and soft beds. The gray light of a winter dawn was beginning to appear in the windows when there was a banging on the heavy west door of the church.

Godwyn tensed. He wished he had been given an extra day or two to consolidate his position.

He signaled that the monks should ignore the knocking and continue with the service. The knocking was then augmented by shouting. Saul stood up to go to the door, but Godwyn made sit-down signs with his hands and, after a hesitation, Saul obeyed. Godwyn was determined to sit tight. If the monks did nothing, the intruders must go away.

However, Godwyn began to realize that persuading people to do nothing was extraordinarily difficult.

The monks were too distracted to concentrate on the psalm. They were all whispering to one another and looking back over their shoulders toward the west end. The singing became ragged and uncoordinated and eventually petered out until only Godwyn's voice was left.

He felt irate. If they had followed his lead, they could have ignored the disturbance. Angered by their weakness, he at last left his place and walked down the short nave to the door, which was barred. "What is it?" he shouted.

"Let us in!" came the muffled reply.

"You can't come in," Godwyn shouted back. "Go away."

Saul appeared at his side. "Are you turning them away from the church?" he said in a horrified tone.

"I told you," Godwyn replied. "No visitors."

The banging resumed. "Let us in!"

Saul shouted: "Who are you?"

There was a pause, then the voice said: "We are men of the forest."

Philemon spoke up. "Outlaws," he said.

Saul said indignantly: "Sinners like us, and God's children, too."

"That's no reason to let them murder us."

"Perhaps we should find out whether that's what they intend." Saul went to the window on the right of the door. The church was a low building, and the window ledges were just below eye level. None of them was glazed: they were closed against the cold by shutters of translucent linen. Saul opened the shutter and stood on tiptoe to look out. "Why have you come here?" he called.

Godwyn heard the reply. "One of our number is sick."

Godwyn said to Saul: "I will speak to them."

Saul stared at him.

"Come away from the window," Godwyn said.

Reluctantly, Saul obeyed.

Godwyn shouted: "We cannot let you in. Go away."

Saul looked at him with incredulity. "Are you going to turn away a sick man?" he said. "We are monks and physicians!"

"If the man has the plague, there is nothing we can do for him. By admitting him, we will kill ourselves."

"That is in God's hands, surely."

"God does not permit us to commit suicide."

"You don't know what is wrong with the man. He may have a broken arm."

Godwyn opened the corresponding window on the left of the door and looked out. He saw a group of six rough-looking characters standing around a stretcher that they had put down in front of the church door. Their clothes were costly but dirty, as if they were sleeping rough in their Sunday best. This was typical of outlaws, who stole fine clothes from travelers and made them shabby very quickly. The men were heavily armed, some with good-quality swords, daggers, and longbows, which suggested they might be demobilized soldiers.

On the stretcher lay a man who was perspiring heavily—even though it was a frosty January morning—and bleeding from his nose. Suddenly, without wishing it, Godwyn saw in his imagination that scene in the hospital when his mother lay dying, and the trickle of blood on her upper lip kept returning, no matter how often the nun wiped it away. The thought that he might die like that made him so distracted that he wanted to throw himself from the roof of Kingsbridge Cathedral. How much better it would be to die in one brief instant of overwhelming pain than over three, four, or five days of mad delirium and agonizing thirst. "That man has the plague!" Godwyn exclaimed, and he heard in his own voice a note of hysteria.

One of the outlaws stepped forward. "I know you," he said. "You're the prior of Kingsbridge."

Godwyn tried to pull himself together. He looked with fear and anger at the man who was evidently the leader. He carried himself with the arrogant assurance of a nobleman, and he had once been handsome, though his looks had been marred by years of living rough. Godwyn said: "And who are you, that comes banging on a church door while the monks are singing psalms to God?"

"Some call me Tam Hiding," the outlaw replied.

There was a gasp from the monks: Tam Hiding was a legend. Brother Jonquil shouted: "They will kill us all!"

Saul rounded on Jonquil. "Be silent," he said. "All of us will die when God wills it, and not before."

"Yes, Father."

Saul returned to the window and said: "You stole our chickens last year."

"I'm sorry, Father," said Tam. "We were starving."

"Yet now you come to me for help?"

"Because you preach that God forgives."

Godwyn said to Saul: "Let *me* deal with this!"

Saul's internal struggle was evident on his face, which looked alternately ashamed and mutinous; but at last he bowed his head.

Godwyn said to Tam: "God forgives those who truly repent."

"Well, this man's name is Win Forester, and he truly repents all his many sins. He would like to come into the church to pray for healing or, failing that, to die in a holy place."

One of the other outlaws sneezed.

Saul came away from his window and stood facing Godwyn, hands on hips. "We cannot turn him away!"

Godwyn tried to make himself calm. "You heard that sneeze—don't you understand what it means?" He turned to the rest of the monks, to make sure they heard what he said next. "They've *all* got the plague!"

They gave a collective murmur of fear. Godwyn wanted them frightened. That way they would support him if Saul decided to defy him.

Saul said: "We must help them, even if they have got the plague. Our lives are not our own, to be protected like gold hidden under the earth. We have given ourselves to God, to use as he wishes, and he will end our lives when it suits his holy purpose."

"To let those outlaws in would be suicide. They'll kill us all!"

"We are men of God. For us, death is the happy reunion with Christ. What do we have to fear, Father Prior?"

Godwyn realized that he was sounding frightened, whereas Saul was speaking reasonably. He forced himself to appear calm and philosophical. "It is a sin to seek our own death."

"But if death comes to us in the course of our holy duty, we embrace it gladly."

Godwyn realized he could debate all day with Saul and get nowhere. This was not the way to impose his authority. He closed his shutter. "Shut your window, Brother Saul, and come here to me," he said. He looked at Saul, waiting.

After a hesitation, Saul did as he was told.

Godwyn said: "What are your three vows, Brother?"

There was a pause. Saul knew what was happening here. Godwyn was refusing to engage with him as an equal. At first, Saul looked as if he might refuse to answer, but his training took over, and he said: "Poverty, chastity, obedience."

"And who must you obey?"

"God, and the Rule of St. Benedict, and my prior."

"And your prior stands before you now. Do you acknowledge me?"

"Yes."

"You may say: 'Yes, Father Prior.'"

"Yes, Father Prior."

"Now I will tell you what you must do, and you will obey." Godwyn looked around. "All of you—return to your places."

There was a moment of frozen silence. No one moved and no one spoke. It could go either way, Godwyn thought: compliance or mutiny, order or anarchy, victory or defeat. He held his breath.

At last, Saul moved. He bowed his head and turned away. He walked up the short aisle and resumed his position in front of the altar.

All the others did the same.

There were a few more shouts from outside, but they sounded like parting shots. Perhaps the outlaws had realized they could not force a physician to treat their sick comrade.

Godwyn returned to the altar and turned to face the monks. "We will finish the interrupted psalm," he said, and he began singing.

Glory be to the Father
And to the Son
And to the Holy Ghost

The singing was still ragged. The monks were far too excited to adopt the proper attitude. All the same, they were back in their places and following their routine. Godwyn had prevailed.

As it was in the beginning
Is now
And ever shall be
World without end
Amen.

"Amen," Godwyn repeated.

One of the monks sneezed.

65

Soon after Godwyn fled, Elfric died of the plague.

Caris was sorry for Alice, his widow; but aside from that she could hardly help rejoicing that he was gone. He had bullied the weak and toadied to the strong, and the lies he had told at her trial almost got her hanged. The world was a better place without him. Even his building business would be better off run by his son-in-law, Harold Mason.

The parish guild elected Merthin as alderman in Elfric's place. Merthin said it was like being made captain of a sinking ship.

As the deaths went on and on, and people buried their relatives, neighbors, friends, customers, and employees, the constant horror seemed to brutalize many of them, until no violence or cruelty seemed shocking. People who thought they were about to die lost all restraint and followed their impulses regardless of the consequences.

Together, Merthin and Caris struggled to preserve something like normal life in Kingsbridge. The orphanage was the most successful part of Caris's program. The children were grateful for the security of the nunnery, after the ordeal of losing their parents to the plague. Taking care of them, and teaching them to read and sing hymns, brought out long-suppressed maternal instincts in some of the nuns. There was plenty of food, with fewer people competing for the winter stores. And Kingsbridge Priory was full of the sound of children.

In the town things were more difficult. There continued to be violent quarrels over the property of the dead. People just walked into empty houses and picked up whatever took their fancy. Children who had inherited money, or a warehouse full of cloth or corn, were sometimes adopted by unscrupulous neighbors greedy to get their hands on the legacy. The prospect of something for nothing brought out the worst in people, Caris thought despairingly.

Caris and Merthin were only partly successful against the decline in public behavior. Caris was disappointed with the results of John Constable's crackdown on drunkenness. The large numbers of new widows and widowers seemed frantic to find partners, and it was not unusual to see middle-aged people in a passionate embrace in a tavern or even a doorway. Caris had no great objection to this sort of thing in itself, but she found that the combination of drunkenness and public licentiousness often led to fighting. However, Merthin and the parish guild were unable to stop it.

Just at the moment when the townspeople needed their spines stiffened, the flight of the monks had the opposite effect. It demoralized everyone. God's representatives had left: the Almighty had abandoned the town. Some said that the relics of the saint had always brought good fortune, and now that the bones had gone their luck had run out. The lack of precious crucifixes and candlesticks at the Sunday services was a weekly reminder that Kingsbridge was considered doomed. So why not get drunk and fornicate in the street?

Out of a population of about seven thousand, Kingsbridge had lost at least a thousand by mid-January. Other towns were similar. Despite the masks Caris had invented, the death toll was higher among the nuns, no doubt because they were continually in contact with plague victims. There had been thirty-five nuns, and now there were twenty. But they heard of places where almost every monk or nun had died, leaving a handful, or sometimes just one, to carry on the work; so they counted themselves fortunate. Meanwhile, Caris had shortened the period of novitiate and intensified the training so that she would have more help in the hospital.

Merthin hired the barman from the Holly Bush and put him in charge of the Bell. He also took on a sensible seventeen-year-old girl called Martina to nursemaid Lolla.

Then the plague seemed to die down. Having buried a hundred people a week in the run up to Christmas, Caris found that the number dropped to fifty in January, then twenty in February. She allowed herself to hope that the nightmare might be coming to an end.

One of the unlucky people to fall ill during this period was a dark-haired man in his thirties who might once have been good-looking. He was a visitor to the town. "I thought I had a cold yesterday," he said when he came through the door. "But now I've got this nosebleed that won't stop." He was holding a bloody rag to his nostrils.

"I'll find you somewhere to lie down," she said through her linen mask.

"It's the plague, isn't it?" he said, and she was surprised to hear calm resignation in his voice in place of the usual panic. "Can you do anything to cure it?"

"We can make you comfortable, and we can pray for you."

"That won't do any good. Even you don't believe in it, I can tell."

She was shocked by how easily he had read her heart. "You don't know what you're saying," she protested weakly. "I'm a nun, I must believe it."

"You can tell me the truth. How soon will I die?"

She looked hard at him. He was smiling at her, a charming smile that she guessed had melted a few female hearts. "Why aren't you frightened?" she said. "Everyone else is."

"I don't believe what I'm told by priests." He looked at her shrewdly. "And I have a suspicion that you don't either."

She was not about to have this discussion with a stranger, no matter how charming. "Almost everyone who falls ill with the plague dies within three to five days," she said bluntly. "A few survive, no one knows why."

He took it well. "As I thought."

"You can lie down here."

He gave her the bad-boy grin again. "Will it do me any good?"

"If you don't lie down soon, you'll fall down."

"All right." He lay on the palliasse she indicated.

She gave him a blanket. "What's your name?"

"Tam."

She studied his face. Despite his charm, she sensed a streak of cruelty. He might seduce women, she thought, but if that failed he would rape them. His skin was weathered by outdoor living, and he had the red nose of a drinker. His clothes were costly but dirty. "I know who you are," she said. "Aren't you afraid you'll be punished for your sins?"

"If I believed that, I wouldn't have committed them. Are *you* afraid you'll burn in Hell?"

It was a question she normally sidestepped, but she felt that this dying outlaw deserved a true answer. "I believe that what I do becomes part of me," she said. "When I'm brave and strong, and care for children and the sick and the poor, I become a better person. And when I'm cruel, or cowardly, or tell lies, or get drunk, I turn into someone less worthy, and I can't respect myself. That's the divine retribution I believe in."

He looked at her thoughtfully. "I wish I'd met you twenty years ago."

She made a deprecatory noise. "I would have been twelve."

He raised an eyebrow suggestively.

That was enough, she decided. He was beginning to flirt—and she was beginning to enjoy it. She turned away.

"You're a brave woman to do this work," he said. "It will probably kill you."

"I know," she said, turning to face him again. "But this is my destiny. I can't run away from people who need me."

"Your prior doesn't seem to think that way."

"He's vanished."

"People can't vanish."

"I mean, no one knows where Prior Godwyn and the monks have gone."

"I do," said Tam.

The weather at the end of February was sunny and mild. Caris left Kingsbridge on a dun pony, heading for St.-John-in-the-Forest. Merthin went with her, riding a black cob. Normally, eyebrows would have been raised by a nun going on a journey accompanied only by a man, but these were strange times.

The danger from outlaws had receded. Many had fallen victim to the plague, Tam Hiding had told her himself before he died. Also, the sudden drop in population had brought about a countrywide surplus of food, wine, and clothing—all the things outlaws normally stole. Those outlaws who survived the plague could walk into ghost towns and abandoned villages and take whatever they wanted.

Caris had at first felt frustrated to learn that Godwyn was no farther than two days' journey from Kingsbridge. She had imagined him gone to a place so distant that he would never return. However, she was glad of the chance to retrieve the priory's money and valuables and, in particular, the nunnery's charters, so vital whenever there was a dispute about property or rights.

When and if she was able to confront Godwyn, she would demand the return of the priory's property, in the name of the bishop. She had a letter from Henri to back her up. If Godwyn still refused, that would prove beyond doubt that he was stealing it rather than keeping it safe. The bishop could then take legal action to get it back—or simply arrive at the cell with a force of men-at-arms.

Although disappointed that Godwyn was not permanently out of her life, Caris relished the prospect of confronting him with his cowardice and dishonesty.

As she rode away from the town she recalled that her last long journey had been to France, with Mair—a real adventure in every way. She felt bereft when she thought of Mair. Of all those who had died of the plague, she missed Mair the most: her beautiful face, her kind heart, her love.

But it was a joy to have Merthin to herself for two whole days. Following the road through the forest, side by side on their horses, they talked continuously, about anything that sprang to mind, just as they had when they were adolescents.

Merthin was as full of bright ideas as ever. Despite the plague, he was building shops and taverns on Leper Island, and he told her he planned to demolish the tavern he had inherited from Bessie Bell and rebuild it twice as big.

Caris guessed that he and Bessie had been lovers—why else would she have left her property to him? But Caris had only herself to blame. She was the one Merthin really wanted, and Bessie had been second best. Both women had known that. All the same, Caris felt jealous and angry when she thought of Merthin in bed with that plump barmaid.

They stopped at noon and rested by a stream. They ate bread, cheese, and apples, the food that all but the wealthiest travelers carried. They gave the horses some grain: grazing was not enough for a mount that had to carry a man or woman all day. When they had eaten, they lay in the sun for a few minutes, but the ground was too cold and damp for sleep, and they soon roused themselves and moved on.

They quickly slipped back into the affectionate intimacy of their youth. Merthin had always been able to make her laugh, and she needed cheering up, with people dying every day in the hospital. She soon forgot to be angry about Bessie.

They were taking a route that had been followed by Kingsbridge monks for hundreds of years, and they stopped for the night at the usual halfway point, the Red Cow Tavern in the small town of Lordsborough. They had roast beef and strong ale for supper.

By this time, Caris was aching for him. The last ten years seemed to have vanished from memory, and she longed to take him in her arms and make love to him the way they used to. But it was not to be. The Red Cow had two bedrooms, one for men and one for women—which was no doubt why it had always been the choice of the monks. Caris and Merthin parted company on the landing, and Caris lay awake, listening to the snores of a knight's wife and the wheezing of a spice-seller, touching herself and wishing the hand between her thighs was Merthin's.

She woke up tired and dispirited, and ate her breakfast porridge mechanically. But Merthin was so happy to be with her that her mood soon lifted. By the time they rode away from Lordsborough, they were talking and laughing as merrily as yesterday.

The second day's journey was through dense woodland, and they saw no other travelers all morning. Their conversation became more personal. She learned more about his time in Florence: how he had met Silvia, and what kind of person she was. Caris wanted to ask: What was it like to make love to her? Was she different from me? How? But she held back, feeling that such questions would trespass on Silvia's privacy, even though Silvia was dead. Anyway, she could guess a lot from Merthin's tone of voice. He had been happy in bed with Silvia, she sensed, even if the relationship had not been as intensely passionate as his with Caris.

The unaccustomed hours on horseback were making her sore, so she was relieved to stop for dinner and get off the pony. When they had eaten, they sat on the ground with their backs to a broad tree trunk, to rest and let their food go down before resuming the journey.

Caris was thinking about Godwyn, and wondering what she would find at St.-John-in-the-Forest, when suddenly she realized that she and Merthin were about to make love. She could not have explained how she knew—they were not even touching—but she had no doubt. She turned to look at him and saw that he sensed it, too. He smiled at her ruefully, and in his eyes she saw ten years of hope and regrets, pain and tears.

He took her hand and kissed her palm, then he put his lips to the soft inside of her wrist, and closed his eyes. "I can feel your pulse," he said quietly.

"You can't tell much from the pulse," she breathed. "You'll have to give me a thorough examination."

He kissed her forehead, and her eyelids, and her nose. "I hope you won't be embarrassed by my seeing your naked body."

"Don't fret—I'm not taking my clothes off in this weather."

They both giggled.

He said: "Perhaps you would be kind enough to lift the skirt of your robe, so that I may proceed with the checkup."

She reached down and took hold of the hem of her dress. She was wearing hose that came up to her knees. She lifted her dress slowly, revealing her ankles, her shins, her knees, and then the white skin of her thighs. She was feeling playful, but in the back of her mind she wondered if he could detect the changes wrought in her body by the last ten years. She had got thinner, yet at the same time her bottom had spread. Her skin was a little less supple and smooth than it had been. Her breasts were not as firm and upright. What would he think? She suppressed the worry and played the game. "Is that sufficient, for medical purposes?"

"Not quite."

"But I'm afraid I'm not wearing underdrawers—such luxuries are considered inappropriate for us nuns."

"We physicians are obliged to be very thorough, no matter how distasteful we find it."

"Oh, dear," she said with a smile. "What a shame. All right, then." Watching his face she slowly lifted her skirt until it was around her waist.

He stared at her body, and she could see that he was breathing harder. "My, my," he said. "This is a very severe case. In fact . . ." He looked up at her face, swallowed, and said: "I can't joke about this anymore."

She put her arms around him and pulled his body to her own, squeezing as hard as she could, clinging to him as if she were saving him from drowning. "Make love to me, Merthin," she said. "Now, quickly."

The priory of St.-John-in-the-Forest looked tranquil in the afternoon light—a sure sign that something was wrong, Caris thought. The little cell was traditionally self-sufficient in food, and was surrounded by fields, moist with rain, that needed plowing and harrowing. But no one was at work.

When they got closer, they saw that the little cemetery next to the church had a row of fresh graves. "It seems the plague may have reached this far," Merthin said.

Caris nodded. "So Godwyn's cowardly escape plan failed." She could not help feeling a glow of vengeful satisfaction.

Merthin said: "I wonder if he himself has fallen victim."

Caris found herself hoping he had, but was too ashamed to say so.

She and Merthin rode around the silent monastery to what was obviously the stable yard. The door was open, and the horses had been let out, and were grazing a patch of meadow around a pond. But no one appeared to help the visitors unsaddle.

They walked through the empty stables into the interior. It was eerily quiet, and Caris wondered if all the monks were dead. They looked into a kitchen, which Caris observed was not as clean as it should be, and a bakery with a cold oven. Their footsteps echoed around the cool gray arcades of the cloisters. Then, approaching the entrance to the church, they met Brother Thomas.

"You found us!" he said. "Thank God."

Caris embraced him. She knew that women's bodies did not present a temptation to Thomas. "I'm glad you're alive," she said.

"I fell ill and got better," he explained.

"Not many survive."

"I know."

"Tell us what happened."

"Godwyn and Philemon planned it well," Thomas said. "There was almost no warning. Godwyn addressed the chapter, and told the story of Abraham and Isaac to show that God sometimes asks us to do things that appear wrong. Then he told us we were leaving that night. Most of the monks were glad to get away from the plague, and those that had misgivings were instructed to remember their vow of obedience."

Caris nodded. "I can imagine. It's not hard to obey orders when they are so strongly in your own self-interest."

"I'm not proud of myself."

Caris touched the stump of his left arm. "I meant no reproof, Thomas."

Merthin said: "All the same, I'm surprised no one leaked the destination."

"That's because Godwyn didn't tell us where we were going. Most of us didn't know even after we arrived—we had to ask the local monks what place this was."

"But the plague caught up with you."

"You've seen the graveyard. All the St. John monks are there except Prior Saul, who is buried in the church. Almost all the Kingsbridge men are dead. A few ran away after the sickness broke out here—God knows what happened to them."

Caris recalled that Thomas had always been close to one particular monk, a sweet-natured man a few years younger than he. Hesitantly she said: "And Brother Matthias?"

"Dead," Thomas said brusquely; then tears came to his eyes, and he looked away, embarrassed.

Caris put a hand on his shoulder. "I'm very sorry."

"So many people have suffered bereavement," he said.

Caris decided it would be kinder not to dwell on Matthias. "What about Godwyn and Philemon?"

"Philemon ran away. Godwyn is alive and well—he hasn't caught it."

"I have a message for Godwyn from the bishop."

"I can imagine."

"You'd better take me to him."

"He's in the church. He set up a bed in a side chapel. He's convinced that's why he hasn't fallen ill. Come with me."

They crossed the cloisters and entered the little church. It smelled more like a dormitory. The wall painting of the Day of Judgment at the east end seemed grimly appropriate now. The nave was strewn with straw and littered with blankets, as if a crowd of people had been sleeping here; but the only person present was Godwyn. He was lying facedown on the dirt floor in front of the altar, his arms stretched out sideways. For a moment she thought he was dead, then she realized this was simply the attitude of extreme penitence.

Thomas said: "You have visitors, Father Prior."

Godwyn remained in position. Caris would have assumed he was putting on a show, but something about his stillness made her think he was sincerely seeking forgiveness.

Then he got slowly to his feet and turned around.

He was pale and thin, Caris saw, and he looked tired and anxious.

"You," he said.

"You've been discovered, Godwyn," she said. She was not going to call him Father. He was a miscreant and she had caught him. She felt deep satisfaction.

He said: "I suppose Tam Hiding betrayed me."

His mind was as sharp as ever, Caris noted. "You tried to escape justice, but you failed."

"I have nothing to fear from justice," he said defiantly. "I came here in the hope of saving the lives of my monks. My error was to leave it too late."

"An innocent man doesn't sneak away under cover of night."

"I had to keep my destination secret. It would have defeated my purpose to allow anyone to follow us here."

"You didn't have to steal the cathedral ornaments."

"I didn't steal them. I took them for safekeeping. I shall return them to their rightful place when it's safe to do so."

"So why did you tell no one that you were taking them?"

"But I did. I wrote to Bishop Henri. Did he not receive my letter?"

Caris felt a growing sense of dismay. Surely Godwyn could not wriggle out of this? "Certainly not," she said. "No letter was received, and I don't believe one was sent."

"Perhaps the messenger died of the plague before he could deliver it."

"And what was the name of this vanishing messenger?"

"I never knew it. Philemon hired the man."

"And Philemon is not here—how convenient," she said sarcastically. "Well, you can say what you like, but Bishop Henri accuses you of stealing the treasure, and he has sent me here to demand its return. I have a letter ordering you to hand everything to me, immediately."

"That's won't be necessary. I'll take it to him myself."

"That is not what your bishop commands you to do."

"I'll be the judge of what's best."

"Your refusal is proof of theft."

"I'm sure I can persuade Bishop Henri to see things differently."

The trouble was, Caris thought despairingly, that Godwyn might well do just that. He could be very plausible, and Henri, like most bishops, would generally avoid confrontation if he could. She felt as if the victory trophy were slipping through her hands.

Godwyn felt he had turned the tables on her, and he permitted himself a small smile of satisfaction. That infuriated her, but she had no more to say. All she could do now was return and tell Bishop Henri what had happened.

She could hardly believe it. Would Godwyn really return to Kingsbridge and resume his position as prior? How could he possibly hold his head up in Kingsbridge Cathedral? After all he had done to damage the priory, the town, and the church? Even if the bishop accepted him, surely the townspeople would riot? The prospect was dire, yet stranger things had happened. Was there no justice?

She stared at him. The look of triumph on his face must be matched, she supposed, by the defeat on her own.

Then she saw something that turned the tables yet again.

On Godwyn's upper lip, just below his left nostril, there was a trickle of blood.

Next morning, Godwyn did not get out of bed.

Caris put on her linen mask and nursed him. She bathed his face in rose water and gave him diluted wine whenever he asked for a drink. Every time she touched him, she washed her hands in vinegar.

Other than Godwyn and Thomas, there were only two monks left, both Kingsbridge novices. They, too, were dying of the plague; so she brought them down from the dormitory to lie in the church, and she took care of them as well, flitting around the dim-lit nave like a shade as she went from one dying man to the next.

She asked Godwyn where the cathedral treasures were, but he refused to say.

Merthin and Thomas searched the priory. The first place they looked was under the altar. Something had been buried there, quite recently, they could tell by the looseness of the earth. However, when they made a hole—Thomas digging surprisingly well with one hand—they found nothing. Whatever had been buried there had since been removed.

They checked every echoing room in the deserted monastery, and even looked in the cold bakery oven and the dry brewery tanks, but they found no jewels, relics, or charters.

After the first night, Thomas quietly vacated the dormitory—without being asked—and left Merthin and Caris to sleep there alone. He made no comment, not even a nudge or a wink. Grateful for his discreet connivance, they huddled under a pile of blankets and made love. Afterward, Caris lay awake. An owl lived somewhere in the roof, and she heard its nocturnal hooting, and occasionally the scream of a small animal caught in its talons. She wondered if she would become pregnant. She did not want to give up her vocation—but she could not resist the temptation of lying in Merthin's arms. So she just refused to think about the future.

On the third day, as Caris, Merthin, and Thomas ate dinner in the refectory, Thomas said: "When Godwyn asks for a drink, refuse to give it to him until he's told you where he hid the treasure."

Caris considered that. It would be perfectly just. But it would also amount to torture. "I can't do that," she said. "I know he deserves it, but all the same I can't do it. If a sick man asks for a drink I must give it to him. That's more important than all the jeweled ornaments in Christendom."

"You don't owe him compassion—he never showed any to you."

"I've turned the church into a hospital, but I won't let it become a torture chamber."

Thomas looked as if he might be inclined to argue further, but Merthin dissuaded him with a shake of the head. "Think, Thomas," he said. "When did you last see this stuff?"

"The night we arrived," Thomas said. "It was in leather bags and boxes on a couple of horses. It was unloaded at the same time as everything else, and I think it was carried into the church."

"Then what happened to it?"

"I never saw it again. But after Evensong, when we all went to supper, I noticed that Godwyn and Philemon stayed behind in the church with two other monks, Juley and John."

Caris said: "Let me guess: Juley and John were both young and strong."

"Yes."

Merthin said: "So that's probably when they buried the treasure under the altar. But when did they dig it up?"

"It had to be when nobody was in the church, and they could be sure of that only at mealtimes."

"Were they absent from any other meals?"

"Several, probably. Godwyn and Philemon always acted as if the rules didn't really apply to them. Their missing meals and services wasn't unusual enough for me to remember every instance."

Caris said: "Do you recall Juley and John being absent a second time? Godwyn and Philemon would have needed help again."

"Not necessarily," Merthin said. "It's much easier to reexcavate ground that has already been loosened. Godwyn is forty-three and Philemon is only thirty-four. They could have done it without help, if they really wanted to."

That night, Godwyn began to rave. Some of the time he seemed to be quoting from the Bible, sometimes preaching, and sometimes making excuses. Caris listened for a while, hoping for clues. "Great Babylon is fallen, and all the nations have drunk of the wrath of her fornication; and out of the throne proceeded fire, and thunder; and all the merchants of the earth shall weep. Repent, oh, repent, all ye who have committed fornication with the mother of harlots! It was all done for a higher purpose, all done for the glory of God, because the end justifies the means. Give me something to drink, for the love of God." The apocalyptic tone of his delirium was probably suggested by the wall painting, with its graphic depiction of the tortures of Hell.

Caris held a cup to his mouth. "Where are the cathedral ornaments, Godwyn?"

"I saw seven golden candlesticks, all covered with pearls, and precious stones, and wrapped in fine linen, and purple, and scarlet, and lying in an ark made of cedarwood, and sandalwood, and silver. I saw a woman riding upon a scarlet beast, having seven heads and ten horns, and full of the names of blasphemy." The nave rang with the echoes of his ranting.

On the following day the two novices died. That afternoon, Thomas and Merthin buried them in the graveyard to the north of the priory. It was a cold, damp day, but they sweated with the effort of digging. Thomas performed the funeral service. Caris stood at the grave with Merthin. When everything was falling apart, the rituals helped to maintain a semblance of normality. Around them were the new graves of all the other monks except Godwyn and Saul. Saul's body lay under the little chancel of the church, an honor reserved for the most highly regarded priors.

Afterward Caris came back into the church and stared at Saul's grave in the chancel. That part of the church was paved with flagstones. Obviously the flags had been lifted so that the grave could be dug. When they had been put back, one of the stones had been polished and carved with an inscription.

It was hard to concentrate, with Godwyn in the corner raving about beasts with seven heads.

Merthin noticed her thoughtful look and followed her gaze. He immediately guessed what she was thinking. In a horrified voice he said: "Surely Godwyn can't have hidden the treasure in Saul Whitehead's coffin?"

"It's hard to imagine monks desecrating a tomb," she said. "On the other hand, the ornaments wouldn't have had to leave the church."

Thomas said: "Saul died a week before you arrived. Philemon disappeared two days later."

"So Philemon could have helped Godwyn dig up the grave."

"Yes."

The three of them looked at one another, trying to ignore the mad mumblings of Godwyn.

"There's only one way to find out," Merthin said.

Merthin and Thomas got their wooden shovels. They lifted the memorial slab and the paving stones around it, and started digging.

Thomas had developed a one-handed technique. He pushed the shovel into the earth with his good arm, tilted it, then ran his hand all the way down the shaft to the blade and lifted it. His right arm had become very muscular as a result of this kind of adaptation.

Nevertheless, it took a long time. Many graves were shallow nowadays, but for Prior Saul they had dug down the full six feet. Night was falling outside, and Caris fetched candles. The devils in the wall painting seemed to move in the flickering light.

Both Thomas and Merthin were standing in the hole, with only their heads visible above floor level, when Merthin said: "Wait. Something's here."

Caris saw some muddy white material that looked like the oiled linen sometimes used for shrouds. "You've found the body," she said.

Thomas said: "But where's the coffin?"

"Was he buried in a box?" Coffins were only for the elite: poor people were interred in a shroud.

Thomas said: "Saul was buried in a coffin—I saw it. There's plenty of wood here in the middle of the forest. All the monks were put in coffins, right up until Brother Silas fell ill—he was the carpenter."

"Wait," said Merthin. He pushed his shovel through the earth at the feet of the shroud and lifted a shovelful. Then he tapped with the blade, and Caris heard the dull thud of wood on wood. "Here's the coffin, underneath," he said.

Thomas said: "How did the body get out?"

Caris felt a shiver of fear.

Over in the corner, Godwyn raised his voice. "And he shall be tormented with fire and brimstone in the sight of the holy angels, and the smoke of his torment will rise up forever and ever."

Thomas said to Caris: "Can't you shut him up?"

"I've got no drugs with me."

Merthin said: "There's nothing supernatural here. My guess is that Godwyn and Philemon took the body out—and filled the coffin with their stolen treasures."

Thomas pulled himself together. "We'd better look in the coffin, then."

First they had to move the shrouded corpse. Merthin and Thomas bent down, grabbed it by the shoulders and knees, and lifted it. When they had raised it to the level of their shoulders, the only way they could get it farther was to toss it out onto the floor. It landed with a thump. They both looked fearful. Even Caris, who did not believe much of what she was told about the spirit world, felt frightened by what they were doing, and found herself glancing nervously over her shoulder into the shadowed corners of the church.

Merthin cleared the earth from the top of the coffin while Thomas went to fetch an iron bar. Then they lifted the lid of the casket.

Caris held two candles over the grave so that they could see better.

Inside the coffin was another shrouded body.

Thomas said: "This is very strange!" His voice was distinctly shaky.

"Let's just think sensibly about this," Merthin said. He was sounding calm and collected, but Caris—who knew him extraordinarily well—could tell that his composure was taking a big effort. "Who is in the coffin?" he said. "Let's look."

He bent down, grabbed the shroud in two hands, and ripped it open along the stitched seam at the head. The corpse was a week dead, and there was a bad smell, but it had not deteriorated much in the cold ground under the unheated church. Even in the unsteady light from Caris's candles, there was no doubt about the identity of the dead man: the head was fringed with distinctively ash blond hair.

Thomas said: "That's Saul Whitehead."

"In his rightful coffin," said Merthin.

Caris said: "So who is the other corpse?"

Merthin closed the shroud around Saul's blond head and replaced the coffin lid.

Caris knelt by the other corpse. She had dealt with many dead bodies, but she had never brought one up from its grave, and her hands were shaky. Nevertheless she opened the shroud and exposed the face. To her horror, the eyes were open and seemed to be staring. She forced herself to close the cold eyelids.

It was a big young monk she did not recognize. Thomas stood on tiptoe to look out of the grave and said: "That's Brother Jonquil. He died the day after Prior Saul."

Caris said: "And he was buried . . . ?"

"In the cemetery . . . we all thought."

"In a coffin?"

"Yes."

"Except that he's here."

"His coffin weighed enough," Thomas said. "I helped carry it . . ."

Merthin said: "I see what happened. Jonquil lay here in the church, in his coffin, prior to burial. While the other monks were at dinner, Godwyn and Philemon opened the coffin and took the body out. They dug up Saul's tomb and tumbled Jonquil in on top of Saul's coffin. They closed the grave. Then they put the cathedral treasures in Jonquil's coffin and closed it again."

Thomas said: "So we have to dig up Jonquil's grave."

Caris glanced up at the windows of the church. They were dark. Night had fallen while they were opening the tomb of Saul. "We could leave it until morning," she said.

Both men were silent for a long moment, then Thomas said: "Let's get it over with."

Caris went to the kitchen, picked two branches from the firewood pile, lit them at the fire, then returned to the church.

As the three of them went outside, they heard Godwyn cry: "And the winepress of the wrath of God was trodden outside the city, and the grapes gave forth blood, and the land was flooded to the height of the horses' bridles."

Caris shuddered. It was a vile image from the Revelation of St. John the Divine, and it disgusted her. She tried to put it out of her mind.

They walked quickly to the cemetery in the red light of the torches. Caris was relieved to be away from that wall painting and out of earshot of Godwyn's mad ravings. They found Jonquil's headstone and began to excavate.

The two men had already dug two graves for the novices and re-dug Saul's. This was their fourth since dinnertime. Merthin looked tired and

Thomas was sweating heavily. But they worked on doggedly. Slowly the hole got deeper and the pile of earth beside it rose higher. At last a shovel struck wood.

Caris passed Merthin the crowbar, then she knelt on the edge of the pit, holding both torches. Merthin prized open the coffin lid and threw it out of the grave.

There was no corpse in the box.

Instead it was packed tightly with bags and boxes. Merthin opened a leather bag and pulled out a jeweled crucifix. "Hallelujah," he said wearily.

Thomas opened a box to reveal a row of parchment rolls, packed tightly together like fish in a crate: the charters.

Caris felt a weight of worry roll off her shoulders. She had got the nunnery charters back.

Thomas put his hand into another bag. When he looked at what he had got hold of, it was a skull. He gave a fearful cry and dropped it.

"Saint Adolphus," Merthin said in a matter-of-fact voice. "Pilgrims travel hundreds of miles to touch the box that holds his bones." He picked up the skull. "Lucky us," he said, and put it back into the bag.

"If I may make a suggestion?" said Caris. "We have to carry this stuff all the way back to Kingsbridge in a cart. Why don't we leave it in the coffin? It's packed already, and the casket may serve to deter thieves."

"Good idea," Merthin said. "We'll just lift the coffin out of the grave."

Thomas returned to the priory and brought ropes, and they lifted the coffin out of the hole. They refixed the lid, then tied the ropes around the box in order to drag it across the ground and into the church.

As they were about to start, they heard a scream.

Caris let out a cry of fear.

They all looked toward the church. A figure was running toward them, eyes staring, blood coming from its mouth. Caris suffered a moment of utter terror when she suddenly believed every foolish superstition she had ever heard about spirits. Then she realized she was looking at Godwyn. Somehow he had found the strength to rise from his deathbed. He had staggered out of the church and seen their torches, and now in his madness he was running toward them.

They watched him, transfixed.

He stopped and looked at the coffin, then at the empty grave, and in the restless torchlight Caris thought she saw a glimmer of understanding on his grimacing face. Then he seemed to lose his strength, and he collapsed.

He fell on the mound of earth beside Jonquil's empty grave, then he rolled down the mound and into the pit.

They all stepped forward and looked into the grave.

Godwyn lay there on his back, looking up at them with open, sightless eyes.

66

As soon as Caris got back to Kingsbridge, she decided to leave again. The image of St.-John-in-the-Forest that stayed with her was not the graveyard, or the corpses Merthin and Thomas had dug up, but the neat fields with no one tilling them. As she rode home, with Merthin beside her and Thomas driving the cart, she saw a lot of land in the same state, and she foresaw a crisis.

The monks and nuns got most of their income from rents. Serfs grew crops and raised livestock on land belonging to the priory and, instead of paying a knight or an earl for the privilege, they paid the prior or prioress. Traditionally they brought a portion of their harvest to the cathedral—a dozen sacks of flour, three sheep, a calf, a cartload of onions—but nowadays most people paid cash.

If no one was cultivating the land, there would be no rent paid, obviously. And then what would the nuns eat?

The cathedral ornaments, the money, and the charters she had retrieved from St.-John-in-the-Forest were stashed safely in the new, secret treasury that Mother Cecilia had commissioned Jeremiah to build in a place where no one could easily find it. All the ornaments had been found except one, a gold candlestick given by the chandlers' guild, the group that represented the wax candle makers of Kingsbridge. That had disappeared.

Caris held a triumphant Sunday service featuring the rescued bones of the saint. She put Thomas in charge of the boys in the orphanage—some of them were old enough to require a strong male presence. She herself moved into the prior's palace, thinking with pleasure how appalled the late Godwyn would be that it was occupied by a woman. Then, as soon as she had dealt with these details, she went to Outhenby.

The Vale of Outhen was a fertile valley of heavy clay soil a day's journey from Kingsbridge. It had been given to the nuns a hundred years ago by a wicked old knight making a last-gasp attempt to win forgiveness for a lifetime of sins. Five villages stood at intervals along the banks of the River Outhen. On either side the great fields covered the land and the lower slopes of the hills.

The fields were divided into strips allocated to different families. As she had feared, many strips were not being cultivated. The plague had changed everything, but no one had had the brains—or perhaps the courage—to reorganize farming in the light of the new circumstances. Caris herself would have to do that. She had a rough idea of what was required, and she would work out the details as she went along.

With her was Sister Joan, a young nun recently out of her novitiate. Joan was a bright girl who reminded Caris of herself ten years ago—not in appearance, for she was black-haired and blue-eyed, but in her questioning mind and brisk skepticism.

They rode to the largest of the villages, Outhenby. The bailiff for the whole valley, Will, lived there in a large timber house next to the church. He was not at home, but they found him in the farthest field, sowing oats; a big, slow-moving man. The next strip had been left fallow, and wild grass and weeds were poking up, grazed by a few sheep.

Will Bailiff visited the priory several times a year, usually to bring the rents from the villages, so he knew Caris; but he was disconcerted to meet her on his home ground. "Sister Caris!" he exclaimed when he recognized her. "What brings you here?"

"I'm Mother Caris now, Will, and I've come to make sure the nuns' lands are being properly husbanded."

"Ah." He shook his head. "We're doing our best, as you see, but we've lost so many men that it's very, very difficult."

Bailiffs always said that times were difficult—but in this case it was true.

Caris dismounted. "Walk with me and tell me about it." A few hundred yards away, on the gentle slope of a hillside, she saw a peasant plowing with a team of eight oxen. He halted the team and looked at her curiously, so she headed that way.

Will began to recover his composure. Walking alongside her, he said: "A woman of God, such as yourself, can't be expected to know much about tilling the soil, of course; but I'll do my best to explain the finer points."

"That would be kind." She was used to being condescended to by men of Will's type. She had found that it was best not to challenge them, but rather to lull them into a false sense of security. That way, she learned more. "How many men have you lost to the plague?"

"Oh, many men."

"How many?"

"Well, now, let me see, there was William Jones, and his two sons; then Richard Carpenter, and his wife—"

"I don't need to know their names," she said, controlling her exasperation. "How many, roughly speaking?"

"I'd have to think about that."

They had reached the plow. Managing the eight-ox team was a skilled job, and plowmen were often among the more intelligent villagers. Caris addressed the young man. "How many people in Outhenby have died of the plague?"

"About two hundred, I'd say."

Caris studied him. He was short but muscular, with a bushy blond beard. He had a cocksure look, as young men often did. "Who are you?" she asked.

"My name is Harry, and my father was Richard, Holy Sister."

"I am Mother Caris. How do you work out that figure of two hundred?"

"There's forty-two dead here in Outhenby, by my reckoning. It's just as bad in Ham and Shortacre, making about a hundred and twenty. Longwater escaped completely, but every soul in Oldchurch is dead but old Roger Breton, which is about eighty people, making two hundred."

She turned to Will. "Out of about how many in the whole valley?"

"Ah, now, let me see . . ."

Harry Plowman said: "A thousand, near enough, before the plague."

Will said: "That's why you see me sowing my own strip, which should be done by laborers—but I have no laborers. They've all died."

Harry said: "Or they've gone to work elsewhere for higher wages."

Caris perked up. "Oh? Who offers higher wages?"

"Some of the wealthier peasants in the next valley," Will said indignantly. "The nobility pay a penny a day, which is what laborers have always got and always should; but there are some people who think they can do as they please."

"But they get their crops sowed, I suppose," Caris said.

"But there's right and wrong, Mother Caris," said Will.

Caris pointed to the fallow strip where the sheep were. "And what about that land? Why has it not been plowed?"

Will said: "That belonged to William Jones. He and his sons died, and his wife went to live with her sister in Shiring."

"Have you looked for a new tenant?"

"Can't get them, Mother."

Harry interjected again. "Not on the old terms, anyhow."

Will glared at him, but Caris said: "What do you mean?"

"Prices have fallen, you see, even though it's spring when corn is usually dear."

Caris nodded. That was how markets worked, everyone knew: if there were fewer buyers, the price fell. "But people must live somehow."

"They don't want to grow wheat and barley and oats—but they have to grow what they're told, at least in this valley. So a man looking for a tenancy would rather go elsewhere."

"And what will he get elsewhere?"

Will interrupted angrily: "They want to do as they please."

Harry answered Caris's question. "They want to be free tenants, paying cash rent, rather than serfs working one day a week on the lord's land; and they want to be able to grow different crops."

"What crops?"

"Hemp, or flax, or apples and pears—things they know they can sell at the market. Maybe something different every year. But that's never been allowed in Outhenby." Harry seemed to recollect himself, and added: "No offense to your holy order, Mother Prioress, nor to Will Bailiff, an honest man as everyone knows."

Caris saw how it was. Bailiffs were always conservative. In good times, it hardly mattered: the old ways sufficed. But this was a crisis.

She assumed her most authoritative manner. "All right, listen carefully, now, Will, and I'll tell you what you're going to do." Will looked startled: he had thought he was being consulted, not commanded. "First, you are to stop plowing the hillsides. It's foolish when we've got good land uncultivated."

"But—"

"Be quiet and listen. Offer every tenant an exchange, acre for acre, good valley bottom instead of hillside."

"Then what will we do with the hillside?"

"Convert it to grazing, cattle on the lower slopes and sheep on the higher. You don't need many men for that, just a few boys to herd them."

"Oh," said Will. It was plain that he wanted to argue, but he could not immediately think of an objection.

Caris went on: "Next, any valley bottomland that is still untenanted should be offered as a free tenancy with cash rent to anyone who will take it on." A free tenancy meant that the tenant was not a serf, and did not have to work on the lord's land, or get his permission to marry or build a house. All he had to do was pay his rent.

"You're doing away with all the old customs."

She pointed at the fallow strip. "The old customs are letting my land go to waste. Can you think of another way to stop this happening?"

"Well," said Will, and there was a long pause; then he shook his head silently.

"Thirdly, offer wages of twopence a day to anyone who will work the land."

"Twopence a day!"

Caris felt she could not rely on Will to implement these changes vigorously. He would drag his feet and invent excuses. She turned to the cocksure plowman. She would make him the champion of her reforms. "Harry, I want you to go to every market in the county over the next few weeks. Spread the word that anyone who is on the move can do well in Outhenby. If there are laborers looking for wages, I want them to come here."

Harry grinned and nodded, though Will still looked a bit dazed.

"I want to see all this good land growing crops this summer," she said. "Is that clear?"

"Yes," said Will. "Thank you, Mother Prioress."

Caris went through all the charters with Sister Joan, making a note of the date and subject of each. She decided to have them copied, one by one—the idea Godwyn had proposed, though he had only pretended to be copying them as a pretext for taking them away from the nuns. But it was a sound notion. The more copies there were, the harder it was for a valuable document to disappear.

She was intrigued by a deed dated 1327 which assigned to the monks the large farm near Lynn, in Norfolk, that they called Lynn Grange. The gift was made on condition the priory took on, as a novice monk, a knight called Sir Thomas Langley.

Caris was taken back to her childhood, and the day she had ventured into the wood with Merthin, Ralph, and Gwenda, and they had seen Thomas receive the wound that had caused him to lose his arm.

She showed the charter to Joan, who shrugged and said: "It's usual for such a gift to be made when someone from a wealthy family becomes a monk."

"But look who the donor is."

Joan looked again. "Queen Isabella!" Isabella was the widow of Edward II and the mother of Edward III. "What's her interest in Kingsbridge?"

"Or in Thomas?" said Caris.

A few days later she had a chance to find out. The bailiff of Lynn Grange, Andrew, came to Kingsbridge on his biannual visit. A Norfolk-born man of over fifty, he had been in charge of the grange ever since it was gifted to the priory. He was now white-haired and plump, which led Caris to believe that the grange continued to prosper despite the plague. Because Norfolk was several days' journey away, the grange paid its dues to the priory in coins, rather than drive cattle or cart produce all that way, and Andrew brought the money in gold nobles, the new coin worth a third of a pound, with an image of King Edward standing on the deck of a ship. When Caris had counted the money and given it to Joan to stash in the new treasury, she said to Andrew: "Why did Queen Isabella give us this grange twenty-two years ago, do you know?"

To her surprise, Andrew's pink face turned pale. He made several false starts at answering, then said: "It's not for me to question Her Majesty's decisions."

"No, indeed," Caris said in a reassuring tone. "I'm just curious about her motive."

"She is a holy woman who has performed many pious acts."

Like murdering her husband, Caris thought; but she said: "However, there must be a reason she named Thomas."

"He petitioned the queen for a favor, like hundreds of others, and she graciously granted it, as great ladies sometimes do."

"Usually when they have some connection with the petitioner."

"No, no, I'm sure there's no connection."

His anxiety made Caris sure he was lying, and just as sure that he would not tell her the truth, so she dropped the subject, and sent Andrew off to have supper in the hospital.

Next morning she was accosted in the cloisters by Brother Thomas, the only monk left in the monastery. Looking angry, he said: "Why did you interrogate Andrew Lynn?"

"Because I was curious," she said, taken aback.

"What are you trying to do?"

"I'm not *trying* to do anything." She was offended by his aggressive manner, but she did not want to quarrel with him. To ease the tension, she sat on the low wall around the edge of the arcade. A spring sun was shining bravely into the quadrangle. She spoke in a conversational tone. "What's this all about?"

Thomas said stiffly: "Why are you investigating me?"

"I'm not," she said. "Calm down. I'm going through all the charters, listing them and having them copied. I came across one that puzzled me."

"You're delving into matters that are none of your business."

She bridled. "I'm the prioress of Kingsbridge, and the acting prior—nothing here is secret from me."

"Well, if you start digging up all that old stuff, you'll regret it, I promise you."

It sounded like a threat, but she decided not to challenge him. She tried a different tack. "Thomas, I thought we were friends. You have no right to forbid me to do anything, and I'm disappointed that you should even try. Don't you trust me?"

"You don't know what you're asking."

"Then enlighten me. What does Queen Isabella have to do with you, me, and Kingsbridge?"

"Nothing. She's an old woman now, living in retirement."

"She's fifty-three. She's deposed one king, and she could probably depose another if she had a mind to. And she has some long-hidden connection with my priory which you are determined to keep from me."

"For your own good."

She ignored that. "Twenty-two years ago someone was trying to kill you. Was it the same person who, having failed to do away with you, paid you off by getting you admitted to the monastery?"

"Andrew is going to go back to Lynn and tell Isabella that you've been asking these questions—do you realize that?"

"Why would she care? Why are people so afraid of you, Thomas?"

"Everything will be answered when I'm dead. None of it will matter then." He turned around and walked away.

The bell rang for dinner. Caris went to the prior's palace, deep in thought. Godwyn's cat, Archbishop, was sitting on the doorstep. It glared at her and she shooed it away. She would not have it in the house.

She had got into the habit of dining every day with Merthin. Traditionally the prior regularly dined with the alderman, though to do so every day was unusual—but these were unusual times. That, at any rate, would have been her excuse, had anyone challenged her; but nobody did. Meanwhile they both looked out eagerly for another excuse to go on a trip so that they could again be alone together.

He came in muddy from his building site on Leper Island. He had stopped asking her to renounce her vows and leave the priory. He seemed content, at least for the moment, to see her every day and hope for future chances to be more intimate.

A priory employee brought them ham stewed with winter greens. When the servant had gone, Caris told Merthin about the charter and Thomas's reaction. "He knows a secret that could damage the old queen if it got out."

"I think that must be right," Merthin said thoughtfully.

"On All Hallows Day in 1327, after I ran away, he caught you, didn't he?"

"Yes. He made me help him bury a letter. I had to swear to keep it secret—until he dies, then I am to dig it up and give it to a priest."

"He told me all my questions would be answered when he died."

"I think the letter is the threat he holds over his enemies. They must know that its contents will be revealed when he dies. So they fear to kill him—in fact they have made sure he remains alive and well by helping him become a monk of Kingsbridge."

"Can it matter, still?"

"Ten years after we buried the letter, I told him I hadn't ever let the secret out, and he said: 'If you had, you'd be dead.' That scared me more than the vow."

"Mother Cecilia told me that Edward II did not die naturally."

"How would she know a thing like that?"

"My uncle Anthony told her. So I presume the secret is that Queen Isabella had her husband murdered."

"Half the country believes that anyway. But if there were proof . . . Did Cecilia say how he was killed?"

Caris thought hard. "No. Now that I think of it, what she said was: 'The old king did not die of a fall.' I asked her if he had been murdered—but she died without answering."

"Still, why put out a false story about his death if not to cover up foul play?"

"And Thomas's letter must somehow prove that there was foul play, and that the queen was in on it."

They finished their dinner in thoughtful silence. In the monastery day, the hour after dinner was for rest or reading. Caris and Merthin usually lingered for a while. Today, however, Merthin was anxious about the angles of the roof timbers being erected in the new tavern, The Bridge, that he was building on Leper Island. They kissed hungrily, but he tore himself away and hurried back to the site. Disappointed, Caris opened a book called *Ars Medica,* a Latin translation of a work by the ancient Greek physician Galen. It was the cornerstone of university medicine, and she was reading it to find out what priests learned at Oxford and Paris; though she had so far found little that would help her.

The maid came back and cleared the table. "Ask Brother Thomas to come and see me, please," Caris said. She wanted to make sure they were still friends despite their abrasive conversation.

Before Thomas arrived, there was a commotion outside. She heard several horses and the kind of shouting that indicated a nobleman wanting attention. A few moments later the door was flung open and in walked Sir Ralph Fitzgerald, lord of Tench.

He looked angry, but Caris pretended not to notice that. "Hello, Ralph," she said as amiably as she could. "This is an unexpected pleasure. Welcome to Kingsbridge."

"Never mind all that," he said rudely. He walked up to where she sat and stood aggressively close. "Do you realize you're ruining the peasantry of the entire county?"

Another figure followed him in and stood by the door, a big man with a small head, and Caris recognized his long-time sidekick, Alan Fernhill. Both were armed with swords and daggers. Caris was acutely aware that she was alone in the palace. She tried to defuse the scene. "Would you like some ham, Ralph? I've just finished dinner."

Ralph was not to be diverted. "You've been stealing my peasants!"

"Peasants, or pheasants?"

Alan Fernhill burst out laughing.

Ralph reddened and looked more dangerous, and Caris wished she had not made that joke. "If you poke fun at me you'll be sorry," he said.

Caris poured ale into a cup. "I'm not laughing at you," she said. "Tell me exactly what's on your mind." She offered him the ale.

Her shaking hand betrayed her fear, but he ignored the cup and wagged his finger at her. "Laborers have been disappearing from my villages—and when I inquire after them, I find they have moved to villages belonging to you, where they get higher wages."

Caris nodded. "If you were selling a horse, and two men wanted to buy it, wouldn't you give it to the one who offered the higher price?"

"That's not the same."

"I think it is. Have some ale."

With a sudden sideswipe of his hand, he knocked the cup from her grasp. It fell to the floor, the ale spilling into the straw. "They're *my* laborers."

Her hand was bruised, but she tried to ignore the pain. She bent down, picked up the cup, and set it on the sideboard. "Not really," she said. "If they're laborers, that means you've never given them any land, so they have the right to go elsewhere."

"I'm still their lord, damn it! And another thing. I offered a tenancy to a free man the other day and he refused it, saying he could get a better bargain from Kingsbridge Priory."

"Same thing, Ralph. I need all the people I can get, so I give them what they want."

"You're a woman, you don't think things through. You can't see that it will all end with everyone paying more for the same peasants."

"Not necessarily. Higher wages might attract some of those who at present do no work at all—outlaws, for example, or those vagabonds who go around living off what they find in plague-emptied villages. And some who are now laborers might become tenants, and work harder because they're cultivating their own land."

He banged the table with his fist, and she blinked at the sudden noise. "You've no right to change the old ways!"

"I think I have."

He grabbed the front of her robe. "Well, I'm not putting up with it!"

"Take your hands off me, you clumsy oaf," she said.

At that moment, Brother Thomas came in. "You sent for me—what the devil is going on here?"

He stepped smartly across the room, and Ralph let go of Caris's robe as if it had suddenly caught fire. Thomas had no weapons and only one arm, but he had got the better of Ralph once before; and Ralph was scared of him.

Ralph took a step back, then realized he had revealed his fear, and looked ashamed. "We're done here!" he said loudly, and turned to the door.

Caris said: "What I'm doing in Outhenby and elsewhere is perfectly legitimate, Ralph."

"It's interfering with the natural order!" he said.

"There's no law against it."

Alan opened the door for his master.

"You wait and see," said Ralph, and he went out.

67

In March that year, 1349, Gwenda and Wulfric went with Nathan Reeve to the midweek market at the small town of Northwood.

They were working for Sir Ralph now. Gwenda and Wulfric had escaped the plague, so far, but several of Ralph's laborers had died of it, so he needed help; and Nate, the bailiff of Wigleigh, had offered to take them on. He could afford to pay normal wages, whereas Perkin had been giving them nothing more than their food.

As soon as they announced they were going to work for Ralph, Perkin discovered that he could now afford to pay them normal wages—but he was too late.

On this day they took a cartload of logs from Ralph's forest to sell in Northwood, a town that had had a timber market since time immemorial. The boys, Sam and David, went with them: there was no one else to look after them. Gwenda did not trust her father, and her mother had died two years ago. Wulfric's parents were long dead.

Several other Wigleigh folk were at the market. Father Gaspard was buying seeds for his vegetable garden, and Gwenda's father, Joby, was selling freshly killed rabbits.

Nate, the bailiff, was a stunted man with a twisted back, and he could not lift logs. He dealt with customers while Wulfric and Gwenda did the lifting. At midday he gave them a penny to buy their dinner at the Old Oak, one of the taverns around the square. They got bacon boiled with leeks and shared it with the boys. David, at eight years of age, still had a child's appetite, but Sam was a fast-growing ten and perpetually hungry.

While they were eating, they overheard a conversation that caught Gwenda's attention.

There was a group of young men standing in a corner, drinking large tankards of ale. They were all poorly dressed, except one with a bushy blond beard who had the superior clothes of a prosperous peasant or a village craftsman: leather trousers, good boots, and a new hat. The sentence that caused Gwenda to prick up her ears was: "We pay twopence a day for laborers at Outhenby."

She listened hard, trying to learn more, but caught only scattered words. She had heard that some employers were offering more than the traditional penny a day, because of the shortage of workers caused by the plague. She had hesitated to believe such stories, which sounded too good to be true.

She said nothing for the moment to Wulfric, who had not heard the magic words, but her heart beat faster. She and her family had endured so many years of poverty. Was it possible that life might get better for them?

She had to find out more.

When they had eaten, they sat on a bench outside, watching the boys and some other children running around the broad trunk of the tree that gave the tavern its name. "Wulfric," she said quietly. "What if we could earn twopence a day—each?"

"How?"

"By going to Outhenby." She told him what she had overheard. "It could be the beginning of a new life for us," she finished.

"Am I never to get back my father's lands, then?"

She could have hit him with a stick. Did he really still think that was going to happen? How foolish could he be?

She tried to make her voice as gentle as possible. "It's twelve years since you were disinherited," she said. "In that time Ralph has become more and more powerful. And there's never been the least sign that he might mellow toward you. What do *you* think the chances are?"

He did not answer that question. "Where would we live?"

"They must have houses in Outhenby."

"But will Ralph let us go?"

"He can't stop us. We're laborers, not serfs. You know that."

"But does Ralph know it?"

"Let's not give him the chance to object."

"How could we manage that?"

"Well . . ." She had not thought this through, but now she saw that it would have to be done precipitately. "We could leave today, from here."

It was a scary thought. They had both lived their entire lives in Wigleigh. Wulfric had never even moved house. Now they were contemplating going to live in a village they had never seen without even going back to say good-bye.

But Wulfric was worrying about something else. He pointed at the hunchbacked bailiff, crossing the square to the chandler's shop. "What would Nathan say?"

"We won't tell him what we're planning. We'll give him some story—say we want to stay here overnight, for some reason, and return home tomorrow. That way, nobody will know where we are. And we'll never go back to Wigleigh."

"Never go back," Wulfric said despondently.

Gwenda controlled her impatience. She knew her husband. Once Wulfric was set on a course he was unstoppable, but he took a long time to decide. He would come around to this idea eventually. He was not closed-minded, just cautious and deliberate. He hated to make decisions in a rush—whereas she thought it was the only way.

The young man with the blond beard came out of the Old Oak. Gwenda looked around: none of the Wigleigh folk was in sight. She stood up and accosted the man. "Did I hear you say something about twopence a day for laborers?" she said.

"That's right, mistress," he replied. "In the Vale of Outhenby, just half a day southwest of here. We need all we can get."

"Who are you?"

"I'm the plowman of Outhenby. My name is Harry."

Outhenby must be a large and prosperous village, to have a plowman all of its own, Gwenda reasoned. Most plowmen worked for a group of villages. "And who is lord of the manor?"

"The prioress of Kingsbridge."

"Caris!" That was wonderful news. Caris could be trusted. Gwenda's spirits lifted further.

"Yes, she is the current prioress," Harry said. "A very determined woman."

"I know."

"She wants her fields cultivated so that she can feed the sisters, and she's not listening to excuses."

"Do you have houses at Outhenby for laborers to live in? With their families?"

"Plenty, unfortunately. We've lost many people to the plague."

"You said it was southwest of here."

"Take the southerly road to Badford, then follow the Outhen upstream."

Caution returned to Gwenda. "I'm not going," she said quickly.

"Ah. Of course." He did not believe her.

"I was really asking on behalf of a friend." She turned away.

"Well, tell your friend to come as soon as he can—we've got spring plowing and sowing to finish yet."

"All right."

She felt slightly dizzy, as if she had taken a draft of strong wine. Twopence a day—working for Caris—and miles away from Ralph, Perkin, and flirty Annet! It was a dream.

She sat back down beside Wulfric. "Did you hear all that?" she asked him.

"Yes," he said. He pointed to a figure standing by the tavern door. "And so did he."

Gwenda looked. It was her father.

ᔕ

"Put that horse in the traces," Nate said to Wulfric around mid-afternoon. "It's time to go home."

Wulfric said: "We'll be needing our wages for the week so far."

"You'll be paid on Saturday as usual," Nate said dismissively. "Hitch that nag."

Wulfric did not move toward the horse. "I'll trouble you to pay me today," he insisted. "I know you've got the money, you've sold all that timber."

Nate turned and looked directly at him. "Why should you be paid early?" he said irritably.

"Because I shan't be returning to Wigleigh with you tonight."

Nate was taken aback. "Why not?"

Gwenda took over. "We're going to Melcombe," she said.

"What?" Nate was outraged. "People like you have no business traveling to Melcombe!"

"We met a fisherman who needs crew for twopence a day." Gwenda had worked out this story to throw any pursuit off the scent.

Wulfric added: "Our respects to Sir Ralph, and may God be with him in the future."

Gwenda added: "But we don't expect to see him ever again." She said it just to hear the sweet sound of it: never to see Ralph again.

Nathan said indignantly: "He may not wish you to leave!"

"We're not serfs, we have no land. Ralph cannot forbid us."

"You're the son of a serf," Nathan said to Wulfric.

"But Ralph denied me my inheritance," Wulfric replied. "He cannot now demand my fealty."

"It's a dangerous thing for a poor man to stand on his rights."

"That's true," Wulfric conceded. "But I'm doing it, all the same."

Nate was beaten. "You shall hear more of this," he said.

"Would you like me to put the horse to the cart?"

Nate scowled. He could not do it himself. Because of his back, he had difficulty with complicated physical tasks, and the horse was taller than he. "Yes, of course," he said.

"I'll be glad to. Would you kindly pay me first?"

Looking furious, Nate took out his purse and counted six silver pennies.

Gwenda took the money and Wulfric hitched up the horse.

Nate drove away without another word.

"Well!" said Gwenda. "That's done." She looked at Wulfric. He was smiling broadly. She asked him: "What is it?"

"I don't know," he said. "I feel as if I've been wearing a collar for years, and suddenly it's been taken off."

"Good." That was how she wanted him to feel. "Now let's find a place to stay the night."

The Old Oak was in a prime position in the market square, and charged top prices. They walked around the little town looking for somewhere cheaper. Eventually they went into the Gate House, where Gwenda negotiated accommodation for the four of them—supper, a mattress on the floor, and breakfast—for a penny. The boys would need a decent night's sleep and some breakfast if they were to walk all morning.

She could hardly sleep for excitement. She was also worried. What was she taking her family to? She had only the word of one man, a stranger, for what they would find when they reached Outhenby. She really ought to have sought confirmation before committing herself.

But she and Wulfric had been stuck in a hole for ten years, and Harry Plowman of Outhenby was the first person to offer them a way out of it.

The breakfast was meager: thin porridge and watery cider. Gwenda bought a big loaf of new bread for them to eat on the road, and Wulfric filled his leather flask with cold water from a well. They passed through the city gate an hour after sunrise and set off on the road south.

As they walked, she thought about Joby, her father. As soon as he learned that she had not returned to Wigleigh, he would remember the conversation he had overheard, and he would guess she had gone to Outhenby. He would not be fooled by the story about Melcombe: he was an accomplished deceiver himself, too experienced to be taken in by a simple ruse. But would anyone think to ask him where she had gone? Everyone knew she never spoke to her father. And, if they did ask him, would he blurt out what he suspected? Or would some vestige of paternal feeling cause him to protect her?

There was nothing she could do about it, so she put him out of her mind.

It was good weather for traveling. The ground was soft with recent rain, and there was no dust; but today was a dry day with fitful sunshine, neither cold nor hot. The boys quickly grew tired, especially David, the younger, but Wulfric was good at distracting them with songs and rhymes, quizzing them about the names of trees and plants, playing number games and telling stories.

Gwenda could hardly believe what they had done. This time yesterday, it had looked as if their life would never change: hard work, poverty, and frustrated aspirations would be their lot for ever. Now they were on the road to a new life.

She thought of the house where she had lived with Wulfric for ten years. She had not left much behind: a few cooking pots, a stack of newly chopped firewood, half a ham, and four blankets. She had no clothes other than what she was wearing, and neither did Wulfric or the boys; no jewelry, ribbons, gloves, or combs. Ten years ago, Wulfric had had chickens and pigs in his yard, but they had gradually been eaten or sold during the years of penury. Their meager possessions could be replaced with a week's wages at the promised Outhenby rates.

In accordance with Harry's directions they took the road south to a muddy ford across the Outhen, then turned west and followed the river upstream. As they progressed, the river narrowed, until the land funneled between two ranges of hills. "Good, fertile soil," Wulfric said. "It'll need the heavy plow, though."

At noon they came to a large village with a stone church. They went to the door of a timber manor house next to the church. With trepidation, Gwenda knocked. Was she about to be told that Harry Plowman did not know what he was talking about, and there was no work here? Had she made her family walk half a day for nothing? How humiliating it would be to have to return to Wigleigh and beg to be taken on again by Nate Reeve.

A gray-haired woman came to the door. She looked at Gwenda with the suspicious glare that villagers everywhere gave to strangers. "Yes?"

"Good day, mistress," Gwenda said. "Is this Outhenby?"

"It is."

"We're laborers looking for work. Harry Plowman told us to come here."

"Did he, now?"

Was there something wrong, Gwenda wondered, or was this woman just a grumpy old cow? She almost asked the question out loud. Stopping herself, she said: "Does Harry live at this house?"

"Certainly not," the woman replied. "He's just a plowman. This is the bailiff's house."

Some conflict between bailiff and plowman, Gwenda guessed. "Perhaps we should see the bailiff, then."

"He's not here."

Patiently, Gwenda said: "Would you be kind enough to tell us where we might find him?"

The woman pointed across the valley. "North Field."

Gwenda turned to look in the direction indicated. When she turned back, the woman had disappeared into the house.

Wulfric said: "She didn't seem pleased to see us."

"Old women hate change," Gwenda commented. "Let's find this bailiff."

"The boys are tired."

"They can rest soon."

They set off across the fields. There was plenty of activity on the strips. Children were picking stones off plowed land, women were sowing seeds, and men were carting manure. Gwenda could see the ox team in the distance, eight mighty beasts patiently dragging the plow through the wet, heavy soil.

They came upon a group of men and women trying to move a horse-drawn harrow that had got stuck in a ditch. Gwenda and Wulfric joined in pushing it out. Wulfric's broad back made the difference, and the harrow was freed.

All the villagers turned and looked at Wulfric. A tall man with an old burn mark disfiguring one side of his face said amiably: "You're a useful fellow—who are you?"

"I'm Wulfric, and my wife is Gwenda. We're laborers looking for work."

"You're just what we need, Wulfric," the man said. "I'm Carl Shaftesbury." He stuck out his hand to shake. "Welcome to Outhenby."

Ralph came eight days later.

Wulfric and Gwenda had moved into a small, well-built house with a stone chimney and an upstairs bedroom where they could sleep separately from the boys. They got a wary reception from the older, more conservative villagers—notably Will Bailiff and his wife, Vi, who had been so rude to them on the day they arrived. But Harry Plowman and the younger set were excited by the changes and glad to have help in the fields.

They were paid twopence a day, as promised, and Gwenda looked forward eagerly to the end of their first full week, when they each got twelve pence—a shilling!—double the highest sum they had ever earned. What would they do with all that money?

Neither Wulfric nor Gwenda had worked anywhere but Wigleigh, and they were surprised to find that not all villages were the same. The ultimate authority here was the prioress of Kingsbridge, and that made a difference. Ralph's rule was personal and arbitrary: appealing to him was hazardous. By contrast, Outhenby folk seemed to know what the prioress would want in most situations, and they could settle disputes by figuring out what she would say if asked to adjudicate.

A mild disagreement of this kind was going on when Ralph came.

They were all walking home from the fields at sundown, the adults work-weary, the children running on ahead, and Harry Plowman bringing up the rear with the unharnessed oxen. Carl Shaftesbury, the man with the burned face, who was a newcomer like Gwenda and Wulfric, had caught three eels at dawn for his family's supper, as it was Friday. The question was whether laborers had the same right as tenants to take fish from the Outhen River on fast days. Harry Plowman said the privilege extended to all Outhenby residents. Vi Bailiff said that tenants owed customary dues to the landlord, which laborers did not, and those who had extra duties should have extra privileges.

Will Bailiff was called upon for a decision, and he ruled against his wife. "I believe the mother prioress would say that if the church wishes people to eat fish, then fish must be provided for them to eat," he said; and that was accepted by everyone.

Looking toward the village, Gwenda saw two horsemen.

A cold wind gusted suddenly.

The visitors were half a mile away across the fields, and heading for the houses at an angle to the path the villagers were taking. She could tell they were men-at-arms. They had big horses, and their clothes looked bulky—men of violence generally wore heavily padded coats. She nudged Wulfric.

"I've seen them," he said grimly.

Such men had no casual reason to come to a village. They despised the people who grew the crops and cared for the livestock. They normally visited only to take from the peasants those things they were too proud to provide for themselves, bread and meat and drink. Their view of what they were entitled to, or how much they should pay, always differed from that of the peasants; so there was invariably trouble.

Within the next couple of minutes all the villagers saw them, and the group went quiet. Gwenda noticed that Harry turned the oxen slightly and headed for the far end of the village, though she could not immediately guess why.

Gwenda felt sure the two men had come to find runaway laborers. She found herself praying they would turn out to be the former employers of Carl Shaftesbury or one of the other newcomers. However, as the villagers came closer to the horsemen she recognized Ralph Fitzgerald and Alan Fernhill, and her heart sank.

This was the moment she had dreaded. She had known there was a chance Ralph would find out where they had gone: her father could make a good guess, and he could not be relied upon to keep his mouth shut. And although Ralph had no right to take them back, he was a knight and a nobleman, and such people generally did as they pleased.

It was too late to run. The group was walking along a path between broad plowed fields: if some of them broke away and fled, Ralph and Alan would immediately see them and give chase; and then Gwenda and her family would lose whatever protection they might gain from being with other villagers. They were trapped in the open.

She called to her boys: "Sam! David! Come here!"

They did not hear, or did not want to, and they ran on. Gwenda went after them, but they thought it was a game, and tried to outrun her. They were almost at the village now, and she found she was too tired to catch them. Almost in tears, she shouted: "Come back!"

Wulfric took over. He ran past her and easily caught up with David. He scooped the boy up in his arms. But he was too late to catch Sam, who ran laughing in among the scattered houses.

The horsemen were reined in by the church. As Sam ran toward them, Ralph nudged his horse forward, then leaned down from the saddle and picked the boy up by his shirt. Sam gave a shout of fright.

Gwenda screamed.

Ralph sat the boy on his horse's wither.

Wulfric, carrying David, came to a stop in front of Ralph.

Ralph said: "Your son, I presume."

Gwenda was appalled. She was afraid for her son. It would be beneath Ralph's dignity to attack a child, but there might be an accident. And there was another danger.

Seeing Ralph and Sam together, Wulfric might realize they were father and son.

Sam was still a little boy, of course, with a child's body and face, but he had Ralph's thick hair and dark eyes, and his bony shoulders were wide and square.

Gwenda looked at her husband. Wulfric's expression showed no sign that he had seen what was so obvious to her. She surveyed the faces of the other villagers. They seemed oblivious to the stark truth—except for Vi Bailiff, who was giving Gwenda a hard stare. That old battleaxe might have guessed. But no one else had—yet.

Will came forward and addressed the visitors. "Good day to you, sirs. I'm Will, the bailiff of Outhenby. May I ask—"

"Shut your mouth, bailiff," said Ralph. He pointed at Wulfric. "What is he doing here?"

Gwenda sensed a slight easing of tension as the other villagers realized they were not the target of the lord's wrath.

Will replied: "My lord, he's a laborer, hired on the authority of the prioress of Kingsbridge—"

"He's a runaway, and he's got to come home," Ralph said.

Will fell silent, frightened.

Carl Shaftesbury said: "And what authority do you claim for this demand?"

Ralph peered at Carl, as if memorizing his face. "Watch your tongue, or I'll disfigure the other side of your face."

Will said nervously: "We don't want any bloodshed."

"Very wise, bailiff," said Ralph. "Who is this insolent peasant?"

"Never you mind who I am, knight," said Carl rudely. "I know who you are. You're Ralph Fitzgerald, and I saw you convicted of rape and sentenced to death at Shiring court."

"But I'm not dead, am I?" Ralph said.

"You should be, though. And you have no feudal rights over laborers. If you try to use force, you'll be taught a sharp lesson."

Several people gasped. This was a reckless way to speak to an armed knight.

Wulfric said: "Be quiet, Carl. I don't want you killed for my sake."

"It's not for your sake," Carl said. "If this thug is allowed to drag you off, next week someone will come for me. We have to stick together. We're not helpless."

Carl was a big man, taller than Wulfric and almost as broad, and Gwenda could see that he meant what he said. She was appalled. If they started fighting, there would be terrible violence—and her Sam was still sitting on the horse with Ralph. "We'll just go with Ralph," she said frantically. "It will be better."

Carl said: "No, it won't. I'm going to stop him taking you away, whether you want me to or not. It's for my own good."

There was a murmur of assent. Gwenda looked around. Most of the men were holding shovels or hoes, and they looked ready to swing them, though they also looked scared.

Wulfric turned his back on Ralph and spoke in a low, urgent voice. "You women, take the children into the church—quickly now!"

Several women snatched up toddlers and grabbed youngsters by the arms. Gwenda stayed where she was, and so did several of the younger women. The villagers instinctively moved closer together, standing shoulder to shoulder.

Ralph and Alan looked disconcerted. They had not expected to face a crowd of fifty or more belligerent peasants. But they were on horseback, so they could get away anytime they wanted.

Ralph said: "Well, perhaps I'll just take this little boy to Wigleigh."

Gwenda gasped with horror.

Ralph went on: "Then, if his parents want him, they can come back where they belong."

Gwenda was beside herself. Ralph had Sam, and he could ride away at any moment. She fought down a hysterical scream. If he turned his horse, she decided, she would throw herself at him and try to drag him off the saddle. She moved a step closer.

Then, behind Ralph and Alan, she saw the oxen. Harry Plowman was driving them through the village from the other end. Eight massive beasts lumbered up to the scene in front of the church, then stopped, looking around dumbly, not knowing which way to go. Harry stood behind them. Ralph and Alan found themselves in a triangular trap, hemmed in by the villagers, the oxen, and the stone church.

Harry had planned this to stop Ralph riding away with Wulfric and herself, Gwenda guessed. But the tactic did just as well for this situation.

Carl said: "Put the child down, Sir Ralph, and go in peace."

The trouble was, Gwenda thought, it was now difficult for Ralph to back down without losing face. He was going to have to do something to avoid looking foolish, which was the ultimate horror for proud knights. They talked all the time about their honor, but that meant nothing—they were thoroughly dishonorable when it suited them. What they really prized was their dignity. They would rather die than be humiliated.

The tableau was frozen for several moments: the knight and the child on the horse, the mutinous villagers, and the dumb oxen.

Then Ralph lowered Sam to the ground.

Tears of relief came to Gwenda's eyes.

Sam ran to her, threw his arms around her waist, and began to cry.

The villagers relaxed, the men lowering their shovels and hoes.

Ralph pulled on his horse's reins and shouted: "Hup! Hup!" The horse reared. He dug in his spurs and rode straight at the crowd. They scattered. Alan rode behind him. The villagers desperately threw themselves out of the way, ending up in tangled heaps on the muddy ground. They were trampled by one another but not, miraculously, by the horses.

Ralph and Alan laughed loudly as they rode out of the village, as if the entire encounter had been nothing more than a huge joke.

But, in reality, Ralph had been shamed.

And that, Gwenda felt sure, meant that he would be back.

68

Earlscastle had not changed. Twelve years ago, Merthin recalled, he had been asked to demolish the old fortress and build a new, modern palace fit for an earl in a peaceful country. But he had refused, preferring to design the new bridge at Kingsbridge. Since then, it seemed, the project had languished, for here was the same figure-eight wall, with two drawbridges, and the old-fashioned keep ensconced in the upper loop, where the family lived like frightened rabbits at the end of a burrow, unaware that there was no longer any danger from the fox. The place must have been much the same in the days of Lady Aliena and Jack Builder.

Merthin was with Caris, who had been summoned here by the countess, Lady Philippa. Earl William had fallen sick, and Philippa thought her husband had the plague. Caris had been dismayed. She had thought the plague was over. No one had died of it in Kingsbridge for six weeks.

Caris and Merthin had set out immediately. However, the messenger had taken two days to travel from Earlscastle to Kingsbridge, and they had taken the same time to get here, so the likelihood was that the earl would now be dead, or nearly so. "All I will be able to do is give him some poppy essence to ease the final agony," Caris had said as they rode along.

"You do more than that," Merthin had said. "Your presence comforts people. You're calm and knowledgeable, and you talk about things they understand, swelling and confusion and pain—you don't try to impress them with jargon about humors, which just makes them feel more ignorant and powerless and frightened. When you're there, they feel that everything possible is being done; and that's what they want."

"I hope you're right."

If anything, Merthin was understating. More than once he had seen a hysterical man or woman change, after just a few calming moments with Caris, into a sensible person capable of coping with whatever should happen.

Her inborn gift had been augmented, since the advent of the plague, by an almost supernatural reputation. Everyone for miles around knew that she and her nuns had carried on caring for the sick, despite the risk to themselves, even when the monks had fled. They thought she was a saint.

The atmosphere inside the castle compound was subdued. Those who had routine tasks were performing them: fetching firewood and water, feeding horses and sharpening weapons, baking bread and butchering meat. Many others—secretaries, men-at-arms, messengers—sat around doing nothing, waiting for news from the sick room.

The rooks cawed a sarcastic welcome as Merthin and Caris crossed the inner bridge to the keep. Merthin's father, Sir Gerald, always claimed to be directly descended from Jack and Aliena's son, Earl Thomas. As Merthin counted the steps to the great hall, placing his feet carefully in the smooth hollows worn by thousands of boots, he reflected that his ancestors had probably trodden on just these old stones. To him, such notions were intriguing but trivial. By contrast his brother, Ralph, was obsessed with restoring the family to its former glory.

Caris was ahead of him, and the sway of her hips as she climbed the steps made his lips twitch in a smile. He was frustrated by not being able to sleep with her every night, but the rare occasions when they could be alone together were all the more thrilling. Yesterday they had spent a mild spring afternoon making love in a sunlit forest glade, while the horses grazed nearby, oblivious to their passion.

It was an odd relationship, but then she was an extraordinary woman: a prioress who doubted much of what the church taught; an acclaimed healer who rejected medicine as practised by physicians; and a nun who made enthusiastic love to her man whenever she could get away with it. If I wanted a normal relationship, Merthin told himself, I should have picked a normal girl.

The hall was full of people. Some were working, laying down fresh straw, building up the fire, preparing the table for dinner; and others were simply waiting. At the far end of the long room, sitting near the foot of the staircase that led up to the earl's private quarters, Merthin saw a well-dressed girl of about fifteen. She stood up and came toward them with a rather stately walk, and Merthin realized she must be Lady Philippa's daughter. Like her mother she was tall, with an hourglass figure. "I am the Lady Odila," she said with a touch of hauteur that was pure Philippa. Despite her composure, the skin around her young eyes was red and creased with crying. "You must be Mother Caris. Thank you for coming to attend my father."

Merthin said: "I'm the alderman of Kingsbridge, Merthin Bridger. How is Earl William?"

"He is very ill, and both my brothers have been laid low." Merthin recalled that the earl and countess had two boys of nineteen and twenty or thereabouts. "My mother asks that the lady prioress should come to them immediately."

Caris said: "Of course."

Odila went up the stairs. Caris took from her purse a strip of linen cloth and fastened it over her nose and mouth, then followed.

Merthin sat on a bench to wait. Although he was reconciled to infrequent sex, that did not stop him looking out eagerly for extra opportunities, and he surveyed the building with a keen eye, figuring out the sleeping arrangements. Unfortunately the house had a traditional layout. This large room, the great hall, would be where almost everyone ate and slept. The staircase presumably led to a solar, a bedroom for the earl and countess. Modern castles had a whole suite of apartments for family and guests, but there appeared to be no such luxury here. Merthin and Caris might lie side by side tonight, on the floor here in the hall, but they could do nothing more than sleep, not without causing a scandal.

After a while, Lady Philippa emerged from the solar and came down the stairs. She entered a room like a queen, aware that all eyes were on her, Merthin always thought. The dignity of her posture only emphasized the alluring roundness of her hips and her proud bosom. However, today her normally serene face was blotchy and her eyes were red. Her fashionably piled hairstyle was slightly awry, with stray locks of hair escaping from her headdress, adding to her air of glamorous distraction.

Merthin stood up and look at her expectantly.

She said: "My husband has the plague, as I feared; and so do both my sons."

The people around murmured in dismay.

It might turn out to be no more than the last remnants of the epidemic, of course; but it could just as easily be the start of a new outbreak—God forbid, Merthin thought.

He said: "How is the earl feeling?"

Philippa sat on the bench next to him. "Mother Caris has eased his pain. But she says he's near the end."

Their knees were almost touching. He felt the magnetism of her sexuality, even though she was drowning in grief and he was dizzy with love for Caris. "And your sons?" he said.

She looked down at her lap, as if studying the pattern of gold and silver threads woven into her blue gown. "The same as their father."

Merthin said quietly: "This is very hard for you, my lady, very hard."

She gave him a wary glance. "You're not like your brother, are you?"

Merthin knew that Ralph had been in love with Philippa, in his own obsessive way, for many years. Did she realize that? Merthin did not know. Ralph had chosen well, he thought. If you were going to have a hopeless love, you might as well pick someone singular. "Ralph and I are very different," he said neutrally.

"I remember you as youngsters. You were the cheeky one—you told me to buy a green silk to match my eyes. Then your brother started a fight."

"I sometimes think the younger of two brothers deliberately tries to be the opposite of the elder, just to differentiate himself."

"It's certainly true of my two. Rollo is strong-willed and assertive, like his father and grandfather; and Rick has always been sweet-natured and obliging." She began to cry. "Oh, God, I'm going to lose them all."

Merthin took her hand. "You can't be sure what will happen," he said gently. "I caught the plague in Florence, and I survived. My daughter didn't catch it at all."

She looked up at him. "And your wife?"

Merthin looked down at their entwined hands. Philippa's was perceptibly more wrinkled than his, he saw, even though there was only four years' difference in their ages. He said: "Silvia died."

"I pray to God that I will catch it. If all my men die, I want to go, too."

"Surely not."

"It's the fate of noblewomen to marry men they don't love—but I was lucky, you see, in William. He was chosen for me, but I loved him from the start." Her voice began to fail her. "I couldn't bear to have someone else . . ."

"You feel that way now, of course." It was odd to be talking like this while her husband was still alive, Merthin thought. But she was so stricken by grief that she had little thought for niceties and said just what was in her mind.

She collected herself with an effort. "What about you?" she said. "Have you remarried?"

"No." He could hardly explain that he was having a love affair with the prioress of Kingsbridge. "I think I could, though, if the right woman were . . . willing. You might come to feel the same, eventually."

"But you don't understand. As the widow of an earl with no heirs, I would have to marry someone King Edward chose for me. And the king would have no thought for my wishes. His only concern would be who should be the next earl of Shiring."

"I see." Merthin had not thought of that. He could imagine that an arranged marriage might be particularly loathsome to a widow who had truly loved her first husband.

"How dreadful of me to be speaking of another husband while my first is alive," she said. "I don't know what came over me."

Merthin patted her hand sympathetically. "It's understandable."

The door at the top of the stairs opened and Caris came out, drying her hands on a cloth. Merthin suddenly felt uncomfortable about holding Philippa's hand. He was tempted to thrust it away from him, but realized how guilty that would look and managed to resist the impulse. He smiled at Caris and said: "How are your patients?"

Caris's eyes went to their linked hands, but she said nothing. She came down the stairs, untying her linen mask.

Philippa unhurriedly withdrew her hand.

Caris took off her mask and said: "I'm very sorry to have to tell you, my lady, that Earl William is dead."

"I need a new horse," said Ralph Fitzgerald. His favorite mount, Griff, was getting old. The spirited bay palfrey had suffered a sprain in its left hind leg that had taken months to heal, and now it was lame again in the same leg. Ralph felt sad. Griff was the horse Earl Roland had given him when he was a young squire, and it had been with him ever since, even going to the French wars. It might serve him a few years longer for unhurried trips from village to village within his domain, but its hunting days were over.

"We could go to Shiring market tomorrow and buy another," Alan Fernhill said.

They were in the stable, looking at Griff's fetlock. Ralph liked stables. He enjoyed the earthy smell, the strength and beauty of the horses, and the company of rough-handed men engrossed in physical tasks. It took him back to his youth, when the world had seemed a simple place.

He did not at first respond to Alan's suggestion. What Alan did not know was that Ralph did not have the money to buy a horse.

The plague had at first enriched him, through the inheritance tax: land that normally passed from father to son once in a generation had changed hands twice or more in a few months, and he got a payment every time—traditionally the best beast, but often a fixed sum in cash. But then land had started to fall into disuse for lack of people to farm it. At the same time, agricultural prices had dropped. The upshot was that Ralph's income, in money and produce, fell drastically.

Things were bad, he thought, when a knight could not afford a horse.

Then he remembered that Nate Reeve was due to come to Tench Hall today with the quarterly dues from Wigleigh. Every spring that village was obliged to provide its lord with twenty-four hoggets, year-old sheep. They could be driven to Shiring market and sold, and they should raise enough cash to pay for a palfrey, if not a hunter. "All right," Ralph said to Alan. "Let's see if the bailiff of Wigleigh is here."

They went into the hall. This was a feminine zone, and Ralph's spirits dropped immediately. Tilly was sitting by the fire, nursing their three-month-old son, Gerry. Mother and baby were in vigorous good health, despite Tilly's youth. Her slight, girlish body had changed drastically: she now had swollen breasts with large, leathery nipples at which the baby sucked greedily. Her belly sagged loosely like that of an old woman. Ralph had not lain with her for many months and he probably never would again.

Nearby sat the grandfather after whom the baby was named, Sir Gerald, with Lady Maud. Ralph's parents were now old and frail, but every morning they walked from their house in the village to the manor house to see their grandson. Maud said the baby looked like Ralph, but he could not see the resemblance.

Ralph was pleased to see that Nate was also in the hall.

The hunchbacked bailiff sprang up from his bench. "Good day to you, Sir Ralph," he said.

He had a hangdog look about him, Ralph observed. "What's the matter with you, Nate?" he said. "Have you brought my hoggets?"

"No, sir."

"Why the devil not?"

"We've got none, sir. There are no sheep left in Wigleigh, except for a few old ewes."

Ralph was shocked. "Has someone stolen them?"

"No, but some have been given to you already, as heriot when their owners died, and then we couldn't find a tenant to take over Jack Shepherd's land, and many sheep died over the winter. Then there was no one to look to the early lambs this spring, so we lost most of those, and some of the mothers."

"But this is impossible!" Ralph said angrily. "How are noblemen to live if their serfs let the livestock perish?"

"We thought perhaps the plague was over, when it died down in January and February, but now it seems to be coming back."

Ralph repressed a shudder of terror. Like everyone else, he had been thanking God that he had escaped the plague. Surely it could not return?

Nate went on: "Perkin died this week, and his wife Peg, and his son Rob, and his son-in-law Billy Howard. That's left Annet with all those acres to manage, which she can't possibly do."

"Well, there must be a heriot due on that property, then."

"There will be, when I can find a tenant to take it over."

Parliament was in the process of passing new legislation to stop laborers flitting about the country demanding even higher wages. As soon as the ordinance became law, Ralph would enforce it and get his workers back. Even then, he now realized, he would be desperate to find tenants.

Nate said: "I expect you've heard of the death of the earl."

"No!" Ralph was shocked again.

"What's that?" Sir Gerald said. "Earl William is dead?"

"Of the plague," Nate explained.

Tilly said: "Poor Uncle William!"

The baby sensed her mood and wailed.

Ralph spoke over the noise. "When did this happen?"

"Only three days ago," Nate replied.

Tilly gave the baby the nipple again, and he shut up.

"So William's elder son is the new earl," Ralph mused. "He can't be more than twenty."

Nate shook his head. "Rollo also died of the plague."

"Then the younger son—"

"Dead, too."

"Both sons!" Ralph's heart leaped. It had always been his dream to become the earl of Shiring. Now the plague had given him the opportunity. And the plague had also improved his chances, for many likely candidates for the title had been wiped out.

He caught his father's eye. The same thought had occurred to Sir Gerald.

Tilly said: "Rollo and Rick dead—it's so awful." She began to cry.

Ralph ignored her and tried to think through the possibilities. "Let's see, what surviving relatives are there?"

Gerald said to Nate: "I presume the countess died, too?"

"No, sir. Lady Philippa lives. So does her daughter, Odila."

"Ah!" said Gerald. "So, whoever the king chooses will have to marry Philippa in order to become earl."

Ralph was thunderstruck. Since he was a lad he had dreamed of marrying Lady Philippa. Now there was an opportunity to achieve both his ambitions at one stroke.

But he was already married.

Gerald said: "That's it, then." He sat back in his chair, his excitement gone as quickly as it had come.

Ralph looked at Tilly, suckling their child and weeping at the same time. Fifteen years old and barely five feet tall, she stood like a castle wall between him and the future he had always yearned for.

He hated her.

Earl William's funeral took place at Kingsbridge Cathedral. There were no monks except Brother Thomas, but Bishop Henri conducted the service and the nuns sang the hymns. Lady Philippa and Lady Odila, both heavily veiled, followed the coffin. Despite their dramatic black-clad presence, Ralph found the occasion lacked the momentous feeling that usually attended the funeral of a magnate, the sense of historical time passing by like the flow of a great river. Death was everywhere, every day, and even noble deaths were now commonplace.

He wondered whether someone in the congregation was infected, and was even now spreading the disease through his breath, or the invisible beams from his eyes. The thought made Ralph shaky. He had faced death many times, and learned to control his fear in battle; but this enemy could not be fought. The plague was an assassin who slid his long knife into people from behind then slipped away before he was spotted. Ralph shuddered and tried not to think about it.

Next to Ralph was the tall figure of Sir Gregory Longfellow, a lawyer who had been involved in suits concerning Kingsbridge in the past. Gregory was now a member of the king's council, an elite group of technical experts who advised the monarch—not on what he should do, for that was the job of Parliament, but on how he could do it.

Royal announcements were often made at church services, especially big ceremonies such as this. Today Bishop Henri took the opportunity to explain the new Ordinance of Laborers. Ralph guessed that Sir Gregory had brought the news and stayed to see how it was received.

Ralph listened attentively. He had never been summoned to Parliament, but he had talked about the labor crisis to Earl William, who had sat with the Lords, and to Sir Peter Jeffries, who represented Shiring in the Commons; so he knew what had been discussed.

"Every man must work for the lord of the village where he lives, and may not move to another village or work for another master, unless his lord should release him," the bishop said.

Ralph rejoiced. He had known this was coming, but he was delighted that at last it was official.

Before the plague there had never been a shortage of laborers. On the contrary, many villages had more than they knew what to do with. When landless men could find no paid work, they sometimes threw themselves on the charity of the lord—which was an embarrassment to him, whether he helped them or not. So, if they wanted to move to another village, the lord was if anything relieved, and certainly had no need of legislation to keep them where they were. Now the laborers had the whip hand—a situation that obviously could not be allowed to continue.

There was a rumble of approval from the congregation at the bishop's announcement. Kingsbridge folk themselves were not much affected, but those in the congregation who had come in from the countryside for the funeral were predominantly employers rather than employees. The new rules had been devised by and for them.

The bishop went on: "It is now a crime to demand, to offer, or to accept wages higher than those paid for similar work in 1347."

Ralph nodded approval. Even laborers who stayed in the same village had been demanding more money. This would put a stop to that, he hoped.

Sir Gregory caught his eye. "I see you nodding," he said. "Do you approve?"

"It's what we wanted," Ralph said. "I'll begin to enforce it in the next few days. There are a couple of runaways from my territory that I particularly want to bring home."

"I'll come with you, if I may," the lawyer said. "I should like to see how things work out."

69

The priest at Outhenby had died of the plague, and there had been no services at the church since; so Gwenda was surprised when the bell began to toll on Sunday morning.

Wulfric went to investigate and came back to report that a visiting priest, Father Derek, had arrived; so Gwenda washed the boys' faces quickly and they all went out.

It was a fine spring morning, and the sun bathed the old gray stones of the little church in a clear light. All the villagers turned out, curious to view the newcomer.

Father Derek turned out to be a well-spoken city clergyman, too richly dressed for a village church. Gwenda wondered whether any special significance was attached to his visit. Was there a reason why the church hierarchy had suddenly remembered the existence of this parish? She told herself that it was a bad habit always to imagine the worst, but all the same she felt something was wrong.

She stood in the nave with Wulfric and the boys, watching the priest go through the ritual, and her sense of doom grew stronger. A priest usually looked at the congregation while he was praying or singing, to emphasize that all this was for their benefit, not a private communication between himself and God; but Father Derek's gaze went over their heads.

She soon found out why. At the end of the service, he told them of a new law passed by the king and Parliament. "Landless laborers must work for the lord in their village of origin, if required," he said.

Gwenda was outraged. "How can that be?" she shouted out. "The lord is not obliged to help the laborer in hard times—I know, my father was a landless laborer, and when there was no work we went hungry. So how can the laborer owe loyalty to a lord who gives him nothing?"

A rumble of agreement broke out, and the priest had to raise his voice. "This is what the king has decided, and the king is chosen by God to rule over us, so we must all do as he wishes."

"Can the king change the custom of hundreds of years?" Gwenda persisted.

"These are difficult times. I know that many of you have come to Outhenby in the last few weeks—"

"Invited by the plowman," the voice of Carl Shaftesbury interrupted. His scarred face was livid with rage.

"Invited by all the villagers," the priest acknowledged. "And they were grateful to you for coming. But the king in his wisdom has ruled that this kind of thing must not go on."

"And poor people must remain poor," Carl said.

"God has ordained it so. Each man in his place."

Harry Plowman said: "And has God ordained how we are to till our fields with no help? If all the newcomers leave, we will never finish the work."

"Perhaps not all the newcomers will have to leave," said Derek. "The new law says only that they must go home if required."

That quieted them. The immigrants were trying to figure out whether their lords would be able to track them down; the locals were wondering how many laborers would be left here. But Gwenda knew what her own future held. Sooner or later Ralph would come back for her and her family.

By then, she decided, they would be gone.

The priest retired and the congregation began to drift to the door. "We've got to leave here," Gwenda said to Wulfric in a low voice. "Before Ralph comes back for us."

"Where will we go?"

"I don't know—but perhaps that's better. If we don't know where we're going, no one else will."

"But how will we live?"

"We'll find another village where they need laborers."

"Are there many others, I wonder?"

He was always slower-thinking than she. "There must be lots," she said patiently. "The king didn't pass this ordinance just for Outhenby."

"Of course."

"We should leave today," she said decisively. "It's Sunday, so we're not losing any work." She glanced at the church windows, estimating the time of day. "It's not yet noon—we could cover a good distance before nightfall. Who knows, we could be working in a new place tomorrow morning."

"I agree," Wulfric said. "There's no telling how fast Ralph might move."

"Say nothing to anyone. We'll go home, pick up whatever we want to take with us, and just slip away."

"All right."

They reached the door and stepped outside into the sunshine, and Gwenda saw that it was already too late.

Six men on horseback were waiting outside the church: Ralph, his sidekick Alan, a tall man in London clothes, and three dirty, scarred, evil-looking ruffians of the kind that could be hired for a few pennies in any low tavern.

Ralph caught Gwenda's eye and smiled triumphantly.

Gwenda looked around desperately. A few days ago the men of the village had stood shoulder to shoulder against Ralph and Alan—but this was different. They were up against six men, not two. The villagers were unarmed, coming out of church, whereas previously they had been returning from the fields with tools in their hands. And, most important, on that first occasion they had believed they had right on their side, whereas today they were not so sure.

Several men met her eye and looked quickly away. That confirmed her suspicion. The villagers would not fight today.

Gwenda was so disappointed that she felt weak. Fearing that she might fall down, she leaned on the stonework of the church porch for support.

Her heart had turned into something heavy and cold and damp, like a clod from a winter grave. A grim hopelessness possessed her completely.

For a few days they had been free. But it had just been a dream. And now the dream was over.

Ralph rode slowly through Wigleigh, leading Wulfric by a rope around his neck.

They arrived late in the afternoon. For speed, Ralph had let the two small boys ride, sharing the horses of the hired men. Gwenda was walking behind. Ralph had not bothered to tie her in any way. She could be relied upon to follow her children.

Because it was Sunday, most of the Wigleigh folk were outside their houses, enjoying the sun, as Ralph had anticipated. They all stared in horrified silence at the dismal procession. Ralph hoped the sight of Wulfric's humiliation might deter others from going in search of higher wages.

They reached the small manor house that had been Ralph's home before he moved to Tench Hall. He released Wulfric and sent him and his family off to their old home. He paid off the hired men, then took Alan and Sir Gregory into the manor house.

It was kept clean and ready for his visits. He ordered Vira to bring wine then prepare supper. It was too late now to go on to Tench: they could not get there before nightfall.

Gregory sat down and stretched out his long legs. He seemed like a man who could make himself comfortable anywhere. His straight dark hair was now tweeded with gray, but his long nose with its flared nostrils still gave him a supercilious look. "How do you feel that went?" he said.

Ralph had been thinking about the new ordinance all the way home, and he had his answer ready. "It's not going to work," he said.

Gregory raised his eyebrows. "Oh?"

Alan said: "I agree with Sir Ralph."

"Reasons?"

Ralph said: "First of all, it's difficult to find out where the runaways have gone."

Alan put in: "It was only by luck that we traced Wulfric. Someone had overheard him and Gwenda planning where to go."

"Second," Ralph went on, "recovering them is too troublesome."

Gregory nodded. "I suppose we have been all day at it."

"And I had to hire those ruffians and get them horses. I can't spend my time and money chasing all over the countryside after runaway laborers."

"I see that."

"Third, what is to stop them running away again next week?"

Alan said: "If they keep their mouths shut about where they're headed, we might never find them."

"The only way it will work," Ralph said, "is if someone can go to a village, find out who the migrants are, and punish them."

Gregory said: "You're talking about a sort of Commission of Laborers."

"Exactly. Appoint a panel in each county, a dozen or so men who go from place to place ferreting out runaways."

"You want someone else to do the work for you."

It was a taunt, but Ralph was careful not to appear stung. "Not necessarily—I'll be one of the commissioners, if you wish. It's just the way the job is to be done. You can't reap a field of grass one blade at a time."

"Interesting," said Gregory.

Vira brought a jug and some goblets, and poured wine for the three of them.

Gregory said: "You're a shrewd man, Sir Ralph. You're not a Member of Parliament, are you?"

"No."

"Pity. I think the king would find your counsel helpful."

Ralph tried not to beam with pleasure. "You're very kind." He leaned forward. "Now that Earl William is dead, there is of course a vacancy—" He saw the door open, and broke off.

Nate Reeve came in. "Well done, Sir Ralph, if I may say so!" he said. "Wulfric and Gwenda back in the fold, the two hardest-working people we've got."

Ralph was annoyed with Nate for interrupting at such a crucial moment. He said irritably: "I trust the village will now be able to pay more of its dues."

"Yes, sir . . . if they stay."

Ralph frowned. Nate had immediately fastened on the weakness in his position. How was he going to keep Wulfric in Wigleigh? He could not chain a man to a plow all day and all night.

Gregory spoke to Nate. "Tell me, bailiff, do you have a suggestion for your lord?"

"Yes, sir, I do."

"I thought you might."

Nate took that as an invitation. Addressing Ralph, he said: "There is one thing you could do that would guarantee that Wulfric would stay here in Wigleigh until the day he dies."

Ralph sensed a trick, but had to say: "Go on."

"Give him back the lands his father held."

Ralph would have yelled at him, except that he did not want to give Gregory a bad impression. Controlling his anger, he said firmly: "I don't think so."

"I can't get a tenant for the land," Nate persisted. "Annet can't manage it, and she has no male relations living."

"I don't care," said Ralph. "He can't have the land."

Gregory said: "Why not?"

Ralph did not want to admit that he still held a grudge against Wulfric because of a fight twelve years ago. Gregory had formed a good impression of Ralph, and Ralph did not want to spoil it. What would the king's counselor think of a knight who acted against his own interests in pursuit of a boyhood squabble? He cast about for a plausible excuse. "It would seem to be rewarding Wulfric for running away," he said finally.

"Hardly," said Gregory. "From what Nate says, you'd be giving him something that no one else wants."

"All the same, it sends the wrong signal to the other villagers."

"I think you're being too scrupulous," Gregory said. He was not the kind of man to keep his opinions tactfully to himself. "Everyone must know you're desperate for tenants," he went on. "Most landlords are. The villagers will see that you're simply acting in your own interest, and consider that Wulfric is the lucky beneficiary."

Nate added: "Wulfric and Gwenda will work twice as hard if they've got their own land."

Ralph felt cornered. He was desperate to look good in Gregory's eyes. He had started but not finished a discussion about the earldom. He could not put that at risk just because of Wulfric.

He had to give in.

"Perhaps you're right," he said. He realized he was speaking through gritted teeth, and made an effort to be nonchalant. "After all, he has been brought home and humiliated. That may be enough."

"I'm sure it is."

"All right, Nate," Ralph said. For a moment words stuck in his throat, he hated so much to give Wulfric his heart's desire. But this was more important. "Tell Wulfric he can have his father's lands back."

"I'll do that before nightfall," Nate said, and he left.

Gregory said: "What were you saying about the earldom?"

Ralph picked his words carefully. "After Earl Roland died at the battle of Crécy, I thought the king might have considered making me the earl of Shiring, especially as I had saved the life of the young prince of Wales."

"But Roland had a perfectly good heir—who himself had two sons."

"Exactly. And now all three are dead."

"Hmm." Gregory took a draft from his goblet. "This is good wine."

"Gascon," said Ralph.

"I suppose it comes into Melcombe."

"Yes."

"Delicious." Gregory drank some more. He seemed to be about to say something, so Ralph remained silent. Gregory took a long time choosing his words. At last he said: "There is, somewhere in the neighborhood of Kingsbridge, a letter that . . . ought not to exist."

Ralph was mystified. What was coming now?

Gregory went on: "For many years, this document was in the hands of someone who could be relied upon, for various complicated reasons, to keep it safe. Lately, however, certain questions have been asked, suggesting to me that the secret may be in danger of getting out."

All this was too enigmatic. Ralph said impatiently: "I don't understand. Who has been asking embarrassing questions?"

"The prioress of Kingsbridge."

"Oh."

"It's possible she may have simply picked up some hint, and her questions may be harmless. But what the king's friends fear is that the letter may have got into her possession."

"What is in the letter?"

Once again, Gregory chose his words warily, tiptoeing across a raging river on carefully placed stepping-stones. "Something touching the king's beloved mother."

"Queen Isabella." The old witch was still alive, living in splendor in her castle at Lynn, spending her days reading romances in her native French, so people said.

"In short," said Gregory, "I need to find out whether the prioress has this letter or not. But no one must know of my interest."

Ralph said: "Either you have to go to the priory and search through the nuns' documents . . . or the documents must come to you."

"The second of those two."

Ralph nodded. He was beginning to understand what Gregory wanted him to do.

Gregory said: "I have made some very discreet inquiries, and discovered that no one knows exactly where the nuns' treasury is."

"The nuns must know, or some of them."

"But they won't say. However, I understand you're an expert in . . . persuading people to reveal secrets."

So Gregory knew of the work Ralph had done in France. There was nothing spontaneous about this conversation, Ralph realized. Gregory must have planned it. In fact it was probably the real reason he had come to Kingsbridge. Ralph said: "I may be able to help the king's friends solve this problem . . ."

"Good."

". . . if I were promised the earldom of Shiring as my reward."

Gregory frowned. "The new earl will have to marry the old countess."

Ralph decided to hide his eagerness. Instinct told him that Gregory would have less respect for a man who was driven, even just partly, by lust for a woman. "Lady Philippa is five years older than I am, but I have no objection to her."

Gregory looked askance. "She's a very beautiful woman," he said. "Whoever the king gives her to should think himself a lucky man."

Ralph realized he had gone too far. "I don't wish to appear indifferent," he said hastily. "She is indeed a beauty."

"But I thought you were already married," Gregory said. "Have I made a mistake?"

Ralph caught Alan's eye, and saw that he was keenly curious to hear what Ralph would say next.

Ralph sighed. "My wife is very ill," he said. "She hasn't long to live."

Gwenda lit the fire in the kitchen of the old house where Wulfric had lived since he was born. She found her cooking pots, filled one with water at the well, and threw in some early onions, the first step in making a stew. Wulfric brought in more firewood. The boys happily went out to play with their old friends, unaware of the depth of the tragedy that had befallen their family.

Gwenda busied herself with household chores as the evening darkened outside. She was trying not to think. Everything that came into her mind just made her feel worse: the future, the past, her husband, herself. Wulfric sat and looked into the flames. Neither of them spoke.

Their neighbor, David Johns, appeared with a big jug of ale. His wife was dead of the plague, but his grown-up daughter, Joanna, followed him in. Gwenda was not happy to see them: she wanted to be miserable in private. But their intentions were kind, and it was impossible to spurn them. Gwenda glumly wiped the dust from some wooden cups, and David poured ale for everyone.

"We're sorry things worked out this way, but we're glad to see you," he said as they drank.

Wulfric emptied his cup with one huge swallow and held it out for more.

A little later Aaron Appletree and his wife Ulla came in. She carried a basket of small loaves. "I knew you wouldn't have any bread, so I made some," she said. She handed them around, and the house filled with the mouthwatering smell. David Johns poured them some ale, and they sat down. "Where did you get the courage to run away?" Ulla asked admiringly. "I would have died of fright!"

Gwenda began to tell the story of their adventures. Jack and Eli Fuller arrived from the mill, bringing a dish of pears baked in honey. Wulfric ate plenty and drank deep. The atmosphere lightened, and Gwenda's mood lifted a little. More neighbors came, each bringing a gift. When Gwenda told how the villagers of Outhenby with their spades and hoes had faced down Ralph and Alan, everyone rocked with delighted laughter.

Then she came to the events of today, and she descended into despair again. "Everything was against us," she said bitterly. "Not just Ralph and his ruffians, but the king and the church. We had no chance."

The neighbors nodded gloomily.

"And then, when he put a rope around my Wulfric's neck . . ." She was filled with bleak despair. Her voice cracked, and she could not go on. She took a gulp of ale and tried again. "When he put a rope around Wulfric's neck—the strongest and bravest man I've ever known, any of us have ever known, led through the village like a beast, and that heartless, crass, bullying Ralph holding the rope—I just wanted the heavens to fall in and kill us all."

These were strong words, but the others agreed. Of all the things the gentry could do to peasants—starve them, cheat them, assault them, rob them—the worst was to humiliate them. They never forgot it.

Suddenly Gwenda wanted the neighbors to leave. The sun had gone down, and it was dusk outside. She needed to lie down and close her eyes and be alone with her thoughts. She did not want to talk even to Wulfric. She was about to ask everyone to go when Nate Reeve walked in.

The room went quiet.

"What do you want?" Gwenda said.

"I bring you good news," he said brightly.

She made a sour face. "There can be no good news for us today."

"I disagree. You haven't heard it yet."

"All right, what is it?"

"Sir Ralph says Wulfric is to have his father's lands back."

Wulfric leaped to his feet. "As a tenant?" he said. "Not just to labor on?"

"As a tenant, on the same terms as your father," said Nate expansively, as if he were making the concession himself, rather than simply passing on a message.

Wulfric beamed with joy. "That's wonderful!"

"Do you accept?" Nate said jovially, as if it were a mere formality.

Gwenda said: "Wulfric! Don't accept!"

He looked at her, bewildered. As usual, he was slow to see beyond the immediate.

"Discuss the terms!" she urged him in a low voice. "Don't be a serf like your father. Demand a free tenancy, with no feudal obligations. You'll never be in such a strong bargaining position again. Negotiate!"

"Negotiate?" he said. He wavered briefly, then gave in to the happiness of the occasion. "This is the moment I've been hoping for for the last twelve years. I'm not going to negotiate." He turned to Nate. "I accept," he said, and held up his cup.

They all cheered.

70

The hospital was full again. The plague, which had seemed to retreat during the first three months of 1349, came back in April with redoubled virulence. On the day after Easter Sunday, Caris looked wearily at the rows of mattresses crammed together in a herringbone pattern, packed so tightly that the masked nuns had to step gingerly between them. Moving around was a little easier, however, because there were so few family members at the bedsides of the sick. Sitting with a dying relative was dangerous—you were likely to catch the plague yourself—and people had become ruthless. When the epidemic began, they had stayed with their loved ones regardless, mothers with children, husbands with wives, the middle-aged with their elderly parents, love overcoming fear. But that had changed. The most powerful of family ties had been viciously corroded by the acid of death. Nowadays the typical patient was brought in by a mother or father, a husband or wife, who then simply walked away, ignoring the piteous cries that followed them out. Only the nuns, with their face masks and their vinegar-washed hands, defied the disease.

Surprisingly, Caris was not short of help. The nunnery had enjoyed an influx of novices to replace the nuns who had died. This was partly because of Caris's saintly reputation. But the monastery was experiencing the same kind of revival, and Thomas now had a class of novice monks to train. They were all searching for order in a world gone mad.

This time the plague had struck some leading townspeople who had previously escaped. Caris was dismayed by the death of John Constable. She had never much liked his rough-and-ready approach to justice—which was to hit troublemakers over the head with a stick and ask questions afterward—but it was going to be more difficult to maintain order without him. Fat Betty Baxter, baker of special buns for every town festivity, shrewd questioner at parish guild meetings, was dead, her business awkwardly shared out between four squabbling daughters. And Dick Brewer had died, the last of Caris's father's generation, a cohort of men who knew how to make money and how to enjoy it.

Caris and Merthin had been able to slow the spread of the disease by canceling major public gatherings. There had been no big Easter procession in the cathedral, and there would be no Fleece Fair this Whitsun. The weekly market was held outside the city walls, in Lovers' Field, and most townspeople stayed away. Caris had wanted such measures when the plague first struck, but Godwyn and Elfric had opposed her. According to Merthin, some Italian cities had even closed their gates for a period of thirty or forty days, called a trentine or a quarantine. It was now too late to keep the disease out, but Caris still thought restrictions would save lives.

One problem she did not have was money. More and more people bequeathed their wealth to the nuns, having no surviving relatives, and many of the new novices brought with them lands, flocks, orchards, and gold. The nunnery had never been so rich.

It was small consolation. For the first time in her life she felt tired—not just weary from hard work, but drained of energy, short of willpower, enfeebled by adversity. The plague was worse than ever, killing two hundred people a week, and she did not know how she was going to carry on. Her muscles ached, her head hurt, and sometimes her vision seemed to blur. Where would it end? she wondered dismally. Would everyone die?

Two men staggered in through the door, both bleeding. Caris hurried forward. Before she got within touching distance, she picked up the sweetly rotten smell of drink on them. They were both nearly helpless, although it was not yet dinnertime. She groaned in frustration: this was all too common.

She knew the men vaguely: Barney and Lou, two strong youngsters employed in the abattoir owned by Edward Slaughterhouse. Barney had one arm hanging limp, possibly broken. Lou had a dreadful injury to his face: his nose was crushed and one eye was a ghastly pulp. Both seemed too drunk to feel pain. "It was a fight," Barney slurred, his words only just comprehensible. "I didn't mean it. He's my best friend. I love him."

Caris and Sister Nellie got the two drunks lying down on adjacent mattresses. Nellie examined Barney and said his arm was not broken but dislocated, and sent a novice to fetch Matthew Barber, the surgeon, who would try to relocate it. Caris bathed Lou's face. There was nothing she could do to save his eye: it had burst like a soft-boiled egg.

This kind of thing made her furious. The two men were not suffering from a disease or an accidental injury: they had harmed one another while drinking to excess. After the first wave of the plague, she had managed to galvanize the townspeople into restoring law and order; but the second wave had done something terrible to people's souls. When she called again for a return to civilized behavior, the response had been apathetic. She did not know what to do next, and she felt so tired.

As she contemplated the two maimed men lying shoulder to shoulder on the floor, she heard a strange noise from outside. For an instant, she was transported back three years, to the battle of Crécy, and the terrifying booming sound made by King Edward's new machines that shot stone balls into the enemy ranks. A moment later the noise came again and she realized it was a drum—several drums, in fact, being struck in no particular rhythm. Then she heard pipes and bells whose notes failed to form any kind of tune; then hoarse cries, wailing, and shouts that might have indicated triumph or agony, or both. It was not unlike the noise of battle, but without the swish of deadly arrows or the screams of maimed horses. Frowning, she went outside.

A group of forty or so people had come onto the cathedral green, dancing a mad antic jig. Some played on musical instruments, or rather sounded them, for there was no melody or harmony to the noise. Their flimsy light-colored clothes were ripped and stained, and some were half-naked, carelessly exposing the intimate parts of their bodies. All those who did not have instruments were carrying whips. A crowd of townspeople followed, staring in curiosity and amazement.

The dancers were led by Friar Murdo, fatter than ever but cavorting energetically, sweat pouring down his dirty face and dripping from his straggly beard. He led them to the great west door of the cathedral, where he turned to face them. "We have all sinned!" he roared.

His followers cried out in response, inarticulate shrieks and groans.

"We are dirt!" he said thrillingly. "We wallow in lasciviousness like pigs in filth. We yield, quivering with desire, to our fleshly lusts. We deserve the plague!"

"Yes!"

"What must we do?"

"Suffer!" they called. "We must suffer!"

One of the followers dashed forward, flourishing a whip. It had three leather thongs, each of which appeared to have sharp stones attached to a knot. He threw himself at Murdo's feet and began to lash his own back. The whip tore the thin material of his robe and drew blood from the skin of his back. He cried out in pain, and the rest of Murdo's followers groaned in sympathy.

Then a woman came forward. She pulled her robe down to her waist and turned, exposing her bare breasts to the crowd; then lashed her bare back with a similar whip. The followers moaned again.

As they came forward in ones and twos, flogging themselves, Caris saw that many of them had bruises and half-healed cuts on their skin: they had done this before, some of them many times. Did they go from town to town repeating the performance? Given Murdo's involvement, she felt sure that sooner or later someone would start collecting money.

A woman in the watching crowd suddenly ran forward screaming: "Me, too, I must suffer!" Caris was surprised to see that it was Mared, the browbeaten young wife of Marcel Chandler. Caris could not imagine that she had committed many sins, but perhaps she had at last seen a chance to make her life dramatic. She threw off her dress and stood stark naked before the friar. Her skin was unmarked; in fact she looked beautiful.

Murdo gazed at her for a long moment then said: "Kiss my feet."

She knelt in front of him, exposing her rear obscenely to the crowd, and lowered her face to his filthy feet.

He took a whip from another penitent and handed it to her. She lashed herself, then shrieked in pain, and red marks appeared instantly on her white skin.

Several more ran forward eagerly from the crowd, mostly men, and Murdo went through the same ritual with each. Soon there was an orgy. When they were not whipping themselves they were banging their drums and clanging their bells and dancing their fiendish jig.

Their actions had a mad abandon, but Caris's professional eye noted that the strokes of the whips, though dramatic and undoubtedly painful, did not appear to inflict permanent damage.

Merthin appeared beside Caris and said: "What do you think of this?"

She frowned and said: "Why does it make me feel indignant?"

"I don't know."

"If people want to whip themselves, why should I object? Perhaps it makes them feel better."

"I agree with you, though," Merthin said. "There's generally something fraudulent about anything Murdo is involved with."

"That's not it."

The mood here was not one of penitence, she decided. These dancers were not looking back contemplatively over their lives, feeling sorrow and regret for sins committed. People who genuinely repented tended to be quiet, thoughtful, and undemonstrative. What Caris sensed in the air here was quite different. It was excitement.

"This is a debauch," she said.

"Only instead of drink, they're overindulging in self-loathing."

"And there's a kind of ecstasy in it."

"But no sex."

"Give them time."

Murdo led the procession off again, heading out of the priory precincts. Caris noticed that some of the flagellants had produced bowls and were begging coins from the crowd. They would go through the principal streets of the town like this, she guessed. They would probably finish up at one of the larger taverns, where people would buy them food and drink.

Merthin touched her arm. "You look pale," he said. "How do you feel?"

"Just tired," she said curtly. She had to soldier on regardless of how she felt, and it did not help her to be reminded of her tiredness. However, it was kind of him to notice, and she softened her tone to say: "Come to the prior's house. It's almost dinnertime."

They walked across the green as the procession disappeared. They stepped inside the palace. As soon as they were alone, Caris put her arms around Merthin and kissed him. She suddenly felt very physical, and she thrust her tongue into his mouth, which she knew he liked. In response, he took both her breasts in his hands and squeezed gently. They had never kissed like this inside the palace, and Caris wondered vaguely whether something about Friar Murdo's bacchanal had weakened her normal inhibitions.

"Your skin is hot," Merthin said in her ear.

She wanted Merthin to pull down her robe and put his mouth to her nipples. She felt she was losing control, and might find herself recklessly making love right here on the floor, where they might so easily be caught.

Then a girl's voice said: "I didn't mean to spy."

Caris was shocked. She sprang guiltily away from Merthin. She turned around, looking for the speaker. At the far end of the room, sitting on a bench, was a young woman holding a baby. It was Ralph Fitzgerald's wife. "Tilly!" said Caris.

Tilly stood up. She looked exhausted and frightened. "I'm so sorry to startle you," she said.

Caris was relieved. Tilly had attended the nuns' school and lived at the nunnery for years, and she was fond of Caris. She could be trusted not to make a fuss about the kiss she had seen. But what was she doing here? "Are you all right?" Caris said.

"I'm a bit tired," Tilly said. She staggered, and Caris caught her arm.

The baby cried. Merthin took the child and rocked him expertly. "There, there, my little nephew," he said. The crying fell to a mild grizzle of discontent.

Caris said to Tilly: "How did you get here?"

"I walked."

"From Tench Hall? Carrying Gerry?" The baby was now six months old, and no easy burden.

"It took me three days."

"My goodness. Has something happened?"

"I ran away."

"Didn't Ralph come after you?"

"Yes, with Alan. I hid in the forest while they went by. Gerry was very good and didn't cry."

The picture brought a lump to Caris's throat. "But . . ." She swallowed. "But why did you run away?"

"Because my husband wants to kill me," Tilly said, and she burst into tears.

Caris sat her down and Merthin brought her a cup of wine. They let her sob. Caris sat on the bench beside her and put an arm around her shoulders while Merthin cradled baby Gerry. When at last Tilly had cried herself out, Caris said: "What has Ralph done?"

Tilly shook her head. "Nothing. It's just the way he looks at me. I know he wants to murder me."

Merthin muttered: "I wish I could say my brother is incapable of that."

Caris said: "But why would he want to do such a terrible thing?"

"I don't know," Tilly said miserably. "Ralph went to Uncle William's funeral. There was a lawyer from London there, Sir Gregory Longfellow."

"I know him," Caris said. "A clever man, but I don't like him."

"It started after that. I have a feeling it's all to do with Gregory."

Caris said: "You wouldn't have walked all this way, carrying a baby, because of something you just imagined."

"I know it sounds fanciful, but he just sits and glares at me hatefully. How can a man look at his wife like that?"

"Well, you've come to the right place," Caris said. "You're safe here."

"Can I stay?" she begged. "You won't send me back, will you?"

"Certainly not," said Caris. She caught Merthin's eye. She knew what he was thinking. It would be rash to give Tilly a guarantee. Fugitives might take refuge in churches, as a general principle, but it was very doubtful whether a nunnery had the right to shelter a knight's wife and keep her from him indefinitely. Moreover Ralph would certainly be entitled to make her give up the baby, his son and heir. All the same, Caris put as much confidence into her voice as she could and said: "You can stay here just as long as you like."

"Oh, thank you."

Caris silently prayed that she would be able to keep her promise.

"You could live in one of the special guest rooms upstairs in the hospital," she said.

Tilly looked troubled. "But what if Ralph should come in?"

"He wouldn't dare. But if it makes you feel safer, you can have Mother Cecilia's old room, at the end of the nuns' dormitory."

"Yes, please."

A priory servant came in to lay the table for dinner. Caris said to Tilly: "I'll take you to the refectory. You can have dinner with the nuns, then lie down in the dormitory and rest." She stood up.

Suddenly she felt dizzy. She put a hand on the table to steady herself. Merthin, still holding baby Gerry, said anxiously: "What's wrong?"

"I'll be fine in a moment," Caris said. "I'm just tired."

Then she fell to the floor.

Merthin felt a tidal wave of panic. For an instant, he was stunned. Caris had never been ill, never helpless—she was the one who took care of the sick. He could not think of her as a victim.

The moment passed like a blink. Fighting down his fear, he carefully handed the baby to Tilly.

The servant girl had stopped laying the table and stood staring in shock at the unconscious form of Caris on the floor. Merthin deliberately made his voice calm but urgent and said to her: "Run to the hospital and tell them Mother Caris is ill. Bring Sister Oonagh. Go on now, as quick as you can!" She hurried away.

Merthin knelt beside Caris. "Can you hear me, my darling?" he said. He picked up her limp hand and patted it, then touched her cheek, then lifted an eyelid. She was out cold.

Tilly said: "She's got the plague, hasn't she?"

"Oh, God." Merthin took Caris in his arms. He was a slight man, but he had always been able to lift heavy objects, building stones and timber beams. He lifted her easily and stood upright, then laid her gently on the table. "Don't die," he whispered. "Please don't die."

He kissed her forehead. Her skin was hot. He had felt it when they embraced a few minutes ago, but he had been too excited to worry. Perhaps that was why she had been so passionate: fever could have that effect.

Sister Oonagh came in. Merthin was so grateful to see her that tears came to his eyes. She was a young nun, only a year or two out of her novitiate, but Caris thought highly of her nursing skill and was grooming her to take responsibility for the hospital one day.

Oonagh wrapped a linen mask over her mouth and nose and tied it in a knot behind her neck. Then she touched Caris's forehead and cheek. "Did she sneeze?" she said.

Merthin wiped his eyes. "No," he answered. He felt sure he would have noticed: a sneeze was an ominous sign.

Oonagh pulled down the front of Caris's robe. To Merthin she looked agonizingly vulnerable with her small breasts exposed. But he was glad to see there was no rash of purple-black spots on her chest. Oonagh covered her up again. She looked up Caris's nostrils. "No bleeding," she said. She felt Caris's pulse thoughtfully.

After a few moments she looked at Merthin. "This may not be the plague, but it seems a serious illness. She's feverish, her pulse is rapid, and her breathing is shallow. Carry her upstairs, lay her down, and bathe her face with rose water. Anyone who attends her must wear a mask and wash their hands as if she had the plague. That includes you." She gave him a linen strip.

Tears rolled down his face as he tied the mask. He carried Caris upstairs, put her on the mattress in her room, and straightened her clothing. The nuns brought rose water and vinegar. Merthin told them of Caris's instructions regarding Tilly, and they took the young mother and baby to the refectory. Merthin sat beside Caris, patting her forehead and cheeks with a rag damped with the fragrant liquid, praying for her to come round.

At last she did. She opened her eyes, frowned in puzzlement, then looked anxious and said: "What happened?"

"You fainted," he said.

She tried to sit up.

"Keep still," he said. "You're sick. It's probably not the plague, but you have a serious illness."

She must have felt weak, for she lay back on the pillow without further protest. "I'll just rest for an hour," she said.

She was in bed for two weeks.

After three days the whites of her eyes turned the color of mustard, and Sister Oonagh said she had the yellow jaundice. Oonagh prepared an infusion of herbs sweetened with honey, which Caris drank hot three times a day. The fever receded, but Caris remained weak. She inquired anxiously about Tilly every day, and Oonagh answered her questions, but refused to discuss any other aspect of life in the nunnery, in case it should tire Caris. Caris was too enfeebled to fight her.

Merthin did not leave the prior's palace. In the daytime he sat downstairs, close enough to hear her call, and his employees came to him for instructions about the various buildings they were putting up or tearing down. At night he lay on a mattress beside her and slept lightly, waking every time her breathing changed or she turned over in her bed. Lolla slept in the next room.

At the end of the first week, Ralph showed up.

"My wife has disappeared," he said as he walked into the hall of the prior's palace.

Merthin looked up from a drawing he was making on a large slate. "Hello, brother," he said. Ralph looked shifty, he thought. Clearly he had mixed feelings about Tilly's disappearance. He was not fond of her, but on the other hand no man likes his wife to run away.

Perhaps I have mixed feelings, too, Merthin thought guiltily. After all, I did help his wife to leave him.

Ralph sat on a bench. "Have you got any wine? I'm parched."

Merthin went to the sideboard and poured from a jug. It crossed his mind to say he had no idea where Tilly could be, but his instinct revolted from the idea of lying to his own brother, especially about something so important. Besides, Tilly's presence at the priory could not be kept secret:

too many nuns, novices, and employees had seen her here. It was always best to be honest, Merthin thought, except in dire emergency. Handing the cup to Ralph, he said: "Tilly is here, at the nunnery, with the baby."

"I thought she might be." Ralph lifted the cup in his left hand, showing the stumps of his three severed fingers. He took a long draft. "What's the matter with her?"

"She ran away from you, Ralph."

"You should have let me know."

"I feel bad about that. But I couldn't betray her. She's frightened of you."

"Why take sides with her against me? I'm your brother!"

"Because I know you. If she's scared, there's probably a reason."

"This is outrageous." Ralph was trying to appear indignant, but the act was unconvincing.

Merthin wondered what he really felt.

"We can't throw her out," Merthin said. "She's asked for sanctuary."

"Gerry's my son and heir. You can't keep him from me."

"Not indefinitely, no. If you start a legal action, I'm sure you'll win. But you wouldn't try to separate him from his mother, would you?"

"If he comes home, she will."

That was probably true. Merthin was casting around for another way of persuading Ralph when Brother Thomas came in, bringing Alan Fernhill with him. With his one hand, Thomas was holding Alan's arm, as if to prevent him from running away. "I found him snooping," he said.

"I was just looking around," Alan protested. "I thought the monastery was empty."

Merthin said: "As you see, it's not. We've got one monk, six novices, and a couple of dozen orphan boys."

Thomas said: "Anyway, he wasn't in the monastery, he was in the nuns' cloisters."

Merthin frowned. He could hear a psalm being sung in the distance. Alan had timed his incursion well: all the nuns and novices were in the cathedral for the service of Sext. Most of the priory buildings were deserted at this hour. Alan had probably been walking around unhindered for some time.

This did not seem like idle curiosity.

Thomas added: "Fortunately, a kitchen hand saw him and came to fetch me out of the church."

Merthin wondered what Alan had been looking for. Tilly? Surely he would not have dared to snatch her from a nunnery in broad daylight. He turned to Ralph. "What are you two plotting?"

Ralph batted the question off to Alan. "What did you think you were doing?" he said wrathfully, though Merthin thought the anger was faked.

Alan shrugged. "Just looking around while I waited for you."

It was not plausible. Idle men-at-arms waited for their masters in stables and taverns, not cloisters.

Ralph said: "Well . . . don't do it again."

Merthin realized that Ralph was going to stick with this story. I was honest with him, but he's not being honest with me, he thought sadly. He returned to the more important subject. "Why don't you leave Tilly be for a while?" he said to Ralph. "She'll be perfectly all right here. And perhaps, after a while, she'll realize you mean her no harm, and come back to you."

"It's too shaming," Ralph said.

"Not really. A noblewoman sometimes spends a few weeks at a monastery, if she feels the need to retire from the world for a while."

"Usually when she's been widowed, or her husband has gone off to war."

"Not always, though."

"When there's no obvious reason, people always say she wants to get away from her husband."

"How bad is that? You might like some time away from your wife."

"Perhaps you're right," Ralph said.

Merthin was startled by this response. He had not expected Ralph to be so easily persuaded. It took him a moment to get over the surprise. Then he said: "That's it. Give her three months, then come back and talk to her." Merthin had a feeling that Tilly would never relent, but at least this proposal would postpone the crisis.

"Three months," said Ralph. "All right." He stood up to go.

Merthin shook his hand. "How are Mother and Father? I haven't seen them for months."

"Getting old. Father doesn't leave their house now."

"I'll come and visit as soon as Caris is better. She's recovering from yellow jaundice."

"Give her my best wishes."

Merthin went to the door and watched Ralph and Alan ride away. He felt deeply disturbed. Ralph was up to something, and it was not simply getting Tilly back.

He returned to his drawing and sat staring at it without seeing it for a long time.

By the end of the second week it was clear that Caris was going to get better. Merthin was exhausted but happy. Feeling like a man reprieved, he put Lolla to bed early and went out for the first time.

It was a mild spring evening, and the sun and balmy air made him light-headed. His own tavern, the Bell, was closed for rebuilding, but the Holly Bush was doing brisk business, customers sitting on benches outside with their tankards. There were so many people out enjoying the weather that Merthin stopped and asked the drinkers if it was a holiday today, thinking he might have lost track of the date. "Every day's a holiday now," one said. "What's the point in working, when we're all going to die of the plague? Have a cup of ale."

"No, thanks." Merthin walked on.

He noticed that many people wore very fancy clothes, elaborate headgear and embroidered tunics that they would not normally have been able to afford. He presumed they had inherited these garments, or perhaps just taken them from wealthy corpses. The effect was a bit nightmarish: velvet hats on filthy hair, gold threads and food stains, ragged hose and jewel-encrusted shoes.

He saw two men dressed all in women's clothing, floor-length gowns and wimples. They were walking along the main street arm in arm, like merchants' wives showing off their wealth—but they were unmistakably male, with big hands and feet and hair on their chins. Merthin began to feel disoriented, as if nothing could be relied on anymore.

As the dusk thickened, he crossed the bridge to Leper Island. He had built a street of shops and taverns there, between the two parts of the bridge. The work was finished, but the buildings were untenanted, with boards nailed across their doors and windows to keep vagrants out. No one lived there but rabbits. The premises would remain empty until the plague died out, and Kingsbridge returned to normal, Merthin supposed. If the plague never went away, they would never be occupied; but, in that eventuality, renting his property would be the least of his worries.

He returned to the old city just as the gate was closing. There seemed to be a huge party going on at the White Horse Tavern. The house was full of lights, and the crowd filled the road in front of the building. "What's going on?" Merthin asked a drinker.

"Young Davey's got the plague, and he has no heirs to bequeath the inn to, so he's giving all the ale away," the man said, grinning with delight. "Drink as much as you can hold, it's free!"

He and many other people had clearly been working on the same principle, and dozens of them were reeling drunk. Merthin pushed his way into the crowd. Someone was banging a drum and others were dancing. He saw a circle of men and looked over their shoulders to see what they were hiding. A very drunk woman of about twenty years was bending over a table while a man entered her from behind. Several other men were clearly waiting their turn. Merthin turned away in distaste. At the side of the building, half-concealed by empty barrels, his eye lit on Ozzie Ostler, a wealthy horse dealer, kneeling in front of a younger man and sucking his penis. That was against the law, in fact the penalty was death, but clearly no one cared. Ozzie, a married man who was on the parish guild, caught Merthin's eye but did not stop, in fact he continued with more enthusiasm, as if excited by being watched. Merthin shook his head, amazed. Just outside the tavern door was a table laden with partly eaten food: joints of roasted meat, smoked fish, puddings, and cheese. A dog was standing on the table tearing at a ham. A man was throwing up into a bowl of stew. Beside the tavern door Davey Whitehorse sat in a big wooden chair with a huge cup of wine. He was sneezing and sweating, and the characteristic trickle of blood came from his nose, but he was looking around and cheering the revelers on. He seemed to want to kill himself with drink before the plague finished him off.

Merthin felt nauseated. He left the scene and hurried back to the priory.

To his surprise, he found Caris up and dressed. "I'm better," she said. "I'm going to return to my usual work tomorrow." Seeing his skeptical look, she added: "Sister Oonagh said I could."

"If you're taking orders from someone else, you can't be back to normal," he said; and she laughed. The sight brought tears to his eyes. She had not laughed for two weeks, and there had been moments when he had wondered whether he would ever hear the sound again.

"Where have you been?" she asked.

He told her about his walk around the town, and the disturbing sights he had seen. "None of it was very wicked," he said. "I just wonder what they'll do next. When all their inhibitions have gone, will they start to kill one another?"

A kitchen hand brought a tureen of soup for their supper. Caris sipped warily. For a long time, all food had made her feel sick. However, she seemed to find the leek soup palatable, and drank a bowlful.

When the maid had cleared away, Caris said: "While I was ill, I thought a lot about dying."

"You didn't ask for a priest."

"Whether I've been good or bad, I don't think God will be fooled by a last-minute change of heart."

"What, then?"

"I asked myself if there was anything I really regretted."

"And was there?"

"Lots of things. I'm bad friends with my sister. I haven't any children. I lost that scarlet coat my father gave my mother on the day she died."

"How did you lose it?"

"I wasn't allowed to bring it with me when I entered the nunnery. I don't know what happened to it."

"What was your biggest regret?"

"There were two. I haven't built my hospital; and I've spent too little time in bed with you."

He raised his eyebrows. "Well, the second one is easily rectified."

"I know."

"What about the nuns?"

"Nobody cares anymore. You saw what it was like in the town. Here in the nunnery, we're too busy dealing with the dying to fuss about the old rules. Joan and Oonagh sleep together every night in one of the upstairs rooms of the hospital. It doesn't matter."

Merthin frowned. "It's odd that they do that, and still go to church services in the middle of the night. How do they reconcile the two things?"

"Listen. St. Luke's Gospel says: 'He that hath two coats, let him impart to him that hath none.' How do you think the bishop of Shiring reconciles that with his chest full of robes? Everybody takes what they like from the teachings of the church, and ignores the parts that don't suit them."

"And you?"

"I do the same, but I'm honest about it. So I'm going to live with you, as your wife, and if anyone questions me I shall say that these are strange times." She got up, went to the door, and barred it. "You've been sleeping here for two weeks. Don't move out."

"You don't have to lock me in," he said with a laugh. "I'll stay voluntarily." He put his arms around her.

She said: "We started something a few minutes before I fainted. Tilly interrupted us."

"You were feverish."

"In that way, I still am."

"Perhaps we should pick up where we left off."

"We could go to bed first."

"All right."

Holding hands, they went up the stairs.

71

Ralph and his men hid in the forest north of Kingsbridge, waiting. It was May, and the evenings were long. When night fell Ralph encouraged the others to take a nap while he sat up, watching.

With him were Alan Fernhill and four hired men, soldiers demobilized from the king's army, fighters who had failed to find their niche in peacetime. Alan had hired them at the Red Lion in Gloucester. They did not know who Ralph was and had never seen him in daylight. They would do as they were told, take their money, and ask no questions.

Ralph stayed awake, noting the passing of time automatically, as he had when with the king in France. He had found that, if he tried too hard to figure out how many hours had gone by, he became doubtful; but, if he simply guessed, what came into his head was always right. Monks used a burning candle, marked with rings for the hours, or an hourglass with sand or water trickling through a narrow funnel; but Ralph had a better measure in his head.

He sat very still, with his back to a tree, staring into the low fire they had built. He could hear the rustle of small animals in the undergrowth and the occasional hoot of a predatory owl. He never felt so calm as in the waiting hours before action. There was quiet, and darkness, and time to think. The knowledge of danger to come, which made most men jumpy, actually soothed him.

The main risk tonight did not in fact come from the hazards of fighting. There would be some hand-to-hand combat, but the enemy would consist of fat townsmen or soft-skinned monks. The real peril was that Ralph might be recognized. What he was about to do was shocking. It would be talked of with outrage in every church in the land, perhaps in Europe. Gregory Longfellow, for whom Ralph was doing this, would be the loudest in condemning it. If the fact ever got out that Ralph was the villain, he would be hanged.

But if he succeeded, he would be the earl of Shiring.

When he judged it was two hours past midnight, he roused the others.

They left their tethered horses and walked out of the woodland and along the road to the city. Alan was carrying the equipment, as he always had when they fought in France. He had a short ladder, a coil of rope, and a grappling iron they had used when attacking city walls in Normandy. In his belt were a mason's chisel and a hammer. They might not need these tools, but they had learned that it was best to be prepared.

Alan also had several large sacks, rolled up tightly and tied with string in a bundle.

When they came within sight of the city, Ralph gave out hoods with holes for the eyes and mouth, and they all put them on. Ralph also wore a mitten on his left hand, to conceal the telltale stumps of his three missing fingers. He was completely unrecognizable—unless, of course, he should be captured.

They all pulled felt bags over their boots, tying them to their knees, to muffle their footsteps.

It was hundreds of years since Kingsbridge had been attacked by an army, and security was slack, especially since the advent of the plague. Nevertheless, the southern entrance to the town was firmly closed. At the townward end of Merthin's great bridge was a stone gatehouse barred with a mighty wooden door. But the river defended the town only on the east and south sides. To the north and west no bridge was needed, and the town was protected by a wall that was in poor repair. That was why Ralph was approaching from the north.

Mean houses huddled outside the walls like dogs at the back of a butcher's shop. Alan had scouted the route several days ago, when the two of them had come to Kingsbridge and inquired about Tilly. Now Ralph and the hired men followed Alan, padding between the hovels as quietly as possible. Even paupers in the suburbs could raise the alarm if awakened. A dog barked, and Ralph tensed, but someone cursed the animal and it fell silent. In another moment they came to a place where the wall was broken down and they could easily clamber over the fallen stones.

They found themselves in a narrow alley behind some warehouses. It came out just inside the north gate of the city. At the gate, Ralph knew, was a sentry in a booth. The six men approached silently. Although they were now within the walls, a sentry would question them if he saw them, and shout for help if he was not satisfied with their answers. But, to Ralph's relief, the man was fast asleep, sitting on a stool and leaning against the side of his box, a stub of candle guttering on a shelf beside him.

All the same, Ralph decided not to risk the man's waking up. He tiptoed close, leaned into the booth, and slit the sentry's throat with a long knife. The man woke up and tried to scream with pain, but all that came out of his mouth was blood. As he slumped, Ralph caught him and held him for the few moments it took him to lose consciousness. Then he propped the body back up against the wall of the booth.

He wiped his bloody blade on the dead man's tunic and sheathed the knife.

The large double door that stopped the gateway had within it a smaller, man-size doorway. Ralph unbarred this little door, ready for a quick getaway later.

The six men walked silently along the street that led to the priory.

There was no moon—Ralph had chosen tonight for that reason—but they were faintly lit by starlight. He looked anxiously at the upstairs windows of the houses on either side. If sleepless people happened to look out, they would see the unmistakably sinister sight of six masked men. Fortunately it was not quite warm enough to leave windows open at night, and all the shutters were closed. Just the same, Ralph pulled up the hood of his cloak and dragged it forward as far as it would go, in the hope of shadowing his face and concealing the mask; then he signed to the others to do the same.

This was the city where he had spent his adolescence, and the streets were familiar. His brother, Merthin, still lived here, although Ralph was not sure exactly where.

They went down the main street, past the Holly Bush, closed for the night and locked up hours ago. They turned into the cathedral close. The entrance had tall ironbound timber gates, but they stood open, not having been closed for years, their hinges rusted and seized up.

The priory was dark except for a dim light in the windows of the hospital. Ralph reckoned this would be the time when the monks and nuns were sleeping most deeply. In an hour or so they would be wakened for the service of Matins, which started and finished before dawn.

Alan, who had reconnoitered the priory, led the team around the north side of the church. They walked silently through the graveyard and past the prior's palace, then turned along the narrow strip of land that divided the east end of the cathedral from the riverbank. Alan propped his short ladder up against a blank wall and whispered: "Nuns' cloisters. Follow me."

He went up the wall and over the roof. His feet made little noise on the slates. Happily, he did not need to use the grappling iron, which might have made an alarming clang.

The others followed, Ralph last.

On the inside, they dropped from the roof and landed with soft thumps on the turf of the quadrangle. Once there, Ralph looked warily at the regular stone columns of the cloisters around him. The arches seemed to stare at him like watchmen, but nothing stirred. It was a good thing monks and nuns were not allowed to have pet dogs.

Alan led them around the deep-shadowed walkway and through a heavy door. "Kitchen," he whispered. The room was dimly lit by the embers of a big fire. "Move slowly so that you don't knock over any pots."

Ralph waited, letting his eyes adjust. Soon he could make out the outlines of a big table, several barrels, and a stack of cooking vessels. "Find somewhere to sit or lie down, and try to make yourselves comfortable," he said to them. "We stay here until they all get up and go into the church."

Peering out of the kitchen an hour later, Ralph counted the nuns and novices shuffling out of the dormitory and heading through the cloisters toward the cathedral, some carrying lamps that threw antic shadows on the vaulted ceiling. "Twenty-five," he whispered to Alan. As he had expected, Tilly was not among them. Visiting noblewomen were not expected to attend services in the middle of the night.

When they had all disappeared, he moved. The others remained behind.

There were only two places where Tilly might be sleeping: the hospital and the nuns' dormitory. Ralph had guessed she would feel safer in the dormitory, and headed there first.

He went softly up the stone steps, his boots still muffled by felt overshoes. He peeped into the dorm. It was lit by a single candle. He was hoping that all the nuns would be in the church, for he did not want miscellaneous people confusing the situation. He was afraid one or two might have stayed behind, because of illness or laziness. But the room was empty—not even Tilly was there. He was about to retreat when he saw a door at the far end.

He padded the length of the dormitory, picking up the candle, and went through the door silently. The unsteady light revealed the young head of his wife on a pillow, her hair in disarray around her face. She looked so innocent and pretty that Ralph felt a stab of remorse, and had to remind himself of how much he hated her for standing in the way of his advancement.

The baby, his son Gerry, lay in a crib next to her, eyes closed, mouth open, sleeping peacefully.

Ralph crept closer and, with a swift movement, clamped his right hand hard over Tilly's mouth, waking her and at the same time stopping her making any noise.

Tilly opened her eyes wide and stared at him in dread.

He put the candle down. In his pocket he had an assortment of useful odds and ends, including rags and leather thongs. He stuffed a rag into Tilly's mouth to keep her quiet. Despite his mask and glove, he had a feeling she recognized him, even though he had not spoken. Perhaps she could smell him, like a dog. It did not matter. She was not going to tell anyone.

He tied her hands and feet with leather thongs. She was not struggling now, but she would later. He checked that her gag was secure. Then he settled down to wait.

He could hear the singing from the church: a strong choir of females and a ragged few male voices trying to match them. Tilly kept staring at him with big, pleading eyes. He turned her over so that he could not see her face.

She had guessed he was going to kill her. She had read his mind. She must be a witch. Perhaps all women were witches. Anyway, she had known his intention almost as soon as he had formed it. She had started to watch him, especially in the evenings, her fearful eyes following him around the room, no matter what he did. She had lain stiff and alert beside him at night while he fell asleep, and in the mornings when he awoke she was invariably up already. Then, after a few days of this, she had disappeared. Ralph and Alan had searched for her without success, then he had heard a rumor that she had taken refuge in Kingsbridge Priory.

Which happened to fit in with his plans very neatly.

The baby snuffled in his sleep, and it occurred to Ralph that he might cry. What if the nuns came back just then? He thought it through. One or two would probably come in here to see if Tilly needed help. He would just kill them, he decided. It would not be the first time. He had killed nuns in France.

At last he heard them shuffling back into the dormitory.

Alan would be watching from the kitchen, counting them as they returned. When they were all safely inside the room, Alan and the other four men would draw their swords and make their move.

Ralph lifted Tilly to her feet. Her face was streaked with tears. He turned her so that her back was to him, then put an arm around her waist and lifted her, hoisting her onto his hip. She was as light as a child.

He drew his long dagger.

From outside, he heard a man say: "Silence, or you die!" It was Alan, he knew, although the hood muffled the voice.

This was a crucial moment. There were other people on the premises—nuns and patients in the hospital, monks in their own quarters—and Ralph did not want them to appear and complicate matters.

Despite Alan's warning, there were several shouts of shock and shrieks of fear—but, Ralph thought, not too loud. So far, so good.

He threw open the door and stepped into the dormitory carrying Tilly on his hip.

He could see by the light of the nuns' lamps. At the far end of the room, Alan had a woman in his grasp, his knife to her throat, in the same pose as Ralph with Tilly. Two more men stood behind Alan. The other two hirelings would be on guard at the foot of the stairs.

"Listen to me," Ralph said.

When he spoke, Tilly jerked convulsively. She had recognized his voice. But that did not matter so long as no one else did.

There was a terrified silence.

Ralph said: "Which of you is treasurer?"

No one spoke.

Ralph touched the edge of his blade to the skin of Tilly's throat. She began to struggle, but she was too small, and he held her easily. Now, he thought, now is the time to kill her; but he hesitated. He had killed many people, women as well as men, but suddenly it seemed terrible to stick a knife into the warm body of someone he had embraced and kissed and slept with, the woman who had borne his child.

Also, he told himself, the effect on the nuns would be more shocking if one of their own died.

He nodded to Alan.

With one strong cut, Alan slit the throat of the nun he was holding. Blood gushed out of her neck onto the floor.

Someone screamed.

It was not merely a cry or a shriek, but a fortissimo yell of pure terror that might have awakened the dead, and it went on until one of the hired men hit the screamer a mighty blow over her head with his club and she fell unconscious to the floor, blood trickling down her cheek.

Ralph said again: "Which of you is treasurer?"

Merthin had woken up briefly when the bell rang for Matins and Caris slipped out of bed. As usual, he turned over and fell into a light doze, so that when she returned it seemed as if she had been away only for a minute or two. She was cold when she got back into bed, and he drew her to him and wrapped his arms around her. They often stayed awake for a while, talking, and usually made love before going to sleep. It was Merthin's favorite time.

She pressed up against him, her breasts squashed comfortably against his chest. He kissed her forehead. When she had warmed up, he reached between her legs and gently stroked the soft hair there.

But she was feeling talkative. "Did you hear yesterday's rumor? Outlaws in the woods north of town."

"It seems a bit unlikely," he said.

"I don't know. The walls are decrepit on that side."

"But what are they going to steal? Anything they want is theirs for the taking. If they need meat, there are thousands of sheep and cattle unguarded in the fields, with no one to claim ownership."

"That's what makes it strange."

"These days, stealing is like leaning over the fence to breathe your neighbor's air."

She sighed. "Three months ago I thought this terrible plague was over."

"How many more people have we lost?"

"We've buried a thousand since Easter."

That seemed about right to Merthin. "I hear that other towns are similar."

He felt her hair move against his shoulder as she nodded in the dark. She said: "I believe something like a quarter of the population of England is gone already."

"And more than half the priests."

"That's because they make contact with so many people every time they hold a service. They can hardly escape."

"So half the churches are closed."

"A good thing, if you ask me. I'm sure crowds spread the plague faster than anything."

"Anyway, most people have lost respect for religion."

To Caris, that was no great tragedy. She said: "Perhaps they'll stop believing in mumbo-jumbo medicine, and start thinking about what treatments actually make a difference."

"You say that, but it's hard for ordinary people to know what is a genuine cure and what a false remedy."

"I'll give you four rules."

He smiled in the dark. She always had a list. "All right."

"One: If there are dozens of different remedies for a complaint, you can be sure none of them works."

"Why?"

"Because if one worked, people would forget the rest."

"Logical."

"Two: Just because a remedy is unpleasant doesn't mean it's any good. Raw larks' brains do nothing for a sore throat, even though they make you heave; whereas a nice cup of hot water and honey will soothe you."

"That's good to know."

"Three: Human and animal dung never does anyone any good. It usually makes them worse."

"I'm relieved to hear it."

"Four: If the remedy looks like the disease—the spotted feathers of a thrush for the pox, say, or sheep's urine for yellow jaundice—it's probably imaginative rubbish."

"You should write a book about this."

She made a scornful noise. "Universities prefer ancient Greek texts."

"Not a book for university students. One for people like you—nuns and midwives and barbers and wise women."

"Wise women and midwives can't read."

"Some can, and others have people who can read for them."

"I suppose people might like a little book that tells them what to do about the plague."

She was thoughtful for a few moments.

In the silence, there was a scream.

"What was that?" Merthin said.

"It sounded like a shrew being caught by an owl," she said.

"No, it didn't," he said, and he got up.

❧

One of the nuns stepped forward and addressed Ralph. She was young—they were nearly all young—with black hair and blue eyes. "Please don't hurt Tilly," she begged. "I'm Sister Joan, the treasurer. We'll give you anything you want. Please don't do any more violence."

"I am Tam Hiding," Ralph said. "Where are the keys to the nuns' treasury?"

"I have them here on my belt."

"Take me there."

Joan hesitated. Perhaps she sensed that Ralph did not know where the treasury was. On their reconnaissance trip, Alan had been able to scout the nunnery quite thoroughly before he was caught. He had plotted their way in, identified the kitchen as a good hiding place, and located the nuns' dormitory; but he had not been able to find the treasury. Clearly Joan did not want to reveal its location.

Ralph had no time to lose. He did not know who might have heard that scream. He pressed the point of his knife into Tilly's throat until it drew blood. "I want to go to the treasury," he said.

"All right, just don't hurt Tilly! I'll show you the way."

"I thought you would," Ralph said.

He left two of the hired men in the dormitory to keep the nuns quiet. He and Alan followed Joan down the steps to the cloisters, taking Tilly.

At the foot of the stairs, the other two hired men were detaining at knifepoint three more nuns. Ralph guessed that those on duty in the hospital had come to investigate the scream. He was pleased: another threat had been neutralized. But where were the monks?

He sent the extra nuns up into the dormitory. He left one hired man on guard at the foot of the stairs and took the other with him.

Joan led them into the refectory, which was at ground level directly under the dorm. Her flickering lamp revealed trestle tables, benches, a lectern, and a wall painting of Jesus at a wedding feast.

At the far end of the room Joan moved a table to reveal a trapdoor in the floor. It had a keyhole just like a normal upright door. She turned a key in the lock and lifted the trapdoor. It gave onto a narrow spiral of stone steps. She descended the stairs. Ralph left the hired man on guard and went down, awkwardly carrying Tilly, and Alan followed him.

Ralph reached the bottom of the staircase and looked around him with a satisfied air. This was the holy of holies, the nuns' secret treasury. It was a cramped underground room like a dungeon, but better built: the walls were of ashlar, smoothly squared-off stones as used in the cathedral, and the floor was paved with closely set flagstones. The air felt cool and dry. Ralph put Tilly, trussed like a chicken, on the floor.

Most of the room was taken up by a huge lidded box, like a coffin for a giant, chained to a ring in the wall. There was not much else: two stools, a writing desk, and a shelf bearing a stack of parchment rolls, presumably the nunnery's account books. On a hook on the wall hung two heavy wool coats, and Ralph guessed they were for the treasurer and her assistant to wear when working down here in the coldest months of the winter.

The box was far too large to have come down the staircase. It must have been brought here in pieces and assembled in situ. Ralph pointed to the clasp, and Joan unlocked it with another of the keys on her belt.

Ralph looked inside. There were scores more parchment rolls, obviously all the charters and title deeds that proved the nunnery's ownership of its property and rights; a pile of leather and wool bags that undoubtedly held jeweled ornaments; and another, smaller chest that probably contained money.

At this point he had to be subtle. His object was those charters, but he did not want that to be apparent. He had to steal them, but appear not to have done so.

He ordered Joan to open the small chest. It contained a few gold coins. Ralph was puzzled by how little money there was. Perhaps more was hidden somewhere in this room, possibly behind stones in the wall. However, he did not stop to ponder: he was only pretending to be interested in the money. He poured the coins into the purse at his belt. Meanwhile, Alan unrolled a capacious sack and began filling it with cathedral ornaments.

Having let Joan see that, Ralph ordered her back up the stairs.

Tilly was still here, watching with wide, terrified eyes, but it did not matter what she saw. She would never have a chance to tell.

Ralph unrolled another sack and began loading the parchment rolls into it as fast as he could.

When they had bagged everything, Ralph told Alan to break up the wooden chests with his hammer and chisel. He took the wool coats from the hook, bundled them up, and held the tip of his candle flame to the bundle. The wool caught fire immediately. He piled wood from the chests on top of the burning wool. Soon there was a merry bonfire, and the smoke caught in his throat.

He looked at Tilly, lying helpless on the floor. He drew his knife. Then, once again, he hesitated.

From the prior's palace, a small door led directly into the chapter house, which itself communicated with the north transept of the cathedral. Merthin and Caris took this route in their search for the source of the scream. The chapter house was empty, and they went into the church. Their single candle was too dim to illuminate the vast interior, but they stood in the center of the crossing and listened hard.

They heard the click of a latch.

Merthin said: "Who's there?" and was ashamed of the fear that made his voice tremble.

"Brother Thomas," they heard.

The voice came from the south transept. A moment later Thomas moved into the light of their candle. "I thought I heard someone scream," he said.

"So did we. But there's no one here in the church."

"Let's look around."

"What about the novices, and the boys?"

"I told them to go back to sleep."

They passed through the south transept into the monks' cloisters. Once again they saw no one and heard nothing. From here, they followed a passage through the kitchen stores to the hospital. The patients lay in their beds as normal, some sleeping and some moving and groaning in pain—but, Merthin realized after a moment, there were no nuns in the room.

"This is strange," said Caris.

The scream might have come from here, but there was no sign of emergency, or of any kind of disturbance.

They went into the kitchen, which was deserted, as they would have expected.

Thomas sniffed deeply, as if trying to pick up a scent.

Merthin said: "What is it?" He found himself whispering.

"Monks are clean," Thomas murmured in reply. "Someone dirty has been here."

Merthin could not smell anything unusual.

Thomas picked up a cleaver, the kind a cook would use to chop through meat and bones.

They went to the kitchen door. Thomas held up the stump of his left arm in a warning gesture and they halted. There was a faint light in the nuns' cloisters. It seemed to be coming from the recess at the near end. It was the reflected gleam of a distant candle, Merthin guessed. It might be coming from the nuns' refectory, or from the flight of stone steps that led up to their dormitory; or both.

Thomas stepped out of his sandals and went forward, his bare feet making no sound on the flagstones. He melted into the shadows of the cloister. Merthin could just about make him out as he edged toward the recess.

A faint but pungent aroma came to Merthin's nose. It was not the smell of dirty bodies that Thomas had detected in the kitchen, but something quite different and new. A moment later Merthin identified it as smoke.

Thomas must have picked it up, too, for he froze in place up against the wall.

Someone unseen gave a grunt of surprise, then a figure stepped out from the recess into the cloister walk, faintly but clearly visible, the weak light outlining the silhouette of a man with some kind of hood covering his entire head and face. The man turned toward the refectory door.

Thomas struck.

The cleaver glinted briefly in the dark, then there was a sickening thud as it sank into the man's body. He gave a shout of terror and pain. As he fell Thomas swung again, and the man's cry turned into a sickening gurgle then stopped. He hit the stone pavement with a lifeless thump.

Beside Merthin, Caris gasped with horror.

Merthin ran forward. "What's going on?" he cried.

Thomas turned to him, making go-back motions with the cleaver. "Quiet!" he hissed.

The light changed in a heartbeat. Suddenly the cloisters were illuminated with the bright glow of a flame.

Someone came running out of the refectory with a heavy tread. It was a big man carrying a sack in one hand and a blazing torch in the other. He looked like a ghost, until Merthin realized he was wearing a crude hood with holes for the eyes and mouth.

Thomas stepped in front of the running man and raised his cleaver. But he was a moment too late. Before he could strike, the man cannoned into him, sending him flying.

Thomas crashed into a pillar, and there was a crack that sounded like his head hitting the stone. He slumped to the ground, out cold. The running man lost his balance and fell to his knees.

Caris pushed past Merthin and knelt beside Thomas.

Several more men appeared, all hooded, some carrying torches. It seemed to Merthin that some emerged from the refectory and others came down the stairs from the dorm. At the same time he heard the sound of women screaming and wailing. For a moment the scene was chaos.

Merthin rushed to Caris's side and tried to protect her, with his body, from the stampede.

The intruders saw their fallen comrade and they all paused in their rush, suddenly shocked into stillness. By the light of their torches they could see that he was unquestionably dead, his neck sliced almost all the way through, his blood spilled copiously over the stone floor of the cloisters. They looked around, moving their heads from side to side, peering through the holes in their hoods, looking like fish in a stream.

One of them spotted Thomas's cleaver, red with blood, lying on the ground next to Thomas and Caris, and pointed at it to show the others. With a grunt of anger, he drew a sword.

Merthin was terrified for Caris. He stepped forward, attracting the swordsman's attention. The man moved toward Merthin and raised his weapon. Merthin retreated, drawing the man away from Caris. As the danger to her receded, he felt more frightened for himself. Walking backward, shaking with fear, he slipped on the dead man's blood. His feet flew from under him and he fell flat on his back.

The swordsman stood over him, weapon raised high to kill him.

Then one of the others intervened. He was the tallest of the intruders, and moved with surprising speed. With his left hand, he grabbed the upraised arm of Merthin's assailant. He must have had authority, for without speaking he simply shook his hooded head from side to side in negation, and the swordsman lowered his weapon obediently.

Merthin noticed that his savior wore a mitten on his left hand, but nothing on the right.

The interaction lasted only as long as it might take a man to count to ten, and ended as suddenly as it had begun. One of the hooded men turned toward the kitchen and broke into a run, and the others followed. They must have planned to escape that way, Merthin realized: the kitchen had a door that gave onto the cathedral green, and that was the quickest way out. They disappeared, and without the blaze of their torches the cloisters went dark.

Merthin stood still, unsure what to do. Should he run after the intruders, go up to the dormitory and find out why the nuns were screaming, or find out where the fire was?

He knelt beside Caris. "Is Thomas alive?" he said.

"I think he's banged his head, and he's unconscious, but he's breathing, and there's no blood."

Behind him, Merthin heard the familiar voice of Sister Joan. "Help me, please!" He turned. She stood in the doorway of the refectory, her face lit up grotesquely by the candle lamp in her hand, her head wreathed in smoke like a fashionable hat. "For God's sake, come quickly!"

He stood up. Joan disappeared back into the refectory, and Merthin ran after her.

Her lamp threw confusing shadows, but he managed to avoid falling over the furniture as he followed her to the end of the room. Smoke was pouring from a hole in the floor. Merthin saw immediately that the hole was the work of a careful builder: it was perfectly square, with neat edges and a well-made trapdoor. He guessed this was the nuns' hidden treasury, built in secrecy by Jeremiah. But tonight's thieves had found it.

He got a lungful of smoke, and coughed. He wondered what was burning down there, and why, but he had no intention of finding out—it looked too dangerous.

Then Joan screamed at him: "Tilly is in there!"

"Dear God," Merthin said despairingly; and he went down the steps.

He had to hold his breath. He peered through the smoke. Despite his fear, his builder's eye noticed that the spiral stone staircase was well made, each step exactly the same size and shape, and each set at precisely the same angle to the next; so that he was able to go down with confidence even when he could not see what was underfoot.

In a second he reached the underground chamber. He could see flames near the middle of the room. The heat was intense, and he knew he would not be able to stand it for more than a few instants. The smoke was thick. He was still holding his breath, but now his eyes began to water, and his vision blurred. He wiped his eyes with his sleeve and peered into the murk. Where was Tilly? He could not see the floor.

He dropped to his knees. Visibility improved slightly: the smoke was less dense lower down. He moved around on all fours, staring into the corners of the room, sweeping with his hands where he could not see. "Tilly!" he shouted. "Tilly, where are you?" The smoke caught in his throat, and he suffered a coughing fit that would have drowned any reply she made.

He could not last any longer. He was coughing convulsively, but every breath seemed to choke him with more smoke. His eyes watered copiously and he was nearly blind. In desperation, he went so close to the fire that the flames began to singe his sleeve. If he collapsed and lost consciousness, he would die for certain.

Then his hand touched flesh.

He grabbed. It was a human leg, a small leg, a girl's leg. He pulled her toward him. Her clothes were smoldering. He could hardly see her face and could not tell whether she was conscious, but she was tied hand and foot with leather thongs, so she could not move of her own accord. Striving to stop coughing, he got his arms under her and picked her up.

As soon as he stood upright the smoke became blindingly thick. Suddenly he could not remember which way the stairs were. He staggered away from the flames and crashed into the wall, almost dropping Tilly. Left or right? He went left and came to a corner. Changing his mind, he retraced his steps.

He felt as if he was drowning. His strength gone, he dropped to his knees. That saved him. Once again he found he could see better close to the floor, and a stone step appeared, like a vision from Heaven, right in front of him.

Desperately holding on to the limp form of Tilly, he moved forward on his knees and made it to the staircase. With a last effort, he got to his feet. He put one foot on the lowest step and hauled himself up; then he managed the next step. Coughing uncontrollably, he forced himself upward until there were no more steps. He staggered, fell to his knees, dropped Tilly, and collapsed on the refectory floor.

Someone bent over him. He spluttered: "Close the trapdoor—stop the fire!" A moment later he heard a bang as the wooden door slammed shut.

He was grabbed under the arms. He opened his eyes for a moment and saw Caris's face, upside-down; then his vision blurred. She dragged him across the floor. The smoke thinned and he began to suck air into his lungs. He sensed the transition from indoors to out, and tasted clean night air. Caris put him down and he heard her footsteps run back inside.

He gasped, coughed, gasped, and coughed. Slowly he began to breathe more normally. His eyes stopped watering, and he saw that dawn was breaking. The faint light showed him a crowd of nuns standing around him.

He sat upright. Caris and another nun dragged Tilly out of the refectory and put her beside him. Caris bent over her. Merthin tried to speak, coughed, and tried again. "How is she?"

"She's been stabbed through the heart," Caris said. She began to cry. "She was dead before you got to her."

72

Merthin opened his eyes to bright daylight. He had slept late: the angle of the sun's rays shining through the bedroom window told him it was the middle of the morning. He recalled the events of the previous night like a bad dream, and for a moment he cherished the thought that they might not really have happened. But his chest hurt when he breathed, and the skin of his face was painfully scorched. The horror of Tilly's murder came back to him. And Sister Nellie, too—both innocent young women. How could God permit such things to happen?

He realized what had awakened him when his eye lit on Caris, putting a tray down on the small table near the bed. Her back was to him but he could tell, by the hunch of her shoulders and the set of her head, that she was angry. It was not surprising. She was grieving for Tilly, and enraged that the sanctity and safety of the nunnery had been violated.

Merthin got up. Caris pulled two stools to the table and they both sat down. He studied her face fondly. There were lines of strain around her eyes. He wondered if she had slept. There was a smear of ash on her left cheek, so he licked his thumb and gently wiped it off.

She had brought new bread with fresh butter and a jug of cider. Merthin found he was hungry and thirsty, and he tucked in. Caris, bottling up fury, ate nothing.

Through a mouthful of bread Merthin said: "How is Thomas this morning?"

"He's lying down in the hospital. His head hurts, but he can talk coherently and answer questions, so there's probably no permanent damage to his brain."

"Good. There will have to be an inquest on Tilly and Nellie."

"I've sent a message to the sheriff of Shiring."

"They will probably blame it on Tam Hiding."

"Tam Hiding is dead."

He nodded. He knew what was coming. His spirits had been lifted by the breakfast, but now they sank again. He swallowed and pushed away his plate.

Caris went on: "Whoever it was that came here last night, he wanted to conceal his identity, so he told a lie—not knowing that Tam died in my hospital three months ago."

"Who do you think it could have been?"

"Someone we know—hence the masks."

"Perhaps."

"Outlaws don't wear masks."

It was true. Living outside the law, they did not care who knew about them and the crimes they committed. Last night's intruders were different. The masks strongly suggested they were respected citizens who were afraid of being recognized.

Caris went on with merciless logic. "They killed Nellie to make Joan open up the treasury—but they had no need to kill Tilly: they were already inside the treasury by then. They wanted her dead for some other reason. And they were not content to leave her to be suffocated by smoke and burned to death: they also stabbed her fatally. For some reason, they had to be sure she was dead."

"What does that tell you?"

Caris did not answer the question. "Tilly thought Ralph wanted to kill her."

"I know."

"One of the hooded men was about to do away with you, at one point." Her voice caught in her throat, and she had to stop. She took a sip of Merthin's cider, composing herself; then she went on. "But the leader stopped him. Why would he do that? They had already murdered a nun and a noblewoman—why scruple to kill a mere builder?"

"You think it was Ralph."

"Don't you?"

"Yes." Merthin sighed heavily. "Did you see his mitten?"

"I noticed he was wearing gloves."

Merthin shook his head. "Only one. On his left hand. Not a glove with fingers, but a mitten."

"To hide his injury."

"I can't be sure, and we certainly couldn't prove anything, but I have a dreadful conviction about it."

Caris stood up. "Let's inspect the damage."

They went to the nuns' cloisters. The novices and the orphans were cleaning the treasury, bringing sacks of charred wood and ashes up the spiral staircase, giving anything not completely destroyed to Sister Joan and carrying the detritus out to the dunghill.

Laid out on a refectory table Merthin saw the cathedral ornaments: gold and silver candlesticks, crucifixes and vessels, all finely wrought and studded with precious stones. He was surprised. "Didn't they take these?" he said.

"Yes—but they seem to have had second thoughts, and dumped them in a ditch outside town. A peasant on his way in with eggs to sell found them this morning. Luckily he was honest."

Merthin picked up a gold aquamanile, a jug for washing the hands, made in the shape of a cockerel, the feathers of its neck beautifully chased. "It's hard to sell something like this. Only a few people could afford to buy it, and most of those would guess it had been stolen."

"The thieves could have melted it down and sold the gold."

"Obviously they decided that was too much trouble."

"Perhaps."

She was not convinced. Nor was Merthin: his own explanation did not quite fit. The robbery had been carefully planned, that was evident. So why would the thieves not have made up their minds in advance about the ornaments? Either to take them or leave them behind?

Caris and Merthin went down the steps and into the chamber, Merthin's stomach clenching in fear as he was grimly reminded of last night's ordeal. More novices were cleaning the walls and floor with mops and buckets.

Caris sent the novices away to take a break. When she and Merthin were alone, she picked up a length of wood from a shelf and used it to prize up one of the flagstones underfoot. Merthin had not previously noticed that the stone was not fitted as tightly as most, having a narrow gap all around it. Now he saw that underneath was a spacious vault containing a wooden box. Caris reached into the hole and pulled out the box. She opened it with a key from her belt. It was full of gold coins.

Merthin was surprised. "They missed that!"

"There are three more concealed vaults," Caris told him. "Another in the floor and two in the walls. They missed them all."

"They can't have looked very hard. Most treasuries have hiding places. People know that."

"Especially robbers."

"So maybe the cash wasn't their first priority."

"Exactly." Caris locked the chest and put it back in its vault.

"If they didn't want the ornaments, and they weren't sufficiently interested in cash to search the treasury thoroughly for hidden vaults, why did they come here at all?"

"To kill Tilly. The robbery was a cover."

Merthin thought about that. "They didn't need an elaborate cover story," he said after a pause. "If all they wanted was to kill Tilly, they could have done it in the dormitory and been far away from here by the time the nuns got back from Matins. If they had done it carefully—suffocated her with a feather pillow, say—we would not even have been sure she had been murdered. It would have looked as if she had died in her sleep."

"Then there's no explanation for the attack. They ended up with next to nothing—a few gold coins."

Merthin looked around the underground chamber. "Where are the charters?" he said.

"They must have burned. It doesn't much matter. I've got copies of everything."

"Parchment doesn't burn very well."

"I've never tried to light it."

"It smolders, shrinks and distorts, but it doesn't catch fire."

"Perhaps the charters have been retrieved from the debris."

"Let's check."

They climbed back up the steps and left the vault. Outside in the cloisters, Caris asked Joan: "Have you found any parchment among the ashes?"

She shook her head. "Nothing at all."

"Could you have missed it?"

"I don't think so—not unless it has burned to cinders."

"Merthin says it doesn't burn." She turned to him. "Who would want our charters? They're no use to anyone else."

Merthin followed the thread of his own logic, just to see where it might lead. "Suppose there's a document that you've got—or you *might* have, or they *think* you might have—and they want it."

"What could it be?"

Merthin frowned. "Documents are intended to be public. The whole point of writing something down is so that people can look at it in the future. A secret document is a strange thing . . ." Then he thought of something.

He drew Caris away from Joan, and walked casually around the cloisters with her until he was sure they could not be overheard. Then he said: "But, of course, we do know of one secret document."

"The letter Thomas buried in the forest."

"Yes."

"But why would anyone imagine it might be in the nunnery's treasury?"

"Well, think. Has anything happened lately that might arouse such a suspicion?"

A look of dismay came over Caris's face. "Oh, my soul," she exclaimed.

"There is something."

"I told you about Lynn Grange being given to us by Queen Isabella for accepting Thomas, all those years ago."

"Did you speak to anyone else about it?"

"Yes—the bailiff of Lynn. And Thomas was angry that I had done so, and said there would be dire consequences."

"So someone is afraid you might have got hold of Thomas's secret letter."

"Ralph?"

"I don't think Ralph is aware of the letter. I was the only one of us children who saw Thomas burying it. He's certainly never mentioned it. Ralph must be acting on behalf of someone else."

Caris looked scared. "Queen Isabella?"

"Or the king himself."

"Is it possible that the king ordered Ralph to invade a nunnery?"

"Not personally, no. He would have used an intermediary, someone loyal, ambitious, and with absolutely no scruples. I came across such men in Florence, hanging around the doge's palace. They're the scum of the earth."

"I wonder who it was."

"I think I can guess," said Merthin.

Gregory Longfellow met Ralph and Alan two days later at Wigleigh, in the small timber manor house. Wigleigh was more discreet than Tench. At Tench Hall there were too many people watching Ralph's every move: servants, followers, his parents. Here in Wigleigh the peasants had their own backbreaking business to do, and no one would question Ralph about the contents of the sack Alan was carrying.

"I gather it went off as planned," Gregory said. News of the invasion of the nunnery had spread all over the county in no time.

"No great difficulty," Ralph said. He was a bit let down by Gregory's muted reaction. After all the trouble that had been taken to get the charters, Gregory might have shown some elation.

"The sheriff has announced an inquest, of course," Gregory said dourly.

"They'll blame it on outlaws."

"You were not recognized?"

"We wore hoods."

Gregory looked at Ralph strangely. "I did not know that your wife was at the nunnery."

"A useful coincidence," Ralph said. "It enabled me to kill two birds with one stone."

The strange look intensified. What was the lawyer thinking? Was he going to pretend to be shocked that Ralph had killed his wife? If so, Ralph was ready to point out that Gregory was complicit in everything that had happened at the nunnery—he had been the instigator. He had no right to judge. Ralph waited for Gregory to speak. But, after a long pause, all he said was: "Let's have a look at these charters."

They sent the housekeeper, Vira, on a lengthy errand, and Ralph made Alan stand at the door to keep out casual callers. Then Gregory tipped the charters out of the sack onto the table. He made himself comfortable and began to examine them. Some were rolled and tied with string, others bundled flat, a few sewn together in booklets. He opened one, read a few lines in the strong sunlight coming through the open windows, then threw the charter back into the sack and picked up another.

Ralph had no idea what Gregory was looking for. He had only said that it might embarrass the king. Ralph could not imagine what kind of document Caris might possess that would embarrass a king.

He got bored watching Gregory read, but he was not going to leave.

He had delivered what Gregory wanted, and he was going to sit here until Gregory confirmed his half of the deal.

The tall lawyer worked his way patiently through the documents. One caught his attention, and he read it all the way through, but then he threw it in the sack with the others.

Ralph and Alan had spent most of the last week in Bristol. It was not likely that they would be asked to account for their movements, but they had taken precautions anyway. They had caroused at taverns every evening except the night they went to Kingsbridge. Their companions would remember the free drinks, but probably would not recall that on one night of the week Ralph and Alan had been absent—or, if they did, they certainly would not know whether it was the fourth Wednesday after Easter or the Thursday but two before Whitsun.

At last the table was clear and the sack was full again. Ralph said: "Did you not find what you were looking for?"

Gregory did not answer the question. "You brought everything?"

"Everything."

"Good."

"So you haven't found it?"

Gregory chose his words carefully, as always. "The specific item is not here. However, I did come across a deed that may explain why this . . . issue . . . has arisen in recent months."

"So you're satisfied," Ralph persisted.

"Yes."

"And the king need no longer be anxious."

Gregory looked impatient. "You should not concern yourself with the king's anxieties. I'll do that."

"Then I can expect my reward immediately."

"Oh, yes," said Gregory. "You shall be the earl of Shiring by harvesttime."

Ralph felt a glow of satisfaction. The earl of Shiring—at last. He had won the prize he had always longed for, and his father was still alive to hear the news. "Thank you," he said.

"If I were you," said Gregory, "I should go and woo Lady Philippa."

"Woo her?" Ralph was astonished.

Gregory shrugged. "She has no real choice in the matter, of course. But still, the formalities should be observed. Tell her that the king has given you permission to ask for her hand in marriage, and say you hope she will learn to love you as much as you love her."

"Oh," said Ralph. "All right."

"Take her a present," said Gregory.

73

On the morning of Tilly's burial, Caris and Merthin met on the roof of the cathedral at dawn.

The roof was a world apart. Calculating the acreage of slates was a perennial geometry exercise in the advanced mathematics class at the priory school. Workmen needed constant access for repairs and maintenance, so a network of walkways and ladders linked the slopes and ridges, corners and gulleys, turrets and pinnacles, gutters and gargoyles. The crossing tower had not yet been rebuilt, but the view from the top of the west facade was impressive.

The priory was already busy. This would be a big funeral. Tilly had been a nobody in life, but now she was the victim of a notorious murder, a noblewoman killed in a nunnery, and she would be mourned by people who had never spoken three words to her. Caris would have liked to discourage mourners, because of the risk of spreading the plague, but there was nothing she could do.

The bishop was already here, in the best room of the prior's palace—which was why Caris and Merthin had spent the night apart, she in the nuns' dormitory and he and Lolla at the Holly Bush. The grieving widower, Ralph, was in a private room upstairs at the hospital. His baby, Gerry, was being taken care of by the nuns. Lady Philippa and her daughter, Odila, the only other surviving relatives of the dead girl, were also staying at the hospital.

Neither Merthin nor Caris had spoken to Ralph when he arrived yesterday. There was nothing they could do, no way to get justice for Tilly, for they could prove nothing; but all the same they knew the truth. So far they had told no one what they believed: there was no point. During today's obsequies they would have to pretend something like normalcy with Ralph. It was going to be difficult.

While the important personages slept, the nuns and the priory employees were hard at work preparing the funeral dinner. Smoke was rising from the bakery, where dozens of long four-pound loaves of wheat bread were already in the oven. Two men were rolling a new barrel of wine across to the prior's house. Several novice nuns were setting up benches and a trestle table on the green for the common mourners.

As the sun rose beyond the river, throwing a slanting yellow light on the rooftops of Kingsbridge, Caris studied the marks made on the town by nine months of plague. From this height she could see gaps in the rows of houses, like bad teeth. Timber buildings collapsed all the time, of course—because of fire, rain damage, incompetent construction, or just old age. What was different now was that no one bothered to repair them. If your house fell down, you just moved into one of the empty homes in the same street. The only person building anything was Merthin, and he was seen as a mad optimist with too much money.

Across the river, the gravediggers were already at work in another newly consecrated cemetery. The plague showed no signs of relenting. Where would it end? Would the houses just continue to fall down, one at a time, until there was nothing left, and the town was a wasteland of broken tiles and scorched timbers, with a deserted cathedral in the middle and a hundred-acre graveyard at its edge?

"I'm not going to let this happen," she said.

Merthin did not at first understand. "The funeral?" he said, frowning.

Caris made a sweeping gesture to take in the city and the world beyond it. "Everything. Drunks maiming one another. Parents abandoning their sick children on the doorstep of my hospital. Men queuing to fuck a drunken woman on a table outside the White Horse. Livestock dying in the pastures. Half-naked penitents whipping themselves then collecting pennies from bystanders. And, most of all, a young mother brutally murdered here in my nunnery. I don't care if we are all going to die of the plague. As long as we're still alive, I'm not going to let our world fall apart."

"What are you going to do?"

She smiled gratefully at Merthin. Most people would have told her she was powerless to fight the situation, but he was always ready to believe in her. She looked at the stone angels carved on a pinnacle, their faces blurred by two hundred years of wind and rain, and she thought of the spirit that had moved the cathedral builders. "We're going to reestablish order and routine here. We're going to force Kingsbridge people to return to normal, whether they like it or not. We're going to rebuild this town and its life, despite the plague."

"All right," he said.

"This is the moment to do it."

"Because everyone is so angry about Tilly?"

"And because they're frightened at the thought that armed men can come into the town at night and murder whomever they will. They think no one's safe."

"What will you do?"

"I'm going to tell them it must never happen again."

ഗ

"This must never happen again!" she cried, and her voice rang out across the graveyard and echoed off the ancient gray walls of the cathedral.

A woman could never speak out as part of a service in church, but the graveside ceremony was a gray area, a solemn moment that took place outside the church, a time when laypeople such as the family of the deceased would sometimes make speeches or pray aloud.

All the same, Caris was sticking her neck out. Bishop Henri was officiating, backed up by Archdeacon Lloyd and Canon Claude. Lloyd had been diocesan clerk for decades, and Claude was a colleague of Henri's from France. In such distinguished clerical company, it was audacious for a nun to make an unscheduled speech.

Such considerations had never meant much to Caris, of course.

She spoke just as the small coffin was being lowered into the grave. Several of the congregation had begun to cry. The crowd was at least five hundred strong, but they fell silent at the sound of her voice.

"Armed men have come into our town at night and killed a young woman in the nunnery—and I will not stand for it," she said.

There was a rumble of assent from the crowd.

She raised her voice. "The priory will not stand for it—the bishop will not stand for it—and the men and women of Kingsbridge will not stand for it!"

The support became louder, the crowd shouting: "No!" and "Amen!"

"People say the plague is sent by God. I say that when God sends rain we take shelter. When God sends winter, we build up the fire. When God sends weeds, we pull them up by the roots. We must defend ourselves!"

She glanced at Bishop Henri. He was looking bemused. He had had no warning of this sermon, and if he had been asked for his permission he would have refused it; but he could tell that Caris had the people on her side, and he did not have the nerve to intervene.

"What can we do?"

She looked around. All faces were turned to her expectantly. They had no idea what to do, but they wanted a solution from her. They would cheer at anything she said, if only it gave them hope.

"We must rebuild the city wall!" she cried.

They roared their approval.

"A new wall that is taller, and stronger, and longer than the broken-down old one." She caught the eye of Ralph. "A wall that will keep murderers out!"

The crowd shouted: "Yes!" Ralph looked away.

"And we must elect a new constable, and a force of deputies and sentries, to uphold the law and enforce good behavior."

"Yes!"

"There will be a meeting of the parish guild tonight to work out the practical details, and the guild's decisions will be announced in church next Sunday. Thank you and God bless you all."

At the funeral banquet, in the grand dining hall of the prior's palace, Bishop Henri sat at the head of the table. On his right was Lady Philippa, the widowed countess of Shiring. Next to her was seated the chief mourner, Tilly's widower, Sir Ralph Fitzgerald.

Ralph was delighted to be next to Philippa. He could stare at her breasts while she concentrated on her food, and every time she leaned forward he could peek down the square neckline of her light summer dress. She did not know it yet, but the time was not far away when he would command her to take off her clothes and stand naked in front of him, and he would see those magnificent breasts in their entirety.

The dinner provided by Caris was ample but not extravagant, he noted. There were no gilded swans or towers of sugar, but there was plenty of roasted meat, boiled fish, new bread, beans, and spring berries. He helped Philippa to some soup made of ground chicken with almond milk.

She said to him gravely: "This is a terrible tragedy. You have my most profound sympathy."

People had been so compassionate that sometimes, for a few moments, Ralph thought of himself as the pitiable victim of a dreadful bereavement, and forgot that he was the one who had slid the knife into Tilly's young heart. "Thank you," he said solemnly. "Tilly was so young. But we soldiers get used to sudden death. One day a man will save your life, and swear eternal friendship and loyalty; and the next day he is struck down by a crossbow bolt through the heart, and you forget him."

She gave him an odd look that reminded him of the way Sir Gregory had regarded him, with a mixture of curiosity and distaste, and he wondered what it was about his attitude to Tilly's death that provoked this reaction.

Philippa said: "You have a baby boy."

"Gerry. The nuns are looking after him today, but I'll take him home to Tench Hall tomorrow. I've found a wet nurse." He saw an opportunity to drop a hint. "Of course, he needs someone to mother him properly."

"Yes."

He recalled her own bereavement. "But you know what it is to lose your spouse."

"I was fortunate to have my beloved William for twenty-one years."

"You must be lonely." This might not be the moment to propose, but he thought to edge the conversation toward the subject.

"Indeed. I lost my three men—William and our two sons. The castle seems so empty."

"But not for long, perhaps."

She stared at him as if she could not believe her ears, and he realized he had said something offensive. She turned away and spoke to Bishop Henri on her other side.

On Ralph's right was Philippa's daughter, Odila. "Would you like some of this pasty?" he said to her. "It's made with peacocks and hares." She nodded, and he cut her a slice. "How old are you?" he asked.

"I'll be fifteen this year."

She was tall, and had her mother's figure already, a full bosom and wide, womanly hips. "You seem older," he said, looking at her breasts.

He intended it as a compliment—young people generally wanted to seem older—but she blushed and looked away.

Ralph looked down at his trencher and speared a chunk of pork cooked with ginger. He ate it moodily. He was not very good at what Gregory called wooing.

ꟿ

Caris was seated on the left of Bishop Henri, with Merthin, as alderman, on her other side. Next to Merthin was Sir Gregory Longfellow, who had come for the funeral of Earl William three months ago and had not yet left the neighborhood. Caris had to suppress her disgust at being at a table with the murdering Ralph and the man who had, almost certainly, put him up to it. But she had work to do at this dinner. She had a plan for the revival of the town. Rebuilding the walls was only the first part. For the second, she had to get Bishop Henri on her side.

She poured the bishop a goblet of clear red Gascon wine, and he took a long draft. He wiped his mouth and said: "You preach a good sermon."

"Thank you," she said, noting the ironic reproof that underlay his compliment. "Life in this town is degenerating into disorder and debauchery, and if we're to put it right we need to inspire the townspeople. I'm sure you agree."

"It's a little late to ask whether I agree with you. However, I do." Henri was a pragmatist who did not re-fight lost battles. She had been counting on that.

She served herself some heron roasted with pepper and cloves, but did not begin to eat: she had too much to say. "There's more to my plan than the walls and the constabulary."

"I thought there might be."

"I believe that you, as the bishop of Kingsbridge, should have the tallest cathedral in England."

He raised his eyebrows. "I wasn't expecting that."

"Two hundred years ago this was one of England's most important priories. It should be so again. A new church tower would symbolize the revival—and your eminence among bishops."

He smiled wryly, but he was pleased. He knew he was being flattered, and he liked it.

Caris said: "The tower would also serve the town. Being visible from a distance, it would help pilgrims and traders find their way here."

"How would you pay for it?"

"The priory is wealthy."

He was surprised again. "Prior Godwyn complained of money problems."

"He was a hopeless manager."

"He struck me as rather competent."

"He struck a lot of people that way, but he made all the wrong decisions. Right at the start he refused to repair the fulling mill, which would have brought him an income; but he spent money on this palace, which returned him nothing."

"And how have things changed?"

"I've sacked most of the bailiffs and replaced them with younger men who are willing to make changes. I've converted about half the land to grazing, which is easier to manage in these times of labor shortage. The rest I've leased for cash rents with no customary obligations. And we've all benefited from inheritance taxes and from the legacies of people who died without heirs because of the plague. The monastery is now as rich as the nunnery."

"So all the tenants are free?"

"Most. Instead of working one day a week on the demesne farm, and carting the landlord's hay, and folding their sheep on the landlord's field, and all those complicated services, they just pay money. They like it better and it certainly makes our life simpler."

"A lot of landlords—abbots especially—revile that type of tenancy. They say it ruins the peasantry."

Caris shrugged. "What have we lost? The power to impose petty variations, favoring some serfs and persecuting others, keeping them all subservient. Monks and nuns have no business tyrannizing peasants. Farmers know what crops to sow and what they can sell at market. They work better left to themselves."

The bishop looked suspicious. "So you feel the priory can pay for a new tower?"

He had been expecting her to ask him for money, she guessed. "Yes—with some assistance from the town's merchants. And that's where you can help us."

"I thought there must be something."

"I'm not asking you for money. What I want from you is worth more than money."

"I'm intrigued."

"I want to apply to the king for a borough charter." As she said the words, Caris felt her hands begin to shake. She was taken back to the battle she had fought with Godwyn, ten years ago, that had ended in her being accused of witchcraft. The issue then had been the borough charter, and she had nearly died fighting for it. Circumstances now were completely different, but the charter was no less important. She put down her eating knife and clasped her hands together in her lap to keep them still.

"I see," said Henri noncommittally.

Caris swallowed hard and went on. "It's essential for the regeneration of the town's commercial life. For a long time Kingsbridge has been held back by the dead hand of priory rule. Priors are cautious and conservative, and instinctively say no to any change or innovation. Merchants live by change—they're always looking for new ways to make money, or at least the good ones are. If we want the men of Kingsbridge to help pay for our new tower, we must give them the freedom they need to prosper."

"A borough charter."

"The town would have its own court, set its own regulations, and be ruled by a proper guild, rather than the parish guild we have now, which has no real power."

"But would the king grant it?"

"Kings like boroughs, which pay lots of taxes. But, in the past, the prior of Kingsbridge has always opposed a charter."

"You think priors are too conservative."

"Timid."

"Well," said the bishop with a laugh, "timidity is a thing you'll never be accused of."

Caris pressed her point. "I think a charter is essential if we're to build the new tower."

"Yes, I can see that."

"So, do you agree?"

"To the tower, or the charter?"

"They go together."

Henri seemed amused. "Are you making a deal with me, Mother Caris?"

"If you're willing."

"All right. Build me a tower, and I'll help you get a charter."

"No. It has to be the other way around. We need the charter first."

"So I must trust you."

"Is that difficult?"

"To be honest, no."

"Good. Then we're agreed."

"Yes."

Caris leaned forward and looked past Merthin. "Sir Gregory?"

"Yes, Mother Caris?"

She forced herself to be polite to him. "Have you tried this rabbit in sugar gravy? I recommend it."

Gregory accepted the bowl and took some. "Thank you."

Caris said to him: "You will recall that Kingsbridge is not a borough."

"I certainly do." Gregory had used that fact, more than a decade ago, to outmaneuver Caris in the royal court in the dispute over the fulling mill.

"The bishop thinks it's time for us to ask the king for a charter."

Gregory nodded. "I believe the king might look favorably on such a plea—especially if it were presented to him in the right way."

Hoping that her distaste was not showing on her face, she said: "Perhaps you would be kind enough to advise us."

"May we discuss this in more detail later?"

Gregory would require a bribe, of course, though he would undoubtedly call it a lawyer's fee. "By all means," she said, repressing a shudder.

The servants began clearing away the food. Caris looked down at her trencher. She had not eaten anything.

"Our families are related," Ralph was saying to Lady Philippa. "Not closely, of course," he added hastily. "But my father is descended from that earl of Shiring who was the son of Lady Aliena and Jack Builder." He looked across the table at his brother Merthin, the alderman. "I think I inherited the blood of the earls, and my brother that of the builders."

He looked at Philippa's face to see how she took that. She did not seem impressed.

"I was brought up in the household of your late father-in-law, Earl Roland," he went on.

"I remember you as a squire."

"I served under the earl in the king's army in France. At the battle of Crécy, I saved the life of the prince of Wales."

"My goodness, how splendid," she said politely.

He was trying to get her to see him as an equal, so that it would seem more natural when he told her that she was to be his wife. But he did not appear to be getting through to her. She just looked bored and a bit puzzled by the direction of his conversation.

The dessert was served: sugared strawberries, honey wafers, dates and raisins, and spiced wine. Ralph drained a cup of wine and poured more, hoping that the drink would help him relax with Philippa. He was not sure why he found it difficult to talk to her. Because this was his wife's funeral? Because Philippa was a countess? Or because he had been hopelessly in love with her for years, and could not believe that now, at last, she really was to be his wife?

"When you leave here, will you go back to Earlscastle?" he asked her.

"Yes. We depart tomorrow."

"Will you stay there long?"

"Where else would I go?" She frowned. "Why do you ask?"

"I will come and visit you there, if I may."

Her response was frosty. "To what end?"

"I want to discuss with you a subject that it would not be appropriate to raise here and now."

"What on earth do you mean?"

"I'll come and see you in the next few days."

She looked agitated. In a raised voice she said: "What could you possibly have to say to me?"

"As I said, it wouldn't be appropriate to speak of it today."

"Because this is your wife's funeral?"

He nodded.

She went pale. "Oh, my God," she said. "You can't mean to suggest . . ."

"I told you, I don't want to discuss it now."

"But I must know!" she cried. "Are you planning to propose marriage to me?"

He hesitated, shrugged, and then nodded.

"But on what grounds?" she said. "Surely you need the king's permission!"

He looked at her and raised his eyebrows briefly.

She stood up suddenly. "No!" she said. Everyone around the table looked at her. She stared at Gregory. "Is this true?" she said. "Is the king going to marry me to *him*?" She jerked a thumb contemptuously at Ralph.

Ralph felt stabbed. He had not expected her to display such revulsion. Was he so repellent?

Gregory looked reproachfully at Ralph. "This was not the moment to raise the matter."

Philippa cried: "So it's true! God save me!"

Ralph caught Odila's eye. She was staring at him in horror. What had he ever done to earn her dislike?

Philippa said: "I can't bear it."

"Why?" Ralph said. "What is so wrong? What right have *you* to look down on me and my family?" He looked around at the company: his brother, his ally Gregory, the bishop, the prioress, minor noblemen, and leading citizens. They were all silent, shocked and intrigued by Philippa's outburst.

Philippa ignored his question. Addressing Gregory, she said: "I will not do it! I will not, do you hear me?" She was white with rage, but tears ran down her cheeks. Ralph thought how beautiful she was, even while she was rejecting and humiliating him so painfully.

Gregory said coolly: "It is not your decision, Lady Philippa, and it certainly is not mine. The king will do as he pleases."

"You may force me into a wedding dress, and you may march me up the aisle," Philippa raged. She pointed at Bishop Henri. "But when the bishop asks me if I take Ralph Fitzgerald to be my husband I will not say yes! I will not! Never, never, never!"

She stormed out of the room, and Odila followed.

When the banquet was over, the townspeople returned to their homes, and the important guests went to their rooms to sleep off the feast. Caris supervised the clearing up. She felt sorry for Philippa, profoundly sorry, knowing—as Philippa did not—that Ralph had killed his first wife. But she was concerned about the fate of an entire town, not just one person.

Her mind was on her scheme for Kingsbridge. Things had gone better than she had imagined. The townspeople had cheered her, and the bishop had agreed to everything she proposed. Perhaps civilization would return to Kingsbridge, despite the plague.

Outside the back door, where there was a pile of meat bones and crusts of bread, she saw Godwyn's cat, Archbishop, delicately picking at the carcass of a duck. She shooed it away. It scampered a few yards then slowed to a stiff walk, its white-tipped tail arrogantly upstanding.

Deep in thought, she went up the stairs of the palace, thinking of how she would begin implementing the changes agreed to by Henri. Without pausing, she opened the door of the bedroom she shared with Merthin and stepped inside.

For a moment she was disoriented. Two men stood in the middle of the room, and she thought, *I must be in the wrong house,* and then *I must be in the wrong room,* before she remembered that her room, being the best bedroom, had naturally been given to the bishop.

The two men were Henri and his assistant, Canon Claude. It took Caris a moment to realize that they were both naked, with their arms around one another, kissing.

She stared at them in shock. "Oh!" she said.

They had not heard the door. Until she spoke, they did not realize they were observed. When they heard her gasp of surprise, they both turned toward her. A look of horrified guilt came over Henri's face, and his mouth fell open.

"I'm sorry!" Caris said.

The men sprang apart, as if hoping they might be able to deny what was going on; then they remembered they were naked. Henri was plump, with a round belly and fat arms and legs, and gray hair on his chest. Claude was younger and slimmer, with very little body hair except for a blaze of chestnut at his groin. Caris had never before looked at two erect penises at the same time.

"I beg your pardon!" she said, mortified with embarrassment. "My mistake. I forgot." She realized that she was babbling and they were dumbstruck. It did not matter: nothing that anyone could say would make the situation any better.

Coming to her senses, she backed out of the room and slammed the door.

⁂

Merthin walked away from the banquet with Madge Webber. He was fond of this small, chunky woman, with her chin jutting out in front and her bottom jutting out behind. He admired the way she had carried on after her husband and children had died of the plague. She had continued the enterprise, weaving cloth and dyeing it red according to Caris's recipe. She said to him: "Good for Caris. She's right, as usual. We can't go on like this."

"You've continued normally, despite everything," he said.

"My only problem is finding the people to do the work."

"Everyone is the same. I can't get builders."

"Raw wool is cheap, but rich people will still pay high prices for good scarlet cloth," Madge said. "I could sell more if I could produce more."

Merthin said thoughtfully: "You know, I saw a faster type of loom in Florence—a treadle loom."

"Oh?" She looked at him with alert curiosity. "I never heard of that."

He wondered how to explain. "In any loom, you stretch a number of threads over the frame to form what you call the warp, then you weave another thread crossways through the warp, under one thread and over the next, under and over, from one side to the other and back again, to form the weft."

"That's how simple looms work, yes. Ours are better."

"I know. To make the process quicker, you attach every second warp thread to a movable bar, called a heddle, so that when you shift the heddle, half the threads are lifted away from the rest. Then, instead of going over and under, over and under, you can simply pass the weft thread straight through the gap in one easy movement. Then you drop the heddle below the warp for the return pass."

"Yes. By the way, the weft thread is wound on a bobbin."

"Each time you pass the bobbin through the warp from left to right, you have to put it down, then use both hands to move the heddle, then pick up the bobbin again and bring it back from right to left."

"Exactly."

"In a treadle loom, you move the heddle with your feet. So you never have to put the bobbin down."

"Really? My soul!"

"That would make a difference, wouldn't it?"

"A huge difference. You could weave twice as much—more!"

"That's what I thought. Shall I build one for you to try?"

"Yes, please!"

"I don't remember exactly how it was constructed. I think the treadle operated a system of pulleys and levers . . ." He frowned, thinking. "Anyway, I'm sure I can figure it out."

⁂

Late in the afternoon, as Caris was passing the library, she met Canon Claude coming out, carrying a small book. He caught her eye and stopped. They both immediately thought of the scene Caris had stumbled upon an hour ago. At first Claude looked embarrassed, but then a grin lifted the corners of his mouth. His put his hand to his face to cover it, obviously feeling it was wrong to be amused. Caris remembered how startled the two naked men had been and she, too, felt inappropriate laughter bubbling up inside her. On impulse, she said what was in her mind: "The two of you did look funny!" Claude giggled despite himself, and Caris could not help chuckling too, and they made each other worse, until they fell into one another's arms, tears streaming down their cheeks, helpless with laughter.

⁂

That evening, Caris took Merthin to the southwest corner of the priory grounds, where the vegetable garden grew alongside the river. The air was mild, and the moist earth gave up a fragrance of new growth. Caris could see spring onions and radishes. "So, your brother is to be the earl of Shiring," she said.

"Not if Lady Philippa has anything to do with it."

"A countess has to do what she is told by the king, doesn't she?"

"All women should be subservient to men, in theory," Merthin said with a grin. "Some defy convention, though."

"I can't think who you mean."

Merthin's mood changed abruptly. "What a world," he said. "A man murders his wife, and the king elevates him to the highest rank of the nobility."

"We know these things happen," she said. "But it's shocking when it's your own family. Poor Tilly."

Merthin rubbed his eyes as if to erase visions. "Why have you brought me here?"

"To talk about the final element in my plan: the new hospital."

"Ah. I was wondering . . ."

"Could you build it here?"

Merthin looked around. "I don't see why not. It's a sloping site, but the entire priory is built on a slope, and we're not talking about putting up another cathedral. One story or two?"

"One. But I want the building divided into medium-size rooms, each containing just four or six beds, so that diseases don't spread so quickly from one patient to everyone else in the place. It must have its own pharmacy—a large, well-lit room—for the preparation of medicines, with a herb garden outside. And a spacious, airy latrine with piped water, very easy to keep clean. In fact the whole building must have lots of light and space. But, most importantly, it has to be at least a hundred yards from the rest of the priory. We have to separate the sick from the well. That's the key feature."

"I'll do some drawings in the morning."

She glanced around and, seeing that they were not observed, she kissed him. "This is going to be the culmination of my life's work, do you realize that?"

"You're thirty-two—isn't it a little early to be talking about the culmination of your life's work?"

"It hasn't happened yet."

"It won't take long. I'll start on it while I'm digging the foundations for the new tower. Then, as soon as the hospital is built, I can switch my masons to work on the cathedral."

They started to walk back. She could tell that his real enthusiasm was for the tower. "How tall will it be?"

"Four hundred and five feet."

"How high is Salisbury?"

"Four hundred and four."

"So it *will* be the highest building in England."

"Until someone builds a higher one, yes."

So he would achieve his ambition too, she thought. She put her arm through his as they walked to the prior's palace. She felt happy. That was strange, wasn't it? Thousands of Kingsbridge people had died of the plague, and Tilly had been murdered, but Caris felt hopeful. It was because she had a plan, of course. She always felt better when she had a plan. The new walls, the constabulary, the tower, the borough charter, and most of all the new hospital: how would she find time to organize it all?

Arm in arm with Merthin, she walked into the prior's house. Bishop Henri and Sir Gregory were there, deep in conversation with a third man who had his back to Caris. There was something unpleasantly familiar about the newcomer, even from behind, and Caris felt a tremor of unease. Then he turned around and she saw his face: sardonic, triumphant, sneering, and full of malice.

It was Philemon.

74

Bishop Henri and the other guests left Kingsbridge the next morning. Caris, who had been sleeping in the nuns' dormitory, returned to the prior's palace after breakfast and went upstairs to her room.

She found Philemon there.

It was the second time in two days that she had been startled by men in her bedroom. However, Philemon was alone and fully dressed, standing by the window looking at a book. Seeing him in profile, she realized that the trials of the last six months had left him thinner.

She said: "What are you doing here?"

He pretended to be surprised by the question. "This is the prior's house. Why should I not be here?"

"Because it's not your room!"

"I am the subprior of Kingsbridge. I have never been dismissed from that post. The prior is dead. Who else should live here?"

"Me, of course."

"You're not even a monk."

"Bishop Henri made me acting prior—and last night, despite your return, he did not dismiss me from this post. I am your superior, and you must obey me."

"But you're a nun, and you must live with the nuns, not with the monks."

"I've been living here for months."

"Alone?"

Suddenly Caris saw that she was on shaky ground. Philemon knew that she and Merthin had been living more or less as man and wife. They had been discreet, not flaunting their relationship, but people guessed these things, and Philemon had a wild beast's instinct for weakness.

She considered. She could insist on Philemon's leaving the building immediately. If necessary, she could have him thrown out: Thomas and the novices would obey her, not Philemon. But what then? Philemon would do all he could to call attention to what Merthin and she were up to in the palace. He would create a controversy, and leading townspeople would take sides. Most would support Caris, almost whatever she did, such was her reputation; but there would be some who would censure her behavior. The conflict would weaken her authority and undermine everything else she wanted to do. It would be better to admit defeat.

"You may have the bedroom," she said. "But not the hall. I use that for meetings with leading townspeople and visiting dignitaries. When you're not attending services in the church, you will be in the cloisters, not here. A subprior does not have a palace." She left without giving him a chance to argue. She had saved face, but he had won.

She had been reminded last night of how wily Philemon was. Questioned by Bishop Henri, he seemed to have a plausible explanation for everything dishonorable that he had done. How did he justify deserting his post at the priory and running away to St.-John-in-the-Forest? The monastery had been in danger of extinction, and the only way to save it had been to flee, in accordance with the saying "Leave early, go far, and stay long." It was still, by general consent, the only sure way to avoid the plague. Their sole mistake had been to remain too long in Kingsbridge. Why, then, had no one informed the bishop of this plan? Philemon was sorry, but he and the other monks were only obeying the orders of Prior Godwyn. Then why had he run away from St. John when the plague caught up with them there? He had been called by God to minister to the people of Monmouth, and Godwyn had given him permission to leave. How come Brother Thomas did not know about this permission, in fact denied firmly that it had ever been given? The other monks had not been told of Godwyn's decision for fear it would cause jealousy. Why, then, had Philemon left Monmouth? He had met Friar Murdo, who had told him that Kingsbridge Priory needed him, and he regarded this as a further message from God.

Caris concluded that Philemon had run from the plague until he had realized he must be one of those fortunate people who were not prone to catch it. Then he had learned from Murdo that Caris was sleeping with Merthin in the prior's palace, and he had immediately seen how he could exploit that situation to restore his own fortunes. God had nothing to do with it.

But Bishop Henri had believed Philemon's tale. Philemon was careful to appear humble to the point of obsequiousness. Henri did not know the man, and failed to see beneath the surface.

She left Philemon in the palace and walked to the cathedral. She climbed the long, narrow spiral staircase in the northwest tower and found Merthin in the mason's loft, drawing designs on the tracing floor in the light from the tall north-facing windows.

She looked with interest at what he had done. It was always difficult to read plans, she found. The thin lines scratched in the mortar had to be transformed, in the viewer's imagination, into thick walls of stone with windows and doors.

Merthin regarded her expectantly as she studied his work. He was obviously anticipating a big reaction.

At first she was baffled by the drawing. It looked nothing like a hospital. She said: "But you've drawn . . . a cloister!"

"Exactly," he said. "Why should a hospital be a long narrow room like the nave of a church? You want the place to be light and airy. So, instead of cramming the rooms together, I've set them around a quadrangle."

She visualized it: the square of grass, the building around, the doors leading to rooms of four or six beds, the nuns moving from room to room in the shelter of the covered arcade. "It's inspired!" she said. "I would never have thought of it, but it will be perfect."

"You can grow herbs in the quadrangle, where the plants will have sunshine but be sheltered from the wind. There will be a fountain in the middle of the garden, for fresh water, and it can drain through the latrine wing to the south and into the river."

She kissed him exuberantly. "You're so clever!" Then she recalled the news she had to tell him.

He must have seen her face fall, for he said: "What's the matter?"

"We have to move out of the palace," she said. She told him about her conversation with Philemon, and why she had given in. "I foresee major conflicts with Philemon—I don't want this to be the one on which I make my stand."

"That makes sense," he said. His tone of voice was reasonable, but she knew by his face that he was angry. He stared at his drawing, though he was not really thinking about it.

"And there's something else," she said. "We're telling everyone they have to live as normally as possible—order in the streets, a return to real family life, no more drunken orgies. We ought to set an example."

He nodded. "A prioress living with her lover is about as abnormal as could be, I suppose," he said. Once again his equable tone was contradicted by his furious expression.

"I'm very sorry," she said.

"So am I."

"But we don't want to risk everything we both want—your tower, my hospital, the future of the town."

"No. But we're sacrificing our life together."

"Not entirely. We'll have to sleep separately, which is painful, but we'll have plenty of opportunities to be together."

"Where?"

She shrugged. "Here, for example." An imp of mischief possessed her. She walked away from him across the room, slowly lifting the skirt of her robe, and went to the doorway at the top of the stairs. "I don't see anyone coming," she said as she raised her dress to her waist.

"You can hear them, anyway," he said. "The door at the foot of the stairs makes a noise."

She bent over, pretending to look down the staircase. "Can you see anything unusual, from where you are?"

He chuckled. She could usually pull him out of an angry mood by being playful. "I can see something winking at me," he laughed.

She walked back toward him, still holding her robe up around her waist, smiling triumphantly. "You see, we don't have to give up everything."

He sat on a stool and pulled her toward him. She straddled his thighs and lowered herself onto his lap. "You'd better get a straw mattress up here," she said, her voice thick with desire.

He nuzzled her breasts. "How would I explain the need for a bed in a mason's loft?" he murmured.

"Just say that masons need somewhere soft to put their tools."

A week later Caris and Thomas Langley went to inspect the rebuilding of the city wall. It was a big job but simple and, once the line had been agreed, the actual stonework could be done by inexperienced young masons and apprentices. Caris was glad the project had begun so promptly. It was necessary that the town be able to defend itself in troubled times—but she had a more important motive. Getting the townspeople to guard against disruption from outside would lead naturally, she hoped, to a new awareness of the need for order and good behavior among themselves.

She found it deeply ironic that fate had cast her in this role. She had never been a rule keeper. She had always despised orthodoxy and flouted convention. She felt she had the right to make her own rules. Now here she was clamping down on merrymakers. It was a miracle that no one had yet called her a hypocrite.

The truth was that some people flourished in an atmosphere of anarchy, and others did not. Merthin was one of those who were better off without constraints. She recalled the carving he had made of the wise and foolish virgins. It was different from anything anyone had seen before—so Elfric had made that his excuse for destroying it. Regulation only served to handicap Merthin. But men such as Barney and Lou, the slaughterhouse workers, had to have laws to stop them maiming one another in drunken fights.

All the same her position was shaky. When you were trying to enforce law and order, it was difficult to explain that the rules did not actually apply to you personally.

She was mulling over this as she returned with Thomas to the priory. Outside the cathedral she found Sister Joan pacing up and down in a state of agitation. "I'm so angry with Philemon," she said. "He claims you have stolen his money, and I must give it back!"

"Just calm down," Caris said. She led Joan into the porch of the church, and they sat on a stone bench. "Take a deep breath and tell me what happened."

"Philemon came up to me after Terce and said he needed ten shillings to buy candles for the shrine of St. Adolphus. I said I would have to ask you."

"Quite right."

"He became very angry and shouted that it was the monks' money, and I had no right to refuse him. He demanded my keys, and I think he would have tried to snatch them from me, but I pointed out that they would be no use to him, as he didn't know where the treasury was."

"What a good idea it was to keep that secret," Caris said.

Thomas was standing beside them, listening. He said: "I notice he picked a time when I was off the premises—the coward."

Caris said: "Joan, you did absolutely right to refuse him, and I'm sorry he tried to bully you. Thomas, go and find him and bring him to me at the palace."

She left them and walked through the graveyard, deep in thought. Clearly, Philemon was set on making trouble. But he was not the kind of blustering bully whom she could have overpowered with ease. He was a wily opponent, and she must watch her step.

When she opened the door of the prior's house, Philemon was there in the hall, sitting at the head of the long table.

She stopped in the doorway. "You shouldn't be here," she said. "I specifically told you—"

"I was looking for you," he said.

She realized she would have to lock the building. Otherwise he would always find a pretext for flouting her orders. She controlled her anger. "You looked for me in the wrong place," she said.

"I've found you now, though, haven't I?"

She studied him. He had shaved and cut his hair since his arrival, and he wore a new robe. He was every inch the priory official, calm and authoritative. She said: "I've been speaking to Sister Joan. She's very upset."

"So am I."

She realized he was sitting in the big chair, and she was standing in front of him, as if he were in charge and she a supplicant. How clever he was at manipulating these things. She said: "If you need money, you must ask me."

"I'm the subprior!"

"And I'm the acting prior, which makes me your superior." She raised her voice. "So the first thing you must do is stand up when you're speaking to me!"

He started, shocked by her tone; then he controlled himself. With insulting slowness he pulled himself out of the chair.

Caris sat down in his place and let him stand.

He seemed unabashed. "I understand you're using monastery money to pay for the new tower."

"By order of the bishop, yes."

A flash of annoyance crossed his face. He had hoped to ingratiate himself and make the bishop his ally against Caris. Even as a child he had toadied unendingly to people in authority. That was how he had gained admission to the monastery.

He said: "I must have access to the monastery's money. It's my right. The monks' assets should be in my charge."

"The last time you were in charge of the monks' assets, you stole them."

He went pale: that arrow had struck the bull's-eye. "Ridiculous," he blustered, trying to cover his embarrassment. "Prior Godwyn took them for safekeeping."

"Well, nobody is going to take them for 'safekeeping' while I'm acting prior."

"You should at least give me the ornaments. They are sacred jewels, to be handled by priests, not women."

"Thomas has been dealing with them quite adequately, taking them out for services and restoring them to our treasury afterward."

"It's not satisfactory—"

Caris remembered something, and interrupted him. "Besides, you haven't yet returned all that you took."

"The money—"

"The ornaments. There's a gold candlestick missing, a gift from the chandlers' guild. What happened to that?"

His reaction surprised her. She was expecting another blustering denial. But he looked embarrassed and said: "That was always kept in the prior's room."

She frowned. "And . . . ?"

"I kept it separate from the other ornaments."

She was astonished. "Are you telling me that *you* have had the candlestick all this time?"

"Godwyn asked me to look after it."

"And so you took it with you on your travels to Monmouth and elsewhere?"

"That was his wish."

This was a wildly implausible tale, and Philemon knew it. The fact was that he had stolen the candlestick. "Do you still have it?"

He nodded uncomfortably.

At that moment, Thomas came in. "There you are!" he said to Philemon.

Caris said: "Thomas, go upstairs and search Philemon's room."

"What am I looking for?"

"The lost gold candlestick."

Philemon said: "No need to search. You'll see it on the prie-dieu."

Thomas went upstairs and came down again carrying the candlestick. He handed it to Caris. It was heavy. She looked at it curiously. The base was engraved with the names of the twelve members of the chandlers' guild in tiny letters. Why had Philemon wanted it? Not to sell or melt down, obviously: he had had plenty of time to get rid of it but he had not done so. It seemed he had just wanted to have his own gold candlestick. Did he gaze at it and touch it when he was alone in his room?

She looked at him and saw tears in his eyes.

He said: "Are you going to take it from me?"

It was a stupid question. "Of course," she replied. "It belongs in the cathedral, not in your bedroom. The chandlers gave it for the glory of God and the beautification of church services, not the private pleasure of one monk."

He did not argue. He looked bereft, but not penitent. He did not understand that he had done wrong. His grief was not remorse for wrongdoing, but regret for what had been taken from him. He had no sense of shame, she realized.

"I think that ends our discussion about your access to the priory's valuables," she said to Philemon. "Now you may go." He went out.

She handed the candlestick back to Thomas. "Take it to Sister Joan and tell her to put it away," she said. "We'll inform the chandlers that it has been found, and use it next Sunday."

Thomas went off.

Caris stayed where she was, thinking. Philemon hated her. She wasted no time wondering why: he made enemies faster than a tinker made friends. But he was an implacable foe and completely without scruples. Clearly he was determined to make trouble for her at every opportunity. Things would never get better. Each time she overcame him in one of these little skirmishes, his malice would burn hotter. But if she let him win he would only be encouraged in his insubordination.

It was going to be a bloody battle, and she could not see how it would end.

*

The flagellants came back on a Saturday evening in June.

Caris was in the scriptorium, writing her book. She had decided to begin with the plague and how to deal with it, then go on to lesser ailments. She was describing the linen face masks she had introduced in the Kingsbridge hospital. It was hard to explain that the masks were effective but did not offer total immunity. The only certain safeguard was to leave town before the plague arrived and stay away until it had gone, but that was never going to be an option for the majority of people. Partial protection was a difficult concept for people who believed in miracle cures. The truth was that some masked nuns still caught the plague, but not as many as would otherwise have been expected. She decided to compare the masks to shields. A shield did not guarantee that a man would survive attack, but it certainly gave him valuable protection, and no knight would go into battle without one. She was writing this down, on a pristine sheet of blank parchment, when she heard the flagellants, and groaned in dismay.

The drums sounded like drunken footsteps, the bagpipes like a wild creature in pain, and the bells like a parody of a funeral. She went outside just as the procession entered the precincts. There were more of them this time, seventy or eighty, and they seemed wilder than before: their hair long and matted, their clothing a few shreds, their shrieks more lunatic. They had already been around the town and gathered a long tail of followers, some looking on in amusement, others joining in, tearing their clothes and lashing themselves.

She had not expected to see them again. The pope, Clement VI, had condemned flagellants. But he was a long way away, at Avignon, and it was up to others to enforce his rulings.

Friar Murdo led them, as before. When he approached the west front of the cathedral, Caris saw to her astonishment that the great doors were open wide. She had not authorized that. Thomas would not have done it without asking her. Philemon must be responsible. She recalled that

Philemon on his travels had met up with Murdo. She guessed that Murdo had forewarned Philemon of this visit, and they had conspired together to get the flagellants into the church. No doubt Philemon would argue that he was the only ordained priest in the priory, therefore he had the right to decide what kind of services were conducted.

But what was Philemon's motive? Why did he care about Murdo and the flagellants?

Murdo led the procession through the tall central doorway and into the nave. The townspeople crowded in afterward. Caris hesitated to join in such a display, but she felt the need to know what was going on, so she reluctantly followed the crowd inside.

Philemon was at the altar. Friar Murdo joined him. Philemon raised his hands for quiet, then said: "We come here today to confess our wickedness, repent our sins, and do penance in propitiation."

Philemon was no preacher, and his words drew a muted reaction; but the charismatic Murdo immediately took over. "We confess that our thoughts are lascivious and our deeds are filthy!" he cried, and they shouted their approval.

The proceedings took the same form as before. Worked into a frenzy by Murdo's preaching, people came to the front, cried out that they were sinners, and flogged themselves. The townspeople looked on, mesmerized by the violence and nudity. It was a performance, but the lashes were real, and Caris shuddered to see the weals and cuts on the backs of the penitents. Some of them had done this many times before and were scarred. Others had recent wounds that were reopened by the fresh whipping.

Townspeople soon joined in. As they came forward, Philemon held out a collection bowl, and Caris realized that his motivation was money. Nobody got to confess and kiss Murdo's feet until they put a coin in Philemon's bowl. Murdo was keeping an eye on the takings, and Caris assumed the two men would share out the coins afterward.

There was a crescendo of drumming and piping as more and more townspeople came forward. Philemon's bowl filled up rapidly. Those who had been "forgiven" danced ecstatically to the mad music.

Eventually all the penitents were dancing and no more were coming forward. The music built to a climax and stopped suddenly, whereupon Caris noticed that Murdo and Philemon had disappeared. She assumed they had slipped out through the south transept to count their takings in the monks' cloisters.

The spectacle was over. The dancers lay down, exhausted. The spectators began to disperse, drifting out through the open doors into the clean air of the summer evening. Soon Murdo's followers found the strength to leave the church, and Caris did the same. She saw that most of the flagellants were heading for the Holly Bush.

She returned with relief to the cool hush of the nunnery. As dusk gathered in the cloisters, the nuns attended Evensong and ate their supper. Before going to bed, Caris went to check on the hospital. The place was still full: the plague raged unabated.

She found little to criticize. Sister Oonagh followed Caris's principles: face masks, no bloodletting, fanatical cleanliness. Caris was about to go to bed when one of the flagellants was brought in.

It was a man who had fainted in the Holly Bush and cracked his head on a bench. His back was still bleeding, and Caris guessed that loss of blood was as much responsible as the blow to his head for the loss of consciousness.

Oonagh bathed his wounds with salt water while he was unconscious. To bring him round, she set fire to the antler of a deer and wafted the pungent smoke under his nose. Then she made him drink two pints of water mixed with cinnamon and sugar, to replace the fluid his body had lost.

But he was only the first. Several more men and women were brought in suffering from some combination of loss of blood, excess of strong drink, and injuries received in accidents or fights. The orgy of flagellation increased the number of Saturday-night patients tenfold. There was also a man who had flogged himself so many times that his back was putrid. Finally, after midnight, a woman was brought in after having been tied up, flogged, and raped.

Fury stoked up in Caris as she worked with the other nuns to tend these patients. All their injuries arose from the perverted notions of religion put about by men such as Murdo. They said the plague was God's punishment for sin, but people could avoid the plague by punishing themselves another way. It was as if God were a vengeful monster playing a game with insane rules. Caris believed that God's sense of justice must be more sophisticated than that of the twelve-year-old leader of a boys' gang.

She worked until Matins on Sunday morning, then went to sleep for a couple of hours. When she got up, she went to see Merthin.

He was now living in the grandest of the houses he had built on Leper Island. It was on the south shore, and stood in a broad garden newly planted with apple and pear trees. He had hired a middle-aged couple to take care of Lolla and maintain the place. Their names were Arnaud and Emily, but they called one another Arn and Em. Caris found Em in the kitchen, and was directed to the garden.

Merthin was showing Lolla how her name was written, using a pointed stick to form the letters in a patch of bare earth, and he made her laugh by drawing a face in the "o". She was four years old, a pretty girl with olive skin and brown eyes.

Watching them, Caris suffered a pang of regret. She had been sleeping with Merthin for almost half a year. She did not want to have a baby, for it would mean the end of all her ambitions; yet a part of her was sorry that she had not become pregnant. She was torn, which was probably why she had taken the risk. But it had not happened. She wondered whether she had lost the ability to conceive. Perhaps the potion Mattie Wise had given her to abort her pregnancy a decade ago had harmed her womb in some way. As always, she wished she knew more about the body and its ills.

Merthin kissed her and they walked around the grounds, with Lolla running in front of them, playing in her imagination an elaborate and impenetrable game that involved talking to each tree. The garden looked raw, all the plants new, the soil carted in from elsewhere to enrich the island's stony ground. "I've come to talk to you about the flagellants," Caris said, and she told him about last night at the hospital. "I want to ban them from Kingsbridge," she finished.

"Good idea," Merthin said. "The whole performance is just another moneymaker for Murdo."

"And Philemon. He was holding the bowl. Will you talk to the parish guild?"

"Of course."

As acting prior, Caris was in the position of lord of the manor, and she could theoretically have banned the flagellants herself, without asking anyone else. However, her application for a borough charter was before the king, and she expected soon to hand over the government of the town to the guild, so she treated the current situation as a transition. Besides, it was always smarter to win support before trying to enforce a rule.

She said: "I'd like to have the constable escort Murdo and his followers out of town before the midday service."

"Philemon will be furious."

"He shouldn't have opened the church to them without consulting anyone." Caris knew there would be trouble, but she could not allow fear of Philemon's reaction to prevent her doing the right thing for the town.

"We've got the pope on our side. If we handle this discreetly and move fast, we can solve the problem before Philemon's had breakfast."

"All right," said Merthin. "I'll try to get the guildsmen together at the Holly Bush."

"I'll meet you there in an hour."

The parish guild was badly depleted, like every other organization in town, but a handful of leading merchants had survived the plague, including Madge Webber, Jake Chepstow, and Edward Slaughterhouse. The new constable, John's son Mungo, attended, and his deputies waited outside for their instructions.

The discussion did not last long. None of the leading citizens had taken part in the orgy, and they all disapproved of such public displays. The pope's ruling clinched the matter. Formally, Caris as prior promulgated a bylaw forbidding whipping in the streets and public nudity, violators to be expelled from the town by the constable on the instructions of any three guildsmen. The guild then passed a resolution supporting the new law.

Then Mungo went upstairs and roused Friar Murdo from his bed.

Murdo did not go quietly. Coming down the stairs he raved, he wept, he prayed, and he cursed. Two of Mungo's deputies took him by the arms and half-carried him out of the tavern. In the street he became louder. Mungo led the way, and the guildsmen followed. Some of Murdo's adherents came to protest and were themselves put under escort. A few townspeople tagged along as the group headed down the main street toward Merthin's bridge. None of the citizens objected to what was being done, and Philemon did not appear. Even some who had flogged themselves yesterday said nothing today, looking a bit shamefaced about it all.

The crowd fell away as the group crossed the bridge. With a reduced audience, Murdo became quieter. His righteous indignation was replaced by smoldering malevolence. Released at the far end of the double bridge, he stumped away through the suburbs without looking back. A handful of disciples trailed after him uncertainly.

Caris had a feeling she would not see him again.

She thanked Mungo and his men, then returned to the nunnery.

In the hospital, Oonagh was releasing the overnight accident cases to make room for new plague victims. Caris worked in the hospital until midday, then left gratefully and led the procession into the church for the main Sunday service. She found she was looking forward to an hour or two of psalms and prayers and a boring sermon: it would seem restful.

Philemon had a thunderous look when he led Thomas and the novice monks in. He had obviously heard about the expulsion of Murdo. No doubt he had seen the flagellants as a source of income for himself independent of Caris. That hope had been dashed, and he was livid.

For a moment, Caris wondered what he would do in his anger. Then she thought: Let him do what he likes. If it were not this, it would be something else. Whatever she did, sooner or later Philemon would be angry with her. There was no point in worrying about it.

She nodded off during the prayers and woke up when he began to preach. The pulpit seemed to heighten his charmlessness, and his sermons were poorly received, in general. However, today he grabbed the attention of his audience at the start by announcing that his subject would be fornication.

He took as his text a verse from St. Paul's first letter to the early Christians at Corinth. He read it in Latin, then translated it in ringing tones: "Now I have written to you not to keep company with anyone who is a fornicator!"

He elaborated tediously on the meaning of keeping company. "Don't eat with them, don't drink with them, don't live with them, don't talk to them." But Caris was wondering anxiously where he was going with this. Surely he would not dare to attack her directly from the pulpit? She glanced across the choir to Thomas, on the other side with the novice monks, and caught a worried look from him.

She looked again at Philemon's face, dark with resentment, and realized he was capable of anything.

"Who does this refer to?" he asked rhetorically. "Not to outsiders, the saint specifically writes. It is for God to judge them. But, he says, you are judges within the fellowship." He pointed at the congregation. "You!" He looked down again at the book and read: "Put away from among yourselves that wicked person!"

The congregation was quiet. They sensed that this was not the usual generalized exhortation to better behavior. Philemon had a message.

"We must look around ourselves," he said. "In our town—in our church—in our priory! Are there any fornicators? If so, they must be put out!"

There was no doubt now in Caris's mind that he was referring to her. And all the more astute townspeople would have come to the same conclusion. But what could she do? She could hardly get up and contradict him. She could not even walk out of the church, for that would underline his point and make it obvious, to the stupidest member of the congregation, that she was the target of his tirade.

So she listened, mortified. Philemon was speaking well for the first time ever. He did not hesitate or stumble, he enunciated clearly and projected his voice, and he managed to vary his usual dull monotone. For him, hatred was inspirational.

No one was going to put her out of the priory, of course. Even if she had been an incompetent prioress the bishop would have kept her on, simply because the scarcity of clergy was chronic. Churches and monasteries all over the country were closing because there was no one to hold services or sing psalms. Bishops were desperate to appoint more priests, monks, and nuns, not sack them. Anyway, the townspeople would have revolted against any bishop who tried to get rid of Caris.

All the same, Philemon's sermon was damaging. It would now be more difficult for the town's leaders to turn a blind eye to Caris's liaison with Merthin. This kind of thing undermined people's respect. They would forgive a man for a sexual peccadillo more readily than a woman. And, as she was painfully aware, her position invited the accusation of hypocrisy.

She sat grinding her teeth through the peroration, which was the same message shouted louder, and the remainder of the service. As soon as the nuns and monks had processed out of the church, she went to her pharmacy and sat down to compose a letter to Bishop Henri, asking him to move Philemon to another monastery.

Instead, Henri promoted him.

It was two weeks after the expulsion of Friar Murdo. They were in the north transept of the cathedral. The summer day was hot, but the interior of the church was always cool. The bishop sat on a carved wooden chair, and the others on benches: Philemon, Caris, Archdeacon Lloyd, and Canon Claude.

"I'm appointing you prior of Kingsbridge," Henri said to Philemon.

Philemon smirked with delight and shot a triumphant look at Caris.

She was appalled. Two weeks ago she had given Henri a long list of sound reasons why Philemon could not be permitted to continue in a responsible position here—starting with his theft of a gold candlestick. But it seemed her letter had had the opposite effect.

She opened her mouth to protest, but Henri glared at her and raised his hand, and she decided to remain silent and find out what else he had to say. He continued to address Philemon. "I'm doing this despite, not because of, your behavior since you returned here. You've been a malicious troublemaker, and if the church were not desperate for people I wouldn't promote you in a hundred years."

Then why do it now? Caris wondered.

"But we have to have a prior, and it simply is not satisfactory for the prioress to play that role, despite her undoubted ability."

Caris would have preferred him to appoint Thomas. But Thomas would have refused, she knew. He had been scarred by the bitter struggle over who was to succeed Prior Anthony, twelve years ago, and had sworn then never again to get involved in a priory election. In fact the bishop might well have spoken to Thomas, without Caris's knowledge, and learned this.

"However, your appointment is fenced about with provisos," Henri said to Philemon. "First, you will not be confirmed in the role until Kingsbridge has obtained its borough charter. You are not capable of running the town and I won't put you in that position. In the interim, therefore, Mother Caris will continue as acting prior, and you will live in the monks' dormitory. The palace will be locked up. If you misbehave in the waiting period, I will rescind the appointment."

Philemon looked angry and wounded by this, but he kept his mouth shut tight. He knew he had won and he was not going to argue about the conditions.

"Secondly, you will have your own treasury, but Brother Thomas is to be the treasurer, and no money will be spent nor precious objects removed without his knowledge and consent. Furthermore, I have ordered the building of a new tower, and I have authorized payments according to a schedule prepared by Merthin Bridger. The priory will make these payments from the monks' funds, and neither Philemon nor anyone else shall have the power to alter this arrangement. I don't want half a tower."

Merthin would get his wish, at least, Caris thought gratefully.

Henri turned to Caris. "I have one more command to issue, and it is for you, Mother Prioress."

Now what? she thought.

"There has been an accusation of fornication."

Caris stared at the bishop, thinking about the time she had surprised him and Claude naked. How did he dare to raise this subject?

He went on: "I say nothing about the past. But for the future, it is not possible that the prioress of Kingsbridge should have a relationship with a man."

She wanted to say: But you live with your lover! However, she suddenly noticed the expression on Henri's face. It was a pleading look. He was begging her not to make the accusation that, he well knew, would show him up as a hypocrite. He knew that what he was doing was unjust, she realized, but he had no choice. Philemon had forced him into this position.

She was tempted, all the same, to sting him with a rebuke. But she restrained herself. It would do no good. Henri's back was to the wall and he was doing his best. Caris clamped her mouth shut.

Henri said: "May I have your assurance, Mother Prioress, that from this moment on there will be absolutely no grounds for the accusation?"

Caris looked at the floor. She had been here before. Once again her choice was to give up everything she had worked for—the hospital, the borough charter, the tower—or to part with Merthin. And, once again, she chose her work.

She raised her head and looked him in the eye. "Yes, my lord bishop," she said. "You have my word."

She spoke to Merthin in the hospital, surrounded by other people. She was trembling and close to tears, but she could not see him in private. She knew that if they were alone her resolve would weaken, and she would throw her arms around him and tell him that she loved him, and promise to leave the nunnery and marry him. So she sent a message, and greeted him at the door of the hospital, then spoke to him in a matter-of-fact voice, her arms folded tightly across her chest so that she would not be tempted to reach out with a fond gesture and touch the body she loved so much.

When she had finished telling him about the bishop's ultimatum and her decision, he looked at her as if he could kill her. "This is the last time," he said.

"What do you mean?"

"If you do this, it's permanent. I'm not going to wait around anymore, hoping that one day you will be my wife."

She felt as if he had hit her.

He went on, delivering another blow with each sentence. "If you mean what you're saying, I'm going to try to forget you now. I'm thirty-three years old. I don't have forever—my father is dying at the age of fifty-eight. I'll marry someone else and have more children and be happy in my garden."

The picture he painted tortured her. She bit her lip, trying to control her grief, but hot tears ran down her face.

He was remorseless. "I'm not going to waste my life loving you," he said, and she felt as if he had stabbed her. "Leave the nunnery now, or stay there forever."

She tried to look steadily at him. "I won't forget you. I will always love you."

"But not enough."

She was silent for a long moment. It wasn't like that, she knew. Her love was not weak or inadequate. It just presented her with impossible choices. But there seemed no point in arguing. "Is that what you really believe?" she said.

"It seems obvious."

She nodded, though she did not really agree. "I'm sorry," she said. "More sorry than I have ever been in my whole life."

"So am I," he said, and he turned away and walked out of the building.

75

Sir Gregory Longfellow at last went back to London, but he returned surprisingly quickly, as if he had bounced off the wall of that great city like a football. He showed up at Tench Hall at suppertime looking harassed, breathing hard through his flared nostrils, his long gray hair matted with perspiration. He walked in with something less than his usual air of being in command of all men and beasts that crossed his path. Ralph and Alan were standing by a window, looking at a new broad-bladed style of dagger called a basilard. Without speaking, Gregory threw his tall figure into Ralph's big carved chair: whatever might have happened, he was still too grand to wait for an invitation to sit.

Ralph and Alan stared at him expectantly. Ralph's mother sniffed censoriously: she disliked bad manners.

Finally Gregory said: "The king does not like to be disobeyed."

That scared Ralph.

He looked anxiously at Gregory, and asked himself what he had done that could possibly be interpreted as disobedient by the king. He could think of nothing. Nervously he said: "I'm sorry His Majesty is displeased—I hope it's not with me."

"You're involved," Gregory said with annoying vagueness. "And so am I. The king feels that when his wishes are frustrated it sets a bad precedent."

"I quite agree."

"That is why you and I are going to leave here tomorrow, ride to Earlscastle, see the lady Philippa, and *make* her marry you."

So that was it. Ralph was mainly relieved. He could not be held responsible for Philippa's recalcitrance, in all fairness—not that fairness made much difference to kings. But, reading between the lines, he guessed that the person taking the blame was Gregory, and so Gregory was now determined to rescue the king's plan and redeem himself.

There was fury and malice in Gregory's expression. He said: "By the time I have finished with her, I promise you, she will beg you to marry her."

Ralph could not imagine how this was to be achieved. As Philippa herself had pointed out, you could lead a woman up the aisle but you could not force her to say "I do." He said to Gregory: "Someone told me that a widow's right to refuse marriage is actually guaranteed by Magna Carta."

Gregory gave him a malevolent look. "Don't remind me. I made the mistake of mentioning that to His Majesty."

Ralph wondered, in that case, what threats or promises Gregory planned to use to bend Philippa to his will. Himself, he could think of no way to marry her short of abducting her by force, and carrying her off to some isolated church where a generously bribed priest would turn a deaf ear to her cries of "No, never!"

They set off early next morning with a small entourage. It was harvest time and, in the North Field, the men were reaping tall stalks of rye while the women followed behind, binding the sheaves.

Lately Ralph had spent more time worrying about the harvest than about Philippa. This was not because of the weather, which was fine, but the plague. He had too few tenants and almost no laborers. Many had been stolen from him by unscrupulous landlords such as Prioress Caris, who seduced other lords' men by offering high wages and attractive tenancies. In desperation, Ralph had given some of his serfs free tenancies, which meant they had no obligation to work on his land—an arrangement that left Ralph denuded of labor at harvesttime. In consequence, it was likely that some of his crops would rot in the fields.

However, he felt his troubles would be over if he could marry Philippa. He would have ten times the land he now controlled, plus income from a dozen other sources, including courts, forests, markets, and mills. And his family would be restored to its rightful place in the nobility. Sir Gerald would be the father of an earl before he died.

He wondered again what Gregory had in mind. Philippa had set herself a challenging task, in defying the formidable will and powerful connections of Gregory. Ralph would not have wished to be standing in her beaded silk shoes.

They arrived at Earlscastle shortly before noon. The sound of the rooks quarreling on the battlements always reminded Ralph of the time he had spent here as a squire in the service of Earl Roland—the happiest days of his life, he sometimes thought. But the place was very quiet now, without an earl. There were no squires playing violent games in the lower compound, no warhorses snorting and stamping as they were groomed and exercised outside the stables, no men-at-arms throwing dice on the steps of the keep.

Philippa was in the old-fashioned hall with Odila and a handful of female attendants. Mother and daughter were working on a tapestry together, sitting side by side on a bench in front of the loom. The picture looked as if it would show a forest scene when finished. Philippa was weaving brown thread for the tree trunks and Odila bright green for the leaves.

"Very nice, but it needs more life," Ralph said, making his voice cheerful and friendly. "A few birds and rabbits, and maybe some dogs chasing a deer."

Philippa was as immune to his charm as ever. She stood up and stepped back, away from him. The girl did the same. Ralph noticed that mother and daughter were equal in height. Philippa said: "Why have you come here?"

Have it your way, Ralph thought resentfully. He half-turned away from her. "Sir Gregory here has something to say to you," he said, and he went to a window and looked out, as if bored.

Gregory greeted the two women formally, and said he hoped he was not intruding on them. It was rubbish—he did not give a hoot for their privacy—but the courtesy seemed to mollify Philippa, who invited him to sit down. Then he said: "The king is annoyed with you, Countess."

Philippa bowed her head. "I am very sorry indeed to have displeased His Majesty."

"He wishes to reward his loyal servant, Sir Ralph, by making him earl of Shiring. At the same time, he will be providing a young, vigorous husband for you, and a good stepfather for your daughter." Philippa shuddered, but Gregory ignored that. "He is mystified by your stubborn defiance."

Philippa looked scared, as well she might. Things would have been different if she had had a brother or an uncle to stick up for her, but the plague had wiped out her family. As a woman without male relations, she had no one to defend her from the king's wrath. "What will he do?" she said apprehensively.

"He has not mentioned the word 'treason' . . . yet."

Ralph was not sure Philippa could legally be accused of treason, but all the same the threat caused her to turn pale.

Gregory went on: "He has asked me, in the first instance, to reason with you."

Philippa said: "Of course, the king sees marriage as a political matter—"

"It *is* political," Gregory interrupted. "If your beautiful daughter, here, were to fancy herself in love with the charming son of a scullery maid, you would say to her, as I say to you, that noblewomen may not marry whomever they fancy; and you would lock her in her room and have the boy flogged outside her window until he renounced her forever."

Philippa looked affronted. She did not like being lectured on the duties of her station by a mere lawyer. "I understand the obligations of an aristocratic widow," she said haughtily. "I am a countess, my grandmother was a countess, and my sister was a countess until she died of the plague. But marriage is not *just* politics. It is also a matter of the heart. We women throw ourselves on the mercy of the men who are our lords and masters, and who have the duty of wisely deciding our fate; and we beg that what we feel in our hearts be not entirely ignored. Such pleas are usually heard."

She was upset, Ralph could see, but still in control, still full of contempt. That word "wisely" had a sarcastic sting.

"In normal times, perhaps you would be right, but these are strange days," Gregory replied. "Usually, when the king looks around him for someone worthy of an earldom, he sees a dozen wise, strong, vigorous men, loyal to him and keen to serve him in any way they can, any of whom he could appoint to the title with confidence. But now that so many of the best men have been struck down by the plague, the king is like a housewife who goes to the fishmonger at the end of the afternoon—forced to take whatever is left on the slab."

Ralph saw the force of the argument, but also felt insulted. However, he pretended not to notice.

Philippa changed her tack. She waved a servant over and said: "Bring us a jug of the best Gascon wine, please. And Sir Gregory will be having dinner here, so let's have some of this season's lamb, cooked with garlic and rosemary."

"Yes, my lady."

Gregory said: "You're most kind, Countess."

Philippa was incapable of coquetry. To pretend that she was simply being hospitable, with no ulterior motive, was beyond her. She returned straight to the subject. "Sir Gregory, I have to tell you that my heart, my soul, and my entire being revolt against the prospect of marrying Sir Ralph Fitzgerald."

"But why?" said Gregory. "He's a man like any other."

"No, he's not," she said.

They were speaking about Ralph as if he were not there, in a way that he found deeply offensive. But Philippa was desperate, and would say anything; and he was curious to know just what it was about him that she disliked so much.

She paused, collecting her thoughts. "If I say rapist, torturer, murderer . . . the words just seem too abstract."

Ralph was taken aback. He did not think of himself that way. Of course, he had tortured people in the king's service, and he had raped Annet, and he had murdered several men, women, and children in his days as an outlaw . . . At least, he consoled himself, Philippa did not appear to have guessed that he was the hooded figure who had killed Tilly, his own wife.

Philippa went on: "Human beings have within them something that prevents them from doing such things. It is the ability . . . no, the compulsion to feel another's pain. We can't help it. You, Sir Gregory, could not rape a woman, because you would feel her grief and agony, you would suffer with her, and this would compel you to relent. You could not torture or murder for the same reason. One who lacks the faculty to feel another's pain is not a man, even though he may walk on two legs and speak English." She leaned forward, lowering her voice, but even so Ralph heard her clearly. "And I will not lie in bed with an *animal.*"

Ralph burst out: "I am not an animal!"

He expected Gregory to back him up. Instead, Gregory seemed to give in. "Is that your final word, Lady Philippa?"

Ralph was astonished. Was Gregory going to let that pass, as if it might be even half-true?

Philippa said to Gregory: "I need you to go back to the king and tell him that I am his loyal and obedient subject, and that I long to win his favor, but that I could not marry Ralph if the Archangel Gabriel commanded me."

"I see." Gregory stood up. "We will not stay to dinner."

Was that all? Ralph had been waiting for Gregory to produce his surprise, a secret weapon, some irresistible bribe or threat. Did the clever court lawyer really have nothing up his costly brocade sleeve?

Philippa seemed equally startled to find the argument so suddenly terminated.

Gregory went to the door, and Ralph had no choice but to follow. Philippa and Odila stared at the two of them, unsure what to make of this cool walkout. The ladies-in-waiting fell silent.

Philippa said: "Please, beg the king to be merciful."

"He will be, my lady," said Gregory. "He has authorized me to tell you that, in the light of your obstinacy, he will not force you to marry a man you loathe."

"Thank you!" she said. "You have saved my life."

Ralph opened his mouth to protest. He had been promised! He had committed sacrilege and murder for this reward. Surely it could not be taken from him now?

But Gregory spoke first. "Instead," he said, "it is the king's command that Ralph will marry your daughter." He paused, and pointed at the tall fifteen-year-old girl standing beside her mother. "Odila," he said, as if there were any need to emphasize who he was talking about.

Philippa gasped and Odila screamed.

Gregory bowed. "Good day to you both."

Philippa cried: "Wait!"

Gregory took no notice, and went out.

Stunned, Ralph followed.

*

Gwenda was weary when she woke up. It was harvesttime, and she was spending every hour of the long August days in the fields. Wulfric would swing the scythe tirelessly from sunrise to nightfall, mowing down the corn. Gwenda's job was to bundle the sheaves. All day long she bent down and scooped up the mown stalks, bent and scooped, bent and scooped until her back seemed to burn with pain. When it was too dark to see, she staggered home and fell into bed, leaving the family to feed themselves with whatever they could find in the cupboard.

Wulfric woke at dawn, and his movements penetrated Gwenda's deep slumber. She struggled to her feet. They all needed a good breakfast, and she put cold mutton, bread, butter, and strong beer on the table. Sam, the ten-year-old, got up, but Davy, who was only eight, had to be shaken awake and pulled to his feet.

"This holding was never farmed by one man and his wife," Gwenda said grumpily as they ate.

Wulfric was irritatingly positive. "You and I got the harvest in on our own, the year the bridge collapsed," he said cheerfully.

"I was twelve years younger then."

"But you're more beautiful now."

She was in no mood for gallantry. "Even when your father and brother were alive, you took on hired labor at harvest time."

"Never mind. It's our land, and we planted the crops, so we'll benefit from the harvest, instead of earning just a penny a day wages. The more we work, the more we get. That's what you always wanted, isn't it?"

"I always wanted to be independent and self-sufficient, if that's what you mean." She went to the door. "A west wind, and a few clouds in the sky."

Wulfric looked worried. "We need the rain to hold off for another two or three days."

"I think it will. Come on, boys, time to go to the field. You can eat walking along." She was bundling the bread and meat into a sack for their dinner when Nate Reeve hobbled in through the door. "Oh, no!" she said. "Not today—we've almost got our harvest in!"

"The lord has a harvest to get in, too," said the bailiff.

Nate was followed in by his ten-year-old son, Jonathan, known as Jonno, who immediately started making faces at Sam.

Gwenda said: "Give us three more days on our own land."

"Don't bother to dispute with me about this," Nate said. "You owe the lord one day a week, and two days at harvesttime. Today and tomorrow you will reap his barley in Brookfield."

"The second day is normally forgiven. That's been the practise for a long time."

"It was, in times of plentiful labor. The lord is desperate now. So many people have negotiated free tenancies that he has hardly anyone to bring in his harvest."

"So those who negotiated with you, and demanded to be freed of their customary duties, are rewarded, while people like us, who accepted the old terms, are punished with twice as much work on the lord's land." She looked accusingly at Wulfric, remembering how he had ignored her when she told him to argue terms with Nate.

"Something like that," Nate said carelessly.

"Hell," Gwenda said.

"Don't curse," said Nate. "You'll get a free dinner. There will be wheat bread, and a new barrel of ale. Isn't that something to look forward to?"

"Sir Ralph feeds oats to the horses he means to ride hard."

"Don't be long, now!" Nate went out.

His son, Jonno, poked out his tongue at Sam. Sam made a grab for him, but Jonno slipped out of his grasp and ran after his father.

Wearily, Gwenda and her family trudged across the fields to where Ralph's barley stood waving in the breeze. They got down to work. Wulfric reaped and Gwenda bundled. Sam followed behind, picking up the stray stalks she missed, gathering them until he had enough for a sheaf, then passing them to her to be tied. David had small, nimble fingers, and he plaited straws into tough cords for tying the sheaves. Those other families still working under old-style tenancies labored alongside them, while the cleverer serfs reaped their own crops.

When the sun was at its highest, Nate drove up in a cart with a barrel on the back. True to his word, he provided each family with a big loaf of delicious new wheat bread. Everyone ate their fill, then the adults lay down in the shade to rest while the children played.

Gwenda was dozing off when she heard an outbreak of childish screaming. She knew immediately, from the voice, that neither of her boys was making the noise, but all the same she leaped to her feet. She saw her son Sam fighting with Jonno Reeve. Although they were roughly the same age and size, Sam had Jonno on the ground and was punching and kicking him mercilessly. Gwenda moved toward the boys, but Wulfric was quicker, and he grabbed Sam with one hand and hauled him off.

Gwenda looked at Jonno in dismay. The boy was bleeding from his nose and mouth, and his face around one eye was inflamed and already beginning to swell. He was holding his stomach, moaning and crying. Gwenda had seen plenty of scraps between boys, but this was different. Jonno had been beaten up.

Gwenda stared at her ten-year-old son. His face was unmarked: it looked as if Jonno had not landed a single blow. Sam showed no sign of remorse at what he had done. Rather, he looked smugly triumphant. It was a vaguely familiar expression, and Gwenda searched her memory for its likeness. She did not take long to recall whom she had seen looking like that after giving someone a beating.

She had seen the same expression on the face of Ralph Fitzgerald, Sam's real father.

Two days after Ralph and Gregory visited Earlscastle, Lady Philippa came to Tench Hall.

Ralph had been considering the prospect of marrying Odila. She was a beautiful young girl, but you could buy beautiful young girls for a few pennies in London. Ralph had already had the experience of being married to someone who was little more than a child. After the initial excitement wore off, he had been bored and irritated by her.

He wondered for a while whether he might marry Odila and get Philippa too. The idea of marrying the daughter and keeping the mother as his mistress intrigued him. He might even have them together. He had once had sex with a mother-daughter pair of prostitutes in Calais, and the element of incest had created an exciting sense of depravity.

But, on reflection, he knew that was not going to happen. Philippa would never consent to such an arrangement. He might look for ways to coerce her, but she was not easily bullied. "I don't want to marry Odila," he had said to Gregory as they rode home from Earlscastle.

"You won't have to," Gregory had said, but he refused to elaborate.

Philippa arrived with a lady-in-waiting and a bodyguard but without Odila. As she entered Tench Hall, for once she did not look proud. She did not even look beautiful, Ralph thought: clearly she had not slept for two nights.

They had just sat down to dinner: Ralph, Alan, Gregory, a handful of squires, and a bailiff. Philippa was the only woman in the room.

She walked up to Gregory.

The courtesy he had shown her previously was forgotten. He did not stand, but rudely looked her up and down, as if she were a servant girl with a grievance. "Well?" he said at last.

"I will marry Ralph."

"Oh!" he said in mock surprise. "Will you, now?"

"Yes. Rather than sacrifice my daughter to him, I will marry him myself."

"My lady," he said sarcastically, "you seem to think that the king has led you to a table laden with dishes and asked you to choose which you like best. You are mistaken. The king does not ask what is your pleasure. He commands. You disobeyed one command, so he issued another. He did not give you a choice."

She looked down. "I am very sorry for my behavior. Please spare my daughter."

"If it were up to me, I would decline your request, as punishment for your intransigence. But perhaps you should plead with Sir Ralph."

She looked at Ralph. He saw rage and despair in her eyes. He felt excited. She was the most haughty woman he had ever met, and he had broken her pride. He wanted to lie with her now, right away.

But it was not yet over.

He said: "You have something to say to me?"

"I apologize."

"Come here." Ralph was sitting at the head of the table, and she approached and stood by him. He caressed the head of a lion carved into the arm of his chair. "Go on," he said.

"I am sorry that I spurned you before. I would like to withdraw everything I said. I accept your proposal. I will marry you."

"But I have not renewed my proposal. The king orders me to marry Odila."

"If you ask the king to revert to his original plan, surely he will grant your plea."

"And that is what you are asking me to do."

"Yes." She looked him in the eye and swallowed her final humiliation. "I am asking you . . . I am begging you. Please, Sir Ralph, make me your wife."

Ralph stood up, pushing his chair back. "Kiss me, then."

She closed her eyes.

He put his left arm around her shoulders and pulled her to him. He kissed her lips. She submitted unresponsively. With his right hand, he squeezed her breast. It was as firm and heavy as he had always imagined. He ran his hand down her body and between her legs. She flinched, but remained unresistingly in his embrace, and he pressed his palm against the fork of her thighs. He grasped her mound, cupping its triangular fatness in his hand.

Then, holding that position, he broke the kiss and looked around the room at his friends.

76

At the same time as Ralph was created earl of Shiring, a young man called David Caerleon became earl of Monmouth. He was only seventeen, and related rather distantly to the dead man, but all nearer heirs to the title had been wiped out by the plague.

A few days before Christmas that year, Bishop Henri held a service in Kingsbridge Cathedral to bless the two new earls. Afterward David and Ralph were guests of honor at a banquet given by Merthin in the guildhall. The merchants were also celebrating the granting of a borough charter to Kingsbridge.

Ralph considered David to have been extraordinarily lucky. The boy had never been outside the kingdom, nor had he ever fought in battle, yet he was an earl at seventeen. Ralph had marched all through Normandy with King Edward, risked his life in battle after battle, lost three fingers, and committed countless sins in the king's service, yet he had had to wait until the age of thirty-two.

However, he had made it at last, and sat next to Bishop Henri at the table, wearing a costly brocade coat woven with gold and silver threads. People who knew him pointed him out to strangers, wealthy merchants made way for him and bowed their heads respectfully as he passed, and the maidservant's hand shook with nervousness as she poured wine into his cup. His father, Sir Gerald, confined to bed now but hanging on tenaciously to life, had said: "I'm the descendant of an earl, and the father of an earl. I'm satisfied." It was all profoundly gratifying.

Ralph was keen to talk to David about the problem of laborers. It had eased temporarily now that the harvest was in and the autumn plowing was finished: at this time of year the days were short and the weather was cold, so not much work could be done in the fields. Unfortunately, as soon as the spring plowing began and the ground was soft enough for the serfs to sow seeds, the trouble would start again: laborers would recommence agitating for higher wages, and if refused would illegally run off to more extravagant employers.

The only way to stop this was for the nobility collectively to stand firm, resist demands for higher pay, and refuse to hire runaways. This was what Ralph wanted to say to David.

However, the new earl of Monmouth showed no inclination to talk to Ralph. He was more interested in Ralph's stepdaughter, Odila, who was near his own age. They had met before, Ralph gathered: Philippa and her first husband, William, had often been guests at the castle when David had been a squire in the service of the old earl. Whatever their history, they were friends now: David was talking animatedly and Odila was hanging on every word—agreeing with his opinions, gasping at his stories, and laughing at his jokes.

Ralph had always envied men who could fascinate women. His brother had the ability, and consequently was able to attract the most beautiful women, despite being a short, plain man with red hair.

All the same, Ralph felt sorry for Merthin. Ever since the day that Earl Roland had made Ralph a squire and condemned Merthin to be a carpenter's apprentice, Merthin had been doomed. Even though he was the elder, it was Ralph who was destined to become the earl. Merthin, now sitting on the other side of Earl David, had to console himself with being a mere alderman—and having charm.

Ralph could not even charm his own wife. She hardly spoke to him. She had more to say to his dog.

How was it possible, Ralph asked himself, for a man to want something as badly as he had wanted Philippa, and then to be so dissatisfied when he got it? He had yearned for her since he was a squire of nineteen. Now, after three months of marriage, he wished with all his heart that he could get rid of her.

Yet it was hard for him to complain. Philippa did everything a wife was obliged to do. She ran the castle efficiently, as she had been doing ever since her first husband had been made earl after the battle of Crécy. Supplies were ordered, bills were paid, clothes were sewn, fires were lit, and food and wine arrived on the table unfailingly. And she submitted to Ralph's sexual attentions. He could do anything he liked: tear her clothes, thrust his fingers ungently inside her, take her standing up or from behind—she never complained.

But she did not reciprocate his caresses. Her lips never moved against his, her tongue never slipped into his mouth, she never stroked his skin. She kept a vial of almond oil handy, and lubricated her unresponsive body with it whenever he wanted sex. She lay as still as a corpse while he grunted on top of her. The moment he rolled off, she went to wash herself.

The only good thing about the marriage was that Odila was fond of little Gerry. The baby brought out her nascent maternal instinct. She loved to talk to him, sing him songs, and rock him to sleep. She gave him the kind of affectionate mothering he would never really get from a paid nurse.

All the same, Ralph was regretful. Philippa's voluptuous body, which he had stared at with longing for so many years, was now revolting to him. He had not touched her for weeks, and he probably never would again. He looked at her heavy breasts and round hips, and wished for the slender limbs and girlish skin of Tilly. Tilly, whom he had stabbed with a long, sharp knife that went up under her ribs and into her beating heart. That was a sin he did not dare to confess. How long, he wondered wretchedly, would he suffer for it in Purgatory?

The bishop and his colleagues were staying in the prior's palace, and the Monmouth entourage filled the priory's guest rooms, so Ralph and Philippa and their servants were lodging at an inn. Ralph had chosen the Bell, the rebuilt tavern owned by his brother. It was the only three-story house in Kingsbridge, with a big open room at ground level, male and female dormitories above, and a top floor with six expensive individual guest rooms. When the banquet was over, Ralph and his men removed to the tavern, where they installed themselves in front of the fire, called for more wine, and began to play at dice. Philippa remained behind, talking to Caris and chaperoning Odila with Earl David.

Ralph and his companions attracted a crowd of admiring young men and women such as always gathered around free-spending noblemen. Ralph gradually forgot his troubles in the euphoria of drink and the thrill of gambling.

He noticed a young fair-haired woman watching him with a yearning expression as he cheerfully lost stacks of silver pennies on the throw of the dice. He beckoned her to sit beside him on the bench, and she told him her name was Ella. At moments of tension she grabbed his thigh, as if captured by the suspense, though she probably knew exactly what she was doing—women usually did.

He gradually lost interest in the game and transferred his attention to her. His men carried on betting while he got to know Ella. She was everything Philippa was not: happy, sexy, and fascinated by Ralph. She touched him and herself a lot—she would push her hair off her face, then pat his arm, then hold her hand to her throat, then push his shoulder playfully. She seemed very interested in his experiences in France.

To Ralph's annoyance, Merthin came into the tavern and sat down with him. Merthin was not running the Bell himself—he had rented it to the youngest daughter of Betty Baxter—but he was keen that the tenant should make a success of it, and he asked Ralph if everything was to his satisfaction. Ralph introduced his companion, and Merthin said, "Yes, I know Ella," in a dismissive tone that was uncharacteristically discourteous.

Today was only the third or fourth time the two brothers had met since the death of Tilly. On previous occasions, such as Ralph's wedding to Philippa, there had hardly been time to talk. All the same Ralph knew, from the way his brother looked at him, that Merthin suspected him of being Tilly's killer. The unspoken thought was a looming presence, never addressed but impossible to ignore, like the cow in the cramped one-room hovel of a poor peasant. If it was mentioned, Ralph felt that would be the last time they ever spoke.

So tonight, as if by mutual consent, they once again exchanged a few meaningless platitudes, then Merthin left, saying he had work to do. Ralph wondered briefly what work he was going to do at dusk on a December evening. He really had no idea how Merthin spent his time. He did not hunt, or hold court, or attend on the king. Was it possible to spend all day, every day, making drawings and supervising builders? Such a life would have driven Ralph mad. And he was baffled by how much money Merthin seemed to make from his enterprises. Ralph himself had been short of money even when he had been lord of Tench. Merthin never seemed to lack it.

Ralph turned his attention back to Ella. "My brother's a bit grumpy," he said apologetically.

"It's because he hasn't had a woman for half a year." She giggled. "He used to shag the prioress, but she had to throw him out after Philemon came back."

Ralph pretended to be shocked. "Nuns aren't supposed to be shagged."

"Mother Caris is a wonderful woman—but she's got the itch, you can tell by the way she walks."

Ralph was aroused by such frank talk from a woman. "It's very bad for a man," he said, playing along. "To go for so long without a woman."

"I think so, too."

"It leads to . . . swelling."

She put her head on one side and raised her eyebrows. He glanced down at his own lap. She followed his gaze. "Oh, dear," she said. "That looks uncomfortable." She put her hand on his erect penis.

At that moment, Philippa appeared

Ralph froze. He felt guilty and scared, and at the same time he was furious with himself for caring whether Philippa saw what he was doing or not.

She said: "I'm going upstairs—oh."

Ella did not release her hold. In fact she squeezed Ralph's penis gently, while looking up at Philippa and smiling triumphantly.

Philippa flushed red, her face registering shame and distaste.

Ralph opened his mouth to speak, then did not know what to say. He was not willing to apologize to his virago of a wife, feeling that she had brought this humiliation on herself. But he also felt somewhat foolish, sitting there with a tavern tart holding his prick while his wife, the countess, stood in front of them looking embarrassed.

The tableau lasted only a moment. Ralph made a strangled sound, Ella giggled, and Philippa said, "Oh!" in a tone of exasperation and disgust. Then Philippa turned and walked away, head held unnaturally high. She approached the broad staircase and went up, as graceful as a deer on a hillside, and disappeared without looking back.

Ralph felt both angry and ashamed, though he reasoned that he had no need to feel either. However, his interest in Ella diminished visibly, and he took her hand away.

"Have some more wine," she said, pouring from the jug on the table, but Ralph felt the onset of a headache, and pushed the wooden cup away.

Ella put a restraining hand on his arm and said in a low, warm voice: "Don't leave me in the lurch now that you've got me all, you know, excited."

He shook her off and stood up.

Her face hardened and she said: "Well, you'd better give me something by way of compensation."

He dipped into his purse and took out a handful of silver pennies. Without looking at Ella, he dumped the money on the table, not caring whether it was too much or too little.

She began to scoop up the coins hastily.

Ralph left her and went upstairs.

Philippa was on the bed, sitting upright with her back against the headboard. She had taken off her shoes but was otherwise fully dressed. She stared accusingly at Ralph as he walked in.

He said: "You have no right to be angry with me!"

"I'm not angry," she said. "But you are."

She could always twist words around so that she was in the right and he in the wrong.

Before he could think of a reply, she said: "Wouldn't you like me to leave you?"

He stared at her, astonished. This was the last thing he had expected. "Where would you go?"

"Here," she said. "I won't become a nun, but I could live in the convent nevertheless. I would bring just a few servants: a maid, a clerk, and my confessor. I've already spoken to Mother Caris, and she is willing."

"My last wife did that. What will people think?"

"A lot of noblewomen retire to nunneries, either temporarily or permanently, at some point in their lives. People will think you've rejected me because I'm past the age for conceiving children—which I probably am. Anyway, do you care what people say?"

The thought briefly flashed across his mind that he would be sorry to see Gerry lose Odila. But the prospect of being free of Philippa's proud, disapproving presence was irresistible. "All right, what's stopping you? Tilly never asked permission."

"I want to see Odila married first."

"Who to?"

She looked at him as if he were stupid.

"Oh," he said. "Young David, I suppose."

"He is in love with her, and I think they would be well suited."

"He's underage—he'll have to ask the king."

"That's why I've raised it with you. Will you go with him to see the king, and speak in support of the marriage? If you do this for me, I swear I will never ask you for anything ever again. I will leave you in peace."

She was not asking him to make any sacrifices. An alliance with Monmouth could do Ralph nothing but good. "And you'll leave Earlscastle, and move into the nunnery?"

"Yes, as soon as Odila is married."

It was the end of a dream, Ralph realized, but a dream that had turned into a sour, bleak reality. He might as well acknowledge the failure and start again.

"All right," he said, feeling regret mingled with liberation. "It's a bargain."

77

Easter came early in the year 1350, and there was a big fire blazing in Merthin's hearth on the evening of Good Friday. The table was laid with a cold supper: smoked fish, soft cheese, new bread, pears, and a flagon of Rhenish wine. Merthin was wearing clean underclothes and a new yellow robe. The house had been swept, and there were daffodils in a jug on the sideboard.

Merthin was alone. Lolla was with his servants, Arn and Em. Their cottage was at the end of the garden but Lolla, who was five, loved to stay there overnight. She called it going on pilgrimage, and took a traveling bag containing her hairbrush and a favorite doll.

Merthin opened a window and looked out. A cold breeze blew across the river from the meadow on the south side. The last of the evening was fading, the light seeming to fall out of the sky and sink into the water, where it disappeared in the blackness.

He visualized a hooded figure emerging from the nunnery. He saw it tread a worn diagonal across the cathedral green, hurry past the lights of the Bell, and descend the muddy main street, the face shadowed, speaking to no one. He imagined it reaching the foreshore. Did it glance sideways into the cold, black river, and remember a moment of despair so great as to give rise to thoughts of self-destruction? If so, the recollection was quickly dismissed, and it stepped forward onto the cobbled roadbed of his bridge. It crossed the span and made landfall again on Leper Island. There it diverted from the main road and passed through low shrubbery, across scrubby grass cropped by rabbits, and around the ruins of the old lazar house until it came to the southwest shore. Then it tapped on Merthin's door.

He closed the window and waited. No tap came. He was wishfully a little ahead of schedule.

He was tempted to drink some wine, but he did not: a ritual had developed, and he did not want to change the order of events.

The knock came a few moments later. He opened the door. She stepped inside, threw back her hood, and dropped the heavy gray cloak from her shoulders.

She was taller than he by an inch or more, and a few years older. Her face was proud, and could be haughty, although now her smile radiated warmth like the sun. She wore a robe of bright Kingsbridge scarlet. He put his arms around her, pressing her voluptuous body to his own, and kissed her wide mouth. "My darling," he said. "Philippa."

They made love immediately, there on the floor, hardly undressing. He was hungry for her, and she was if anything more eager. He spread her cloak on the straw, and she lifted the skirt of her robe and lay down. She clung to him like one drowning, her legs wrapped around his, her arms crushing him to her soft body, her face buried in his neck.

She had told him that, after she left Ralph and moved into the priory, she had thought no one would ever touch her again until the nuns laid out her cold body for burial. The thought almost made Merthin cry.

For his part, he had loved Caris so much that he felt no other woman would ever arouse his affection. For him as well as Philippa, this love had come as an unexpected gift, a spring of cold water bubbling up in a baking-hot desert, and they both drank from it as if they were dying of thirst.

Afterward they lay entwined by the fire, panting, and he recalled the first time. Soon after she moved to the priory, she had taken an interest in the building of the new tower. A practical woman, she had trouble filling the long hours that were supposed to be spent in prayer and meditation. She enjoyed the library but could not read all day. She came to see him in the mason's loft, and he showed her the plans. She quickly got into the habit of visiting every day, talking to him while he worked. He had always admired her intelligence and strength, and in the intimacy of the loft he came to know the warm, generous spirit beneath her stately manner. He discovered that she had a lively sense of humor, and he learned how to make her laugh. She responded with a rich, throaty chuckle that, somehow, led him to think of making love to her. One day she had paid him a compliment. "You're a kind man," she had said. "There aren't enough of them." Her sincerity had touched him, and he had kissed her hand. It was a gesture of affection, but one she could reject, if she wished, without drama: she simply had to withdraw her hand and take a step back, and he would have known he had gone a little too far. But she had not rejected it. On the contrary, she had held his hand and looked at him with something like love in her eyes, and he had wrapped his arms around her and kissed her lips.

They had made love on the mattress in the loft, and he had not remembered until afterward that Caris had encouraged him to put the mattress there, with a joke about masons needing a soft place for their tools.

Caris did not know about him and Philippa. No one did except Philippa's maid and Arn and Em. She went to bed in her private room on the upper floor of the hospital soon after nightfall, at the same time as the nuns retired to their dormitory. She slipped out while they were asleep, using the outside steps that permitted important guests to come and go without passing through the common people's quarters. She returned by the same route before dawn, while the nuns were singing Matins, and appeared at breakfast as if she had been in her room all night.

He was surprised to find that he could love another woman less than a year after Caris had left him for the final time. He certainly had not forgotten Caris. On the contrary, he thought about her every day. He felt the urge to tell her about something amusing that had happened, or he wanted her opinion on a knotty problem, or he found himself performing some task the way she would want it done, such as carefully bathing Lolla's grazed knee with warm wine. And then he saw her most days. The new hospital was almost finished, but the cathedral tower was barely begun, and Caris kept a close eye on both building projects. The priory had lost its power to control the town merchants, but nevertheless Caris took an interest in the work Merthin and the guild were doing to create all the institutions of a borough—establishing new courts, planning a wool exchange, and encouraging the craft guilds to codify standards and measures. But his thoughts about her always had an unpleasant aftertaste, like the bitterness left at the back of the throat by sour beer. He had loved her totally, and she had, in the end, rejected him. It was like remembering a happy day that had ended with a fight.

"Do you think I'm peculiarly attracted to women who aren't free?" he said idly to Philippa.

"No, why?"

"It does seem odd that after twelve years of loving a nun, and nine months of celibacy, I should fall for my brother's wife."

"Don't call me that," she said quickly. "It was no marriage. I was wedded against my will, I shared his bed for no more than a few days, and he will be happy if he never sees me again."

He patted her shoulder apologetically. "But still, we have to be secretive, just as I did with Caris." What he was not saying was that a man was entitled, by law, to kill his wife if he caught her committing adultery. Merthin had never known it to happen, certainly not among the nobility, but Ralph's pride was a terrible thing. Merthin knew, and had told Philippa, that Ralph had killed his first wife, Tilly.

She said: "Your father loved your mother hopelessly for a long time, didn't he?"

"So he did!" Merthin had almost forgotten that old story.

"And you fell for a nun."

"And my brother spent years pining for you, the happily married wife of a nobleman. As the priests say, the sins of the fathers are visited upon the sons. But enough of this. Do you want some supper?"

"In a moment."

"There's something you want to do first?"

"You know."

He did know. He knelt between her legs and kissed her belly and her thighs. It was a peculiarity of hers that she always wanted to come twice. He began to tease her with his tongue. She groaned, and pressed the back of his head. "Yes," she said. "You know how I like that, especially when I'm full of your seed."

He lifted his head. "I do," he said. Then he bent again to his task.

The spring brought a respite in the plague. People were still dying, but fewer were falling ill. On Easter Sunday, Bishop Henri announced that the Fleece Fair would take place as usual this year.

At the same service, six novices took their vows and so became full-fledged monks. They had all had an extraordinarily short novitiate, but

Henri was keen to raise the number of monks at Kingsbridge, and he said the same thing was going on all over the country. In addition five priests were ordained—they, too, benefiting from an accelerated training program—and sent to replace plague victims in the surrounding countryside. And two Kingsbridge monks came down from university, having received their degrees as physicians in three years instead of the usual five or seven.

The new doctors were Austin and Sime. Caris remembered both of them rather vaguely: she had been guest master when they left, three years ago, to go to Kingsbridge College in Oxford. On the afternoon of Easter Monday she showed them around the almost-completed new hospital. No builders were at work as it was a holiday.

Both had the bumptious self-confidence that the university seemed to instill in its graduates along with medical theories and a taste for Gascon wine. However, years of dealing with patients had given Caris a confidence of her own, and she described the hospital's facilities and the way she planned to run it with brisk assurance.

Austin was a slim, intense young man with thinning fair hair. He was impressed with the innovative new cloisterlike layout of the rooms. Sime, a little older and round-faced, did not seem eager to learn from Caris's experience: she noticed that he always looked away when she was talking.

"I believe a hospital should always be clean," she said.

"On what grounds?" Sime inquired in a condescending tone, as if asking a little girl why Dolly had to be spanked.

"Cleanliness is a virtue."

"Ah. So it has nothing to do with the balance of humors in the body."

"I have no idea. We don't pay too much attention to the humors. That approach has failed spectacularly against the plague."

"And sweeping the floor has succeeded?"

"At a minimum, a clean room lifts patients' spirits."

Austin put in: "You must admit, Sime, that some of the masters at Oxford share the mother prioress's new ideas."

"A small group of the heterodox."

Caris said: "The main point is to take patients suffering from the type of illnesses that are transmitted from the sick to the well and isolate them from the rest."

"To what end?" said Sime.

"To restrict the spread of such diseases."

"And how is it that they are transmitted?"

"No one knows."

A little smile of triumph twitched Sime's mouth. "Then how do you know by what means to restrict their spread, may I ask?"

He thought he had trumped her in argument—it was the main thing they learned at Oxford—but she knew better. "From experience," she said. "A shepherd doesn't understand the miracle by which lambs grow in the womb of a ewe, but he knows it won't happen if he keeps the ram out of the field."

"Hm."

Caris disliked the way he said: "Hm." He was clever, she thought, but his cleverness never touched the world. She was struck by the contrast between this kind of intellectual and Merthin's kind. Merthin's learning was wide, and the power of his mind to grasp complexities was remarkable—but his wisdom never strayed far from the realities of the material world, for he knew that if he went wrong his buildings would fall down. Her father, Edmund, had been like that, clever but practical. Sime, like Godwyn and Anthony, would cling to his faith in the humors of the body regardless of whether his patients lived or died.

Austin was smiling broadly. "She's got you there, Sime," he said, evidently amused that his smug friend had failed to overwhelm this uneducated woman. "We may not know exactly how illnesses spread, but it can't do any harm to separate the sick from the well."

Sister Joan, the nuns' treasurer, interrupted their conversation. "The bailiff of Outhenby is asking for you, Mother Caris."

"Did he bring a herd of calves?" Outhenby was obliged to supply the nuns with twelve one-year-old calves every Easter.

"Yes."

"Pen the beasts and ask the bailiff to come here, please."

Sime and Austin took their leave, and Caris went to inspect the tiled floor in the latrines. The bailiff found her there. It was Harry Plowman. She had sacked the old bailiff, who was too slow to respond to change, and she had promoted the brightest young man in the village.

He shook her hand, which was overfamiliar of him, but Caris liked him and did not mind.

She said: "It must be a nuisance, your having to drive a herd all the way here, especially when the spring plowing is under way."

"It is that," he said. Like most plowmen, he was broad-shouldered and strong-armed. Strength as well as skill was required for driving the communal eight-ox team as they pulled the heavy plow through wet clay soil. He seemed to carry with him the air of the healthy outdoors.

"Wouldn't you rather make a money payment?" Caris said. "Most manorial dues are paid in cash these days."

"It would be more convenient." His eyes narrowed with peasant shrewdness. "But how much?"

"A year-old calf normally fetches ten to twelve shillings at market, though prices are down this season."

"They are—by half. You can buy twelve calves for three pounds."

"Or six pounds in a good year."

He grinned, enjoying the negotiation. "There's your problem."

"But you would prefer to pay cash."

"If we can agree the amount."

"Make it eight shillings."

"But then, if the price of a calf is only five shillings, where do we villagers get the extra money?"

"I tell you what. In future, Outhenby can pay the nunnery either five pounds or twelve calves—the choice is yours."

Harry considered that, looking for snags, but could find none. "All right," he said. "Shall we seal the bargain?"

"How should we do that?"

To her surprise, he kissed her.

He held her slender shoulders in his rough hands, bent his head, and pressed his lips to hers. If Brother Sime had done this she would have recoiled. But Harry was different, and perhaps she had been titillated by his air of vigorous masculinity. Whatever the reason, she submitted to the kiss, letting him pull her unresisting body to his own, and moving her lips against his bearded mouth. He pressed up against her so that she could feel his erection. She realized that he would cheerfully take her here on the newly laid tiles of the latrine floor, and that thought brought her to her senses. She broke the kiss and pushed him away. "Stop!" she said. "What do you think you're doing?"

He was unabashed. "Kissing you, my dear," he said.

She realized that she had a problem. No doubt gossip about her and Merthin was widespread: they were probably the two best-known people in Shiring. While Harry surely did not know the truth, the rumors had been enough to embolden him. This kind of thing could undermine her authority. She must squash it now. "You must never do anything like that again," she said as severely as she could.

"You seemed to like it!"

"Then your sin is all the greater, for you have tempted a weak woman to perjure her holy vows."

"But I love you."

It was true, she realized, and she could guess why. She had swept into his village, reorganized everything, and bent the peasants to her will. She had recognized Harry's potential and elevated him above his fellows. He must think of her as a goddess. It was not surprising that he had fallen in love with her. He had better fall out of love as soon as possible. "If you ever speak to me like that again, I'll have to get another bailiff in Outhenby."

"Oh," he said. That stopped him short more effectively than the accusation of sin.

"Now, go home."

"Very well, Mother Caris."

"And find yourself another woman—preferably one who has not taken a vow of chastity."

"Never," he said, but she did not believe him.

He left, but she stayed where she was. She felt restless and lustful. If she could have felt sure of being alone for a while, she would have touched herself. This was the first time in nine months that she had been bothered by physical desire. After finally splitting up with Merthin she had fallen into a kind of neutered state, in which she did not think about sex. Her relationships with other nuns gave her warmth and affection: she was fond of both Joan and Oonagh, though neither loved her in the physical way Mair had. Her heart beat with other passions: the new hospital, the tower, and the rebirth of the town.

Thinking of the tower, she left the hospital and walked across the green to the cathedral. Merthin had dug four enormous holes, the deepest anyone had ever seen, outside the church around the foundations of the old tower. He had built great cranes to lift the earth out. Throughout the wet autumn months, oxcarts had lumbered all day long down the main street and across the first span of the bridge to dump the mud on rocky Leper Island. There they had picked up building stones from Merthin's wharf, then climbed the street again, to stack the stones around the grounds of the church in ever-growing piles.

As soon as the winter frost was over, his masons had begun laying the foundations. Caris went to the north side of the cathedral and looked into the hole in the angle formed by the outside wall of the nave and the outside wall of the north transept. It was dizzyingly deep. The bottom was already covered with neat masonry, the squared-off stones laid in straight lines and joined by thin layers of mortar. Because the old foundations were inadequate, the tower was being built on its own new, independent foundations. It would rise outside the existing walls of the church, so no demolition would be needed over and above what Elfric had already done in taking down the upper levels of the old tower. Only when it was finished would Merthin remove the temporary roof Elfric had built over the crossing. It was a typical Merthin design: simple yet radical, a brilliant solution to the unique problems of the site.

As at the hospital, no builders were at work on Easter Monday, but she saw movement in the hole and realized someone was walking around on the foundations. A moment later she recognized Merthin. She went to one of the surprisingly flimsy rope-and-branch ladders the masons used, and clambered shakily down.

She was glad to reach the bottom. Merthin helped her off the ladder, smiling. "You look a little pale," he said.

"It's a long way down. How are you getting on?"

"Fine. It will take many years."

"Why? The hospital seems more complicated, and that's finished."

"Two reasons. The higher we go, the fewer masons will be able to work on it. Right now I've got twelve men laying the foundations. But as it rises it will get narrower, and there just won't be room for them all. The other reason is that mortar takes so long to set. We have to let it harden over a winter before we put too much weight on it."

She was hardly listening. Watching his face, she was remembering making love to him in the prior's palace, between Matins and Lauds, with the first gleam of daylight coming in through the open window and falling over their naked bodies like a blessing.

She patted his arm. "Well, the hospital isn't taking so long."

"You should be able to move in by Whitsun."

"I'm glad. Although we're having a slight respite from the plague: fewer people are dying."

"Thank God," he said fervently. "Perhaps it may be coming to an end."

She shook her head bleakly. "We thought it was over once before, remember? About this time last year. Then it came back worse."

"Heaven forbid."

She touched his cheek with her palm, feeling his wiry beard. "At least you're safe."

He looked faintly displeased. "As soon as the hospital is finished we can start on the wool exchange."

"I hope you're right to think that business must pick up soon."

"If it doesn't, we'll all be dead anyway."

"Don't say that." She kissed his cheek.

"We have to act on the assumption that we're going to live." He said it irritably, as if she had annoyed him. "But the truth is that we don't know."

"Let's not think about the worst." She put her arms around his waist and hugged him, pressing her breasts against his thin body, feeling his hard bones against her yielding flesh.

He pushed her away violently. She stumbled backward and almost fell. "Don't do that!" he shouted.

She was as shocked as if he had slapped her. "What's the matter?"

"Stop touching me!"

"I only . . ."

"Just don't do it! You ended our relationship nine months ago. I said it was the last time, and I meant it."

She could not understand his anger. "But I only hugged you."

"Well, don't. I'm not your lover. You have no right."

"I have no right to touch you?"

"No!"

"I didn't think I needed some kind of permission."

"Of course you knew. You don't let people touch you."

"You're not *people.* We're not strangers." But as she said these things she knew she was wrong and he was right. She had rejected him, but she had not accepted the consequences. The encounter with Harry from Outhenby had fired her lust, and she had come to Merthin looking for release. She had told herself she was touching him in affectionate friendship, but that was a lie. She had treated him as if he were still available to her, as a rich and idle lady might put down a book and pick it up again. Having denied him the right to touch her all this time, it was wrong of her to try to reinstate the privilege just because a muscular young plowman had kissed her.

All the same, she would have expected Merthin to point this out in a gentle and affectionate way. But he had been hostile and brutal. Had she thrown away his friendship as well as his love? Tears came to her eyes. She turned away from him and went back to the ladder.

She found it hard to climb up. It was tiring, and she seemed to have lost her energy. She stopped for a rest, and looked down. Merthin was standing on the bottom of the ladder, steadying it with his weight.

When she was almost at the top, she looked down again. He was still there. It occurred to her that her unhappiness would be over if she fell. It was a long drop to those unforgiving stones. She would die instantly.

Merthin seemed to sense what she was thinking, for he gave an impatient wave, indicating that she should hurry up and get off the ladder. She thought of how devastated he would be if she killed herself, and for a moment she enjoyed imagining his misery and guilt. She felt sure God would not punish her in the afterlife, if there was an afterlife.

Then she climbed the last few rungs and stood on solid ground. How foolish she had been, just for a moment. She was not going to end her life. She had too much to do.

She returned to the nunnery. It was time for Evensong, and she led the procession into the cathedral. As a young novice she had resented the time wasted in services. In fact Mother Cecilia had taken care to give her work that permitted her to be excused for much of the time. Now she welcomed the chance to rest and reflect.

This afternoon had been a low moment, she decided, but she would recover. All the same she found herself fighting back tears as she sang the psalms.

For supper the nuns had smoked eel. Chewy and strongly flavored, it was not Caris's favorite dish. Tonight she was not hungry, anyway. She ate some bread.

After the meal she retired to her pharmacy. Two novices were there, copying out Caris's book. She had finished it soon after Christmas. Many people had asked for copies: apothecaries, prioresses, barbers, even one or two physicians. Copying the book had become part of the training of nuns who wanted to work in the hospital. The copies were cheap—the book was short, and there were no elaborate drawings or costly inks—and the demand seemed never-ending.

Three people made the room feel crowded. Caris was looking forward to the space and light of the pharmacy in the new hospital.

She wanted to be alone, so she sent the novices away. However, she was not destined to get her wish. A few moments later Lady Philippa came in.

Caris had never warmed to the reserved countess, but sympathized with her plight, and was glad to give sanctuary to any woman fleeing from a husband such as Ralph. Philippa was an easy guest, making few demands, spending a lot of time in her room. She had only a limited interest in sharing the nuns' life of prayer and self-denial—but Caris of all people could understand that.

Caris invited her to sit on a stool at the bench.

Philippa was a remarkably direct woman, despite her courtly manners. Without preamble, she said: "I want you to leave Merthin alone."

"What?" Caris was astonished and offended.

"Of course you have to talk to him, but you should not kiss or touch him."

"How dare you." What did Philippa know—and why did she care?

"He's not your lover anymore. Stop bothering him."

Merthin must have told her about their quarrel this afternoon. "But why would he tell you . . . ?" Before the question was out of her mouth, she guessed the answer.

Philippa confirmed it with her next utterance. "He's not yours, now—he's mine."

"Oh, my soul!" Caris was flabbergasted. "You and Merthin?"

"Yes."

"Are you . . . Have you actually . . ."

"Yes."

"I had no idea!" She felt betrayed, though she knew she had no right. When had this happened? "But how . . . where . . . ?"

"You don't need to know the details."

"Of course not." At his house on Leper Island, she supposed. At night, probably. "How long . . . ?"

"It doesn't matter."

Caris could work it out. Philippa had been here less than a month. "You moved fast."

It was an unworthy jibe, and Philippa had the grace to ignore it. "He would have done anything to keep you. But you threw him over. Now let him go. It's been difficult for him to love anyone else, after you—but he has managed it. Don't you dare interfere."

Caris wanted to rebuff her furiously, tell her angrily that she had no right to give orders and make moral demands—but the trouble was that Philippa was in the right. Caris had to let Merthin go, forever.

She did not want to show her heartbreak in front of Philippa. "Would you leave me now, please?" she said with an attempt at Philippa's style of dignity. "I would like to be alone."

Philippa was not easily pushed around. "Will you do as I say?" she persisted.

Caris did not like to be cornered, but she had no spirit left. "Yes, of course," she said.

"Thank you." Philippa left.

When she was sure Philippa was out of earshot, Caris began to cry.

78

Philemon as prior was no better than Godwyn. He was overwhelmed by the challenge of managing the assets of the priory. Caris had made a list, during her spell as acting prior, of the monks' main sources of income:

1. *Rents*
2. *A share of profits from commerce and industry (tithing)*
3. *Agricultural profits on land not rented out*
4. *Profits from grain mills and other, industrial mills*
5. *Waterway tolls and a share of all fish landed*
6. *Stallage in markets*
7. *Proceeds of justice—fees and fines from courts*
8. *Pious gifts from pilgrims and others*
9. *Sale of books, holy water, candles, etc.*

She had given the list to Philemon, and he had thrown it back at her as if insulted. Godwyn, better than Philemon only in that he had a certain superficial charm, would have thanked her and quietly ignored her list.

In the nunnery, she had introduced a new method of keeping accounts, one she had learned from Buonaventura Caroli when she was working for her father. The old method was simply to write in a parchment roll a short note of every transaction, so that you could always go back and check. The Italian system was to record income on the left-hand side and expenditure on the right, and add them up at the foot of the page. The difference between the two totals showed whether the institution was gaining or losing money. Sister Joan had taken this up with enthusiasm, but when she offered to explain it to Philemon he refused curtly. He regarded offers of help as insults to his competence.

He had only one talent, and it was the same as Godwyn's: a flair for manipulating people. He had shrewdly weeded the new intake of monks, sending the modern-minded physician, Brother Austin, and two other bright young men to St.-John-in-the-Forest, where they would be too far away to challenge his authority.

But Philemon was the bishop's problem now. Henri had appointed him and Henri would have to deal with him. The town was independent, and Caris had her new hospital.

The hospital was to be consecrated by the bishop on Whitsunday, which was always seven weeks after Easter. A few days beforehand, Caris moved her equipment and supplies into the new pharmacy. There was plenty of room for two people to work at the bench, preparing medicines, and a third to sit at a writing desk.

Caris was preparing an emetic, Oonagh was grinding dried herbs, and a novice, Greta, was copying out Caris's book, when a novice monk came in with a small wooden chest. It was Josiah, a teenage boy usually called Joshie. He was embarrassed to be in the presence of three women. "Where shall I put this?" he said.

Caris looked at him. "What is it?"

"A chest."

"I can see that," she said patiently. The fact that someone was capable of learning to read and write did not, unfortunately, make him intelligent. "What does the chest contain?"

"Books."

"And why have you brought me a chest of books?"

"I was told to." Realizing, after a moment, that this answer was insufficiently informative, he added: "By Brother Sime."

Caris raised her eyebrows. "Is Sime making me a gift of books?" She opened the chest.

Joshie made his escape without answering the question.

The books were medical texts, all in Latin. Caris looked through them. They were the classics: Avicenna's *Poem on Medicine,* Hippocrates' *Diet and Hygiene,* Galen's *On the Parts of Medicine,* and *De Urinis* by Isaac Judaeus. All had been written more than three hundred years ago.

Joshie reappeared with another chest.

"What now?" said Caris.

"Medical instruments. Brother Sime says you are not to touch them. He will come and put them in their proper places."

Caris was dismayed. "Sime wants to keep his books and instruments here? Is he planning to work here?"

Joshie did not know anything about Sime's intentions, of course.

Before Caris could say any more, Sime appeared, accompanied by Philemon. Sime looked around the room then, without explanation, began unpacking his things. He moved some of Caris's vessels from a shelf and replaced them with his books. He took out sharp knives for opening veins, and the teardrop-shaped glass flasks used for examining urine samples.

Caris said neutrally: "Are you planning to spend a great deal of time here in the hospital, Brother Sime?"

Philemon answered for him, clearly having anticipated the question with relish. "Where else?" he said. His tone was indignant, as if Caris had challenged him already. "This is the hospital, is it not? And Sime is the only physician in the priory. How shall people be treated, if not by him?"

Suddenly the pharmacy did not seem so spacious anymore.

Before Caris could say anything, a stranger appeared. "Brother Thomas told me to come here," he said. "I am Jonas Powderer, from London."

The visitor was a man of about fifty dressed in an embroidered coat and a fur hat. Caris noted his ready smile and affable manner, and guessed that he made his living by selling things. He shook hands, then looked around the room, nodding with apparent approval at Caris's neat rows of labeled jars and vials. "Remarkable," he said. "I have never seen such a sophisticated pharmacy outside London."

"Are you a physician, sir?" Philemon asked. His tone was cautious: he was not sure of Jonas's status.

"Apothecary. I have a shop in Smithfield, next to St. Bartholomew's Hospital. I shouldn't boast, but it is the largest such business in the city."

Philemon relaxed. An apothecary was a mere merchant, well below a prior in the pecking order. With a hint of a sneer he said: "And what brings the biggest apothecary in London all the way down here?"

"I was hoping to acquire a copy of *The Kingsbridge Panacea.*"

"The what?"

Jonas smiled knowingly. "You cultivate humility, Father Prior, but I see this novice nun making a copy right here in your pharmacy."

Caris said: "The book? It's not called a panacea."

"Yet it contains cures for all ills."

There was a certain logic to that, she realized. "But how do you know of it?"

"I travel a good deal, searching for rare herbs and other ingredients, while my sons take care of the shop. I met a nun of Southampton who showed me a copy. She called it a panacea, and told me it was written in Kingsbridge."

"Was the nun Sister Claudia?"

"Yes. I begged her to lend me the book just long enough to make a copy, but she would not be parted from it."

"I remember her." Claudia had made a pilgrimage to Kingsbridge, stayed in the nunnery, and nursed plague victims with no thought for her own safety. Caris had given her the book in thanks.

"A remarkable work," Jonas said warmly. "And in English!"

"It's for healers who aren't priests, and therefore don't speak much Latin."

"There is no other book of its kind in *any* language."

"Is it so unusual?"

"The arrangement of subjects!" Jonas enthused. "Instead of the humors of the body, or the classes of illness, the chapters refer to the pains of the patient. So, whether the customer's complaint is stomachache, or bleeding, or fever, or diarrhea, or sneezing, you can just go to the relevant page!"

Philemon said impatiently: "Suitable enough for apothecaries and their *customers,* I am sure."

Jonas appeared not to hear the note of derision. "I assume, Father Prior, that you are the author of this invaluable book."

"Certainly not!" he said.

"Then who . . . ?"

"I wrote it," Caris said.

"A woman!" Jonas marveled. "But where did you get all the information? Virtually none of it appears in other texts."

"The old texts have never proved very useful to me, Jonas. I was first taught how to make medicines by a wise woman of Kingsbridge, called Mattie, who sadly left town for fear of being persecuted as a witch. I learned more from Mother Cecilia, who was prioress here before me. But gathering the recipes and treatments is not difficult. Everyone knows a hundred of them. The difficulty is to identify the few effective ones in all the dross. What I did was to keep a diary, over the years, of the effects of every cure I tried. In my book, I included only those I have seen working, with my own eyes, time after time."

"I am awestruck to be speaking to you in person."

"Well, you shall have a copy of my book. I'm flattered that someone should come such a long way for it!" She opened a cupboard. "This was intended for our priory of St.-John-in-the-Forest, but they can wait for another copy."

Jonas handled it as if it were a holy object. "I am most grateful." He produced a bag of soft leather and gave it to Caris. "And, in token of my gratitude, accept a modest gift from my family to the nuns of Kingsbridge."

Caris opened the bag and took out a small object swathed in wool. When she unwrapped the material she found a gold crucifix embedded with precious stones.

Philemon's eyes glittered with greed.

Caris was startled. "This is a costly present!" she exclaimed. That was less than charming, she realized. She added: "Extraordinarily generous of your family, Jonas."

He made a deprecatory gesture. "We are prosperous, thanks be to God."

Philemon said enviously: "That—for a book of old women's nostrums!"

Jonas said: "Ah, Father Prior, you are above such things, of course. We do not aspire to your intellectual heights. We do not try to understand the body's humors. Just as a child sucks on a cut finger because that eases the pain, so we administer cures only because they work. As to why and how these things happen, we leave that to greater minds than ours. God's creation is too mysterious for the likes of us to comprehend."

Caris thought Jonas was speaking with barely concealed irony. She saw Oonagh smother a grin. Sime, too, picked up the undertone of mockery, and his eyes flashed anger. But Philemon did not notice, and he seemed mollified by the flattery. A sly look came over his face, and Caris guessed he was wondering how he could share in the credit for the book—and get some jeweled crucifixes for himself.

The Fleece Fair opened on Whitsunday, as always. It was traditionally a busy day for the hospital, and this year was no exception. Elderly folk fell ill after making a long journey to the fair; babies and children got diarrhea from strange food and foreign water; men and women drank too much in the taverns and injured themselves and each other.

For the first time, Caris was able to separate the patients into two categories. The rapidly diminishing number of plague victims, and others who had catching illnesses such as stomach upsets and poxes, went into the new building, which was officially blessed by the bishop early in the day. Victims of accidents and fights were treated in the old hospital, safe from the risk of infection. Gone were the days when someone would come into the priory with a dislocated thumb and die there of pneumonia.

The crisis came on Whitmonday.

Early in the afternoon Caris happened to be at the fair, taking a stroll after dinner, looking around. It was quiet by comparison with the old days, when hundreds of visitors and thousands of townspeople thronged not just the cathedral green but all the principal streets. Nevertheless, this year's fair was better than expected after last year's cancellation. Caris figured that people had noticed how the grip of the plague seemed to be weakening. Those who had survived so far thought they must be invulnerable—and some were, though others were not, for it continued to kill people.

Madge Webber's cloth was the talking point of the fair. The new looms designed by Merthin were not just faster—they also made it easier to produce complex patterns in the weave. She had sold half her stock already.

Caris was talking to Madge when the fight started. Madge was embarrassing her by saying, as she had often said before, that without Caris she would still be a penniless weaver. Caris was about to give her customary denial when they heard shouts.

Caris recognized immediately the deep-chested sound of aggressive young men. It came from the neighborhood of an ale barrel thirty yards away. The shouts increased rapidly, and a young woman screamed. Caris hurried over to the place, hoping to stop the fight before it got out of control.

She was a little too late.

The fracas was well under way. Four of the town's young tearaways were fighting fiercely with a group of peasants, identifiable as such by their rustic clothing, and probably all from the same village. A pretty girl, no doubt the one who had screamed, was struggling to separate two men who were punching one another mercilessly. One of the town boys had drawn a knife, and the peasants had heavy wooden shovels. As Caris arrived, more people were joining in on both sides.

She turned to Madge, who had followed her. "Send someone to fetch Mungo Constable, quick as you can. He's probably in the basement of the guildhall." Madge hurried off.

The fight was getting nastier. Several town boys had knives out. A peasant lad was lying on the ground bleeding copiously from his arm, and another was fighting on despite a gash in his face. As Caris watched, two more townies started kicking the peasant on the ground.

Caris hesitated another moment, then stepped forward. She grabbed the nearest fighter by the shirt. "Willie Bakerson, stop this right now!" she shouted in her most authoritative voice.

It almost worked.

Willie stepped back from his opponent, startled, and looked at Caris guiltily. She opened her mouth to speak again, but at that instant a shovel struck her a violent blow on the head that had surely been intended for Willie.

It hurt like hell. Her vision blurred, she lost her balance, and the next thing she knew she hit the ground. She lay there dazed, trying to recover her wits, while the world seemed to sway around her. Then someone grabbed her under the arms and dragged her away.

"Are you hurt, Mother Caris?" The voice was familiar, though she could not place it.

Her head cleared at last, and she struggled to her feet with the help of her rescuer, whom she now identified as the muscular corn merchant Megg

Robbins. "I'm just a bit stunned," Caris said. "We have to stop these boys killing each other."

"Here come the constables. Let's leave it to them."

Sure enough, Mungo and six or seven deputies appeared, all wielding clubs. They waded into the fight, cracking heads indiscriminately. They were doing as much damage as the original fighters, but their presence confused the battleground. The boys looked bewildered, and some ran off. In a remarkably few moments the fight was over.

Caris said: "Megg, run to the nunnery and fetch Sister Oonagh, and tell her to bring bandages."

Megg hurried away.

The walking wounded quickly disappeared. Caris began to examine those who were left. A peasant boy who had been knifed in the stomach was trying to hold his guts in: there was little hope for him. The one with the gashed arm would live if Caris could stop the bleeding. She took off his belt, wound it around his upper arm, and tightened it until the flow of blood slowed to a trickle. "Hold that there," she told him, and moved on to a town boy who seemed to have broken some bones in his hand. Her head was still hurting but she ignored it.

Oonagh and several more nuns appeared. A moment later, Matthew Barber arrived with his bag. Between them they patched up the wounded. Under Caris's instructions, volunteers picked up the worst victims and carried them to the nunnery. "Take them to the old hospital, not the new one," she said.

She stood up from a kneeling position and felt dizzy. She grabbed Oonagh to steady herself. "What's the matter?" said Oonagh.

"I'll be all right. We'd better get to the hospital."

They threaded their way through the market stalls to the old hospital. When they went in, they saw immediately that none of the wounded were here. Caris cursed. "The fools have taken them all to the wrong place," she said. It was going to take a while for people to learn the importance of the difference, she concluded.

She and Oonagh went to the new building. The cloister was entered through a wide archway. As they went in, they met the volunteers coming out. "You brought them to the wrong place!" Caris said crossly.

One said: "But, Mother Caris—"

"Don't argue, there's no time," she said impatiently. "Just carry them to the old hospital."

Stepping into the cloisters, she saw the boy with the gashed arm being carried into a room where, she knew, there were five plague victims. She rushed across the quadrangle. "Stop!" she yelled furiously. "What do you think you're doing?"

A man's voice said: "They are carrying out my instructions."

Caris stopped and looked around. It was Brother Sime. "Don't be a fool," she said. "He's got a knife wound—do you want him to die of the plague?"

His round face turned pink. "I don't propose to submit my decision to you for approval, Mother Caris."

That was stupid and she ignored it. "All these injured boys must be kept away from plague victims, or they'll catch it!"

"I think you're overwrought. I suggest you go and lie down."

"Lie down?" She was outraged. "I've just patched up all these men—now I've got to look at them properly. But not here!"

"Thank you for your emergency work, Mother. You can now leave me to examine the patients thoroughly."

"You idiot, you'll kill them!"

"Please leave the hospital until you have calmed down."

"You can't throw me out of here, you stupid boy! I built this hospital with the nuns' money. I'm in charge here."

"Are you?" he said coolly.

Caris realized that, although she had not anticipated this moment, he almost certainly had. He was flushed, but he had his feelings under control. He was a man with a plan. She paused, thinking fast. Looking around, she saw that the nuns and volunteers were all watching, waiting to see how this would turn out.

"We have to attend to these boys," she said. "While we're standing here arguing, they're bleeding to death. We'll compromise, for now." She raised her voice. "Put every one down exactly where they are, please." The weather was warm, there was no need for the patients to be indoors. "We'll see to their needs first, then decide later where they are to be bedded."

The volunteers and nuns knew and respected Caris, whereas Sime was new to them; and they obeyed her with alacrity.

Sime saw that he was beaten, and a look of utter fury came over his face. "I cannot treat patients in these circumstances," he said, and he stalked out.

Caris was shocked. She had tried to save his pride with her compromise, and she had not thought he would walk away from sick people in a fit of petulance.

She quickly put him out of her mind as she began to look again at the injured.

For the next couple of hours she was busy bathing wounds, sewing up gashes, and administering soothing herbs and comforting drinks. Matthew Barber worked alongside her, setting broken bones and fixing dislocated joints. Matthew was in his fifties now, but his son Luke assisted him with equal skill.

The afternoon was cooling into evening when they finished. They sat on the cloister wall to rest. Sister Joan brought them tankards of cool cider. Caris still had a headache. She had been able to ignore it while she was busy, but now it bothered her. She would go to bed early, she decided.

While they were drinking their cider, young Joshie appeared. "The lord bishop asks you to attend on him in the prior's palace at your convenience, Mother Prioress."

She grunted irritably. No doubt Sime had complained. This was the last thing she needed. "Tell him I'll come immediately," she said. In a lower voice she added: "Might as well get it over with." She drained her tankard and left.

Wearily she walked across the green. The stallholders were packing up for the night, covering their goods and locking their boxes. She passed through the graveyard and entered the palace.

Bishop Henri sat at the head of the table. Canon Claude and Archdeacon Lloyd were with him. Philemon and Sime were also there. Godwyn's cat, Archbishop, was sitting on Henri's lap, looking smug. The bishop said: "Please sit down."

She sat beside Claude. He said kindly: "You look tired, Mother Caris."

"I've spent the afternoon patching up stupid boys who got into a big fight. Also, I got a bang on the head myself."

"We heard about the fight."

Henri added: "And about the argument in the new hospital."

"I assume that's why I'm here."

"Yes."

"The whole idea of the new place is to separate patients with infectious illnesses—"

"I know what the argument is about," Henri interrupted. He addressed the group. "Caris ordered that those injured in the fight be taken to the old hospital. Sime countermanded her orders. They had an unseemly row in front of everyone."

Sime said: "I apologize for that, my lord bishop."

Henri ignored that. "Before we go any farther, I want to get something clear." He looked from Sime to Caris and back again. "I am your bishop and, ex officio, the abbot of Kingsbridge Priory. I have the right and power to command you all, and it is your duty to obey me. Do you accept that, Brother Sime?"

Sime bowed his head. "I do."

Henri turned to Caris. "Do you, Mother Prioress?"

There was no argument, of course. Henri was completely in the right. "Yes," she said. She felt confident that Henri was not stupid enough to force injured hooligans to catch the plague.

Henri said: "Allow me to state the arguments. The new hospital was built with the nuns' money, to the specifications of Mother Caris. She intended it to provide a place for plague victims and others whose illnesses may, according to her, be spread from the sick to the well. She believes it is essential to compartmentalize the two types of patient. She feels she is entitled, in all the circumstances, to insist that her plan be carried out. Is that fair, Mother?"

"Yes."

"Brother Sime was not here when Caris conceived her plan, so he could not be consulted. However, he has spent three years studying medicine at the university, and has been awarded a degree. He points out that Caris has no training and, apart from what she has picked up by practical experience, little understanding of the nature of disease. He is a qualified physician, and more than that, he is the only one in the priory, or indeed in Kingsbridge."

"Exactly," said Sime.

"How can you say I have no training?" Caris burst out. "After all the years I've cared for patients—"

"Be quiet, please," Henri said, hardly raising his voice; and something in his quiet tone caused Caris to shut up. "I was about to mention your history of service. Your work here has been invaluable. You are known far and wide for your dedication during the plague that is still with us. Your experience and practical knowledge are priceless."

"Thank you, Bishop."

"On the other hand, Sime is a priest, a university graduate . . . and a man. The learning he brings with him is essential to the proper running of a priory hospital. We do not want to lose him."

Caris said: "Some of the masters at the university agree with my methods—ask Brother Austin."

Philemon said: "Brother Austin has been sent to St.-John-in-the-Forest."

"And now we know why," Caris said.

The bishop said: "I have to make this decision, not Austin or the masters at the university."

Caris realized that she had not prepared for this showdown. She was exhausted, she had a headache, and she could hardly think straight. She was in the middle of a power struggle, and she had no strategy. If she had been fully alert, she would not have come when the bishop called. She would have gone to bed and got over her bad head and woken up refreshed in the morning, and she would not have met with Henri until she had worked out her battle plan.

Was it yet too late for that?

She said: "Bishop, I don't feel adequate to this discussion tonight. Perhaps we could postpone it until tomorrow, when I'm feeling better."

"No need," said Henri. "I've heard Sime's complaint, and I know your views. Besides, I will be leaving at sunrise."

He had made up his mind, Caris realized. Nothing she said would make any difference. But what had he decided? Which way would he jump? She really had no idea. And she was too tired to do anything but sit and listen to her fate.

"Humankind is weak," Henri said. "We see, as the apostle Paul puts it, as through a glass, darkly. We err, we go astray, we reason poorly. We need help. That is why God gave us His church, and the pope, and the priesthood—to guide us, because our own resources are fallible and inadequate. If we follow our own way of thinking, we will fail. We must consult the authorities."

It looked as if he was going to back Sime, Caris concluded. How could he be so stupid?

But he was. "Brother Sime has studied the ancient texts of medical literature, under the supervision of the masters at the university. His course of study is endorsed by the church. We must accept its authority, and therefore his. His judgment cannot be subordinated to that of an uneducated person, no matter how brave and admirable she may be. His decisions must prevail."

Caris felt so weary and ill that she was almost glad the interview was over. Sime had won; she had lost; and all she wanted to do was sleep. She stood up.

Henri said: "I'm sorry to disappoint you, Mother Caris . . ."

His voice tailed off as she walked away.

She heard Philemon say: "Insolent behavior."

Henri said quietly: "Let her go."

She reached the door and went out without turning back.

The full meaning of what had happened became clear to her as she walked slowly through the graveyard. Sime was in charge of the hospital. She would have to follow his orders. There would be no separation of different categories of patient. There would be no face masks or hand washing in vinegar. Weak people would be made weaker by bleeding; starved people would be made thinner by purging; wounds would be covered with poultices made of animal dung to encourage the body to produce pus. No one would care about cleanliness or fresh air.

She spoke to nobody as she walked across the cloisters, up the stairs, and through the dormitory to her own room. She lay facedown on her bed, her head pounding.

She had lost Merthin, she had lost her hospital, she had lost everything.

Head injuries could be fatal, she knew. Perhaps she would go to sleep now and never wake up.

Perhaps that would be for the best.

79

Merthin's orchard had been planted in the spring of 1349. A year later most of the trees were established and came out in a scatter of brave leaves. Two or three were struggling, and only one was inarguably dead. He did not expect any of them to bear fruit yet, but by July, to his surprise, one precocious sapling had a dozen or so tiny dark green pears, small as yet and as hard as stones, but promising ripeness in the autumn.

One Sunday afternoon he showed them to Lolla, who refused to believe that they would grow into the tangy, juicy fruits she loved. She thought—or pretended to think—that he was playing one of his teasing games. When he asked her where she imagined ripe pears came from, she looked at him reproachfully and said: "The market, silly!"

She, too, would ripen one day, he thought, although it was hard to imagine her bony body rounding out into the soft shape of a woman. He wondered whether she would bear him grandchildren. She was five years old, so that day might be only a decade or so away.

His thoughts were on ripeness when he saw Philippa coming toward him through the garden, and it struck him how round and full her breasts were. It was unusual for her to visit him in daylight, and he wondered what had brought her here. In case they were observed, he greeted her with only a chaste kiss on the cheek, such as a brother-in-law might give without arousing comment.

She looked troubled, and he realized that for a few days now she had been more reserved and thoughtful than usual. As she sat beside him on the grass he said: "Something on your mind?"

"I've never been good at breaking news gently," she said. "I'm pregnant."

"Good God!" He was too shocked to hold back his reaction. "I'm surprised because you told me . . ."

"I know. I was sure I was too old. For a couple of years my monthly cycle was irregular, and then it stopped altogether—I thought. But I've been vomiting in the morning, and my nipples hurt."

"I noticed your breasts as you came into the garden. But can you be sure?"

"I've been pregnant six times previously—three children and three miscarriages—and I know the feeling. There's really no doubt."

He smiled. "Well, we're going to have a child."

She did not return the smile. "Don't look pleased. You haven't thought through the implications. I'm the wife of the earl of Shiring. I haven't slept with him since October, haven't lived with him since February, yet in July I'm two or at most three months pregnant. He and the whole world will know that the baby is not his, and that the countess of Shiring has committed adultery."

"But he wouldn't . . ."

"Kill me? He killed Tilly, didn't he?"

"Oh, my God. Yes, he did. But . . ."

"And if he killed me, he might kill my baby, too."

Merthin wanted to say it was not possible, that Ralph would not do such a thing—but he knew otherwise.

"I have to decide what to do," said Philippa.

"I don't think you should try to end the pregnancy with potions—it's too dangerous."

"I won't do that."

"So you'll have the baby."

"Yes. But then what?"

"Suppose you stayed in the nunnery, and kept the baby secret? The place is full of children orphaned by the plague."

"But what couldn't be kept secret is a mother's love. Everyone would know that the child was my particular care. And then Ralph would find out."

"You're right."

"I could go away—vanish. London, York, Paris, Avignon. Not tell anyone where I was going, so that Ralph could never come after me."

"And I could go with you."

"But then you wouldn't finish your tower."

"And you would miss Odila."

Philippa's daughter had been married to Earl David for six months. Merthin could imagine how hard it would be for Philippa to leave her. And the truth was that he would find it agony to abandon his tower. All his adult life he had wanted to build the tallest building in England. Now that he had at last begun, it would break his heart to abandon the project.

Thinking of the tower brought Caris to mind. He knew, intuitively, that she would be devastated by this news. He had not seen her for weeks: she had been ill in bed after suffering a blow on the head at the Fleece Fair, and now, though she was completely recovered, she rarely emerged from the priory. He guessed that she had lost some kind of power struggle, for the hospital was being run by Brother Sime. Philippa's pregnancy would be another shattering blow for Caris.

Philippa added: "And Odila, too, is pregnant."

"So soon! That's good news. But even more reason why you can't go into exile and never see her, or your grandchild."

"I can't run, and I can't hide. But, if I do nothing, Ralph will kill me."

"There must be a way out of this," Merthin said.

"I can think of only one answer."

He looked at her. She had thought this out already, he realized. She had not told him about the problem until she had the solution. But she had been careful to show him that all the obvious answers were wrong. That meant he was not going to like the plan she had settled on.

"Tell me," he said.

"We have to make Ralph think the baby is his."

"But then you'd have to . . ."

"Yes."

"I see."

The thought of Philippa sleeping with Ralph was loathsome to Merthin. This was not so much jealousy, though that was a factor. What weighed most with him was how terrible she would feel about it. She had a physical and emotional revulsion toward Ralph. Merthin understood the revulsion, though he did not share it. He had lived with Ralph's brutishness all his life, and the brute was his brother, and somehow that fact remained no matter what Ralph did. All the same, it made him sick to think that Philippa would have to force herself to have sex with the man she hated most in the world.

"I wish I could think of a better way," he said.

"So do I."

He looked hard at her. "You've already decided."

"Yes."

"I'm very sorry."

"So am I."

"But will it even work? Can you . . . seduce him?"

"I don't know," she said. "I'll just have to try."

The cathedral was symmetrical. The mason's loft was at the west end in the low north tower, overlooking the north porch. In the matching southwest tower was a room of similar size and shape that looked over the cloisters. It was used to store items of small value that were used only rarely. All the costumes and symbolic objects employed in the mystery plays were there, together with an assortment of not-quite-useless things: wooden candlesticks, rusty chains, cracked pots, and a book whose vellum pages had rotted with age so that the words penned so painstakingly were no longer legible.

Merthin went there to check how upright the wall was, by dangling a lead pointer on a long string from the window; and while there he made a discovery.

There were cracks in the wall. Cracks were not necessarily a sign of weakness: their meaning had to be interpreted by an experienced eye. All buildings moved, and cracks might simply show how a structure was adjusting to accommodate change. Merthin judged that most of the cracks in the wall of this storeroom were benign. But there was one that puzzled him by its shape. It did not look normal. A second glance told him that someone had taken advantage of a natural crack to loosen a small stone. He removed the stone.

He realized immediately that he had found someone's secret hiding place. The space behind the stone was a thief's stash. He took the objects out one by one. There was a woman's brooch with a large green stone; a silver buckle; a silk shawl; and a scroll with a psalm written on it. Right at the back he found the object that gave him the clue to the identity of the thief. It was the only thing in the hole that had no monetary value.

A simple piece of polished wood, it had letters carved into its surface that read: "M:Phmn:AMAT."

M was just an initial. *Amat* was the Latin for "loves." And Phmnn was surely Philemon.

Someone whose name began with M, boy or girl, had once loved Philemon and given him this; and he had hidden it with his stolen treasures.

Since childhood Philemon had been rumored to be light-fingered. Around him, things went missing. It seemed that this was where he hid them. Merthin imagined him coming up here alone, perhaps at night, to pull out the stone and gloat over his loot. No doubt it was a kind of sickness.

There had never been any rumors about Philemon having lovers. Like his mentor Godwyn, he seemed to be one of that small minority of men in whom the need for sexual love was weak. But someone had fallen for him, at some time, and he cherished the memory.

Merthin replaced the objects, putting them back exactly the way he had found them—he had a good memory for that sort of thing. He replaced the loose stone. Then, thoughtfully, he left the room and went back down the spiral staircase.

Ralph was surprised when Philippa came home.

It was a rare fine day in a wet summer, and he would have liked to be out hawking, but to his anger he was not able to go. The harvest was about to begin, and most of the twenty or thirty stewards, bailiffs, and reeves in the earldom needed to see him urgently. They all had the same problem: crops ripening in the fields and insufficient men and woman to harvest them.

He could do nothing to help. He had taken every opportunity to prosecute laborers who defied the ordinance by leaving their villages in search of higher wages—but those few who could be caught just paid the fine out of their earnings and ran off again. So his bailiffs had to make do. However, they all wanted to explain their difficulties to him, and he had no choice but to listen and give his approval to their makeshift plans.

The hall was full of people: bailiffs, knights and men-at-arms, a couple of priests, and a dozen or more loitering servants. When they all went quiet, Ralph suddenly heard the rooks outside, their harsh call sounding like a warning. He looked up and saw Philippa in the doorway.

She spoke first to the servants. "Martha! This table is still dirty from dinner. Fetch hot water and scrub it, now. Dickie—I've just seen the earl's favorite courser covered with what looks like yesterday's mud, and you're here whittling a stick. Get back to the stables where you belong and clean up that horse. You, boy, put that puppy outside, it's just pissed on the floor. The only dog allowed in the hall is the earl's mastiff, you know that." The servants were galvanized into action, even those to whom she had not spoken suddenly finding work to do.

Ralph did not mind Philippa issuing orders to the domestic servants. They got lazy without a mistress to harry them.

She came up to him and made a deep curtsy, as was only appropriate after a long absence. She did not offer to kiss him.

He said neutrally: "This is . . . unexpected."

Philippa said irritably: "I shouldn't have had to make the journey at all."

Ralph groaned inwardly. "What brings you here?" he said. Whatever it was, there would be trouble, he felt sure.

"My manor of Ingsby."

Philippa had a small number of properties of her own, a few villages in Gloucestershire that paid tribute to her rather than to the earl. Since she had gone to live at the nunnery, the bailiffs from these villages had been visiting her at Kingsbridge Priory, Ralph knew, and accounting to her directly for their dues. But Ingsby was an awkward exception. The manor paid tribute to him and he passed it on to her—which he had forgotten to do since she left. "Damn," he said. "It slipped my mind."

"That's all right," she said. "You've got a lot to think about."

That was surprisingly conciliatory.

She went upstairs to the private chamber, and he returned to his work. Half a year of separation had improved her a little, he thought as another bailiff enumerated the fields of ripening corn and bemoaned the shortage of reapers. Still, he hoped she did not plan to stay long. Lying beside her at night was like sleeping with a dead cow.

She reappeared at suppertime. She sat next to Ralph and spoke politely to several visiting knights during the meal. She was as cool and reserved as ever—there was no affection, not even any humor—but he saw no sign of the implacable, icy hatred she had shown after their wedding. It was gone, or at least deeply hidden. When the meal was over, she retired again, leaving him to drink with the knights.

He considered the possibility that she was planning to come back permanently, but in the end he dismissed the idea. She would never love him or even like him. It was just that a long absence had blunted the edge of her resentment. The underlying feeling would probably never leave her.

He assumed she would be asleep when he went upstairs but, to his surprise, she was at the writing desk, in an ivory-colored linen nightgown, a single candle throwing a soft light over her proud features and thick dark hair. In front of her was a long letter in a girlish hand, which he guessed was from Odila, now the countess of Monmouth. Philippa was penning a reply. Like most aristocrats, she dictated business letters to a clerk, but wrote personal ones herself.

He stepped into the garderobe, then came out and took off his outer clothing. It was summer, and he normally slept in his underdrawers.

Philippa finished her letter, stood up—and knocked over the jar of ink on the desk. She jumped back, too late. Somehow it fell toward her, disfiguring her white nightdress with a broad black stain. She cursed. He was mildly amused: she was so prissily particular that it was funny to see her splashed with ink.

She hesitated for a moment, then pulled the nightdress off over her head.

He was startled. She was not normally quick to take off her clothes. She had been disconcerted by the ink, he realized. He stared at her naked body. She had put on a little weight at the nunnery: her breasts seemed larger and rounder than before, her belly had a slight but discernible bulge, and her hips had an attractive swelling curve. To his surprise, he felt aroused.

She bent down to mop the ink off the tiled floor with her bundled-up nightgown. Her breasts swayed as she rubbed the tiles. She turned, and he got a full view of her generous behind. If he had not known her better, he would have suspected her of trying to inflame him. But Philippa had never tried to inflame anyone, let alone him. She was just awkward and embarrassed. And that made it even more stimulating to stare at her exposed nakedness while she wiped the floor.

It was several weeks since he had been with a woman, and the last one had been a very unsatisfactory whore in Salisbury.

By the time Philippa stood up, he had an erection.

She saw him staring. "Don't look at me," she said. "Go to bed." She threw the soiled garment into the laundry hamper.

She went to the clothespress and lifted its lid. She had left most of her clothes here when she went to Kingsbridge: it was not considered seemly to dress richly when living in a nunnery, even for noble guests. She found another nightdress. Ralph raked her with his eyes as she lifted it out. He stared at her uplifted breasts, and the mound of her sex with its dark hair, and his mouth went dry.

She caught his look. "Don't you touch me," she said.

If she had not said that, he would probably have lain down and gone to sleep. But her swift rejection stung him. "I'm the earl of Shiring and you're my wife," he said. "I'll touch you anytime I like."

"You wouldn't dare," she said, and she turned away to put on the gown.

That angered him. As she lifted the garment to put it on over her head, he slapped her bottom. It was a hard slap on bare skin, and he could tell that it hurt her. She jumped and cried out. "So much for not daring," he said. She turned to him, a protest on her lips, and on impulse he punched her in the mouth. She was knocked back and fell to the floor. Her hands flew to her mouth, and blood seeped through her fingers. But she was on her back, naked, with her legs spread, and he could see the triangle of hair at the fork of her thighs, with its cleft slightly parted in what looked like an invitation.

He fell on her.

She wriggled furiously, but he was bigger than she, and strong. He overcame her resistance effortlessly. A moment later he was inside her. She was dry, but somehow that excited him.

It was all over quite quickly. He rolled off her, panting. After a few moments he looked at her. There was blood on her mouth. She did not look back at him: her eyes were closed. Yet it seemed to him that there was a curious expression on her face. He thought about it for a while until he worked it out; then he was even more puzzled than before.

She looked triumphant.

*

Merthin knew that Philippa had returned to Kingsbridge, because he saw her maid in the Bell. He expected his lover to come to his house that night, and was disappointed when she did not. No doubt she felt awkward, he thought. No lady would be comfortable with what she had done, even though the reasons were compelling, even though the man she loved knew and understood.

Another night went by without her appearing, then it was Sunday and he felt sure he would see her in church. But she did not come to the service. It was almost unheard of for the nobility to miss Sunday mass. What had kept her away?

After the service he sent Lolla home with Arn and Em, then went across the green to the old hospital. On the upper floor were three rooms for important guests. He took the outside staircase.

In the corridor he came face-to-face with Caris.

She did not bother to ask what he was doing here. "The countess doesn't want you to see her, but you probably should," she said.

Merthin noted the odd turn of phrase: Not "The countess doesn't want to see you," but "The countess doesn't want *you* to see *her.*" He looked at the bowl Caris was carrying. It contained a bloodstained rag. Fear struck his heart. "What's wrong?"

"Nothing too serious," Caris said. "The baby is unharmed."

"Thank God."

"You're the father, of course?"

"Please don't ever let anyone hear you say that."

She looked sad. "All the years you and I were together, and I only conceived that one time."

He looked away. "Which room is she in?"

"Sorry to talk about myself. I'm the last thing you're interested in. Lady Philippa is in the middle room."

He caught the poorly suppressed grief in her voice and paused, despite his anxiety for Philippa. He touched Caris's arm. "Please don't believe I'm not interested in you," he said. "I'll always care what happens to you, and whether you're happy."

She nodded, and tears came to her eyes. "I know," she said. "I'm being selfish. Go and see Philippa."

He left Caris and entered the middle room. Philippa was kneeling on the prie-dieu with her back to him. He interrupted her prayers. "Are you all right?"

She stood up and turned to him. Her face was a mess. Her lips were swollen to three times their normal size and badly scabbed.

He guessed that Caris had been bathing the wound—hence the bloody rag. "What happened?" he said. "Can you speak?"

She nodded. "I sound queer, but I can talk." Her voice was a mumble, but comprehensible.

"How badly are you hurt?"

"My face looks awful, but it's not serious. Other than that, I'm fine."

He put his arms around her. She laid her head on his shoulder. He waited, holding her. After a while, she began to cry. He stroked her hair and her back while she shook with sobs. He said: "There, there," and kissed her forehead, but he did not try to silence her.

Slowly, her weeping subsided.

He said: "Can I kiss your lips?"

She nodded. "Gently."

He brushed them with his own. He tasted almonds: Caris had smeared the cuts with oil. "Tell me what happened," he said.

"It worked. He was fooled. He will be sure it's his baby."

He touched her mouth with his fingertip. "And he did this?"

"Don't be angry. I tried to provoke him, and I succeeded. Be glad he hit me."

"Glad! Why?"

"Because he thinks he had to force me. He believes I would not have submitted without violence. He has no inkling that I intended to seduce him. He will never suspect the truth. Which means I'm safe—and so is our baby."

He put his hand on her belly. "But why didn't you come and see me?"

"Looking like this?"

"I want to be with you even more when you're hurt." He moved his hand to her breast. "Besides, I've missed you."

She took his hand away. "I can't go from one to the other like a whore."

"Oh." He had not thought of it that way.

"Do you understand?"

"I think so." He could see that a woman would feel cheap—although a man might be proud of doing exactly the same thing. "But how long . . . ?"

She sighed, and moved away. "It's not how long."

"What do you mean?"

"We've agreed to tell the world that this is Ralph's baby, and I've made sure he'll believe that. Now he's going to want to raise it."

Merthin was dismayed. "I hadn't thought about the details, but I imagined you would continue to live in the priory."

"Ralph won't allow his child to be raised in a nunnery, especially if it's a boy."

"So what will you do, go back to Earlscastle?"

"Yes."

The child was nothing yet, of course; not a person, not even a baby, just a swelling in Philippa's belly. But all the same Merthin felt a stab of grief. Lolla had become the great joy of his life, and he had been looking forward eagerly to another child.

But at least he had Philippa for a little while longer. "When will you go?" he asked.

"Immediately," she said. She saw the look on his face, and tears came to her eyes. "I can't tell you how sorry I am—but I would just feel wrong, making love to you and planning to return to Ralph. It would be the same with any two men. The fact that you're brothers just makes it uglier."

His eyes blurred with tears. "So it's over with us already? Now?"

She nodded. "And there's another thing I have to tell you, one more reason why we can never be lovers again. I've confessed my adultery."

Merthin knew that Philippa had her own personal confessor, as was appropriate for a high-ranking noblewoman. Since she came to Kingsbridge, he had been living with the monks, a welcome addition to their thinned ranks. So now she had told him of her affair. Merthin hoped he could keep the secrets of the confessional.

Philippa said: "I have received absolution, but I must not continue the sin."

Merthin nodded. She was right. They had both sinned. She had betrayed her husband, and he had betrayed his brother. She had an excuse: she had been forced into the marriage. He had none. A beautiful woman had fallen in love with him and he had loved her back, even though he had no right. The yearning ache of grief and loss he was feeling now was the natural consequence of such behavior.

He looked at her—the cool gray-green eyes, the smashed mouth, the ripe body—and realized that he had lost her. Perhaps he had never really had her. In any case it had always been wrong, and now it was over. He tried to speak, to say good-bye, but his throat seemed to seize up, and nothing came out. He could hardly see for crying. He turned away, fumbled for the door, and somehow got out of the room.

A nun was coming along the corridor carrying a jug. He could not see who it was, but he recognized Caris's voice when she said: "Merthin? Are you all right?"

He made no reply. He went in the opposite direction and passed through the door and down the outside staircase. Weeping openly, not caring who saw, he walked across the cathedral green, down the main street, and across the bridge to his island.

80

September 1350 was cold and wet, but all the same there was a sense of euphoria. As damp sheaves of wheat were gathered in the surrounding countryside, only one person died of the plague in Kingsbridge: Marge Taylor, a dressmaker of sixty years old. No one caught the disease in October, November, or December. It seemed to have vanished, Merthin thought gratefully—at least for the time being.

The age-old migration of enterprising, restless people from countryside to town had been reversed during the plague, but now it recommenced. They came to Kingsbridge, moved into empty houses, fixed them up, and paid rent to the priory. Some started new businesses—bakeries, breweries, candle manufactories—to replace the old ones that had disappeared when the owners and all their heirs died off. Merthin, as alderman, had made it easier to open a shop or a market stall, sweeping away the lengthy process of obtaining permission that had been imposed by the priory. The weekly market grew busier.

One by one Merthin rented out the shops, houses, and taverns he had built on Leper Island, his tenants either enterprising newcomers or existing tradesmen who wanted a better location. The road across the island, between the two bridges, had become an extension of the main street, and therefore prime commercial property—as Merthin had foreseen, twelve years ago, when people had thought he was mad to take the barren rock as payment for his work on the bridge.

Winter drew in, and once again the smoke from thousands of fires hung over the town in a low, brown cloud; but the people still worked and shopped, ate and drank, played dice in taverns and went to church on Sundays. The guildhall saw the first Christmas Eve banquet since the parish guild had become a borough guild.

Merthin invited the prior and prioress. They no longer had the power to overrule the merchants, but they were still among the most important people in town. Philemon came, but Caris declined the invitation: she had become worryingly withdrawn.

Merthin sat next to Madge Webber. She was now the richest merchant and the largest employer in Kingsbridge, perhaps in the whole county. She was deputy alderman, and probably should have been alderman but for the fact that it was unusual to have a woman in that position.

Among Merthin's many enterprises was a workshop turning out the treadle looms that had improved the quality of Kingsbridge Scarlet. Madge bought more than half his production, but enterprising merchants came from as far away as London to place orders for the rest. The looms were complex pieces of machinery that had to be made accurately and assembled with precision, so Merthin had to employ the best carpenters available; but he priced the finished product at more than double what it cost him to make, and still people could hardly wait to give him the money.

Several people had hinted that he should marry Madge, but the idea did not tempt him or her. She had never been able to find a man to match Mark, who had had the physique of a giant and the disposition of a saint. She had always been chunky, but these days she was quite fat. Now in her forties, she was growing into one of those women who looked like barrels, almost the same width all the way from shoulders to bottom. Eating and drinking well were now her chief pleasures, Merthin thought as he watched her tuck into gingered ham with a sauce made of apples and cloves. That and making money.

At the end of the meal they had a mulled wine called hippocras. Madge took a long draft, belched, and moved closer to Merthin on the bench. "We have to do something about the hospital," she said.

"Oh?" He was not aware of a problem. "Now that the plague has ended, I would have thought people didn't have much need of a hospital."

"Of course they do," she said briskly. "They still get fevers and bellyaches and cancer. Women want to get pregnant and can't, or they suffer complications giving birth. Children burn themselves and fall out of trees. Men are thrown by their horses or knifed by their enemies or have their heads broken by angry wives—"

"Yes, I get the picture," Merthin said, amused by her garrulousness. "What's the problem?"

"Nobody will go to the hospital anymore. They don't like Brother Sime and, more importantly, they don't trust his learning. While we were all coping with the plague, he was at Oxford reading ancient textbooks, and he still prescribes remedies such as bleeding and cupping that no one believes in anymore. They want Caris—but she never appears."

"What do people do when they're sick, if they don't go to the hospital?"

"They see Matthew Barber, or Silas Pothecary, or a newcomer called Marla Wisdom who specializes in women's problems."

"So what's worrying you?"

"They're starting to mutter about the priory. If they don't get help from the monks and nuns, they say, why should they pay toward building the tower?"

"Oh." The tower was a huge project. No individual could possibly finance it. A combination of monastery, nunnery, and city funds was the only way to pay for it. If the town defaulted, the project could be threatened. "Yes, I see," said Merthin worriedly. "That is a problem."

It had been a good year for most people, Caris thought as she sat through the Christmas Day service. People were adjusting to the devastation of the plague with astonishing speed. As well as bringing terrible suffering and a near-breakdown of civilized life, the disease had provided the opportunity for a shake-up. Almost half the population had died, by her calculations; but one effect was that her remaining peasants were farming only the most fertile soils, so each man produced more. Despite the Ordinance of Laborers, and the efforts of noblemen such as Earl Ralph to enforce it, she was gratified to see that people continued to move to where the pay was highest, which was usually where the land was most productive. Grain was plentiful and herds of cattle and sheep were growing again. The nunnery was thriving and, because Caris had reorganized the monks' affairs as well as the nuns' after the flight of Godwyn, the monastery was now more prosperous than it had been for a hundred years. Wealth created wealth, and good times in the countryside brought more business to the towns, so Kingsbridge craftsmen and shopkeepers were beginning to return to their former affluence.

As the nuns left the church at the end of the service, Prior Philemon spoke to her. "I need to talk to you, Mother Prioress. Would you come to my house?"

There had been a time when she would have politely acceded to such a request without hesitation, but those days were over. "No," she said. "I don't think so."

He reddened immediately. "You can't refuse to speak to me!"

"I didn't. I refused to go to your palace. I decline to be summoned before you like a subordinate. What do you want to talk about?"

"The hospital. There have been complaints."

"Speak to Brother Sime—he's in charge of it, as you well know."

"Is there no reasoning with you?" he said exasperatedly. "If Sime could solve the problem I would be talking to him, not you."

By now they were in the monks' cloisters. Caris sat on the low wall around the quadrangle. The stone was cold. "We can talk here. What do you have to say to me?"

Philemon was annoyed, but he gave in. He stood in front of her, and now he was the one who seemed like a subordinate. He said. "The townspeople are unhappy about the hospital."

"I'm not surprised."

"Merthin complained to me at the guild's Christmas dinner. They don't come here anymore, but see charlatans like Silas Pothecary."

"He's no more of a charlatan than Sime."

Philemon realized that several novices were standing nearby, listening to the argument. "Go away, all of you," he said. "Get to your studies."

They scurried off.

Philemon said to Caris: "The townspeople think you ought to be at the hospital."

"So do I. But I won't follow Sime's methods. At best, his cures have no effect. Much of the time they make patients worse. That's why people no longer come here when they're ill."

"Your new hospital has so few patients that we're using it as a guest house. Doesn't that bother you?"

That jibe went home. Caris swallowed and looked away. "It breaks my heart," she said quietly.

"Then come back. Figure out a compromise with Sime. You worked under monk-physicians in the early days, when you first came here. Brother Joseph was the senior doctor then. He had the same training as Sime."

"You're right. In those days, we felt that the monks sometimes did more harm than good, but we could work with them. Most of the time we didn't call them in at all, we just did what we thought best. When they did attend, we didn't always follow their instructions exactly."

"You can't believe they were always wrong."

"No. Sometimes they cured people. I remember Joseph opening a man's skull and draining accumulated fluid that had been causing unbearable headaches—it was very impressive."

"So do the same now."

"It's no longer possible. Sime put an end to that, didn't he? He moved his books and equipment into the pharmacy and took charge of the hospital. And I'm sure he did so with your encouragement. In fact it was probably your idea." She could tell from Philemon's expression that she was right. "You and he plotted to push me out. You succeeded—and now you're suffering the consequences."

"We could go back to the old system. I'll make Sime move out."

She shook her head. "There have been other changes. I've learned a lot from the plague. I'm surer than ever that the physicians' methods can be fatal. I won't kill people for the sake of a compromise with you."

"You don't realize how much is at stake." He had a faintly smug look.

So, there was something else. She had been wondering why he had brought this up. It was not like him to fret about the hospital: he had never cared much for the work of healing. He was interested only in what would raise his status and defend his fragile pride. "All right," she said. "What have you got up your sleeve?"

"The townspeople are talking about cutting off funds for the new tower. Why should they pay extra to the cathedral, they say, when they're not getting what they want from us? And now that the town is a borough, I as prior can no longer enforce the payment."

"And if they don't pay . . . ?"

"Your beloved Merthin will have to abandon his pet project," Philemon said triumphantly.

Caris could see that he thought this was his trump card. And, indeed, there had been a time when the revelation would have jolted her. But no longer. "Merthin isn't my beloved anymore, is he," she said. "You put a stop to that, too."

A look of panic crossed his face. "But the bishop has set his heart on this tower—you can't put that at risk!"

Caris stood up. "Can't I?" she said. "Why not?" She turned away, heading for the nunnery.

He was flabbergasted. He called after her: "How can you be so reckless?"

She was going to ignore him, then she changed her mind and decided to explain. She turned back. "You see, all that I ever held dear has been taken from me," she said in a matter-of-fact tone. "And when you've lost everything—" Her facade began to crumble, and her voice broke, but she made herself carry on. "When you've lost everything, you've got nothing to lose."

The first snow fell in January. It formed a thick blanket on the roof of the cathedral, smoothed out the delicate carving of the spires, and masked the faces of the angels and saints sculpted over the west door. The new masonry of the tower foundations had been covered with straw to insulate the new mortar against winter frost, and now the snow overlaid the straw.

There were few fireplaces in a priory. The kitchen had fires, of course, which was why work in kitchens was always popular with novices. But there was no fire in the cathedral, where the monks and nuns spent seven or eight hours every day. When churches burned down, it was usually because some desperate monk had brought a charcoal brazier into the building, and a spark had flown from the fire to the timber ceiling. When not in church or laboring, the monks and nuns were supposed to walk and read in the cloisters, which were out of doors. The only concession to their comfort was the warming room, a small chamber off the cloisters where a fire was lit in the most severe weather. They were allowed to come into the warming room from the cloisters for short periods.

As usual, Caris ignored rules and traditions, and permitted nuns to wear woolen hose in the winter. She did not believe that God needed his servants to get chilblains.

Bishop Henri was so worried about the hospital—or rather, about the threat to his tower—that he drove from Shiring to Kingsbridge through the snow. He came in a charette, a heavy wooden cart with a waxed canvas cover and cushioned seats. Canon Claude and Archdeacon Lloyd came with him. They paused at the prior's palace only long enough to dry their clothes and drink a warming cup of wine before summoning a crisis meeting with Philemon, Sime, Caris, Oonagh, Merthin, and Madge.

Caris knew it would be a waste of time, but she went anyway: it was easier than refusing, which would have required her to sit in the nunnery and deal with endless messages begging, commanding, and threatening her.

She looked at the snowflakes falling past the glazed windows as the bishop drearily summarized a quarrel in which she really had no interest. "This crisis has been brought about by the disloyal and disobedient attitude of Mother Caris," Henri said.

That stung her into a response. "I worked in the hospital here for ten years," she said. "My work, and the work of Mother Cecilia before me, are what made it so popular with the townspeople." She pointed a rude finger at the bishop. "You changed it. Don't try to blame others. You sat in that chair and announced that Brother Sime would henceforth be in charge. Now you should take responsibility for the consequences of your foolish decision."

"You must obey me!" he said, his voice rising to a screech in frustration. "You are a nun—you have taken a vow." The grating sound disturbed the cat, Archbishop, and it stood up and walked out of the room.

"I realize that," Caris said. "It puts me in an intolerable position." She spoke without forethought, but as the words came out she realized they were not really ill-considered. In fact they were the fruit of months of brooding. "I can no longer serve God in this way," she went on, her voice calm but her heart pounding. "That is why I have decided to renounce my vows and leave the nunnery."

Henri actually stood up. "You will not!" he shouted. "I will not release you from your holy vows."

"I expect God will, though," she said, scarcely disguising her contempt.

That made him angrier. "This notion that individuals can deal with God is wicked heresy. There has been too much of such loose talk since the plague."

"Do you think that might have happened because, when people approached the church for help during the plague, they so often found that its priest and monks . . . ," here she looked at Philemon, ". . . had fled like cowards?"

Henri held up a hand to stifle Philemon's indignant response. "We may be fallible but, all the same, it is only through the church and its priests that men and women may approach God."

"You would think that, of course," Caris said. "But that doesn't make it right."

"You're a devil!"

Canon Claude intervened. "All things considered, my lord bishop, a public quarrel between yourself and Caris would not be helpful." He gave her a friendly smile. He had been well disposed toward her ever since the day she had caught him and the bishop kissing and had said nothing about it. "Her present noncooperation must be set against many years of dedicated, sometimes heroic service. And the people love her."

Henri said: "But what if we do release her from her vows? How would that solve the problem?"

At this point, Merthin spoke for the first time. "I have a suggestion," he said.

Everyone looked at him.

He said. "Let the town build a new hospital. I will donate a large site on Leper Island. Let it be staffed by a convent of nuns quite separate from the priory, a new group. They will be under the spiritual authority of the bishop of Shiring, of course, but have no connection with the prior of Kingsbridge or any of the physicians at the monastery. Let the new hospital have a lay patron, who would be a leading citizen of the town, chosen by the guild, and would appoint the prioress."

They were all quiet for a long moment, letting this radical proposal sink in. Caris was thunderstruck. A new hospital . . . on Leper Island . . . paid for by the townspeople . . . staffed by a new order of nuns . . . having no connection with the priory . . .

She looked around the group. Philemon and Sime clearly hated the idea. Henri, Claude, and Lloyd just looked bemused.

At last the bishop said: "The patron will be very powerful—representing the townspeople, paying the bills, and appointing the prioress. Whoever plays that role will control the hospital."

"Yes," said Merthin.

"If I authorize a new hospital, will the townspeople be willing to resume paying for the tower?"

Madge Webber spoke for the first time. "If the right patron is appointed, yes."

"And who should it be?" said Henri.

Caris realized that everyone was looking at her.

A few hours later, Caris and Merthin wrapped themselves in heavy cloaks, put on boots, and walked through the snow to the island, where he showed her the site he had in mind. It was on the west side, not far from his house, overlooking the river.

She was still dizzy from the sudden change in her life. She was to be released from her vows as a nun. She would become a normal citizen again, after almost twelve years. She found she could contemplate leaving the priory without anguish. The people she had loved were all dead: Mother Cecilia, Old Julie, Mair, Tilly. She liked Sister Joan and Sister Oonagh well enough, but it was not the same.

And she would still be in charge of a hospital. Having the right to appoint and dismiss the prioress of the new institution, she would be able to run the place according to the new thinking that had grown out of the plague. The bishop had agreed to everything.

"I think we should use the cloister layout again," Merthin said. "It seemed to work really well for the short time you were in charge."

She stared at the sheet of unmarked snow and marveled at his ability to imagine walls and rooms where she could see only whiteness. "The entrance arch was used almost like a hall," she said. "It was the place where people waited, and where the nuns first examined the patients before deciding what to do with them."

"You would like it larger?"

"I think it should be a real reception hall."

"All right."

She was bemused. "This is hard to believe. Everything has turned out just as I would have wanted it."

He nodded. "That's how I worked it out."

"Really?"

"I asked myself what you would wish for, then I figured out how to achieve it."

She stared at him. He had said it lightly, as if merely explaining the reasoning process that had led him to his conclusions. He seemed to have no idea how momentous it was to her that he should be thinking about her wishes and how to achieve them.

She said: "Has Philippa had the baby yet?"

"Yes, a week ago."

"What did she have?"

"A boy."

"Congratulations. Have you seen him?"

"No. As far as the world is concerned, I'm only his uncle. But Ralph sent me a letter."

"Have they named him?"

"Roland, after the old earl."

Caris changed the subject. "The river water isn't very pure this far downstream. A hospital really needs clean water."

"I'll lay a pipe to bring you water from farther upstream."

The snowfall eased and then stopped, and they had a clear view of the island.

She smiled at him. "You have the answer to everything."

He shook his head. "These are the easy questions: clean water, airy rooms, a reception hall."

"And what are the difficult ones?"

He turned to face her. There were snowflakes in his red beard. He said: "Questions like: Does she still love me?"

They stared at one another for a long moment.

Caris was happy.

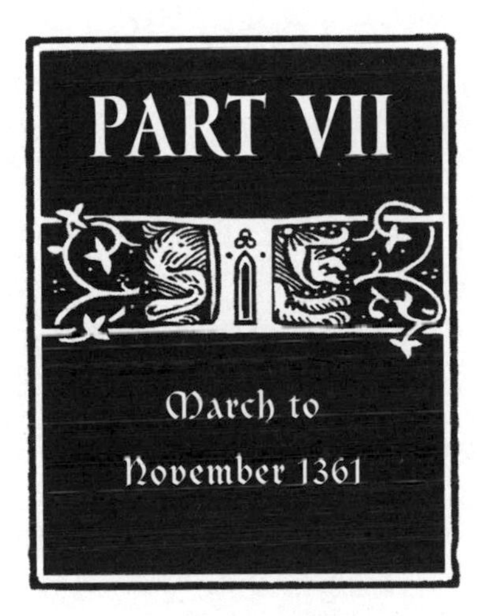

PART VII

March to
November 1361

81

ulfric at forty was still the handsomest man Gwenda had ever seen. There were threads of silver now in his tawny hair, but they just made him look wise as well as strong. When he was young his broad shoulders had tapered dramatically to a narrow waist, whereas nowadays the taper was not so sharp nor the waist so slim—but he could still do the work of two men. And he would always be two years younger than she.

She thought she had changed less. She had the kind of dark hair that did not go gray until late in life. She was no heavier than she had been twenty years ago, although since having the children her breasts and belly were not quite as taut as formerly.

It was only when she looked at her son Davey, at his smooth skin and the restless spring in his step, that she felt her years. Now twenty, he looked like a male version of herself at that age. She, too, had had a face with no lines, and she had walked with a jaunty stride. A lifetime of working in the fields in all weathers had wrinkled her hands, and given her cheeks a raw redness just beneath the skin, and taught her to walk slowly and conserve her strength.

Davey was small like her, and shrewd, and secretive: since he was little, she had never been sure what he was thinking. Sam was the opposite: big and strong, not clever enough to be deceitful, but with a mean streak that Gwenda blamed on his real father, Ralph Fitzgerald.

For several years now the two boys had been working alongside Wulfric in the fields—until two weeks ago, when Sam had vanished.

They knew why he had gone. All winter long he had been talking about leaving Wigleigh and moving to a village where he could earn higher wages. He had disappeared the moment the spring plowing began.

Gwenda knew he was right about the wages. It was a crime to leave your village, or to accept pay higher than the levels of 1347, but all over the country restless young men were flouting the law, and desperate farmers were hiring them. Landlords such as Earl Ralph could do little more than gnash their teeth.

Sam had not said where he would go, and he had given no warning of his departure. If Davey had done the same, Gwenda would have known he had thought things out carefully and decided this was the best way. But she felt sure Sam had just followed an impulse. Someone had mentioned the name of a village, and he had woken up early the next morning and decided to go there immediately.

She told herself not to worry. He was twenty-two years old, big and strong. No one was going to exploit him or ill-treat him. But she was his mother, and her heart ached.

If she could not find him, no one else could, she figured, and that was good. All the same she yearned to know where he was living, and if he was working for a decent master, and whether the people were kind to him.

That winter, Wulfric had made a new light plow for the sandier acres of his holding, and one day in spring Gwenda and he went to Northwood to buy an iron plowshare, the one part they could not make for themselves. As usual, a small group of Wigleigh folk traveled together to the market. Jack and Eli, who operated the fulling mill for Madge Webber, were stocking up on supplies: they had no land of their own, so they bought all their food. Annet and her eighteen-year-old daughter, Amabel, had a dozen hens in a crate, to sell at the market. The bailiff, Nathan, came too, with his grown son Jonno, the childhood enemy of Sam.

Annet still flirted with every good-looking man that crossed her path, and most of them grinned foolishly and flirted back. On the journey to Northwood she chatted with Davey. Although he was less than half her age, she simpered and tossed her head and smacked his arm in mock reproach, just as if she were twenty-two rather than forty-two. She was not a girl any more, but she did not seem to know it, Gwenda thought sourly. Annet's daughter, Amabel, who was as pretty as Annet had once been, walked a little apart, and seemed embarrassed by her mother.

They reached Northwood at mid-morning. After Wulfric and Gwenda had made their purchase, they went to get their dinner at the Old Oak Tavern.

For as long as Gwenda could remember there had been a venerable oak outside the inn, a thick, squat tree with malformed branches that looked like a bent old man in winter and cast a welcome deep shade in summer. Her sons had chased one another around it as little boys. But it must have died or become unstable, for it had been chopped down, and now there was a stump, as wide across as Wulfric was tall, used by the customers as a chair, a table, and—for one exhausted carter—a bed.

Sitting on its edge, drinking ale from a huge tankard, was Harry Plowman, the bailiff of Outhenby.

Gwenda was taken back twelve years in a blink. What came to her mind, so forcefully that it brought tears to her eyes, was the hope that had lifted her heart as she and her family had set out, that morning in Northwood, to walk through the forest to Outhenby and a new life. The hope had been crushed, in less than a fortnight, and Wulfric had been taken back to Wigleigh—the memory still made her burn with rage—with a rope around his neck.

But Ralph had not had things all his own way since then. Circumstances had forced him to give Wulfric back the lands his father had held, which for Gwenda had been a savagely satisfying outcome, even though Wulfric had not been smart enough to win a free tenancy, unlike some of his neighbors. Gwenda was glad they were now tenants rather than laborers, and Wulfric had achieved his life's ambition; but she still longed for more independence—a tenancy free of feudal obligations, with a cash rent to pay, the whole agreement written down in the manorial records so that no lord could go back on it. It was what most serfs wanted, and more of them were getting it since the plague.

Harry greeted them effusively and insisted on buying them ale. Soon after Wulfric and Gwenda's brief stay at Outhenby, Harry had been made bailiff by Mother Caris, and he still held that position, though Caris had long ago renounced her vows, and Mother Joan was now prioress. Outhenby continued to be prosperous, to judge by Harry's double chin and alehouse belly.

As they were preparing to leave with the rest of the Wigleigh folk, Harry spoke to Gwenda in a low voice. "I've got a young man called Sam laboring for me."

Gwenda's heart leaped. "My Sam?"

"Can't possibly be, no."

She was bewildered. Why mention him, in that case?

But Harry tapped his wine-red nose, and Gwenda realized he was being enigmatic. "This Sam assures me that his lord is a Hampshire knight I've never heard of, who has given him permission to leave his village and work elsewhere, whereas your Sam's lord is Earl Ralph, who never lets his laborers go. Obviously I couldn't employ your Sam."

Gwenda understood. That would be Harry's story if official questions were asked. "So, he's in Outhenby."

"Oldchurch, one of the smaller villages in the valley."

"Is he well?" she asked eagerly.

"Thriving."

"Thank God."

"A strong boy and a good worker, though he can be quarrelsome."

She knew that. "Is he living in a warm house?"

"Lodging with a good-hearted older couple whose own son has gone to Kingsbridge to be apprenticed to a tanner."

Gwenda had a dozen questions, but suddenly she noticed the bent figure of Nathan Reeve leaning on the doorpost of the tavern entrance, staring at her. She suppressed a curse. There was so much she wanted to know, but she was terrified of giving Nate even a clue to Sam's whereabouts. She needed to be content with what she had. And she was thrilled that at least she knew where he could be found.

She turned away from Harry, trying to give the impression of casually ending an unimportant conversation. Out of the corner of her mouth she said: "Don't let him get into fights."

"I'll do what I can."

She waved perfunctorily and went after Wulfric.

Walking home with the others, Wulfric carried the heavy plowshare on his shoulder with no apparent effort. Gwenda was bursting to tell him the news, but she had to wait until the group straggled out along the road, and she and her husband were separated from the others by a few yards. Then she repeated the conversation, speaking quietly.

Wulfric was relieved. "At least we know where the lad has got to," he said, breathing easily despite his load.

"I want to go to Outhenby," Gwenda said.

Wulfric nodded. "I thought you might." He rarely challenged her, but now he expressed a misgiving. "Dangerous, though. You'll have to make sure no one finds out where you've gone."

"Exactly. Nate mustn't know."

"How will you manage that?"

"He's sure to notice that I'm not in the village for a couple of days. We'll have to think of a story."

"We can say you're sick."

"Too risky. He'll probably come to the house to check."

"We could say you're at your father's place."

"Nate won't believe that. He knows I never stay there longer than I have to." She gnawed at a hangnail, racking her brains. In the ghost stories and fairy tales that people told around the fire on long winter evenings, the characters generally believed one another's lies without question; but real people were less easily duped. "We could say I've gone to Kingsbridge," she said at last.

"What for?"

"To buy laying hens at the market, perhaps."

"You could buy hens from Annet."

"I wouldn't buy anything from that bitch, and people know it."

"True."

"And Nate knows I've always been a friend of Caris, so he'll believe I could be staying with her."

"All right."

It was not much of a story, but she could not think of anything better. And she was desperate to see her son.

She left the next morning.

She slipped out of the house before dawn, wrapped in a heavy cloak against the cold March wind. She walked softly through the village in pitch darkness, finding her way by touch and memory. She did not want to be seen and questioned before she had even left the neighborhood. But no one was up yet. Nathan Reeve's dog growled quietly then recognized her tread, and she heard a soft thump as he wagged his tail against the side of his wooden kennel.

She left the village and followed the road through the fields. When dawn broke, she was a mile away. She looked at the road behind her. It was empty. No one had followed her.

She chewed a crust of stale bread for breakfast, then stopped at midmorning at a tavern where the Wigleigh-to-Kingsbridge road crossed the Northwood-to-Outhenby road. She recognized no one at the inn. She watched the door nervously as she ate a bowl of salt-fish stew and drank a pint of cider. Every time someone came in she got ready to hide her face, but it was always a stranger, and no one took any notice of her. She left quickly, and set off on the road to Outhenby.

She reached the valley around mid-afternoon. It was twelve years since she had been here, but the place had not changed much. It had recovered from the plague remarkably quickly. Apart from some small children playing near the houses, most of the villagers were at work, plowing and sowing, or looking after new lambs. They stared at her across the fields, knowing she was a stranger, wondering about her identity. Some of them would recognize her close up. She had been here for only ten days, but those had been dramatic times, and they would remember. Villagers did not often see such excitement.

She followed the River Outhen as it meandered along the flat plain between two ranges of hills. She went from the main village through smaller settlements that she knew, from the time she had spent here, as Ham, Shortacre, and Longwater, to the smallest and most remote, Oldchurch.

Her excitement grew as she approached, and she even forgot her sore feet. Oldchurch was a hamlet, with thirty hovels, none big enough to be a manor house or even a bailiff's home. However, in accordance with the name, there was an old church. It was several hundred years of age, Gwenda guessed. It had a squat tower and a short nave, all built of crude masonry, with tiny square windows placed apparently at random in the thick walls.

She walked to the fields beyond. She ignored a group of shepherds in a distant pasture: shrewd Harry Plowman would not waste big Sam on such light work. He would be harrowing, or clearing a ditch, or helping to manage the eight-ox plow team. Searching the three fields methodically, she looked for a crowd of mostly men, with warm hats and muddy boots and big voices to call to one another across the acres; and a young man a head taller than the others. When she did not at first see her son, she suffered renewed apprehension. Had he already been recaptured? Had he moved to another village?

She found him in a line of men digging manure into a newly plowed strip. He had his coat off, despite the cold, and he was hefting an oak spade, the muscles of his back and arms bunching and shifting under his old linen shirt. Her heart filled with pride to see him, and to think that such a man had come from her diminutive body.

They all looked up as she approached. The men stared at her in curiosity: Who was she and what was she doing here? She walked straight up to Sam and embraced him, even though he stank of horse dung. "Hello, Mother," he said, and all the other men laughed.

She was puzzled by their hilarity.

A wiry man with one empty eye socket said: "There, there, Sam, you'll be all right now," and they laughed again.

Gwenda realized they thought it funny that a big man such as Sam should have his little mother come and check on him as if he were a wayward boy.

"How did you find me?" Sam said.

"I met Harry Plowman at Northwood market."

"I hope no one tracked you here."

"I left before it was light. Your father was to tell people I went to Kingsbridge. No one followed me."

They talked for a few minutes, then he said he had to get back to work, or the other men would resent his leaving it all to them. "Go back to the village and find old Liza," he said. "She lives opposite the church. Tell her who you are and she'll give you some refreshment. I'll be there at dusk."

Gwenda glanced up at the sky. It was a dark afternoon, and the men would be forced to stop work in an hour or so. She kissed Sam's cheek and left him.

She found Liza in a house slightly larger than most—it had two rooms rather than one. The woman introduced her husband, Rob, who was blind. As Sam had promised, Liza was hospitable: she put bread and pottage on the table and poured a cup of ale.

Gwenda asked about their son, and it was like turning on a tap. Liza talked unstoppably about him, from babyhood to apprenticeship, until the old man interrupted her harshly with one word: "Horse."

They fell silent, and Gwenda heard the rhythmic thud of a trotting horse.

"Smallish mount," blind Rob said. "A palfrey, or a pony. Too little for a nobleman or a knight, though it might be carrying a lady."

Gwenda felt a shiver of fear.

"Two visitors within an hour," Rob observed. "Must be connected."

That was what Gwenda was afraid of.

She got up and looked out of the door. A sturdy black pony was trotting along the path between the houses. She recognized the rider immediately, and her heart sank: it was Jonno Reeve, the son of the bailiff of Wigleigh.

How had he found her?

She tried to duck quickly back into the house, but he had seen her. "Gwenda!" he shouted, and reined in his horse.

"You devil," she said.

"I wonder what you're doing here," he said mockingly.

"How did you get here? No one was following me."

"My father sent me to Kingsbridge, to see what mischief you might be making there, but on the way I stopped at the Cross Roads Tavern, and they remembered you taking the road to Outhenby."

She wondered whether she could outwit this shrewd young man. "And why should I not visit my old friends here?"

"No reason," he said. "Where's your runaway son?"

"Not here, though I hoped he might be."

He looked momentarily uncertain, as if he thought she might be telling the truth. Then he said: "Perhaps he's hiding. I'll look around." He kicked his horse on.

Gwenda watched him go. She had not fooled him, but perhaps she had planted a doubt in his mind. If she could get to Sam first she might be able to conceal him.

She walked quickly through the little house, with a hasty word to Liza and Rob, and left by the back door. She headed across the field, staying close to the hedge. Looking back toward the village, she could see a man on horseback moving out at an angle to her direction. The day was dimming, and she thought her own small figure might be indistinguishable against the dark background of the hedge.

She met Sam and the others coming back, their spades over their shoulders, their boots thick with muck. From a distance, at first sight, Sam could have been Ralph: the figure was the same, and the confident stride, and the set of the handsome head on the strong neck. But as he talked she could see Wulfric in him, too: he had a way of turning his head, a shy smile, and a deprecating gesture of the hand that exactly imitated his foster father.

The men spotted her. They had been tickled by her arrival earlier, and now the one-eyed man called out: "Hello, Mother!" and they all laughed.

She took Sam aside and said: "Jonno Reeve is here."

"Hell!"

"I'm sorry."

"You said you weren't followed!"

"I didn't see him, but he picked up my trail."

"Damn. Now what do I do? I'm not going back to Wigleigh!"

"He's looking for you, but he left the village heading east." She scanned the darkening landscape but could not see much. "If we hurry back to Oldchurch, we could hide you—in the church, perhaps."

"All right."

They picked up their pace. Gwenda said over her shoulder: "If you men come across a bailiff called Jonno . . . you haven't seen Sam from Wigleigh."

"Never heard of him, Mother," said one, and the others concurred. Serfs were generally ready to help one another outwit the bailiff.

Gwenda and Ralph reached the settlement without seeing Jonno. They headed for the church. Gwenda thought they could probably get in:

country churches were usually empty and bare inside, and generally left open. But if this one should turn out to be an exception, she was not sure what they would do.

They threaded through the houses and came within sight of the church. As they passed Liza's front door, Gwenda saw a black pony. She groaned. Jonno must have doubled back under cover of the dusk. He had gambled that Gwenda would find Sam and bring him to the village, and he had been right. He had his father Nate's low cunning.

She took Sam's arm to hurry him across the road and into the church—then Jonno stepped out from Liza's house.

"Sam," he said. "I thought you'd be here."

Gwenda and Sam stopped and turned.

Sam leaned on his wooden spade. "What are you going to do about it?"

Jonno was grinning triumphantly. "Take you back to Wigleigh."

"I'd like to see you try."

A group of peasants, mostly women, appeared from the west side of the village and stopped to watch the confrontation.

Jonno reached into his pony's saddlebag and brought out some kind of metal device with a chain. "I'm going to put a leg iron on you," he said. "And if you've got any sense you won't resist."

Gwenda was surprised by Jonno's nerve. Did he really expect to arrest Sam all on his own? He was a beefy lad, but not as big as Sam. Did he hope the villagers would help him? He had the law on his side, but few peasants would think his cause just. Typical young man, he had no sense of his own limitations.

Sam said: "I used to beat the shit out of you when we were boys, and I'll do the same today."

Gwenda did not want them to fight. Whoever won, Sam would be wrong in the eyes of the law. He was a runaway. She said: "It's too late to go anywhere now. Why don't we discuss this in the morning?"

Jonno gave a disparaging laugh. "And let Sam slip away before dawn, the way you sneaked out of Wigleigh? Certainly not. He sleeps in irons tonight."

The men Sam had been working with appeared, and stopped to see what was going on. Jonno said: "All law-abiding men have a duty to help me arrest this runaway, and anyone who hinders me will be subject to the punishment of the law."

"You can rely on me," said the one-eyed man. "I'll hold your horse." The others chuckled. There was little sympathy for Jonno. On the other hand, no villager spoke in Sam's defense.

Jonno moved suddenly. With the leg iron in both hands, he stepped toward Sam and bent down, trying to snap the device onto Sam's leg in one surprise move.

It might have worked on a slow-moving older man, but Sam reacted quickly. He stepped back then kicked out, landing one muddy boot on Jonno's outstretched left arm.

Jonno gave a grunt of pain and anger. Straightening up, he drew back his right arm and swung the iron, intending to hit Sam over the head with it. Gwenda heard a frightened scream and realized it came from herself. Sam darted back another step, out of range.

Jonno saw that his blow was going to miss, and let go of the iron at the last moment.

It flew through the air. Sam flinched away, turning and ducking, but he could not dodge it. The iron hit his ear and the chain whipped across his face. Gwenda cried out as if she herself had been hurt. The onlookers gasped. Sam staggered, and the iron fell to the ground. There was a moment of suspense. Blood came from Sam's ear and nose. Gwenda took a step toward him, stretching out her arms.

Then Sam recovered from the shock.

He turned back to Jonno and swung his heavy wooden spade in one graceful movement. Jonno had not quite recovered his balance after the effort of his throw, and he was unable to dodge. The edge of the spade caught him on the side of the head. Sam was strong, and the sound of wood on bone rang out across the village street.

Jonno was still reeling when Sam hit him again. Now the spade came straight down from above. Swung by both Sam's arms, it landed on top of Jonno's head, edge first, with tremendous force. This time the impact did not ring out, but sounded more like a dull thud, and Gwenda feared Jonno's skull had cracked.

As Jonno slumped to his knees, Sam hit him a third time, another full-force blow with the oak blade, this one across his victim's forehead. An iron sword could hardly have been more damaging, Gwenda though despairingly. She stepped forward to restrain Sam, but the village men had had the same idea a moment earlier, and got there before her. They pulled Sam away, two of them holding each arm.

Jonno lay on the ground, his head in a pool of blood. Gwenda was sickened by the sight, and could not help thinking of the boy's father, Nate, and how grieved he would be by his son's injuries. Jonno's mother had died of the plague, so at least she was in a place where grief could not afflict her.

Gwenda could see that Sam was not badly hurt. He was bleeding, but still struggling with his captors, trying to get free so that he could attack again. Gwenda bent over Jonno. His eyes were closed and he was not moving. She put a hand on his heart and felt nothing. She tried for a pulse, the way Caris had shown her, but there was none. Jonno did not seem to be breathing.

The implications of what had happened dawned on her, and she began to weep.

Jonno was dead, and Sam was a murderer.

82

On Easter Sunday that year, 1361, Caris and Merthin had been married ten years.

Standing in the cathedral, watching the Easter procession, Caris recalled their wedding. Because they had been lovers, off and on, for so long, they had seen the ceremony as no more than confirmation of a long-established fact, and they had foolishly envisaged a small, quiet event: a low-key service in St. Mark's Church and a modest dinner for a few people afterward at the Bell. But Father Joffroi had informed them, the day before, that by his calculation at least two thousand people were planning to attend the wedding, and they had been forced to move it to the cathedral. Then it turned out that, without their knowledge, Madge Webber had organized a banquet in the guildhall for leading citizens and a picnic in Lovers' Field for everyone else in Kingsbridge. So, in the end, it had been the wedding of the year.

Caris smiled at the recollection. She had worn a new robe of Kingsbridge Scarlet, a color the bishop probably thought appropriate for such a woman. Merthin had dressed in a richly patterned Italian coat, chestnut brown with gold threads, and had seemed to glow with happiness. They both had realized, belatedly, that their drawn-out love affair, which they had imagined to be a private drama, had been entertaining the citizens of Kingsbridge for years, and everyone wanted to celebrate its happy ending.

Caris's pleasant memories evaporated as her old enemy Philemon mounted the pulpit. In the decade since the wedding he had grown quite fat. His monkish tonsure and shaved face revealed a ring of blubber around his neck, and the priestly robes billowed like a tent.

He preached a sermon against dissection.

Dead bodies belonged to God, he said. Christians were instructed to bury them in a carefully specified ritual; the saved in consecrated ground, the unforgiven elsewhere. To do anything else with corpses was against God's will. To cut them up was sacrilege, he said with uncharacteristic passion. There was even a tremor in his voice as he asked the congregation to imagine the horrible scene of a body being opened, its parts separated and sliced and pored over by so-called medical researchers. True Christians knew there was no excuse for these ghoulish men and women.

The phrase "men and women" was not often heard from Philemon's mouth, Caris thought, and could not be without significance. She glanced at her husband, standing next to her in the nave, and he raised his eyebrows in an expression of concern.

The prohibition against examining corpses was standard dogma, propounded by the church since before Caris could remember, but it had been relaxed since the plague. Progressive younger clergymen were vividly aware of how badly the church had failed its people then, and they were keen to change the way medicine was taught and practised by priests. However, conservative senior clergy clung to the old ways and blocked any change in policy. The upshot was that dissection was banned in principle and tolerated in practice.

Caris had been performing dissections at her new hospital from the start. She never talked about it outside the building: there was no point in upsetting the superstitious. But she did it every chance she got.

In recent years she had usually been joined by one or two younger monk-physicians. Many trained doctors never saw inside the body except when treating very bad wounds. Traditionally, the only carcasses they were allowed to open were those of pigs, thought to be the animals most like humans in their anatomy.

Caris was puzzled as well as worried by Philemon's attack. He had always hated her, she knew, though she had never been sure why. But since the great standoff in the snowfall of 1351 he had ignored her. As if in compensation for his loss of power over the town, he had furnished his palace with precious objects: tapestries, carpets, silver tableware, stained-glass windows, illuminated manuscripts. He had become ever more grand, demanding elaborate deference from his monks and novices, wearing gorgeous robes for services, and traveling, when he had to go to other towns, in a charette that was furnished like a duchess's boudoir.

There were several important visiting clergymen in the choir for the service—Bishop Henri of Shiring, Archbishop Piers of Monmouth, and Archdeacon Reginald of York—and presumably Philemon was hoping to impress them with this outburst of doctrinal conservatism. But to what end? Was he looking for promotion? The archbishop was ill—he had been carried into the church—but surely Philemon could not aspire to that post? It was something of a miracle that the son of Joby from Wigleigh should have risen to be prior of Kingsbridge. Besides, elevation from prior to archbishop would be an unusually big jump, a bit like going from knight to duke without becoming a baron or an earl in between. Only a special favorite could hope for such a rapid rise.

However, there was no limit to Philemon's ambition. It was not that he felt himself to be superbly well qualified, Caris thought. That had been Godwyn's attitude, arrogant self-confidence. Godwyn had assumed that God made him prior because he was the cleverest man in town. Philemon was at the opposite extreme: in his heart he believed he was a nobody. His life was a campaign to convince himself that he was not completely worthless. He was so sensitive to rejection that he could not bear to consider himself undeserving of any post, no matter how lofty.

She thought of speaking to Bishop Henri after the service. She might remind him of the ten-year-old agreement that the prior of Kingsbridge had no jurisdiction over the Hospital of St. Elizabeth on Leper Island, which came under the bishop's direct control; so that any attack on the hospital was an attack on the rights and privileges of Henri himself. But, on further reflection, she realized that such a protest would confirm to the bishop that she was conducting dissections, and turn what might now be only a vague suspicion, easily ignored, into a known fact that must be dealt with. So she decided to remain silent.

Standing beside her were Merthin's two nephews, the sons of Earl Ralph: Gerry, age thirteen, and Roley, ten. Both boys were enrolled in the monks' school. They lived in the priory but spent much of their free time with Merthin and Caris at their house on the island. Merthin had his hand resting casually on the shoulder of Roley. Only three people in the world knew that Roley was not his nephew but his son. They were Merthin himself, Caris, and the boy's mother, Philippa. Merthin tried not to show special favor to Roley, but found it hard to disguise his true feelings, and was especially delighted when Roley learned something new or did well at school.

Caris often thought about the child she had conceived with Merthin and then aborted. She always imagined it to have been a girl. She would be a woman now, Caris mused, twenty-three years old, probably married with children of her own. The thought was like the ache of an old wound, painful but too familiar to be distressing.

When the service was over, they all left together. The boys were invited to Sunday dinner, as always. Outside the cathedral, Merthin turned to look back at the tower that now soared high over the middle of the church.

As he examined his almost-finished work, frowning at some detail visible only to him, Caris studied him fondly. She had known him since he was eleven years old, and had loved him almost as long. He was forty-five now. His red hair was receding from his brow, and stood up around his head like a curly halo. He had carried his left arm stiffly ever since a small carved stone corbel, dropped from the scaffolding by a careless mason, had fallen on his shoulder. But he still had the expression of boyish eagerness that had drawn the ten-year-old Caris to him on All Hallows Day a third of a century ago.

She turned to share his view. The tower appeared to stand neatly on the four sides of the crossing, and to be exactly two bays square, even though in fact its weight was held up by massive buttresses built into the exterior corners of the transepts, which themselves rested on new foundations separate from the old original ones. The tower looked light and airy, with slender columns and multiple window openings through which you could see blue sky in fine weather. Above the square top of the tower, a web of scaffolding was rising for the final stage, the spire.

When Caris brought her gaze back down to ground level she saw her sister approaching. Alice was only a year older at forty-five, but Caris felt she was from another generation. Her husband, Elfric, had died in the plague, but she had not remarried, becoming frumpy, as if she thought that was how a widow should be. Caris had quarreled with Alice, many years ago, over Elfric's treatment of Merthin. The passage of time had blunted the edge of their mutual hostility, but there was still a resentful tilt to Alice's head when she said hello.

With her was Griselda, her stepdaughter, though only a year younger than Alice. Griselda's son, known as Merthin Bastard, stood beside her, towering over her, a big man with superficial charm—just like his father, the long-gone Thurstan, and about as different from Merthin Bridger as could be. Also with her was her sixteen-year-old daughter, Petranilla.

Griselda's husband, Harold Mason, had taken over the business after Elfric died. He was not much of a builder, according to Merthin, but he was doing all right, although he did not have the monopoly of priory repairs and extensions that had made Elfric rich. He stood next to Merthin now and said: "People think you're going to build the spire with no formwork."

Caris understood. Formwork, or centering, was the wooden frame that held the masonry in place until the mortar dried.

Merthin said: "Not much room for formwork inside that narrow spire. And how would it be supported?" His tone was polite, but Caris could tell from its briskness that he did not like Harold.

"I could believe it if the spire was going to be round."

Caris understood this, too. A round spire could be built by placing one circle of stones on top of another, each a little narrower than the last. No formwork was needed because the circle was self-supporting: the stones could not fall inward because they pressed on one another. The same was not true of any shape with corners.

"You've seen the drawings," Merthin said. "It's an octagon."

The corner turrets on the top of the square tower faced diagonally outward, easing the eye as it progressed upward to the different shape of the narrower spire. Merthin had copied this feature from Chartres. But it made sense only if the tower was octagonal.

Harold said: "But how can you build an octagonal tower without formwork?"

"Wait and see," said Merthin, and he moved away.

As they walked down the main street Caris said: "Why won't you tell people how you're going to do it?"

"So that they can't fire me," he replied. "When I was building the bridge, as soon as I'd done the hard part they got rid of me, and hired someone cheaper."

"I remember."

"They can't do that now, because no one else can build the spire."

"You were a youngster then. Now you're alderman. No one would dare sack you."

"Perhaps not. But it's nice to feel they can't."

At the bottom of the main street, where the old bridge had stood, there was a disreputable tavern called the White Horse. Caris saw Merthin's sixteen-year-old daughter, Lolla, leaning on the wall outside, with a group of older friends. Lolla was an attractive girl, with olive skin and lustrous dark hair, a generous mouth and sultry brown eyes. The group was crowded around a dice game, and they were all drinking ale from large tankards. Caris was sorry, though not surprised, to see her stepdaughter carousing on the street at midday.

Merthin was angry. He went up to Lolla and took her arm. "You'd better come home for your dinner," he said in a tight voice.

She tossed her head, shaking her thick hair in a gesture that was undoubtedly meant for the eyes of someone other than her father. "I don't want to go home, I'm happy here," she said.

"I didn't ask what you wanted," Merthin replied, and he jerked her away from the others.

A good-looking boy of about twenty detached himself from the crowd. He had curly hair and a mocking smile, and he was picking his teeth with a twig. Caris recognized Jake Riley, a lad of no particular profession who nevertheless always seemed to have money to spend. He sauntered over. "What's going on?" he said. He spoke with the twig sticking out of his mouth like an insult.

"None of your damn business," Merthin said.

Jake stood in his way. "The girl doesn't want to leave."

"You'd better get out of my way, son, unless you want to spend the rest of the day in the town stocks."

Caris froze with anxiety. Merthin was in the right: he was entitled to discipline Lolla, who was still five years short of adulthood. But Jake was the kind of boy who might punch him anyway, and take the consequences. However, Caris did not intervene, knowing it might make Merthin angry with her instead of with Jake.

Jake said: "I suppose you're her father."

"You know perfectly well who I am, and you can call me Alderman, and speak respectfully to me, or suffer the consequences."

Jake stared insolently at Merthin a moment longer then turned aside, casually saying: "Yes, all right."

Caris was relieved that the confrontation had not turned into fisticuffs. Merthin never got into fights, but Lolla was capable of driving him to distraction.

They walked on toward the bridge. Lolla shook herself free of her father's grasp and walked on ahead, arms folded under her breasts, head down, frowning and muttering to herself in a full-dress sulk.

This was not the first time Lolla had been seen in bad company. Merthin was horrified and enraged that his little girl should be so determined to seek out such people. "Why does she do it?" he said to Caris as they followed Lolla across the bridge to Leper Island.

"God knows." Caris had observed that this kind of behavior was more common in youngsters who had suffered the loss of a parent. After Silvia died, Lolla had been mothered by Bessie Bell, Lady Philippa, Merthin's housekeeper Em, and of course Caris herself. Perhaps she was confused about whom she should obey. But Caris did not voice this thought, as it might seem to suggest that Merthin had somehow failed as a parent. "I had terrible fights with Aunt Petranilla when I was that age."

"What about?"

"Similar things. She didn't like me spending time with Mattie Wise."

"That's completely different. You didn't go to low taverns with rogues."

"Petranilla thought Mattie was bad company."

"It's not the same."

"I suppose not."

"You learned a lot from Mattie."

Lolla was undoubtedly learning a lot from handsome Jake Riley, but Caris kept that inflammatory thought to herself—Merthin was furious enough already.

The island was entirely built up now, and an integral part of the city. It even had its own parish church. Where once they had wandered across waste ground, they now followed a footpath that ran straight between houses and turned sharp corners. The rabbits had long gone. The hospital occupied most of the western end. Although Caris went there every day, she still felt a glow of pride when she looked at the clean gray stonework, the large windows in regular rows, and the chimneys lined up like soldiers.

They passed through a gate into Merthin's grounds. The orchard was mature, and blossoms covered the apple trees like snow.

As always, they went in through the kitchen door. The house had a grand entrance on the river side which no one ever used. Even a brilliant architect can make a mistake, Caris thought with amusement; but, once again, she decided to give the thought no voice today.

Lolla stamped upstairs to her room.

From the front room a woman called: "Hello, everyone!" The two boys rushed into the parlor with glad cries. It was their mother, Philippa. Merthin and Caris greeted her warmly.

Caris and Philippa had become sisters-in-law when Caris married Merthin, but their past rivalry had continued to make Caris feel awkward in Philippa's presence for some years. Eventually the boys had brought them together. When first Gerry then Roley enrolled at the priory school, it was natural for Merthin to look after his nephews, and then it became normal for Philippa to call at Merthin's house whenever she was in Kingsbridge.

At first, Caris had felt jealous of Philippa for having attracted Merthin sexually. Merthin had never tried to pretend that his love for Philippa had been merely superficial. He clearly still cared about her. But Philippa nowadays cut a sad figure. She was forty-nine and looked older, her hair gray and her face lined with disappointment. She lived now for her children. She was a frequent guest of her daughter, Odila, the countess of Monmouth; and when she was not there she often visited Kingsbridge

Priory to be close to her sons. She managed to spend very little time at Earlscastle with her husband Ralph.

"I've got to take the boys to Shiring," she said, explaining her presence here. "Ralph wants them to attend the county court with him. He says it's a necessary part of their education."

"He's right," Caris said. Gerry would be the earl, if he lived long enough; and if he did not Roley would inherit the title. So they both needed to be familiar with courts.

Philippa added: "I intended to be in the cathedral for the Easter service, but my charette broke a wheel and I made an overnight stop."

"Well, now that you're here, let's have dinner," Caris said.

They went into the dining hall. Caris opened the windows that looked onto the river. Cool, fresh air came in. She wondered what Merthin would do about Lolla. He said nothing, leaving her to stew upstairs, to Caris's relief: a brooding adolescent at the dinner table could bring down everyone's spirits.

They ate mutton boiled with leeks. Merthin poured red wine, and Philippa drank thirstily. She had become fond of wine. Perhaps it was her consolation.

While they were eating, Em came in looking anxious. "There's somebody at the kitchen door to see the mistress," she said.

Merthin said impatiently: "Well, who is it?"

"He wouldn't mention his name, but he said the mistress would know him."

"What kind of person?"

"A young man. By his clothes a peasant, not a town dweller." Em had a snobbish dislike of villagers.

"Well, he sounds harmless. Let him come in."

A moment later, in walked a tall figure with a hood pulled forward to cover most of his face. When he drew it back, Caris recognized Gwenda's elder son, Sam.

Caris had known him all his life. She had seen him born, had watched his slimy head emerge from the small body of his mother. She had observed him as he grew and changed and became a man. She saw Wulfric in him now, in the way he walked and stood and raised a hand slightly as he was about to speak. She had always suspected that Wulfric was not in fact his father—but, close as she was to Gwenda, she had never mentioned her doubt. Some questions were better left unasked. However, the suspicion had inevitably returned when she heard that Sam was wanted for the murder of Jonno Reeve. For Sam when born had had a look of Ralph.

Now he came up to Caris, lifted his hand in that gesture of Wulfric's, hesitated, then went down on one knee. "Save me, please," he said.

Caris was horrified. "How can I save you?"

"Hide me. I've been on the run for days. I left Oldchurch in the dark and walked through the night and I've hardly rested since. Just now I tried to buy something to eat in a tavern and someone recognized me, and I had to run."

He looked so desperate that she felt a surge of compassion. Nevertheless, she said: "But you can't hide here, you're wanted for murder!"

"It was no murder, it was a fight. Jonno struck first. He hit me with a leg iron—look." Sam touched his face in two places, ear and nose, to indicate two scabbed gashes.

The physician in Caris could not help noting that the injuries were about five days old, and the nose was healing well enough though the ear really needed a stitch. But her main thought was that Sam should not be here. "You have to face justice," she said.

"They'll take Jonno's side, they're sure to. I ran away from Wigleigh, for higher wages in Outhenby. Jonno was trying to take me back. They'll say he was entitled to chain a runaway."

"You should have thought of that before you hit him."

He said accusingly: "You employed runaways at Outhenby, when you were prioress."

She was stung. "Runaways, yes—killers, no."

"They will hang me."

Caris was torn. How could she turn him away?

Merthin spoke. "There are two reasons why you can't hide here, Sam. One is that it's a crime to conceal a fugitive, and I'm not willing to put myself on the wrong side of the law for your sake, fond though I am of your mother. But the second reason is that everyone knows your mother is an old friend of Caris's, and if the Kingsbridge constables are searching for you this is the first place they will look.

"Is it?" Sam said.

He was not very bright, Caris knew—his brother, Davey, had all the brains.

Merthin said: "You could hardly think of a worse place than this to hide." He softened. "Drink a cup of wine, and take a loaf of bread with you, and get out of town," he said more kindly. "I'll have to find Mungo Constable and report that you were here, but I can walk slowly." He poured wine into a wooden cup.

"Thank you."

"Your only hope is to go far away where you aren't known and start a new life. You're a strong boy, you'll always find work. Go to London and join a ship. And don't get into fights."

Philippa said suddenly: "I remember your mother . . . Gwenda?"

Sam nodded.

Philippa turned to Caris. "I met her at Casterham, when William was alive. She came to me about that girl in Wigleigh who had been raped by Ralph."

"Annet."

"Yes." Philippa turned back to Sam. "You must be the baby she had in her arms at the time. Your mother is a good woman. I'm sorry for her sake that you're in trouble."

There was a moment of quiet. Sam drained the cup. Caris was thinking, as no doubt Philippa and Merthin were too, about the passage of time, and how it can change an innocent, beloved baby into a man who commits murder.

In the silence, they heard voices.

It sounded like several men at the kitchen door.

Sam looked around him like a trapped bear. One door led to the kitchen, the other outside to the front of the house. He dashed to the front door, flung it open, and ran out. Without pausing he headed down toward the river.

A moment later Em opened the door from the kitchen, and Mungo Constable came into the dining hall, with four deputies crowding behind him, all carrying wooden clubs.

Merthin pointed at the front door. "He just left."

"After him, lads," said Mungo, and they all ran through the room and out the door.

Caris stood up and hurried outside, and the others followed her.

The house was built on a low, rocky bluff only three or four feet high. The river flowed rapidly past the foot of the little cliff. To the left, Merthin's graceful bridge spanned the water; to the right was a muddy beach. Across the river, trees were coming into leaf in the old plague graveyard. Pokey little suburban hovels had grown up like weeds either side of the cemetery.

Sam could have turned left or right, and Caris saw with a feeling of despair that he had made the wrong choice. He had gone right, which led nowhere. She saw him running along the foreshore, his boots leaving big impressions in the mud. The constables were chasing him like dogs after a hare. She felt sorry for Sam, as she always felt sorry for the hare. It was nothing to do with justice, merely that he was the quarry.

Seeing he had nowhere to go, he waded into the water.

Mungo had stayed on the paved footpath at the front of the house, and now he turned in the opposite direction, to the left, and ran toward the bridge.

Two of the deputies dropped their clubs, pulled off their boots, got out of their coats, and jumped into the water in their undershirts. The other two stood on the shoreline, presumably unable to swim, or perhaps unwilling to jump into the water on a cold day. The two swimmers struck out after Sam.

Sam was strong, but his heavy winter coat was now sodden and dragging him down. Caris watched with horrid fascination as the deputies gained on him.

There was a shout from the other direction. Mungo had reached the bridge and was running across, and he had stopped to beckon the two non-swimming deputies to follow him. They acknowledged his signal and ran after him. He continued across the bridge.

Sam reached the far shore just before the swimmers caught up with him. He gained his footing and staggered through the shallows, shaking his head, water running from his clothing. He turned and saw a deputy almost on him. The man stumbled, bending forward inadvertently, and Sam swiftly kicked him in the face with a heavy waterlogged boot. The deputy cried out and fell back.

The second deputy was more cautious. He approached Sam then stopped, still out of reach. Sam turned and ran forward, coming out of the water onto the turf of the plague graveyard; but the deputy followed him. Sam stopped again, and the deputy stopped. Sam realized he was being toyed with. He gave a roar of anger and rushed at his tormentor. The deputy ran back, but he had the river behind him. He ran into the shallows, but the water slowed him, and Sam was able to catch him.

Sam grabbed the man by the shoulders, turned him, and head-butted him. On the far side of the river, Caris heard a crack as the poor man's nose broke. Sam tossed him aside and he fell, spurting blood into the river water.

Sam turned again for the shore—but Mungo was waiting for him. Now Sam was lower down the slope of the foreshore and hampered by the water. Mungo rushed at him, stopped, let him come forward, then raised his heavy wooden club. He feinted, Sam dodged, then Mungo struck, hitting Sam on the top of his head.

It looked a dreadful blow, and Caris herself gasped with shock as if she had been hit. Sam roared with pain and reflexively put his hands over his head. Mungo, experienced in fighting with strong young men, hit him again with the club, this time in his unprotected ribs. Sam fell into the water. The two deputies who had run across the bridge now arrived on the scene. Both jumped on Sam, holding him down in the shallows. The two he had wounded took their revenge, kicking and punching him savagely while their colleagues held him down. When there was no fight left in him, they at last let up and dragged him out of the water.

Mungo swiftly tied Sam's hands behind his back. Then the constables marched the fugitive back toward the town.

"How awful," said Caris. "Poor Gwenda."

83

The town of Shiring had a carnival air during sessions of the county court. All the inns around the square were busy, their parlors crowded with men and women dressed in their best clothes, all shouting for drinks and food. The town naturally took the opportunity to hold a market, and the square itself was so closely packed with stalls that it took half an hour to move a couple of hundred yards. As well as the legitimate stallholders there were dozens of strolling entrepreneurs: bakers with trays of buns, a busking fiddle player, maimed and blind beggars, prostitutes showing their breasts, a dancing bear, a preaching friar.

Earl Ralph was one of the few people who could cross the square quickly. He rode with three knights ahead of him and a handful of servants behind, and his entourage went through the melee like a plowshare, turning the crowd aside by the force of their momentum and their carelessness for the safety of people in their way.

They rode on up the hill to the sheriff's castle. In the courtyard they wheeled with a flourish and dismounted. The servants immediately began shouting for hostlers and porters. Ralph liked people to know he had arrived.

He was tense. The son of his old enemy was about to be tried for murder. He was on the brink of the sweetest revenge imaginable, but some part of him feared it might not happen. He was so on edge that he felt slightly ashamed: he would not have wanted his knights to know how much this meant to him. He was careful to conceal, even from Alan Fernhill, how eager he was that Sam should hang. He was afraid something would go wrong at the last minute. No one knew better than he how the machinery of justice could fail: after all, he himself had escaped hanging twice.

He would sit on the judge's bench during the trial, as was his right, and do his best to make sure there was no upset.

He handed his reins to a groom and looked around. The castle was not a military fortification. It was more like a tavern with a courtyard, though strongly built and well guarded. The sheriff of Shiring could live here safe from the vengeful relatives of the people he arrested. There were basement dungeons in which to keep prisoners, and guest apartments where visiting judges could stay unmolested.

Sheriff Bernard showed Ralph to his room. The sheriff was the king's representative in the county, responsible for collecting taxes as well as administering justice. The post was lucrative, the salary usefully supplemented by gifts, bribes, and percentages skimmed off the top of fines and forfeited bail money. The relationship between earl and sheriff could be fractious: the earl ranked higher, but the sheriff's judicial power was independent. Bernard, a rich wool merchant of about Ralph's age, treated Ralph with an uneasy mixture of camaraderie and deference.

Philippa was waiting for Ralph in the apartment set aside for them. Her long gray hair was tied up in an elaborate headdress, and she wore an expensive coat in drab shades of gray and brown. Her haughty manner had once made her a proud beauty, but now she just looked like a grumpy old woman. She might have been his mother.

He greeted his sons, Gerry and Roley. He was not sure how to deal with children, and he had never seen much of his own: as babies they had been cared for by women, of course, and now they were at the monks' school. He addressed them somewhat as if they were squires in his service, giving them orders at one moment and joshing them in a friendly way the next. He would find them easier to talk to when they were older. It did not seem to matter: they regarded him as a hero whatever he did.

"Tomorrow you shall sit on the judge's bench in the courtroom," he said. "I want you to see how justice is done."

Gerry, the elder, said: "Can we look around the market this afternoon?"

"Yes—get Dickie to go with you." Dickie was one of the Earlscastle servants. "Here, take some money to spend." He gave them each a handful of silver pennies.

The boys went out. Ralph sat down across the room from Philippa. He never touched her, and tried always to keep his distance so that it would not happen by accident. He felt sure that she dressed and acted like an old woman to make sure he was not attracted to her. She also went to church every day.

It was a strange relationship for two people who had once conceived a child together, but they had been stuck in it for years and it would never change. At least it left him free to fondle servant girls and tumble tavern wenches.

However, they had to talk about the children. Philippa had strong views and, over the years, Ralph had realized it was easier to discuss things with her, rather than make unilateral decisions and then have a fight when she disagreed.

Now Ralph said: "Gerald is old enough to be a squire."

Philippa said: "I agree."

"Good!" said Ralph, surprised—he had expected an argument.

"I've already spoken to David Monmouth about him," she added.

That explained her willingness. She was one jump ahead. "I see," he said, playing for time.

"David agrees, and suggests we send him as soon as he is fourteen."

Gerry was only just thirteen. Philippa was in fact postponing Gerry's departure by almost a year. But this was not Ralph's main worry. David, earl of Monmouth, was married to Philippa's daughter, Odila. "Being a squire is supposed to turn a boy into a man," Ralph said. "But Gerry will get too easy a ride with David. His stepsister is fond of him—she'll probably protect him. He could have it too soft." After a moment's reflection, he added: "I expect that's why you want him to go there."

She did not deny it, but said: "I thought you would be glad to strengthen your alliance with the earl of Monmouth."

She had a point. David was Ralph's most important ally in the nobility. Placing Gerry in the Monmouth household would create another bond between the two earls. David might become fond of the boy. In later years, perhaps David's sons would be squires at Earlscastle. Such family connections were priceless. "Will you undertake to make sure the boy isn't mollycoddled there?" Ralph said.

"Of course."

"Well, all right then."

"Good. I'm glad that's settled." Philippa stood up.

But Ralph was not finished. "Now what about Roley? He could go too, so that they would be together."

Philippa did not like this idea at all, Ralph could tell, but she was too clever to contradict him flatly. "Roley's a bit young," she said, as if thinking it over. "And he hasn't properly learned his letters yet."

"Letters aren't as important to a nobleman as learning to fight. After all, he is second in line to the earldom. If anything should happen to Gerry . . ."

"Which God forbid."

"Amen."

"All the same, I think he should wait until he's fourteen."

"I don't know. Roley's always been a bit womanish. Sometimes he reminds me of my brother, Merthin." He saw a flash of fear in her eyes. She was afraid of letting her baby go, he guessed. He was tempted to insist, just to torture her. But ten was young for a squire. "We'll see," he said noncommittally. "He'll have to be toughened up sooner or later."

"All in good time," said Philippa.

The judge, Sir Lewis Abingdon, was not a local man, but a London lawyer from the king's court, sent on tour to try serious cases in county courts. He was a beefy type with a pink face and a fair beard. He was also ten years younger than Ralph.

Ralph told himself he should not be surprised. He was now forty-four. Half his own generation had been wiped out by the plague. Nevertheless, he continued to be startled by distinguished and powerful men who were younger than he.

They waited, with Gerry and Roley, in a side chamber at the Court House Inn, while the jury assembled and the prisoners were brought down from the castle. It turned out that Sir Lewis had been at Crécy, as a young squire, though Ralph did not recall him. He treated Ralph with wary courtesy.

Ralph tried subtly to probe the judge, and find out how tough he was. "The Statute of Laborers is difficult to enforce, we find," he said. "When peasants see a way to make money, they lose all respect for the law."

"For every runaway who is working for an illegal wage, there is an employer who is paying it," the judge said.

"Exactly! The nuns of Kingsbridge Priory have never obeyed the statute."

"Difficult to prosecute nuns."

"I don't see why."

Sir Lewis changed the subject. "You have a special interest in this morning's proceedings?" he asked. He had probably been told that it was unusual for Ralph to exercise his right to sit beside the judge.

"The murderer is a serf of mine," Ralph admitted. "But the main reason I'm here is to give these boys a look at how justice works. One of them is likely to be the earl when I give up the ghost. They can watch the hangings tomorrow, too. The sooner they get used to seeing men die, the better."

Lewis nodded agreement. "The sons of the nobility cannot afford to be softhearted."

They heard the clerk of the court bang his gavel, and the hubbub from the next room died down. Ralph's anxiety was not allayed: Sir Lewis's conversation had not told him much. Perhaps that in itself was revealing: it might mean he was not easily influenced.

The judge opened the door and stood aside for the earl to go first.

At the near end of the room, two large wooden chairs were set on a dais. Next to them was a low bench. A murmur of interest arose from the crowd as Gerry and Roley sat on the bench. The people were always fascinated to see the children who would grow into their overlords. But more than that, Ralph thought, there was a look of innocence about the two prepubescent boys that was strikingly out of place in a court whose business was violence, theft, and dishonesty. They looked like lambs in a pigpen.

Ralph sat in one of the two chairs and thought of the day, twenty-two years ago, when he had stood in this very courtroom as a criminal accused of rape—a ludicrous charge to bring against a lord when the so-called victim was one of his own serfs. Philippa had been behind that malicious prosecution. Well, he had made her suffer for it.

At that trial, Ralph had fought his way out of the room as soon as the jury pronounced him guilty, and then had been pardoned when he joined the king's army and went to France. Sam was not going to escape: he had no weapon, and his ankles were chained. And the French wars seemed to have petered out, so there were no more free pardons.

Ralph studied Sam as the indictment was read. He had Wulfric's build, not Gwenda's: he was a tall lad, broad across the shoulders. He might have made a useful man-at-arms if he had been more nobly born. He did not really look like Wulfric, though something about the cast of his features rang a bell. Like so many accused men, he wore an expression of superficial defiance overlaying fear. That's just how I felt, Ralph thought.

Nathan Reeve was the first witness. He was the father of the dead man but, more importantly, he testified that Sam was a serf of Earl Ralph's and had not been given leave to go to Oldchurch. He said he had sent his son Jonno to follow Gwenda in the hope of tracking down the runaway. He was not likeable, but his grief was clearly genuine. Ralph was pleased: it was damning testimony.

Sam's mother was standing next to him, the top of her head level with her son's shoulder. Gwenda was not beautiful: her dark eyes were set close to a beaky nose, and her forehead and chin both receded sharply, giving her the look of a determined rodent. Yet there was something strongly sexual about her, even in middle age. It was more than twenty years since Ralph had lain with her, but he remembered her as if it were yesterday. They had done it in a room at the Bell in Kingsbridge, and he had made her kneel up on the bed. He could picture it now, and the memory of her compact body excited him. She had a lot of dark hair, he recollected.

Suddenly she met his eye. She held his gaze and seemed to sense what he was thinking. On that bed she had been indifferent and motionless, to begin with, accepting his thrusts passively because he had coerced her; but, at the end, something strange had come over her, and almost against her own will she had moved in rhythm with him. She must have remembered the same thing, for an expression of shame came over her plain face, and she looked quickly away.

Next to her was another young man, presumably the second son. This one was more like her, small and wiry, with a crafty look about him. He met Ralph's gaze with a stare of intense concentration, as if he was curious what went on in the mind of an earl, and thought he might find the answer in Ralph's face.

But Ralph was most interested in the father. He had hated Wulfric since their fight at the Fleece Fair of 1337. He touched his broken nose reflexively. Several other men had wounded him in later years, but none had hurt his pride so badly. However, Ralph's revenge on Wulfric had been terrible. I deprived him of his birthright for a decade, Ralph thought. I lay with his wife. I gave him that scar across his cheek when he tried to stop me escaping from this very courtroom. I dragged him home when he tried to run away. And now I'm going to hang his son.

Wulfric was heavier than he used to be, but he carried it well. He had a salt-and-pepper beard that did not grow over the long scar of the sword wound Ralph had given him. His face was lined and weatherbeaten. Where Gwenda looked angry, Wulfric was grief-stricken. As the peasants of Oldchurch testified that Sam had killed Jonno with an oak spade, Gwenda's eyes flashed defiance, whereas Wulfric's broad forehead creased in anguish.

The foreman of the jury asked whether Sam had been in fear for his life.

Ralph was displeased. The question implied an excuse for the killer.

A thin peasant with one eye responded. "He wasn't in fear of the bailiff, no. I think he was ascared of his mother, though." The crowd tittered.

The foreman asked whether Jonno had provoked the attack, another question that bothered Ralph by indicating sympathy for Sam.

"Provoked?" said the one-eyed man. "Only by hitting him across the face with a leg iron, if you call that provoking." They laughed loudly.

Wulfric looked bewildered. How can people be amused, his expression said, when my son's life is at stake?

Ralph was feeling more anxious. The foreman seemed unsound.

Sam was called to testify, and Ralph noticed that the young man resembled Wulfric more when he spoke. There was a tilt of the head and a gesture of the hand that immediately brought Wulfric to mind. Sam told how he had offered to meet Jonno the following morning, and Jonno had responded by trying to put an iron on his leg.

Ralph spoke to the judge in an undertone. "None of this makes any difference," he said with suppressed indignation. "Whether he was in fear, whether he was provoked, whether he offered to meet the following day."

Sir Lewis said nothing.

Ralph said: "The bare fact is that he's a runaway and he killed the man who came to fetch him."

"He certainly did that," said Sir Lewis guardedly, giving Ralph no satisfaction.

Ralph looked at the spectators while the jury questioned Sam. Merthin was in the crowd, with his wife. Before becoming a nun Caris had enjoyed dressing fashionably, and after renouncing her vows she had reverted to type. Today she wore a gown made of two contrasting fabrics, one blue and the other green, with a fur-trimmed cloak of Kingsbridge Scarlet and a little round hat. Ralph remembered that Caris had been a childhood friend of Gwenda's, in fact she had been there the day they all saw Thomas Langley kill two men-at-arms in the woods. Merthin and Caris would be hoping, for Gwenda's sake, that Sam would be treated mercifully. Not if I have anything to do with it, Ralph thought.

Caris's successor as prioress, Mother Joan, was in court, presumably because the nunnery owned Outhenby Valley and was therefore the illegal employer of Sam. Joan ought to be in the dock with the accused, Ralph thought; but when he caught her eye she gave him an accusing glance, as if she thought the murder was his fault more than hers.

The prior of Kingsbridge had not shown up. Sam was Prior Philemon's nephew, but Philemon would not want to draw attention to the fact that he was the uncle of a murderer. Philemon had once had a protective affection for his younger sister, Ralph recalled; but perhaps that had faded with the years.

Sam's grandfather, the disreputable Joby, was present, a white-haired old man now, bent and toothless. Why was he here? He had been at odds with Gwenda for years, and was not likely to have much affection for his grandson. He had probably come to steal coins from people's purses while they were absorbed in the trial.

Sam stood down and Sir Lewis spoke briefly. His summing-up pleased Ralph. "Was Sam Wigleigh a runaway?" he asked. "Did Jonno Reeve have the right to arrest him? And did Sam kill Jonno with his spade? If the answer to all three questions is yes, then Sam is guilty of murder."

Ralph was surprised and relieved. There was no nonsense about whether Sam was provoked. The judge was sound after all.

"What is your verdict?" the judge asked.

Ralph looked at Wulfric. The man was stricken. This is what happens to those who defy me, Ralph thought, and he wished he could say it out loud.

Wulfric caught his eye. Ralph held his gaze, trying to read Wulfric's mind. What emotion was there? Ralph saw that it was fear. Wulfric had never shown fear to Ralph before, but now he crumbled. His son was going to die, and that had weakened him fatally. A profound satisfaction filled Ralph's being as he stared into Wulfric's frightened eyes. I have crushed you at last, he thought, after twenty-four years. Finally, you're scared.

The jury conferred. The foreman seemed to be arguing with the others. Ralph watched them impatiently. Surely they could not be in doubt, after what the judge had said? But there was no certainty with juries. It can't all go wrong at this stage, Ralph thought, can it?

They seemed to come to a resolution, though he could not guess who had prevailed. The foreman stood up.

"We find Sam Wigleigh guilty of murder," he said.

Ralph kept his eyes fixed on his old enemy. Wulfric looked as if he had been stabbed. His face went pale and he closed his eyes as if in pain. Ralph tried not to smile in triumph.

Sir Lewis turned to Ralph, and Ralph tore his gaze away from Wulfric. "What are your thoughts about the sentence?" said the judge.

"There's only one choice, as far as I'm concerned."

Sir Lewis nodded. "The jury has made no recommendation for mercy."

"They don't want a runaway to get away with murdering his bailiff."

"The ultimate penalty, then?"

"Of course!"

The judge turned back to the court. Ralph locked his gaze on Wulfric again. Everyone else looked at Sir Lewis. The judge said: "Sam Wigleigh, you have murdered the son of your bailiff, and you are sentenced to death. You shall be hanged in Shiring market square tomorrow at dawn, and may God have mercy on your soul."

Wulfric staggered. The younger son grabbed his father's arm and held him upright; otherwise he might have fallen to the floor. Let him drop, Ralph wanted to say; he's finished.

Ralph looked at Gwenda. She was holding Sam's hand, but she was looking at Ralph. Her expression surprised him. He expected grief, tears, screams, hysterics. But she stared back at him steadily. There was hatred in her eyes, and something else: defiance. Unlike her husband, she did not look crushed. She did not believe the case was over.

She looked, Ralph thought with dismay, as if she had something up her sleeve.

84

Caris was in tears as Sam was taken away, but Merthin could not pretend to be grief-stricken. It was a tragedy for Gwenda, and he felt desperately sorry for Wulfric. However, it was no bad thing, for the rest of the world, that Sam should be hanged. Jonno Reeve had been carrying out the law. It might well be a bad law, an unjust law, an oppressive law—but that did not give Sam the right to kill Jonno. After all, Nate Reeve was also bereaved. The fact that nobody liked Nate made no difference.

A thief was brought up before the bench, and Merthin and Caris left the courtroom and went into the parlor of the tavern. Merthin got some wine and poured a cup for Caris. A moment later, Gwenda came up to where they sat. "It's noon," she said. "We have eighteen hours to save Sam."

Merthin looked up at her in surprise. "What do you propose?" he said.

"We must get Ralph to ask the king to pardon him."

That seemed highly unlikely. "How would you persuade him to do that?"

"I can't, obviously," Gwenda said. "But you can."

Merthin felt trapped. He did not believe Sam deserved a pardon. On the other hand, it was hard to refuse a pleading mother. He said: "I intervened with my brother on your behalf once before—do you remember?"

"Of course," Gwenda said. "Over Wulfric not inheriting his father's land."

"He turned me down flat."

"I know," she said. "But you have to try."

"I'm not sure I'm the best person."

"Who else would he even listen to?"

That was right. Merthin had little chance of success, but no one else had any.

Caris could see that he was reluctant, and she threw her weight in on Gwenda's side. "Please, Merthin," she said. "Think how you would feel if it was Lolla."

He was about to say that girls don't get into fights, then he realized that in Lolla's case it was all too likely. He sighed. "I think this is a doomed enterprise," he said. He looked at Caris. "But, for your sake, I'll try."

Gwenda said: "Why don't you go now?"

"Because Ralph is still in court."

"It's almost dinnertime. They'll be finished soon. You could wait in the private chamber."

He had to admire her resolve. "All right," he said.

He left the parlor and walked around to the back of the tavern. A guard was standing outside the judge's private room. "I'm the earl's brother," Merthin said to the sentry. "Alderman Merthin of Kingsbridge."

"Yes, Alderman, I know you," the guard said. "I'm sure it will be all right for you to wait inside."

Merthin went into the little room and sat down. He felt uncomfortable asking his brother for a favor. The two of them had not been close for decades. Ralph had long ago turned into something Merthin did not recognize. Merthin did not know the man who could rape Annet and murder Tilly. It seemed impossible that such a one could have grown from the boy Merthin had called his brother. Since their parents had died, they had not met except on formal occasions, and even then they spoke little. It was presumptuous of him to use their relationship as justification for asking for a privilege. He would not have done it for Gwenda. But for Caris, he had to.

He did not wait long. After a few minutes the judge and the earl came in. Merthin noticed that his brother's limp—the result of a wound suffered in the French wars—was getting worse as he aged.

Sir Lewis recognized Merthin and shook hands. Ralph did the same and said ironically: "A visit from my brother is a rare pleasure."

It was not an unfair jibe, and Merthin acknowledged it with a nod. "On the other hand," he said, "I suppose that if anyone is entitled to plead with you for mercy, I am."

"What need do you have of mercy? Did you kill someone?"

"Not yet."

Sir Lewis chuckled.

Ralph said: "What, then?"

"You and I have known Gwenda since we were all children together."

Ralph nodded. "I shot her dog with that bow you made."

Merthin had forgotten that incident. It was an early sign of how Ralph was going to turn out, he realized with hindsight. "Perhaps you owe her mercy on that account."

"I think Nate Reeve's son is worth more than a damn dog, don't you?"

"I didn't mean to suggest otherwise. Just that you might balance cruelty then with kindness now."

"Balance?" Ralph said, with anger rising in his voice, and Merthin knew then that his cause was lost. "Balance?" He tapped his broken nose. "What should I balance against this?" He pointed a finger aggressively at Merthin. "I'll tell you why I won't give Sam a pardon. Because I looked at Wulfric's face in the courtroom today, as his son was declared guilty of murder, and do you know what I saw there? Fear. That insolent peasant is afraid of me, at last. He has been tamed."

"He means so much to you?"

"I'd hang six men to see that look."

Merthin was ready to give up, then he thought of Gwenda's grief, and he tried once more. "If you've conquered him, your work is done, isn't it?" he argued. "So let the boy go. Ask the king for a pardon."

"No. I want to keep Wulfric the way he is."

Merthin wished he had not come. Putting pressure on Ralph only brought out the worst in him. Merthin was appalled by his vengefulness and malice. He never wanted to speak to his brother again. The feeling was familiar: he had been through this with Ralph before. Somehow it always came as a shock to be reminded of what he was really like.

Merthin turned away. "Well, I had to try," he said. "Good-bye."

Ralph became cheery. "Come up to the castle for dinner," he said. "The sheriff lays a good table. Bring Caris. We'll have a real talk. Philippa's with me—you like her, don't you?"

Merthin had no intention of going. "Let me speak to Caris," he said. Caris would rather have dinner with Lucifer, he knew.

"I may see you later, then."

Merthin made his escape.

He returned to the parlor. Caris and Gwenda looked expectantly at him as he crossed the room. He shook his head. "I did my best," he said. "I'm sorry."

Gwenda had expected this. She was disappointed but not surprised. She had felt she had to try through Merthin. The other remedy she had at her disposal was so much more drastic.

She thanked Merthin perfunctorily and left the inn, heading for the castle on the hill. Wulfric and Davey had gone to a cheap tavern in the suburbs where they could get a filling dinner for a farthing. Wulfric was no good at this sort of thing anyway. His strength and honesty were useless in negotiations with Ralph and his kind.

Besides, Wulfric could not be allowed even to know about how she hoped to persuade Ralph.

As she was walking up the hill she heard horses behind her. She stopped and turned. It was Ralph and his entourage with the judge. She stood still and looked hard at Ralph, making sure he caught her eye as he passed. He would guess she was coming to see him.

A few minutes later she entered the courtyard of the castle, but access to the sheriff's house was barred. She made her way to the porch of the main building and spoke to the marshal of the hall. "My name is Gwenda from Wigleigh," she said. "Please tell Earl Ralph I need to see him in private."

"Yes, yes," said the marshal. "Look around you: all these people need to see the earl, the judge, or the sheriff."

There were twenty or thirty people standing around the courtyard, some clutching rolls of parchment.

Gwenda was prepared to take a terrible risk to save her son from hanging—but she would not get the opportunity unless she succeeded in speaking to Ralph before dawn.

"How much?" she said to the marshal.

He looked at her with a little less disrespect. "I can't promise he'll see you."

"You can give him my name."

"Two shillings. Twenty-four silver pennies."

It was a lot of money, but Gwenda had all their savings in her purse. However, she was not yet ready to hand over the money. "What is my name?" she said.

"I don't know."

"I just told you. How can you give Earl Ralph my name if you can't remember it?"

He shrugged. "Tell me again."

"Gwenda from Wigleigh."

"All right, I'll mention it to him."

Gwenda slipped her hand into her purse, brought out a handful of little silver coins, and counted twenty-four. It was four weeks' wages for a laborer. She thought of the backbreaking work she had done to earn the money. Now this idle, supercilious doorkeeper was going to get it for doing next to nothing.

The marshal held out his hand.

She said: "What's my name?"

"Gwenda."

"Gwenda from where?"

"Wigleigh." He added: "That's where this morning's murderer came from, isn't it?"

She gave him the money. "The earl will want to see me," she said as forcefully as she could.

The marshal pocketed the coins.

Gwenda retreated into the courtyard, not knowing whether she had wasted her money.

A moment later she saw a familiar figure with a small head on wide shoulders: Alan Fernhill. That was a piece of luck. He was crossing from the stables to the hall. The other petitioners did not recognize him. Gwenda stood in his way. "Hello, Alan," she said.

"It's Sir Alan now."

"Congratulations. Will you tell Ralph that I want to see him?"

"I don't need to ask you what it's about."

"Say I want to meet him in private."

Alan raised an eyebrow. "No offense, but you were a girl last time. You're twenty years older today."

"Do you think perhaps we should let him decide?"

"Of course." He grinned insultingly. "I know he remembers that afternoon at the Bell."

Alan had been there, of course. He had watched Gwenda take off her dress, and stared at her naked body. He had seen her walk to the bed and knelt on the mattress, facing away. He had laughed coarsely when Ralph said she was better looking from behind.

She hid her revulsion and shame. "I was hoping he would remember," she said as neutrally as she could.

The other petitioners realized Alan must be someone important. They began to crowd around, speaking to him, begging and pleading. He pushed them aside and went into the hall.

Gwenda settled down to wait.

After an hour it was clear Ralph was not going to see her before dinner. She found a patch of ground that was not too muddy and sat with her back to a stone wall, but she never took her eyes off the entrance to the hall.

A second hour passed, and a third. Noblemen's dinners often went on all afternoon. Gwenda wondered how they could keep on eating and drinking for such a long time. Why did they not burst?

She had eaten nothing all day, but she was too tense to feel hungry.

It was gray April weather, and the sky began to darken early. Gwenda shivered on the cold ground, but she stayed where she was. This was her only chance.

Servants came out and lit torches around the courtyard. Lights appeared behind the shutters in some of the windows. Night fell, and Gwenda realized there were about twelve hours left until dawn. She thought of Sam, sitting on the floor in one of the underground chambers beneath the castle, and wondered if he was cold. She fought back tears.

It's not over yet, she told herself; but her courage was weakening.

A tall figure blocked the light from the nearest torch. She looked up to see Alan. Her heart leaped.

"Come with me," he said.

She jumped to her feet and moved toward the hall door.

"Not that way."

She looked inquiringly at him.

"You said privately, didn't you?" Alan said. "He's not going to see you in the chamber he shares with the countess. Come this way."

She followed him through a small door near the stables. He led her through several rooms and up a staircase. He opened a door to a narrow bedchamber. She stepped inside. Alan did not follow her in, but closed the door from the outside.

It was a low room almost completely filled by a bedstead. Ralph stood by the window in his undershirt. His boots and outer clothing were piled on the floor. His face was flushed with drink, but his speech was clear and steady. "Take off your dress," he said with a smile of anticipation.

Gwenda said: "No."

He looked startled.

"I'm not taking my clothes off," she said.

"Why did you tell Alan you wanted to see me in private?"

"So that you would think I was willing to have sex with you."

"But if not . . . why are you here?"

"To beg you to ask the king for a pardon."

"But you're not offering yourself to me?"

"Why would I? I did that once before, and you broke your word. You reneged on the deal. I gave you my body, but you didn't give my husband his land." She allowed the contempt she felt to be heard in her tone of voice. "You would do the same again. Your honor is nothing. You remind me of my father."

Ralph colored. It was an insult to tell an earl that he could not be trusted, and even more offensive to compare him with a landless laborer who trapped squirrels in the woods. Angrily he said: "Do you imagine this is the way to persuade me?"

"No. But you're going to get that pardon."

"Why?"

"Because Sam is your son."

Ralph stared at her for a moment. "Hah," he said contemptuously. "As if I would believe that."

"He is your son," she repeated.

"You can't prove that."

"No, I can't," she said. "But you know that I lay with you at the Bell in Kingsbridge nine months before Sam was born. True, I lay with Wulfric, too. So which of you is his father? Look at the boy! He has some of Wulfric's mannerisms, yes—he has learned those, in twenty-two years. But look at his features."

She saw a thoughtful expression appear on Ralph's face, and knew that something she had said had hit the mark.

"Most of all, think about his character," she said, pressing home. "You heard the evidence at the trial. Sam didn't just fight Jonno off, as Wulfric would have done. He didn't knock him down then help him up again, which would have been Wulfric's way. Wulfric is strong, and quick to anger, but he's tenderhearted. Sam is not. Sam hit Jonno with a spade, a blow that would have knocked any man senseless; then, before Jonno fell, Sam hit him again, even harder, although he was already helpless; and then, before Jonno's limp form reached the ground, Sam hit him a third time. If the Oldchurch peasants hadn't jumped on Sam and restrained him, he would have continued to lash out with that bloody spade until Jonno's head was smashed to a pulp. He wanted to kill!" She realized she was crying, and wiped the tears away with her sleeve.

Ralph was staring at her with a horrified look.

"Where does the killer instinct come from, Ralph?" she said. "Look in your own black heart. Sam is your son. And, God forgive me, he's mine."

When Gwenda had gone, Ralph sat on the bed in the little chamber, staring at the flame of the candle. Was it possible? Gwenda would lie, if it suited her, of course; there was no question of trusting her. But Sam could be Ralph's son as easily as Wulfric's. They had both lain with Gwenda at the crucial time. The truth might never be known for sure.

Even the possibility that Sam might be his child was enough to fill Ralph's heart with dread. Was he about to hang his own son? The dreadful punishment he had devised for Wulfric might be inflicted on himself.

It was already night. The hanging would take place at dawn. Ralph did not have long to decide.

He picked up the candle and left the little room. He had intended to satisfy a carnal desire there. Instead he had been given the shock of his life.

He went outside and crossed the courtyard to the cell block. On the ground floor of the building were offices for the sheriff's deputies. He went inside and spoke to the man on guard duty. "I want to see the murderer, Sam Wigleigh."

"Very good, my lord," the jailer said. "I'll show you the way." He led Ralph into the next room, carrying a lamp.

There was a grating set in the floor, and a bad smell. Ralph looked down through the grating. The cell was nine or ten feet deep with stone walls and a dirt floor. There was no furniture: Sam sat on the floor with his back against the wall. Beside him was a wooden jug, presumably containing water. A small hole in the floor appeared to be the toilet. Sam glanced up, then looked away indifferently.

"Open up," said Ralph.

The jailer unlocked the grating with a key. It swung up on a hinge.

"I want to go down."

The jailer was surprised, but did not dare argue with an earl. He picked up a ladder that was leaning against the wall and slid it into the cell. "Take care, please, my lord," he said nervously. "Remember, the villain has nothing to lose."

Ralph climbed down, carrying his candle. The smell was disgusting, but he hardly cared. He reached the foot of the ladder and turned.

Sam looked up at him resentfully and said: "What do you want?"

Ralph stared at him. He crouched down and held the candle close to Sam's face, studying his features, trying to compare them with the face he saw when he looked into a mirror.

"What is it?" Sam said, spooked by Ralph's intense stare.

Ralph did not answer. Was this his own child? It could be, he thought. It could easily be. Sam was a good-looking boy, and Ralph had been called handsome in his youth, before his nose got broken. In court earlier, Ralph had thought that something about Sam's face rang a bell, and now he concentrated, searching his memory, trying to think who Sam reminded him of. That straight nose, the dark-eyed gaze, the head of thick hair that girls would envy . . .

Then he got it.

Sam looked like Ralph's mother, the late Lady Maud.

"Dear God," he said, and it came out as a whisper.

"What?" said Sam, his voice betraying fear. "What is this?"

Ralph had to say something. "Your mother . . . ," he began, then he trailed off. His throat was constricted with emotion, making it difficult for him to get words out. He tried again. "Your mother has pleaded for you . . . most eloquently."

Sam looked wary and said nothing. He thought Ralph had come here to mock him.

"Tell me," Ralph said. "When you hit Jonno with that spade . . . did you mean to kill him? You can be honest, you have nothing more to fear."

"Of course I meant to kill him," Sam said. "He was trying to take me in."

Ralph nodded. "I would have felt the same," he said. He paused, staring at Sam, then said it again. "I would have felt the same."

He stood up, turned to the ladder, hesitated, then turned back and put the candle on the ground next to Sam. Then he climbed up.

The jailer replaced the grating and locked it.

Ralph said to him: "There will be no hanging. The prisoner will be pardoned. I will speak to the sheriff immediately."

As he left the room, the jailer sneezed.

85

When Merthin and Caris returned from Shiring to Kingsbridge, they found that Lolla had gone missing.

Their long-standing house servants, Arn and Em, were waiting at the garden gate, and looked as if they had been stationed there all day. Em began to speak but burst into incoherent sobs, and Arn had to break the news. "We can't find Lolla," he said, distraught. "We don't know where she is."

At first Merthin misunderstood. "She'll be here by suppertime," he said. "Don't upset yourself, Em."

"But she didn't come home last night, nor the night before," Arn said.

Merthin realized then what they meant. She had run away. A blast of fear like a winter wind chilled his skin and gripped his heart. She was only sixteen. For a moment he could not think rationally. He just pictured her, halfway between child and adult, with the intense dark-brown eyes and sensual mouth of her mother, and an expression of blithe false confidence.

When rationality returned to him, he asked himself what had gone wrong. He had been leaving Lolla in the care of Arn and Em for a few days at a time ever since she was five years old, and she had never come to any harm. Had something changed?

He realized that he had hardly spoken to her since Easter Sunday, two weeks ago, when he had taken her by the arm and pulled her away from her disreputable friends outside the White Horse. She had sulked upstairs while the family ate dinner, and had not emerged even when Sam was arrested. She had still been in a snit a few days later, when Merthin and Caris had kissed her good-bye and set out for Shiring.

Guilt stabbed him. He had treated her harshly, and driven her away. Was Silvia's ghost watching, and despising him for his failure to care for their daughter?

The thought of Lolla's disreputable friends came back to him. "That fellow Jake Riley is behind this," he said. "Have you spoken to him, Arn?"

"No, master."

"I'd better do that right away. Do you know where he lives?"

"He lodges next to the fishmonger's behind St. Paul's Church."

Caris said to Merthin: "I'll go with you."

They crossed the bridge back into the city and headed west. The parish of St. Paul took in the industrial premises along the waterfront: abattoirs, leather tanners, sawmills, manufactories, and the dyers that had sprung up like September mushrooms since the invention of Kingsbridge Scarlet. Merthin headed for the squat tower of St. Paul's Church, visible over the low roofs of the houses. He found the fish shop by smell, and knocked at a large, run-down house next door.

It was opened by Sal Sawyers, poor widow of a jobbing carpenter who had died in the plague. "Jake comes and goes, Alderman," she said. "I haven't seen him for a week. He can do as he pleases, so long as he pays the rent."

Caris said: "When he left, was Lolla with him?"

Sal warily looked sideways at Merthin. "I don't like to criticize," she said.

Merthin said: "Please just tell me what you know. I won't be offended."

"She's usually with him. She does anything Jake wants, I'll say no more than that. If you look for him, you'll find her."

"Do you know where he might have gone?"

"He never says."

"Can you think of anyone who might know?"

"He doesn't bring his friends here, except for her. But I believe his pals are usually to be found at the White Horse."

Merthin nodded. "We'll try there. Thank you, Sal."

"She'll be all right," Sal said. "She's just going through a wild phase."

"I hope you're right."

Merthin and Caris retraced their steps until they came to the White Horse, on the riverside near the bridge. Merthin recalled the orgy he had witnessed here at the height of the plague, when the dying Davey Whitehorse had given away all his ale. The place had stood empty for several years afterward, but now it was once again a busy tavern. Merthin often wondered why it was popular. The rooms were cramped and dirty, and there were frequent fights. About once a year someone was killed there.

They went into a smoky parlor. It was mid-afternoon, but there were a dozen or so desultory drinkers sitting on benches. A small group was clustered around a backgammon board, and several small piles of silver pennies on the table indicated that money was being wagered on the outcome. A red-cheeked prostitute called Joy looked up hopefully at the newcomers, then saw who they were and relapsed into bored indolence. In a corner, a man was showing a woman an expensive-looking coat, apparently offering it for sale; but when he saw Merthin he folded the garment quickly and put it out of sight, and Merthin guessed it was stolen property.

The landlord, Evan, was eating a late dinner of fried bacon. He stood up, wiping his hands on his tunic, and said nervously: "Good day to you, Alderman—an honor to have you in the house. May I draw you a pot of ale?"

"I'm looking for my daughter, Lolla," Merthin said briskly.

"I haven't seen her for a week," said Evan.

Sal had said exactly the same about Jake, Merthin recalled. He said to Evan: "She may be with Jake Riley."

"Yes, I've noticed that they're friendly," Evan said tactfully. "He's been gone about the same length of time."

"Do you know where he went?"

"He's a close-lipped type, is Jake," said Evan. "If you asked him how far it was to Shiring, he'd shake his head and frown and say it was none of his business to know such things."

The whore, Joy, had been listening to the conversation, and now she chipped in. "He's openhanded, though," she said. "Fair's fair."

Merthin gave her a hard look. "And where does his money come from?"

"Horses," she said. "He goes around the villages buying foals from peasants, and sells them in the towns."

He probably stole horses from unwary travelers, too, Merthin thought sourly. "Is that what he's doing now—buying horses?"

Evan said: "Very likely. The big fair season is coming up. He could be acquiring his stock-in-trade."

"And perhaps Lolla went with him."

"Not wishing to give offense, Alderman, but it's quite likely."

"It's not you who has given offense," Merthin said. He nodded a curt farewell and left the tavern, with Caris following.

"That's what she's done," he said angrily. "She's gone off with Jake. She probably thinks it's a great adventure."

"I'm afraid I think you're right," Caris said. "I hope she doesn't become pregnant."

"I wish that was the worst I feared."

They headed automatically for home. Crossing the bridge, Merthin stopped at the highest point and looked out over the suburban rooftops to the forest beyond. His little girl was somewhere out there with a shady horse dealer. She was in danger, and there was nothing he could do to protect her.

When Merthin went to the cathedral the next morning, to check on the new tower, he found that all work had stopped. "Prior's orders," said Brother Thomas when Merthin questioned him. Thomas was almost sixty years old, and showing his age. His soldierly physique was bent, and he shuffled around the precincts unsteadily. "There's been a collapse in the south aisle," he added.

Merthin glanced at Bartelmy French, a gnarled old mason from Normandy, who was sitting outside the lodge sharpening a chisel. Bartelmy shook his head in silent negation.

"That collapse was twenty-four years ago, Brother Thomas," Merthin said.

"Ah, yes, you're right," said Thomas. "My memory's not as good as it used to be, you know."

Merthin patted his shoulder. "We're all getting older."

Bartelmy said: "The prior is up the tower, if you want to see him."

Merthin certainly did. He went into the north transept, stepped through a small archway, and climbed a narrow spiral stair within the wall. As he passed from the old crossing into the new tower, the color of the stones changed from the dark gray of storm clouds to the light pearl of the morning sky. It was a long climb: the tower was already more than three hundred feet high. However, he was used to it. Almost every day for eleven years he had climbed a stair that was higher each time. It occurred to him that Philemon, who was quite fat nowadays, must have had a compelling reason to drag his bulk up all these steps.

Near the top, Merthin passed through a chamber that housed the great wheel, a wooden winding mechanism twice as high as a man, used for hoisting stones, mortar, and timber up to where they were needed. When the spire was finished the wheel would be left here permanently, to be used for repair work by future generations of builders, until the trumpets sounded on the Day of Judgment.

He emerged on top of the tower. A stiff, cold breeze was blowing, though none had been noticeable at ground level. A leaded walkway ran around the inside of the tower's summit. Scaffolding stood around an octagonal hole, ready for the masons who would build the spire. Dressed stones were piled nearby, and a heap of mortar was drying up wastefully on a wooden board.

There were no workmen here. Prior Philemon stood on the far side with Harold Mason. They were deep in conversation, but stopped guiltily when Merthin came into view. He had to shout into the wind to make himself heard. "Why have you stopped the building?"

Philemon had his answer ready. "There's a problem with your design."

Merthin looked at Harold. "You mean some people can't understand it."

"Experienced people say it can't be built," Philemon said defiantly.

"Experienced people?" Merthin repeated scornfully. "Who in Kingsbridge is experienced? Who has built a bridge? Who has worked with the great architects of Florence? Who has seen Rome, Avignon, Paris, Rouen? Certainly not Harold here. No offense, Harold, but you've never even been to London."

Harold said: "I'm not the only one who thinks it's impossible to build an octagonal tower with no formwork."

Merthin was about to say something sarcastic, but stopped himself. Philemon must have more than this, he realized. The prior had deliberately chosen to fight this battle. Therefore he must have weapons more formidable than the mere opinion of Harold Mason. He had presumably won some support among members of the guild—but how? Other builders who were prepared to say that Merthin's spire was impossible must have been offered some incentive. That probably meant construction work for them. "What is it?" he said to Philemon. "What are you hoping to build?"

"I don't know what you mean," Philemon blustered.

"You've got an alternative project, and you've offered Harold and his friends a piece of it. What's the building?"

"You don't know what you're talking about."

"A bigger palace for yourself? A new chapter house? It can't be a hospital, we've already got three. Come on, you might as well tell me. Unless you're ashamed of it."

Philemon was stung into a response. "The monks wish to build a Lady chapel."

"Ah." That made sense. The cult of the Virgin was increasingly popular. The church hierarchy approved because the wave of piety associated with Mary counterbalanced the skepticism and heresy that had afflicted congregations since the plague. Numerous cathedrals and churches were adding a special small chapel at the east end—the holiest part of the building—dedicated to the Mother of God. Merthin did not like the architecture: on most churches, a Lady chapel looked like an afterthought, which of course it was.

What was Philemon's motive? He was always trying to ingratiate himself with someone—that was his modus operandi. A Lady chapel at Kingsbridge would undoubtedly please conservative senior clergy.

This was the second move Philemon had made in that direction. On Easter Sunday, from the pulpit of the cathedral, he had condemned dissection of corpses. He was mounting a campaign, Merthin realized. But what was its purpose?

Merthin decided to do nothing more until he had figured out what Philemon was up to. Without saying anything further, he left the roof and started down the series of staircases and ladders to the ground.

Merthin arrived home at the dinner hour, and Caris came in from the hospital a few minutes later. "Brother Thomas is getting worse," he said to Caris. "Is there anything that can be done for him?"

She shook her head. "There's no cure for senility."

"He told me the south aisle had collapsed as if it had happened yesterday."

"That's typical. He remembers the distant past but doesn't know what's going on today. Poor Thomas. He'll probably deteriorate quite fast. But at least he's in a familiar place. Monasteries don't change much over the decades. His daily routine is probably the same as it has always been. That will help."

As they sat down to mutton stew with leeks and mint, Merthin explained the morning's developments. The two of them had been battling Kingsbridge priors for decades: first Anthony, then Godwyn, and now Philemon. They had thought that the granting of the borough charter would put an end to the constant jockeying. It had certainly improved matters, but it seemed Philemon had not given up yet.

"I'm not really worried about the spire," Merthin said. "Bishop Henri will overrule Philemon, and order the building restarted, just as soon as he hears. Henri wants to be bishop of the tallest cathedral in England."

"Philemon must know that," Caris said thoughtfully.

"Perhaps he simply wants to make the gesture toward a Lady chapel, and get the credit for trying, while blaming his failure on someone else."

"Perhaps," Caris said doubtfully.

In Merthin's mind there was a more important question. "But what is he really after?"

"Everything Philemon does is driven by the need to make himself feel important," Caris said confidently. "My guess is he's after a promotion."

"What job could he have in mind? The archbishop of Monmouth seems to be dying, but surely Philemon can't hope for that position?"

"He must know something we don't."

Before they could say any more, Lolla walked in.

Merthin's first reaction was a feeling of relief so powerful that it brought tears to his eyes. She was back, and she was safe. He looked her up and down. She had no apparent injuries, she walked with a spring in her step, and her face showed only the usual expression of moody discontent.

Caris spoke first. "You're back!" she said. "I'm so glad!"

"Are you?" Lolla said. She often pretended to believe that Caris did not like her. Merthin was not fooled, but Caris could be thrown into doubt, for she was sensitive about not being Lolla's mother.

"We're both glad," Merthin said. "You gave us a scare."

"Why?" said Lolla. She hung her cloak on a hook and sat at the table. "I was perfectly all right."

"But we didn't know that, so we were terribly worried."

"You shouldn't be," Lolla said. "I can take care of myself."

Merthin suppressed an angry retort. "I'm not sure you can," he said as mildly as possible.

Caris stepped in to try to lower the temperature. "Where did you go?" she asked. "You've been away for two weeks."

"Different places."

Merthin said tightly: "Can you give us one or two examples?"

"Mudeford Crossing. Casterham. Outhenby."

"And what have you been doing?"

"Is this the catechism?" she said petulantly. "Do I have to answer all these questions?"

Caris put a restraining hand on Merthin's arm and said to Lolla: "We just want to know that you haven't been in danger."

Merthin said: "I'd also like to know who you've been traveling with."

"Nobody special."

"Does that mean Jake Riley?"

She shrugged and looked embarrassed. "Yes," she said, as if it were a trivial detail.

Merthin had been ready to forgive and embrace her, but she was making that difficult. Trying to keep his voice neutral, he said: "What sleeping arrangements did you and Jake have?"

"That's my business!" she cried.

"No, it's not!" he shouted back. "It's mine, too, and your stepmother's. If you're pregnant, who will care for your baby? Are you confident that Jake is ready to settle down and be a husband and father? Have you talked to him about that?"

"Don't speak to me!" she yelled. Then she burst into tears and stomped up the stairs.

Merthin said: "Sometimes I wish we lived in one room—then she wouldn't be able to pull that trick."

"You weren't very gentle with her," Caris said with mild disapproval.

"What am I supposed to do?" Merthin said. "She talks as if she's done nothing wrong!"

"She knows the truth, though. That's why she's crying."

"Oh, hell," he said.

There was a knock, and a novice monk put his head around the door. "Pardon me for disturbing you, Alderman," he said. "Sir Gregory Longfellow is at the priory, and would be grateful for a word with you, as soon as is convenient."

"Damn," said Merthin. "Tell him I'll be there in a few minutes."

"Thank you," the novice said, and left.

Merthin said to Caris: "Perhaps it's just as well to give her time to cool off."

"You, too," Caris said.

"You're not taking her side, are you?" he said with a touch of irritation.

She smiled and touched his arm. "I'm on your side, always," she said. "But I remember what it was like to be a sixteen-year-old girl. She's as worried as you are about her relationship with Jake. But she's not admitting it, even to herself, because that would wound her pride. So she resents you for speaking the truth. She has constructed a fragile defense around her self-esteem, and you just tear it down."

"What should I do?"

"Help her build a better fence."

"I don't know what that means."

"You'll figure it out."

"I'd better go and see Sir Gregory." Merthin stood up.

Caris put her arms around him and kissed him on the lips. "You're a good man doing your best, and I love you with all my heart," she said.

That took the edge off his frustration, and he felt himself calm down as he strode across the bridge and up the main street to the priory. He did not like Gregory. The man was sly and unprincipled, willing to do anything for his master the king, just as Philemon had been when he served Godwyn as prior. Merthin wondered uneasily what Gregory wanted to discuss with him. It was probably taxes—always the king's worry.

Merthin went first to the prior's palace where Philemon, looking pleased with himself, told him that Sir Gregory was to be found in the monks' cloisters to the south of the cathedral. Merthin wondered what Gregory had done to win himself the privilege of holding audience there.

The lawyer was getting old. His hair was white, and his tall figure was stooped. Deep lines had appeared like brackets either side of that sneering nose, and one of the blue eyes was cloudy. But the other eye saw sharply enough, and he recognized Merthin instantly, though they had not met for ten years. "Alderman," he said. "The archbishop of Monmouth is dead."

"Rest his soul," Merthin said automatically.

"Amen. The king asked me, as I was passing through his borough of Kingsbridge, to give you his greetings, and tell you this important news."

"I'm grateful. The death is not unexpected. The archbishop has been ill." The king certainly had not asked Gregory to meet with Merthin purely to give him interesting information, he thought suspiciously.

"You're an intriguing man, if you don't mind my saying so," Gregory said expansively. "I first met your wife more than twenty years ago. Since then I've seen the two of you slowly but surely take control of this town. And you've got everything you set your hearts on: the bridge, the hospital, the borough charter, and each other. You're determined, and you're patient."

It was condescending, but Merthin was surprised to detect a grain of respect in Gregory's flattery. He told himself to remain mistrustful: men such as Gregory praised only for a purpose.

"I'm on my way to see the monks of Abergavenny, who must vote for a new archbishop." Gregory leaned back in his chair. "When Christianity first came to England, hundreds of years ago, monks elected their own superiors." Explaining was an old man's habit, Merthin reflected: the young Gregory would not have bothered. "Nowadays, of course, bishops and archbishops are too important and powerful to be chosen by small groups of pious idealists living detached from the world. The king makes his choice, and His Holiness the Pope ratifies the royal decision."

Even I know it's not that simple, Merthin thought. There's usually some kind of power struggle. But he said nothing.

Gregory continued: "However, the ritual of the monks' election still goes on, and it is easier to control it than to abolish it. Hence my journey."

"So you're going to tell the monks whom to elect," Merthin said.

"To put it bluntly, yes."

"And what name will you give them?"

"Didn't I say? It's your bishop, Henri of Mons. Excellent man: loyal, trustworthy, never makes trouble."

"Oh, dear."

"You're not pleased?" Gregory's relaxed air evaporated, and he became keenly attentive.

Merthin realized that this was what Gregory had come for: to find out how the people of Kingsbridge—as represented by Merthin—would feel about what he was planning, and whether they would oppose him. He collected his thoughts. The prospect of a new bishop threatened the spire and the hospital. "Henri is the key to the balance of power in this town," he said. "Ten years ago, a kind of armistice was agreed between the merchants, the monks, and the hospital. As a result, all three have prospered mightily." Appealing to Gregory's interest—and the king's—he added: "That prosperity is of course what enables us to pay such high taxes."

Gregory acknowledged this with a dip of his head.

"The departure of Henri obviously puts into question the stability of our relationships."

"It depends on who replaces him, I should have thought."

"Indeed," said Merthin. Now we come to the crux, he thought. He said: "Have you got anyone in mind?"

"The obvious candidate is Prior Philemon."

"No!" Merthin was aghast. "Philemon! Why?"

"He's a sound conservative, which is important to the church hierarchy in these times of skepticism and heresy."

"Of course. Now I understand why he preached a sermon against dissection. And why he wants to build a Lady chapel." I should have foreseen this, Merthin thought

"And he has let it be known that he has no problem with taxation of the clergy—a constant source of friction between the king and some of his bishops."

"Philemon has been planning this for some time." Merthin was angry with himself for letting it sneak up on him.

"Since the archbishop fell ill, I imagine."

"This is a catastrophe."

"Why do you say that?"

"Philemon is quarrelsome and vengeful. If he becomes bishop he will create constant strife in Kingsbridge. We have to prevent him." He looked Gregory in the eye. "Why did you come here to forewarn me?" As soon as he had asked the question, the answer came to him. "You don't want Philemon either. You didn't need me to tell you what a troublemaker he is—you knew already. But you can't just veto him, because he has already won support among senior clergy." Gregory just smiled enigmatically—which Merthin took to mean he was right. "So what do you want me to do?"

"If I were you," Gregory said, "I'd start by finding another candidate to put up as the alternative to Philemon."

So that was it. Merthin nodded pensively. "I'll have to think about this," he said.

"Please do." Gregory stood up, and Merthin realized the meeting was over. "And let me know what you decide," Gregory added.

Merthin left the priory and walked back to Leper Island, musing. Who could he propose as bishop of Kingsbridge? The townspeople had always got on well with Archdeacon Lloyd, but he was too old—they might succeed in getting him elected only to have to do the whole thing again in a year's time.

He had not thought of anyone by the time he got home. He found Caris in the parlor and was about to ask her when she preempted him. Standing up, with a pale face and a frightened expression, she said: "Lolla's gone again."

86

The priests said Sunday was a day of rest, but it had never been so for Gwenda. Today, after church in the morning and then dinner, she was working with Wulfric in the garden behind their house. It was a good garden, half an acre with a hen house, a pear tree, and a barn. In the vegetable patch at the far end, Wulfric was digging furrows and Gwenda sowing peas.

The boys had gone to another village for a football game, their usual recreation on Sundays. Football was the peasant equivalent of the nobility's tournaments: a mock battle in which the injuries were sometimes real. Gwenda just prayed her sons would come home intact.

Today Sam returned early. "The ball burst," he said grumpily.

"Where's Davey?" Gwenda asked.

"He wasn't there."

"I thought he was with you."

"No, he quite often goes off on his own."

"I didn't know that." Gwenda frowned. "Where does he go?"

Sam shrugged. "He doesn't tell me."

Perhaps he was seeing a girl, Gwenda thought. Davey was close about all sorts of things. If it was a girl, who was she? There were not many eligible girls in Wigleigh. The survivors of the plague had remarried quickly, as if eager to repopulate the land; and those born since were too young. Perhaps he was meeting someone from the next village, at a rendezvous in the forest. Such assignations were as common as heartache.

When Davey came home, a couple of hours later, Gwenda confronted him. He made no attempt to deny that he had been sneaking off. "I'll show you what I've been doing, if you like," he said. "I can't keep it secret forever. Come with me."

They all went, Gwenda, Wulfric, and Sam. The Sabbath was observed to the extent that no one worked in the fields, and the Hundredacre was deserted as the four of them walked across it in a blustery spring breeze. A few strips looked neglected: there were still villagers who had more land than they could cope with. Annet was one such—she had only her eighteen-year-old daughter Amabel to help her, unless she could hire labor, which was still difficult. Her strip of oats was getting weedy.

Davey led them half a mile into the forest and stopped at a clearing off the beaten track. "This is it," he said.

For a moment Gwenda did not know what he was talking about. She was standing on the edge of a nondescript patch of ground with low bushes growing between the trees. Then she looked again at the bushes. They were a species she had never seen before. It had a squarish stem with pointed leaves growing in clusters of four. The way it had covered the ground made her think it was a creeping plant. A pile of uprooted vegetation at one side showed that Davey had been weeding. "What is it?" she said.

"It's called madder. I bought the seeds from a sailor that time we went to Melcombe."

"Melcombe?" Gwenda said. "That was three years ago."

"That's how long it's taken." Davey smiled. "At first I was afraid it wouldn't grow at all. He told me it needed sandy soil and would tolerate light shade. I dug over the clearing and planted the seeds, but the first year I got only three or four feeble plants. I thought I'd wasted my money. Then, the second year, the roots spread underground and sent up shoots, and this year it's all over the place."

Gwenda was astonished that her child could have kept this from her for so long. "But what use is madder?" she said. "Does it taste good?"

Davey laughed. "No, it's not edible. You dig up the roots, dry them, and grind them to a powder that makes a red dye. It's very costly. Madge Webber in Kingsbridge pays seven shillings for a gallon."

That was an astonishing price, Gwenda reflected. Wheat, the most expensive grain, sold for about seven shillings a quarter, and a quarter was sixty-four gallons. "This is sixty-four times as precious as wheat!" she said.

Davey smiled. "That's why I planted it."

"Why you planted what?" said a new voice. They all turned to see Nathan Reeve, standing beside a hawthorn tree as bent and twisted as he was. He wore a triumphant grin: he had caught them red-handed.

Davey was quick with an answer. "This is a medicinal herb called . . . hagwort," he said. Gwenda could tell he was improvising, but Nate would not be sure. "It's good for my mother's wheezy chest."

Nate looked at Gwenda. "I didn't know she had a wheezy chest."

"In the winter," Gwenda said.

"A herb?" Nate said skeptically. "There's enough here to dose all Kingsbridge. And you've been weeding it, to get more."

"I like to do things properly," Davey said.

It was a feeble response, and Nate ignored it. "This is an unauthorized crop," he said. "First of all, serfs need permission for what they plant—they can't go raising anything they like. That would lead to total chaos. Secondly, they can't cultivate the lord's forest, even by planting herbs."

None of them had any answer to that. Those were the rules. It was frustrating: often peasants knew they could make money by growing nonstandard crops that were in demand and fetched high prices: hemp for rope, flax for expensive underclothing, or cherries to delight rich ladies. But many lords and their bailiffs refused permission, out of instinctive conservatism.

Nate's expression was venomous. "One son a runaway and a murderer," he said. "The other defies his lord. What a family."

He was entitled to feel angry, Gwenda thought. Sam had killed Jonno and got away with it. Nate would undoubtedly hate her family to his dying day.

Nate bent down and roughly pulled a plant out of the ground. "This will come before the manor court," he said with satisfaction; and he turned and limped away through the trees.

Gwenda and her family followed. Davey was undaunted. "Nate will impose a fine, and I'll pay it," he said. "I'll still make money."

"What if he orders the crop destroyed?" Gwenda said.

"How?"

"It could be burned, or trampled."

Wulfric put in: "Nate wouldn't do that. The village wouldn't stand for it. A fine is the traditional way to deal with this."

Gwenda said: "I just worry about what Earl Ralph will say."

Davey made a deprecatory gesture with his hand. "No reason why the earl should find out about a little thing like this."

"Ralph takes a special interest in our family."

"Yes, he does," Davey said thoughtfully. "I still don't understand what made him pardon Sam."

The boy was not stupid. Gwenda said: "Perhaps Lady Philippa persuaded him."

Sam said: "She remembers you, Mother. She told me that when I was at Merthin's house."

"I must have done something to endear myself to her," Gwenda said, extemporizing. "Or it could be that she just felt compassion, one mother for another." It was not much of a story, but Gwenda did not have a better one.

In the days since Sam had been released they had had several conversations about what might account for Ralph's pardon. Gwenda just pretended to be as perplexed as everyone else. Fortunately Wulfric had never been the suspicious type.

They reached their house. Wulfric looked at the sky, said there was another good hour of light left, and went into the garden to finish sowing peas. Sam volunteered to help him. Gwenda sat down to mend a rip in Wulfric's hose. Davey sat opposite Gwenda and said: "I've got another secret to tell you."

She smiled. She did not mind him having a secret if he told his mother. "Go on."

"I have fallen in love."

"That's wonderful!" She leaned forward and kissed his cheek. "I'm very happy for you. What's she like?"

"She's beautiful."

Gwenda had been speculating, before she found out about the madder, that Davey might be meeting a girl from another village. Her intuition had been right. "I had a feeling about this," she said.

"Did you?" He seemed anxious.

"Don't worry, there's nothing wrong. It just occurred to me that you might be meeting someone."

"We go to the clearing where I'm growing the madder. That's sort of where it started."

"And how long has this been going on?"

"More than a year."

"It's serious, then."

"I want to marry her."

"I'm so pleased." She looked fondly at him. "You're still only twenty, but that's old enough if you've found the right person."

"I'm glad you think so."

"What village is she from?"

"This one, Wigleigh."

"Oh?" Gwenda was surprised. She had not been able to think of a likely girl here. "Who is she?"

"Mother, it's Amabel."

"No!"

"Don't shout."

"Not Annet's daughter!"

"You're not to be angry."

"Not to be angry!" Gwenda struggled to calm herself. She was as shocked as if she had been slapped. She took several deep breaths. "Listen to me," she said. "We have been at odds with that family for more than twenty years. That cow Annet broke your father's heart and never left him alone afterwards."

"I'm sorry, but that's all in the past."

"It's not—Annet still flirts with your father every chance she gets!"

"That's your problem, not ours."

Gwenda stood up, her sewing falling from her lap. "How can you do this to me? That bitch would be part of our family! My grandchildren would be her grandchildren. She'd be in and out of this house all the time, making a fool of your father with her coquettish ways and then laughing at me."

"I'm not going to marry Annet."

"Amabel will be just as bad. Look at her—she's just like her mother!"

"She's not, actually—"

"You can't do this! I absolutely forbid it!"

"You can't forbid it, Mother."

"Oh, yes I can—you're too young."

"That won't last forever."

Wulfric's voice came from the doorway. "What's all the shouting?"

"Davey says he wants to marry Annet's daughter—but I won't permit it." Gwenda's voice rose to a shriek. "Never! Never! Never!"

Earl Ralph surprised Nathan Reeve when he said he wanted to look at Davey's strange crop. Nate mentioned the matter in passing, on a routine visit to Earlscastle. A bit of unlicensed cultivation in the forest was a trivial breach of the rules, regularly dealt with by a fine. Nate was a shallow man, interested in bribes and commissions, and he had little conception of the depth of Ralph's obsession with Gwenda's family: his hatred of Wulfric, his lust for Gwenda, and now the likelihood that he was Sam's real father. So Nate was startled when Ralph said he would inspect the crop next time he was in the neighborhood.

Ralph rode with Alan Fernhill from Earlscastle to Wigleigh on a fine day between Easter and Whitsun. When they reached the small timber manor house, there was the old housekeeper, Vira, bent and gray now but still hanging on. They ordered her to prepare their dinner, then found Nate and followed him into the forest.

Ralph recognized the plant. He was no farmer, but he knew the difference between one bush and another, and on his travels with the army he had observed many crops that did not grow naturally in England. He leaned down from his saddle and pulled up a handful. "This is called madder," he said. "I've seen it in Flanders. It's grown for the red dye that has the same name."

Nate said: "He told me it was a herb called hagwort, used to cure a wheezy chest."

"I believe it does have medicinal properties, but that's not why people cultivate it. What will his fine be?"

"A shilling would be the usual amount."

"It's not enough."

Nate looked nervous. "So much trouble is caused, lord, when these customs are flouted. I would rather not—"

"Never mind," Ralph said. He kicked his horse and trotted through the middle of the clearing, trampling the bushes. "Come on, Alan," he said. Alan imitated him, and the two of them cantered around in tight circles, flattening the growth. After a few minutes all the shrubs were destroyed.

Ralph could see that Nate was shocked by the waste, even though the planting was illegal. Peasants never liked to see crops despoiled. Ralph had learned in France that the best way of demoralizing the population was to burn the harvest in the fields.

"That will do," he said, quickly getting bored. He was irritated by Davey's insolence in planting this crop, but that was not the main reason he had come to Wigleigh. The truth was that he wanted to see Sam again.

As they rode back to the village, he scanned the fields, looking for a tall young man with thick dark hair. Sam would stand out, because of his height, among these stunted serfs hunched over their spades. He saw him, at a distance, in Brookfield. He reined in and peered across the windy landscape at the twenty-two-year-old son he had never known.

Sam and the man he thought was his father—Wulfric—were plowing with a horse-drawn light plow. Something was wrong for they kept stopping and adjusting the harness. When they were together, it was easy to see the differences between them. Wulfric's hair was tawny, Sam's dark; Wulfric was barrel-chested, oxlike, where Sam was broad-shouldered but lean, like a horse; Wulfric's movements were slow and careful, but Sam was quick and graceful.

It was the oddest feeling to look at a stranger and think: my son. Ralph believed himself immune to womanish emotions. If he had been subject to feelings of compassion or regret, he could not have lived as he had. But the discovery of Sam threatened to unman him.

He tore himself away and cantered back to the village; then he succumbed again to curiosity and sentiment, and sent Nate to find Sam and bring him to the manor house.

He was not sure what he intended to do with the boy: talk to him, tease him, invite him to join them for dinner, or what. He might have foreseen that Gwenda would not leave him free to choose. She showed up with Nate and Sam, and Wulfric and Davey followed them in. "What do you want with my son?" she demanded, speaking to Ralph as if he were an equal rather than her overlord.

Ralph spoke without forethought. "Sam was not born to be a serf tilling the fields," he said. He saw Alan Fernhill look at him in surprise.

Gwenda looked puzzled. "Only God knows what we are born for," she said, playing for time.

"When I want to know about God, I'll ask a priest, not you," Ralph said to her. "Your son has something of the mettle of a fighting man. I don't need to pray to see that—it's obvious to me, as it would be to any veteran of the wars."

"Well, he's not a fighting man, he's a peasant, and the son of a peasant, and his destiny is to grow crops and raise livestock like his father."

"Never mind his father." Ralph remembered what Gwenda had said to him in the sheriff's castle at Shiring, when she had persuaded him to pardon Sam. "Sam has the killer instinct," he said. "It's dangerous in a peasant, but priceless in a soldier."

Gwenda looked scared as she began to divine Ralph's purpose. "What are you getting at?"

Ralph realized where this chain of logic was leading him. "Let Sam be useful, rather than dangerous. Let him learn the arts of war."

"Ridiculous, he's too old."

"He's twenty-two. It's late, but he's fit and strong. He can do it."

"I don't see how."

Gwenda was pretending to find practical objections, but he could see through her simulation, and knew that she hated the idea with all her heart. That made him all the more determined. With a smile of triumph he said: "Easily enough. He can be a squire. He can come and live at Earlscastle."

Gwenda looked as if she had been stabbed. Her eyes closed for a moment, and her olive-skinned face paled. She mouthed the word "No," but no sound came out.

"He's been with you for twenty-two years," Ralph said. "That's long enough." Now it's my turn, he thought, but instead he said: "Now he's a man."

Because Gwenda was temporarily silent, Wulfric spoke up. "We won't permit it," he said. "We are his parents, and we do not consent to this."

"I didn't ask for your consent," Ralph said contemptuously. "I'm your earl, and you are my serfs. I don't request, I command."

Nate Reeve put in: "Besides, Sam is over the age of twenty-one, so the decision is his, not his father's."

Suddenly they all turned and looked at Sam.

Ralph was not sure what to expect. Becoming a squire was something many young men of all classes dreamed about, but he did not know whether Sam was one of them. Life in the castle was luxurious and exciting, by comparison with breaking your back in the fields; but, on the other hand, men-at-arms died young, or—worse than that—came home crippled, to live the rest of their miserable days begging outside taverns.

However, as soon as Ralph saw Sam's face he knew the truth. Sam was smiling broadly, and his eyes gleamed with eagerness. He could hardly wait to go.

Gwenda found her voice. "Don't do it, Sam!" she said. "Don't be tempted. Don't let your mother see you blinded by an arrow, or mutilated by the swords of French knights, or crippled by the hooves of their warhorses!"

Wulfric said: "Don't go, son. Stay in Wigleigh and live a long life."

Sam began to look doubtful.

Ralph said: "All right, lad. You've listened to your mother, and to the peasant father who raised you. But the decision is yours. What will you do? Live out your life here in Wigleigh, tilling the fields alongside your brother? Or escape?"

Sam paused only for a moment. He looked guiltily at Wulfric and Gwenda, then turned to Ralph. "I'll do it," he said. "I'll be a squire, and thank you, my lord!"

"Good lad," Ralph said.

Gwenda began to cry. Wulfric put his arm around her. Looking up at Ralph, he said: "When shall he go?"

"Today," Ralph said. "He can ride back to Earlscastle with me and Alan after dinner."

"Not so soon!" Gwenda cried.

No one took any notice of her.

Ralph said to Sam: "Go home and fetch anything you want to bring with you. Have dinner with your mother. Come back and wait for me in the stables. Meanwhile, Nate can requisition a mount to carry you to Earlscastle." He turned away, having finished with Sam and his family. "Now, where's my dinner?"

Wulfric and Gwenda went out with Sam, but Davey stayed behind. Had he already found out that that his crop had been trampled? Or was it something else? "What do you want?" Ralph said.

"Lord, I have a boon to ask."

This was almost too good to be true. The insolent peasant who had planted madder in the woods without permission was now a supplicant. What a satisfying day this was turning out to be. "You can't be a squire, you've got your mother's build," Ralph told him, and Alan laughed.

"I want to marry Amabel, the daughter of Annet," said the young man.

"That won't please your mother."

"I will be of age in less than a year."

Ralph knew all about Annet, of course. He had nearly been hanged for her sake. His history was entwined with hers almost as much as with Gwenda's. He recalled that all her family had died in the plague. "Annet still has some of the lands her father held."

"Yes, lord, and she is willing for them to be transferred to me when I marry her daughter."

Such a request would not normally have been refused, although all lords would charge a tax, called an entry fee, on the transfer. However, there was no obligation on a lord to consent. The right of lords to refuse such requests on a whim, and blight the course of a serf's life, was one of the peasants' greatest gripes. But it provided the ruler with a means of discipline that could be extraordinarily effective.

"No," said Ralph. "I will not transfer the land to you." He grinned. "You and your bride can eat madder."

87

Caris had to prevent Philemon becoming bishop. This was his boldest move yet, but he had made his preparations carefully, and he had a chance. If he succeeded, he would have control of the hospital again, giving him the power to destroy her life's work. But he could do worse than that. He would revive the blind orthodoxy of the past. He would appoint hard-hearted priests like himself in the villages, close schools for girls, and preach sermons against dancing.

She had no say in the choice of a bishop, but there were ways to exert pressure.

She began with Bishop Henri.

She and Merthin traveled to Shiring to see the bishop in his palace. On the way, Merthin stared at every dark-haired girl that came into view, and when there was no one he scanned the woods at the side of the road. He was looking for Lolla, but they reached Shiring without seeing any sign of her.

The bishop's palace was on the main square, opposite the church and beside the Wool Exchange. It was not a market day, so the square was clear but for the scaffold that stood there permanently, a stark warning to villains of what the people of the county did to those who broke the law.

The palace was an unpretentious stone building with a hall and chapel on the ground floor and a series of offices and private apartments upstairs. Bishop Henri had imposed upon the place a style that Caris thought was probably French. Each room looked like a painting. The place was not decorated extravagantly, like Philemon's palace in Kingsbridge, where the profusion of rugs and jewels suggested a robber's cave. However, there was something pleasantly artful about everything in Henri's house: a silver candlestick placed to catch the light from a window; the polished gleam of an ancient oak table; spring flowers in the cold fireplace; a small tapestry of David and Jonathan on the wall.

Bishop Henri was not an enemy, but he was not quite an ally either, Caris thought nervously as they waited for him in the hall. He would probably say that he tried to rise above Kingsbridge quarrels. She, more cynically, thought that whatever decision he had to make, he remained unshakably focused on his own interests. He disliked Philemon, but he might not allow that to affect his judgment.

Henri came in followed, as always, by Canon Claude. The two of them did not seem to age. Henri was a little older than Caris, and Claude perhaps ten years younger, but they both looked like boys. Caris had noticed that clergy often aged well, better than aristocrats. She suspected it was because most priests—with some notorious exceptions—led lives of moderation. Their regime of fasting obliged them to eat fish and vegetables on Fridays and saints' days and all through Lent, and in theory they were never allowed to get drunk. By contrast, noblemen and their wives indulged in orgies of meat-eating and heroic wine-drinking. That might be why their faces became lined, their skin flaky, and their bodies bent, while clerics stayed fit and spry later into their quiet, austere lives.

Merthin congratulated Henri on having been nominated archbishop of Monmouth, then got straight to the point. "Prior Philemon has stopped work on the tower."

Henri said with studied neutrality: "Any reason?"

"There's a pretext, and a reason," Merthin said. "The pretext is a fault in the design."

"And what is the alleged fault?"

"He says an octagonal spire can't be built without formwork. It is generally true, but I've found a way around it."

"Which is . . . ?"

"Rather simple. I will build a round spire, which will need no formwork, then give its exterior a cladding of thin stones and mortar in the shape of an octagon. Visually, it will be an octagonal spire, but structurally it will be a cone."

"Have you told Philemon this?"

"No. If I do, he'll find another pretext."

"What is his real reason?"

"He wants to build a Lady chapel instead."

"Ah."

"It's part of a campaign to ingratiate himself with senior clergy. He preached a sermon against dissection when Archdeacon Reginald was there. And he has told the king's advisors that he will not campaign against taxation of the clergy."

"What is he up to?"

"He wants to be bishop of Shiring."

Henri raised his eyebrows. "Philemon always had nerve, I'll give him that."

Claude spoke for the first time. "How do you know?"

"Gregory Longfellow told me."

Claude looked at Henri and said: "Gregory would know if anyone does."

Caris could tell that Henri and Claude had not anticipated that Philemon would be so ambitious. To make sure they did not overlook the significance of the revelation, she said: "If Philemon gets his wish, you as archbishop of Monmouth will have endless work adjudicating disputes between Bishop Philemon and the townspeople of Kingsbridge. You know how much friction there has been in the past."

Claude said: "We certainly do."

"I'm glad we're in agreement," Merthin said.

Thinking aloud, Claude said: "We must put forward an alternative candidate."

That was what Caris had hoped he would say. "We have someone in mind," she said.

Claude said: "Who?"

"You."

There was a silence. Caris could tell that Claude liked the idea. She guessed he might be quietly envious of Henri's promotion, and wondering whether it was his destiny always to be a kind of assistant to Henri. He could easily cope with the post of bishop. He knew the diocese well and handled most of the practical administration already.

However, both men were now surely thinking about their personal lives. She had no doubt they were all but husband and wife: she had seen them kissing. But they were decades past the first flush of romance, and her intuition told her they could tolerate a part-time separation.

She said: "You would still be working together a good deal."

Claude said: "The archbishop will have many reasons to visit Kingsbridge and Shiring."

Henri said: "And the bishop of Kingsbridge will need to come to Monmouth often."

Claude said: "It would be a great honor to be bishop." With a twinkle in his eye he added: "Especially under you, archbishop."

Henri looked away, pretending not to notice the double meaning. "I think it's a splendid idea," he said.

Merthin said: "The Kingsbridge guild will back Claude—I can guarantee that. But you, Archbishop Henri, will have to put the suggestion to the king."

"Of course."

Caris said: "If I may make one suggestion?"

"Please."

"Find another post for Philemon. Propose him as, I don't know, archdeacon of Lincoln. Something he would like, but that would take him many miles from here."

"That's a sound idea," Henri said. "If he's up for two posts, it weakens his case for either one. I'll keep my ear to the ground."

Claude stood up. "This is all very exciting," he said. "Will you have dinner with us?"

A servant came in and addressed Caris. "There's someone asking for you, mistress," the man said. "It's only a boy, but he seems distressed."

Henri said: "Let him come in."

A boy of about thirteen appeared. He was dirty, but his clothes were not cheap, and Caris guessed he came from a family that was comfortably off but suffering some kind of crisis. "Will you come to my house, Mother Caris?"

"I'm not a nun anymore, child, but what's the problem?"

The boy spoke fast. "My father and mother are ill and so is my brother, and my mother heard someone say you were at the bishop's palace and said to fetch you, and she knows you help the poor but she can pay, but will you please come, please?"

This type of request was not unusual, and Caris carried a leather case of medical supplies with her wherever she went. "Of course I'll come, lad," she said. "What's your name?"

"Giles Spicers, Mother, and I'm to wait and bring you."

"All right." Caris turned to the bishop. "Go ahead with your dinner, please. I'll join you as soon as I can." She picked up her case and followed the boy out.

Shiring owed its existence to the sheriff's castle on the hill, just as Kingsbridge did to the priory. Near the market square were the grand houses of the leading citizens, the wool merchants and sheriff's deputies and royal officials such as the coroner. A little farther out were the homes of moderately prosperous traders and craftsmen, goldsmiths and tailors and apothecaries. Giles's father was a dealer in spices, as his name indicated, and Giles led Caris to a street in this neighborhood. Like most houses of this class, it had a stone-built ground floor that served as warehouse and shop, and flimsier timber living quarters above. Today the shop was closed and locked. Giles led Caris up the outside staircase.

She smelled the familiar odor of sickness as soon as she walked in. Then she hesitated. There was something special about the smell, something that struck a chord in her memory that for some reason made her feel very frightened.

Rather than ponder it, she walked through the living room into the bedroom, and there she found the dreadful answer.

Three people lay on mattresses around the room: a woman of her own age, a slightly older man, and an adolescent boy. The man was farthest gone in sickness. He lay moaning and sweating in a fever. The open neck of his shirt showed that he had a rash of purple-black spots on his chest and throat. There was blood on his lips and nostrils.

He had the plague.

"It's come back," said Caris. "God help me."

For a moment fear paralyzed her. She stood motionless, staring at the scene, feeling powerless. She had always known, in theory, that the plague might return—that was half the reason she had written her book—but even so she was not prepared for the shock of once again seeing that rash, that fever, that nosebleed.

The woman lifted herself on one elbow. She was not so far gone: she had the rash and the fever, but did not appear to be bleeding. "Give me something to drink, for the love of God," she said.

Giles picked up a jug of wine, and at last Caris's mind started to work and her body unfroze. "Don't give her wine—it will make her thirstier," she said. "I saw a barrel of ale in the other room—draw her a cup of that."

The woman focused on Caris. "You're the prioress, aren't you?" she said. Caris did not correct her. "People say you're a saint. Can you make my family well?"

"I'll try, but I'm not a saint, just a woman who has observed people in sickness and health." Caris took from her bag a strip of linen and tied it over her mouth and nose. She had not seen a case of the plague for ten years, but she had got into the habit of taking this precaution whenever she dealt with patients whose illness might be catching. She moistened a clean rag with rose water and bathed the woman's face. As always, the action soothed the patient.

Giles came back with a cup of ale, and the woman drank. Caris said to him: "Let them have as much to drink as they want, but give them ale or watered wine."

She moved to the father, who did not have long to live. He was not speaking coherently and his eyes failed to focus on Caris. She bathed his face, cleaning the dried blood from around his nose and mouth. Finally she attended to Giles's elder brother. He had only recently succumbed, and was still sneezing, but he was old enough to realize how seriously ill he was, and he looked terrified.

When she had finished, she said to Giles: "Try to keep them comfortable and give them drinks. There's nothing else you can do. Do you have any relations? Uncles or cousins?"

"They're all in Wales."

She made a mental note to warn Bishop Henri that he might need to make arrangements for an orphan boy.

"Mother said to pay you," the boy said.

"I haven't done much for you," Caris said. "You can pay me sixpence."

There was a leather purse beside his mother's bed. He took out six silver pennies.

The woman raised herself again. Speaking more calmly now, she said: "What's wrong with us?"

"I'm sorry," said Caris. "It's the plague."

The woman nodded fatalistically. "That's what I was afraid of."

"Don't you recognize the symptoms from last time?"

"We were living in a small town in Wales—we escaped it. Are we all going to die?"

Caris did not believe in deceiving people about such important questions. "A few people survive it," she said. "Not many, though."

"May God have mercy on us, then," said the woman.

Caris said: "Amen."

All the way back to Kingsbridge, Caris brooded on the plague. It would spread, of course, just as fast as last time. It would kill thousands. The prospect filled her with rage. It was like the senseless carnage of war, except that war was caused by men, and the plague was not. What was she going to do? She could not sit back and watch as the events of thirteen years ago were cruelly repeated.

There was no cure for the plague, but she had discovered ways to slow its murderous progress. As her horse jogged the well-worn road through the forest, she thought over what she knew about the illness and how to combat it. Merthin was quiet, recognizing her mood, probably guessing accurately what she was thinking about.

When they got home, she explained to him what she wanted to do.

"There will be opposition," he warned. "Your plan is drastic. Those who did not lose family and friends last time may imagine they are invulnerable, and say you're overreacting."

"That's where you can help me," she said.

"In that case, I recommend we divide up the potential objectors and deal with them separately."

"All right."

"You have three groups to win over: the guild, the monks, and the nuns. Let's start with the guild. I'll call a meeting—and I won't invite Philemon."

Nowadays the guild met in the Cloth Exchange, a large new stone building on the main street. It enabled traders to do business even in bad weather. It had been paid for by profits from Kingsbridge Scarlet.

But before the guild convened, Caris and Merthin met individually with the leading members, to win their support in advance, a technique Merthin had developed long ago. His motto was: "Never call a meeting until the result is a foregone conclusion."

Caris herself went to see Madge Webber.

Madge had married again. Much to everyone's amusement, she had enchanted a villager as handsome as her first husband and fifteen years her junior. His name was Anselm, and he seemed to adore her, though she was as plump as ever and covered her gray hair with a selection of exotic caps. Even more surprising, in her forties she had conceived again and given birth to a healthy baby girl, Selma, now eight years old and attending the nuns' school. Motherhood had never kept Madge from doing business, and she continued to dominate the market in Kingsbridge Scarlet, with Anselm as her lieutenant.

Her home was still the large house on the main street that she and Mark had moved into when she first began to profit from weaving and dyeing. Caris found her and Anselm taking delivery of a consignment of red cloth, trying to find room for it in the overcrowded storeroom on the ground floor. "I'm stocking up for the Fleece Fair," Madge explained.

Caris waited while she checked the delivery, then they went upstairs, leaving Anselm in charge of the shop. As Caris entered the living room she was vividly reminded of the day, thirteen years ago, when she had been summoned here to see Mark—the first Kingsbridge victim of the plague. She suddenly felt depressed.

Madge noticed her expression. "What is it?" she said.

You could not hide things from women the way you could from men. "I walked in here thirteen years ago because Mark was ill," Caris said.

Madge nodded. "That was the beginning of the worst time of my life," she said in her matter-of-fact voice. "That day, I had a wonderful husband and four healthy children. Three months later I was a childless widow with nothing to live for."

"Days of grief," Caris said.

Madge went to the sideboard, where there were cups and a jug, but instead of offering Caris a drink she stood staring at the wall. "Shall I tell you something strange?" she said. "After they died, I couldn't say Amen to the paternoster." She swallowed, and her voice went quieter. "I know what the Latin means, you see. My father taught me. *Fiat voluntas tua:* 'Thy will be done.' I couldn't say that. God had taken my family, and that was sufficient torture—I would not acquiesce in it." Tears came to her eyes as she remembered. "I didn't want God's will to prevail, I wanted my children back. 'Thy will be done.' I knew I'd go to Hell, but still I couldn't say Amen."

Caris said: "The plague has come back."

Madge staggered, and clutched the sideboard for support. Her solid figure suddenly looked frail, and as the confidence went from her face she appeared old. "No," she said.

Caris pulled a bench forward and held Madge's arm while she sat on it. "I'm sorry to shock you," she said.

"No," Madge said again. "It can't come back. I can't lose Anselm and Selma. I can't bear it. I can't bear it." She looked so white and drawn that Caris began to fear she might suffer some kind of attack.

Caris poured wine from the jug into a cup. She gave it to Madge, who drank it automatically. A little of her color came back.

"We understand it better now," Caris said. "Perhaps we can fight it."

"Fight it? How can we do that?"

"That's what I've come to tell you. Are you feeling a little better?"

Madge met Caris's eye at last. "Fight it," she said. "Of course that's what we must do. Tell me how."

"We have to close the city. Shut the gates, man the walls, prevent anyone coming in."

"But the city has to eat."

"People will bring supplies to Leper Island. Merthin will act as middleman, and pay them—he contracted the plague last time and survived, and no one has ever got it twice. Traders will leave their goods on the bridge. Then, when they have gone, people will come out from the city and get the food."

"Could people leave the city?"

"Yes, but they couldn't come back."

"What about the Fleece Fair?"

"That may be the hardest part," Caris said. "It must be canceled."

"But Kingsbridge merchants will lose hundreds of pounds!"

"It's better than dying."

"If we do as you say, will we avoid the plague? Will my family survive?"

Caris hesitated, resisting the temptation to tell a reassuring lie. "I can't promise," she said. "The plague may already have reached us. There may be someone right now dying alone in a hovel near the waterfront, with nobody to get help. So I fear we may not escape entirely. But I believe my plan gives you the best chance of still having Anselm and Selma by your side at Christmas."

"Then we'll do it," Madge said decisively.

"Your support is crucial," Caris said. "Frankly, you will lose more money than anyone else from the cancellation of the fair. For that reason, people are more likely to believe you. I need you to say how serious it is."

"Don't worry," said Madge. "I'll tell them."

ᔕ

"A very sound idea," said Prior Philemon.

Merthin was surprised. He could not remember a time when Philemon had agreed readily with a proposal of the guild's. "Then you will support it," he said, to make sure he had heard aright.

"Yes, indeed," said the prior. He was eating a bowl of raisins, stuffing handfuls into his mouth as fast as he could chew them. He did not offer Merthin any. "Of course," he said, "it wouldn't apply to monks."

Merthin sighed. He might have known better. "On the contrary, it applies to everyone," he said.

"No, no," said Philemon, in the tone of one who instructs a child. "The guild has no power to restrict the movements of monks."

Merthin noticed a cat at Philemon's feet. It was fat, like him, with a mean face. It looked just like Godwyn's cat, Archbishop, though that creature must be long dead. Perhaps it was a descendant. Merthin said: "The guild has the power to close the city gates."

"But we have the right to come and go as we please. We're not subject to the authority of the guild—that would be ridiculous."

"All the same, the guild controls the city, and we have decided that no one can enter while the plague is rife."

"You cannot make rules for the priory."

"But I can for the city, and the priory happens to be in the city."

"Are you telling me that if I leave Kingsbridge today, you will refuse me admission tomorrow?"

Merthin was not sure. It would be highly embarrassing, at a minimum, to have the prior of Kingsbridge standing outside the gate demanding admission. He had been hoping to persuade Philemon to accept the restriction. He did not want to put the resolve of the guild to the test quite so dramatically. However, he tried to make his answer sound confident. "Absolutely."

"I shall complain to the bishop."

"Tell him he can't enter Kingsbridge."

The personnel of the nunnery had hardly changed in ten years, Caris realized. Nunneries were like that, of course: you were supposed to stay forever. Mother Joan was still prioress, and Sister Oonagh ran the hospital under the supervision of Brother Sime. Few people came here for medical care now: most preferred Caris's hospital on the island. Those patients Sime did have, devoutly religious for the most part, were cared for in the old hospital, next to the kitchens, while the new building was used for guests.

Caris sat down with Joan, Oonagh, and Sime in the old pharmacy, now used as the prioress's private office, and explained her plan. "People outside the walls of the old city who fall victim to the plague will be admitted to my hospital on the island," she said. "While the plague lasts, the nuns and I will stay within the building night and day. Nobody will leave, except those lucky few who recover."

Joan asked: "What about here in the old city?"

"If the plague gets into the city despite our precautions, there may be too many victims for the accommodation you have. The guild has ruled that plague victims and their families will be confined to their homes. The rule applies to anyone who lives in a house struck by plague: parents, children, grandparents, servants, apprentices. Anyone caught leaving such a house will be hanged."

"It's very harsh," Joan said. "But if it prevents the awful slaughter of the last plague, it's worthwhile."

"I knew you'd see that."

Sime was saying nothing. The news of the plague seemed to have deflated his arrogance.

Oonagh said: "How will the victims eat, if they're imprisoned in their homes?"

"Neighbors can leave food on the doorstep. No one may go in—except monk-physicians and nuns. They will visit the sick, but they must have no contact with the healthy. They will go from the priory to the home, and from the home back to the priory, without entering any other building or even speaking to anyone on the street. They should wear masks at all times, and wash their hands in vinegar each time they touch a patient."

Sime was looking terrified. "Will that protect us?" he said.

"To some degree," Caris said. "Not completely."

"But then it will be highly dangerous for us to attend the sick!"

Oonagh answered him. "We have no fear," she said. "We look forward to death. For us, it is the longed-for reunion with Christ."

"Yes, of course," said Sime.

The next day, all the monks left Kingsbridge.

88

Gwenda felt murderously angry when she saw what Ralph had done to Davey's madder plants. Wanton destruction of crops was a sin. There should be a special place in Hell for noblemen who despoiled what peasants had sweated to grow.

But Davey was not dismayed. "I don't think it matters," he said. "The value is in the roots, and he hasn't touched them."

"That would have been too much like work," Gwenda said sourly, but she cheered up.

In fact the shrubs recovered remarkably quickly. Ralph probably did not know that madder propagated underground. Throughout May and June, as reports began to reach Wigleigh of an outbreak of the plague, the roots sent up new shoots, and at the beginning of July, Davey decided it was time to harvest the crop. One Sunday Gwenda, Wulfric, and Davey spent the afternoon digging up the roots. They would first loosen the soil around the plant, then pull it out of the ground, then strip its foliage, leaving the root attached to a short stem. It was back-aching work of the kind Gwenda had done all her life.

They left half the plantation untouched, in the hope that it would regenerate itself next year.

They pulled a handcart piled with madder roots back through the woods to Wigleigh, then unloaded the roots into the barn and spread them in the hayloft to dry.

Davey did not know when he would be able to sell his crop. Kingsbridge was a closed city. The people still bought supplies, of course, but only through brokers. Davey was doing something new, and he would need to explain the situation to his buyer. It would be awkward to do that through an intermediary. But perhaps he would have to try. He had to dry the roots first, then grind them to a powder, and that would take time anyway.

Davey had said no more about Amabel, but Gwenda felt sure he was still seeing the girl. He pretended to be cheerfully resigned to his fate. If he had really given her up, he would have moped resentfully.

All Gwenda could do was hope he would get over her before he was old enough to marry without permission. She still could hardly bear even to think of her family being joined to Annet's. Annet had never ceased to humiliate her by flirting with Wulfric, who continued to grin foolishly at every stupid coquettish remark. Now that Annet was in her forties, with broken veins in her rosy cheeks and gray streaks among her fair ringlets, her behavior was not just embarrassing but grotesque; yet Wulfric reacted as if she were still a girl.

And now, Gwenda thought, my son has fallen into the same trap. It made her want to spit. Amabel looked just like Annet twenty-five years ago, a pretty face with flyaway curls, a long neck and narrow white shoulders, and small breasts like the eggs that mother and daughter sold at markets. She had the same way of tossing her hair, the same trick of looking at a man with mock reproach and hitting his chest with the back of her hand in a gesture that pretended to be a smack but was in fact a caress.

However, Davey was at least physically safe and well. Gwenda was more worried about Sam, living now with Earl Ralph at the castle, learning to be a fighting man. In church she prayed he would not be injured hunting, or learning to use a sword, or fighting in a tournament. She had seen him every day for twenty-two years, then suddenly he had been taken from her. It's hard to be a woman, she thought. You love your baby with all your heart and soul, and then one day he just leaves.

For several weeks she looked for an excuse to travel to Earlscastle and check on Sam. Then she heard that the plague had struck there, and that decided her. She would go before the harvest got under way. Wulfric would not go with her: he had too much to do on the land. Anyway, she had no fear of traveling alone. "Too poor to be robbed, too old to be raped," she joked. The truth was that she was too tough for either. And she carried a long knife.

She walked across the drawbridge at Earlscastle on a hot July day. On the battlements of the gatehouse a rook stood like a sentry, the sun glinting off its glossy black feathers. It cawed a warning at her. It sounded like: "Go, go!" She had escaped the plague once, of course; but that might have been luck: she was risking her life by coming here.

The scene in the lower compound was normal, if a little quiet. A woodcutter was unloading a cart full of firewood outside the bakehouse, and a groom was unsaddling a dusty horse in front of the stables, but there was no great bustle of activity. She noticed a small group of men and women outside the west entrance of the little church, and crossed the baked-earth ground to investigate. "Plague victims inside," a maidservant said in answer to her inquiry.

She stepped through the door, feeling dread like a cold lump in her heart.

Ten or twelve straw mattresses were lined up on the floor so that the occupants could face the altar, just as in a hospital. About half the patients seemed to be children. There were three grown men. Gwenda scanned their faces fearfully.

None of them was Sam.

She knelt down and said a prayer of thanks.

Outside, she approached the woman she had spoken to earlier. "I'm looking for Sam from Wigleigh," she said. "He's a new squire."

The woman pointed to the bridge leading to the inner compound. "Try the keep."

Gwenda took the route indicated. A sentry at the bridge ignored her. She climbed the steps to the keep.

The great hall was dark and cool. A big dog slept on the cold stones of the fireplace. There were benches around the walls and a pair of large armchairs at the far end of the room. Gwenda noticed that there were no cushions, no upholstered seats, and no wall hangings. She deduced that Lady Philippa spent little time here and took no interest in the furnishings.

Sam was sitting near a window with three younger men. The parts of a suit of armor were laid out on the floor in front of them, arranged in order from faceplate to greaves. Each of the men was cleaning a piece. Sam was rubbing the breastplate with a smooth pebble, trying to remove rust.

She stood watching him for a moment. He wore new clothes in the red-and-black livery of the earl of Shiring. The colors suited his dark good looks. He seemed to be at ease, talking in a desultory way with the others while they all worked. He appeared healthy and well fed. It was what Gwenda had hoped for, but all the same she suffered a perverse pang of disappointment that he was doing so well without her.

He glanced up and saw her. His face registered surprise, then pleasure, then amusement. "Lads," he said, "I am the oldest among you, and you may think I'm capable of looking after myself, but it's not so. My mother follows me everywhere to make sure I'm all right."

They saw her and laughed. Sam put down his work and came over. Mother and son sat on a bench in a corner near the staircase that led to the upstairs rooms. "I'm having a wonderful time," Sam said. "Everyone plays games here most days. We go hunting and hawking, we have wrestling matches and contests of horsemanship, and we play football. I've learned so much! It's a bit embarrassing to be grouped with these adolescents all the time, but I can put up with that. I just have to master the skill of using a sword and shield while riding a horse at the same time."

He was already speaking differently, she noticed. He was losing the slow rhythms of village speech. And he used French words for "hawking" and "horsemanship." He was becoming assimilated into the life of the nobility.

"What about the work?" she said. "It can't be all play."

"Yes, there's plenty of work." He gestured at the others cleaning the armor. "But it's easy by comparison with plowing and harrowing."

He asked about his brother, and she told him all the news from home: Davey's madder had regenerated, they had dug up the roots, Davey was still involved with Amabel, no one had fallen sick of the plague yet. While they were talking, she began to feel that she was being watched, and she knew her feeling was not fanciful. After a moment, she looked over her shoulder.

Earl Ralph was standing at the top of the staircase in front of an open door, evidently having stepped out of his room. She wondered how long he had been looking at her. She met his gaze. His stare was intense, but she could not read it, did not understand what it meant. She began to feel the look was uncomfortably intimate, and she glanced away.

When she looked back, he had gone.

The next day, when she was on the road and halfway home, a horseman came up behind her, riding fast, then slowed down and stopped.

Her hand went to the long dagger in her belt.

The rider was Sir Alan Fernhill. "The earl wants to see you," he said.

"Then he had better come himself, instead of sending you," she replied.

"You've always got a smart answer, haven't you? Do you imagine it endears you to your superiors?"

He had a point. She was taken aback, perhaps because in all the years he had been Ralph's sidekick she had never known Alan to say anything intelligent. If she was really smart she would suck up to people such as Alan, not poke fun at them. "All right," she said wearily. "The earl bids me to him. Must I walk all the way back to the castle?"

"No. He has a lodge in the forest, not far from here, where he sometimes stops for refreshment during a hunt. He's there now." He pointed into the woods beside the road.

Gwenda did not much like this but, as a serf, she had no right to decline a summons from her earl. Anyway, if she did refuse she felt sure Alan would knock her down and tie her up and carry her there. "Very well," she said.

"Jump up on the saddle in front of me, if you like."

"No, thanks, I'd rather walk."

At this time of year the undergrowth was thick. Gwenda followed the horse into the woods, taking advantage of the path it trampled through the nettles and ferns. The road behind them swiftly disappeared into the greenery. Gwenda wondered nervously what whim had caused Ralph to arrange this forest meeting. It could not be good news for her or her family, she felt.

They walked a quarter of a mile and came to a low building with a thatched roof. Gwenda would have assumed it to be a verderer's cottage. Alan looped his reins around a sapling and led the way inside.

The place had about it the same bare, utilitarian look Gwenda had noted at Earlscastle. The floor was beaten earth, the walls unfinished wattle-and-daub, the ceiling nothing more than the underside of the thatch. The furniture was minimal: a table, some benches, and a plain wooden bedstead with a straw mattress. A door at the back stood half-open on a small kitchen where, presumably, Ralph's servants prepared food and drink for him and his fellow huntsmen.

Ralph was sitting at the table with a cup of wine. Gwenda stood in front of him, waiting. Alan leaned against the wall behind her. "So, Alan found you," Ralph said.

"Is there no one else here?" Gwenda said nervously.

"Just you, me, and Alan."

Gwenda's anxiety went up a notch. "Why do you want to see me?"

"To talk about Sam, of course."

"You've taken him from me. What else is there to say?"

"He's a good boy, you know . . . our son."

"Don't call him that." She looked at Alan. He showed no surprise: clearly he had been let in on the secret. She was dismayed. Wulfric must never find out. "Don't call him our son," she said. "You've never been a father to him. Wulfric raised him."

"How could I raise him? I didn't even know he was mine! But I'm making up for lost time. He's doing well, did he tell you?"

"Does he get into fights?"

"Of course. Squires are supposed to fight. It's practice for when they go to war. You should have asked whether he wins."

"It's not the life I wanted for him."

"It's the life he was made for."

"Did you bring me here to gloat?"

"Why don't you sit down?"

Reluctantly, she sat opposite him at the table. He poured wine into a cup and pushed it toward her. She ignored it.

He said: "Now that I know we have a son together, I think we should be more intimate."

"No, thank you."

"You're such a killjoy."

"Don't you talk to me about joy. You've been a blight on my life. With all my heart I wish I had never set eyes on you. I don't want to be intimate with you, I want to get away from you. If you went to Jerusalem it wouldn't be far enough."

His face darkened with anger, and she regretted the extravagance of her words. She recalled Alan's rebuke. She wished she could say no simply and calmly, without stinging witticisms. But Ralph aroused her ire like no one else.

"Can't you see?" she said, trying to be reasonable. "You have hated my husband for, what, a quarter of a century? He broke your nose and you slashed his cheek open. You disinherited him then you were forced to give him back his family's lands. You raped the woman he once loved. He ran away and you dragged him back with a rope around his neck. After all that, even having a son together cannot make you and me friends."

"I disagree," he said. "I think we can be not just friends, but lovers."

"No!" It was what she had feared, in the back of her mind, ever since Alan had reined in on the road in front of her.

Ralph smiled. "Why don't you take off your dress?"

She tensed.

Alan leaned over her from behind and slipped the long dagger out of her belt with a smooth motion. He had obviously premeditated the move, and it happened too quickly for her to react.

But Ralph said: "No, Alan—that won't be necessary. She'll do it willingly."

"I will not!" she said.

"Give her back the dagger, Alan."

Reluctantly, Alan reversed the knife, holding it by the blade, and offered it to her.

She snatched it and leaped to her feet. "You may kill me but I'll take one of you with me, by God," she said.

She backed away, holding the knife at arm's length, ready to fight.

Alan stepped toward the door, moving to cut her off.

"Leave her be," Ralph said. "She's not going anywhere."

She had no idea why Ralph was so confident, but he was dead wrong. She was getting out of this hut and then she was going to run away as fast as she could, and she would not stop until she dropped.

Alan stayed where he was.

Gwenda got to the door, reached behind her, and lifted the simple wooden latch.

Ralph said: "Wulfric doesn't know, does he?"

Gwenda froze. "Doesn't know what?"

"He doesn't know that I'm Sam's father."

Gwenda's voice fell to a whisper. "No, he doesn't."

"I wonder how he would feel if he found out."

"It would kill him," she said.

"That's what I thought."

"Please don't tell him," she begged.

"I won't . . . so long as you do as I say."

What could she do? She knew Ralph was drawn to her sexually. She had used that knowledge, in desperation, to get in to see him at the sheriff's castle. Their encounter at the Bell all those years ago, a vile memory to her, had lived in his recollection as a golden moment, probably much enhanced by the passage of time. And she had put into his head the idea of reliving that moment.

This was her own fault.

Could she somehow disabuse him? "We aren't the same people we were all those years ago," she said. "I will never be an innocent young girl again. You should go back to your serving wenches."

"I don't want serving girls, I want you."

"No," she said. "Please." She fought back tears.

He was implacable. "Take off your dress."

She sheathed her knife and unbuckled her belt.

89

The moment Merthin woke up, he thought of Lolla.

She had been missing now for three months. He had sent messages to the city authorities in Gloucester, Monmouth, Shaftesbury, Exeter, Winchester, and Salisbury. Letters from him, as alderman of one of the great cities of the land, were treated seriously, and he had received careful replies to them all. Only the mayor of London had been unhelpful, saying in effect that half the girls in the city had run away from their fathers, and it was no business of the mayor's to send them home.

Merthin had made personal inquiries in Shiring, Bristol, and Melcombe. He had spoken to the landlord of every tavern, giving them all a description of Lolla. They had all seen plenty of dark-haired young women, often in the company of handsome rogues called Jake, or Jack, or Jock; but none could say for sure that they had seen Merthin's daughter, or heard the name Lolla.

Some of Jake's friends had also vanished, along with a girlfriend or two, the other missing women all some years older than Lolla.

Lolla might be dead—Merthin knew that—but he refused to give up hope. It was unlikely she had caught the plague. The new outbreak was ravaging towns and villages, and taking away most of the children under ten. But survivors of the first wave, such as Lolla and himself, must have been people who for some reason had the strength to resist the illness, or—in a very few cases, such as his own—to recover from it; and they were not falling sick this time. However, the plague was only one of the hazards to a sixteen-year-old girl running away from home, and Merthin's fertile imagination tortured him, in the small hours of the night, with thoughts of what might have happened to her.

One town not ravaged by the plague was Kingsbridge. The illness had affected about one house in a hundred in the old town, as far as Merthin could tell from the conversations he held, shouted across the city gate, with Madge Webber, who was acting as alderman inside the city walls while Merthin managed affairs outside. The Kingsbridge suburbs, and other towns, were seeing something like one in five afflicted. But had Caris's methods overcome the plague, or merely delayed it? Would the illness persist, and eventually overcome the barriers she had put up? Would the devastation be as bad as last time in the end? They would not know until the outbreak had run its course—which might be months or years.

He sighed and got up out of his lonely bed. He had not seen Caris since the city was closed. She was living at the hospital, a few yards from Merthin's house, but she could not leave the building. People could go in but not come out. Caris had decided she would have no credibility unless she worked side by side with her nuns, so she was stuck.

Merthin had spent half his life separated from her, it seemed. But it did not get any easier. In fact he ached for her more now, in middle age, than he had as a youngster.

His housekeeper, Em, was up before him, and he found her in the kitchen, skinning rabbits. He ate a piece of bread and drank some weak beer, then went outside.

The main road across the island was already crowded with peasants and their carts bringing supplies. Merthin and a team of helpers spoke to each of them. Those bringing standard products with agreed prices were the simplest: Merthin sent them across the inner bridge to deposit their goods at the locked door of the gatehouse, then paid them when they came back empty. With those bringing seasonal produce such as fruits and vegetables he negotiated a price before allowing them to deliver. For some special consignments, a deal had been made days earlier, when he placed the order: hides for the leather trade; stones for the masons, who had recommenced building the spire under Bishop Henri's orders; silver for the jewelers; iron, steel, hemp, and timber for the city's manufacturers, who had to continue working even though they were temporarily cut off from most of their customers. Finally there were the one-off cargoes, for which Merthin would need to take instructions from someone in the city. Today brought a vendor of Italian brocade who wanted to sell it to one of the city's tailors; a year-old ox for the slaughterhouse; and Davey from Wigleigh.

Merthin listened to Davey's story with amazement and pleasure. He admired the lad for his enterprise in buying madder seeds and cultivating them to produce the costly dye. He was not surprised to learn that Ralph had tried to scuttle the project: Ralph was like most noblemen in his contempt for anything connected with manufacture or trade. But Davey had nerve as well as brains, and he had persisted. He had even paid a miller to grind the dried roots into powder.

"When the miller washed the grindstone afterward, his dog drank some of the water that ran off," Davey told Merthin. "The dog pissed red for a week, so we know the dye works!"

Now he was here with a handcart loaded with old four-gallon flour sacks full of what he believed to be precious madder dye.

Merthin told him to pick up one of the sacks and bring it to the gate.

When they got there, he called out to the sentry on the other side. The man climbed to the battlements and looked down. "This sack is for Madge Webber," Merthin shouted up. "Make sure she gets it personally, would you, sentry?"

"Very good, Alderman," said the sentry.

As always, a few plague victims from the villages were brought to the island by their relatives. Most people now knew there was no cure for the plague, and simply let their loved ones die, but a few were ignorant or optimistic enough to hope that Caris could work a miracle. The sick were left outside the hospital doors, like supplies at the city gate. The nuns came out for them at night when the relatives had gone. Now and again a lucky survivor emerged in good health, but most patients went out through the back door, and were buried in a new graveyard on the far side of the hospital building.

At midday Merthin invited Davey to dinner. Over rabbit pie and new peas, Davey confessed he was in love with the daughter of his mother's old enemy. "I don't know why Ma hates Annet, but it's all so long in the past, and it's nothing to do with me or Amabel," he said, with the indignation of youth against the irrationality of parents. When Merthin nodded sympathetically, Davey asked: "Did your parents stand in your way like this?"

Merthin thought for a moment. "Yes," he said. "I wanted to be a squire and spend my life as a knight fighting for the king. I was heartbroken when they apprenticed me to a carpenter. However, in my case it worked out quite well."

Davey was not pleased by this anecdote.

In the afternoon access to the inner bridge was closed off at the island end, and the gates of the city were opened. Teams of porters came out and picked up everything that had been left, and carried the supplies to their destinations in the city.

There was no message from Madge about the dye.

Merthin had a second visitor that day. Toward the end of the afternoon, as trading petered out, Canon Claude arrived.

Claude's friend and patron, Bishop Henri, was now installed as archbishop of Monmouth. However, his replacement as bishop of Kingsbridge had not been chosen. Claude wanted the position, and had been to London to see Sir Gregory Longfellow. He was on his way back to Monmouth, where he would continue to work as Henri's right-hand man for the moment.

"The king likes Philemon's line on taxation of the clergy," he said over cold rabbit pie and a goblet of Merthin's best Gascon wine. "And the senior clergy liked the sermon against dissection and the plan to build a Lady chapel. On the other hand, Gregory dislikes Philemon—says he can't be trusted. The upshot is, the king has postponed a decision by ruling that the monks of Kingsbridge cannot hold an election while they are in exile at St.-John-in-the-Forest."

Merthin said: "I assume the king sees little point in selecting a bishop while the plague rages and the city is closed."

Claude nodded agreement. "I did achieve something, albeit small," he went on. "There is a vacancy for an English ambassador to the pope. The appointee has to live in Avignon. I suggested Philemon. Gregory seemed intrigued by the idea. At least, he didn't rule it out."

"Good!" The thought of Philemon being sent so far away lifted Merthin's spirits. He wished there were something he could do to weigh in on Claude's side; but he had already written to Gregory pledging the support of the guild, and that was the limit of his influence.

"One more piece of news—sad news, in fact," Claude said. "On my way to London, I went to St.-John-in-the-Forest. Henri is still abbot, technically, and he sent me to reprimand Philemon for decamping without permission. Waste of time, really. Anyway, Philemon has adopted Caris's precautions, and would not let me in, but we talked through the door. So far, the monks have escaped the plague. But your old friend Brother Thomas has died of old age. I'm sorry."

"God rest his soul," Merthin said sadly. "He was very frail toward the end. His mind was going, too."

"The move to St. John probably didn't help him."

"Thomas encouraged me when I was a young builder."

"Strange how God sometimes takes the good men from us and leaves the bad."

Claude left early the next morning.

As Merthin was going through his daily routine, one of the carters came back from the city gate with a message. Madge Webber was on the battlements and wanted to talk to Merthin and Davey.

"Do you think she'll buy my madder?" Davey said as they walked across the inner bridge.

Merthin had no idea. "I hope so," he said.

They stood side by side in front of the closed gate and looked up. Madge leaned over the wall and shouted down: "Where did this stuff come from?"

"I grew it," Davey said.

"And who are you?"

"Davey from Wigleigh, son of Wulfric."

"Oh—Gwenda's boy?"

"Yes, the younger one."

"Well, I've tested your dye."

"It works, doesn't it?" Davey said eagerly.

"It's very weak. Did you grind the roots whole?"

"Yes—what else would I have done?"

"You're supposed to remove the hulls before grinding."

"I didn't know that." Davey was crestfallen. "Is the powder no good?"

"As I said, it's weak. I can't pay the price of pure dye."

Davey looked so dismayed that Merthin's heart went out to him.

Madge said: "How much have you got?"

"Nine more four-gallon sacks like the one you have," Davey said despondently.

"I'll give you half the usual price—three shillings and sixpence a gallon. That's fourteen shillings a sack, so exactly seven pounds for ten sacks."

Davey's face was a picture of delight. Merthin wished Caris were with him just to share it. "Seven pounds!" Davey repeated.

Thinking he was disappointed, Madge said: "I can't do better than that—the dye just isn't strong enough."

But seven pounds was a fortune to Davey. It was several years' wages for a laborer, even at today's rates. He looked at Merthin. "I'm rich!" he said.

Merthin laughed and said: "Don't spend it all at once."

The next day was Sunday. Merthin went to the morning service at the island's own little church of St. Elizabeth of Hungary, patron saint of healers. Then he went home and got a stout oak spade from his gardener's hut. With the spade over his shoulder, he walked across the outer bridge, through the suburbs, and into his past.

He tried hard to remember the route he had taken through the forest thirty-four years ago with Caris, Ralph, and Gwenda. It seemed impossible. There were no pathways other than deer runs. Saplings had become mature trees, and mighty oaks had been felled by the king's woodcutters. Nevertheless, to his surprise there were still recognizable landmarks: a spring gurgling up out of the ground where he remembered the ten-year-old Caris kneeling to drink; a huge rock that she said looked as if it must have fallen from Heaven; a steep-sided little valley with a boggy bottom where she had got mud in her boots.

As he walked, his recollection of that day of childhood became more vivid. He remembered how the dog, Hop, had followed them, and Gwenda had followed her dog. He felt again the pleasure of having Caris understand his joke. His face reddened at the recollection of how incompetent he had been, in front of Caris, with the bow he had made—and how easily his younger brother had mastered the weapon.

Most of all, he remembered Caris as a girl. They had been preadolescent, but nevertheless he had been bewitched by her quick wits, her daring, and the effortless way she had assumed command of the little group. It was not love, but it was a kind of fascination that was not unlike love.

Remembrance distracted him from pathfinding, and he lost his bearings. He began to feel as if he was in completely unfamiliar territory—then, suddenly, he emerged into a clearing and knew he was in the right place. The bushes were more extensive; the trunk of the oak tree was even broader; and the clearing in between was gay with a scatter of summer flowers, as it had not been on that November day in 1327. But he was in no doubt: it was like a face he had not seen for years, changed but unmistakable.

A shorter and skinnier Merthin had crawled under that bush to hide from the big man crashing through the undergrowth. He remembered how the exhausted, panting Thomas had stood with his back to that oak tree and drawn his sword and dagger.

He saw in his imagination the events of that day played out again. Two men in yellow-and-green livery had caught up with Thomas and asked him for a letter. Thomas had distracted the men by telling them they were being observed by someone hiding in a bush. Merthin had felt sure he and the other children would be murdered—then Ralph, just ten years old, had killed one of the men-at-arms, showing the quick and deadly reflexes that had served him so well, years later, in the French wars. Thomas had dispatched the other man, though not before receiving the wound that had ended in his losing his left arm—despite, or perhaps because of, the treatment given him in the hospital at Kingsbridge Priory. Then Merthin had helped Thomas bury the letter.

Just here, Thomas had said. *Right in front of the oak tree.*

There was a secret in the letter, Merthin knew now; a secret so potent that high-ranking people were frightened of it. The secret had given Thomas protection, though he had nevertheless sought sanctuary in a monastery and spent his life there.

If you hear that I've died, Thomas had said to the boy Merthin, *I'd like you to dig up this letter and give it to a priest.*

Merthin the man hefted his spade and began to dig.

He was not sure whether this was what Thomas had intended. The buried letter was a precaution against Thomas's being killed by violence, not dying of natural causes at the age of fifty-eight. Would he still have wanted the letter dug up? Merthin did not know. He would decide what to do when he had read the letter. He was irresistibly curious about what was in it.

His memory of where he had buried the bag was not perfect, and with his first try he missed the spot. He got down about eighteen inches and realized his mistake: the hole had been only about a foot deep, he was sure. He tried again a few inches to the left.

This time he got it right.

A foot down, the spade struck something that was not earth. It was soft, but unyielding. He put the spade to one side and scrabbled with his fingers in the hole. He felt a piece of ancient, rotting leather. Gently, he dislodged the earth and lifted the object. It was the wallet Thomas had worn on his belt all those years ago.

He wiped his muddy hands on his tunic and opened it.

Inside was a bag made of oiled wool, still intact. He loosened the drawstring of the bag and reached in. He pulled out a sheet of parchment, rolled into a scroll and sealed with wax.

He handled it gently, but all the same the wax crumbled as soon as he touched it. With careful fingertips he unrolled the parchment. It was intact: it had survived thirty-four years in the earth remarkably well.

He saw immediately that it was not an official document but a personal letter. He could tell by the handwriting, which was the painstaking scrawl of an educated nobleman, rather than the practised script of a clerk.

He began to read. The salutation ran:

From Edward, the second of that name, King of England, at Berkeley Castle; by the hand of his faithful servant, Sir Thomas Langley; to his beloved eldest son, Edward; royal greeting and fatherly love.

Merthin felt scared. This was a message from the old king to the new. The hand holding the document shook, and he looked up from it and scanned the greenery around him, as if there might be someone peering at him through the bushes.

My beloved son, you will soon hear that I am dead. Know that it is not true.

Merthin frowned. This was not what he had expected.

Your mother, the queen, the wife of my heart, has corrupted and subverted Roland, earl of Shiring, and his sons, who sent murderers here; but I was forewarned by Thomas, and the murderers were killed.

So Thomas had not been the assassin, after all, but the savior of the king.

Your mother, having failed to kill me once, would surely try again, for she and her adulterous consort cannot feel safe while I live. So I have changed clothes with one of the slain murderers, a man of my height and general appearance, and I have bribed several people to swear that the dead body is mine. Your mother will know the truth when she sees the body, but she will go along with the pretense; for if I am thought to be dead, I will be no threat to her, and no rebel or rival to the throne can claim my support.

Merthin was amazed. The nation had thought Edward II to be dead. All Europe had been fooled.

But what had happened to him afterward?

I will not tell you where I plan to go, but know that I intend to leave my kingdom of England and never return. However, I pray that I will again see you, my son, before I die.

Why had Thomas buried this letter instead of delivering it? Because he had feared for his own life, and had seen the letter as a powerful weapon in his defense. Once Queen Isabella had committed herself to the pretense of her husband's death, she had needed to deal with those few people who knew the truth. Merthin now recalled that while he was still an adolescent, the earl of Kent had been convicted of treason and beheaded for maintaining that Edward II was still alive.

Queen Isabella had sent men to kill Thomas, and they had caught up with him just outside Kingsbridge. But Thomas had disposed of them, with the help of the ten-year-old Ralph. Afterward, Thomas must have threatened to expose the whole deception—and he had proof, in the form of the old king's letter. That evening, as he lay in the hospital at Kingsbridge Priory, Thomas had negotiated with the queen, or more likely with Earl Roland and his sons as her agents. He had promised to keep the secret, on condition that he was accepted as a monk. He would feel safe in the monastery—and, in case the queen should be tempted to renege, he had said that the letter was in a safe place and would be revealed on his death. The queen therefore needed to keep him alive.

Old Prior Anthony had known something of this, and as he lay dying had told Mother Cecilia, who on her own deathbed had repeated part of the story to Caris. People might keep secrets for decades, Merthin reflected, but they felt compelled to tell the truth when death was near. Caris had also seen the incriminating document that gave Lynn Grange to the priory on condition Thomas was accepted as a monk. Merthin now understood why Caris's disingenuous inquiries about this document had caused such trouble. Sir Gregory Longfellow had persuaded Ralph to break into the monastery and steal all the nuns' charters in the hope of finding the incriminating letter.

Had the destructive power of this sheet of vellum been lessened by the passage of time? Isabella had lived a long life, but she had died three years ago. Edward II himself was almost certainly dead—if alive, he would be seventy-seven now. Would Edward III fear the revelation that his father had remained alive when the world thought him dead? He was too strong a king now to be seriously threatened, but he would face great embarrassment and humiliation.

So what was Merthin to do?

He remained where he was, on the grassy floor of the forest among the wildflowers, for a long time. At last he rolled up the scroll, replaced it in the bag, and put the bag back in the old leather pouch.

He put the pouch back into the ground and filled up the hole. He also filled in his first, erroneous hole. He smoothed the earth on top of both. He stripped some leaves off the bushes and scattered them in front of the oak tree. He stood back and looked at his work. He was satisfied: the excavations were no longer visible to the casual glance.

Then he turned his back on the clearing and went home.

90

At the end of August, Earl Ralph made a tour of his landholdings around Shiring, accompanied by his long-term sidekick, Sir Alan Fernhill, and his newfound son, Sam. He enjoyed having Sam along, his child yet a grown man. His other sons, Gerry and Roley, were too young for this sort of thing. Sam did not know about his paternity, but Ralph nursed the secret with pleasure.

They were horrified by what they saw as they went around. Hundreds of Ralph's serfs were dead or dying, and the corn was standing unharvested in the fields. As they rode from one place to the next, Ralph's anger and frustration grew. His sarcastic remarks cowed his companions, and his bad temper turned his horse skittish.

In each village, as well as the serfs' landholdings, some acres were kept exclusively for the earl's personal use. They should have been cultivated by his employees and by serfs who were obliged to work for him one day a week. These lands were in the worst state of all. Many of his employees had died; so had some of the serfs who owed him labor; other serfs had negotiated more favorable tenancies after the last plague, so that they no longer had to work for the lord; and, finally, it was impossible to find laborers for hire.

When Ralph came to Wigleigh, he went around the back of the manor house and looked into the big timber barn, which at this time of year should have been filling with grain ready for milling—but it was empty, and a cat had given birth to a litter of kittens in the hayloft.

"What will we do for bread?" he roared at Nathan Reeve. "With no barley to make ale, what will we drink? You'd better have a plan, by God."

Nate looked churlish. "All we can do is reallocate the strips," he said.

Ralph was surprised by his surliness. Nate was usually sycophantic. Then Nate glared at young Sam, and Ralph realized why the worm had turned. Nate hated Sam for killing Jonno, his son. Instead of punishing Sam, Ralph had first pardoned him, then made him a squire. No wonder Nate looked resentful.

Ralph said: "There must be one or two young men in the village who could farm some extra acres."

"Ah, yes, but they aren't willing to pay an entry fee," Nate said.

"They want land for nothing?"

"Yes. They can see that you have too much land and not enough labor, and they know when they're in a strong bargaining position." In the past Nate had been quick to abuse uppity peasants, but now he seemed to be enjoying Ralph's dilemma.

"They act as if England belongs to them, not to the nobility," Ralph said angrily.

"It is disgraceful, lord," said Nate more politely, and a sly look came over his face. "For example, Wulfric's son Davey wants to marry Amabel and take over her mother's land. It would make sense: Annet has never been able to manage her holding."

Sam spoke up. "My parents won't pay the entry fee—they're against the marriage."

Nate said: "Davey could pay it himself, though."

Ralph was surprised. "How?"

"He sold that new crop he grew in the forest."

"Madder. Obviously we didn't do a sufficiently thorough job of trampling it. How much did he get?"

"No one knows. But Gwenda has bought a young milking cow, and Wulfric has a new knife . . . and Amabel wore a yellow scarf to church on Sunday."

And Nate had been offered a fat bribe, Ralph guessed. "I hate to reward Davey's disobedience," he said. "But I'm desperate. Let him have the land."

"You would have to give him special permission to marry against his parents' will."

Davey had asked Ralph for this, and Ralph had turned him down, but that was before the plague decimated the peasantry. He did not like to revisit such decisions. However, it was a small price to pay. "I shall give him permission," he said.

"Very well."

"But let's go and see him. I'd like to make the offer in person."

Nate was startled, but of course made no objection.

The truth was that Ralph wanted to see Gwenda again. There was something about her that made his throat go dry. His last encounter with her, in the little hunting lodge, had not satisfied him for long. He had thought about her often in the weeks since then. He got little satisfaction nowadays from the kind of women he normally lay with: young prostitutes, tavern wenches, and maidservants. They all pretended to be delighted by his advances, though he knew they just wanted the present of money that came afterward. Gwenda, by contrast, made no secret of the fact that she loathed him and shuddered at his touch; and that pleased him, paradoxically, because it was honest and therefore real. After their meeting in the hunting lodge he had given her a purse of silver pennies, and she had thrown it back at him so hard that it had bruised his chest.

"They're in Brookfield today, turning their reaped barley," Nate said. "I'll take you there."

Ralph and his men followed Nate out of the village and along the bank of the stream at the edge of the great field. Wigleigh was always windy, but today the summer breeze was soft and warm, like Gwenda's breasts.

Some of the strips of land here had been reaped, but in others Ralph despaired to see overripe oats, barley rank with weeds, and one patch of rye that had been reaped but not bundled, so that the crop lay scattered on the ground.

A year ago he had thought that all his financial troubles were over. He had come home from the most recent French war with a captive, the Marquis de Neuchatel, and had negotiated a ransom of fifty thousand pounds. But the marquis's family had not been able to raise the money. Something similar had happened to the French king, Jean II, captured by the prince of Wales at the battle of Poitiers. King Jean had stayed in London for four years, technically a prisoner, though living in comfort at the Savoy, the new palace built by the duke of Lancaster. The king's ransom had been reduced, but still it had not been paid in full. Ralph had sent Alan Fernhill to Neuchatel to renegotiate his prisoner's ransom, and Alan had reduced the price to twenty thousand, but again the family had failed to pay it. Then the marquis had died of the plague, so Ralph was insolvent again, and had to worry about the harvest.

It was midday. The peasants were having their dinner at the side of the field. Gwenda, Wulfric, and Davey were sitting on the ground under a tree eating cold pork with raw onions. They all jumped to their feet when the horses came near. Ralph went over to Gwenda's family and waved the rest away.

Gwenda wore a loose green dress that hid her shape. Her hair was tied back, making her face more ratlike. Her hands were dirty, with earth under the nails. But, when Ralph looked at her, in his imagination he saw her naked, ready, waiting for him with an expression of resigned disgust at what he was about to do; and he felt aroused.

He looked away from her to her husband. Wulfric stared back at him with a level gaze, neither defiant nor cowed. There was a little gray now in his tawny beard, but still it would not grow over the scar of the sword cut Ralph had given him. "Wulfric, your son wants to marry Amabel and take over Annet's land."

Gwenda responded. She had never learned to speak only when spoken to. "You've stolen one son from me—will you take the other now?" she said bitterly.

Ralph ignored her. "Who will pay the heriot?"

Nate put in: "It's thirty shillings."

Wulfric said: "I haven't got thirty shillings."

Davey said calmly: "I can pay it."

He must have done very well out of his madder crop, Ralph thought, to be so cool about such a large sum of money. "Good," he said. "In that case—"

Davey interrupted him. "But on what terms are you offering it?"

Ralph felt his face redden. "What do you mean?"

Nate intervened again. "The same terms as those upon which Annet holds the land, of course."

Davey said: "Then I thank the earl, but I will not accept his gracious offer."

Ralph said: "What the devil are you talking about?"

"I would like to take over the land, my lord, but only as a free tenant, paying cash rent, without customary dues."

Sir Alan said threateningly: "Do you dare to haggle with the earl of Shiring, you insolent young dog?"

Davey was scared but defiant. "I've no wish to offend, lord. But I want to be free to grow whatever crop I can sell. I don't want to cultivate what Nate Reeve chooses, regardless of market prices."

Davey had inherited that streak of stubborn determination from Gwenda, Ralph thought. He said angrily: "Nate expresses my wishes! Do you think you know better than your earl?"

"Forgive me, lord, but you neither till the soil nor go to market."

Alan's hand went to the hilt of his sword. Ralph saw Wulfric glance at his scythe, lying on the ground, its sharp blade gleaming in the sunlight. On Ralph's other side, young Sam's horse skittered nervously, picking up its rider's tension. If it came to a fight, Ralph thought, would Sam fight for his lord, or for his family?

Ralph did not want a fight. He wanted to get the harvest in, and killing his peasants would make that harder. He restrained Alan with a gesture. "This is how the plague undermines morality," he said disgustedly. "I will give you what you want, Davey, because I must."

Davey swallowed drily and said: "In writing, lord?"

"You're demanding a copyhold, too?"

Davey nodded, too frightened to speak.

"Do you doubt the word of your earl?"

"No, lord."

"Then why demand a written lease?"

"For the avoidance of doubt in future years."

They all said that when they asked for a copyhold. What they meant was that if the lease was written down the landlord could not easily alter the terms. It was yet another encroachment on time-honored traditions. Ralph did not want to make a further concession—but, once again, he had no option if he wanted to get the harvest in.

And then he thought of a way he could use this situation to gain something else he wanted, and he cheered up.

"All right," he said. "I'll give you a written lease. But I don't want men leaving the fields during the harvest. Your mother can come to Earlscastle to collect the document next week."

Gwenda walked to Earlscastle on a baking hot day. She knew what Ralph wanted her for, and the prospect made her miserable. As she crossed the drawbridge into the castle, the rooks seemed to laugh derisively at her plight.

The sun beat down mercilessly on the compound, where the walls blocked the breeze. The squires were playing a game outside the stables. Sam was among them, and too absorbed to notice Gwenda.

They had tied a cat to a post at eye level in such a way that it could move its head and legs. A squire had to kill the cat with his hands tied behind his back. Gwenda had seen the game before. The only way for the squire to achieve his object was to head-butt the wretched animal, but the cat naturally defended itself by scratching and biting the attacker's face. The challenger, a boy of about sixteen, was hovering near the post, watched by the terrified cat. Suddenly the boy jerked his head. His forehead smashed into the cat's chest, but the animal lashed out with its clawed paws. The squire yelped with pain and jumped back, his cheeks streaming blood, and all the other squires roared with laughter. Enraged, the challenger rushed at the post and butted the cat again. He was scratched worse, and he hurt his head, which they found even funnier. The third time he was more careful. Getting close, he feinted, making the cat lash out at thin air; then he delivered a carefully aimed strike right at the beast's head. Blood poured from its mouth and nostrils, and it slumped unconscious, though still breathing. He butted it a final time to kill it, and the others cheered and clapped.

Gwenda felt sickened. She did not much like cats—she preferred dogs—but it was unpleasant to see any helpless creature tormented. She supposed that boys had to do this sort of thing to prepare them for maiming and killing human beings in war. Did it have to be that way?

She moved on without speaking to her son. Perspiring, she crossed the second bridge and climbed the steps to the keep. The great hall was mercifully cool.

She was glad Sam had not seen her. She was hoping to avoid him as long as possible. She did not want him to suspect that anything was wrong. He was not notably sensitive, but he might detect his mother's distress.

She told the marshal of the hall why she was here, and he promised to let the earl know. "Is Lady Philippa in residence?" Gwenda asked hopefully. Perhaps Ralph would be inhibited by the presence of his wife.

But the marshal shook his head. "She's at Monmouth, with her daughter."

Gwenda nodded grimly and settled down to wait. She could not help thinking about her encounter with Ralph at the hunting lodge. When she looked at the unadorned gray wall of the great hall she saw him, staring at her as she undressed, his mouth slightly open in anticipation. As much as the intimacy of sex was a joy with the man she loved, so much was it loathsome with one she hated.

The first time Ralph had coerced her, more than twenty years ago, her body had betrayed her, and she had felt a physical pleasure, even while experiencing a spiritual revulsion. The same thing had happened with Alwyn the outlaw in the forest. But it had not occurred this time with Ralph in the hunting lodge. She attributed the change to age. When she had been a young girl, full of desire, the physical act had triggered an automatic response—something she could not help, although it had made her even more ashamed. Now in her maturity her body was not so vulnerable, the reflex not so ready. She could at least be grateful for that.

The stairs at the far end of the hall led to the earl's chamber. Men were going up and down constantly: knights, servants, tenants, bailiffs. After an hour, the marshal told her to go up.

She was afraid Ralph would want sex there and then, but she was relieved to find that he was having a business day. With him were Sir Alan and two priest-clerks sitting at a table with writing materials. One of the clerks handed her a small vellum scroll.

She did not look at it. She could not read.

"There," said Ralph. "Now your son is a free tenant. Isn't that what you always wanted?"

She had wanted freedom for herself, as Ralph knew. She had never achieved it—but Ralph was right, Davey had. That meant that her life had not been completely without purpose. Her grandchildren would be free and independent, growing what crops they chose, paying their rent and keeping for themselves everything else they earned. They would never know the miserable existence of poverty and hunger that Gwenda had been born to.

Was that worth all she had been through? She did not know.

She took the scroll and went to the door.

Alan came after her and spoke in a low voice as she was going out. "Stay here tonight, in the hall," he said. The great hall was where most of the castle's residents slept. "Tomorrow, be at the hunting lodge two hours after midday."

She tried to leave without replying.

Alan barred her way with his arm. "Understand?" he said.

"Yes," she said in a low voice. "I will be there in the afternoon."

He let her go.

She did not speak to Sam until late in the evening. The squires spent the whole afternoon at various violent games. She was glad to have the time to herself. She sat in the cool hall alone with her thoughts. She tried to tell herself that it was nothing for her to have sexual congress with Ralph. She was no virgin, after all. She had been married for twenty years. She had had sex thousands of times. It would all be over in a few minutes, and it would leave no scars. She would do it and forget it.

Until the next time.

That was the worst of it. He could go on coercing her indefinitely. His threat to reveal the secret of Sam's paternity would terrify her as long as Wulfric was alive.

Surely Ralph would tire of her soon, and go back to the firm young bodies of his tavern wenches?

"What's the matter with you?" Sam said when at dusk the squires came in for supper.

"Nothing," she said quickly. "Davey's bought me a milking cow."

Sam looked a bit envious. He was enjoying life, but squires were not paid. They had little need of money—they were provided with food, drink, accommodation, and clothing—but, all the same, a young man liked to have a few pennies in his wallet.

They talked about Davey's forthcoming wedding. "You and Annet are going to be grandmothers together," Sam said. "You'll have to make your peace with her."

"Don't be stupid," Gwenda snapped. "You don't know what you're talking about."

Ralph and Alan emerged from the chamber when supper was served. All the residents and visitors assembled in the hall. The kitchen staff brought in three large pike baked with herbs. Gwenda sat near the foot of the table, well away from Ralph, and he took no notice of her.

After dinner she lay down to sleep in the straw on the floor beside Sam. It was a comfort to her to lie next to him, as she had when he was little. She remembered listening to his childish breathing, soft and contented, in the silence of the night. Drifting off, she thought about how children grew up to defy their parents' expectations. Her own father had wanted to treat her like a commodity to be traded, but she had angrily refused to be used that way. Now each of her sons was taking his own road through life, and in both cases it was not the one she had planned. Sam would be a knight, and Davey was going to marry Annet's daughter. If we knew how they would turn out, she thought, would we be so eager to have them?

She dreamed that she went to Ralph's hunting lodge and found that he was not there, but there was a cat on his bed. She knew she had to kill the cat, but she had her hands tied behind her back, so she butted it with her head until it died.

When she woke up she wondered if she could kill Ralph at the lodge.

She had killed Alwyn, all those years ago, sticking his own knife into his throat and pushing it up into his head until its point had come out through his eye. She had killed Sim Chapman, too, holding his head under the water while he wriggled and thrashed, keeping him there until he breathed the river into his lungs and died. If Ralph went to the hunting lodge alone, she might be able to kill him, if she chose her moment well.

But he would not be on his own. Earls never went anywhere alone. He would have Alan with him, as he had before. It was unusual for him to travel with only one companion. It was unlikely he would have none.

Could she kill them both? No one else knew she was going to meet them there. If she killed them and simply walked on home she would not even be suspected. No one knew of her motive—it was a secret, that was the whole point. Someone might realize she had been near the lodge at the time, but they would only ask her whether she had seen any suspicious-looking men in the vicinity—it would not occur to them that big strong Ralph might have been murdered by a small middle-aged woman.

But could she do it? She thought about it, but she knew in her heart it was hopeless. They were experienced men of violence. They had been at war, off and on, for twenty years, most recently in the campaign of the winter before last. They had quick reflexes and their reactions were deadly. Many French knights had wanted to kill them, and had died trying.

She might have killed one, using guile and surprise, but not two.

She was going to have to submit to Ralph.

Grimly she went outside and washed her face and hands. When she came back into the great hall, the kitchen staff were putting out rye bread and weak ale for breakfast. Sam was dipping the stale bread into his ale to soften it. "You've got that look again," he said. "What's the matter?"

"Nothing," she said. She drew her knife and cut a slab of the bread. "I've got a long walk ahead of me."

"Is that what you're worried about? You shouldn't really go on your own. Most women don't like to travel alone."

"I'm tougher than most women." She was pleased that he showed concern for her. It was something his real father, Ralph, would never have done. Wulfric had had some influence over the boy, after all. But she was embarrassed that he had read her expression and divined her state of mind. "You don't need to worry about me."

"I could come with you," he offered. "I'm sure the earl would let me. He doesn't need any squires today—he's going off somewhere with Alan Fernhill."

That was the last thing she wanted. If she failed to keep her rendezvous, Ralph would let out the secret. She could readily imagine the pleasure Ralph would take in that. He would not need much provocation. "No," she said firmly. "Stay here. You never know when your earl will call for you."

"He won't call for me. I should come with you."

"I absolutely forbid it." Gwenda swallowed a mouthful of her bread and stuffed the rest into her wallet. "You're a good boy to worry about me, but it's not necessary." She kissed his cheek. "Take care of yourself. Don't run unnecessary risks. If you want to do something for me, stay alive."

She walked away. At the door, she turned. He was watching her thoughtfully. She forced herself to give what she hoped was a carefree smile. Then she went out.

∽

On the road, Gwenda began to worry that someone might find out about her liaison with Ralph. Such things had a way of getting out. She had met him once, she was about to do so a second time, and she feared there might be more such occasions. How long would it be before someone saw her leaving the road and heading into the woods at a certain point in her journey, and wondered why? What if someone should stumble by accident into the hunting lodge at the wrong moment? How many people would notice that Ralph went off with Alan whenever Gwenda was traveling from Earlscastle to Wigleigh?

She stopped at a tavern just before noon and had some ale and cheese. Travelers generally left such places in a group, for safety, but she made sure to wait behind so that she would be alone on the road. When she came to the point where she had to turn into the woods, she looked ahead and behind, to make sure there was no one watching. She thought she saw a movement in the trees a quarter of a mile back, and she peered into the hazy distance, trying to make out more clearly what she had seen; but no one was there. She was just getting jumpy.

She thought again about killing Ralph as she waded through the summer undergrowth. If by some lucky chance Alan was not here, might she find an opportunity? But Alan was the one person in the world who knew she was meeting Ralph here. If Ralph were killed, Alan would know who had done it. She would have to kill him, too. And that seemed impossible.

There were two horses outside the lodge. Ralph and Alan were inside, sitting at the little table, with the remains of a meal in front of them: half a loaf, a ham bone, the rind of a cheese, and a wine flask. Gwenda closed the door behind her.

"Here she is, as promised," Alan said with a satisfied air. Clearly he had been given the job of getting her to come to the rendezvous, and he was relieved she had obeyed orders. "Just perfect for your dessert," he said. "Like a raisin, wrinkled but sweet."

Gwenda said to Ralph: "Why don't you get him out of here?"

Alan stood up. "Always the insolent remark," he said. "Will you never learn?" But he left the room, going into the kitchen and slamming the door behind him.

Ralph smiled at her. "Come here," he said. She moved obediently closer to him. "I'll tell Alan not to be so rude, if you like."

"Please don't!" she said, horrified. "If he starts being nice to me, people will wonder why."

"As you please." He took her hand and tried to draw her closer. "Sit on my lap."

"Couldn't we just fuck and get it over with?"

He laughed. "That's what I like about you—you're honest." He stood up, held her shoulders, and looked into her eyes; then he bent his head and kissed her.

It was the first time he had done this. They had had sex twice without ever kissing. Now Gwenda was revolted. As his lips pressed against hers she felt more violated than when he had thrust his penis into her. He opened his mouth, and she tasted his cheesy breath. She pulled away, disgusted. "No," she said.

"Remember what you stand to lose."

"Please don't do this."

He started to become angry. "I will have you!" he said loudly. "Get that dress off."

"Please let me go," she said. He started to say something, but she raised her voice to speak over him. The walls were thin, and she knew that Alan in the kitchen could hear her pleading, but she did not care. "Don't force me, I beg you!"

"I don't care what you say!" he shouted. "Get on that bed!"

"Please don't make me!"

The front door flew open.

Both Gwenda and Ralph turned and stared.

Sam stood there.

Gwenda said: "Oh, God, no!"

The three of them were frozen still for a split second, and in that moment Gwenda guessed, all at once, what had happened. Sam had been worried about her, and—disobeying her orders—he had followed her from Earlscastle, staying out of sight but never far behind. He had seen her leave the road and head into the woods—she had caught a flash of movement when she looked behind, but she had dismissed it. He had found the hut, arriving a minute or two after her. He must have stood outside and heard the shouting. It must have been obvious that Ralph was in the process of forcing Gwenda to submit to unwanted sex—although, recalling in a flash what they had said, Gwenda realized they had not mentioned the true reason she had to submit. The secret had not been revealed—yet.

Sam drew his sword.

Ralph leaped to his feet. As Sam rushed at him, Ralph managed to get his own sword out. Sam swung at Ralph's head, but Ralph raised his sword just in time to parry the stroke.

Gwenda's son was trying to kill his father.

Sam was in terrible danger. Hardly more than a boy, he was up against a battle-hardened soldier.

Ralph shouted: "Alan!"

Then Gwenda realized Sam was up against not one but two veterans.

She dashed across the room. As the kitchen door came open, she stood on the far side of the doorway and flattened herself against the wall. She drew the long dagger from her belt.

The door flew wide and Alan stepped into the room.

He looked at the two fighters and did not see Gwenda. He paused for an instant, taking in the scene in front of him. Sam's sword swept through the air again, aimed at Ralph's neck; and again Ralph took the blow on his own sword.

Alan could see instantly that his master was under furious attack. His hand went to the hilt of his sword, and he took a pace forward. Then Gwenda stabbed him in the back.

She thrust the long dagger in and upward as hard as she could, pushing with a field-worker's strength, thrusting through the muscles of Alan's back, up through kidneys and stomach and lungs, hoping to reach his heart. The knife was ten inches long, pointed and sharp, and it sliced through his organs; but it did not kill him immediately.

He roared with pain then suddenly went silent. Staggering, he turned and grabbed her, pulling her to him in a wrestler's embrace. She stabbed him again, in the stomach this time, with the same upward stroke through the vital organs. Blood came out of his mouth. He went limp and his arms fell to his sides. He stared for a moment with a look of utter incredulity at the contemptible little woman who had ended his life. Then his eyes closed and he fell to the floor.

Gwenda looked at the other two.

Sam struck and Ralph parried; Ralph stepped back and Sam advanced; Sam struck again and Ralph parried again. Ralph was defending himself vigorously, but not attacking.

Ralph was fearful of killing his son.

Sam, not knowing that his opponent was his father, had no such scruples, and pressed forward, slashing with his sword.

Gwenda knew this could not go on for long. One of them would hurt the other, and then it would become a fight to the death. Holding her bloody knife ready, she looked desperately for a chance to intervene, and stab Ralph the way she had stabbed Alan.

"Wait," Ralph said, holding up his left hand; but Sam was angry, and thrust at him regardless. Ralph parried and spoke again. "Wait!" He was gasping from exertion, but he managed to get a few words out. "There's something you don't know."

"I know enough!" Sam yelled, and Gwenda could hear the note of boyish hysteria in his big man's voice. He swung again.

"You don't!" Ralph shouted.

Gwenda knew what Ralph wanted to tell Sam. He was going to say *I am your father.*

It must not happen.

"Listen to me!" Ralph said, and at last Sam responded. He stepped back, though he did not lower his sword.

Ralph panted, catching his breath in preparation for speaking; and, as he paused, Gwenda ran at him.

He spun around to face her, at the same time swinging his sword to the right in a flat arc. His blade hit hers, knocking the knife out of her hand. She was completely defenseless, and she knew that if he slashed at her with the return stroke she would be killed.

But, for the first time since Sam had drawn his sword, Ralph's guard was open, leaving the front of his body undefended.

Sam stepped forward and thrust his sword into Ralph's chest.

The pointed tip of the blade passed through Ralph's light summer tunic and entered his body on the left side of his breastbone. It must have slipped between two ribs, for the blade sank farther in. Sam gave a bloodthirsty cry of triumph and pushed harder. Ralph staggered backward under the impact. His shoulders hit the wall behind him, but still Sam came forward, pushing with all his might. The sword seemed to pass all the way through Ralph's chest. There was a strange thud as the point came out of his back and stuck into the timber of the wall.

Ralph's eyes looked into Sam's face, and Gwenda knew what he was thinking. Ralph understood that he had been wounded fatally. And, in the last few seconds of his life, he knew that he had been killed by his own son.

Sam let go of the sword, but it did not fall. It was embedded in the wall, impaling Ralph gruesomely. Sam stepped back, aghast.

Ralph was not yet dead. His arms waved feebly in an effort to grab the sword and pull it out of his chest, but he was not able to coordinate his movements. Gwenda realized in a ghastly flash that he looked a bit like the cat the squires had tied to the post.

She stooped and quickly picked up her dagger from the floor.

Then, incredibly, Ralph spoke.

"Sam," he said. "I am . . ." Then blood spurted from his mouth in a sudden flood, cutting off his speech.

Thank God, Gwenda thought.

The torrent stopped as quickly as it had started, and he spoke again. "I am—"

This time he was stopped by Gwenda. She leaped forward and thrust her dagger into his mouth. He made a gruesome choking noise. The blade sank into his throat.

She let go of the knife and stepped back.

She stared in horror at what she had done. The man who had tormented her for so long was nailed to the wall as if crucified, with a sword through his chest and a knife in his mouth. He made no sound, but his eyes showed that he was alive, as they looked from Gwenda to Sam and back again, in agony and terror and despair.

They stood still, staring at him, silent, waiting.

At last his eyes closed.

91

The plague faded away in September. Caris's hospital gradually emptied, as patients died without being replaced by new ones. The vacant rooms were swept and scrubbed, and juniper logs were burned in the fireplaces, filling the hospital with a sharp autumn fragrance. Early in October, the last victim was laid to rest in the hospital's graveyard. A smoky red sun rose over Kingsbridge Cathedral as four strong young nuns lowered the shrouded corpse into the hole in the ground. The body was that of a crookbacked weaver from Outhenby, but as Caris gazed into the grave she saw her old enemy, the plague, lying on the cold earth. Under her breath, she said: "Are you really dead, or will you come back again?"

When the nuns returned to the hospital after the funeral, there was nothing to do.

Caris washed her face, brushed her hair, and put on the new dress she had been saving for this day. It was the bright red of Kingsbridge Scarlet. Then she walked out of the hospital for the first time in half a year.

She went immediately into Merthin's garden.

His pear trees cast long shadows in the morning sun. The leaves were beginning to redden and crisp, while a few late fruits still hung on the boughs, round-bellied and brown. Arn, the gardener, was chopping firewood with an axe. When he saw Caris, he was at first startled and frightened; then he realized what her appearance meant, and his face split in a grin. He dropped his axe and ran into the house.

In the kitchen, Em was boiling porridge over a cheerful fire. She looked at Caris as at a heavenly apparition. She was so moved that she kissed Caris's hands.

Caris went up the stairs and into Merthin's bedroom.

He was standing at the window in his undershirt, looking out at the river that flowed past the front of the house. He turned toward her, and her heart faltered to see his familiar, irregular face, the gaze of alert intelligence and the quick humor in the twist of his lips. His golden-brown eyes looked lovingly at her, and his mouth widened in a welcoming smile. He showed no surprise: he must have noticed that there had been fewer and fewer patients arriving at the hospital, and he would have been expecting her to reappear any day. He looked like a man whose hopes have been fulfilled.

She stood beside him at the window. He put his arm around her shoulders, and she put hers around his waist. There was a little more gray in his red beard than six months ago, she thought, and his halo of hair seemed to have receded a little farther, unless it was her imagination.

For a moment, they both looked out at the river. In the gray morning light, the water was the color of iron. The surface shifted endlessly, mirror-bright or deep black in irregular patterns, always changing and always the same.

"It's over," Caris said.

Then they kissed.

ഗ

Merthin announced a special Autumn Fair to celebrate the reopening of the town. It was held during the last week of October. The wool dealing season was over, but anyway fleeces were no longer the principal commodity traded in Kingsbridge, and thousands of people came to buy the scarlet cloth for which the town was now famous.

At the Saturday night banquet that opened the fair, the guild honored Caris. Although Kingsbridge had not totally escaped the plague, it had suffered much less than other cities, and most people felt they owed their lives to her precautions. She was everyone's hero. The guildsmen insisted on marking her achievement, and Madge Webber devised a new ceremony in which Caris was presented with a gold key, symbolizing the key to the city gate. Merthin felt very proud.

Next day, Sunday, Merthin and Caris went to the cathedral. The monks were still at St.-John-in-the-Forest, so the service was taken by Father Michael from St. Peter's parish church in the town. Lady Philippa, countess of Shiring, showed up.

Merthin had not seen Philippa since Ralph's funeral. Not many tears had been shed for his brother, her husband. The earl would normally have been buried at Kingsbridge Cathedral but, because the town had been closed, Ralph had been interred in Shiring.

His death remained a mystery. His body had been found in a hunting lodge, stabbed through the chest. Alan Fernhill lay on the floor nearby, also dead of stab wounds. The two men appeared to have had dinner together, for the remains of a meal were still on the table. Obviously there had been a fight, but it was not clear whether Ralph and Alan had inflicted fatal wounds on one another, or someone else had been involved. Nothing had been stolen: money was found on both bodies, their costly weapons lay beside them, and two valuable horses were cropping the grass in the clearing outside. Because of that, the Shiring coroner inclined to the theory that the two men had killed one another.

In another sense, there was no mystery. Ralph had been a man of violence, and it was no surprise that he had died a violent death. They that live by the sword shall die by the sword, Jesus said, although that verse was not often quoted by the priests of King Edward III's reign. If anything was remarkable, it was that Ralph had survived so many military campaigns, so many bloody battles, and so many charges by the French cavalry, to die in a squabble a few miles from his home.

Merthin had surprised himself by weeping at the funeral. He wondered what he was sad about. His brother had been a wicked man who caused a great deal of misery, and his death was a blessing. Merthin had not been close to him since he murdered Tilly. What was there to mourn? In the end, Merthin decided he was grieving for a Ralph that might have been—a man whose violence was not indulged but controlled; whose aggression was directed, not by ambition for personal glory, but by a sense of justice. Perhaps it had once been possible for Ralph to grow into such a man. When the two of them had played together, aged five and six, floating wooden boats on a muddy puddle, Ralph had not been cruel and vengeful. That was why Merthin cried.

Philippa's two boys had been at the funeral, and they were with her today. The elder, Gerry, was Ralph's son by poor Tilly. The younger, Roley, was believed by everyone to be Ralph's son by Philippa, though in fact he was Merthin's. Fortunately, Roley was not a small, lively redhead like Merthin. He was going to be tall and dignified like his mother.

Roley was clutching a small wooden carving, which he presented solemnly to Merthin. It was a horse, and he had done it rather well for a ten-year-old, Merthin realized. Most children would have sculpted the animal standing firmly on all four feet, but Roley had made it move, its legs in different positions and its mane flying in the wind. The boy had inherited his real father's ability to visualize complex objects in three dimensions. Merthin felt an unexpected lump in his throat. He bent down and kissed Roley's forehead.

He gave Philippa a grateful smile. He guessed she had encouraged Roley to give him the horse, knowing what it would mean to him. He glanced at Caris and saw that she, too, understood its significance; though nothing was said.

The atmosphere in the great church was joyful. Father Michael was not a charismatic preacher, and he went through the mass in a mumble. But the nuns sang as beautifully as ever, and an optimistic sun shone through the rich dark colors of the stained-glass windows.

Afterward they walked around the fair in the crisp autumn air. Caris held Merthin's arm and Philippa walked on his other side. The two boys ran on ahead while Philippa's bodyguard and lady-in-waiting followed behind. Business was good, Merthin saw. Kingsbridge craftsmen and traders were already beginning to rebuild their fortunes. The town would recover from this epidemic faster than from the last.

Senior members of the guild were going around checking weights and measures. There were standards for the weight of a woolsack, the width of a piece of cloth, the size of a bushel, and so on, so that people knew what they were buying. Merthin encouraged guildsmen to perform these checks ostentatiously, so that buyers could see how carefully the town monitored its tradesmen. Of course, if they really suspected someone of cheating, they would check discreetly and then, if he was guilty, get rid of him quietly.

Philippa's two sons ran excitedly from one stall to the next. Watching Roley, Merthin said quietly to Philippa: "Now that Ralph has gone, is there any reason why Roley should not know the truth?"

She looked thoughtful. "I wish I could tell him—but would it be for his sake, or ours? For ten years he's believed Ralph to be his father. Two months ago he wept at Ralph's graveside. It would be a terrible shock to tell him now that he is another man's son."

They were speaking in low voices, but Caris could hear, and she said: "I agree with Philippa. You have to think of the child, not of yourself."

Merthin saw the sense of what they were saying. It was a small sadness on a happy day.

"There is another reason," Philippa said. "Gregory Longfellow came to see me last week. The king wants to make Gerry earl of Shiring."

"At the age of thirteen?" Merthin said.

"The title of earl is always hereditary, once it has been granted, although baronies are not. Anyway, I would administer the earldom for the next three years."

"As you did all the time Ralph was away fighting the French. You'll be relieved the king isn't asking you to marry again."

She made a face. "I'm too old."

"So Roley will be second in line for the earldom—provided we keep our secret." If something should happen to Gerry, Merthin thought, my son will become earl of Shiring. Fancy that.

"Roley would be a good ruler," Philippa said. "He's intelligent and quite strong-willed, but not cruel like Ralph."

Ralph's mean nature had been obvious at an early age: he had been ten, Roley's age now, when he shot Gwenda's dog. "But Roley might prefer to be something else." He looked again at the carved wooden horse.

Philippa smiled. She did not smile often, but when she did it was dazzling. She was still beautiful, he thought. She said: "Give in to it, and be proud of him."

Merthin recalled how proud his father had been when Ralph became the earl. But he knew he would never feel the same way. He would be proud of Roley whatever he did, as long as he did it well. Perhaps the boy would become a stonemason, and carve saints and angels. Perhaps he would be a wise and merciful nobleman. Or he might do something else, something his parents had never anticipated.

Merthin invited Philippa and the boys to dinner, and they all left the cathedral precincts. They walked over the bridge against the flow of loaded carts coming to the fair. They crossed Leper Island together and went through the orchard into the house.

In the kitchen they found Lolla.

As soon as she saw her father, she burst into tears. He put his arms around her and she sobbed on his shoulder. Wherever she had been, she must have got out of the habit of washing, for she smelled like a pigsty, but he was too happy to care.

It was a while before they could get any sense out of her. When at last she spoke, she said: "They all died!" Then she burst into fresh tears. After a while she calmed down, and spoke more coherently. "They all died," she repeated, suppressing her sobs. "Jake, and Boyo, Netty and Hal, Joanie and Chalkie and Ferret, one by one, and nothing I did made any difference!"

They had been living in the forest, Merthin gathered, a group of youngsters pretending to be nymphs and shepherds. The details came out gradually. The boys would kill a deer every now and again, and sometimes they would go away for a day and come back with a barrel of wine and some bread. Lolla said they bought their supplies, but Merthin guessed they had robbed travelers. Lolla had somehow imagined they could live like that forever: she had not thought about how things might be different in the winter. But, in the end, it was the plague rather than the weather that brought the idyll to an end. "I was so frightened," Lolla said. "I wanted Caris."

Gerry and Roley listened with mouths agape. They idolized their older cousin Lolla. Although she had come home in tears, the story of her adventure only enhanced her in their eyes.

"I never want to feel like that again," Lolla said. "So powerless, with my friends all sick and dying around me."

"I can understand that," Caris said. "It's how I felt when my mother died."

"Will you teach me to heal people?" Lolla said to her. "I want to really help them, as you do, not just sing hymns and show them a picture of an angel. I want to understand about bones and blood, and herbs and things that make people better. I want to be able to do something when a person is sick."

"Of course I'll teach you, if that's what you want," Caris said. "I would be pleased."

Merthin was astonished. Lolla had been rebellious and bad-tempered for some years now, and part of her rejection of authority had been a pretense that Caris, her stepmother, was not really her parent, and need not be respected. He was delighted by the turnaround. It was almost worth the agony of worry he had been through.

A moment later, a nun came into the kitchen. "Little Annie Jones is having a fit, and we don't know why," she said to Caris. "Can you come?"

"Of course," Caris said.

Lolla said: "Can I go with you?"

"No," said Caris. "Here's your first lesson: you have to be clean. Go and wash now. You can come with me tomorrow."

As she was leaving, Madge Webber came in. "Have you heard the news?" she said, her face grim. "Philemon is back."

ꕥ

On that Sunday, Davey and Amabel were married at the little church in Wigleigh.

Lady Philippa gave permission for the manor house to be used for the party. Wulfric killed a pig and roasted it whole over a fire in the yard. Davey had bought sweet currants, and Annet baked them in buns. There was no ale—much of the barley harvest had rotted in the fields for want of reapers—but Philippa had sent Sam home with a present of a barrel of cider.

Gwenda still thought, every day, about that scene in the hunting lodge. In the middle of the night she stared into the darkness and saw Ralph with her knife in his mouth, the hilt sticking out between his brown teeth, and Sam's sword nailing him to the wall.

When she and Sam had retrieved their weapons, pulling them grimly out of Ralph, and the corpse had fallen to the floor, it had looked as if the two dead men had killed one another. Gwenda had smeared blood on their unstained weapons and left them where they lay. Outside, she had loosened the horses' tethers, so that they could survive for a few days, if necessary, until someone found them. Then she and Sam had walked away.

The Shiring coroner had speculated that outlaws might have been involved in the deaths, but in the end had come to the conclusion Gwenda expected. No suspicion had fallen on her or Sam. They had got away with murder.

She had told Sam an edited version of what had happened between her and Ralph. She pretended that this was the first time he had tried to coerce her, and she said he had simply threatened to kill her if she refused. Sam was awestruck to think that he had killed an earl, but he had no doubt that his action had been justified. He had the right temperament for a soldier, Gwenda realized: he would never suffer agonies of remorse over killing.

Nor did she, even though she often recalled the scene with revulsion. She had killed Alan Fernhill and finished Ralph off, but she had not a twinge of regret. The world was a better place without both of them. Ralph had died in the agony of knowing that his own son had stabbed him through the heart, and that was exactly what he deserved. In time, she felt sure, the vision of what she had done would cease to come to her by night.

She put the memory out of her mind and looked around the hall of the manor house at the carousing villagers.

The pig was eaten, and the men were drinking the last of the cider. Aaron Appletree produced his bagpipes. The village had had no drummer since the death of Annet's father, Perkin. Gwenda wondered whether Davey would take up drumming now.

Wulfric wanted to dance, as he always did when he had had a bellyful of drink. Gwenda partnered him for the first number, laughing as she tried to keep up with his cavorting. He lifted her, swung her through the air, crushed her to his body, and put her down again only to circle her with great leaps. He had no sense of rhythm, but his sheer enthusiasm was infectious. Afterward she declared herself exhausted, and he danced with his new daughter-in-law, Amabel.

Then, of course, he danced with Annet.

His eye fell on her as soon as the tune ended and he let go of Amabel. Annet was sitting on a bench at one side of the hall of the manor house. She wore a green dress that was girlishly short and showed her dainty ankles. The dress was not new, but she had embroidered the bosom with yellow and pink flowers. As always, a few ringlets had escaped from her headdress, and they hung around her face. She was twenty years too old to dress that way, but she did not know it, and nor did Wulfric.

Gwenda smiled as they began to dance. She wanted to look happy and carefree, but she realized her expression might be more like a grimace, and she gave up trying. She tore her gaze away from them and watched Davey and Amabel. Perhaps Amabel would not turn out quite like her mother. She had some of Annet's coquettish ways, but Gwenda had never seen her actually flirting, and right now she seemed uninterested in anyone but her husband.

Gwenda scanned the room and located her other son, Sam. He was with the young men, telling a story, miming it, holding the reins of an imaginary horse and almost falling off. He had them spellbound. They probably envied his luck in becoming a squire.

Sam was still living at Earlscastle. Lady Philippa had kept on most of the squires and men-at-arms, for her son Gerry would need them to ride and hunt with him, and practise with the sword and the lance. Gwenda hoped that, during the period of Philippa's regency, Sam would learn a more intelligent and merciful code that he would have got from Ralph.

There was not much else to look at, and Gwenda's gaze returned to her husband and the woman he had once wanted to marry. As Gwenda had feared, Annet was making the most of Wulfric's exuberance and inebriation. She gave him sexy smiles when they danced apart, and when they came together she clung to him, Gwenda thought, like a wet shirt.

The dance seemed to go on forever, Aaron Appletree repeating the bouncy melody endlessly on his bagpipes. Gwenda knew her husband's moods, and now she saw the glint in his eye that always appeared when he was about to ask her to lie with him. Annet knew exactly what she was doing, Gwenda thought furiously. She shifted restlessly on her bench, willing the music to stop, trying not to let her anger show.

However, she was seething with indignation when the tune ended with a flourish. She made up her mind to get Wulfric to calm down and sit beside her. She would keep him close for the rest of the afternoon, and there would be no trouble.

But then Annet kissed him.

While he still had his hands on her waist she stood on tiptoe and tilted her face and kissed him full on the lips, briefly but firmly; and Gwenda boiled over.

She jumped up from her bench and strode across the hall. As she passed the bridal couple, her son Davey saw the expression on her face and tried to detain her, but she ignored him. She went up to Wulfric and Annet, who were still gazing at one another and smiling stupidly. She poked Annet's shoulder with her finger and said loudly: "Leave my husband alone!"

Wulfric said: "Gwenda, please—"

"Don't you say anything," Gwenda said. "Just stay away from this whore."

Annet's eyes flashed defiance. "It's not dancing that whores are paid for."

"I'm sure you know all about what whores do."

"How dare you!"

Davey and Amabel intervened. Amabel said to Annet: "Please don't make a scene, Ma."

Annet said: "It's not me, it's Gwenda!"

Gwenda said: "I'm not the one trying to seduce someone else's husband."

Davey said: "Mother, you're spoiling the wedding."

Gwenda was too enraged to listen. "She always does this. She jilted him twenty-three years ago, but she's never let him go!"

Annet began to cry. Gwenda was not surprised. Annet's tears were just another means of getting her way.

Wulfric reached out to pat Annet's shoulder, and Gwenda snapped: "Don't touch her!" He jerked back his hand as if burned.

"You don't understand," Annet sobbed.

"I understand you all too well," Gwenda said.

"No, you don't," Annet said. She wiped her eyes and gave Gwenda a surprisingly direct, candid look. "You don't understand that you have won. He's yours. You don't know how he adores you, respects you, admires you. You don't see the way he looks at you when you're speaking to someone else."

Gwenda was taken aback. "Well," she mumbled, but she did not know what else to say.

Annet went on: "Does he eye younger women? Does he ever sneak away from you? How many nights have you slept apart in the last twenty years—two? Three? Can't you see that he will never love another woman as long as he lives?"

Gwenda looked at Wulfric and realized that all this was true. In fact it was obvious. She knew it and so did everyone. She tried to remember why she was so angry with Annet, but somehow the logic of it had slipped her mind.

The dancing had stopped and Aaron had put down his pipes. All the villagers now gathered around the two women, mothers of the bridal couple.

Annet said: "I was a foolish and selfish girl, and I made a stupid decision, and lost the best man I've ever met. And you got him. Sometimes I can't resist the temptation to pretend it happened the other way around, and he's mine. So I smile at him, and I pat his arm; and he's kind to me because he knows he broke my heart."

"You broke your own heart," Gwenda said.

"I did. And you were the lucky girl who benefited from my folly."

Gwenda was dumbfounded. She had never looked at Annet as a sad person. To her, Annet had always been a powerful, threatening figure, ever scheming to take Wulfric back. But that was never going to come to pass.

Annet said: "I know it annoys you when Wulfric is nice to me. I'd like to say it won't happen again, but I know my own weakness. Do you have to hate me for it? Don't let this spoil the joy of the wedding and of the grandchildren we both want. Instead of regarding me as your lifelong enemy, couldn't you think of me as a bad sister, who sometimes misbehaves and makes you cross, but still has to be treated as one of the family?"

She was right. Gwenda had always thought of Annet as a pretty face with an empty head, but on this occasion Annet was the wiser of the two, and Gwenda felt humbled. "I don't know," she said. "Perhaps I could try."

Annet stepped forward and kissed Gwenda's cheek. Gwenda felt Annet's tears on her face. "Thank you," Annet said.

Gwenda hesitated, then put her arms around Annet's bony shoulders and hugged her.

All around them, the villagers clapped and cheered.

A moment later, the music began again.

Early in November, Philemon arranged a service of thanksgiving for the end of the plague. Archbishop Henri came with Canon Claude. So did Sir Gregory Longfellow.

Gregory must have come to Kingsbridge to announce the king's choice of bishop, Merthin thought. Formally, he would tell the monks that the king had nominated a certain person, and it would be up to the monks to elect that person or someone else; but, in the end, the monks usually voted for whomever the king had chosen.

Merthin could read no message in Philemon's face, and he guessed that Gregory had not yet revealed the king's choice. The decision meant everything to Merthin and Caris. If Claude got the job, their troubles were over. He was moderate and reasonable. But if Philemon became bishop, they faced more years of squabbling and lawsuits.

Henri took the service, but Philemon preached the sermon. He thanked God for answering the prayers of Kingsbridge monks and sparing the town from the worst effects of the plague. He did not mention that the monks had fled to St.-John-in-the-Forest and left the townspeople to fend for themselves; nor that Caris and Merthin had helped God to answer the monks' prayers by closing the town gates for six months. He made it sound as if he had saved Kingsbridge.

"It makes my blood boil," Merthin said to Caris, not troubling to keep his voice down. "He's completely twisting the facts!"

"Relax," she said. "God knows the truth, and so do the people. Philemon isn't fooling anyone."

She was right, of course. After a battle, the soldiers on the winning side always thanked God, but all the same they knew the difference between good generals and bad.

After the service, Merthin as alderman was invited to dine at the prior's palace with the archbishop. He was seated next to Canon Claude. As soon as grace had been said, a general hubbub of conversation broke out, and Merthin spoke to Claude in a low, urgent voice. "Does the archbishop know yet who the king has chosen as bishop?"

Claude replied with an almost imperceptible nod.

"Is it you?"

Claude's head shake was equally minimal.

"Philemon, then?"

Again the tiny nod.

Merthin's heart sank. How could the king pick a fool and coward such as Philemon in preference to someone as competent and sensible as Claude? But he knew the answer: Philemon had played his cards well. "Has Gregory instructed the monks yet?"

"No." Claude leaned closer. "He will probably tell Philemon informally tonight after supper, then speak to the monks in chapter tomorrow morning."

"So we've got until the end of the day."

"For what?"

"To change his mind."

"You won't do that."

"I'm going to try."

"You'll never succeed."

"Bear in mind that I'm desperate."

Merthin toyed with his food, eating little and fighting to keep his patience, until the archbishop rose from the table; then he spoke to Gregory. "If you would walk with me in the cathedral, I would speak to you about something I feel sure will interest you deeply," he said, and Gregory nodded assent.

They paced side by side up the nave, where Merthin could be sure no one was lurking close enough to hear. He took a deep breath. What he was about to do was dangerous. He was going to try to bend the king to his will. If he failed, he could be charged with treason—and executed.

He said: "There have long been rumors that a document exists, somewhere in Kingsbridge, that the king would dearly love to destroy."

Gregory was stone-faced, but he said: "Go on." That was as good as confirmation.

"This letter was in the possession of a knight who has recently died."

"Has he!" said Gregory, startled.

"You obviously know exactly what I'm talking about."

Gregory answered like a lawyer. "Let us say, for the sake of argument, that I do."

"I would like to do the king the service of restoring that document to him—whatever it may be." He knew perfectly well what it was, but he could adopt a cautious pretense of ignorance as well as Gregory.

"The king would be grateful," said Gregory.

"How grateful?"

"What did you have in mind?"

"A bishop more in sympathy with the people of Kingsbridge than Philemon."

Gregory looked hard at him. "Are you trying to blackmail the king of England?"

Merthin knew this was the point of danger. "We Kingsbridge folk are merchants and craftsmen," he said, trying to sound reasonable. "We buy, we sell, we make deals. I'm just trying to make a bargain with you. I want to sell you something, and I've told you my price. There's no blackmail, no coercion. I make no threats. If you don't want what I'm selling, that will be the end of the matter."

They reached the altar. Gregory stared at the crucifix that surmounted it. Merthin knew exactly what he was thinking. Should he have Merthin arrested, taken to London, and tortured until he revealed the whereabouts of the document? Or would it be simpler and more convenient to the king just to nominate a different man as bishop of Kingsbridge?

There was a long silence. The cathedral was cold, and Merthin pulled his cloak closer around him. At last Gregory said: "Where is the document?"

"Close by. I'll take you there."

"Very well."

"And our bargain?"

"If the document is what you believe it to be, I will honor my side of the arrangement."

"And make Canon Claude bishop?"

"Yes."

"Thank you," said Merthin. "We'll need to walk a little way into the woods."

They went side by side down the main street and across the bridge, their breath making clouds in the air. A wintry sun shone with little warmth as they walked into the forest. Merthin found the way easily this time, having followed the same route only a few weeks earlier. He recognized the little spring, the big rock, and the boggy valley. They came quickly to the clearing with the broad oak tree, and he went straight to the spot where he had dug up the scroll.

He was dismayed to see that someone else had got here first.

He had carefully smoothed the loose earth and covered it with leaves but, despite that, someone had found the hiding place. There was a hole a foot deep, and a pile of recently excavated earth beside it. And the hole was empty.

He stared at the hole, appalled. "Oh, hell," he said.

Gregory said: "I hope this isn't some kind of charade—"

"Let me think," Merthin snapped.

Gregory shut up.

"Only two people knew about this," Merthin said, thinking aloud. "I haven't told anyone, so Thomas must have. He was getting senile before he died. I think he spilled the beans."

"But to whom?"

"Thomas spent the last few months of his life at St.-John-in-the-Forest, and the monks were keeping everyone else out, so it must have been a monk."

"How many are there?"

"Twenty or so. But not many would know enough about the background to understand the significance of an old man's mumblings about a buried letter."

"That's all very well, but where is it now?"

"I think I know," said Merthin. "Give me one more chance."

"Very well."

They walked back to the town. As they crossed the bridge, the sun was setting over Leper Island. They went into the darkening cathedral, walked to the southwest tower, and climbed the narrow spiral staircase to the little room where the costumes for the mystery play were kept.

Merthin had not been here for eleven years, but dusty storerooms did not change much, especially in cathedrals, and this was the same. He found the loose stone in the wall and pulled it out.

All Philemon's treasures were behind the stone, including the love note carved in wood. And there, among them, was a bag made of oiled wool. Merthin opened the bag and drew from it a vellum scroll.

"I thought so," he said. "Philemon got the secret out of Thomas when Thomas was losing his mind." No doubt Philemon was keeping the letter to be used as a bargaining counter if the decision on the bishopric went the wrong way—but now Merthin could use it instead.

He handed the scroll to Gregory.

Gregory unrolled it. A look of awe came over his face as he read. "Dear God," he said. "Those rumors were true." He rolled it up again. He had the look of a man who has found something he has been seeking for many years.

"Is it what you expected?" Merthin said.

"Oh, yes."

"And the king will be grateful?"

"Profoundly."

"So your part of the bargain . . . ?"

"Will be kept," said Gregory. "You shall have Claude as your bishop."

"Thank God," said Merthin.

Eight days later, early in the morning, Caris was at the hospital, teaching Lolla how to tie a bandage, when Merthin came in. "I want to show you something," he said. "Come to the cathedral."

It was a bright, cold winter's day. Caris wrapped herself in a heavy red cloak. As they were crossing the bridge into the city, Merthin stopped and pointed. "The spire is finished," he said.

Caris looked up. She could see its shape through the spiderweb of flimsy scaffolding that still surrounded it. The spire was immensely tall and graceful. As her eye followed its upward taper, Caris had the feeling that it might go on forever.

She said: "And is it the tallest building in England?"

He smiled. "Yes."

They walked up the main street and into the cathedral. Merthin led the way up the staircase within the walls of the central tower. He was used to the climb, but Caris was panting by the time they emerged into the open air at the summit of the tower, on the walkway that ran around the base of the spire. Up here the breeze was stiff and cold.

They looked at the view while Caris caught her breath. All Kingsbridge was laid out to the north and west: the main street, the industrial district, the river, and the island with the hospital. Smoke rose from a thousand chimneys. Miniature people hurried through the streets, walking or riding or driving carts, carrying tool bags or baskets of produce or heavy sacks; men and women and children, fat and thin, their clothing poor and worn or rich and heavy, mostly brown and green but with flashes of peacock blue and scarlet. The sight of them all made Caris marvel: each individual had a different life, every one of them rich and complex, with dramas in the past and challenges in the future, happy memories and secret sorrows, and a crowd of friends and enemies and loved ones.

"Ready?" Merthin said.

Caris nodded.

He led her up the scaffolding. It was an insubstantial affair of ropes and branches, and it always made her nervous, though she did not like to say so: if Merthin could climb it, so could she. The wind made the whole structure sway a little, and the skirts of Caris's robe flapped around her legs like the sails of a ship. The spire was as tall again as the tower, and the climb up the rope ladders was strenuous.

They stopped halfway for a rest. "The spire is very plain," Merthin said, not needing to catch his breath. "Just a roll molding at the angles." Caris realized that other spires she had seen featured decorative crochets, bands of colored stone or tile, and windowlike recesses. The simplicity of Merthin's design was what made it seem to go on forever.

Merthin pointed down. "Hey, look what's happening!"

"I'd rather not look down . . ."

"I think Philemon is leaving for Avignon."

She had to see that. She was standing on a broad platform of planks, but all the same she had to hold on tight with both hands to the upright pole to convince herself that she was not falling. She swallowed hard and directed her gaze down the perpendicular side of the tower to the ground below.

It was worth the effort. A charette drawn by two oxen was outside the prior's palace. An escort consisting of a monk and a man-at-arms, both on horseback, waited patiently. Philemon stood beside the charette while the monks of Kingsbridge came forward, one by one, and kissed his hand.

When they had all done, Brother Sime handed him a black-and-white cat, and Caris recognized the descendant of Godwyn's cat Archbishop.

Philemon climbed into the carriage and the driver whipped the oxen. The vehicle lumbered slowly out of the gate and down the main street. Caris and Merthin watched it cross the double bridge and disappear into the suburbs.

"Thank God he's gone," said Caris.

Merthin looked up. "Not much farther to the top," he said. "Soon you will be higher off the ground than any woman in England has ever stood." He began to climb again.

The wind grew stronger but, despite her anxiety, Caris felt exhilarated. This was Merthin's dream, and he had made it come true. Every day for hundreds of years people for miles around would look at this spire and think how beautiful it was.

They reached the top of the scaffolding and stood on the stage that encircled the peak of the spire. Caris tried to forget that there was no railing around the platform to stop them falling off.

At the point of the spire was a cross. It had looked small from the ground, but now Caris saw that it was taller than she.

"There's always a cross at the top of a spire," Merthin said. "That's conventional. Aside from that, practise varies. At Chartres, the cross bears an image of the sun. I've done something different."

Caris saw that, at the foot of the cross, Merthin had placed a life-size stone angel. The kneeling figure was not gazing up at the cross, but out to the west, over the town. Looking more closely, Caris saw that the angel's features were not conventional. The small round face was clearly female, and looked vaguely familiar, with neat features and short hair.

Then she realized that the face was her own.

She was amazed. "Will they let you do that?" she said.

Merthin nodded. "Half the town thinks you're an angel already."

"I'm not, though," she said.

"No," he said with the familiar grin that she loved so much. "But you're the closest they've seen."

The wind blustered suddenly. Caris grabbed Merthin. He held her tightly, standing confidently on spread feet. The gust died away as quickly as it had come, but Merthin and Caris remained locked together, standing there at the top of the world, for a long time afterward.

ACKNOWLEDGMENTS

My principal historical consultants were Sam Cohn, Geoffrey Hindley, and Marilyn Livingstone. The weakness in the foundations of Kingsbridge Cathedral is loosely based on that of the cathedral of Santa Maria in Vitoria-Gasteiz, Spain, and I'm grateful to the staff of the Fundación Catedral Santa Maria for help and inspiration, especially Carlos Rodriguez de Diego, Gonzalo Arroita, and interpreter Luis Rivero. I was also helped by the staff of York Minster, especially John David. Martin Allen of the Fitzwilliam Museum in Cambridge, England, kindly allowed me to handle coins from the reign of Edward III. At Le Mont St. Michel in France I was helped by Soeur Judith and Frère François. As always, Dan Starer of Research for Writers in New York City helped with the research. My literary advisors included Amy Berkower, Leslie Gelbman, Phyllis Grann, Neil Nyren, Imogen Taylor, and Al Zuckerman. I was also helped by comments and criticisms from friends and family, especially Barbara Follett, Emanuele Follett, Marie-Claire Follett, Erica Jong, Tony McWalter, Chris Manners, Jann Turner, and Kim Turner.

ABOUT THE AUTHOR

Ken Follett is the author of seventeen bestselling books, from the groundbreaking *Eye of the Needle* to, most recently, *Jackdaws, Hornet Flight,* and *Whiteout.* He lives in England with his wife, Barbara Follett.